"[Kaga's] criticism of the criminal justice system of mid-century Japan could just as well have been written about the United States today, and Anglophone readers interested in the subject will find Kaga's work here highly rewarding, though it is quite divorced from the racial conditions that underlie the prison-industrial complex in the United States ... Readers interested in a brilliant, high-definition portrait of postwar Japan will find little to compare to this that is readily available in the English language."
—Jack Rockwell, *Words Without Borders*

"Here, we see the other side of industrial Japan—not just the economic miracle but also how the stifling constraints of space in Tokyo inevitably categorize people into types—as Kaga wonderfully illustrates in his depictions of the various criminals and pickpockets that Atsuo meets in prison."
—Iona Tait, *Asymptote Journal*

FURTHER PRAISE FOR OTOHIKO KAGA:

"Kaga skillfully reveals the friction between the Japanese military command, who were eager to start a war with America, and the Japanese diplomats who felt their country could not win such a confrontation ... [Riding the East Wind] delivers a powerful message about the consequences of war."
—*Publishers Weekly*

"...Otohiko Kaga, in Riding the East Wind, confidently claims a fictional territory that ranges across the Pacific. ... Riding the East Wind is above all an honest work — humane in intent, generous in spirit and movingly rendered."
—Dianne Highbridge, *The New York Times*

"Although told on an epic scale uncharacteristic of modern Japanese fiction, [Riding the East Wind] does deal with the classically postwar Japanese themes of duty and loyalty. Most readers know what will happen, but they will still be gripped by the political intrigue and tales of the ongoing war. ... A welcome addition to World War II literature; recommended for larger fiction collections and anywhere historical fiction is in demand."
—Tom Cooper, *Library Journal*

"[Riding the East Wind] offers a convincingly detailed picture of urban Japan on the eve of WWII, while focusing memorably on three members of a deeply conflicted family: diplomat Suburo Kurushima, who arrives in Washington on a peace-seeking mission just as the bombs are falling on Pearl Harbor; his fully Easternized, American-born wife Alice; and their son, Ken, an idealistic aeronautical engineer whose skills and vision are co-opted and corrupted by Japan's vainglorious military bureaucracy. A familiar story, movingly retold in a way that will be new to American readers."
—*Kirkus Reviews*

BOOKS BY OTOHIKO KAGA IN
ENGLISH TRANSLATION:

Riding the East Wind: A Novel of War and Peace
Marshland

Deep Vellum | Dalkey Archive Press
3000 Commerce Street
Dallas, Texas 75226

www.dalkeyarchive.com

Support for this publication has been provided in part by grants from the National
Endowment for the Arts, the Texas Commission on the Arts, the City of Dallas Office
of Arts and Culture, the Communities Foundation of Texas,
and the Addy Foundation.

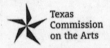

Paperback: 9781628974041
Ebook: 9781628974331

LCCN: 2024012051

Cover design by Daniel Benneworth-Gray
Cover photograph by Kzaral
Interior design by Anuj Mathur

Printed in Canada

Marshland

Otohiko Kaga

Translated by Albert Novick

DALKEY ARCHIVE PRESS

Dallas, TX

Contents

Marshland

Chapter 1

Fingers

People swarmed into Shinjuku Station like a great army on emergency call up. The men, uniformed in business suits selected from a narrow range of color lines, raced after one another up the stairway, hastening to fulfill their missions of service to their respective companies. The women's dress showed real variety, but no other distinctions were evident among them as they followed close after the men, like pale shadows.

This familiar morning spectacle always inspired a kind of awe. The multitude would shortly station itself at corporate posts around the city and commence its work. The world turned on the grand total of these people's labor. They were the movers of this world, exactly like individual soldiers who carry out their respective duties, making it possible to wage a colossal war.

As the train arrived, bodies rushed into spaces vacated by exiting passengers. The packed car was an anonymous mass of textile and flesh. Abandoning himself to the pressure of the bodies around him, Atsuo Yukimori let his gaze fall on the man ahead of him.

He was a successful-looking gentleman, perhaps approaching fifty, in other words, Atsuo's contemporary, wearing a starched shirt and brand new striped necktie. Probably a section chief or assistant section chief, he was the type who minds his appearance and does his work competently. An air of confidence wafted about his clean-shaven jaw.

A university graduate, employed by a leading corporation, living in a fine apartment. The father of one boy and one girl. The owner of an automobile. His salary . . . .

3

Looking at the man, Atsuo imagined a life based on a level of income different than his own. Most of what this man possessed, he, Atsuo Yukimori, did not. He was an auto mechanic who had not gone beyond elementary school. His home was a rented room in a wooden building. At age 49, he was still without wife and children.

Nevertheless, his external appearance was as nice as the gentleman's. The fabric of his English-made suit was even better than what the gentleman wore, and his Italian silk necktie, carefully selected at an uptown department store, certainly out-priced the gentleman's. At a glance, he, too, could be taken for a section chief at a major company, or maybe even an executive.

But Atsuo knew well that his hands gave him away. The strong joints of his fingers and grease-stained nails conclusively marked him as an auto mechanic. The contrast with this man's plump hands — innocent of labor — was unmistakable. Moreover, Atsuo's rawboned chest and broad shoulders testified to his history of manual labor by making uncouth distortions in his suit. Evidently, business suits were designed for this sort of man, with his fine bone structure covered by fat and soft flesh.

As the train arrived at Yotsuya Station, the pressure of moving bodies began again. Atsuo abruptly braced his legs to resist the inertia. His rock-hard shoulder pressed into the weak breast of the gentleman, eliciting a grimace. Atsuo let the pressure continue for a beat. As he was relaxing his posture, his senses were assailed by a sinister presence, like death lurking on a battlefield.

There was something unnatural about the manner of the man who had just boarded the train and was standing next to the well-fed gentleman. He had opened a newspaper, but his eyes did not follow the printed lines. They darted about his surroundings. Then, from below the newspaper held up by his left hand, his right hand was inching forward. As it rose slowly across the gentleman's jacket, the wallet in the inside pocket crept upward. When it fell from inside the coat, the hand was waiting to receive it. Then the wallet was gone. It had all happened in a moment. The man blandly read his newspaper.

It was a brilliant maneuver, so brilliant it kept Atsuo looking on in admiration, as if watching a masterful scene in a silent movie. For one moment, his feelings had been at one with the man, praying that his fingers would do their job well, and no one would catch on.

Pickpockets who work trains call themselves *hakoshi*. This man seemed to be a master of the art. He looked to be over fifty, maybe even significantly older. Perfectly outfitted for his pose as a businessman on his way to the office, his approach startled no one. His sense of timing was keen, using the moment when the people who had just boarded the train were jostling about to settle into place. The job was done during the fleeting instant when the gentleman was distracted by the jostling.

Using a newspaper to cover your work was a classic ploy called "drawing a curtain." Extracting a wallet from an inner pocket by pushing it upward was called "inside out." This maneuver is even more difficult than undoing a button and slipping one's fingers into the pocket because the mark might easily feel the pressure on his chest.

Who on earth was this man?

He remembered his face. They had met before somewhere. Then he knew, after he had mentally removed the large-frame glasses and the pomade that made the hair gleam like ink, cropped the hair to fully reveal the face and smoothed out the wrinkles of fifteen or sixteen years. They had once been to-gether in a common cell in Fuchu prison. He had forgotten the man's name, but everyone had called him "boss."

One day "the boss" had picked the pocket of a guard who was marching him somewhere. His objective had been cigarettes, but he had mistakenly lifted the guard's official notebook. He was puzzling over how to return it when the deed was discovered. That earned him a stretch in solitary confinement, followed by a ban on reading for a number of days — punishments that inflict suffering through isolation and tedium.

He had been grumbling before they took him away to solitary . . . Now he remembered. The man's name was Ginji. That was it — Ginji Sato. "Boss Ginji," they had called him.

Boss Ginji had been muttering, "Must be getting old, taking a notebook for cigarettes. Amateurs don't mess up that bad. I've had it. Forty's too old for this game. Time to go straight."

But fifteen, sixteen years had passed and old Ginji was as crooked as he had ever been.

The gentleman was still unaware he had been robbed. His taut, clean-shaven jowls radiated confidence. Perhaps sensing that he was being watched, he darted a contemptuous glance at Atsuo.

That was just fine, he could give all the dirty looks he liked. Shortly he would be running panic-stricken for a police booth.

Atsuo tasted revenge, a barbaric glee that rose up in his breast.

It was a return of the long forgotten mind set of the criminal. You develop X-ray vision to pick out objects in their pockets, briefcases, handbags or belly bands — wallets, cash jewelry, watches and other things they believe to be their own. Suddenly he was looking at the world from the other side, where people are nothing more than a flock of prey. You size a person up. Their social standing, age, or gender don't matter.

As he gripped the hand strap, his eyes turned toward a faint impression at the base of his right index finger. It was a scar from a burn he had received as a child. In the past, he would sometimes gaze at that scar after he had committed some crime, feeling it held a clue to why he had become the sort of person he was.

He must have been about four. His mother had been furious. She grabbed his hand and dragged him, resisting, into a small, dark room. Waiting there was a woman from the neighborhood who often came to their family diner. As the two held him tightly, a white substance was placed on his right index finger. His mother held a burning match to it.

He finally understood what was happening. He was receiving *o-kyu* — moxa burning. The soft moxa powder burned down until his finger was seared by pain. He sobbed piteously, unable to understand why he was being subjected to this agony. Much later, his mother explained, "I placed a charm on you so you won't do wrong."

He had done wrong, she said, by stealing a few copper coins from the change basket that hung from a post in the family's diner. He couldn't remember doing this, but could clearly recall the rule against taking things from the basket. He had probably reached for the basket one day in childish delight at violating a taboo. What remained was a scar and a memory of punishment.

He was among the vast wave of passengers getting off at Ochanomizu Station. He caught sight of Ginji's retreating figure on the platform. He followed behind as Ginji nimbly threaded his way through openings in the crowd.

At the bottom of the stairway he tried calling out, "Boss!" but got no reaction. When he called "Boss Ginji!" the shoulders jumped angrily. Ginji looked back, but he didn't stop, turning instead into the shadow of a steel supporter beam.

"It is Boss Ginji, all right," Atsuo said warmly, inclining his head in greeting. "Atsuo Yukimori. We were together at Fuchu."

The eyes gleamed hard and cold from the shadows, simultaneously taking in Atsuo and warily watching a girl at a nearby newspaper stand.

"Who's that you say? I don't recognize your name. What do you want with me?"

"I don't especially want anything with you. It's just nice to see an old friend."

"I don't know you." Ginji looked straight ahead while his eyes angrily traveled up and down Atsuo's face once, then a second time. "You are . . ."

"Atsuo Yukimori." Then he remembered to pull out a business card and offer it.

The next train pulled in. As the doors opened Ginji turned to board it,

6

but when he was enveloped by the wave of alighting passengers, he relaxed his shoulders and his expression softened.

"I remember all right. Couldn't forget you. But what do you want with me?"

"Don't want nothing, like I said." Like Ginji, Atsuo was talking prisoner style. "Just wanted to say the job you just did was a real beaut."

Ginji gave a short laugh through his nose. "You could tell, eh?"

"What do you think? You do it wide open right in front of me, cool as ice. What if I squealed?"

"You wouldn't do nothing like that. I knew it was you. You were my shield."

A "shield" is an accomplice who helps cover up a crime.

"Oh, come on."

"No lie. I spotted you, so I thought, okay, I can use him. So I came over. But I sure didn't expect to see you looking so respectable. Since when you been like that?"

"Since I got out. It's almost ten years."

"That's really something," Ginji said admiringly as he measured up Atsuo's appearance with a critical eye. "You seem to be doing pretty well. Must be about fifty thousand in that wallet in your left inside pocket."

"On the mark," Atsuo said respectfully, patting his wallet. "That's almost exactly what I have."

"Is that an appointment book in your right inner pocket? It's pretty fat. Must be one of those 'business diary' jobs."

"Can't hide a thing from you," Atsuo laughed. Then, with a teasing look, he said, "Hey, boss, didn't you say you were going to go straight?"

Ginji snorted and cast a sharp eye about. He was watching out for undercover detectives. "No other way to keep eating. But I have to quit. Losing my touch."

"You're doing fine."

"No, sometimes I mess up. I pulled it off today, though, thanks to your shield." Atsuo looked at his watch. It was a little past eight. He would have to hurry. "Got to go. Hey, let's meet up again."

Ginji followed him up the stairway. He stopped in front of a restroom. "My little habit," he said, tapping his left arm and closing one eye. He meant he was shooting *shabu* — methamphetamine. Atsuo remembered he had been addicted, every vein of both arms like swollen worms, covered with needle tracks. He seemed to be living exactly the same kind of life he had lived years ago.

~

From the entrance to the station came a strident voice like a barrage of needles.

7

About thirty youths wearing construction helmets, their faces masked with towels, were standing together, arms linked. Before them, their leader was shouting into a portable loudspeaker. The volume was turned up beyond the microphone's capacity, so only snatches of the speech were comprehensible.

"We denounce . . . university authorities . . . now is the hour! . . . bourgeois democracy's lies and deceptions . . ."

Atsuo couldn't understand why the university students had suddenly become so excited. Since the spring campuses had been ablaze, as if a flash fire had been fanned by a strong wind until it surged across the entire country. The universities had become sites of an endless cycle of demonstrations, occupations, mass negotiations, and riots. Professors and intellectuals were on the side of the students. To read the newspapers or watch the news, you would think the country was on the brink of revolution.

To a man whose domestic circumstances had not permitted anything beyond an elementary school education, not even being able to attend middle school, much less university, higher education seemed like the best of all possible worlds. He couldn't imagine what could make the fortunate students become so dissatisfied as to riot. Atsuo had attended an army aircraft mechanics' school during the war. That was the whole of his post-elementary school academic career. In the mechanics' school he had been no match for the university graduates, who had made great fun of his ignorance of English, physics, and chemistry. They were a bunch of privileged brats who held the likes of Atsuo Yukimori in contempt.

The startling sight of a girl among the youths made Atsuo stop. Boys on either side had their arms about her shoulders, and she was literally being lifted off her feet. Her hands were delicate, her skin fair. Her fingers looked as if the slightest force might snap them in two. Her round bottom strained her jeans provocatively when the mass of bodies swayed. Because the lower half of her face was masked with a cloth, Atsuo couldn't be sure, but she resembled Wakako Ikéhata, the university co-ed he had met at the skating rink.

In his mind he stripped the girl, put a short skirt on her and set her to whirling across the ice of a skating rink.

Legs long and slim seem immature until they kick at the ice with startling strength. She lowers her hips and begins to spin. Steel blades atop a crystal circle of light gliding round and round and round . . .

Atsuo went to figure skating lessons every Sunday morning. He often met Wakako because they both had the same instructor. But this girl was not Wakako. Atsuo left the scene with a feeling of great relief. He reassured himself that the student radicals who had the schools in an uproar were different from a student who would go ice skating.

The army of office workers formed a dark river flowing down the slope of the boulevard. Here and there students from two or three private universities in the area could be seen. Atsuo was suddenly conscious of a stern gaze, like the beam of a flashlight cutting through the dark of night. The source was a police booth on the other side of the broad thoroughfare.

It was an utterly familiar sight. Standing in front of the police booth was a young patrolman in an oversized cap, looking for all the world like a middle school boy in his uniform. But the patrolman's eyes were trained squarely on Atsuo, singling him out from the throng, identifying him as different from the average worker, a suspicious man, a criminal. Atsuo tried shifting his position a few steps. The eyes followed.

He had an impulse to fly in front of the patrolman and shout "Who do you think you're looking at? You got something to say to me? Yeah, I met that thief, Ginji. All I did was meet him. I didn't do nothing."

That look! He hated it! He could slam his fist into a face looking at him that way.

Before he realized what he was doing, he had cried aloud, "Whadaya' lookin' at me like that for!"

People turned in surprise. Now I've done it, he thought. Raising his voice at the wrong time was a bad habit he had acquired recently. He would always feel chagrined when it happened. He put on a bland face and made as if he had been singing to himself.

"Why do you look at me that way?
Why do you look at me that way?
Oh-oo, why do you look at me,
Why do you look at me that 'a waaay? . . ."

People got out of his way. They looked back disdainfully, probably thinking he was drunk.

Reaching the building of a major printing company, Atsuo turned onto a narrow street. The crowd thinned out as he passed book binders and printing shops. The buildings were all small, two-story wooden structures.

"Why, oh, why da'ya looo-ook that a-waaaay . . ."

He had shaped it into a semblance of a song. The winding road led to a main thoroughfare. On the corner was Fukawa Motors, where Atsuo worked. A gas station faced the main road. In back was a parking lot and an auto repair shop, where several young men were raising shutters and tidying up the premises. As he entered, they grunted and lowered their heads in unison, as if on signal. This was a bit of military style decorum Atsuo had taught them — a kind of salute soldiers give to an officer. He returned it with a "Ya!" and a brisk nod, then headed for the locker room at a corner of the shop.

He took off his suit and picked up a work uniform. It had a big grease stain on the belly. He clucked his tongue and selected another. He couldn't be comfortable if he didn't start the day with a clean, freshly ironed uniform. It was bound to become soiled over the course of working, but starting off completely clean in the morning was his rule. So he had bought five uniforms in addition to the two the company issued. He rotated them through the laundry. It ran up expenses, but he looked sharp every morning. That was the important thing. He had decided he would be that way when he first started working at the shop.

It was part of the resolutions he had made upon his return to "the world," after finishing his last prison term. "You're almost forty," he had told himself. "You can't go on the way you have. No matter what happens, you're not going back to prison."

Atsuo had set out for himself a program of duties designed to deter further lawbreaking. They didn't really amount to much. You might call them a set of charms. First, he sent New Year greeting cards to everyone he owed a debt of gratitude. It was an annual renewal of his resolve to inform his former lawyer, his rehabilitation counselor, his younger sister, and her husband that he had passed the year with no untoward incident. Second, his clothing was always sharp; a first-class business suit and tie or a clean uniform. Third, he did no work that involved handling cash, no back office work, and no collecting of proceeds — only shop work. Fourth was regular exercise. That was the ice skating, which he had learned as a boy, and recently had re-learned from the basics under an instructor. Number five, he was always at work on time. Number six . . .

Oh well, there were several other charms. Atsuo felt that they supported him, body and soul, somehow making it possible to live in this world. He lived in dread that violating even a single one would somehow relax the tension keeping his world from falling apart, the way a single puff on a cigarette can make a mockery of years of abstention from smoking.

He knew how others regarded him: strong willed, punctilious, studious, a dependable worker, a lover of cleanliness, exacting in his work, quiet, gentle. Various words were used to describe Atsuo Yukimori, but he knew that none of them reflected his true self. He considered himself dissolute, weak willed, frivolous, wayward, cold, brutal — although those negative appraisals didn't get to the whole truth either.

Eight twenty-seven. He went from the locker room to the break room and fixed his eyes on his watch. It was a hard rule that he made his appearance in the shop at precisely eight thirty. At twenty seconds before zero, he began walking at a sure, steady pace. The young men had formed themselves into a single rank and awaited him. Thus began "morning call."

Atsuo called roll, then pushed a bell on an upright post three times. There was an expectant pause before the company president, Ichiro Fukawa, opened the door of his office with a vigorous push. Fukawa gave the impression of someone who came rolling in. He was bald, and the belly of his work uniform, in tatters from too many washings, protruded like a watermelon. His presence was far from authoritative, but no one laughed. This was the man who had founded Fukawa Motors, single-handedly navigating the wave of Japan's motorization to build up a successful business with an outstanding record. He was president, chairman of the board and chief engineer. The day's work could not begin until his orders were given.

Fukawa's orders were meticulous. He divided the shop workers into three groups — for sheet metal painting, servicing cars to meet inspection requirements and engine overhaul. He gave a minute explanation of his estimates of the times required for the day's workload. The outside jobs he took for himself — picking up a car from a customer, transporting another car to an inspection station, collecting payments, etc. Atsuo, the shop foreman, would be solely occupied with directing the shop work schedule.

When morning call was finished Fukawa flashed Atsuo an eye signal, then invited him into the president's office. This was a room situated between the workshop and the gas station. It doubled as the reception and administration office for both.

Fukawa mopped away sweat with a damp towel and heaved a sigh.

"Go on, pull up a chair," he told Atsuo. Clearing his throat vigorously he went to the sink and gargled noisily. "I'm out of shape. Got to start doing some sort of exercise. You still skating?"

"Yes, every once in a while."

"Good for you, that's great. I really have to start doing something like that too. Here I am ten yours younger than you, and I weigh too much for my own good."

Atsuo smiled. Fukawa was sensitive about his baldness and obesity. He was pleased to refer to these things himself, but any mention from others would plunge him into a black mood.

Atsuo changed the subject for him. "The arrangements for the Hokkaido trip are all set." This comment moved Fukawa to joy. His eyes opened wide and his body seemed to pulse with waves of contentment.

"Ah, Hokkaido. Can't wait to go! Hope the birds aren't scarce this year."

"I had a phone conversation with my brother-in-law, and he was saying he's spotted a lot of duck and snipe. He says the grouse are breeding, too."

"That grouse is fine eating. Nothing like it under the sun." Fukawa licked his lips. He had sampled Hokkaido's own Ezo grouse for the first time the previous year. Since then, he had said repeatedly that the taste had been unforgettable and that he looked forward to sampling it again this year.

"He says the wild grape wine couldn't have turned out better."

"That's the stuff. Grouse and wild grape wine. Some of the great joys in this life. Oh, yes, that American-made rifle came the day before yesterday."

"At last!" said Atsuo with feeling.

"The order took two years to come through. Barrel by Hart — a Winchester Model 70, pre-64 mechanism and Conjure custom trigger."

"That's tremendous. Nothing but the world's finest parts."

"Yep, this year I'm going to be shooting in style with that baby."

A customer of the gas station came in. Kimiko Fujiyama, who handled office work, went to receive him. Fukawa followed, undergoing an instant transformation to the persona of the humble merchant, lavishing civilities on the customer.

Everyone sensed that office worker-cum-private secretary Kimiko Fujiyama was Fukawa's mistress. The times they would go off together supposedly to collect money from clients were apparently spent at "companion" tea rooms with semi-private booths, or at hotels. They seemed to take trips together on holidays as well. Rumor had it that Mrs. Fukawa was the only one who wasn't on to them.

Atsuo was earnestly regarding Kimiko's ample bosom and substantial bottom when he was startled by a tap on the shoulder from Fukawa. But the courteous smile for the customer remained at the corners of the boss's eyes, and he spoke agreeably.

"Got a minute? There's something I want to talk over."

"Right."

"Kimiko, I'm going out. Take care of things, will you?"

Kimiko Fujiyama responded with a musical "*Okaay!*" like an obedient child. Her voice was so youthful no one would guess she was in her mid-thirties. Fukawa got into the driver's seat of the truck. Atsuo climbed in beside him. As soon as they were in motion, Fukawa began speaking rapidly, as if impatient to get through everything he had to say.

"This is something I've really got to discuss with you. Can't talk about it in the shop with everyone around. Fact is, there's been a theft. An envelope containing 170,000 yen in cash disappeared from a drawer in my office. I realized it was missing three days ago, on Tuesday morning. There's a lock on the drawer, but it looks like I forgot to lock it the day before. On Monday, Kimiko was in the office all day. If it was stolen, it probably happened during the evening, while she was out for a moment. I've done my own investigating. I'm certain it wasn't Kimiko. I've had her in charge of the cash for two years and she hasn't made any mistakes. There's one strange thing. Kimiko says when she came back she saw Jinnai slip quietly out of the office."

"Yukichi?" Atsuo felt as if a cold blade had been drawn across his heart. Yukichi Jinnai was his younger sister's second son, from Nemuro, Hokkaido. He had been working there since the spring. Yukichi had come to Fukawa's attention over the New Year holiday, while the president was visiting Nemuro for some hunting. Yukichi had been working in the lunchroom run by Atsuo's sister and brother-in-law. Atsuo had put in a good word for him, and Yukichi had joined the auto maintenance crew at Fukawa Motors in the spring. Atsuo had neglected to mention Yukichi's police record.

The boy's habit of pilfering had been with him since elementary school. He had been caught several times taking money from change purses or the cash register. Upon finishing middle school, a friend of the family had found him a job at a plant processing walleye pollack in Raúsu, Hokkaido, but it had not lasted for long. Another friend set him up with a crew fishing for salmon by fixed shore net. That time, he had stolen the salary of another man in the dormitory. He was caught and sent to a juvenile reformatory. After his discharge, he was put to work at his parents' diner.

"There's no proof. It's not as if Kimiko caught him in the act. But the door to the office in the gas station was locked at closing time, so the only way to get in was from the shop. When you think about that . . ."

"Yukichi's not the only one who might have a reason for doing something like that."

"Sure, that's true." Fukawa gave this affirmation without hesitation. He stopped at a red light, put on the handbrake and turned, smiling.

"I'm not suspecting Jinnai. After all, he's your nephew. I think he's a steady, good kid. However . . ." The smile clouded, and he rolled his goggle eyes upward. The light turned green and the car sped ahead.

"There are a couple of other things. Maybe they're just coincidences, I don't know. I didn't say anything to you, but some money turned up missing from the dormitory about a week ago. Tomoyama's wallet, with 30,000 yen in it, disappeared."

Atsuo was silent. Tomoyama was a shop employee who shared Yukichi's room in the dormitory. "Now get this. Yesterday, I heard from Sonoko, the dormitory housemother. She said Jinnai suddenly bought a stereo and had it turned up so loud others could hardly hear the TV. I talked to him on the phone and told him to have some consideration."

"Well, I will look into this fully," said Atsuo with a heavy heart.

Atsuo kept a casual watch on Yukichi at work all that morning, but there was nothing about him that seemed out of the ordinary. Seen from certain angles, his short, square-shouldered figure was startlingly similar to his father, Torakichi Jinnai. Yukichi was spraying steam to clean an engine. The others had covered their faces with towels, but he calmly exposed his face to the white steam. His expression of stoic indifference had been inherited intact from his mother, Suéko.

Breakfast and supper were served at the dormitory, but the workers had to buy their own lunch. When the young men all trooped out to a local ramen shop, Atsuo used the brief period of their absence to head for the dormitory, which adjoined the auto repair shop. The first floor consisted of a kitchen, the superintendent's room and the dining room. Housemother Sonoko Kanéhara was in the kitchen, slicing vegetables. Atsuo asked her to show him to the second floor.

At the head of the stairs was a TV room with large zabuton cushions scattered about. The rooms where the young men lived, two to a six-mat tatami room, faced one another along the corridor, four on a side. Yukichi's room was on the far right. The fusuma door panels were open. Inside, the imposing silver stereo set clashed with the small desks and cheap shelving units that comprised the only other furnishings in the room.

"I hear there was quite an uproar yesterday," said Atsuo, as he peered at a map of Southeast Asia on the wall.

"There certainly was." Sonoko creased her brows as she patted down stray black hairs that showed traces of white at the ends.

"The noise was so sudden I thought we'd been hit by lighting. Somebody asked me to make him turn it down. I talked to him, but he wouldn't listen. He said war songs don't have the right impact if they aren't played loudly. I had to get the boss on the phone before he would stop. This dormitory is no place for a big stereo."

Yukichi's room was rather orderly. Surprisingly, there were a number of books in his bookcase. It was somewhat disconcerting that most were war tales or references on the old imperial army and navy.

Thinking this odd, Atsuo took another look at the map on the wall. It was a reproduction of a wartime map, labeled "Greater East Asia Co-Prosperity Sphere."

"Very peculiar taste," Atsuo muttered to himself. There hadn't been much opportunity to talk with Yukichi since he had started working at Fukawa Motors. This was Atsuo's first look at Yukichi's room. Their relationship was more shop foreman and worker than uncle and nephew.

"Since when has he been reading books like these?"

"Why, from the beginning. I don't know, I guess you would call him a militarist. He likes those songs. He's been asking me about army life ever since he found out my husband was killed in action in Manchuria. He really knows those war songs well. Sings them every night."

"Every night."

"Yes, indeed. With the other boys, it's nothing but rock. With him, it's nothing but war songs. Once he said he wanted to join the Self-Defense Forces. He brought back an application, but either his schooling or his scholastic ability wasn't enough. He was very annoyed."

Atsuo heaved a dismayed sigh, then shifted to a businesslike tone. "I understand Tomoyama's wallet disappeared last week."

"Oh, that," Sonoko said carelessly. "There's no telling where he lost it. Mr. Tomoyama says it was in his room, but he may have lost it outside somewhere. He's always doing something like that. If he hasn't forgotten his umbrella on the train, he's left his jacket at some pub or lost his commutation ticket somewhere in the subway."

"Do you know money was stolen from the office?"

"Sure I know." This time, Sonoko's eyes gleamed brightly, her expression serious. "Is Mr. Jinnai suspected of that?"

"That isn't what I meant, but Kimiko says she saw Yukichi going out of the president's office."

"I hope you don't think you think you can go by that." Sonoko wrinkled her nose as at a loathsome sight. "Kimiko says a lot that doesn't add up. Either she took the money, or, well, even if she didn't take it and simply lost it somehow, she is looking to put the blame on someone. What is she supposed to be, the president's private secretary? I would like to know how a woman with a husband and children can carry on the way she does!"

Sonoko's eyes blazed more intensely still. Atsuo was impressed. Men's eyes don't smolder this way, he thought. This phenomenon is unique to women.

Sonoko launched into a story, recounting events as if they were unfolding before her eyes.

The relationship between Kimiko and the president had recently become extremely blatant. Just the other day, Sonoko had seen signs of activity beyond the drawn curtains of the president's office. She tried the door, but it was locked from the inside. She called out and the president answered. "I thought it might be a burglar," she told him and withdrew. But there was something strange about the situation, so she went to watch from the window of the dormitory's lavatory that overlooked the president's office. After a time, Kimiko came sneaking out with one sock down around her ankle.

Last Saturday — no, the Saturday before — the president took Kimiko on a drive to Hakone. Fukawa had told his wife he was going on a company outing. Not having heard of any such outing, Sonoko followed their car.

"Eh? You followed them?"

"Sure. I can drive, too, you know. They would have spotted me if I took the company car, so I rented one. I put on dark glasses and a hat as a disguise. Followed them all the way to Hakone. They stayed at a hotel in Miyanoshita."

Once again, a sigh escaped Atsuo as he listened with a helpless feeling. Sonoko had started working for Ichiro Fukawa over ten years before, when he had just started his business. Now she was perhaps forty-four or forty-five. She hadn't remarried, she said, because she was too busy with her job. Previously, she had handled the office work, so she knew the business well. Though her status had fallen, she claimed Fukawa would listen to whatever she might have to say. She was wont to tell anyone who would listen that with only two years in at Fukawa Motors, Kimiko Fujiyama was an employee of little significance.

Actually, Fukawa had no great regard for Sonoko. He had once described her as "a troublesome battle-axe" and said she was far out of touch with present-day businesses practices. He had exiled her to the easy job of housemother when Kimiko Fujiyama joined the company. But Sonoko had rallied to the challenge by mounting a campaign to win support from the dozen or so boys in the dorm who worked in the body shop and the gas station. Her success in this effort had secured for her a certain status in the business. She had the boys call her "Mom" and cultivated popularity with them by communicating their grievances to the boss. She was an essential contact for Atsuo in his effort to get to the bottom of the questions about Yukichi.

Sonoko finally returned to the point. "Kimiko is the suspicious one. Mr. Jinnai didn't do it."

The boys arrived back from lunch. Atsuo called Yukichi over. "Got something to talk to you about."

Sonoko helpfully suggested they use the superintendent's room, so Atsuo and Yukichi went into her eight-mat room. The dresser and tea table bespoke a feminine presence. A simple arrangement of fragrant olive blossoms was on display in the tokonoma. Its heavy fragrance filled the room.

Atsuo took the head of the table, before the flowers, and gestured Yukichi to sit.

"I'll ask without beating around the bush. Where did you get the money for that stereo?"

"That's a funny way of asking," Yukichi answered defensively, stiffening his shoulders.

"Was it your own money?"

"Yeah, sure it was my own money."

"That's an expensive piece of merchandise."

"Got it in Akihabara for a hundred and twenty thousand. Twenty percent discount."

Yukichi was making around 50,000 yen a month. The cost was more than two months salary. "That for sure?"

"Is what for sure!"

"That you got it with your own money."

"Yeah, for sure," Yukichi said, in a surly tone. "But what's this all about?"

"I was worried," Atsuo said, forcing a smile. "Thought maybe you went into debt over it."

"Thanks. Sorry to worry you." Yukichi bowed his head politely, without sarcasm. "I saved up for it. I wanted it for a long time."

"Okay, good. Now there's one more thing."

"It's too noisy, right?" Yukichi broke in. "Yesterday 'Mom' scolded me about it. I'll get a pair of headphones. I won't play it again until I do."

"All right."

"Well, gotta' go. A guy's waiting to play catch."

Yukichi sprang up. Atsuo said to his retreating figure, "What do you say tonight we go out to eat? Maybe have a little to drink."

Yukichi thought it over for a moment then answered in a small voice, "Yeah, sure."

Fukawa was waiting for Atsuo at the shop. "What happened?" he asked. "You went into the dorm, so I suppose you talked to Jinnai. Right?"

Atsuo answered politely, with a distressed smile at Fukawa's impatience. "That's right. But please give me a little more time. I still don't know."

"A lot of money is missing. That puts me in a bind. I don't want to notify the police if I can help it."

"Of course. I'll investigate thoroughly." Atsuo said with a bow of his head. Fukawa nodded and bustled away.

Atsuo's outing that night with Yukichi was convened at a bistro located behind the second-hand bookstore quarter of Jimbocho. The giant size red paper lantern hanging outside was a signboard proclaiming a place offering drinks and dinner on the cheap. Its target clientele was students, but it was also frequented by many people on their way home from work. In his sweater, Yukichi could have been taken for a student cultivating the business suited Atsuo as a valuable contact in his chosen career.

For Atsuo, it was a rare event to be out drinking. Part of the reason was that his considerable expenditures on clothes, shooting, and skating left little extra spending money, but the main issue was that he couldn't relax in a crowd. He was feeling distinctly uncomfortable to be perched on a stool with his back exposed to the stares and voices of people all around. Yukichi seemed accustomed to places like this. His eyes narrowed like a contented cat upon his second glass of shochu and hot water.

"I see you can handle that stuff. That's heredity for you— just like your papa," Atsuo said, reflecting that this was the first time he had ever been out drinking with Yukichi.

Yukichi had still been in grade school when Atsuo returned to Hokkaido after his last release from prison. The boy was athletically inclined, like his father. He had been on his middle school's speed skating team. It seemed phenomenal how he had grown in a few short years. Working as a fixed-net fisherman had broadened his shoulders and chest. After taking him to Tokyo, Atsuo had been startled the first time he saw Yukichi smoking. It had looked to him like a little boy playing grownup.

"So what do you think of Tokyo?" he asked, affection in his voice.

"What do I think of Tokyo? Well . . ." Yukichi's expression showed he was pondering what to make of the question.

"When you first got here, you said the crowds made you tired," Atsuo prompted. Yukichi answered only with a vague "Yeah," and tossed down more shochu.

When Yukichi had first arrived in Tokyo in April, Atsuo had taken him to Uéno Park to see the cherry blossoms by night. Yukichi had complained repeatedly that he couldn't stand the throngs of people. His complaints that the sounds of traffic kept him awake at night had continued for the first two or three weeks.

"It's been six months. I expect you've gotten used to the big city. You've learned your job pretty well, too, kid."

"Yeah," Yukichi said, swallowing more shochu. There wasn't much left of his second glass. Like his father, Yukichi was normally not very taciturn, but occasionally something would send him into a silent mood, suddenly revealing stark discontent, like a reef emerging at ebb tide.

"Hey, listen." Atsuo smiled at Yukichi, his eyes seeing past the reef. "Your uncle wants to see you standing on your own feet by and by. Fortunately, you learn quickly. You're good with your hands, and you really are suited to the job."

"I can't even learn the basics," Yukichi muttered. He was stroking his empty glass. Atsuo ordered a third round.

"Basics? What basics?" he asked gently.

Yukichi raised his head. His eyes were points that moved restlessly. "I can't learn the English words. I don't understand electricity. I don't get the theory. It's just no good."

"That's nothing to worry about. Your uncle didn't know any English or electricity either. I didn't know anything at first. But cars just aren't that complicated. The only English you need is just some words. No big thing. You'll pick it up."

"This job isn't for me. I tried it for six months and I know."

"Not yet you don't. You have to stay with it longer. Look, you're a fast learner. Faster than Tomoyama, and he graduated high school. He's been here a year longer than you and he still doesn't know the parts of the engine." Atsuo had decided to disparage Tomoyama as a way of encouraging Yukichi.

"He's slow and he gives up too easily. He said he was going to get a ham license and set up a station. The next thing you know he started electric guitar. Then it was English conversation. The last I heard, he was going on and on about yoga like he knew all about it.

He talks big, then forgets about it. You're not like that. I hear you know a lot of war songs."

"Yeah. Those songs are great." At last, Yukichi was smiling. "Makes me feel good to sing 'em."

"And that's why you bought that stereo."

Yukichi's expression became earnest.

"Uncle, I want to join the Self-Defense Forces. But I can't because I didn't graduate high school. You can get in as a student after middle school, but that's only up to age seventeen."

"And you're nineteen."

"You can't do nothin' if you didn't go to high school."

"That's the way it is," said Atsuo, as much to himself as his nephew. Suddenly, he felt as if he and Yukichi were enclosed in a thick glass capsule, sealed off from the clamor of the surrounding crowd. A warmth only they could share flowed between them.

"Now listen to me. You don't have any choice. You have to stay with this job whether you like it or not. Uncle won't do you wrong. Stick with it, kid."

Instead of answering, Yukichi took a vigorous swallow of shochu, laid the glass down and nodded agreement by letting his head fall, like a marionette. He was obviously quite drunk.

Yukichi's behavior problem was partly why he hadn't been sent to high school, but the central factor was his family's poverty. Torakichi was basically a hunter, whose income was limited to the hunting season in fall and winter. The diner that was started as a side business was located on a back street where few customers strayed. The eldest son, Tetsukichi, had been sent to a fisheries high school. It had taken much scraping to manage his tuition costs. There simply hadn't been anything left for Yukichi's education.

At the end of the counter was an old-fashioned black-and-white television set tuned to the news. The scene showed a vast assembly of students wearing construction helmets, with towels tied around the lower halves of their faces. Each brandished a long piece of building timber. The sticks swayed like a field of reeds in a strong wind. The picture changed to an old-fashioned, fortress-like building with an imposing tower that belonged to a national university. The announcer's voice resonated pathos, reminiscent of the style once used for news reports from the battle front.

" . . . the situation at T. University, which has been the scene of continuing disturbances, has reached the outcome that had been most feared. The forces of Zenkyoto, the Japan Federation of Student Joint Struggle Committees, who are in opposition to a number of sects aligned with the Japan Communist Party, have rejected a call from the university for a meeting of all sides and declared that the talks have broken down. Last night, Zenkyoto began sealing off two or three school buildings, and is in the process of surrounding the entire campus with a barricade. A force of JCP aligned sects is posed to prevent completion of the barricade. They have approximately 600 members, including about 500 students from campuses all over Tokyo. There have been clashes between the two sides, starting with a melee this evening in front of the university library, in which construction timbers were wielded as weapons. It appears that numerous casualties have resulted on both sides. Now we bring you live coverage from the scene of the disturbances."

The scene switched back to the Tower. It had the aura of a western style citadel from the Middle Ages, bathed in a whitish light, timeless and cold. At its base were signs bearing hand-painted slogans, flags and a group of helmeted figures sitting on the ground. Next, the outside of the library was shown. In the foreground were countless splintered construction spars and battered helmets. Behind it was a mob of helmeted youths restlessly bounding about.

"What in blazes are they trying to do?" Atsuo muttered. "Do you understand it?" Yukichi seemed interested in this question. He gave a drunken nod.

"A little, yeah. The point is, see, they want to bust things up. Blow everything away."

Actually, Atsuo knew something about that game. He had a vivid mental flash of a scene in a northern wilderness; a white light racing across a field, then an explosion.

The link between those campus scenes on the TV screen and the field featured in the theater of Atsuo's mind lay in an experiment he had conducted the previous fall. On the way back from hunting in the wooded environs of a lake, he had stuffed smokeless powder taken from shotgun shells into a Coke bottle, wired it up, and set it among the reeds by a river. He had used a battery to detonate the bomb by remote control. As far as he was concerned, it was just idle play, but it had set off a violent explosion that flattened the reeds and tilted back an alder tree some distance away. Atsuo had experienced a wave of pleasure at having unleashed such a force from a mere Coke bottle. It was an electrifying sensation that pulsed throughout the body, like what one feels upon ejaculation.

"Hey Uncle, what's the matter?" said Yukichi, giving Atsuo a worried look. This jarred Atsuo back to reality. He thrust his chin at the television set.

"Just trying to imagine how those guys must feel about wanting to blow things up. How do you think it feels?"

"Don't ask me," Yukichi said with an awkward shrug. He was silent for a moment. Then he began speaking, sounding like a tape recorder that had been switched on abruptly.

"I caused some trouble in the reformatory. Broke rules — porking a younger kid. So I was punished. They locked me up in a little room. I was there for days and days. All that time I was thinking, I want to blow this place up. You know? Bust it all. Everything."

"And now how do you feel?" asked Atsuo, leaning back a bit to avoid Yukichi's fists, which he had begun brandishing to punctuate his recitation. "Do you feel like smashing something right now?"

"Yeah, I do," he said, slamming the table hard enough to raise the proprietor's eyebrows and elicit a restraining "Hey!" from him.

"What on earth do you want to smash?"

"Dunno."

"Listen to me," said Atsuo. "There's nothing you need to smash now."

"If there isn't anything, then I'll find something," Yukichi said with an exaggerated wave of his arm, clearly drunk, his voice unnecessarily loud.

"Uncle, there's no fun in just breaking things. It's no good if you don't have an explosion. See? If you want to get an explosion, there's got to be some kind of strong resistance. Yeah, that's it. That's what they're up to," he said, pointing to the television. "First they get the riot police mad, see? Set up the resistance for the big bang!"

Yukichi sounded like he knew what he was talking about, Atsuo reflected admiringly. He recalled his second explosion experiment. By using an iron pipe with a screw down stopper, he had produced a terrific blast that blew away a large alder and caused a plume of smoke and earth to rise several meters high. The stronger the resistance, the bigger the explosion. He wished he could have shown that blast to someone. He longed to make the world know that one man, Atsuo Yukimori, could wield power on such a scale.

Atsuo cut Yukichi off before he could call for a fourth round.

"Forget it," said Atsuo waving a restrictive hand. He made the mistake of adding, "That's too much for a kid."

"I'm no kid," said Yukichi, truculently. "I pay my own way, not like those college kids. They're living off their parents while they act big." He jabbed a scornful thumb at the television screen, where a student was standing at a lectern, giving a speech. The face that filled the screen was that of a youth Yukichi's age.

"Okay, you support yourself. But you still have a lot to learn about life."

"I know how to cut the gills from a walleye pollack. I can scale it and clean out the guts. I know what it's like to stand all day doing that. I know how to pull in a salmon net. I know all that stuff good. Not like the college brats. All they know is what's in a book."

Yukichi was again speaking loudly enough to catch the attention of the proprietor, who looked as if he was about to say something. Before Atsuo could tell Yukichi to pipe down, five or six youths who looked like students came in. They were talking loudly to one another, making a considerable racket. Taking a tatami room in the back, they immediately began clapping and singing. They started with the "Internationale," then launched into labor movement songs.

Yukichi kept quiet for a time, as if intimidated. But then he bellowed, "Too damn noisy!" This produced no reaction of any kind. His voice had been drowned out.

"Shit!" he yelled, and stood up.

Atsuo pulled him back. "Leave them be. They sound like they want to blow something up too. You were sympathizing with that a minute ago."

"I wasn't sympathizing with them. It was just interesting to watch."

"So sit back and enjoy."

"Ain't nothin' to enjoy here." He called for a fourth round. The proprietor looked inquiringly at Atsuo.

"You heard me order. Give it to me!" Yukichi yelled. The proprietor returned a hostile glare, and Atsuo hastily intervened.

"Let's just make it beers. I'll take a break with one too." He winked at the proprietor, who looked over to the youths in the back room.

"Full of pep, aren't they? These days it looks like we old folks don't count for much."

A man sitting next to Atsuo chimed in, "You can say that again. The kids cry and make a fuss and they get their way. That's the kind of world it is." The man was past middle age. He was among a group of older people who looked like his coworkers.

"All right!" said Yukichi abruptly, with a loud hand clap. Without further ado, he began singing.

Under falling snow our troops advance o'er the ice
No way to know which course a river, which a road
Though horses fall, they cannot be left behind
This is the land of the enemy."

One after another, faces turned to Yukichi with startled expressions. Someone said, "Hey, I haven't heard that for years." A few sang along. Pretty soon, half the guests in the place were clapping time. The students' revolutionary songs were drowned out.

But the accompaniment petered out in the second and third chorus, leaving Yukichi to carry on alone. He continued in a ringing voice through to the fourth and final chorus. There was applause. Atsuo had been surprised at how well Yukichi knew the lyrics, but was even more surprised at the quality of his voice. It was both resonant and expressive.

Yukichi jumped atop his stool, took a bow and surveyed his audience. "Thank you folks, you're so kind. As a token of my gratitude, I will be glad to take anyone's request. As long as it's a war song, anything goes."

"Anything at all?"

"Yes, my friend. You name it and I'll sing it from memory."

Atsuo was worried. There was no graceful way to stop the boy now. There was nothing to do but sit back and let events proceed. It was rather pleasant to see his quiet nephew so enlivened.

The first request was an easy one, "Battlefield Compatriots." Atsuo joined in for all fourteen verses and received praise from on high.

"Uncle, you got it all perfect!"

Many of the requests were for long ballads. Yukichi breezed through "Courageous Bombers Three" and "March of the Kwantung Army" without fudging a line. By then he was getting hoarse. The other customers, enthusiastic at first, were now talking among themselves, no longer looking his way.

When Yukichi started on "Colonel Tachibana," Atsuo could tell it was time to bring the curtain down. He, too, had learned that song, long ago. It consisted of thirty-two verses; nineteen to part one and thirteen to part two. It was not the time for such an endurance test.

"Hey, let's go," he said, slapping Yukichi's knee. He paid the bill, and out they went. Yukichi walked with brisk, sure steps. The singing seemed to have sobered him up.

"You've got quite a memory, kid. Where did you pick up those songs?"

"Long time ago in the reformatory. There was this guy who liked them."

"So that's what you learn in a reformatory. With a memory like that, you shouldn't have any trouble with English words."

"Nope. I just can't get into English, so I can't learn it."

"And war songs you like."

"Yeah. Actually, what I really like is war. Just destroy everything. That's what I call a party!"

Atsuo was thinking "War is no party," but he kept his mouth shut. Never had he spoken to Yukichi about the war. It wasn't an easy subject, and there was much he wanted to keep under wraps. Besides that, Yukichi had not been the sort of child to ask adults to tell him about things. He was prone to melancholy, to going off quietly into a corner.

They threaded their way through a back street behind the bookstore district. The houses were all shuttered, to a slightly eerie effect. Half scrambling to keep up with his sure-footed nephew, Atsuo brushed against the handlebar of a bicycle leaning against a telephone pole, and knocked it over.

"Drunk," said Yukichi humorously as he righted the bicycle.

"Confounded twerp! You drank four times as much as I did."

"That's youth for you," Yukichi laughed.

"No, it's heredity," Atsuo answered back. Speaking these words filled him with warm feelings he associated with that blood relationship.

Yukichi came up shoulder to shoulder with Atsuo. "Uncle, listen," he said. "Money was stolen from the office, right? It wasn't me. I've got no reason to do anything like that."

"You knew about it?"

"Everyone knows. 'Mom' was squawking about it. But I got that stereo with my own money. You can take a look at my bankbook. That's proof."

"That's okay. I believe you."

"Thanks," said Yukichi with a laugh. It was the same guileless laugh that he had as a small child.

They reached Ochanomizu Station. Atsuo was expecting to see his nephew off to his dorm at the subway entrance, then get on the national railway line for the ride back to his own apartment. But before he could get out a word of farewell, Yukichi said, "Let's go see what's up at the campus."

"Campus? You mean T. University?"

"Yeah. It said on the news those two sects might tussle tonight. If I go back to the dorm I can't listen to the stereo, and everybody just wants to watch stupid TV programs. There's nothing to do."

"Well . . ." As Atsuo hesitated Yukichi was already walking. His retreating figure exuded confidence that his uncle would follow. That is what Atsuo did, with a pained smile. When he caught up, Yukichi again burst into song.

Striking down the unrighteous, in Heaven's service
Soldiers without peer, brave and true
Send them forth with exultant cries!
Land of our fathers and mothers, the hour has arrived!

This kid is starting to get to me, Atsuo thought with annoyance. He too had memorized that song once upon a time. He seemed to recall that people from his neighborhood council had been singing it for the new recruits when he enlisted. His head a fuzzy billiard ball, he had stood amidst cheers and cries of "Banzai!" before the rising sun flag and a banner with the words "Congratulations to enlistees!"

He was looking backward down a thirty-year tunnel to his youth. As a non-commissioned officer, he had taught the troops to use this song for pacing. From the second verse on, first the scouts, then the engineers, gunners, infantry, cavalry, transport corps, and finally, the medics would each sing in turn. It was supposed to take exactly five minutes to go through all ten verses; thirty seconds for each six-line verse, at five seconds per line. So the song could be used to count off blocks of time. Yukichi wouldn't know this, Atsuo thought as he sang along.

When they had finished, Atsuo sighed pensively.

"Great singing, Uncle!"

"Damn right. You're talking to a former army sergeant."

"An NCO! Uncle, you had rank!"

"You've got to show a little respect."

"I do respect you, Uncle. Hey, tell me — how many you killed."

"What do you need to ask questions like that for?"

"Well, you were in combat, right?"

"Yeah, I was in combat. But my company was machine gunners and the enemy was far away. So I don't really know."

"A machine gun company! You must've done some real shooting!" Yukichi mimed squeezing a trigger and provided the sound effects: "*Da-da-da-da-da-da!*"

Within a cavernous space in Atsuo's mind a vision appeared of enemy troops being mowed down. He had killed people, no doubt about it. Maybe a substantial number, but he wasn't sure. War is like that. Not like hunting. If you are after duck or deer, records of kills are kept. The meat and bones from the carcasses are consumed as food. In war, there is no limit to the number of people you kill, according to your strategy for winning. The killing is a military achievement on the way to the goal. The dead serve no purpose after they have been killed. You just leave them to rot or be discarded.

"There's nothing fun about war," Atsuo said lamely, and again stopped. He was pained by Yukichi's clowning, but he had no idea how to make his wartime experiences understandable to the boy. War was a subject too big, too complicated, too uncanny to express in terms Yukichi would understand.

~

A pushing, jostling mob had materialized from somewhere on the sidewalk outside T. University. Under the circles of light from the streetlamps it was possible to pick out the faces of office workers, housewives, students and old people, but beyond that the faces quickly dissolved into a uniform flow of anonymous bodies. A line of helmeted students, the anointed ones of the hour, surged through this crowd. They had the bearing of a privileged class that expects the masses to make way for them.

Metropolitan Police Department riot control officers bearing Duralumin shields formed a ring around the outer walls of the university, a somber force standing as an additional barrier. A line of gray buses with wire mesh covered windows, like these used to transport prisoners, were parked nearby. More armored police could be discerned in their shadowy interiors, looking like robots waiting to be switched on.

At the main gate was a sign with the words "Absolutely no admittance to non-university personnel." This was the university's way of saying it would solve its problems by itself, but it could also be taken as an assertion that its problems were of no concern to ordinary people. Atsuo felt resentment at this implication, forgetting that he was only there as a curiosity seeker.

The iron central gate was drawn across the broad promenade leading into the campus. The side gate was flanked by regular university guards who held back the crowd pushing forward to gather there. The guards occasionally admitted people who appeared to be students, faculty members or press.

Atsuo was disappointed by the sight of this checkpoint as they emerged at the gate. He assumed they wouldn't gain admission, but Yukichi whispered, "Don't worry. You're a professor and I'm a student. We just walk in."

Atsuo hesitated. He was conditioned to be in awe of state institutions. From his point of view, a national university was like the army, prisons, and the police, in that it had authority. He had a gut fear that this authority might be brought to bear on him at any time. The university guards projected the same aura of power as policemen.

Yukichi hissed, "Here we go. Look unconcerned," and strode confidently toward the wall of guards. Like magic, he passed through unmolested. Atsuo followed, as if swept along by Yukichi's momentum.

Lights from inside buildings and streetlamps made the campus surprisingly bright. The ginkgo trees had turned bright yellow, contributing to a festive mood. People swarmed in every direction. Yukichi struck out toward some destination he evidently had in mind. Atsuo hurried after him with an uneasy feeling there would be trouble if he lost sight of his nephew.

The Tower that was so familiar from the recent TV news reports rose up from the darkness, its outline eerily sharp, as if hidden lights were trained on it. On television it had appeared white, but now he saw it was made of blood-red brick.

The quadrangle in front of the Tower was filled with helmeted students, all sitting on the ground. Against a background of signboards and banners bearing slogans, a frenzied speech was being delivered in monotonous bursts, like savage howls. It sounded for all the world like a Hitler speech from an old newsreel.

Yukichi threaded his way among this sea of helmeted youths, deftly avoiding construction staves scattered everywhere. Atsuo followed, taking care to imitate Yukichi's footwork, all the while wondering if the students beneath those helmets were truly normal people. Why weren't they challenging him and his nephew as interlopers? How could they sit there expressionlessly, listening submissively to such a tedious harangue?

They reached the edge of the woods, and their ears were filled with a nearly deafening mid-autumn chorus of locusts. Even the unintelligible noise blasting from loudspeakers around the Tower, on rooftops and over pathways were no match for the power of the locusts' lucid tones. Yukichi scrambled up an embankment, then extended a hand to pull Atsuo up beside him. This elevated position afforded an excellent view of the entire quadrangle.

"How come you know this campus so well?" Atsuo asked.

"Been coming every night. Here, let me show you something." Yukichi searched for a moment in the shrubbery that covered the embankment. Finally, he extracted a helmet and put it on his head. It bore the name of some sect. Next, Yukichi produced a towel and adroitly tied it around the bottom of his face. Now he looked like all the other student activists.

"You're just full of surprises. Where'd you steal the helmet?"

"Picked it up somewhere. They get scattered all around after a battle."

"You'll be pegged a radical."

"That's okay. Everyone's afraid of radicals now. I'll get respect."

"What a numbskull! At least you don't intend to join in any rioting, right?"

"Just once. I want to see what it's like to go berserk."

"Damn fool. What do you do when they find out you're not a student here?"

"First of all, no one is going to find out, and it wouldn't matter anyway. There aren't all that many kids from this school in that crowd over there. Everyone came from outside. You put on the right helmet and presto, you're a comrade. Un-oh, looks like action is brewing."

The youths in the plaza were all standing, their sticks upraised. Yukichi removed his helmet and carefully returned it to its hiding place in the brush.

"Wonder what happens now."

"There's going to be a brawl."

"With who, for goodness sake?"

"The enemy."

"What enemy?"

"Who cares? It's a rival sect. Let's go check out the forces on the other side."

Yukichi slid down the dark side of the embankment with practiced movements. Atsuo hesitated, unsure of his footing in the pitch darkness. Yukichi shined a flashlight at his feet, well prepared by his nightly visits to the campus.

Treading on fallen leaves, they made their way along a narrow footpath that wound around a pond and over a hill. As they emerged from the trees, a large building came into view. It was the library that had been shown on the news, but, like the Tower, it lacked the strange charm it had when seen on television. In real life it was just an ordinary building, yellow with age.

There was a group of youths in the front plaza. Half wore helmets. All kinds of clothing were in evidence, including black high school uniforms, dress jackets and overalls. It hardly seemed like a coherent group.

The broad staircase to the library was packed with a helmeted group armed with sticks, about two hundred strong. As if on command, they gave a war cry and brought their sticks down in unison. Again a cry, and the sticks rose. The action was repeated a number of times. Presumably, this was supposed to be a kind of military drill, but there was no uniformity in the troops' movements. They didn't assume any particular stance when they brought their weapons down. The exercise hardly amounted to useful preparation for battle.

Atsuo thought rifle and bayonet drills should be done more intensively than that. He recalled the attack drills he had put new recruits through, years before. Given an hour with these youths, he could turn them into a top outfit.

"Here, this way."

Atsuo followed Yukichi to the edge of the wood. By a set of concrete pillars joined at the top by a bridge,— probably a wisteria trellis — was a gathering of about a hundred men in dress suits, looking like faculty. One had a portable loudspeaker he was using to make an appeal to the students. Enough violence, he was saying, let's talk it over and work things out. But his words were lost amid angry outcries from the students. The speech was having no effect at all.

Then, unexpectedly, the students broke into cheers. A large sound truck equipped with a speakers' platform had pulled up. In a moment, someone had begun a speech from atop its roof. The volume was turned up to a level painful to the ears. The sound dominated the area. The speaker atop the truck began to lead the students in choral chanting. The students raised their fists and yelled "No!" to something from the leader that Atsuo wasn't able to make out.

As if on signal, the youths fell into formation. Then, laying their sticks down, they formed a colossal single file line that zig-zagged back on itself again and again as it slowly moved around the quadrangle. Just before their eyes, a girl at one end of a segment that had changed direction was being tossed about helplessly amidst the surging male bodies as she went by.

"Here they come!" Yukichi cried jubilantly, with the excitement of a fan at a horse race. It was the Phantom Trooper Corps from the Tower, mounting a charge. There was no bugle, but there were bloodcurdling battle cries, exactly like those Atsuo remembered from his army days. The force at the library, which had been advancing, quickly responded for the counterattack by falling back to the stairway to yield the forward position to their shock troops, who wielded signboards like shields, using them to push back the assault force. From behind the shields they struck out with their sticks.

Howls of rage, savage shouts, wails of anguish, taunts, police whistles, sounds of collisions and wreckage. News photographers appeared from nowhere, darting about and setting off flashes that highlighted tableaux of distorted faces, bulging eyes, masked faces, hatred, excitement, anguish, and blood.

Moments before the clash, the band of faculty members had tried to head off the battle. They were beaten off by students from both sides. Now, as the fury of the battle intensified and blood began to flow freely, the school authorities began shouting: "Stop!" "Enough violence!" "You'll be killed!" "Talk it over." They were attacked again and fled.

Since no one was wearing a uniform, there was no way to be sure who one's enemy was. Several youths clustered around one who had fallen, showering him with blows. The fallen youth's shirt became sodden with his blood, but the blows continued to fall. When his helmet flew off, his head was beaten. He put his hands over his head and soon they, too, were covered with blood. Sticks were used to poke at his head and eyes. Even when the victim stopped moving, the beating continued relentlessly.

Atsuo recalled a newspaper article he had read recently. A radical student of a certain university had been captured by a rival sect. His hands were bound with wire. He was punched, kicked, and beaten with an iron pipe. Every one of his fingers was methodically broken. Water was dumped on his head when he lost consciousness, over and over. The reporter had asked some students who were involved if the object of this torture was to get information. The reply was no, it was to make the prisoner suffer. At the time he read the article, Atsuo had thought the reporter had been exaggerating. Now, his own eyes saw evidence that there had been no exaggeration.

The situation resolved itself into a win for the Phantom Trooper Corps. The forces from the library fled. The winning side gathered on the library stairway and raised whoops of victory. It was the same scene regularly played out by crowds who gather at the imperial palace gate draped with the rising sun flag to shout their banzais to the emperor.

The victorious students were picking up signboards, helmets and other war trophies. About ten prisoners, hands bound behind their backs, were marched to the top of the stairs for all to see. Though it was off in the distance and hard to be sure, it seemed to Atsuo that one of the prisoners was a girl. Since there were women in both of the radical camps, it was not really surprising that a woman should turn up among prisoners. Nevertheless, Atsuo found it amazing, because, as far as he had been able to see, everyone trading blows in battle had been male. He thought of the girl student with the slender, fragile-looking fingers he had seen in front of the station that morning. This girl also looked like a small, slender child.

"Is that a girl there, among the prisoners?"

"Where? Too far away to tell."

"Let's get closer and find out."

"Uh-uh. It's time to clear out."

Trouble was again brewing. The radicals had gotten into a shouting match with the faculty. The portable loudspeaker that had been in the hands of one faculty member was snatched from his hands and he was sent reeling. The radicals formed themselves into a line, their sticks poised to charge. Forced to retreat step by step, the faculty members finally bolted into the woods.

Atsuo was convinced. "Yeah. If we're going to make our break, now's the time."

Yukichi took his uncle by the arm, leading him at a run through the trees. At that moment, the students all set upon the fleeing group of faculty members. Yukichi's flashlight was a godsend that helped several of the other running people pick their way along the uneven pathway in the darkness.

They reached the pond. Crossing a stone bridge, they followed an upward path, and were up on a hill when they had run themselves out of breath. They sat down on the slope, surrounded by the chirping of locusts in the deep grass. There was no one else around. The night was chilly. The effects of the alcohol they had consumed had disappeared.

31

Twenty after eleven. It was too late to catch a bus, but if they hurried, they could reach the station in time for their respective last trains running that day.

"I don't know about you," Atsuo said, "but I'm going home."

"Right." Yukichi rose alongside Atsuo.

"How do you get out of here?"

"Easy. You just walk out any gate. They don't check people going out. Same as a movie theater."

They emerged from the woods. Wending their way through a maze of paths winding among buildings large and small, they finally arrived at one of the campus gates. Atsuo headed for it, but Yukichi stopped.

"I'm going to check things out a little more," he said. The next moment he had disappeared.

It was already one a.m. when Atsuo was back at his apartment. There was a thick envelope in the box under his front door mail slot. Its bulk instantly told him the sender was his younger sister in Nemuro.

"Forgive my long silence. This is the first time I've had a chance to write since your last letter. That must have been before the Bon festival, around June, I guess, because I remember we were having a cold, foggy summer and you said it was the rainy season in Tokyo. I keep thinking how I wanted to write, but, you know how it is — no money and no spare time. The diner isn't doing any business, which is not good, but I have my hands full with piecework. Tailoring and mending clothes for little girls takes up a lot of time.

"Our shop is forlorn. We aren't running it as a diner. The city's population is continually shrinking, so we get fewer and fewer customers. That's just the way things are now. The days when the Kurile Islands were Japanese and Nemuro was a busy gateway city seem like a long-lost dream. Being a remote outpost isn't the half of it — people I know keep disappearing. It's like we're the only ones left. I don't mean to complain, but your leaving for Tokyo seven years ago was really sad. It is such an empty feeling to see your last blood relative leave.

"Now what was I going to tell you about? This always happens. I have one thing in mind, then my letter goes off in some other direction, all by itself. It's very frustrating. Oh, yes. I was going to tell you that since the hunting season started in October, Torakichi is out shooting every day, so we finally have a steady income. We are working hard to make sure everything is ready for you and Mr. Fukawa when you come to

Nemuro in November. Torakichi went to check out the hunting ground I don't know how many times.

"We haven't had a large number of guests yet, but hunters from Tokyo and Osaka are starting to come on Saturdays and Sundays. I guess we've had more than twenty so far. Most of our fishing customers are from Hokkaido. We have to turn them away if their plans interfere with the hunting calendar. We are looking forward to seeing you and Mr. Fukawa. You know, it has been a year since I've seen you. It would be so nice to have you visit during the Bon festival at least one more time. Excuse me, I'm grumbling again. I'll stop.

"Speaking of fishing. A big huchen salmon, all of 123 centimeters, was taken from the Furen River. It weighed twenty-one kilograms! It's been years since anyone caught a huch longer than a meter. This is about the second time in ten years. The person who caught it was the wife of a man who works in Nemuro. It was the first time she had ever been fishing. What's more, it just suddenly bit while she was practicing how to cast her lure. It just about pulled her into the river! She screamed for help. Fortunately, Torakichi was right there. He could tell it was a huch by the way it was fighting so hard and bending the rod so sharply. He let it run with the line so it would tire out. It took forty minutes before it tired enough to net. Imagine, 123 centimeters! He was afraid it would tear the net.

"Isn't that the most fantastic story you ever heard? I'm pretty sure the biggest huch you ever caught was about 80 centimeters, so that was really something.

"There I go, drifting off again. The main thing I wanted to talk about was Yukichi. I'm ever so grateful to you for getting Mr. Fukawa to hire that a boy like that. The thing that bothers me is that he hasn't written me a letter even once.

"I write him two or three times a month. Its not fair, and he's not doing right by his parents. I'm worried as I can be. When fall came, I wanted to know what he would need for the cold weather, so I wrote and told him to at least call to tell me what to send. He called that one time. He just said he didn't have the money for the pay phone, told me to call back and hung up. So I called him back and then all he had to say was he needed two sweaters and nothing else, goodbye. That was it. He was so brusque, like he wanted me to be upset. That worries me.

"That rude tone of voice reminded me of an unpleasant thing that happened. I apologize for keeping this from you until now. Last year, some money turned up missing from the cash register. I'd locked it up as always, but when I counted the proceeds, about 20,000 yen was missing. The boy's father voiced his suspicions and Yukichi suddenly took that brusque tone with his father. Then, before I knew it, they were going at each other. Yukichi had never been violent before, but he went after his father with everything he had. Torakichi is pretty strong himself from hunting and fishing and being out in the mountains, but he was no match for that boy. I thought he would be killed. Yukichi was that violent.

"So when I heard him take that tone on the phone, I could tell that something was going on inside him. A mother has a sense for these things, and I have a scary feeling. Please teach him. Show him the the way. You are the only one in Tokyo I can turn to.

"Sometimes when I'm sitting here, looking out over the Okhotsk Sea on days when the wind brings the cold into the pit of your stomach, I wonder how a boy like Yukichi came into the world. Tetsukichi is a good boy. He doesn't cause any worries. As you know, he has been in Akkeshi all along, working as a fisherman. He must be doing good work because in May they made him captain of a ten-man vessel. You know, as long as a boat is out at sea, the captain's word is absolute. They say even the boat's owner has to follow Tetsukichi's orders. And how he has filled out! He is really a fine-looking man now, with his suntan, and a bright look in his eyes. We think it is about time he found a wife, but he says first he wants to get his fishing license so he can go into business for himself.

"The only trouble is that a fishing license costs tens of millions of yen. I don't know where he is going to get that kind of money. I suppose having a dream about a huge fortune is just taking after his father. I just hope his big dreams aren't like his father's, which don't seem to be coming to anything.

"Tetsukichi says his ship recently ran into a Soviet patrol boat when they were within 200 miles south of Shikotan Island, inside Soviet waters. In other words, they were poaching. He says they got off by giving the Russians pantihose and disposable cigarette lighters. The boat could have been seized. That has actually happened several times. It worries me.

"In salmon fishing, you can't turn a profit if you worry about territorial waters. Tetsukichi says he's not bending the rules any more than what everyone else in the business is doing, and if he didn't he would never be able to get his license. I suppose it's the same with anything — the rules are one thing and the real world is something else again. But if he bends the rules too far and his ship is seized he would lose the boat. That would be a major loss, and he would be held for six months or a year, living on disgusting food. So I want him to be careful. He'll end up like Yukichi if he goes too far.

"Forgive me. I didn't particularly have you in mind in bringing all this up, but I guess it looks as if I did, so let me just come out and tell you what I'm really thinking about you. I just want you to know how thrilled I am that you have straightened out and are doing so well there in Tokyo. I know I have no right to be talking to you like a mother. It's just that now Mother is gone and I've reached her age I understand her feelings so well it hurts. Just about everything you did hurt her, but she forgave you everything and never got angry. That was the difference with Father, and his way of raising his hands whenever he got angry.

"I have something... Oh, I guess I might as well just write everything that is on my mind. I wanted to say this to you in person, but anyway, here goes.

"What do you think about the idea of getting married? There, I said it. I knew it would shock you if I wrote that right at the start. I suppose you think it's none of my business. I guess I should have eased into it more indirectly, but that's me. I just can't hide what I'm thinking. At least I held off until the end, even though I had it in mind right from the beginning, so please excuse me.

"It won't be long until you're fifty. That's not young, but it isn't very old either.

"You're living the best years of a man's life now. I know of someone. She's thirty-seven, a widow with no children. She lives here in Nemuro, and she's really beautiful. Her husband worked in a bank. He died unexpectedly two years ago, of cancer. She's all alone. She's the older sister of that woman who caught the 123-centimeter huch. After she caught the fish I was helping her make an ink rubbing print of it and telling her about a taxidermist, so we got to talking. She asked if I knew any nice available men. I said, well, there's my brother. I just meant it as a joke, but she took it seriously. She sent me her sister's picture afterwards. So I'm enclosing it. Please don't be angry. If you have someone else in mind you can laugh it off, or if you don't like the picture, you could just send it back."

Atsuo shook the envelope and a picture fell out. It was an amateur snapshot, a full-length view of a woman standing at a slight angle to the camera. She didn't look thirty-seven, but more like thirty. The only impression he received from the picture was that she had a large face.

"What do I think of this woman?" Atsuo grumbled in a loud voice as he prepared for bed. "Nothing! What am I supposed to think?" Though tired and sleepy, he did not forget to check that his alarm clock was set.

~

An insistent trumpet blast assaults his ears. Emergency muster! His mind frantically tries to leap from bed, but his body does not awaken. Sleep has saturated his muscles as if they were filled with mercury, making his movements sluggish. He must get his uniform on properly: the shirt, the trousers, then wrap the leggings. The leggings must be wrapped so the last triangles formed are perfectly aligned with the trouser seams. He wraps and re-wraps the leggings, but they won't come out right. A squad leader can't dress like a slovenly private. The troops have all gone. Sergeant Yukimori sits alone in the dark, struggling with his puttees.

The soldiers are lined up in the pale light of day outside the barracks. The commanding officer glares angrily at late arriving Sergeant Yukimori, the squad leader. Atsuo bellows commands, intent on making up for his tardiness. Tenhut! Eyes front! The commanding officer gives his return salute. Parade rest.

Atsuo notices something strange about the CO. He is an old guy with white hair. What's going on? Why, the face beneath the army cap is that of Ginji Sato. When did that old weasel get to be an officer? Oh, well, an officer is an officer. Know ye that a superior officer's commands are the direct pronouncements of the Emperor Himself. Old Ginji's word is law.

Commanding officer Ginji issues an order with solemn grandeur. "You will now undergo a special battle drill. Today we have specially provided a living person for your benefit. You will learn what it is to deal with living flesh. You will pay careful attention to this lesson."

This is a machine gun corps. The troops carry no rifles. If it comes to close fighting, they use short swords. Therefore, they have put in many hours of short sword drill.

The exercise now to be conducted is stabbing a human being with that short sword. The target is a prisoner bound with wire between a pair of posts in the middle of the assembly ground. A white spotlight shines upon the prisoner.

"There are eleven of you. To make sure everyone has a chance, you are to stay away from the throat and the heart. For everyone's sake, the prisoner will be kept alive for as long as possible. Sergeant Yukimori! You will provide the example for these troops!"

"Yessir!" Sergeant Yukimori vigorously extracts his short sword from its sheath on his waist. He strikes a spirited stance. All eyes are on him. He has put long hours into the upkeep of his sword. There are no sloppy traces of spindle oil on the guard. His puttees are in perfect adjustment, his stance — perfected through short sword drills — beautiful. As he charges with a homicidal cry, he tells himself that he will thrust into the target exactly as he has practiced numerous times with straw bags. But then the strength disappears from his arms. The target seems to be Ichiro Fukawa.

"Well, Sergeant Yukimori?"

"Yessir!" That was an order from the supreme commander-in-chief. It is not me who is doing this. With this thought, he regains control of his limbs. His sword sinks into the right side of the chest and Fukawa screams in anguish. Dark blood wells up, soaking his work uniform.

Sergeant Yukimori returns to direct the troops. Each of their swords flash in turn. Though his clothing is matted with heavy, oozing blood, Fukawa lives on. He looks outward, eyes opened wide. One of the soldiers thrusts off the mark. He sinks his sword into the left side of Fukawa's chest.

The head lolls, the body goes limp. Fukawa has died. Sergeant Yukimori bawls at the transgressor. "Jackass! What kind of simpleton stabs the heart?" he bellows.

But the private doesn't reply. He snickers. It is Yukichi Jinnai. Private Jinnai has disobeyed an order from the high command.

"Why didn't you obey the command?"

"He was going to die anyway. I put him out of his misery."

"But what about the others? They . . . they need their practice!"

Private Jinnai laughs scornfully. His laughter is like a crash of cymbals, but it doesn't die out. The crash goes on and on, filling the assembly ground.

Atsuo turned off his alarm clock, but he still heard that ringing laughter. Yukichi's laughing expression had been odious. No doubt he had been wearing such an expression the day he wrapped his fingers around his father's neck.

Sitting on his bed, Atsuo slapped the back of his neck several times to clear away the bad dream. His head was muzzy from lack of sleep. His temples throbbed. Several pages of the letter from his sister had fluttered from the bed and lay scattered on the tatami mat floor. There was the photo of the woman. Was marriage reasonable at his age? He looked about the room. Signs of an orderly bachelor's existence were everywhere.

The apartment consisted of one eight-mat room, dining-kitchen and bath-toilet. His combination living room and bedroom had a rug, with a bed, desk, bookcase, television set and gun cabinet squeezed into the available space. Nothing in this arrangement presupposed cohabitation with a woman. This room met the needs of him alone.

Atsuo shook his head crossly, meaning that he saw little chance of getting married. It would be risking too much change after he had finally gotten his life running smoothly. Besides, he had the feeling that any little alteration of his living pattern would be enough to wreck the system of charms that protected against recidivism. Those charms were carefully laid bricks in the walls around his daily life. I am a prisoner of these walls. They make me feel secure, the way any prisoner feels inside the walls that surround him.

He set about his morning tasks to get back on track. He had a daily routine to fulfill between five thirty when he awoke until his departure at seven o'clock. Wash, shave, then have toast and coffee while reading the paper. Make the bed, clean the room, do laundry, and hang it up by the window. Then, as necessary, perform maintenance on his guns or fishing gear. Maybe read a book. Nothing should be left undone to prey on his peace of mind after leaving the apartment.

When Atsuo checked his refrigerator, he clucked his tongue. No bread. He had meant to buy some on the way back from his outing with Yukichi. The adventure had ended so late he had forgotten. He could make rice and miso soup instead of toast and coffee, but the extra time required would interfere with the rest of his schedule. He decided to make do with rice crackers and coffee. But he couldn't get over the loss of his toast. It was a rent in the fabric of a day just begun. Dourly, he opened his newspaper.

The melee at T. University was on the front page. It occupied a lot of space there, as well as on the inside back page. Photos showed scenes he had witnessed. Atsuo was absorbed in the article, comparing his own observations with the reporting. He had to hand it to the reporters for getting the big picture and giving clear explanations of the events. The students in the Tower had been Zenkyoto students from the New Left, consisting of various groups who had broken with the Japan Communist Party line. The students at the library were led by keepers of the JCP faith. Their policy differences had spawned the violent clash. Um-hum. Atsuo nodded to himself, satisfied with this explanation.

But there was a fundamental question he still didn't understand. What makes students hate fellow students with such venom as to make them brutally beat one another? Atsuo had formerly engaged in the theft of other people's property. Documents written by prosecutors and judges handling his case had said, "desire for money drove him to theft," but he himself couldn't really say if he had been feeling a need for money prior to his thefts, or if there had ever been a decisive moment when he had decided to commit a crime. He didn't understand his former self any more than the officials who had judged him. This central issue had always been remained an unsolved riddle.

As usual, the article was accompanied by comments from intellectuals. The season of revolution is upon the universities, they said. The winds of youthful rebellion are sweeping the world. The fundamental problem is that the people running the universities are mired in the past. They are constitutionally unable to understand the revolution's significance. The universities are so out of tune with the times they should be dismantled and done away with. See the shining fruits of victory of the May Revolution in France. Learn from the great achievements of the Red Guard in China. The great Cultural Revolution is the key to a new future.

Dear me! Everyone has a consuming interest in revolution at the universities. It seems that the role of the intellectuals is to deliver heroic pronouncements that serve the students. Atsuo muttered sarcasms as he nibbled his rice crackers.

"That stuff ain't war; it's just child's play. A bunch of kids break windows and beat up their classmates. When they start ragging their professors, it puts all the adults in a panic. The newspapers and TV make a big deal about it, and the intellectuals get excited. The students get a charge out of this, so they really go wild breaking things."

Atsuo drank his coffee. He stood, folded his hands behind his back and took a few steps to the mirror. He nodded at the glass. "That's all it comes to. The first time I picked a guy's pocket, I did it because it was fun to see him get excited and make a fuss. You can't be a pickpocket if you don't get that rush."

Ginji's well-honed maneuver the day before had been a thrill, just as the battle of the student factions had been. Everyone gets a kick out of watching the kids, so they go crazy. The intellectuals say it's revolution. They make a big show about how seriously they take it, but nobody knows why students rebel, any more than they know why people commit crimes — or so it seems to me.

According to his wont of late, Atsuo opened his gun cabinet. The previous Sunday, he had broken down and thoroughly cleaned his two rifles and three shotguns in preparation for the trip to Hokkaido scheduled for the middle of November. The guns were all cheap and practical. He had long made loving use of them, and knew their idiosyncrasies well.

He removed a rifle. He knew there were no shells in the chamber, but checked it anyway before assuming a firing stance. He held the butt firmly against his right shoulder, cradling the barrel on the flat of his left hand. At this moment the gun became an extension of his body. He aligned the sight with a photograph of an Ezo deer on the wall. He crooked his finger, and recalled countless moments of gratification experienced upon firing.

Atsuo had been known as a sharpshooter from his days as a private. He had always placed first or second in his regiment in drills with the model 92 machine gun. In actual combat, he had outshone everyone in the machine gun corps. For some reason, he was perfectly suited for handling these instruments of death, as if his body had been especially made to order for that purpose. He didn't know why he had the ability, while others didn't. For example, it didn't matter how hard Ichiro Fukawa practiced shooting or how many millions of yen he spent on top quality rifles with precision scope sites. He couldn't match Atsuo with his cheap rifles equipped with nothing more than simple notch sights. This ability of Atsuo's had deepened his relationship with Fukawa far beyond that of the usual employer-employee relationship. To Atsuo, that bond was a very important element of the walls he had built about his present life.

Unexpectedly, Atsuo's left palm began to shake. The photograph of the deer jumped about. He couldn't align the sight. The muzziness in the core of his brain had spread to his cranium and now permeated the room. His temples hurt. He lowered the gun and returned it to its cabinet.

It was lack of sleep. Between staying out late and his bad dream, his brain had been given no chance to rest. It had been a dreadful dream that brought back a long forgotten wartime experience. The actual victim had been a China-man village chief. Atsuo was a buck private. It was the first time he had taken a sword to a human being. He felt as if there had been another dream before the one about the stabbing, but he couldn't quite recall. It was lurking somewhere in the dark core of his brain, sending out a gray cloud that brooded enigmatically in his consciousness.

As his mind groped after the elusive dream, he turned up something quite different, a recent memory that floated up from a corner of his mind. One day during the rainy season, Atsuo had been abruptly roused from his sleep in the early morning by an unexpected visit from a police detective. The policeman wanted to see his guns and ammunition. He said it was a routine inspection of gun licensees. Atsuo had never before undergone such an inspection, so he was suspicious of that explanation. Afterwards, he found out that on the day of the officer's visit, June sixteenth, there had been a bombing of a train on the Yokosuka line, which runs south from Tokyo. It was a terrible event. A time bomb placed on an overhead luggage rack had exploded, leaving one dead and eleven injured.

Atsuo kept a log book with meticulous accounting of ammunition. Every expended bullet was recorded, specifying the type and quantity of the charge and the place where it had been fired. The log had no shortcomings for the detective to fault. Moreover, Atsuo was cleared of any suspicion of involvement in the incident (which had taken place on a Sunday) when the detective learned he had been trout fishing with Fukawa that day and the day before at the Yugashima hot springs, on the Izu Peninsula. But it bothered Atsuo that there had been no investigation of Fukawa, who was also a gun owner. There was no doubt that Atsuo was questioned because he was the one with a police record.

The fact is, Atsuo had not told the detective the whole truth. He did not mention his bomb experiment by Lake Furen in the fall of the previous year. He had juggled his log to account for the extra expenditure of smokeless powder. He was not foolish enough to volunteer information to a detective about this forbidden use of gunpowder.

In any case, it was unpleasant to have been suspected. The detective's expression was disquieting; a cordial smile that did not quite conceal disdain. He put on a show of friendly belief with eyes that suggested hidden suspicion.

A series of bombing incidents had been occurring. A bomb had exploded in a lavatory of Hanéda Airport in February of the previous year. In March of that year, there was an explosion near the ticket reservation window at Kyoto Station. In April, a time bomb concealed in a book had been discovered on a super-express Shinkansen train. There was an explosion in July on the Boso-Nishi line. The explosion on the Yokosuka line in June drew the most attention because there had been loss of life and injuries. The police had mounted a sweeping investigation. Atsuo was just one of many bystanders caught up. Still, it bothered him.

Atsuo left his apartment at three minutes to seven. Descending the iron staircase, he looked up to a sky of glowering clouds, and wondered if he should go back to grab an umbrella. The weather report had said bad weather was in store the next day, but no rain before then. Okay, he decided, let's go by that.

He lived in a newly developed residential area. Its former field and woods were now nearly extinct, barely hanging on as doleful reminders of a rural past, still bearing trees whose yellowed leaves were stirring in the breeze with an authentic feeling of autumn. On the far side of the field was a psychiatric hospital, an eerie-looking building with iron-latticed windows. At that moment, some nurses were herding patients out into the garden. It wasn't very cold, but the patients were bundled up like ungainly spacemen. They gathered in the garden, taking cautious footsteps and looking more like they were balancing on moving ground than walking. A nurse unceremoniously dragged the last patient outside, then locked the door. It was too far to hear, but Atsuo distinctly sensed the authoritative click of the lock.

Suddenly, Atsuo was seized with worry about whether he had locked his gun cabinet. Given his regular habits, he could hardly have failed to do so. In addition to guns and ammo, the cabinet held cash and his bank book. He was always scrupulously cautious about keeping the cabinet locked. Normally he had a fail-safe custom of going back and checking so he could leave his apartment with the memory of having checked the lock. But this morning his thoughts had been elsewhere, so he didn't have that reassuring memory.

Atsuo stopped, cold sweat on his brow. The 7:08 bus from the stop in front of the shrine would get him to work with time to spare. The next bus was at 7:22, which meant there was a possibility of arriving late. If he went back now, he might not make his bus. It was 7:02. I must have locked it, he told himself. He meant to calm his mind, but thinking these words only had the opposite effect of fanning his anxiety. Overwhelmed, he broke into a run back to his apartment.

The cabinet was locked, as were the locks to the ammo and cash drawers inside. He turned the key again, this time registering the act on his consciousness to appease his anxiety. Then he checked the propane gas safety cock and window lock. Finally, he gave a lingering look at his hand turning the key to the apartment.

He sprinted for the bus stop. Running at full speed would get him there in five minutes. Conditioned by daily exercise, he could normally count on his body's performance, but not this day. Weariness and lack of sleep made his joints sluggish, as if overdue for an oil change. He missed the bus. Breathless, sweaty, his head aching, the sight of the bus's rear end in the distance made him groan aloud.

Traffic flowed with maddening fitfulness, like a clogged pipe. At the station, a train had just departed. The next train was delayed with point trouble, or some blasted thing. It was past eight thirty when he got to Ochanomizu Station. He bounded up the staircase. At the exit he stumbled, hit his side and was temporarily immobilized. He arrived at the shop, bathed in sweat, ten minutes late. Fukawa had already begun the morning roll call.

"Pretty unusual for you to be late for work."

"My train was running late from a breakdown."

"We have a big day ahead. Got to do something with this wreck," said Fukawa, pointing with his chin at a car with a missing hood and a bashed-in roof. The body was also badly battered, but there was nothing wrong with the engine or the frame.

Atsuo took a look underneath and said "This was no traffic accident. What happened? Vandals?"

Fukawa nodded. "That's about it. Students. They were scuffling with the police around here yesterday. They turned over cars to make a blockade."

"They really smashed it up."

"Yeah, well, you might say it's good business for us. We have orders to pick up four others bashed up in the same way. Bring 'em in with the wrecker, will you?"

Jobs were assigned and the workers went to their stations. Yukichi was with Atsuo in the wrecker. Atsuo went into Fukawa's office to get the key. There, all by herself, was Kimiko Fujiyama, a woman whose spectacular bust drew the eyes like a magnetic field. Probably conscious of this effect, she gave a saucy toss of her head as if she was being caressed.

"You met with Sonoko yesterday," she said. Atsuo didn't reply.

"She said nasty things about me, didn't she?"

"Nah."

Kimiko clapped her hands and laughed. "So you did see her. Of course she said nasty things about me. She always does. Did you check up on Mr. Jinnai?"

"What do you mean by that?"

"The theft, of course. You heard about it from the boss. He says Mr. Jinnai is a suspect." She spoke as if she herself had pushed Fukawa into launching an investigation. Her attitude annoyed Atsuo. Until then, he had assumed Fukawa had confided in him alone.

"Yukichi didn't do it. That's for sure."

"My goodness, such confidence!" Kimiko's eyes were still smiling. Smiles so became her wide-open features it was easy to be taken in by them, even though her smiles always held a shade of mockery.

"I can tell. I've known that kid since he was a baSmiles so became her wide-open features it was easy to be taken in by them, even though her smiles always held a shade of mockeryby."

"Maybe that makes you partial. After all, Mr. Yukichi Jinnai does have a police record."

"What!"

Atsuo checked himself a hairline ahead of falling into Kimiko's trap and exclaiming, "How did you know that?"

"I know all about it. I called Raúsu. I'm responsible for our personnel. It's my job to check on the records of new employees. I know he was in a reformatory too."

Atsuo caught his breath. Of course Fukawa knew about Yukichi's past too. He felt betrayed.

Fukawa had said nothing of this. He had consistently displayed an attitude of faith in Atsuo.

If Yukichi's past had been investigated, the same should be true for Atsuo. Prior to his employment by Fukawa Motors, he had submitted a personal history that was entirely fabricated. He had filled in the names of trucking companies and auto repair shops in Kobe, Urawa, and Tokyo as his employers to coincide with the times spent in prisons in those cities. It would only take calls to each of those companies to uncover his lies.

That was not the only potential source of suspicion against Atsuo. Kimiko's predecessor, Sonoko Kanéhara, was herself exceedingly fond of checking up on people. Small chance that a woman who would tail someone all the way to Hakone wouldn't have been interested in the employees' pasts. Was Sonoko's friendliness also a sham? And what if Kimiko had investigated Yukichi on Fukawa's orders, rather than her own initiative? Fukawa would have given her the same orders about himself, that's what.

"You seem lost in thought," Kimiko giggled. "Your forehead's wrinkled."

"Was it your idea to check up on Yukichi?" asked Atsuo.

"Me?" Kimiko reflected for a beat, then put on her ebullient expression again. "Orders from the boss, of course. He's very particular. He's obsessive about investigating things thoroughly."

"That's true enough," Atsuo said, eyeing the bookcases and steel file cabinets in the office. "He is obsessive," he said as if explaining to himself. Fukawa kept records of everything. He had pamphlets on almost every car manufactured in Japan since the end of the war. They were filed by manufacturer. His collection was well known in the trade. He even received requests from manufacturers to view it. Fukawa had numerous books on his hobbies — fishing and hunting — as well. His collection was particularly strong on Hokkaido. It included references methodically collected from local publishers based in Sapporo, Nemuro and Kushiro. But Fukawa was no mere collector, satisfied just by having the publications. Fukawa read it all, savoring every word. His obsession was not in the collecting, but in researching.

There was no question but that he would have files somewhere on each of his employees. At least, so it seemed to Atsuo. A vivid image appeared in his mind of Fukawa poring over a report with every last detail on his past. It was an unpleasant thought.

Another suspicion occurred to Atsuo. Maybe he had been questioned on the day of that bombing incident on the Yokosuka line because Fukawa had informed on him to the police. His police record was the probable cause, rather than the simple fact that he was a gun owner. It now seemed to Atsuo it was a good thing he hadn't told Fukawa about the explosions he had set off in Hokkaido.

Fukawa poked his head in the door. "Oh, there you are." Instead of answering, Atsuo held up the key to the wrecker and headed for the door. Fukawa followed.

"Wait a minute. You look a little green around the gills."

"Yeah. A little hung over from last night. Drank too much."

"Hmm, that's unusual for you," said Fukawa, mopping the sweat from his bald head. The round head and semi-circle eyebrows recalled to Atsuo his dream that morning. It is an uneasy feeling to confront someone you murdered in a dream. He thought it odd that there was a dark stain around the breast pocket of Fukawa's shirt, just where the sword had gone in. Then he realized he'd noticed that stain two or three days before. Maybe that was the source of the dream.

"By the way, about Jinnai. He didn't do it. That's for sure. I checked it all out yesterday."

"Yeah? Okay, if you say so, then it's settled." Fukawa clapped Atsuo on the shoulder to show he trusted him.

"It is very likely that Tomoyama lost his wallet by himself. He's a very disorganized kid. As for the stereo, Jinnai bought it with his own savings."

"I see." Fukawa nodded again and again. "So we're back to where we started."

"Will you notify the police?"

"The trouble with doing that is if there is a suspicion that someone in the shop did it, it would play hell with morale. It wasn't a tremendous amount of money. Let's wait and see."

Fukawa laughed heartily. Atsuo knew very well he was faking. A mere one hundred yen turning up missing would be enough to aggravate Fukawa to the point of mounting a search.

Atsuo rapidly changed the subject. "Oh, yeah, I meant to tell you, I got a letter from my sister saying a whopper huch was caught in the Furen River."

"No kidding?" Fukawa's eyes opened wide. Huchen was a subject dear to his heart.

"One hundred and twenty-three centimeters. Twenty-one kilos."

"That's really big. Seven, eight years ago there was an article in the Hokkaido newspaper about a huch, I believe, 115 centimeters long."

"Yeah, this was one of the biggest in ten years. Some housewife caught it. My sister says it was the first time she had ever been fishing."

"Damn! That's what you call beginners luck. I've been going after huch for ten years and haven't caught one yet. Sure would like to. Just once. Wonder what you have to do to net one of those babies. What kind of bait did she use?"

"A lure. It seems she was practicing casting with it when the huch bit."

"I'd like to see it. Wonder what color it was."

"The guide was Torakichi Jinnai. He'll know. It was probably one of his lures. Let's use it this time and go fishing for huch in the Furen."

"That's perfect! Nothing could hold me back."

Having set Fukawa quivering with pleasure, Atsuo gave a respectful nod and went to the wrecker. Yukichi was waiting in the passenger seat. There was a patch of gauze taped to his forehead.

"What happened to you?" Atsuo asked.

"It's nothing. I fell."

"Get a little too breezy for you?"

Yukichi let the jest pass without expression. Atsuo shifted to a serious expression and asked, "So what'd you do last night?"

"I was in there."

"What time you stay 'til?"

"Ah, I left pretty soon after."

Atsuo went back to clowning mode. "Well, of course you weren't in on that riot, now were you?"

"Actually, I was," Yukichi said with a glimmer of a smile. "Got in some good licks. It was fun."

"Uh-oh," said Atsuo in a strained voice. He started the engine. "Which side did you beat up?"

"Who knows? It was pitch dark."

"You're looking for trouble, if you ask me. By the way, I got a letter from your mother. She wants to know what it takes to get you to write. Please send her a postcard once in a while."

No response.

"You hear me?"

"Yeah, I hear, but I don't have anything to write."

This time Atsuo fell silent. He could understand the boy's point of view.

Life in the city was monotonous. You do your job and go home. Every day is the same, totally unlike the countryside, where there is color, where your whole way of living changes with the seasons. The fact was, Atsuo himself only wrote his sister once in a great while.

The wrecker reached a broad thoroughfare in front of the main gate of a private university, where seven wrecked automobiles were strewn about like toys from an upended toy chest. Three cars laying on their sides were burned black. Traffic had been sealed off. There were numerous policemen on the scene, their patrol cars flashing red lights.

Atsuo muttered, "They really tore things up." Fragments of paving stones were scattered in such profusion as to prevent passage of the truck. Presumably, they had been thrown by students at riot police.

Atsuo and Yukichi got out of the truck. An old man who looked like a shop owner came up and said he'd been waiting. He showed them his damaged vehicle. It was a pickup truck with the name of a fruit and vegetable store painted on it. The loading platform was bent and the windshield was cracked.

"The police had to write a report. They just now got finished with me. How about it? Can you fix it?"

Atsuo had Yukichi assist him as he conducted a spot inspection of the damage. The engine wouldn't start. No apparent damage to the chassis. The cooling and lube systems seemed okay. There was a worrisome dent in the clutch cover, with oil seeping along the seam, meaning the transmission would have to be replaced.

"Got to get it in the shop before we can say anything for sure. But the chassis and axle are okay, so it can be fixed."

"I suppose it will be expensive," the shop owner said anxiously.

"The insurance will cover it," Atsuo answered with professional aplomb.

As the front of his truck was being hoisted by the wrecker, the shop owner suddenly vented his anger. He had been dealing with students for years and had never suffered such violence. Without his truck he couldn't get to the market to buy produce, so he couldn't do business. Big shot revolutionaries! All they did was make trouble for little people. Damned radicals, they should all be strung up.

"You can say that again." Atsuo said as he started the engine. "Trashing cars is too much. I don't want to see them break into our parking lot."

"They will, eventually," said Yukichi. "They're going to turn this area into a liberated zone."

"A liberated zone?"

"Set up barricades, seal the area off, take it over."

"They can't do something like that."

"They can. They put out a plan, 'Project Liberation and Occupation.' I read it. They mean business."

"The cops will stop them."

"The cops can't keep up with them. Did they stop them from busting up this truck?"

"No, but still . . ."

"We have to look out for ourselves. Form our own Fukawa Motors Self-Defense Force. Get out and defend the shop and the parking lot."

"We can't do something like that. To begin with, it isn't necessary."

Yukichi didn't reply. From the corner of his eye, Atsuo saw him draw up his broad shoulders and glare at his uncle through narrowed eyes.

They returned to the shop and went out again right away to pick up two other damaged cars. It was an unusually hectic day. No time for meal breaks. Fukawa sent out for lunches and dinners. Under his direction, all personnel toiled tirelessly. They didn't finish up until past nine o'clock at night.

Chapter 2

Rain

On Sunday morning Atsuo invited Yukichi to the Korakuen skating rink. They were there waiting when the doors opened, and it happened they were the only customers at the time, even though the rink was sure to fill up, as it always did on weekends.

A milky fog hugged the blue-white ice surface. This phenomenon occurred when the air was damp, as it was that cloudy morning, before the ventilation system went on. Atsuo liked this sight; it was exhilarating to glide through the mist.

Yukichi sped off on his rented speed skates and promptly disappeared into the fog. A moment later he suddenly reemerged from the opposite direction like a dark projectile and whizzed past Atsuo at extraordinary speed. He was an accomplished skater, who had earned a championship record during his middle school years in Nemuro. He circled the rink three times and stopped in front of Atsuo, kicking up a spray of ice crystals.

"So how's it feel?"

"Okay, I guess, but the ice is like, too perfect. There's no wind. This place is too comfortable. It ain't real."

"Yeah, I suppose it's not the same as an outdoor rink."

"Don't compare at all."

Yukichi sped off again and disappeared. Atsuo's figure skates took him to the center of the rink with a single kick. The world's squalor fell behind the moment he began gliding atop the ice. That sensation of instant transformation was itself one of the indescribable pleasures of skating.

A more technical way to explain the feeling would be to attribute it to being released from the effects of gravity. Walking requires expenditure of your own power at every step, but on skates you just let the ice take you. The smoothness of the ice surface nullifies the effects of gravity. That is why the skater's experience is much like that of a bird with wings spread, soaring through the air. The ice is nothing but sheer, simple flatness. In the kindred sport of skiing, one deals with uneven snow surfaces and every kind of slope. In ice skating, the medium is always exactly the same. That makes every action depend entirely on what the skater does. That autonomy is a great source of satisfaction. Gaining mastery of the many skating techniques brings the thrill of having greater freedom.

Surrendering himself to the world of flight, Atsuo began to trace a figure eight. One of the sixty-nine "compulsory figures" in competition skating set out by the International Skating Union, the figure eight requires the skater to describe a pair of circles whose diameters are three times his or her height. There are four varieties that use combinations of the blade's outer and inner edges and backward or forward skating.

You only have to trace simple circles, but it's very hard to do. They bend out of shape or you end up in a different spot from where you started, leaving an erratic track. When beginners repeat a figure several times, they blemish the ice surface with tangles of ugly lines. Atsuo was in his fourth year of learning and cutting a nice-looking figure, but not like a competition skater who could go round and round any number of times, leaving tracks that waver by no more than a centimeter or two.

By the time he had finished his figure eight practice, there were more people around him. One was a conspicuously good skater. That was Wakako Ikéhata.

Launching herself from the rinkside into an approach run, she jumped when she arrived in the center, turned one and a half times and came out skating backwards; an Axel Paulsen jump. On her approach, she flashed Atsuo a bright smile of recognition. After that, she tried a Double Axel, but it was unsuccessful and she landed on her rear end. She rose instantly, and, brushing ice from her short skirt, came up to Atsuo. "Good morning," she said, swelling her chest to slow her breathing.

"Isn't the coach here yet?"

"No, I wonder what's holding him up." Wakako looked up at a wall clock. It read 9:12. Her lessons were supposed to be from 9:00 to 9:30, after which Atsuo was scheduled from 9:30 to 10:00, but sometimes the coach came a little late.

"Who's that you came with?" Wakako asked.

"Oh, did you see him? It's just my nephew, my younger sister's boy."

"He's really good — like a pro," said Wakako with eyes fixed on Yukichi as he executed a precise cross-stroke to turn a corner.

"Yeah, he was on the skating team in middle school. I think this may be his first time at an indoor rink, though."

The ventilation system was on, and the mist over the ice had disappeared. Yukichi's speeding figure was reflected in the mirror surface. There were two or three other fast gliders in speed skates or hockey skates, but Yukichi zipped past them at a speed they couldn't match.

"I meant to tell you I was at T. University the day before yesterday. You know, a riot started there in the evening and kept up all night. We went to see it."

"Oh, is that a hobby of yours?"

"Not exactly. I was watching television with that nephew of mine and he wanted to go. I was dragged into it. But I was amazed at how rowdy students are nowadays. Well, not you, I'm sure. You go to a private university. I don't suppose you're like that."

"You never know," said Wakako with a mysterious, tight-lipped smile.

"Well, you're not a radical."

"..."

Wakako's smile disappeared. She was looking at Atsuo with a direct stare.

"Um, if you are, sorry. I seem to have said something wrong."

Wakako shook her head and retained her intense look.

"I don't like that word, 'radical.' The papers throw around those categories — 'radicals,' 'Zenkyoto,' 'Yoyogi faction' — but it's all malarkey. The reality is more complex, more involved. It has warmth and feeling. It's human, in other words."

"Okay, I was wrong. I apologize. I don't know anything about universities. I was just a curiosity seeker. But I really would like to know what makes young people want to riot."

"And what if you found out the reason?" asked Wakako with a blink of her gracefully curved eyelids. She had a habit of keeping her eyes fixed on people she was addressing. Atsuo had often felt she was annoyed with him before he realized that.

"Well . . ." Averting her gaze, Atsuo's eyes fell on the woman's well-formed legs extending from her short skirt. The figure of Yukichi flitted across the corner of his vision.

"Look, they're out to destroy something, right? Why do they want to?"

"At first, no one thought destruction was really possible. But when they raised their voices a little, it began to look as if it could happen. So everyone got serious about it."

"In other words, they think they can bring down the whole system? That's pretty naive." Atsuo was surprised at the bitterness of his own words.

"Naive."

"Yes." Atsuo chose his words carefully to avoid sounding offensive. "This world is build on solid rock. Nothing you or I do is going to really change anything. They talk as if that war we went through destroyed everything, but the truth is even that much of a war didn't change a single thing about how the world works. Pretty much everything there was during the war is still here, the same as always, whether its factories, universities or prisons."

"Prisons." Wakako took a step, as if to avoid a pile of dog waste.

"Maybe that's funny, I don't know. But it's true. No matter what happens — war, revolution or what have you — there will never be an end to prisons."

"Because there are always criminals."

"Exactly. If you take that a little further, you come to the fact that anyone could be a criminal. That is why the criminal population will never die out."

"Could you be a criminal too?"

"Sure I could."

"That's a little scary," Wakako said, drawing her head back uneasily. "But fascinating."

"Good heavens," Atsuo said, unconsciously imitating her startled gesture. "Whatever made me say such a strange thing?"

They had stopped moving on the ice to carry on their conversation, allowing the cold to penetrate to an uncomfortable degree. Atsuo crossed his arms for warmth, and Wakako was striking a similar pose when the coach, dressed in a bulky down jacket, appeared at rinkside. In an instant, Wakako had skated up to him as if launched from a slingshot, and was bowing in greeting.

Yukichi must have been waiting for the opening, for the next moment he appeared beside Atsuo, his face red and glistening with sweat. The bandage on his forehead was conspicuous.

"I'm goin'."

"Already?"

"It's crowded. You can't skate."

An oval-shaped yellow line divided the rink into two zones. Outside the oval was the zone for doing laps around the rink; inside was for practicing figures. There was still room in the inner zone, but the outside track was filled with numerous beginners "polishing the handrail" or doing the "penguin walk." Youths in hockey skates were zipping through these skaters.

"So long." Yukichi turned to go, then asked over his back, "Who's that girl?"

"A university student."

"That so?" Yukichi faced in the direction of Wakako, who was having her lesson. She was in the process of turning an admirable Double Axel.

"She's pretty good, isn't she?"

"That's the kind of girl I hate."

"How come?"

"They put on that 'Oh, I'm So Nice' act." Yukichi squared his shoulders and shot off at top speed in a path that crossed directly in front of a youth in hockey skates, who let out a startled cry. With a sidelong glance at the youth, Yukichi bounded up to rinkside. Noticing the youth flush with anger and chase after Yukichi, Atsuo moved in closer.

"You know that's dangerous?" said the youth threateningly as he blocked Yukichi's path. He was an imposing figure, towering a good twenty centimeters over Yukichi. Atsuo recognized him. He belonged to a motorcycle gang and wore the flamboyant clothes of such groups. He amused himself in the skating rink by intentionally cutting in front of girls and jeering at them or standing in the paths of people in the center zone practicing their figures. One day when Atsuo was tracing a circle backwards, he had collided with the youth, who had stopped squarely in his path, and been told menacingly, "Watch where you're goin'!"

"What's dangerous?" asked Yukichi expressionlessly.

"Cutting in front! You almost ran into me!"

"But I didn't, did I? I was timing your drag-ass speed so I wouldn't."

"Who you calling drag-ass? Nobody talks to me like that!" The youth clenched his fists and glared.

Two observers, whose job was to patrol the rink, approached. A crowd gathered.

Yukichi suddenly raised his voice. "Anyhow, I didn't run into you." Conditioned to delivering war songs, Yukichi's voice was alarmingly loud. The youth's shoulders flinched.

"Yeah, but what you did was dangerous." The tone of confidence had disappeared.

"Well, I'll tell you something," said Yukichi, oratorically, looking over the crowd with a nod. "What do you call the way you skate? Going out of your way to cut people off, making ladies scream, is that dangerous or what? I suppose you think you're good, so there's no danger. Well, it's the same with me. I'm better than you, so there's nothing dangerous, is there?"

Yukichi took a step forward and the youth backed off. He seemed to have noticed for the first time the bandage on Yukichi's forehead — possibly the result of brawling — the swelling muscles of his shoulders and the strength evident in his sturdy frame. He himself was merely tall, but otherwise weak, hardly a match for Yukichi if it came to a fight.

"Ah, shit! You better remember this," was the youth's parting shot as he retreated over the ice. Atsuo followed Yukichi to the locker room.

"You better watch out. That's the kind who tries to get even."

"I won't be coming here again. This indoor rink ain't for me. There's no wind, it's crowded and on top of that they keep playing those candy-ass pop songs." Yukichi returned his rented skates and strode out.

Atsuo returned to the center of the rink and continued practicing figures. The next step up from the figure eight is the three-turn, in which the skater turns around halfway through a circle to trace out a figure three. This figure also has four variations that use the runner's outer or inner edge while moving forward or in reverse.

Atsuo traced out the figure with deliberation as he thought over Yukichi's words. It was certainly true that the indoor rink differed from outdoor rinks. It shut out the open air with walls and ceiling, used electricity to make the ice and a resurfacing machine to polish it into a shining mirror. Every nook and corner of this brightly lit skating rink was fashioned by human hands. The municipal rink at Nemuro offered a naturally frozen pond at the foot of a hill, where cold winds from the Sea of Okhotsk blow in powdered snow that nips at skaters' faces like a hail of fine needles.

Leisurely practice of skating figures would not be possible in Nemuro. But that environment is just right for flat-out speed skating against the wind and snow. In Nemuro, elementary and middle school students like Yukichi were taught speed skating exclusively.

Atsuo had started skating when he returned to Nemuro nine years before. There, speed skating was all he practiced. Then when he arrived in Tokyo, he realized that the intricate forms of figure skating were best suited to the indoor rinks he found there. He had made the big decision four years ago to reinvent himself as a figure skater, and had begun receiving weekly private lessons from a coach.

Around that time he had become acquainted with Wakako Ikéhata. She had come to the rink one day with a group of other girls. They were all beginners, taking penguin steps on the ice. Wakako approached him to request that he teach them to skate. He gave a demonstration of how to achieve forward motion, and Wakako had acquired the knack pretty well. He said the best thing to do if you really want to learn is have a coach right from the start, so she asked him to introduce her to one. That was how they came to have the same coach.

As the years went by, Wakako was the one who progressed by leaps and bounds. Now she was doing difficult figures and jumps, while Atsuo was barely equal to the easy figures, and couldn't jump at all. He reflected that youth provided an unbeatable advantage, but at the same time, it seemed to him from his experience with shooting that the mysterious quality of innate ability must be at work. Not that he was envious of the girl. He had no ambition to be a better skater than the next person. The freedom of winging over the ice satisfied him.

At the moment, Wakako was doing a Salchow jump, which requires leaping from the back edge of the right skate, doing two full midair turns and landing on the left skate. She extended her long legs smartly and they traced a beautiful arc, but her knees were shaky, a sign of inadequate stability. The coach was showing her how to correct the problem. Atsuo applied himself to his own practice.

Then it was time for his lesson. The coach was in his early thirties, almost twenty years younger than Atsuo, but he had to his credit a national championship, superb skills and a reputation as a good teacher. Atsuo skated a circle as the coach directed. When they had gone through a series of compulsory figures, it was freestyle time. He chose a spin.

To get started you twist your whole body to the left, then snap your left leg straight at the axis of the spin. Accelerate by pulling in your extended arms and right leg to focus the momentum on your axis. Now you're turning around like a top, with an audible whiz. In this state, from his point of view the entire rink was revolving around Atsuo at a very fast clip. Building, people, and ice all lost their shapes. They flew about him, a diaphanous, sparkling vision; a wondrous spectacle you could never experience back down on the ground, in everyday life.

To pull out of the spin, you need only jump into reverse with your right leg. In the beginning, he would experience dizziness at this point, but he seemed to have become accustomed to the maneuver, because now everything returned to normal the instant he stopped.

The coach gave him some pointers on the weak points of his form. He repeated the spin a number of times, and then his lesson was over. Thirty minutes had gone by before he knew it. He looked around to find a packed rink. There were elementary school children in the center having a group lesson, with little girls hopping about. A vast space was occupied by a skating team doing figures.

The oval track was so crowded one had to search for little patches of ice to keep moving foward. The surface of the ice was so slashed up it was no longer good for the delicate maneuvers figure skating requires. Deciding to call it quits, Atsuo went to rinkside.

There was a couple in the locker room engaged in a whispered conversation. Though he was facing the woman's back, he recognized her as Wakako. She was talking to a youth who wasn't wearing skates. He was of slight stature and thin, with long hair hanging just above sickle-shaped eyes that peered incisively. He had a vague aura like a low-level yakuza. Wakako sat hunched over, as if weary. When the youth saw Atsuo, he abruptly ended the conversation with the words, "Well, so long. Think it over," and departed.

"Hey."

Wakako gave a start at Atsuo's greeting, and turned around.

"It's too crowded. I'm leaving." Atsuo opened the locker he rented by the month and started undoing his skates. Wakako sat with a vacant expression, eyes turned to inner thoughts.

"Who was that?"

"Ah ..."

She finally looked at him. "A friend. He goes to T. University."

"T.U. huh? Doesn't seem interested in skating."

Wakako stood. "I'm leaving too." She opened her locker, then asked suddenly, "Hey, Mr. Yukimori, let's go for coffee."

"Okay, fine." To date, his association with Wakako had been as an acquaintance at the skating rink. They had both attended skaters' parties at a restaurant and get-togethers at coffee houses, but never had they been together alone. He was especially pleased that this occasion came at her invitation.

He started to head for the skating rink coffee shop, but Wakako rejected that choice because, she said, she didn't like being recognized by people. They went into a basement coffee shop in a building near Suidobashi.

Wakako revealed what she had in mind. "Actually, I have a favor to ask. I want you to take me to Shinjuku."

"Shinjuku." Atsuo was startled. "How come?"

"I'm sure you know that tomorrow is International Anti-War Day."

"I recall something in the paper about that. I haven't paid much attention though. Wasn't the police chief warning people away from Shinjuku Station because the students might cause trouble?"

"You seem well informed. That's right, tomorrow will be a day of burning glory."

"What's going to burn?"

56

"Young people."

"Yeah?"

"To be precise, my generation, although I won't be directly involved."

"I get it. That long-haired guy from T. University will be at Shinjuku, won't he? He asked you along, you wavered and finally refused. But you really want to see what's going on."

Wakako dropped her gaze, which was unusual for her. The next moment, like withered flower petals suddenly revived, she directed her widely opened eyes to Atsuo.

"Please go with me to Shinjuku."

"Okay, sure I will. But I do have just one question. Why didn't you ask one of your other friends? Why me?"

"Do I have to say?"

"You don't have to, but I'd be happy if you did."

"You'll be disappointed."

"I won't be disappointed, so tell me."

"Because I'll be safe with you."

Atsuo sighed.

"Angry?"

"Not angry, but something like it. It's certainly an honor to be seen by you as safe. But I don't really know if I measure up to that estimate."

"Oh, I see, you took my meaning differently. Well, that's one consideration, I guess, but I meant 'safe' in another way. Tomorrow, it could be dangerous for a group of students to be walking together. You'll be my father. A daughter walking with his father will be safe."

"So that's it."

"Disappointed?"

"No, I'm glad. I certainly am of the age to be your father. That's an honor."

"How old are you?"

"Forty-nine. How old're you?"

"Twenty-four. I'm pretty old too."

"Nonsense. You could be my daughter."

"For a student, I'm old. I didn't start college until two years out of high school."

"So what? You're young. That's wonderful."

"Father, is it all right to smoke?"

"Be my guest."

Wakako reached into a red handbag and extracted a cigarette case and lighter. When the cigarette was between her slim, white fingers, Atsuo gave her a light.

"Don't you smoke?"

"I quit nine and a half years ago."

"Why do you say nine and a half years?" Wakako asked in an amazed tone.

"What's wrong with that?"

"Nobody says 'nine and a half years.' You say 'almost ten years' or something."

"Well, you see I was a heavy smoker. I kept trying to quit and couldn't. It was nine and a half years ago that I finally succeeded. So I keep track of the time as a warning to myself. To be exact, it's been nine years, seven months and fifteen days."

"That's amazing." Wakako was shaking her head and blowing smoke at the table at the same time. "You're really strict with yourself."

"It's a sad story, really," Atsuo said with a mirthless smile. "I'm weak-willed, so I take the trouble to count the days. It's a ritual to keep the spell from breaking."

"Cast a spell, did you?" As Wakako laughed, the legs in her jeans convulsed. This body language of a young woman was a tantalizing novelty to Atsuo.

"Anyway, let me offer to be your safe escort tomorrow. But I do have to work during the day."

"Nighttime is fine. Nothing will catch fire until then anyway."

"Night burners are they? So what do you say we meet here at five thirty?"

"Great. Thanks very much. You don't have to spend money on me. All I want to do is walk around the town."

"As you wish. If you travel under guard, you must obey the captain of the guard's orders implicitly. Aside from that, though, I wonder if it would cause you any problems if you were seen walking with me, say, by that long-haired fellow."

"Oh, him." Wakako's tiny tongue appeared and flitted over her lips, as if savoring the aftertaste of a kiss.

"I wonder, is he your lover?"

" . . ." Her expression became stern.

Now I've done it, thought Atsuo. Hastily he said, "Right, you don't like the word 'lover.' I'm sorry. I could tell by your expression. You made the same face when I said 'radical.'"

Wakako began laughing. The laughter continued until she was shaking and tears welled up in her eyes. Atsuo watched helplessly. He felt as if all eyes in the coffee shop were turned their way, like a great net falling over them.

"Forgive me," Wakako said when her laughter finally died down. "You see, when someone says exactly what I'm thinking, it makes me want to laugh. You're like a mind reader. He's my boyfriend. We've slept together. But he isn't a lover, and, no, I don't like that word."

"Hmmm." The woman's smoke had gotten into his eyes. He blinked. "It's nice to be young and free."

"And you are a very understanding person. You know how other people feel."

"Humph. It's evening already. Would you join me for something to eat?"

"No, not today." She abruptly rose, bowed and departed.

~

There was a chilly, on-again-off-again drizzle that night. The crowd filling Shinjuku Station's east exit plaza was so great it was hardly possible to move around. Most of the people gathered were there as curiosity seekers, hoping something interesting would happen. They didn't want to miss any spectacles, but at the same time they were wary about staying safe.

Helmeted students pushed through the crowd, formed ranks and marched to the cadences of whistle blasts and choral chanting. Exhortations from the station PA speakers to "Please keep moving," and "Please clear the area." had no effect at all. The crowd continued to grow, and cries of "Don't push!" arose everywhere, along with angry voices and excited screams.

Atsuo and Wakako were swept by the crowd against a column of the station building. Realizing they would be crushed if something set the crowd surging back on them, he took the girl by the hand and they set out to edge across the station front until they emerged into a side street.

"You okay?" Atsuo asked.

"Yes, I'm all right." A camera flashed, capturing Wakako, in sunglasses with a scarf over her head.

Explosions like mortar fire came from the direction of the station. This set off a commotion in the crowd.

"Is that gunfire?"

"No, they're firing tear gas."

"Ah, the kids are beating a drum."

"It sounds like bombs."

Rain began falling in earnest. She turned up the hood on her parka. He pulled his beret down low to eye level.

The explosions were getting closer, and shouting could be heard. He deduced they were hearing the sound of tear-gas rifles being fired by riot police to drive the students their way. He grabbed her arm and they ran down a back street. The next moment there was chaos in the plaza as the crowd surged backward like a wall of violently displaced water.

"What do you suppose happened?"

"The riot police and the students collided."

"I want to see that."

"That way is too dangerous. You're too delicate — you'd be squashed. Let's try going this way." They emerged to the main thoroughfare that dips under the railroad bridge and leads to the west side of the station. Helmeted figures had gathered on the bridge. They were throwing rocks from the tracks at the policemen below. The police were responding with liberal barrages of tear gas shells and streams of high-pressure water. Smoking gas canisters were being thrown back at the police. Eyes smarting from the gas, Atsuo instinctively gauged the wind direction and led the girl upwind. They climbed across a pile of paving stones deposited around a utility pole that had presumably been collected by students for use as ammunition.

The police forces were relentlessly pressing down on the helmeted youths, inch by inch. It was obvious that an untrained band armed with no more than rocks and sticks could not stand up to a professional organization equipped with formidable clubs, Duralumin shields and strong helmets with face guards. Nor was the occasional Molotov cocktail any match for water cannon and tear gas.

"Well, that battle's decided," Atsuo said.

Wakako said, "We don't know that yet."

"It will take another hour. Then the students will drift apart and take up sporadic guerrilla activities. Of course, we want to be around to see that. You must be hungry."

"You said it. I certainly am!" Wakako replied, laughing.

Though they were standing on a darkened street, a walk of only a dozen or so meters brought them as if through a parted curtain to a world of illuminated streets jammed with shops peacefully doing booming business. There was no sign of the rioting in progress one street over. The pachinko parlors, go-go coffee shops, ordinary coffee shops, restaurants, neon, music, passersby and sidewalk touts were the same as ever.

When Atsuo said apologetically, "I don't come to Shinjuku much," Wakako responded, "Oh, I know a good place." She led him back of Hanazono Shrine, to a realm of tiny food and drink stalls where customers shared intimate space.

"Hey, this is the old blue line quarter," he remarked.

"Now it's called Golden Lane," she replied.

A brothel he had frequented just after the war was there just the same as ever, except that the sign at the entrance said it was a bar. This area's appearance had not changed much in the past twenty years. His nose twitched, as if trying to sniff out the old times.

She opened a wooden door. It was a little bar, consisting of a single counter that was filled to capacity with customers. "Well, well, come right in!" The bar's proprietress gave them a professionally effusive greeting. "Unfortunately," she continued with a gesture at the full counter, "all I can offer is a place in the back."

"That's fine," said Wakako. "This is Mr. Yukimori. He was one of my teachers in high school." The bar's "mama" gave a reverential bow. "Welcome, Mr. Yukimori. Very glad to have you."

The space in the back was a tiny tatami alcove whose three walls were occupied by shelves of dishes. They each pulled up a zabuton, barely managing to squeeze in on either side of the foot-high table.

"I'll bring you something in a jiffy, Mr. Yukimori." Wakako sprang up and busied herself behind the counter. She helped Mama serve customers — whom she seemed to know — with a practiced hand. Finally, she returned with a bottle of whiskey, water, and dishes of meat-and-potatoes, *oden*, and cuttlefish. They had a toast with whiskey and water.

"Come here often?"

"I used to work here part time. Well, I still do, when I run out of money."

"It gave me a jolt to be introduced as a teacher."

"You have the air of a schoolteacher. What do you really do?"

He had told her he worked for a company, but not that he was a mechanic. "I work with automobiles."

"Oh, a motor corporation." Evidently satisfied with that answer, Wakako abruptly leaned her back against the wall. "Today was disappointing. I mean really disappointing."

"How so?"

"That's no revolution. Throwing rocks at policemen, tossing gasoline bombs, waving sticks . . . That's not going to destroy the system. All they did was a little damage around the station, and not much of that. There isn't a scratch anywhere on the station building or the outside plaza. Nothing was destroyed anywhere between Yasukuni Street and here. Look around Golden Lane! No damage at all!"

This exasperated torrent of words was unlike anything he had seen in Wakako before. It was adorable.

"Don't you agree?" she continued. "It was just a show. 'Step right up, folks! See the big revolution, right before your eyes!' What do you think, Mr. Yukimori?"

"That was my opinion from the beginning," said Atsuo.

"They have to get more serious about it."

"More serious?"

"If you're going to have a revolution, you have to be properly armed. You need guns, bazookas, cannons, tanks. And you've got to be serious enough to kill all the reactionary elements."

"Well, yeah, I suppose that's true, but . . . you know . . ." Atsuo was flustered by the woman's bellicose rhetoric.

"They've got to! If they don't, the system won't break down. And that's no good!"

"That's what I don't get." Imitating Wakako, he looked straight into her comely eyes as he said this, but immediately began to feel as if he was in a staring contest, so he ended up looking away sheepishly as he muttered, "What's the good of wanting to destroy everything?"

"Yeah, it's really funny," she said, also muttering. "You see, the reasons come later. Wanting destruction comes first. There's a million reasons for doing it, but none of them are for real. Mao Zedong, Jiang Qing, Guevara, spontaneous worldwide revolution, direct democracy . . . All of that is jive talk."

"That stuff is just a fad."

This he said with feeling. For a time after the war, everyone had been carried away with Stalin. Interesting stories about Stalin were hot items, but that craze was soon dropped. Now, instead of Stalin, the young people were carried away with Mao Zedung, Jiang Qing, and Che Guevara. No doubt they were fascinated with these characters, but his take was that it amounted to nothing more than a momentary trend.

"I remember how you were saying yesterday that no matter what happens in the world there will always be prisons."

"Yep."

"That kept going around in my head. Later on I told it to him, you know, the one with the long hair — his name's Moriya — and he was really interested. He's out there now, raising hell around Shinjuku Station. He was saying maybe he'd be arrested. Maybe he has been already."

"That's a concern."

"No, not a bit. He was arrested once before. They let him go for lack of evidence. He was disappointed."

"Why?"

"He said he wanted to go to prison once to see what it is like."

"Well, there is nothing in the least bit interesting about prison."

"Oh, do tell me what prison is like!"

Atsuo realized he had blurted out too much. Curiously, however, he wasn't regretting his blunder. To the contrary, he strongly desired to answer the girl's question, simply because her expression was so devoid of ulterior purpose, so intent on knowing.

"A long time ago, back during the war, I was in an army prison," he said in a low voice. He glanced along the line of backsides at the counter to make sure the other customers didn't overhear.

"Wow!" Wakako shrieked, her mouth opened wide. Beyond the white teeth, he could see the epiglottis pulsing with a life of its own. This display of surprise touched Atsuo's heart. He wanted to teach this child everything he knew.

"I was locked up for desertion. I didn't like the army, so I ran away. You know what the punishment for that is when the country is at war?"

"A firing squad." Wakako drew in her breath at her own words.

"No, the sentence was one year and six months. Handed down by a court-martial. They said it was due to a lack of military spirit."

"So what's an army prison like?"

"Okay, I'll tell you." Atsuo pondered how to approach this question and how much to say. It was hard enough to communicate to young people just what the military was like, let alone present a clear picture of life in a prison.

"During the day I worked in a leather shop. We made ammunition belts. They are hand-sewn. At night, you return to your cell and sit facing the wall. You sit *seiza* for thirty minutes, then you can cross your legs for the next thirty minutes, then back to *seiza* again and so on. You can't move at all, not so much as change the position of your hands. So, say your nose gets itchy. You call out your number to the guard; 'Number 12.' 'What is it?' he says. 'Sir, my nose is itchy,' you say. If he tells you, 'All right,' you've finally got permission to scratch your nose."

Wakako's expression was composed. She was clearly intent on not missing a single word. That was gratifying to Atsuo, who was adept at talking with earnest young people.

"You need permission to use the toilet. You have to say, 'Sir, I want to urinate.' After you finish, you have to report. 'Sir, I'm finished urinating.' Under no circumstances can you talk to your neighbor. Bedtime is at nine o'clock. Bed is the wooden floor, with a single blanket over you. The cells are infested with lice and fleas. That makes you itch all over. And it's cold. There's an electric light on all night, but you get tired and so you sleep. The next day would be all the worse if you didn't. This isn't a pretty subject. I don't suppose you want to hear any more."

"I want to hear ugly things. Tell me more."

"Well, all right. You can't use the toilet at all during the day when you're in the shop. Defecation is done at night. If you can't hold it during the day, you do it in your pants."

"Wow."

"You're human, so what can you do? Sometimes you have to go during the day. You get diarrhea. No excuses, so you do it in your pants. Ahh, this is too disgusting to talk about."

"It's interesting. I like to hear things like this."

"Army prison exerts one hundred percent control over its inmates. The individual doesn't have any kind of freedom. They conduct inspections when you leave the shop. They make you take off all your clothes and straddle a bar."

"A bar?"

"An iron bar. You put your leg up over it, stark naked. That way the guards can see inside your body, right? They're checking to see if you've anything hidden up there. You open your mouth so they can look in. You march naked in front of the guards."

Wakako pursed her lips, lost in thought. Finally, she asked, "How come you deserted?"

"I didn't like the army anymore."

"That's great!" she said with a clap of her hands. "That's anti-war activity."

"'Anti-war,' you say," Atsuo smiled ironically. "There wasn't anything heroic about it. I just didn't have the guts to stay."

"It isn't everyone who could get up the nerve to run away from the army. You were brave. Being imprisoned for it is an honor."

"No it isn't. It's shameful. It really is."

"One thing I wanted to ask was, why you said no matter what else happens there would never be an end to prisons. When the war ended, there weren't any more army prisons, right?"

"I was transferred from the army prison to a regular prison before then. My conscription was up. I wasn't a soldier anymore. When you lost your military status the rule was that they put you in civilian prison. Civilian prisons are always there, war or no war."

"Uh-huh." Wakako nodded thoughtfully.

"What are you two talking about?" Mama had come over. "Seats at the counter have opened up. Come on, it's cramped and cold back here."

"Shall we?" Wakako asked brightly, as she stood up. He would have preferred continuing their private talk for a while, but instead followed her to the counter.

Someone who had witnessed the rioting was talking excitedly. Buses and cars were on fire. Windows of the trains in the station had been broken. Railroad ties were burning. Onlookers had joined with the rioting students. The riot police meant business. They were hauling in large numbers of people. Most of those who had left the bar were going to see the riot.

"Don't you two want to go see the commotion?" Mama asked Wakako. "We saw a little before. That was enough. It all seems so . . . meaningless."

"Uh, oh. Looks like Wakako's in one of her moods. That's what she says when something sets her off. Tell her anything and she says it's meaningless."

"Well, that's what it is! What good does burning cars do? They just keep producing new ones. So what if a few railroad ties get ruined? Nothing's permanently destroyed and nothing changes. Nothing!"

"Someone's a little drunk."

"She certainly is," said Wakako. "Say, there's something that wants roasting." She went behind the counter and began roasting ginkgo nuts in an earthenware dish.

"What subject do you teach?" Mama asked Atsuo.

"I . . . uh . . ." Atsuo began hesitantly.

"Social studies," Wakako replied. "Mr. Yukimori knows all about crime and prisons."

"How interesting! I guess you've studied about all this rioting going on now."

"He has. He knows about war and revolution and armies and everything. You really do, Mr. Yukimori!"

Someone called for a whiskey and water. Wakako poured it out from the customer's reserved bottle. Then she produced a shaker and made a cocktail for another customer. She seemed popular with the customers, getting into conversations with everyone. Left to himself, Atsuo had one drink after another.

As the whiskey took hold, he dozed off for a while. He awakened to ringing laughter from Wakako, engaged in high-spirited exchanges with the young men at the bar. She instantly spotted Atsuo yawning.

"You okay, Mr. Yukimori?"

"Just fine. Drinking makes me sleepy these days. What time is it anyway?"

"A little past twelve. We're stuck. The trains aren't running. We probably won't be able to snag a taxi. Where do you live?"

"Chofu, near Jindai Temple."

"A taxi would be the only way to get there now, but that's unlikely. Mama says she'll stay open until daybreak, so we could stay here."

"Nah, I'm going." Atsuo rose.

"Wait, then I'm leaving too." She followed him out.

The streets were as busy as ever; times were prosperous and the hour of day no long longer mattered. There were long queues at every taxi stand. He tried waving down a vacant taxi, but they all ignored him.

"We're getting nowhere."

"I'm hungry. Let's go for ramen," she said.

The couple went into an alley lined with ramen shops along Shinjuku Station's west exit. The area near the railroad bridge was so littered with rocks thrown by the rioters that walking was difficult. Though the air was acrid with lingering tear gas that stung the eyes, the back street rows of humble stalls dispensing inexpensive ramen — unchanged from the early postwar days — were doing bustling business as usual.

The shop proprietor greeted them heartily as he served out steaming bowls of ramen. "Seats right here for the young lady and papa!" Atsuo interpreted this as sarcasm, but he realized they must certainly look an odd pair.

They emerged from the ramen shop.

"Still no good," said Wakako. "C'mon, let's go somewhere else for a drink. There'll be taxis available soon enough."

"It's time for you to be getting home. Where do you live?"

"No need to concern yourself with other people's business. Worry about yourself." Wakako was walking unsteadily.

"You seem to have had quite a lot to drink. Look out!" She was weaving so dangerously he took her arm. Then he had an unreasoning fear his rough hand might crush her delicate limb, so he loosened his grip. The touch of her skin had an effect he hadn't felt at the start of the evening when he had taken her hand as they walked through the darkness. This time her hand conveyed a sweet sensation that suddenly coursed through him and spread to his loins.

"Now tell me where you live."

"Sendagaya. It's close by. I can walk home."

They walked in a wide arc around the station to avoid the ongoing disorder there. That took them to the Meiji-dori boulevard, one side of which was occupied by armored police vehicles. The police had set up a checkpoint to question pedestrians. A young officer looked the two of them over with a demeanor that mixed official authority with male curiosity, then he nodded them by.

The rain had momentarily ceased, but there was a strong wind, so he supported her as they walked, lest she be blown over and shatter. He tried waving down a taxi, and it stopped.

"Sendagaya, then Chofu," Atsuo said, as he climbed in ahead of her. "Now tell me how to get there," he said to Wakako, but she had closed her eyes.

"Where in Sendagaya?" asked the driver. Wakako didn't answer, so Atsuo shook her awake.

Yawning, with eyes running, she answered, "Four chomé."

The taxi passed Sendagaya Station and entered a narrow road that wound down an incline. Wakako's house was located midway down the hill. It had a great stone entryway. The two-story house was surrounded by a grove of stately trees and bushes. The ceramic nameplate at the entrance read "Kotaro Ikéhata."

"Well, g'night" said Atsuo, but the girl responded by muttering, "I'm not getting out."

"Why not?"

"I don't want to go home. Let me stay at your place."

"You can't do that. Now get out," he said forcefully, but she continued to balk. They were at an impasse.

"What are you people going to do?" asked the driver impatiently.

"All right, let's get out." He pushed her from the taxi and got out himself.

"Sorry it turned out to be a short trip," Atsuo told the driver, who regarded him with a stony expression as he received his payment.

"Look, this is no good. You've got to go home," Atsuo said, looking half at the house and half at the woman. The house was darkened, and she was glowering. The stark difference from the cheerful Wakako, chatting and laughing a short time ago was both shocking and troubling.

"You have a key, don't you?" He said, looking up at the sturdy iron gate.

"We don't go in that way. Here's the entrance," Wakako said. She took a key from her handbag and headed for the side entrance set into the stone wall that surrounded the property. She turned the key, the door opened and she started in. Then she turned around.

"It's no good. I really don't want to be here."

"Why?"

"Family matters. It's too weird to explain."

"But it's late. You run along now and go to bed." Wakako giggled.

"See, you're laughing. Things aren't so bad after all."

"'Run along and go to bed.' You really do sound like a teacher. All right, sir. Good night."

Wakako disappeared inside. Atsuo started off down the hill. Next to the Ikéhata residence the silhouettes of gravestones and the roof of a big temple beyond them were discernible. The hushed street along the mansion-like residences with their luxuriant gardens was brightly illuminated by lamp posts. When he reached the main road, he heard footsteps behind. It was Wakako.

"I couldn't stay. I will not return to that household."

"What am I going to do with you? It's late!"

"All the more reason why I can't show up there."

He flagged down a taxi, intending to get in and leave her there. He told the driver his destination.

As he was squeezing into the seat, Wakako pushed her way inside.

The door slammed shut and the car went into motion. Now he didn't have the option of ordering her out. She was wearing a fierce pout once again, biting her lower lip and glaring at him.

Atsuo glared back. "Well, let's hear about those family matters."

"Later," she said in a low voice, giving his leg a pinch. She jerked her chin in the direction of the driver. Realizing she meant that she wanted to talk when they were alone, the pain where she had pinched him became a warm glow.

In a moment she was asleep. The alcohol still seemed to have a hold on her. But sleep evaded him. Lately, even having a drink with a young woman was a rare experience. Now he had one in a taxi heading for his apartment. What lay ahead? It seemed as though he had gone through the looking glass into a different world, so he really couldn't imagine.

The sleeping woman's head was resting on his shoulder. Her hair had a pleasant fragrance. Gradually, drowsiness came upon him. To his consternation, sleep brought the sudden reappearance of something that had been shut away deep in his consciousness, as if a tightly rusted hatchway had sprung open spontaneously. It was that forgotten dream of two days before, the one that had preceded the dream about the brutal killing of the prisoner.

His squad had attacked and taken a Chinese village. The troops dragged a young woman from under the straw in a shed where she had been hiding. Told by the squad leader to have the first honors, he had stripped the clothes from the protesting woman, raped her, then cast her aside indifferently. The woman's face was familiar. He couldn't clearly remember if was Wakako's face, but most likely it was.

Atsuo endeavored to put the dream away once again by sleeping more soundly. He awakened when they reached the street that runs by Jindai Temple, not far from his apartment. For better or worse, they had arrived. He maneuvered the inert Wakako onto the sidewalk and finally managed to rouse her with a slap to her cheek. Mindful that the driver was watching suspiciously, he casually took her arm and took his time climbing the iron stairway.

"Come on in." Atsuo took a fresh look at his own apartment as he invited her in. There was little free space. A bookcase sat atop the TV set, laundry was suspended over a desk and the gun locker placed conspicuously in the middle of the room was piled with boxes and bags. Things were heaped atop one another everywhere, leaving little room for moving around. For one man living alone it was adequate, but for two people, it was cramped.

"Bet you're surprised. It's like living in a submarine."

In lieu of a chair, Wakako sat on the bed. She was shivering.

"It's cold in here. Let me get it warmed up." He turned on his kerosene heater. Deftly sweeping away underpants and shirts that had been hung up to dry, he went to the kitchenette to search the refrigerator. There wasn't much. He thought wistfully of what might have been on hand had he expected company. Fortunately, there was dried cod his brother-in-law Torakichi Jinnai had sent from Akkeshi and some salmon caviar. He also had beer and shochu. He applied himself to preparing snacks.

Atsuo raised his glass and Wakako joined him in a toast. The inebriation that had dissipated some time before rose up from his stomach to envelope him once again. Wakako's cheeks flushed and her big eyes turned liquid.

"Cold?" he asked, still concerned.

"I'm fine," she smiled. "It's perfectly warm here." She looked around. A photograph on the wall attracted her attention.

"That's an Ezo deer. Plenty of them on the Konsen wilderness. Here, look at this." He took out the horn of an Ezo deer.

"It's really hard," she said, stroking it.

"At first it's soft, all bloody. Eventually it gets hard like this."

"You shot the deer?"

"Right. The year before last."

"With a rifle?"

"Hunting is my only . . . no, that and fishing are my only two hobbies. You see, my father was a hunter. So I still go hunting once in a while. I'll be going again in November."

"Where do you go?"

"Hokkaido. There's a lake near Nemuro, Lake Furen. In that area."

"That's wonderful. I'd like to try shooting a rifle. I'd like to go hunting too."

"No kidding?" He was surprised by this statement. He thought women generally hated hunting because it's bloody, and they're frightened by gunfire. "Hunting isn't pretty. You get animal blood and guts on your hands."

"I wouldn't mind getting my hands dirty. I'd like to try the dirty life, like primitive people lived."

"You are certainly a peculiar one." He removed a rifle from the gun cabinet, set it on the bed and proceeded to give an explanation. Rifles have grooves inside the bore to make the bullet spin, improving its accuracy. The advantage of shotguns is they cover a wide area. Japan's former army used rifles. After a rifle has been fired, you must break it down for a good cleaning. Otherwise, you can't count on it in battle.

Wakako picked up the rifle, gingerly at first, then, gathering her nerve, she struck a shooting pose. She went through the motions of loading the gun and pulled its trigger.

He talked about stalking deer. Their hearing is fifty times sharper than humans. Deer can pick up the sound of human voices far behind them, so they are long gone by the time hunters arrive. You must approach silently, from downwind. Sometimes you can attract them with a deer call. But once a deer knows humans are around, it will immediately flee downwind. The ability to pursue and kill this elusive animal is the real test of one's mettle as a hunter.

"That's fascinating. I'd like to try it."

"Hey, I've been doing all the talking. I was supposed to be listening to your story. Tell me why you don't want to go home. What are the family matters you mentioned?"

"Let that be," she said sharply. "Let's not talk about it now. Go on with what you were saying. I've never heard this kind of talk before. It's fifty times more interesting than university lectures."

"It's late, almost four." He returned the rifle to its cabinet, thinking, What do I do next? No, make that, What happens next?

"What time do you get up?" Wakako asked, falling backwards into the space on the bed the gun had occupied.

"Five thirty. I leave here at seven. That gets me to work at eight thirty."

"Every day?"

"Yep."

"Including tomorrow, of course. I mean, today. If you're going to work today, you'd better get some sleep. You'll only get an hour and a half, though."

"That's enough. You sleep on the bed. I'm sleeping on the floor."

Atsuo pulled the bed cover over Wakako. The young woman tumbled about atop the blankets and stretched her jeans-clad legs. The graceful body he had observed spinning atop the ice lay before him. Molten desire surged up inside. He could have her this moment. But it was no good. He still didn't know why she had come. He had no idea what would make a woman come in the dead of night to the home of a man twice her age. He made a bed for himself on the floor in the space between the TV and dining table with a few cushions and blankets.

"You can shower if you want. There's hot water." She said she wanted to shower, so he turned on the heater, then lay down, just as he was. Thanks to the alcohol he had consumed, sleep claimed him immediately.

He awakened to the sound of rain on the roof. It was full daylight. He had overslept, having forgotten to set the alarm clock. He looked at his watch, which he was still wearing. It was past eight. No way to make it to work on time. After all these years at Fukawa Motors, he was suddenly late for work repeatedly.

Overcome with the need to rise quickly, it took a moment to remember he wasn't in his bed, but Wakako was. Her head was buried beneath a blanket. Twenty-five past eight. Better call in, he thought, and overturned the bottle of shochu on the table as rushed for the telephone. It wasn't capped, and the contents spilled out. He dialed the number and the stentorian voice of Ichiro Fukawa abruptly began blaring from the receiver. Atsuo hastily pinched his nose as he spoke.

"Guess I caught a cold. I have a fever."

"That's unusual for you."

"I'm running thirty-nine degrees. Going to have a doctor look at me."

"This really puts us in a fix. Thanks to the rioting in Shinjuku the trains aren't running and three men can't get to work. On top of that we've got another wreck to fix. The students got to it. We're running around here like crazy. We don't have enough hands."

"I'll come in when my fever goes down."

"Nah, not if you got a thirty-nine degree temperature. Don't take the chance. Oh, by the way, Jinnai got hurt. Like a fool, he was in Shinjuku. Looks like someone hit him. He won't say who — police or students. These kids like to live dangerously."

"So how is he?"

"He wasn't hurt bad. He's working, just limping on his left leg."

Putting down the receiver he found Wakako's eyes fixed steadily upon him. He smiled. "Looks like I woke you up. Go ahead, sleep as long as you like. I'm taking off from work today."

"You mustn't do that. You have to go to work." Using the back of her hand to brush aside a tear caused by yawning, she slowly arose from the bed, emerging from the blanket in the same jeans and sweater she had been wearing the previous night.

"I just got tired of being a work-horse. Today I'll be with you."

"Oh, okay," she responded, lightly accepting the situation. She went to a mirror on a door-frame post and began combing her hair. It was cut short, revealing an elegant neck.

"Ohhh . . . I didn't bring any makeup," she said, patting a cheek.

"Did you have makeup on?"

"Of course. I may not be much, but I am female."

"You're beautiful just as you are, without makeup."

"Thank you," she said, turning to face him. Her expression wasn't one of gratification, but the offhand attitude of a woman accustomed to being told how beautiful she is.

Atsuo set to smoothing out his jacket, much crumpled from rain and being slept in the previous day. "I suppose we're in for some misunderstanding from people," he said.

Wakako was silent for a time before she asked, "About what?"

"You and me spending the night in the same room. People draw conclusions about that sort of thing."

She didn't answer, so Atsuo grabbed an umbrella and went out for groceries. He bought bread, butter, cheese, and jam. Normally, he would have made do with bread and margarine alone. When he returned, coffee was brewing and two servings of fried eggs were on the table.

As they ate, she said abruptly, "There's nothing for you to worry about. I came here of my own free will. Yesterday, going home was really repellent to me. I had a big fight with my mother — I mean an argument — in the morning. Then my father came and started yelling at me to keep quiet. It was an awful scene, so I went flying out the door and decided I wouldn't come back."

"But still . . ."

"I've done that more times than I can count. My mother and father are probably just thinking, 'Here we go again.' I'm not going back home. Let me stay. I'll stay inside all the time."

"No, that's not . . ."

"I'll pay for my meals. I'll pay for board too."

"That's no problem. But if you stayed here, that would make me like a kidnapper or something."

"You kidnapping me?" Wakako was indignant. "I'm not a minor!"

"But you're so young, compared to me! Maybe not a minor, but the next thing to it."

"Is that how I look to you? How can you say that? That's just as bad as my parents — they don't treat me like an adult either. So when you brought me here last night, did you think you were kidnapping a minor?"

Suddenly, she was overcome with emotion. Tears streamed from her eyes as if a tap had been opened. This was highly upsetting to Atsuo, who was at a loss when it came to dealing with young women.

"I'm sorry. Forgive me. That isn't how I meant it. I just felt like I was responsible for separating you from your parents."

"It's all right." Now Wakako was laughing. "You don't have to make a big apology. I just wanted to worry you a little."

"That's a relief." Atsuo sighed. "I can't stand watching you cry. It has to do with all the times I made my mother and sister cry, years ago. Now I try to watch myself so I won't be like that any more."

"How did you make them cry?"

"By getting into trouble. I was pretty wild when I was young. Went to army prison and all." Atsuo looked down at the scar on his index finger. He had far worse things in his past than that. He had been imprisoned time and again. If he told her that she would of course be stunned, and feel disdain for him. This young lady and he unquestionably belonged to separate worlds.

"There is one thing I can say. I did try desperately not to make my mother cry. But I kept sliding back into trouble. It was like sinking into quicksand. I couldn't pull myself out."

"I know why you can look at things that way. Your mother deserves the credit. With me, it's just the opposite. My parents make me cry. They put me into a mental hospital twice."

" . . ."

"It was really awful." Wakako placed some cheese between two bread slices and proceeded to rip off huge chunks until it was all crammed into her mouth. Then she washed it down with coffee. It was a kind of self-administered forced feeding.

"When I get provoked, I eat like crazy. I gained ten kilos in the hospital."

"When was that?"

"The year before last. Remember when I was away from the skating rink for six months?"

He did. She had suddenly disappeared. When next she showed up, her explanation was that she had been in the hospital with a broken leg. She did seem to have gained some weight.

"After I get out of the hospital, my weight goes down to normal again right away. I'm like an air pillow."

"When was the other time?"

"This spring, when I said I had been overseas. That was a lie. I was in the hospital."

"What was the matter with you?"

"Everything was despicable, meaningless. I wanted to die, I wanted to cry, I wanted to run away somewhere. I couldn't stand being where I was."

Wakako cast her eyes down. Her hair was fragrant. She was like a flower wilted by the rain. The shadow over her heart seemed to have fallen over his as well, for he was seized with an overwhelming feeling of anxiety. Every now and then the world looked hateful and meaningless to himself as well.

Wakako continued quietly, as if to herself.

"One day I escaped from my hospital. It was a five-story building, in the middle of town. The windows didn't have bars, but they were made of reinforced glass and would only open a little way. I went down the fire escape from the roof. A nurse saw me when I went past the front entrance. She chased after me as I ran. First it was just her, but when I looked back again there were three people running after me. It was broad daylight and people were everywhere. There I was in my pajamas, barefoot — so of course they all thought I was a lunatic. I stopped at a crossing. The light was red. I just stood there, thinking everything was pointless. That's how they caught me."

"That's a feeling I can understand. I was in the same boat, in prison."

"Yes . . ." Wakako smiled sadly. For some reason, her cheerfulness of the previous night had completely evaporated. Even physically, she seemed thin and enervated. Women's minds and bodies are a mystery, he thought. He wanted to say something comforting. What would be comforting to her?

"The reason they put me into army prison was because I ran away. I ran away because I didn't like the army, but the joke was on me. If you run away they put you in a prison that's the same as the army, but worse. It's like you, running away because the crazy world gets you down and they put you in a mental hospital."

"Yes, that's it. That's it exactly." This time Wakako's expressive eyes were shining.

"It's weak people who run away," Atsuo continued with feeling. "But the world doesn't tolerate weak people. The ones who run away always get locked up somewhere as punishment."

"Exactly. You've got it."

"What the weak ought to do is help each other out, but they are the ones least able to get together. So they lose out."

"But you seem awfully strong."

"I'm not, though, not at all. In fact, I'm weak. All it takes is a little push and I go down."

The rain began falling much harder. Didn't Wakako have classes to attend?

74

He knew he probably wouldn't be going to work that day. A whole day off! He would like to spend all day like this, talking with her. He wondered if he could.

"Don't you have to go to the university?"

"We're locked out. The administration closed the school and won't let the students in."

"Just the reverse of the situation with T. University. All very complicated. You did say you go to R. University, right? What's your major?"

"Ah, yes, a background check. Chemistry major. Department of Science and Engineering."

"That's a surprise. I thought it would be literature or something."

"I've liked physics and science since I was little," Wakako said. "I definitely am an odd one."

They went out in the rain for a walk, after she accepted Atsuo's proposal that they visit Jindai Botanical Garden. There was a psychiatric hospital on the way. Wakako stopped to look it over. The hospital confined all its patients in their wards. They could be seen restlessly moving about behind the barred windows, like fish in a tank.

"What are you thinking?" he asked.

"That all the people inside are the weak ones. That they are all suffering."

"Yes, I guess they must be." He looked at the hospital from her point of view. Those patients had always seemed so very remote, like people from outer space. He was suddenly able to see them as warm, approachable human beings.

"Oh, look," said Wakako with the excitement of having discovered something. "See that little window set high up at the corner of the building?"

"I see it."

"That's a seclusion room. It's a cell for patients who get excited. They're completely solid. I was put into seclusion once."

"No kidding."

"I wrapped my arms around a nurse and started choking her. I was faking, but the doctor said my condition was worsening and I was dangerous, so they threw me in there."

"Awful thing to do to a person."

"No, actually, the seclusion room is the best place. When you are in a regular hospital room the other patients bother you. When I want to be by myself I let my condition take a bad turn."

"The doctors should be able to see through a pretense like that."

"There isn't one who can . . . Ahh, I want to be by myself. Talking about seclusion rooms made me feel like I want to be in one."

"That's quite a statement coming from someone who hates mental hospitals."

"A contradiction. That's me, just one big mass of contradictions."

From the grass came feeble sounds of crickets, their energy sapped by the rain. The wind drove water droplets from the bamboo grass. An artificial green color at the far end of a cabbage patch was a golf driving range. There were no players. The botanical garden was also deserted, except for a groundskeeper wearing a plastic poncho. Atsuo strolled along without hesitation about which path to take.

"Do you come here often?"

"Well, it is so close by. But this is my first time coming on a rainy day."

The wind was blowing great beads of water from the treetops. The yellow leaves fluttered heavily. Finally they reached the rose garden. Though past their prime, the roses were still blooming, casting a cool fragrance across the grounds. Under the dark sky, the brightness of the flowers seemed fluorescent. The couple retreated from the rain under the eaves of a shuttered shop, and from there gazed about tirelessly. Wakako took Atsuo's arm and nestled close.

"I'm frightened."

"Of what?"

"Someone's watching."

"There isn't anyone here."

"Over there," said Wakako, pointing to a dry fountain in the middle of the rose garden.

The aging yellow flowers were nodding to one another, a gaggle of wizened faces. That was all. There was no trace of human presence.

"There isn't anyone there," Atsuo said, flatly dismissing her suspicion.

"He's hiding. That's always the way. As soon as you spot them, they disappear."

"For goodness sake, who?"

"A spy. From the organization." It was evident from her voice it was that she was trembling. Perhaps it wasn't only because of the cold that she had been trembling since the previous day.

"I don't really understand. What kind of organization do you mean?"

"Look, organizations manipulate the world, right? There are invisible organizations set up everywhere. They manage people. Isn't that right?"

"Well, yes, you could say that. Like, for instance . . ."

He was going to say states, laws, police, but then it seemed to him none of those things precisely fit what she had in mind.

"Those organizations have tremendous power, but they are very suspicious. And they're scared of people who want to destroy them. Right?"

"That's true . . ."

"That's why they are always sending out spies to watch those people. I'm one of the dangerous ones, so they're always watching me."

"..."

"Don't you understand what I'm saying?" Wakako's lovely face was creased at the brow.

"Sure I understand," he said gently. He didn't understand at all, but wanted to be caring.

"You do understand. That's it. That's why I'm frightened."

"I'll look after you. Come on, let's get going."

The rain had let up. They set out walking through a wooded area. Leaves burdened by raindrops fell and struck their foreheads. There was a playground, its jungle gym and slide cold and gleaming. Taking the rear exit and walking a short distance brought them to a tea shop, and, next to that, an entrance gate with a wooden sign that said "All Souls Monument: Jindai Temple Domestic Animal Cemetery."

"What might this be?" Wakako asked.

"A cemetery for dogs and cats. They call that spire the All Souls Monument. There are shrines for animals all around it," Atsuo replied.

"Let's go see."

Around the towering steeple was a hexagonal building housing numerous little shelves upon which were aligned mortuary urns, tablets, artificial flowers and, here and there, photographs of animals. Each memorial identified the departed pet and its owner. "In memory of our beloved dog, Lucky" . . . "Spirit of our beloved cat, Hina-chan." Though the bad weather was keeping visitors away, the heavy scent of memorial incense permeated the building. Atsuo suddenly recalled Torakichi Jinnai making memorial tablets for animals he killed and enshrining them in his household Buddhist altar.

"My brother-in-law makes memorials for dead animals too."

"He does?"

"He's a hunter. Remember my nephew at the skating rink? His father. He regrets having to kill animals for his livelihood, so he prays for them."

Wakako silently turned from the monument. Atsuo continued talking.

"My brother-in-law loves animals. Deer, foxes, whatever — he really likes being around them, and wouldn't kill them if it could be avoided. But that's his work."

"He should find some other work."

"Yeah, if he could. It would be better if there was something else he was suited for, but he's a born hunter. It's the only way he can live."

"What it all comes to is he likes hunting. That's why he can't stop."

"Maybe so." Atsuo thought about this as he and Wakako descended the stone stairway. (Torakichi was born in Tokyo and became an average company employee, but he loved roaming through the mountains and hunting. Finally, he settled in eastern Hokkaido. Just the opposite of me, leaving behind that land to live in the big city. I was born there, but now it's where Torakichi belongs and I'm the Tokyoite.)

There was a path along the base of a precipice that was accessed by a side gate to Jindai Temple. After the downhill route that continued for a time, the way to the main shrine was again uphill.

There was no one around. The priests' living quarters were a forlorn sight, with their discolored plaster walls. They gazed at the wooden votive tablets displayed outside the shrine. Upon each one was written some visitor's orison to the gods: "Watch over our home." . . . "Give us a child soon." . . . "Bring success on my exam." . . . "Make my grades better."

"Everyone is looking for happiness," Atsuo commented.

"Everything is about home and school. Why doesn't anyone pray for something bigger?"

"Well, home and school is the whole world as far as most people are concerned. If you're like me, with no family, no schooling, they look like very big wishes. You have both, so I guess average people's wishes look small to you. You should count your blessings."

"With my family, there's nothing to count. Those dogs and cats over there got more consideration than I do."

"That isn't . . ." Atsuo trailed off. He didn't think he could persuade her of his point of view and he had no desire to argue with her. "Let's get something to eat," he proposed. She nodded.

The street outside the main temple entrance was lined with shops offering souvenirs and noodles, but all were closed. Finally, they found a restaurant that was open. It had a fishing pond outside stocked with rainbow trout.

"We're in luck. They serve great herb tempura here."

They were the only two customers. Behind the fishing pond a waterfall issued from a miniature mountain. Trout were cavorting happily at the rain-lashed water surface. A television set was turned on, apparently intended as a customer service.

"Typhoon 19 is now over the ocean, far south of Shikoku, moving at a relatively slow speed to the northeast. There is a strong possibility this typhoon will follow a course a little more to the south than initially expected. Because the autumnal rain front is stationary over Japan's southern coastline, there is a chance of heavy rains in some areas. For details on the path of the typhoon . . ."

"Typhoon, eh? I thought that was a pretty strong wind in the street."

"I hope it comes soon. I love typhoons." Wakako said this with sudden cheerfulness.

"That sounds pretty brave to me," Atsuo said to encourage this display of high spirits.

"I just really like typhoons! When I was a child I'd put on a swim suit and run out in the garden when a typhoon came. It's not just rain falling. The wind blows in leaves, branches, boards, paper, pieces of roofing. It's great fun."

"Dangerous too. There are people who have been killed by falling trees in typhoons."

"I can't think of a better way to die."

A silvery haired man came in with a young woman dressed in kimono. They sat down at a table far away. Wakako suddenly lapsed into an uneasy silence. With counterfeit lightness, Atsuo remarked, "Wonder if he's her father."

"No, they're completely unalike. They're lovers."

"Their ages are too far apart."

"Oho," Wakako laughed. "Well, what about us?"

"Yeah, you could say that."

"That couple is wondering about us. They're saying, 'They're completely unalike. Do you suppose they're lovers?'"

Atsuo nodded as if seeking her agreement. "Yeah, they probably are."

"Ahh, who knows?" Wakako's smile was gone, as if it had been extinguished by the wind.

Atsuo tasted bitter disappointment. He had been pondering the question of their relationship since the previous day, but the riddle remained. Why hadn't she returned home? Why stay at his place? What was she thinking now? It was all incomprehensible. At the same time, the desire for her he had felt the night before came back, together with regret over a lost opportunity. Maybe she had come to his apartment because she was counting on his desire for her. Maybe she was even more disappointed than himself that nothing had happened.

Their order came: Tempura of *ikema*, *yuki-no-shita*, *yomogi*, and bamboo shoots, served on a bamboo basket tray.

"Tastes best when it's hot," he said, pulling apart a pair of wooden chopsticks. Wakako suddenly stood up.

"I have to make a phone call."

She was gone before he could say, "Why not have your meal first?" He slowly chewed on a piece of tempura as she stood about twenty meters away, speaking on a pay phone. What if I could marry Wakako? I'm an eligible bachelor. So what if she's so young, if she goes to university! Wouldn't it be wonderful if we could be together? That horse-faced widow from Kushiro my sister wants to fix me up with is certainly no consideration. But there is a problem, and I'm it. Could she really just accept someone like me, with such a long record of repeat offenses? Could a woman so easily hurt, so plagued by anxiety, who has been in a mental hospital, cope with someone with a past like mine?

Wakako returned. Without a word, she began eating the now cold tempura with gusto. He reflected once again, as he had so many times, that to him, this woman was incomprehensible.

"Did you call home?" Atsuo asked.

Wakako shook her head and answered with her mouth full. "Him."

"Who's 'him?'"

"Makihiko Moriya."

"Am I supposed to know that name?"

"Did you forget? I told you about him in Shinjuku. My boyfriend. You know, the one with the long hair who goes to T. University. He said he didn't get arrested and was all right."

"Oh, him."

"Drinking makes you forgetful, doesn't it? Don't you remember you talked about yourself? You said you're a foreman at a big plant, that you go on classy hunting expeditions and you've got more money than you know what to do with."

"Eh?" He had no recollection. It seemed to him he had said something when they were in Golden Lane, but he couldn't remember what. He'd fallen into a deep, alcohol-induced slumber.

"That was the whiskey talking. As you saw, I live a humble life. I work at an auto repair shop. I'm just a mechanic. For someone who only went to elementary school, what else could you expect?"

"Why do you talk about yourself that way?"

"Why? I'm only stating the facts. I don't want you to have the wrong idea about what kind of person I am. I don't amount to anything. I'm an ex-con."

"You were in army prison. That couldn't be helped. The real crime was the war."

"That's not the whole story." A masochistic impulse rose up inside, a desire to spill out his whole sordid tale, to turn himself inside-out. It was the same powerful impulse that arose during police interrogations. He began speaking, the words spewing out as if from a small opening under air pressure. "You see, I'm . . ." he began, then was stopped by an opposing feeling that proved even more powerful; the conviction that this young girl couldn't possibly be made to understand. This despair made him pause.

". . ." She was waiting, eyes wide.

"Aw, it's just that I'm worthless. Couldn't go to school. That's always kept me on the bottom of the heap. You've got to dislike that kind of man."

"No." She spoke in a low tone, but with the strength of conviction. "I like you."

"Really?"

"Yes, I really do. You're honest. You're for real."

"Thank you," Atsuo said quietly, profoundly affected. "I am what I am. Let's keep this secret. Just between us."

"Right. That's how I want it too."

"Okay, we have each other's secret. Now what are you going to do today?"

"Guess for today I'll go home."

"That's for the best. We can meet again."

Wakako smiled. This was somewhat of a relief to Atsuo, but he remained troubled that he had been unable to tell her the truth. The rain blew across the windowpane, distorting the image of the garden outside. "Let me see you off," he said in a somber voice.

Chapter 3

Marsh

Milky white brightness crept into a gray world, announcing the night's passing. The fog thinned occasionally to unveil a rolling vista of golden reeds stretching to the horizon, before dropping its heavy shroud once again.

Finally, a shack appeared, phantom-like, in the mist. Rippling, blue-black water became visible. They had reached the Furen River salmon roe extraction station. The jeep plunged into a tall clump of grass and stopped. Then Torakichi Jinnai emerged.

"We're going to leave the car here. I have to drop in and say hello." He threw back his shoulders and, taking slow and purposeful strides with his short legs, he went inside.

Atsuo emerged from the back seat and began removing sets of rubber boots, ponchos and coverall bottoms. "Well, let's get ready to move," he called to Ichiro Fukawa and Kimiko Fujiyama.

Fukawa responded with a hearty "Yo!" and emerged somewhat unsteadily from the back seat. His hunting jacket, with its massive pockets on the back, bulged near to bursting under the pressure of too many layers of underwear and sweaters worn against the cold.

Kimiko was dressed in a bright red ski outfit that no serious hunter would consider wearing. As the couple donned their rubber boots, Torakichi and Atsuo went to an aluminum boat resting ashore and lowered it to the water. Torakichi deftly attached the boat's rudder and screw assembly. It was full daylight by the time the guns and gear had been loaded in and the boat was under way, the fog merely hovering low over the water.

Fukawa sat in the prow, one moment scanning the surroundings with his binoculars, the next opening his gun case to stroke his rifle, then checking the fit of the ammunition belt on his waist, his restless movement never ceasing. Whenever a bird rose from the reeds he emitted loud exclamations and asked Torakichi their names. In this way, a crow, a black-backed gull, and a sandpiper were identified. The first duck was yet to be sighted.

"That's an awful lot of dead alder," Atsuo commented to Torakichi.

"Yeah. It gets worse every year. Salinization does it."

Fallen treetops lined the river like cactuses. There were withered trees extending back inland, making the scenery resemble a vast graveyard.

"Do you suppose cow dung has anything to do with it?"

"Who knows? There are more cattle ranches now upriver, and they just throw their dung away."

The river widened, affording a clear view across the reed bed. The thin fog made reed tips glisten like crystal. Suddenly, gunshots from somewhere resounded under the cloudy sky.

"Damn! They're at it already." Fukawa's tone was bitter. His eyes darted to the new American-made gun he'd ordered, as if eager to start shooting soon.

The boat was heading toward a sandbank. A black shadow passed overhead. Atsuo couldn't tell if it was a wild duck or a goosander.

"There's a duck," Torakichi said.

"Where?" Fukawa asked excitedly. The boat rocked.

"Over there," said a composed Kimiko, pointing to a dot in the sky.

Torakichi eased the boat onto the sandbank whose reeds rose above human height, offering far better cover than the waist-high clumps of bamboo grass scattered throughout the marsh.

"Here's where we shoot." Torakichi extended his hand to Fukawa and helped him ashore.

Kimiko stepped out and her feet sank into the mire. Atsuo reached to steady her, commenting, "You have to be careful here. Some places are bottomless holes that will suck you right in."

"This place is kind of scary," she answered, edging meekly over to the dry bamboo grass. Atsuo had made his ominous comment for the fun of seeing the bravery evaporate from one so given to egotism back in the company president's office. During the airplane ride he had filled her with hair-raising stories of the marshland. Much of the territory from Nemuro to Kushiro is underlain with semisolid peat — once you sink in, there's no getting out again under your own power. There are only a few riverbanks that are safe to walk along, and even there you have to be on guard because water underlies the strata of solid ground. That danger keeps humans out of the area, and makes it a bounteous fish reserve, home to the legendary giant huchen salmon, as well as regular chum salmon, cherry salmon, Sakhalin trout, rainbow trout, dolly varden trout, dace, flounder, pond smelt, stickleback . . . and many, many more, all there for the taking.

"That's for me," Kimiko had enthused. "I'd love to go fishing there."

Fukawa had been taking Kimiko on ocean fishing trips since the previous year, and now she wanted to try her hand at river fishing. Accordingly, Atsuo had proposed that for the next Hokkaido trip they plan plenty of time for fishing as well as hunting.

"I'm going to scout around," said Torakichi, and he went out in the boat by himself.

Atsuo made himself useful by hauling the gear to the reed-covered dry ground, taking the guns from their bags and sorting the cartridges by size. Fukawa picked up his gun and walked off to the middle of the sandbar, heedlessly splashing through puddles. Atsuo was thinking Fukawa was creating enough of a disturbance to startle any birds around when one rose up from somewhere underfoot. Fukawa fired while it was leisurely moving its wings, still close to the ground, but he missed. At the same moment, five wild ducks flew off. Fukawa returned to their outpost.

"Missed, dammit! Crazy bird takes off right in front of me, where I least expect!"

"That was awfully loud," Kimiko said reproachfully. "You might have given some warning."

"Better put your fingers in your ears, or you'll get a broken eardrum," Atsuo said ominously.

"Pretty soon there's going to be a whole lot of shooting."

Tetsukichi returned in the boat to report that a sizable number of ducks were on the water downstream and would doubtlessly be flying their way presently.

The fog had retreated to the sea. A pair of red-crested cranes sounded their distinctive *karroo! karroo!* as they searched for food. A cluster of black specks moving low in the sky suddenly reversed direction: sandpipers. The hunters waited amidst the reeds. Water lapped softly at the riverbank.

A single bird, flying upwind, appeared overhead. Its path was crossed by another bird — perhaps a duck, perhaps a goosander. It was flying slowly. Fukawa fired and the bird fell writhing into the steam.

Bleeding, the bird raised its wings above the water and barely managed to gain flight. Flapping desperately, it proceeded for a while like a butterfly, then fell again. Fukawa fired again, but missed, so Atsuo finished it off with another shot. Torakichi took the boat to bring it in. It was a red-breasted merganser — similar to a mallard, but with a slenderer bill, and not especially good eating.

"That's no great prize," said Fukawa regretfully. Atsuo nevertheless split open the bird's belly and gutted it to insure the odor from the intestine wouldn't reach the meat.

"Sure would be nice to have duck stew tonight."

"All right, let's be sure to bag enough for dinner." Atsuo picked up a double-barreled gun and crept off cautiously through the bamboo grass.

As he approached the end of the sandbar he sensed motion in a pool just beyond some bushes. Looking back, he realized that Fukawa and the others had become tiny far-off figures. He slowed his breathing and waited impassively. A cold wind rustled the grasses. It came from the southwest, wind force two ... no, probably three. A large flock of sandpipers passed by. It was beautiful the way such a large group could change its direction in an instant, in perfect order. No troop leader's command could elicit a formation that sharp. Scholars said this behavior pattern originated in the sympathetic nervous system. However the phenomenon worked, it was amazing.

Atsuo felt greatly relieved to be finally off by himself. He had been continually preoccupied with attending to Fukawa and Kimiko. Fukawa hadn't announced that she would be part of the outing until the last moment. Her inclusion required additional flight and hotel reservations and Torakichi's okay. Then it was necessary to prevent the suspicious tale telling that could be expected from Sonoko Kanéhara by explaining to her that Kimiko was going along on the trip to recruit new personnel to hire. This excursion was proving to be one headache after another for Atsuo. He had reserved separate hotel rooms for Fukawa and Kimiko, but when Fukawa switched to a room with twin beds, it was clear they would be spending their nights together. When Torakichi caught on to this relationship, he developed a loathing for Kimiko that he expressed by speaking to her with gratuitous curtness. High-strung as ever, Fukawa fussed over this perceived ill humor, while Kimiko baited Torakichi with unnecessary questions. It was getting to be more than Atsuo could stand.

From somewhere, a shot rang out. It wasn't Fukawa's gun. A pair of cranes were standing by, quite calmly, as if they knew that they weren't hunters' quarry.

Atsuo sensed a presence. His gun was already raised by the moment the sound of wings reached his ears. There were two birds. He fired a hair in front of the one in the lead. As it went down, he hit the other one full on. He'd killed them before they could escape to the water. Shouldn't boast, he thought, but that was some nice shooting.

He picked up the birds, blood spurting; each had been shot through the heart. There was no need for any thought as his hands moved of their own accord to open the bellies and pull out the entrails.

"Here's dinner," he said, holding up the two birds.

"Oho," said Fukawa, licking his lips. "Very glad to see these plump little fellows."

Atsuo tossed the birds at Kimiko's feet. She jumped aside and gave a theatrical shriek. "So how do you like hunting?"

"Oh, it's scary, but fun," she said, shrilly.

Torakichi cut her off with a sharp "Shh!" A good number of ducks were flying their way in a disorderly V-formation.

"C'mon, let's give them the business," Atsuo said to encourage Fukawa, who was quaking with anticipation. He reached for his new rifle, then thought better of it and armed himself with a shotgun. Poised like an anti-aircraft gunner awaiting the approach of enemy planes, he aimed carefully, but the flock of ducks suddenly veered off to flee in the opposite direction.

"Now!" said Atsuo.

Fukawa fired once, then a second time, but in vain. "A little too far off," he said regretfully. "How come they broke off course like that?"

"It's no good to wear red. It stands out too much," said Torakichi curtly.

"He means me," said Kimiko defensively. "Well, what am I supposed to do? It's cold!"

Atsuo held out a gray-colored windbreaker. He had offered it to her when the party set out, but had been rebuffed on the grounds that she found it too unsightly. "Hurry up and get it on," he said, glaring at her. Dourly, Kimiko put the windbreaker over her red ski outfit.

All sorts of birds passed by as they waited in the thick reed cover. There were gulls, goosanders, crows and others, but there was no more magnificent spectacle than the white-tailed eagle in flight carrying a large fish, its massive wings reflected on the water.

"Isn't this great?" said Fukawa. "There's nobody around. You can't even imagine this in Tokyo."

"You can say that again," Atsuo replied agreeably. "All those people in Tokyo can really wear you down."

"Getting pretty chilly. Could do with a little alcohol about now."

Atsuo pulled out a small bottle of whiskey from a pocket and handed it over. Fukawa drank off two capfuls, poured a third and offered it to Atsuo, who refused, so he drank that too. Then he carefully wiped condensation from the barrel of his gun, counted cartridges, reshuffled the contents of his hunting jacket pockets and lit a cigarette, never once keeping still. By the time he had finished off the bottle, he was tipsy enough to have lost his inhibitions. He drew Kimiko close, nestling his cheek against hers. She made a mumbled protest and pulled away, but eventually gave in and moved close to Fukawa, while Torakichi and Atsuo pretended not to notice.

After about an hour's time, Torakichi announced to Fukawa, "I'm sorry, boss, but this is no good. The birds don't like us. Let's go shooting from the boat."

"Shoot from the boat? Okay, fine!" Fukawa was delighted. He patted his watermelon belly and walked unsteadily to the water's edge, where he unleashed a robust stream of urine.

Kimiko made a face. "Ugh! I wish you'd go further away when you do that," she said, pushing back some stray hairs.

About a kilometer beyond the sandbar, the river came to an end and they entered the vast expanse of Lake Furen. A brisk wind was blowing, waves rolling across the water. The shallow lake was host to vast beds of eelgrass that could easily snarl a boat's screw. Successful navigation required keeping to a charted boating channel where the current was fast. Torakichi of course maneuvered the boat handily, without the slightest letup on speed. The low-lying land around them was like a green line applied by brush. The contour of the line was defined entirely by the height of a coniferous forest.

"There're ducks," said Torakichi.

"Where?" Fukawa excitedly grabbed his binoculars.

"Over there," said Torakichi, pointing.

There was a yellowish-brown promontory extending out into the water like a flattop tanker. Out beyond it one could barely make out indistinct forms swimming on the water. At that distance, it took an eye like Torakichi's to have spotted them.

"Hey, no kidding they are ducks! Looks like mallards, lots of them. I can almost taste them." Fukawa was beside himself with joy.

"Okay, how's this strategy? This current will take us right along from down-wind heading upwind. So we cut the engine and just let the boat drift up close."

"Okay, great," said Fukawa, in instant agreement.

"The reeds are thick out there," said Atsuo thoughtfully. "If you lie prone in the boat you won't be seen — that's for sure. But there are too many people for everyone to do that. I'll get off on the land spit and wait there. In case you miss, I might even be able to down some birds as they fly away."

"Good idea!" said Fukawa. "Do that, will you?"

"That still leaves too many people. Ms. Fujiyama, please get out too."

"Me, too?" said Kimiko. Clearly dissatisfied, she cast a searching look at Fukawa. The promontory was a desolate scene of dead trees and dried-up weeds. She didn't seem to like the prospect of being left alone in such a lonely place with Atsuo.

The boat reached a shore overlooked by withered alders. Atsuo alighted. With no intervention from Fukawa forthcoming, Kimiko followed resignedly. The boat's engine was silenced, supplies were removed from the boat and the two men positioned themselves prone in the boat's bottom. Atsuo gave the boat a shove, and it drifted slowly away.

"I have to get ready for battle too," said Atsuo, as he strapped on an ammunition belt and shouldered a gun. His plan was to creep out to the end of the promontory to back up Fukawa after he fired. "The ground's soft, so let's be careful walking," he said, and turned to find Kimiko with her back against a tree trunk, legs stretched out.

"I'll be waiting here. Is there anything to eat? I'm hungry."

He took out a couple of sandwiches and some juice from the supplies. As he was handing them to her, she took his hand. Startled by the cold, moist grip, he pulled his hand away. She burst out laughing. "Don't worry, I won't eat it. I just wanted to touch your hand. It's so like you — warm and strong."

"I have to go."

"That's all right. You can just leave me here. This is all just playtime for the boss, anyway. No need to entertain me." Kimiko yawned. "So sleepy. I was up at five o'clock this morning. Hunting certainly isn't for lazy people. Oh, come on, won't you sit down for a minute and chat with me? Here we are, finally alone!"

Atsuo took care to seat himself a good two meters away from her. The layers of thick clothing she wore paradoxically set off the generous curves of her breasts and hips. The prominence of her lips made her nose seem a little small, but it had a gentle outline that was exceedingly graceful.

"To tell the truth, you're looking at an unhappy woman," said Kimiko dejectedly.

"Really," Atsuo replied, with a hint of irony. "I was thinking you are about as happy-looking a woman as anyone could find."

He didn't really know much about Kimiko Fujiyama. Her husband belonged to some company or other and they had three children. When the youngest started middle school, Kimiko had taken a job with Fukawa Motors to help out with family expenses. She was a junior college graduate, had a class one qualification in abacus, and could speak English well enough that she never had difficulty dealing with American customers who came into the shop.

"No, I really am unhappy. I got married at nineteen, while I was still in college. The next thing I knew I was having one baby after another. I was so preoccupied with the children, youth passed me by. Now I'm an old lady."

"Well, you seem to be doing just what you want to do," Atsuo said with a hint of irony.

"With the boss, you mean," Kimiko said, without anger. She continued in her despondent tone. "He's the one who kept chasing after me. I kept resisting for the longest time. Finally, I told my husband the whole story. I said I wanted to quit the job. What do you think he told me?"

"He must have been angry."

"Not a bit. I wish he had gotten mad, but he liked the situation. He said it proved I'm attractive. He told me to play around as much as I wanted."

"Well, I guess that's one way of looking at things."

"That husband of mine, he was hitting forty and there just wasn't any zip left in him. I guess that's why he wasn't jealous. Maybe some people would call that being a good sport, but I don't like it at all!"

Atsuo was incensed by this comment. "You don't like it, do you? You're married, have children — that is quite a lot to call your own, but it doesn't stop you from running around. Then you blame it all on your husband. That's way too self-centered!"

Kimiko would not be angered. She sighed. "Is it?" she said sadly. "Actually, he's more self-centered than I am. He doesn't so much as glance at the children. He won't lift a finger at home. He's always claiming to be busy with his job, but finds plenty of time to go drinking at bars and taking off on golfing trips. He doesn't give a thought to what might make his wife happy."

"So does the boss think about making you happy?"

"Hmm, does he now?" Kimiko yawned. She really did seem to be sleepy. "He isn't dependable at all. He doesn't want to wreck his marriage, so he's careful about not doing anything to wreck mine. That's all there is to it. In other words, it's all just recreation. That makes for a lukewarm relationship. It's boring."

"Humph. I see. Okay, you are an unhappy woman."

"That's the truth. I'm glad I could get you to understand."

In a single instant a flock of birds rose up in the distance like an expanding fireball, and shots rang out. It was too far off to be able to tell if any ducks had been hit. A number were coming their way; an easy target, flying low. Atsuo raised his gun and fired into empty sky.

"Oh, you missed," Kimiko said with disappointment.

"I missed on purpose. We've already bagged two ducks. That's already plenty for dinner, and the boss probably got one. I don't want to destroy any more life than necessary."

"Spoken like a real man! That's what I like about you."

He was mentally groping for a way to extricate himself from the woman's insistent gaze as the sound of the boat's engine neared. Soon, Fukawa was before them with a bird in each hand, displaying his inimitable smile. "Bagged me a couple of big ones!" he shouted.

"Great, congratulations." Atsuo grasped the hawser and pulled the boat ashore.

"You fired too, didn't you? Down any?"

"Nah, I missed."

"You mean you really do miss sometimes?"

"Sure. Only human, you know." Atsuo poked a dry stick into each bird's anus in turn, twisted it around and pulled out the intestines. They were large, female ducks. Cast into a pool, the intestines floated, gleaming bluish-black.

Fukawa looked at the sky. "Wonder if it'll clear?" The sun was enveloped in a white cocoon of downy clouds. The water of the lake was clear, affording an unobstructed view of its coffee-colored bottom.

"No, it's going to shower," Torakichi replied. "That's good for fishing. Shall we go?"

"Sure, of course, let's hit the river," Fukawa said cheerfully.

The gear was transferred back to the boat, and soon the four were back on the lake and had returned as far as the roe extraction station. There, they stopped off to stow the kill in their car's ice box, then headed the boat for the river's upper reaches.

It began to rain, as Torakichi had predicted, according to the pattern in the late autumn. Luminous clouds appeared from nowhere, and soon cold raindrops were lashing their faces without letup. Fukawa and Kimiko pulled up the hoods of their windbreakers over their heads. The bare trees along the shore traced an intricate latticework against the white clouds. The reed bed swayed heavily under the weight of the rain. Wherever they passed, they saw the same stark loneliness of a moorland in autumn.

The dark river wound on and on. The boat had reached a point where a large poplar extended over the water's surface. The fishing party landed there and set out, rods on shoulders, along a trail by the water's edge.

"This is where someone caught a huchen salmon," explained Torakichi. His remark set Fukawa feverishly scanning the river, as if his gaze could part the veil of water and pursue the fish that swam within. "Right on that neck over there. The lady cast a lure, supposedly toward the far bank. Basically, she was a beginner who'd maybe practiced a little bit, so her line wasn't going to go beyond about the middle of the river. Well, that's where it bit."

"When you think about that, once the big one was landed, there probably won't be any more around now."

"Uh-uh," said Torakichi, his stubbly face brightening into a sly smile. "That huchen was female. There'll be males yet, for sure. Runt huchen come up to these parts pretty regularly."

"So there's hope? What kind of lure did she use?"

Torakichi indicated a black-speckled orange spinner and attached it to Fukawa's rod. It was Kimiko's first time river fishing, so Atsuo gave her a rundown on the rudiments: The first rule is to position yourself where you have sure footing. Second, watch out for branches and bushes that can snarl your line, and take your time when you cast. This briefing notwithstanding, Kimiko came close to falling in the river on her first cast, and on her second, gave a loud, girlish shriek as her hook caught in the top of an alder. Torakichi and Atsuo wordlessly exchanged pained expressions.

After a while, Atsuo, picked up his gun, cast a meaningful glance at Torakichi, then set out to explore the surroundings.

There had been a report that at dawn the previous day someone had spotted a bear cross the road and head upriver near the point where the Furen and Jintaro Rivers merged, hardly three hundred meters from their present location. It was a time when migrating bears foraging for food should be moving downstream — upstream movement would be abnormal behavior. Might the cause be that this year the bushes hadn't yielded much monkey pear? Bears were especially fond of that sort of berry. When they're in short supply, pre-hibernation hunger might drive bears to do unusual things.

Atsuo had never once encountered a bear, even though he had been roaming the region since childhood. Nevertheless, he had a very healthy fear of bears, having heard enough stories of the experiences of his father Ishizo, a seasoned bear hunter. Ishizo had said that bears foraging for food as winter approaches were especially dangerous.

The day before, Torakichi had taken Atsuo aside to tell him about the reported bear sighting. This information raised the question of whether it might be advisable to find some other place to angle for huchen, but both men agreed that such a last-minute change in plans would only disappoint Fukawa, who had a long-standing request for the spot where the massive 1 meter, 23 cm. fish had been landed. They had decided that Atsuo would stand watch on the perimeter while Torakichi tended to their two clients.

A vast bed of reeds extended beyond the river. The pearly tips of countless grass stems bowed under the weight of absorbed rainwater. Rain continued to fall, lightly now, but Atsuo's collar was getting soaked. A dark alder loomed up in his path. Water was falling in drops large and small from each twig and branch, as if welling up from somewhere within the tree itself. Water permeated everything, from heaven to earth. He fancied he could feel the dampness penetrate to his soul.

His path was cut off by a rivulet that sliced through the reed bed. It was surrounded by peat moss, and his feet only sank into the ground when he stepped forward. It didn't seem advisable to continue on that path, so he doubled back along what firm ground there was in areas occupied by the roots of dead trees, thinking that not even bears would venture into territory where the ground was so soft and yielding.

When he reappeared, Torakichi approached him. "It's all right. This area seems safe," Atsuo reported.

"That so?" Torakichi rubbed his coarse growth of whiskers expressionlessly. "No bear's shown up in the thirty years I've been here. Guess yesterday's report wasn't so reliable after all. It came from a forestry bureau car, so it sounded pretty official, but maybe they just couldn't see very well in the fog."

"So how's the fishing going?"

"Nowhere. No one's caught anything. And that's not good, with that impatient boss of yours." The two walked over to the anglers at their stations.

"Mr. Yukimori, would you give me a hand? My hooks keep getting caught. This is the fifth one I've ruined."

"My, my, this fishing doesn't seem to go as smoothly as keeping the books," Atsuo remarked as he straightened out the tangled line for her.

"I did get one pretty strong bite, but that was all," Fukawa said bitterly as he cast his line. An hour passed without as much as a nibble.

They unpacked boxes of food and set them out them along the riverbank. Fukawa drank some whiskey and his mood mellowed. They moved to a spot a little upstream for their afternoon fishing. Torakichi and Atsuo joined in.

The rain lifted and rifts opened in the mint sherbet clouds. Just then, Kimiko screamed. Atsuo came running. "What happened?"

"I felt like something pulling hard," said Kimiko, handing over the rod.

"Maybe you snagged a root."

But the heavy line was bending the rod like an archer's bow under the insistent pull of what could only be a living thing. He began reeling in the line. A silvery fish about forty centimeters long fought steadily as it was drawn from the water and landed with a net.

"That's what you call beginner's luck," Fukawa commented, with evident displeasure.

"It's a white spotted char. Pretty big," said Atsuo as he pulled in the struggling fish.

When Torakichi shouted, "Wait a minute . . . that babe's a huchen!" Fukawa bounded over to see, his face a frozen study in envy.

"This a huchen? Damn! Yeah, it really is a huchen, the lord of Lake Furen!"

"Well, not quite," said Atsuo wryly. "It's just a little kid."

"It's quite a catch, anyway. Good going, ma'am!"

"What lure did she have? Probably the one I was using . . . Yeah, sure enough. That was the one to go with, all right."

"If you just kept it a little longer, you'd have caught it," Atsuo said consolingly.

"Yeah, that's my trouble — no persistence. Always losing out."

Fukawa laid the fish on a plain towel and took several pictures. In about thirty seconds, the silver belly began to blacken and the pink color of the fins to fade. The fish had been a chromatic splendor for just a fleeting moment.

"You caught it for me, Kimiko. I'm thankful for that. Still . . ."

"Boss, do I hear a note of sarcasm?" Atsuo teased him.

"Aw, now I know the buggers are in there. That just adds to the fun next time, when I haul one in."

As it happened, that one huchen was the entire catch of the day. They agreed to have supper at Torakichi's restaurant. It was past seven when Torakichi and Atsuo arrived at the restaurant, after dropping off Fukawa and Kimiko at the hotel to change.

Torakichi's enterprise, "Jinnai Diner," was located close to the harbor, in an area of warehouses and offices that were mostly deserted by night. Next door to the restaurant was a garage; both establishments had second-floor private residences.

Inside the restaurant were several customers. Suéko was serving them. She smiled and greeted her husband and brother when they appeared.

"O-kaeri. So how did it go?" She had rounded cheeks that set off to advantage the fair skin she shared with Atsuo.

"Caught a huchen," said Atsuo, holding it up by the tail.

"No!" Suéko exclaimed, fixing widened eyes on the fish. Awed sighs could be heard from the guests as well, and a couple came over to examine the prize catch. Atsuo gave everyone an account of the landing of the fish. It was a region where interest in such a story ran high.

"Yo!" Torakichi addressed his wife. He had donned his proprietor's uniform; a livery coat bearing the restaurant name and a dot-patterned headband. "Tonight we close up at eight, then we serve supper for the boss."

"Tetsukichi's here to help out," Suéko said, addressing Atsuo. She was buoyant as she delivered this information to her brother. "He said he wanted to stay around so he could see you."

The tall young man in the kitchen cooking up a large salmon was Tetsukichi. The last time Atsuo had seen him, he had a gentle air, mild eyes and his mother's light complexion. Now his deep tan and muscles taut as a bear's gave him a strikingly different appearance. Atsuo greeted him with a resonant, "Yo!"

Tetsukichi replied "Hi!" and smiled, completing the preliminary formalities.

"Been hearing good things about you on the job."

"Getting by, I suppose."

"Did you get chased by a Soviet patrol boat?"

"That was no big thing." Tetsukichi hands continued busily at the cutting board as he spoke.

"Yukichi's doing just fine. Looks to me like he's beyond his old problems. There's one thing that's got me wondering, though. Lately it's like he's gone right-wing — always singing war songs."

"That's nothing new. He gets it from his father."

"His father likes war songs?"

"Sure does. He's crazy about them."

"Oh, okay, that explains it." Atsuo couldn't imagine dour Torakichi singing any kind of song.

Skillfully wielding a broad bladed carving knife, Tetsukichi was setting out neat piles of salmon roe, oysters, sea urchin roe, and various other kinds of sliced fish and meat along the sink. Atsuo laid Kimiko's catch alongside this.

"Hmm, a huchen. Today we have plenty of ocean sashimi, so what do you say we broil it?" said Tetsukichi.

"Okay, please do." Tetsukichi had long experience working in his father's restaurant and was a pro when it came to preparing fresh seafood. There was no reason not to leave everything to him.

Suéko came into the kitchen. "What should we serve the boss to drink?"

"He's had plenty of whiskey today," Atsuo answered. "I suppose what he wants tonight is Torakichi's homemade fruit wine and the local brand of saké."

"What's the plan for tomorrow?"

"Didn't Torakichi tell you?"

"He doesn't tell me anything, and if I ask, he just tells me to keep quiet."

"He's going to take the boss and Ms. Fujiyama into the mountains to shoot deer. I'm going to stay behind and take care of some business."

Suéko nestled her cheek against her son's shoulder; she almost had to stand tiptoe to reach it. "He's grown into a fine young man, don't you think?"

"He's looking good, all right. Hasn't he found himself a wife yet?"

"No, his parents are the only ones in a hurry about that. He says he's going to wait until he's on his own as a fisherman . . . That reminds me, what are you going to do about, you know, that matter I mentioned?"

" . . . " Atsuo glared querulously at his sister. Undaunted, Suéko returned an intense gaze and beckoned him into the next room.

"I showed her your picture and she liked what she saw. When I said you were coming to Nemuro she said she wanted to meet you. Can't you make some time tomorrow?"

"No, I can't!" Atsuo replied flatly. "I don't have the slightest intention of getting married."

"Really? Well, that's a shame, it really is. This looked like it could have been a good match. You know, when I told her about your job and your good prospects, she seemed pleased." Suéko spoke insinuatingly, resolved to win over her brother.

"What makes you so bound and determined to get me married?" said Atsuo, with a show of anger.

"Why do you say a thing like that?" Suéko protested, shrinking back. "I'm only doing this for your good."

"You mean I'd better settle down and get married, for my own good?"

"No, not exactly."

"Get a wife to keep me out of trouble?"

"No, no!" Suéko seemed to be blinking back tears.

"All right, let me ask you this. Did you tell her about my past? Did you tell her I've got a record?"

"Not yet," Suéko answered in a small voice. "But I fully intend to."

"You didn't tell her! Now look . . ." Atsuo kept his voice down, mindful that Tetsukichi was nearby. "Who would say okay to that kind of deal? Just suppose we did get married. She would just be taking on that past of mine, and it would haunt her all her life. There's just no way I could do that to someone. I'm not getting married now, or ever. So will you please tell her no?"

"All right." Suéko wiped her eyes with her apron. "I understand now. Don't be angry with me."

"I'm not angry," Atsuo said, laying his big hands tenderly onto his sister's slight shoulders. "I'm happy you think so much of me. I'm thankful, really. But I'm a man who just isn't qualified to get married."

Suéko nodded and left. Atsuo's thoughts turned to Wakako Ikéhata.

That rainy day, he had seen her off as far as the front gate of her home. "Come on, let's go in together," she said, but he refused. Until that moment, he had been thinking it would be all right to meet Wakako's family; perhaps her mother or her younger sister or brother. But when confronted with the actual prospect, he found himself overwhelmed with shyness. What would they think of some strange older man suddenly showing up? And how could he explain the events of the previous night?

It had continued raining for the next several days; cold, autumn rain, the product of a typhoon hovering out at sea, south of Japan. When he telephoned her house, the youngish voice that answered — presumably her mother — insisted on establishing exactly who he was. "Name of Yukimori. We attend the same skating rink," he had answered. He had been thinking about trying to call a second time, but was having difficulty summoning the courage after recalling what an imposition her mother seemed to find him. His vacillation continued until he met Wakako again at the rink one Sunday.

There were clues that she wasn't her normal self. Normally she would skate confidently in the middle of the rink, but that day she kept to the perimeter, and her hard expression did not change when she noticed him. He tried, "Hi, howareya" and "How've you been?" but he might just as well have been a stranger, from the way she looked back at him, so he tried asking, "Aren't you well?" She shook her head, seeming to shudder as she did so. At that moment, the instructor appeared and Atsuo greeted him. Then when he looked back, she was nowhere to be seen.

"Hey, where'd she go?" the instructor asked, looking about with a baffled expression.

"She was here a minute ago. I'll go see if I can find her," said Atsuo.

When he came to the skate rental counter, he spotted Wakako sitting on a bench in front of the rental lockers. She had removed one of her skates.

"The coach is waiting for you."

"I don't feel like having a lesson today. Sorry, but could you please give my apologies to him?"

"Not feeling good?"

"Not at all."

"Okay, I'll go tell him."

But as he started to go, she stopped him. "No, wait. I'll have my lesson after all." She refastened the one skate she had removed and bounded back to the ice the next moment, with a polite nod of her head to the instructor.

First she did a rocker, which is a bracketed turn on a circle. Then she did a series of Salchow jumps. She had no difficulty executing several back edge double rotations. Next up in the lesson was the triple rotation. Atsuo noticed that Wakako's movements were uncharacteristically awkward. There was too much tension in the shoulders, and her whole body seemed stiff. It only takes a little bit of anxiety, nervousness, low confidence, or any other kind of mental distress to cause that kind of unnatural stiffness of the shoulders. It diminishes strength in the legs and upsets body balance. He was worrying about this when Wakako fell. Her legs hit the ice with visibly painful force. Now she was dragging one leg. The next jump was executed without enough power, and she fell over. The alarmed instructor pulled her to her feet. Atsuo skated to the scene at full speed.

"What's the trouble today?" asked the instructor.

"I didn't get any sleep. I was up all night writing a report."

"You shouldn't skate on days like that. It's dangerous," the instructor declared prudently. "Let's call it quits for today."

Atsuo addressed Wakako. "Are you okay?"

"No, I'm not okay. My knee hurts."

"Well, it looks like you can walk, so you'll be alright. But I could see the tension in your shoulders."

"That's it exactly. I'm tense all over. Body and soul. There's something wrong with me."

When Atsuo finished his lesson and went rinkside, Wakako was there waiting. They went outside together. Milky light filled the street. She walked with a slight limp. They started down the stairs to the basement level coffee shop they had visited before. It was quite crowded, with many families there for the amusement park. "I won't go into a place like that!" she said angrily, turning on her heel. "Everyone's staring! Don't they have any common courtesy?"

They strolled up the hill alongside the National Noh Theatre. The route provided a sweeping view of wooden homes nestled along the sidewalks with towering buildings interspersed among them, like a claque of unfriendly giants.

"I called your home once," said Atsuo.

"I know. My mother kept asking, 'Who is this Mr. Yukimori?'"

"So what did you say?"

"I said that's my new lover."

"Oh, righto," Atsuo said in a joking tone as he searched Wakako's expression — but her face remained inscrutable, so he shut up. Their respective footsteps sounded in complementary cadence — his leather shoes and her rubber-soled sneakers. There was a park, tiny and deserted, next to an elementary school, with a sign by the entrance identifying it as Motomachi Park. Atop a little knoll was a bench that afforded an unimpeded view of the city below. They sat down. A train was running on the far side of the river. Lights shone in the windows of hilltop houses, suggesting that someone might be watching from within.

"I had a big fight with my mother."

"About me?"

"About all kinds of things. We fight all the time."

"What did your mother say about me?"

"She stopped talking about you when I said you were my lover."

"I don't want her to really believe that."

"Why not? What if she does?"

"It's not . . ." He gazed at her left hand. Her slender fingers were perfectly still. The youthful skin had a sheen like porcelain.

"I guess we can be together today."

"No, I have to go." Wakako arose, as if she was scheduled to catch the train just coming into the station platform that could be seen across the river.

"When can I see you again?"

" . . . I don't know," she replied softly, and began to walk away, still favoring the hurt leg. She hobbled down a stone stairway. "No, don't follow me," she commanded and Atsuo froze in his tracks.

That was the last time he had seen her. She wasn't at the skating rink the next Sunday. He had come to Hokkaido without being able to contact her.

~

"Of all the places to find you," said Torakichi as he entered the room. "Got a favor to ask.

Would you take a look at the car? I've been having trouble starting the engine."

"Okay, I'm on it." Atsuo headed for the garage in buoyant spirits. The battery had an adequate charge, and the fan belt wasn't loose. A careful inspection showed that the trouble was worn spark plugs. He replaced them.

When preparations for the meal were complete he took the jeep to pick up Fukawa and Kimiko at the hotel.

The main course was duck stew, with options of broiled huchen, salmon sashimi, and large oysters from Akkeshi Bay, fried in butter. The first round of drinks were the pride of Nemuro, *Kita-no-katsu* saké, followed by Torakichi's fruit wines, each with a distinctive color and bouquet: mountain grape, cowberry, black crowberry, monkey pear, and magnolia blossom. Fukawa was fond of the wild grape wine, drinking enough to become quite tipsy. Kimiko started out shy and quiet, but Atsuo's praise for the excellence of the salt-broiled huchen was enough to set her off on a spirited account of its landing, complete with pantomime. Atsuo had nothing to drink, mindful that he had to drive the guests back to their hotel, which he did, late that night.

Early the next morning Torakichi set off in the jeep with Fukawa and Kimiko. Fukawa's parting words to Atsuo had been, "I'm counting on you. I want at least two boys, and if at all possible, four." He wanted Atsuo to handle recruitment of four boys due to graduate junior high school the following March to hire as new Fukawa Motors employees. Before leaving Tokyo, Atsuo had contacted Yuji Harazaki, a middle school teacher who had been a classmate back in elementary school. When he called again to check on the appointment, Harazaki had said he would be free during the first class period. Atsuo set out after a hasty breakfast.

He wore his English trench coat over an Italian suit, donning a soft cap so his hair wouldn't be disturbed by the strong wind. Though the school was within easy walking distance, he was seeking a taxi for the sake of appearances when a bus rolled up.

Squat houses were laid out chockablock in lines that continued on and on to the seashore. A tiny island far out from the harbor named Benten-jima wavered in and out of visibility. Time might just as well have been standing still for this little, unassuming town by the sea, for the scant changes it had endured since the end of the war. Things were different in Nemuro, a prospering city that had undergone spectacular growth. Atsuo preferred his hometown for the peace that came with its modest existence.

The white oaks on the grounds of the junior high school all leaned south, probably because of strong northerly winds from the sea. A chilly wind was blowing that morning. He went to the reception office, asked to be announced, and was shown to a visitors' room. Harazaki appeared, short, stout, hair thinning, and turning white. He had the bearing of a man prudent in all things, without a trace of the mischievous little boy he had once been. Atsuo stood and politely presented his business card.

"Gosh, how many years has it been?" Harazaki motioned for Atsuo to be seated, closing each finger of one hand in turn, as he mentally calculated. With this gesture, his face showed the glimmer of a familiar expression from the distant past. "It's been thirty-six years since we finished grade school. We haven't met in all that time."

"I was in Honshu the whole time." Atsuo was consciously keeping the talk on a formal plane by avoiding local jargon, but his voice resonated with his own feeling of familiarity toward an old friend.

"You've got the same black mane on your head. You haven't changed at all."

"And you're the same old Harazaki, just like back when you were class president."

"Think so?" Harazaki laughed and opened a cigarette box, pushing it forward. When Atsuo declined, he removed a cigarette for himself and lit it.

His smoke ring trailed in the air like a symbol of the long years that had passed. Atsuo had been friends with Harazaki from the time they started elementary school. Their houses were close by, so they would walk to school together, and had many opportunities to play together. But the main thing between them was that they both did well in class and had a lot to say to one another. The son of a doctor, Harazaki was in a position to lend Atsuo picture books and storybooks from his plentiful supply at home. Atsuo's father was a hunter, so could show Harazaki exotic things like a dried deer penis or a stuffed fox. After school they would head for a pasture, the seashore, or perhaps the station to look at trains. It all came to an end in the sixth grade, when the classes were divided into two tracks, one for the students bound for middle school and one for all the others. Harazaki was in the former group, staying in school for extra lessons from the teachers. That gave him little occasion to associate with Atsuo. Once Harazaki was in middle school and Atsuo in higher elementary school, they no longer had any chance meetings.

Atsuo well remembered their last encounter. It was during the winter break of his second year in senior elementary school. There was a pharmacy nearby that had hired him to hawk their wares. He had been given a paper lantern bearing the store's name and a wooden box of medicines to carry on his back as he cruised the village streets after dark.

On that particular night the ice floes seemed to have reached the harbor. It was cold enough to freeze the marrow. Walking from a cluster of shops toward a residential area, he found himself in front of Harazaki Hospital. With his happy memories of the many times he had visited this home, it seemed to Atsuo that Harazaki might be willing to buy some of his medicines. He went inside through the back entrance. The maid did not conceal her distaste when he announced that he was selling medicine.

"This is a doctor's home. We don't need any medicine," she said. He tried explaining that he had been a classmate of Yuji in elementary school and asked to see him. "You can't," she rebuffed him. "He's studying now."

As this exchange was playing out, Harazaki showed up at the back entrance. His stylish appearance in woolen sweater and slacks was very different from Atsuo, who was casually dressed in a working kimono of rough serge. Harazaki couldn't make out who it was standing there on the dirt floor of the gloomy chamber. Since the maid wouldn't introduce him, it was left to Atsuo to announce, "It's me, Yukimori!" Finally, realization registered in Harazaki's expression.

"I'm helping out at the pharmacy. Won't you buy some medicine?"

But Harazaki only countered, "Are you kidding? This is a doctor's house. We've got tons of medicine already!" He turned away, drank some water, then said, "Look, I'm busy now." The next moment he had disappeared back inside. The maid shooed away the boy she saw as a loathsome peddler.

"And your father?" Atsuo asked.

"He's been dead a long time," Harazaki answered.

"What became of the hospital?"

"My older brother took it over."

"Oh, I see, your brother." He recalled a big signboard for a hospital along the national highway that listed departments of internal medicine and surgery. The name had indeed been Harazaki Hospital. But now the moment for business talk had come.

"Well, now, about my company. We would like to hire about four students up for graduation next year." He handed over a sheaf of papers from a Japanese typewriter with information on the company's size, business record, number of employees and the like. He added that automotives was a growing industry, its shares in high demand, and he stressed that the company had living accommodations for all its employees.

"This isn't the kind of thing . . ." Harazaki began, then took a deep drag on his cigarette. He was clearly annoyed by the request.

"I'm afraid it's a little late. Just about all our students have already been placed. Most go on to high school now, so there aren't all that many who start working after middle school. Besides that, being minors, they want to go to work in Sapporo, Kushiro, or somewhere else in Hokkaido. Tokyo's too far away."

"Sure, I know that, but still there must be some who want to go to Tokyo."

"Yes, that's true. But usually then it's a case of being in a group that is all hired by a big corporation, not like your . . ." His voice trailed off, but it was clear he had something like "back-alley workshop" in mind.

"Well, in any case, please put our company on your list of employers that are hiring," said Atsuo earnestly. His shop really was short of hands, and it would be so much easier to relate to new workers if they came from his own part of the country. He also wanted to score a success to show Fukawa.

But Harazaki wasn't finished raising objections. "I can do that, but . . . I'm sorry to have to say this, but I will. Yukichi Jinnai works for your company, I believe. He was recruited this spring."

"With your kindness." Atsuo recited this conventional phrase with feeling, as he remembered that Harazaki had signed Yukichi's letter of recommendation.

"Oh, yes. His mother was saying that Jinnai is a relation of yours."

"I'm his uncle."

"Then that makes it easier to say this. The fact is, Jinnai was a notorious bad apple. As an educator, I would be very concerned about arranging employment where he would be the student's senior."

"Is that it?" Atsuo felt both discouraged and a little offended. "Yukichi Jinnai is completely reformed. He's doing honest, decent work."

"Well, I suppose he is, but still . . ."

"How about this? I'll take personal responsibility for the students. This is my hometown too. Let me help them become good, dependable workers."

"You?" Harazaki set to scratching a thin patch of hair over his forehead as he thought about this. He seemed to know about Atsuo's police record. Since his first run-in with the law, Atsuo had avoided elementary school class reunions and generally kept hidden in hopes that rumors would not spread beyond those people who had been involved, but in small towns rumors travel fast and come in rich detail.

"Look, in any case, I would appreciate your doing what you can."

"Well, I will see if any students are interested."

Sunlight shone in through the window, but it was pale, like a florescent light, and brought little warmth. Chill spread through the room implacably, despite a kerosene heater. Unlike Harazaki in his thick sweater, Atsuo was wearing only a suit jacket. He felt cold, through and through.

He emerged from the school into the streets of the old town. For no particular reason, he headed down toward the sea. He noticed the abandoned remains of a brothel he had frequented in his youth. Traces of its former existence remained in lattice windows facing the road and a fancy balustrade on the second floor. Its tin roof, broken and corroded, was the vestige of a bygone era. Time erodes everything — a town and its ways; the hearts of its people.

He recalled that a number of friends in elementary school had lived in the area. The parents of one grade-school buddy (he couldn't remember his name) had a grocery store. He went there, but now it was a flower shop. As he was gazing at some yellow and white chrysanthemums, he abruptly decided to visit his parents' grave.

Carrying a bouquet of flowers, he started back in the direction from which he had come. Going west along the national highway took him to a slope on the left leading to the municipal cemetery. As he ascended, the wind seized the back of his neck in an icy grip. The dark sea rose up over the town and hung suspended from a pale blue sky. He had considerable difficulty finding the little plot that faced away from the sea because it had been many years since he had been to the cemetery, and new graves had appeared in the interim.

There was only a three-tiered slab of granite marked "Yukimori Family Tomb," with no gravestones, no enclosure, and no foliage around it, looking bleak in the cold wind. Wanting to cleanse the memorial, he searched the area for a time until he found a water outlet and ceremonial wooden pail there for that purpose. He painstakingly scrubbed the monument until it looked like new. As he set the flowers before it, he realized he had forgotten to get incense. He placed his palms together in prayer.

His parents had died twenty years before, his father in the spring, his mother two months later, as if following her husband to the next world. He had not been able to attend the bedside of either parent as death approached because he was in prison. His prison was in Urawa, Saitama Prefecture. That was too far from Nemuro for him to have had even a single visitor, until one day, his little sister Suéko had suddenly shown up. He could still hear her voice as she announced their parents' deaths. No tears had come during their exchange. She had traveled far to visit him, but he could hardly find any words to say to her. Finally, he had risen abruptly and fled the visiting room before the time limit was up. The guard monitoring the visit had chased after him and reprimanded him for acting without permission by walking away without supervision. Those violations had earned him solitary confinement. Left alone, he had wept uncontrollably.

Later on, he was told that his father had died of a stroke, but his mother's cause of death was undetermined. The story was that she had eaten little because of her grief, becoming increasingly feeble until her death. Atsuo believed he had caused her death by failing to abandon the behavior that had landed him in prison. She had born six children, and every one of the four boys had been a source of sorrow. Shinichi, the eldest, had died in battle at Guadalcanal, the second boy, Keiji, had died of tuberculosis at an early age, and Yuzo, the third, had died of accidental drowning in infancy. Atsuo, the youngest boy, had fallen into a life of crime. Yoshiko, the oldest girl, had married a fisherman in Kushiro, and the youngest child, Suéko, had married Torakichi Jinnai. Both girls had made respectable lives for themselves, but the boys had all brought disappointment.

His palms together, blown by a wind that chilled him to his marrow, Atsuo reported to his parents that he had somehow managed to reform himself.

It was the face of his mother rather than his father that emerged clearly in his mind. He thought that if only she were alive now, she would be overjoyed about the life he had made for himself.

When he returned, he said to Suéko, "I went to Father's and Mother's grave."

"My, that's an event," she said, pursing her lips as she deep fried pork cutlets for the day's luncheon menu.

"The stone was pretty dirty. I cleaned it up."

"I'm glad you went. So how did the recruiting go?"

"Not good. I was counting on Mr. Harazaki to help out an old classmate. I appealed to him, but he's not going to help. He doesn't see any value in a company as small as ours."

He couldn't very well tell her that her son Yukichi was the obstacle.

"Maybe Mr. Harazaki doesn't like my husband," she said quietly. "That teacher is very big on with saving the environment. He belongs to several organizations. The *Hokkaido Shimbun* published his letter criticizing hunters. He says they kill living creatures in the natural world."

"They do what? Hunters kill animals for a living. So what do you do about fisherman who kill fish?"

"Yeah, right," said Suéko, stepping aside to avoid spattering oil. "Well, fish aren't animals."

"Father was a respectable hunter. So is Torakichi. What is bad about that?" Atsuo suddenly found himself peeved.

"Well, you see, Mr. Harazaki thinks hunters are evil because they destroy nature. He's against killing animals, even if a bear kills somebody or foxes raid people's fields or crows carry off fish from the harbor. But he doesn't mind when developers tear up natural forest for dairy farms. It's okay to take salmon and walleyes by the hundreds of thousands. He doesn't have any problem with eating meat from slaughtered cows and pigs, but if you shoot one deer with a rifle, he makes a big fuss about how cruel it is. How many hunters does he think there are in Nemuro? Including my husband, there are maybe five or six. Even if you take tourist hunting into account, there just aren't very many animals being shot. With salmon, a fixed net hauls in hundreds and hundreds at a time."

Suéko delivered this speech without pausing, hands never faltering as she laid out plates of cutlets and dressed them with waiting piles of fine-shredded cabbage.

"When Yukichi went wrong and was called in to the school for stealing money from a friend, it was Mr. Harazaki who handled it. You know what he said? 'I'm sorry to say this, but the occupation of the father has something to do with the boy turning out like this. Seeing his father kill animals from the time he was little prevented development of his reverence for life. That is the whole basis of morality.' That's what he said! What he doesn't know is that no one grieves the death of an animal more than my husband. He gives numbers to every animal he has killed and writes them on memorial tablets he keeps in the family altar. Can you imagine a fisherman making memorials for the souls of every fish he catches? My husband always says 'I destroy animal life only because it is necessary for living. I pray for forgiveness every time I place my finger on the trigger.' When I heard what Mr. Harazaki said, I took Yukichi right out of that school."

"But Mr. Harazaki is the one who wrote a letter of recommendation for Yukichi."

"I wrote that letter. I had someone else make the final copy. I carved the school seal out of a wood block myself."

"That's what you call forgery of an official document."

"I did it for Yukichi's sake. That school wasn't doing anything to help him."

"Well, I suppose you may be right."

"You know how those college kids are rioting now? I can understand it. The college professors are all a bunch of phony educators."

Customers were coming in for lunch, so Suéko quit talking. Atsuo helped himself to a lunch tray and started eating before the place became crowded. There were four customers, regulars apparently, based on the way Suéko chatted familiarly with them as she took their orders. The two who wore numbered caps and rubber boots glittering with fish scales would be from the fish market. The other two looked liked clerks of some kind, both in threadbare suits. It was clear from the sharp glances flashed Atsuo's way that they were conscious of his presence. Who's the fancy-looking gentlemen? Don't know the face — he's a stranger. Maybe he's some bigwig from one of the paper manufacturers in Kushiro. Nah, no reason for someone like that to come here. Their expressions bespoke curiosity and consciousness of his alien presence.

After lunch, Atsuo went up to the second floor. Next to the living room was the altar room, dominated by a big family altar. In it, memorial tablets of unfinished wood, brown with age, were arranged in neat rows, like a miniature graveyard. Each bore an inscription one would find on a gravestone: Ezo Deer Soul, Northern Fox Soul, Field Rabbit Soul, Mallard Soul, etc. On the backs were numbers for each animal, together with its sex and a date, written in angular characters that reflected Torakichi's personality. The reading of morning and evening sutras for the animals he had killed was a ritual that Torakichi never neglected. For the Bon Festival he would have a monk come to give a prayer service for their eternal happiness. Atsuo had attended one such service.

"Human beings cannot live without killing animals. We live in deep sin. Some of us have to kill animals. I am one. My sin is great." Torakichi was wont to say these things. His words could be taken as pompous, but coming as they did in a soft voice from a man of such reserve as Torakichi, they seemed to hold some truth.

The room was near to overflowing with stuffed animals placed in the tokonoma, above the fusuma and on the tatami, including two enormous specimens: a sea lion and a brown bear. There was a huchen that looked about 140 cm long. Atsuo wondered when it had been caught. The night before, Fukawa's face had been a study in contentment as he ate the meat of a forty-centimeter huchen, but they hadn't been able to finish the whole fish. How in the world had Torakichi managed to consume a 1.4 meter huchen?

There was also an antique gun collection, including a matchlock, an old Winchester, and a Model 99 Imperial Army infantry rifle.

Atsuo picked up the latter and trained it on an imaginary target. Looking into the bore, he saw rifling that gleamed as brightly as the imperial chrysanthemum crest on the barrel. Not surprisingly, the crest impression was worn down, but this weapon was well maintained, without a speck of rust. It was ready for use at a moment's notice.

In his own less than articulate way, Torakichi had spoken of how hard it had been to obtain that rifle. Someone had brought it back from the army and kept it hidden away in a storehouse for twenty years. It had changed hands since then, he said, so tracking it down had taken much effort.

The presence of Torakichi Jinnai the hunter was stifling in the room. His creed, discipline, and temperament hung in the air and clung to the pillars, floor, and wall. As Atsuo opened a window for a deep breath, a question popped into his mind. Why wouldn't a man who had spent as much money as Torakichi had on a gun collection not send his son Yukichi to high school? Of course, Yukichi himself had invited his father's anger with his rebelliousness and neglect of schoolwork. But to Atsuo it seemed clear that Yukichi had turned on his father and run away from home because he hadn't been able to stand these suffocating surroundings. Atsuo himself was feeling an urge to go off somewhere that very moment.

He went into the four-and-a-half-mat room that was his sleeping quarters and began to change clothes. He took off his suit and put on the same jacket he had worn the previous day for fishing. Into his rucksack he packed several items he had assembled that were needed for a blasting experiment: a three-way water hose coupler, electric wire, a timer, and black gunpowder. Then he packed a rod and fishing gear, went downstairs, and checked out with Suéko.

"I'm borrowing the bike."

"The bike? Where're you headed?"

"Going fishing in the Furen River."

The road petered out forlornly, and before him was the bridge to the base of the Nemuro Peninsula crossing the stretch of water known as Nemuro Bay on one side and the salt lake, Onneto, on the other. Lake Furen, long and narrow, lies west of Nemuro, stretching southeast to northwest alongside Nemuro Bay. It is bordered on the west and south by the gently rising Nemuro terrace, which is covered with a conifer forest, and by low sand shoals to the east and north, with a gap open to the bay in between. More than ten rivers empty into the lake, including the Furen and Bettoga rivers. Their banks form a vast peat bog. This abundance of river water dilutes the sea water, providing a semi-saline environment for a community of sea plants and fish not found elsewhere. In winter, the marsh freezes over into a sheer ice plain.

Atsuo had been coming to Lake Furen for fun since childhood. Now he was looking out across the long sand shoal called Shunkunitai that divides Nemuro Bay and Lake Furen. He was especially fond of this spot. Many times he had explored the length of its larch woods or launched a small boat from its shores to go fishing. Salinization was taking its toll here, too, among the larch trees; the shoal was on the road to becoming just a flat, featureless island.

Atsuo gunned the bike's 250 cc engine again. There weren't many cars on the road, so he let it roar as he sped through a dark forest of Sakhalin fir and Jezo spruce. When there was no one to see, he tried a little stunt riding. After doing a few wheelies, he turned off the highway and plunged into the trackless wood. Dead branches snapped, and dried leaves flew by as he plowed a path through bamboo grass, sailing past trunks of white birch. The tamarisk, Japanese oak, and hazel were bereft of their leaves. For some reason, winter's approach had left only the oaks with dead leaves still attached to branches, as the forest's last, wind-blown adornment. The tires slipped on a patch of wet moss as the bike headed down a slope, but Atsuo didn't reduce his speed. The pulsing engine had called forth a hidden cache of youthful energy from within. Descending the hill took him near the salmon and trout roe extraction station he had visited the day before. With its hill rising directly from the Furen River, this area was a good base for entering the marsh.

He spotted Torakichi's aluminum boat, but its engine had been removed, rendering it useless. Atsuo hid the bike in the woods and set out into the marsh on foot. It would take considerable toil to travel the same distance they had quickly closed by boat the previous day, but Atsuo had confidence in his legs. He pushed ahead vigorously, opening a path through the grass and avoiding pools of water. Then he found himself cut off by a narrow stream, only about a meter wide. He could jump it, but there would be dire consequences if the ground on the far bank was soft. The viscous peat would only suck in his legs as he moved, making him sink inexorably into the bottomless mire. Searching about the bank of the stream, he discovered a place where a large alder's branch extended to the far side. He suspended himself from it and jumped off into a thicket of bush clover. Progressing in this way, he finally arrived at the place where his group had been casting.

Features of the surroundings that had been obscured by the misty rain could now be discerned clearly. It was an endless vista of flat marsh, with only a few scattered trees. There wasn't another soul anywhere, no one between heaven and earth but himself. All there was to hear were flowing water and the sounds of wind. No bird cried in the quiet light.

Atsuo felt an impulse to bellow lustily like a wild beast set free. There was no one to witness any event that might take place here, be it sublime act or hideous crime. That marked the major difference between here and cities, where one becomes entangled in intricate meshes of human relationships. He had spent long years at labor in prison, but in essence there wasn't much difference between penal servitude and working for Fukawa Motors. Either way, you get ordered around, you are watched, you do your daily tasks and get paid a pittance in return. That goes on and on until your sentence is up or you retire. Just keep working and grow old. Now he was completely removed from labor. Free. For just a brief moment in time, he was free.

Atsuo took off his pack, thinking of doing some fishing right there. Then he changed his mind, re-shouldered the pack and started off again. Heading away from the river, he pushed into the depths of the vast marsh, moving with cautious steps. The soft ooze of the ground pulled at his boots. He advanced one step at a time, patiently extracting his legs over and over again as they sunk into the tenacious mire.

Having walked this region many times since childhood, Atsuo was able to pick out the safe spots. The bottom of this marsh consisted of a sludgy peat layer, the sediment of plants accumulated over — he didn't know if it was thousands or tens of thousands of years, but in any case, a ridiculously long time. It was that coffee-colored deposit one could see by peering into the river or lake. There was no telling its actual thickness. His father, Ishizo, had taught him it was bottomless, and added that when any large animal like a cow or a bear falls in, it's swallowed up in no time. The adhesiveness of the peat makes it impossible to swim. Of course, human beings are no exception to the rule.

Communities of tall reeds form along rivers and lakes. There, great deposits of peat slowly build. One feature of these deposits are "eyes of the bog," or bottomless potholes that form wherever water accumulates — virtually everywhere. Despite these obstacles, it is possible to pick one's way forward by keeping to places where the roots of the reeds are densely matted. Pushing yellow stems left and right, Atsuo checked his footing with every step. Alders, many with multiple trunks, were scattered about the desolate reed bed, their branches like bony hands that beckoned. Now, they were bare, but in spring and summer their foliage gave welcome shade. It was sure the ground was firm wherever these trees grew. Atsuo knew them as welcome signposts.

Finally, he reached a spot where sedge grass had withered into rounded clumps, like sheaves of harvested rice. The local name for this dried brush was "marsh monks" because it supposedly resembled the unkempt heads of monks who come from the mountains to beg for food. Atsuo seated himself there.

He had walked almost an hour without seeing another person. There were neither birds nor flowers, much less people. For a moment, memories of bird song and the rustling of red and white flowers in spring and summer came to mind, but they were quickly dispelled by the bleak silence of the scene. His father Ishizo had warned incessantly against coming here, since it was very dangerous for children. Those warnings effectively heightened his urge to slip secretly into the marshland.

He had carved a flat-bottomed dugout boat for himself from a Sakhalin fir. The size was just enough for one child. Modeled after a canoe, it was propelled by paddle. He had enthusiastically gathered all the items that seemed necessary to a child's mind: a bamboo fishing pole, needle and thread, rice balls, mosquito repellent, salve. He waited for a time when Ishizo struck out into the mountains, knowing his father would not be back for several days. He left the house on his bicycle early one morning. Upon reaching the riverbank, he had stealthily retrieved his hidden boat and launched it, waving a hand toward an imaginary crowd gathered at the riverbank to see him off on the great adventure.

What had been the objective of that expedition? Ah yes, to meet the "Furen hermit." One winter, when Atsuo was very young, perhaps six or seven, Ishizo had told him the story before a crackling wood burning stove.

The Furen hermit was the lord of the marshland. Both his long hair and the beard that fell to his chest were snowy white. No one knew his real age. He looked like an eighty-year-old man, but ran as fast as a deer, so it was simply beyond belief that he could be that old. He wore the same bearskin jacket and sealskin boots in summer and winter. A dozen or more dried salmon hung from his waist like a skirt. He walked the marsh carrying an old-fashioned rifle on his shoulder and a short fishing pole. He didn't like people, and kept hidden when he saw them, but he was friendly with Ishizo and a few other hunters. When he got to talking, he would warm to his subject and teach his listeners many things about the mountains and fields. He was well educated, knowing the names of many animals and plants, and all about their places in the scheme of nature. In his shoulder sack was a notebook where he would write down his own observations in a fine hand. But he would never speak about where he had come from or what kind of life he had led. No one even knew where he stayed at night. In summer, it might be all right to camp out in the open, but what do you do in the ice and snow of winter? Why on earth would anyone choose such a life all by himself? It was all a great riddle.

"Father, you met him?"

"Many times."

"Is he scary?"

"No, he's kindhearted and gentle, like the Buddha himself."

"Does he come to town?"

"No, never."

"I want to meet the Furen hermit."

"You can't. The marsh is no place for children."

"But I want to meet him!"

"Dumb kid!"

With that, Ishizo lapsed into smoldering silence punctuated by sips of *doburoku*. Whenever something would lead Ishizo to start talking to one of the children, the standard pattern was that his mood would abruptly sour when he finished what he had to say. Persisting with questions beyond that point would only get you a walloping. It was better to give up without trying.

From that time on, Atsuo had all sorts of fantasies about the Furen hermit. Somewhere in the marsh a great craggy mountain had sunk, leaving only a tiny entrance way to a giant cavern under the ground. There, the Furen hermit had outfitted a palatial residence. On the surface he seemed like nothing more than an old beggar, but he really had vast riches. He must have been a notorious thief down in Honshu, stealing everything in sight. They tried to chase him down, but he got away to that cave, where he lived under cover. Come what may, Atsuo wanted to meet this man and discover his secrets. That was what had led him to fashion a boat to venture into the marshland.

One summer, Atsuo went upriver in his boat. A truly memorable rebuking from his father the night before had left him dispirited. The next morning he slipped away from the house, resolved never to return. Accordingly, he brought along some rice and miso. His scolding had indeed been fully justified; it was for lifting money from his brother's wallet. In his breast was hatred, not for his father, but for himself. There was also room to reflect that his death would probably gratify his father.

A summer fog from the sea that was a specialty of the region had come in and turned into a chilly, milky-white wind hugging the surfaces of river and marsh. Fortunately, it was a tail wind; the fog helped him paddle his boat. The river flowed gently enough that a child's strength was sufficient to move the boat along. When he came to a small river branch, he shouldered his mooring line and walked the boat along the bank.

He walked on and on, dogged every step by the pernicious fog. His shirt and trousers went from damp to drenched. Paddling the boat had kept up his body warmth, but now chill was gaining the upper hand, and he was hungry. He washed some rice in his kettle, then took out the Sakhalin fir branches brought from home, added some white birch bark and tried to start a fire, but the sodden matches wouldn't light. At that moment, it began to rain. It was a mighty downpour, as if from a great hole that had suddenly opened up in the colorless sky.

Shivering, he decided to return home. He got into the boat and let the current take it as he used the kettle to bail out water. Having reached his present location by paddling upriver against the current, he assumed that going with the current would return him to his point of departure. The river soon showed him how mistaken that reasoning was. It had risen beyond the bounds of its banks. The reed bed he had walked only minutes before was now at lake bottom. All around him was a single surface of seething water, with only the tops of alders protruding above it. The water wasn't so much flowing as swirling about wildly in random directions. When the boat seemed to move ahead, the next moment it was being pulled back, then turning in circles. He lost his sense of direction and simply drifted. Unable to see anything but water, he had no idea where he was. The handmade boat had poor stability. When it was assailed by waves from the side it nearly overturned, and Atsuo's paddle and food supplies were lost. Only the kettle remained, and this he used to desperately bail out water.

There was no telling how long the aimless journey continued, since he was probably unconscious for part of it. It ended when a large tree loomed into view like a ship in a dream. He had reached the edge of a stand of fir. Atsuo crawled onto the land and fell flat, hugging the earth. Then he walked for about two hours, until he was finally rescued by hunters.

Atsuo knew well that the marsh is not really land at all. There was no way to know when the very spot on which he sat would be inundated and returned to its original condition. It was a home for the wild goose alone, a land floating atop a bottomless lake.

After his encounter with this flood, Atsuo stopped believing there could be such a person as the Furen hermit. It seemed to him that human beings simply could not live where such floods occurred, nor could there be large caves under the ground. One cold winter night when a snowstorm raged, Atsuo addressed these doubts to Ishizo.

"What do you suppose the Furen hermit is doing now?"

"Humph."

"He must get awful cold when it snows like this."

"Humph."

No matter what he tried saying, it was only answered by another "Humph."

His backside was getting wet from water seeping up through the marsh monks upon which his sat. He arose and regarded them. They were a droll sight, all alone with their wild hair. He bid them adieu, having decided it was time to move on.

A flock of geese came his way. They were birds who kept in flawless formation, unlike the chaotic flight patterns of ducks. He was struck by a feeling of admiration for their orderly movement. A little while later, a large flock of crows came by, flying scatter shot, and calling to one another in their crass way. The goose, Atsuo reflected, is beauty, the crow, ugliness; we do not know who made it so, but it is a world of beauty and ugliness.

Atsuo walked the "fisherman's trail" along the riverbank with stealthy steps. The river undercut the edge of the bank, so it was actually flowing beneath his feet. Fish lurking in that water would quickly flee at the faintest sound of human footsteps. In particular, the huchen could move at astounding speed. If you were out to catch fish, it behooved you to tread very softly. It seemed to Atsuo that the poor showing for the previous day's angling was due to the boat's motor and Fukawa's reckless way of walking. The place where the river took a gradual bend Atsuo recognized as "The Spot." Here, he began casting. The sun was going down, and darkness crept over the water. After about thirty minutes, he was reeling in his lure when it was suddenly seized by a fish that leaped from the water almost at his feet. Taking care not to let the line go slack, he let it swim, waited until it tired and finally scooped it from the water with his net. It was a white spotted char, about 14 centimeters long.

He was standing at a point not five meters from the place where Kimiko had caught her huchen the day before, so this indeed seemed an authentic Spot. There was a forked stick someone had thrust into the ground as a fishing rod support, a clear sign that anglers sought out this location.

Atsuo decided to remain where he was. Having made that decision, he gave no further thought to strategy. He gave his fishing rod a light flick that bent it almost enough to tap the water surface, while the line sped outward like an extension of the rod until the lure sunk into the river, raising a little column of water just in front of the far bank. Then he wound the reel, making the lure swim back to him like a living thing, just under the surface. There was nothing to be done except repeat this process, nothing to listen to but the faint plopping sound of the lure and the soft whine of the reel. Thought being unnecessary, thinking stopped of its own accord. The flow of untroubled time cleansed his mind like clear water.

At another level, his perceptions were keen, apprehending the particulars of each event occurring around him: the spread of darkness over the water as the sun descended beyond the forest, a flock of mallards approaching close enough for a sure kill had there been a gun at hand, the small face of an Ezo squirrel appearing, then disappearing on the other bank of the river . . . He was quite aware of these events, and they did not cause the slightest disturbance of his consciousness.

When he had raised his third spotted char, he switched to a hair fly for catching dolly varden. Setting the lure to swimming where the current was slow, a greenish white fish leaped from the shadow of a rock. In a very short time he had netted eleven more fish. In the next interval he caught two cherry salmon. But no huchen showed itself.

Twilight had gathered. Atsuo collected his tackle and began walking through the dense reed growth. His path took him to a scene so extraordinary it stopped him cold.

The reeds before his eyes had been flattened down to an even surface. Dry reeds being brittle, they bend and break when people walk through them, but he was looking at ten square meters of reeds neatly pressed to the ground. That was far too large an area to be accountable as the result of people bedding down. A bear had done this — a very large brown bear, enjoying itself by rolling about in the reeds.

With bated breath, Atsuo scanned the scene for other signs. There were no droppings or footprints. The rain could have washed away such traces. There had been nothing unusual in this area the day before. The bear had been here since then, maybe just a little while ago. Or maybe only a minute ago. He sensed something move nearby and a foul odor reached his nostrils. His mouth went dry and he tried unsuccessfully to swallow. He moved forward slowly. A black shape suddenly loomed in front of him.

It was a dead tree. Part of the trunk had broken off, leaving a stump that slightly resembled a furry ear. It had given him such a jolt it perversely made him find his courage. He berated himself. Getting scared out of your wits is for little kids. He thought, Oh, well. At least I didn't scream. Getting old must have done some good.

It was a sure bet the bear was nearby and was aware of him. Two days before, a bear sighting in the area had in fact been reported. The "old man of the mountain" in person, ravenous as he faced hibernation. Atsuo regretted not taking his gun. There was movement from deep inside the reeds, and the wind was not the cause.

He suddenly remembered the three-way water hose coupler he had brought along. Until that moment he had forgotten packing it into his rucksack with the idea of setting off an experimental explosion somewhere. Hastily, he made preparations by packing black gunpowder into the coupler, connecting a wire to a blasting cap and letting it trail outside, then hooking up a 6-volt detonator consisting of four D-size batteries and a windup timer. He planted the coupling at the roots of a dead tree, set the timer for five minutes and ran. There was a large alder about a hundred meters away. He shinnied up and watched.

Exactly five minutes later there was a flash and a roar. A vast circle of reeds billowed, a column of white smoke rising from its center that was pierced by countless arrows of mud streaking outwards. Atsuo estimated that he had used about fifty grams of gunpowder. The resulting explosion had been much greater than his two previous experiments. No doubt one very surprised bear was fleeing at full speed.

The dead tree had been knocked over and flung five meters away. There was a crater three meters across and a meter deep, with water already bubbling up from the bottom. There were no fragments of the coupling or timer to be seen. Only some wire remained, at the edge of the crater. One gets a bigger bang with an iron pipe than a cola bottle, and bigger still with a multichannel coupling, that is, by increasing the resistance of the gunpowder container. But, unlike the previous two explosions he had set off, this time he derived no pleasure. Given a big enough rig, you can increase the size of a blast all you want, but so what?

"Today was really disappointing." That was what Wakako had said. He finished the thought as she might put it. "Just a big pop that didn't destroy the marsh even a little bit. One more phony performance!"

He was riding the motorcycle along the forest road when the last rays of the sun had expired. Darkness flowed liquid from the yawning woods. The craving for speed that had seized him on the journey to the marsh was gone now. He rode along leisurely as night fell. Stars in the frozen sky were brighter and far more numerous than ever seen in Tokyo. A light came up from behind and a car passed him. He wondered who it might be, at such an hour. It wasn't the car from the roe extraction station. Perhaps it was someone like him, savoring the pleasure of going fishing on a weekday.

The jeep was in the garage, covered with mud. The thought popped into his mind that he had to give Fukawa a report on his visit to the middle school. Going around to the restaurant, he found it without customers. Torakichi, his wife, and Tetsukichi were sitting around the stove drinking, with a big bottle of saké and an array of dishes set out before them. Torakichi was already well under the influence of the saké.

"Didn't expect to see you this early. How's the boss?"

But Torakichi exercised his "right to silence" instead of answering Atsuo's question. Suéko filled in for him. "He and Ms. Fujiyama went to Raúsu," she said with a wry expression indicating that something was not to her liking.

"For goodness sakes why?" asked Atsuo, surprised.

To this, Torakichi responded, "Humph. Sorry, but I got the boss mad."

Atsuo waited for clarification, but none came. Finally, Suéko broke the silence.

"Well, this husband of mine is so unsociable, it was partly his fault, but that . . . Ms. Fujiyama, it was her fault too, blabbing on and on about everything. She was interfering with the hunt, and I guess he lost his temper."

"She doesn't even realize what she's doing," Torakichi corrected her. "She would talk to the boss just the same as if she were back in Tokyo. Trouble is, deer can hear ten times better than we can. Soon as they hear a human voice, they run away. And when they run, it's always downwind. They're smart enough to run in the direction where their own stink won't trail behind. That's what they do when they hear a sound. We spent the whole morning in Ashoro in the mountains walking around, but not a single trace of a deer. But, see, I'd been up there time and again checking around until I finally found a place up there where there's a lot of bamboo grass, sure to attract deer. So I said to her, look, will you keep quiet — just like that, speaking normally. Next thing you know, she bursts out crying."

"Well, of course, what sounds normal to him might sound to someone else like he was angry," Suéko explained. "I guess she felt like he was beating up on her."

"Anyway, the boss objected. He said I should say things more gently. Then he says, 'That's my woman, you know.'"

"That's what got him angry for real," Suéko continued. "He started yelling how it takes a lot of cheek for a man with a wife and children to talk that way. So the boss started yelling right back, and that ended everything."

"It ended everything?" Atsuo asked plaintively.

"That's about it," said Torakichi rubbing his whiskers with the back of his hand. "I'm finished with him. I'm sorry to have to tell you I won't deal with him any more."

"You can't just say that . . ." Atsuo began, but couldn't find the words to continue the thought, so he bowed his head as if pleading with his brother-in-law and tried again. "This is no good. Can't you see what it does to me?"

"It doesn't have anything to do with you," Torakichi answered and took a swallow of cold saké from his glass.

"Well, what about Yukichi?"

"I'll have him quit that job. I don't want him having anything to do with that man either."

"No! I'm against that" Atsuo said, decisiveness entering his voice for the first time. He took a big swallow of the saké Suéko had brought him and continued. "Look, Torakichi, this is as good a time as any to tell you this. Yukichi happens to be doing a very good job. For his father to wreck it all for his own personal reasons just when his kid is doing well, I'm against that. To begin with, he won't listen to what you say anyway."

"You have done a lot for Yukichi. That's the truth. I suppose it's not up to me to say anything," said Torakichi, softening his stance a bit. "But how do you think I would feel, having him work for a man I had a fight with?"

"As far as that goes, I guess you'd feel pretty much the same as me," Atsuo answered with a mirthless smile. "I wouldn't particularly enjoy working for a man who had a fight with my brother-in-law either."

"You know, you really should apologize," Suéko said. "Why don't you, for everyone's sake?"

"What do you expect me to say?" Torakichi answered, deftly separating off a piece of raw venison with his chopsticks and dipping it into soy sauce. "I ain't in the wrong."

"Fukawa's the type who's quick to anger, but he gets over it just as quickly. That's a big help," Atsuo offered.

"This one's just the same," said Suéko.

"In that case, you might as well make up. I'll be the go-between." Atsuo scraped together a bite-sized gob from a bowl of red caviar and consumed it. "When will they be back from Raúsu? There must be some message for me."

"Oh, that's right, there was! He said he wanted you to call tonight. Here's the number of the hotel in Raúsu." Suéko produced not one, but two crumpled scraps of paper from a pocket in her apron. "There's another thing I forgot. Mr. Harazaki called. Sounds like he found one student interested in your job offer."

"That's good to hear." Atsuo called Harazaki's home immediately. He repeated his thanks over and over and said he wanted to visit the school again the following day. Harazaki replied he would arrange for him to meet the student. When he put down the receiver, Suéko laughed.

"You kept bowing at the telephone the whole time you were talking. Whatever else you might say, when it comes to talking to somebody important, you're like a puppy dog."

"We're short of hands. I would be very happy to get one new man, if not more. And I certainly don't want to lose Yukichi either, especially now that we've taught him the basics. He's finally at the point where he can be really useful. I don't care what Torakichi says, I won't have him quitting."

He telephoned the hotel in Raúsu, but Fukawa and company hadn't arrived yet. That was to be expected as they hadn't left until late afternoon. He left a message that a job applicant had turned up.

"Uncle," Tetsukichi addressed him abruptly. It was the first word Atsuo had heard from him that evening. "Actually, Yukichi says he wants to quit Fukawa Motors."

Torakichi, Suéko and Atsuo converged around the young man and stared.

"Yes, he's said that to me, too, something about the work not suiting him," said Atsuo with a show of confidence. "It doesn't mean much. It's natural for a young man to be unsure about what he wants."

"He says he plans to be back in Nemuro in April for the ice break-up," Torakichi continued calmly. "We're going to pair up as fisherman. It's all decided."

"What do you mean, it's all decided? When was this?" Atsuo asked, his displeasure showing. It was the first he had heard about this matter.

"We talked it over a lot. Listen, Uncle, Father, Mother, I want you to listen to what I have to say, too. I've had it with Akkeshi. You know as well as me that herring just isn't being caught at all. No one knows why. It's like something made all the herring disappear. Everyone in Akkeshi depended on herring. With that gone, it's all over. Everyone's saying, okay, we'll go for kelp or surf clams or oysters. But if you don't have the money to buy fish farm equipment and wait out the five years it takes before you start getting mature stock, you're out of luck.

"I was thinking about what to do this summer when — who knows why — all of a sudden everyone was getting unbelievable sardine catches. I couldn't understand it. They'd come in giant waves, whipping up the surface, and we just kept pulling them in. You could make fantastic hauls with gill nets for herring. The catches were too big — it brought the price down to thirty yen a kilo, and that don't pay. This year's just abnormal."

Torakichi nodded. "Yeah, abnormal. That's what you call it when the old man of the mountain shows up on the Furen River."

Atsuo was about to tell them about encountering bear tracks only a short time ago when Tetsukichi continued.

"For now, there is no herring to catch and you can't fall back on sardines. I decided to come back to Nemuro and work with my own boat."

Torakichi inclined his head skeptically. "You don't have the money to buy a boat."

"Yeah, I do. There's a guy with a fast 5-ton boat who'll sell cheap."

Torakichi lifted his head heavily and glared. "You wouldn't just be thinking about doing a little crooked business on the sly, would you?"

"Now, Father! Tetsukichi doesn't do that kind of thing," Suéko interrupted. "He's not like Yukichi."

"Hog swill!" Torakichi angrily pounded his fist on the table, looking exactly the same as Yukichi when he used that manner of expression. "He says Yukichi's in this with him. You don't think that's suspicious? I'm telling you, I won't have you two running a *reposen* racket."

"*Reposen*," meaning "reporting boat," was the term for Japanese fishing boats that passed information about domestic matters and gave home appliances or other goods to Soviet patrol boats in waters around Etorofu, Kunashiri, or the other Kuril Islands — former Japanese territory taken over by the Soviet Union in 1945. In return, these fisherman — many of whom were from Nemuro and Raúsu — were allowed to poach in those waters of abundant fish and crustaceans. Soviet patrol boats would seize other Japanese craft that strayed into their territory, but "reporting boats" went unmolested. That privileged status made the fishing all the better.

"It would be good to have Yukichi back home," Suéko said.

"Nah, he and I are renting a house" said Tetsukichi bluntly. "That's all been taken care of."

"When you say you talked it over with Yukichi, you mean by letters?" Atsuo asked.

"Yeah, letters," Tetsukichi replied. "The kid loves to write. I get long letters from him."

"And not a word to his parents. That's infuriating." Suéko interrupted.

"Did he have anything to say about wanting to join the Self-Defense Forces?"

"He mentioned that a lot. He wants most of all to get into the Maritime SDF so he can be on a battleship and tangle with Soviet patrol boats."

"So that's it . . ." Atsuo was getting a hazy understanding of what Yukichi had in mind.

"Father." Tetsukichi straightened his large frame, the better to overlook his short statured father. "I've been wanting to say this for a while, so let me say it now."

"Well, what?" Torakichi glowered drunkenly, but seemingly cowed by his son's aggressive attitude, he uncharacteristically shrank back.

"You call poaching crooked business on the sly, but we're talking about territory that was originally Japanese. And it just happens the fishing is unbelievable there. I don't care if it's scallops, sea urchin, mackerel, crab, salmon, or sea trout, there's plenty for the taking. The Soviets put fishermen in little outfits like us out of work when they grabbed that territory. So we don't have any choice if we want to make a living."

"That is not what I'm talking about." Torakichi washed down a mouthful of food with saké and continued. "If you got to poach, you got to poach — that's just the way it is. What I'm saying is, paying for it with reporting is no good. It's selling out your country. That's unforgivable."

"It is, huh?" Tetsukichi wore a faintly contemptuous smile. For a young man generally regarded as a model of probity, the expression made him look singularly villainous.

"No information a bunch of fisherman can give the Soviets amounts to anything. They know everything from their satellites anyway. It ain't about information, it's about goods — TVs, cameras, typewriters, copy machines, yeah, and women too. We give 'em what they want and they let us fish. That's all."

"You don't know what you're talking about!" Torakichi roared. He raised a clenched fist, but instead of directing it at his son, he dragged the palm across his stubbled jowl. "*Repo* boats pass on high quality information, sometimes even state secrets. I know 'cause I know someone in the police. Sure, the little guys want the goods you're carrying, but that stuff doesn't cut any ice with the Soviet higher-ups. You know it's the higher-ups who have the say about letting you poach. I'm telling you, once you get mixed up in that business, you've had it. It's like the 'eyes of the bog,' — there ain't no bottom to it."

As his father delivered this excited torrent of words, Tetsukichi had fixed a cold gaze upon him. "Okay, what do you think we should do? We don't have big ships, we don't have fixed salmon nets, we don't get the same fishing rights as the big operators. We're just young fishermen on our own, and the herring are gone from the sea. So how do we make a living?"

"Well, that's . . ." Torakichi trailed off without a rebuttal.

"Everyone does a certain amount of poaching. But if we ever get our boat seized and confiscated, that's the end for us. We either find a way to get around that or we can't work."

Until then, Tetsukichi had touched neither food nor drink, but now he downed a glass of saké in a single drought and chased it with two or three pieces of raw venison, without bothering to dip it in soy sauce.

The silence in the little restaurant slowly drove up the voltage level until it seemed sparks might fly at any moment. Suéko sniffled. Tetsukichi and Torakichi ate and drank with a vengeance. When a wistful sigh escaped Atsuo's lips, Suéko moved to his side.

"Why don't we get my brother's opinion?" she said. "Yukichi's his concern too, you know."

"Ah, I don't know much about any of this," Atsuo said.

"Well, what do you think about Yukichi being a fisherman?"

"I don't know . . . But if that is what he really means to do, I guess it can't be helped. It is a shame, though, now that he's up to speed in the shop. I was thinking about getting him qualified as a Class Three auto mechanic."

"What has me worried is how easy it is for that boy to get into trouble. It seems to me if he starts straying outside the law again, this time it will be for good."

"From my own experience . . ." Atsuo began, knowing full well what his sister had in mind. This was a question for the man with the police record. Tetsukichi had been in high school when Atsuo had finished his last prison term, so he had some knowledge of his uncle's criminal past. On that point, he differed from Yukichi, who had been in grade school. Atsuo chose his words with a mind to inform Tetsukichi about the lesson of his own experiences.

"Once you get involved in the underworld, it's no easy thing to get out again. You get pulled in, whether you like it or not. Forces beyond your control are at work. That was what happened to me, and it cost me twenty-some years hardship — almost half my life. The key to the whole thing is what you do at the beginning. If you two really know what you're getting into and you don't mind that kind of hardship, go ahead, but if you don't like what you see, it's best to quit cold right at the start."

"That's right," Torakichi said, having finally discovered his talking point. "He's telling you to think ahead. You go chasing after any gain you can see, but you don't know what's coming. Politics can change, anything can change. You shouldn't get mixed up in that kind of business."

"Live honestly, even if you're poor," Suéko said.

"The problem ain't being poor," Tetsukichi retorted. "I'm up to my neck in debt. I can't even make enough to pay off the interest. And I might as well tell you, I've been dealing with crooks a long time. About five years. There's no going back."

"Son, listen . . ." Suéko sniffled plaintively.

"Yukichi knows about it too," Tetsukichi continued implacably. "Might as well tell you, he decided on being a fisherman 'cause it ain't straight."

"Dammit, dammit . . . A couple of damn criminals!" Torakichi swung his fist downward. "Tetsukichi, you too? Hah! Bad heritage is what it is. A bad bloodline. This one or that one, they're both the same."

"Now you just stop that, you hear?" said Suéko, cutting him off for Atsuo's sake.

"Humph." Torakichi closed his mouth. He was breathing heavily enough for his mustache whiskers to shake.

Tetsukichi rose abruptly. "I'm leavin'," he announced.

"It's late, why don't you stay over?" Suéko implored.

"No, if I can't talk, I'm leaving," he said adamantly. "The whole reason I came was to talk to Father."

He walked to the front door while his mother followed, arguing with him. Atsuo interceded on his sister's behalf.

"Come on, Tetsukichi, talk it over a little more."

"Father doesn't want to."

"Well, then, talk to me."

This produced a flicker of mellow light in Tetsukichi's eyes, but they quickly glazed over.

"No, it can't be with you, Uncle. This is between me and Father." He walked away with resolute steps.

"Come on, will you please?" Suéko said, but the pace of the footsteps did not waver. Their precise rhythm continued as the distance lengthened. There was a brief silence, followed by a motorcycle engine roaring to life.

Torakichi was leaning weakly against a wood column, like a balloon whose air had escaped. "I shouldn't have said what I did. I'm sorry." He spoke in an uncharacteristically small voice.

"I don't mind. There's something to what you say. Wrongdoing really does run in the Yukimori line."

"No it don't. I apologize."

"Facts are facts. That's all there is to it."

"All right, you two, that's enough," Suéko interrupted. "Enjoy your drinks. My brother's here for a visit. Let's forget all that dismal talk."

"I'll apologize to the boss, too. Should have kept my mouth shut. There wasn't any reason to get him angry like that."

"That is a good idea," said Suéko, well pleased. "You ought to call Raúsu right now."

"Now that you mention it, I have to call there myself." Atsuo dialed the number. This time, he got Fukawa.

"Yukimori here. Sorry about that business with my brother-in-law. He's terribly sorry about it. He says he wants to apologize over the phone."

The response came back so loud he had to move the receiver a distance from his ear.

"Far as I'm concerned there's no problem — I'm not annoyed about it. Kimiko's the problem. There's nothing like an angry woman to hold a grudge. It's enough to scare you. She's not here now, she's gone to the bath. But whatever happened between us men, there's no hard feelings. No need for Mr. Jinnai to get on the phone. You tell him."

Atsuo gave his report about the single middle school job applicant. Fukawa told him: Conduct an interview tomorrow, the decision to hire is up to you, I'm going to be traveling for about another two days. You go back to Tokyo ahead of me . . . talking on and on without pausing to listen, until he abruptly hung up.

"The boss doesn't seem to be angry," Atsuo informed Torakichi. "I can smooth it all over later on. There's Yukichi to consider too."

"Do look after him, won't you? Try to make him stay on in Tokyo," said Suéko, with a humble bow of her head.

~

His plane arrived at Hanéda in the late afternoon. It was early evening when he reached his apartment. A cardboard box placed under the door to catch postal deliveries during his absence held a stack of newspapers and junk mail. A postcard with a hastily scrawled message in pencil caught his eye.

"i was put into this mental hospital address on other side please come visit mother comes on sunday so make it a weekday if you can hours are until four thirty p.m. i slipped this letter to a patient with outside privileges wakako."

The hospital's address was in Ushigomé. He checked a map and quickly identified the location. So she's been in the hospital! Have to pay her a visit tomorrow, for sure.

He had been aware that something was not quite right with Wakako. He couldn't say just what was wrong or how it was wrong, only that he did have the impression that her "illness" (whatever that might mean) had come over her once more. But he definitely had not thought it was the sort of condition that would require hospitalization. "I was put into this mental hospital," she had written. Did that mean against her will? The poor kid . . .

Atsuo left his baggage unpacked and lapsed into thought. Feeling travel weary, he unceremoniously fell back on the bed and gazed idly at a stain on the ceiling. It had sinuous curves, like a nude drawing. It was simply unbelievable that Wakako had spent a night in this bed. There was no trace of her presence anywhere in the small room. She had made her unexpected approach, then departed, like a landed fish that promptly escaped back into the river, leaving the line and the lure just the same as it had been before the catch and the river flowing placidly, as if nothing had happened.

It occurred to him to check the postmark. It was dated five days before, the very day he had left for Hokkaido. So when had she been hospitalized? And why was the penciled writing in such an unsteady hand, like one might expect from a very elderly person? The lines were cockeyed, and the characters varied in size.

He arose ponderously and showered. Then, wearing pajamas, he poured himself a nightcap of shochu and began sipping it. Switching on the television, more of the same old coverage of T. University campus disturbances appeared on the screen. There was a close-up shot of students holding iron pipes that were a good three meters long. On command, they brandished the pipes with an impassioned "Waaaa!" The students were rejecting a call by university officials inviting them to an open meeting on reconstituting the school's administration. At the moment, "military maneuvers" were being conducted by the two mutually opposed factions, each side's forces incorporating outside supporters.

He had never been sympathetic to the students' predilection for confrontation and violence. Now, back from communing with nature in eastern Hokkaido, his view was that these youths were overly preoccupied with trivial matters. Better to confront the wonder of a peat strata, built up from countless tons of decayed plants over thousands, or tens of thousands of years. You could beat the marsh or poke it with an iron pipe; you could even set off an explosion, but that wouldn't change the marsh one bit.

The face of a student addressing the crowd appeared on the screen. Atsuo thought that face belonged to Wakako's boyfriend. To the best of his recollection, the name was Morita, or something like that. The young man had removed the towel obscuring his face and was screaming into the mike. He had the piercing look of an absolute believer. Atsuo had seen that look many years before, in the eyes of graduates of boys' imperial army officer training schools. Or Hitler Youth, as seen in news reels. It was the eye of the fanatic. Long, disorderly hair flowing from his helmet swayed like seaweed. His genitals swelled in his jeans.

Wakako had telephoned a student that rainy day. What had they talked about? He hardly gave it a second thought at the time, but now it suddenly bothered him. She had been going with him a long time. Then she said she had told her mother Atsuo was "my new lover." That meant there was an "old lover," who, it seemed, would be this student.

Preoccupied with these thoughts, Atsuo noted with little interest from the corner of his eye that the TV program had changed to "Tales from the Inner Palace." Normally, a certain amount of alcohol would send him off to sleep, but not this night. He was still drinking past midnight when he was finally able to drift off.

Fukawa still hadn't returned the next day, so it was up to Atsuo to run the shop, making it an uncommonly busy day for him. He heard reports on jobs received during his absence, supervised the disassembly of an engine that had been on hold, then personally redid a poorly executed paint spray job on a car that had been in an accident. It was already evening by then. He put half the crew on overtime and kept up work until close to 10 p.m. There was no time for talking with Yukichi about his future.

It wasn't until afternoon on the following day when he finally managed to find time to visit the hospital. He changed into his business suit and carefully washed his oil-stained hands and face. He sprinkled some cologne on his sleeves, hoping to overcome the machine oil smell. Having achieved more or less the appearance of a gentleman, he set off, driving a car of foreign make that was in for a safety inspection.

The hospital was a five-story ferroconcrete building with no iron grills over any of its windows. It had a grandiose canopy for arriving automobiles. If it wasn't for the white uniformed nurses visible beyond the well-polished glass doors, he might easily have mistaken the building for a hotel. At the reception counter he was given a paper asking for his name and relationship to the patient. He thought about that and wrote "acquaintance."

After a time his name was called. A girl on the far side of a reception window put her head out and told him, "Ms. Ikéhata is not receiving visitors now."

"Is her condition that bad?"

"I'm afraid I can't say."

"But I came here because I am concerned about her condition."

"And because of her condition it has been decided she should not see anyone."

"Who decided that?"

"The doctor."

She uttered this phrase with such assurance it was clear the "doctor" imprimatur carried absolute authority within the hospital.

"But the patient herself wants to see me." Atsuo persisted. He thought of showing Wakako's postcard as proof, but abandoned the idea when he realized there might be trouble if it was known the message had been secretly sent without the doctor's knowledge.

An older male clerk took the girl's place. "This is a hospital. Therefore the patient's welfare is of foremost concern." He was polite, but his attitude asserted strong refusal. Atsuo could find no more words of protest.

He was heading for the exit in resignation when someone tapped him on the shoulder. He immediately recognized Wakako's friend, the university student. Nevertheless, he asked, "You are . . .?"

"Wakako Ikéhata's friend," came the straightforward reply.

"Yes? Do you have something to say?" Atsuo asked cautiously.

"They wouldn't let you see her, right? Let's discuss that."

Before Atsuo could answer, the young man had fallen in step beside him. It gave him an unpleasant feeling of being led somewhere. He took confidence, however, in the fact that the lad was smaller than he was, slim and rather weak looking.

"Where do we go?"

"There's a cafe over that way. Would that be OK?"

"All right."

There were no other customers in the small shop. The young man spoke loudly enough for the waitress to overhear.

"I don't have any money on me."

" . . . That's all right," Atsuo said in surprise.

They sat facing each other, at last giving Atsuo an opportunity to look the student over closely. The most outstanding feature were eyes, single-lidded and narrow, that became a V-shaped pair of isosceles triangles when opened wide. He had a long face and a pointed chin. With his delicate-looking frame, one solid punch would probably suffice to flatten him. Long, shoulder-length hair and a red sweater made him look like a girl. It was surprising that such a fellow would be associating with Wakako, but even more surprising that he was a militant who shouted fiery speeches into microphones.

The young man blinked. "Is there something strange about my face?"

"No," Atsuo replied, smiling. He felt at ease because of his physical superiority. "I was just thinking it's kind of amazing I should be sitting like this with a young person. But let me introduce myself," he said, proffering his business card. Accepting it, the young man said he was Makihiko Moriya, and wrote the name out in pencil on a napkin.

The waitress appeared. Atsuo ordered coffee, Moriya hot chocolate and a sandwich plate. Atsuo got to the point. "Now, you had something to talk about."

"Yes," Moriya nodded, impatiently brushing back the hair that fell across his forehead. "First, I would like to get our standpoints clear."

"Our standpoints."

"Wakako Ikéhata and I are friends. We've known each other for about three years and we've slept together. Whether or not we are in love isn't something that can be quantified, so I can't give a measure of that. We haven't made any vows about the future. We both keep the relationship completely free."

"Uh-huh," Atsuo's responded in a slightly disheartened tone.

"That's it for my part. Now please clarify your standpoint, Mr. Yukimori."

"Well, I wouldn't really know what to call my own standpoint."

"Just your relationship with Wakako Ikéhata. That's enough."

"My relationship? Just a friend. We met at the skating rink. We both take lessons from the same figure skating instructor."

"Have you slept together?"

"That's not the kind of thing . . ."

"Of course, there's no need to say if it's a matter of privacy. It's just that Wakako Ikéhata has confided to me that she spent a night in your apartment."

"Did she say that?"

"It isn't anything to worry about. She maintains a free relationship with me, so she can reveal anything at all. I relate to her in exactly the same way."

"Free relationship . . ."

"Now that we have confirmed our standpoints, we can proceed."

"Not so fast, please. Just what is wrong with Ms. Ikéhata?"

"That is exactly our next issue," said Moriya, narrowing his eyes. It was a curious expression that could either be taken as ridiculing his elder or just laughing innocently. "We share an interest in this problem. I think we both want very much to solve it."

"Yes, that's true. So what happened to her?"

"Wakako Ikéhata was hospitalized on October twenty-eighth."

"The twenty-eighth? That was Monday," Atsuo said, consulting his appointment book calendar. It was the day after they had taken their stroll from the skating rink to the National Noh Theatre. "It's been over three weeks."

"The last time I met Wakako Ikéhata was October twenty-seventh. She called me and we met in Shinjuku. We were walking around there, debating about revolution. Typically, we find ourselves on subtly different sides of an issue, and that is what happened then. I won't go into the details of it all, but it came down to her disagreeing with my argument that all criminals are revolutionaries."

"Now, there's a puzzler to chew over."

"Yes. It is a difficult issue," Moriya said without smiling. "But everything she said was perfectly clear throughout. There wasn't anything muddled about her reasoning. She was not in the least mentally unbalanced."

" . . ."

"Nevertheless, she was put in the hospital. That's the problem. I want to get to the truth of it. I have been demanding a visit every day since her hospitalization, but they have been unjustly refusing because they say it would disturb her treatment."

Makihiko Moriya assaulted the sandwich plate that was placed before him. He devoured the food savagely, like a starving man, then gulped the chocolate with evident satisfaction. When Atsuo had drunk less than a third of his coffee, Moriya had finished his meal and was licking his lips as he leaned forward in his seat, ready to resume the business at hand.

"I met with the doctor in charge of her case and demanded an explanation of just what sort of sickness she has. He wouldn't deal with me. He says a patient's condition is confidential information that cannot be shared with anyone but the parents. As a mere friend, my relationship isn't good enough. Now, you are interested in her condition, aren't you Mr. Yukimori?"

"Yes. Well, more worried than interested, I would say."

"Worried is a variation of interested. What do you say we mount a joint operation? Go to meet the doctor in charge together and get him to state her diagnosis."

"My going wouldn't help any. I'm still just an acquaintance."

"That's enough. You're an acquaintance, I'm a friend. Acquaintances and friends have a right to know too."

"Yeah, but . . ."

"Collective bargaining is more effective than solitary demands. Besides, you're older than me and you make a very good impression. That's even more effective."

"Ahh, I don't know."

"I'm a student in the Joint Struggle. That makes me a radical, a dangerous figure as far as that head doctor is concerned. He's had me investigated. I have the power to intimidate, but no credibility. You don't pose any problems. You're respectable looking and you've got the credibility that comes with social standing. You couldn't get a better combination than us."

"I'm not so sure about this," Atsuo muttered.

"Whether you feel confident or you don't," said Moriya, "there's nothing to stop you from acting." He brushed back his long hair, unleashing a sparkling shower of dandruff. "Look, we're talking about rescuing Wakako Ikéhata, who happens to be an adult woman being unlawfully confined under the collusion of her parents and this doctor. So would you please drop your defeatist attitude?"

"Just a moment." Atsuo raised a hand to check the exuberant youth's torrent of debating points. He had finally arrived at his own view on the issue. "I do have the impression there's something not quite right with Ms. Ikéhata. She was frightened about something, and depressed. There wasn't anyone around, but she thought someone was watching her. She said an organization was after her."

"What's strange about that?" said Moriya, tiny pupils shining in the triangles of his eyes. It was the stare of an animal preparing to attack.

"Well, I hardly think there's an organization following people around and reporting on them to someone."

"There certainly is such an organization. That's a well-known fact." Moriya fixed a sharp gaze at the view from the window. "I'm being watched by the same organization. See that guy standing behind that utility pole? He's one of them."

Atsuo followed Moriya's gaze. Unquestionably, there was someone standing behind a utility pole beside a bus stop. Just a shoulder was visible, sticking out from behind the pole. But wasn't that just someone waiting for his bus? Moriya answered the thought.

"He isn't waiting for the bus. Two buses have come and gone since he's been there."

Atsuo wasn't about to concede his position, but he gave a little ground. "Well, even supposing there is some group of spies, there really was something strange about Ms. Ikéhata. I don't know about that kind of sickness, so I can't say exactly what the trouble was, though."

"That isn't saying much." Moriya's tongue slid over a thin upper lip. "Oh, well. No point in arguing the matter. Let's just drop it and go see about meeting with that doctor. How's that?"

"Okay, fine." Atsuo drank off his remaining coffee, now cold. Though acutely conscious he had to get back to the shop soon, he thought seeing the doctor might tell him something about Wakako's condition.

While he was paying at the counter, Moriya was already out the door of the coffee shop, as if it was only natural to leave Atsuo with the bill. Following outside, Atsuo glanced over at the utility pole. There was only empty sidewalk behind it, but all the people coming and going on the street looked as if they might be clandestine watchers of marked individuals. Atsuo wondered if his own mind might be playing tricks.

The same girl was at the reception counter. Atsuo told her they wanted to see the attending physician. After having them write out their names, she said the doctor was seeing patients and asked them to wait.

The waiting room benches were filled. As time passed, names were called and people went into the examination room or received prescriptions from the dispensary. Presumably, all these people were psychiatric patients, but Atsuo wasn't able to pick out anyone who seemed to especially fit that role. He had seen people who acted quite strangely among the patients of the psychiatric hospital near his apartment, but that wasn't the case here. He wondered if different hospitals had different classes of patients.

"They'll keep us waiting," said Moriya. "Just so we know they're in charge. Last time I had to wait two hours."

"I can't be waiting here very long." Atsuo glanced at a public phone. He was thinking about calling in to reschedule a difficult job awaiting his return when their names were called.

"That was quick," said Moriya. "Probably because you're in on it. See, that does make a difference."

They were admitted to the outpatient clinic. The doctor was in his forties. He had a name plate on the breast of his white coat. With his neatly parted hair and rimless glasses, he had an air of refinement. Perhaps due to limited experience with doctors, having been healthy all his life, Atsuo felt intimidated by his host, who so looked the part of the scientist. He bowed his head repeatedly as he took one of the seats being offered. Atsuo faced the doctor, with Moriya sitting at an angle to one side.

"Let me tell you to begin with, I'm in the midst of outpatient examinations, so I only have ten minutes to spare."

"Understood." With this reply, Atsuo had finally resolved himself to deal with the doctor.

"I see you are acquaintances of Wakako Ikéhata," said the doctor, with a look at the appointment forms they had filled out. "Have you known her for long?" he asked, his gaze fixed equally on Atsuo and Moriya.

"I've known her about four years," Atsuo replied.

"Really?" The doctor looked down at what seemed to be Wakako's medical record and used a ball point to write in something that was not in Japanese.

"We both have the same skating instructor."

"I see. I did hear that Ms. Ikéhata ice skates. Is she a good skater?"

"She's very good. We both started at the same time, but she is way beyond my level. But do tell us about her condition."

"Well, it's not at all serious. It will take more time to make a firm diagnosis. I am now putting together information on her condition before and after the appearance of the disorder. What's your view? When did you became aware of unusual behavior on her part?"

"Let me see." Atsuo thought about it. He couldn't pin down a particular time. Normally she was playful, but once in a while she would be blue. She had suddenly quit coming to skating lessons for two or three months. These things were unusual, but not abnormal. What he did think was abnormal was that rainy day at Jindai Botanical Park.

"This happened just recently. We were walking together and she suddenly started saying 'I'm afraid. There's an organization watching me.'"

"When was this?" asked the doctor, nodding intently as his marshmallow-soft hand busily wielded the pen.

"I guess it was around the middle of October."

"Where were you walking?"

"In a park."

"What park?"

"Jindai Botanical Garden." Saying this, Atsuo glanced at Moriya beside him and added, "I think Ms. Ikéhata made a call to Mr. Moriya immediately afterwards."

"Well, well." The doctor faced Moriya. "And what did she say to you?"

"Eh?" Moriya blurted this out like a very loud cough. "That's in the realm of private matters."

"That may be so," said the doctor, motionless, as he peered coolly through his rimless glasses. "I'm asking as a doctor. Be assured that I will not reveal to anyone else confidential information gained in the course of professional work."

"Very well." Moriya assumed a triumphant expression. "I'll tell you what she said, but it won't meet your expectations, doctor. There wasn't anything abnormal about what she had to say. She was perfectly logical. It is a fact that she is being targeted by people belonging to an organization."

"What kind of organization?"

"That I cannot say."

Moriya turned to Atsuo. "She was feeling desperate that day. She'd been followed for days on end, so she used your apartment as a hideout. I might as well tell you, she doesn't love you. She was only using you."

"What is all this?" asked the doctor.

Disconcerted, Atsuo leaned forward. "Nothing," he began and trailed off.

Moriya had been speaking loudly, and now he stepped up the volume as he threw back his slim shoulders.

"Sorry, but there is nothing ambiguous about this. That day was October twenty-first, a Monday. It was International Anti-War Day. Shinjuku was the scene of actions taken in that struggle. She walked around Shinjuku with Mr. Yukimori. That night she stayed at his apartment. Now, when you . . ."

"Wait a minute," Atsuo interrupted.

"No, it's all right," Moriya said with a knowing smile. "I won't say anything. The only thing that matters is the fact that she stayed at your apartment. The organization was following her, so she couldn't return home. Her parents don't recognize the seriousness of her situation. That led to their mistakenly thinking she was mentally unbalanced. She has been confined illegally with the cooperation of psychiatrists like you, doctor, whose one-sided decisions come from listening to the parents' viewpoint alone . . . What is it, doctor, do you see something funny about this?"

"I really appreciate your opinion. It's very interesting. I certainly want to ask her parents more about this. Do you know her father?"

"I've met him. To be precise, I've argued with him."

"What kind of argument?"

"Before I get into that I have to explain something about her mother. It would take some time."

"Go right ahead. There's still eight minutes left."

"Eight minutes. Not much, but okay. As you know, doctor, she is the oldest of three siblings. She has a sister and a brother. Their mother was completely dedicated to raising her children, but that dedication made her try to anticipate everything, with the result that the children had no freedom. That was more than Wakako could take. She would occasionally run away from home, as a way of seeking her freedom. Her father reacted to that by suddenly casting himself as the chief disciplinarian, even though he had been apathetic about his children's education until then. That's the basic paradigm of Wakako's household."

"That's an excellent summary. A bit oversimplified, though."

"'Oversimplified?'" Moriya repeated with evident dissatisfaction, but hurried on to his next point. "The first time she ran away, I accompanied her back home and confronted that overbearing father of hers."

"Just a moment," the doctor interrupted. "I believe that 'overbearing father' you speak of so disdainfully happens to be a teacher to whom you owe a debt of gratitude. You are a student of T. University's law department, are you not? That is Professor Ikéhata's department."

"How does his being a professor in the law department give me a debt of gratitude?"

"Very well. If there's no such relationship, there isn't. But you got to know Wakako because you had occasion to visit the Ikéhata home, as a law department student, didn't you?"

"Yeah, sure."

"In that case, don't you at least see him as your teacher, even if he hasn't done something for you?"

"Why do you make a fuss over details like that?"

"Because it seems to me your feelings about Professor Ikéhata are too cold. As a psychoanalyst, intuition tells me that points to a problem."

"I just can't believe a doctor, a supposed man of science, believes in such an unscientific thing as intuition." For the first time, Moriya's face showed consternation.

"Mr. Moriya," began the doctor with a gentle expression, as if comforting a baby. "Intuition is an important function of human psychology. You are the one who is being unscientific if you deny that."

Moriya glowered and shrank back like a cornered fox.

"I would be very interested to hear the basis for your finding Professor Ikéhata to be an over-bearing father."

"He doesn't realize the harm he has caused. That is why he believes his daughter has delusions of victimization when she tells him she is suffering because of her parents."

"Just a moment," the doctor interrupted. "What harm have her parents caused?"

"I have been telling you," Moriya replied with exasperation. "Her mother interferes excessively. Her father condemns obsessively. Neither recognizes that Wakako Ikéhata is an individual who has individual needs."

"Be a bit more specific," asked the doctor.

"If I get to specifics, there would never be enough time to cover everything."

"Just give one example, please."

"One example. Okay, her mother doesn't like her associating with me. So a simple telephone call from me sends her into hysterics. Her father berates her mother for letting his daughter get away with seeing someone of my ilk and lectures his daughter."

"In short, both Wakako Ikéhata's parents dislike you."

"They hate me."

"What might be the reason?"

"How would anyone know such a thing? The father was haranguing me for enticing his daughter to run away from home. He says my radical ideas are bad for her."

"Are your ideas radical?"

"According to him, they are. My political thought can't be contained by tired old adjectives like that. I suppose he was pretty well provoked over our occupying the professors' offices."

"What did you do that for?" Atsuo interrupted.

"It would take all day to answer that," said Moriya, and, with no further attention to Atsuo's question, he again addressed the doctor.

"Doctor, does she have some kind of disorder? Isn't the real problem with her parents?"

"I haven't reached the stage where that can be answered."

"That's not fair, doctor." Moriya looked at the medical record on the desk, trying to read it.

The doctor closed it deftly.

"Doctor," Atsuo interjected again. "If you can't tell us anything about her condition, please allow us a visit."

"Right! Let us visit her!" Moriya joined in hastily, as if he'd just remembered that point. The doctor took an inconspicuous glance at his watch as he frowned.

"Ms. Ikéhata is not being denied visits. She herself has said that she doesn't want to see anyone," he said, rising from his seat.

Atsuo withdrew the postcard from his inner pocket and placed it in front of the doctor. "She wrote this herself. See, it says 'please visit.'"

"I see it's postmarked a week ago. The situation has changed since then."

"Wait a minute. I came a week ago for a visit, and was turned away then, too." Moriya said.

"She wrote that she wanted Mr. Yukimori to visit. She hasn't written that she wanted to see you. All right now, your time is up."

The doctor opened the door, gestured them out by raising his chin and instructed the nurse to call in the next patient.

Atsuo and Moriya exited the building together.

"He sure knows how to get rid of people," Atsuo signed.

"It was the same thing last time. They give you the runaround, then they brush you off," said Moriya with a bitter smile. "He's a smooth operator. He wouldn't tell us anything, but he got what he wanted from us. I suppose he had us pegged as a good information source."

Atsuo opened the car door. "I'm going back to my company. Where are you headed?"

"The university."

"I'll take you as far as I'm going in that direction."

Moriya got into the passenger seat, without a word of thanks. There was no one outside the coffee shop or near the bus stop, but Moriya scanned the surroundings ceaselessly.

"Are there any watchers from that organization?" Atsuo asked playfully.

"They're not in sight now. They'll show up by and by," Moriya replied confidently.

"Is Ms. Ikéhata really in your organization?"

"There isn't any organization to join."

"But you're a major player in the student struggle, aren't you?"

"I'm a member of one sect. It doesn't amount to anything you could call an organization. Wakako Ikéhata participates strictly on an individual basis, not as a member. She hates sects and organizations."

"So why would that organization want to follow her?"

"It's the people who do not belong to organizations who become targeted by organizations."

"Oh, by the way, I saw you on TV the other day. You were giving a speech."

Moriya didn't bother to deny this. He turned to look at the procession of cars behind them. A young woman was driving a red car. Countless windows shone from lines of cars large and small.

The traffic slowed. They had hit a road repair project. Tramcar railing was being removed. Trolley lines were being phased out everywhere because they posed an obstacle to the growing numbers of cars on the roads. Removal of trolley routes didn't ease traffic jams in the least, however. Cars just kept filling up all available space.

"Mr. Yukimori, I hear you were in an army prison," Moriya said unexpectedly.

"So what?" Atsuo answered, tasting bitterness. Something he had confided to Wakako as a secret between them was coming back to him from the lips of another person.

"I heard it from Wakako Ikéhata. Please don't blame her for telling me. We maintain a free relationship based on a policy of no secrets between us. If there were secrets, there would be no freedom to the relationship."

Atsuo was silent.

"I am very interested to hear about prisons. They are on the underside of society. When you look at society from the underside you get to see how the system works in fine detail. I was held in police detention once. I got busted during the Oji struggle. They didn't have anything on me, and I didn't talk, so they had to let me go. That was when I realized what an interesting place a police station is. You can really see what the bosses want to protect and what they are afraid of. A police station jail is a good place to learn about the system's power structure and its weak points. Of course police jails are just prep schools. The ultimate academy has got to be prison. I'm thinking about committing some kind of crime so I can get into prison for some real learning."

"There isn't any room for learning in a prison. It's just forced labor, every day. Nobody cares about what you want to do. There's no freedom at all."

"Exactly! That's the essence of the power structure. That's why I think it's important to know prison firsthand. Power fears individual freedom. That is why it oppresses. Big authoritarian states always have vast prison systems. Look at the Nazis, the Soviets, America, China — you might as well include Japan too."

"There is one very important thing you're forgetting. If you go to prison, you get a prison term. Look, theft is the most common crime. You can get up to ten years for that. That's not just losing your freedom — you're losing a big chunk of your life. One day of confinement is enough to find out about the power structure. What's to learn from ten years of that life, day in and day out? If anything, it will make you stupid."

Moriya was taking this in with a serious expression. He nodded thoughtfully. "Yeah. I can understand that."

"Time is the most precious thing a person has. You talk about freedom, learning, revolution. Well, if you are going to make any of that a reality, it's going to take time, isn't it? That's what you lose when you do a prison term. In prison you do forced labor. That's not the same as work done on the outside. There are shops where they put you to work during the day. You might be working with leather or wood or metal. There's print shops and body shops too. Different prisons have different kinds of work. But whatever you do, you might as well call it unpaid labor. Actually, they do give you a little money which they call work compensation, but the amount is way out of line with modern standards. And strikes for higher wages aren't allowed. Because you aren't a worker, you're a prisoner. It isn't work that you are doing. It's punishment."

"That is really interesting," Moriya said. His arrogant tone had vanished, his voice now surprisingly unaffected, like a youth truly eager to learn.

"Glad you find it interesting," Atsuo said, as if explaining to a child. "But get this. You can afford to say that because it isn't happening to you. If you want to find out for yourself, go ahead and become a convict and get turned out day after day to do work you don't want to do and you're not doing for the pay. It's just working to kill time."

"There's a novel by Dostoevsky, *The House of the Dead*. Do you know it?"

"Nah. I've read some war stories and period novels. That's about all. Novels are just a pack of lies. That stuff doesn't interest me. I like to read something that talks about the way things really are. That's what I like about tanka and haiku."

"Sometimes novels tell the truth. There are truths that stand above the truth. *The House of the Dead* is one of those novels." Like the student he was, Moriya was warming to his topic.

"It's about life in a prison camp for exiles in Siberia. There's a place where he talks about what happens when you give a prisoner meaningless work to do. Say you make him keep pouring the same water from one bucket into another. He ends up either hanging himself or going crazy and committing some crime. It says there's no other way out."

"Yeah, that's what forced labor in prison is. Tormenting the prisoner with meaningless labor. The present day penal confinement system works on that principle."

"Pouring water from one bucket to another. That would be brutal. It would be enough to drive me crazy."

"That's it. Prisoners are all crazy. You come to believe your meaningless work has some kind of meaning, so you won't be bored by doing the same thing over and over, day after day. It happens automatically. You aren't really in your right mind."

"That's fascinating. No it isn't, it's terrifying. Mr. Yukimori, you really know prisons, and not just army prisons."

Atsuo did not reply.

"Here I am telling people that all criminals are revolutionaries, but I've never met a criminal. Mr. Yukimori, are you a criminal?"

"You just hit a sore spot. That's all in the long-gone past."

"Tell me, how does it feel the moment you do the deed?"

"I don't remember. It happened long, long ago."

They had reached the vicinity of Ochanomizu Station. A left turn would lead to T. University. "I'll take you as far as your school," said Atsuo, turning left.

Armored police wagons were parked along the road, turning it into a fortified battle line. Behind mesh-covered windows were riot police in full gear looking like robots in storage. The cold sheen from their shields and visors seemed all the colder for its stunning contrast with the brilliant yellows of the ginkgo trees lining the boulevard.

Inside the university entrance the students were having a demonstration. Helmets and sticks on display, they were zig-zagging around the plaza in a tight line. Their privileged status lent weight to the spectacle. They were yelling "Go home, go home!" to the riot police outside. Traffic soon slowed to a crawl.

"Aren't they your friends?" said Atsuo.

"Hardly." Moriya replied disdainfully. "They're just playing revolutionary because it's a big thing now. You don't get anything done if all you've got is helmets and sticks. They look the part on the outside, but there's nothing inside."

"Those are hard lines. Don't you wear a helmet?"

"Sure I do, but only to protect my head, which is thinking about something besides playing stupid games. I don't wear it just to be seen wearing it. Ah, would you let me out there?" Moriya pushed the door open.

"Going to the hospital again?" Atsuo asked quickly.

"Yes, every day."

His long hair swaying as he walked, Moriya could easily be taken for a slightly built girl. In a moment he was swallowed up by the crowd of pedestrians.

Atsuo's thoughts snapped back to his immediate concerns. There was no time to lose. He had to get back to the shop. The episode featuring student radical Moriya already seemed to him like a bizarre fantasy from another world.

The sight of Ichiro Fukawa wearing his work uniform in back of the gas station set him to worrying how suspicious he must seem, having left the shop to go wandering off dressed up in his business suit. He was hoping to roll past unnoticed, but their eyes met, so there was nothing to do but get out of the car.

Fukawa mopped his forehead and pate with a handkerchief. "Just got back. Can't believe how warm it is in Tokyo. You know you're back in the south."

"Welcome back." Atsuo lowered his head in greeting. He felt Fukawa taking in his suit. "A friend of mine is in the hospital. I just went to pay a visit."

"Oh, okay." Fukawa tugged uncomfortably at a stiffly starched cuff of his uniform. "How's the shop?"

"Everything's going well. The senior men put the youngsters to good use, so we were covered. There was just one tough job, an engine overhaul, that was on hold."

"You mean the wheels keep turning whether the old man and the foreman are there or not? I guess that's good news, even if it sounds a little sad."

Kimiko Fujiyama appeared in a blue work jacket and headed for her desk, ignoring Atsuo. He wasn't about to let her off the hook. "Hi!" he called out breezily. Kimiko's expression remained frozen.

"It was quite a trip, that's for sure," Fukawa said as he continued wiping away sweat. He seemed much affected by the heat outside, even though the office was extremely cool. "The hunting was great, though."

"I'm really sorry about what happened with Torakichi."

"You know, when I got home, there was a long letter from his wife. Much too long to get through."

"Torakichi and his wife are both sincerely sorry about it. He's not much of a talker, so I guess she wrote that letter to put his feelings into words."

"I don't have any hard feelings. One thing led to another, that's all. Couldn't be helped. Only thing is . . ." Fukawa winked, using the eye that was beyond Kimiko's line of sight.

Atsuo changed the subject.

"I met that middle school lad. His marks are in the low end of the middle range, but he's looks fit and he's a good boy. He's the second son of a fisherman from Otaru. I'll bring his resume."

"If you say he's okay, that's enough. Let's hire him. We can use every hand we can get. Oh, by the way, I got some big news for you." Fukawa said this in good humor. "That 170,000 yen you know, that we thought was stolen. Well, it turned up."

"Where?"

"I hate to admit it, but it was in the drawer of my desk. Somehow it got into a letter case."

"Very glad to hear it."

"It's a tale of a dimwit. Getting old, I guess. I emptied out the drawer and looked through everything, but not inside that letter case." Fukawa was all smiles, evidently enjoying the story.

Unexpectedly, Kimiko's bright red mouth opened in laughter. "I don't know about you. I wish you'd pay a little more attention to what you're doing. I was one of the suspects too!"

"Yeah, it's a good thing the matter is settled," Atsuo said, but he was frowning. He had a distinctly unpleasant feeling he had been lied to. Questions remained. What was the fuss over the supposed theft really all about? Yukichi had been the suspect. He'd spent days on end with a heavy heart, probing Yukichi while having to defend him to the suspicious Fukawa. The investigation of Yukichi's delinquent record had probably gotten back to Torakichi, who would have been quick to sense Kimiko's evident disdain for him. Was that the real reason behind the altercation? If all this had been caused by Fukawa's carelessness, there was a lot Fukawa should answer for. But there he was laughing, with no sign he recognized any personal responsibility.

A suspicion rose up in Atsuo's mind like the enigmatic shadow of a tree glimpsed in a fog. What if the affair had been nothing but a malicious prank by Fukawa? Casting suspicion on Yukichi was one way to put Atsuo on the burner. Why do that? Well, why not? He wouldn't put it past Fukawa to take pleasure in using his power to make him suffer, just to show he had that power. That contented laughter just might be ridicule directed at him.

"Okay, that's one happy ending." Atsuo forced a sunny smile as he repeated the sentiment he didn't feel. He gave a bow of his head and made a show of hurrying busily from the room before his happy expression faded.

He changed clothes quickly and headed for the shop, where he immediately commenced the engine overhaul awaiting his return. Soon he was covered with oil stains. After the young shop workers had finished their jobs, Atsuo continued the overhaul with one of the older men. It was past eight o'clock when they had gotten far enough to call it a day. Fukawa's office was already dark, and the shop's outer shutter had been lowered. They walked through the darkened shop cautiously to avoid stumbling over machine parts scattered about. It was like finding one's way through a forest at night.

After showering, Atsuo went to the shop workers dorm. A group of workers lying about on the tatami floor before a television were startled by the unexpected appearance of the shop foreman. A couple scrabbled to their feet to watch curiously as he passed. Others conspicuously ignored the spectacle as they pored over comic books or porn magazines. From somewhere, the clatter of Mahjong tiles could be heard. Smells of cigarettes, saké, armpits and machine oil relentlessly assaulted the nostrils.

Yukichi was in his room facing the stereo with his headphones on, keeping time with his right hand. What could be heard sounded like war songs. Yukichi's roommate Tomoyama was in a yoga pose, standing on his hands with his ankles tucked behind his neck. Sensing another presence in the room, Yukichi turned around and removed his headphones.

"There you go — goodies from home. Share it with the other guys." Atsuo handed over a bag of dried saffron cod and a large package of salted salmon that he had brought back from Hokkaido. Yukichi silently accepted them with a nod of thanks.

"Your papa and mama were looking good."

No response.

"I saw Tetsukichi."

This at least elicited what looked like a flicker of interest. The scar on Yukichi's forehead was unexpectedly big, a splotch about three centimeters across.

"What do you say we go out for a while?" Tomoyama did not break his exotic pose as he watched uncle and nephew leave the dormitory.

As they reached the bottom of the stairway they were caught by Sonoko Kanéhara.

"You certainly are a rare sight," she said with a toss of her head, which she had wrapped in a towel, having washed her hair. "I hear you got back the day before yesterday. You might have dropped by to say hello."

"We've got backlog work on top of backlogs to do. It's enough to make your head spin. I only got off just a little while ago. Oh, yes. I have a gift I brought back for you in my locker. I'll give it to you tomorrow."

"Oh, my! Thanks for remembering me." There was no irony in Sonoko's tone — she was sincerely pleased. She cast a meaningful glance down the hall toward her office, a sign she wanted Atsuo to join her there for a private word. Yukichi was left to wait.

"So now the story is that money turned up. Somebody's got an awful lot of nerve."

"Yeah, that's how it sounds to me, too."

"The boss says he misplaced it. Well, who would buy that story? He's covering up for Kimiko. She's the one who took it. There just isn't any other explanation. That's the way it is. It didn't look like that money was going to be found, so I played informer. I told the police."

Atsuo received this information in startled silence. He looked at Sonoko Kanéhara, finding her aging skin a less than pleasant sight, its darkness unmitigated by powder because she was fresh from the bath.

"Actually, I don't know if you would call it informing. I certainly didn't go sneaking into the police box to report it. I didn't let the boss know, though. So I guess it was a kind of informing."

"I'd call it taking the bull by the horns."

"I got tired of seeing him fret over it. Everyone under suspicion. That's too much to take."

"Yeah."

"So today I called the Kanda police station to let them know the boss was back and an inspector called him. Next thing you know he was making a big fuss that he found the money."

"There's something funny about that," Atsuo muttered.

"There certainly is." Sonoko Kanéhara gave a victorious twitch of her small nose. "That pretty much proves Kimiko's the culprit."

"Hey, where's Yukichi?"

"He went outside. He'll be waiting out there. He hates to hear people talking when he's not in on the conversation. But tell me what went on between the boss and Kimiko in Hokkaido." Sonoko's eyes were wide with curiosity.

"Just as you expect. Doing what they always do."

Sonoko was ready with a stream of detailed questions. Did they stay in the same hotel room? What did Kimiko wear? Did she go hunting? Did she catch any fish? Atsuo knew there was no point in trying to discourage Sonoko with curt responses. Time went by as he dealt with her. Wanting to get back to Yukichi, he finally broke off and was heading for the door when Sonoko's insistent voice assailed him from behind.

"I hear Mr. Jinnai and Kimiko had quite a scrap." Startled, Atsuo turned to face her again in spite of himself.

"You certainly are well-informed."

"I know everything that goes on here, even though I'm not meant to. Don't be surprised. Mr. Jinnai got a phone call from his brother. I just listened in on that."

"He had a call from Hokkaido?"

"That's right."

"And did Yukichi say anything about it to you?"

"Not a word. But it is bothering him a lot. So please do have a good talk with him about it."

Yukichi was standing at the entrance to the parking lot with one hand on the chain link fence and the other on the rail-mounted steel gate to the entrance, shaking them both.

"What are you doing?"

"Uncle, we need something stronger than this fence and this gate."

"Why?"

"The students are going to attack it. They can bust through here in no time."

"Yeah? You were saying that before."

"I got good information. They have a plan to occupy Kanda and make it a liberated zone. There's a lot of universities around here. They can do it easy."

They went to a low-priced eatery. Atsuo had a pork cutlet set and Yukichi had a beer with meat and potatoes. There was a counter in the back set up bistro style, with customers in small groups.

"Tetsukichi says you want to quit here and be a fisherman."

Yukichi was on his guard immediately. His broad shoulders stiffened as if he faced an opponent in a bare-knuckle fight.

"Any chance of changing your mind? Or are you set on quitting?"

"I'm set on being a fisherman. I want to help my brother."

"That's a good thing to do, but there's a lot of danger to that job. You know about that?"

Yukichi didn't answer. His tiny eyes opened to the bursting point as he drank off his beer in a single swallow.

Chapter 4

Tower

11:05 a.m.

Makihiko Moriya gazed down at the wave of riot police advancing on the Tower beneath the branches of the bare trees, a malignant blue effluence on the midday promenade. They were following behind an armored personnel carrier. Each officer wore the same helmet, the same riot gloves, the same chest protector, and the same confident expression of one wielding the power of the state. The force was a formidable sight, moving to the attack, row upon row, in tight ranks. The enemy had begun sporadic attacks at dawn. Accompanied by the sounds of explosions, frenzied cries, raucous loudspeakers and property being destroyed, the morning light had revealed white smoke from tear gas, arcs of water cannon and flames from Molotov cocktails. Thus far, the enemy had not approached this Tower. Now he was coming.

The other liberated zones around the city had most likely already fallen, leaving only this Tower still in the hands of the free. The enemy knew what he was doing. He recognized this Tower as the symbol of the revolutionaries. He would take it as a trophy of our eradication for the world to see. That was why his troops had fanned out to install TV cameras on rooftops and in windows so they covered every possible shooting angle, insuring a plentiful supply of evidentiary footage later on. Helicopters converged like flies swarming to rotting meat. "Watch the Tower," they urged. "Get the story on what happens there!"

The personnel carrier reached the front driveway to meet an angry rain of Molotov cocktails. Flames danced across the pavement and spread, proclaiming our burning hatred of the oppressor. Rocks hurtle downward and set off a variety of sound effects, from dull thuds to ringing crashes — a stirring song of revenge for our oppression. The cumbersome vehicle retreats, no match for the onslaught.

The main entryway was barricaded by a complex structure of oak painstakingly designed by the architectural students' team. No simple tool set would suffice to breach it. This wall was sturdy, like the ramparts of our resolve. Even if you did get beyond the oak beams, you would only meet a solid barricade of steel desks, lockers, and chairs.

Makihiko Moriya surveyed his surroundings. He was in a room five meters square, at the summit of the Tower. A hole had been punched through the low ceiling to provide passage to the roof. The backs of the giant clocks on all four sides of the Tower were visible. On the floor were stacks of munitions — rocks, Molotov cocktails, and wooden staves.

Their laborious preparations notwithstanding, chances were the siege would end by early evening. The enemy had eight thousand troops, armored vehicles, water cannons, tear gas, and who knows what new high-tech police equipment. He could crush us with sheer volume of resources. That was beside the point. We have never sought victory. We take satisfaction in the symbolism of holding out through a long siege.

Glass shattered and a smoking tear gas canister flew inside. "Throw it back!" someone shouted. He picked up the tube with smoke pouring out and threw it back outside. The roar of a helicopter paralyzed him for several interminable moments. He saw the face of a newspaper reporter behind a plastic windshield in the passenger seat. He projected burning curiosity and the self-assurance of the anointed reporter on his mission of serving the people's right to know with strictly neutral reporting.

Makihiko Moriya mounted a steel chair and stepped out onto the Tower roof. T. University's entire campus appeared before him like a ship floating upon a sea of city streets. Two red banners unfurled to the winds. At his side were a dozen or so crouching youths. Moriya faced the loudspeaker system they had installed, drew a deep breath and began speaking, as if to address the entire world.

11:36 a.m.

Wakako Ikéhata walked as a full member of the Movement. Until this day, she had only participated in demonstrations that had for the most part circulated

144

tamely within the campus. Never before had she ventured out into the streets among such a large group of people, much less in the radical student uniform of construction helmet and facecloth. It felt bizarre, as if she had become someone else. She was even armed with a wooden staff. Having forgotten to bring work gloves, she had borrowed someone else's. They were oil-stained, with some kind of residue inside that was unpleasant to the touch.

"Wasshoi!" You're supposed to shout "Wasshoi!" in time to the leader's whistle. I don't suppose anyone is going to hear my feeble voice — but, anyway . . . "Wasshoi!"

Oh, well. The important thing is that our private university at Surugadai came forth in support of the comrades at the national university, under siege in the Tower. The only trouble is, this feels more like a festival than a militant action. "Wasshoi!" — Well, well. That time, I could finally hear my own shrill voice.

The procession stopped moving forward. There seemed to be something ahead blocking their path. Suddenly the boys in front were backing up, and at the same time a terrific surge of forward pressure came from behind.

Wakako Ikéhata went down, striking her elbow hard on the pavement. She felt the weight of bodies falling across her head, back and hips. The fear of having this terrific weight bearing down upon her was worse than the pain from her elbow. A voice called — "Look out there! Get her up before she gets trampled to death!" But she didn't hear it. All that reached her mind was the crushing weight. She lost consciousness for just a moment before she realized someone had pulled her out and her body was in motion.

The boys had given her a hand. She was on her feet and running. For a time, there was nothing to do but just run. The street was overwhelmed with riot police five and six abreast, moving decisively against the students. They were driven back, scattered, chased away. They fled to the Tower without a trace of the vengeful ferocity they had shown when advancing in attack squads and brandishing fighting sticks. Reaching a crossing, they joined with another group of students who had also been routed as they approached T. University's rear gate. The great thoroughfare was flooded to capacity with helmeted students.

Wakako Ikéhata ran without knowing where she was going, only that she was going with everyone else, which meant that danger and excitement lay ahead. She ran with increasing anticipation that something would happen. She wasn't particularly frightened by the riot police chasing them. They were a ridiculous sight, running in their blue-and-black helmets, silver shields and heavy body armor. There was no chance they would catch the lightly clad students, who were already pulling away from the police and regarding the streets of the city and all it held as theirs alone.

When they ran out of breath, they began walking. In a moment, they were back in formation and proceeding like a proper demonstration in time to whistle blasts. Someone said they should return to their own university. Everyone thought that was the best destination for them. Wakako Ikéhata thought so too.

The campus of Wakako's university was thronged with students. Helmeted figures filled the quadrangles, hallways, and rooftops. They were all comrades, no matter that she didn't know their names or faces. Wakako Ikéhata realized that she wasn't the same person she had been when she had set out earlier that morning. She was a part of the movement, living her life as one of these people who comprised it.

11:40 a.m.

Choking and coughing, eyes streaming from tear gas, Kotaro Ikéhata gazed up at the Tower, but its Gothic Sham facade swam before his eyes. His office was inside, and in his office were all his research papers, files, books, and notebooks; notes and references culled from twenty-five years of research. Driven by ambition, he had conducted his research diligently, enthusiastically, stubbornly. When rumors circulated that the students would occupy the faculty offices, he had scoffed at colleagues who moved their own research materials to their homes. In conversations and at faculty meetings he had consistently argued for trusting the students. "This is a seat of learning, and those talented young people are here to study," he would say. "Those who assume the worst of them from the start aren't qualified to be teachers."

The police were breaking windows as the first step to forcing their way into the building. The students' resistance was fierce. They rained chairs, bottles and rocks down upon the officers. The police directed streams from water hoses into some windows and fired volleys of tear gas into others. Books inside would be soaked. Wasn't there a less obnoxious way of breaking in? Kotaro Ikéhata approached the commanding officer.

"Please stop using that water hose! It will damage valuable papers."

This protest elicited a sarcastic laugh from the chief. "Those kids have gasoline bombs. If they start a fire, the damage will be a lot worse." Then he turned up the pressure on the water stream issuing from a hose.

Kotaro Ikéhata bit his lip as he retreated to his position of safety, taking care to avoid as best he could the rocks being hurled down by the angry students. Suddenly, his thoughts were on his daughter, Wakako. Her whereabouts had been unknown since she had run away from the hospital about ten days before. She had evidently scaled a wire fence on the roof and climbed down to the ground. When she called his wife three days ago, she had neglected to say where she was. It was highly probable she was with Makihiko Moriya, that ingrate of a student. The thought was too much to bear.

Kotaro Ikéhata walked in the direction of the Tower. He was stopped by one of the police guards posted around this strategic zone and granted entry upon showing his "faculty" armband. This is like having your homeland occupied by a hostile army, he thought. He was a professor here, but he might as well have been a stranger from the street, as far as the riot police were concerned. Two or three arcs of high-pressure water streams played about the Tower, which was completely surrounded by riot police. Inside the Tower was a large auditorium, a venue for student ceremonies and the presentation of addresses by renowned scholars. Located at the very center of T. University, the Tower symbolized the proud history of Japan's most important institution of learning. He thought of the auditorium's magnificent "Harvest" mural and its chandelier. The Tower had survived devastating air raids on Tokyo. It was heartbreaking to be witnessing bit-by-bit destruction inflicted upon it by students and policemen. It was of course up to the police to successfully defeat and arrest all the students. As a leader, Makihiko Moriya, would probably be held responsible and put on trial. But what would happen to Wakako?

Kotaro Ikéhata looked away from the Tower and considered the question. Suppose she was arrested as a student radical and charged. What were the chances of winning a not guilty decision by pleading insanity?

12:00 p.m.

Atsuo Yukimori switched on the TV. It was a color model Ichiro Fukawa had purchased two years before, as soon as color news broadcasts had begun. The red brick Tower at T. University abruptly appeared on the screen. The announcer's voice was an octave too high, breaking with the excitement and urgency of reporting dramatic events in progress. A group soon assembled around the television set — Ichiro Fukawa and Kimiko Fujiyama joined with the young shop workers to watch. Engulfed in smoke and jetting water, the Tower was the color of oozing blood.

"This is one hell of an event," Ichiro Fukawa said. "Show of the century, that's what it is." When the announcer said they would continue the broadcast into the afternoon, Fukawa said, "You can't miss something like this. Looks like we'll get no damn work done today." He rubbed his watermelon belly.

Atsuo Yukimori put on his jacket and went out to lunch. The restaurants had put up "closed today" signs and all the storefronts were shuttered — very unusual for a Saturday, especially in view of crowds so heavy it was almost impossible to move forward, as if a festival was in progress. The sea of students occupying the roads included self-styled guerrillas in helmets and facecloths, but they were outnumbered by students in their usual colorful student dress, suitable mainly for activities like picnicking. A curtain of dry dust hung about an area issuing forth the heavy sounds of rock-splitting. Students were digging up paving stones and breaking them down into rocks for throwing.

Atsuo Yukimori had the feeling that Wakako Ikéhata was somewhere among the students. He was carefully watching for her. A letter she had written in a tidy hand on proper letter stationary had arrived two days before.

"i escaped from the hospital i would never get better as long as i was there i'm in a certain place in tokyo i can't go back home i won't go back home a nurse told me you came to visit i'm grateful but it was better you didn't see me they made me take medicine i was in a daze i ate too much i was enormous it was awful now that i'm back in the real world a week my head is clear i lost all that weight i finally felt like a person again so i decided to write isn't it funny you stop taking medicine and you feel great!!! my depression is all gone my body is back to normal i can't say where i am now it would be big trouble if the organization found out where i am so it's a secret the reason i am writing is i want to see you but i don't know how i'm scared of getting close to the skating rink or your home in chofu wakako."

It was likely that Wakako Ikéhata had fled the hospital to be with Makihiko Moriya. He had probably engineered her escape. So did that mean she was at T. University? Atsuo Yukimori had been taking every opportunity to look at the TV set since early that morning, but the students on the screen were all so alike he could hardly tell one from another. His conviction that she had joined the revolutionary students was growing. He scrutinized each student as he made his way through the milling crowd.

12:10 p.m.

As Ginji Sato pushed through the throngs of people, he was accurately identifying locations, shapes, thicknesses, and even contents of wallets. His fingertips were his most finely tuned sensors. Fleeting contact with a hip pocket or breast pocket was enough to obtain a clear assessment, just as if the wallets had been extracted and closely examined. But apart from this skill set, Ginji had a special talent all his own. He could identify wallets with fair accuracy through arm or shoulder contact. "S'cuse me," he'd mutter and check the mark's breast pocket with his shoulder as he passed. He could do the same with both arms as he worked his way through the crowd, as if hurrying to some destination. This gift enabled him to perceive valuables carried by the people around him as if they were on display in a shop.

Only rarely would Ginji Sato actually make a move. He waited patiently for the moment when the fleeting conditions necessary for an operation would materialize. There had to be a fat wallet. There couldn't be any plainclothes in the vicinity. The mark had to be off guard. There had to be some kind of "curtain" or "shield." There had to be a viable exit path. Such exacting conditions don't come together very often. It is basically a matter of chance. Conditions on commuter trains favor the chances, which was why Ginji Sato had chosen the career of a *hakoshi*. Today was special in that the trains weren't running, and he wasn't about to pass up the chances offered by so many wallets floating about the streets. Thanks to the frequent student demonstrations of late, there had been many occasions when the right conditions presented themselves. The riot in Shinjuku of the previous fall had netted him seventeen wallets. He had lived high for two months. Ginji Sato was strongly in favor of student riots. Pushing and shoving through the crowd, he kept an accurate memory of his route to ensure that he would never pass the same place twice.

The streets were alive with plainclothes. He could pick them out by their builds and the way they looked at the crowd. Another sign was the pocket bulges produced by handcuffs and ropes. But Ginji Sato never looked them in the eye. That was to be absolutely avoided. The light of the eyes holds the truth of human intentions. Knowing this, he avoided all eye contact, not only with detectives. When he had to look at people, he did it surreptitiously, from the corner of his vision. He had practiced that art well enough to be able to distinguish faces that way.

Besides plainclothes, there were plenty of pickpockets in this crowd too.

They weren't as easy to spot as detectives, but they, too, could be picked out by subtle mannerisms or traces of strategically positioned accomplices. Like himself, they kept eyes downcast and concentrated on fingertip awareness, awaiting their chance. If it was too obvious one was doing that, you knew he was a rookie. If you really know your business you can look stupid while your nerve ends are working overtime.

Some students began throwing rocks at approaching riot police. People in front started backing up to avoid the missiles. That created a moment of confusion for Ginji Sato to spring into action. He undid the button on a certain inner pocket he had located. Then he extracted a wallet made of kangaroo skin, simultaneously refastening the button. The name for this rapid maneuver is "badge unpinning" — the thumb and index finger undo the button, then refasten it after the wallet is lifted and dropped by the ring finger and little finger.

He felt a glow of pride. "Ain't lost my touch yet — still Boss Ginji."

He counted the take, now inside his own pocket. It was a satisfying wad of 10,000 yen bills — close to thirty of them. Savoring the afterglow of the tactile sensations he had received upon executing the deed, he turned right into one alley, then left into another to distance himself from the scene.

That is how a master plays the game, he thought. I don't need any blade, like they use in Kansai. There was a special miniature knife that was held between the fingers. Slashing the mark's clothing made it easy to take the goods, so you have a higher success rate. But it was a clumsy way of doing your work, and if you were caught holding that little knife, that was sure evidence against you. No, a real pickpocket is an aristocrat. He does beautiful work, perfect work that doesn't leave behind any trace. You can't do that without years of practice.

The real third-raters in the business were the thugs. In prison, Ginji Sato had regarded violent criminals with contempt. That is what he thought of anyone so inept he couldn't steal without drawing blood.

The sight of a burly figure in a leather jacket up ahead was enough to overcome his self-satisfaction and set off wariness, and a feeling of abjection. Was it a detective? No, it was Atsuo Yukimori.

Uncertain if he should let his presence be known, he kept quiet and followed behind him. Atsuo Yukimori walked along the sidewalk's edge with his head high, looking about like a scout on patrol. The sidewalk was becoming congested with office workers whose work week ended on Saturday afternoon. The boundary between them and the students in the street was blurring. A patrol car was repeatedly issuing commands: "You are creating a dangerous situation. Go back to your homes." . . . "You are obstructing traffic. Please do not loiter."

Ginji Sato approached Atsuo Yukimori. "Hey, how are you?"

"If it isn't the boss! What are you doing around here?"

"Just saying hello. And why the hell are you here?"

"This is where I work. I came out to get lunch, but everything's closed."

"There are places open near the station."

"Let's go check them out."

Ginji Sato and Atsuo Yukimori followed a back street to a station front area. There the diners, restaurants and lunch counters were mostly open, with no regard for the commotion playing out on the nearby thoroughfares. They went into a grilled meat shop. Both men ordered bowls of Korean style noodles and kimchi.

The breast of Atsuo Yukimori's oil-stained coveralls was visible under his leather jacket. His nails were black with grease. Ginji Sato kept quiet, waiting for the other man to talk. As long as nothing was said to him, he had nothing to say. He wasn't hungry either; he was there because he had been invited, and in his view, it was up to the one who did the inviting to do the talking and pay the bill. Having been on his feet plying his trade all day, he was glad for the break. The back of Atsuo Yukimori's hand was flaccid and covered with wrinkles. It looked every bit the hand of a fifty-year-old working man.

"Looks like T. University is going nuts," Atsuo Yukimori said as he looked up at the TV. Ginji Sato's response was an apathetic, "Yeah?"

"There's a private university back of my shop. The kids in there took it over this morning and they've been raising hell ever since."

"Yeah? Don't know a thing about it, but it's okay with me. Let 'em keep raising hell. Gets people out on the street. That's good for business."

Atsuo Yukimori looked at his watch. It was 12:42.

He's always looking at his watch — that was the third time, Ginji Sato thought. "What time you got to be back?" he asked.

"At one. It's hard, working for the Man."

Some minutes past 2:00 p.m.

Wakako Ikéhata was with all the others, sitting around their school quadrangle. Blood vessels dilated by prolonged running, the blood coursed through her body like a full throated song. It was pleasantly cool there in the shadows of the buildings.

I can't believe what I just did. But we really upended that car. It was like a beautiful fantasy. Someone was trying to light a match, but couldn't because the matches were all wet from the water cannon. He said, "Anyone got a lighter?" So

I lent him my lighter, and the car was set aflame. It ballooned up to three times normal size, burning beautifully.

The cops shot tear gas bombs to chase us away. My eyes were hurting and my nose was running, but I couldn't stop looking at what the flame from my lighter had done. There was my battle victory. It was a joy to behold.

Wakako Ikéhata lay back on the ground, her head on the breast of a boy already lying down. In a moment, another boy's head was on her stomach. It felt very good indeed to be among this tangle of bodies looking up at the sky. Everything blended into that wonderful song from within.

The sky looked pathetically squarish, its blue color made turbid by lifeless clouds sullying the sun. The boy whose head was on Wakako Ikéhata's stomach handed her a cigarette that was being passed around. The end was wet with spit, but it didn't feel dirty. She took a deep drag, filling her breast with the smoke they all shared. She felt expansive. Whatever it was that ailed her seemed to have disappeared.

Was it really some kind of illness? The doctor said it was depression. I really did feel melancholy — heavy hearted. It was like having mind and soul pulled down into a dark, bottomless hole. Still, maybe it wasn't exactly depression, not if depression is wanting to sob and cry or letting out long sighs and being so sad you just want to leave the world. It wasn't like that. I never felt like crying. I wasn't even sad. To the contrary, I had been hoping for that kind of real emotion. It would have made me feel like a human being.

One day in the hospital I had a strange dream. The ground in the garden at home had a big hole. When my eyes fell on it, I saw it was a long way down to the bottom. At the very bottom was a circular stage, like in a Greek theatre. I went down a stairway in the wall and found the stage rapidly expanding until I was suspended in the air over a colossal seating section. A single actor was on the stage. He extended his right hand and made beckoning motions, as if entreating me to come forth. I descended from the stairway on a rope ladder, like a circus dancer, to the stage in front of the actor. As I looked to his face, I was suddenly overcome with fear, but I looked anyway. His face was featureless and smooth, exactly like a boiled egg with the shell removed.

I told the doctor about my dream. That was in accordance with his orders. He was very insistent on finding out who the actor was. He pressed me to tell him who I associated with the actor, so I said my father. That satisfied him. He said my illness was the product of father-daughter conflict. He seemed very confident about that pronouncement. But I think that egg-faced actor was not my father. He was probably someone else I know.

Looking into the luminous whitish blue sky, Wakako Ikéhata thought of the face of Atsuo Yukimori. The stories of life in army prison he had told her when they were in Shinjuku had the kind of real detail you wouldn't know if you hadn't experienced it yourself. Just imagine a place where it is forbidden to defecate during the daytime. There might be places like that even today. Prisons exist on the hidden side of the world. He is on this side now, but once he was on the other side.

That is one pale face to see on a man. Kind of amazing, lifeless, almost like a really dead person. He didn't touch me that night. You go strolling in to a man's home all by yourself, of course you expect something is going to happen — I'd already decided that would be okay. Strangely, the expected didn't happen. But there is something about him . . . Makihiko Moriya certainly wouldn't have hesitated to lay his hands on me. But he isn't like Makihiko Moriya, is he? He is older — he knows a lot that I don't know.

There was applause. Everyone who had been lying about was getting to their feet and forming a line. Wakako Ikéhata applauded along with everyone else, without knowing why. Finally she saw a red-faced rag doll being carried in by several people. It had on a riot policeman's uniform. Are they going to burn it? . . . Wait a minute. That's no doll. It's a policeman, bloody and barely breathing. Fists struck at his chest and belly. Wood staves came down on him. Wakako Ikéhata looked away. He was on the way to being killed. I am against killing people. But the next moment she was realizing she was one of many accomplices there. The lurid light from that burning car had exposed in minute detail what was in her heart. She was an arsonist. Just think! The daughter of Professor Ikéhata, the student, Wakako Ikéhata, distinguishes herself as a criminal.

She recalled the angry look that came so often from those eyes like slits carved in a mask that belonged to Makihiko Moriya.

"All crime is revolutionary," he would declare. "Crime is the product of a perverted social order that says no to that society."

"Well, I think crime is wrong. It hurts people."

"It hurts bourgeois society."

"If somebody gets killed, that's a real person dying, not society."

"In a revolution the ruling elite's dogs get killed. That's how it should be."

That was what Makihiko Moriya said, very clearly. I really think he could kill without turning a hair.

Would it really be okay to kill that riot policeman? . . . (Hey, he's gone! They've taken him somewhere.) . . . He might not even be twenty yet. He's just as young as all the students here. He's probably in the police because he couldn't go to a university. That makes him the rulers' dog and okay to kill. Makihiko Moriya's logic doesn't make sense to me.

Wakako Ikéhata was simultaneously thinking about Makihiko Moriya, now under siege in the Tower, and her father, who was among the faculty that had called out the riot police now assaulting the Tower.

The first time he visited the house I went into the parlor to serve coffee and cake. It was a perfectly normal visit — he was in Father's criminal law seminar. I talked with him about something. I don't remember what was said, only that it was all very ordinary and quiet. Now it seems like something from another world.

After that, the student revolt erupted, for who knows what reason. (Well, actually, there were lots of reasons. Like opposition to disciplinary actions against student leaders. They were demanding the right to run their own affairs and the dissolution of the faculty council. There were other things, too. I just don't know what was the real cause of it all.) Makihiko Moriya emerged as a fighter against the pro-faculty side of the confrontation, making him Father's enemy. They closed off access to the faculty office and chased all the professors and associate professors from their offices.

He was expelled from the school and Father laid down a ban on him coming to our home or meeting me. Of course I wasn't going to accept that passively — absolutely not. Father's attitude was unforgivable. The official relationship between him and Makihiko Moriya as professor and former student had nothing to do with our rights as individuals to associate with whomever we pleased. I stormed out of that house and went knocking on the door of the room where Makihiko Moriya was living. That's how everything started — the trouble at home, my "sickness" — everything. Something just exploded inside.

I was away from home for a long while. One day I came back to find a big stack of dirty dishes in the kitchen. My mother is completely incapable of housekeeping. For years, my younger sister Kikuko and I had split up doing the cooking, cleaning and washing. We managed to keep the house in some semblance of order. Then Kikuko had university entrance exams coming up. That left housekeeping up to me. When I left home, nothing got done. Everything was a mess. I spent half the day doing dishes and cleaning the kitchen and living room. I had just finished when Mother came home.

You might think she would be happy to see me, but no, she started carping at me for neglecting my house duties. She said, You just disappear for days on end. Is that any way for a daughter to behave? I answered in kind, and we were going at each other when Kikuko got back from exam prep school. She told

Mother she wanted dinner and was told, If you're hungry, you fix dinner. Pretty soon all three of us were howling at each other like stray dogs.

That was the scene Father walked in on. He became indignant over the quarreling, the fact that no preparations had been made for supper and because the head of the household was not being shown respect. He started shouting. As far as he was concerned, it all came down to me turning my back on my parents and family because I was under the influence of radicals like that miserable excuse for a student, Makihiko Moriya.

A sigh escaped Wakako Ikéhata. The quadrangle was as cold and forlorn as the bottom of a well. The band of young classmates and comrades had been left behind by the student movement. At that moment, someone said. "Hey, we need more hands to set up a relief kitchen." A plot was afoot to make rice balls in the basement student cafeteria. Wakako Ikéhata arose. That's a swell idea! she said. I'll make the best rice balls you've ever tasted. With this turn of the conversation, she realized she hadn't had anything to eat since morning. She felt as hungry as could be.

3:30 p.m.

Yukichi Jinnai raised the hulk of a small truck with the wrecker. Then he and several of his fellow workers maneuvered it onto its side. They had emptied the fuel tank beforehand, but a little bit of gasoline had leaked out. After carefully wiping the spot with a rag, he put his nose to the ground like a bloodhound, to check how strong the smell was.

"It's okay." He sprang up agilely and joined the others, who were stacking oil drums atop the wrecked truck, then lashing them down tightly with wire. The purpose of this was to fashion a barricade at the entrance to the parking lot. At the same time, they were raising and lowering the shutter as necessary to let gas station customers pass through.

Yukichi Jinnai had reason to be well pleased with this operation; it had been his idea. It was gratifying that everyone was working to implement his proposal. A student demonstration in the boulevard that morning had drawn such a large crowd of spectators that it was decided not to open the gas station. By noon, they were closing down the shutters on the service station as well. Foreman Yukimori and his crew were on standby in the dormitory. That was when Yukichi Jinnai stood up to address the others. He argued that the student demonstrators might break in if nothing was done to block the entrance. A listener countered, "That's not a problem. We're on a back street."

That objection was squelched by Atsuo Yukimori.

"No, that parking lot has other people's cars we're taking care of. Let's not take chances."

From that support for Yukichi Jinnai's proposal, the talk turned to the latest event reported on the three o'clock TV news. Some students had overturned a car in the middle of the street and set it on fire to block traffic. The parking lot really could be in danger. When it was revealed that students had already stolen one of the oil drums stacked up in back of the gas station, everyone agreed there wasn't a moment to lose in securing the entrance. Yukichi Jinnai's plan to erect a barricade was unanimously accepted.

That plan had not materialized on the spur of the moment. Pamphlets and speeches from the students had been mentioning a plan to set up "liberated zones" in Kanda since fall of the year past. Yukichi Jinnai had been pondering how to respond. He hatched his idea on the basis of materials available in the shop. The other shop workers knew nothing of this background; they were simply impressed by the proposal. Tomoyama said, "Man, you got brains," with an amazed expression.

"So what's next?" Atsuo Yukimori inquired.

Yukichi Jinnai replied without hesitation. "Stack up lockers in back of the oil drums, then stand up tires, desks, and chairs against them — just jam 'em all together."

"That sounds good." His uncle was impressed with the answer, which was merely a description of how the students were barricading university buildings.

Their barricade was about eighty percent complete when a band of students came rushing down the street, riot police in hot pursuit. Another mob of students appeared from the side and ambushed those police they could hit with rocks. Some of the rocks flew in the direction of the parking lot and bounced off the oil drums.

"Our fort's holding up fine," someone said. That got a hearty laugh from everyone but Yukichi Jinnai, who was scowling.

"If those students get serious about it, they could bust right through this barricade. We need a Plan B in case that happens." Yukichi Jinnai raised his formidable voice. "We got to organize a Fukawa Motors Self-Defense Force!"

"That's a little too heroic," someone said, setting off a ripple of snickers. Yukichi Jinnai's temper flared.

"If those students want to get in here, they're going to get in unless we stop them. And if we don't stop them, they'll wreck every car in this place," he shouted.

Once again, it was Atsuo Yukimori who listened soberly to the words of Yukichi Jinnai. "Well, what's to be done?" he asked.

"Everyone carries an iron bar, puts on a helmet and mask and stands guard at the entrances to the parking lot and the dorm."

This drew many dubious reactions. "I don't want any part in violence."

"Its pointless."

"You won't catch me in a getup like those students!"

Everyone realized the proposal could be easily implemented, there being no shortage in the shop of helmets and iron bars suitable for such use.

Ichiro Fukawa appeared, wearing a dark expression.

"Oh, hi boss," Atsuo Yukimori said, respectfully inclining his head. But Ichiro Fukawa was in no mood for polite exchanges.

"Whose idea was it to put up this strange thing?" he demanded.

"Forgive us. It's an emergency situation. We couldn't wait for you to return."

Atsuo Yukimori explained about the theft of the oil drum. He said he took it upon himself to put up the barricade to prevent damage to the customers' cars. At last, Ichiro Fukawa's dour expression dissipated, but he still wasn't convinced.

"I'm against this. Seems to me it might end up causing trouble with the students. We're just ordinary people. They aren't going to come attacking us. Well, what's done is done. But see that you get things back to normal as soon as possible." His saucer eyes flashed fiercely as he issued this order.

Atsuo Yukimori stood his ground. "Actually, boss, it seems to me we have to organize a self-defense force," he said.

"Why?"

"A barricade by itself isn't enough security for the parking lot."

"What do you mean, 'self-defense force?' Exactly what do you have in mind?"

Atsuo Yukimori explain the proposal made by Yukichi Jinnai. Ichiro Fukawa's expression immediately clouded upon mention of the name "Jinnai." The frown remained etched in his face while a suspicious stare steadily intensified.

Just then, a tumultuous noise rose from the street. There was a ferocious volley of explosions. Then a student came scrambling into the parking lot over the barricade. Two more followed. The three students were running between the cars. Then there were five, then seven students. They all leapt atop the roofs of a line of cars parked at the edge of the lot along a fence bordering an adjacent private home. Finally, they jumped down into the house's backyard, leaving behind a series of caved in car roofs.

The extraordinary scene had played out in mere moments. The entire

Fukawa Motors crew watched in stunned silence. Ichiro Fukawa's entire body trembled in shock. Then he ran to one of the damaged cars and began stroking its bent roof.

"Damned, stinking students! Treating people's property like dirt!" he roared. "Set up that self-defense force immediately!"

Kiyoshi Tomoyama commented, "Boy, you never know where the boss is coming from."

"You can say that again," Yukichi Jinnai said, nodding in agreement. "He doesn't understand something big is going on these days. Those crazy students will stop at nothing. If we don't set up a defense now, we're going to get hit bad."

4:30 p.m.

Atsuo Yukimori was issuing orders to his workers. He had them bearing steel bars in place of rifles. They had just completed a run-through of basic drill — standing at attention, marching in formation, forming ranks and squads. It was a pleasure to oversee the transformation of a bunch of ragtag youths into coordinated troops. He was experiencing vivid recollections of his time as a non-commissioned officer, when he did this regularly with new recruits.

Then it was time to get down to business — close combat drill. He taught them basic bayonet techniques for wielding the steel bars. You support the weapon lightly with the left hand and thrust with the right. The most important thing is positioning your hips. The effectiveness of your thrust depends on having a stable stance and facing the enemy dead on.

In the course of giving explanations and bawling out his troops, he began feeling a sense of mission to instruct them in his own way of dealing with everyday work.

"Now get this. Whether it's bayonet fighting or working in the shop or whatever, the most important thing is your stance — how you face whatever it is you are dealing with. You do that by planting your feet and your butt down solid, square in front of your target.

"Take engine repair. First you loosen all the screws, then you remove the cover. If you think it's too much trouble to do the preliminaries and you force open the cover, it's going to break, isn't it? You've got to start with the right approach to the job. All right! charge! — Tomoyama! Your weapon is off target because you don't plant your butt straight!

"Whatever you do — fishing, ice skating or anything else — it all comes down to how you use your pelvis. Whether you want to execute a decent fly cast or a spin on the ice, you've got to start with a firm stance and give it a strong, sure follow-through."

As he went on with his instructions, Atsuo Yukimori began wondering if he wasn't doing a bit too much talking. Maybe that's what happens when people past a certain age get enthusiastic about something. He called an end to the drill when he caught sight of one of the youngsters yawning. He divided them up into four squads, appointed squad leaders, issued orders for 24-hour rotating guard duty and dismissed them.

He went back to the TV room in the dorm. Ichiro Fukawa, Kimiko Fujiyama, Sonoko Kanéhara, the cook and the chief gas station attendant were sitting around the television. Ichiro Fukawa was commenting on developments on the T. University campus.

"Doesn't look as if they're going to take back the Tower today. The police should be allowed to use guns. Shoot to kill! Take out every one of 'em. That's how they'd do it in America . . . Well, well, here's the chief of our self-defense force. How'd the training go?"

"Okay, I guess."

"They're raising hell in this neighborhood, too. We don't have the manpower to stop them. That barricade's no good. It's just asking for trouble with those apes."

"Well, I would say it is better than nothing. At a time like this, we ought to put up the best security we can manage."

"If you can't guarantee you'll keep them out, it's better not doing anything."

This reply left Atsuo Yukimori blinking speechlessly. He couldn't understand what Ichiro Fukawa wanted of him.

Elsewhere, also at 4:30 p.m.

The eyes of Makihiko Moriya beheld a sun dripping blood that drenched his body and penetrated to the bottom of his soul. A microphone was before him. He strained an already hoarse voice.

"The bricks of this Tower that symbolize the power structure now shine red with our blood! We stand here filled with joy to be living out this moment of blood! We, the living, are alive with full corporeal existence! We feel the power of that physical existence and know it is the bond between us and our comrades throughout the world!

"Comrades of the world, hear me! For five hours we have resisted the police forces, the running dogs of state power! In that time we have not retreated a single step, nor have they encroached upon us by a single step!

"We stand here in a Tower that was once a symbol of state power, raising our voices loudly with the dignity of the living! Once this was the ivory Tower of a university that gave the state its elite slaves! The action that we have taken today disavows that status in the most concrete terms, transforming this Tower into a new symbol of liberty!

"Comrades throughout this country and throughout the world — now is the time to arise! Arise and crush state power and universities that train the elite slaves of the state!

"At this moment a sun wet with our life-blood is setting! Let our lives burn unto glory! Hasten the night! The night, our friend, be with us!"

Comments were heard from comrades in Makihiko Moriya's immediate vicinity. "Wasn't that a trifle too literary?"

"Nah, that's okay. It was a great speech. Our struggle is part literary anyway."

"What's going on downstairs?"

"They got past the entrance and now they're stuck there."

The riot police had finally breached the oaken barricade on the main entranceway using a chain saw and a big wooden hammer. They were stopped by the equally robust secondary barricade of lockers, chairs, desks, bookshelves, and other objects that had been painstakingly fitted together. Ultimately, they were driven back by a continuing barrage of Molotov cocktails and bottles of nitric, hydrochloric, and sulfuric acid. No other strategies at hand, the police resumed their water cannon attack, as if they believed soaking everything inside would render the students' weapons useless. Several trucks surrounded the Tower directing high pressure streams at each side of the building. One stream reached the rooftop.

It was like being in the basin of a waterfall. Makihiko Moriya had on a plastic poncho, but was nevertheless soaked to the skin and shivering. It was past sundown. Beneath a sky of embers, the sea of streets had the pallor of death. The Tower seemed to be tilting, like the one in Pisa. The riot police withdrew some of the numerous cars they had positioned along the gingko lined boulevard as attack reinforcements. They were standing in file for roll call. Makihiko Moriya reckoned they had given up operations for the day.

"I give you the voice of the people from the Tower! We are victorious! Depart, depart you running dogs of state power, you dogs in human form! We join in solidarity with comrades from all over this country and around the world! Comrades who would dismantle and abolish state power, who demand your freedom, whose struggle brings liberty for all, accept our heartfelt greetings to you! The struggle of the people shall spread from this Tower to the far corners of the world!"

5:45 p.m.

Kotaro Ikéhata was gripped by the kind of anxiety felt by a patient informed by his doctor of a malignancy as he pulled open the drawers of a steel filing cabinet in a corner of his office. Inside was one sheet of damp straw paper and nothing else. Handwritten notes, survey data, unfinished papers, and book manuscripts collected over twenty-five years of research, from the time he was a young graduate studying in Europe and America and thereafter — all gone. The single sheet of damp paper bore a blurred scrawl:

"Everything associated with reactionary Professor Ikéhata hereupon liquidated"

Unwilling to believe that all his time and effort of the past twenty-five years had come to nothing, Kotaro Ikéhata frantically looked about the wreckage within the room, turning over books and magazines that had been scattered and torn and trampled. All he found was a sodden floor and the smell of tear gas. It took him a little longer to realize that the filing cabinet that formerly contained his research records had been left on prominent display like a mangled corpse, but every single item of his other belongings, including desk, chair, bookshelves, and locker, had vanished.

Otherwise, there were a few books and magazines scattered about, but the vast majority of publications, whose collection by the university had begun a century before, were nowhere to be seen. There was, however, a mound of black ash in the center of the room that clearly indicated they had been incinerated on the spot. Noting this, Kotaro Ikéhata uttered a low-pitched moan, a sound of lamentation for the loss of long years of research and the office that had made his studies possible, things that he had believed never could be lost.

Reports began coming in from associate professors, lecturers, and teaching assistants. They said that every office had been systematically vandalized, leaving only wreckage and graffiti. Each and every faculty member had lost all their research papers.

Kotaro Ikéhata didn't know how to console them. He learned from a young lecturer in his thirties that this was a time for anger to displace words of comfort. "They're not students, they're apes, savages," he shouted with clenched fists.

His outcry resonated in Kotaro Ikéhata's heart. He told himself he should feel anger and he did. But despair over his loss was by far the stronger and deeper feeling. With the assistance of the young instructor, he walked unsteadily out into the night.

A battleground encampment scene met his eyes as riot police built bonfires in preparation for an overnight stay in their armored vehicles. They were now the authorities on the campus. It was only by their grace Kotaro Ikéhata, in his suit, greatcoat and "Personnel" armband was finally cleared to be on the premises.

"Makihiko Moriya is in the Tower, for sure," a young lecturer commented with assurance. "He's the one who was making those 'voice of liberation' speeches all day. That was his voice, for sure. It was his style, too, with those old-fashioned romantic touches."

"That troublemaker!" This response marked the first moment when dark anger erupted from the depths of Kotaro Ikéhata's heart. It was the degenerate Moriya who had destroyed both the peace of his household and the fruits of his research.

The anger swelled within Kotaro Ikéhata and merged with a core of darkness inside. The students were trying to get their way through violence — vandalizing faculty offices and destroying research papers. (The image of a damp sheet of crude paper with a scrawled message flashed in his mind.) They demanded the entire faculty's resignation and dismantling of the university. If those demands were met, the dispute would be over. They wouldn't be students anymore and the market would be flooded with unemployed former students. They would be the primary victims, but of course they knew it would never come to that, no matter how many things they smashed to pieces. They carried on their rampage in the security of that knowledge. Theirs was the psychology of infants who know the worst tantrum they can throw will not move their parents to abandon them. There was a breed of youngster who could become a university student and still be nothing more than a baby. That Makihiko Moriya was the prime example.

Makihiko Moriya first came to the attention of Kotaro Ikéhata as a zealous asker of questions. During a lecture in Introduction to Criminal Law, a hand had shot up from far in the back row of the capacious lecture hall.

"Just what is it that causes crime?"

"The entire history of criminal law bears on such weighty questions. Their solution is what criminal law is all about."

That answer didn't satisfy the student. Nor did any subsequent answers dissuade him from persistently pressing his argument on the professor in the form of questions.

"You've got penalties that define the crimes, so wouldn't crime disappear if you abolish the penalties?"

"Penalties were established because crime exists."

"Well then, who decides what is a crime, and by what authority?"

This chicken-and-egg exchange was getting an amused reaction from the other students, but Makihiko Moriya didn't crack a smile. He continued to bore in on Kotaro Ikéhata until the professor ran out of answers and retreated by inviting the stubborn youth to discuss the matter individually. Soon after the lecture ended Makihiko Moriya made his first visit to the office of Kotaro Ikéhata.

It turned out to be the first of many visits to that office. A mere student, Makihiko Moriya didn't hesitate to occupy a desk there for the use of an associate professor. He behaved as if he was a faculty member. Kotaro Ikéhata accepted this presumption as the style of the new generation of students.

Thus, Makihiko Moriya gained the status of favored student. As such, he became a regular visitor to the professor's home, where he soon was on familiar terms with one of the professor's daughters, Wakako. Then, for some reason, he abruptly began neglecting his studies. He was no longer showing up in the faculty room either. The next time Kotaro Ikéhata saw him, he was leading a strike.

Kotaro Ikéhata could not forgive Makihiko Moriya for filling Wakako's head with the infantile whining that he considered revolutionary theory. One day, Wakako had said to him, "You know, Father, that criminal code you think so highly of doesn't do anything but protect the capitalist class. Teaching that kind of thing is a criminal act in itself!"

That angered him to the point of yelling at his daughter with such abandon he was later ashamed of himself. He ended up by shouting, "Get out!" At that, Wakako really did leave the house.

5:45 p.m.

Yukichi Jinnai spotted a trio of students standing atop the oil drum barricade. He gave the order "Charge!" to his four-man squad. The students were caught off guard. One fell to the ground inside the barricade. The other two leaped to the ground outside and were immediately arrested by riot policemen. Seeing his friends handcuffed and roped about the waist, the student inside the barricade tried to flee, but was grabbed by the Fukawa Motors crew.

"Hey, you! Hand him over!" one of the officers commanded loudly.

Yukichi Jinnai had the student firmly by the arm, but made no move to comply. Instead, he glared back wordlessly, his anger rising in the face of the policeman.

Another officer addressed Yukichi Jinnai in a placating tone. "Hey, buddy, would you please let us have him? We'd appreciate it."

Kiyoshi Tomoyama whispered, "Hand him over! Let's be done with it!"

The other officer didn't seem to know any way of speaking other than yelling. "You are obstructing officers performing official duty! Get the hell out of our way!"

When the police began climbing the barricade, Yukichi Jinnai released the student's arm. "Go on out there, will ya?" he said and gave the student's back a strong push. The student returned a pleading look, but Yukichi Jinnai resolutely shook his head. When the other shop workers began prodding his backside with their steel bars, the student scrambled atop the barricade in desperation and was seized by the two waiting policemen, who held him fast by both shoulders, like an unfortunate rabbit suspended by the legs in a hunter's grasp.

"Thanks, buddy," said the friendly officer in the same soothing tone. "Good work! Is this a neighborhood patrol?" he asked with a respectful tilt of his head.

"Dumb-ass!" Yukichi muttered, turning his back angrily. He returned to patrolling the parking lot, poking the asphalt with his steel bar as he walked. "No, we ain't no damn neighborhood patrol!" he continued in disgust, to no one in particular.

He despised those riot police. He hated the students, but it seemed to him he hated the police even more. How much better it would be to dump this stupid hard hat and steel bar, put on a real battle helmet, pick up a sidearm and engage the enemy as a real soldier. That scuffling between the students and police, always careful not to kill each other, was a load of crap. You got an enemy, you kill him. Death to the enemy — that's how it's done.

6:00 p.m.

When it came time to change guards, Yukichi Jinnai turned over his post to the next squad and he went with his companions back to the dorm. The off-duty crew was circled about the television, tirelessly watching the battle for T. University's Tower.

"Hasn't the Tower been taken yet?" Kiyoshi Tomoyama asked.

"Not yet," one of the young men answered. "They called off the attack for the day. It'll all start up again tomorrow." There was delight in his voice as he added, "Another TV day!" and pumped a triumphant fist at the ceiling.

The private university located directly behind Fukawa Motors appeared on the screen. "Hey, that's right over there!" someone said excitedly.

"Yeah, it is! Wow!" said anothfer. It was an image of some nervous-looking students screaming "Get out of here!" at a force of police encircling the school's perimeter.

"Bunch of jerks," Yukichi Jinnai commented contemptuously and went into his room. To Kiyoshi Tomoyama, who was already there, he said, "I'm going to quit this place. Cheap pay, the boss thinks about nothing but making money, the job's boring . . . ain't nothing good about it."

Kiyoshi Tomoyama nodded. "Yeah, that's right. I'd like to quit myself."

7:20 p.m.

Wakako Ikéhata slipped away from her private university. Someone had warned her there were cops galore outside, but she went out anyway because she felt like being alone.

The streets were dark, like the bottom of the hole in the ground of her dream. There wasn't anyone on the streets, not even a single cat. Enjoying the sense of moving among deserted ruins, she walked briskly from alleyway to alleyway. But as the university grew more distant, she began having uneasy thoughts of plainclothes policemen lurking in dark corners. Now she was regretting venturing out alone.

There's no denying the fire from my lighter set a car aflame. That makes me an accessory to the crime of "setting fire to objects other than structures," which is to say I am myself guilty of the crime. What I did seemed perfectly natural when I was with everyone else. Actually, I was proud and pleased with myself at the time, but now, being alone, I feel like a wanted criminal . . .

That moment the flames had caught, they brought uplift, joy, brightness — it felt like the organizations, father, mother, household, university, the world's expectations of a professor's daughter — everything had burned away to nothingness. Now it seems more like it was a pointless thing to do. Guess that's like an arsonist looking at the ashes when the fire is over and being disappointed. No, it isn't like that, it's precisely that. Nothing changes just because you burned one car — they make new ones by the thousands, millions — every day. All that stuff about liberated zones and barricades is nothing but illusions. Just look around this town. All that rampaging, and nothing has changed — not a single wall, not one utility pole is any bit different.

The only effect it had, she thought — by accelerating her footsteps Wakako Ikéhata had quickened her blood, stimulating her brain — was to get me banned from this town. It is armed to the teeth against arsonists like myself. Those steel shutters, blinds, storm doors and spiked fences are there to shut us out in the cold.

Someone, somewhere must have seen me do it — I was out on the street in broad daylight, and people were all around. Someone — either a newspaper or police photographer — must have taken a picture of that moment. The police probably have me on their wanted list — they've already got the hard proof.

Thinking of her dreadful prospects — arrest, time in a pigsty, then prison — she recalled the face of Makihiko Moriya. The seven o'clock TV news had reported many arrests at T. University. It wouldn't be long until the Tower was captured. Sooner or later, he, too, would be arrested.

The previous evening she had helped deliver vegetables to the Tower. The group had shouldered rucksacks and taken a tow cart. Makihiko Moriya's face had appeared in a window.

He waved to me. He was so far away, at the top of the Tower, I couldn't read his expression, but I knew it was him so I waved back. Three days ago when he went into the Tower he said, "You'd better not come. Everyone's just going to get arrested," sounding like he wanted to be arrested. I ran away from the hospital because I hated being under guard, but that is just what he wanted to have happen to him . . .

Wakako Ikéhata stopped suddenly, startled. Her eye had been caught by the sight of Atsuo Yukimori on the far side of a glass window.

He was deep in conversation with someone. It might have been the lighting, but his face was ruddy, unlike the pale face of her recollection. He seemed excited, his face flushed. He had thick eyebrows and a flat, wide forehead. It was a face formed by a sturdy bone structure. His blue work uniform was becoming. He would be a good model for a socialist realism style portrait of a hardy laborer.

Wakako Ikéhata surveyed her surroundings and realized she was on the grounds of a gas station. She drew near the window. His eyes were looking in her direction, but they moved on without noticing her. He was looking upward at the man he was speaking with. The back of the man's head came into view. It was balding. His rounded, heavyset shoulders were shaking, as if he was laughing.

Hearing the sound of footsteps, Wakako Ikéhata peered into the darkness. It was a number of men, perhaps detectives. Wakako Ikéhata ran. She ran toward her university as fast as she could.

7:40 p.m.

Atsuo Yukimori's hands were clenched into tight fists.

Ichiro Fukawa's voice suddenly took on a resolute tone. " . . . I don't care. I'm having Jinnai leave this company. He's been hanging around radical students lately. That's dangerous. I can't have it."

"Excuse me, I think you've got it wrong," Atsuo Yukimori countered. "Jinnai hates all university students. He was the one who proposed the self-defense force that stopped students from getting in today."

"That was a dangerous thing to do. Putting up that barricade just invited them to come around. First of all, it gets in the way of customers coming and going."

"They can use the back entrance to the stand."

"You have to keep rolling down the shutter and closing it up again. It's too much trouble. We got three complaints from customers, didn't we?"

"If a big force of students came storming in here, we'd have big trouble. They would just drag out any car they could lay their hands on for their barricades."

"We've not going to get a huge number of them way back where we are."

"Well, we have had students in here, not once but twice."

"It was just a few who got in, that's all. What are you trying to sell me?" Ichiro Fukawa glared. "I'm telling you Jinnai has to go! Every night he's been going over to T. University. I hear he was in with those demonstrators who rioted in Shinjuku last year. Sonoko says he's a right-winger who likes war songs, but I'll tell you something. There's both left and right behind those student riots. It doesn't matter which side those troublemakers are coming from. They're all the same. There's another thing. He's still suspect in that theft of 170,000 yen."

"Didn't you say you found the money?"

"I was lying. Had to. Didn't want the police sniffing around."

"Jinnai didn't do it. That's certain."

"Just because his bankbook shows he took money out for the stereo, that's not proof. He could just be hiding the money somewhere."

Atsuo Yukimori started framing his rebuttal, but this time the words didn't come. He was no match for this adversary, who parried every objection with more force than he could muster.

"Now look," Ichiro Fukawa said, lifting a scotch bottle by the neck and pouring some into a glass. "Jinnai has a record. Yeah, he was in a juvenile reformatory. Wasn't he? I understand he was sent there for theft. And it wasn't just one or two times, either. I'd call that evidence!" Ichiro Fukawa's voice reverberated like a cross-examiner's.

"Sorry to be argumentative," Atsuo Yukimori began cautiously. His gaze fell upon the other's head, balding and brightly flushed from the scotch. He sensed no suggestion his words would get a receptive listening. "Transfer to a juvenile reformatory is not a criminal record. He wasn't criminally charged . . . It was only delinquency, not a crime, so . . ."

"That's not the point. Stealing is stealing. And they send a kid to a reformatory because there's something wrong with the household. The parents are at fault — that no-good Torakichi Jinnai. You could expect an uncouth character like him would have that kind of kid."

Previous denials notwithstanding, it appeared that Ichiro Fukawa bore a grudge over his quarrel with Torakichi Jinnai.

"What gets me," Ichiro Fukawa said, his eyes agape, the veins within meandering like a marshland river, "is I don't know why you wanted to stick me with a kid like that. Why'd you cover up that he has a record? Is that any way for you to deal with me? We're supposed to be a lot closer than that! If you came right out and said he had a record, I still would have hired him!"

"I see." Atsuo Yukimori had decided his only course was to apologize. "Forgive me. I was intending to tell you eventually, but I never got around to it."

"I wanted you to say it right up front, not eventually. I don't like there be secrets between you and me."

"I'm sorry." That single word, "secrets" was a stinging barb that went through Atsuo Yukimori's heart. It carried a nasty hint that Ichiro Fukawa knew of his own criminal record.

"Oh, well. Sonoko says it looks like Jinnai wants to quit anyway, so it's okay all around. Help him find another job."

"All right, I get the message." Atsuo Yukimori bowed his head in resignation. "I would like to request that you give him until the end of March."

"Sure, that's fine." Now Ichiro Fukawa was smiling affably. "Fact is, I found a hunter in Raúsu. He knows the Shiretoko peninsula backwoods like his own house. I'm going to use him as guide, starting next year. Going for bear. Really want to bag 'the old man of the mountains' one time. That's the trouble with Furen — no bear."

Actually, there was a bear on the scene at the time Fukawa was there, but there would be no point in saying so. Ichiro Fukawa doesn't want to hire Torakichi Jinnai as a guide again under any circumstances. Now that he's cut ties with Yukichi Jinnai and Torakichi Jinnai, doesn't that put firing me next on his list?

Until that moment, Atsuo Yukimori had believed his own position in life rested on solid ground. Now the reality confronted him that the opposite was true, that his job security depended entirely on the whims of Ichiro Fukawa.

8:00 p.m.

Makihiko Moriya swigged vodka from a bottle, taking pleasure from the burning sensation in his throat. The university had cut the power supply, immersing the great assembly hall in darkness broken by points of light from candles that revealed flickering images of its occupants, looking like groups of early Christians gathered in caves. Rather than offering up quiet prayers, however, they were in high spirits. The scene was an original sort of youth festival, with everyone merrymaking as they would, clapping and singing, dancing to music from tape recorders, laughing shrilly, drinking and socializing. No one doubted that tomorrow held arrest for all, meaning that each would gain recognition as a revolutionary. They were celebrating that inevitable future.

Just beside him, a man and woman, completely naked, were locked in embrace. Skin warmed by an oil stove and aglow with perspiration, they were moaning in pleasure without reserve. They went about it so naturally it was easy to take as an onstage performance, not indecent, but rather infused with the beauty of youth. Makihiko Moriya was thinking he would be glad to give them a rousing hand of applause.

The man was Ryujiro Nakajima, a medical student who had been a militant from the very beginning of the great T. University struggle. Though he belonged to a different sect than Makihiko Moriya, friendship had rapidly blossomed between the two after they came together in the takeover of the Tower. The point in Ryujiro Nakajima's ideology that Makihiko Moriya most admired was his idea that deeds have an independent, eternal existence, irrespective of human mortality. He said that the Bolsheviks disappeared, but the people's revolutionary acts in the Russian Revolution were remembered as imperishable facts; there was no more Japanese army, but the bloodletting wrought by a band of young officers one snowy day in Tokyo would not fade from history.

Makihiko Moriya had asked, "You mean every little thing we do belongs to eternity?"

"Not at all," was Ryujiro Nakajima's answer. "Strict conditions must be met for an act to be immortalized. It has to be outrageous, creative, it has to grab people accustomed to the ordinary and totally blow their minds. The Russian Revolution and Japan's February Twenty-Sixth incident meet those conditions. Our occupation of the Tower clearly qualifies too. Maybe we will be arrested, tried and convicted. Decades later, we'll disappear from this earth, but our act will be remembered and our story will be told forever."

Everyone received this pronouncement from Ryujiro Nakajima with wild enthusiasm. His words served a useful purpose of establishing a glorified vision of a legend in the making, the takeover of a Tower, built with money from a corporate conglomerate, rising high above the center of the country's supreme seat of learning as its symbol for almost fifty years, taken over by students, destroyed and reborn as a symbol of revolution. What could be more outrageously creative than that? No one would have thought of it, but now the tale belonged to the ages. Hundreds of years hence, the Tower may have crumbled away without a trace, but what was done there will live on and on.

At the moment when the naked body of Ryujiro Nakajima convulsed in ecstasy and suddenly relaxed, face-down, back and buttocks shining, Makihiko Moriya thought of himself embracing Wakako Ikéhata.

Makihiko Moriya thought it would have been beautiful if she was with him in the Tower, but he himself had decided she shouldn't come. Now he was no longer a part of her. Ten days before, she had run away from the hospital and come to him a changed woman. She surprised him by refusing when he wanted to make love. Wondering if her illness was the cause of her changed temperament, he had put her up at the inn next door to his apartment without having reached any understanding.

Makihiko Moriya took another drink of vodka, thinking it was lonely that Wakako Ikéhata wasn't here, that she had left for the world outside. The flames of the candles were burning low. Everyone was asleep, their steady breathing like a soft rustling in the darkness. A small band of about three hundred oppressed souls, driven here, taking their rest for the final night.

Loneliness gave way to black hatred for traitors of the revolution, like a rapacious monster springing upward from a lead-gray lake, water cascading from its scales. When the movement for reform and revolution in T. University began, it was betrayed at the start by the members of the establishment party posing as the revolutionary vanguard. They were supposedly against the university officials, but they branded our revolutionary sect as counter-revolutionary because we didn't follow their directives. So they opposed us and ended up cooperating with the university officials. Then, the ones who started out with us as the true revolutionaries caused discord and broke up into a number of sects. The K. Sect betrayed us right before we holed up in the Tower. They left us alone in the Tower and hid out somewhere, to the benefit of the university and the police. There were also one or two, or maybe about ten traitors who just ran off or dropped out.

The reason Makihiko Moriya had strongly insisted Wakako Ikéhata not join in the Tower takeover was that he did not want her getting mixed up in the treachery that occurred over and over. Already Ryujiro Nakajima had caught someone from the K. Sect trying to get away. He hit him with a stick, knocking him off his feet, and in turn received a savage blow over the eye from an iron pipe wielded by another K. Sect confederate.

Ryujiro Nakajima had recounted the incident with a grim expression. "They meant business. They were trying to kill me, plain and simple. None of that pulling your punches like the police do." Then he broke into a sly smile. "Actually, I wanted to kill those guys myself. Guess we're birds of a feather."

Makihiko Moriya believed traitors had to be killed. Like the Russian revolutionaries of old, he stoked his hatred for them by taking some vodka, which left him gasping.

5:50 a.m.

Makihiko Moriya awoke to find the suggestion of a glow within the luminous ceiling high above.

An engine roared to life and something big began moving. The sounds merged into a rumbling of the ground that shook the building's concrete foundation.

It could only be the police again on the scene, with everyone defenselessly sprawled across the floor like produce in a marketplace. Getting rid of all the chairs for use in the barricade had provided them with a very spacious roost.

It grew quiet. The source of the earth-shaking was probably not a police vehicle, but a big truck brought in via the road running by the main entrance to the university. Everyone was sleeping soundly, even though their noses and throats burned from lingering tear gas they had been breathing throughout the night. Ryujiro Nakajima was snoring especially loudly, with enough force to send ripples through a growth of beard of about two centimeters.

Makihiko Moriya arose, his face showing displeasure at the clammy feel of his still-damp shirt. Ryujiro Nakajima had dressed at some unnoticed moment. His woman was no longer in sight. Some of the faces Makihiko Moriya recognized from classes, but most were unfamiliar. The only thing in common among this group was that they were young students. They came from different parts of the country, belonged to different universities and different sects and had different majors. T. University students were only a minority.

What's more, T. University student Makihiko Moriya found that no one seemed to want to have much to do with him. The ones who took delight at ripping chairs from the floor, spray-painting walls with graffiti and wreaking general destruction were students of other universities. Just the day before he had hastily intervened to prevent one from taking a can of spray paint to the "Harvest" mural that surrounds the speaker's lectern in the front of the main hall, depicting in profoundly elegant style female figures gathering fruit. He had been jeered at by the thwarted student. "Yeah, what can you expect from someone who belongs to this place. You like dear old T. University, don't you?"

He told himself he had done that for the sake of the picture, not the university — that he didn't want to engage in meaningless destruction. But he really couldn't deny that somewhere inside he regarded the school as his own.

The great chandelier hanging from the ceiling sparkled as it swayed almost imperceptibly. Once it had shone above enrollment and graduation ceremonies presided over by the university chancellor and the department deans, seated together on the podium. All who took part in occupying, dismantling, and liberating this famed hall could be proud of their creativity. To be sure, this zone of liberation would be recaptured shortly. Only the actions taken by this band of liberators would remain, and those actions would never fade.

6:45 a.m.

Once again Makihiko Moriya was roused by the ground shaking under him. The approaching roar unmistakably signified the reappearance of the police. "Everybody up!" The command spontaneously arose from a chorus of voices. Representatives of the respective sects yelled "Everyone get to your positions!" into their power megaphones. Cracker and milk breakfasts were abruptly abandoned. Face cloths were wetted down and fastened before the helmets were donned. The fighters picked up their wooden staves and ran to their appointed posts.

Makihiko Moriya went out into the hallway. There stood the sturdy barricade, intricately constructed of desks, lockers and chairs stacked to the ceiling, an impossibly extraordinary object, like a fantasy from a different world. Indeed, thought Makihiko Moriya, we have ascended to a realm far removed from the ordinary!

A piercing whine of machinery outside rent the air. Amid this sound was the thud-thud of an object being pounded. They were out there on the other side, the inhabitants of the ordinary world, living under the powerful protection of the establishment. Everyone sprang into work shoring up the barricade. Back in the main hall, six comrades were at work fashioning an "iron wall" from metal chairs. Ryujiro Nakajima was in general command at that post.

Makihiko Moriya mounted the stairway and dropped in on "general command headquarters." Formerly it had been the office of the chancellor. Every effort had been made to scour away all vestiges of the authority attached to that station in order to claim full possession of that room. Manifestations of authority resting on the bookshelves — *Fifty Year History of T. University, Building the*

Tower: An Illustrated Chronicle, Guest Book, etc. — were removed and dumped upon the floor for all to tread upon. The walls were decorated with graffiti in red spray: "First Army Headquarters," "Victory in the Battle of T. University," "Long live world revolution," "It is right to rebel."

Next door was the "emergency room," formerly known as the secretary's office. Several injured comrades were receiving care from medical department students. One was in serious condition, with injuries to both eyes from the impact of a teargas canister. There were burns, abrasions and some other kinds of injuries.

Water began flooding the floor. The enemy had begun its water cannon attack. Makihiko Moriya made his way against the flow of the rushing water, now ankle-deep, to a narrow stone staircase and began climbing it at a run. Many others were running up this stairway as well. On the way was a landing being used for assembly of Molotov cocktails, equipped with oil drums, cans of kerosene, and piles of bottles. Signs saying "Keep all fire away" were posted everywhere. The staircase became still more narrow. Finally, there was only the spiral stairs to the top of the Tower. Then they were in the observation room on the second floor from the top, with windows spaced between the backs of the four Tower clocks that looked out in every direction. A window had been broken and a shaft of water several centimeters across was gushing in through the opening with ferocious force. Makihiko Moriya was soon soaked to the skin.

Outside, numerous armored vehicles, surrounded by row upon row of police bearing shields, were slowly advancing. It was a bigger force than the day before. Then, the enemy had been scattered about several locations within the campus. Today his forces were all concentrated on the Tower. Four helicopters were scouting the area from high overhead. Someone who had been listening to a transistor radio said, "The enemy has begun a full-scale offensive."

"Well, this is it," Makihiko Moriya said to him.

"Yeah, this is it," he replied, nodding.

The red light of the dawn sped across the sea of buildings and streets surrounding the university, sending out dazzling flashes as it raced from window to window. This Tower, our Tower, here at the heart of the vast city! The eyes of the world now turned up it, turning our action into undying legend!

Elsewhere, also at 6:45 a.m.

Wakako Ikéhata had been dreaming. She had cut through the iron grate on the windows of the mental hospital and escaped, only to run into another iron grate. She cut through that too and there was yet another beyond it. As she had begun to tire and despair, she dove underground as a last resort. Luckily, the particles of earth were like tiny feathers she could swim through. Down, down she went until she reached the bottom, where it was completely dark, but she could make out little points of light. Going closer to investigate, she found a window covered by an iron grating. It was a cramped prison cell and Atsuo Yukimori was inside. In fact, it was a prison, a giant prison with countless barred windows, all exactly the same, and all holding prisoners. An overwhelming feeling of hopelessness overcame her. No matter where you go, where you run to, the same iron bars await. There was a sound of running footsteps. It was a mob of white uniformed nurses coming this way. She was just about to scream, "Those aren't nurses, it's the riot police!" when she awoke.

The lingering effects of the dream and anxiety at being shut in on all sides made Wakako Ikéhata dread opening her eyes. Cautiously, she opened them just a crack. It was full daylight in the classroom. She looked about furtively.

Alighting from the desks she had been using for a bed, she wondered if her feeling of gloom and emptiness meant a relapse of illness, but was somewhat reassured to find the cause was the simple fact that no one else was in her immediate vicinity. There were only about ten people in the entire room, whereas it had been packed the night before when she fell asleep.

Wakako Ikéhata looked into the room next door. The number of occupants had decreased considerably overnight. A sect leader outside on the quad laughed ironically.

"They all skipped out. What a pack of deadheads."

As she was heading for the washroom to wash her face, he called after her.

"The unified rally for victory at T. University is at eleven. Hope to see you there!"

A little past 7:00 a.m.

Kotaro Ikéhata said to his wife, "We still don't know where Wakako is?"

"The last word we got was when she called four days ago. I'd really like to know where she is."

"You don't suppose she's with Moriya?"

"There's no way of knowing . . . But he's in the Tower."

"He's been there for the past four days. What has me worried is Wakako might be in the Tower too."

"And if she is?"

174

"She would be arrested on charges of damaging buildings and property, obstructing the discharge of official duties and arson, among other things, I suppose. The daughter of a T. University professor a criminal — that's sure to raise a scandal." Kotaro Ikéhata sighed.

According to the doctor, she had been getting over her illness and probably could have been discharged in another couple of weeks. She didn't have to run away, straight into the middle of the campus turmoil.

"Oh, I don't think Wakako is in the Tower," his wife said. "She doesn't have that much nerve."

"Nerve . . ." Kotaro Ikéhata thought about that.

It wouldn't take much nerve to hole up in the Tower. Besides that, Wakako has always done eccentric things. That Tower takeover would be just the kind of stunt she would join.

Kotaro Ikéhata counted up Wakako's eccentricities: propensity to run away from home, excitability, depression, paranoia.

What it all comes down to is that she's unwell. Being unwell keeps her from knowing what she is doing, so she behaves erratically. No, it's worse than that. Shutting yourself up in that Tower so you can battle the whole Metropolitan Police Department is sheer insanity. The students have fallen prey to mass hysteria. People with low resistance levels like Wakako are the ones most likely to become infected with hysteria.

If it comes to facing a trial, the thing to do is present the fact that Wakako was in a mental hospital undergoing treatment when she escaped, in hopes of winning a not guilty decision by proving criminal incompetency by virtue of mental incapacity. Then, when she's done with the trial, she will have to be put into a mental hospital for long-term treatment.

Koaro Ikéhata went to the front door. His wife followed to see him off.

"Today will be another long day. If the Tower is retaken by evening, there will probably be so many problems to deal with I won't be able to get away tonight at all."

12:00 p.m.

Wakako Ikéhata was working together with everyone else on a barricade. Four cars had been overturned. Chairs, lockers, bicycles, oil drums, and anything else at hand or stolen were being piled up. It was great fun to be building this strange and startling stack of things in the middle of the road. She was also getting a pleasantly warm sensation from being the object of countless burning gazes, wide-eyed with curiosity, from the station nearby, the windows and roof of a hospital, and the sidewalks. Since morning, all signs of depression seemed to have disappeared. Her mind was clear and fully engaged with detailed thoughts, textured and nuanced.

Tossing a child's tricycle, Wakako Ikéhata was surprised at how easily it went sailing through the air. She put up a red flag and a streamer that said "Liberated Zone." She hauled cardboard boxes and gunny sacks of rocks for throwing. She unloaded the tow cart full of Molotov cocktails and made neat piles of plastic sacks for protection against water cannon. Everyone was consumed with accomplishing the same objective. That feeling was marvelous.

Even if it all disappears in a few moments, even if it turns out futile — well, to be more accurate, even though it will turn out futile — this moment right now is beautiful. Nothing in life goes on forever anyway. I am twenty-four, already an old lady. Youth fades. Let it go in a blaze of glory.

"What's going to burn?" Atsuo Yukimori had asked. He'd shown an envious expression when I answered "Youth — my generation's." Wonder what kind of youth he had. He's from Hokkaido. That's a cold place. They have lots of bear and deer. What must it be like to be young there? He said his youth was all about war and army prisons.

When Wakako Ikéhata walked close by a sidewalk, she drew calls from lookers-on.

"Check out the girl!" . . . "Hey, miss! You're awesome!" . . . "Can I give you a hand?" Looking from the corner of her eye, she saw it was a group of men — not the same as a crowd of people. The flocks of curiosity seekers were like riot police squads in that they were all male.

4:10 p.m.

"Hey, you! Stop!"

Turning around at the sound of this voice, Ginji Sato was horrified to see a row of five men who looked a lot like detectives, grasping handcuffs in their pockets and coming his way fast. Like a rat scrambling into a hole, he dove into the throng of people and ran, pushing aside the bodies, soft and limp, that lay beyond the facade of fabric, leather, and buttons. After he had been running a good while, he turned and saw the same five, still coming at him, shoulder to shoulder in a solid line with grins that said, "The party's over."

When the detectives began morphing into double and triple images Ginji Sato suddenly snapped to, as if awakening from a dream. He realized there

176

weren't any detectives. He had been hallucinating. Reassured, he walked on, weaving and pushing his way through the crowd.

Ginji Sato rapped his head with a fist. Time to shoot up. If you don't do it soon, you're going to be right back in the funny pages again.

The trains weren't running. Coffee houses and restaurants were all closed. Ginji Sato's annoyance mounted as he searched for a rest room that was open. He headed for the hospital, but a student picket line had it sealed off. He returned to the crowded sidewalk.

"You over there! Halt!"

"Yeah, you, Ginji! You ain't getting away this time!"

It was the five detectives, after him again. He told himself urgently it was just an illusion. He had to do some meth, and he had to do it right away.

The strength went out of Ginji Sato's limbs as if under anesthesia. He was on the verge of collapsing on the ground like a mass of jelly. As sleepiness assaulted his brain, he began yawning uncontrollably. The world was shrouded in gray fog. His preternatural powers gone, the rushing crowd tossed him from side to side and swept him along as he frantically sought a place where he could inject himself with a dose of methamphetamine.

He stepped over an iron railing onto a tree-lined greensward and went tumbling down the slope along the Kanda River to the shelter of a fortuitously located overhead girder. He took out a syringe and an ampule, which he broke open with quavering hands. In a moment he was jabbing the needle into his arm.

There was something strange going on in the station on the other side of the river. Riot police were running toward some students gathered on the platform. Taken by surprise, the students had no chance to mount a resistance. They jumped onto the tracks and ran into the arms of more police lying in wait, who arrested them, one after another. Other students on the bridge overlooking the platform and on the riverbank commenced a vigorous rock-throwing counterattack. A storm of rocks from above and below beat steadily on duralumin shields, forcing the police back, inch by inch. Delighted cheers arose from the students.

A band of what looked like students had brought a cardboard carton of rocks close to where Ginji Sato was standing. They began heaving rocks across the river. Before he knew it, Ginji Sato was in on the action. A former pitcher on prison ball teams, his aim and range put the young people's performance to shame.

"Geez, mister, that's some arm you've got!"

Brightening at this praise from the students, Ginji Sato went on throwing stones more and more effectively. He was getting a shabu boost from every blood vessel in his body, his muscle tone and mental clarity drum tight. Ginji Sato exulted with the feeling of being double sized. Further emboldened, he took aim at the apparent leader of a squad of police that had appeared on the rim of the embankment. The man was standing in the front and center of the squad, directing its advance on the students' forward line. Ginji Sato unleashed a fastball that landed squarely on his shoulder, evoking a howl of rage.

The distant voice resonated in Ginji Sato's ear. "You son of a bitch, Ginji!" it said. He suspected it belonged to one of the five detectives who had been on his tail a little while before. Listening closer, he realized it was the voice of the police sergeant who had arrested him on his last offense. This was for real.

Ginji Sato burned with vengeful rage. "Now you're going to die," he told the officer telepathically.

The squad leader's expression changed. Ginji Sato could hear him say, "Ginji, you're a fool."

When Ginji Sato threw his third pitch at the squad leader, he was rushed by a contingent of officers, who handcuffed him.

Elsewhere, also at 4:10 p.m.

Wakako Ikéhata burst out laughing as several armored police vans suddenly appeared on the far side of the barricade, in front of the hospital and on a street corner, like a fleet of spaceships from an evil galactic empire. The great gray vehicles had wire nets way up on top, like little bird cages, with robot-like people in iron hats and iron suits. It was just such so much overkill, so ridiculous looking, she couldn't help laughing.

I've got it! That's the ultimate organization. Right out of a comic book. Except they've jumped off the pages into the street, and they look a lot more intimidating than people from outer space in comic books. You know these guys are for real.

Everyone began throwing rocks. Cans of kerosene were brought and poured onto the barricade. An angry curtain of flame arose. Spectators cried aloud as they retreated. Visors affixed against the pelting stones, the police banged their duralumin shields on the ground rhythmically and fired volleys of tear gas. A stream of water reached like an arm through the white smoke and fell onto the flames.

The combination of heat, chill, and acrid smell hanging in the air invited visions. Instead of joining in throwing rocks, Wakako Ikéhata turned to cast a fascinated look at the spectacle, with the result that her face was enveloped in the white smoke. She was withdrawing, eyes burning and streaming tears, as the police finished putting out the fire and began crossing the barricade in force. A number of students had already been randomly struck with police batons. A hulking man in uniform struck Wakako Ikéhata on her left shoulder once, then again, and then a third time. The third blow evoked an extraordinary pain in the scapula, causing it to swell. Wakako Ikéhata screamed. At that moment, the students began a counterattack with sticks and iron pipes. The burly police officer wavered, giving Wakako Ikéhata a moment to flee, leaning on a supporting arm extended by someone.

4:40 p.m.

Makihiko Moriya watched the sun going down between Mt. Fuji and a high-rise. For its finale, the last orange arc flickered, faded, and left behind a stunning chromatic arrangement of Fuji in purple, clouds golden and buildings coral red. Makihiko Moriya forgot the chorus of the "Internationale" being sung by a group on the balcony, their arms across each others' shoulders; he forgot the armored vehicles and water cannon surrounding the Tower, he forgot the violence and the noise below. He forgot everything as he gazed upon the dance of colors across the mountain and city. The Tower's fall drew closer by the moment. The police had invaded the main lecture hall in the morning. At three in the afternoon they reached the outside of the sole iron door that led to the Tower. That door was sturdy, and the spiral staircase behind it had been jammed tightly with every available object so that it would not be breached by any half measures. Thus far, the Tower had been safe for an hour and a half. But inside was much distress, groaning, and a presentiment that the walls were about to burst apart. Makihiko Moriya wondered why it was that yesterday's sun had appeared to be dripping blood, but today it seemed tranquil and at peace. The insane passions, hatred and fever pitch excitement of yesterday were gone. For the past two days in the Tower he had watched the struggle between police and students in lurid detail. But that sun made it all — the fighting, the screaming, the impassioned speeches — look small, inconsequential, empty.

5:00 p.m.

Atsuo Yukimori was watching warily as students threw rocks at riot police not far from the entrance to the parking lot. Inside the barricaded entrance the "Fukawa Motors Self-Defense Force" had formed a line, each man wearing his own distinctive hard hat, his face tied with a wet towel and holding a steel bar. Two tear gas canisters fell inside the parking lot. Yukichi Jinnai picked them up and threw them out among the gathered students. From that moment, rocks that had been directed at the police began to fly at the "self-defense force." The tear gas canisters were thrown back inside as well. While the Fukawa Motors hands fell back in confusion, a great multitude of students scaled the barricade, overturning the steel fencing beyond and invading the parking lot. The self-defense force of only twenty men was useless against that many opponents.

Atsuo Yukimori shouted, "All men withdraw! Get into the dorm!" but his voice was lost in the thunderous uproar. Nevertheless, most of the young workers ran to the dorm, leaving behind Yukichi Jinnai and a few others. They each faced off with several foes at once, swinging their bars, but they were so heavily outnumbered, they began breaking away and running for the dorm, one or two at a time. Finally, Yukichi Jinnai was left alone to receive a concentrated attack. His helmet flew off and he went down. Immediately, wooden sticks began beating his prone body.

Atsuo Yukimori ran to intercede. Sonoko Kanéhara was at his side. "Stop! You're going to hurt him!" she yelled.

"Please, he works here. He's just a kid. Let him go, please." Atsuo Yukimori bowed politely and whisked his injured nephew off to the dormitory the moment the students turned to look at him.

Yukichi Jinnai was taken to the housemother's room for treatment of his injuries. He had a large bruise over his right eye. This eye injury was a concern, and he had pain in the ribs, which could indicate a fracture, but the patient was irrepressible. He spoke bitterly of wanting to go back right away to take down at least one of those students. Ichiro Fukawa appeared at this point and addressed Atsuo Yukimori.

"We've got trouble. Those damn students are having a rally in the parking lot and they're spouting off about making it a base for their liberated zone."

"I'd like to get them out of here, fast," Atsuo Yukimori said, folding his arms with a preoccupied expression.

"If no one provoked them to begin with, none of this would have happened. You go after them with iron clubs, of course they're going to bust things up." Ichiro Fukawa cast a sharp glance at Yukichi Jinnai with his bandage.

Kimiko Fujiyama came in with a report. "Those students are walking on the roofs of the cars. They'll bend them out of shape!"

"What next?" Ichiro Fukawa groaned. "That's customers' property. Can't we get them out of here? Where's the police when you need them?"

"If the police came in here and got into it with the students, the damage would be worse."

"Well, yeah, that's true too."

"I'll go out and have a talk with them." Casting aside his hard hat and face towel, Atsuo Yukimori opened the door and plunged into the crowd of students gathered there, shooing them out of the way with an authoritative, "'scuse me!" Feeling someone pushing from behind, he turned to see his nephew Yukichi, lending momentum to the drive through the crowd. They headed for the center of the assembled students.

The students were uncertain what to make of the two garage shop workers who had appeared suddenly in their midst. They looked at the pair in surprise, leaving them unmolested and hovering about like a cloud of mosquitoes, emitting an aroma compounded from tear gas, sweat and urine. They were tired, wet, and rumpled, looking less like warriors than stragglers from a battleground defeat. The most noticeable thing about the scene was the army of onlookers that followed after the students, whom they outnumbered. Loathe to miss any new development, they had climbed atop the barricade, the roofs of cars and were even clinging to utility poles; tightly packed clusters of ravenous faces.

Atsuo Yukimori and Yukichi Jinnai strode toward a student who looked like a leader. He had just finished addressing the crowd, wearily letting his power megaphone fall to his side. Several injured students were lying on the ground before him, groaning in pain. There was at least one serious injury, a youth with a makeshift bandage about his head through which blood was seeping. "This man's got to be taken to a hospital right away," said Atsuo Yukimori to the leader. He was of delicate build, a bit like Makihiko Moriya, the very model of a studious youth.

"We're surrounded by the police."

"Suppose we put him up in our dormitory for the time being." Atsuo Yukimori pointed to the company dormitory. "We work in this shop. We'll take him to a hospital when the police leave."

The leader went to confer with his companions, then returned and said, "We'd appreciate that," with a polite bow of his head.

"Actually, there something we'd like to ask, in return, so to speak. We would like for you to leave the parking lot as soon as possible. You see, these cars belong to our customers."

That dispelled the youth's courtesy. "That's tough shit. We're not going anywhere. The cops are all around here!"

"I understand that. But if you want to brawl, we want you to do it outside."

"Let's get him inside," Yukichi Jinnai said, placing his hands on the shoulders of the student with the head wound, who was softly moaning. "Somebody get his legs." Three volunteers sprang to help. Atsuo Yukimori also lent a hand. As they began carrying the student, slowly and carefully, a group of other students some distance behind raised an outcry.

"Hey, where are you taking him?" . . . "They're cops!" . . . "Get your hands off him!"

As the leader tried to explain, the crowd moved into action. Angry students returned the wounded student to the spot on the ground where he had been. Others grabbed at Atsuo Yukimori and Yukichi Jinnai, now targeted by a hail of hostile glares. From the parking lot entrance, there was an audible snap as the overburdened roof of a car caved in, sending the people who had been standing on its roof tumbling to the ground.

"Dammit! Hey, lemme use this, okay?" Yukichi Jinnai growled as he snatched the megaphone from the hand of the leader. He began speaking in a booming voice.

"Students, hear me out! I am a laborer! I got hurt by you guys a little while ago. You beat me up. You came in and messed this place up. This is where I work! I was only trying to protect this place, and got beat up for it! Don't you think it's natural for a laborer to protect his workplace? Look, I got one request for you! Clear out! That's all. Clear out and do it now!"

Students were listening in stunned silence to the unexpected show of oratory. A conspicuous figure with his bandaged head, Yukichi Jinnai was commanding the crowd's attention.

"I got another thing to say. You guys took a lot of casualties, including some life-threatening cases that need hospital treatment right away. We can put them in our shop's dorm to rest until we get an ambulance. Okay? Why not do that?"

Someone called out, "No way! Ambulances call the cops!" That broke the silence. Other voices joined in. The ensuing shouting match drowned out the rest of Yukichi Jinnai's speech. The leader took back his megaphone and tried to speak, but the tumult only grew louder and louder.

"Yukichi, time to get back to the dorm," Atsuo Yukimori said and set off. He was thinking that if he only had the kids to deal with, he might have been able to talk them into leaving, but with all those spectators gone wild, no one was listening to reason.

A woman's voice called, "Mr. Yukimori." He stopped. He knew immediately that the student in a hard hat and face cloth who addressed him was Wakako Ikéhata.

"What are you doing in this mob!" Atsuo Yukimori exclaimed in the reproachful tone of a worried elder.

"You can see for yourself what I'm doing here."

"It's dangerous for a girl!"

"I know. I'm a schoolgirl with a destructive bent."

"Yukichi, go on back ahead of me," he said, but when he turned, Yukichi Jinnai had already distanced himself and was on his way to the dorm.

Wakako Ikéhata's complexion was faintly white in the evening darkness. She had an abrasion on her forehead and the corner of her right eye had been blackened. "Hey, you really are hurt. Better take care of that."

"That's nothing. It's my shoulder. I got clubbed with a nightstick." As Wakako Ikéhata used her left hand to grasp her right shoulder, she grimaced in pain.

"That's not good. Come to our dormitory. We'll put a compress on it."

There was an outbreak of ominous noises. Alarm flashed through the crowd. People were scrambling up the fence around the parking lot and crawling over the roofs of the house and shop next door, each running frantically to escape. Cars trampled upon by numerous panicked feet were reduced to wretchedly misshapen hulks. Police were pouring over the barricade and indiscriminately nabbing everyone slow to escape, be they student or onlooker. Piteous pleas from middle-aged men in handcuffs fell upon deaf ears.

"Let's get out of here." Atsuo Yukimori hustled Wakako Ikéhata away, taking care not to touch her injured shoulder. As the pair dashed inside the dormitory door, two apparent students unceremoniously followed in behind them. Several of the young shop workers sprang to eject these two, but Atsuo Yukimori stopped them.

"Let them stay. Call it "samurai compassion." And lock that door now. See that no one else gets in."

Wakako Ikéhata and the two others were hurriedly chased upstairs, sparing no time for removal of shoes. As they reached the top of the stairs there was a rapping on the door.

"Police! Please open up!"

Yukimori Atsuo raised an index finger over his lips, signaling to all to keep quiet. Then he opened the door. He was confronted by several police officers. A large group of fellow shop workers were behind him, looking on with a show of mild surprise.

"Did any students come in here?" asked an officer who seemed to be the squad leader.

"No," Atsuo Yukimori said flatly.

"Well," the officer replied, with a skeptical expression and a hard look down the corridor, "if you find any, please turn them over to the Kanda police station. It's dark now, so we'll hold off our site inspection until morning. Please leave everything untouched until then. It's okay if you just do a sight survey of your damage, though."

"Understood. We appreciate your help."

An officer came running up. He whispered something to the squad leader, who responded "Good!" with a nod. He saluted Atsuo and left with his men.

With the disappearance of the mob of people, the parking lot looked bigger than normal. Every car there had suffered major damage, with engine hoods bashed in, windows cracked, and bodies contorted. The shop wasn't liable for damage to cars in rental parking spaces, but they would certainly have to fully restore cars they had received for repairs or mandatory inspections.

Atsuo casually picked up an object underfoot and got a shock. It was a Molotov cocktail — a 600 ml bottle filled with gasoline. Looking around, he saw Molotov cocktails fashioned from coke bottles or other kinds of bottles all over the place. There would have been a catastrophe if someone had lit a fire.

He went into the dorm up to the second floor and found a strange scene in the TV room. Everyone was gathered there. Wakako Ikéhata and the two students were in a corner, surrounded by the young shop workers. Ichiro Fukawa was leaning back in a chair and eyeing the three outsiders with an imperious expression, as if inspecting prisoners of war.

"What's happening here?"

"Not a damn thing. I'm telling these characters they should turn themselves in."

"What do you mean, 'turn themselves in?' That's not funny." Atsuo was yelling as if being choked. "That isn't why I let them in here!"

"I'm not trying to be funny!" Ichiro Fukawa's whole body stiffened with anger. "The cars in that parking lot are all wrecked! Who's going to pay for that? The troublemakers who did it, that's who!"

"Well, that wasn't the students. It was that mob of spectators who climbed all over the cars so they could see what was going on. As of now, the only damage we've got is to the cars."

"There's major damage to the gas station and the shop too! The roof of the shop is all ripped up too! All because of these students!"

"The student leaders, yes. These kids were just tagging along. They don't have any responsibility in this."

"We do too have responsibility!" Wakako Ikéhata said.

She was the only one of the students Atsuo Yukimori was really concerned about. The two boys were hanging their heads dejectedly, while she was sitting cross-legged and fixing a keen eye on this exchange between Ichiro Fukawa and Atsuo Yukimori.

"You do not have responsibility," Atsuo Yukimori answered hastily.

"Yes we do. We weren't tagging along. We participated in the demonstration of our own free will."

"Quiet down!" Atsuo Yukimori shot a meaningful look to her, but Wakako Ikéhata's great eyes only shined brighter.

"I won't quiet down! This is my personal issue!"

To Wakako Ikéhata, this room full of males with its spermatic odor was suffocating. She was annoyed at Atsuo Yukimori for bringing her into such a place, and of a mind to say anything at all to discomfit him. She didn't like this fat, balding, middle-aged company president, gloating with self-importance, or the men, including Atsuo Yukimori, who fawned over him. She was in rebellion against them, her professors, her school dean, her father, her mother, her doctor, and most other older people who stood above her and held conceits about their own importance. As she saw it, they all lived by the false rules of a bygone past.

"Whew!" The President, with baggy eyes and lecherous face, affected a bogus smile. "Students come nice and spunky nowadays."

"What! Who are you to be critiquing my temperament?" Wakako Ikéhata was shrieking, a voice that was effective when she crossed swords with her father. "First you leer at us, then you start preaching about surrendering. Who are you to tell us what to do? We joined the demonstration of our own accord, so we take responsibility for anything we do, but it so happens we didn't tear up your parking lot. We didn't have anything to do with that. I didn't lay a finger on any car. And they didn't either, right?"

The two boys nodded. She didn't know them, but they didn't look like fighting sect members, just follower types who couldn't be counted on to stand up to anyone.

"Uh-uh," said the President, moving to the offensive, his eyes flashing. Wakako Ikéhata thought, "Those eyes are the one thing about him that are intimidating."

"There wouldn't have been any damage if you students didn't get into the parking lot. Even if you didn't do it, your buddies did. You've got collective responsibility."

"This guy over here just told you," she said, pointing with her chin at Atsuo Yukimori, "it was the spectators who did it, not us."

"No, look . . ." the President said, and gestured at Atsuo Yukimori to weigh into this verbal joust, but he was ignored.

"Let us out of here! If you don't, we will bring a suit against you for unlawful confinement!"

"Boss, let's turn them loose," said Atsuo Yukimori. "We don't have the authority to arrest them or hold them."

"Look at the loss to us! They have collective responsibility."

"There's no such thing in law as collective responsibility. There is what you call being an accomplice to a crime, but you have to prove it. How are we going to prove the students and the spectators conspired to commit the crime?"

Wakako Ikéhata was impressed. Mr. Yukimori knows law, she thought. The daughter of a law professor, she had been absorbing legal jargon from early childhood. She had acquired a habit of leafing through the *Complete Six Codes of Law* as a diversion from her studies while prepping for university entrance exams.

The President fell silent. After the shop workers had quit their positions around the intruding students and drifted off to other rooms, Atsuo Yukimori came over to address Wakako Ikéhata.

"How's your shoulder?"

"It's no big deal," said Wakako Ikéhata, regarding him sullenly.

"They arrested everyone in sight out in the parking lot," Atsuo Yukimori offered, but Wakako Ikéhata wasn't buying it. To her mind, it sounded like a flimsy excuse for bringing her into a place like this, to be put on display and badgered about surrendering to the police. And he hadn't rushed to the rescue when that fat slob of a president started grilling her.

"You know her?" the President asked incredulously.

"Yes. This student takes skating lessons from the same instructor I have. Her father is a professor at T. University."

"Is that right? You should have told me that in the first place, for heaven's sake! Sure, let her go home. Just be careful there aren't any police still hanging around. Hey, miss, I'm sorry. I just got a little excited. We took a big loss. It got me upset."

Wakako Ikéhata looked elsewhere, ignoring him. Atsuo Yukimori caught her eye and the two of them, accompanied by the other two students, headed toward the staircase. Before they could descend, they were stopped by an excited voice from the television set, sounding like a sportscaster announcing a home run that just turned the ball game around.

" . . . The police came rushing out onto the Tower roof. There are dozens of students, offering no resistance at all. They just now placed their hands on their heads, all at once, and are quietly submitting to handcuffs. It is dark, hard to see, but it looks like they are being linked together, two by two. At this moment a student who was waving the red flag up to the last has set the flag down. The moment of surrender! The Tower has been retaken! The time is five forty-five by the big Tower clock. The end of a long, fierce battle . . ."

Floodlights illuminated the Tower's summit. Reflections flashed from handcuffs, but faces were not distinguishable. The student who waved the red flag until the end was the right height to be Makihiko Moriya, but there was no way to be sure.

As Wakako Ikéhata descended the stairway, she was assailed by the same apprehension she had felt in her dream of falling into a dark abyss. She decided to write it off to exhaustion and hunger. Indeed, she had spent the entire day running, dodging, and throwing rocks, without having anything to eat.

Atsuo Yukimori cast a critical eye over the three students standing at the dormitory entrance. "You're too easy to spot as a battle refugee. At least take off the helmet and blinker and wash your face."

"I'm okay the way I am," Wakako Ikéhata said. "But let me have a glass of water, will you?"

But once she had finished her drink of water, she wanted to use the toilet. That led to washing up and wiping off some of the dirt from her jeans. By then, she was ready to comply with Atsuo Yukimori's offer to have her hurt shoulder attended to. Meanwhile, the mistress of the dormitory exchanged one of the boys' thoroughly soaked shirt for a dry one. Then the three students were treated to rice balls and miso soup. The two male students kept quiet while Wakako Ikéhata negotiated with the housemother and Atsuo Yukimori.

Then Atsuo Yukimori called her aside. "Got something to talk to you about." He invited her into a room with a sign over it saying "Housemother."

"Do you have any place to go back to?"

"Sure," she said, but the reply came out in an unintentionally small voice. Actually, she had nowhere to go.

"I've been worried ever since I got your letter. You said you were staying in 'a certain place' in Tokyo. Does that mean his place?"

"No. An inn, right next door to the apartment he's renting."

"What's he doing now?"

"He was in the Tower. He must have been arrested a little while ago."

"If so, that inn might come under suspicion of the police. There's no question they'll search his room. I've been wanting to ask you, were you in his sect?"

"No."

"What about today's demonstration?"

"I joined in completely on my own. Actually, yesterday was the first time I ever was in a demonstration."

"Well, it would be best for you to keep quiet about being in yesterday's and today's demonstrations."

"Keep it from who?"

"Everyone. Especially the police."

"Do you suppose the police will come asking questions?"

"It's very likely. You can expect they will follow up this episode at the Tower with a security sweep of radicals. That means going after everyone they can find who has anything to do with the ones they just arrested. Your name is bound to come up. That's why you should be careful not to give them anything that will lead to misunderstandings."

"But all I did was take part in a demonstration. I didn't do anything. Except throw a few rocks." Wakako Ikéhata recalled that she had given her lighter to someone when the car was set on fire. What happened to that lighter?

"Just the fact of your having taken part in a demonstration is enough for you to be charged. Even if you say you didn't break anything or set anything on fire, just because you were there they can get you for assembling with dangerous weapons."

"Well, it is true that I took part. I don't want to hide that. It would be cowardly."

"Don't worry about being cowardly. The point is that Japan is no place to get mixed up with the police. They think nothing of blowing up any little thing into a major crime. They can do it."

"Have you had that experience?"

"Having something blown up into a big crime?"

Atsuo Yukimori suddenly lost his composure. He frowned and rubbed his hands together. Wakako Ikéhata's question seemed to have hit a weak spot. Maybe he had bad experiences with police in his past.

"You might say that." A slightly crooked smile appeared on his delicately featured face. "I know a good bit about police. Being a lot older than you."

"Okay, I get it. I'll keep quiet."

"Yes, do that. And the thing for you to do is to go home. At a time like this, that's really for the best."

"Go home . . ." The thought hadn't occurred to her. Coming from Atsuo Yukimori, this solution caught her unaware. Makihiko Moriya had been paying her bill at the inn since her escape from the hospital. If he wasn't going to be available, there weren't any alternative ways to meet the expense. "I guess I have no choice," she murmured.

"Okay, then, give your mother a call. She must be waiting to hear from you." Atsuo Yukimori pushed the telephone on the table toward her.

Chapter 5

Ice

Atsuo Yukimori looked at the pale green florescent clock hands. It was five thirty-five, past time to get up. He was sure the alarm hadn't rung; he had, once again, forgotten to set it the night before. Turning on the light, he headed for the washstand, then stopped with a sheepish smile when he noticed the paper bag on the table. (Ah yes, I was fired.) The bag contained everything that had been in his locker at Fukawa Motors: the five extra uniforms he had purchased, travel kit, underwear, Class Two auto mechanic certification, an English-Japanese dictionary. While collecting these items into the bag, he had reflected that this was all it took to expunge every trace of his presence at the shop. He had left the shop with that bag, just as if he was leaving a hotel stayed at on a single night of a journey elsewhere.

Shortly after the day's work had begun yesterday morning, Kimiko Fujiyama had come in with a message that the boss wanted to see him. That in itself was suspiciously out of the ordinary. If Fukawa had something to say, he could have said it at morning roll call. Any orders he might have about jobs he customarily issued himself. When he asked "What is it?" Kimiko looked a bit discomfited.

"I don't know. He just now told me to go call you," she said, with the expression of one who knows, but doesn't want to say.

In his office, Fukawa was accompanied by Tatsuro Shiomi, the young engineer hired about two weeks before. Fukawa spoke in an unusual, formal way. He was wiping away sweat even though the room wasn't especially warm. "Sorry to say this, but the fact is, I want you out."

"Aha, you mean . . ." Atsuo said, in the spirit of a gag, as he pretended to decapitate himself with the side of his hand.

"I'm not joking," said Fukawa, with such an effort to intimidate that his eyes bulged. "I mean business. You're through with this company."

"All right, I can see you mean it," Atsuo said with a nod, quite composed. Abrupt as his firing had come, there had been many signs that it could happen. "Okay to ask a few questions?"

"You want to hear the reasons? You ought to know!"

"Well, I don't."

"You shouldn't say that when you know very well. Look, you and I just aren't on the same wavelength. That's fatal, in a small business like this. I think you understand that."

Atsuo was dismayed to see that the long-familiar face of Ichiro Fukawa, a face that had shown such friendship, with censure and disapproval etched in every line. But that expression was probably the real face of Ichiro Fukawa. It now seemed likely he had seen Atsuo Yukimori as contemptible all along, a piece of trash the wind blew in.

But it had been the invasion of the parking lot in mid-January that set off a strange sort of friction between Fukawa and Atsuo. They had differing views on how to deal with the damage suffered by cars in the lot. There had been some damage to almost every vehicle, including forty using parking spaces paid for by the month and twenty the shop had received for servicing. Body and window damage was especially heavy to cars that were parked along the fence and jumped upon by the fleeing mob. Fukawa said the shop had no obligation to repair any damage, on the grounds that the crowd's invasion was the same as a natural disaster. Atsuo's view was that they couldn't very well avoid paying a certain amount of compensation.

"How much is 'a certain amount?'"

"Well, all maintenance for the vehicles in for service and the ones next to the fence that got banged up the worst."

"That means twenty cars to fix and Fukawa Motors goes bankrupt."

"No, the chassis and the engines are okay. Most of the damage is to bodies. It won't cost us much."

"Still, we aren't liable for it. Those students did all the damage. They didn't have any business being here."

"We had custody of the cars. It seems to me we're at fault for not taking adequate care of them."

"Oh, yeah? Well then, since you bring that up, who's at fault for stupidly stirring up the students and making them come in here in the first place? Whose idea was it to have a self-defense force for them to attack?"

"I don't think that has anything to do with the issue at hand."

"It has plenty to do with it. To put it plainly, it's the cause of the problem. If somebody's going to pay compensation, it should be the one's who caused the damage. That's the students, but if we can't get them to pay, then it comes down to the one who let the students in. That's you."

"How can you . . ." Atsuo Yukimori looked in amazement at Ichiro Fukawa, now flushed bright red and sweating profusely, reminding him of a boiled octopus.

"The students came in here because they were being chased by the police. I don't think they came in because we stirred them up."

"Then why didn't they go into any other property around here? There're other open lots and people's yards. They came in here because there was a barricade. They thought they'd be safe here, didn't they?"

"But . . ."

"There you are! You can't deny that, can you? You don't take responsibility, the students don't take responsibility, then you want this business to take responsibility? You're not just knocking on the wrong door, mister, you're living in the wrong world!"

With that, Atsuo fell silent.

A period of about ten days followed that kept Atsuo preoccupied in negotiations with the owners of damaged cars from morning until night. It was up to him to dicker with angry car owners by presenting Fukawa's theory of student riots as a "natural disaster," with the objective of shifting as much of the repair expenses as possible to the car insurance companies or the owners. Fukawa was utterly incapable of this kind of negotiation. He couldn't advance his own position, being entirely focused on pleasing the customer. Thus, all matters that required having the customer share the burden of payments were left to Atsuo's humble, but confident and well-reasoned arguments.

One day, near the end of January, when this business was well on its way to completion and daily operations were back to normal, Fukawa used the morning roll call to introduce a pale faced young man to all the employees.

"Name of Shiomi. From now on he works here as an engineer."

In no time at all, rumors were circulating about the new engineer, Tatsuro Shiomi. According to the information tirelessly accumulated by Sonoko Kanéhara, Shiomi was a distant relative of Fukawa on his father's side. He had graduated from Fukawa's alma mater, the private K. University, four or five years earlier, then gone to work as an automotive and electronics engineer for a major dealer. Fukawa had lured him away with a high salary. Sonoko whispered the amount to Atsuo — more than twice his salary as shop foreman and over ten times what Yukichi was getting as a common shop worker.

"That can't be right," Atsuo muttered. There was no reason on earth why a green employee in his twenties should draw a higher salary than the foreman of Fukawa Motors.

"But it's true." This day, Sonoko was youthful, hair nicely dyed, speaking with a charming pout of the lips. "I got it from Kimiko when I brought some plum blossoms to the president's office. She was bragging about what a brilliant student he had been in school. It seems he wrote his graduation thesis on computer control of engines."

"Computers," Atsuo said with a sigh. Computerized fuel control units were being used in new cars. Atsuo was at a loss when they came in for repair. He didn't have any choice but to seek help from specialists with dealers who handled the models. He had read a few introductory books on these systems, but it was a field in which he was so poorly grounded he couldn't understand them. That gave him the same helpless feeling that had ultimately landed him in military prison for fleeing army aircraft mechanic school in desperation because his lack of basic knowledge of physics and chemistry made him unable to digest the lessons.

"And he has Class Two auto mechanic certification, too."

"Yeah?" Atsuo sighed again. Without any post-elementary school education at all, he had leveraged his on-the-job experience to pick up all three types of Class Three certification (chassis, gasoline engine, and diesel engine) and another three years of work at that level to finally acquire Class Two qualification, just two years before. Getting that far had been a tough slog that involved running directly from the job, with no time to eat before night classes began at a transportation ministry approved school of maintenance engineering. And this kid easily made Class Two mechanic just by graduating a university.

"Be careful," Sonoko elaborated further, "or that Shiomi will end up in your place!"

"So what can I do about it? There's a demand for knowledge and skill. Times are past for a guy who can't do anything but crawl under cars and get covered with grease."

"Don't underestimate yourself! You're the most valuable man in the shop. Everyone has faith in you. The work wouldn't get done right without you."

"I wonder about that." Atsuo looked down and made a show of thinking it over, but in fact no ideas were coming to him. All he was got was a feeling like the strength draining from his neck muscles.

Meanwhile, Yukichi Jinnai turned up missing one night, along with all his possessions from his room in the dormitory. He hadn't said a word to anyone about leaving.

The morning after his disappearance Atsuo called Torakichi Jinnai in Nemuro to ask if Yukichi was at home and was told that he wasn't. A call to Tetsukichi revealed that Yukichi's things had arrived by post, but not Yukichi. Atsuo reported this to Fukawa, who responded by bringing up the disappearance of 170,000 yen. Yukichi had walked off the job because he was the thief, Fukawa declared flatly.

"There isn't any proof he took that money," Atsuo answered.

"I wouldn't be so sure," Fukawa said, with a look at Kimiko Fujiyama. Atsuo was thinking they seemed to have hit on some other evidence when Ichiro Fukawa made a sensational revelation.

"The monthly proceeds from the gas station are missing. This time it's a big deal — 427,000 yen. The collector put the bag down while he was washing his face and that's when someone grabbed it."

"When was this?"

"Yesterday afternoon, about four o'clock." Yukichi had gone missing that night.

"That doesn't prove Jinnai did it."

"Still want proof? Why did he vanish the night the money was stolen?"

"Jinnai put his things together and sent them home a week ago. He didn't just decide to leave yesterday."

"That makes it worse. It's almost proof the crime was planned for the day he knew was collection day. This time we're talking about a lot of money. I've reported it to the police. They'll be searching the dormitory and everyone's lockers."

The police arrived shortly. Yukichi's room was the first to be investigated. They dusted the desk and wardrobe case for fingerprints. Everything in the locker room was examined, including Atsuo's possessions. Of course, no clues to the theft emerged. What they did find was a fountain pen in a corner that Atsuo had lost years before and a plentiful supply of porn books and masturbation goods among the shop workers' possessions that drew sardonic smiles from the investigators.

That evening, Fukawa called Atsuo to his office. "The police say they want to search your apartment. See that you cooperate with them."

"Why search my place?" Atsuo asked angrily.

"Aw, it's not like you're a suspect." Fukawa said, timidly scratching his head. This gesture contrasted with his aggressive front a short while before, revealing a very fainthearted interior. "It's just that since you're Jinnai's uncle, they think they might find something informative."

"I suppose that's what you told them."

Fukawa neither acknowledged nor denied it. Instead, he turned a studiously sober, good citizen's countenance to the policeman sitting next to him.

After the shop was closed down, two young detectives visited Atsuo's apartment and spent two hours questioning him on a variety of matters. They seemed to know he had a criminal record because their tone was extremely ill-mannered, addressing him exactly the way guards talk to prisoners. Atsuo answered politely, without attempting to keep anything secret, although he found it unpleasant to be treated like a suspect. He made it a point to demand numerous revisions of the examination record before he signed and affixed his seal to it. Each passing day seemed to wreak a little more damage to the solid walls of protection he had built up around himself.

The only reason Fukawa gave for firing Atsuo was they weren't "on the same wavelength." Atsuo surmised the real explanation lay in a long string of recent events. There was no simple cause that might be overcome with an apology, no way out of the predicament. He had no recourse but to accept his sentence.

"When do you want me to leave?" Atsuo asked Fukawa.

"Stay until the March payday. That would be fine."

Payday was the twenty-sixth of every month. There was more than a month's time until then. "Who's the new foreman?"

Fukawa looked over at Tatsuro Shiomi. "Do I get retirement pay?"

"Of course. A month's pay for every year worked."

He had been there for seven years. Seven month's pay, plus unemployment insurance and his savings would be enough to get by for a year. He would have to find another job in that time.

"All right, I'll leave right away," Atsuo said. He had no desire to work for another month and a half, certainly not as a common shop hand under Shiomi, with everyone feeling sorry for him.

He went back into the shop, where word of his fall from grace had spread. The workers attitudes were changed. They answered him with exaggerated amenability, pretended not to hear his directions, exchanged meaningful glances. All of this made it extremely uncomfortable to be there. He did a tear down and rebuild of a frame and was tired out by lunchtime. In the afternoon, he couldn't bring himself to return to the shop, so he went to the locker room, put his personal belongings together, delivered a brief notice of parting to the workers and went to the dormitory, where Sonoko Kanéhara cornered him.

"I heard about it. Our boss is inhuman! Casually firing the most valuable worker out of the blue! The one who made that shop what it is! It's outrageous! I want to get everyone's name on a petition demanding your job back!"

"No, don't do that. I made up my mind to leave. I wouldn't want to work here any more."

"It's Kimiko who's behind it all. She had a big fight with Mr. Jinnai's father, didn't she? So now she resents Mr. Jinnai and you. She couldn't stand having you around. This way, she's rid of you. For all we know, maybe she's the one who took that 170,000 yen before and this latest 400,000 yen. She had charge of the money in both cases. Is that suspicious or not?"

"Just let it go."

"I won't let it go! There's more to the story!" A tear ran down Sonoko's cheek. She continued, speaking rapidly. "That Kimiko, first she said that Shiomi character was a distant relative of the boss. Well, the latest is that he's actually her cousin. She put her own relative in your job! She wants to take over the company! Where does her scheming end?"

"Goodbye. Thanks for everything," said Atsuo, softly patting her on the shoulder. Then he left the dormitory.

Atsuo looked back when he reached the parking lot exit. The shop, gas station and parking lot all looked utterly different from what had been until that moment their normal appearance. In the morning they had been part of his company, where he thought he naturally belonged. He had considered himself on good terms with his workplace, believing he had a relationship with it that would go on and on. That had all been counterfeit, or at least an illusion that could be dispelled with a word from the company president. Having been expelled, he now saw the shop as someone else's workplace. Tomoyama and the other young men appeared outside the shop and waved to him. He wasn't their foreman any more, just an outsider. They would continue working as the times changed under their new foreman, Shiomi. Eventually, they would fall behind the changing times and be cast aside as he had been.

Beholding this scene, Atsuo recalled the last time he had felt this way. Yes, this was exactly the same feeling as when he got out of prison. He had taken a final look back when he was being released to the freedom of ordinary life, after serving out the long years of his term inside high walls, where life was dominated by guards, bars, cells and prison rules.

His baggage was unbelievably light — a crummy paper bag from the big bookstore, S. Books, was enough to hold all the gear for the seven years he had spent at Fukawa Motors. For all it weighed, it might have been his lunch for that day.

Atsuo ran his fingers over the paper bag on his table and went to the wash-stand to shave. Then he stopped himself. If he wasn't going to work, there was no need to shave. Okay, he thought, why not grow a beard to commemorate getting sacked? It was a royal pain having to shave day after day for the sake of dealing with customers and co-workers. What was surprising was that he had never gotten sick and tired of it. Normally, he would be going through his morning tasks, taking care to get everything right, finally putting on his suit so he could make the 7:08 bus. Now there was no need to do any of that. Not being particularly hungry, he didn't bother fixing breakfast either.

He brought the newspaper to the bed and lay down, but he couldn't get in-terested in reading, lacking his customary enthusiasm for scanning the morning paper to stay informed for conversations in the shop. He pushed the newspaper aside, and was absentmindedly looking at the Ezo deer on the wall when he no-ticed a pack of cigarettes on the top of the television set, forgotten by Wakako. Examining the cigarettes, he found them a bit damp with mildew, but servicea-ble, so he put one in his mouth and lit it.

He had completely forgotten the taste of smoke. Harsh and bitter, it made him cough as if something had caught in his throat. Once again, it was a replay of a familiar experience; having his first cigarette after getting out of prison, where smoking is absolutely prohibited. The sting in his throat and the cough-ing parted the curtain to a new existence. His body was used to the nicotine by the time he had finished his first smoke, and it demanded another one.

Atsuo had started his second cigarette when he noticed that the newspa-per's front page headline was in extra-large type: "Bomb Explodes On Shin-kansen — Two Die, Injury Count is High." It was too much trouble to get up for his reading glasses, so he just looked at the sub-headlines: "Radical Sect In-volved?" . . ."Witnesses See Young Couple"

A photo showed a train interior hit by an explosion. Realizing this was a big event, he went for his reading glasses and sat down on the bed to read.

An explosion had occurred the day before in Coach No. 2 of a Shinkansen "Hikari" train departing at four in the afternoon, immediately after it had passed through Shimbashi Station. It was believed that an explosive placed on an overhead rack was the cause of the blast. That would make it an exact copy of the bombing of the Yokosuka Line train in June of the previous year.

It takes a hopeless jerk to commit a crime like that, Atsuo reflected. Putting a bomb on a train isn't going to change anything anyway, and this job couldn't have been botched more if you tried. (My career covers theft, embezzlement and robbery causing injury, but not murder. I didn't mind filching other people's property when it came to doing the deed, but I wouldn't have had the nerve to kill the owners if that was what it took to rob them). All the bomb did was mess up the front half of one car — it didn't flip the train over or even derail it. The bomb just blew up the overhead rack it was sitting on. Glass and fragments of the rack did fall on the road below, but, by chance, no debris hit any passersby or cars. This attack had turned out on the same scale as the previous year's Yokosuka line bombing, which it was imitating.

Watching the drifting stream of purple smoke, Atsuo had a disagreeable recollection of the two detectives who had visited after the Yokosuka train bombing. He could fully expect to see them again, or someone just like them, coming to question him on the pretense of a routine check of gun owners. It would be more than he could stand if police were going to show up every time there was an explosion somewhere. There was nothing for them to find the previous year, but he was cautioned not to keep his guns and ammunition together in the same gun locker. He had completely forgotten about that rule. It was a new legal requirement that had gone into effect in June 1966. There weren't any penalties for violations, so the detectives had just told him about it and left. He still wasn't in compliance because he didn't have any room for a new gun locker.

Well, now he was in a position to take care of the matter, so he thought about securing the ammunition somewhere else. Where to put a new gun locker? What about putting the TV on top of the refrigerator and moving the china closet into the kitchen? Or how about getting rid of the cardboard box under the bed and putting a small safe in its place? It was very annoying to have to do this. Things were so densely arranged in the room you couldn't move one item without having to shift two or three others. But that wasn't the real issue. Every fixture was located in its most convenient place, as far as he was concerned. Nothing could be relocated without disrupting his lifestyle. There was a power outage once, and the room went to total darkness, but he got by with virtually no inconvenience. He could just reach out in any direction and know with fair accuracy what would be there.

While he was making coffee and toast in the kitchen, Atsuo had an attack of anxiety as he considered what to do that day. His daily agenda had gone from being neatly divided up between commuting, working, and going home to a blank slate. It was like being deposited in the middle of a great wilderness and trying to decide which direction to go. He didn't think there was anything wrong with taking it easy in bed and loafing all day, but that wasn't in his nature. It would be distressing to even try. He liked being occupied all the time. Anything was fine — reading, cleaning, walking around, working, skating — just keep going until it's time to quit.

Well, there you have it, he decided. It's a good day to go skate as much as I want. The rink opens at ten o'clock. Get there when it's just opened and it shouldn't be crowded at all. I can skate to my heart's content.

Making up his mind emboldened him. Numerous things came to mind that needed doing before leaving the apartment at eight thirty. Industriously, he vacuumed, did laundry, and cleaned his rifles. When the alarm he had set for eight thirty sounded, he strode promptly out the front door.

The sight of the quonset style skating rink put Atsuo at ease. It was a place where one could be out of work and still feel welcome. Riding the bus, and then the train to get there had placed him among crowds of commuters in suits and neckties who made him acutely conscious that he had been expelled from the working world they inhabited. The great mixed brigade of Japanese workers was advancing, its troops resolutely en route to their posts, and he was the lone deserter from his unit.

He arrived a little before ten o'clock. There were only three housewives who looked like regulars, waiting at the admissions ticket window. They were shortly joined by a tall foreigner. At his appearance the three women all bowed to him in unison. From their conversion, he learned the foreigner was a pastor who was a fellow member of their ice dance class. These people were the only ones entering the capacious rink when it opened. When they dispersed inside, it was as good as having an empty space. Atsuo occupied part of the center and began doing circle eights, three turns and other compulsory figures.

His skates etched a sharp record of his path in the mirror surface, ruthlessly disclosing every bit of mental stress, physical imbalance, and lack of experience. Nevertheless, he moved gracefully, powered by ice and gravity, his mind focused on simple geometric forms. Gradually, he traced the forms with greater consistency, his mind at ease and fully engaged with each moment as it came.

"Ooh, Mr. Yukimori!"

Accosted suddenly by this cry, he nearly toppled in surprise. It was a stout woman in her sixties he met occasionally at the rink on Sundays. She had told him her career there spanned forty years. In other words, she had started coming before the beginning of Japan's fifteen-year war.

"How unusual to see you on a weekday! Off from work?"

"Yes, worked on Sunday, so I got today off."

"You certainly have become a good skater!"

"No, no. I can't get anything right."

"You're shifting your weight a little too much on those three turns. See, your tracks are uneven." The lady pointed to Atsuo's figure tracings on the ice. In the three turn, you go from skating forward to backward or backward to forward as you trace out a figure three. It is hard to keep both halves of the figure symmetrical. He didn't need this woman to tell him it was a weak point; his coach had hammered that home time and again. It was the very thing he had been working on.

"Right. Thanks," Atsuo said, inclining his head politely and thinking she was a nuisance.

The lady gave a satisfied smile and moved to the side, as if to say, "All right, let's see you try it again."

It was awkward to practice while being watched. He was wishing she would go somewhere else when she launched into a critique of the pastor's ice dancing.

"Foreign people have such nice long legs, but the trouble with that pastor is he doesn't flex them enough. He's much too stiff, and he kicks at the ice. He'll never have good balance that way. Look how he wavers."

Once again, she was on the mark, but her criticism was hardly necessary. Most likely, the pastor knew his own shortcomings very well and was trying to improve. This lady specialized in critiquing other people's skating without providing her own example. Atsuo had never seen her skate. She wore flashy skating outfits with short skirts fit for a first-class competition skater, now pink, now purple, now yellow. But she never skated. She spent her time either in the middle of the rink engaging people in conversation or at rinkside watching other people skate.

There was another meddlesome character who frequented the rink, a self-styled skating guru, in her forties, whose skating abilities didn't really match her self-confidence. Dressed in slacks, she was patrolling the rink, eyes greedily scanning the crowd for anyone a little below her level who looked ripe for a gratuitous lesson. Atsuo watched her approach a group of girls in uniforms that suggested they all belonged to the same university skating club. Fairly good skaters, they had been circling the rink at a fast clip. They were doing jumps. Their self-appointed coach was explaining something, probably giving pointers about the takeoff. Then she demonstrated a jump that was hardly better than what the girls had been doing. To the contrary, her legs were cocked at an odd angle that spoiled her form.

A trill of laughter escaped the "critic" standing beside Atsuo. "Why on earth does she think she can teach those girls anything? Look, you can see they want her to go away. Oh, by the way, you'll never guess who showed up the other day — Ms. Ikéhata!"

"Is that right?" The lady finally said something of interest to him, but he intentionally kept curiosity out of his tone. The last time he had seen Wakako was during the battle over the Tower in mid-January. That night, he had accompanied her as far as the Ogawa-machi streetcar stop on her way home. He had heard nothing of her since. A confluence of things preying on his mind had kept Atsuo from his Sunday lessons, leaving no opportunity to meet Wakako.

"She is really good. Of all Mr. I.'s students, she is the best." Mr. I. was Wakako and Atsuo's instructor.

"That's really true. She has an innate talent."

"Well, she's really dedicated. She never missed a day's practice. Then she suddenly just stopped coming. I was really worried, until she showed up again."

"When was that?"

"Ummm, wait a minute . . . Two weeks ago, maybe Wednesday or Thursday . . . Oh, I know. It was the Bunkyo Skate Club's lesson day, so it must have been Wednesday. Exactly two weeks ago. And the interesting thing about it was she always skates in the middle of the rink, but that day she just kept going round and round with a boy on speed skates. Later on I asked her who the boy was and she said it was your nephew."

She gave him a look that said she assumed Atsuo would know this so he answered, "Yup, that was him," with a self-deprecating smile.

This was unforeseen information, but it made some sense. During the police search of Yukichi's room, his roommate Tomoyama had handed over a notebook he had been keeping for Yukichi. Its lines were crammed with poetry in Yukichi's small, inept handwriting. Some of it was waka, a form Atsuo knew a bit about. One poem stuck in his mind:

A long-legged maiden circles o'er the ice"
There blooms a flower red"
Bringing autumn fragrance"

It was surprising enough to find Yukichi writing waka, but more surprising still that he should be attracted to Wakako, whose trim legs were indeed long. Yukichi had met her at the rink wearing a red costume in the fall of the previous year. Thinking back to that night when the police were storming the Tower at

T. University, he now reckoned that Yukichi must have been happy to fetch a wet towel for Wakako and serve her a meal. At the time, he had assumed his nephew was annoyed about being told to do this, since it was he who had said, "That's the kind of girl I hate. They put on that 'Oh, I'm So Nice' act." But that assessment seemed to have been mistaken.

Two weeks before, Yukichi had suddenly announced he wanted to use one of his leave days. That in itself wasn't at all unusual. Everyone in the shop had been doing the same, to compensate for Sundays worked and the many overtime hours they had been putting in.

The "critic" deserted him to engage in conversation with the roving instructor she had been disparaging a moment before. They were soon chatting cozily like old friends about the group of girls. As they saw it, those poor girls were slaves to the completely outmoded skating style taught by one of the instructors. They agreed it was beyond understanding why any instructor would inflict such tired old techniques on young people.

Being collared by the "critic" had soured Atsuo on compulsory figures. He impulsively headed for the outer track and began barreling forward at top speed. Even figure skates have the potential to get up to a respectable speed. Atsuo was soon whizzing past others on hockey skates and speed skates, a stiff wind nipping at his earlobes. He switched between forward and backward skating a few times, described curves to the left and right, did spins, skated spread eagle. By the time he had been around the track about twenty times he had worked up enough sweat to soak his undershirt. Free style skating uses up incomparably more energy than figure skating. He was out of breath, so he went to rinkside for a break.

A middle-aged man in a business suit approached and said, "That was terrific speed skating." Atsuo wasn't in the mood for chit-chatting. He shot a cold sidelong glance at the speaker, and was surprised to find a good-natured sort of face. The man went on talking. He was sniffling as he smiled.

"I skated in grade school so I thought I'd be okay here, but it's no good when you let thirty years go by. 'Scuse me for saying, but for a man your age you're a good skater. Have you been at it long?"

Atsuo didn't want to start discussing skating again, so he pretended not to hear and asked instead, "Are you working?"

"Hoo!" The man blew out his breath as if a bad odor had reached his nostrils. He fingered a necktie whose knot seemed to have been tied and retied enough times to wear it down to a string. "Friend, you just got me where it hurts. No point in hiding anything. Fact is, I'm out of work. I'm in the futon business.

No, I don't have my own shop — I'm a cotton stuffer. We work in other people's stores, putting the cotton inside the futon. Well, there's a lot of products made with synthetics going around these days, so they don't need cotton stuffers any more. I was doing work for two stores. Both gave me the ax. Do you understand what I'm staying?" The man sniffled to catch his breath.

Atsuo's sweaty underwear was turning cold. He invited the man to join him in the heated lounge. His original revulsion at what had seemed to be a drunk-ard was replaced by interest in the man's confession to being unemployed.

"Mmm, it's warm in here." The cotton stuffer was delighted. "After one turn around the rink I was already tired out, and getting cold too. I was thinking about leaving, but it's warm here. You could stay all day."

"Go on, have a seat." Atsuo seated himself on a bench and idly looked out at the rink. The "critic" was standing before that group of girls.

"So, like I was saying," the cotton stuffer began, but then he stopped short. "Wait a minute, how far did I get?" With that, he gave himself a rap on the head with his fist with enough force to raise a lump. "I forget things. This pumpkin head of mine is no good."

"You said you were out of work."

"I sure am. Told it to the mountain god, but I can't tell my brat. I have a little girl. She's in second grade. Every morning she says, 'Bye-bye Papa.' She thinks her old man's working. You can't be told that and stay in the house all day, now can you? So I wave to her and say 'Bye-bye' and leave, but there's nowhere to go. So I have to kill time until evening. What do you think I should do?"

"That's a tough question."

"Pachinko, coffee shops, movies — they all cost money. I was going to the zoo for a while because admission is cheap. When it rains you can go in the aquarium. They have the reptiles up on the second floor. There's a big tank with lots of turtles inside. Turtles don't move much. They just hug that floor like nothing's going to move them. Maybe ten minutes goes by and one will bend his neck just a little. Twenty more minutes go by and some other turtle crawls like, two or three steps. And I'm watching, waiting for one to move. Once I was there for a whole day. I watched the turtles all morning and went to the cafeteria for ramen. In the afternoon I took in the snakes, just for a change, then back to the turtles, just waiting for one to move." The man did an imitation of a turtle moving its head.

"Did you go looking for work?"

"Did I look for work? Did I look for work?" The cotton stuffer's shoulders rose angrily as if he was about to rain blows on the questioner. "Did I ever look for work! I couldn't count all the referral offices I've been to. You know where I was just a little while ago? The Iidabashi job security office, that's where! Sure, they have lots of different jobs, especially in sanitation and management. But I'm a cotton stuffer. I take pride in my profession. I couldn't take any other job. I just couldn't, you understand? The trouble is, futoners just aren't hiring! Not one ad for a cotton stuffer! Not one!"

"Okay, get this," Atsuo said melodramatically. "The fact is, I'm out of work myself."

"Really?" The cotton stuffer leaped to his feet. The next moment he sat down again, dejected. "No, of course not. You shouldn't make fun of people like that."

"It's true. I was fired yesterday. I'm still a raw recruit in the army of the unemployed."

"It really is true!" The cotton stuffer sniffled and a tear appeared in his eye. "So you're here, skating in the day like me, so your kids will think Dad is working."

"No, that's not me. I have no wife and no kids."

"What? Why not?" the man asked, shaking his head in wonderment at the idea of a grown man not having his own family. "Did you separate?"

"I've always been a bachelor."

"Oho!" Elated again, the man clapped his hands. "I see. You're an avowed bachelor. I've heard of that. Hey, that's great! The truth is having a family just weighs you down. To be all by yourself — how wonderful! But you certainly are a mystery. At first I thought you must be a college professor. See, because there are only three kinds of men who could be out skylarking all day — guys out of work, like me, or else they must be either retired, or college professors. The three great men of the leisure classes. You look important, so I figured you wouldn't be unemployed, and you're too young to be retired, so you must be a college professor."

"Yeah, I do seem to give that impression, but the truth is, I was a mechanic. Just a lowly car mechanic."

"That's not lowly! It's a proud profession!"

"What do you say we do a little skating?" Atsuo stood up. His underwear had dried and the room was getting stuffy.

The cotton stuffer rose too. "Fine. Let's go."

The rink had filled up considerably, not as jammed as it became on Sundays, but the center was largely occupied, the right side with groups of college-age kids, and the left half with housewife groups. About twenty youths belonging to a university hockey team were hurtling around the outer track at terrific speed, urged on by angry shouts from their coach. A few elderly patrons from the re-tired ranks were gliding along timorously in the hockey team's wake.

"Here you see a microcosm of our world," Atsuo said.

"Yes?" answered the cotton stuffer, bewilderment written on his face.

"There are men slaving at their jobs to pay for these people to come here and play. Here you see their wives, sons, and daughters. The old ones slaved away long years, but now they are reduced to unimportant nobodies. The ones who were thrown out of their jobs are free, but there isn't any place for them."

"Right, I see. You really are like a scholar."

"See there? She's what you call a critic," Atsuo said, his eyes on the lady wear-ing the flamboyant red skating costume, ostentatiously engaged in conversation with the coach of a housewives' group. "Critics don't do anything themselves. They just look at little pieces of the world and make comments about it. They don't care about the larger context, and they have no idea what will come of the things they criticize."

"No kidding, you really are a scholar."

"Then there's the self-styled teachers. Fancy themselves educators or gurus or something. Spouting off about how people should live their lives, but their own lives don't amount to anything. Yeah, they're a damn waste of space. Here I go!"

"Hey, wait up!"

Disregarding the cotton stuffer, Atsuo took off after the hockey team that was speeding along in single file, raising low-pitched rasps as its members slashed earnestly at the ice. He overtook the team and left it behind. At this, the coach bawled "Faster!" at his charges and the rasping sounds became a cacoph-ony. But Atsuo was faster still, overtaking them once again on his third time around the track. He was about to pass them again when he noticed the cotton liner, soaking wet for some reason, skating along and looking miserable.

"What's wrong?"

"Everything! One of those fool hockey players clipped my skate as he came around and I went down. He didn't even apologize — just made like he had nothing to do with it. I was thinking about telling him off, but you know, college kids these days are worse than yakuza, so I kept my cool. Next it was those col-lege girls. They came jumping around and one kicked me. So does she say she's sorry? Hah! She says, 'You're in the way, bub! Quit blocking the road!' They're a bunch of thugs too!"

"That's just awful. Actually, I'm leaving now."

"Yeah? Me too. I've had it with this place! Let's go somewhere cheap to eat. Neither of us has money, so we split the bill."

"Good idea." Atsuo took a look around the rink just to make sure Wakako wasn't there. Now that he was leaving, he realized he had been longing to see her all along. He watched one of the college girl's graceful ballet-like movements. It seemed like it was Wakako herself performing in disguise. The girl jumped and went into a camel spin, arms and legs parallel to the ground as she went round. Atsuo stroked the well-formed legs with his eyes, ardently taking in glimpses of their place of juncture that was revealed when she spun. Then he was suddenly seized with a desire to meet Wakako and hold her. He averted his eyes.

The two unemployed men headed for the shopping district around the nearest train station. It was lunchtime and the area was filled with employed people in their business suits and work uniforms. Feeling like refugees, they fled into a back street, found an unprepossessing lunch room in a dank, sunless alley and went through the curtain.

"How about having a drink?" the cotton liner proposed.

"Alcohol? I've never been one to start drinking during the day."

"Today's special. We have to commemorate the day you and me met."

They had croquettes and broiled cuttlefish with shochu, refreshments much to Atsuo's taste.

His partner was clearly in his element as well. They each downed several drinks as they talked. "Been out of work two months now. We can get by for a while on unemployment insurance and my wife's part-time job. What really gets to me is all this time on my hands. You try to while it away and it just gets longer and longer. But you know what? All you need is alcohol and whoosh! It burns the time up. I hate to admit it, but I was on fire when I went up to you. Started in the morning. Three cans of beer and two cups of second grade. Got me to thinking about the old days. You know, skating. Understand what I'm saying?"

"Yeah, I sure do." Atsuo nodded sympathetically. The corners of the cotton liner's eyes and cheeks were flaccid. His entire face somehow looked as if all the muscles had loosened and were drooping.

"You can tell my nose is funny, can't you? It's an occupational disease. You breathe in cotton and it messes up something in there. Masks get in the way so I don't wear them. I've had two operations on my nose. They cut out some of the bone."

The cotton liner sniffled and blew his nose vigorously. Atsuo had the feeling wads of cotton would come flying out. He laughed.

"Aha, you laughed. Finally. That's good. People have to laugh. I could see you're depressed. Really down. Look, there's no sense in crying just because you're out of work. Me, I've been through this lots of times. Cotton futons are in decline, you see. Wasn't always like that. About ten years back there was a dog year when purple futons were all the rage. Did you know that?"

"No, I didn't."

"Somehow the word got out that old people who sleep in purple futons have long lives. It spread across the whole country. Purple futons were selling like blazes. This is high quality futons we're talking about — only the best cotton is used. Well, every futon shop in Japan was frantic to get cotton liners. And this is not the kind of work some college kid can do part time. No way! Cotton liners work by annual contract. Well, let me tell you, I had my hands full that whole year. Working right through every night. So I was making good money. It was a really lucky year. Hit the urban development housing lottery that year too. Never had it better! But, you know how it is when You're at the top. The next thing just has to be the fall. Luck's like youth — over in no time. Well, here I am now, at rock bottom. You too."

"That's true enough."

"So when you are at the bottom, the only way to go next is up, right? So get happy!"

"Sometimes you think you are at rock bottom, but the next thing that happens is you fall further. People can see up to the top, but they can't see all the way down to the bottom. That's because there is no limit to how far you can fall."

"You sure say scary things. I thought I was down as far as I could get. Do you suppose things could get worse?"

"Yeah, it's entirely possible. Things can always fall apart for anyone."

"You sound like it's happened to you."

"And you sound very wet behind the ears." The talk was getting a trifle on Atsuo's nerves, so he tried the same trick the cotton liner had used a while before of a sudden show of anger. "I know about disaster. I've been there. It's a place where you only look like a human being, but you're nothing, because they take everything away from you. Everything."

"Please, stop looking at me like that!" The cotton liner's palms were pressed together prayerfully, his head pulled in between his shoulders, like a turtle.

"Humph." With a glance that confirmed the lone waitress-cum-cashier was absorbed in laughing at a quiz show on the television and there were no other customers in the lunch room, Atsuo sprang the following upon the now cringing cotton liner: "I'm an ex-con. I did time in jail. Inmates don't have rights. None. No dignity, no nothing. That's where the bottom is. So don't give me that posh crap about your god of the mountain and your brat. You don't know what you're talking about."

"Boss! Forgive me!" The cotton liner looked ready to burst into tears. He pressed his hands together and moved them up and down, beseeching mercy.

"Aw, I was only joking," Atsuo said, relenting. Verbalizing had triggered an eruption of anger from within. He became alarmed that it might really explode at any moment.

"Was it a joke? You sure can give a guy a scare, boss" the cotton liner said, wringing his hands. "I thought I was about to be killed."

"I'm sorry. Things have been getting to me lately. Makes me get brutal, shoot off my mouth."

"That feeling I can understand. What do you say we have another drink, boss?"

"Enough of that 'boss' stuff. Call me Yuki, as in 'snow.'"

"Okay, Yuki. My name's Yamamura."

The two went on drinking. When they went out together, arms across each others' shoulders and walking unsteadily, the sun had fallen low, immersing the street in shadow. A cold wind was blowing. Passersby spotted them as drunks and avoided them.

They reached a crossroad whose left branch went past Fukawa Motors. Atsuo turned right without hesitation. Shortly, they were walking up an incline. They looked up at a giant torii, black as pitch, that stood atop the hill.

"Yasukuni Shrine," Atsuo said.

"No kidding. That sure brings back memories. Came here a lot during the war," the cotton liner said and gave a military style salute.

"Mr. Yamamura, were you a soldier? In the war?"

"Well, of course I was! Army private first class Takeshi Yamamura went to war."

"A pfc, huh? I was a sergeant. Where were you? I was in central China."

"I was in the south — the Philippines, Sergeant Yuki." The two marched proudly in step up the hill.

Shrines are built atop elevations. There is an uphill road to Gokoku Shrine in Nemuro. The day Atsuo was inducted into the army the people of his village all turned out to send him off. They formed lines to mount the hill. Banzai! Banzai! Atsuo Yukimori, private second class, banzai! Our precious soldiers fighting for Country, His Majesty's Country, land of the gods Nippon, banzai! Peerless army of the emperor, banzai! Our gratitude to our troops!

It was a raucous sendoff, with Atsuo at the head of the procession. He was proud to be marching ahead of the village people. At the time, he thought he had put an end to his life of crime and indolence. To him, no distinction could exceed the glory of becoming a soldier in the Japanese army. He believed that by dying for his country he would become a guardian spirit of Japan, a fallen hero to be celebrated at Yasukuni Shrine. He had climbed that hill with buoyant steps, filled with the strange feeling that dying was something to be happy about.

Passing through the great torii took them to a promenade lined with gingko and cherry blossom. All the leaves were gone. The pair beheld a cold-looking procession of bare trees silhouetted over a broad expanse of white pebbles. There was no one else to be seen. A bronze figure of the founder of the Japanese army stood atop a stone pedestal, clad in hakama and haóri, head shaved but for an elaborate topknot. The duo stood before the statue and gave formal salutes.

"Well, let's go visit the guardian heroes."

"Sergeant Yuki, first I request leave for a drink of water."

Searching for water, they came to the shrine's water basin. Drinking from the fragrant plain wooden dippers was refreshing, and it put them in the mood for paying respects in the hallowed sanctuary.

"Lost a lot of buddies."

"Yeah, so did I. Lots and lots of them. More than I can count."

"Makes me feel like I got no right to still be alive."

Facing the main sanctuary, Atsuo performed the ritual signs of respect to the enshrined spirits: two bows, two claps of the hands, and one more bow. He peered inside. As the wind cooled down the radiance in his head induced by alcohol, thoughts came to him of various comrades in arms who had died.

One night on the march in China they were traversing the ridges between rice paddies, feeling their way in pitch darkness, when an orange pillar of flame suddenly arose. They raced to battle positions to face the enemy's attack, but there was only silence and darkness. Eventually a voice was heard announcing that a land mine had been hit and urgently calling for the medics. Atsuo shined his flashlight and found a man down, his left arm missing from the shoulder. Next to him a superior private complained, "I'm cold." As Atsuo was helping him up, blood gushed from the top of his leg. Alarmed, Atsuo pressed a towel on the wound. A squishy mass of something covered his hands. It was the man's intestines, still warm with life.

"I was just now thinking about how a guy died," Atsuo said.

"So was I," Yamamura said. "Sergeant Yuki, I got to take a leak."

"Me too." Atsuo said. He scanned the surroundings with the piercing gaze of a sentry and discovered a sign that said "Rest Rooms." They followed the arrow past a line of bronze cannon from the Tokugawa era and found the staircase they were seeking next to a Type 97 medium tank, a familiar sight during the war.

When they emerged, their attention was captured by a building identified as a "Repositorium."

"Shall we go in?"

"Yeah, let's." They both wanted to see the war relics. The exhibits were on the second floor, arranged in chronological order by war: Boshin War, Satsuma Rebellion, First Sino-Japanese War, Russo-Japanese War, Mukden Incident, January Twenty-Eighth Incident, Second Sino-Japanese War — artifacts of people killed in a long succession of conflicts. They were the only visitors. Atsuo read the written commentary out loud as they peered closely at each article of military clothing, sword, Japanese flag, photograph, will, and letter.

When they finished this process, they looked at one another and heaved a spontaneous sigh. "Sergeant Yuki, there is something wrong here."

"Yeah, I definitely get that feeling. What do you suppose it is?"

"There's no memorabilia from soldiers."

"Yeah, that's it. All this is just stuff from the big shots!" Atsuo thundered, realizing that the exhibits consisted almost exclusively of items from generals. Memorabilia of the men he knew in the war — NCOs and privates — were nowhere to be seen.

"Private Yamamura! We will now conduct a general inspection of these exhibits! Let us begin by counting the possessions of non-commissioned officers."

The pair began a careful reexamination of the premises. Items from non-commissioned officers were not entirely absent, but very few in number. They found a private's valuables bag and a corporal's thousand-stitch sash, but these items were largely obscured by the swords, papers and uniforms from the likes of generals and regiment commanders. There was a framed display of insignias worn by army and navy personnel, from full generals and admirals down to privates and seamen. They counted seventeen ranks. As a sergeant, Atsuo was number six up from the bottom and superior private Yamamura was number three.

"Yeah, it's always been like that for me," Atsuo muttered. "In the service or on the outside, always a noncom."

"Sergeants are a lot more important than privates, like me. I'm always a private, wherever I am. Except that now I'm a bum because they threw me out of the service."

"It's the same for you and me no matter what. We don't get anywhere."

They went outside. It was six o'clock and dark. Night had come, they were not really drunk anymore, and feeling hungry. They shortly found their way to Shinjuku, teeming with people, its neon streets raucous with commercials streaming from countless loudspeakers. After fortifying themselves with ramen and gyoza, they resumed drinking shochu, talking together with the warm fraternity of troopers from the same company who have fought hard battles together. What they actually said was just so much drunken banter, spoken and soon forgotten. They roamed the streets, stopping at one place after another. After Private Yamamura ran out of money, responsibility for picking up the tabs fell to Atsuo, who had a sound instinct for choosing low-cost, non-predatory establishments.

They wandered into the frenzied neon streets of gaudy, sleazy Kabukicho, passing underground theatres, army canteen style cabarets, "studios" offering private nude modeling sessions, jazz coffee shops, sing-along coffee shops and some establishments whose nature they could not ascertain and therefore could not muster the courage to enter. Then Atsuo remembered the bar in Golden Lane that Wakako had taken him to one night. He soon found his way inside its wooden door. Fortunately, there were a pair of unoccupied stools. They sat down.

"Whoa! Aren't you the mellow one! Something good come your way?" Mama said this to Yamamura, whom she evidently recognized.

"This here's my old war buddy. Last time I saw him was thirty years back," said Yamamura. His words came out in a drunken slur. Even the muscles of his face were loose and baggy from the alcohol coursing through his veins.

"And this is . . ." Mama said to Atsuo, searching his face for something to trip her memory.

"Does Wakako Ikéhata still come by?" Atsuo asked.

"Oh, right, You're Mr. Yukimori, the high school teacher who is really an auto shop foreman!"

"You remember!"

"I certainly do! All that talk about stalking deer on the Konsen plain was very interesting."

Though he seemed to have given her an earful, Atsuo could remember none of it. "And does Wakako come around?"

"She comes in now and then. Now that you mention it, she gave me a message for you. She said to give it to you if you came by. Here it is."

She handed him a tiny scrap of paper that looked like a page ripped from a pocket diary. It was a map in Wakako's handwriting showing the way to a coffee shop named "If."

"Hmm, wonder if she might be there."

"From what I hear, she's become a permanent fixture."

Atsuo paid the bill and grabbed Yamamura's arm. Now quite bent out of shape, the cotton liner reeled along behind, his mouth emitting flecks of foam.

It was a five-minute walk to If. Its lavish interior, divided up by glass partitions, was so tony-looking Atsuo hesitated before going inside. When he turned around, the cotton liner was not in sight. Atsuo went back outside, searched about the sidewalk, then gave up when he failed to locate his friend. He headed back for the inner reaches of If with the resolve of an army scout in enemy territory.

Strange young people swarmed about round tables. They were truly strange, outlandish, eccentric, bizarre young people. Some had very long hair that hung freely, some wore heavy makeup and necklaces or patchwork coats, some were of indeterminate gender. The air was oppressively thick with a mist of nicotine laced with alcohol, perfume, essence of armpit, oil, coffee, medicine, and gasoline. The coffee shop was long and narrow. As he moved toward the back, there were more and more foreign people about — white, black, and sundry shades in between. It didn't feel like Japan anymore.

There was a stairway to the second floor. As he was going up, he was hailed from above: "Mr. Yumikori." It was Wakako's voice.

The voice was the only thing about her that he could recognize as Wakako. She was wearing a red and yellow braided headband, bone earrings, oversize "dragonfly" glasses and some kind of strangely shimmering skin-tight garment that was red on the right and black on the left. Atsuo gaped. "What are you doing in that get-up?" he exploded.

"Never mind about that. Come on, this way." Wakako led the way to a dimly lit corner. Glimpsed from behind, her slim, softly curved hips were enticing.

Several couples were sitting around the kind of large circular tables one finds in any corporate meeting room. There was a huge white man with an arm around a classical Japanese beauty, an oriental man next to a blonde woman and two clearly intimate male-male couples.

"Are you working here?" Atsuo asked.

"No." Wakako shook her head, then ordered a couple of whiskey-and-waters from a waiter who had appeared before them.

"It's been quite a while. I was wondering how you were doing since . . . you know . . ."

"It's been almost exactly a month. You were a life saver." Wakako said, lowering her head in gratitude. A scent like honey wafted from hair that was gracefully waved. Previously he had always seen her with short hair. It was quite different now — long and luxurious.

"You did go home, didn't you?"

"Yes. I was a good girl for about two weeks. My father and my mother kept quiet too, like I was a sore spot they didn't want to touch. We had a couple of visits from detectives. They asked me a bunch of questions about — him. They wanted to know about our relationship, when I met him and where."

"Did you tell them the truth?"

"I didn't really have any choice. They had already checked at the inn where I was staying. There wasn't any room for lying. But I kept quiet about being in the demonstration. I said I was at the inn watching TV that day."

"That was good."

"After the detectives came my father suddenly started ordering me to go to the hospital. He said I wasn't over my sickness yet. My mother started in too. 'Go apologize to the doctor, get readmitted,' she said. They wouldn't leave me alone, so I left home again."

"How do you keep eating?"

"Work part time at the bar, teach Japanese to foreigners. Jean over there is one of my students," Wakako said, pointing with her nose toward the big white man, who acknowledged the gesture by pulling at his brown whiskers and performing a bow that came across as an impersonation of a man bowing.

"Well, how about you?" Wakako asked. "Business must be good for your shop these days."

"Me? Ah, the fact is . . ." Atsuo refreshed himself by downing his entire whiskey-and-water, then continued. "I was fired. The boss didn't like me. It happened just yesterday."

"Oh. Oh, dear." Creases formed in Wakako's young forehead. It was an expression of real distress.

"It's nothing to worry about. I have savings. I can get along for a while. Another job will turn up eventually."

"Is there really nothing to worry about?"

"Sure, I'm okay."

"That's a relief." A smile spread over her face like a wilting flower invigorated by a spring.

"The fact is, it feels pretty good to be out of work and free. Maybe that's something like how you feel being away from home."

"Unemployed man meets runaway girl," Wakako laughed. Her slight shoulders joined in the laughter. "Let me introduce you to Jean and Yumi."

The large man repeated his artificial bow. Atsuo returned the gesture, but commented to Wakako with a strained expression, "I'm no good at English."

At this, Jean said, "I'm no good at English either."

"Oh, you speak Japanese well," Atsuo replied.

"Oh, you speak Japanese well too," said Jean, repeating his bow again.

Wakako laughed. "Jean's French. He's only been in Japan for about six months."

"Getting that good in six months is an accomplishment."

Jean raised up the face of the woman he had his arm around. Her cheeks and forehead were smeared all over with something bright yellow that looked like clay pigment. When Jean removed his hand, the woman's head flopped down just as if she were dead.

"Do you suppose she's drunk?"

"She's zonked on sleeping pills."

Wakako said something to Jean in a foreign language and Jean took a bottle from an inside pocket of his leather jacket and put it on the table. There were white pills inside. He urged Atsuo to help himself. Atsuo refused, but instead extracted a cigarette from Wakako's pack and used Jean's lighter to get it going. Jean extracted five or six pills with a hairy hand and popped them into his mouth.

The crowd of patrons, white, black, and Japanese, had swelled alarmingly by the time Atsuo was tipsy on his fourth whiskey and water. As he sat at the big table, enveloped in smoke and body odors, he wondered if his fate was to be crushed beneath this talkative, multicolored crowd.

Wakako stood up. "Let's go someplace interesting." Jean also arose, along with his girlfriend and several others. Atsuo followed Wakako and they all trooped out of "If."

They crossed a main thoroughfare and turned into a back street. The procession entered a building via an unlit passageway. Groping their way forward, they came to a stairway leading down below street level. A door was opened, and their ears were assailed by unnaturally loud music.

The forms of numerous dancing couples were revealed in disconnected tableaus by frenzied light flashes, while a multicolored mirror ball turned reflections of the couples, the walls and the curtains into countless deep-sea fishes that swam round and round the room.

Wakako said, "Let's dance."

"I don't know how to dance."

"There's nothing to know. Just move to the music," she laughed.

He imitated her as she wriggled hips and shoulders, and was presently dancing. Her position changed moment by moment, compelling him to keep up, lest
someone come between them. Finally, he was holding her tightly and enjoying
the sensation of her breasts in rhythmic motion against his chest.

It was like being in an aquarium of people, colors and music floating together in a confused mass. There were all kinds of people, the black ones most
conspicuous. Most of the people were young, but there were some middle aged
and old men too. "You were right about this place being interesting," Atsuo said,
but his voice was drowned out by the noise.

Atsuo and Wakako had a beer at the bar. He was charged several times the
normal rate for beers, but he took it as a not unreasonable alternative to free
admission. A number of couples seated on chairs were embracing. The flashing
light created sharply etched images of their kissing figures, making them look
like sculptures on exhibit. Atsuo felt Wakako's warm breath at his ear: "You're a
marvelous dancer. I know a place even more interesting. Let's go."

She took him by the hand and pushed aside a heavy curtain, behind which
was a door. When the door closed behind them, they were suddenly in a very
different kind of room, quiet and peaceful. Red light emanated from somewhere
above. There was a gentle murmuring of air. About ten people were lying about
on the floor.

Wakako led Atsuo to a man siting on a sofa at the entrance and whispered,
"He gets the money." Atsuo counted out the named number of ten thousand
yen notes and the man gave them a small dish with four sugar cubes on it and
a couple of glasses of water. Wakako took the dish, raising it like a sacramental
offering and went to arrange cushions for them against a wall.

"There we are. Now we relax and suck on our sugar cubes."

"What is it?"

"LSD."

"Huh?"

"Never mind, just do as you're told. You have a high tolerance for liquor, so
three cubes for you and one for me. You can buy more if it isn't enough."

Atsuo reclined on his back as directed. Wakako lay down at his left side. He
fulfilled her orders by putting three of the sugar cubes in his mouth. They tasted
like nothing other than ordinary sugar cubes. He didn't like sweet things, so he
washed them down with water.

"Feel any different?"

"No, not really."

The red light emanated from an arm-shaped lamp projecting from the wall, illuminating floral wallpaper and casting its color across the people lying in various positions on cushions, sofas, and davenports. A nearly naked woman with fantastic patterns painted on her breasts and arms was being embraced by a completely naked black man whose torso and backside were painted white. There was also a man impeccably dressed in a suit with a well-adjusted necktie puffing on a cigar. Subdued conversations carried along the floor. The ticking of a heart-shaped clock on the wall was distinctly audible. It read twelve minutes past one.

When Wakako asked, "How're you doing?" and he began to reply, he suddenly found it difficult to exert the effort required to speak.

"Now that you mention it, it's like . . . well, like everything's too much trouble to bother with."

"That means it's working."

The surface of his body was hot. His face, arms, and chest were covered with some kind of hot film. It seemed that the film would slip right off if he just started peeling it. Beneath the skin he could feel the muscles and bones separate from one another, as if they had been dissected apart. He was afraid to move, lest the whole assembly of skin, flesh and bone fall apart. Cautiously, he tried moving one leg ever so slightly and discovered that his socks, underpants and trousers were tightly bound about his legs like iron hoops. He thrust his limbs straight out in an effort to burst open the hoops. With that, the surface of his body went from hot to cold. This was a pleasant, cooling sensation, like being coated in mint. A delicious shiver spread from inside his chest downwards. It was the same feeling as when he had sex. He caught sight of Wakako's face; the sight was so extraordinarily funny that he burst out laughing. Her nose was long and pointed like a Tengu, but her eyes were nested deep inside pits scooped out of the bottoms of her dragonfly glasses, and her neck was ridiculously long and thin, like it was made of silly putty.

"What the . . . !" Atsuo sputtered, laughing, but before he could get his mind around the oddness of the sight, he was distracted by another extraordinary sight. The floral pattern on the wall was bathed in hues of blue and purple, while the flowers themselves had floated off the wall and were swaying in the wind. Looking closer, he noticed that the surface of the wall was pulsing and warping, as if made of soft rubber. The floor and ceiling were also kind of rubbery . . . no, they didn't have the tautness of rubber — it was more like soft human flesh. But everything around him was changing so fast he didn't have time to marvel over any one remarkable event.

The vast expanse of a red sea appeared. Waves rising from its surface were bristly hard and pointed, like rose thorns. The water turned the bright cyan blue of a tropical sea. Then it was no longer a sea, but a cloud of blue glass beads silently expanding through space. The glass beads turned to velvety powder. Atsuo glided through this powder with the feeling that a core of pleasure within him was being caressed by powdered hands. The powder began to shine with dazzling brightness, each particle a minute blazing light bulb. The center of the light burst into blackness, revealing a colossal rock that contained numerous chambers on its surface, each one with luxurious furnishings inside. He thought this was surely the very same secret residence of the Furen hermit he had imagined as a child. The rock changed into a right-angled tall building that climbed up and up, like one of those New York skyscrapers he'd seen in pictures. Atsuo's body gained lift that sent him rising upward as well.

The images came faster and faster. Absurd forms appeared and vanished. Women large and small, like dolls, sailed through space, broke apart and scattered. A naked woman stood up, her ovaries visible; they had a bumpy surface like sea urchin roe. An undersea exploration scene. Underwater ruins. Prison bars. A mountain of bones. Cans of something. Headless men. A storm in a desert.

Days and months flew by at a mad pace. His body and mind were flying along at the same, somewhat frightening speed. The only trouble was that Atsuo wasn't sure whether or not all this was happening to him because his self had been divided up among a number of other people, and each one of those selves was having its own experiences, so there was no way to tell which of those experiences were really his. When his shoulder was shaken by Wakako and his eyes opened, that self and the self that continued to keep his eyes closed both reacted at the same time. He didn't even know if it was really Wakako or just an apparition of Wakako.

"How was it?"

"Kind of crazy."

"Is it still going on?"

"It's a lot less intense now, but it's still happening."

"What time do you think it is now?"

"Hmmm. Guess at least February must be over by now." The clock said it was a little past two thirty. "I wonder what day it is. Is that time morning or afternoon?"

"Wow! You really are out of it," Wakako laughed. "Only about one hour has gone by."

With that laugh, the span of several months that had passed ran backwards and found himself back in the present. Now he clearly recognized that Wakako still wore her dragonfly glasses and Indian headband and was lying right by his side.

He rose to his feet. His bones were leaden. The joints of his knees felt completely unreliable, like hinges that had lost their pins. He tried walking a couple of steps, but the air rasped so painfully against his cheeks he felt that if he continued walking they would be rubbed raw.

"Still feel funny," Atsuo said, and gave himself a violent rap on the head with his fist just as a certain cotton liner had done.

"It's late, come on, let's go," Wakako said and started walking. Atsuo saw her back rapidly receding in the distance. It looked as if he would be left behind, so he hastily followed after her. The doorknob stuck out like a club. The corridor outside it was like an extraordinarily long tunnel. Wakako turned, her nose projecting out so far it threatened to stab him, so he leaned back to get out of the way.

"It still feels funny."

"You'll come out of it, little by little."

They went through some rooms and hallways. He couldn't tell if they were the same places they had been the previous day. It was dark, and there wasn't another soul around. It seemed like they were going through a complex labyrinth. When they went up the stairs, each step was like a high wall that took his breath away just to bring one leg up to its top.

There were cars on the broad street. They all sped along at terrifying speed on a road that was all bumps. Some cars floated off the street and sailed up into the air, coming at Atsuo and forcing him to jump aside, again and again.

"You really are in a weird state," Wakako said, laughing. "You'd better give up and stay at my place. I'm renting an apartment off the west exit."

"I'm going home. All I've gotta do is get in a taxi. I'll be fine."

"Well, then I'll see you off."

Atsuo got into a taxi, under Wakako's guidance. As soon as the car was in motion, sweat began to pour from his body as if a tap had been turned on. He was assailed by a ferocious headache and nausea.

"Stop the car, please!" Atsuo screamed. He got out and began vomiting into the curb. Wakako was there, reassuringly patting him on the back. Nevertheless, his nausea didn't subside.

"Maybe it would be too much to try to make it all the way back home," Atsuo gasped weakly.

"I'm sorry. It was too big a dose." Wakako said. She supported him as they went into a hotel framed in pink neon that loomed before their eyes.

There was a double bed in the middle of the room. The walls and curtains were all pink. He continued sweating profusely and his head was splitting, but at least the nausea had subsided.

"This'll fix you up," Wakako said, bringing him a white pill and water. "What's this?"

"Chloropromazine. It stops the effects of LSD."

Atsuo took the pill as directed. He closed his eyes and soothing drowsiness overtook him. He slept.

The first thing he saw when he woke was Wakako's face wearing a worried expression. There was a damp towel on his forehead. Wakako readjusted it and smiled.

"How do you feel?"

"Just great!" Atsuo raised himself up on the bed. Actually, there was still some sleepiness in the core of his brain, but the headache was gone. He was thinking that he wanted to change out of his sweat-soaked shirt.

"There's a bath. Go get cleaned up and you'll feel better still."

"Good idea." Atsuo arose. His legs were back to normal. He had the strange feeling of having returned from a long journey.

Easing into the hot bathtub, the residual effects of the previous day's liquor and drug seemed to melt away. He did feel a lot better. He wrapped a towel around his waist and stepped out to find Wakako sitting on the bed. Her hair was in disarray and she looked sleepy.

"It looks like you didn't get any sleep last night."

"I got some," she said, pointing to the sofa.

"You were looking after me all that time."

"I just checked you out every now and then." She smiled, but her eyelids were swollen.

"Guess I must have been a handful. Thanks."

"You went through all that pain because I gave you too big a dose. It was my fault."

"Not at all. It was really fun. Honestly, it was wonderful, like being in a dreamworld. It stands to reason you would have to pay the consequences after having that much fun. Whatever that stuff is, it's dynamite. And I thought it was just sugar."

"They call them cubes. It's sugar impregnated with fifty microns of a drug called LSD. They come from Switzerland."

"I was completely out of my mind. You seemed okay, though."

"Uh-uh, I was crazy too. Your hands were chalk-white. I could see the bones."

"Now I've had it. She's seen though me!"

"I'm going to go have a bath too."

With a light skip, Wakako disappeared into the bathroom. The sound of water flowing began. He put his underwear on a hanger and suspended it from an air vent, then opened the curtain and looked outside. It was broad daylight, with bright rays of sunlight glancing from the windows of numerous buildings. It must have been around three a.m. when they arrived here. Now it was twelve thirty. He had slept nearly ten hours. He felt hungry and thought of going with Wakako somewhere for a meal. The telephone rang. He was informed that it was checkout time and that guests wanting to stay another day had to pay in advance. He said that was what he would do and in no time there was a bellhop at the door to collect. After paying, he reflected that this was a love hotel and he was staying with a young woman.

Having finally awakened fully, Atsuo gazed, cigarette in mouth, at Wakako's small shoes and green poncho. The mint-coated thrill of cool pleasure he had felt the day before stirred again in his nether regions.

Wakako was standing before the mirror, combing her damp hair. Perhaps she was aware he was watching as her slender fingers slowly moved the comb. Eyes radiant, she cast an inviting look from below her upraised arms. He arose lightly and approached, embracing her shoulders with both arms. He turned her to face him and kissed a pair of lips beside which a small mole resided. The next moment he lifted her — light and damp — and carried her to the bed. He began to undo the belt of her yukata. "No!" she protested, but moved close when he pulled it open and smiled when his lips went to a nipple that had hardened. She had shapely hips that narrowed to become a pair of gracefully long legs. He was having difficulty coming to terms with the unbelievable reality of having such a beauty in his arms. In an effort to check that it was really true, he said, "How lovely."

Without opening her eyes, she asked, "What's lovely?"

"You are more lovely than I can say." He entered into her, his own body pulsing with joy.

Afterwards, he was stroking her eyelid with the tip his tongue and admiring its shape. With this, her eyes opened, but they had a dreamy look.

"Let's go somewhere. Somewhere far away."

"Like where?"

"Like your home town in Hokkaido."

Then she closed her eyes again and was still.

~

Hills and forests slipped by the window. Snow covered hillsides that shone silver, white, and gray were sectioned off by wood fencing into plots that looked like pastures. The hills rose and fell, quite as if they were alive and breathing. Each of the dark trees was a giant. Wrapped in snow, they together formed a picturesque Christmas landscape. Occasionally one would give an angry shake that sent clumps of snow from its branches like flour being dumped from huge sacks.

Everywhere she looked, Wakako was struck by the breadth and depth to the hills and forests. They were quite unlike the hillocks and scattered woods of the Kanto Plain that she knew. It was harsh scenery, uninviting and lonely, but at the same time there was a feeling of human warmth. Just like Atsuo Yukimori, she thought, turning her gaze to the seat opposite hers.

"You aren't cold?" he asked. (It's the third time he's asked that question, she thought. First was when we arrived at Kushiro Airport, then he asked when we were in the train station waiting room. He seems taken with the idea that people from the south like me can't stand the cold.)

"No," she said, smiling. That raised a smile from Atsuo Yukimori. (His face changes to match my expression. It's like looking in a mirror.)

Forest emerged once again. Many of its trees evoked sympathy; with their broad trunks and bark in tatters, they looked like defiant beings dug in with grim determination against the cold.

"What are these trees?"

"Mainly Ezo spruce, with some Sakhalin fir here and there."

"They're awesome. And it's such a deep forest. Do animals live in it?"

"Of course," he said nodding.

He was looking at the forest as if seeing the distant past. Wakako liked that look. (It goes beyond what is there before your eyes, into the far distance. It sees things I can't see.)

"Once I ran into a fish owl in the forest somewhere around here. That was just before I went for my army recruitment physical."

"What's a fish owl?"

"A very big owl. It's the lord of the forest, an amazing bird. It comes out at night — huge, but the wings don't make any sound at all. I was walking in the forest all by myself. When it gets dark, you start feeling very alone. You get to wondering if you're going to run into a bear. That was what I was thinking when I spotted this bird up in a Sakhalin fir. I was about to jump out of my skin. I started running away, and it came after me. It comes diving straight down, without a sound. It hit me in the face with one of those big wings and disappeared."

"It must have been have been really scary."

221

"It was scary all right."

"Did you meet any bears?"

"No, never. I've been going for walks in the forest since I was little. I've met a lot of different animals — Ezo deer, red fox, otter, striped squirrel, Ezo flying squirrel . . . but I've never seen a bear. My father did though. He was one of the best when it came to hunting bear."

"It's like your real home is the forest."

"That's me. The forest and the marsh and the mountains and the sea."

"That kind of upbringing is as different as it gets from mine in the big city."

(He is built solid and strong, like one of those trees in the forest, that forever has to push back against its own environment just to live.)

He is old, twice Wakako's age, or about the same age as her father, but young compared to professor Ikéhata, whose stooped shoulders and habits were those of an old man. His hair is black, his back is straight, he moves agilely and his face, now ornamented with stubble, has a healthy sheen. He also has a wonderful sex drive. Wakako thought of the moment in his embrace when she had melted away to transparency. Being before him now, she felt as if she were about to be drawn whole inside him, and her pulse quickened in anticipation.

(This is something I never felt in the presence of the likes of Makihiko Moriya. Here is a man of substance. *Atsuo* — he could not have a more appropriate name. His body is certainly substantial, but there is more to it than that. He has a depth, the kind that only comes with time. There is so much there that I can't read. With Makihiko Moriya one glance is enough to see everything inside him — the defenses, the experiences, the feelings. Which is why he's not interesting.)

"Your whole upbringing was in Tokyo, wasn't it?"

"Yep. Born in Sendagaya, fourteen years at a private school in Yotsuya — nursery school through high school. Then I got into R. University, which is also in Yotsuya. All this time I've been shuttling between three stations on the same Chuo Line."

"It sounds wonderful to me. A trouble-free life is a good thing."

"Really? When nothing ever happens? I don't know anything. Not much, anyway. Sure, I have a little knowledge in chemistry and science, but nothing that's mine, nothing that you can only get by living your own life."

"That'll come. Your life is just beginning."

"I don't see that. It looks more to me like it's all over. Look, I've already tried to commit suicide."

"Suicide? . . . I wanted to die once too. Not once. Lots of times."

"You did?"

Wakako sighed. (He seems to have experienced everything. I get the feeling he's gone through so much complicated stuff, and the experiences I've had just don't compare.)

"You've suffered, too, haven't you? My suicide and all that don't amount to much. Listen . . ."

"No, don't go into it. Put that kind of talk away." Atsuo surreptitiously cast his eyes about their surroundings. There were few passengers in the car. The seats across the aisle from them were empty, but a conversation of high-pitched female voices could be heard from behind Wakako's seat. This was certainly no place to be discussing suicide.

"But I do want to talk about everything. With you," Wakako said with quiet sadness.

(This is someone who would accept me for what I am. Everyone else has their own take on me and they all get it wrong — my parents, the psychiatrists, Makihiko Moriya, my friends. Then the police show up and ask me a million questions about my relationship with Makihiko Moriya and my "political ideology." They all come after me with their questions. Why do you do that. Why do you think that. What's the reason. Then what did you do. And it always ends with criticism of me for being all wrong. You don't understand. You don't have common sense. You have a persecution complex. You think like a petty bourgeois. Radical students bring shame to their families. You should keep quiet and study. You should be a proper daughter. Everything I think is wrong, so I have to correct everything about myself. In other words, they order me, plead with me, demand that I become somebody else. I've had it with all of that. I can't keep living with it.)

"You seem troubled," Atsuo Yukimori said apprehensively.

"Fed up is what I am. Fed up with human beings."

"I know what you mean. I'm fed up with human beings too," he said, echoing her sigh. His face showed fine traces of suffering endured. It seemed to affirm that he accepted her inner being to its deepest recesses.

"That's Lake Akkeshi. It's all frozen now. They call it a lake, but that narrow channel over there connects to the sea. There's Akkeshi Bay over on the other side."

There were horse-drawn sleighs and automobiles on the lake. "That's convenient. You can just ride over the ice and back."

"Only in winter. That channel divides Akkeshi in two. When the ice melts you've got to take the ferry to cross. I have a nephew who works here as a fisherman."

"I know. That's Tetsukichi." Enjoying seeing him blink in surprise, Wakako continued. "Yukichi told me all kinds of things. Like about his father and mother in Nemuro. About you, too."

"Humph."

When something surprised Atsuo Yukimori his voice would come out in a gasp, as if something had cut off his air supply.

"He sent me a letter asking me to meet him. I answered, okay, as long as it's at the skating rink. He sent me back a self-addressed postcard with spaces to write in place, time and length of meeting. So I filled it in and met him for fifteen minutes. We went around and around the rink for fifteen minutes and when the time was up he left."

"So what did he have to say?"

"A lot more than I can easily summarize. He talked unbelievably fast and just kept talking on and on through the whole fifteen minutes. He said he was used to talking fast because there was always a fifteen-minute limit on visits, whether he was at the police station or in the reformatory."

"He told you about the reformatory? So what did he say about me?"

"Oh, I see. That's what's really bothering you. He told me lots of things. It was all very informative."

Atsuo Yukimori's eyes moved uneasily. Wakako found such expressions of his both amazing and charming. That kind of person was easier to like than someone who was always calm and unruffled. She recalled the expressionless professor's face always worn by her father, Kotaro Ikéhata. This face was just the opposite.

"Don't worry," Wakako giggled. "He didn't say anything bad. In fact, he said everyone looks up to his uncle, and he does too. He wants to be like you. There was only one thing . . ."

That was all it took for Atsuo Yukimori to regain his anxious expression. She intentionally drew out her response for a long moment to maximize the suspense, then smiled reassuringly when the worried look was at critical level.

"He said the only thing about his uncle is that he is very hard to understand. He could figure out his father and his brother and that president what's-his-name, but with his uncle it was a different story."

"Oh, is that it?"

"You look relieved, all of a sudden."

"No, it's just that I don't understand myself either. That isn't anything to be proud of, for someone my age."

"Not at all," Wakako said, offering an idea she thought she had read some-where with an air of certitude. "People who say they don't understand themselves are the ones who are giving serious thought to what they are. It's the ones who don't think about anything who believe they understand themselves. They assume their opinions are absolutely right and can't imagine why anyone would believe otherwise." An image floated up in her mind of her father, Kotaro Ikéhata, the intellectual-scholar-professor, determined never to show uncertainty.

"Yeah, that's quite right. Anyone your age who can understand that deserves credit. At my age I get to remembering what I've been doing all this time and wondering what it all means. I don't really know what kind of person I am, so all I can do is think about what I've actually done."

"I'd say that's important all by itself. A person's past is the most precious thing they have."

"And I just assumed young people thought only about now and the future. You're really different."

"That's because I'm always getting dragged back into my past. There's only a little more than twenty-four years' worth, but it's what I'm all about. It's all I have."

The sun fell into shadow. Desolate forest rolled on and on.

"That's snow break forest. It helps dispel fog too. They purposefully left it untouched all along the rail line," he said.

Silver-gray snow covered leaves the color of steel. What's missing from this scene is color, she thought. No reds, yellows, greens — none of the colors you see in print fabrics for spring wear.

Finally they were beyond the forest. A dark and rugged sea was in view. There was a band of whiteness on its surface that started near the horizon and traced a meandering line like a river that reached to the nearby vicinity.

"What's that?"

"Glacier."

"Is that what it is! This is the first I've ever seen it." Wakako pressed her forehead to the window to gaze upon the sight. As they sped along, more and more ice floes covered the sea, taking up the surface area, right up to the shore. Having thought of ice until this moment in terms of the uniformly flat skating rink, her eyes were caught by the unexpected variety of forms taken by the vast glacial sheets. There were triangular, square and round floes, grill-like networks of cracks, ice mesas and obelisks, smooth and jagged surfaces that were colored white, silver, pale blue and deep blue.

"It comes in from the Sea of Okhotsk and breaks up along the coast, and the fragments push against each other and pile up," Atsuo said.

"Can you get up on that ice?"

"You sure can. Let's try it some time."

They arrived at Nemuro Station, the last stop on the line. A dismally small handful of passengers alighted from the train's two cars and were soon gone from the station. Atsuo picked up all their luggage in both hands and started off first, easily carrying the load. It had been a spontaneous decision to make this journey, so packing had been simply a matter of gathering up items close at hand, but they had agreed on taking skates for a trip to the cold country. They exited the platform gate, passing cold-looking people sitting around a stove.

"I was expecting something a bit more impressive than this, for the terminal station of the Nemuro trunk line," Wakako said, and ran outside to look over the station building exterior. It was a squat wooden structure, with icicles hanging like teardrops, that stretched across the frozen ground of an abandoned plaza. The station seemed to sigh mournfully, looking less like the jumping off point of a journey than the end of everything.

Atsuo Yukimori came up beside her, issuing long, white breath trails as he spoke.

"Nemuro is a has-been town. It was in good shape during the war when it was a military base town for the Kuriles. But it was hit by an air raid. It's been losing population ever since the northern territories were lost after the war."

"Did your house burn down?"

"Yes, it did. A new one was built after the war, but it was sold off after my parents died, so now . . ."

"I know. Your sister and her family are the only ones here."

"Yukichi told you? That's right. We could go straight to her house . . . but I don't really feel like seeing her now."

"Because you're with me."

"No." Atsuo shook his head in discomfited denial, then nodded affirmation. "To be honest, that's part of it. But there's a lot more to it. The main thing is I got fired. That's a little awkward. So . . ."

"I want just the two of us together, too. So how about showing me around this town."

"There's not much to see."

"That's all right. I want to walk around the place where you grew up."

He checked their baggage, and they set out. Some snow remained along the roadside and in shady places, but the streets were clear.

It was only a short downhill walk to the harbor. A great many people were there fishing through holes they had opened in the solid sheet of ice that covered the sea. Wakako learned that they were fishing for surf smelt, and that an island with a red torii visible from shore was called Benten Island. Thick clouds in rapid transit above opened occasionally to let sunlight through. Stopping before a building made of tin sheeting that looked like a warehouse, he explained it was the site of the home he had lost in the air raid. Now it was a ship repair shop whose tin walls were corroding. The view inside through a half-rotted door revealed machinery bearing a heavy coating of dust.

They climbed a flight of stone steps and passed through a torii to a shrine that overlooked the harbor, now covered to the horizon with glacial ice. This was Konpira Shrine, where he had often played as a child. "That's about it. This is where I come from."

Wakako gazed down over the town. "You get the feeling it barely managed to crawl up out of the sea."

They retraced their path back to the station and got into a taxi. In scant moments the rows of houses gave way to a vast expanse of ice on the left. Atsuo told the driver to stop. "Let's look at the swans," he said, then explained that they were on the shore of Lake Onneto.

It was Wakako's first acquaintance with wild swans. She ran to the shoreline and looked intently at the great flock of birds on the water. Piercing cries of *kooo-kooo* cut through the breeze off the lake. A pair of swans took flight, their regal white forms winging across a bridge in the distance, over the forest and into the clouds. When a bird descended, legs like a pair of black boots effortlessly came forward as it settled contentedly on the water surface.

"Swans are really lovely birds."

"Like them, do you? There's lots more on Lake Furen."

"Let's go see."

"That's where we're headed."

Partway up a hill overlooking Lake Furen was house with a small sign in front that said "Traveler's Lodge — Peken." They alighted from the taxi at the bottom of the hill and encountered four large brown dogs tied up in front of the lodge. Wakako reflexively backed away, but the dogs didn't bark, merely turning surprisingly placid gazes upon them as they approached the building.

Atsuo announced himself at the entrance, but there was no answer. They went around to the back to find a man in a Russian style wool cap crouched by a sled. His sun-tanned skin was glistening with sweat.

"Can you put us up?" Atsuo asked him.

The man stood up and stretched with both hands on his back while he carefully scrutinized the pair, as if sizing up their worth. He was the same height as Atsuo, but pudgy, with short legs.

"Sure can. But there's no fishing, this time of year."

"That's okay. We'll have a room." Atsuo put down the baggage and bent over the sled.

"What's this?"

"A snowmobile."

"That's a novelty ... Well, what do you know! It's Japanese made."

"This is the first domestic model on the market. I bought it because it's more convenient than a dog sled, but it broke down yesterday. I don't know how to fix it."

"Let me have a look." Atsuo put his face close to the machine.

"Careful, sir. You'll get dirty," said the man, gesturing for him to stop.

"Let me at it! I'm an auto mechanic," Atsuo said, laughing. He borrowed a pair of work gloves and set to work, selecting wrenches and a hammer from a toolbox.

The man said to Wakako, "It's cold here. Go on inside," but she shook her head and looked on admiringly at Atsuo's practiced movements as loosened bolts and tapped engine parts.

He went through a process of dismantling and reassembling a number of times, then stood up and said, "Okay, let's give it a try," as he pulled a cord. The engine fired auspiciously and then was running.

"It's fixed! You sure know what you're doing, sir." The man made a gesture of amazement like Westerners often do, spreading both arms and opening his hands. Wakako spontaneously clapped her hands in celebration.

"It was the connecting rod, piston, and crankshaft. They were just a tiny bit out of line. The principle's just the same as a car. Nothing to it." Atsuo took off the work gloves. The man offered him some soap. He took it and washed his hands in the snow.

The man stood up straight on the snowmobile and gripped the handlebars. He checked the movement of the vehicle's two runners, then abruptly sped off with a stunning display of power as the back caterpillar treads kicked up a blizzard. He took the vehicle to the far end of the snow-covered field and returned with impressive speed. Then it was Atsuo's turn. He careened left and right, tracing arcs with the same relish he knew from gliding over ice on skates.

Wakako ran forward. "Let me ride too." Atsuo stood and she sat, her arms tight around his waist. The moment they took off, the man shouted after them, "Be careful around the *shiokiri* — the ice is thin there!"

"What does that mean?" Wakako shouted over the thunderous roar of the engine.

"*Shiokiri* is the current. Don't worry. I know this lake inside out."

The machine vibrated fiercely as the speed mounted. Wakako held her arms tightly around his waist, determined not to be thrown off. His broad back was strong, dependable. Pressed against it, she felt enveloped by its strength. The lodge fell off into the distance and the sweeping snowscape stretched outward in all directions. Up ahead, an island covered with a dark woods was approaching. It seemed they were somewhere in the lake's center. The snowmobile bore left to avoid the island. A needle-like spray of snow dust stung her face.

"Hold on tight!" he said. At the same moment the snowmobile shook violently, bucked into the air and came whizzing down onto the ice again.

"Wrinkle in the ice. I couldn't swerve clear in time," he said. He slowed down and steered carefully to the banks of the lake. It was a desolate spot, all the trees dead and blackened as if burned.

"We're at one end of Shunkunitai Island. This is Fox Forest. There used to be beautifully dense growth of Sakhalin fir, with fox living here. Now look at it — Sakhalin straw. It's a sad sight." He ran his fingers over one of the tree trunks, sunk in fond recollection of days gone by.

"They call that spit of land Benzai point. I used to play here a lot as a kid. I made a little boat and crossed over to here."

"You made a boat by yourself?"

"Yeah. A dugout — a hollowed out Sakhalin fir. It must have taken about two months to build. I was in the sixth grade."

"Still in grade school!"

"Yeah, I was just a little kid. They filled me with stories about how it's so dangerous for little kids to go on the river or the lake or into the marsh. So, being a little kid, that was naturally exactly where I wanted to go."

Again and again, his eyes slowly traveled up and down the delicate interplay of lake and hills that formed the landscape, teasing out one memory at a time. She had been thinking they were all alone on the lake, but now she could make out little black specks moving about, back near the middle of the ice.

"There're people here."

"They're fishing."

"Do they poke holes through the ice?"

"That's it. Let's go check them out. This time you drive." He gave her a rundown on how to run the snowmobile.

It was as easy to drive as an amusement park go-cart. Turn the right handlebar and — wheee! you go faster. With his strong arm across her back and no obstacle on the wide-open snow field, there was no reason not to go zooming straight down the middle, spewing clouds of snow dust left and right.

Everything was white brilliance that sparkled in the sunshine. The throbbing of the engine resonated through Wakako's body, rippled through her breasts to her brain and emerged as a spontaneous cry of joy. When she turned, he held her waist fast — wordless support that reassured. She ran the vehicle across the lake in one direction, crossed once again at right angles to the first path, then drove up near the people she had spotted.

Two young fishermen were raising a net from a hole in the ice about three meters long and twenty centimeters wide. Fish small and large were being tossed one after another into a plastic basket.

"Okay to look?" Wakako asked as she peered into the basket. Atsuo told her the fishes' names — surf smelt, pond smelt, great sculpin, and cucumber fish. She gave the latter a sniff and discovered it really did smell like a cucumber.

Yukimori addressed the fishermen. "Catching any good ones?"

"Nah, nothing at all. Fishing's terrible these days."

"Still, this here's a good take. You even got sculpin."

"Hardly ever getting big ones. A little while back we weren't doing so bad, though."

It was hard for Wakako to make out their vernacular speech, but fascinating to listen to him instantly revert to being one of the local folk.

The young men gave him several fish. "Let's have this served up tonight in some sculpin soup. Great stuff!" he said happily.

They went back to Fox Forest, but this time came off the lake and crossed over to the seashore. The water was covered over with ice floes. Immense ice blocks of all shapes were closely jostling one another. They extended far back to the open sea. Wakako ran from the beach onto a floe and into a grotesquely shaped labyrinth. She dashed down corridors, through gateways, past walls, crags, and pillars, and climbed stairways and mountains.

"Hey, that's dangerous!" he yelled, chasing after her. She let him get close, then dashed away out of his reach. Frustrated, he took off again, determined to catch her. She pulled away and ducked out of sight into a yawning cavern. He ran past and she revealed herself with her laughter. But this time she was backed into a corner.

"Now I've got you!" Wakako was captured, held tightly so she couldn't move and kissed full on the lips. They reclined against a fortuitously placed ice slab shaped like a sleeping berth. There they embraced for a long time. Their backs and buttocks were chilled by the ice while lips, breasts, and loins burned hot. Having one's body so divided between warmth and cold was an altogether curious feeling. The cold wind chafed at their ears. The ice floes groaned loudly as they scraped together.

Wakako flinched at the shrill sound. "The ice is jealous of us."

The ice floe was shaking slightly. He looked closely at the vast white vista and noted that it was undulating ever so slightly. Each vertical movement was producing squeaking sounds, like a rising chorus of chirping insects.

"C'mon, let's go out to the end of this ice floe!"

"No, let's go back. When the wind's up, the ice could take us out to sea," he said and took her hand to urge her along.

They went back toward the land. About a meter's width of water had opened up between the shore and the ice they were standing on. He jumped across first, then reached out to take Wakako's hand.

"That was close. A little while longer and we might have been heading out to sea."

"That's what I wanted to happen. I wanted us to go far away together."

"That's no joke. There's been a lot of people who went fishing from ice floes and ended up disappearing."

"I want to disappear," Wakako persisted. She was more than half serious. Once she had tried suicide, but the attempt failed for lack of enough sleeping pills. Had the option of dying on an ice floe been available, she would have gone for it.

The sun went down shortly after they arrived back at the lodge. Dinner was served in a large room with an old-fashioned potbellied stove in its center. There was a luster to the darkness beyond windows that were misted on their outsides. Sticks crackled in the fire as they were fed in by the master of the house. The two guests were enveloped by warmth and the charm of the pastoral setting. The master brought a steaming soup kettle and place it on the stove.

"Hoo! Sculpin soup!" Atsuo Yukimori clapped his hands in delight. At the same time, his knees were jiggling. Wakako was amused to note that he had been infected with her own mannerism.

The firm flesh of the sculpin was delicately flavored from just enough immersion in miso. "Mmmm, good," Wakako said with feeling.

Yukimori delivered a commentary on how the region prepares sculpin soup. Only freshly caught fish can be used. It should be cut into large chunks, discarding only the liver and intestine, rubbed in salt to firm the meat and let stand for thirty minutes before cooking. Potatoes, green onions, carrots, and burdock root should be cooked separately, then mixed in with the miso.

"You sound like you're from these parts," the master said. He didn't wear a cap, but his hair, thinning and going white, had the charm of a cap especially made for his tanned face.

"That's right. I come from Nemuro."

"Yes, that follows. I'm from Tokyo, myself."

"Is that so!" Wakako exclaimed.

"Would you be from Tokyo, too, ma'am?"

"Right again," Wakako said in a small voice.

For an instant the master's eyes darted inquisitively over the middle-aged man and his young woman.

"Why did you come here from Tokyo?" Wakako asked.

"For the simple reason that I was sick of Tokyo. I quit my job and moved to Hokkaido. I worked at a ranch for about five years, then I opened this lodge the year before last. I guess I'm what you would call a salaryman dropout."

"You're lucky to live in such a beautiful place."

"I think so, too. I certainly don't regret leaving behind the boring job I had, and that murky air in Tokyo, and the people who never stop giving you a hard time. Not a bit."

"Are you single?" Atsuo Yukimori asked.

"Yes. Actually, I was living with a woman in Tokyo, but she didn't want to leave the big city, so we split up."

The wind blew harder. There was a sound like scattered beans hitting the window glass. It was snow being blown from the surface of the lake. A panorama of stars blazed across open sky.

"It's like millions of cut jewels!" Wakako whispered.

"There's nothing like it in Tokyo, is there?" the master said. "That hit me when I first came to Hokkaido. I was thinking, 'So that's how a night sky really looks!'"

The flames in the stove painted the master's face red on one side. Atsuo Yukimori became a silhouette in front of a bookshelf. When Wakako moved beside him, his arm went around her shoulders. Every volume was a reference work or picture book about the natural environment of the region — its birds, animals, grasses, flowers, edible plants, sea plants, fish of the northern seas, rivers, plains, marshes, forest, trees, insects, the night sky, the weather.

"I see we've come to a house of learning," she said.

The master took a book from a shelf. "I wrote this one," he said. Entitled *The Four Seasons of Furen*, its title page bore the name of a publishing house in Kushiro.

"It's a journal of my own observations and research on this region's natural environment. But it hasn't sold at all. It all comes down to my being an outsider — someone who sees things differently than the natives."

"What's different?"

"To me, nature is something precious, to be preserved. The people who were born here see land as a resource that should be developed. They want to open up unproductive marshland and turn it into pastures or residential tracts that turn profits. There is a national and prefectural plan now in the works to go into the virgin forest around Lake Furen and cut down everything in sight to make way for new dairy farms. If they go ahead with it, we will lose one of the few virgin forests left in Japan. It will be taken over by humans and cows. That inevitably leads to release of cow dung that spreads pollution through the rivers. I spoke out against that in my book. Someone organized a boycott. I was getting threatening telephone calls. Someone put up a sign in front of the house that said, 'Outsiders, get out!'"

"They're not doing right by their own beautiful heritage."

"That way of thinking is regarded as outsider sentimentalism."

"I'm from this territory. I know what's in their heads. It's true that you pick up a kind of hostility toward nature. There's fog in summer, it's cold in winter — there's wind and snow and not much sun. Nature comes down on you hard in a place like this. It makes you want to conquer nature, make life easy, turn things around, promote business, have money coming in. But you also want to preserve nature, harsh as it is, because it's your home. You want to pass it on to the next generation. You have those two conflicting feelings, and they're both strong."

Wakako looked out at the moonlit night sky once again. "You would think there would be a way to work out some balance between the two." She opened the glass door and stepped outside.

Atsuo Yukimori came running after her. "You'll catch cold!" The two stood in the pitilessly frigid night air. "Aren't you cold?" he asked.

"Yes, I am!" she said, stiffening. Then she burst into laughter. "You've been asking me that over and over, and this is the first time I really am cold."

They went back inside. Once in a while the firewood snapped loudly and scattered live ashes. The master brought in a selection of homemade wines — cowberry, black crowberry, monkey pear, mountain grapes. Wakako took to the fragrant, ruby-red cowberry wine.

"Young folks generally like cowberry wine," said the master, as he refilled her empty glass. "There's a group of girl students who have been coming here every year just so they can have it." The master talked about hunting for cowberries in the forest. There was a secret spot he had found where they grew in profusion, providing him with a supply year after year. There were well-heeled folk in Sapporo who prized the berry as a longevity tonic. He could sell to them for three thousand yen per kilogram. He could easily pick twenty kilos in a day, meaning sixty thousand for a day's work.

The master was drinking along with them. Eventually, his bald pate reddened. When Wakako began feeling rattled at being the object of frequent lustful glances, she seized the first opportunity to beckon Atsuo Yukimori to their room.

"Sleepy, are you?" he asked, looking at his wristwatch. It was about five minutes past eight o'clock.

"No, not at all. I just wanted to be alone with you."

"Fine. Let's talk. Just wait while I get us some drinks and snacks."

"Don't. Let's not drink any more tonight, so we can talk. You always forget what was said while you were drinking."

"Now that you mention it, that's true. Okay, no more saké tonight. Let's just talk for hours and hours."

"I know what you're going to say next. 'Are you sleepy? Are you cold? Are you tired?'"

"I think you're right again. Okay, I give up."

"Ain't sleepy, cold or tired. Not me."

"That's a good girl." He turned off the light and sat next to Wakako. There was a kerosene heater before them, a blue flame flickering within. Somewhere in the distance a thunderous snap reverberated for an instant and was swallowed up in the stillness of night.

"What do you suppose that was?"

"One of the trees in the forest split apart. It happens a lot when the temperature gets down around thirty below. The moisture in the trunk freezes and it just rips open the whole tree."

"That's enough to make your hair stand on end." The next moment, Wakako cried out, "Ooh!" as a star flashed a yellow streak and fell out of view.

"That's a shooting star," he said, in surprise. "Was that the first you've seen?"

"The first. Everything that's happening is new to me," Wakako said, brushing her face against his stout arm. "First experiences are wonderful. I want to see and hear and touch lots and lots of new things."

"What do you say we borrow that snowmobile again tomorrow, cross the lake and take a trip up the Furen River?" He put his arm softly on her shoulder. "There's an immense marsh around Lake Furen that you normally can't get into, but in winter it freezes all over so you can go in pretty much wherever you want. You could drive a truck through it. But you do have to be careful where the current flows. Lots of people have taken their cars in to fish and they fall in and that's it, they're dead."

"What's under the ice?"

"Eel grass. Once your legs get tangled up in it, there's no getting out. You go missing until spring comes." He quit talking. After several drags on his cigarette, he began anew. "Fact is, my nephew Yukichi has gone missing. Have you heard anything from him?"

"No. What makes you think he would get in touch with me?"

"No particular reason," he said brushing some ash that had fallen onto his shirt. "I was just wondering if he might."

"When did he disappear?"

"Just a few days ago. Look, did Yukichi say anything to you? You know, something that might suggest a reason for him to drop out of sight."

"Hmmm . . ." Wakako pondered. "Well, he was saying being a mechanic was all wrong for him. He said he wanted to be a fisherman. And he said he wanted to go to Raúsu. That was because they need men in Raúsu in winter for the walleye pollack season."

"Raúsu? He didn't say Nemuro?'"

"No, he said Raúsu. I'm sure of it."

"Thanks. That makes sense."

"Do we have to go to Raúsu to look for him?"

"I've got to find him. You see, four hundred thousand yen of company money turned up missing the same time Yukichi disappeared. They think he took it."

"That's awful. He's a good person. He really is."

"Yes, he is, but he's got weaknesses. That's what landed him in a reformatory."

"I'll help you look for him. He said he loved me, I'm sorry to say."

"Yukichi loves you." Yukimori looked out into the darkness, a complicated expression on his face. The wind suddenly seemed to be blowing harder.

"I don't love Yukichi. There are no second thoughts about that. I'm in love with . . ."

"Listen, there are some things I have to confess to you," Yukimori said, interrupting her for some reason. "A whole lot of things. Much more than I can possibly cover in just a day or two."

"Such a long confession? But I don't have to hear it to know what kind of person you are. I know that very well."

"No. No, you don't." Yukimori sighed a deep sigh born of inner torment.

"You don't know about me at all. I have a hideous past. There are a lot of terrible things . . ."

"Actually, my past is ugly too," Wakako said. "My confession would be pretty short, though."

"There isn't anything you have to say," Yukimori said sympathetically. "A lot of times you only cause grief for yourself because of something you said."

"No, do you know what's worse than that? Speaking your mind and not having anyone understand. That's what always hurts me the most."

"Well, all right then. Let's hear it." He lit a cigarette. Wakako took it and used the burning end to light her own cigarette. A wind arose that pushed against the windows with such force snowflakes came into the room. In her mind, Wakako confronted the twenty-four years she had passed at the old house in Sendagaya. The seasons had come and gone, rapidly in some ways, but interminably long in others. She could make no more sense of those years than she could sort out a box of worthless junk.

~

The layout of the house where I was born and raised is quite simple. On the south side is a garden with many trees. There is also a pond. It's a traditional Japanese garden in something-or-other style. While my grandfather was alive he had a gardener come in to take care of it. That garden is a point of pride with my father. He has a high-minded speech about it for students who come to the house, but it hasn't really been tended at all since my grandfather died. It's gone pretty much wild. My father says it's a "recreation of the Musashino natural environment" as if it was something special.

A parlor and my father's study look out over the garden. Then there are four rooms at the end of the corridor, one each for me, my younger sister, my younger brother and my parents. That arrangement comes from my father's educational philosophy. The idea is children become independent thinkers when they have their own rooms. I had my grandfather's old room, right next to the toilet. The smell penetrated the wall and so did everyone's toilet noises. That's the room where I grew up. It's on the north side, where it's dark. My brother's room faced south. He had a much better room, but I never once raised a complaint about it. I wasn't a very demanding child, from infancy on. Always the well-behaved child, satisfied with what she was given.

I grew up as what is generally called a good little girl. I started in private schools from kindergarten. My traditional girls' education was piano and Japanese dance. I was totally devoted to all of it. My grades were up near the top of the class. I was happy when I was quietly reading science fiction about outer space. Being the eldest girl, I babysat for my sister and my brother. In middle school, I became interested in home economics and started helping my mother with the cooking. In high school I was in the tennis club. Got a suntan. Healthy as could be, and a sunny personality too.

I had good handwriting, so by my second year of high school my father was having me write the final drafts of his research papers. He said I was very useful. I learned a lot of legal terms and little-known kanji. I could amaze my friends with legal jargon. Like, for example, anyone would understand if I said something like "stolen goods" or "willful negligence." Well, lawyers don't use those words, even though they are perfectly good. Lawyers have their own special words that mean the same things, but are used by no one in the world but them. Then there are legal concepts the average person might not know. Ever heard of "mistaken self-defense?" That is what you say when you decide that someone acting in self-defense stepped over the line and committed a criminal offense.

My good girl persona started to crumble in my third year of high school. Very suddenly I became interested in doing chemical experiments. I got retorts, a gas burner, and a whole shelf full of chemicals in bottles. I was having great fun in my room doing all kinds of experiments. One day I was analyzing an inorganic sample of something. Every kid who is into chemistry does it. I got carried away and didn't come out for dinner — it was a rule that the whole family gathers for dinner. I mistakenly ignited a bottle of ethyl ether and it exploded. The fire spread to the shoji, I screamed and my mother and brother came with buckets and pails. They threw water on the fire, but the water got into a bottle of concentrated sulfuric acid and that made the fire blaze up worse.

Fortunately, a neighbor called in a fire truck. Firemen know their business. It was all over in no time. The outcome was my room and the toilet next door burned and there was a flood in the corridor and entryway. My father came home when he heard about the emergency. He took one look at me and started bawling me out.

"My research papers are kept here! Don't you know they can't be replaced?"

I was burned in the fire, I lost textbooks and other books and my diary — most of all, the chemical equipment and supplies I bought with money saved from jobs worked on school vacations were damaged or lost. He didn't show any concern about me at all. All he could think about was his research papers. As a matter of fact, the first thing he did when he returned home was rush into his study to check that his papers and books were safe. He kept glaring at me and shouting.

I rebelled when he said "You're only a girl! You've got no business doing chemistry experiments!"

"Why shouldn't girls do chemistry experiments?"

"That's for men to do!"

I guess he realized for himself that comment was going too far, because he kept quiet after that, but I didn't. I was incensed. I had a lot to say, so I started screaming. It's wrong to make gender distinctions about kinds of work. You tell me some department of literature is enough for a girl's education, but that's just prejudice. I'm going to get into an engineering school and study chemistry.

That was too much for my father. He said, "That's enough!" and slapped my face.

That one senseless act blew away all my confidence in him. It was the end of my career as a good girl. Of course, the fire was my fault. He had every right to criticize my carelessness. The fire department gave me quite a lecture. They made me write out a letter of apology. I don't have any resentments about that. I was in the wrong. But I couldn't forgive Professor Kotaro Ikéhata's attitude, from his "You're only a girl!" comment to that slap in the face. I didn't cry when he did that. I just glared back at him.

I flunked my university entrance exams. I think the shock from the fire had something to do with it, but I wasn't upset about that failure because I was determined to get into engineering school to spite my father. I enrolled in an exam prep school and concentrated on my goal.

About that time my mind started to become disorganized. I don't know why. It was the first time I ever experienced mental problems. Mornings were the worst. I would wake up feeling like the insides of my head were all mixed up and stinking, covered with excrement. When that started, it would just go on and on until late afternoon. There was no point in going to classes because I couldn't concentrate on what was being said. On those days there wasn't anything else to do but go to a coffee shop. I got to know Sa, a tall fellow in my prep school who frequented the same coffee shop. Sa was in his third year studying for entrance exams. He had vowed to get into a national medical school by the time he was thirty. He was always carrying word cards — he would glance at them once in a while, even while talking with me. I went along when he invited me to a hotel. He was surprised that I was a virgin. I refused the next time he wanted to go to a hotel. I didn't want to — there wasn't any particular pleasure in doing it with him. Sa invited me again a few times after that, then gave up. Pretty soon he was into smooching with another girl, and he wasn't shy about it when I was around.

Men followed me around. There was a middle-aged man with silver hair who was staring at me on the train. I changed cars, and he followed me. He stayed behind me until I went into the prep school. He was waiting when I came out. He started following me again. I was really angry. I told him I was going to report him to the police. He said I was adorable when I got mad. He bowed his head very politely and asked me to go with him. There was another young man who sidled up and started stroking my backside. I don't mean furtively, but aggressively. He said, "Don't play hard to get, just follow me." Men followed me with their eyes. Their expressions and the way they acted were like they had nets and were waiting for the chance to throw them over me.

Basically, this was annoying, but at the same time there was a small element of gratification. Then one day it hit me that my body was emitting a special kind of odor that was causing my presence to have some kind of effect on men. I thought that because I had spent my whole existence steeped in the odor from the toilet next door, that was the odor coming from my body. To a certain kind of man that was sexually attractive, but most people found it unpleasant. That explained why people would hold their noses when I approached, or groan or look away, or be standoffish.

I hated going outdoors. I shut myself up in my room. Pretty soon I was in there all the time. I stayed shut up in my room until one day my parents came barging in like policemen with an arrest warrant. They lectured, admonished, entreated, and finally brought me to a psychiatrist.

The psychiatrist said there was nothing to worry about, that there were many patients like me. He gave me pills that make you sleepy and drain away all your energy. In that state, it was too much for me to even be bothered about how I smelled. The doctor said, there now, your condition has improved. He told my parents, your daughter is sexually frustrated. He advised them to get me married. They followed his advice and set up a meeting with a prospective husband for me. I had to go to the lobby of the Imperial Hotel to meet the man. As usual, I was groggy and listless on my pills. He took me to a Kabuki play. The next day I told them I never wanted to see him again. We went through the same thing three more times. Each time they had me meet a different man and each time I refused after one meeting.

I started ice skating on pure happenstance. It was a hot day in the middle of summer. I was going to a swimming pool, but I got to thinking my body odor would make it unpleasant for people. I couldn't bring myself to go into the pool entrance. I turned back and caught sight of the skating rink signboard. It was a burning hot outside and I was imagining cool ice. And there probably wouldn't be that many people at the skating rink. That's better than a swimming pool, with everyone bobbing around together like potatoes in a tub for washing. But what made me most happy about the idea of a skating rink was there would always be a wind to blow away my body odor. I was tottering around on my skates when a middle-aged man came up and showed me the basics. That was you.

After two years of prepping, I passed the exam for the chemistry department of R. University's school of science and engineering. I started classes at the Yotsuya campus. That body odor neurosis wasn't bothering me anymore, but something else started up that was real trouble, and it ended up getting me put into a mental hospital.

The students of the science and engineering school are mostly male. The two or three female students in the classes were conspicuous. The students interact a lot in experiments and exercises. Several male friends were always hovering around me. There was always an uncomfortable feeling that someone was staring at me. One day we were making models of molecules for inorganic chemistry experiments. You make the molecules by putting together plastic balls with sticks. Suddenly the body of the guy standing next to me got on my nerves. The sight of his right hand holding a plastic ball looked creepy, like it was a lizard, or maybe an alligator. And his chin stuck out. I don't know why, but it looked like a rotten apple. It was so startling I jumped back away from him. Then I took a good look at his face. He was asking "What's the matter?" like he didn't understand, but that's not what his expression said. He had a sardonic smile and spite in his eyes. It looked to me like he was gloating over my distress. I tried really hard to concentrate on making the model and forget about him, but it was no good. My eyes kept going back. The parts of his body looked grotesque. They reminded me of all kinds of horrible plants and animals.

Something had gone wrong with my equipment for perceiving the world. I can say that now, but at the time I believed it was the world that was all wrong. I didn't know what to make of it. I looked at that guy's body, then I looked at the bodies of all my classmates in the room. It was like their clothes all fell off so they were stark naked. Those naked bodies were really ugly. I hadn't realized before how grotesque the human body was. Faces, hands — they all looked so weird. More than anything else I was wondering why in the world men should have such an unsightly thing as a dangling penis.

The laboratory wasn't a laboratory. It looked like a strange warehouse with the columns, walls, and ceiling all hideously distorted. I laughed out loud. I suppose my laugh was quite unexpected, under the circumstances. The professor was writing chemical symbols on the blackboard and everyone was paying attention. That laugh went sailing through the silence in the room like bird shit falling from the sky. The professor drew back, surprised, like he was trying to avoid the shit. That looked so funny I laughed again. I was convulsing to the point of getting a stomach cramp. That hurt, so I screamed.

"That stuff about everything around you changing, was it like when we had those sugar cubes the other day?"

"Something like it, but it's not the same thing. With LSD everything looks changed, but the changes keep going on and on. My condition was more stable. The professor seemed to think I was joking around with all those male students. I said 'Excuse me,' and went outside, but everything out there was changed just the same as in the classroom. The students were walking around, like they were naked, and it was all just so funny."

It seemed more like a Nazi concentration camp than a university, as if there was a signboard somewhere that said "Learning is strength," and all the men and women wore the same prisoner clothes and were shooting around aimlessly, like the steel balls in a pachinko machine.

All of a sudden I couldn't understand what it is that makes a university a university. Do buildings and professors and students make a university? Or is it that everyone thinks it's a university, so it is? That brought me to this idea — it's an organization of arbitrary human relationships formed for the purpose of having a university. All you have to do to join is answer the questions on a test sheet. That seemed pretty funny to me. You are safe and secure in the organization as long as you don't think about anything, but the minute you start having doubts, or you start questioning the organization or want to destroy it, you become a traitor, a fugitive, a rebel, an outsider, unnecessary, alien. The organization denounces you and you are watched and persecuted. I don't know why, but organizations have that kind of cruelty, that precision mercilessness, like machines have. Once you are pushed out from the organization, you aren't forgiven.

All of this has something to do with why I joined the demonstrations on the day of the Tower— or more to the point, why I got so caught up with Makihiko Moriya and all those people with their "revolution" and why my excitement about it quickly cooled, as excitement usually does. I wanted revenge on organizations. I think that was my number one motive for joining.

I stopped going to classes and holed up in my room. They had a new one built right after the fire. It was chintzy, but the walls were thick and it was quiet — you couldn't hear the toilet noises. I put three padlocks on the door, covered the window with paper and stayed buried under my futon. I only got up to go to the toilet or for meals. As always happens when my head gets screwed up, I developed a ravenous appetite. I wanted to eat something hard — like crunching on a pile of rice crackers. I realized I was getting fatter by the day. Swelling up into an ugly lump gave me an excuse for not going outside. One day my father suddenly came in and ordered me to go to a mental hospital. Yes — "Go to the hospital," just like that, an absolute order. I said okay, I would. That was the last reaction he was expecting. He was ready for another bout of lecturing, persuading, demanding, and pleading. Professor Ikéhata was so surprised at his daughter's compliance, he gave what was for him a record performance as a caring father. He said, "Yes, go. You are sick. The best thing to do for sickness is let the doctor cure you."

There were four patients in my room, including me.

Ah spent the whole day lying down in her futon, covered up over her head. She wasn't sleeping at all, though. She peeped out bright-eyed from the corner of her futon at everything around her. Nurses making their rounds called out to her, but she wouldn't so much as twitch in response. She got up when mealtime was announced, like she had been waiting all along for that moment to arrive. That was when I realized Ah was a young girl like me, who had gotten heavy. She had been doing the same things I was doing at home, so I felt friendly toward her.

Eh sat at a small desk by the window reading a book. Her hair was disorderly. She must have been past fifty — It was half white. Her face had a ladylike sort of look. She was totally absorbed in reading. Whenever her reading glasses slid down, she pushed them firmly back into place with her left index finger. I tried speaking to her, but she just said, "I'm reading now," like I was being terribly annoying. But she didn't hesitate to say to things to me out of the blue like, "Hey, what time is it?"

Uh was hardly ever in the room. She would either be out, tirelessly walking up and down the hallways, or watching the TV in the lobby that was always on. She laughed a lot and talked a lot, but the conversations would go like this:

"So what's your name?"

"Me? I'm Uh!"

"And how old are you?"

"Gosh, I wonder how old I am."

"When did you come to the hospital?"

"I don't know. A long time ago. No, that's not right. It was yesterday."

One day, early in the morning, suddenly there was loud singing from somewhere, like a radio had been switched on. It turned out to be Uh. She had quite a good voice, and she carried the melody very well. She went through three full stanzas of a song. I clapped and said "Great singing!" and she parroted it right back — "Great singing!" — and went off walking all the way down the corridor. A nurse came and scolded her for disturbing the other patients who were still sleeping. She came back quietly into the room and dropped right off to sleep.

Another morning at wake-up time, I got out of my futon and my brassiere, slip, and suit were gone. Uh had filched them and put them on. I said "Give me my clothes back!" and she laughed and said, "Give me my clothes back!" A nurse came and made her take them off, after she had gone tripping off down the hall, ignoring the fact that I was really upset, wearing my clothes and imitating my manner of walking. She looked just like me walking up and down the hallway.

Eh had permission to leave the hospital on her own to go borrow books from the public library. One day she came back with an armful of large roses. She went around collecting flower vases, bottles and cans and put the flowers in them. The head nurse came in and started scolding her, as well she might. She had cut off half the roses in the flower bed by the hospital entrance. As punishment, they took away her permission to leave the hospital premises. She ran out of books to read immediately, so she just sat idly at her desk, talking to herself a lot. It sounded like she was talking to someone, maybe in outer space or some faraway country. I found this interesting, so I asked her who she was speaking with. She said, "I'm talking now" and waved me away with her hand, as if I was being terribly annoying.

As far as my own condition was concerned, I didn't have the slightest idea what was wrong with me. The doctor interviewed me time and again, but I never gave really meaningful answers. I didn't tell him about the weird happenings in my laboratory class or anything about organizations. I just said I felt depressed and didn't feel like going to class. He gave me his verdict after several of these sessions. "You have melancholia. It's called 'May depression syndrome' — you become disenchanted with university shortly after you start classes." He guaranteed I would get over it if I took medicine. The medicine was pills that made me so sleepy I couldn't get out of bed all day.

"I wonder if that doctor was the one I met. At the hospital in Ushigomé."

"Yes, that was him."

"He was wearing a name tag and rimless glasses. He came on like the most distinguished doctor you could find."

"He's been my attending doctor all along. But he doesn't know anything about me. There's no way he could. I've never once told him what I was really thinking."

Probably because I was so sleepy, I couldn't think of anything, like my mind was weighed down with sandbags. It was too much for me to be bothered by things, but that didn't take away the anxiety one little bit. Rather, it got worse and worse by the day. I was also scared the medicine was disintegrating my mind. But the world outside was scarier still. From the windows the streets looked like a concentration camp or the yard of a prison with a million stone walls, where everyone inside was under watch. All day long I heard horrible howling noises coming from the organizations that sounded like monster watchdogs.

The only comfort to be had in such a place came from the other patients. I was free to go downstairs from the women's ward to the men's ward. I became friends with Tsu, who was in his thirties. He heard voices from a faraway star and he talked about them to me in a soft voice.

"I just heard from the star. They say we needn't worry about them because everything is at peace there. They wanted to know how things are on the earth. When I told them we're still fighting wars, they laughed. They said earth people are really dumb. We're still in the stone age, as far as they are concerned."

Later on, he said he told the star people about me.

"When I told them there was a beautiful girl here who was unhappy, they said that is not good — beautiful girls must be happy. They want us to see that you get happy."

Madam Eh in my room seemed to be communicating with someone, but she wouldn't reveal a single word of her conversations. Tsu spoke to me very frankly about his voices. He said he wanted to go visit the star, but one has to die to do that. There is no way to get a living body someplace tens of millions of light years away, but the spirit can travel faster than light. There was infinite warmth in Tsu's eyes as he told me these things.

Uh, walking around, singing and laughing without a care in the world; Eh resuming trips to the public library when her travel ban was lifted, consumed with her desire to read all the books it held; Ah responding only when it came to eating; Tsu communicating with the stars — they were all completely honest about expressing their views of the world, and each one lived according to her or his own will. You look at these patients and notice something about the people on the outside, like people who work for companies, students, professors (including my father), or housewives. You see how they get themselves tied into knots just so they can conform to their organizations' uniforms and attitudes and customs and I don't know what else. They hide their own thoughts, they spend their whole lives being obedient to organizations against their own wills, and the irony of it all is they have complete contempt for these patients (myself included), who are the only ones living free and honestly. They call us crazy and think they are the sane ones.

Little by little, a kind of beautiful glow came welling up inside. One day I went to Tsu, talking about his star, and pressed my face into his breast. "You're right, Tsu," I said. "If being a slave to organizations is normal, I don't want to be normal. You are abnormal, but you are free, you are caring and honest. You are a wonderful person."

Tsu stroked my head and sighed. "All right. I will pass this message on to the star. I am sure everyone there will be overjoyed," he said.

"I'm starting to understand what you mean about organizations."

"I wonder if you do. Personally, I understand less now about organizations than ever."

The wind beat violently against the window. The sky was howling like a thousand rags being ripped apart. Cold was settling into the room despite the kerosene stove. Sounds of dishes being washed no longer came from the kitchen, which was now dark and still. The master seemed to have withdrawn to somewhere else.

Wakako recalled the time she was in Tsu's embrace. The nurses' station had an unobstructed view of the entire corridor to ensure that everyone passing through it could be seen. Tsu took Wakako into the room where futons were stored. There, in pitch darkness, amid smells of cotton, sweat and something fermenting, Tsu undressed her with infinite care, as if handling delicate crystal. He had none of Sa's rough mannerisms. He said something she couldn't quite catch.

"You have . . . inside."

"What do I have?"

"The stars. So peaceful and warm. You do, you have them inside."

These were words Wakako could accept. He moved inside her. The hot fluid issuing from him felt like the liquefied stars of the skies that filled his head.

I don't know if Tsu loved me. I think the stars were more important to him than I was. His love for them exceeded love for any human being. But he rubbed back tears with the palm of his hand when the summer ended and they decided to release me from the hospital. He said, "I will report back to the stars when you are gone. I'm sure everyone there will be sad."

I went back to classes again in the fall. My sickness certainly seemed to have gone. No more awful things happened in the lecture rooms or the lab classes, and I wasn't worrying about organizations watching me. In place of all that, everything was miserably dreary and boring. I couldn't get interested in anything that had to do with study. There is a main street that runs all the way from the university's front entrance to the rear gate. That used to look like a really long way, like there was so much that it traveled through, but now it was like a super telephoto picture, with the front entrance touching the back gate. It was like everything inside the university, including me, was being squeezed in from opposite directions and had lost its depth. I felt thin as paper.

It seemed to me I was worse off than I had been before. The sickness I had was gone, but it was replaced by a different one. The doctor said I was self-delusional. He called my condition "melancholia." None of his labels ever matched what was actually wrong with me. I supposed he would have some label for the latest development — maybe "delusional compression syndrome" or some such thing.

What bothered me the most were regular classes. I didn't want to sit where people could see me, fat as I now was, so I sat in the back row. The professor should have been far away, but his face got closer and closer, until his mouth was close enough to kiss mine. I was getting really shaken. I looked away and applied myself to my notes, but as soon as I looked up I saw the professor's mouth, targeting me with an obscene expression. In the end, I didn't absorb a single thing from the lecture.

I visited the hospital once a week to get medicine. The doctor corrected me when I reported to him about my "delusional compression syndrome." He said that disorder is called "depersonalization." His way of pinning new labels on me all the time made me feel like goods in a shop with different price stickers pasted one on top of the other.

After that examination, I went to the men's ward to visit Tsu. He talked about the stars, as usual. I enjoyed seeing his eyes glimmer like stones in a clear stream. He put his arm gently around my shoulders and started walking down the corridor, then he stopped suddenly and picked up a book from the floor. It was a paperback I had left at the hospital. He handed it to me without a word. I said, "I want you to have it." He took it back reverently and turned the pages. It was the Iwanami pocket edition of *The Notebooks of Malte Laurids Brigge*. I had been reading and re-reading it since high school. I always carried it around in my handbag, and it would eventually fall apart. The one I gave to Tsu was the third copy I had bought. When I visited him the following week he said he'd read it and found it interesting. He talked about Rilke. It was pretty funny to hear this coming from someone who had never talked about anything but the stars. It turned out that Tsu was a serious reader. He had read a lot of poetry and literature. He said he was thirty-four years old and had been a high school

Japanese teacher. I started giving him books after that. I was always looking forward to hear what he had to say about them.

One day — it was a clear afternoon in the middle of winter — when I went to visit Tsu, the head nurse told me he had been released. That was startling. She refused to give me his address, "to protect the patient's privacy." I was regretting not having asked him his address. The next week I asked the doctor in charge and he said very simply, "He committed suicide." He explained that Tsu had hanged himself in the futon storage room. The shock was like being caught in an intense flash of light — everything went white. It wasn't until I was on the streetcar on my way home that I was finally able to start thinking again. What I thought was that he must have decided it was time to leave for his star. Grief didn't come welling up until I went for my hospital visit the following week. There had been a time when the world outside the windows of that hospital had looked like a vast graveyard to me. That was how that hospital looked after he was gone.

For whatever reason, my "depersonalization" started getting better about then, a little at a time. Thickness and depth came to the world, like ten thousand dried flowers magically restored. I took classes and went skating when I had free time. Eventually, the weekly visits to the hospital and the doctor started feeling oppressive. One day I realized I had forgotten an appointment. That seemed as good a reason as any to quit going, so I did, and I quit taking the medicine too. The next day I was so tired I could hardly move. I was nauseous and couldn't eat. That made me afraid I must still be sick after all, but all those symptoms went away in a few days. It felt wonderful, like all the old blood was changed to fresh new blood. The tenth day after I quit taking the medicine, my period started. I hadn't had one since I was hospitalized. At the beginning, the doctor had said the psychological effects of hospitalization were the cause of it stopping. After my release, he said it was a side effect of the medicine.

As long as I was going to classes and cheerful, my parents didn't have anything to say. That was all it took to make them stop worrying. For about a year I was a normal, average, serious student. In other words, I was back to being a good little girl.

~

Wakako abruptly fell silent. Her mind had gone blank. That had been happening occasionally ever since her hospitalization. Even if she tried to go on talking it was if someone had taken her thoughts away and nothing more would emerge. It was like walking along a road without a care in the world and suddenly finding the land cut off by a vast ocean disappearing in a hazy distance.

The stars shone brightly, looking like pieces of ripe fruit ready to fall at any moment, but hanging quietly. Atsuo Yukimori lay on the bed. At some point he had begun snoring lightly. (I wonder when he dozed off. I never realized, being so caught up in chattering on and on all by myself.)

His chest rose and fell with the slowness of that glacier outside.

Then she recalled Makihiko Moriya. In that instant, the blank vanished and her consciousness was replete. (He is in police detention, keeping silent under interrogation. I didn't tell the police anything about him. I said only that he was one of my boyfriends. I got to know him when he came to the house to visit my father, who is his professor. That was all I told them. The police didn't ask anything else. With more than five hundred suspects to investigate — if you count everyone who was arrested, detained or indicted — they aren't going to go digging up everything about them all.)

That Shinkansen bombing three days before was a matter of concern. The newspapers were reporting that it looked like the work of Makihiko Moriya's Q. Sect. The reasoning behind this theory was that after the "day of the Tower," when Moriya, who was officially a member of the central executive committee, but actually the sect's de facto leader, was arrested along with the secretary and operations squad chief, the few Q. Sect officials who were still free resorted to terrorism as their response to the police offensive. Unfortunately, this theorizing by the media didn't sound at all unlikely. Q. Sect was fully capable of committing atrocities.

The confrontation that had surfaced between the K. Sect and the Q. Sect the previous fall had led to frequent outbreaks of violence. One day, the Q. Sect operations squad had captured a female member of K. Sect and tortured her in a sealed off basement room of T. University that had steel pipes running across its ceiling. The door was covered with blankets to prevent the sound of screams from being heard outside. The girl was a student who looked scarcely out of childhood. She was surrounded by four youths who pushed her to the floor and stripped off her clothes while she cried and screamed. When she was completely naked she was stretched out face up atop a steel desk and tied down by the hands and feet. She struggled desperately to free herself as the youths pinched her immature vulva and small breasts.

Four of the assailants removed their belts to mete out punishment under the eyes of a group of about thirty Q. Sect members and "sympathizers" like Wakako who stood around them in a circle. They called out numbers, as they flogged her: *Ichi! Ni! San! Shi!* Deep red welts quickly emerged across the girl's pale skin, but the flogging continued. The floggers stayed their hands when the skin broke and blood was flowing. The girl had lost consciousness. She was revived with water poured over her from a bucket at the ready for this use. Then she was turned over and her bonds were retied for flogging of her back and buttocks. When Wakako began to retch in revulsion to the sight, Makihiko Moriya led her from the room. When she had first become acquainted with the members of Q. Sect, she knew them as intellectuals, genial and earnest. What had caused their transformation?

Wakako recalled vividly recalled Yukichi Jinnai's massive shoulders and the contours of his lips constricting and relaxing as words cascaded from them in impatient streams. The vision was so realistic she drew in her legs in a reflexive gesture of self-protection. He had made his ideas very clear as they circled the skating rink.

"You can't destroy anything with a 'Self-Defense Force.' We've got to build up real armed forces — army, navy air force, with state-of-the-art weaponry — and use it to kill off all the opposition. Then we have power. What do those students think they are doing?"

He had fixed a fierce, beady-eyed gaze upon Wakako. It was the same look he had given her on the day of the Tower, as he wiped the mud from her helmet. "You shouldn't be doing this," was his comment then.

Wakako's interest was piqued by Yukichi Jinnai's vision of armies. He didn't think they were for protecting Japan against foreign invasion, but to kill off "the opposition." This was not standard militant nationalism.

"Well, I don't like killing. It's inhuman," she answered.

He laughed. "Sure it is. That's how politics works. It's the way of the world. My uncle's killed people."

Atsuo Yukimori had killed. What did that mean? He killed in the war? Or had he committed murder? She had been on the verge of asking Yukichi Jinnai about this when he launched into passionate talk of the right-wing ideologues who had been executed for their role in the plot that culminated in the assassination of four government ministers at the beginning of the Showa era. He had read all their works. They were the true revolutionaries, he declared. Have you read them? he asked, and his face showed heartfelt regret when she answered "No."

Atsuo Yukimori was snoring in full measure — powerfully, from the depths of his breast. He had killed. (How? How many? Shall I ask him tomorrow? Or wait until he tells me? No, I don't care, even if he did kill someone. Nothing matters except that I love him. I feel like at least snuggling up beside him now, if I can't take shelter inside that strong breast.)

Wakako rose, groped her way to the bed and crawled in beside him, beside Atsuo Yukimori, warm, strong and dependable. The memories that remained of Makihiko Moriya, Tsu, Sa, Yukichi Jinnai, and every other male were already faded and blurry.

Wakako rested her head on Atsuo Yukimori's chest. Rocked by his breathing, she thought about crossing the ocean on an ice floe. Then a sturdy arm closed gently about her shoulders. No storm would overturn this ice vessel. It was safe for sailing.

"Woke you up, didn't I?"

"I was awake the whole time, listening to you."

"Fibber. You were snoring."

"No, I heard everything. You were saying your period came when you stopped taking your medicine."

"Oh, great, you heard most of it."

"I was completely focused on what you were saying. You've been through a lot, for someone so young." He snuggled close to Wakako.

~

The stout girl was greedily devouring a sweet bun the size of a watermelon. When she finished it all, a snake-like tongue emerged to lick off traces of filling from her forehead and neck. This was Ah.

"Was it good?" Wakako asked.

"Of course not. Why should it be? It tastes terrible. I'm forcing myself to eat it," was Ah's reply.

In her mind, Wakako superimposed her own body upon Ah's, then looked out at the hospital room from a corner of the futon with Ah's eyes and heart. People came and went, it was morning, it was evening, flowers bloomed, snow fell, but nothing that happened had any more meaning than the pages of a comic book turned one after the other without being read. Nevertheless, time went on; you could tell by the hands of the clock and the days marked off on the calendar — you were getting older and older. The doctor tells you get up, read something, pull weeds, walk around. Do something, anything at all. But Ah doesn't have the will to do anything. Life is too hard to face. Ah has been driven down to doing nothing but having her three meals a day, and that is hard, too, because she doesn't have much appetite. She clings to her hunger, the one human desire she retains, and endeavors to get all the way through each meal. Wakako understands heart and soul the sorrow of this stout woman who idles life away, and her sympathy is with Ah. (Have your wretched-tasting sweet bun, Sister Ah! Eat it all and be a human being.)

~

Wakako was hungry. She patted her stomach, wondering when she last had such a wonderful appetite, and filled her lungs with bitingly chilly air. Dogs were barking. The roar of some kind of engine sounded like the ground being cut away.

Wakako sprang from the bed, looked for Atsuo Yukimori and experienced a touch of anxiety when she didn't find him. She changed hurriedly, brushed her hair and applied just a little bit of makeup. Outside, the master in his lamb's-wool cap was feeding his huskies. Out on the lake the snowmobile was running, with Atsuo Yukimori in the driver's seat. He was going around and around in an elliptical path, pulling an iron snow rake with a net that left smooth, gleaming ice in its wake.

"We're making a skating rink," the master explained. "There's a college skating team that comes for training on the New Years' break, so I prepared a lake-top rink for them. You use that thing to clear the snow, lay on a new ice layer and you've got a championship rink."

"It's beautiful!" Wakako said with an exuberant jump. She kicked up some snow, skipped and broke off an icicle hanging from the lodge's eaves. Then she went to pet the dogs.

"Mornin'!"

Atsuo Yukimori approached, wearing a big smile. Eyebrows and whiskers frozen white, he looked like a comical old codger.

The master began streaming water over the ice with a long hose. The couple went inside to find breakfast laid out in the main hall.

An agreeable fragrance rose from a coffee pot on the stove. There was black bread, natural cheese from Betsukai, and an assortment of homemade jam: cowberry, monkey pear, gooseberry, Kamchatka bilberry. For the coffee, there was extra-rich milk straight from a nearby dairy farm. Everything tasted good. Wakako ate voraciously.

Wakako put on her skates impatiently and was soon gliding over the ice. The thick cloud cover picked that time to open up enough to admit a spotlight of sun on the lake that penetrated the blue-black ice, illuminating green seaweed swaying beneath. This view made skating seem like flying above a field of grass. One turn around the lake was sufficient for her to grow accustomed to the taut hardness that distinguishes a natural ice surface. After going around a second time, she had a sense of how wind direction affects stability. The wind was coming from exactly the same direction as the sunshine, making conditions very easy to assess. She crossed one foot behind her skating foot, went into a backward glide and concentrated on aligning the center of her body with the center of the light, wind, ice, and gravity. It was like deftly climbing aboard an invisible turntable that whirls about at high speed; what the pro skaters call "defining an axis," as you begin to spin. Drawing legs and arms into the axis made her spin faster still, until the field of snow, clouds, sun, Atsuo Yukimori, and everything else ran together and became streaks of light. The centrifugal force yanked her breasts back, sending a pleasant sensation throughout her body.

She could make out the form of Atsuo Yukimori approach and begin to spin right next to her. Wakako let up on her own speed to match his and they spun together. Then they jumped from their respective axes and began tracing a giant circle like a waterwheel. After a while, they noticed that the master had brought out a tape recorder that was providing music for them. They began ice dancing. Both knew the steps for each piece that came, and were able to continue through the "Dutch Waltz," "Canasta Tango," "Swing Dance," and "Fiesta Tango" without a glitch.

As she glided, jumped, spun and danced, power began to surge through Wakako's body. The many days she had devoted to skating practice seemed embedded in each muscle and tendon.

(For me, "going to classes" was a matter of heading straight for the rink for three hours of blissful skating, then dropping in for a lecture or lab class before going back to the rink for another three or four hours on the ice. At six hours practice a day, day after day, I could tell I was getting better and better. Atsuo Yukimori went skating for a couple of hours on Sundays alone. With that much more practice time in, of course I would surpass him. He said "You have natural ability," but that's not right. I reached a certain level through lots of practice. Top pros get to where they are through practice on top of natural ability. I know — I've watched others who started the same time I did and were outdoing me in no time. They just kept getting better and better, and then they came in number one or number two in some national competition.)

The couple continued skating until Atsuo Yukimori ran out of breath, threw up his hands, said "I surrender," and quit skating. "Can't win against youth," he said with a pained smile as he wiped his face and neck with a towel. They went to their room, showered and changed their sweat-drenched underwear.

"Shall we take a rest?" he asked, but she shook her head.

"No, let's go out. C'mon, let's go someplace far away."

They got onto the snowmobile, with him driving. This time they were pulling a sled behind, packed with fishing gear and lunches prepared for them by the master. The clouds were black and heavy, but the great expanse of snow was bright. The couple sped through its radiance, past Fox Forest, where they had been the previous day, to the center of the lake. Once in a while, they would hit a bump, as if the ice had wrinkles in it, causing Wakako to scream histrionically. Suddenly the vehicle stopped. Looking in the direction his finger was pointing, she saw a great flock of swans.

Some birds were blending in with the snow, some were breaking away and some were swimming upon water between cracks in the ice. They flew, lined up in order, crying *kooo-kooo*. There were many hundreds, gathered together in territory that was their own. It was a far more impressive sight than the much smaller number she had seen on Lake Onneto.

"Oh, look. Some of them are dancing!"

One bird would spread its wings and fly up a little way and then another would strut one step forward on the snow. The first bird descended to the ground and the other took off. This give and take had a kind of pleasant rhythm. Wakako tried keeping time and discovered the swans were moving in triple meter. It was a waltz!

The swan waltz had a sizable audience. One could almost expect a rousing applause. In fact, the pair was getting appreciative whoops. One bird started to cry and was followed by all the others in a mighty chorus of *koo-koo*.

But there were two birds sulking by themselves, far away from the crowd.

"Look, there's a couple of birds like us. They don't give a damn about the others."

"Those are red-crowned cranes. See, the ends of their feathers and necks are black."

"Wow, you have good eyesight! I can hardly tell."

"Hey, there's a sea eagle!" He was pointing to a great, black shadow of a bird in flight, its strong wings churning the cold air currents. It receded into the distance beyond the cape and disappeared over the sea. That sea had been packed with ice floes just the day before. They were all gone now, leaving only grayish water.

"The ice floes are gone."

"The wind must have carried them out to sea."

They went along the coast as far as they could, to where the ice on the lake ended. Beyond that was the sea, black and expansive, with countless slabs of ice tossing in the waves and rattling together like a frigid chorus of crickets.

"This is coastal ice in the making. See how slushy it is, like it's about to freeze solid? The local word for sea water in that state is *teshiroppu*. They call those plates of ice 'lotus leaf ice.'"

Wakako went from the beach to the water's edge and dipped a finger in. It felt gluey, as if it was pulling on her finger. She snatched it back hastily. Waves came to the shore but the water was thick as mercury, with no foam.

"There's Kunashir Island — one of the Northern Territories."

"Is this the Sea of Okhotsk?"

"The people of Nemuro think so. They say Nemuro has two ports — Port Hanasaki, on the Pacific, which never freezes up and Port Nemuro, on the Sea of Okhotsk, which does."

"What do you mean, 'they think so'?"

"Well, it's a matter of opinion. There are books that say the Sea of Okhotsk is north of where the Kuril Islands start, but the question is, are the Habomai and Shikotan islands part of the Kuriles? If they are, then this is the Sea of Okhotsk."

"Count me with the people of Nemuro. I declare these waters the Sea of Okhotsk."

Say "Okhotsk" and pretty soon someone is bound to mention places like Sakhalin, Kamchatka, Siberia, or the North Pole. The words signify ice, cold, uninhabited territory, the farthest reaches, where all is frozen, stationary or dead. Wakako licked her finger. It tasted of north sea salt. The kind of taste that invites shivers.

"Cold?"

"Yes, but I'm okay. Let me drive this thing." She twisted the throttle and roared off over the white field of ice and snow. The vehicle responded with exhilarating speed, spewing smokey snow clouds left and right. He jabbed a warning index finger toward the current running under the ice. There was a patch of water in the middle of the lake. Far away, swans were gathered. She headed after them, steering around the unsafe region of the current. She amused herself by swerving one way and another every once in a while. Where there didn't seem to be any obstacles ahead, she gunned the engine to full speed. He was trying to tell her something but she couldn't hear over the engine. She was turning her head the better to listen when she saw a blue-black opening in the ice looming ahead. Panicking, she tried steering around, but lacked the strength to make it respond. This snowmobile didn't have a brake; all one could do was gear down, but it was too late for that. There was a three meter pool of dark water five meters ahead. She accelerated full speed, hoping for a successful jump. As the vehicle sailed over the gap, she though she caught a glimpse of lake bottom, seaweed and a face that might have been the god of death. She turned off the engine and looked back. They were inside a hollow in the ice. Their vehicle's hurtling speed had carried them several meters beyond the open water. The surface of the ice around them had cracked from the impact of their landing.

"That was close," he said, laying a hand on her shoulder.

"Sure was," she said, putting out her tongue, while shuddering visibly.

"You are one young lady with a serious weakness for speed."

"Still, it was fun."

"Didn't that jump scare you?"

"Not as much as I was expecting. But I did see the god of death. It was a really creepy man with a ghastly pale face." As she said this, Wakako had the feeling she really had seen such a face. It was cold and smiling, with skin the color of grass, the man's seaweed hair swaying in the current. It was probably from a dream of long ago.

He took over the driving and they came to the mouth of the river. There were trucks and horse-pulled sleighs with camping gear set out. A sizable crowd of people engaged in ice fishing gave the scene the air of a festival in progress.

"They're fishing for pond smelt. Let's join 'em!"

"No, I don't want to. I don't want to be where there are so many people around. Let's go to the far end of somewhere where there's no one else."

The couple headed up the Furen River. Vast expanses of marsh stretched out on either side. The sandbar visited the previous year for duck shooting with Ichiro Fukawa and Kimiko Fujiyama went gliding past. The reeds, dried brown, were half buried in snow. The tops of the alders formed intricate lace patterns encased in shining glazes of ice.

They reached the salmon roe extraction station. Knowing that the hill in back of the station afforded a magnificent view, Atsuo alighted from the snowmobile and led Wakako to its top.

The sight prompted a rapturous cry from her. "Wow! It's gorgeous!"

The river wound like a sinuous tentacle from the white lake across the vast brown-colored marsh. Withered forms of Sakhalin fir and beds of reed lent a touch of warmth to the landscape of snow and ice. Amid this bleakness, a myriad of frost-covered twigs and clover gleamed in the sun. Beyond the marsh-land, a pasture could be seen on a hill. A silo against a clear blue sky gave testa-ment to human habitation.

"What is this building for?"

"It's a plant that captures salmon when they swim upriver. They extract the roe and fertilize it."

This left Wakako with a puzzled expression. It occurred to Atsuo an explanation of the migratory behavior of the salmon was in order.

The migration that starts in late August or mid-September brings them to the rivers of eastern Hokkaido around the beginning of November. Heading from the ocean back to the places where they were spawned, they churn up rivers like the Kaorigi, Nishibetsu, Furen, or Bettoga. I watched the spectacle countless times since childhood. One day the sea is suddenly teeming black with them. You can see tails and fins on the surface. They are swarming toward the mouths of their respective rivers. All the streams fill up with silver and black bodies. They pile up on one another in the shoals. When they get into rapids they can make powerful leaps. They scrape their heads and teeth and bellies on rocks as they go, getting bloodier and bloodier, single-mindedly pushing on and on upstream.

The goal of course is spawning roe and fertilizing it. That's how they have sex. There is no natural phenomenon that makes the point more blatantly that the coupling of male and female is the thing of ultimate importance to living be-ings. The males swim guard protectively around the females, swollen with roe. Each female is guarded by a number of rival males, who keep predators away by thrusting their crooked snouts and fiercely baring their formidable teeth. When they reach the destination in the upper sand shoals, the females spawn and victorious males deposit their milt onto the roe. For the next several days, the females stand guard over the fertilized eggs. The males and females all die after spawning. They call salmon who have finished with spawning *hocchare*. They are an awful sight. Their mouths are white where the skin has worn off, and they are covered with scars.

When Atsuo finished this explanation, Wakako looked out at the river sur-face, as if it was filled with salmon at that moment. Her eyes shone.

"What a wonderful story. The life of the salmon ends giving everything for love. Dying for love — that's the happiest way to go."

"It would be, if the Lord Homo Sapien didn't steal their happiness for his own purposes," said Atsuo. "He hauls them all in here on their way upstream, separates the males and females, kills them all, slits open the female's bellies for the roe — caviar — and pours in the milt from the males to fertilize it. Their lives journeys end without any consummation of love."

"How sad."

"That's done to preserve the resources. You lose them if you don't hatch the fry and release them."

"The salmon are a resource."

"To feed us humans. Just another resource, like oil."

Atsuo recalled scenes of fisherman killing salmon by knocking them on the head with truncheons. Salmon filled with the dream of ending their lives in the act of love fall into darkness, spewing blood from their eyeballs. Raised from the ocean in nets and dumped into the holds of ships like so much garbage, writhing in agony as they die of suffocation. Salmon fry are nurtured and released for the sole reason of insuring there will be more mature resources to kill again.

(There is no difference between the cruelty of the fisherman bludgeoning the salmon to death and the person who gladly has the salmon for dinner. The fisherman does the deed on behalf of the consumer. It' is merely a matter of role division. As a hunter, he had shot to death countless Ezo deer, wild duck, and Ezo grouse. Yes, there is blood on my hands, but it's just the same for those who like the taste of those animals' meat. It's the same with butchers of pigs and cow and consumers of their meat. The point is that human beings live by consuming animals — plants too. Being born, we are fated to being cruel. As Torakichi Jinnai puts it, our sins are deep.

(With me, that is not the half of it. I have killed many human beings. It was done in wartime; the persons killed were enemy, but they were no less human for that. The killing was done with machine guns. I killed more than I could count. I killed prisoners, civilians; raped a woman. It was all done under the sanction of a just war, a sacred war. The more you killed, the more respect you got for heroism. But once it was over, it was immediately condemned as barbaric, as aggression. I defended it to myself by saying the killing was ordered by senior officers — ordinary troopers didn't have any say. But the truth is I myself justified the killing at the time, as a Japanese national. This isn't pious talk about "deep sins." It's about real criminal acts.)

Atsuo came out of his reverie, feeling warm breath at his face. He saw Wakako's great eyes up close.

"Whatever it is, you're really thinking seriously about it."

"I was thinking about one thing and another. Now let's go upriver some more. The end of the earth is up there."

"Let's go." Wakako went down the slope at a gallop, Atsuo chasing after, damned if he'd be bested.

He took advantage of the snowmobile to take a route out on the ice not along the river itself. It was clear which part of the surface was river and which was land, but it was all the same surface. The blending of river and field offered interesting possibilities. As long as he avoided the highly ridged patches of ice where the river bent, he was free to go into the reed beds or go shooting to the top of snow drifts. There was no one else around. Atsuo was glad to be alone with Wakako. He stopped the snowmobile at the place called "Big Bend," where the river angled off.

"Okay here's the end of the earth," he said, alighting. He unloaded fishing gear from the sled. "Here's where we fish."

Atsuo had the satisfaction of being watched in amazement as he made preparations. First thing was to put a hole in the ice with a large drill. The job required prodigious effort. The muscles in his arms and shoulders swelled. He was soon sweating. Wakako put out her hands. "Let me give it a try." She took the drill, but it wouldn't so much as turn for her, so she gave up.

He used a big spoon to extract the crushed ice every so often, then continued drilling. Finally, he got through, having opened a hole about ten centimeters across. It was instantly flooded with water. He had a measure that told him the ice was sixty-four centimeters thick.

He set an empty can atop a board on the ice and started a fire in it. Fire wood prepared for them by the master was dry and easily set ablaze. Mess kits holding rice for their lunches he set upon the fire, then prepared to fish. He attached a line holding five No. 4 fish hooks to a short pole only fifty centimeters long. After lightly affixing maggots to the hooks, he trailed the line into the hole and got a bite almost immediately. he pulled in a pair of pond smelt ten centimeters long as Wakako gave a clap of admiration.

"Here, try your luck," he said, passing her the pole.

"This is my first time fishing."

"Pretty fancy, fishing for the first time at the end of the earth."

"I'll say." In no time, Wakako had pulled in a fish.

"All right, we've found a Spot," Atsuo said, and set to drilling another hole next to Wakako. He joined her with another line in the water. The fishing continued to be good. For a time, the couple were absorbed in this diversion. They arranged their instantly frozen fish in rows of ten fish each as a convenient way of keeping count of their catch. When it reached thirty-four Wakako inquired about the time. It was eleven-thirty. The rice was done shortly thereafter. They had it with fish roasted on skewers.

"This is delicious. I've never had lunch in a mess kit before."

"You've having all kinds of first time experiences. In the army I had a tanker load of mess kit meals. These are cooked right. I could do it in my sleep."

Atsuo explained how to cook rice in a mess kit. You measure out the rice to go into the inner tin. Fill the outer tin with water up to the line. You can tell when it's done by the sound it makes when you tap on the cover.

"You really know a lot of useful things," Wakako said, leaving rice grains sticking to the side of her mouth. "Everything that's practical and useful."

"Practical stuff is about all I do know. With the kind of life I've lived, you can't get by any other way. But you can get so preoccupied with practical things you end up boxed into a little world of your own. I don't understand anything that's academic or abstract."

"Living practically is a wonderful way to live. It's a lot better than anything academic or abstract." Wakako said this with quiet conviction.

Snow began falling. Clouds loaded with great cargoes of snow appeared, one after another. Wind began blowing. It was a north wind, with a force of four, enough to raise snow from the ground and make it dance in the air. The weather report had predicted a snowstorm beginning in the evening. The clouds were coming in a bit early.

"Shall we start back?"

"No," Wakako said forcefully. "I don't want to quit when we're finally all alone together."

They finished their meal and packed their gear and fish on the sled, ready for departure. Then they sat down by the blistering red tin can stove. It gave off radiant heat that kept them quite warm.

"I had a funny dream this morning," Wakako said, slowly moving her slender fingers before the fire. "About Ah, that stout girl I was with in the hospital. She never had any appetite, but she was forcing herself to eat a great big sweet bun. That's how she kept gaining weight. I understand why she did it. I knew how she felt so well, it was getting to me. She was so much like me."

"How's that?"

"You want to be a normal person, but you can't, so you get desperate."

"Okay, that I understand. It's the same with me. I wanted to be a normal person, but I couldn't do it."

"How's that?"

Atsuo stopped talking, although an impulse to confess swelling up inside was threatening to break through the hard shell containing it.

Wakako smiled helpfully. "Remember yesterday, how I was pouring out everything from my past? It seems to have done me a world of good. Today I feel really at peace. It's like all that gruesome history has disappeared and it's just me, light as a feather with no baggage. That's not all, either. Now, instead of hating my father and mother, it's more like I feel sorry for them. When you think about it, it isn't completely their fault that they got to be someone's parents. I can understand that a little. Being a parent is something like those *hoccharé* salmon. That's what I thought when you were telling me about them."

"That's a good thing," Atsuo said. "To be honest, It was painful for me to hear you speak badly about your parents. That has to do with me and my parents. I caused nothing but trouble for them, especially my mother. I'm in no position to hate my parents. They're the ones who should have hated me. It would have been easier if they did, but they wouldn't. Not at all."

"Maybe I wasn't in any position to hate my parents either. At least that's how it seems now."

"Is that the salmon's influence?"

"The salmon, the Furen River, the snowmobile, Atsuo Yukimori. The influence from all of it."

"That's a good thing," Atsuo said again.

The snow was falling heavily, while gusts of wind lifted up patches of surface snow into the air, putting heaven and earth into a turmoil of swirling snowflakes. The wind fanned the fire in the stove and blew sparks in every direction.

"I'd like to forget the past and be light as a feather too. But that's a tall order in my case."

"Why?"

"There's a lot of things, an awful lot. It's not the kind of past you can leave behind. It's worse than I could say, no matter how much I talked." Atsuo held his head in both hands.

"Don't go into it. Put that kind of talk away."

"Is that what I said to you? In my case, it's not something that can be put away. More than any one else, you're the one I have to confess it to . . . Look, I've got a record, a criminal record. It's not a matter of one time or two times. It's a long record of repeat offenses. I was put in jail time after time. That's the kind of man I am."

"But you gave up crime, right?"

"Why do you say that?"

"You gave it up for nine years, seven months and fifteen days. You told me that last year, on October twentieth. So now it's been nine years, eleven months and ten days since you quit."

"Did you know about my past?"

"How could I have? I found out just now. That's another first-time experience. The only thing is, I could feel that the reason you quit smoking was that you wanted desperately to break away from something in the past so you could be normal. That was just intuition — there wasn't any reason for thinking that. Then when we met in "If" suddenly you were smoking. I was wondering what it was that made you break down after nine years and eleven months abstinence. I was worried that maybe you were in some kind of big trouble."

"Think maybe I committed some crime?"

"I just told you I couldn't possibly know about that. I can see that subject really bothers you, but it doesn't matter to me whether you are a criminal or not."

"Yeah, but . . ."

"Stop. Don't keep saying you were a criminal, as if you were never anything but a criminal. You are first and foremost Mr. Atsuo Yukimori. The same goes for me. I'm Wakako a lot more than I am some mental patient, some crazy person. Look, we had a great time ice dancing a little while ago. That wasn't the crook and the screwball dancing, it was you and me. I'm sick of doctors putting labels on me with the names of diseases. So how about you just throw away the label some judge pinned on you!"

"I'd like to, if I could."

"You can."

"That's not how it works in the real world. Those labels carry weight. Sure, you'd like to throw them away, but the world won't let you."

"Who cares about the world!"

"You can say that because you're young. You don't know what the world can do. They've got lots of ways to clobber you. As you would put it, it's a great big organization. It works like fixed nets for salmon. Once they've got you, there's no escape, and they have all kinds of smart, mean ways to get you."

"So let's fight them. Fight them together."

"You want to fight them? . . . You are one strong woman."

"Hardly. It's because of weakness that I go flying over the edge."

"Just having the spirit to fight is being strong. Looking back, there wasn't a single time I fought back. Too scared. It doesn't even occur to me to fight. The first thing that comes to mind is run away."

The wind was wailing. It blew a white coating over them. Atsuo was thinking they should be getting away from there fast, but Wakako's eyes were aglow; he didn't want to interrupt her cascade of words, so he sat feeding firewood into the fire to keep it burning.

Atsuo was unable to say what he wanted most to say. Should he come out and say it, or would saying it hurt her? The thing that scared him most of all was the prospect of doing something that would destroy the happiness that was theirs at that moment. I am a coward, he thought. This is how I let a lot of precious women get away. Been doing it since I was young.

There was something in the sky, barely visible because it was stationary amid the frenzied turmoil of wind and snow. Slightly mystified, he fixed his eyes on the spot. It was a large bird, sheer white, painted whiter still by the blowing snow, wings fully outstretched against a white sky. It faced into the blustery wind, keeping nearly motionless by adroit adjustments of its wings. It had the sharp beak, black eyes and deeply notched wings of the gyrfalcon. Using, rather than fighting the blizzard to hunt its prey, the great falcon was a mighty presence. He told Wakako about it. She looked and looked, but couldn't spot the bird until it finally flew laterally to a lower position, where it again hung onto the wind motionlessly, but this time discernible to her as well.

"It's awesome to think it lives in that kind of snow."

"It is awesome. That bird is a hellacious fighter."

Atsuo drew Wakako close. He brushed snow from the top of her head and pressed his lips upon hers. The passion between them was no less intense than the ice and snow about them was cold. As they stood in the blizzard, each felt an urgent need to communicate that passion.

The next moment a thick blanket of snow blew around them with such force they were both knocked down to the ice. They scrambled to their feet, wondering if they had been hit by an avalanche. Stinging cold snow got inside their collars. Visibility was less than ten meters ahead. It was just barely possible to make out the poplars along the riverbank. Moving quickly, he prepared for their departure. Their tin can stove had been blown away to parts unknown. He threw their pond smelt, frozen solid, into a bag and started the engine.

The snow was driving directly against the vehicle, making it extremely difficult to steer. The caterpillar treads could hardly engage with the soft, newly fallen snow, uselessly slipping most of the time, so they could only inch ahead. As they were making their very slow progress, they ran into a snowbank on the dark side of a piece of driftwood. Gunning the engine only raised clouds of snow. They got off the snowmobile and tried pushing it, but that only made it sink deeper. Atsuo braced his legs and tried lifting with all his strength, but he only sunk into the snow.

"You're not getting anywhere. What do we do now?"

"I wasn't expecting the snow to be drifting this much. The only thing to do is clear the way in front and run the thing out at top speed."

He picked up the board that had been the base for their stove and used it as a snow shovel. There was a great load of snow to move. Fortunately, Atsuo's arms and back were equal to the task. He applied himself like a bulldozer to opening a path.

The snowmobile bolted ahead, and he concentrated on steering around snow-banks without reducing their speed. The driving snow was hitting them broad-side. That ribbon of white he could see broke off momentarily to become a row of dead Sakhalin fir stumps, gray like grave markers. That told him they were up to the river mouth. There was no sign of the fisherman who had gathered there. Faintly visible forms of pine trees made it possible to discern the riverbank.

Finally, they reached the reed-fringed marsh. The wind was blowing snow from the ground surface, leaving a hard, thin ice surface that made the snow-mobile glide as if in a dream, and they had a back wind as well. Occasionally, a flock of swans would fly by, their long necks extended. A jackrabbit, probably startled by the engine's roar, was suddenly in flight, and the next instant was being chased by a red fox, who must have been lurking. The animals went about their affairs as usual in the midst of the snowstorm.

Wakako, who was clinging tightly to Atsuo's waist, made a sign with her hand. "I hear bells," she said.

He let up on the accelerator and caught the unmistakable sound of bells, their rhythm out of place against the sound of the wind. Four dogs, followed by the master on his sleigh came into view.

"You two had me worried," he said. "It was getting later and later. The people who were out for pond smelt said you had gone up the Furen River. So I came looking for you."

Atsuo gave a grateful bow. "I'm sorry. We ran into a snowdrift and got stuck. That held us up for quite a time."

"There was one accident. A car went through the ice. It looks like they couldn't make out where the current was in this snow."

"Was anyone killed?" Wakako asked.

"They're missing. I don't suppose it will be possible to mount a search party before the spring thaw."

With the dogsled in the lead, they took off at full speed, sticking to the most direct route. The dogs bounded straight ahead, the blinding snow no particular inconvenience to them. They sun went down while they were en route. The snow scattered their headlight beam. They might easily have missed seeing the sled. Atsuo did not doubt but that he would have lost his way if the master had not come looking for them.

They arrived back to find the lodge lit by flickering candles — the power was out — and the main hall filled with men and women laughing and talking loudly. It was an itinerant theatre troupe staying for the night.

Quite unlike the previous night, the setting for the evening meal was lively. People were clustered around the stove. Dampness from too many bodies clouded the windows. Laughter, shouts, and jests were being exchanged. The talk ran the gamut from vulgar gossip to intellectual discussion. Off by themselves at their little table, where it was cold and otherwise none too comfortable, Atsuo and Wakako were musing about making an early departure to their room when a fortyish man approached, carrying a large bottle of saké. Moments before, his clowning had been eliciting roars of laughter at the other tables. He had a technique of wiggling his nose, which was red and nubby, like the legs of a boiled crab, as he talked. He explained that his troupe was touring Hokkaido, putting on plays in community centers and fishermen's association centers. Winter was the season for touring in Hokkaido, where ice floes prevent fishermen from plying their trade. They would go back to Honshu in the spring. He mentioned a number of plays they performed, but to Atsuo the titles meant nothing, so he promptly forgot them.

"If you will forgive my abruptness," he said, rubbing his red nose with the sleeve of his Russian rubashka shirt. "What kind of relationship do you two have?"

"We're lovers," Wakako said, defiantly. "What of it?"

"I win!" The red-nosed man said, raising his arms in a kind of banzai. "The fact is, people over there were placing bets. Let's see, I think the bets covered professor and student, father and daughter, uncle and niece, lovers, and engaged. Hey," he called over to the others, flashing a V-sign, "I win!"

At that, a round of applause went up. Someone said, "Don't it make you jealous?" The answer to that was, "It's lovely!"

"Won't you come over and join us? Everyone's easy to get along with. We come from all over the country, we have people of every age, from every background and everyone has their own philosophy. The only thing we have in common is we're all poor."

"Let's go," Wakako urged.

Atsuo was generally lukewarm about meeting people, but he noticed a few men about his age, so he rose.

Wakako was chatting and laughing with the young members of the company in short order, just as if they were school classmates. Sitting next to Atsuo was an elderly man in dark glasses, strangely subdued. His hand groped for a glass of cold saké, which he sipped at slowly. He was sightless. A young woman was looking after him, bringing a big plate of food and refilling his glass. "This is my wife," he said, closing his hand over that of the young woman, who smiled as if pleased. She was perhaps twenty-seven or twenty-eight, slightly older than Wakako. Her hair hanging freely over a broad forehead, she appeared to have a healthy constitution.

The guy with the red nose called to the one with dark glasses, demanding that he play the guitar. Accepting the instrument brought by the young woman, the man casually began to play. A young couple stood and began singing. Everyone else kept time by clapping or by striking their tables.

It was a nice tune, but the words were in English. Then Wakako was singing too, along with the standing couple. Everyone but Atsuo knew the lyrics.

"What song is this?" Atsuo asked the young woman.

"It's a Beatles song."

"Oh, so that's the Beatles."

Wakako's voice carried well. Atsuo suddenly thought of Yukichi's beautiful voice. It would be fun to pair off those two as a duet. Or is there too much distance between Beatles and war songs? Ah, well, he thought, it's good to be young. My voice doesn't have that kind of luster anymore. All that stuff that has these young people so delighted is beyond me.

Atsuo felt lonely, as if Wakako had abandoned him. At the same time, he had qualms about the future. (Could she and I really go through life together? There are just too many differences between us.)

Atsuo stood up and went to the windows. He rubbed away some of the mist from the glass with the palm of his hand and peered into the howling darkness. The lake, the marsh, the forest, too, were completely buried in ice and darkness. But it only looked cold and dead. In fact, life was present in abundance. The great huchen would be still, its powerful body awaiting the appearance of its prey. A storm meant nothing to swans and gyrfalcons. The wail of the rampaging wind caused him to shiver and reflect on his own feeble existence. Suddenly he noticed the master in the kitchen standing in the shadow of a wooden post casting a strangely sharp-eyed look at Wakako.

There was no hard evidence that the master's attention was focused on

Wakako. He might just have been taking in the general scene of merrymaking. Atsuo didn't care. He was overwhelmed at that moment with jealousy strong enough to want to kill the master. He faced the object of his hatred, drawn to his attention like iron filings to a magnet. The moment his violent impulse to begin shouting reached the boiling point, the master turned a friendly smile to him. Until that moment, such friendliness had been missing from the master's attitude. Now it deflected Atsuo's antagonism, but at the same time, deepened his suspicion. Morosely, he turned away.

"They're a lively bunch," the master said, with an artificial smile. "They stayed here last year, too. That fellow playing the guitar was single then, so he got married just recently. Isn't his wife lovely? It's a shame he can't see her face. The troupe leader — he's the fat man with the red nose — says she was the one to fall in love with him. He says she saw one of their productions in Shibetsu — or maybe it was Teshikaga — and she's been with him ever since."

Atsuo said nothing. The master went on talking unconcernedly.

"She plays piano. I hear she makes up all his music sheets in Braille for him. The troupe leader was saying what a beautiful couple they are."

The master dashed toward a table with startling agility. Someone had upset a candle. After replacing it with a new one, the master went to the stove and threw a massive log inside. Wakako came weaving her way through the people. Clearly, she had been liberally sampling the alcoholic refreshments between songs.

"Hey, quit hiding out in your corner. Come over and sing with us."

"Aah, I don't know those *keto* songs."

"That's okay. Sing songs you know."

"If it was war songs, I'd know them."

"War songs! Great!" said the red-nosed troupe leader. "I'll join you. Let's sing a salute to the war generation. The hell with the Beatles."

But Atsuo would not budge. The more cheer bubbled around him, the greater was the emptiness that loomed in his heart and pushed any playful thoughts beyond his reach. He well understood that his ill humor bespoke old age, and felt sure that it could only be distressing to young Wakako, who would not understand. Nevertheless, he could not become one with his companions.

"You don't look well," said Wakako with concern. "You must be tired."

"That's it," Atsuo said, with a forced smile. "I am tired."

"Let's go to bed," Wakako said firmly, taking Atsuo's hand and leading him to the corridor as she pushed people aside, without the slightest attention to the eyes upon them.

Atsuo spoke up the moment they were in their room.

"Let's leave this place tomorrow. We'll go north. I want to go where it's just you and me. I don't care if there's a raging blizzard, we're going. Right, it's decided."

"Funny, now you don't sound tired at all." She looked at him in wonderment, her attractive eyes wide.

The next afternoon, Atsuo and Wakako went for a walk from their new lodge in Raúsu. The previous day's storm had miraculously given way to a clear sky. Sunlight sparkled upon the powdered crystalline surface of the road. A strong wind still prevailed, however, and it was numbingly cold.

They came to a bridge. Below it, the river's clear water washed its snow-covered banks. Wakako ran to the railing and cried out in delighted wonder. "This river isn't frozen! How come?"

"That's a good question." Atsuo thought about it. Back in Nemuro, all the rivers were frozen under a thick sheets of ice. So why wasn't the Raúsu River ninety kilometers to the north frozen as well? Did the Shiretoko peninsula act as a break to the north wind? Maybe a hot spring was emptying into the river upstream. He had been in Raúsu in winter numerous times, but never had this question from Wakako entered his mind.

"Oh, well, it's just warmer around here than it is in Nemuro," Wakako said, dismissing the issue and taking hold of Atsuo's arm as she began walking ahead rapidly. The town was a long ribbon that straddled the national highway along the shoreline, pushed up against the sea by mountainous terrain. Wherever one might be in the town, it was just a short walk from the highway to the sea.

The couple went to the harbor, where several trawlers were docked and unloading their catches of walleye pollack. Great nets of fish were extended over plastic bins and opened by fishermen using hooks. Pulled from the depths of the northern seas to be laid out there in the sun, the reddish-brown colored fish had large eyes and uncouth shapes.

The powerful fish odor brought to Atsuo's mind images of the thatched cottage by the sea where he had been born and raised, of his father as a fisherman and of himself, who had also been a fisherman in youth. It reminded him as well of Tetsukichi and Yukichi. He knew the life of the fisherman, his physical suffering, what it is like to work long hours or all day without a moment's rest, even while emptying one's bladder or bowels; how the sweat inside your rubber raincoat never really dries, but just stays clammy while it ferments; how you go on standing in the stinking air, fighting sleepiness and fatigue.

At first glance, these young fishermen boisterously yelling to each other were pretty much the same as Atsuo had been. Wakako was watching them curiously.

Of course, she wouldn't have any more understanding of their sensual orientation than children have of the suffering endured by soldiers in war when they view battle scenes in comics or on TV.

The dock was approached by a group of market bidders wearing yellow plastic number tags on their hats. In a very short time, the walleyes in the plastic bins were all graded as first, second, or third class goods. The fruits of their long, arduous labor thus appraised, the fishermen would receive but a small part of the prices paid out for the fish.

Atsuo inspected the faces of each fisherman, going from one boat to the next. He thought Yukichi would be in there somewhere. He couldn't ask for Yukichi by name, not when he was wanted by the police on suspicion of stealing four hundred thousand yen.

"Looking for Yukichi?"

"Yes. He must be in this town somewhere."

"I'll look too."

Wakako approached the fishermen to get a close look at their faces. The objects of her scrutiny were delighted, laughing and waving at the young woman in her eye-catching parka.

Atsuo approached a fisherman with a cigarette dangling from his lips. "How's the fishing?" he asked, in the local dialect.

Recognizing Atsuo as a native, the fisherman gave a friendly response.

"Take a look. We did all right, but that's all for a while. Ice pack is in. Had to hustle back. Won't be leaving port again for a while."

"Ice floes, eh?"

"Yeah. We started hitting 'em. It was getting really hairy. Damn shame, too, just when the fishing was good, but it was a question of getting back in one piece. Take a look out there."

The fisherman cast a significant glance at the sea. There was a white band of ice just beyond the end of the jetty. About three vessels were hovering out beyond the band of ice, unable to return to port.

"There you go, miss." An older man, probably the skipper, threw five or six fish in Wakako's direction and a young man gathered them up, put them in a plastic bag and handed it to her.

That set off a chorus of gleeful comments. "Are you a school girl?" . . . "Sure are pretty!" . . . "Sleep with me!" Wakako smiled brightly in return, with no show of bashfulness. Atsuo threw out a proud response.

"This is my daughter. She goes to college in Tokyo. She's here on pre-examination break."

"Fabulous. Give her to me. I want to marry her." The young one delivering this line, stood up and executed a theatrical bow. His body language said he was joking, but his expression was dead serious. Atsuo felt a stab of jealously as he read the lust in that snub-nosed face. He shot a look at Wakako to signal her it was time to move on.

Along the streets off the side of the highway opposite the harbor were small warehouses and workshops. Frozen-over puddles made the walking treacherous. With his burden of fish, Atsuo almost lost his footing, but Wakako steadied him. The touch of her delicate arm momentarily set off his desire for her. By this reaction he realized the jealously toward the fisherman a short time before was a reflection of his desire.

At a corner plant walleye pollack was being processed. Men clad in waders sat in one sectioned off space beside piles of fish, cutting away gills with knives. In the next section over the fish were gutted in a stream of water, then women washed the fish in sinks. A thick odor of blood and fish oil filled the cramped, gloomy hive of activity and seemed to leave a viscous coating in the nostrils. While Atsuo hesitated at the entrance, Wakako calmly walked inside with a friendly "Hi!" to everyone. She went once around the floor and reported back.

"Uh-uh. Yukichi isn't here."

They inspected every fish processing plant in the town without discovering Yukichi. Finally they were back at the point where they had started their quest.

"What should we do?" Wakako asked, looking up at Atsuo with a worried expression.

"Take a break. I know! Let's go see the luminous moss." Abruptly he began walking briskly, as if to shake off the fish odor hanging around them.

Inside the cave, Wakako wasn't able to pick out the luminous moss. Maybe it was those green places on the ground deep inside, where the light was dim. It sort of looked like luminous moss. For some reason, she suddenly thought of the points of Makihiko Moriya's eyes. Was it because his eyes had darkness in them that had caused her to think of his peculiar way of looking at a person? No, I've got it, she thought. She had once been with him on an outing with the same objective as now — examining luminous cave moss. It was in Onioshi-dashi volcanic park in Gumma prefecture. It had been in summer, just two years before, but now it seemed like ten years in the past, if not a dim memory from early childhood, spotty, out of focus, and far distant.

The truly interesting thing about the present cave was the icicles. They were an overwhelming presence, a hundred ice sculptures formed by frozen water droplets from the roof of the cave, looking like a cavalcade of life-size stone

Bodhisattvas. They had shoulders, necks, eyes, and noses, each with its own expression. (They should have more tourist value than any luminous moss. But there aren't any tourists, just the two of us, alone here in this natural Hall of Thirty-Three Spans. Such luxury!)

"Aw, in the summer you can see better how it shines," Atsuo said regretfully.

Wakako's eyes widened impatiently. "The icicles are better. Look, they're alive, they grow, they have souls," she said.

Those columns of ice really did each take on individual forms as they grew over time, forms that were ever changing; forms that expressed — something. Some kind of will, the will that set nature in motion. That was the thing. This was not human will. There was too much variety there. It was beyond what people could make. In Tokyo the will that moves nature was in hiding. It was hidden by concrete and steel and cars and glass — the things made by people. But the stars showed the will of the creator of the natural world. So did the forest, the sea, the lake.

A thunderous noise from behind shook the ground. It came from the sea wall on the far side of the road outside. Spontaneously, they both started running. He was the fastest up the embankment, then he offered a muscular arm that lightly pulled Wakako up.

A great cluster of ice floes was advancing to the shore. This time they were not immobile, but crashing into one another and breaking asunder or rising up, then falling heavily down atop one another. The massive ice sheets were rapidly moving in, with dull rumbles as they collided, sometimes raising a delicate clatter, exactly like the sound of shattering glass, as they fell to pieces. The thin crust of ice that had formed along the shoreline was broken up and crushed into gruel. Massive ice sheets pushed against the base of the concrete embankment where the couple stood, and were pushed upward almost in their faces.

Atsuo yelled to Wakako, "Let's get back down!"

"Yeah, but . . . just a minute."

Wakako wanted to see more of this. She stood, braving the wind, unable to turn away. She had never before seen nature demonstrate its power in this awesome way. Every one of the countless ice floes pressing toward the shore had a different shape. Tossed and tormented by the waves, sunlight glittering from their facets like a million glaring eyes, their assault was relentless.

"There's God," Wakako said.

"Eh?" Atsuo asked. "What did you say?"

"The ice floes are looking at us." Disregarding his question, Wakako strained to speak over a wind so powerful as to constrict the throat. "They all have eyes and they are all staring at us."

"They have eyes? You certainly have an original way of seeing things."

"See for yourself. They're like human faces, each one different. There are politicians. They are always conspiring and bribing. There are company workers. They worry about what everyone else in the company thinks about them. There are housewives. They don't care about anything but their own children. There are radical students resisting oppression. There are babies, old people . . ."

"Since you put it that way, it does make some kind of sense. I can see men way down at the bottom who can never rise to the top. Those ones over there are keeping away from the crowd, off all by themselves. There are criminals who don't play by the rules. There are killers . . ."

"It is awesome how God can just whip up so many sculptures."

"Oh, I see. You said 'God' before." Atsuo put his arms around Wakako's waist. The cold wind whipped at the couple standing there, carrying away the meager warmth of day that had remained.

"Don't you believe in God?"

"I do think there is some being more powerful than people. I don't know if that is God or what."

"Yeah, that's the same as me. There's another thing . . . Did you ever kill anybody?"

"Yes." Unusually for him, this answer came out clearly. "I killed a lot of people in the war. I was a soldier and they were enemies. I was an outstanding member of the military organization, because I was totally loyal to the cause. Of course, I regret it now. I think it was criminal. Hey, it's getting cold. Let's go where it's warm. I know just the place. What about going to a hot spring?"

"I don't want to go anywhere that has other people."

"Don't worry. It's a completely deserted hot spring." Atsuo Yukimori brushed a bewhiskered jaw across Wakako's forehead.

They went back to their lodge, and put together a set of towels, soap, and changes of clothing. Then he went out and came back in a car he had rented somewhere. Wakako got in and they set out on an uphill road.

A mountain stream came into view, running beside the road. The snow was deep, making driving difficult. Time after time, the car hit sections where the tires spun futilely. The mountain was rising precipitously. "Mt. Raúsu," he said simply. It was completely covered in snow, its top looking like the head of someone who had little hair.

A snowslide blocked further progress on the road. There was only one recourse. "We go on foot from here," Atsuo said. They put on rubber boots and set out, Atsuo in the lead. They picked they way across rocks in the stream to the other side, then followed a branch of the stream into the woods along a narrow backwoodsman style trail. Atsuo took care to trample down the ground to make the way easier for Wakako.

"Here we are," he said at last, pointing to a waterfall issuing from a crevice in a large rock and running down to the river below. Rocks were laid out to pool the hot water in a space suitable for bathing.

"Wow, just like you said. A private hot spring!" Wakako leaped in delight. "You sure do know a lot of great stuff!"

"A long time ago before the war I came here fishing. There used to be a little hut a ways up from here. There was an old guy living in it. I guess he was like a hermit. He was the one who made this stone pool."

Atsuo went looking around the place where the hut had been, but couldn't find a trace of it. "People fade away, nature goes on," he muttered.

Wakako promptly threw off her clothes onto the snow and dipped a foot into the water. It was comfortably hot, but the slick moss on the rocks was unpleasant to the touch. Ignoring this, she plunged on in and settled into the water, to discover that the moss now felt like luxurious velvet. Letting her legs float, she looked upward. The bare treetops and blue sky wove a delightful pattern. The surface of the stream shimmered brightly at the edge of vision. Atsuo Yukimori was standing there. This was the first time she saw his body in the full light of day. It was a dazzling sight. Pale skin covered a sturdy frame. The hair on his chest and limbs was luxurious. It had taken time to produce that splendid body. Wakako's eyes narrowed in fascination. He stepped into the water slowly and took a place beside her, letting his legs float up. The sound of the wind through the mountain came softly from far away. The rushing of the stream was a satisfying melody. The joy of being together with him in this tranquility was such that she felt that her body might melt away. The next moment she felt a stirring of apprehension, as if someone's eyes were upon them. She consciously recalled the image from a while ago of ice floes with a thousand eyes. The last time she had taken LSD she had seen an ocean covered with eyes. Most likely that vision had influenced her to see eyes on those ice floes. But there was no reason to believe someone else might be here. She cast a frightened look around. His finger was pointing to a spot in the forest. "Deer," he whispered. She took at hard look. There were several doe among the trees, overlooked by a stag, whose head was visible in profile. It looked as if they had come to drink, but they did not approach the water's edge. The stag's antlers were inclined as he stood guardedly looking for danger. Finally, he slowly lowered his head and began to drink. The doe gathered to join him. Some were still baby fawns. "Oh, how cute!" Wakako said spontaneously. At that, the entire herd stiffened. The next moment, the stag had turned to show his white backside and was running away, with all the doe following behind. Then they were gone. "Aaah!" Wakako signed regretfully.

Atsuo laughed. "Just goes to show how skittish deer are about human voices."

"They come right up to a place like this."

"This mountain is full of them. It has plenty of one of their favorite foods — bamboo grass."

"Are there bears too?"

"Sure are, but we won't see them. They're hibernating now."

They were silent for a while. Then Wakako faced him straight on and said, "Sorry for asking about that. Killing people."

"It's okay. I'm glad you did ask. I'd been thinking I had to tell you. I don't want to keep anything from you. I have war buddies who keep everything from their wives and kids, it seems. But I think that is something you ought to bring out. I don't mean to everyone, just certain people."

Wakako thought about mentioning what Yukichi had said. "My uncle has killed people." But it seemed to her that would just hurt Atsuo and Yukichi both, so she kept it to herself.

"I'm thinking about putting my own past on paper — writing a memoir. As soon as I get it done I want you to read it."

"Please do write it. That's something I want to read."

"Since I'm out of work, for better or worse I have free time. And I have you to read it. It is definitely something worth doing right."

Atsuo cupped his hands in the hot water and sent out little waves. It was an indirect way of caressing Wakako's young body. The ripples went out and around her, the maiden eluding his touch. The mountain's shadow rose over the sun. Darkness was growing over the snow-covered forest floor. There was sleek darkness between the stones from which algae extended, blending with the darkness of the ground.

Wakako laughed brightly in the warmth above. He could not share her brightness. He did not doubt she associated no guilt with his admission to having taken human life. She had no way of grasping the terrible reality behind that admission. War was all about killing people, the greatest crime there is, and soldiers were the instrument of that crime. He did not think it possible to convey the meaning of it all to this maiden in the course of a short conversation. So he had to write it down.

Atsuo enjoyed writing. He had written poetry in prison and had already written down his experiences as a non-commissioned officer. So, he decided, then and there, he would write his memoir for the eyes of Wakako Ikéhata alone. That would be the mission to dedicate his efforts for the time it took to find another job. The decision made, Atsuo felt relieved at having a job to do once again. The blankness of his future had been oppressive. Now the blankness was replaced with a firm agenda.

"You smiled. You finally smiled!" Wakako said, slapping the water. "You get that way sometimes, like you fell into a dark hole and you don't come out. I really get worried."

"I have a lot to think about."

"You mean Yukichi?"

"Well . . ." That issue had not been in mind. He scratched at some moss with a finger. "Yeah, him too . . . Where the devil did he run off to? But more than that, I'm worried about you and me. About what's coming down the road next."

"What's there to worry about?"

"There's too much that's different for you and me. You're going to continue on in school back in Tokyo."

"I want to quit school and live right here, with the stars and the sea and the marsh and the snow and Mr. Yukimori."

"No. That's no good. I want you to continue your studies."

"I don't want me to continue my studies. I've had enough of forcing myself to do things I don't want to do. Here I can listen to what the stars have to say. I heard the stars' voices the other day when I saw a shooting star for the first time."

"What?" Atsuo sputtered.

"I told you about Tsu, right? That patient who got messages from the stars. I can understand what he meant, at least sort of."

"How?"

"There aren't any limits to the universe. There are more things about the universe than human beings can possibly understand. You can use computers to put together all human knowledge, but it's limited, it's just a tiny speck of all there is to know about the whole universe. That is the message from the stars."

"Okay, that makes sense."

"There's something I want to ask you about. What do you think about God?"

"God." He looked at her fair body shimmering below the water surface and felt stuck for an answer. God had been the farthest being of all from him. The familiar companions of his life had been crime, violence, labor, and hunting, all polar opposites of God. People, he could not have faith in. There had been no end to the betrayals he had met. Ichiro Fukawa's betrayal was only the latest, and the pain of that was still very fresh. As for himself, he carried a full load of sins committed for the sake of unreasoning violence and cruelty.

"You don't have to make such a sad face." Wakako flipped over and started swimming. Steam rose above her like a nimbus.

"It's because I'm sad. God has forsaken me."

"Me too. I'm the prodigal daughter. The lost sheep."

Wakako slipped away from him. Feeling more abandoned than ever, Atsuo was seized with a desire to capture her. She dove under the steaming water and grinned up at him from inside a dark forest of duckweed. (C'mere you!) Atsuo pulled her by the neck towards him. Kissing underwater, they rose upwards. As they swam with legs intertwined, he penetrated her. They rose and sank down, one and then the other in the upper position. This operation continued for a time. Finally, he pulled her onto the snow and ejaculated on melting snow. Wakako's loins trembled with joy.

"This is what you call happy," she said.

"Me too."

"Don't go anywhere. Stay just as you are forever."

"We'll freeze."

"That's all right. Let's die together."

And she really would not release him. Their embrace went on and on as in the cold as darkness fell, until they very nearly did freeze to death.

That night Atsuo made a call to Nemuro from their lodge. Suéko seemed startled at the unexpected call from her brother. Her voice quavered.

"Where are you?"

"Raúsu. Came looking for Yukichi."

"He's been arrested. They picked him up yesterday, in Akkeshi. Detectives were staked out at Tetsukichi's place."

"I see."

"They came around here. Not just once. They kept showing up. They were looking for him. And for you too."

"Me? I don't know what they would want with me. I haven't done anything wrong."

"I don't know what's going on. But, look, why did you suddenly disappear? They seem suspicious about that."

"I'm just traveling around. There's a reason, but I don't want to say over the phone. I'll tell you when I see you. I'll be there tomorrow."

"No, you mustn't come. They'll arrest you too. There are detectives waiting outside our place too. Maybe they're listening on this line."

"Listen, I haven't done anything wrong! Believe me!"

"They're telling me you quit Fukawa Motors. That president called here too. For heaven's sake what happened?" Suéko's voice was tearful.

Chapter 6

Darkness

Atsuo was arrested the morning after he returned to Tokyo.

He had unpacked his baggage the night before and gone to bed early, but thoughts of Wakako and Yukichi had kept him awake. Finally, he had resorted to drinking a few glasses of shochu for a nightcap, until he fell onto the bed in deep, drunken slumber. He awakened with an aching head and parched mouth to the sound of someone pounding on the door. He got up, put on his robe and called out, "Who is it?"

"Telegram for Mr. Yukimori!"

He opened the door and two men pushed their way inside. They were watching him with a guarded intensity that told his instincts they were police. He had been confronted by men this way many times before. By experience, he had learned that it comes to this if you did something wrong. What was different this time was that he had not done anything wrong, and so was not expecting to be arrested.

The older detective spoke. "We'd like for you to come with us." It was a flat tone that said it was an order, not a request.

Atsuo's response was polite. "Who might you be?" His voice was steady. He was steeling himself to be calm, but it was unpleasant to realize that his old habit of subservience in this situation was asserting itself.

"Police." He displayed the black leather police ID. Atsuo's headache spread through his entire brain as if he had received a blow on the head. But his sleepiness had vanished and he knew this was really happening. Having often dreamed of detectives walking in on him, he had until that moment been thinking this too might be a dream.

"There must be some mistake." Now his voice was quavering and he began to sweat profusely — more pathetic habits of his that emerged when addressing a police officer.

"We'll get you to the station and you'll find out then," the detective said with finality. Atsuo changed clothes like a soldier upon receiving marching orders. It was six-ten a.m. He took out some pain reliever medicine and asked permission to take the pills. His throat was parched, so he drank three glasses of water. A bit calmer, he noticed the older officer had a fleshy nose and a swollen jaw.

"May I see the arrest warrant?"

"There is no arrest warrant," the officer responded with a trace of politeness.

"Then what is the reason?"

"Go voluntarily. You'll be told the reason at the station."

"Voluntary accompaniment" supposedly means you can refuse, but if you do, there is nothing to prevent them from making a warrantless arrest. There was a young man standing guard outside the door, blocking the exit. He looked the type to hold about a fifth dan level in judo. Atsuo abandoned any intention of offering futile resistance.

Outside, the older officer led the procession down the stairs, the young ones behind Atsuo. There was a cold wind, and a drizzling rain was falling. Parked in the rainy mist was a light van, looking out of place for the neighborhood. A cigarette glowed beside the van — another man waiting. He threw away his cigarette as Atsuo approached, and quickly got into the driver's seat. The van was a 2,000 cc model by N. Corporation, bearing a license plate beginning with the number 8, meaning it was a special use vehicle, order made for police use. Atsuo was placed in the back seat, between two men.

The van started rolling without delay. The engine must have been warm, because it immediately began running smoothly. Atsuo turned to look back at the two-story apartment that had been his home for many years. The windows were all shut up, still slumbering. It was a small relief that he had been taken away quietly, with no one else knowing.

He pulled a cigarette out from his breast pocket. The older man to his right reflexively struck a match and held the flame in front of his nose. The sharp odor of the sulfur assailed his nostrils, making him cough. The cigarette tasted bad, for some reason. He watched the smoke curl, feeling baleful gazes turned upon him from both sides.

The car was traveling east along the Chuo Expressway. It was past daybreak, but the rows of high-rise buildings were dark and wet. The numbers of cars on the road driven by people on their way to work increased steadily. Traffic jams were starting by the time they were on the Shuto Expressway. The young detective answered a call on the car radio. To Atsuo, what he was saying might as well have been in a foreign language. His attention was claimed by the shapes of buildings and rooftop advertisements. There was nothing usual about these sights, but he had a presentiment he would not be seeing them again.

Why did they pick him up? Probably, they thought he was Yukichi's accomplice. If so, there wouldn't be any problem at all in clearing up the matter. To begin with, there wasn't even any possibility that Yukichi might have been the thief. These thoughts ran through Atsuo's mind again and again, as he smoked one bad-tasting cigarette after another.

The car took the exit ramp for Shiba Park and entered the Hibiya-bound flow of traffic, making Atsuo wonder where the devil they were taking him. The van turned into a narrow street, and presently he saw characters reading "Onarimon Police Station" along the length of a pillar the size of a lamp post outside a building about ten stories high. He hadn't been expecting anything quite this intimidating. The next moment, something more astounding occurred.

A swarm of people assembled in front of the police station building as if for a demonstration rushed the van en masse as it approached. A squad of police officers stood between the crowd and the van, but many people were nevertheless able to get close. Flashes from a battery of cameras went off again and again. Feeling something cold, Atsuo discovered that a pair of handcuffs bound his left hand to the right hand of the man on his left. A rope was wound about his waist. From the moment he stepped from the van, there was a continuing fusillade of clicks and flashes from the cameras. As he began to walk, he thought to cover his face with his right hand. What was the reason for all this commotion? Atsuo went into shock, and his mind stopped working. He walked in a daze. Led by the handcuff, he stumbled on the stairway.

He was taken to the Criminal Investigation section, a big room with uniformed patrolmen and women in plain clothes sitting at desks. The abrupt transition to quiet after the clamor outside made the setting quite peaceful.

Atsuo was taken to an interrogation room whose window was covered over by a black curtain. There, they removed his waist rope and handcuffs. Then he was made to sit before a desk for fingerprinting. Black ink was applied to the fingertips, then each finger was rolled, not pressed, upon the record paper. As he underwent the procedure, Atsuo felt as if it was all happening to someone else. It was hardly his first time; he had been fingerprinted countless times before, but this time there was no reason for these acts to be forced upon him. Next, his footprints were recorded, he was photographed, then given a strip search, in which the examining officer peered into his anus. He couldn't believe he was being subjected to all this. He was annoyed to realize he was not experiencing any of the reactions to these indignities one would expect a person to have — neither defiance, anger, nor self-hatred. I am not myself, he thought, even though I want to be myself.

His clothes back on and seated once again, Atsuo gazed at the ashtray on the table. It was a cheap piece of glass, thoroughly coated with cigarette residue. He stared hard at the nicotine stains, determined to calm himself. There was some mistake, but what was it? That gang of photographers didn't show up because they suspected he was in on some theft with Yukichi. It must be something big. So what about that . . . No, it couldn't be that.

"Here, take a break."

He was being addressed. He looked up. It was the older detective, holding out his cigarette pack.

"Thanks." Atsuo took a cigarette and the officer struck a match. He drew in deep and exhaled a cloud of smoke.

"Please tell me the reason for taking me here. I haven't . . ."

"You haven't done anything wrong? Nothing to get excited about. We'll be taking down your statements pretty soon. Tell us about it then."

"But this is voluntary accompaniment. You told me you would explain the reason at the station."

"Yeah, I did." The man appeared to lapse into thought, the sheen of his nose highlighting the black specks of the pores. His expression said he wasn't about to reveal any information. His broad shoulders backed the message like an unspoken threat of violence. It was clear that no questions would be answered.

The two-tatami mat room was like being in a hole. Not a glimpse of the outside world penetrated the black curtained windows. Bare light bulbs on the high ceiling assailed the eyes with their bright glare. A small steel table and some plain chairs were enough to fill the room. The door could not have been of ordinary construction, because no sound could be heard from the large room beyond. Atsuo was annoyed that he had completely lost track of the time, but he could not see the watch beneath the sleeve of the man's white shirt.

When he finished his cigarette, there was nothing else to do. Atsuo would normally use such a time to jot down matters that occurred to him in his notebook diary, but those items had been taken from him. He would have had another cigarette, but his own cigarettes had also been taken away. The man lit himself another cigarette. His gestures demonstrated he was enjoying it. But he didn't offer another one to Atsuo.

The man smoked in silence, ignoring Atsuo. He finished his second cigarette. Presently, he lit a third and suddenly asked, "You hungry?"

"Yes," Atsuo answered. The question made him realize that he was very hungry indeed. But the man did not follow up his question with any indication that Atsuo would be fed.

"I want to use the toilet," Atsuo said. Fortunately, the pills had eradicated his headache, but the three glasses of water were now sending an insistent message. He was accustomed to moving his bowels every morning and had not yet done so. Moreover, his stomach was unsettled. But the man did not answer. Atsuo was about to voice his request again when the door opened and two more men entered. They were, respectively, an assistant police inspector and a police sergeant. The three men surrounded Atsuo.

The inspector spoke, or, rather bellowed, very loudly, "Atsuo Yukimori, I'm talking to you!" His tone exuded arrogance. "You know why you're here, don't you?"

When Atsuo replied, "No, I have no idea," the sergeant took out a notebook. Realizing that interrogation had begun, Atsuo braced himself, resolving not to say a single word more than necessary.

"This isn't your first time with police. You know we don't pick up anybody unless there's a reason, right?" The last was yelled into Atsuo's ear.

"You better start talking now," the inspector continued. "It'll be worse for you if we have to say it first. You know that much, don't you? Don't you!"

"I'm afraid not." The pressure in Atsuo's bladder was making him wince. His bowels were also threatening to release themselves. "Excuse me. I need to use the toilet," he said, bowing his head in supplication.

"Don't try to change the subject. I'm asking you a serious question, Yukimori. We got a lot of other cases to handle, but there's three of us here just to take care of you. Understand? So start talking now!"

"I really do have to use the toilet."

The assistant inspector leaned over Atsuo menacingly and yelled "Damn fool!" sending flecks of spittle into his face. "I just told you not to change the subject. This is a big moment in your life, so don't play dumb!"

"Come on now, Yukimori," said the older plainclothes detective. He was purring agreeably, as if his attitude hadn't been threatening just moments before. "Just be honest and say it, that's all. If you do that, we let you go to the toilet."

"What do you mean, 'Say it?' Say what?"

"That's for you to think about. It's your own issue."

"I've really got to go." Atsuo was shivering. Cold sweat broke out on his face.

"I'll just try one question. Where'd you run away to before you got back home yesterday?"

"I wasn't running away from anything. I was on vacation."

"Where?"

Waves of pain were shuttling between Atsuo's solar plexus and anus. He thought of Wakako. If he started talking about where he went he would have to mention her name. He had to keep her out of this no matter what. Desperately holding back the urge to evacuate, he vividly remembered the times in the army prison workshop waiting for permission to urinate and, even worse, holding back diarrhea. All he had to do was concentrate, and he could hold on for close to an hour. The best course was keeping his mind off it.

"Well?" The assistant inspector banged the table with his fist. "I asked you where you went on that vacation!"

Atsuo closed his eyes. He recalled scenes of his trip with Wakako that began with their arrival at Kushiro Airport. Conversations as they sat in the train and views from the train windows came back with crystal clarity. The agony in his gut receded into the distance. Then the men standing before him receded into the background. Questions were raining down upon him, but did not seem to have much to do with him. "You going to keep quiet?" . . . "Why don't you answer?" . . . He realized they were annoyed with him.

The assistant inspector struck the table. This display of latent violence was not as impressive as Torakichi could perform it. "You went to meet Yukichi Jinnai, didn't you?" he said.

"Is Yukichi here?" Atsuo asked, opening his eyes as if awakening from a deep dream.

"Yeah, you met Yukichi! Didn't you?"

"Just say yes and you can go to the toilet," the elder detective, still affecting a soothing voice.

"Yukichi is here, isn't he? Take me to him."

"Why do you want to see him?" the assistant inspector asked.

"He's my nephew. Just an uncle wanting to see his nephew, that's all."

"The question is, did you meet Yukichi in Hokkaido? We know you went to Hokkaido with Wakako Ikéhata. You stayed in that lodge Peken on Lake Furen, then two nights at the Takasago lodge in Raúsu."

The mention of Wakako's name abruptly raised Atsuo's anxiety. Why did the police know about their confidential journey?

"What about Wakako Ikéhata?"

"You want to know about Wakako Ikéhata? Okay, I'll tell you. She's your accomplice, isn't she?"

"Accomplice?" This statement so surprised Atsuo he almost lost control of his bladder. "What are you talking about? She's just a girl who isn't involved in any kind of crime."

"Yeah? So why were you traveling together?"

"Is there anything wrong with a man going on a trip with his girl?"

"Oh, she's your girlfriend, huh? That's nice. Except that you're forty-nine and she's twenty-four. Well, maybe age doesn't matter in affairs of the heart, but you happen to be an ex-con and she happens to be a student radical in the Q. Sect. That's quite a pair to be taking a trip together. You want me to tell you what brought you together? It's got to do with a lot more than romance. You were traveling together to Hokkaido because that was the getaway plan. And you were going to meet Yukichi Jinnai because he was in on it."

"That doesn't make sense. What getaway plan?"

"That's exactly what we want you to tell us. You are Yukichi Jinnai's uncle and you are a key figure in this case who suddenly took off for parts unknown. If that isn't making a getaway, you tell me what it was."

"This is ridiculous." Atsuo was suddenly on his feet, pushing past the police sergeant. He opened his trouser front before the far wall and began urinating against it. The sergeant jumped aside to avoid the stream.

Next, he dropped his pants and was preparing to finish his business when the elder detective said, "Wait. I'll take you to the toilet."

The door to the toilet stayed wide open, as Atsuo had his bowel movement under watch by the plainclothes detective and the assistant inspector. The situation itself was nothing new to him. In detention centers and prisons it's considered utterly normal for guards to observe inmates during defecation. But this time he felt burning humiliation, unable to accept being yanked into the status of prisoner for no reason.

Back in the interrogation room, the assistant inspector bawled out Atsuo for the mess, handed him rags, a mop, and a bucket and ordered him to clean up the urine. Atsuo took the chore as a refreshing diversion. He made liberal use of the water, scrupulously scrubbing the places on the wall and floor that had taken the spray. That left a conspicuous discrepancy between the freshly cleaned places and the rest of the room. "Looks funny this way. Shall I finish the job?" Atsuo asked.

"That's enough," the assistant inspector said with disgust.

"Supposedly, I came here voluntarily. The visit is over. I'm leaving," Atsuo said, bowing.

The assistant inspector opened a drawer and pulled out a single sheet of paper. "Fact is, we got an arrest warrant," he said.

The charge was robbery. Atsuo Yukimori was suspected of conspiring with Yukichi Jinnai to commit two thefts from the office of the president of Fukawa Motors, of 170,000 yen and 427,000 yen, respectively, in cash, to provide funding for the radical Q. Sect student group. Furthermore, he was suspected of "fleeing" together with Wakako Ikéhata, an active member of Q. Sect, for the purpose of destroying evidence.

"This is crazy. There's no grounds for any of this," Atsuo said. Since he'd been questioned about Yukichi's disappearance, it wasn't unexpected that his connection with his nephew might fall under suspicion, but this allegation that Wakako could somehow be involved took him by surprise. "Especially this stuff about Wakako Ikéhata. She hasn't done anything."

"Does that mean Yukichi Jinnai did something?"

"Yukichi isn't the kind of man who seals money."

"He already confessed. He said he gave the money to Wakako Ikéhata."

"I don't believe it."

"We know every place Yukichi was, right up to where we caught him. But we haven't recovered the cash. Where'd he stash it? You know, so let's hear it."

"I haven't met him once since he disappeared. Wakako Ikéhata and I went to Hokkaido alone. It was nothing more than a simple, private trip."

"So you admit you traveled with Wakako and the destination was Hokkaido."

Atsuo regretted his words. He had fallen for a leading question. Still, they even knew the name of the places they had stayed at. They would have checked the sign-in records and found "Atsuo and Wakako Yukimori" in his handwriting. Of course they would also have checked the passenger lists on their air flights. Maybe they even found that taxi driver in Nemuro. They knew everything about where he and Wakako had been. Well, what of it? If he just laid it all out himself, he could show there wasn't any time when they could have met Yukichi. When he called Nemuro from Raúsu, Suéko had said Yukichi was arrested "the day before yesterday." That meant the day they had taken a flight from Hanéda to Kushiro, then immediately taken the train to Nemuro. All he had to do was give proof of everything they had done that day, and it would be evident there had been no opportunity to meet Yukichi . . . No, that was no good. If Yukichi had been in Nemuro, it would just show they could have met.

Atsuo decided to keep his mouth shut. There wasn't anything he had to say, so he just wouldn't say anything . . . Well, were they going to arrest Wakako too? What was all this for? What were they up to?

Atsuo kept stubbornly silent, no matter what questions they asked. Eventually, the assistant police inspector seemed to give up. After about two hours, he was taken in handcuffs and waist rope to the station holding center. It was located in back of the kendo gym, behind a massive steel door at the end of a narrow passageway, next to a tiny room marked "Attorneys' Conference Room."

After the steel door had clanged shut behind him, a guard came on his rounds and removed Atsuo's handcuffs and waist rope. Before him was a row of four cells, with another one off to the side. They were barred, exactly like animal cages. The eyes of the men under watch inside gleamed exactly like those of caged animals. Dark windows high up on the wide walls of the building left no doubt that the space was a prison. He had been in such holding centers in many police stations, and had vowed he would never return. Nevertheless, he was there once again. Put inside his cell, Atsuo hung his head and sighed deeply.

The cell was long and narrow, with wood flooring. There were three other occupants. A middle-aged man was at the far end of the cell, squatting over the hole in the floor that served as the toilet. A tall, thin young man nodded to Atsuo at the entrance. As he walked along the wall he came to a short man with long hair. Physically, he so closely resembled Makihiko Moriya that Atsuo turned to check, but it was someone else. The man returned no smile. He walked past Atsuo, then turned around and walked in another direction. The man who had finished wiping his backside suddenly yelled out, "Boss! Finished with the toilet. Please flush!"

The guard turned a handle and there was a rush of water. Atsuo remembered this system, unique to police station prisons, for preventing inmates from disposing of evidence. The middle-aged man noticed Atsuo and averted his eyes apprehensively. He went to a corner, sat down and kept still. The lanky youth drew near Atsuo.

"S'cuse me, mister. What are you here for?"

"I'm innocent. There was some mistake."

"Innocent." The youth closed a pair of tiny eyes and began to laugh. He laughed wholeheartedly, belly heaving and tears coming to his eyes. "That's what everyone says. It's so funny."

"Well, what did you do?"

"I didn't do anything. I was framed. The guy says I pinched his stuff, but I didn't take nothing. That dick over there with the long hair is in for a rollover job. He's not talking. He'll probably say he's innocent too. That old guy, he's got face. He's a big man in the Asakusa yakuza."

A voice from another cell called out, "Boss! Finished peeing. Please flush." The guard turned a handle and there was a flushing sound. There was a constant murmur of low voices, but the only time anyone spoke out loud was for a toilet flushing request.

"If you don't mind me saying, I get the feeling you're up for offing somebody. You don't have to get mad about it. You got that killer look, and the build for it too. I figured that's got to be it. Are you in a family?"

Atsuo glared at the man. "You are a stupid punk who don't know etiquette. You don't go up to a man in this place and start nosing into his past. You look like a stooge in some pickpocket gang, with that callus on your right middle finger, so don't hand me any half-assed lies."

"Sorry, boss." The tall one backed off and assumed a formal sitting posture before Atsuo and bowed his head. "Guess you must have men like me under you."

"Keep quiet. I got things to think about."

Atsuo turned his back to the tall one and folded his arms. That arrest warrant was crazy. He couldn't see how they could prove any of it, if they actually tried to prosecuted him. It bothered him, though, that they thought Wakako was an active member of Q. Sect and that Yukichi stole large sums of money twice to fund it. Was it possible Yukichi had secretly met Wakako? No, not that girl. No reason on earth to think she would . . . As his thoughts reached that point, Atsuo moaned aloud.

It was ridiculous to think that Yukichi would steal twice to get money for Q. Sect. He was a right-wing zealot who loved war songs. On the other hand, he seemed to have visited T. University quite often to be in on the rioting there. So what about him meeting Makihiko Moriya or somebody from Q. Sect? And maybe Wakako too? . . . No, the first time Yukichi met her was last October at the Korakuen skating rink, right? "That's the kind of girl I hate. They put on that 'Oh, so nice' act," he'd said, with a disgusted expression. The next time was in January this year. It was the second day of that battle at the Tower with the riot police. Wakako had fled into the Fukawa Motors workers' dorm. Yukichi was running to get things for the girl he supposedly hated, serving her like she was a princess and he was her servant . . . That certainly did not look as if they knew each other well. They next time they met was at the Korakuen skating rink, which they circled fifteen times, according to the rink "skating critic" and Wakako. He loved her, as she said, so it would make no sense at all for him to do something that had to do with Q. Sect. That arrest warrant was laughably absurd. They said Yukichi confessed, but that was unbelievable. There wasn't anything for him to confess to. But one thing that was beyond understanding was why Yukichi disappeared suddenly, immediately after the four-hundred-thousand yen was stolen. He could have formally quit the job. There wasn't any need for him to run away or go into hiding when the money disappeared . . . And where was Wakako now? She couldn't have been arrested. Could she?

The night before, he had accompanied Wakako as far as the outside of her house. Had he not talked her into going home, she would have gone back to her apartment off the west exit of Shinjuku Station. She had wanted him to go inside with her and meet her parents, brother, and sister, but he resisted on the grounds it was getting late and he wasn't very presentable after the long journey. She smiled, waved her hand and said, "Well, see ya' again." By the time he had run back to the doorstep, wanting to give her another embrace, she had disappeared inside. Back in his apartment, he was running his washing machine when Wakako called. She was speaking in a low voice, but he heard her with bell-like clarity.

"Naturally, showing up after two weeks was a big surprise to everybody. But my mother is used to this, so she just said, 'Oh, welcome back.' Sorry to be talking so quiet. My mother's at the door, listening. My father came home early enough for dinner, which is unusual. So we all had dinner together. No, not all of us — my sister stayed in her room. She didn't want to lose the time a normal meal takes this close to her entrance exam. She says she's too busy to talk to us. My father asked me where I went. I said I went to Hokkaido with a man. Then I said I'm going to marry him, and my mother — she's listening outside the door, I can hear her breathing — my mother dropped her chopsticks, like she had a heart attack. Later, my father came to my room. He said the police kept coming while I was away, asking where I was. He said he told them I'm not right in the head and I have a habit of straying from home, and that's a big problem. Then he said I should go back to the mental hospital."

"Go to the hospital for what? There's nothing wrong with you. I'll vouch for that."

"I don't think there's anything wrong with me either. But my father thinks what I do is abnormal — not going to class, running away from the hospital, running away from home, wandering off to Hokkaido, and most especially traveling with a man as an unmarried woman. 'That's abnormal,' he says. So I yelled at him, if you're going to put me in the hospital again I'll leave home for good. Then he said, 'They think you're in with the radicals. You'll be arrested if you run away from home again. You'll be safe in the hospital.' He says they have detectives posted around the house all the time. I tell you, this is scary! They are saying it is either the joint or the hospital for me. It's really scary!"

"Wait a minute. If the police have your house staked out they might be listening in on this conversation. I better hang up now. I'll get in touch later."

He had already known that Yukichi was under suspicion for those thefts of 170,000 and 400,000 yen and that Wakako was suspected of being a student radical because of her relationship with Makihiko Moriya. But he hadn't seen himself as a link between them, liable to be arrested. Since they had arrested him, he was worried Wakako had been arrested too.

The anxiety was an oppressive weight, a lurking beast that threatened to tear him apart. Wakako was guilty of absolutely nothing. She hadn't done anything wrong.

"Boss!" The tall youth was rubbing his hands together as he approached. "You got busted this morning, right? What was it like outside? Were there a lot of reporters and photographers?"

"Huh?" Atsuo heard what was being said to him without grasping the meaning. The youth's face seemed to swim in the gray murk of his thoughts. His eyes were perfect circles on a long, featureless face that bespoke sheer curiosity.

"See, I've been in here two weeks. The past week has been crazy. They keep hauling in student radicals they busted. Some were girls. Blows me away. This morning there was a big uproar outside. It was still dark when it started up. I figured they must have caught some big wig. I wanted to see his face, but no one showed up. Then you came in."

"Yeah? So what's it all about?"

"Ah, come on! There's only one thing it could be!"

"What's that? Haven't read any papers for a while."

"The Shinkansen bombing last week. Student radicals did it — some group named Q. Those students are getting really vicious. They go busting people up. They don't care if they kill someone. Maybe I'm a crook, but I never hurt no one."

"Me neither." Atsuo decided to talk with the tall one. He could supply needed information. "Actually, I'm in the pickpocket line too."

"Might have known it!" The tall one flexed his fingers like a pianist at the keyboard. "That makes us buddies. Pleased to meet you." The last was delivered with a respectful inclination of the head.

"So where did you do your prior?" Atsuo asked, motioning the tall one to join him at the far end of the cell. The middle-aged yakuza and the long-haired mugger were by the barred entrance door.

"Urawa."

"Yeah? Still new in the business!" The prison in the city of Urawa is for first offenders.

"Where you been, boss?"

"I was at Fuchu." Fuchu Prison, in greater Tokyo, is for repeat offenders. "Everybody there has a record long as your arm."

"Aah, Fuchu." The tall one repeated the name with utmost respect.

"But I never messed up bad enough to land in Chiba." Chiba prison houses inmates who are serving long terms, usually for homicide.

"Nah, that place is for losers," the tall one said, laughing.

"The worst losers are in the tank in Tokyo, waiting to get their necks stretched. That's where they're putting the radicals."

"They don't know their asses from their elbows," the tall one said, with a furtive laugh and a side glance in the direction of the guard. "A bunch of rich little boys and girls. Some of 'em started crying. Pathetic. If they want to start a revolution, they better learn how to hustle on the street first."

"Girls been coming in too?"

"There was one, in that protection cell over there," the tall one said, pointing with his right finger. All detention centers have protection cells with tatami rather than wood floors for holding women and minors separately. Unfortunately, the protection cell was the farthest one from Atsuo's location. He thought, She might be in there. The impulse to shout out her name burned hot in his throat.

All of a sudden, the guard began shouting. "Hey, you two over there! You're talking too much. Keep quiet!"

Atsuo and the tall one looked at one another and laughed derisively. They continued their conversation, speaking softly. The guard's command notwithstanding, the murmur of conversations from the cells increased. It would take more than one guard to maintain strict control over all the prisoners.

Atsuo went to the hole in the floor that served as the toilet, urinated and yelled out "Boss, need a flush please!" He thought Wakako would know it was him if she could hear his voice. "Turn on the water please," he called out once again.

"And how many of those student radicals are there?"

"Guess they must have brought in about ten. But they're all out in two or three days. They probably sent them to the tank at Met HQ. There's maybe two here now — three if you count the girl."

"Is it easy to tell if it's a student?"

"You can tell by how long the interrogation lasts. They're public security cases. They get pulled out of here early in the morning and they ain't back until nine, ten at night. That's like torture, man. It'd be more than I could take. Me, I was done quick because I admitted everything. The prosecutor just read out the police records, I said, 'Yeah,' and that was it."

The steel door opened and an officer came inside, pushing a meal cart. Aluminum trays were being passed out, beginning with the cell at the end. Atsuo immediately felt ravenous. He had been hauled in at daybreak without breakfast. Now it was lunch time. Some men received box lunches or lunch bowls purchased with their own money from a caterer. The yakuza boss got a sumptuous meal of broiled eel in nested lacquered boxes. The fillets glistening sweet kabayaki sauce were a tasty-looking sight to be envied. The tall one brought Atsuo's portion to him. As he was lifting a piece of fried fish with his chopsticks, his name was called.

"Atsuo Yukimori! Interrogation! Get up!"

At the cell's entrance he was handcuffed and a rope was tied around his waist. Two policemen led him to the interrogation room. Seated inside were the same assistant police inspector, police sergeant, and the elder plainclothesman, now wearing the uniform of a police sergeant. The two officers who had escorted Atsuo stood to his rear. He was feeling the oppressiveness of being handcuffed and surrounded by five men as the assistant inspector began the session by yelling in his face.

"Atsuo Yukimori! You're not getting away with playing stupid anymore! We've got a lot of questions, and we're not going to go easy on you. I'll tell you right off, you are suspected of putting a bomb on the Hikari Shinkansen. You must know about it. It was big news. February eleventh, last Tuesday. The bomb went off at four-oh-two in the afternoon, when the train was at Shimbashi. Two dead and twenty-eight injured."

"I think there is some mistake. I haven't . . ."

"You did it, mister!" The assistant inspector glared at him with bloodshot eyes. The ironic tone, the roundabout way of questioning he had affected a short while ago was completely gone.

"Certainly not. I had nothing to do with it."

"You must have read about it in the papers."

"I read something about it. Not much. I don't really know about it."

"Yeah? They're covering it every day on the front page."

"I didn't read any papers while I was traveling."

"You didn't read any papers. You didn't read anything about the job you did. That's too much to swallow. But okay, just skip that. Since you didn't do the job, let's hear you prove your alibi. What did you do that day? Tell me what you did that day, starting in the morning."

"That's a little hard to remember, all of a sudden."

"The eleventh! National Foundation Day!"

"Oh." That was the day he lost his job at Fukawa Motors. "I went to work, at Fukawa Motors."

"It was a holiday."

"Yes. We had a lot of car repairs to do. Everyone came to work that day. It's a small outfit. Everyone was giving up their time off to get the work done."

"So you went to the shop. What did you do?"

"I worked."

"Dummy! I didn't think you went to your shop to play! I want to know what work you did."

"A chassis had to be broken down and reassembled. I did that until noon. I had vegetable and pork fried rice for lunch at a place near the shop. After that, I left the shop."

"Why?"

"Because I was fired."

"Well, it seems the company president, Ichiro Fukawa, said you could stay on until payday in March." This question projected assurance, acquired from records of interviews with Fukawa and other company employees.

"I didn't want to work there any more after being fired. There wasn't any big difference in leaving then and staying around through March."

"Getting another month and a half of pay is a big difference. Why didn't you take that? Your story isn't very convincing. So, what time did you leave the shop?"

"After lunch, I took out all my things from my locker and left with them. I guess it was a little before two."

"What did you do with your stuff from the locker?"

"I put it in a paper bag and took it with me."

"What color was this paper bag? Describe it."

"It was light brown. Like a tote bag. I got it from a bookstore, S. Books, when I bought books there."

"Tell me everything you put into that bag."

"What does that matter? . . . Ah, whatever. Everything that was in the locker

— five work uniforms, shaving kit, mechanic's license, English-Japanese dictionary . . . That's about it."

"Must've been pretty heavy."

"It was light. As a matter of fact, I was thinking it was too light to be all I had there, after working in that shop seven years."

"We've got testimony that it looked like a heavy paper bag. Of all the bags you could use, you picked a sturdy bag like you get from a bookstore. That must mean you were going to put something heavy inside."

"That's not right. S. Books is close by Fukawa Motors. I go there a lot to buy books."

"Where did you go after you left the shop?"

"I went directly home to my apartment."

"Where did you go from, and how? Train? Subway? Bus? Name the places and times of departure."

"I went from Ochanomizu Station. Took the rapid service train to Mitaka. Must have been about two☒thirty when I got there. Then I took the Chofu-bound bus from the south exit and got off at Nozaki. Arrived at my apartment about three o'clock. Then I went for a walk."

"A walk? That means you left that apartment again."

"I can't go for a walk inside the apartment."

"I didn't ask you for jokes, mister, I'm asking you serious questions. Where did you go for a walk? How did you go? No, before we get to that, why did you go for a walk at a time like that? That's no time to take a walk."

"Who says there's only certain times when it's okay to go for a walk? I like to go for walks. I was just fired, out of the blue. I was in a bad mood. Going for a walk is just the thing to do at a time like that. I went to Jindai Botanical Garden Park. It's close by. I go there a lot."

"Who did you meet?"

"In the park? It was filled with people. It was a holiday and the plum trees were in full bloom. I wasn't expecting to see so many people. That park has a beautiful grove of plum trees with a bamboo grove in back. The sky was overcast, and you could see both the light green of the bamboo and the red and white plum blossoms."

"Were you still in the park around four in the afternoon?"

"I would think so. No, I know I was because I heard the announcement at four thirty that the park closes at five, and then I left at closing time. It must have been five thirty when I was back in my apartment. It was getting dark."

"Got it. Now, is there anyone who can verify your story? Did you meet anyone you know going back home? Anyone at all, in the park, on the way back or at your apartment?"

"Someone I know? . . . No, I didn't meet anyone I know. Crossed paths with a lot of people I don't know, though."

"In other words, you can't prove this story you just handed me. That's because it's a pack of lies."

"I haven't said a thing that isn't true. I gave you honest answers, as complete as I could."

"Sure was complete. A lot too complete! You expect us to believe you could remember everything you did on a day eight days back, in that much detail? You're giving us all this stuff for your alibi, but it won't work."

"No, certainly not. I was fired that day. It wasn't any ordinary day. There's plenty of reason for me to remember everything that happened that day."

"Yeah, but you don't have any witnesses backing your story. You didn't pass by anyone you know, no one who lives in that apartment building — no one. It doesn't add up. Unless it's a story you made up that just happens to have no witnesses, so you could cover up your lies. I can't think of any other explanation."

"You see, we have a number of witnesses. They told about what they saw at about three thirty p.m. in Tokyo Station, on a Shinkansen platform. To be more precise, on Platform Eighteen, near the south exit stairwell. They saw a man about fifty years old, with a hefty build, wearing a brown coat and carrying a light brown paper bag that looked heavy. And he was standing there with a young woman in her twenties. That's what the witnesses say!"

"A young woman?"

"That's right. And we know she was Wakako Ikéhata. We showed her picture to witnesses who said it looks exactly like the woman they saw."

"Well, they're completely mistaken. First of all, I never met Wakako Ikéhata on that day."

"Why do you insist that was the one day you didn't meet her? From what I hear, you two are tight. Looks like you were meeting every day. You met her on the following day, at the 'If' coffee shop in Shinjuku. They next day you stayed together at a hotel. Then the day after that you went on the lam together to cover up your tracks. So don't expect us to believe the only day you didn't meet was the day the crime occurred."

"Wakako Ikéhata has nothing to do with it. We traveled together for purely personal reasons."

"Yeah, right. You did the job for your politics, then you went on the lam for purely personal reasons. Can't you come up with better lies than that?"

"Neither one of us has anything to do with that crime."

"All right, then, prove your alibi. Give us the proof you were in Jindai Botanical Garden, or wherever, between three thirty and four o'clock, which is when Hikari Number 33 blew up. You can't, can you? Wakako Ikéhata can't either. So it was you two on the platform at Tokyo Station . . ."

"Was Wakako Ikéhata arrested?"

"Don't interrupt. You two were on the platform at Tokyo Station, before that bomb went off, and you were carrying a heavy paper bag."

"That's ridiculous. It's completely unfounded."

"What? You know what you just said? Our organization put all its effort into an investigation that you just called ridiculous. Don't you know any civility? Apologize!"

"Sorry, I shouldn't have said that, but . . ."

"All you have to do is get straight and admit it, that's all. Do that and things get easy for you. The questions get simple. You can skate through all this. You're an ex-con, you been around the block a few times. You're just making it hard on yourself. Soon as it looks like we're getting somewhere, we'll let you have some ramen. You must be hungry." The last was spoken by the assistant inspector in an unexpectedly courteous tone.

Atsuo was suddenly acutely conscious that he had been hungry for a very long time. He was weak and hungry. An officer placed a bowl of ramen before him. It was cold, with lumps of congealed fat floating in the soup, but it carried a wonderful smell that sent inviting signals to his stomach. Atsuo swallowed. He was a fish becoming more and more entangled as it struggled in a mesh net. He wanted to get a grip on himself, but lacked the will do so. He sighed, and his handcuffs clattered.

"Well, let's try getting back to the day of the crime. That bomb was made with black gunpowder. It so happens you have black gunpowder, don't you, Yukimori?"

"Yes, I have a little for hunting . . ."

"Oh, for hunting? Okay, let's see about that. You used black powder in the explosion you set off on the banks of the Furen River on November eighteenth last year. Were you hunting then? What's the matter, can't answer that? There were witnesses to that experiment. It was quite a big blast. When the guard from the salmon roe extraction station came running to see what happened, he saw you up in a tree, watching it. Afterwards, a crime scene investigator determined that black gunpowder and a three-way coupler had been used. At the time, all that was known was the culprit fled the scene on a bike. A district forestry office car passed the culprit on that bike. When we were checking on you, it turned up that on November eighteenth of last year — the day of that explosion — you took a bike to the Furen River from Torakichi Jinnai's house in Nemuro. That right? You were responsible for that explosion."

"And that's not all. You conducted two test explosions the year before last, also in November. The first time, you stuffed a bottle with smokeless gunpowder into the banks of the Furen River. The second time you put smokeless powder into an iron pipe and exploded it by Lake Furen. There are witnesses for that, too. Ichiro Fukawa overheard you talking in a low voice, telling Torakichi Jinnai about your first experiment. He was in the next room. You were witnessed fleeing the scene in an aluminum boat immediately after the second explosion.

"So there isn't anything left for you to hide. We know you conducted three test explosions, and that you set off each one using a spring-driven timer. We know your tests showed you that the billowing smoke you get from black gunpowder is more terror inducing than smokeless powder. And we know that after this careful series of tests you picked National Foundation Day for your bomb attack to make a big statement of opposition to the emperor."

"No, that's all wrong."

"What's wrong? There are witnesses and sure proof to all three test explosions and the train bombing. It doesn't seem to me like there's anything wrong."

Atsuo couldn't find a rejoinder. He fell to thinking. They had all the facts about his experiments with explosives. But if he admitted to them, it would amount to admitting to the train bombing. At the same time, he knew from long experience that denying the three experiments was no good either. Once you start lying, you are bound to be tripped up by your own statements, over things that don't square, until ultimately everything falls in on you.

"I suppose you want that ramen. You're suddenly quiet. Trying to think up a new set of lies? It won't work. All the evidence is against you. It's time to own up and get it off your chest. Then for dinner we'll get you broiled eel or sushi or whatever you want."

Atsuo remained silent. The assistant inspector chose to refrain from pressing him further. Suddenly, he rose and left the room. The police sergeant who was acting as recording secretary and the other two officers followed him out. The older police sergeant — the one who had been in plain clothes for Atsuo's arrest — was the only one who remained behind in the room with Atsuo. He worked his expansive jaw while exhaling heavily, releasing a steady stream of smoke from the cigarette protruding from his mouth that drifted against Atsuo's face. He pulled at the black curtains covering the window for a peek outside, then shot a glance at his wristwatch. After a while, he began muttering as if to himself, as he looked away from Atsuo.

"You know, Yukimori, I feel sorry for you, I really do. We know everything. Everything about that long record of yours, about your history of hunting, that you were in the machine gun corps and you know how to use explosives, given those three bomb experiments and the Shinkansen bombing. We know it from third-party witness testimony and hard evidence. If you deny it, you're still going to be indicted, and then what happens? You're a repeat offender — you know well and good what's going to happen. Overturning a train resulting in death, homicide, attempted homicide, causing injury, illegal use of explosives — that's the death penalty, no question about that. But if you get straight and confess, express deep regret in your testimony, then you're looking at life, maybe even a limited term. You really ought to think about that like a grownup and do the sensible thing. Hey, I don't want to see you get death. You know what's even sadder? Wakako Ikéhata. Yeah. To think of that beautiful young girl going to the gallows with you, that's just awful. Oh, incidentally, you can have your ramen. Looks like it got cold, though."

Atsuo was handcuffed and tied up with a rope, making him unable to pick up the chopsticks that lay beside the bowl of noodles. The inspector released his right hand, leaving the handcuffs attached to the left hand. Atsuo picked up the chopsticks. The noodles, cold and soggy, entered Atsuo's famished belly in the capacity of supremely welcome nutrition. It was necessary to lay the chopsticks down and pick up the bowl to drink the soup. He was half finished when the assistant inspector and recording secretary sergeant reentered, together with a new addition, an inspector, elegantly tall and slim. When Atsuo hastily put his bowl down, the inspector said in a ringing tenor,

"Go ahead and eat! Meals are a right!"

Atsuo had to continue eating under those four pairs of eyes. He was beginning to get a bitter taste on the tip of his tongue, but he was focused on getting nourishment inside, so he drank off the broth of soy sauce and oil to the last drop. Of course, there was no tea for cleansing the palate. His right hand was shackled once again.

"He's the investigation chief," said the assistant inspector, indicating the inspector. Atsuo bowed his head and then looked closely at the man standing directly before him, as he swallowed repeatedly to clear the dregs of ramen soup from his throat. The officer appeared to be still in his twenties. He had a face that projected intelligence. The impression Atsuo received was that this man belonged to a different class of persons from those like the assistant inspector, who only advance up the ladder slowly, one rung at a time.

"Atsuo Yukimori," he said, speaking rapidly, as if further identification of the suspect was necessary. "I have a few points to confirm. Please answer the questions. What is your relationship with Makihiko Moriya?"

When Atsuo did not respond, the inspector cracked the kind of bright smile one gets from a highly competent salesman.

"Oh, perhaps you don't recall. He's a student at T. University. He's intimate with Wakako Ikéhata. Guess you could say he's your love rival."

The inspector leaned against the back of his chair, which seemed too small for his rangy torso, and brushed a hand against a sleeve of his uniform, as if removing dust specks. He seemed to be a career specialist in public security. It was ominous to be questioned by such an official about the prominent Q. Sect figure, Makihiko Moriya. Atsuo's gaze slipped away from the inspector and fixed upon a grease spot in an ashtray that looked like a bearded old man.

"You don't want to answer?" the inspector continued smoothly. "Well, you have a right to stay silent, if that's what you want to do, but Makihiko Moriya is telling us he knows you very well. He says he's been in contact with you a good many times. He told us about detailed discussions he had with you about the Shinkansen bomb job. Wakako Ikéhata has confirmed that. If you don't have anything to say about that, that's the same as affirming their testimony. You listening to what I'm saying?"

Atsuo looked up and his eyes met the large eyes, round, unblinking and opened wide, of the inspector. Atsuo realized they gleamed because he was wearing contact lenses.

"From what they tell us, it seems that Q. Sect was planning to use bombs in its revolutionary campaign from the time it was founded in the spring of 1967. The story is that Wakako Ikéhata struck up a relationship with you at the skating rink — she'd already known you for a while. You wanted to be in on Q. Sect's revolution, so you decided to conduct test explosions that you then carried out in mid-November, 1967. Actually, we have the exact dates. The sites of two tests were the banks of the Furen River and one was by Lake Furen. You reported the results to Makihiko Moriya, Wakako Ikéhata, and other key Q. Sect players. That's how it was, right? Well? Can I take your silence to mean those are the facts?

"There was a string of bombings in 1967. One went off in a rest room of Hanéda Airport on February fifteenth, there was another explosion by the

Shinkansen ticket counter in Tokyo Station on March thirty-first and an attempted bombing of the Shinkansen Hikari on April fifteenth. That job was a lot like the one you were arrested for. No doubt you were looking at it closely. That's clear from the way you so carefully made newspaper clippings for your scrap book. Then there was the bombing of the Sanyo Railway Line on April eighteenth — Oh! I see from your expression that one got to you! That's because there's a close link between the Sanyo Line bombing and this one ... Let's see ... There was a failed bombing attempt on the Sobu West Line on July thirteenth.

"So by the time you were testing bombs in November, 1967, you had learned a lot on the subject from past bombings. We can see you were completely in the spirit of the times doing such careful, scientific testing. Why? Because you like new things, Atsuo Yukimori. You're on the cutting edge with your knowledge of automotive engineering, you're fascinated with the bombings done by the revolutionary superstars. That's where you fit right in with the revolutionary line of Q. Sect. As far as they were concerned, I would say they found a very valuable partner in you. That Makihiko Moriya was smart, the way he used Wakako Ikéhata to bring you in with their team. If it's a skating rink, right out in public, no one's going think it strange for a young woman to be with a much older man.

"So you operated under direction from Q. Sect. The bomb attack plans were moving right along by 1968, but then the political situation changed for Q. Sect. They became very busy when the student struggle broke out across the whole country, so they put your bombing operation on hold for a while."

The inspector abruptly fell silent and scrutinized Atsuo's face, as if looking for signs of his words' effect. The speech was delivered in a rapid monotone, expressionless, like a rote reading of a newspaper article, but its meaning was quite clear. Atsuo had been listening cautiously, in an effort to learn what these policemen were up to. His mouth had opened, his entire face registering frank astonishment at the preposterous allegations being made against him.

"From the looks of you, it seems like I have your attention, so I'll continue. Nineteen sixty-eight was quite a year for us doing police work. We were swamped with one mysterious case after another. But, you know, it makes me want to sympathize with the student radicals when I think about how it must have been for them, with all the battles they were fighting. I don't suppose Q. Sect really had the time, or even the need to go testing bombs, but the Yokosuka Line explosion on June sixteenth was the one big exception. Death and injuries combined, there were thirty-nine victims, and it was done with a three-way coupler packed with smokeless gunpowder. Yeah, Atsuo Yukimori, it's clear that was connected to your test bomb on the Furen River on November eighteenth last year. You used a three-way coupler too. The only difference is you used black gunpowder because it's more effective. From the way you clipped out articles on the Yokosuka Line bombing so as not to miss a single detail, I'm sure you learned a lot from it. Q. Sect was very excited about that case. They decided to go ahead with that bomb attack plan they had set aside.

"So you ended up going to Hokkaido in November for bomb testing. There aren't many good places for doing that kind of thing in Honshu. Hokkaido's good, and you could make like you were going hunting to cover the extra gunpowder you took along. The test went off perfectly. Makihiko Moriya was thrilled to hear your report. Q. Sect was focused on working out the particulars for pulling off a Shinkansen bombing in the near future when the Tower takeover rolled around on January eighteen and nineteen, 1969, and Makihiko Moriya was arrested. The sect had to act fast with a show of its power to take back their leader, so they picked National Foundation Day for the attack. Springing Wakako Ikéhata from the hospital, working out an operation plan — including the getaway to Hokkaido after the attack — was all decided on by you, in consultation with Q. Sect. Yeah, we know all about it, Atsuo Yukimori. We don't just know about it, we have witnesses, evidence, and confessions from the ones who were in on it, backing up each fact. So what do you think you we should do about it?"

The inspector puckishly batted his eyes and gently inflated his cheeks. His expression said, We are so well-informed, your downfall will come easy. Atsuo felt the need to rebuff his assurance. He smiled broadly and said with a light laugh.

%exuded self-confidence that

"This is pure fabrication. It's just a made-up story. There are hardly any real facts to it at all. I don't have anything at all to do with that crime."

"But you are very tight with Makihiko Moriya, aren't you? You were having meetings with him all the time."

"Sorry, no. I met that person only once and that is all."

"Only once, he says. Okay, if you met him just once you must know when and where. Let's hear it."

"That would be the fall of last year. I met him at the hospital in Ushigomé."

"You mean S. Psychiatric Hospital, where Wakako Ikéhata was admitted?"

"Correct. I went to visit Wakako Ikéhata. Makihiko Moriya was there for the same reason. That's when I met him."

"What did you talk about?"

"We had both asked to visit Wakako Ikéhata and been refused. We went together to meet her doctor and find out about her condition, but the doctor wouldn't tell us anything. He asked us a lot of questions instead. All we got from the visit was to be examined ourselves."

"Do you remember when that day was?"

There was no reason to cover up anything. Even if he tried to do that, it would just make him look more suspicious in his examiner's eyes. He thought, I really did meet Makihiko Moriya once and once only. If I prove that, it should be possible to overturn that ridiculous tale he was telling. "As I recall, it was around November twentieth. I went hunting in Hokkaido with the company president and I came back to Tokyo alone two days early. I went to the hospital, not the next day, but one day later. I'm sure of the day we went to Hokkaido. We left Tokyo on November fifteenth, which is the first day of the deer hunting season. The most hunters are always out on the first day, so I make it a rule not to start until the second or third day. That would make it about the twentieth when I went to the hospital, I think."

"When did you conduct the explosion?"

"Umm . . ."

The inspector took out a pocket notebook and began turning pages covered top to bottom with handwriting.

"As I said before, you conducted your test explosion on November eighteenth, Monday, in the evening. That morning you visited Hakuryo Middle School for a visit with a teacher at that school, Yuji Harazaki, your elementary school classmate, to recruit students up for graduation in the spring. In the afternoon, you took a motorcycle to the Furen River pretending you were going fishing and you secretly conducted your test explosion. At least it was supposed to be secret, but the fact is, it was observed by a worker from the salmon harvest station and two or three hunters. The next day, the nineteenth, you went to Hakuryo Middle School again and met the boy scheduled to be hired by Fukawa Motors the next April. In the evening you returned to Tokyo. Two days later you went to the hospital. That was the twenty-first, Thursday."

"Oh, was it?"

"Yep, that was it. November twenty-first was a very important day. T. University's Hongo campus was filled with students in the Joint Struggle, there from all over Japan for the big national rally in support of the strikes at T. and N. universities due to be held there the following day, November twenty-second. After Makihiko Moriya got your report on the success of your explosion test, he had a secret meeting with Q. Sect officials that ended with the decision to hit the Shinkansen on February eleven."

"That is the first I've heard anything about what the students were doing."

"Be that as it may, it is a fact that you reported the success of your explosion test to Makihiko Moriya on November twenty-one. Given the other facts about what happened, it is inconceivable that you didn't."

"I am sorry, but I met that student for the first time on that day. It occurs to me now that I gave him my business card that day. One does not hand out a business card to someone he had met before."

"Oh, I guess you must mean this card." The inspector pulled out a business card from his breast pocket, apparently prepared for this moment. Though it was unmistakably Atsuo's business card, it was not the brand new card he had given Moriya, but dirty and yellow-stained, evidently quite old.

"It was newer than this."

"This was the only card of yours that Makihiko Moriya had. There is certainly no reason to believe you gave it to him brand new, only three months ago, is there, Mr. Atsuo Yukimori?" the inspector asked with a jovial wink as he pinched the card between two fingers and fluttered it like a bit of rag to show how soft it was.

"Since you can't deny conducting the test explosion on November eighteen, the only thing left you can say in your own defense is your motive. Our determination is you did it in preparation for the Shinkansen bomb attack, but I would assume you have some other explanation, and that is what I would like to hear from you. Of course, if you don't have anything to say about that, it means you have no objection to our determination that you are the culprit."

Atsuo fell silent. The ashtray was filled with a foul mass of cigarette butts the assistant inspector had been successively drowning in it. It is customary in holding cells and prisons to fill ashtrays with water, lest inmates pilfer smokable butts. The assistant inspector went on smoking, the inspector made entries in his pocket notebook and the senior policeman in charge of writing out examination reports read over his notes. Atsuo wondered what the time was, then told himself he would have to get used to the insecurity of not being able to know the time. His head began to hurt, maybe because the pills he had taken were no longer working. It felt like it was something worse than a headache from lack of sleep or being hung over — more like the migraines he got on damp, rainy days that hurt like the top of his head was in a vise and shattered his thoughts into tiny fragments. For the sake of his own well-being, he tried moving his head, but it hurt too much. If he could have, he would gone back to his cell and lay down. After a while (he thought about twenty minutes passed), the inspector spoke.

"Well, what's the matter. I'm waiting for you to answer my question. Why did you set off that explosion on November eighteenth?"

Some more time went by (maybe about ten minutes). The inspector repeated the question, then added, "You know, I've noticed something about you. When you want to deny something, you deny it right away, but when it's something you just don't want to affirm, you clam up. And there's one thing that you never respond to — your bomb experiments. You shut up when you don't want to deny it, but you don't want to affirm it either . . . Oho! You turned a little red at that. Looks like what's going on inside shows up on your face."

The inspector continued talking on and on in this glib tenor. Atsuo was careful to keep his face expressionless and not pay attention. Unfortunately, however, he was unable to maintain complete indifference. He wanted to know what was being plotted against him and it was in his nature to pay attention to what people said. He couldn't help being concerned about something being said in his presence by anyone. Eventually, the words "prior offenses" caught his attention. That grabbed his attention.

"You know, I don't have any particular prejudice against a man just because he has a record. Quite the contrary, in your case. I have great respect for the fact that from the time you were paroled from Chiba prison on March fifth, 1958 until February of this year, you stayed out of trouble. Nearly ten years with no crimes! That's the first time that's happened in your life! I know it took effort, real commitment to turn over a new leaf. I sincerely think you should be commended for it. Just look at what it got you! Foreman of Fukawa Motors, a top position with a good salary, and you earned it.

"That's why I just can't understand why you would fall in with radical students, pick up their dangerous ideas and get yourself involved with this bombing. I am simply amazed. I really wish you would tell me, but it doesn't look as if you will, so I'll just mention what seems reasonable to me. I guess part of it comes from your falling in love with Wakako Ikéhata. Here's this girl twenty-five years younger than you. The only way to make her happy is to sympathize with her politics. You know, just agree to her ideas, but then pretty soon you're accepting her plans. I, for one, can understand how you felt, a man in your place, Foreman Yukimori, age forty-nine, deeply in love. Not only do I understand, I have complete respect for your feelings!

"Another part of it I guess would have to be Yukichi Jinnai, who was an undercover member of the Q. Sect. I suppose he must have been some sort of influence, as your nephew — a young guy, pure of heart. It seems to me like it came down to him infecting his uncle with his extremism, but to be honest, that is just my conjecture. I'd like to get your backing on that.

"There's another thing, I think I ought to add for the sake of your honor. I believe money had nothing to do with your involvement in this case. For you, it was all about love and your political beliefs. None of that 597,000 yen Yukichi Jinnai stole went to you. I just don't think you are that kind of person. Well, anyway, the one thing I want to make clear is it wasn't your own idea that got you going into a crazy stunt like blowing up a Shinkansen car. You were just going along with Wakako Ikéhata and the ideas of the Q. Sect behind her. In other words, you weren't a full partner in the crime, but an accessory. Therefore, if Wakako Ikéhata gets the death penalty for this, your sentence is one level below that, maybe life, maybe about fifteen years — that's about what they're giving in cases like this. At least, that's the way I see this case. Of course, if it wasn't like that . . ."

Words, words, words. Empty words, words with no substance, words of papier-mâché and lies, but they threatened Atsuo with death. They might be capable of killing him and Wakako too. How to escape the invisible, clinging net being cast over him? Atsuo hung his head and groaned as pain shot through the inside of his head once again. The four men around him were a stifling presence. He hung his head, nostrils quivering at the suffocating sensation.

Having finished speaking for the moment, the inspector abruptly arose, as if bound for the toilet. For a man of such imposing height, he seemed somewhat weak physically. If he wasn't in uniform, no one would expect him to be a policeman. He left with a nod to the assistant inspector and police sergeant, and did not return.

Unexpectedly, the assistant inspector radiated a genial smile.

"Yukimori, you are one stubborn son of a gun, I'll give you that. It takes guts to just deny everything like that. It was getting me nervous to watch you stiffing the inspector when he was saying he would help you get a light sentence. Go on, stand up and stretch a little. You must need it. You've been sitting in that hard chair a long time. That's the way. Take a deep breath. You ain't finished — not by a long shot. It's going to be a long night. We have a lot more to talk about."

Atsuo stood and stretched his back, twisted his waist and moved his neck, his handcuffs rattling at every movement. Reduced to the status of a performing monkey with a rope tied about its waist, he could not believe his present self was the same man who had been a free member of society until the morning of this day. He had been manacled countess times in the past, but this time he could not become reconciled to it. He must not become reconciled to it.

"I really didn't do anything. I'm truly not guilty," Atsuo said, his voice strained. He was hoarse, as if he had been talking for a long stretch.

"If that's so," the assistant inspector said without cutting off his smile, "prove it! Let's have your alibi! What's your alibi for February eleven?"

"I've told you. That was the day I was fired. I went for a walk in Jindai Botanical Garden."

"You sure about that? You're the kind that forgets what he did once in a while. Especially when you're drinking. You got fired, you were riled about it, you hit the bottle and forgot everything. Isn't that what happened?"

"I didn't drink that day."

"No, that doesn't wash. There are witnesses who say you were walking around Shinjuku and drinking. They say you were stinking drunk. Isn't that proof you started drinking during the day?"

"Who said that? I went drinking in Shinjuku the next day. I went to a bar in Golden Lane."

"Yeah, you went to a bar named 'The Hammer.' The mama-san from that bar says you were there on the night of the eleventh."

"No, it was the twelfth."

"Sorry. Mama-san's account book has your business entered in there for the eleventh."

"There is something that's wrong."

"Sure! Isn't it your memory that's mistaken? Look, I'm in public security, but I came up through criminal investigation. You know how we work? We wear out our shoes checking up on the facts of a case. I got the facts on you. Mama-san testified that when you get drunk you forget everything. That's what she said."

"But it wasn't . . ."

The assistant inspector nodded, and his smile became a pleased grin. "Give it some thought! This is a very important issue for you."

Was it the eleventh or the twelfth when he went to Golden Lane? Atsuo's recollections were in disarray. Little confidence in his memory was one of his major weak points. The officer had scored a direct hit upon it.

Atsuo kept silent in the face of all questions thereafter. It must have been well past eight, perhaps about nine o'clock when he was given another meal that had long turned cold. He had to eat it with handcuffs on one wrist.

There was no way of knowing what time it was when he was returned to the cell, but he got a glimpse through a window in the corridor and saw that all buildings outside had darkened windows, showing it must have been very late. He had sitting in the interrogation room for many more than ten hours since morning. When he took the blankets he was given and lay down in a corner of the cell, contact with the floor sent pain through his back that made him groan.

Without a sound of warning, the face of the tall one appeared, whispering. He had crawled serpent-like across the wafer-thin mat on the cell floor.

"It's late, Boss. They get you on a security rap? I don't suppose it had anything to do with the radicals."

"Nah, it's just 'cause I don't confess." This man could be a spy. Can't trust anyone. His mental guard on full alert, Atsuo struck a conversational tone. "They keep screaming I killed someone. They got the wrong man. Why should I confess? But they're like flies on shit. They don't let you be."

"You can say that again. I'm innocent, but they were the same with me."

"Wait a minute. Which one of your stories is on the level? First you said you were innocent, then you said you got off easy because you admitted everything and now you're innocent again. You ain't making a lot of sense, kid."

"You have a good head, boss," the tall one purred, then he sniggered. "That innocent stuff was a lie. I got caught dealing hot goods. There was no way out — they found the goods because a son of a bitch in Fuchu ratted on me."

"Yeah? You said you were in Urawa before."

"Oh, did I? I forgot. Sorry. Something's wrong with my head." The tall one lowered his deficient head contritely.

From the cell next door, an angry young voice yelled out. "Hey! Tell me what time it is!"

"I told you I'm not allowed to say" the guard shot back. "Go to sleep!"

"That sad-ass," said the tall one. "He don't know enough to keep his trap shut. He's a student. They brought him in around lunch time. Every half-hour he yells 'tell me what time it is.' He ain't no revolutionary. He's a jerk."

A guard on patrol stopped outside the cell. The tall one fell silent.

"Hey you two! Separate!" he ordered. The tall one withdrew from Atsuo's side. But the guard's eyes were on the yakuza boss and the long-haired man, who were both naked from the waist down, their legs entwined. The boss had crawled atop the other, but the chances were nil that he could fulfill his intended act in a cell where every movement could be observed. The boss cursed the guard in a low voice.

Atsuo turned toward the wall to avoid the glaring light bulb. He was tucked in between the three blankets he had been given, but the cold from the wood floor easily penetrated the thin mat and his bedding. The hard floor made his shoulders stiff. He turned over, and that sent sharp pains from his hip to his spine. But the mental distress was worse than the physical pain. The soft comfort of his inner being had been subjected to a thousand cuts that stung and bled.

"What time is it? Tell me!"

"Keep quiet!"

"Boss! Please flush the toilet!"

"Break it up, you two!"

The chorus went on and on. Distressed in mind and body, he was unable to sleep at all.

Presently, the sounds of traffic from outside increased and he knew the night had passed. "Everyone up and on their feet!"

As the order boomed, the guard, accompanied by another officer, went around unlocking each cell and ordering the occupants outside to wash hands and faces.

The tall one looked at Atsuo and said, "Boss, your eyes are red as cherries!"

The protection cell was visible from the washstand, but it was too dark to make out if the woman inside was Wakako. A Spartan meal was served, and immediately following the end of the brief time allotted for eating, a voice called out.

"Atsuo Yukimori!"

As Atsuo was being handcuffed and tied with a rope outside his cell, the student who had persistently demanded to know the time thoughtfully yelled encouragement to him. "Power to you, brother! Viva world revolution!"

This time, he was taken past the interrogation room and outside into the parking lot, filled with row upon row of armored vehicles and patrol cars. He was put into the same light van that had taken him to Onarimon police station. With a squeal of rubber, it circled around to the parking area in front of the station and sped past a gaggle of photographers who had stationed themselves to wait. When they sprang for the van, it already out on the street and accelerating.

It was another dark, rainy street scene, just the same as the previous day. The windshield wipers of all the vehicles around them were on. The busy monotony of their movement set Atsuo's nerves on edge. The van turned inside the back entrance of the Tokyo Metropolitan Police headquarters and glided to a stop. He was hustled through the cold rain into the building and down a flight of stairs to a basement interrogation room. There, his handcuffs and waist rope were removed. He was confronted by the same team as the day before, consisting of the tall young inspector, the short older assistant inspector and the police sergeant acting as recording secretary. He now realized they were not middle level officers from a branch police station but belonged to the number one police force of Japan.

The inspector crossed his long legs and spoke affably. "How about it? Now that you've had a night to think it over, do you feel up to confessing?" His voice reverberated because it was a bigger room.

"No. I'm innocent. I didn't do anything."

"Well, that's a shame." The smile changed to a look of concern. "I feel sorry for you. The fact is, Makihiko Moriya made a full confession yesterday afternoon. We found out quite a bit. What it comes down to is the Q. Sect thought up the Shinkansen attack and you did it at their request. It looks like that makes you a complete accessory to the crime. In that case, even though I was talking about an indefinite sentence yesterday, you ought to be able to get by with something lighter than that. Would you care to make any comments?"

"I didn't have anything to do with it."

The inspector sighed. "Still saying that, are you? What are we going to do with you? You're about as hard-headed as they come! If you keep it up, we're never going to get anywhere, and there will be nothing to save you from ending up with the same charge as Wakako Ikéhata, which is principal offender, because she is the biggest activist in Q. Sect . . . And to think you were just being used by her . . ."

Atsuo paid no attention, having decided to just let him talk. He was only repeating the same things from the day before. That proved he had no new ammunition.

The assistant inspector removed a booklet of lined report paper from a paper bag on his desk. "Read this. It's Yukichi Jinnai's statements."

Atsuo turned over the booklet. He recognized Yukichi's signature beside a thumb print.

"I was born on February 1, 1949 in residence at my family register address. I am now twenty years of age.

"I gained employment as an apprentice mechanic at the above-mentioned Fukawa Motors Corp., located at 3 chomé, Ogawa-machi, Chiyoda Ward, Tokyo, on April 5, 1965. I had been working as a cook at the Jinnai Diner operated by my father, Torakichi Jinnai, located at the above-mentioned family register address. I had a bad relationship with my father and argued constantly with him, day and night. I was thinking that I wanted an opportunity to escape from my family register address to Tokyo or Osaka, so I was happy to gain employment at the above-mentioned Fukawa Motors, where my uncle, Atsuo Yukimori, worked as foreman. However, when I met the president of Fukawa Motors, Ichiro Fukawa, in his office on April 5 of the same year, he surprised me by saying,

"'This company will not discriminate against you because you were once in a juvenile reformatory. Forget the past and do a good job.'

"This was a surprise to me. It meant that my father or my uncle had told my secret to the president. I realized that my father and uncle had decided to get me the job at Fukawa Motors to keep watch on me. That dampened my interest in working there, but I always did like machinery and I was interested in auto mechanics, so I did come around to working hard at the job.

"Next I will testify about the theft in October, 1968. There was a lot of rioting at T. University, beginning in the spring of that year. It was on TV every night. I wanted to see it in person, so I starting going to the campus every night, after work. Eventually, I became friends with Shinichi Tagawa and Akito Fukaya, who are students belonging to Q. Sect. We went to coffee shops to talk, and also went drinking. Makihiko Moriya and Wakako Ikéhata, who were friends with Shinichi Tagawa and Akito Shinya, were part of the same group.

"Wakako Ikéhata was sitting next to me one day when I mentioned that I am from Nemuro. She said that someone she knew from her skating rink was also from Nemuro. I questioned her and it turned out that she was talking about my uncle, Atsuo Yukimori. She said she had known him for three or four years and that Atsuo Yukimori and Makihiko Moriya had become well acquainted with one another after she had introduced them. I don't know why my uncle was associating with radical students, but my guess is that it had to do with the fact that the students were interested in him because he was a hunter who had gunpowder and knew a lot about guns and the fact that he lusted after Wakako Ikéhata.

"One day in October — I don't recall the exact day, but it was several days before International Antiwar Day on October 21 — Makihiko Moriya, Shinichi Tagawa and Akito Shinya called and asked me to meet them at a coffee house named 'Bonn,' in front of T. University. They asked me if there was anything I could steal from Fukawa Motors that could be turned into funding for their sect. I agreed to do what they wanted. For myself, I am devoted to the philosophies of Ikki Kita and Hitler, and cannot go along with the Marxist line of simultaneous world revolution followed by Q. Sect, but I strongly believe in the goal of destroying present-day Japan and installing a completely new system. That was where I could see eye to eye with the Q. Sect members.

"Besides that, to be honest, I was in love with Wakako Ikéhata. I was willing to do anything at all for her. Naturally, I never did anything to show that in front of Makihiko Moriya's group.

"It was Monday, October 14 of that year, at approximately five minutes past five o'clock when I was passing by the president's office, just after I finished work. I happened to notice that no one was inside, not even Kimiko Fujiyama, a clerk who was always there. I sneaked inside. The drawer in Kimiko Fujiyama's desk was slightly open and I could see what looked like ten-thousand-yen bills inside. I opened it and found a kraft paper envelope with more than ten bills sticking out. I put the whole envelope into the pocket of my work uniform and went back to the dormitory as if nothing special was happening.

"That night, at eight thirty, I visited Q. Sect headquarters on the second floor of T. University and handed 170,000 yen to Makihiko Moriya. I wanted to see Wakako Ikéhata, but she wasn't there. I expected there would be a commotion at Fukawa Motors the next day over the theft of 170,000 yen, but nothing happened at all.

"The first time I heard anything about that theft was on Friday, October 18, during the noon break, when my uncle Atsuo Yukimori called me to the dorm mother's room to ask me the source of the money I used to buy a stereo at Akihabara. My uncle seemed to have received word from Q. Sect about the situation. He told me to be very careful not to do anything to arouse suspicions that I might be the thief. Both my uncle and I had been secretly associating with the Q. Sect, but that was the first time we acknowledged to one another that we were both secret Q. Sect operators. We vowed to do everything we could to make it look as if the clerk Kimiko Fujiyama was the one who stole the 170,000 yen. After that, I was watching for another opportunity to steal, but security was tightened in the president's office after the first theft. Any time the clerk Kimiko Fujiyama left the room for even a brief time to use the toilet, she was careful to lock the drawer, leaving no openings for another theft.

"The year ended, and then came the occupation of the Tower on January 18 and 19, 1969. Makihiko Moriya and other Q. Sect members had informed me that Surugadai in Kanda would be occupied by students and turned into a 'liberated zone.' At meetings I had with Shinichi Tagawa, Akito Shinya, and Wakako Ikéhata we planned to use the Fukawa Motors parking lot as a hideout for students pursued by the Metropolitan Police riot division. I discussed this with my uncle Atsuo Yukimori, and he agreed.

"On the afternoon of Saturday, January 18, I worked with the other employees to overturn a wrecked vehicle to serve as a barricade to the parking lot entrance on the false pretense that it was to protect against student attacks. I don't know if you could say what happened the next day, January 19, at a little past five p.m. was according to expectation or according to plan. Q. Sect members Shinichi Tagawa, Akito Shinya, and Wakako Ikéhata were among a group of students surrounded by forces of the Metropolitan Police riot division who fled inside the Fukawa Motors parking lot, so it served as their final 'liberated zone.' Our plan was to have a line of cars parked along the fence to enable students to jump on top of them and into the grounds of the house next door in an emergency, but the riot squad made such a swift assault it wasn't possible for all the students to escape. The best we could manage was to hide Shinichi Tagawa, Akito Shinya, and Wakako Ikéhata inside the dormitory.

"Q Sect's organization took a major hit by the arrests of Makihiko Moriya and other key figures over those two days. Whenever the other members got together, they would get into heated arguments over what to do. Besides the loss of their leaders, they had very little funding for sect operations, so they pressed me to commit another theft. I had been wanting to quit Fukawa Motors and work somewhere else, so I thought this time I would take a large amount of money for the sect and just run away. I decided a good time for the theft would be the beginning of the month, on a collection day for proceeds from gas and car wash ticket sales and car servicing. I packed my bags and sent them to the house of my brother Tetsukichi Jinnai in Akkeshi and waited for my chance. On Friday, February 7, at about four p.m. I spotted a black bag stuffed with collected money in the gas station office. I grabbed it and fled.

"Two days before this, I had met Wakako Ikéhata at the Korakuen Skating Rink some time past ten a.m. and discussed with her how I would hand over the stolen money. In accordance with the plan we decided on, I took the money to Wakako Ikéhata's apartment in the Fujimi-so building at Nishi-Shinjuku 7 chomé, Shinjuku Ward near the west exit of Shinjuku Station. (I should have mentioned that Wakako Ikéhata left the home of her father, Kotaro Ikéhata, at Sendagaya 2 chomé, Shibuya Ward on February 2 of the same year.) I gave her the black bag and we opened it together. It contained ten thousand, one thousand and five hundred-yen notes, for a total of 427,540 yen, one book of Shuto Expressway toll tickets, and invoices to customers. I told her that I thought it would be dangerous to go to the house of my brother, Tetsukichi Jinnai, in Akkeshi, or my father, Torakichi Jinnai, in Nemuro, so I would flee to Raúsu, where I had worked in a walleye pollack processing plant and as a salmon fixed net fisherman before going to juvenile reformatory. That night I stayed in Wakako Ikéhata's room and had sexual intercourse with her for the first time.

"I will answer the question concerning my uncle Atsuo Yukimori's relationship to the theft of 420,000 yen. I did not consult directly with my uncle concerning the theft itself, the same as with the previous theft of 170,000 yen. My uncle knew what I was doing from his contacts with Q. Sect. He told me that the collections for the previous month would be made on the seventh and when I stole the black bag on February 7, he distracted the clerk in charge of the gasoline stand by engaging him in conversation by the water hoses.

"Concerning the question about the Shinkansen bombing on February 11 of this month, I do not know anything, but I often heard from Q. Sect members that they wanted to blow up some big public facility. My uncle Atsuo Yukimori is a man who is usually quiet, but sometimes something will make him suddenly become all excited and blow up. There is something in him that could make him do something like set a bomb."

"So what do you think of that?" the assistant inspector demanded in his obnoxious growl, as he took back the examination records.

Atsuo shook his head. "These — Yukichi's statements? I can't believe this. I don't believe it."

"It's authentic, whether you believe it or not. That's Yukichi Jinnai's confession. You read it yourself. It's full of facts no one else but him would know. No one could just make up a story like this."

"Besides that," the officer said, returning to his well-modulated tone, "There is nothing in Yukichi Jinnai's testimony that conflicts with the testimonies from Makihiko Moriya, Shinichi Tagawa, Akito Shinya, Wakako Ikéhata, Ichiro Fukawa, Kimiko Fujiyama, Sonoko Kanéhara, Kiyoshi Tomoyama, or Torakichi, Suéko, and Tetsukichi Jinnai. It all checks out as true. So I'd like to know what part of this testimony you say is unbelievable."

"Just about all of it. It's lies, through and through."

"You know, an extreme, all-inclusive statement like that is no different than not saying anything. Just like it's meaningless to say, 'Oh, I didn't do that bombing.' You're not going to convince anyone if you don't give specifics about what you were doing that day to prove your alibi. It's the same with this. Prove what's untrue in this statement by Yukichi Jinnai, how it's untrue. Refute it!"

"For one thing, that stuff about me knowing Makihiko Moriya from way back."

"But when Makihiko Moriya, Shinichi Tagawa, and Wakako Ikéhata have all testified you did, it's useless for you to deny it. Not without giving some kind of statement with real meaning."

"I didn't have anything to do with taking 170,000 yen or 420,000 yen, and I didn't know a thing about it."

"No, it's the same thing. We have testimony from so many different people that confirms you had long association with Q. Sect, so it just doesn't make sense that you wouldn't know anything about crimes done at the direction of the Q. Sect. We have to use common sense about something like this. It's an iron principle of criminal investigations that all crime follows common sense rules."

"Be that as it may . . ." Atsuo's thoughts were disordered. Every issue had to do with retracing the past, and his recollections were not at all clear. He was no longer sure of anything. He didn't know anything about this Q. Sect, but it seemed to him that some essential place in his memory must have gone fuzzy, that he really did know this organization well. It was just recently that he had met Makihiko Moriya, in the waiting room of the Ushigomé Mental Hospital, but it also seemed that he had met him someplace else before that, perhaps the locker room at the skating rink.

The outside world had receded to the far distance. From where he was in the present, anything he may have really done or not done in the outside world was open to doubt. To begin with, the fact of his having been brought by detectives the morning before seemed like an event that had occurred two or three months in the past. He tried to remember if he had locked the door to his apartment, but could not recall. Maybe the detectives had turned the key, maybe he himself had done it, maybe neither, but he had absolutely no recollection of it. If he couldn't even recall what had happened the previous day, he couldn't have any confidence at all about his memory of things further in the past.

Suddenly, the assistant inspector drew close and began to yell in Atsuo's face, spraying it with spittle. "Yukichi Jinnai acts like a man. Not like you. He didn't try to hide anything. He owned up to his crime, confessed everything and now he's ready to take his medicine. When are you going to stop your sniveling and shilly-shallying? It's pitiful to look at you. You hear me? That Yukichi Jinnai, he's protecting Wakako Ikéhata. He says he's the one who did the theft, Wakako Ikéhata was only a simple contact, all she did was give the goods to Q. Sect. He talks straight. You hear me?"

"You said that Wakako Ikéhata testified." Though Atsuo had spoken little, his voice had grown husky for some reason. He strove to clear his throat as he said this.

"Oh, yes indeed," the inspector said with a smile. "She confessed to everything."

"Please show me her examination statements. Then I will rethink things."

"You whiney-ass!!" This time the assistant inspector sent a discharge of spit smelling of halitosis onto Atsuo's lips. "We let you see Yukichi Jinnai's testimony as a special favor to you, out of our own good will. That was our consideration of human rights, to give you full opportunity for your own defense. And you turn around and start crying to see Wakako Ikéhata's examination statements on top of that. You are way out of line, boy!"

"Tell you what," the inspector said gently, still smiling. "Let's do this by give-and-take. We gave you Yukichi Jinnai's examination record. In return, we want a little bit of a statement from you. That's our take. When we get that, let's say we give you Wakako Ikéhata's statements — no, we'll do better than that. We'll let you meet with Wakako Ikéhata. Then you can ask her about it directly."

"Do you really mean that?"

"Yes, I do. That will be our exchange," the inspector said, nodding. His fair complexion was uncreased. It was the face of a young man in his twenties, projecting vigor and self-confidence, but the expression had the force of one much older than that.

As Atsuo struggled to order his confused memories of past events, the inspector softly began a recitation that blended into the stream of his thoughts.

"I know you've been trying to remember this and that, but you know the way memory works, you've got to pick out some point to focus on. If you don't do that, it's like looking through fog. So what do you say you focus on this one thing. One day the year before last, some time between November sixteenth and nineteenth, 1967 — did you conduct an experimental explosion or not? Just answer about that one thing."

"I did no such thing."

"You didn't do it. Okay, that's the first time you came out and clearly denied it. So how about the explosion last year, on November eighteen, 1968?"

"I didn't do that. Why would I do a crazy thing like that? Hunters are forbidden to do any kind of blasting, not for clearing out moles or anything else."

"Well, your denial presents a problem. You see, there are unimpeachable witnesses. If you are going to deny facts that have been determined to be true by criminal investigation, that shows all your denials are false."

The assistant inspector turned to the inspector and asked, "Shall we let him read the rest?"

"All right. It's a good time to let him read a little more," The inspector replied. Though he had the higher rank, his manner showed respect for an elder.

The assistant inspector felt around inside the paper bag, extracted two documents and placed them in front of Atsuo.

"There, this is another special favor for you. We don't normally do this. Since you don't say anything, we're giving you this to chew on. Understand?"

Examination Record of Testimony by Torakichi Jinnai,
in his home in Nemuro

". . .Next, I will answer the question concerning the actions of Atsuo Yukimori on November 18, 1968.

"That day, I was the guide for the Fukawa Motors president, Mr. Fukawa,
and his secretary, Kimiko Fujiyama, on a trip to the mountains in Ashoro for
deer hunting. We left early in the morning, but could not sight any deer, so we
left Ashoro about noontime. I think we returned to my home at about three
o'clock.

"After seeing off the president and his secretary in a taxi for Raúsu, I went to
work with my wife Suéko and my eldest son Tetsukichi in the diner we operate
at our home. Suéko said that Atsuo Yukimori had gone fishing in the Furen
River, and that he had taken our 250-cc motorcycle. He had still not returned
home by dark. I became concerned because the Furen River is surrounded by a
swamp where even local hunters can become lost.

"Then I thought of something that made me go to the second floor and
examine Atsuo Yukimori's baggage. I suppose it sounds strange that I should
examine someone's baggage, even though it belonged to my brother-in-law, but
the fact is I was extremely concerned about the strange objects that were in
Atsuo Yukimori's baggage. He had a clock timer, a three-way coupler for gas or
water lines and a screw cap.

"He had them in a cloth bag when I first showed him to the room. My wife
Suéko found these suspicious things while she was cleaning. She said, 'What on
earth might these things be!' I took one look at them and recalled the explosion
that Atsuo Yukimori was boasting about just one year before, in the middle of
November, 1967. It seems he had packed smokeless gunpowder for rifles into
a coke bottle and set it off with a spark from batteries. He said he was pleased
to have gotten a bigger explosion than he had been expecting. When I warned
him that the police would come after someone for committing that kind of a
violation, Atsuo Yukimori became agitated, and said 'Torakichi, please don't tell
anyone. I wasn't doing blasting to kill animals, and I didn't hurt anyone.'

"But two days later, he was at it again. A hunter named Rentaro Watanabé
witnessed that explosion. He is a man I have been good friends with for years.
He served as chairman of the Nemuro Hunting Association. I heard about it
from him. And those strange things in my brother-in-law's baggage were gone.

" . . . Why was Atsuo Yukimori interested in explosions? I will state what comes to mind about this. To my mind, Atsuo Yukimori is a bad person, through and through. Since he was young, the police have had to deal with him countless times, and now he has finally arrived at the ultimate stage . . .

" . . . It was in the spring of 1946 when I married the youngest daughter of Ishizo Yukimori, Suéko. My understanding at the time was that Ishizo Yukimori's fourth son Atsuo was in Tokyo. After we had been married about three years Suéko suddenly got a New Year's card from Atsuo. It was from the Urawa prison. I confronted Suéko about this and found out he had been court-martialed during the war for desertion because he didn't like the army and was sentenced to breaking rocks in an army prison. I was shocked to discover I had married the sister of a criminal. As I was addressing this issue, Suéko began crying. She apologized, but it was a crisis in our marriage.

"Atsuo Yukimori's life after that was a complete mess — fraud, theft, embezzlement, robbery — I can't remember everything. Anyway, he ended up with a bunch of pickpockets. He is just hopelessly no good.

"Anyway, that so and so seemed to be living his own life of crime down in Tokyo. Maybe he was too ashamed of his degeneracy to stay in his homeland of Nemuro. I had just forgotten I even had such a brother-in-law. But blood will tell. My second son Yukichi was the same as Atsuo. He had a habit of stealing right from the beginning. As you know, they finally put him in a reformatory. Now this — stealing money to fund a radical group. It's outrageous. If you ask me what the cause of it is, I think Yukichi was touched by the bad blood of the Yukimori line.

" . . . Concerning Atsuo Yukimori's personality, on the surface he seems like a nice fellow, a bit argumentative, but he looks like the quiet, steady type. When you first meet him, he seems like a very good person, trustworthy, like a schoolteacher, but his true nature is that he doesn't stick to anything he starts doing. If he gets a job, he won't have it for long. If he doesn't run off with the company's money, he'll steal money from the home of people who took him in, or something else. Unfortunately, my boy Yukichi is exactly the same.

"I hear he killed a lot of people in China during the war. When you're around him it can be scary when he's angry. You feel like this is a treacherous man with murder in his heart. I think it's a miracle that a man like that went for close to ten years living like a true human being, without committing more crimes. I think part of that has to do with the goodness of Mr. Fukawa and the encouragement my wife and I gave him.

"At the instigation of Atsuo Yukimori, my son got mixed up with radicals and stole for them. Atsuo Yukimori blew up an important public railroad and destroyed human life. These are acts that cannot be forgiven by heaven or by man. I will have nothing more to do with him. I ask that he be put to strict justice."

Examination Record of Testimony by Ginji Sato
at the Metropolitan Police Department

"I was surprised to hear that Atsuo Yukimori was the culprit in that Shinkansen bombing. Knowing it was a heinous crime that caused death or injury to a great many people, I would like to tell everything I know that might serve as helpful information.

" . . . It was last year, that is, one morning in mid-October, 1968, at about eight a.m., I was on a platform in the national railways Ochanomizu Station when Atsuo Yukimori stopped me. I hadn't seen him in sixteen years so I didn't realize it was him right away.

" . . . Atsuo Yukimori and I were making small talk. He said 'Nothing interesting is happening. I want to do something big to shake things up.' He didn't let on what he meant by 'something big,' but knowing Yukimori, I could tell it was some kind of crime, like a robbery or a bomb or something that would get everybody talking.

"Yukimori kept telling me to join up with him. We were on the station platform with people all around. After my last term at Fuchu prison, I quit being a pickpocket and went straight. I am engaged in collection of cardboard boxes at the fruit and vegetable market in Akihabara. I am living respectably now, and have no interest in going back to the evil life.

"At first I told him I wasn't interested, but Atsuo Yukimori kept insisting so strongly that I finally decided to pretend to go along and listen to what he had to say, then go to a policeman and tell on him. I started acting like a criminal. I told him I was still picking pockets. He said he was in with radical students. I said it's risky to talk about that kind of thing on the train platform, that we should go outside. I left the station with Atsuo Yukimori and we talked while walking toward Juntendo University. Then, unfortunately, the effects of the stimulant drug I had injected wore off. I am ashamed to say that I had started injecting stimulants because my work at the market begins early in the morning. At that time I would become too sleepy to continue working if I did not inject ten 5 cc ampules per day intravenously.

"Yukimori followed me when I went to a roadside public rest room to inject myself. He was watching closely as I did this. He probably felt reassured to see I was the type of person who uses drugs. He began boasting proudly that his student radical friends had plans to bomb universities, railroads, big corporations, or police. He invited me to join the group and take part. He said the police were concentrating on radical students, so it was safer for them to use old people like himself or me to do bombings. I just made a noncommittal answer and then we parted for the day.

"I ran into Atsuo Yukimori a number of times after that, always in the same place, when I was talking a walk around Ochanomizu. He always found me. It was like he was always there, walking around. He took me to T. University two or three times. I don't know the first thing about the student movement. I was spooked when I saw all those students in their helmets, carrying fighting sticks, but that Yukimori was real chummy with the radicals in his sect. He could go into the Tower whenever he wanted, like he was a sect boss. I know the exact day when he told me it was getting close to it the time for that big job. It was January 18, 1969, the day of the showdown at the Tower . It was on the street in Surugadai. The reason I was caught throwing rocks at the police on January 19 was because Atsuo Yukimori got me drinking and urged me on. I only tried it because it seemed like fun. Yes, really, that was all there was to it.

"I will answer the question of what Atsuo Yukimori meant when he said a big job. I realized it meant a bombing when I met him on the day of the Tower . He said he could pull it off easy as pie, all he had to do was blow away the riot police with a bomb. Yes, that is what he said. He said it while were in a Korean lunch house near Ochanomizu Station, while we were looking at TV. It sounded like a joke, so I said, yeah, sure, talk is cheap. Yukimori looks at me, like real fierce, and says, I can make a bomb easy, I used to be a bomb specialist in the machine gun corps. It raised the hairs on the back of my neck.

" . . . The fact that Atsuo Yukimori bombed a Shinkansen train reminds me of something I will state for your reference. I was with him in a common cell at Fuchu Prison between spring and fall, 1952. He had a reputation for being a master tinder box maker. As I am sure you know, tinderboxes can be made by tightly wrapping bits of glass and celluloid toothbrush bristles around cotton and then used inside prison cells to make fire for lighting cigarettes. The ones he made were guaranteed to light a fire on the first try.

"We were working at a motor pool. One day Yukimori started talking seriously about starting a fire in the shop. I couldn't believe it. The place had plenty of fuel and gasoline and oil. Of course, if a fire got started it would blow the walls away. I was in a panic to talk him out of it. Starting fires, blowing things up, it's like that kind of thing is in Yukimori's blood. From the time I spent in prison, I would say the typical guy who commits arson or plants bombs is clumsy, gutless and frustrated. That description fits him to a tee."

When he finished reading, Atsuo drew a heavy sigh. All three of the records were a mixture of falsehood and truth. Even knowing the truth of the matters discussed, Atsuo found it difficult to parse it from the lies that were so adroitly woven in. Yukichi mixing with Q. Sect, friendly with Makihiko Moriya and Wakako, stealing money to fund Q. Sect operations was all just inconceivable, but given this detailed confession from him, perhaps he did have some kind of involvement. Yukichi said he had sex with Wakako. If so, the things she had said to him were not true — she had deceived him. An almost imperceptible hint of doubt stirred from inside. Atsuo suppressed it, but it felt like something that would tear him apart.

The statements of Torakichi Jinnai revealed a brother-in-law harboring an unexpected reserve of aversion and disdain. His bias made him sure Atsuo was a despicable criminal who had dragged his son into a den of radicals. His testimony on the explosion experiment by Lake Furen was accurate. It would be nearly impossible to overturn it.

Ginji Sato's words were about eighty percent lies. No matter much he wracked his brain, Atsuo couldn't recall saying anything to him of sympathy for the Q. Sect or student radicals. But the scary thing about it was the aura of realism surrounding the composite portrait of Atsuo Yukimori the radical that emerged from the testimonies of Yukichi, Torakichi, and Ginji.

Atsuo shook his head and arched his back in an effort to invigorate his thought processes, which had slowed to a crawl from lack of sleep. He had been getting shooting pains from his back to his tail bone since the day before. He sighed repeatedly, and then yawns escaped him of their own accord. He wiped away tears with his sleeve. He knew he was fidgeting and he knew the inspector and assistant inspector saw into his inner turmoil, but he simply did not have control over his body or his thoughts.

He had managed somehow to endure until lunch time. After the interrogators left the room, he ate his meal of red beans and reflected. He faced grillings day after day, being pressed to confess to his crimes. But there wasn't anything to confess. He could probably get by by just agreeing to whatever they said. That would doubtlessly make things much easier. That was probably what had led Yukichi to give his false confession.

The following day Atsuo was referred to a Tokyo prosecutor's office for suspicion of theft, in advance of the expiration of the forty-eight-hour limit to police detention on unindicted suspects. The referral consisted of a document describing the evidence the police had of Atsuo's involvement in theft, meaning the interrogation records obtained from Yukichi. On receiving this, the prosecutor requested a court order for Atsuo's continued detention for investigation of the theft to which he had not yet confessed, even though his interrogation had actually consisted mainly of pressing him to confess to the Shinkansen bombing, and the media was reporting on his suspected connection to that crime. As expected, the court granted an additional ten days of police detention, and when that term was about to expire, it again granted another ten-day extension. This was the legal basis for detention that was used to interrogate Atsuo on the Shinkansen case.

A special headquarters for investigating the Shinkansen bombing was established in the Onarimon police station. Officially, it was headed by the station chief, but in reality it was police superintendent Noseh, the first division supervisor of the Tokyo Metropolitan Police Public Security Department, who held responsibility for directing all aspects of the investigation. The team assigned to interrogate Atsuo Yukimori consisted of two members of the Public Security Department's first division, who enjoyed the confidence of superintendent Noseh, Police Inspector Magara, Police Sergeant Semba, and Assistant Inspector Hino of the Onarimon police station.

For his previous offenses, Atsuo had usually been questioned by only one officer, so he was quite disoriented at first to be interrogated day after day by three officers, but he gradually learned to distinguish them, and came to realize that he, Wakako Ikéhata, and a large number of students from the Q. Sect were all undergoing interrogation on the same Shinkansen bombing case.

Interrogation began at nine or ten o'clock in the morning and continued until ten or eleven o'clock at night. It took place mainly in the basement of the Metropolitan Police Department building, but on days when no interrogation rooms were available there, the Onarimon police station was used. Atsuo arose every morning uncertain where he would be taken for twelve hours or more of the same questions repeated over and over until it was time to be returned to a cell for a night spent on a hard floor, where cold and noise made sleep impossible. Under normal circumstances Atsuo could rely on his own physical strength, but not after days and days of sleep deprivation and enforced fatigue. He fell victim to waves of dizziness while walking, making him totter on his feet. When seated, his spine threatened to buckle under his weight.

While Atsuo's weakening progressed, the interrogators' vigor was undiminished. Assistant Inspector Hino, the up-from-the-ranks constable, outshone the others in terms of stamina, tenacity, and zeal. Though Inspector Magara would occasionally leave the room, Assistant Inspector Hino continued sitting opposite Atsuo in his chair from morning to night, tirelessly repeating the same questions over and over, his composure never fraying. When Atsuo grew sick of giving the same answers and fell silent, Assistant Inspector Hino continued his litany like a devout believer. It was an uncanny mystery to Atsuo where the force came from that drove the slightly built inspector whose hair was already half white.

It happened in the afternoon of March 11, when there were only two more days left before the order for Atsuo's detention on the theft charge was due to expire. Inspector Magara did not return to the Onarimon interrogation room in the afternoon, leaving only Assistant Inspector Hino and Sergeant Semba to conduct the questioning. The monotonous stream of questions had Atsuo's head drooping like a plant in need of water. At the insistence of Assistant Inspector Hino, Sergeant Semba left the room.

The assistant inspector drew close to Atsuo, gave him a cigarette, took one for himself and lit them both with his lighter. His voice hoarse from the morning session, he said, "Yukimori, you got me fagged out. I admit it. Three weeks have gone by like this, me giving up Sundays, doing nothing but handling your case. I don't know what to do. If you don't confess, you will get charged on the physical evidence and witness testimony. What does the prosecutor think when he looks at that? That you are the worse kind of case there is — showing no remorse at all. So that's how he's going treat you. If you ask me, you're going to lose out big that way, but it's your problem. There's no point in me talking about it. I'm too tired anyway.

"What the hell, I might as well talk about myself. I'm a different animal than that Inspector Magara. He's what you call elite. He passed the advanced level public service exam and, bang, he was assistant inspector. Six months later he was inspector. Pretty soon he's going to be a superintendent, then a chief superintendent, while he's still in his thirties. In other words, he's heading straight to being a station chief.

"Me, I'm fifty-four. I hit retirement the March after next. I'm not going any higher than what I am — assistant inspector. I could care less about taking some test for inspector, so kiss off. I don't want to be no manager. I'll tell you what I am. I spent all my time on violent crime cases, and I take second place to no one in hands-on police work. I've brought in the worst kinds of criminals, more than I can count and I made 'em talk. Every one. They call me 'father confessor.' That's right. You don't have enough fingers to count all the outstanding service awards I got.

"Anyway. Yukimori, you were a sergeant in the Army. I was a sergeant major. Noncoms can't ever be officers. So there I am, thirty years old, and I have to jump when some twenty-year-old second lieutenant, fresh out of officer's school give the order. Now I'm a cop and still a non-com. Spent my whole life that way. Of course noncoms got their own pride. Know what they have to be proud of? That they can't be officers. They got their sorrow too. You what that is? They can't be officers.

"Now this here Shinkansen bomb case is the end for me. After this, I'm out. So the sendoff I get is up to you, Yukimori. Ball is in your court. If you want to give a fellow noncom a hand, if you have some human warmth in you, just say one thing for me. You are responsible for the explosion on the Furen riverbank in November last year, aren't you? If you deny even that, when Torakichi Jinnai and a whole pack of other witnesses say it happened, nobody in the world is going to believe a word you say."

"I did it." Atsuo spoke with a vague feeling of being in a dream.

"Is that right?" The assistant inspector relaxed his shoulders and pressed another cigarette on Atsuo. "Thank you. It's so good to hear you say that," he said, blinking back tears. One would think it was a sham, but two, three tear streaks etched silver lines across his cheek.

"It's so good to hear that," the assistant inspector said with a friendly slap on Atsuo's shoulder. "I am very glad. Sergeant Yukimori, you can become a real human being with this."

Assistant Inspector Hino telephoned Sergeant Semba and asked him to prepare for taking down testimony. Then he addressed Atsuo with a friendly laugh.

"Hey, Sergeant Yukimori. I need to get you to say what you just said once more for this police sergeant. See, we have to write up the examination record. You've been around, so I guess you know the '7W1H rule' — When? Where? Who? What? Why? How? to Whom? with Whom? Cover that, with all the detail you can. You don't have to worry about complete sentences. Just the true facts."

"Right." Atsuo smiled back at the assistant inspector, thinking it was just a matter of spitting out something he had gone through a lot of unnecessary anguish to hold back, for the sake of this hardworking NCO. It couldn't do him any harm.

"Okay, now, by the 7W1H rule. November eighteenth, 1968. The 'why' of that explosion experiment. In other words, what was the motive?"

"There was a bear around. Well, actually, there were traces of a bear rolling around in the reeds. Very scary. I set off the gunpowder to scare him away."

"Ahh, that's too small to be a motive. You can't satisfy the 'why?' article without a bigger motive than that. What about it? You knew Makihiko Moriya and Wakako Ikéhata, right?"

"I knew Wakako Ikéhata."

"Okay, that's good enough. How's this? 'I was on friendly terms with Wakako Ikéhata and other students in Q. Sect. On November eighteen, 1968, I conducted an experimental explosion in order to realize their plans concerning explosions.'"

"Oh well, if you think so, that's fine." Exhausted, Atsuo's thoughts were in a haze as he said this. He was taken with a glorious feeling of having his confused thoughts picked up and transformed into sonorous phrases of a document that cast him in the lead role.

"Next off, you give the whole story on the equipment for that blast. Talk about when and where you got the three-way coupler, the timer and the black powder."

Atsuo mentioned these details randomly, as he recalled them, while the assistant inspector took notes that he afterwards referred to as he read out formal sentences for the sergeant to record.

"Good! Now we have the examination record for the November eighteen, 1968 explosion experiment out of the way. I promise you, we won't be asking you about that any more."

"No more questions about that, right?"

"Correct. You've got that item behind you. Congratulations. Well, what do you say you get another thing off your chest? That explosion experiment near Lake Furen two years ago, in 1967. It'll do you a world of good!"

Atsuo confessed to that as well. There was satisfaction in knowing that his statements would put an end to the subjects of interrogation, one by one, akin to the removal of numerous thorns piercing his psyche. He gave statement after statement, according to instructions. There was no more stopping him than there would be a way to stop the leaking of an earthen vessel cracked by repeated blows.

A great number of personnel assigned to the case, representing the investigation, crime lab and general affairs departments sat at rows of desks arranged against the wall inside the Onarimon police station security division room awaiting the appearance of Assistant Inspector Hino with Atsuo Yukimori's full confession. The previous afternoon Assistant Inspector Hino had requested

Inspector Magara to let himself handle the next day's questioning by himself, with Sergeant Semba as the recording secretary, saying that he would be at it from morning and have the examination records complete by evening.

"We got a present," said one of a party of three officers carrying in a colossal barrel of saké dressed in rice straw. A decorative paper tied to it said, "Regards to headquarters staff — Press Club."

Superintendent Noseh addressed Inspector Magara. "I don't suppose there've been any leaks to the press about a certain full confession in the works."

"No, of course not. It's just that these reporters are good at smelling things out. They're here in droves out front. Looks like they think there has been some break in the investigation."

"I'm worried about information leaks," Superintendent Noseh said, biting a slightly curled lower lip. He repeated cautions about reporters again and again at morning briefings, and still they had managed to pick up on every move in the investigation. They were swarming around Onarimon station from early in the morning when Atsuo Yukimori and Wakako Ikéhata had been brought in for voluntary questioning. That night, the evening editions had covered the story extensively, casting the pair as extremely suspicious. The worst of it was that the investigators showed signs of being affected by this "public opinion."

Those two were arrested on the theft charge. They were not actually suspects, but merely important witnesses on the Shinkansen bombing. This was the cautious line on the investigation Superintendent Noseh had laid out. They would accumulate evidence and wait for confessions. The nominal chief of the investigation agreed to this. There was, to begin with, no decisive evidence against them.

There was nothing to rule out their alibis on the day of the crime. Atsuo Yukimori maintained he was in his apartment around three in the afternoon that day, then went to Jindai Botanical Garden and was there until it closed at five o'clock. Thus far, no one had shown up to substantiate that, but there wasn't any evidence deing it either. Wakako Ikéhata had been completely unresponsive from the time of her arrest, so there was no information from that source, but she had been given a vague sort of alibi by the superintendent of her apartment building, who said it seemed to him he had seen her return to her apartment at about four in the afternoon.

Whoever placed the time bomb on the Shinkansen Hikari No 33, there had been only ten minutes to do the job — from 3:50 until 4:00 p.m. What was needed was some kind of incontrovertible evidence placing the suspects on Platform Eighteen in Tokyo Station during that time frame. What they actually had was testimony from a salesgirl at a platform concession stand and two passengers on the train that they had seen a middle-aged man and a young woman together, but when asked to identify the faces, the response from one witness was "I don't know," one said it wasn't Yukimori or Ikéhata, and one said "I am not sure if those two were the couple I saw."

Their motives looked pretty thin too. According to the testimony from Makihiko Moriya and some other Q. Sect members, as well as Yukichi Jinnai and Ginji Sato, Atsuo Yukimori and Wakako Ikéhata were active sect members who held to the Marxist simultaneous world revolution line. But some of the students denied that. Moreover, there was separate information on Wakako Ikéhata to the effect that she was nonpolitical and not a formal sect member. So it was a little hard to see Wakako Ikéhata getting somebody with so little ideology in his background as Atsuo Yukimori to develop a bomb. What would make an auto shop foreman with that many years under his belt go for those students' half-baked ideas and take it all the way to making a deadly bomb?

Superintendent Noseh wasn't quite convinced. He couldn't abandon the suspicion that someone else was responsible for the crime. As the man with the main responsibility for the investigation, the superintendent's need to avoid dampening his subordinates' esprit de corps made him consistently avoid emphasizing his doubts. Instead, he questioned them carefully, and confronted them with any inadequacies he found. It was a way of testing his own doubts. So far, he had found no decisive evidence to clear them up.

By order of the metropolitan police commissioner, the Onarimon police station served as headquarters for investigating the Shinkansen bombing. That made the Onarimon station chief the titular head of the investigation. Within a few hours of the crime, superintendent Noseh, first division supervisor of the Tokyo Metropolitan police public security department assumed responsibility as the senior officer on the case. At that point, none of the investigators had any firm notions about the perpetrators. It was the newspapers and TV reporters who had little reluctance to speculate the bombing was the work of radicals. They reported the existence at the scene of "a suspicious looking young couple." They didn't get any of this from the investigation spokesman. It was the media's own opinions, mixed with quotes from reporters' questioning of witnesses.

With the cooperation of the National Research Institute of Police Science, it was determined that the gunpowder used in the bomb was black powder for hunters' shotguns, that the container was a cast iron T-shaped three-way coupler used in water, gas or steam pipe systems, and that the device was triggered by a spring type timer.

The first persuasive eyewitness information came from a vendor at a newsstand on Platform Eighteen who had seen a middle-aged man and a young woman loitering on the platform, then leaving the scene without getting onto the train. Of course, there were other witness statements, as well, that told of young men dressed like students, teenagers, and young women, but the story of the couple caught the attention of investigation HQ, coming as it did from three different witnesses. According to them, they looked like a middle-aged gentleman with his young girlfriend going on a trip because their faces seemed too unlike one another for them to have been father and daughter. The girl wore jeans, and the man, a suit and a brown trench coat. He was carrying a light brown, heavy-looking paper bag.

The investigators began thinking in terms of looking for a middle-aged man who owned a hunting rifle and associated with a young woman. Nevertheless, superintendent Noseh thought students were behind the bombing. His suspicion was the product of a long career in dealing with public safety offenses, and an encyclopedic knowledge of what radical factions were up to. He had handled the International Anti-War Day riot of October 11 the previous year and the unlawful occupation of T. University's Tower on January 18 and 19.

The Q. Sect was a new force on the radical front, formed in the spring of 1967. It had a small membership, but the great swell of support nationally for the student movement raised its popularity among ordinary students, who admired its fiercely uncompromising rhetoric calling for simultaneous world revolution and abolition of the state. This group was gaining adherents. Superintendent Noseh's main concern with it came from his information that Q. Sect had a secret program for bombing public facilities that logically followed from its declarations that revolution would not be won with sticks and Molotov cocktails alone, but that production of really effective bombs was necessary. According to his intelligence, the group was researching bomb making and collecting the necessary materials. In his view, Q. Sect was a likely suspect in the Shinkansen bombing.

It was not Superintendent Noseh, but Assistant Inspector Hino, of the Onarimon station's security division, who turned up Atsuo Yukimori as a suspect by mobilizing his forces to comb through every possible information source from the environs of the crime scene. The statements from three witnesses at the crime scene had him convinced the crime was the work of a middle-aged man and a young woman. He sifted through evidence on radical groups maintained by the metropolitan police public security division, looking for that connection and turned up Atsuo Yukimori's business card among items confiscated from

Makihiko Moriya. He went to Fukawa Motors with the intention of interviewing this Yukimori. The date was February 14.

The visit produced valuable information from the company president, Ichiro Fukawa. Atsuo Yukimori was an ex-con who hunted for a hobby, had been in a machine gun company during the war, had professional level knowledge of explosives and was on friendly terms with a student radical named Wakako Ikéhata.

"When the battle of the Tower was going on, he hid three radicals in here," Ichiro Fukawa said. "One of them was the daughter of that famous Professor Ikéhata. He was buddy-buddy with her. I don't know where Yukimori is now. I fired him for bad behavior the day before yesterday."

Assistant Inspector Hino's triumphant manner of advancing his theory of Atsuo Yukimori as the culprit was etched in Superintendent Noseh's memory. Short and round-shouldered, he strode up proudly, his arms briskly slashing the air. "I found our suspect," he intoned basso profundo. "Name of Atsuo Yukimori."

His report presented many points substantiating his thesis. The superintendent asked about his alibi.

"He got fired from his job the day of the crime. He left his shop carrying a heavy-looking light brown paper bag. That was a little past two in the afternoon. That shop is in Ochanomizu. You can get from there to Tokyo Station in about ten minutes. What's more, he and Wakako Ikéhata went on the lam after the crime."

"'Went on the lam.'"

"Right. I went to Yukimori's apartment yesterday. His landlady said he left on a trip somewhere."

"Maybe he went by himself."

"He didn't," Assistant Inspector Hino said, exuding confidence. "I guessed if he's going to run away he'd go back where he came from. I checked passenger logs for flights to Kushiro and out popped the names of Atsuo Yukimori and Wakako Ikéhata on the same flight."

The investigation team adopted Assistant Inspector Hino's view that Atsuo Yukimori should be sought out. His nephew, Yukichi Jinnai, was arrested in Akkeshi and sent to Kanda Station in Tokyo for questioning. Inspector Hino lost no time in visiting him, and soon extracted his confession to conspiring with Atsuo Yukimori and Wakako Ikéhata to steal money to fund activities by Q. Sect.

The assistant inspector performed brilliantly. In his hands, a miscellany of events merged into a master plan of interdependent parts. He was a virtuoso, a wizard. Superintendent Noseh laid out a plan to arrest Atsuo Yukimori and Wakako Ikéhata on suspicion of robbery to provide ample time for investigating their involvement in the bombing. This was adopted by a meeting of senior investigators.

The media was already assuming the suspects' guilt. It was especially fascinated by Wakako Ikéhata, the eldest daughter of well-known criminal law scholar, T. University professor Kotaro Ikéhata, as student radical and engineer of a heinous bombing. A flood of articles about her appeared in the newspapers and weekly magazines:

"Made explosives in high school — Accidental blast nearly demolished home"

"Rebellion against father, Kotaro — Violence at home"

"Twice committed to mental hospital"

"Habitual runaway"

"Beautiful face — hideous heart"

"Middle-aged man meets his Lolita"

The articles featured comments from psychologists, psychiatrists and criminologists. Superintendent Noseh had every one of these articles he encountered clipped out and collected. Using any and every means to define Wakako Ikéhata as a modern criminal archetype, they represented a kind of "public opinion" that exerted an unnerving sort of pressure on him.

~

It happened that Wakako Ikéhata had not spoken a single word since she was arrested and placed in detention within the Metropolitan Police headquarters, to the extreme frustration of the officers charged with interrogating her. According to her head psychiatrist at S. Psychiatric Hospital, Doctor K., she suffered from "strongly dysthymic depersonalization disorder." He said the condition could be expected to recur, so for precaution's sake, Superintendent Noseh had asked a domestic court psychiatrist to examine her. That doctor returned a tentative diagnosis of "mutism," and said there was a need to monitor its progress.

"Wakako Ikéhata still hasn't said a word?" Superintendent Noseh asked Inspector Magara. "She's still keeping quiet. Women don't give up easy, that's for sure."

"Tell me what you really think of her."

"What do I think?" The inspector blinked back, in an effort to discern the question's meaning. The contact lenses over his eyeballs glinted sharply. "I don't believe that stuff from the doctor and what they write in the press. I think she's just keeping her mouth shut, and there isn't anything else to it."

"The doctor says she has mutism disorder."

"I don't think you can just show up for a thirty-minute examination and expect to know anything. We have been with her morning to night for twenty days now, and we are having her watched all night. We can tell. She is just clammed up is all. That's everyone's opinion."

"I am aware of that," the superintendent said, nodding. This young man had graduated the psychology department of T. University. He knew a lot about psychiatry. That field was a mystery to the superintendent, and so he relied upon various comments from the inspector on those matters. "I know what mutism disorder is." Inspector Magara kept his head low to show deference to his senior, but spoke flatly, with no hesitation about demonstrating his competence. "Basically, it means not speaking, but there is more to it than that. It is a kind of schizophrenia. The patient loses the capacity to think, and therefore can't speak. In other words, it isn't just a matter of nothing being said — there is nothing going on inside either. That is not the case with Wakako Ikéhata. There is a great deal going on in her head. You can tell that. Her eyes follow every change in people's expressions. She is clearly very much aware of what is going on around her."

"So you don't think she's mentally ill?"

"I do not."

"That's one big issue. If she were mentally ill, she might not be charged. Let's hope the prosecutor goes along with your view. I'm going to take you along for an oral briefing with the prosecutor to go with the written report on the investigation. I want you to win him over."

"Yes sir." Captain Magara's expression showed full confidence as he nodded. Coming from him, this did not seem affected to Deputy Inspector Noseh, but reassuring. This man had the makings of a future key person in the police force. He had started his career as an assistant inspector, having passed the advanced level national civil service examination. Now at twenty-seven, he was a captain. He would be a superintendent in two or three years, and make chief superintendent by thirty-five or thirty-six, meaning he would make police station chief, the dream of every policeman. His career advanced at a different speed than mine, Noseh thought. He had started as a patrolman straight out of the police academy, then taken one administrative exam at a time for sergeant, lieutenant, captain, finally making deputy inspector at forty. What's more, Captain Magara had performed beautifully on this case. Unlike Assistant Inspector Hino, who was apt to go charging ahead recklessly, he was there every step of the way to find witness testimony or hard evidence to back up whatever statement came out of Atsuo Yukimori and feed it back to Hino. Captain Magara stored information like a computer that could instantly recall any event and the date and time when it happened. Rather than read through the documentation, Noseh found it much quicker to simply ask Captain Magara. Noseh regarded the great pile of papers on his desk to be sent to the prosecutor's office, feeling overwhelmed by the terrific amount of documentation it took to conduct a criminal investigation. This included crime scene assessment reports and photos, records of police examinations of numerous witnesses, reports from each and every one of the army of investigators on the case and the records of Atsuo Yukimori's interrogation. Those records had started out as useless — the most important figure in the case denying everything. Thanks to Assistant Inspector Hino's efforts, the confession was finally obtained. With that, the investigation was concluded. All that was left was to send the report on the facts of the criminal offenses committed by Atsuo Yukimori and Wakako Ikéhata, together with the report on the investigation, to the prosecutor's office.

A cheer arose as Assistant Inspector Hino came in the room, visibly quivering with pride and joy. His expression was tense as he presented a thick stack of examination records to the chief of the investigation.

"It's finished. Here's the full confession." There was applause. The press spokesman came running in.

"The reporters are getting nervous. They need an announcement in time for the morning editions."

"Simmer down. That comes after I read through all this," said Inspector Noseh calmly, fixing a stern glance upon his fidgeting subordinates.

~

(The organization flunkies puff on their cigarettes, bored to distraction. Every one of them must have gone through two whole cartons of ciggies since morning. They draw upon them slowly, dragging out the time as best they can. When one is down to the butt and threatening to burn their fingers, they put it out and light another one. But the only thing that happening is the gray cloud in the room gets thicker and thicker. The flunkies let out long sighs, read every word in a sports newspaper with a dour expression or fall into a daze, like so many weary passengers on a commuter train. Well, guess what folks? This train isn't going anywhere, so get good and bored, you organization slaves!)

Wakako Ikéhata sat atop a chair, hands and legs in full lotus posture, her back not touching the backrest. She was positioned for Zen meditation, but not really meditating. She sat that way simply because when she was in this posture, she was untroubled by the passage of an hour or two. Actually, she did go into meditation once in while, and when she did, another hour or two would go by in a breeze.

It had never occurred to her back when she was in the university zazen club that what she learned there would come in handy in a place like this. She had spent a week as a visitor at the temple Eiheiji during the February 15th services marking the Buddha's death and supreme enlightenment. The days were spent in steady meditation from dawn until late at night upon a spare straw mat, snowbound in the temple's outer meditation hall, with only a feeble charcoal stove for warmth.

(That hall was filled with the dauntless spirit of the Zen monks, those voyagers on cloud and water. It enveloped us and made it possible to carry on. Compared to that, doing zazen here is no big thing. I can keep it up any number of hours. Though it is a little tough not being able to do *kinhin* breaks.)

After Wakako Ikéhata finished a turn of zazen, she began listening to Mozart piano sonatas. She played them herself, on the piano in her mind. The sound reverberated inside her head, so it wasn't really different from listening to it coming from the outside.

K. 330 in C Major: Allegro moderato (Lovely, full, elegant, refreshing happiness. A pleasure the organization flunkies don't know. All tied up taking orders, enforcing rules, obeying laws, following customs. Look at them in those stupid uniforms. There's something of the slave's chains in uniforms. Business suits for company workers, military suits, Mao suits, prisoner suits. Wouldn't you rather go for a ride with Mozart? It would do you a world of good!)

Wakako Ikéhata recalled the hot spring deep in the mountains at Raúsu. (Music was caressing the white vapor and blending with it as it rose above the water. Vapor clouds are forever changing into different shapes. I was like a great, weightless cloud of vapor making love with Atsuo Yukimori and looking at the stars. There was music that night, far away in the mountains, in the secret hot spring known only to the two of us.)

She finished the Allegro moderato and went into the Andante cantabile. She could go on this way forever. She had started piano as a small child. Delighted to find that one could see marvelous scenes by playing piano, she had stayed with it, learning one piece after another. She knew every Mozart piano sonata. Now she played her favorites, one after another: K. 330, K. 331, K. 332, K.

333 . . . 457, 545, 570. (This program takes exactly two hours, and I am not going to be the least bit bored playing through it any number of times.)

Wakako Ikéhata giggled inwardly at the sight of the organization flunkies working their mouths at her like feeding goldfish. They were telling her to eat the prisoner food on an aluminum tray. (No, I won't eat that. I decided that I would only eat prisoner food once a night, in the cage. That is quite enough for their lousy food. It doesn't have a soul and it stinks of organization.

(. . . So the organization made a fuss about me not getting the mandated nourishment. They sent in a quack doctor in a white uniform, stuck a rubber tube through my nose into my stomach and pumped in feeding liquid. Of all the nervy things to do to a person . . . I spouted it right back out. It hit the ceiling and left a nice, filthy spot. I damn well have a right not to eat. Force-feed me and I'll gush it right back out every time. The quack in the white gown stopped showing up, so I guess he figured that out and gave up. Then one day they dragged me out to some other organization's hospital. That staff was frantic. They took off all my clothes and started checking things like weight and blood pressure. They even took out some blood. All with very sober expressions. They couldn't understand why one meal a day was all the nourishment I need. If they weren't idiots they would know that people whose minds are at peace don't burn up all that many nutrients when they meditate. During a zazen retreat, Zen priests get by on little bowls of rice gruel and vegetables, so I don't need that stinking tray of prison food. Get it out of my sight.)

Thereafter, Wakako Ikéhata continued holding her zazen posture. This did not prevent her from closely watching the organization flunkies perform. Their behavior patterns did not vary. They smoked cigarettes, shifted positions with evident boredom, and once in a while worked their mouths, reciting the same questions. All the while, they were incessantly checking their wristwatches. Their frustration with the tedium was very clear. One was writing some kind of report, but he didn't have anything to write, so he wrote the date, he wrote the time, and he wrote the name of some officer. In other words, the important things are what year, month, day, hour, and minute, and what flunky from what section. Organizations are fanatical about calendars, clocks, departments, and that's all. Once you've written down that stuff, there isn't anything else left to do.

(Still, what Mr. Yukimori said is really true. Organizations have the power to catch people like fish in a net. We don't have any way of resisting that power. Fish just don't have the strength to rip through a fishing net. But organizations have one weakness. They run on time filled up with numbers. Refuse to recognize that, and they can't make out their documents. Organizations don't work without their documents. So I win, ha-ha. Every time the flunkies look at their watches, they get the word that they are losing.)

Wakako Ikéhata was put into a cage. After the evening meal, she lay down and became immersed in dreams of her own past performances of the kabuki dances "Dojo Temple Maiden" and "Wisteria Maiden." Then she relived performing "Heron Maiden" on stage, draped in white, and wielding an infinitely expressive parasol, dancing madly all the while. The organization flunkies showed up during this performance, and dragged her outside the cage. They were in a festive mood and stinking of alcohol. Documents were held up in front of her face, and they were bleating about Atsuo Yukimori's full confession. (So what? No, I am not going to read those papers stuffed with numbers. They are your weakness, not mine.)

~

"Well, then." Prosecutor Onuki rubbed his petite hands together, as a surgeon might don a pair of rubber gloves for an operation. "No meetings this afternoon. Don't admit anyone. I will not take any calls either." Then he hastily added, "That does not apply to any top officials from the Office."

"Understood." Mr. Kishi, the prosecutors' secretary, had a complexion pale enough to have been powdered white. The effect was heightened by a flat, nearly featureless face.

"Other than that . . ."

At this, Prosecutor Onuki broke off and rose to look down through the window to Hibiya Park, where people strolled beneath cherry trees halfway on to full bloom and willows by the banks of the pond sporting cascades of new green raiment. He tore his gaze from the exhilarating spectacle of spring warmth outside and shifted it to the icy piles of documents on his desk. The stacks were arranged chronologically, from left to right and divided between forms from the police and prosecutors' examination records. Suspects' examination records had red tags. Witness examination records had white tags. Other papers with black tags were investigation reports from police and prosecution officers. Crime scene examination reports, photographs, diagrams and maps were arranged in neat piles to the sides, ready for instant reference. In the center of the desk were his own records: a timeline, diagrams of relationships between persons, and a grand index of all documents. There were Number 4B pencils available for writing in or erasing notes as ideas came to mind. Prosecutor Onuki regarded all this with proprietary satisfaction, not unlike a child directing the traffic of toy cars on the roads of a tabletop kingdom.

Then he remembered Mr. Kishi, who was looking at his face like a dog told to sit. He finished his sentence. " . . . there isn't anything for you to do. I'll take care of this. I want to concentrate on this for a while."

"Shall I leave the room?"

"No, no," prosecutor Onuki said with a wave of the hand. "Please wait here. I might have something for you to help with. This is a big case. Quite a handful. Just have a seat, please."

Prosecutor Onuki was pacing around his desk. The issue was whether to issue indictments for Atsuo Yukimori, Wakako Ikéhata, Makihiko Moriya, and other Q. Sect members. Of course, his decision to do that had already been made. It was, in fact, his intention to have them done by the evening. Nevertheless, it was necessary to re-enact the entire movie of this case in his mind one more time, scene by scene. He had to know exactly how far he could rebut the defense attorneys at trial, how well his case would hold up in court. It was hard to get a handle on the big picture of the case, for a couple of reasons. There was a terrific volume of examination records involving relationships between suspects that didn't always match up between different testimonies. And one of the key defendants, Wakako Ikéhata, was still keeping quiet. It was troubling, too, that he was getting noise and pressure about this case from every direction.

In the course of this vigorous pacing, prosecutor Onuki's elbow struck the wall. He frowned and abruptly recalled his encounter the day before with the Tokyo district chief prosecutor after being summoned to his office.

"Are the indictments ready?"

"Not yet. I will write them up tomorrow. It's just that there are still some unanswered questions, and I am thinking about doing a supplementary investigation."

At this, the senior prosecutor's expression lost the detachment one expects from the commandant, to register displeasure.

"Hasn't that investigation been completed?" The district chief ground the ash end of his cigar in his ash tray, as if to express irritation at Onuki's indolence.

"Basically, it was completed, as I reported to the Conference on Measures for Public Order."

"That was two weeks ago." the chief prosecutor said, heavily emphasizing the "two weeks." Then he added, tersely "There was an understanding of all parties at that point that all the evidence was in, and the investigation was about wrapped up."

The conference had been called in the wake of the riot that had taken place in Shinjuku on November 2 of the previous year. It had provided a forum for prosecutors in charge of public security from the national and local levels to meet with their counterparts in the Tokyo police headquarters and the justice ministry to discuss such matters as interrogations, arrests, and ways to prevent disturbances. The conference had viewed the Shinkansen bombing as the work of radicals, much like the rioting in Shinjuku had been. Discussions had been held on the progress of the investigation and the possibilities for issuing indictments. People from the justice ministry had expressed concerns from the government about possible copycat bombings by other radical groups. They had asked for stern punishment of those responsible for the Shinkansen bombing, as a warning. Prosecutor Onuki understood exactly what the chief had in mind. His own thoughts at the moment were framed by some deeply impressive advice he had been given when he was just starting off as a prosecutor, more than a decade before. A senior prosecutor had been offering him words of encouragement while he was hesitating on the handling of a case of theft that would have to be prosecuted on circumstantial evidence because the suspect had not confessed. "I would deny I ever said it, but it isn't up to you to worry about whether the suspect is guilty. The only question is, can you be sure he'll be convicted if you charge him. Let the judges worry about the rest. You can go with the case if there is a sixty percent chance he did the deed. His attorney can run with the other forty percent. The prosecutor represents the public's interest on his sixty percent and the defendant's human rights are protected with the other forty percent. That's how it works."

"In any case," the district chief said with a puff on his cherished cigar, "I want this case prosecuted ASAP. That is what the prosecutor-general wants too."

"Right."

"You were at the crime scene when it happened. You know very well what a savage, appalling act it was."

"I do."

It was the policy of the Tokyo district chief prosecutor that staff members in charge of cases were to be in on crime scene investigations, not only to cooperate with the police, but to direct and advise them as well. Under current law, prosecutors and police officers are equal partners, but he saw things in the light of the old criminal procedures code, in effect until 1949, when police and criminal investigations were entirely run by prosecutors.

Accordingly, Prosecutor Onuki always made certain to show up at crime scenes. He had covered various crime scene investigations, including campus disturbances, the Shinjuku riot and the tower takeover. At the time of the Shin-kansen bombing, his office had been contacted by police headquarters people in both the Serious Crimes and Public Order divisions. He had hurried to the scene together with his secretary, Mr. Kishi. Officers from the Onarimon police station had sealed off traffic in the Shimbashi Station area. The train was stopped on the Chuo-dori overpass. The second car was sitting at a slight angle, glass from its windows scattered about. The area was alive with policemen and fire department personnel carrying away blast victims. Ambulance and patrol car lights flashing red, sirens and emergency traffic instructions from loudspeakers at full blast left no doubt that the incident that had just occurred would have an impact on a major scale. As always happens at crime scenes, people were streaming in from the environs, the crowd filling the sidewalks and overflowing into the street.

A policeman escorted Onuki and Kishi at a run from the street up to the tracks by a ladder and inside the car where the bomb had gone off. They were greeted by a plain clothed Assistant Inspector Hino, who briefed them. Persecutor Onuki had previously met this short, baritone voiced officer at a seminar on radical sects held at Tokyo police headquarters. He recalled him as the very picture of a police officer who had risen through the ranks; speaking infrequently, but when he expressed his views, he conveyed the impression they were backed by solid personal experience. "They just now finally got the casualties out of here. We've got two dead," the inspector said, pulling down the blankets over a pair of dead bodies on stretchers. There was a man in a dark colored jacket, the left side of his face blown away, a red mass of brain matter visible. The other corpse was a little girl about seven years old whose right arm was missing.

"They appear to be father and daughter. They were sitting together. The father was in seat 19B and the child in A. It is presumed the explosive went off in the luggage rack over their heads." The luggage rack had been torn away and the two seats were bashed in. A crime scene examiner was squatting on the floor, carefully picking up pieces of metal and glass. The three men withdrew to the car's entry door so as not to obstruct the investigation.

"Twenty-eight casualties were taken to Toranomon hospital. Three are seriously injured. One of those is a young girl whose face was blown off. She might live, but they probably won't be able to save her eyes and nose. Mr. Prosecutor, the ones who did this are the worst of the worst. Whatever reasons they might have for this, there's no excuse for killing a little kid." Hino's muscular shoulders jumped angrily.

A young patrolman addressed the officer. "Sir, the press photographers say they want to shoot this interior."

"All right. They get five minutes. See that they work from the door and don't come inside."

A detachment of photographers who had been busily shooting the train from afar surged to the door. For several long moments their flash units lit up the car's interior, vividly exposing splashes of red on the ceiling and floors. Blood was spattered everywhere. Audible gasps of surprise escaped the photographers at the spectacle of the bomb's fearsome efficacy, and they jostled one another all the harder in their efforts to capture the scene. A reporter addressed Prosecutor Onuki, mistaking him for a detective. "Inspector! Do you have any suspects?"

Assistant Inspector Hino hastily intervened. "We don't have any information yet. Please get back so you don't get in the way of the investigation." He hustled all the reporters and photographers out the door, then in a warm tone resumed speaking to Prosecutor Onuki.

"We don't have any sure proof of this at the moment, but our gut feeling is radicals did this. That goes for the criminal investigation division and me, in the security division. Don't you agree sir?"

It just so happened that Prosecutor Onuki did agree with that assessment. He was attached to the public order division of the Tokyo district prosecutor's office, not the criminal investigation division. He and the lieutenant shared a common view of the matter.

Upon returning to his own office from his meeting with the Tokyo district chief prosecutor the previous day, Onuki had once again gone out for a solitary stroll in the park before lunch. It was his custom on such occasions to remove his prosecutor's badge from his lapel as a way of putting aside his persona of state inquisitor to become an ordinary citizen.

He entered Hibiya Park and walked a path beneath trees warmed by sunlight and spring breezes. Naturally enough for the upper west side of Hibiya park, he encountered a number of familiar faces belonging to lawyers and various officials, but he avoided them by putting on a show of being preoccupied with personal matters. Entering Matsumoto Tower, he went up to the French restaurant on the third floor. A window seat was fortunately available. He ordered raw oysters for as an appetizer, followed by soup and Chateaubriand, then gazed outside as he awaited his meal. The high-rise buildings of Ginza overshadowing the freshly verdant keyaki trees like great walls around the park seemed in terribly bad taste. After what he had been told by the Tokyo district chief prosecutor, he would have to have the indictments and opening statements written up by the following day. But there were things on his mind making him hesitant about getting to the task.

Prosecutor Onuki had visited the crime scene when it occurred, then left the investigation to the police, opting to disengage and see how things developed. Deputy Inspector Noseh was second to none in the Tokyo police department when it came to getting a job done, and besides, he was a personal friend. The field work was in good hands with such an experienced and dedicated man as Assistant Inspector Hino, so Prosecutor Onuki was of a mind to let the police investigate in their own way. His confidence proved justified when Atsuo Yukimori and Wakako Ikéhata turned up as suspects and were arrested in an unprecedentedly short period for the type of crime.

Prosecutor Onuki had issued a request to the court for their detention upon receiving the investigation chief's request to arrest them on the unrelated charge of robbery in order to insure plenty of time to conduct a thorough investigation. Atsuo Yukimori had made a full confession on the twenty-first day of detention, and the pair were rearrested on the basis of it. But Wakako Ikéhata continued to maintain silence. Aside from witness statements and deductive reasoning, nothing was known of her motives, nor what she did on the day of the crime. What if she starts talking in court and says something that isn't good for the case? That was the big sticking point in his mind.

His raw oysters arrived. As he ate them, Prosecutor Onuki recalled the unexpected visit he had received three days before from Professor Ikéhata. He himself had summoned the professor four times or so in the course of his witness examinations, but that day's interview was at the professor's request. His face had become quite familiar, having appeared so frequently in newspapers and magazines since his daughter's arrest. It was aging at an amazingly rapid pace for a man fifty-four years of age, the skin creases deepening by the day, while the hair grew steadily whiter. He entered the room and bowed to Prosecutor Onuki, wearing the expression of a man driven to despair. From the beginning he spoke in a pleading tone.

"Wakako is insane."

Prosecutor Onuki was silent. Professor Ikéhata inclined his head to Secretary Kishi as in supplication. Then he spoke again with a trifle more restraint.

"She has delusions of being victimized. She was in the hospital because she thought she was being persecuted by some kind of organization. Then she ran away from the hospital. She was living in a daze with no one to look after her when that convict Yukimori got his hands on her. He's twenty-five years older. She didn't know what was happening. He tricked her into going along with his deviant behavior. Wakako was delusional. She didn't know what she was doing. She just did what that man told her to."

"One moment, please." Prosecutor Onuki interrupted with elaborate courtesy toward the eminent legal scholar. "Your daughter escaped from the hospital on January tenth. The police raid on the Tower happened after that. She was back living at home on that day, I believe. I recall you saying she stayed at home for a while, and then left home at the beginning of February."

"She was at home for a while, but she was completely abnormal. She shut herself up in her room, avoiding me and my wife. She was incapable of normal behavior when she left home. I'm telling you she wasn't in control. She couldn't tell right from wrong and act accordingly."

"Yes, you covered that same point in your prior testimony," Prosecutor Onuki said curtly. "I understand your views insofar as they are the same as in your examination records."

"No, no," Professor Ikéhata said, dismayed by the cold response. "I just thought I would request to see you today to inquire if you intend to indict Wakako. I was here on a visit with Mr. —— —— The professor named a chief prosecutor who had been in his T. University graduating class.

"I haven't decided that yet," Persecutor Onuki answered quickly, his gaze plowing through the piles of papers on his desk. "I am reviewing the papers on the case now."

"Forgive me for interfering with your work," Professor Ikéhata said, rising.

"Not at all," Prosecutor Onuki said, shifting to warm geniality. He smilingly saw Professor Ikéhata to the door. "It is an honor to have you visit. Incidentally, I was deeply impressed by your article in defense of prosecutors in the March issue of *Criminology Magazine*. It is very important to have your voice of reason at a time when student radicalism has made it fashionable to criticize prosecutors and journalism raises a fuss about supposed abuse of powers or overreaching in investigations."

"You are very kind," Professor Ikéhata said, sheepishly bowing his head. Then he whispered into Prosecutor Onuki's ear, "I want to save my daughter. I am her father. I want you to know how I feel. That is the only reason I came."

After his meal at Matsumoto Tower, Prosecutor Onuki walked to Tokyo police headquarters. He was taken by the chief of the first public security division to the room where the interrogation of Wakako Ikéhata was in session. At the prosecutor's sudden appearance, the three interrogating officers on duty all bolted upright, put away magazines they had been reading and hastily emptied ashtrays. Wakako Ikéhata sat silently before them, ankles on calves, face expressionless. The fairness of her complexion without makeup was striking. The down on her cheeks stirred faintly. With her big, serene eyes, she looked more like a teenaged girl than a woman of twenty-four. Compared to them, the eyes of the three policemen, sullied with nicotine, alcohol, and age, had looked grotesque.

Now, as Prosecutor Onuki busily paced about his desk, as he thought about Wakako Ikéhata's eyes, then thought about words whispered into his ear by Professor Ikéhata, the sharply focused mental image he had of this case seemed to go a trifle gauzy. Wakako Ikéhata. What's that girl's game? What is she thinking? Is it really going to be possible to bring off a case built against her without getting a single word from her?

The next moment, Prosecutor Onuki was striving to banish these thoughts like a dog shakes off water. He had examined the documents scrupulously, not once, but many times. He had investigated for himself, until he was satisfied. Even though he had intimated thinking otherwise by telling the chief prosecutor that he was considering a supplementary investigation, in truth, there was nothing more for him to do at this point.

Two days after obtaining Atsuo Yukimori's full confession, the police team on the case had sent all their evidence against Atsuo Yukimori and Wakako Ikéhata to the prosecutor's office. Onuki had devoted an entire day to poring over the record of the investigation and report. It had left him with admiration for the team's efforts. He particularly admired that they had managed to zero in on the suspects so quickly, although there really was a big problem with that very fact. This was the kind of case where you should be picking up every tile you can find and deciding if it fits in the mosaic or not.

These investigators were gung-ho when it came to getting the goods on Atsuo Yukimori, but it seemed to Onuki they had skimped on checking if there wasn't someone else who could fill the bill even better than he. That was what he had in mind when he asked the director of the investigation, Deputy Inspector Noseh, for an additional explanation. Noseh had shown up with Captain Magara and Assistant Inspector Hino. Onuki knew Noseh and Hino, but had never met Captain Magara. It was a bit surprising to see a young fellow who looked like a student sporting the three-bar captain insignia. Onuki gave the three a slight bow and abruptly got to the point.

"So what do we have on this Atsuo Yukimori character? He's a hunter who uses black gunpowder, he's an ex-con, he was a machine-gunner in the army, he pals around with radicals, he fits descriptions from witnesses on the train platform, he conducted three bomb experiments and he has no alibi for the day of the crime. All that adds up to proof he did it. Is that it?"

"There's more." Assistant Inspector Hino's basso voice resounded with grave urgency. "There is the newspaper used to wrap the explosive, and the paper bag that was used to carry it, to name two other items."

"Quite so." Prosecutor Onuki nodded. The fragments of newspaper that had been recovered belonged to the January 10 morning edition of the *A. Shimbun*. They carried advertisements that pointed to the edition of the newspaper targeting the San-Tama region of greater Tokyo. The paper bag belonged to S. Books, located in Jimbocho 1 chōmé in Kanda. Atsuo Yukimori lived in the San-Tama region, and Fukawa Motors was located next to S. Books. "But the problem with all this is that it was entirely too easy to find this guy," Onuki said, looking directly at Assistant Inspector Hino.

"For somebody who pulled off this big a crime, he leaves an awful lot of evidence laying around. Take that bag from S. Books. You found that when you searched his house. Inside there were five work uniforms, a shaving kit, a mechanic's license and an English-Japanese dictionary, which is exactly what he told you."

"He planned it that way, of course." Assistant Inspector Hino was livid with excitement. "He did that to use in his alibi. Yukimori could get all the bags he wanted from S. Books."

"I think that's exactly what is wrong. Would a man commit a major crime using a paper bag that could be easily tied to him? Now, what about the witnesses? The lady in the newspaper stand and two passengers said they saw a middle-aged man and a young woman, but only one identified the suspects."

At this, Captain Magara spoke up. "Concerning that point, more than ten people were lined up outside the door to board the rear entrance to car No. 2 at approximately 15:40. Two passengers noticed that at 15:50, moments before the door opened, a middle-aged man and a young woman who were together joined the end of the line. The two witnesses were men, aged twenty-five and thirty-two. They said the young woman was a good-looking girl wearing jeans and the man had on a brown trench coat and looked like somebody important. Two of witnesses testimonies agree that the middle-aged man was carrying a heavy-looking paper bag.

"The other witness was the woman in the south exit news stand, which was in front of car No. 5. She said a middle-aged man in a brown trench coat and a young woman who looked like they were a couple bought a couple of cans of soft drink and drank them in front of the stand. She said she remembered the young woman was quite attractive."

"But suspect identifications were mostly negative."

"Well, all three witnesses said they didn't see the middle-aged man's face, but they did see the woman's. Of those three, the one who said it wasn't Wakako Ikéhata was the news stand saleswoman."

"Hmmm." While Prosecutor Onuki ruminated, Captain Magara continued in a resonant voice. "The news stand lady only saw the couple having canned soft drinks. I think it only natural she would give a denial in suspect identification. But all three witnesses confirmed the middle-aged man wore a brown trench coat. Atsuo Yukimori doesn't wear his mechanics uniform except on the job. Anywhere else he went it was his habit to wear high quality foreign made suits and coats. He was wearing an English style brown trench coat on the day of the bombing."

"There must have been other suspicious looking people sighted, but the papers you sent my office didn't include examination reports on them."

"We omitted the negative evidence," Deputy Inspector Noseh replied. "I will send it if you like."

"Excuse me," Captain Magara said, self-consciously inclining his tall frame forward in a gesture of humility. "It is hard to say who really qualifies as suspicious-looking. We have reports of a hippy-style youth, a boy of about middle school age who wasn't with an adult and a woman of about thirty restlessly wandering around the platform without getting in any line. But the passengers in car No. 2 include people who match every one of these descriptions, so those reports don't point anywhere. There were sixty-three people inside car No. 2 when the bomb went off, and we know the names and addresses of every one. We also know what the relationships were between all the people riding together, and we know they don't include any couple who happened to be a middle-aged man and a young woman."

"Isn't it possible they did get on Car No. 2, then decided they wanted to sit someplace else? Did you at least check the passengers on car No. 1 and 3?"

"That was something we didn't check," said Captain Magara.

"Mr. Prosecutor," Assistant Inspector Hino broke in. His expression was seething. "You are chasing after faint possibilities. It is not a faint possibility, but a very strong probability that Atsuo Yukimori and Wakako Ikéhata were on that platform. Besides that, Yukimori has confessed to being there."

"Of course the confession is very important. I am the first to pay respects to the man who got a confession out of an old weasel who's been sent up as many times as that one has." With this, Onuki executed an awkward bow.

"It was no easy thing to take him down. Spent three whole weeks on that job, doing nothing but that, morning til night."

"Yeah." Once again, Onuki gave a stiff nod of his head in ceremonious tribute to the officer. "Your delivery of a full confession in this case was exemplary work." After offering this praise, he asked abruptly, "I don't suppose there was any coercion, leading questioning, torture or abuse involved, was there?"

"That's ridiculous!" Hino shot back angrily in spite of himself, then realizing the irony in the prosecutor's manner, he chortled. "There's nothing to worry about on that score. No coercion, no leading, no torture was used. We didn't lay a finger on the suspect. He confessed of his own accord, as the result of much persuasion and hard questioning. That confession was one hundred percent voluntary."

"It's a relief to hear that. We know very well the first thing the defense always does is raise doubts about the voluntary nature of the confession.

"Now, on the subject of lawyers, there is something I want to get straight. Your investigation report shows Atsuo Yukimori engaged a lawyer after he had given his full confession. Why is that? Can I assume you got down his explanation when you arrested him, according to procedure?"

Under Article 203 of the criminal procedure code, police officers are required to inform a suspect of the reason for arrest, take a record of any explanation the suspect offers and inform the suspect he or she can engage a lawyer. Police occasionally overlook the procedure, which can lead to claims from the defense that the defendant did not have the freedom to appoint a lawyer or didn't know that option was available. It was getting common for attorneys to use this defense in the many recent cases of arrests on charges of endangering public safety.

Assistant Inspector Hino was at a loss for an answer. Inspector Noseh leaned forward to come to the defense of his subordinate. His lower lip slipped upward to wet the upper lip, then he scratched the back of his head with his right hand, a gesture he frequently used to indicate his favor for a man.

"Let me explain that point. Atsuo Yukimori has a rich background of experience with the police. We didn't want him playing games with us, so we tried a bit of psychological pressure. We had an arrest warrant on February nineteen when we took him in, but rather than present it and give the notification of suspicion we just had him accompany us voluntarily."

"That is the number one problem. There have been decisions that recognized taking in the suspect under watch by three police officers as an arrest."

"I know that, but Atsuo Yukimori did not ask the reason for voluntary accompaniment. He came to the station submissively. We notified him he was coming voluntarily. Anyone with a record as long as his would know he didn't have to go if he didn't want to. The thing is, we ran into an unexpected situation outside the station house. There was a big media stake out. We couldn't take the chance of letting him escape in the confusion, so we put a handcuff on one hand and took him into the station. Then we immediately showed him the arrest warrant on the theft charge."

"Okay, you had an emergency situation, so you did an emergency arrest. Is that it?"

"No, if we did that Code of Criminal Procedure Article 210 would apply — we'd have to ask for a warrant, but in that case we already had one, so . . ."

"In that case, there wasn't the slightest need for voluntary accompaniment . . . Well, it's no big thing, but defense lawyers can raise a fuss about it. Chief, this is how it should be. From the beginning Atsuo Yukimori was arrested on suspicion of robbery and his explanation concerning the reason for arrest was recorded."

"Yes sir. That is how it should have been."

"No, that is how it was," Onuki said with a playful wink at Inspector Noseh. "Atsuo Yukimori was arrested on suspicion of robbery on February twenty-ninth according to procedure. He was rearrested during detention on this charge when he voluntarily confessed to the Shinkansen bombing. The suspect was informed of his right to remain silent in the course of the interrogation. He denied the charge initially and then confessed, without exercising his right to remain silent. Let's be sure of this now. The officers who did the arrest and the questioning did nothing unlawful. Please make sure everyone who was involved is perfectly clear on this point so we don't have any slip-ups if someone is called to testify at trial."

"Understood. You know how it is, these guys get so gung-ho on the job, sometimes they go a little too far."

"They couldn't catch the bad guys if they didn't go at it that hard. Your team has my full support on this case." Onuki turned a warm smile upon Assistant Inspector Hino, who had turned rigid and assumed a worried expression when his lapse was being discussed. Now he cast a relieved look at Captain Magara.

Onuki had himself questioned Atsuo Yukimori to ascertain his memory of being taken from that apartment in back of Jindai Temple. Yukimori had replied, "I was agitated at the time so I don't really remember. I think maybe they told me I was a suspect in the train bombing." Asked about notification of the right to remain silent, his answer was, "They did say that, but I thought if I kept quiet, I'd look guilty, so I answered the questions." On the point of engaging an attorney, he said, "I knew about that, but I was much too occupied with answering questions to be able to think about it until the confession was out of the way." He did not think the police officers' illegal tactics would come to light in court through questioning of this defendant. The important thing was to establish the defendant's guilt — he did not want to be tripped up by procedural technicalities over the arrest or the questioning.

"Now there is one other question," Onuki said to Inspector Noseh. "Atsuo Yukimori does not seem to have much in the way of politics in his background. What is your take on this?"

"That was a big sticking point for us in the beginning, but his confession cleared it up. He was very careful to never have political books or things like provocative leaflets in his apartment. When he was at work or talking to people on the outside he kept his dangerous ideas to himself."

"Okay, he kept up a cover. But, look, the suspect himself keeps saying, 'I don't know anything about that stuff' when you ask him about the Q. Sect or worldwide Marxist revolution."

"Excuse me," Captain Magara began with utmost hesitancy, but the next moment was speaking with the smooth assurance of a seasoned announcer reading from a script. "Atsuo Yukimori is no amateur when it comes to Marxism. He was imprisoned during the war for desertion and after the war he was recognized as a pro-Communist Party, antiwar resistance activist. The fact that he repeatedly engaged in criminal activities thereafter can be taken as confirmation of his fundamental opposition to the social order. I myself don't have experience in this field, so I would like for you to hear the views of Assistant Inspector Hino, but I will just say that Atsuo Yukimori doesn't fit the pattern of the usual repeat offender larcenist. He's neither stupid nor shiftless. On the contrary, his personality traits are obsessive neatness and a seriousness of purpose."

Assistant Inspector Hino continued. "He is dead serious. He is a man who knows what he is doing. You do not see any trace of the man who engaged in larceny, embezzlement and picking pockets."

"You are saying he is an ideology-driven criminal?" Onuki asked, searching the two officers' faces.

"Yes, that's right," Captain Magara answered. "He keeps to himself, works hard and he's very particular about getting everything right. He did a very good job for seven years as the foreman of that body shop. He was always well dressed — loved to have everything neat and clean. He's the type who's always worrying about locking up, so he keeps going around checking all the doors. The thing about him is he wants to make sure he remembers everything he did. He is what is called an obsessive personality. I would say he is very typical of that personality type.

"Now, his *locus minoris resistente* — excuse me, that is a term used in psychology that means 'place of less resistance.' With him, that is his memory. You see with people like him who always want to be able to recall every single thing they did, as soon as they find they have forgotten something, they immediately become very uncertain about the entire memory. In the beginning, when he was denying the charges, I kept pressing him on that very point. At first, he tried to give the alibi he made up for his recollections of February eleven, the day of the crime, but his recollection was imperfect and it fell apart. So he finally told the truth, which is a completely different story."

"That's for sure." Encouraged by Captain Magara's explanation, Assistant Inspector Hino nodded three times. "He doesn't remember things very well. He makes a lot of vague comments that are different every time he talks about it. Basically, he's really forgetful. He remembers what he puts his mind to remembering. It's plain as could be everything he says is from his made-up alibi."

Captain Magara proceeded with his explanation evenly. "Concerning his politics, it is clear that Atsuo Yukimori is well informed about the latest New Left positions. The students all testified to this, most especially Makihiko Moriya and Shinichi Tagawa. Moriya even confided that he picked up a thing or two from Atsuo Yukimori about using bombs as a tactic in urban style revolution."

"All right, your additional explanations have pretty much answered the questions I had." Onuki bowed to the three police officers. After they were gone, he had turned to his own investigation. Once again, he read through examination records of witnesses and suspects. He met with witnesses to confirm his own impressions of them. The police had conducted a near-perfect investigation. There was hardly anything for him to change or add, but there was one single item in Atsuo Yukimori's statements that required special attention. Concerning his actions at Platform Eighteen in Tokyo Station on the day of the crime, Yukimori had given the following responses.

"Wakako and I went up the stairway onto the Shinkansen platform and got in line outside the door."

"Are you talking about the South Exit stairway? It's the stairway at the far end of the platform, facing the direction the train is going."

"Yes."

"How many people were waiting in that line?"

"Fifteen or sixteen. No, maybe it was more like twenty."

"What could you see from there?"

"The train came in, the door opened. There was an old cleaning lady inside working."

"What did you see after that?"

"Well, there was a newsstand."

"What! That newsstand is not next to car No. 2. It is in front of car No. 5!"

"Oh, yes. That is where it was. We went to the newsstand and we both had soft drinks."

"Then did you go back in line?"

"No. Before we got in line we drank our soft drinks."

"Didn't you see anything else before you got in line? Besides passengers, did you see someone selling lunches or a push cart or something?"

"Oh, yes, there was a push cart. A push cart with a big stack of lunches on it. There were soft drinks and vegetables and things."

With this statement, Onuki had succeeded in extracting a new piece of oral evidence not previously appearing in the police examination records. It described conditions at Platform Eighteen in Tokyo Station witnessed shortly before the departure at 1600 of Hikari No. 33.

Hikari No. 26 arrived at the platform at 1510, the passengers disembarked, the doors were closed for cleaning and inspection of the interior. Cleaning women with brooms and dusters cleaned the floors, turned the seats around to their default positions, and changed pillows and sheets. The train would depart as Hikari No. 33. Passengers began lining up outside the doors at approximately 1530. At around this time, a push cart operated by Nippon Restaurant Enterprise bearing soft drinks, vegetables and other items rolled past car No. 2 on its way to the buffet in car No. 9.

In other words, Atsuo Yukimori had mentioned a fact that could only be known to the ones who had committed the crime. It was one fact that was not known to the interrogating officers, therefore it was proof that the confession was the truth. When Onuki conducted an investigation that substantiated the facts concerning the push cart he satisfied himself that Atsuo Yukimori, and therefore Wakako Ikéhata as well, were the ones who had placed the Shinkansen bomb. He was fully confident the case would withstand the defense attorneys' attempts to cast doubt on the voluntary nature of the confessions or claim they were framed. The defendants' conviction was assured.

Onuki stopped pacing around his desk, sat in his chair, took up a pencil and began jotting down some essential points as the whole of the case emerged in his mind with vivid clarity.

An unusually heavy snowfall that had begun the night brought Tokyo more than ten centimeters of snow for the first National Foundation Day on February 11, 1967. In this reinstatement of the former Empire Day was the realization of a fond dream for right-wing and nationalist organizations, who staged a celebration in Hibiya Park with a parade of rising sun banners. Radical students saw it as a revival of militarism. They held a demonstration rally in Shimizudani Park to raise opposition to Empire Day. At this point in time Q. Sect did not exist as an organization. Makihiko Moriya (age 22) involved himself with such anti-Communist Party groups as the K. Sect and the B. Faction, listening to speeches given by others and joining the loud voices chanting slogans against Empire Day and militarism.

From that day on, Makihiko Moriya dedicated himself to realizing his ideal of abolishing nation-states by forming a new sect with a mission of armed revolution to that end. He spoke of his plans to his friend in the T. University law department, Shinichi Tagawa. They began getting other students in the law department, and eventually recruited students in the departments of literature, science and engineering. By mid-April, they finally were in a position to hold the first meeting of the Q. Sect.

As these plans were coming to fruition, a series of events were occurring that stirred the imagination

of this young man from a desolate village on the Noto Peninsula, who had grown up experiencing the region's snows and rough seas.

On the night of February 15, a time bomb exploded in a men's room in the terminal building of Tokyo International Airport at Hanéda, seriously injuring two people. An unemployed twenty-two-year old from Ibaraki prefecture was arrested and charged with the crime.

On March 31 at approximately 4:45 p.m., an explosion from a steel trash basket near the Shinkansen ticket window at the Yaésu Central Entrance to Tokyo Station caused serious to light injuries to fifteen people.

A volume of *The Tale of Genji* someone had left on seat 16D in car No. 7 of Tokai Shinkansen Hikari No. 21 bound for Osaka was suspected of being a bomb. Nagoya Station was contacted and the book was removed at the station and taken to the Aichi Prefecture police shooting range, where an examination found it was a bomb consisting of dynamite, batteries, and an electrical detonator.

On April 22, nearly fifty students responded to invitations from Makihiko Moriya and Shinichi Tagawa to gather at a Japanese-style hotel, the H. Inn, located at Hongo 1 chomé in Tokyo's Bunkyo ward to establish Q. Sect. The organization formed on this occasion consisted of Moriya and Tagawa at the central executive committee, Akito Shinya (age 21), Mitsuko Akizuki (age 19) and Wakako Ikéhata (age 22) serving as the operations corps and forty-seven other members. The important point here is the fact that Wakako Ikéhata was a sect member at

347

that time. She became acquainted with Makihiko Moriya in the fall of the previous year when he visited her father, professor Kotaro Ikéhata, at the Ikéhata home. An intimate relationship subsequently developed between the couple.

Wakako Ikéhata started R. University in April, 1965, but was admitted to S. Psychiatric Hospital in May for a neurotic condition. She recovered in mid-September and was released. At the time of the formation of Q. Sect. on April 22, 1967 she had returned to a normal condition. Makihiko Moriya asked Wakako Ikéhata to work out a method for manufacturing time bombs because she was in a chemistry department and had detailed knowledge of explosives and gunpowder. She agreed to the request.

Shown photographs of the students, the front desk clerk and room cleaners testified Makihiko Moriya and Wakako Ikéhata had been present at the meeting that day. They said there were only three female students among the group and Wakako Ikéhata's slim, long-legged appearance stood out. Makihiko Moriya's testimony that she had not participated then lacked credibility. The students had rented the room for the stated purpose of a party, but little alcohol was consumed. His suspicions aroused, the head clerk listened in to their hushed conversation and was astounded to hear incendiary talk about plans for blowing things up, armed struggle, killing members of the Communist Party youth wing, bloody revolution and dismantling the universities.

On June 18, at approximately 2:05 p.m. as a local passenger train of the Sanyo Railways bound for Himeji was stopping at Shioya Station in Kobe's Tarumi ward, a package placed on a luggage rack near the forward entrance of the rear car on the side facing sea suddenly emitted a thunderous whooshing noise and then exploded, propelling a metal fragment that struck the head of a woman (age 22), killing her and causing heavy to light injuries to seventeen other people. The bomb consisted of a steel canister packed with smokeless gunpowder. It used an alarm clock as a detonator. Two objects presumed to be dynamite harmlessly exploded atop a section of railway between Nagaura Station and Anegasaki Station on the Boso-Nishi Line in Kimitsu (Chiba Prefecture) on July 13 at approximately 11:13 p.m., after the last train from Tokyo had passed through. Six days later two seventeen-year-olds from Kochi Prefecture were arrested and confessed to the crime.

It isn't hard to imagine the students in Q. Sect taking inspiration from the media sensation created by this series of bombings or attempted bombings and applying themselves to carry out their their own bombing plan.

Now to Wakako Ikéhata. She began learning figure skating at the Korakuen skating rink in the summer of 1964 with an instructor there named Mr. I. (age

32). She became acquainted with Atsuo Yukimori (age 45), who took lessons from the same instructor. In the course of conversations with him, she learned that he hunted for pleasure, a hobby that allowed him to freely purchase gunpowder, and that he had been in a machine gun company during the war, which had given him a great deal of knowledge about gunpowder and bombs. She became increasingly friendly toward him. With the complicity of her boyfriend, Makihiko Moriya, she seduced Atsuo Yukimori and tried to persuade him to make a bomb for the Q. Sect.

Wakako Ikéhata (age 23) requested Atsuo Yukimori (age 48) to manufacture a bomb in early fall, 1967. He was the foreman of Fukawa Motors, a gasoline filling station and automobile repair shop. He did his work more or less responsibly, hiding from his fellow workers his dealings with Wakako Ikéhata and Makihiko Moriya of Q. Sect. Eventually, he adopted their radical ideas. Though he may have once sought only to please Wakako Ikéhata, he now applied himself enthusiastically to bomb manufacture, secretly making careful preparations to conduct test explosions in east Hokkaido on the occasion of hunting trips taken there when he served as guide for Ichiro Fukawa, the president of Fukawa Motors, in early November when the deer hunting season began.

Fukawa Motors secretary to the president Kimiko Fujiyama testified as follows:

"I had heard from Mr. Fukawa about Atsuo Yukimori's dark history as a former convict. He said, 'There is no telling what that ex-con might try. Don't trust him.' He said that to me, as his secretary. I kept it from the other employees that he had a criminal record. Mr. Fukawa recognized his leadership as the shop foreman. He said 'You can tell he's an old non-com. He knows how to keep the troops in line.'

"Atsuo Yukimori likes to read. He was always reading paperbacks on the train or during the lunch break in the shop. One day, I think it was in the fall of 1967, he was reading a book during lunch and he tried to hide it. I thought it was odd, so I took it away from him and was astonished to see it was a manual about explosives. Yes, it was in mid-November, before he and Mr. Fukawa went to Hokkaido."

Sonoko Kanéhara, Fukawa Motors dorm mother at the workers' dormitory testified as follows: "Everyone knew that Mr. Yukimori had a criminal past. They couldn't help but know — Kimiko Fujiyama blabbed about it to everyone. There was something creepy about knowing someone who seemed so respectable had been a pickpocket. It was like food that fell into the garbage. You don't want to have it anymore, no matter how much it was washed. That feeling."

Kiyoshi Tomoyama, Fukawa Motors mechanic, testified as follows:

"Mr. Yukimori is very good with his hands. He did everything himself — cutting pipe, turning threads — whatever. He could troubleshoot a car's electrical system and fix the problem in no time. Yes, I don't think he would have any problem at all rigging a timer for a bomb."

On November 15, Atsuo Yukimori traveled with Fukawa Motors president Ichiro Fukawa to Hokkaido, where they stayed at the Nemuro Grand Hotel. The following day, November 16, they went duck shooting in the Lake Furen area with Yukimori's brother-in-law, Torakichi Jinnai as hunting guide. On November 17, Ichiro Fukawa and Torakichi Jinnai went duck shooting together. Yukimori used that time to conduct a test explosion, as he had been discussing with the Q. Sect. Using an aluminum boat owned by Torakichi Jinnai that was ashore near the Furen salmon roe extraction station, he ran it down river to a sandbar at the river mouth and went ashore. At approximately 4:00 p.m. on November 17, he connected four size D batteries to a windup timer set for detonation five minutes later. He waited face down on the ground approximately fifty meters away until the explosion occurred, according to plan. It was a bigger explosion than he had been expecting, sending waves through the reeds and causing an alder three meters away to tip partly over. His experiment had been a big success.

Ichiro Fukawa testified as follows:

"Yukimori wasn't in his room next to mine in the hotel when I got back there from shooting deer. I talked with Torakichi Jinnai for a while, then went into the bath. Yukimori came in and I guess he thought I couldn't hear because he was bragging to Jinnai about what a big explosion he had set off in the marsh. He told him not to talk about it to anyone. I was suspicious of why he would want to do something against the law like that on the sly. It was scary, like I was seeing the real Yukimori and he was up to something."

The above testimony from Ichiro Fukawa is substantiated by testimony from Torakichi Jinnai. Ichiro Fukawa came down with a cold following his early-morning deer hunting and stayed in bed for the next couple of days, leaving Atsuo Yukimori with time on his hands. On November 19, he announced he was going fishing, and took the above-mentioned aluminum boat onto Lake Furen to a location in the marsh approximately six hundred meters south of Honmoshiri Island near the northern end of the lake. At approximately 3:00 p.m. on November 19 he packed twenty grams of smokeless gunpowder into a sealed chamber he had fashioned from iron pipe, and set a wind-up spring detonator with a five-minute delay. He then drove the boat away at full speed and watched from out on the lake an explosion bigger than he had achieved before. This experiment demonstrated that a bigger explosion could be obtained with the same amount of smokeless gunpowder when using a strong steel pipe. He confirmed that once again the blast had pushed back an alder tree located about three meters from the explosion, but this time the tree had been completely overturned.

It happened that this explosion was heard by a hunter named Rentaro Watanabé, who was duck hunting at the mouth of the Yaushibetsu River to the west end of Honmoshiri Island at approximately 3:00 p.m.. Suspicions aroused, he went to investigate the site of the explosion and witnessed a flat-bottomed aluminum boat racing toward the mouth of the Furen River at full speed. This made him more suspicious still. Searching the lakefront marsh, he found a crater about one meter across and fifty centimeters deep, with the reeds flattened around. He judged someone had used a baited explosive for the purpose of killing red fox, a practice that is banned. He reported this to the Nemuro police station. An examination of the scene by officers from the station determined that the above mentioned iron pipe, smokeless gunpowder and spring-wind timer had been used.

The investigation of the November 19 explosion was terminated because it was not a case of using exploding bait, moreover it took place in the marsh, causing no damage. Nevertheless, Torakichi Jinnai was suspected because he was the only person in the Lake Furen areas who used a flat-bottomed aluminum boat. From his testimony from the current investigation it was discovered that the crime had been committed by Atsuo Yukimori.

Two successful experimental explosions convinced Atsuo Yukimori of his ability to make time bombs. In late November, he reported his success to Wakako Ikéhata and Makihiko Moriya. Q. Sect members discussed bombing objectives, taking cues from recent bomb attacks like the Sanyo railways bombing. They considered a moving train to be a good objective, likely to attract popular attention, and concluded that the Shinkansen was the best target because it symbolized the government policy of pursuing a high economic growth rate. Technology students in Q. Sect led the group in a study of the structural weaknesses of Shinkansen cars. It was suggested that because Shinkansen cars are airtight like aircraft cabins, an explosion within a car could turn the car itself into a kind of bomb that would set off a secondary explosion.

On February 11, 1968, the second National Foundation Day since its establishment, a rally of Empire Day opponents was held in the Hibiya Open Air Concert Hall. Q. Sect mobilized three hundred of its supporters and tried to wrest control of a gathering of the K. Sect, there with a membership five hundred strong, by engaging its leader in an onstage shouting match with power megaphones. Makihiko Moriya had matured since the last such rally he had attended on a snowy day in Shimizudani Park the previous year. He addressed the crowd of two thousand sympathetic students from around the country with the confidence of a sect leader. He captivated his listeners by howling into the microphone in a style reminiscent of Hitler as he waved his shoulder-length hair like a Kabuki lion dancer.

The K. Sect resisted fiercely. They attacked the Q. Sect members with fighting sticks and flagpoles, knocking helmets from heads and turning the confrontation into a very bloody clash. The two sides went through several cycles of physical confrontations followed by interims when each side would fall back until, ironically, their brawl was put down by a mixed crowd of nationalists, rightists and various political groups affiliated with the governing party who had come to the open-air concert hall to celebrate National Foundation Day to the tune of military marches. The Q. and K. sects, and a string of other sects then organized themselves into demonstration marches. The Q. Sect went to Tokyo Station, entered the terminal building through the Yaésu entrance and jumped onto the tracks to halt movement of Shinkansen trains and throw stones at them before scattering.

That evening, fifty key members of the Q. Sect assembled in Number 3 assembly hall of T. University's law school. They had much to discuss. The surprise attack from the K. Sect had left more than ten of their members with injuries that included one who lost sight in one eye, one completely paralyzed and several who lost consciousness. Among the matters agreed upon at that meeting was a resolution to always conduct operations wearing helmets and face cloths and be armed with sticks. They vowed to retaliate against the K. Sect for its attack. It was agreed that a range of campus issues, most notably opposition to Empire Day, tuition hikes and the system of internship for medical students had raised the student movement to such a high pitch they had better concentrate on building up their organization. Accordingly, it was decided to put aside their bombing plans for the time being.

The campus disturbances that erupted suddenly across the country in 1968 burst forth with energy that had been building up for many years, like jets of vapor from a liquid that had reached its boiling point. The key to dealing with such situations is to cool it down below the boiling point by even a tiny bit; that is all it takes to restore quiet as if nothing had happened. Stronger riot control does the job very easily. That is the consistent lesson from the history of periods of political strife and how they were settled. The authorities charged with maintaining public order adopted a policy of subduing student violence with overwhelming force and numbers of policemen. This was a dispassionate response that reflected the best available knowledge of riot control.

If there was anything more preposterous than the press being carried away with the idea that student riots were ushering in some kind of new era that was going to change everything, it was the self-styled intellectuals who handed the reporters what they were looking for in the form of asinine pronouncements they seemed to consider courageous. Onuki felt revulsion at the popular press and the progressive intellectuals. The feeling was physical, like real nausea. There arose within him a desire to banish from his mind all traces of their foolish preoccupations, and at the same time, a strong will to do battle with those who advocated them.

He had been born shortly after the Showa emperor's reign began, early on the road to war and hardship. After the war ended, he had spent his teens witnessing grownups perpetually befuddled by the new truisms of life. When he was a child, imperial Japan was the latest and the greatest cause. Japan was the country of the gods, its emperor a living god, the commander of a mighty army that would rightfully place him as the leader of a confederation of East Asia and the world. Pundits, novelists, and poets were no less eager than journalists to extol this self-assured doctrine of Japan as a great world power. He had gone to a rally at Uéno Park, where he had seen a student giving a speech punctuated with raised fists, screams and tears. The nation is in crisis. The autumn of our fate is at hand. We students gladly offer ourselves up to the empire. We can do no less than the heroes who have fallen in its defense, to die and join them in everlasting watch over these shores. Nay! To die but once for the empire is not enough! National guardians must be reborn seven times to make the ultimate sacrifice seven-fold!

For his impassioned screaming, Makihiko Moriya was a dead ringer to that student in Uéno Park, long ago. The similarities didn't stop there. All that distinguished the students back then from today's radicals was their dress. Then it was student caps and storm trooper style leggings, but the frenzied eyes and their way of falling into tight formations hadn't changed much. During the war, students had denounced their professors for parroting the antiquated doctrines of liberalism and democracy pushed by Japan's enemies in America and England. They chased the offending professors from their lecterns and demanded they be expelled from the universities. The leaders would shout a demand and their followers circled around them would chorus back a low, rumbling, "OHHHH!"

Essentially the same scene was being played out right now on campuses across the country, this time in the name of leftist revolution.

When the war ended, most militarism disappeared like the morning fog. Now everyone believed the emperor had always been a mere mortal. Journalists, the cultural elite, the students, too, were all either silent, or, if they had something to say, their reversals on everything they had stood for were pathetic to hear.

These people were a dispiriting sight. He did not want to be like them. The lesson he had taken from them was to distrust trendy ideas. That had been his motto when he started university. He consistently shunned the student movements springing up on every campus. They seemed to him nothing but a one hundred eighty degree reversal of the wartime dogma that the Japanese empire was the paragon for humankind. Now it was communism, and Lenin, Stalin, and Mao were the world's most advanced ideologues. Their solutions were the only correct ones. Everything else was to be bitterly opposed.

He developed an abhorrence for both extremes. After a period of agonizing over where he belonged, he began attending the church of a certain Christian sect and underwent baptism while he was a student. It was just at this time that he decided he wanted to be a prosecutor.

He was asked the reason for that decision more times than he could count. He was denounced by classmates who were communists or communist sympathizers, of whom there were many. They called him an apologist for the power establishment and a betrayer of the people. He was never angered by this kind of treatment, but he never revealed what he had in mind when he decided he wanted to be a prosecutor.

There is a story of a poisoned arrow told by the Buddha to a disciple in a sutra called the "Shorter Discourse to Malunkya." A man is shot with a poisoned arrow. When the doctor comes, the foolish man declares he does not want the arrow removed before he knows the caste of the man who shot it, what kind of person he is, his nationality, and the type of bow he used. A good doctor will ignore these irrelevant questions and promptly remove the arrow. If he did otherwise, the man would die. In the justice system, it is the prosecutor whose role is to remove the poisoned arrow. Of course, the judges and lawyers have a part in this, but judges can't initiate the process and lawyers take the part of the one who shot the poisoned arrow. Neither of those professions were right for him.

Feeling aversion and something like heartburn, Onuki frowned as he inspected the papers on Atsuo Yukimori, Wakako Ikéhata and Makihiko Moriya. When he looked away, he noticed Kishi at the corner of his vision, anxiously looking his way.

"Got something for me?"

"Yes. There was a call from your home. It was your daughter."

"My daughter . . ." Onuki looked even more annoyed as he realized he had forgotten his promise to his only daughter. Today was her seventh birthday. He had promised to bring her a present that night. His promise had been on his mind the day before, then banished after the chief prosecutor had pressed him for the indictment drafts. Tactfully, Kishi had left the office, so Onuki dialed his home phone number. His wife answered, then he heard the little one's childish voice, bringing with it the living warmth of the household. It was a disconcerting contrast to the grisly facts spelled out in the papers piled high on his desk, and also a reminder that the two people killed in this case were a father and his daughter. Onuki tasted hatred for the two who had done this deed, Atsuo Yukimori and Wakako Ikéhata, and this only increased the softness in his voice as he apologized to the child for breaking his promise.

On April 5, 1968, Yukichi Jinnai (age 19) took up residence in the dormitory of Fukawa Motors, where he began working as an apprentice mechanic. When off the job he was a passionate devotee of military songs and the writings of Ikki Kita and Yukio Mishima, identifying himself as a strongly right-leaning youth. He became interested in the student disturbances that were taking place on the campuses of T. University and a private university located nearby Fukawa Motors. He began visiting the campuses of various universities after work. In late April, these visits brought him in contact with Shinichi Tagawa, Akito Shinya, Makihiko Moriya, and Wakako Ikéhata, all members of the Q. Sect. The question of why radical leftists would accept a right-wing youth like Yukichi Jinnai is partially answered by the fact that he confided to them that he wanted to destroy Japan's present system and install a completely different system. It is probably more to the point, however, that he shared with them an ambition to use military force to accomplish his goal.

Yukichi Jinnai maintained his contact with the Q. Sect, and at the same time began visiting the office of the ultra-nationalist Y. Brotherhood, where he worked as an assistant to members. He received military training from this association using wooden replicas of firearms. He dreamed of becoming a full-fledged member, and worshiped its leader, Masayoshi Taniguchi (age 46).

Onuki had sent Taniguchi to jail before, in October 1965, on an indictment for assault causing injury. The sentence had been the full one year, six-month prison term for him he requested, though in truth the defendant's own behavior had guaranteed that outcome. Taniguchi was really more of a plain yakuza than an ultra-nationalist. He had begun his career as a thug on the streets of Asakusa in his boyhood. His entire body was covered with tattoos. He was loud, outspoken and had strong arms, qualities that quickly gained him distinction. Displacing the boss of the gang that controlled most of the black market operations in Asakusa after the war, he used the ultra-nationalism he had learned in the army as the gang's spiritual support when it made the rounds of its territory collecting "operations fees" through extortion, assault and battery or simple theft.

Masayoshi Taniguchi showed no contrition in the courtroom. To the contrary, he unleashed a tirade in stentorian tones that brought an eye-catching flush to his trademark scar on the left cheek. He was demanding the formation of an army led by the emperor to dismiss the Diet, proclaim marital law over all Japan, shoot all the corrupt politicians, and round up all Communist Party members to be put into forced labor camps. His removal was ordered and he was charged with contempt of court when he bared his upper torso to display his tattoos: "carp climbing waterfall" on his back, "Hannya, the female demon" on his right arm and a death skull on his left arm. He had offered pious words to Onuki: "I'm really a meek person. I basically mean well." Tearfully, he added, "I accept my punishment for doing wrong. I will serve my sentence with honor."

It was easy to see how someone like Yukichi Jinnai, who was simply a rebellious youth, would be attracted enough to Taniguchi's phony heroism to want to serve under him. Jinnai's head was filled simultaneously with heroic visions of Masayoshi Taniguchi and Makihiko Moriya's radical philosophy. No matter that this pair was like oil and water; this lad accepted both with the greatest of ease. As far as he was concerned, desire for unification of Asia under the emperor's benevolent rule was but a variation of the Marxist line on simultaneous world revolution. Both sides regarded crime as revolutionary activity to be proud of, meaning that street racketeers and radical students had much in common.

"Wait a minute! That's not right." Muttering, Onuki cast a sharp look at the great piles of documents on his desk as if he could scan through them from above. Something had told him there was something wrong with this take on the connections between these characters. He read through a few of the relevant statement records, laid them out in chronological order, penciled underlines into his notes and pondered.

Atsuo Yukimori was the one who got Yukichi Jinnai a job at Fukawa Motors. He was already tight with the Q. Sect when he did this, so he must have been the one who recruited Jinnai into the sect. Couldn't very well have them both falling in with the radicals on their own. That would be too much of a coincidence.

Here's how it should be. Atsuo Yukimori brokered Yukichi Jinnai into employment at Fukawa Motors, starting on April 5, 1968. Jinnai was a youth who loved war songs and had received military training using wooden rifles from the ultra-nationalist Y. Brotherhood. Yukimori showed him that he could do some real bashing, with fighting sticks, as a member of the militant Q. Sect. Gradually, he guided his nephew from the radical right to the radical left. Even though Jinnai had deep respect for the Y. Brotherhood leader Masayoshi Taniguchi as a "man of direct action," he took pleasure in associating with the students of Q. Sect, who were his own age. His love for Wakako Ikéhata was another factor. Eventually, he left the Y. Brotherhood and embraced the goals of the Q. Sect. The standoff between the student body and the administration at T. University was intensifying.

In January, medical students began an indefinite strike in protest against the intern system. In February, striking students held one of the university hospital's head doctors prisoner. In March, the school administration expelled, suspended or issued reprimands to seventeen student activists; the students responded with a boycott of the graduation ceremony later that month and a demand that the actions against the seventeen be withdrawn. The students disrupted the April 12 enrollment ceremony, and the Q. Sect organized a joint action with other sects to take over the Tower as a show of support for the strikers. On June 17, the university called in the police, who recaptured the Tower with a force of one thousand officers. The Tower was reoccupied on July 2 by the All-Campus Joint Struggle Committee. This time, the administration expelled ten students, including Makihiko Moriya, Shinichi Tagawa, and Akito Shinya of Q. Sect. This precipitated an open-ended strike by the law department students, who were subsequently joined by other departments. By October, the entire student body was on indefinite strike.

All the members of the Q. Sect were elated by these unprecedented developments, and turned their efforts to expanding their organization. Sorely needing funding for printing pamphlets and getting supplies for occupying buildings, they decided to secure it by whatever means possible. On October 13, Makihiko Moriya, Shinichi Tagawa and Akito Shinya summoned Yukichi Jinnai to meet them at the coffee shop "Bonn," located outside the entrance to T. University and instructed him to steal money from Fukawa Motors. On the following evening, October 14, Jinnai stole an envelope containing 170,000 yen that was in a drawer in the president's office of Fukawa Motors. That night he brought it to the Q. Sect headquarters on the second floor of the T. University Tower, where he handed it over to Makihiko Moriya.

On the morning of October 18, while going to his job, Atsuo Yukimori met Ginji Sato (age 57) on the platform of Ochanomizu Station. Because Sato was a former inmate of a prison where he had been held, Yukimori felt friendly enough to confide his plan to bomb a railway. From this, it can be inferred that the Q. Sect had made the go-ahead decision on the Shinkansen bombing plan that had been pending for approximately one year.

Q. Sect's entire membership turned out for the disturbances in Shinjuku on October 21, International Antiwar Day. Rocks and gasoline bombs were thrown at police officers (thereby interfering with the performance of duties by public officials), barricades were constructed in the street (obstructing traffic) and from 8:45 p.m. until approximately 1:00 a.m. on the morning of the following day, October 22, riotous behavior, including the throwing of rocks and setting of fires, was repeated on platforms in Shinjuku Station, on the tracks, inside the station building and in the immediate external surroundings of the station (unlawful acts, including engaging in riotous behavior, forcible obstruction of lawful business and assisting riotous behavior).

Due to the scale of the rioting at Shinjuku, the police were not able to determine what members of Q. Sect had participated, other than those arrested on the scene. Nevertheless, the testimony of N. (age 45), proprietor of the bar "The Hammer," located in Shinjuku ward, Sanko-cho, which is known popularly as "Golden Lane," makes it clear that Atsuo Yukimori and Wakako Ikéhata were in that bar from 10:00 p.m. on October 21 until 12:00 a.m. It is entirely possible that they joined in the rioting in Shinjuku with other Q. Sect members, at which time they would have probably set fire to a National Railways passenger coach, thereby obtaining information on flammable properties of materials used in its construction. Then after this, they would have escaped to "The Hammer" and pretended to be ordinary people out for a night of drinking. That night, Wakako Ikéhata stayed at Atsuo Yukimori's apartment near Jindai Temple and the following day, October 22, contacted Makihiko Moriya at approximately 1:00 p.m. She met him on the evening of that day in the T. University Tower to report on the results of the previous day's "investigation." At that meeting it was decided that Atsuo Yukimori would conduct a final experimental explosion on his upcoming hunting trip to east Hokkaido in mid-November.

The Shinjuku riot resulted in the arrest of sixty-five Q. Sect members and much media attention to the group's colorful behavior. It also aroused resentment from other sects, most especially the K sect, at Q. Sect's clear intention to become the leading radical group by using the most provocative tactics. During the predawn hours of October 25 more than twenty K. Sect members armed with wooden sticks and steel pipes burst into the Q. Sect headquarters and attacked the seven members who were sleeping there, inflicting serious injuries, including one who lost sight in both eyes, a brain contusion, and an abdominal rupture. Word of the attack soon reached Q. Sect, which showed up with a force of fifty members. After taking their wounded comrades to the T. University hospital, they invaded the K. Sect headquarters on the second floor of the T. University student cafeteria, to find that all but one member of K. Sect, a female student, had vacated the premises. They took her prisoner and brought her to a storage room in the basement of the law department building. She was stripped completely naked and beaten with a belt until she had lost consciousness. This torture was being closely watched by Wakako Ikéhata, who was suddenly seized with a fit of retching, convulsions, and fainting. Makihiko Moriya and Shin-ichi Tagawa decided to escort her to her home in Sendagaya. Wakako Ikéhata's condition continued to be abnormal even at home, however, causing her father, Kotaro Ikéhata, to obtain her admission as a patient at S. Psychiatric Hospital in Ushigomé.

Comments from the attending physician, Dr. K.

"Ms. Wakako Ikéhata has a history of occasionally falling into neuroses. Her defenses are weak, and she has trouble adapting even to slight changes in her environment. She could not deal with failing university entrance exams, and then, once she did get into a university, she was overcome with feelings of disappointment in the university itself. The recent campus disturbances were also too much for her. Each event led to more neuroses. Her problems in the fall of 1968 probably had to do with the intensifying conflict between the Q. and K. sects. The best treatment for that was to get her away from it all, by putting her in the hospital."

On November 15, Atsuo Yukimori accompanied Ichiro Fukawa, the company president, and Kimiko Fujiyama, his secretary, on a hunting vacation to Hokkaido, an excursion that had gained the status of an annual event. Fukawa and Fujiyama stayed in the Nemuro Grand Hotel, while Yukimori stayed at the home of brother-in-law, Torakichi Jinnai. On the morning of November 17, Torakichi Jinnai took Yukimori, Fukawa and Fujiyama duck hunting on the Furen River in his aluminum boat. That afternoon, they fished in the river. On November 18, Torakichi Jinnai went with Fukawa and Fujiyama to the mountains in Ashoro to hunt deer.

Yukimori seized the opportunity alone to conduct a test explosion in preparation for the Shinkansen bomb, according to his agreement with the Q. Sect. Telling his sister, Suéko Jinnai, he was going fishing, he took a 250 cc motorcycle to the vicinity of the local salmon roe extraction station, then slipped into the brush to avoid notice. He walked along the riverbank, heading back in the direction he had come, and did some fishing as a cover. Possibly because it was a Monday, there was no one in sight fishing or hunting. Picking a time a bit past 3:30, when dusk was settling, as a good condition for observing the effects of an explosion, he packed five grams of black gunpowder into a cast iron three-way coupler and connected four size D batteries and a windup spring timer as detonator that he set for five minutes. He then climbed a large alder about a hundred meters distant to watch. The explosion carried a dead tree a distance of five meters and left a crater three meters across and a meter deep. In order to establish the viability of the bomb for use in attacking a Shinkansen train, he continued observing the effects of the explosion until past six o'clock and then finally took the above-mentioned motorcycle to depart the scene. He arrived back at the residence of Torakichi Jinnai at approximately 7:30 p.m.

The explosion was heard by three personnel of the salmon roe extraction station, and two hunters observed the flash and white smoke from it. A car driven by personnel from the district forestry office passed Atsuo Yukimori on the motorcycle heading toward Nemuro at approximately 6:27 p.m. They testified as follows:

"We thought it was suspicious that someone would be out on a motorcycle at such a time, so we went by him slowly to take a good look. It was unmistakably this man in the photo. He wasn't wearing a helmet, and he seemed to be afraid of something. He looked our way, then hastily looked away. We had heard the explosion in the marsh two hours before so we thought he might be the perpetrator. We were thinking about stopping to question him, but we were afraid he might have another bomb, so we didn't."

Atsuo Yukimori returned to Tokyo on November 19. Using the pretext of visiting Wakako Ikéhata, he met with Makihiko Moriya in the waiting room of S. Psychiatric Hospital on November 21 to report the success of his experiment. Then he drove Moriya to the front gate of T. University.

Two officers of Onarimon police station belonging to the No. 2 Public Safety Unit of the Security Division observed Makihiko Moriya getting out of a large car of foreign make driven by Atsuo Yukimori. They followed the car in a taxi and were able to confirm that it entered the parking lot of Fukawa Motors. Makihiko Moriya disappeared into a large crowd of students there from across the country, eluding the police tail. It was, however, later confirmed by an undercover police officer from the metropolitan police Public Safety Division, Unit One in front of the Tower that he entered the headquarters of the Q. Sect in the Tower.

Students aligned with the Japan Communist Party and the opposing All-Campus Joint Struggle coalition assembled at T. University campus from the entire country, intent on mobilizing their supporters for massive rallies to be held the following day. The university administration responded to the crisis situation by putting the entire faculty on standby alert. Unanimous approval was voiced for a proposal from Professor Kotaro Ikéhata of the law department that faculty members armed with foam rubber cushions interpose themselves between the opposing factions to prevent bloodshed.

Q. Sect leaders held a planning session at their Tower headquarters at 11 p.m., during which they decided on the plan to bomb a Shinkansen train on the occasion of National Foundation Day on February 11. The meeting went on for some time, due to a difference of opinion about who should carry out this operation.

Makihiko Moriya wanted to leave the manufacture of the time bomb and its placement to Atsuo Yukimori, on the grounds that one person working alone would be the least noticeable. Many sect members opposed this view because they were suspicious of a middle-aged man with a criminal record. They argued that he might double cross them if there was no one watching him. They voted to have Wakako Ikéhata accompany him, since she had established intimacy with him. It was therefore decided to spring her from the hospital where she was a patient, in early January.

These facts can be inferred from testimony by Makihiko Moriya, Shinichi Tagawa, and Akito Shinya, although the whole truth of the story is not clear because their accounts are inconsistent on various points. Let us simply recognize the point that the Shinkansen bombing was scheduled at this meeting. It is probably safe to say that Moriya, Tagawa, and Shinya were key in deciding. We know that the job was carried out by Yukimori and Ikéhata.

The All-Campus Joint Struggle students stole a march on the JCP faction on the morning of November 22 by taking over the library. That was the first of a series of successful occupations and lockouts of buildings on campus, a blatant use of violence that angered many ordinary students, as well as the JCP faction. In January 1969, those students got together and breached the building lockouts one after another, leaving the Joint Struggle students isolated and in control of only a few buildings, most prominently including the Tower, by January 18, the first day of the two-day standoff with police that resulted in the end of all the building occupations.

Makihiko Moriya was one of the key figures who conceived the occupation of the Tower and guided its consistently radical course. He had already been arrested along with other Q. Sect leaders when their siege of the Tower was ended. They were charged with trespassing, assembling with dangerous weapons and interfering with the discharge of duties by public officials. Now the time has come for bringing him to justice, together with Shinichi Tagawa and Akito Shinya, as a full conspirator behind the Shinkansen bombing.

On January 10, Wakako Ikéhata escaped from S. Psychiatric Hospital by climbing over the chain link fence on the roof and descending the fire escape. She hid out in the N. Inn, located nearby the room Makihiko Moriya had in Hongo, Kikuzaka. This escape was made possible by the planning of Moriya and the financial support of Atsuo Yukimori. It was their intention to immediately begin preparing for the Shinkansen bombing, but they had to switch their first priority to preparing for battle with the riot police when they received information that the police would be called in to break the occupation of the Tower.

The Q. Sect feverishly set to buying up the supplies of food and gasoline for making petrol bombs that it needed for holing up in the Tower. Atsuo Yukimori and Yukichi Jinnai plotted to turn the Fukawa Motors parking lot into a hideout for rioting students when they set up a "liberated zone" in Kanda-Surugadai. On the afternoon of January 18, they built a barricade inside the parking lot. At some point past 5:00 p.m. on January 19, they led a number of students, mainly from the Q. Sect, inside their barricade. Then, when Wakako Ikéhata, Shinichi Tagawa and Akito Shinya were unable to make their escape outside again, they secreted them in the company dormitory.

With the fall of their Tower stronghold, the arrests of Makihiko Moriya and other leaders, among a total of over one hundred arrests of Q. Sect members, was a major blow to the organization. Shinichi Tagawa, Akito Shinya, and other members who had avoided arrest hastened to promote the Shinkansen bomb project as a means of advertising their organization to attract new membership. Wakako Ikéhata returned to her home in Sendagaya on the night of January 19, then ran away from home again on February 2 and established a hideout in apartment number 202 of the Fujimi-so building in Nishi-Shinjuku 7 chome. From there, she pressed her demands on Atsuo Yukimori to manufacture a bomb and also conducted a preliminary inspection of the Shinkansen platforms in Tokyo Station.

An important point here is that after the arrest of her lover, Makihiko Moriya, Wakako Ikéhata was quick to develop an intimate relationship with Atsuo Yukimori. According to Yukimori's confession, he claims to have had sex with her for the first time on February 11, on the night they placed the bomb, but that had little credibility. She had already stayed in his apartment on October 21, the night of the Shinjuku riot, at which time it can naturally be surmised they had sex. Although she was ostensibly importuning Yukimori to make the bomb, in fact she was carrying out the directives of the Q. Sect leaders who wanted him kept under observation until the bomb was planted. To put it plainly, she was making her body available as she advanced her idea of a "revolution." Unable to discern her true motives, he regarded her simply as a lover.

Wakako Ikéhata also came to be on very familiar terms with Yukichi Jinnai for the purpose of asking him on two occasions to steal money from Fukawa Motors to fund the Q. Sect's revolutionary activities. She consulted with him frequently, meeting him at the Korakuen skating rink and elsewhere. He carried out her wishes at about 6:00 p.m. on February 7, stealing 427,540 yen from the Fukawa Motors office and giving it to her. It is likely that this money was eventually used to fund her escape with Atsuo Yukimori, although the remaining money has not been located. It may be that they concealed it in the mountains of Raúsu while they were in hiding there.

It was chilling to behold the cunning employed by Wakako Ikéhata in manipulating two men, one to steal for her and the other to plant a bomb. Even though Onuki had little regard for the half-baked stereotypes being turned out by the newspapers and weekly magazines about the case, he did think there was a kernel of truth in the ways they characterized this woman:

"Evil-Hearted Beauty Plots Revolution" / "The Woman Behind the Crimes" / "Child Upbringing Gone Awry in Elite Household of T. University Professor," etc., etc. Maybe they were exaggerating, maybe they were distorting the facts, but professor Kotaro Ikéhata's claims that she wasn't in her right mind notwithstanding, the truth was that Wakako Ikéhata knew exactly what she was doing and there was no doubt at all that she was looking on with the utmost calm to ensure that her criminal intents were carried out as planned.

Atsuo Yukimori worked as foreman for more than seven years at Fukawa Motors, from the time his employment there began in April, 1961. The company's body repair business grew over those year, as it became commonplace for ordinary people to own cars. His achievements as foreman made the company what it is today. The company president, Ichiro Fukawa, readily acknowledges this, but was always a bit wary of the fact that Yukimori had a criminal record.

His concerns were raised considerably when he learned that Yukimori had set off an explosion in the fall of 1967 when they were in Hokkaido. He finally decided to terminate Yukimori's employment on February 11, 1969.

Statement from Ichiro Fukawa

"When I heard him bragging about setting off a bomb, that was the end of my confidence in him. I admit he was a good worker. He was more than good. He'd put in hours after hours on his back on the cold concrete floor fixing engines. He never asked for overtime pay and he'd work until midnight if there was a rush job. But there was too much on the personal level that was objectionable about him. It made me think there really must be something wrong with a person in the first place for him to end up with a criminal record.

"I hired Yukichi Jinnai in April, 1968 on Yukimori's request. According to him, Jinnai was completely dependable, but when I checked with his middle school home room teacher, Yuji Harazaki, I found out he was a juvenile delinquent, as bad as they come. There was a letter of recommendation supposedly from that teacher, but the signature was completely different from his real one. It was clear Yukimori forged it. I hired Jinnai anyway, though. At the time we were badly short staffed, and as long as Yukimori was the foreman, I thought it was best to let him have his way on his recommendation.

"Jinnai was good with his hands. He could do fine tuning kinds of jobs very well. He was strong, even if he was short, so he didn't have any trouble moving heavy equipment around. That was fine, but what wasn't good was that he didn't get along with the other boys very well, and he never worked past the regular quitting time. He'd just disappear somewhere outside, no matter how much the workload was backed up. This is just a small shop. We have to pamper our customers, even if have to bend over backwards. But that never got through to Jinnai.

"June 16, 1968, the day the Yokosuka line train was bombed, was a Sunday. I had been staying at the Yugashima hot springs with Atsuo Yukimori since the day before, fishing for ayu. We were live decoy fishing, but we only caught maybe two or three fish each all day and they had already gone bad, so in the evening we switched to sinker fishing and that got forty-two fish between us. We went drinking at the inn to celebrate. We happened to catch the news of the train bombing when I switched on the television. Yukimori suddenly went sharp-eyed. He forgot the saké and was taking in the news report like it was the most important thing in the world. It gave me the creeps when I remembered he'd been bragging about setting off an explosion on the Furen River. I said, 'Maybe the guy who did that was some hunter who knows all about gunpowder.'

"Yukimori answered, like he was joking, 'At least it wasn't you or me. We've got an alibi.'

"So I said, 'That was a time bomb. Maybe he set it yesterday.' That got Yukimori worried. He shut up and looked like he was thinking about something."

Atsuo Yukimori's scrapbook testifies to the extreme degree of interest he had in the Yokosuka train bombing. From the time of his release from Chiba prison in March 1959, Yukimori kept a scrapbook of newspaper articles with mind-boggling meticulousness. The articles he collected were exclusively about crimes. When it came to the "Jiro Kusaka" serial bombings that began in August 1963, he assembled articles from assorted newspapers with astonishing thoroughness, and it was the same with the Yokosuka train bombing. Among the points in common between that bomb attack and the Shinkansen bombing were that both used gunpowder for hunting, a three-way coupler and a windup timer. Undeniably, he must have taken some important ideas away from those articles.

Ofuna police station officers arrested Mikio Wakabayashi (age 25), a carpenter living in the city of Hino, for the Yokosuka train bombing on November 9, 1968. The things Atsuo Yukimori has in common with Wakabayashi need to be alluded to, if not directly pointed out at trial. Both had completed no more than middle school compulsory education, meaning they had to live their lives at the bottom of the social ladder, but both had a drive to work to work their up, so one became a licensed carpenter, the other, a licensed mechanic. Enjoying a substantial income, they could indulge in a common fondness for dressing in white collar style suits and ties rather than typical working-class clothing. They both wore only upscale foreign made name brand apparel and they both had a passion for hunting, which is a rich man's diversion. Both had a talent for hand craftsmanship involving electrical wiring or metal work. Both were loner types who avoided forming deep relationships with fellow workers, and that tendency turned anti-social to the point of a desire to wreak destruction. When Wakabayashi was arrested, Atsuo Yukimori probably muttered, "I am Mikio Wakabayashi."

Ichiro Fukawa's testimony continues

"On the morning of Tuesday, October 15, 1968, Kimiko Fujiyama realized when she came to work that an envelope containing 170,000 yen that had been inside the drawer of a steel office desk in the president's office was missing. I questioned her about it and she told me that the previous evening, after five o'clock, when she was returning from a trip to the toilet she saw someone hastily exiting the president's office. It was dark and she couldn't tell who it was, but she said it was someone short and square-shouldered, and from the back looked like Yukichi Jinnai. She said she thought it was something he might do, since he had a record of delinquency. Still, we didn't know that for sure, so I told Kimiko to keep quiet about it. For the time being, I kept an eye on Jinnai. Two days later I got a report from the dorm mother, Sonoko Kanéhara, that he suddenly bought an expensive stereo set. That sounded suspicious. Yukimori being the foreman, I had him investigate the situation and he said Jinnai bought it with his own savings. That didn't leave me with any real options to pursue the matter any further. I was worried that if it got out someone in the shop was a thief that might not be good for the workers' morale, so I pretended it didn't happen, although I wasn't at all happy about Yukimori covering up for Jinnai's crime. Then Sonoko Kanéhara upset everything by taking it upon herself to report the theft to the Kanda police station while I was away hunting in Hokkaido. When I got back, I got a call from the station about it. The last thing I wanted to do at that point was start an uproar about a theft and subject the workers to a search, so I said I was mistaken, the money turned up and told them not to investigate."

Ichiro Fukawa

"What made me decide to terminate Atsuo Yukimori was what he did on the day of the Tower, January 18, 1968. Without consulting me, the company president, he had a barricade built in the company parking lot, then let in radical students who inflicted major damage on the cars parked inside. He not only denied any responsibility for this, he said the company should pay for repairs to the cars because he said we didn't take proper care of them.

"I made Tatsuro Shiomi (age 27) the foreman after dismissing Yukimori. I gave him a big salary to hire him away from the automotive division of H. Corporation at the end of January. I was trying to decide when I should inform Yukimori of his dismissal when we had the theft of 420,000 yen on February 7. Yukichi Jinnai disappeared at the same time. He was already under suspicion of the previous theft, so I didn't have any doubt he was the thief. I called the Kanda police station, and they did a thorough investigation of Yukimori, too, since he was probably in on the theft. But the money wasn't found. I informed Yukimori of his dismissal on the morning of February 11. I told him he could stay until the end of March, but for some reason he said he would leave right away. So he packed his things and left."

Wakako Ikéhata received the stolen 427,540 yen from Yukichi Jinnai at her apartment in the Fujimi-so building in Nishi-Shinjuku on the night of February 7. This provided funds for fleeing after the bomb attack.

On February 11, National Foundation Day, at approximately 2:00 p.m. Atsuo Yukimori, who had been notified of the termination of his employment that morning, put on a brown trench coat, then placed an explosive device he had prepared inside a light brown paper bag from S. Books. This device contained a three-way coupler packed with 50 grams of black gunpowder, a detonator using four D size batteries and a spring timer set to detonate at 4:02.

He took a National Railways train from Ochanomizu Station to Tokyo Station, and there met Wakako Ikéhata at a coffee shop on the second floor on the Yaésu exit side of the station building. Wakako Ikéhata wore beige colored jeans, a red sweater and an orange half coat and was carrying a brown Boston bag. The couple had coffee and carried on an idle conversation to pass the time. At 3:30 p.m. they purchased two over-sized platform tickets, passed through the platform wicket and ascended to No. 18 platform. They bought and drank cans of orange juice at a platform kiosk near the south staircase, passing the time and watching what was happening around them.

With the actual bomb attack now at hand, Atsuo Yukimori was smiling with the confidence gained through three successful test explosions as he beckoned Wakako Ikéhata toward the line of passengers at the rear door of car No. 2.

Testimony from passengers identify a middle-aged gentleman with a young woman who was smiling cheerfully.

It was approximately 3:48 p.m. when the two reached the rear entrance door to car No. 2. The door opened two minutes later and they went inside. Because it was a reserved seats only car, they had to pretend to be looking for their seats. Atsuo Yukimori placed the paper bag containing the explosive device on the steel luggage rack above seat 19A. Then the two exited the car back onto the platform, as if to buy something from a kiosk, and immediately distanced themselves from the scene. They went to No. 2 platform of the National Railways Chuo Line, during which time the Shinkansen Hikari No. 33 departed on schedule at 4:00 p.m. At approximately 4:02, when it had passed through Shimbashi Station and reached the Chuo-Boulevard overpass, the above mentioned explosive device detonated, causing an explosion that damaged the train, including destruction of or damage to eight steel and alloy metal plates, eight passenger seats, the luggage rack, seven window glass panes and nine car components, and fulfilling its objective by causing the deaths of two passengers, D. (age 32), whose proximity to the explosion resulted in brain concussion, and D.'s daughter (age 7), who suffered severing of the right arm, and injuries to twenty-eight other passengers. Atsuo Yukimori and Wakako Ikéhata got on a train of the National Railways local Chuo line. Ikéhata got off at Shinjuku Station at approximately 4:30 and returned to her apartment. Yukimori got off at Mitaka Station and took the bus to the stop at the rear of Jindai Temple, returning to his apartment at 5:30 p.m.

The superintendent of Ikéhata's apartment testified that she returned at approximately 4:00 p.m., but a discrepancy of thirty minutes in a witness's recollection of an event is possible. The wife (age 62) of the landlord on the first floor of the Yukimori's apartment building heard sounds of Yukimori entering the room at approximately 5:30 p.m.

On the night of February 12, Atsuo Yukimori drunkenly appeared in the bar "The Hammer," located in Sanko-cho, Shinjuku Ward, and inquired from the female proprietor of the whereabouts of Wakako Ikéhata, on the pretense of not having met her for a long time. From there, he proceeded to the coffee shop "If" in Shinjuku 3 chomé, where he met Ikéhata. The two visited bars in Shinjuku, staying at a hotel in the vicinity for two days. On February 14, at 8:40 a.m. they boarded a flight on a domestic airliner from Hanéda Airport to Kushiro, via Obihiro, landing at Kushiro Airport at noon. Thereafter, they took a taxi to Kushiro Station and boarded an eastbound train on the Nemuro trunk line departing at 12:25 p.m. and arriving in Nemuro at 3:32 p.m. They took a taxi from there to the "Peken" lodge on Lake Furen, where they hid out for two days. On February 16, the proprietor of Peken (age 36) took them in his jeep to Nemuro-Shibetsu Station. From there they took the Akan bus departing at noon and arrived at Raúsu at 1:35 p.m., where they stayed at the Takasago Inn for two days.

They were on the run from the crime scene, so the pair must have been keeping a close eye on the newspaper and TV news. Presumably, they were well aware that the Q. Sect was suspected of the bombing and that Yukichi Jinnai had been arrested for robbery at his brother's home in Akkeshi on February 15. They had 400,000 yen stashed for their getaway, but it makes sense that they chose to stay at stay at low cost guest houses in out-of-the-way places that don't attract many tourists. They probably buried the cash somewhere around Lake Furen or in the mountains in Raúsu, but Atsuo Yukimori stubbornly denied it.

On the night of February 15, when a blizzard was in progress, the Troupe P., a traveling theater company, stayed overnight at the Peken lodge and met Atsuo Yukimori and Wakako Ikéhata. The troupe leader (age 42) testified that Yukimori was unable to engage in conversation with other guests, that he seemed frightened of something and ran off to his room.

The two decided to return to Tokyo on February 8 because they knew they were wanted by the police from the telephone calls Yukimori made on the night of February 26 to his sister in Nemuro, Suéko Jinnai. They reasoned that continuing to hide out would only raise suspicions further. They took the 7:00 a.m. Akan bus, arriving at Nemuro-Shibetsu Station at 8:35 and took a Shibetsu line train departing at 9:13 that arrived at Kushiro at 11:50. They boarded domestic fight 272, departing at 1:30 p.m. and arriving at Hanéda Airport at 5:00 p.m. An officer of Onarimon police station posted outside the Sendagaya residence of Wakako Ikéhata observed her return there at 6:30 p.m. An officer of the Chofu City police station at the apartment of Atsuo Yukimori near Jindai Temple observed his return at 7:40 p.m.

Officers of the Onarimon police station arrested the two on the early morning of February 19. Prosecutor Onuki took his time reading over his notes once more. He had items for the indictment marked in red and items for the opening statement in blue. Once he had that bird's eye view of the affair sharply etched in his mind, writing up the papers became a very easy task. The Q. Sect chiefs, Makihiko Moriya, Shinichi Tagawa, and Akita Shinya hatched the plot, had Yukimori and Ikéhata carry it out, leaving procurement of the money for their getaway to Yukichi Jinnai. That was the whole story, and it was backed up in numerous testimonies from witnesses.

Onuki experienced the exhilaration of the nonfiction novelist who has assembled all of his reference material and is about to embark on chronicling a major crime. There was one big exception, however, between himself and the author, who merely retraces the facts of the crime, with no attempt to remove the poisonous arrow. That is the job for the prosecutor. Every word, every line of what he wrote up in the indictment and the opening and concluding statements was a hard-edged sword with the power to banish the toxin. As the prosecutor wrote his draft, he felt its lethal power against the malefactors.

Back when he was in university, Onuki had been an avid reader of novels. Something drew him to crime fiction from Europe, America, and Russia. He was fascinated by their depictions of the world of killers, prisons, and thieves. These novels taught one about the nature of evil and the cruelty lurking in people's souls. There was one single reason why he had no interest at all in contemporary Japanese literature. Those books didn't portray crimes. Japan's novelists liked to show the world of underdogs, drinkers, and womanizers. Maybe they were all such righteous people they couldn't see into the nature of evil. He was no longer reading novels after prosecuting for a while, after he had come into contact with numerous criminals in the course of bringing them to justice. No novel, however detailed, however cleverly written, could match the impact of real-life events.

Onuki believed in reality and reality alone. What is reality? It is the totality of that which we feel, see, and do. It cannot be recreated just as it was. Some medium is required, like the written word (witness statements, testimony, reports) or images (photos, film, video), and the use of these modes of expression necessarily involves the possibility some constraint will be imposed, exaggeration will occur, or falsehood intrude. That being the case, Onuki placed his faith only in that reality that lay beyond the limits of words and images. His confidence came from his ability to see that far, with near-perfect clarity.

Of course, one is only human, and humans can make mistakes. He prayed to God and strove to hold mistakes to the minimum. When he finished writing up the indictment, he bowed his head to God and held the posture of prayer for a time. Then he added this appendix at the end of the indictment:

Offenses and applicable penal statutes	
Overturning railway car, causing injury and death	Penal code, 126-1 and 126-3
Homicide, attempted homicide	Penal code, 199 and 203
Injury	Penal code, 204
Explosives Control Law violation	Explosives Control Law, 1
Theft	Penal code, 235

Not having been directly involved in the plot, Yukichi Jinnai would have to be tried for indirect involvement through theft and abetting flight from the crime scene. The Q. Sect leaders were conspirators in charge of the principal offenders, Yukimori and Ikéhata. According to precedent, conspiracy made them principal offenders. Jinnai aside, the penalties for each of the five principles would be death or indefinite imprisonment. Each would have to suffer the consequences. Failure to impose the penalties would be failure to remove the poisoned arrow. In the face of a steadily mounting threat of terrorist bombings by radicals, it was necessary to demand capital punishment for their crimes, for the sake of guarding against the deadly threat they posed.

On March 20, just a short while ago, the defendant in the Yokosuka train bombing, Mikio Wakabayashi, was sentenced to death, as the prosecution had requested. That crime was much the same, except that this one was more serious — it caused the death of one additional victim. The social impact was greater still because the target of the bomb was not a local train line, but the Shinkansen, a national institution. It would not do to ask for anything less than capital punishment for this crime.

Onuki recalled the haggard face of Professor Ikéhata, when he came to ask that his daughter not be indicted. It wasn't hard to imagine the despondency of this renowned legal scholar at his daughter condemned to death, but bending the law out of sympathy was out of the question. The criminal code stood above all, immutable. In his writings, Professor Ikéhata himself expounded the absolute authority of the law. There were no exceptions for young women. Having committed the crime, Wakako Ikéhata would be sent to the gallows.

Onuki had been in attendance at many hangings. No matter how many times one witnessed it, it was never possible to grow accustomed to the sight of a condemned person with a rope wrapped about his neck falling, and then hanging at its end. He recalled the sight now and frowned. As a Christian, he did not favor capital punishment. But he could not shirk his responsibility as a prosecutor who represented the public interest. (Lord, forgive me, and let there be not a single evil thought or doubt in my mind.)

When he finished writing up the indictment, Onuki directed Kishi to type it up. Then he applied himself to putting away the papers he no longer needed and rearranging the remaining piles of documents on his desk in the order most convenient for writing the opening statement to the court, which he would begin doing the next day. At last, he settled back in his chair. It was only a little past five, still light outside. There was time to get over to Ginza and buy a birthday present for his daughter. It would be a nice change to be home early enough to have dinner with his whole family. When he called his wife, their conversation was interrupted by a jubilant child listening in.

"Papa! Are you really bringing a present?"

"I sure am! I'll bring a cake too."

Though slightly embarrassed by his seven-year-old daughter's delighted voice, her vexation forgotten, a trace of a smile lingered on Onuki's face as he descended to the lobby of the Supreme Public Prosecutors Office building. He nodded politely to a guard's salute and was greeted with a pleasant spring breeze outside. Feeling a sudden urge to see cherry blossoms, he set out in the direction of the Imperial Palace and walked along the busy thoroughfare beyond the palace moat, beside which a long line of cherry trees were in full bloom.

(The street is alive with cherry blossom viewers. The world is at peace. Preserving the peace is the ultimate public interest requirement. There can be no mercy for those who seek to disturb the peace, whether they are political radicals or common criminals. Hmmm, can't even stop being a prosecutor when I go cherry blossom viewing.)

A group of men in business suits coming from the direction of the metropolitan police building all bowed their heads toward him, as if on cue. It was Inspector Noseh and his men — Captain Magara, Assistant Inspector Hino, Sergeant Semba and six or seven others.

"Well, well, the gang's all here," Onuki said. "Is this a cherry blossom viewing party?"

"Yessir," Noseh replied, with an abashed head scratching gesture. "That's part of it. It's more like a going away party for Captain Magara. He's been promoted to deputy inspector and reassigned to Osaka police headquarters. We would be honored to have you join us."

"No, no. I still have work to do," Onuki replied with a congenial shake of his head. "I can see you have a lot to deal with," said Noseh.

"Sir," Assistant Inspector Hino interrupted abruptly, as if ejecting a bit of phlegm from his throat. "Have you decided on indicting that pack of radicals?"

When Onuki nodded, Hino struck his hands together and breathed, "Glad to hear it" and looked up at Magara, the newly anointed deputy inspector, who gave him a friendly slap on his massive shoulders.

"Phew," Magara continued, with a roll of one shoulder. "They really had me going. Haven't been able to think of anything else for the past two months."

"I really appreciate the job you did," the prosecutor said, smiling. "You deserve special credit for it. It isn't often a major case like that is solved so simply."

"I'm just wondering what happens next," Hino said in a fainthearted tone that sounded decidedly odd, coming from one with such an intimidating bearing as his. "I'm worried they might get up in court and start denying everything."

"Sure, that's possible. They claim their confessions were forced. The police tortured them, the police threatened them. That's what they always say. It's okay. We've got all the proof we need."

Prosecutor Onuki gave a parting wave of his hand to the police officers and followed in the wake of a passing flower viewing party.

Chapter 7

Walls

First hearing

We hit the road a little past 9:00 a.m. Thirty minutes later, they had me in a holding cell in Tokyo District Court. I was hit with a barrage from the newspaper photographers' flash units as I stepped out of the police van. A police line surrounded the building, and was holding back the crowd. Some people were waving red flags. Angry shouts were being exchanged.

Then I was all by myself in the holding cell, where it was quiet. That made it all the harder, because I was imagining the moment I would be facing Wakako. I had confessed to a pack of lies that implicated her. How could I possibly make up for that?

The moment came at the defendants' seats. I couldn't do any better than to cast a look at her with a stone face. But those big eyes of hers weren't looking at me. They were shining, but the light was focused on something inside. I was searching for a trace of a smile, anything. I blinked, she looked away and that was it. We didn't see each other again after that.

Makihiko Moriya's long hair was totally unkempt and his face was so buried in whiskers I might have taken him for someone else, but I recognized his features. There were two other young fellows I did not recognize. They had to be Shinichi Tagawa and Akito Shinya, but of course, I didn't know who was who. Yukichi was the last one into the courtroom. He flashed me a grin, the first smile seen among the defendants that day.

The visitors' gallery was filled to overflowing. I could make out Suéko's pale features and Tetsukichi, towering above everyone else. I couldn't find Torakichi, but I had the feeling he was there somewhere, watching me.

The presiding judge went into verification of the defendants' identities. Wakako was the only one who wouldn't give her name. The judge pressed her to answer and was ignored, Wakako looking calmly out the window, with all eyes upon her. With a pained smile, the judge asked the female guard who brought Wakako in to vouch for her identity. Someone from the spectators' section shouted "Right on!" It was a young kid, probably a student. The judge ordered the bailiff to remove him from the courtroom.

The prosecutor read out his indictment. I didn't know about the Q. Sect or Yukichi, but I knew that everything he was saying Wakako and I did was utter nonsense. I wanted to stand up and say so in a very loud voice, and I probably would have, if my lawyer, Mr. Iino, hadn't already told me to keep my mouth shut.

Next up was defendants' pleas. Moriya, Tagawa and Shinya all denied everything. Then it was my turn. I said, "None of the allegations are true," but I suppose I was too tensed up from waiting so long for that moment to come. It came out sounding like I was coughing.

Again, Wakako wasn't saying anything. Yukichi denied the charges. The prosecutor's eyes blinked delicately every time a defendant pleaded innocence, as if he was having none of it, but he kept a completely blank expression. Shigétaké Onuki, thirty-five years old, of the Tokyo District Prosecutors' Public Security Division. Medium height, slightly dark complected, prominent nose, piercing gaze. Those eyes had crinkled up with laughter time after time when he was examining me. He said he had been at a military prep school during the war, so he could understand how it was for an old army sergeant like me. He brought up things like the war in China for no obvious reason. I couldn't feel comfortable with a man like that. I hated the phony smile and the over-privileged sneer that lay behind it.

Onuki began reading out his opening statement. It was mind-boggling they could just make up phony evidence that way. I was hearing my name pinned on to someone else who did all that stuff. True enough, I had said something like that. At the time my mind was in a fog from exhaustion. It felt like being in a dream. All I wanted was for the interrogation to stop, so I said to Assistant Inspector Hino what he wanted me to say, which was only, "Yeah, that's right," after having said, "No, that's all wrong" about a million times. When the police sent me to the prosecutor, I was thinking, "Okay, here's my chance to overturn all that, tell him it was all lies." But when the time came, I knew very well Hino and company would get me in their clutches again. I didn't want to go through that wringer again, so I just parroted back the answers I had been taught me to give. I told myself all I had to do was tell the truth at trial.

Yeah, sure. I realized how ridiculous that idea was just by looking at Onuki rolling out his case against me like he knew from the start it was all sewn up. There was a mountain of evidence to back it up. Anybody who didn't know better, like those judges sitting up there, would certainly be apt to think it all must be true.

I know nothing about the Q. Sect. There isn't any reason why I should. I met Moriya once at the hospital. I had never so much as heard the names of Tagawa and Shinya before. Seeing them in court confirmed that they were complete strangers to me. The three explosions? Two were just fun and games. The last one was to scare off a bear. All they had to do was check on it and they could easily confirm that there had been a string of bear sightings in the marsh around that date. But this prosecutor didn't mention that — he was too cocksure all three explosions were dry runs for the Shinkansen bomb. If I could only prove my alibi. If there is someone I don't know about who saw me walking around in Jindai Botanical Garden that day, all of this could be cleared up if they would just come forward and testify.

All of a sudden Wakako was giggling. No she wasn't, she was shrieking with laughter. The prosecutor gave her the evil eye. The judge said, "Stop that laughing!" but she went on and on, in increasingly higher tones. I felt like laughing myself at that string of ridiculous lies. Undertones came from the spectator section. The judge ordered Wakako removed from the courtroom. The prosecutor resumed talking as if there had been no interruption.

I watched her being led away. Her hair had gotten much longer, down to her shoulders. She seemed to have lost a little weight. Her pantsuit set off those long legs nicely.

I became so preoccupied wondering what was going on in her mind and what she thought of me I didn't hear the rest of what the prosecutor was saying. I had written her about twenty letters after they sent me from Onarimon Police Station to the detention center and I got permission to write letters, but I didn't get any answers. I didn't write anything about the case against us so I don't think they were withheld over a censorship issue. I couldn't get over the look she cast my way. It was like a heavy curtain draw behind a window. And I kept hearing the piercing laughter that mocked the prosecutor.

They set the second hearing for twenty days later. Knowing I would get to see her again made me look forward to the next day in court.

~

Back in my cell, I gazed at a horizontal bar of blue sky through a crevice in the window. The sky that was visible from the police van had seemed like an amazingly wide vista. Never before had I thought of the sky over Tokyo as being particularly big.

They have me shut up in a three-mat room. The window is covered over with iron bars, so that almost nothing of the outside world can be seen. The walls are painted a yellowish color. You can see that the countless messages written on them have been painted over. I am one of countless souls who have been locked up in this room.

I was awakened by the sound of someone pacing. Outside, it was still night, the scene lit by a silvery bar of light from a mercury lamp. Someone was pacing the floor of the cell over mine at this hour, restlessly, heels coming down heavy. The other day this man was crying. He cried all day. He hit his head against the wall too. Later on, I was awakened again. It was still night. The sound of pacing had stopped. Now it was the sound of water being flushed away. The sounds that guards make don't even bother me. Two months on, their presence had become as natural as the air. But the prisoners do get to me.

~

Got a visit from Suéko. She immediately started crying. When she said she had just come from a visit to Yukichi, the guard cut her off. He said "That's not an appropriate conversation topic." That stopped her tears.

"You didn't do it, did you? That's the truth, right?"

"It's true. Believe me, it is."

"I believe you, but . . ."

"No one else does, do they?"

Last week, Suéko had sent me a long letter. She had been getting chilly looks around the neighborhood ever since Yukichi and I were arrested. Jinnai Diner had lost its customers. Torakichi found a live-in fishing job at a stationary salmon net post in Betsukaicho. Tetsukichi had bought a fast five-ton boat, and was out fishing since the start of the season. He had invited his father to join him, but of course stubborn Torakichi declared he would never be looked after by his own son.

" . . . So you're all by yourself."

Suéko nodded. Grayness stood out among the stray hairs hanging over her forehead. As far as Torakichi was concerned, I was completely responsible for what had happened, and he wasn't about to forgive Suéko for being my sister. The marital relationship had broken down. Her quivering expression bespoke a woman whose sons had turns their backs to her.

~

Slightly warm early summer breezes blow in. It gets stuffy if I keep the window closed, so I open it and have to listen to conversations from nearby cells. You're not allowed to talk at a normal conversational level, but the buzzing starts up like water from a faucet every time the guard walks past on his rounds. The talk is random gab or about things like shogi, or pop songs . . . I wish they would keep quiet.

At Mr. Iino's prompting, I've started writing down everything I can remember about what I did from the time Wakako and I went to Shinjuku last October. The damn talking is distracting.

I am in the four-two block — the second floor of building four. This is where they put the big losers, here for major crimes, and maybe up for the death penalty or life. Our numbers all end with a zero. I'm number 70. When I first arrived, it sounded like a good number — easy to remember — but it turned out to be very unlucky.

Next door is a killer named Furukawa. He is uncommonly high spirited, and doesn't stop talking. I don't understand how so much energy can keep pouring out from his pint-sized body. He is going on and on right now, sounding like he's hawking candy apples at a circus.

" . . . I gotta tell'ya about Shinko. She had the nicest little flower petals down there, like a sweet camellia. Tight as they come. My little deep-sea anemone. Oh, my, how she could squeeze on down. Take you right to heaven. That's my little Shinko. We did it, I don't know how many times, and it was always the greatest."

Of course, Shinko was the name of Furukawa's woman. He told every new arrival about his case. He starting spouting it to me the first time I met him in the exercise yard.

"You're talking to the man behind the Shinkokyu case. *Shin*, that's for my girl Shinko, *ko* is me, Furukawa and *kyu* is for Hisako. She was the victim. It was the most spectacular murder case of the whole high growth era. The Shinkokyu killer, that's me."

Furukawa had met Shinko in his hometown in Yamanashi Prefecture, several years ago. He fell in love with her. She was eighteen, with fair skin and large breasts. He proposed marriage to her, but he was twenty-six, with no steady job and a history of overindulgence in frivolous pastimes. Shinko agreed with her parents that he was worthless, and she turned him down. Resolving to get a steady job, Furukawa went to Tokyo and worked making sushi deliveries, doing janitorial work and other jobs, but he never stayed long at any one. He returned to his hometown and started chasing Shinko again. He would hug her when he saw her on the street or call out to her in a loud voice in the shopping district. He was so persistent that Shinko went into hiding. Furukawa tried to find out where she was from her parents, but of course they wouldn't tell him.

He didn't give up searching for her. Walking the streets one autumn night, a women passed ahead of him. In the moonlight, he was sure it was Shinko. The hairdo, the set of the shoulders and her height matched Shinko perfectly. He followed her outside the town as far as an upland rice field and caught sight of her profile. Convinced it was Shinko, he grabbed her neck with both hands and squeezed until she collapsed to the ground. "You are the one I loved," he thought. "If all you will do is run away, I'll fix it so you can't run anymore." He wrapped a towel around her neck and kept tightening it until he was certain she was dead. Even then his anger was not sated. He cut away her breasts and mons veneris. When he read the following day's newspaper, he learned that the woman he had killed was a stranger to him by the name of Hisako.

That is a summary of the story that Furukawa would tell endlessly, embellished with pantomime, gesture, and meticulous description of the murder scene.

"Used a folding straight razor for the cutting. Kept it good and sharp, 'cause I promised myself I'd cut out her you-know-what when I killed her. I worked at a saw and knife honing shop, so I know how to put an edge on a blade. Put her two cupcakes and her sweet camellia together in a plastic bag. That made me feel right, 'cause then I knew Shinko was my woman. Put the rest of her into a straw bag I found outside a farmhouse and threw it away. I had the most important parts of any woman, so, you know, I thought I didn't need the rest."

Furukawa got a life sentence at his original trial. He was willing to settle for that, but when the prosecutor appealed for a death sentence, Furukawa became incensed, and filed his own appeal without consulting his lawyer. The appeal trial was the scene of an unusual court room event.

Shinko appeared as a witness. The moment she testified that she and Furukawa had never had sexual relations, Furukawa leaped to the witness stand with a bamboo stick he had been concealing and plunged it into her left breast. Suddenly the courtroom became the scene of screams, chaos, and bloodletting, with the guards thunderstruck.

"Damn woman, Shinko, saying she didn't do it with me. Couldn't let her get away with it. My whole life came to nothing out of that broad's camellia petals. She was good, all right, time after time after time. That's how it was."

The courtroom witness stabbing incident must have given the judges a bad impression. They returned a death sentence in the first appeal trial. That was this past March. It happened that my acquaintance with Furukawa began just after he received his death sentence. The way he told me about it, he might have been speaking of someone else.

"Hey, you've got to die anyways. They hang me, that's a one-stop solution to every problem. Do me a damn favor. The truth be told, I only stabbed Shinko to get a quicker death. The judges did exactly what I wanted."

With this introduction, Furukawa continued on to his regular theme. "That woman Shinko, let me tell you, she had the greatest . . ."

There is a Himalayan cedar outside the window, that I cannot see very well through the iron grill. A fledgling sparrow is perched on a branch. Some pigeons are foraging the ground. The fledgling mimics its parent flying, but loses confidence and perches on a lower branch. The parent goes back to urge another try. I do not tire of watching the fledgling's flying practice. I only wish this dismal grill wasn't in the way so I could see clearly.

I closed the glass pane of the window to shut out Furukawa's yammering, but, surprise, surprise, suddenly there is a loud rumbling that doesn't stop, and pretty soon there is steam rising from the bath hall. I forgot it's Friday — the day we get bathed. The boiler will be shaking the whole building all day. I can't write with the pen jumping under my fingers, at least not when my mind is on the verge of unhinging anyway. I can't do anything. I can't even lie down, because you can't do that without permission, which would not be given if requested. When I lean back against the wall, I can tell there is someone, somewhere hitting his head against the same wall. I suppose it is the man directly above me, who paces at night. (Hey, man, you know this wall doesn't care what you do to it. The walls here are quite thick. Not you or anyone else can break them down. The state built them to last forever.)

I had three visitors. The guard named three names I had never heard before. It all seemed suspicious, but I went to meet them. It was my would-be support group, from the Q. Sect. They said the whole sect would stand by me. They wanted me to fire Mr. Iino and let the Q. Sect lawyers represent me. I did not hesitate about turning down that proposal. I don't have anything to do with the Q. Sect, and therefore I do not want it doing me any favors. I told them the lawyer I had hired was sufficient for me. They were clearly troubled by my refusal. As things stand, most of the defendants have separate legal representation.

Wakako's father recruited Mr. Tsukioka as her counsel, Torakichi has hired Mr. Natsuki to represent Yukichi. Moriya, Tagawa, and Shinya are being jointly represented by the two Q. Sect lawyers. The Q. Sect view is that we can't win the case if we don't get together with a common legal strategy.

I told them what I thought.

"The prosecution is saying we all conspired together. The truth is there never was any conspiracy, or anything else between us, so I don't mind there being different lawyers having different opinions. The thing for us to do is show that we are just a random group of people."

Our monitor-guard tried to cut off this line of conversation. He said conversation about trial proceedings is forbidden. All three visitors argued in turn that they were talking about their attorney appointments, with the result that we managed to finish our exchange.

I could hardly be less inclined to try to win an acquittal by having supporters who go around waving red flags and staging demonstrations and mass actions. I made a false confession. My struggle is first and foremost with myself. There isn't much chance of beating those absurd accusations being made against me if I can't even overcome my own weaknesses.

~

Exercise time. They chase out four of us like so many pigs into a narrow, fan-shaped pen. Normally, we would pair off and play catch or kick around a big ball, but today nobody felt like working out. It is getting close to the rainy season. The sky was clouded over, and the air was like a steam bath.

Furukawa started up about Shinko again, but Mitsuo Takasaki cut him off. "You keep quiet. I'm not going to listen to that noise."

Takasaki was a very good-looking young fellow with a history of working in a foundry and a coal mine, and a reputation as a formidable opponent. Moreover, he had received multiple punishments for assaulting guards. Furukawa was certainly not about to answer him back. He put on a sullen expression and approached Yusuké Okayasu, who normally heard out Furukawa patiently. As it happened, though, Okayasu was talking to me, so I took it upon myself to tell Furukawa to butt out. It startled him enough to make him jump backward. Atsuo Yukimori has his own stock of prestige as a former army sergeant, supposedly turned passenger train bomber, with an extravagant record of ordinary crimes to his credit as well.

Furukawa went off by himself in despair to kick the canvas ball against the fence and raise lamentations.

"Give me some lovin', Shinko!" . . . "Damn shitheads!"

Okayasu is around forty, I suppose. He was wearing a mournful look as he told me his kid sister had come to visit. He spoke in such a small voice, I could hardly make out his words.

"She took the trouble to come see me, and I let her down. Couldn't tell her half what I was thinking. My sister's got a big scar on left cheek. I gave it to her. Just seeing it tears me up."

"A kid sister's a nice thing to have. Mine paid me a visit too."

"You got a little sister too? Well, I guess you know what I'm talking about. I caused mine enough grief to hate me, but she doesn't. She still likes me."

"Yeah, that's pretty much the same as me."

"I didn't just cause her trouble. I hit her bad enough to leave a scar. And she still doesn't hate me."

Okayasu sighed and turned tear filled eyes to a line of buildings visible under the pale sky — the world beyond the high wall around us.

Furukawa sidled up. "Is somebody talking about a kid sister? Did you slip it to her? Nobody cares about women who didn't get poked!"

Like a fly undeterred by being twice driven away, he was back clowning again. Takasaki addressed him.

"Don't pay any attention to Okayasu. Let's you and me kick that ball around."

"Ah, it's too hot for that," Furukawa said, but received the ball with his foot and returned it back to Takasaki, setting the pace for their game.

Okayasu remained silent, still gazing tearfully at the town outside.

He had killed his father and injured his younger sister. No longer able to bear the sight of his drunken father beating his mother every night, he had lunged at his father with a kitchen knife. His sister had suffered a serious wound while attempting to stop the attack. The father died of massive bleeding from a chest wound. The original trial found Okayasu guilty of homicide of a lineal ascendant and bodily injury to a collateral ascendant. Okayasu was received a life sentence. His sister never missed a visiting day to see her brother, sympathetic, as she was to what he had done.

I consoled Okayasu, at the same time thinking what a crazy situation it was. It is tragic how he ended up killing his father, but he did commit the crime. I am the one who is here for something he didn't do.

Furukawa quit returning the ball to Takasaki. "I'm out," he said, and strutted off, yelling his trademark Shinkokyu mantra.

Takasaki yelled, "Hey, let's see that ball," but Furukawa wasn't listening. He ran to the far end of the fence and started saying something to the guard.

"Don't that beat all," Takasaki said with an exasperated laugh. Then he turned to me and said in a softened tone, "You're right, what you said about little sisters. I got one too."

Takasaki's light complexion had flushed to a handsome pink shade. His red polo shirt set off his facial profile and bare arms well. He carried himself with the grace of an athlete. Compared to Okayasu, wearing a grimy shirt or shaggy and faded prison clothes, Takasaki looked like the product of a well-to-do household. Maybe my preference for clean clothes and suits made him feel a kind of kinship with me. That would explain why he approached me so warmly. He wanted to reminisce about his sister and mother with me, without ever mentioning his crimes. I found out about Takasaki's background from Furukawa, who knew the inside details about everyone.

"He worked in a die casting plant, but he couldn't stay away from the massage parlors. He kept running out of money and taking out loans to pay off his tabs. It got to be more than he could cover, so he ran off to Hokkaido and got a job in a coal mine. The mine shut down and he started hanging out with Yakuza. Pretty soon he was in a reformatory for assault. He got seriously handy with his fists and built up a rep from Hokkaido all the way to Aomori. He was with a gang in Omiya when a fight broke out and he took out the other side's boss. They say he hit him once and the guy dropped dead, just like that. Then he made bad enough a lot worse by taking the guy's wallet. So they hit him with a robbery-murder rap."

Takasaki got a death sentence at his original trial. He appealed that, and his second trial is in progress now. His story about taking the wallet is that it wasn't the reason for the killing. He says he just saw it lying on the ground and thought somebody must have dropped it, so he picked it up as he was getting away from the scene. In other words, he is claiming he wasn't guilty of robbery and murder, but only injury resulting in death and simple theft, crimes that are not heinous enough for the death penalty.

Eiji Furukawa first got a life term, then death. Yusuké Okayasu got life. Mitsuo Takasaki got death. They were all charged with serious crimes, and they all admitted their own guilt. I haven't committed any crime, but I am being prosecuted for something that will return either a life term or death. This doesn't make any sense to me.

I had a dream just as dawn was breaking. Men in blue prison clothes were sitting in a big mess hall, eating from aluminum pans. The food was yellow rice gruel that looked like feces — stinking, horrible tasting stuff not fit to eat. The warden was sermonizing the inmates. You all are not human beings, so you are fed human waste. It is better than starving, so eat it and be grateful you are getting your fill of nourishment.

That is what every day here is really like. Day after day, I wake up feeling fear and repugnance. It was a dream about my reality, except that my real situation is even worse than being allowed to live on a diet of excrement. Maybe I won't even be allowed to live. I may be heading for the gallows, and for no reason at all.

6:00 is get-up time. Inspection at 7:00, then breakfast (though it's called "ration") is at 7:20. There is an exercise hour sometime during the morning. Lunch is at 11:30. Supper and inspection is at 4:30. "Pre-bedtime," when it's OK to recline, starts at 5:15. Bedtime is 9:00.

Postal (letter sending) days are Tuesday, Thursday, and Saturday. Special permission is required to send a letter on other days.

Bath day is Friday.

There is no no exercise hour on Sundays.

Day after day, week after week, the simple routine is repeated with machine-like precision. I had previously believed I was used to prison life, but I was mistaken. Until now, my longest period of detention before sentencing was about two or three months. When you're a convict, you have some kind of work to do every day. No matter what kind of work it is, the time passes when you have a job to perform. Working at Fukawa Motors for seven years passed the time for me, but for the three months I have been here as an unsentenced detainee, time stands still. Stagnant, muddy, fetid time is more than I can stand.

I finished the notes Mr. Iino told me to write. I have been reading up on tanka bit by bit, but writing a tanka or two does not make the time pass. This is a tragic situation for a man who has spent his life performing manual labor.

~

Today I started work at the job I had applied for — making baggage tags. At first, I couldn't loop the cord the right way to make the two ends turn out the same length. But at least I was doing something with my hands, and time began at last to flow again, dispelling that awful stagnant, rotten feeling. Doing that job all day is no hardship at all. The norm for this nursery school task is three thousand tags a day. I get paid thirty yen if I meet the norm, about enough to buy a paper cup of ice cream. There is no extra pay for exceeding the norm, but I don't care. I amuse myself by seeing how many I can do. There is a joy to working. I turn out about 3,500 tags in a day. I spend the thousand yen I get for a month's work on envelopes and stamps to write letters to Wakako. It is a one-way flow, with no replies.

Mr. Iino's attorney's fee comes out of my savings. When that is gone, there will be nothing to do but dismiss Mr. Iino and get a nationally compensated lawyer. Suéko said she can cover attorney fees for me, but I am sure it is all she can manage to cover that cost for Yukichi. I have lived this far on my own, and I want to continue that way, without anyone's help.

We are fully into the rainy reason. I know it's raining every day, but I can't hear it. I can tell only because I can see that the Himalayan cedar's needles are wet, and because the sounds from the town are louder than usual.

There is a driving school very close by. I have a partial view of its maintenance shop. I get a familiar feeling seeing the workers there. It is still only four months ago that I was just like them, peaceably doing my work — before I was suddenly out of a job, and, shortly thereafter, arrested.

I reread the indictment and the opening statement, and it is still incomprehensible. All I know for sure is that I have suddenly found myself walled in and unable to escape, like a mouse in a trap.

In the middle of the night I look at the electric light that burns all night. I cannot sleep, feeling myself watched persistently by malicious eyes from above.

~

Visit from Mr. Iino. We talked in the attorneys visiting room to the side of the corridor. I am so used to being watched I cannot get over being able to talk freely with someone from the outside without a guard monitoring the conversation.

This attorney is well past sixty. His gray hair is cropped short, and he has elderly-looking round shoulders. I thought I wanted my own private lawyer as long as I had money to pay for one. I picked a name at random from the Japan Federation of Bar Associations register and he showed up. Fortunately, he said he was a criminal law specialist and had handled homicide cases before, but he had a way of mumbling indistinctly that did little to assure me of his dependability.

This visit was to prepare for the second hearing. There were two items he wanted to discuss:

1. Why did I give a false confession to the police and prosecutor?
2. Are there any witnesses who can testify in support of my alibi on the day of the crime?

Concerning the first point, I had already explained repeatedly, but he still did not seem convinced. I went back over the same dreary details once again. He looked at me askance with a dubious expression as he listened. I was saying exactly the same things I had said previously, but he prompted me on with surprised responses — "Oh, I see!" "Is that right?" — as if he had never heard it before. Then he reacted by saying the same things he had said previously. I should have denied the charges when I went before the prosecutor. Why didn't I? He seemed to have completely forgotten that we had gone through it all before.

Second point: I said maybe the landlady of my apartment house, who lived directly below me had heard my footsteps on the day of the crime. Mr. Iino pointed out that the elderly woman who was my landlady had testified only that she thought I had returned home past five thirty.

On that day I had been among many people, on a train, in a bus, in Jindai Park. Wasn't there anyone among all those people could be a witness? Mr. Iino said he would make efforts to see about that, but he didn't say what kind of efforts he would make.

It was raining outside while this interview was taking place. Unlike my cell, the windows of this room weren't obscured by bars. It looked out over the courtyard between the cell houses, affording a good view of two lines of Himalayan cedar.

It was the fifth day of continuous rain. Think as I might, nothing occurred to me that might be helpful for the upcoming hearing. All I could do was leave everything up it to the attorney. It was like a sick person leaving his sickness up to a doctor, but I couldn't shake my misgivings that I had fallen into the hands of a full-blown quack.

Clothes don't dry when you hang them out. I have no fresh shirt to change into, which is unpleasant.

The only joy today is that the rain has lowered the temperature, so I can get by with the window closed. Tag-making all day, and when I reach three thousand, I will quit and spend the rest of my time reading.

The days are getting longer, but supper is, as always, at four thirty. Haven't gotten any exercise because of the rain, so I am not hungry, but I shut up and force myself to eat because I will get hungry later, in the middle of the night.

We get fed a lot of rice curry here — watery roux over rice, with no meat in it. The other menus are meatless stew, oden, pork broth and grilled mackerel — that's about all. Everything tastes of cooking oil. The greatest treat here is buying a fancy box lunch once a week, with your own money.

Second hearing

The prosecutor, Onuki, led off. Wakako Ikéhata has maintained silence, and all the other defendants have denied the charges against them. That is to say the official record of their statements under pretrial interrogation is inconsistent with their statements in court — they have given "self-contradictory testimony." Onuki asked to have the defendants' records of police and prosecutorial examination admitted as evidence. The chief defense counsel (one of the two Q. Sect lawyers) objected on the grounds that those documents do not meet the requirement that testimony be given voluntarily because it was all obtained under compulsion, torture, and coercion, but they were accepted into evidence without hesitation by the judges.

Next phase — establishment of the facts of the crime. Onuki had slides shown of the scene after the Shinkansen bombing. One appalling shot after another, of the train wreckage, the corpses, and the injured people. I hadn't seen or known any of it before.

It weighed heavily on my mind thereafter. That was the crime they were pinning on me and Wakako. Where were the real perpetrators? Who were they? From the bottom of my heart, I wanted the police to look for them, to restart their investigation.

Third hearing

Attorney Tsukioka asked to have psychiatric testing of Wakako conducted for trial evidence, and the presiding judge accepted. She just keeps a blank expression without saying a word — I don't know, but I can't help but think there is something wrong with her. I nod to her, look at her, but she never reacts, and I feel miserable for being rejected again.

Onuki is still reading out my interrogation records. It is excruciating to be sitting there listening to myself being quoted saying what amounts to identifying Wakako as complicit with my crimes. Then on top of that I get questioned in front of her from both sides — prosecution and defense.

Onuki has handed the court reams of interrogation records that have the defendants all laying blame on each other. Tagawa and Shinya say Yukimori planned the bombing and came touting it to Q. Sect. He sold them on it. All they did was say, Oh, okay. Yukimori is the ringleader and they are just accessories. Moriya says pretty much the same thing, but gives Wakako cover. She wasn't a Q. Sect member, and she didn't have anything to do with planting the bomb. Onuki was quoting eyewitness testimony from the day of the crime to pin down Moriya's part.

Hearing number . . .

I don't know which number hearing it was. Onuki plays up what a barefaced liar I am. I give voluntary testimony before the police, and then to the prosecutor, and then I turn around and tell the court it was all a lie. You see, he admits it himself. You can't believe anything this guy says.

Onuki puts me on the stand and makes profitable use of my long past record of misappropriating funds.

"Has the defendant ever told a lie?"

"Yes . . ."

"Isn't it true that the defendant has committed fraud, that is to say, made false statements for the purpose of defrauding other people's money?"

"Yes."

"You have taken money that was entrusted to you on false pretenses and run off with it, haven't you?"

"Yes."

"So it can be said that you had no difficulty in facing people and telling them falsehoods, isn't that right?"

". . . yes."

I am simply not in a position to counter the crazy logic that my present denial of guilt is a lie, and my previous confession is the truth. I am stuck in the ooze of a bottomless marsh.

August 10

I have turned fifty. I once had plans to celebrate this day with a trip to China.

August 15

The twenty-fourth anniversary of the end of the Pacific War. Fifty and twenty-four years — you would think those numbers would be very meaningful, but they aren't.

It's hot. I had forgotten how hot a room without air conditioning can get. Sweat streams down. The mat beneath my butt is all wet. I do my voluntary work every day, and the time passes. My sweat and my time flow away in the heat of the days.

Maybe it was because the heat unhinged Mitsuo Takasaki's mind that he bit his own arm. That fellow has teeth as strong looking as any dog's. They were sharp enough to sink deep into the flesh and cause the blood to gush out. A doctor came, the security division chief came, and the commotion was heard beyond the walls of his cell. Furukawa picked up the news instantly, and broadcast it throughout the cell house.

"Takasaki bit his arm! He bit his own arm!"

I understand very well how that good-looking kid, so calm and collected, could bite his own arm so ferociously. I could do it too. You get to feeling like you want to just open your veins and let all the blood flow away. Completely comprehensible.

Went to the barber and got a buzz cut. They give it to you for free. The last time I had this monk's hairdo was also in prison. It makes you feel very much like a prisoner. I got a teasing from Furukawa at exercise time. Okayasu was consoling. He said he thought the style was becoming to me. Men who have shaved heads belong either in monasteries, armies or prisons. All three are closed societies that call the outside world *shaba*.

Mitsuo Takahashi was placed in a punitive cell. In his place, Shunta Uéda joined our group. He didn't offer any kind of greeting on his first encounter with us. He just stood facing the wall. I was going to say something to him, but Furukawa stopped me.

"Don't say anything, it's no good. He's weird. He doesn't talk to anyone."

"So what'd he do?"

"Rape-murder. One of his victims was fifty. He killed her and dumped the body on a mountainside. He raped another twenty-five-year-old girl, but he didn't kill her."

Okayasu said, "That is one sad-looking face." He had a ghastly pale profile. His head hung as if the neck was broken. He pressed his forehead against the wall. Then Uéda unexpectedly turned to glare at the three of us.

"You were bad-mouthing me, wasn't you?"

Furukawa laughed. "Nah, not a word. I got better things to do than bad-mouth you. Allow me to inform you, I am the one and only Shinkokyu Killer."

"You're bad-mouthing me," Uéda's face flushed red.

Suddenly Uéda let fly a fist at Furukawa's face. Furukawa dodged the moment before it landed. He grabbed Uéda by the collar and tried to throw him down, but Uéda's second punch caught Furukawa on the jaw. Taken aback, the smaller man went down.

"Damn bastard." Furukawa was up again, and something gleamed in his hand. It was a five-inch nail filed down to a knife. Two guards ran into the cell, and the knife was knocked to the ground with a police stick. As Furukawa stood passively, Uéda punched him squarely on the eye. Furukawa fell and did not get up again. He was unconscious, blood flowing from his eyelid.

I was taken to the main office for questioning by the cell house warden. I told the whole story, just as it happened. I said the fight started because Uéda wasn't acting normally, and he had the mistaken impression we were saying insulting things about him. The warden was a young chief guard, probably a university graduate. He peppered me with questions like Magara, the Tokyo Met police inspector. It was a major task to answer everything. The office was an intimidating place, with guards going in and out, and rows of handcuffs and police clubs on the wall. You could look out from it over the entire three stories of the cell house. The bars covering the cells looked like a giant abacus. I belonged inside one of the beads, the tiny capsule where I was monitored and managed around the clock.

Furukawa's wound didn't amount to much. It seemed as if he had only been faking unconsciousness. The winner and loser of the fight both got reading privileges taken away for ten days, and ten days disciplinary confinement. And, just so we wouldn't feel left out, Okayasu and I were deprived of exercise privileges for ten days. Shut up day after day inside these walls in the heat, the air around you gets thick as mud. It is just times like that when guys start screaming or hitting their heads on the wall, because they can't stand that thick air any more.

Wakako's psychiatric testing expert witness was sworn in. Professor Matsuda, from the psychiatric department at N. University, has thinning hair and a mild-looking round face. He says testing will take until the end of next March. That means hearings will be held up for a while. They were saying she will be transferred to the N. Medical University hospital.

A clear sky and fresh autumn breeze were calling, so Furukawa and I were fired up for a game of catch. In no time, I sprained my middle finger. Now it is crooked and swollen. I can't make baggage tags. I started that work in the middle of April, and went four months without taking a day off. Being cut off from my work is like being dammed up. I am in suspended animation again.

I am reading all day. I never felt like reading during the day when I had work to do.

Tuesday, October 21 (weather: cloudy)

It was exactly one year ago on this day, International Antiwar Day, that Wakako and I went to Shinjuku to watch the crowd, but it feels like an event ten years in the past. It was fun going out and doing something together with a young woman. Neither of us had any way of knowing that would be the beginning of all that befell us.

My finger has stopped hurting, so I am back to work, but now the whole hand is clumsy, and the operation isn't proceeding with much efficiency. At the day's end, I had turned out two thousand tags. Twenty yen for me.

We are feeling signs of winter. It is cold enough that I wake up shivering.

Getting near to year's end. The wind gets strong enough by around midnight to set the tops of the Himalayan cedars to groaning. Some combination of conditions makes them all resonate together. I once saw this phenomenon in the woods in eastern Hokkaido. I was half awake all night with that sound echoing in my ears. My head was heavy all the next day.

Showa 44, you were the worst year of my life. Hurry up and be gone forever . . . The wind is howling and ripping across the concrete with the ferocity of an attacking wolf.

Now it is the first day of the new year. Not that it is much different from any other day in my life here. There is nothing to make it any different. There is no heating. Surrounded by cold concrete and iron, I continue making baggage tags as I blow on my numbed fingers in white puffs. I am wearing two shirts, two pairs of long johns, two sweaters, and I am still cold, shivering cold.

I can hear amplified speeches being made outside the prison walls. They are talking about the security treaty with America, a new university law and how important 1970 will be. Their speeches are followed up with slogan-chanting by countless voices. It's the students, safe, warm, sitting pretty and playing revolution. They have nothing to do with me. Thanks to a bunch of guys just like you, my destiny took a nosedive. They testified that I was the one who thought up a plan for revolution by urban bombing. Me — the guy who hates politics.

I just can't believe the story that Wakako was their spy. The one thing in the world she detests most is what she calls "organization spies." They framed her up the same as they did to me.

Besides them, the people at Fukawa Motors, Torakichi and Yukichi Jinnai — they have all turned against me. Suéko is on my side, but she doubts that I am innocent too. I am the only one who understands the meaning of Wakako's silence. Silence is the only way to speak the truth when you are in a police holding cell, that special place where the police lock you up and leave your human rights behind.

Three interrogators worked on me steadily day after day, from morning to late at night. I had no rest when they were leaning on me to confess. For them to insist that wasn't coercion, it wasn't torture, there weren't any threats must mean that police officers and prosecutors are some species of fiend who can't understand the human mind. I have learned to be submissive to all representatives of national authority, be it officer, guard, police, or prosecutor, during my long career in the army, and all the more while in prison. That is how I have survived, including all that has happened to me this time around. I did what they wanted to escape duress, torture and threats. There was absolutely nothing voluntary about my confession.

I believe Wakako. From now on I will deny the charges, for her sake. She is innocent, and so am I. Until we were arrested, we were as happy as two people can get.

My fingers get numb as I work, so I blow on them to restore some sensation, and notice the middle finger and pinkie of both hands are red and swollen. That is frostbite. I had forgotten about this when I grew accustomed to life in heated rooms. The old scar from the burn at the base of my right index finger is abnormally big. That awful scar I got as a small child is back, and hurting me again. My life started with this pain, and look at me now, on a slope sliding down toward some insane destination.

Got a new year's card from Suéko. It is the only one I received this year.

The iron cell door opened suddenly, and in walked a short, middle-aged man in a business suit, wishing me a happy new year. I was astonished. He was introduced to me by the guard accompanying him.

"This is the education officer."

Naturally, I listened to all this in *seiza* position, with eyes downcast. "I want you to tell me if there is anything troubling you."

The education officer was making the rounds of zero block. I had seen him a number of times, passing by in the corridors. One rumor had it he was a True Pure Land monk. He gave counseling to condemned prisoners. Furukawa says he is here to teach you to go quietly to the gallows without any fuss, but that isn't my take on the man. I would say he feels sorry for people marked for execution. What I saw in the wrinkles in his forehead and the light in his eyes was a will to help out a fellow human being.

There is an unbreachable gulf between prisoners and guards. Prisoners instinctively despise guards, and guards will never open themselves to prisoners, so there is little room for friendship or trust between the two sides. Nevertheless, it is true that there are guards who have warmth and goodness in them. In fact, there are many such guards on zero block, the place for defendants sentenced to death or life terms and condemned prisoners whose appeals have run out and are simply waiting to be executed. My impression is that the people running this detention center are interested in avoiding unnecessary accidents and conflicts, so they send in the most competent veteran guards. Having been in many prisons, I am used to guards who are jealous of their authority and don't know any tactics apart from ways to turn up the pressure, but here I didn't see many of that type.

This head guard, Otsuki, who introduced the education officer, is very much the understanding, gentle type, good at handling the many demands and emotional outbursts from zero block inmates. He drops in on me, for example, on days I have a hearing, to say encouraging things.

"Yukimori, you're claiming innocence, right? Well, just relax, go in there and let 'em see where you stand."

He came in on New Year's Eve too. Told me to greet the new year without catching cold. Basically, I am not the type who can fully believe in people. I've been betrayed too many times.

Even if I try to believe in someone, the effort runs into that bad feeling you get from betrayal that is always there, nesting inside. But now that pretty much everyone has turned against me, any small words of kindness from the education officer or Officer Otsuki really do resonate. It is a slight bit of warmth that means a lot. It helps fire me up to continue making my baggage tags.

Earthquake! It must be sometime between 3:15 and 3:20 p.m. now. No clocks here, but I usually know pretty well about what time it is. Will check if tomorrow's newspaper confirms my estimate. The walls are creaking. This entire concrete building is swaying. Thinking how nice it would be if it just split apart . . . But, no. It's all over. Not as much as a crack in a wall, of course — not in this sturdy container, this human crypt.

Yesterday's earthquake occurred at 3:17 p.m. Magnitude 3 — epicenter in the Izu Peninsula.

I had a dream at daybreak. Wakako and I were birds sailing through a blizzard that was blowing in from the sea. Snow came at us like darts of ice, but she navigated the onslaught effortlessly. I could see her, slender and naked inside the form of the bird. Aroused, I tried to hold her. Someone's voice yelling "Liar!" resounded to the heavens, and I suddenly lost my lift. I watched her longingly, as she flew off into the distance while I went plunging downward, head-first.

I awoke to the sound of a strong wind blowing. The window was still a silvery bar. I reflected on the dream until the bar disappeared under the brightness of day. She had looked exactly like that gyrfalcon, seen once upon a time. The bird flew in complete silence, strong and beautiful. But I am not worthy of her. Thanks to my gutlessness, it takes only someone's voice — say, a prosecutor's voice — to bring me down. She is beyond my reach. That is why I want her so much. Every part of me wants her.

Now she is in a hospital, but it doesn't matter to me whether she is crazy or whatever she is. I love her for being who she is, and that doesn't change.

It is so cold that exercise time was mostly spent loitering in the sunlight. Great fun, listening to "Shinkokyu" Furukawa's gabbing and Okayasu sighing about his sister's scar, all the while trying to get warm in the winter sun. By and by, the shadows crept up on us and it was too cold to stand still, so we spent the rest of the time playing catch to try to keep warm.

On the way back from the exercise yard I saw Mikio Wakabayashi. He was among another group of four out for exercise at the same time as us. Mister Information, Furukawa, pointed him out to me. Wakabayashi is the defendant in the Yokosuka Line train bombing. He received a death sentence last March at his original trial. Now his appeal is in the works. Physically, he was like Yukichi — a brawny right shoulder, short legs, and a restless, impatient way of walking. I don't know if he recognized me. I imagine the detention authorities are consciously keeping us, the two bomb defendants, apart, but I really would like to talk with him.

I saw the news of the Yokosuka train bombing on the TV at the Yugashima Hot Springs inn where we were staying on June 16, the year before last. Rain had muddied up the river that day and we weren't catching anything with live decoys, so in the evening we switched to lures and pulled in forty-two ayu. We drank to our jackpot, and after that I was watching the news, loaded with saké. I don't know why, but the strange idea came over me that I was the one who had caused that train explosion. It got me interested in the power of explosives. My hidden attraction to explosions is purely an individual quirk. I wish that prosecutor would understand that. It has nothing to do with anything heroic, be it revolution or rebellion or whatever. It is all about my desire to bring myself down, to blow myself to smithereens.

I became enthusiastic about saving clippings on the Yokosuka train bombing in scrapbooks. I was enthusiastic about many things, one of which was keeping scrapbooks of articles about crimes. It was a way of warning myself to keep straight. It belonged to the string of rituals I worked out for myself, involving dress, ice skating and sending new years greeting cards. They were magic charms to keep me too occupied to slip back into my old ways. The prosecutor's claim that I was preparing to bomb the Shinkansen is just plain wrong.

Mikio Wakabayashi was arrested in November of the year before last, just before we left for our annual duck-shooting trip. I was interested in what was going on in the mind of this young fellow of twenty-five. He came from a small agricultural village in the northeast deep snow territory. He wanted to go to high school, but poverty made him go from middle school to become an apprentice carpenter. He had a hard life that brought him to Tokyo. I knew instinctively what kind of feelings he was having. One day he decides to set off a bomb. To his great misfortune, he chose to plant it on a train. He would have been well advised to set it off in a swamp, like I did. It would have delighted him no end to experience the feeling I got from a number of experiments with explosives — the power unleashed when a small piece of iron suddenly assumes gigantic proportions.

Wakabayashi didn't seem to understand what made me nod to him. He only glared back suspiciously and walked past me abruptly. He had been utterly respectable, a man with no criminal record. I am a worse crook than he will ever be. I suppose he doesn't like facing the fact that he is not only a criminal, but one who has been handed a death sentence for a heinous crime. He had a proud-looking walk and an ill-tempered expression that said he didn't belong in such a place as this.

I work in a space that might as well be a meat refrigerator, shivering as I make my baggage tags, but I don't even feel that cold anymore. Well, I do feel cold, but it is just that it isn't such a hardship as it was. I don't know if you would call it the nervous system losing sensitivity or just learning to endure. To put it simply, I got used to being cold.

I am used to a lot of things that would be abnormal in the world outside. Mercury lamps lighting up the night to deter escape attempts. Plastic panel over the window to prevent intercommunication between inmates. Light burning inside the cell all night to make it easy for guards to keep watch. Wide observation slot in the iron door. A radio that might suddenly start blaring announcements any time. Wash basin with a lid so it can double as a desk. Toilet with a lid so it can double as a chair. Release from this cell for one hour only on days when it isn't raining. Guard posted in a high-backed chair like a pulpit, where he sits between his rounds of the cells that he makes like clockwork.

It isn't that I wouldn't savor having time not being observed, to go for a walk somewhere, to defecate in peace and in private, to be in a quiet place where there is no need to listen to talk from someone I would rather not hear. Or that I don't wish I didn't live in a world where a person who hasn't done anything wrong can be arrested anyway, locked up and put on trial.

Hey, everybody out there! What happened to me could happen to you. It is entirely possible that one day, you too, could be arrested for no reason that makes any sense.

It is just one year ago that three detectives got me out of bed and barged into my apartment. I wasn't even particularly troubled about getting into their car because I assumed there was some kind of simple misunderstanding that would soon be cleared up. Little did I know that was the first step on the way to hell. It was raining that day. The weather is nice today, though.

My claim of innocence seems to go down as weakness here. Cowardice. Eiji "Shinkokyu" Furuawa was riding me about it.

"If you ask me, you did the deed. You're just scared to die, so you lie about it. Guys like you are a disgrace to zero block."

I do not become angry. Long years of incarceration have taught me the wisdom of not giving in to anger in prison.

Hearing

Limited afternoon court session for testimony by Professor Matsuda, Wakako's psychiatric examiner. The court, prosecutors and defense attorneys had already received his report. Instead of reading it all out in court, the presiding judge just gave a quick run-through of the conclusion, without any fanfare. It used the terminology psychiatrists use — some long names of mental conditions that I couldn't remember after hearing them only once. It came down to schizophrenia. He said she was non compos mentis — not of sound mind at the time of the crime, meaning she didn't have legal responsibility.

Well, the eminent doctor spent a long time reaching that conclusion, so you have to accept it. That bombing occurred on the day I met her at the If coffee shop. It was a party atmosphere, and she was as playful as anyone, up to and through the time she had us both taking LSD. Was she abnormal then? If so, I don't know what to make of it. Was I making love to her, or was she out of her mind, and it was really some schizophrenic other person I was making love to? What throws me into deeper confusion is the thought that while we were traveling in Hokkaido and I saw her almost glittering with happiness so intoxicating the spell fell over me too, that in fact she was non compos mentis — some other person without any responsibility for what she was doing. Do I have to accept that, too?

She was the last one to enter the courtroom today, looking like a little schoolgirl between the two husky female guards who led her in. Slender fingers rubbed slender wrists when her handcuffs were removed. She might have been feeling my gaze upon her when her big eyes brightened for just a moment and a faint smile flickered across the corners. It felt like a brilliant light flooding over me.

The spectator seats had been deserted lately, but they were filled today, and I noticed what looked like reporters taking notes. The daughter of the T. University professor on trial for lurid crimes was a hot news item, and the report from her court-appointed psychiatrist was choice feed for reporters. A pair of eyes exactly like Wakako's told me the gentleman in the first row patting down whitening hairs was Professor Kotaro Ikéhata. I didn't notice anyone there to see me. Neither Suéko nor Tetsukichi had been coming for a long time. Tora-kichi had not come even once.

The presiding judge started off by asking Professor Matsuda for his report's diagnosis. The judge seemed not to have much understanding of mental illness. Even I could tell that his questions were pretty basic, like, for example, "What's the difference between schizophrenia and neurosis?"

Then Wakako's lawyer, Mr. Tsukioka, went into direct questioning of the witness. Mr. Tsukioka had requested Professor Matsuda as an expert witness to examine Wakako.

"Was the defendant cooperative during the period she was in your custody for examination?"

"She was not at all defiant."

"The defendant maintained complete silence throughout the periods she was held for interrogation in the police station and the prosecutor's office. Did she respond to your questions?"

"At certain times and in certain cases."

"Please answer in greater detail."

"The report gives all the particulars. In general, she answered my examining questions." This raised a slight stir in the spectators' section.

"There was no indication of refusal to answer, although she did lapse into complete silence at times. These silences might continue for days, a week or ten days."

"What sort of silences were they?" Mr. Tsukioka asked.

"I don't quite understand the question," Professor Matsuda returned, blinking his mild eyes.

"Was she keeping silent of her own free will, or was her silence the unavoidable result of some kind of symptom of illness?"

"The latter. Her silence was selective mutism, a symptom common to schizophrenia. The defendant's thought process would suddenly stop, be incomplete or contain gaps, making it impossible to verbally express her thoughts."

"Is it conceivable that her silence at the police station and the prosecutor's office was not a willed silence but selective mutism due to schizophrenia?"

The prosecutor, Onuki, rose to object. He said the defense had asked a leading question. The presiding judge recognized this and cautioned the defense attorney. Mr. Tsukioka directed a piercing gaze upward at the presiding judge through tinted glasses.

"Your honor, the expert witness was appointed to examine the mental condition of the defendant from the time of the crime to the present. That naturally includes examination of her mental condition during the time of detention for interrogation at the police station and the prosecutor's office. Our accurate understanding of this period is crucially important for getting at the truth. Of the six defendants, the examination records of all but Wakako Ikéhata have been entered into evidence. It is essential to the defense of my client that we bring to light the truth of the silence she has maintained."

The judge was leaning back in his chair. He seemed overwhelmed by Tsukioka's articulate appeal.

"Proceed with your questioning, counsel, please."

"Thank you, your honor," Tsukioka said with a slight bow of his head and turned to the witness stand. "Professor, please tell me if this is a fair statement. The defendant was unable to give voluntary statements when she was in the police station and prosecutor's office. Her silence was not willful, but rather the result of selective mutism, which is a condition that comes with schizophrenia."

"That is correct. As I wrote in the examination report, the defendant's schizophrenia began in 1964, while she was attending a private school to study for university exams. In the beginning she had a delusion that her body smelled of feces. She was convinced that the odor emanated only from her own body and not from other people. A professional society has agreed to identify this as 'self-odor delusion.'

"A disorder like self-odor delusion can appear independently, but it is established theory that they often emerge as early symptoms of schizophrenia. Ms. Ikéhata began attending the chemistry department of R. University in April, 1964. By May, she had gone from elation at successfully matriculating into her chosen course of studies to neurotic refusal to attend classes, showing symptoms of abulia and autism resulting from disappointment with the university. Because she had shown clear evidence of schizophrenia, the defendant underwent treatment at S. Psychiatric Hospital in Ushigomé from May 10 through the last day of August. Her attending physician was Dr. K. His diagnosis was schizophrenic melancholia . . ."

Professor Matsuda swallowed and cleared his throat. He had been introduced as a psychiatrist and authority on criminal psychology. He enunciated his words clearly and his voice carried, but I had trouble picking up all the technical language he used. It was tiring to keep straining to listen, but it was about Wakako, and I was burning to hear it. He was giving his professional interpretation of those uncanny experiences I vividly recalled her telling about in the darkness on that land spit in Lake Furen. The only trouble was that her account of personal experiences had a real-life, vital quality that was lost when it was transposed into abstract scientific jargon.

"In September, 1964 the defendant's condition was in remission, she was out of the hospital and attending classes at R. University, but her recovery was not complete. She continued receiving outpatient treatment from Dr. K. in the form of psychiatric therapy and medication. As I said, the symptoms of the defendant's schizophrenia were generally less intense, but they did continue, in the form of depersonalization. She had a strong perception of the outside world as a set of extraordinary phenomena in which she existed as a social outcast. This perception developed into a persecutory delusion that cast her as being targeted by an organization. It should be taken as a matter of particular importance that the defendant came into contact with the Q. Sect students, most notably, the defendant Makihiko Moriya, during the period when her delusion was active."

"Why is it a matter of importance?" Tsukioka asked.

"The Q. Sect has an ideology that the capitalist system oppresses the people, and on the surface, that belief accommodated the defendant's delusion of persecution. It is very important that she was not a student radical, but only suffering from delusion. She was again hospitalized from October 28, 1968 through January 10, 1969 under the supervision of Dr. K. for treatment of persecutory delusion. She was clearly suffering from this delusion on February 11, the day of the crime, and as she was from the time of her arrest, throughout the term of my examination and the present."

Prosecutor Onuki rose to begin cross-examination.

"I see from your report the defendant has made a number of statements concerning her actions before and after the day of the crime, February 11. Under what circumstances did she make these statements?"

"During the process of medical examination."

"As voluntarily answers to questions?"

"Yes. She answered voluntarily."

"The defendant denies involvement with the crime. What is your view as an expert witness?"

"What do you mean?"

"Do you accept her statement as the truth?"

"I do. She says that on February 11 she went to R. University in the morning, read chemistry magazines in the library, had lunch in the student cafeteria and after that returned to her apartment at three thirty."

There were audible reactions to this statement among the spectator seats. The prosecutor fixed Professor Matsuda with a stare.

"We are to understand that the defendant was suffering from schizophrenia when she made this statement?"

"Yes."

"Being under a persecutory delusion, she was unable to distinguish right from wrong or control her behavior on the basis of such a distinction, is that correct?"

"As a schizophrenic she may have hallucinations or delusions, but beyond that . . . for example, she could clearly recall memories of what she did in the past."

"What are the criteria for deciding how much of a statement by a mentally ill person is delusion and how much is the truth?"

"That is something that comes from many years of clinical experience."

"Does that mean it is a matter of subjective judgment?"

"No, not subjective."

"Well then, what objective evidence did you use to determine the truth of the defendant's statement that she was not present at the scene of the crime that occurred on February 11?"

Professor Matsuda was stuck, driven down by the prosecutor's relentless questions. He may have been an able psychiatrist, but he gave the impression of not being at home in a courtroom. He was sweating and mopping his brow with a handkerchief.

Wearing a fierce expression like a hunter who has scored a kill, Onuki faced the judge and asked for Wakako Ikéhata as a witness. He said he wanted to cross-examine her statements recorded in the expert witness's report. Tsukioka agreed to this, and Wakako was led to the witness stand.

And she sat there quietly. She would not read the oath and would not answer questions. So she was sent back to her original seat and the court recognized that she had refused to testify. Onuki then asked for and received permission to make a statement. His ramrod posture and sharply defined facial features made for a statuesque presence.

"The witness's refusal to testify makes it impossible to cross-examine the statements in the expert witness's examination report. Therefore, her denial of committing the crime must be taken as nothing more than hearsay, with no probative value. I ask that the court recall that eyewitnesses have given positive identification that the defendant, together with Atsuo Yukimori, were present at Platform eighteen in Tokyo Station between three thirty and four o'clock on the afternoon of February 11, that is, immediately before the bomb exploded inside the Shinkansen car."

"Your honor," Tsukioka began, but was cut off by Onuki.

"I have not yet finished my statement. Similarly, the expert witness's report mistakenly affirms the defendant's denial of guilt to the crime despite the fact of her presence at the scene of the crime that has been objectively established. Other parts of the report as well, for example, the medical diagnosis, can only be regarded as having little probative value. The expert witness diagnoses the defendant as having persecutory delusion without making any rigorous distinction between delusion and fact."

Tsukioka again called Professor Matsuda for direct questioning. He obtained answers that stressed the accuracy of the report's medical diagnosis, but it didn't sound very compelling after the prosecutor's forceful accusations. Processor Matsuda was perspiring more than ever. It looked as if his handkerchief needed a wringing.

There was nothing subtle about Onuki's points. Wakako's mental health was normal — you couldn't claim she had no responsibility for her actions, which included blowing up that Shinkansen car, in partnership with me. Onuki wanted to bury that psychiatrist's report, with its claim that Wakako didn't do the deed.

I didn't know which side to back. I don't want to believe she is crazy. But if being labeled crazy and not responsible is what it takes to get her off this charge, that would make me very happy.

Got a visit from my lawyer, Mr. Iino. He says the conflicting claims between the defense lawyers are irreconcilable.

The two lawyers for the three Q. Sect defendants, Moriya, Tagawa and Shinya, now are saying the crime was committed by Yukimori and Ikéhata, with no Q. Sect involvement — there was no conspiracy to begin with. The new version of their story is that their confessions were lies and that Yukimori was implicating them to take away some of the weight from his own culpability.

Ikéhata's lawyer, Tsukioka, is focused on the argument that his client has no legal responsibility because she is schizophrenic. When the prosecutor clashes with him on the facts concerning denial of guilt, he doesn't even dispute the issue. He appears dedicated to the proposition that she is feeble-minded.

The attorney for Jinnai, Natsuki, came out disputing everything — not only the Shinkansen bombing, but the theft charge as well.

Discomfiture was written all over the wrinkled face of Mr. Iino, my attorney. "Well, what will be your argument?" I asked him.

"Of course, I will dispute all the charges. But, look, the situation is bad for you."

"Why is that?"

"Because Tsukioka is saying Wakako Ikéhata has this delusion she's persecuted, she can't tell right from wrong and in walks Atsuo Yukimori and lures her into pulling off his crime."

"That is ridiculous. Neither of us had anything to do with it."

"It looks as if Professor Ikéhata has Tsukioka convinced on several points. Ikéhata's view is his daughter was seduced into criminal activity by the crafty ex-con, twenty-five years older than she is. It is an easy story to believe, now that so many newspapers and magazines have written it up that way."

"I am in love with her. The age difference and my dark past are beside the point."

"Yeah, that is true . . . I might as well tell you, I am having a hard time, too. There are people who take offense at my defending you. I keep getting threatening phone calls. There is one who had called again and again. He yells at me that claiming a villain like Atsuo Yukimori is innocent stands in the way of justice. Most of the time those callers don't say anything. You just hear them breathing on the other end, which is quite unpleasant in itself."

I was about to argue with him, but the sight of the old lawyer with both elbows on the desk, listless and stoop-shouldered, made me think twice. I decided on a pep talk instead.

"Mr. Iino, don't let them get to you! I'm innocent. That is the truth, no matter what the prosecutor, Professor Ikéhata or the press say, I didn't do it!"

"Yes, I understand that."

"No, you don't, not yet. You shy away from threatening calls and Mr. Tsukioka because you don't believe me. If you really believe in my innocence, please, look for the real culprits who planted that bomb."

"The real culprits . . . " Iino's eyes widened. He had been caught unawares.

"Yes, the real culprits." I was becoming annoyed. "That was a major crime, and there is someone out there who did it. I don't know how, but that police investigation went off the rails. It's all wrong! Will you please do a really thorough examination of the investigation records? Find out exactly where they are wrong!"

"Do you have any idea how many records you are talking about? Besides, attorneys don't have the right to examine everything."

"There are five lawyers, aren't there? Work together and you can do it. When you find the real culprits, that's proof every one of the defendants is innocent."

"Five lawyers? What five lawyers could do wouldn't get anywhere close to what that investigation did, with all the money and manpower that went into it. Lawyers don't even have authority to investigate."

Mr. Iino shriveled before my eyes, like a balloon with the air let out. He had nothing more to say and was showing no further reactions. That disheartened me so completely I kept quiet too.

~

My stomach has been acting up for over a week. I was feeling nauseous. I tried to eat, but the rice would hardly go down, and I ended up vomiting. I was thinking what a relief it would be if I could reach inside and just pull everything out.

I went to the medical section for an examination. I vomited again in the waiting room and the medical orderly showed open revulsion. He had a bad attitude. He considers himself a cut above me for being a defendant, while he is a sentenced prisoner in a blue prison uniform.

Hearing . . . (I don't remember what number hearing it was.)

Because the defense is atomized, evidence taking proceeds exactly as the prosecution desires.

There is a cast iron three-way coupler made by N. Corporation. This product was available for purchase along the Kanda "hardware road" — a district where such products have always been manufactured — located not far from Fukawa Motors. The S. Books paper shopping bag could have been obtained from the S. Books outlet that I frequented, and, indeed, such a bag was found on the table in my apartment. The newspaper — *A. Shimbun* — used to wrap the bomb was the Mitama District edition, a newspaper I could have purchased. The windup timer was a product that is available in the Akihabara electrical appliance shopping district — also not far from Fukawa Motors. All this evidence merely shows that I could have acquired those items, nothing more, but the prosecutor delivers a wordy spiel that makes it sound like he's proving I am the one who went around collecting them, even though he doesn't — cannot — actually say that.

Unfortunately, not one piece of evidence has turned up to show that Wakako and I are not the culprits.

June 1

A great downpour has continued since morning. No one caught in that torrent could become any more muddied than my spirits.

June 2

I have been moved to another cell, according to the standard rotation schedule in June and December. When they brought me here I was placed on the west side, and now I have migrated east, where sunlight enters for only a very short time in the morning. I am getting a cool breeze. My biggest headache is that everything that had been to my right is now to my left — shelf, chair/toilet, and desk/washbasin. I sit down to write my diary and keep expecting the window to be on the right, but it isn't there — it is on the left. So I tire myself out spending the day trying to reverse my mental map of this cell.

My neighbor to the south is Katsumi Kamimura. Yoshio Yamaishi is on the north side. Kamimura received a death sentence and is appealing. Yamaishi is at the same stage as I am — still a defendant at his first trial. On the other side of the corridor are the "confirmed condemned" prisoners — their appeals have run out.

My new cell is relatively quiet. I am no longer bothered by Furukawa running off at the mouth next door. Once in a while Kamimura breaks the rule against "intercommunication" with another cell, but Yamaishi doesn't say a word. Even if I try some aural reconnaissance by putting my ear to the wall, it is nearly impossible to detect any sound of movement. This is not to say Yamaishi is not communicative. He uses the guard call fairly often. On those occasions, I can peep through the observation window and hear him saying he wants to buy some supply that ran out, or be shown the list of books available in the detention center library.

The guard call is a wooden box that with a button that will loudly drop a plastic tag outside the cell door, as a signal to the guard on duty. It is the only recourse a prisoner has for communication with guards, but I have never used it. I don't have the courage to summon a guard as you would a delivery man, or to ask one to get me something.

I obey the rules, submit to orders from guards like a pet dog, and don't make any demands. Ever the model prisoner, I have never once committed an "intercommunication" infraction, which just about every prisoner does at least once in a while. I seem to have a prisoner personality hidden inside me, one that blooms afresh whenever I'm locked up. Perhaps the many times I have been imprisoned since the time I was a green army recruit has taught me to be happy being ordered around.

Tea time. The meal slot opens and the tea kettle spout pokes inside. I deftly reach for my cup and receive the lukewarm, flavorless beverage.

Next comes the meal — curry rice. As always, soupy, yellow roux with no meat sitting atop the rice. It has little taste and it smells of cooking oil.

My stomach is in good condition now, and I have my meal. I don't leave a speck, that being a prisoner's duty, and, coincidentally, good sense as well, because I get hungry at night. The stretch between the evening meal at four-thirty and breakfast at seven-twenty the next morning is too long. I hear other prisoners ordering snacks every night, but I don't have the money for that. I have to cut down on "living" expenses to pay for my private lawyer.

At night, I put up with hunger and make my baggage tags. I am past the stage where I must think about what I'm doing. My hands move on their own.

We have been shut in for over a week because the rain won't let up. Got to bathe once in that time. The bathing room is pretty small, but it seemed spacious after being hemmed into my tiny square isolation cell. The feeling of being crammed inside those four walls makes it harder and harder to even imagine the world outside.

There was a break in the rain, and we got out for exercise. Despite clouds like dirty washrags hanging over, it was the wide, wide sky and nothing else overhead, and that was a wonderful blessing to be thankful for.

Eiji Furukawa was in the group. He hadn't shown up for six months. The rest of the group consisted of Katsumi Kamimura, Yoshio Yamaishi, and me.

Kamimura and Furukawa took off their shirts and had a sumo match. Kamimura had the height and physical strength advantages, but undersized Furukawa was fast, and after they grappled for a while, he managed to get behind Kamimura and throw him down. Kamimura sprang up, covered with mud and charged after Furukawa with a vengeance, but it ended with an increasingly frustrated Kamimura futilely chasing Furukawa around and around the yard.

Kamimura has a tattoo of a nude woman on his arm he can move enticingly by rippling the muscles. I don't know what crimes are in his past, but he looks every bit the part of a fearsome killer, including a lurid scar from a sword above his navel. It resembles an uncommonly large mouth, like a frog's.

Yamaishi was acting strangely. It was hot and humid, but he was crossing his arms, hunching over, and shivering. I called to him, "Hey, what's up?" but got no response. I tried once more.

"Yamaishi, what the matter?"

"I'm sorry, please forgive me!" he blurted out, like someone being whipped. Suddenly, he was on his knees, pressing his head to the ground like he was begging for pardon from some unseen lord.

Startled by this, Kamimura and Furukawa came running.

"Hey, what's wrong?" Furukawa squatted down in front of Yamaishi. "You're okay! It's me, 'Shinkokyu,' the legendary killer from Japan's high-growth golden age! C'mon, let's see your face. Show us your damn mug!" But Yamaishi would not raise his face from the ground.

"This sucker's just putting on!" Kamimura grabbed Yamaishi under the arms and flipped him over. Yamaishi made like a turtle, all fours moving helplessly in the air, but Kamimura pinned his hands behind him by the wrists.

"Help me! Give me a break! I didn't do it!" Yamaishi was crying piteously.

"What the hell are you talking about?"

"I'm innocent! That's what! It wasn't me that did it!"

"Oh, you're innocent, are you?" Kamimura licked his ample lips and laughed. "If you're innocent, act like it, instead of simpering like a brat." Kamimura clamped down hard on the two wrists, while tears ran down Yamaishi's face.

"This is getting interesting. Let him tell us about it." Furukawa clapped Kamimura on the shoulders. "Go on, explain! I'll decide if you're innocent or not."

"Go ahead and tell us. I'll leave you be." Kamimura released his hold and Yamaishi sank to the ground like a jellyfish thrown up on the sand.

"What it comes down to is I was arrested for something I didn't do," Yamaishi began. Suddenly, he was talking in a sure, level voice, as if he had never been a grown man bawling like a child. He seemed pleased that his story was being heard. There was even a trace of a smile.

"Two men by the name of Shinkai and Mitsumoto did it. Shinkai's a Chinaman who moves a lot of meth. Mitsumoto works for him. I am ashamed to say I was hooked on shabu. I got it from Mitsumoto. There's a pachinko parlor in Akabané where he dealt the stuff. The owner of the place, Mr. Nakané, would stand watch. There's a room in the back where you go to get it . . ."

"Wait a minute, let's check this out. Lemme see your arm." Kamimura pulled up the sleeve of Yamaishi's right arm. Black veins were clearly visible. The skin was swollen up as if stretched by a rod embedded inside, and it was riddled with countless needle marks, as if sprinkled with sesame seed.

"Yeah, this is a genuine shabu head." Kamimura released Yamaishi's arm.

"Come on, tell us how you're innocent," Furukawa demanded.

Yamaishi nodded, gestured with an uplifted right pinkie, and began to speak.

"This is no lie I'm telling you. One night I was out of shabu. It was the middle of the night. I went to that pachinko parlor. You see, when the dealer Mitsumoto wasn't around you could ask Mr. Nakané to give you some. I rang the bell, but no one came, so I went around back. Shinkai and Mitsumoto came out. I asked Mitsumoto for some shabu and he said to go inside. I was heading for the usual room when all of a sudden a pachinko machine falls over, and there's Mr. Nakané on the floor with his head split open. I panicked and tried to run, but Mitsumoto gets in my face and says, You going nowhere, you've seen too much. I tell him, hey, don't do me, I won't say nothing to nobody.

"Well, he takes me in Shinkai's car to his apartment and he says we're going to do a deal. I take the rap and he'll give me ten million yen, then he'll get me away from the cops inside of a month. If I don't like the deal I get killed, he says, so I say okay.

"Now, what really happened is Mr. Nakané said he didn't want any more dealing inside his business. He got into a fight with Shinkai, and Mitsumoto busted him up with a hammer. That got changed to me asking Mr. Nakané for shabu and he wouldn't give it to me I got mad and killed him. Mitsumoto told me how I did it. We went over that again and again until I knew it backwards and forwards.

"Next day, I turn myself in to the police. Pretty soon I find out around half a million was taken from Mr. Nakané's cash box, so the rap wasn't just a fight where someone died, it was robbery-murder. I told the cops and the prosecutor exactly what Mitsumoto said but everything was going wrong. I could see that death sentence coming, so when the trial started, I denied everything. I submitted a statement, too, saying Shinkai and Mitsumoto were the real killers.

"Well, guess what. The prosecutor says there's no such persons as Shinkai and Mitsumoto, nobody like that has ever been in that apartment building. Yeah. I know what happened. They got their butts out — disappeared. Poof! So now what do I do?"

As Yamaishi finished talking, impressively large teardrops welled from his eyes, and his whole frame quivered as he wept.

~

Yamaishi didn't go out for exercise today. That was Furukawa's cue to report that his story had been a pack of lies.

"The real story is he did it alone. The pachinko parlor owner was getting on him to pay up on his loans. Of course, the loans were his shabu bill. So one night he was out of shabu, had the shakes bad. He went to the owner for a fix and got turned down. That ticked him off, so he beat the guy to death with a hammer and ran away with all the meth and the day's pachinko proceeds. That's what you call a classic robbery-murder case. There's plenty of evidence. Employees on the second floor heard him and the owner yelling at each other and they have bloodstains on his shirt and pants that match the owner's blood type. If that's not robbery-murder, nothing is, and it's what they hang you for. He's scared of that, so he made up that cheesy 'Shinkai and Mitsumoto' story. That's all there is to it."

"Yeah? You talk like you saw it. Where'd you get all that inside stuff?" Kamimura asked, fixing Furukawa with a dubious expression.

"A certain source. The great 'Shinkokyu' Furukawa has many sources. I can't reveal them. They're a professional secret."

"That damn punk!" Kamimura glared in the direction of Yamaishi's cell house and held up a fist. "He had me convinced he was innocent. I was feeling sorry for him! Next time he's going to be feeling pain! I'll make him talk straight."

"Don't bother. He doesn't even know how to talk straight."

"Just a damn minute, you! Who told you all that stuff?" Kamimura said warily.

"Like I just told you, that's secret," Furukawa said, backing away as Kamimura loomed over him.

My suspicions were growing too, as I watched the scene play out. Furukawa seemed to know the criminal past of everyone on zero cell block, like a guard who had access to the inmates' personal information register. Maybe he was a spy telling the prison officials about conversions between inmates and getting information about their criminal backgrounds and family relationships in return. It is best to be careful about what you say to such a man.

It looked as if Kamimura had reached the same conclusion. His face now showing apprehension, he drew closer to Furukawa.

"Hey, you ain't no . . ."

"I ain't no creep" Furukawa said as he stepped aside. "And I got a good story for you. This here Yukimori's claiming he's innocent too. He's the guy that blew up a Shinkansen car, but he's scared of hanging, so he's crying they framed him."

"You did that Shinkansen job?" Kamimura asked me. Snaggled, yellowed teeth were visible beyond the thick lips. The smell of his breath was not pleasant.

"I heard about you from that Yokosuka Line guy," he continued.

"Yokosuka Line . . . You mean Mikio Wakabayashi?" I asked.

"Of course! Who else?"

"He said something about me? Wha'd he say?" Suddenly I was filled with anticipation. Kamimura flexed his upper arm and a cartooned pair of breasts shimmied.

"Said he's interested in you. Sounded like he really felt for you. Said he'd probably do the same thing if he were in your place."

I was about to say something when Furukawa interrupted.

"Yukimori won't own up to his own crime and Yokosuka admits he did it. That's not being in the same boat, not by a long shot."

"You shut up. I got a message from Yokosuka Line to Shinkansen. He said to give it if I saw him." Kamimura licked his ample lips and darted a glance toward the guard, then a good distance away. The guard was looking at the sky because rain had begun to fall.

"Give it, don't keep us waiting," Furukawa urged.

"Not in front of a stoolie like you, I won't!"

"You think that's what I am?"

"No, I know you're that!" Kamimura said, pushing my back to get us separated from Furukawa, who followed, but was chased off by a shaking fist brandished in his face.

"The message is 'Take good care of your woman.'"

"Is that all of it?" I felt let down.

"He wants you to know he had no intention of killing people he'd never met. He did it because of his woman. He wants to meet you. Says he's got a lot to tell you."

"I feel exactly the same! Tell him I said so. But where do you get to meet him?"

"In the chapel. He goes to Saturday Christian sermons every other week. You could meet him there if you want. There's only three or four guys who show up."

Furukawa had snuck back by this time. "Might as well skip it. That Christian stuff will bore you to death."

"That did it!" Kamimura angrily grabbed Furukawa's wrists, spun him around and applied a take-down sweep with one leg. Furukawa's small body sped across the ground like a soccer ball. He rose, wincing in pain and began to slap his buttocks to knock off some of the mud that covered him almost head to foot. This time he seemed conscious he was no match in a fight. He kept his distance while cursing Kamimura.

"Look out, you phony Christian. Something's going to come down on you! I know you're just going there to get goodies from the chaplain. 'Blah-blah-blah, amen. Now gimme a cookie.' Some Christian! How come you go to the Buddhist shrine? Then it's 'Namu-amida-butsu' Peace, enlightenment and get two cans of spam. Shit! I think I'll go to the chapel myself and tell the chaplain what you're doing the other two Saturdays in the month."

"Quiet down!" the guard bellowed, and Furukawa finally quit squawking. The rain had reached penetration level, falling quietly, but persistently.

~

Rain has us cooped up. Ten days have gone by with no exercise.

It has been raining steadily for a full two weeks. The windshield wiper in the car on the way to the courthouse is getting me down. I can't stand the monotony — tens of thousands of cars on the road, every single one with a rubber arm tediously stroking the front glass.

The hearings are going exactly as the prosecution likes. The defense attorneys haven't produced one piece of counter-evidence. I was astounded by the sound of snoring behind the defendants' seats. I turned around to see it was old Iino. At this rate, there is no way to expect anything from our side to disprove all that evidence from the prosecution.

I make my baggage tags as usual, but the time isn't going by. Confinement in this tiny box makes it hard to breathe. I come to the realization that time cannot be left to flow by itself. Time is really like an army of cockroaches. I have to force my hands to keep moving; it is like making myself squash cockroaches, one at a time. By my calculations, it takes one hundred finished tags to squash one cockroach.

In another three days, it will be August. The rains have finally stopped and the mid-summer sun has begun to bake the concrete of this wonderful place. In a few days it should be hot on the third floor, then, after that, my own second floor will be hot, too.

Exercise hour, at long, long last. The old gang hasn't changed a bit. Furukawa is noisy, Kamimura is rowdy and Yamaishi simpers about his innocence. Kamimura seemed to have forgotten what Furukawa had said about him and Mikio Wakabayashi, because he was trading sarcasms with Furukawa today about the Christian chaplain.

Even in weather as hot as it is now, or maybe because it is so hot and there is nothing else you want to do, people become absorbed in talking, whether they are in the exercise yard or in their cells. They go on and on, like a car's windshield wiper, monotonous and untiring. I cannot stand it and there is nothing I can do to spare myself from having to listen to it.

There is a group betting postage stamps on horse races in raucous voices. Games of shogi are being played between contenders ten cells apart. In the distance I hear Furukawa describing to someone in excruciating detail scenes of sexual intercourse with Shinko. When the level of intercommunication gets this high, the guards don't generally bother much about enforcing the rule against it. Some insist on laying down the law, while others keep quiet. It might be that the heat has burned off the guards' enthusiasm, but there could also be a will to cut some slack for zero block inmates.

The incessant chatter on the second floor of building four seems to be too much for the prisoners in the cell house opposite ours. Occasionally they howl at us things like, "Shut up and get in your pine boxes!" or "Quiet down, so we can light your incense."

It is just not possible to read in the midst of all this talking. I keep at my cockroach squashing operation, making tags. Now I am making price tags with the words "high quality, low price" printed in white on red. They must be threaded through a hole one millimeter in diameter, an operation I can perform without even looking at the tag. I am a skilled worker, ha-ha.

August 10

Now I am fifty-one. Five hundred thirty seven days since I was arrested. Mind you, that's not five hundred thirty seven days of my life that have passed — it is five hundred thirty seven days of my life killed.

August 15

The twenty-fifth anniversary of the end of the war. As far as I am concerned it was twenty-five years of no particular returns, no quality, no substance. My whole life has come to nothing.

I haven't written to Wakako for a long time. I tried to write when that psychiatric testing was finished, was unable to do it and haven't tried writing any more since then. She was found to be mentally ill and therefore not legally competent. If the judges accept that, she'll be found not guilty. The last thing I want to do is send her something that might be used as evidence that that assessment was wrong. Much as I want to contact her, I will not do so until her not guilty status is confirmed. I think of her every day. In the early morning hours I dream of holding her. Sometimes as I work, her image will appear in my cell for just a moment. It is only those moments when I feel her presence nearby that time regains its savor and substance. But it is just a pale vision that soon vanishes.

I have given up my tag-making work ever since I spent the money earned from it to buy a map of Japan and a train timetable book. I can't tear my eyes from these items because I am absorbed in calculating departure and arrival times. Which pair of trains will pass by one another, and when, where and for how many seconds will it happen? Change from one train to another, connect up with a third on a journey through the mountains and across plains. I recall I have been playing this game ever since I was in elementary school. Geography was my favorite subject. I got to know cities, villages, mountains and rivers all over Japan as if they were my hometown. Whenever I was running away with misappropriated money, I never had doubts about where to go. The first time I committed a crime and fled Tokyo all the way to the far end of Kyushu, I was going to a place I knew well.

After I finished my last prison term, I shifted the focus of my map-gazing hobby from Japan to the whole world. I took imaginary journeys to foreign countries by reading airline timetables and world maps — my crystal ball for viewing scenes of faraway mountains, forests and cities.

This is my third day playing with my maps and timetables.

Wrote out a request to send off around thirty books of mine to Tetsukichi. The books aren't in my cell. They are kept in custody by the prison.

There is a special prison word for holding a prisoner's property in custody, another one for discarding it and yet another for sending it elsewhere. These words are not generally used by people in the outside world. The terminology comes from the Prison Law, promulgated with the emperor's sanction in the year Meiji 41 — 1909. Japan has no shortage of intellectuals who invent phony truisms like "the post-war era is over." They are neither as thoughtful nor as well informed as they think. The part of Japan I inhabit, together with guards, policemen, and prosecutors, is no different than it was in the wartime era, the prewar era and far back before then. Modern Japan has a living fossil of a judicial system, and with so few people concerned about that contradiction, there is no hope in sight the system will change for the better.

Along the opposite side of the corridor are the cells holding prisoners whose death sentences have been finalized. The iron doors of their cells are painted the same yellow as mine, but theirs look like the doors of a crematorium. The guards come for them after breakfast. You know they are consciously treading as silently as possible, but you hear them anyway, and their soft footsteps are the giveaway about what they are coming for. They all stop together outside one of the cells, and at that moment conversation ceases, as all prisoners on zero block wait with baited breath.

The sound of the lock turning, the door being opened, notification being given in a low voice, the sound of footsteps. One of us has been taken away, never to return. Sometime after that, one on our side will have his death sentence finalized by a high court and be moved to fill the empty cell on the other side.

It is extremely rare for a convict's death sentence to be finalized at the original trial; only when some perverse soul refuses to appeal is he taken to the scaffold at that stage. The vast majority go through two appeals, pleading that their sentence be reduced to a life term. Their appeals are in vain, and one day, they, too, acquire "affirmed sentence" status and are sent to a "pre-crematorium" cell.

A prisoner who acquires finalized condemned status receives certain kinds of special treatment. Though he is a sentenced prisoner, his sentence is not to serve a penal term, but be executed, and as long as that sentence isn't carried out he is in many ways treated the same as unsentenced prisoners. He doesn't have to do odd jobs for the guards, he can let his hair grow out, he doesn't have to wear a blue prison uniform. Visits and letters are subject to far less restrictions. He isn't subjected to forced labor, and can even see a movie once a month. Then, one morning, he is suddenly taken away to the scaffold, where he is blindfolded before the rope is wrapped around his neck and he is dropped into a pit for a fall that does not quite reach the ground below. It is about the most degrading form of death that a person gets nowadays, but until it is meted out, he receives special treatment, like a favorite pet animal.

Mitsuo Takahashi, the good-looking young man who savagely bit his own arm, was recently given residence on the other side of the corridor. He has much more of the convict's pallor now than when he was still a defendant. The magnetic power of the condemned draws my eyes to his face. Just the other day he was being hurried by a guard before me as I was on my way back inside from the exercise yard. The sight made me stop to witness his withdrawal. It was like watching a wraith making its exit from the stage.

For some condemned prisoners, execution does not come for a long time. That was the case for Keiichi Morita, the former National Railways worker convicted of causing a train wreck, resulting in multiple deaths. Thin and fragile, he shuffled his slippers along the floor with stooping shoulders as if they bore a heavy load. The odor of garlic hung in the corridor for a time after he passed by. He consumed great quantities of garlic as a health building measure. Despite this, however, he always seemed to have something wrong with him, and paid daily visits to the medical office, asking the visiting health assistant for medicine to treat vertigo, chest pains or poor appetite.

Fifteen years has passed since Morita's death sentence was affirmed, so why hasn't he been executed? It seems to me that defense motions to revise one of the decisions and order a new trial have met with some understanding among national leaders who have their own skepticism that Morita is the real culprit.

Keiichi Morita confessed to the police and prosecutor, then claimed innocence at trial. He received a life sentence at his original trial and that was bumped up to death on appeal. The death sentence was affirmed at the third trial. The press voiced suspicions about the case against him, while intellectuals were speculating someone else had caused the train wreck.

The thing that interested me about him was that he was originally arrested along with nine others for plotting and carrying out the crime together. That was how the indictment read. Morita switched to denying the charges when all the others were found not guilty, but when he testified, his basic claims and his accounts of the facts of the case were wildly different from hearing to hearing. When I was on the outside, I collected articles on the case. I believed his alibi for when the crime took place and believed in his innocence.

I was charged with being one of the joint principals in a conspiracy, the same as Keiichi Morita. My denial of the charges is taken as fixing the blame on Q. Sect, and their denial supposedly means Wakako and I did the job, or that it was just me. Morita provided an example of how helpless one becomes by trying to disprove the charges when there are many defendants.

Next spring, the Tokyo Detention Center is due to move from Sugamo to Kosugé. Rumor has it that Kosgé has the latest equipment for better efficiency in carrying out executions. If that is so, you would think they would wait until after relocation, then clear up their execution schedule, but the fact is there have been frequent executions right here since the start of autumn. Out in the exercise yard, I got this from Furukawa in a whisper.

"The blitz hit Mitsuo Takasaki too."

That made me realize I hadn't seen him lately. On the way back to my cell I confirmed his name and number were no longer on the door to his cell. But Keiichi Morita still lives. Will the latest blitz pass him over once again?

~

The blitz continues to rage — an average of three men a week are being executed. That is an abnormal pace. In one short month, a third of all affirmed sentence prisoners have been liquidated. Everyone has something to say about what is happening, whether it makes sense or not.

"It's population control. They're doing it now, while they can. Kosugé doesn't have a lot of cells for affirmed cons."

"There's a new cabinet. The new justice minister likes executions."

"No, they want to get rid of anyone who might cause trouble or try to escape before they move to Kosugé."

A typhoon was forecast to land around Tokyo, but it has veered south over the sea. Now it is raining on and off, totally unpredictably. That kind of half-baked condition gets on my nerves. If there is going to be a typhoon, let it blow everything away. If lightning's coming, I want to see it dancing on the ground.

About this time two years ago, Wakako and I were walking from Jindai Botanical Garden to Shindai Temple in the wind and rain as a typhoon was approaching. She said she loved typhoons — "I couldn't think of a better way to die" is the way she put it, with a big smile. That must have been the moment I started liking typhoons too.

Today's hearing was completely frustrating to me and, I am sure, very satisfying to the prosecutor, because my attorney's lame cross-examination didn't get to the truth of anything. It helped create an illusory sense that the prosecution's claims must be all true.

Assistant police inspector Hino came to the stand to testify on the voluntary nature of the confessions. To my ears, his voice resonated with insincerity, but maybe that's only because I know what a liar he is. He swore that every word of my confession was spoken voluntarily. He said my examination records met every standard for use as evidence.

Attorney Iino's cross-examination of Assistant Inspector Hino:

"During your examination of the defendant, did you pound the desk with your fist or threaten him in a loud voice?"

"Nothing of the kind occurred even once."

"Did you fail to provide the defendant with meals at meal times, leaving him with an empty stomach?"

"Of course not. He was given meals every day, on schedule."

"Was he questioned while handcuffed or tied with a waist rope or otherwise subjected to undue pressure?"

"Certainly not. Handcuffs and the waist rope are always removed during questioning in respect of the suspect's human rights."

"When you asked the defendant about his three experiments with explosives in the Lake Furen area, did you ask leading questions? For example, did you ask questions that contained information on dates and times of the experiments or ways of actually conducting the experiments?"

"No," assistant inspector Hino replied, emphatically shaking his half-whitened head. "Excuse me, sir, but the awkward sort of question just asked — perhaps a leading question in itself — is something that police officers do not ever engage in."

Hino was followed to the witness stand by the long-legged police superintendent, Magara (who had been an inspector when he was interrogating me). He, too, who strongly affirmed that my confessions had been completely voluntary, that there had been no coercion, torture or threats to the investigation.

~

Hiki-atari. That is police jargon for bringing suspects or defendants to the crime scene to check their testimony about commission of the crime against the facts on the ground. Wakako and I were taken in handcuffs and waist-ropes to Tokyo Station for corroboration of the facts connected with our supposedly having been together on Shinkansen Platform Eighteen on the day of the crime. Since neither of us was admitting to the charges, this exercise seemed useless to me, but it was done in accordance with Onuki's request, in the company of the judges and defense attorneys.

Onuki pointed to the stairway and sales kiosk.

"You came up onto the platform from this stairway, then bought canned drinks from the kiosk. That right?"

Of course, I did not answer. Numerous waiting photographers sprang into frenzied action. Their desire to catch our attention was palpable. There were jeers from onlookers: "Murdering creeps!" "You don't deserve to live!" etc. Maybe the reason for having this nonsensical investigation was to offer up the two of us to those people who thought of themselves as righteous citizens.

Outside car No. 1 of the train were four pushcarts bearing cans of beer and drinks and vegetables piled up in boxes. As we watched, the carts were moved to the buffet car. The prosecutor turned back to the judges.

"We have just witnessed the transfer of the pushcarts. This event does not appear in the police examination records. It was only mentioned during my own questioning. That point is therefore strong evidence that the defendant was indeed present at the scene of the crime," he explained.

It is true that I said to him something about a pushcart bearing a load of things. I was just guessing about it, because I was making an effort to tell him what he very clearly wanted to hear. What I had in mind was one pushcart used by Red-Cap porters to transport passengers' baggage. The idea came from my own experiences of what one sees on train station platforms. What I was now seeing was not one, but four carts, and they weren't being pushed by Red Cap porters but employees of the Nippon Restaurant Enterprise Company, and the carts were laden with food and drink. But of course, Japanese does not make distinctions between singular and plural, and that helped Onuki embellish my words to convince the judges that I had accurately identified these four pushcarts.

The trial has finished with examination of evidence. No more hearings this year. In January, the prosecutor will give his closing argument and sentence recommendation.

I have no way of knowing what Makihiko Moriya, Shinichi Tagawa, and Akito Shinya may have plotted together, or anything else about the inner workings of the Q. Sect. Both I and Wakako had nothing to do with the Shinkansen bombing. God — if there is a god — tell those judges that we are innocent.

I doubt that there is any god. That is why I have not taken up Katsumi Kamimura's invitation to visit the Christian chapel. If I must go there to meet Mikio Wakabayashi, I won't meet him. I want to put God to the test. If he exists, Wakako and I should get a not guilty decision. Otherwise, I would not have faith in people, country, God or anything else.

Be that as it may, I bought a Bible and started reading Genesis. Now I am up to Kings. I thought Japan's leaders did absurd things, but if anything, Israel's kings in those days were even crazier. Nevertheless, it says God really existed. Supposing that is true, then the question is, am I wrong to want to put God to the test? In other words, maybe the real truth is a paradox; God has to exist because you can't believe in people or nations.

Cold all day, even with a little snow. Furukawa, Kamimura and I knocked ourselves out having sumo matches. Thanks to that workout, I returned to my cell warmed to the core. I didn't mind the cold for about two hours after that. Then I was back to freezing in this icebox.

New Year's Day, Showa 46 (1971)

Six hundred eight-one days since I was arrested. Nothing about this day is the slightest bit different than life has always been here. New Year's Day does not penetrate inside the human crypt.

It was raining all day. During the night I suddenly found myself awake and saw a pale light at the window. I wondered if it was a new kind of warning light, but it was too high up for that. I realized it was the moon. A three-day moon, pure and clear. Wind rustling the treetops' silver needles, by turns, hiding and revealing the moon. A wild mismatch of beauty in jail, a tiny bit of nature in the artificial prison world.

Today's district court hearing was set to start at three in the afternoon. I was sent out on their early morning shuttle run, then kept waiting six hours in the district courthouse holding cell. Police in full riot gear were stationed outside. The students chanting slogans at them sounded pathetically weak in the face of an overwhelming police force. The demonstration only demonstrated the youths' helplessness against the power of the state. They were shouting, "Go home! Go home!" as the police effortlessly backed them out of their way.

The spectators' gallery was filled. Prosecutor Onuki radiated self-confidence as he played to his audience. By then, his refrains were well known to everyone in the house. His closing argument was no different than the opening statement. Every argument advanced by the defendants was simply ignored.

Each count of the indictment was substantiated by numerous pieces of evidence, he said. It proved that Q. Sect leaders Makihiko Moriya, Shinichi Tagawa, Akito Shinya, and Atsuo Yukimori conspired to place a bomb on a Shinkansen passenger train; that, upon conducting three experimental explosions, Yukimori, together with Wakako Ikéhata, set the date for the attack on National Foundation Day, February eleven, 1969, then proceeded to carry out the plan; that on the appointed day they placed a time bomb in a car of Hikari 33 that exploded at approximately 4:02 p.m., inflicting damage to Car 2 of Hikari 33, causing the deaths of two passengers and slight to serious injury to twenty-eight passengers; and that Yukichi Jinnai committed theft from Fukawa Motors on two occasions — October fourteen, 1968 and February seven, 1969, for a total of 597,540 yen, to provide funds for the manufacture of the bomb and the conspirators' escape.

Onuki added a salacious touch to his catalog of accusations by accusing me of using "sexual seduction" to draw a young woman having only vague ideas about revolution into a "world of violent revolution."

I couldn't very well avoid listening anxiously when the moment came for Onuki's sentencing demands. For Moriya, Tagawa, Shinya and Yukimori as principals in the conspiracy, he demanded death. For Ikéhata, he said, life imprisonment, and for Jinnai, five years, were appropriate sentences.

How crazy can the world be? I haven't done anything and yet the law wants to hang me. What a fine country to have been born into!

Returning to my cell, I felt that my body was already marked by the black shadow of the condemned prisoner. The walls, window and iron bars held a different significance than they had that morning. I had taken the first step toward crossing the corridor to join the class of prisoners having finalized death sentences. I imagined myself walking into the execution chamber and my final moments on the gallows. Now it was no longer grim fantasy, but the true picture of my future.

The one consolation was that Wakako had not been marked for death.

The news of the prosecutor's call for my death sentence ran through zero block like rolling thunder. The next day, in the exercise yard, Furukawa greeted me gleefully.

"You didn't really think that frame-up story of yours would fly, did you? I guess yesterday knocked some sense into you. Now start acting like a man with a death sentence! Blowing up a Shinkansen — hey, that's going down in history! It's way bigger than the Shinkokyu Murder! Don't mess things up. Claim the title — it's yours! You can bet every newspaper and weekly will send someone to get the story. This is your big opportunity! That's how you go down in history!"

Kamimura had the same point of view, but he ended up sounding like a priest giving benediction. "Listening to you talking about being innocent . . . To be honest, it was making me sick. That stuff is for wimps like Yamaishi, not you. You got guts. Don't forget that. Time is past for crying innocent so they won't ask for death. Now you got it, it's real and you can walk tall. Congratulations, buddy!"

Instead of being in high spirits like Furukawa and Kamimura, Yamaishi seemed distressed. He spoke in a soft whisper.

"You need to find the real culprits. It's the same as me, you just have to get the prosecutor to understand who the real criminals are. Those prosecutors are nobody's patsy, I know, but I do believe they will always investigate when they know there are crooks out there. One of these days they're going to arrest Shinkai and Mitsumoto, and I will be exonerated."

The final statements of our defense attorneys have begun. They never did get their acts together, so the final statements were, once again, at odds with one another.

The attorneys for the Q. Sect rejected the joint conspiracy-joint enterprise charge; their clients knew nothing about any plan to attack a Shinkansen train — Atsuo Yukimori dragged the Q. Sect into it.

At first, I had thought Wakako Ikéhata's lawyer, Tsukioka, was going to argue exclusively that she's not guilty by reason of being non compos mentis, but to this he has added an alibi for the day of the crime. In other words, he is advancing the theory that Atsuo Yukimori committed the crime alone.

Yukichi Jinnai's lawyer, Natsuki, says his client had nothing to do with the bombing and he did not commit either of the thefts.

Iino — my lawyer — did an okay job of covering what I told him, in other words, denying all the charges, but then he ended making a deep bow to the judges and telling them he hopes for their leniency. I don't need leniency! I need the world to know I had nothing to do with the crime.

That was the end of the trial. The decision comes Tuesday, April sixth.

I guess the day for moving the whole detention center to Kosugé is coming soon. They told us to get our personal items together. My personal items don't amount to very much. I had Suéko sell off everything in my apartment in Shindaiji. Now I've got one dictionary, the *Complete Six Codes of Law*, the Bible, the *Manyoshu*, both the old and new *Collection of Ancient and Modern Japanese Poetry*, several notebooks, some clothes and toiletries. It all fits into a medium sized cardboard box. Just like when I was in the army, I could easily put everything I own into a backpack and be ready to roll any time.

Perhaps because of the impending relocation, there was no semi-annual changing of cells that would normally have occurred last December. The guards are furiously at work cleaning up their districts. The smell of dust and dirt is drifting through the cells. We have 1,700 unsentenced detainees and four hundred prison employees, How are they going to manage the move of such a big outfit?

March 20

Relocation marching orders came together with the morning get-up radio broadcast — a surprise attack style announcement. Still groggy and in ill humor, I set to getting my things together without even bothering to wash my face.

They separated off the prisoners with confirmed death sentences from the defendants, put on the handcuffs, strung us together with waist ropes and marched us across the yard, where a staggering number of police wagons and well-armed guards were waiting for us. They kept driving us on, making sure we kept moving and stayed too busy to find openings to hold back or even complain. One more wholly successful strategy of officialdom. They bullied us to go right and go left until we were packed tight inside the vans.

We received proper VIP treatment with a full escort of motorcycles and patrol cars. Looking around, I saw Eiji Furukawa, Yusuké Okayasu, Shunta Uéda, Katsumi Kamimura, and Yoshio Yamaíshi. It isn't often one sees the entire zero cell block population out on the road. It began feeling like an excursion and it put us in high spirits. We started chatting together. That prompted the guards to tell us to keep quiet, but it didn't have much effect. Pretty soon everyone was talking and there was no hope we would be orderly again.

I realized I was sitting next to Mikio Wakabayashi, the man responsible for the bomb that went off on the Yokosuka Line train. I tried talking to him, and discovered he knew me. We got into conversation without the need for introductions.

"Kamimura gave me your message. Thanks."

"Message? What message?" Wakabayashi's bony jaw lifted in a show of puzzlement.

"He said you told him to tell me to treat my woman right."

"Nah, I didn't say anything like that."

"Well, Kamimura said you wanted to give me that message."

"That's some kind of mistake. 'Take care of your woman.' Who says shit like that?"

"No one! I was thinking there was something funny about it," I answered, laughing.

Wakabayashi also laughed, then he suddenly took on a serious expression. He was skinny enough to show the underlying skeleton, with eyes peering out from deep in their sockets.

"I just remembered talking to Kamimura about your job. He said you have a lot more reasons to be happy than he does. He thinks that because you and your woman are together on the same rap. Me, I caused trouble for my women by blowing up a train and now she hates me."

"It's probably the same with me. It was my lying confession that dragged her into it."

"But that ain't the truth, is it? Neither one of you did it."

"That's it, but the prosecutor won't buy it. He won't believe anything I say."

"I believe you're innocent."

That was a surprise to hear. All the others on zero cell block sneer when I say I am innocent. It was the first time anyone here said he believed me.

"How do you know I'm innocent?"

"Hard to say. I just know, somehow. Lots of guys here say they're innocent. Most of them are lying. You are one of the very few telling the truth."

Mikio Wakabayashi blinked at me with eyes like lights at the bottom of a well.

"Would you guys quiet down?" the young guard standing beside the driver's seat reproved us. The uncertainty in his own voice only intensified his fear of the unsentenced prisoners and the volume level of their conversations.

As always, Eiji Furukawa was enthusiastically reciting "Shinkokyu" obscenities in a loud voice. Yoshio Yamaishi was explaining tearfully that Shinkai was the real culprit. Shunta Uéda was scanning his environment closely, ready to confront anyone who might be uttering disparaging words about himself. Yusuké Okayasu looked sorrowfully into space and sighed, most likely recalling the scar he had inflicted on his sister. I came to a sudden realization.

Prisoners have only a very limited range of thoughts that chase around and around in their minds endlessly. Mikio Wakabayashi was no exception. He was forever tied to the crime he had committed. The crime gets into your mind in an instant and stays there stubbornly, unmoving. If you could actually remove the crimes from the prisoners' heads, they would probably all be empty and none would be able to think of anything at all.

The streets slipped by. Everyone stopped to look back at us because our prison van convoy was so unusual. Speeding through traffic signals, patrol cars with sirens screaming lead the way; state power in the form of a glorious prison squadron, on parade.

A willow lined boulevard, the parking lot of a credit bank, a bakery, a restaurant, a sushi house. The morning hush of the city at peace. In order to preserve the city's peace and tranquility, the people built a prison and locked up all the felons inside. Then they forgot the prison and its prisoners, to live out their lives as if such things did not exist.

Nevertheless, we are living human beings, every one of us inside this gray prisoner transfer wagon. The sole connection to this city for each is his crime, and that will have an important place in his mind for the rest of his life; were it not for the crime, there would never have been anything between him and the city.

But what about me? I once saw myself as a criminal, in prison for good reason. That made for a strong tie between me and the world outside my prison. This time I am not even a criminal, but the city has quite arbitrarily exiled me anyway. Such gloomy thoughts filled my mind.

We crossed a bridge — the Senju-Shimbashi bridge, across the Arakawa River. A dark, extraordinary-looking building on the far side of the river came into view. The central watchtower loomed like the rising neck of a monster. I could smell the water. It had a dank tang, more like the sea than a river. There were gulls in the air. It felt like we were at the seashore.

"Like to see you again sometime." I said to Mikio Wakabayashi. "Any way to do that?"

"Come to Father Okuda's sermons. They're twice a month."

"Isn't that the Christian sermons Kamimura goes to?" I glanced at Eiji Furukawa happily chatting with Katsumi Kamimura.

"No, he hasn't been coming for a while."

"In that case, I'll go have a look." I said.

Wherever you turn, there are only concrete buildings to see, with no greenery at all. No flowers, no birds. It feels like being in a garret amidst a cluster of factories in the middle of a desert.

I had a bath. Being new, the bath hall is clean, but the hot water smelled of concrete.

At night I heard the sound of a steam locomotive. It made me think of the Nemuro Main Line. When I was a child, I loved to go see the trains up close. I would still go to look when trains pulled in when I was working for Kushiro Railways.

I wrote postcard notices of my new location to Suéko, Tetsukichi, and Mr. Iino.

My new cell has a big window with no metal screen. There are no Himalayan cedars blocking the sky, either. I have a good view of the sky. I look for stars every night, but so far I haven't been able to see any. Where I am is a far cry from that brilliant view of the heavens Wakako and I had at Lake Furen.

With the decision coming soon, it is my intention to remain composed, but I must be getting irritable. There is a stinker in the cell above me who is getting me very annoyed by running water in his sink early in the morning. He starts opening the tap full blast at about four a.m. He does this about six times. It is not a matter of washing up or drinking water. His only purpose is to bother me.

Three days until the decision. My fate will be decided less than seventy hours from now. So if it's death, as Onuki demanded, do I appeal? The first trial took two years, and I'm fed up. I would rather get it over and let them hang me. That's better than rotting in this cell through an appeal and then another appeal. I am fifty-one, nothing good has happened until now, and there is no way anything better will be coming.

I am praying to the god I suspect does not exist. Please make the truth come out. Please fix things so I can have some faith in this country, and, above all, so I can have faith in you.

~

Forty hours until the decision.

~

Notice has been delivered that the day of my sentencing hearing has been rescheduled.

> "To: Hon. Warden, Tokyo Detention Center, on behalf of the Defendant
> "Defendant Atsuo Yukimori
>
> "Having heard the views of the prosecutors and defense attorneys concerning the charges against the above person of (1) overturning and destroying an electric railway train, resulting in death, and (2) homicide, the presiding judge of this court has decided the following:
>
> "Hearing of April 6, Showa 46 (1971) 1:10 p.m. (sentencing hearing) shall be changed to April 22, Showa 46 (1971) 2:40 p.m.
>
> "Tokyo District Court, Criminal Division Presiding Judge"

In this way, the hearing that was supposed to be tomorrow has been suddenly changed. I sent two urgent telegrams, to Suéko and Tetsukichi. It may be too late, and they are already in Tokyo. The notice shows that the court recorder made a phone call to the attorneys about the change, asking for their approval. Why didn't Iino notify me immediately? I can't get to sleep, thinking over what might be the reason for the postponement. Does it take time for judges to decide to give out death sentences?

April 22

Today was bath day, and I got to take the first bath before leaving for my court appearance. Kept going to take a pee — more than ten times during the four hours they had me waiting in the holding cell. Not that I had much to pass, mind you. I kept getting the urge because I couldn't sit still.

Got a tasteless croquette in my lunch that I was unable to eat. My body is reacting honestly, with fear of the coming sentence.

The door just opened and the guard called me. I went out and there was a court reporter with a notice that the sentencing hearing was postponed again. He wanted my signature and seal. It seems now the hearing will be May 11.

These repeated delays of the sentencing are infuriating. Important dates being put off at the convenience of the judges. Those pampered, privileged boys with their university degrees have no idea what it feels like to be a pitiful defendant getting ready for one of those dates. In normal human relations, it is common courtesy to give a reason when you reschedule doing something you are committed to do. All the more so when it's a matter of life and death.

Suéko and Tetsukichi came to visit this afternoon. Being shut up indoors for the winter has Suéko looking white as a sheet, not much different than the prisoners here. Tetsukichi was suntanned to begin with and he came in red-faced on top of that, no doubt from alcohol. He said he had had been out fishing since mid-April when the ice floes were gone.

They were visiting Yukichi in the morning. Then they got tickets to visit me. There are a limited number of visiting rooms, and many visitors, so they had to wait their turn. There was a thick Plexiglas panel between them and me, with sound holes for conversation. The effect is less to muffle the sound of their voices than to make it like listening to some kind of artificially produced sound. Suéko spoke restlessly, conscious of the guard beside her, taking down the conversation.

"We came to Tokyo the day before yesterday. We went to the courthouse yesterday, but nobody was there. Then three other people showed up. They looked like students. We went to an office to see what the problem was, and that's when we found out about the schedule change. There we were, after coming all the way from Hokkaido, feeling kind of beat, you know. It's not as if they didn't know good and well there was a schedule change."

"That was the second time they did it. It's enough to tear you to pieces."

"Why do they do it?"

"I don't know. Something that makes the judges want to hold off the decision for a while, I guess."

"Hope it's something in your favor."

"I just want to get my sentence, get it over with and finish with that trial. I'm sick of being an unsentenced prisoner."

"It has to be not guilty."

"I don't care what it is — death, anything"

"No!" Suéko said vehemently. "I don't want to hear any more of that nonsense! You're not guilty, and that's all there is to it! I believe completely in that."

"You mean you believe in the judges?"

"I believe in you."

"That's no help. I'm up against the state, and that is something you can't believe in."

"You mustn't give up. The truth is the truth as far as anyone is concerned, including the state."

"No, this country doesn't care about the truth. I've had it with this country."

I didn't mean to start an argument with Suéko, but that is what it turned into. When a woman loses talking logic, she starts crying. Suéko wept, her noticeably thinned shoulders quavering.

I wanted to say something to Tetsukichi, but found myself at a loss for words. My well-built nephew had been sitting expressionless, looking down at his uncle and mother arguing. From the looks of the diamond wristwatch on his sturdy arm, his fishing boat must have been doing well. As he was leaving with his mother, he muttered scornfully.

"Shit! To hell with this country."

I don't know who those words were directed at. Suéko and I were both astonished. The eyes of the guard monitoring our visit narrowed, as if he thought he personally had been vilified.

~

I went to Father Okuda's sermon. Mikio Wakabayashi and I were the only ones sitting before the pastor. He began the first chapter of the Acts of the Apostles, reading about Jesus's resurrection. Then he sang Hymn 188. His voice was powerful. Having just seen Tetsukichi's magnificent physique, I was all the more conscious of what a small, lightweight body Father Okuda has. (My habit of appraising people's physiques keeps asserting itself.) It only served to increase my admiration for his impressive voice.

"Have you ever come to a Christian sermon before now?"

"I am ashamed to say I have not. This is the first time."

"Do you read the Bible often?"

"I have read it only once. Actually, I read from Genesis straight through to the Apocalypse of John."

"Straight through . . ."

The father looked surprised. Of course, I didn't understand the first thing

425

about the Bible, not from a single reading, having zipped through it, the same as I would read a novel. It must have seemed surprising to him that someone like that would show up at a Christian sermon. I kept quiet about the fact that I had started my second Bible reading marathon. I guess one is supposed to read passages here and there from the Bible, just like in today's sermon, but I like reading books straight through, start to finish. Sometimes I'll even do it all over again.

When the session was over, Mikio Wakabayashi and I had about fifteen minutes of free time to talk together until the guard came. He said that having been a carpenter, he always felt irritable in bad weather, so he didn't like to do volunteer labor on rainy days. As hobbies, he wrote tanka and submitted articles to religious periodicals and newspapers. He recited his latest tanka for me.

To touch this desk where sat the condemned
Anguish resounds through my hand

I could have offered a critique, but didn't. I just said I also liked to compose tanka, and would show him my own recent efforts sometime. It was the first time since arriving at the detention center that I met someone I could have a quiet, serious conversation with.

~

Father Okuda's sermon. This time Yusuké Okayasu was there, as well as Mikio Wakabayashi.

"Are you reading the Bible?"

"Yes."

"Do you read it every day?"

"Yes, I do read it every day."

That's a lie. For the past two weeks I did nothing but make baggage tags. Woe to him who speaks falsely without qualm!

Mikio Wakabayashi had something very interesting to tell me. He got a death sentence the year before last at his first trial, then, last year the decision on his second trial dismissed his appeal. He said the hearing for that decision was twice postponed, the same as happened to me. He said postponements like that happen only because they have a lot of pending cases to examine, not because they have any special interest in your case and want to look at it carefully.

The morning of May 11, sentencing day, arrived. I would have hopes and anxieties when I was facing a one or two year sentence on a theft or embezzlement charge, but this time, being up for a death sentence, the pressures of conflicting feelings were enough to rip me apart. I sat in the prisoner transport bus like a patient on his way to find out if he has cancer. I had gotten this far twice before only to learn of a postponement, but this time I had a strong feeling there would be no cancellation.

A great crowd of people gathered around the courthouse bore out my hunch. There were media people, student radicals, sensation seekers, riot police . . . the whole constellation of people interested in what judgment the state would mete out to us, all under the watch of the crowd controllers.

As usual, I was alone in the holding cell. Normally, waiting defendants are held three or five together in a cell, but I am always kept alone. On this day, my wait was only long enough to restlessly go have a leak three times. I could neither make baggage tags nor read, but just pass the tedium by glaring at some air vents that looked like they could be used for eavesdropping.

I just could not believe that I faced a charge that could bring the death penalty. I found myself running my hands over my arms, my face and legs as if they were not mine, but instead belonged to some other person. I would have examined my face if I had a mirror. It would be a nasty shock if I saw myself looking half dead, but even so, I would have wanted to confirm that I still existed.

Guards arrived — it must have been time for the hearing to begin. They clamped an icy pair of handcuffs around my wrists. Instead of being led inside by two guards as usual, this time there were four — to my left and right, in front of and behind me. While I was marveling over that, I saw that Wakako was ahead of me, surrounded by four women guards. Moriya, Tagawa, Shinya, and Yukichi were also in sight. For six defendants there was a total procession of twenty-four guards, making for a high-profile show of force that was unprecedented. Previously, they would just bring each of us separately into the courtroom.

The reason for the extraordinary situation became clear when the doors to the main courtroom were opened. The space between the doors and the defendants' seats was jammed with media photographers, who commenced a hail of bursts with their flash units.

"Move out of the way!"

"Please get back!"

The guards' yelling had no effect. The photographers were pressing in like stray dogs fighting over fresh meat. They trained their cameras on us from above and below, snapping without pause. They poked their lenses in our faces, pushed us and squatted down at our feet, so that we were unable to move. When we finally managed to get to our seats, we were again hemmed in by a ring of photographers. There must have been close to a hundred, wielding still and video cameras or 16mm movie cameras.

The court clerk ordered the guards to remove our handcuffs. It was one more unusual thing about this day, for handcuffs to be removed before the judges appeared. Once again, the photographers began shooting. The flashes were blinding and the spotlights were uncomfortably hot. My eyes hurt so I closed them and looked downward.

"Open your eyes please!"

"Ah, c'mon. Open your eyes will you?"

I ignored these requests from the media, keeping my eyes firmly shut, while the sound of whirling motors and shutter clicks assaulted my ears.

"You people stop annoying us!" came Wakako's voice. I looked to find her standing and glaring at the photographers.

"You're being offensive. We are human beings, not a spectacle to gawk at!"

Her beautiful eyes were shining. The photographers enthusiastically seized on that image and happily kept shooting. That continued for a time and the sound suddenly ceased. The media dispersed. Again I was handcuffed.

Massive doors built as if to accommodate giants opened, highlighting the smallness of the three judges who stepped through. Their self-important manner was comical. I could sense that everyone in the courtroom behind me had risen to their feet. When the judges took their seats, everyone in the spectator's gallery could see our handcuffs being removed as we continued standing.

"The defendants will come forward."

At this command from the presiding judge, the six of us were brought to stand before the bench. Speaking in a low voice, the presiding judge began by reading out the reasons for the decision. (Hey, what is this?)

The decision was quite simply parroting the prosecutor's argument. It was not long before I was quite certain the decision was heading toward "guilty as charged."

The spectators' gallery was buoyant. The door kept opening and closing. At one point I heard this clearly from out in the corridor:

"Yep! It's guilty. Get it into the evening edition."

The judge's tone didn't change, and the murmuring from behind made it hard to make out his words. I did understand that he gave Moriya and me death, and life terms to Tagawa, Shinya, and Ikéhata. Jinnai got five years (or maybe he said six).

"The penalty of death for Atsuo Yukimori as stated in the main text of this judgment is therefore considered unavoidable."

"Penalty of death." The words became a resounding echo, a slim shaft going through my heart, making the blood spurt out and drain away. It was all I could do to continue standing, feeling as I did, as if my veins had been emptied.

A Chinese prisoner was digging a hole — a square hole, two by four meters, one meter, fifty centimeters deep. He dug with full knowledge his corpse was to be buried in the hole, raw fear driving him to work with all his might. Finally, his hands were tied behind his back and he was made to kneel with his neck extending over the hole.

The second lieutenant unsheathed his army sword. At the time, I was interested to see how the officer's sword would sever the prisoner's head from his body. When it came down on the back of the prisoner's neck and blood began flowing, I felt pain on the back of my own neck. Either the officer's skill or the sword itself was not up to the job, because the head did not fall off at the second or third blow, and the prisoner continued to wail.

I was somewhat relieved that Wakako did not receive a death sentence, but my relief soon turned to black rage. By what perverted thinking did those judges conclude that she had contrived to blow up a train? I had the idea they were not real people at all, not the middle-aged presiding judge wearing glasses and neither of the other two, slightly younger, associate judges. They were nothing more than moving parts in the machinery of the state.

For a time after the judges and the prosecutor had left, the five lawyers remained seated, like stones against the current, their faces studies in conflicting feelings. Then Mr. Iino rose, as if returning to his senses. Slouching unconcernedly, he thrust a paper at me. The action was so abrupt I turned aside reflexively, as if kicked.

"Here, sign this please."

"What is it?"

"It's an appeal request. The decision was unjust. We have to appeal and get it overturned."

"It's all right. I am tired of this. I don't want to appeal. I just want to let it stand and be executed."

"No, you aren't allowed to waive the right of appeal when the sentence is death or undetermined term."

"I don't care. No more hearings. I mean it."

"Aah . . ." Mr. Iino seemed determined, but uncertain how to proceed. He stood stroking his white hair, then a broad smile abruptly spread across his wrinkled face.

"The time limit on filing your appeal is two weeks. After that, the sentence is final."

"I know that," I answered shortly. I was thoroughly annoyed with this incompetent lawyer who would only go through the motions of defending me. I didn't want to see his face any more . . . To add a little more detail to that, I wouldn't be able to meet him anymore because I had no money left to pay his fees.

Once again, we were hit by frenzied picture snapping. This time, the flash units weren't even particularly bright. Being surrounded by media cameramen wasn't much different than being on a crowded commuter train. Wakako and I were the center of attention. Tears came to my eyes, and I didn't care what anyone thought of me. I wept openly. She was so small, so weak and defenseless, just like a little girl.

I keep thinking here, in between the walls. I haven't even been out for exercise. I found in the *Complete Six Codes of Law* that the appeal procedure on a sentence of death or indeterminate imprisonment is automatic, but then you can withdraw it if you want to. A wish to let the death sentence be finalized, to die and be at peace, rose up like an overwhelming black cloud.

How do I describe the life I have led? War, thievery, prison stretch after prison stretch, and now, after all that, I am to die at the end of a rope. Sure, I can appeal and go on living X number of years, but always under the threat of execution. I have taken the pain and shame of existence as an unsentenced prisoner for 812 days. I don't want to go on like that for another 2,000 or 3,000 days.

Paying for my own private lawyer didn't buy me much more concern for defending my rights than I might have gotten from that lying police inspector, Hino. I certainly couldn't expect any spectacular courtroom performance from one of those lawyers the state appoints for poor people. Once the state has driven home a judgment to send a man to the gallows, it would take a lot more than a halfhearted courtroom struggle to overturn it.

Apart from all that, the thing that weighs heaviest on my dark thoughts is resignation that capital punishment is fit for me. That phantom scene that popped into my mind when I heard my sentence was tied to much, much more. I myself have killed people. I killed countless human beings we called "the enemy." The Model 92 heavy machine guns used by my unit shot to death fleeing enemy troops on a hillside without mercy. I saw human beings falling under a hail of bullets from my weapon far more times than I want to recall. I am a murderer. I am condemned by the numerous souls I sent to their deaths. It makes perfect sense that a man as sinful as myself should be put to death.

The guard on duty comes to check on me more frequently than usual. That is because they are afraid I will commit suicide . . . Uh-oh, the door is opening.

It was Otsuki, the chief guard. "You got a new visitor. He's a Christian!"

The name was Shiro Kirikaé, a name I had never heard of before. I was grievously despondent, and the prospect of meeting a stranger was not welcome, but an annoyance. Nevertheless, I did not get many visitors, so there was some element of curiosity. I entered the visiting room to find a thin man somewhere beyond thirty sitting on the other side of the Plexiglas. He inclined his head politely and smiled. I saw kindness in his eyes.

"I know it isn't really good manners to drop in out of the blue like this, but I came anyway after reading about your decision in the newspaper. I really wanted to meet you."

Not being able to grasp just what it was that brought him, I kept quiet. The man continued to speak at an unhurried pace.

"I would like to pray for you. Will you permit me?"

I still did not know what to make of it. Feeling a little confused, I told him to go ahead. It was my first experience being told such a thing by a person I didn't even know.

The man placed his fingers together, closed his eyes, inclined his head downward, and prayed for a long time. I could make out a few muttered phrases here and there: "Lord . . ." " . . . for our brothers . . ." " . . . Thy blessings."

I could not relate to some guy I didn't know suddenly launching into such a demonstration. It seemed vaguely insulting. Finally he said, "Amen."

"What was that all about?" I asked, showing my annoyance.

"I prayed for your peace of mind."

"Well, there is no peace of mind for me. I have been handed an unjust sentence. I am innocent of the crime."

"I believe that."

"Oh, you do? Well, then, why didn't you pray that the truth be known?"

"That is a struggle to be won. But before that, peace of mind is necessary."

"No," I said reprovingly. "It's just the opposite. I won't have any peace of mind unless that struggle is won."

The man didn't reply, but gave me a sympathetic look that changed to sadness when I glared back at him antagonistically. He sighed, and began speaking quietly.

"Well, I have to apologize for taking it upon myself to start praying and giving you my opinions. But I really did want to see you before me and pray for you. I am an assistant professor at R. University. Ms. Wakako Ikéhata is my student, and I know her well. She was in my seminar."

Surprised and overjoyed at the sudden mention of Wakako's name, I could only stare stupidly.

"That is why I can't believe she is involved in this crime. I don't believe you are either."

"Have you seen her?" I asked, shifting my tone to polite discourse.

"Yes, I have just come from visiting her. She was gossiping about you, saying you had absolutely nothing to do with the bombing."

"She did? She said that?"

"She did."

I was elated. It was like the ice floes breaking up to a view of the beautiful blue sea. "How is she?"

"I am pleased to say she is quite well," Professor Kirikaé said, with an encouraging nod.

"To be frank, I was refraining from visiting her until that decision and her sentence. Her attorney was arguing non compos mentis, so I didn't want to do anything that might interfere with the hearings."

"Same here. I wasn't sending her any letters."

Professor Kirikaé smiled broadly. "We had the same thing in mind."

"I will send her letters now. There is just one thing that worries me. I wonder if she doesn't bear a grudge against me. It was my false confession that got her arrested."

"Certainly not. She didn't become a suspect only because of your statements, but those of the other defendants as well. The fact that she remained silent during questioning was part of it as well."

"Well, it would be a good thing if that was the case."

"There is nothing to worry about concerning that. She doesn't hold anything against you." Kirikaé had a long goatee that flapped up and down. His face and gestures made him seem less like a university professor than someone you would pay to read your fortune.

When I returned to my cell, I found that my spirits had risen considerably. Now I wanted to try to make things better again, not for me, but for her. I set to writing Wakako a letter straight away. When I finished I decided I couldn't wait until the next day, Thursday, when letters are normally posted. I requested special handling to send it express. The officer in charge looked at the address and said correspondence between prisoners was not allowed. I protested that they sent my letters at Sugamo and he explained how their system works. The district office confiscates all such communications. In other words, Wakako has not received even one of the letters I have sent her. Another of my hopes was crushed.

It must have been the influence of Professor Kirikaé that made me pick up my long abandoned Bible and start reading it. This time, I am reading slowly, the way Professor Kirikaé speaks. The last time, I had been speeding through the text, following the plot, like in a novel. Now I can feel each line rising up from the page.

"Which of you by taking thought can add one cubit unto his stature?" (Mathew 6:27) When I reached that, it set me to thinking. Then I felt comforted, and at that moment, sunlight entered the cell at an angle. There wasn't much of it, due to interference by the roof of the cell house next to this one. It moved across the floor for about thirty minutes, then disappeared. All that time, my hand was extended to it.

Attorney Iino came with an application for an appeal trial and told me to sign and seal it. I did as he asked. Then I explained that I didn't have any more money for defense fees. He stared in surprise. Then he grumbled, "The only thing you can do is choose a court-appointed attorney." I thanked him for his work and we parted.

People bearing the titles of newspaper reporter, magazine writer, and free writer have asked for interviews. I refused them all, having a vague idea of the kinds of things being written about me and Wakako in the press. The publications I get to read are all blacked out where our names appear. I get what I do know from Furukawa and other prisoners.

A certified copy of my decision arrived by post. It's a hefty document, typewritten on lined paper and bound. In form, it looks like a proper legal paper, but it is filled with falsehoods and unwarranted conjecture that distorts the facts of the case. It is frightening that such a thing would come from judges who represent the state. The first time I read through it, the impression was a detailed record of the actions of some stranger. It bore so little relationship to me that it made me laugh. But however insipid this document may be, its "main text" reading "The defendant shall be punished by death" gives this document the power to send me to the gallows.

It includes a list of reasons why I should receive the death penalty. The words have menacing overtones to common people like me:

+ The crime posed a danger to society
+ It had grave human consequences

- ♦ It had a major social impact
- ♦ It provided a model for imitative crimes
- ♦ It was committed with willful negligence
- ♦ The defendant was psychologically normal when committing the crime

In sum, it says, the crime was meticulously planned, and, given the law specifying the death penalty for the crime of overturning or destroying an electric railway train resulting in death, application of the death penalty is unavoidable.

Professor Kirikaé's visit was like a glimpse of blue skies, but I only had to go through all the abstruse terminology and self-importance of that decision once more to become depressed again. Even supposing Wakako came out denying the charges, just how much effect would that have? That goggle-eyed prosecutor with the big nose, Onuki, came to mind. He had no trouble ripping to shreds every argument and every piece of counter-evidence the defense put out. I lost confidence and began to feel like one who had fallen into a deep, pitch-black crater. My outlook careens between bright and bleak outlooks, moment by moment.

It's very cold for the middle of May. The cold walls have me cold to the core. I want to contact Wakako somehow. There is no doubt that Professor Kirikaé would convey my words to her, but I want to talk to her directly. No I don't. I want to write her letters and get letters from her.

It got so cold I went out for exercise. As could be expected, Eiji Furukawa set upon me, spouting commentary nonstop.

"Hey, you got the rope! That's great! Congratulations, man! That puts you and me in the same boat. The man who bombed the Shinkansen — that's one for the history books, no doubt about it. I heard about that reporter coming to see you. You got to get your story down on paper, how you put a bomb on the bullet train, the most famous symbol of the high growth era. Write it up big! Mix in some lies — whatever sounds good. You got to write a lot. There's money in every word. Pretty soon you'll be buying first class meals every night. Feast big, build up that paunch. Then you get an easy death when they hang you. You'll have so much weight, your neck bone will pop right in two, nice and clean. One snap and it's over, yeah!"

To escape Furukawa I went beside Yoshio Yamaishi, who was standing in the sun, where it was warmer. It was a very different Yamaishi than usual. He was all smiles and looking exultant.

"Guess what? I got life! My sentence came down last week. I decided to leave it at that. They're not ever going to catch the real culprits anyway."

I couldn't bring myself to congratulate him. I was jealous because he was someone who had robbed and killed his victim and got a life sentence for it. Containing my impulse to knock him down, I moved into the shade and went into a squat.

Chapel with Father Okuda. I thought it strange for Mikio Wakabayashi not to be there, and found out from Yusuké Okayasu that the decision of Wakabayashi's second appeal had finalized his death sentence. It is prison policy to separate condemned prisoners after their appeals have run out from prisoners whose cases are still pending. Henceforth, Wakabayashi will be kept isolated.

After the sermon and hymn, the father went aside to let me and Okayasu speak freely. Okayasu's face was ashen and wet with tears. He spoke in a whisper.

"I asked my sister if her scar hurt. She said, 'A little.' It might be hurting her now since spring is so cold this year. It gets to me that I gave her that scar. She's living on welfare. Can't afford to eat meat. She's surviving on brown rice and tofu. Brown rice is more nourishing, but it costs more than white rice, and that difference is a big deal — I just remembered. There's something I just have to do today."

Okayasu called to the father. He asked me to listen, then inclined his head and began a confession.

"There was Hansen's disease in my mother's family. I heard she had it too. My father hated her for it. She ended up dying much too young because he was mean to her. No one in the family talked about it — I mean about the disease — in my mother's family. But the people in the neighborhood could tell, somehow. My sister and I both would get spit on by the other kids in grade school."

"When my father tried to bring vegetables to the farmer's cooperative to sell, they pushed them back at him. That kind of thing happened all the time.

"By and by, my father quit working in the field and started drinking full time. He treated me and my sister like dirt. He said he couldn't make a living raising vegetables because we had bad blood. That's what led up to what happened. I stabbed my father to death with a kitchen knife. My sister tried to stop it and I put a scar on her face. But I didn't say anything about the disease at the trial. If I had, it would just make the judges prejudiced and cause more trouble for my sister, so I kept quiet. Neither one of us has the disease anyway. We got examined over and over, so we know. Even if we did have it, today's medicine can completely cure it, and it's not contagious, but people think it is. They think, 'They're lepers, keep away!' like we were poison snakes. The guards right here caught on about it just recently. When my sister comes to visit they think her scar is the disease. They look at her likes she's some kind of filth."

"Have you spoken to anyone about your mother's disease?" the father asked.

"No, not to anyone from the time I was arrested until now. You are the first one I have mentioned it to."

"In that case, couldn't it be that you are imagining things?"

"No, it's the truth. Everyone in the cell house knows about it. They all talk about it."

"I haven't heard any rumor like that," I said.

Instantly, Yusuké Okayasu went from kneeling before the father to confront me with a look of hatred. Then he was shouting at me.

"Yukimori! You better not tell anyone what I just said! I just wanted to confess to the father and there's no confessional here. That's the only reason I said it in front of you!"

~

I received this letter from Suéko:

"You must be feeling down about the sentencing, but I want you to know I don't believe you planted that bomb. There is something wrong with the police, prosecutors and judges to think you did. It is the same with Yukichi. He didn't have anything to do with that bombing or those thefts. It is just outrageous that they are blaming you.

"I was in that courtroom quite a bit. I watched a lot of the goings on there from start to finish, and I can't understand why people are so willing to make such a fuss as they did. It is inhuman the way those reporters and cameramen take such delight in other people's misfortune, like they were too stupid to know any better. Back home in Nemuro, people from one newspaper or magazine or other keep calling or showing up at the door. They want to get everything they can from me about Yukichi's past — police record, reformatory, school, work — any and everything. So I don't answer the phone and keep the door locked, and then they take pictures of our place. They follow me when I go out shopping so they can get my picture, all the time sneering about how I am the sister of a radical bomber, laughing because they think I look like some kind of fiend. When people get like that, there is no limit to how nasty they can be.

"You and the others said you didn't do any of those things through the whole trial, but that didn't make one bit of difference. As far as they were concerned, you were all guilty anyway. What's the point of having a trial if everyone's mind is made up before it even begins? A trial is supposed to be about deciding if someone is guilty or not. Isn't it up to everyone else to keep their minds open, to wait and see what develops?

"Of course it is. People can be so mean spirited and so narrow-minded, all it does is give me confidence about believing in your innocence. It seems to me that the police, prosecutors and judges are not a whit better that those ordinary people who are spiteful enough to want to make you into a criminal.

"The evening newspaper on the day of the sentencing was worse than the lowest level of journalism you might imagine. I suppose they black out articles about trials at the detention center so you wouldn't have seen the kinds of things they are writing. No doubt the reporters know that, so they don't mind a bit writing the wildest things they can come up with to smear you. You are a wily seducer of women, a hardened criminal, a radical, split personality, an insane bomber. There was a lot more of that crazy nonsense, and I can tell you, it burns me up no end. The articles about Yukichi were hardly any different, and none of it has anything to do with reality. Yukichi is about as inept and unpolished as any boy can be, and they make him out to be some kind of master criminal.

"If you think I'm furious about all this, you should see Tetsukichi, loudly ripping the newspaper to shreds, then getting plastered out of frustration.

"This is what Tetsukichi has to say. He says the trial wasn't worth a bucket of bilge, so we should fight it all the way.

"The truth is, he and I both believed the police at first when they said you and Yukichi had done a terrible thing. Then, around the time that psychiatric test report on Ms. Wakako Ikéhata came out, Tetsukichi started having suspicions. He went to Tokyo to see Professor Matsuda at N. Medical University. He came back convinced the trial was getting everything wrong because Ms. Ikéhata, you, and Yukichi had nothing to do with the bombing, and the whole thing is a miscarriage of justice.

"The thing is, now that the first trial is over and things have come this far, it will be no easy matter to get things right. That is the same as Yukichi's lawyer, Mr. Natsuki, was saying.

"Tetsukichi thinks Mr. Natsuki is no good. He wants another lawyer. He told me to tell you the same goes for Mr. Iino, and you should have another lawyer too.

"And that finally brings me to the most important reason for my writing this letter. As usual, I had to beat around the bush before I got to it.

"Tetsukichi says he wants to hire a decent lawyer for you and Yukichi. I know very well that you always want to do things by yourself and you don't like the idea of us helping you out, but this is just as much for Yukichi as for you. And it is for Ms. Ikéhata too. We want you all to get not guilty decisions. Tetsukichi wants to get a really good private lawyer who can do that. He has the money. Tetsukichi has a good income from going out fishing on his own swift boat. Please leave this to us.

"I went back to Nemuro without visiting you this time. It would have been too much for me. I knew if I went to see you right after you were sentenced to death I would break out in tears. Please forgive me.

"Tetsukichi stayed in Tokyo. He went to see Mr. Jun Akutsu. He and Tetsukichi were in the same classes in elementary school and middle school. He went on to study law at C. University. After he graduated, he was a legal apprentice, and then he became a lawyer last spring. He said he would accept the case, and he would pay a visit to the detention center soon, and asked for a letter of introduction to you. That is what this letter is.

"I remember Jun Akutsu very well. His house was near the forestry office building up on the hill. He would come down to visit our place. His father worked at Nemuro city hall, if my memory serves me right. Even though he came from a good family, he got into all kinds of mischief, so naturally, he got right along with Tetsukichi, who was the king-pin mischief maker. They were good friends. Once he started going to high school in Sapporo, he and Tetsukichi didn't cross paths anymore, but they kept in touch by letter. Since this business with your arrest brought Tetsukichi to Tokyo now and then, it was mentioned in their letters.

"So I have a favor to ask. Let Mr. Iino go so you can be represented by Mr. Akutsu. (I really want to call him 'Jun-chan,' but he is a lawyer, and that means I should call him '-sensei.') Mr. Akutsu works at the law office of a well-known attorney by the name of Sadanosuké Ishikawa. That law office attracts talented young lawyers, and it is good to know that if we needed some kind of support, it would be there in that office."

I thought it over for one night, then wrote Suéko agreeing to go along. By the time I had gone through the experiences of the first trial, I had developed an instinctive understanding of the importance of a competent lawyer when it comes to a case of false charges like ours. If I had a court appointed lawyer, it would be him, not me in the driver's seat. The way things stand, everybody in the world treats us as the worst kinds of criminal. They criticize, they condemn, they pay no attention to what we say. Under those circumstances, there is little chance that some courageous lawyer will come forth to represent us. This is a time to choose a private lawyer and put up a fight, for the sake of Yukichi, but above all, for Wakako.

~

Mr. Akutsu came to visit. He is quite young. Being from the same class as Tetsukichi, he must be twenty-five or six, but he hardly looks twenty. A funny thing that stands out is the gold attorney's badge pinned to his suit's lapel. The one Mr. Iino wore was grayish and losing its plating. This one is shiny and new. It looked to me like some cheap bauble you would buy one night from an outdoor stall at a festival.

We made our introductions. He has tiny eyes that he was blinking nervously all the while. He is so slender he gives an impression of being unsteady on his feet. But his voice was reassuring.

"I have just finished reading through all the case documents. I think we have two courses for presenting our counter-evidence. One is to show that the confession was not given voluntarily. This means pursing the line that the police officers and the prosecutor conducted your interrogation in ways that did not meet the requirements of law. Our other path is to prove your alibi. That means finding witnesses who can testify that you were somewhere other than at the scene of the crime on the day it occurred."

"That's all true enough, but we weren't able to find any witnesses or any material evidence in either of those categories in the first trial," I said. I said this with a slightly sarcastic smile. It seemed to me I was pointing out something too obvious to have to mention.

"You were arrested at your home."

"Yes, in my apartment. They drove me from there to the Onarimon police station."

"Did they handcuff you immediately?"

"No. The detectives were still being nice to me at that point. They didn't handcuff me, as if they trusted me. It was a case of voluntary accompaniment."

"Voluntary accompaniment. So it wasn't an arrest?"

It suddenly came back to me that I had said to a detective, "Please show me my arrest warrant," and was told "There is no arrest warrant. This is a voluntary accompaniment."

When I explained this to Mr. Akutsu, his eyes gleamed. He had long eyelashes and puffy eyelids. "That is not what you said to the prosecutor. You testified that you were told you were being arrested on suspicion of planting a bomb."

"That was my mistake . . . For heaven's sake! Why didn't I remember that? I completely forgot! They wouldn't show me an arrest warrant. I spent the whole time in the car wondering why I was being taken to the police station."

"It was a completely unlawful detention. To take a person away in a car without giving any reason. What is even more serious is that an arrest warrant had actually been issued for you, on a charge of theft, and they didn't show it to you."

"I just remembered! I was shown that arrest warrant when I was in the detective's interrogation room. I was supposedly there voluntarily, and time went on and on and they still wouldn't give any reason, so I finally said, 'I will take my leave now.' That was when he suddenly pulled the arrest warrant out of a drawer."

"A drawer? That was a peculiar place for it to have been. Did the detective who brought you to the station take the arrest warrant from his pocket and put it in that drawer?"

"That detective was watching me every minute. I don't think he had any opportunity to do such a thing."

"You know what? That statement you just made contains an important discovery!" Mr. Akutsu blinked his bright eyes. "Who pulled the arrest warrant from that drawer?"

"It was assistant inspector Hino."

"Aha. He was a witness at the trial. He was on your interrogation the whole time, wasn't he?"

"That's right. I gave him my false confession. Well, actually, he forced it out of me."

"Did he arrest you? Or should I say 'voluntarily accompanianize' you?"

"No, that was someone else — three others. One was older, a sergeant with a red nose, a young patrolman and the driver."

"Those three brought you in under the pretense of voluntary accompaniment, and they didn't even have the arrest warrant that was issued on a theft charge!"

" . . . What was the point of that?"

"There is no point. It makes no sense. They had themselves convinced, on the basis of nothing but speculation and preconceptions, that you were the culprit in the Shinkansen bombing. The theft charge was a classic example of using a separate charge arrest as an excuse for a fishing expedition. And they didn't even remember to bring the arrest warrant!"

"Yes, that fits." The young lawyer's reasoning had me impressed.

"There's something else. Photographs taken of you outside the Onarimon police station — they appeared in the evening newspapers — show you were handcuffed. It is against the law to put handcuffs on a person who is not under arrest."

"They put the handcuffs on in a hurry because there was a big crowd of press people."

"You see, everything they did before they even began questioning you was illegal!"

"Wait, there's more. They took my fingerprints, footprints and strip-searched me, including an anal examination — all before I was shown that arrest warrant."

"Right out of a comic book. They were out to prove you were the culprit, and the only way to do it was force a confession. They used all kinds of techniques to build up psychological pressure on you to get it."

"Well, why? What is the point of pinning the crime on me, when I didn't do it?"

"Your confession is really the only evidence in the case. I would say assistant inspector Hino was the ringleader. He retired in the second year after the crime, in other words, this year, in March. He wanted credit for solving some major crime before he retired, but nothing big enough to satisfy him was in the cards — until you came into his sights. That is why he considered it necessary to make you into the key criminal of the case."

"He was all over me in that interrogation room. I didn't get any peace."

"He had a reputation to live up to. He was known as the 'make-'em-sing maestro.' That reputation was on the line when he interrogated you, and he committed a number of unlawful acts in his haste to achieve your downfall. We're going to confront him with evidence of his misdeeds in the second trial. Those three detectives who brought you in, the newspaper photographs and the arrest warrant inside the drawer are all sources of viable counter-evidence. Of course, we will also have to put together some kind of evidence to present to the prosecutor on how your interrogations were conducted . . . Now, then, about your alibi."

"Oh, that's hopeless. There isn't a single person to say he saw me." A mournful sign escaped me as I thought of my meager prospects.

"February 11, 1969, four in the afternoon. To be more precise, the ten minute period beginning at three fifty-four, when the doors of the Hikari 33 Shinkansen were open on the platform. All we have to do is show that you weren't there during those ten minutes." Mr. Akutsu nodded at me encouragingly.

He was young enough to be my son. I could only mumble a hoarse reply from under my downcast gaze, like a failure as a father, unable to give his son anything.

"I was in Jindai Botanical Garden at that time. The plum blossoms were in full bloom, it was very crowded. No one who saw me would remember. It looked as if everyone there belonged to a group that was being led around."

"Guided tours?"

"Yes. I suppose they all came on tour buses for plum blossom viewing on the holiday. The parking lot in front of the garden was full of buses."

"What kinds of groups?"

"All kinds. Let's see . . . there was a line of people who looked like they came from some retirement home, there were, I guess, housewives — different kinds of groups. Of course I wouldn't know any of the group names."

"Any group that stood out? Maybe a religious group, people dressed in black, right-wing nationalists out to celebrate Empire Day? Didn't you see something memorable about any of those groups?"

"Hmmmmm . . . It was such an assortment . . . All right, how's this? There was a group of psychiatric hospital patients being led around by a nurse."

"A nurse. In a white uniform?"

"No. I could tell she was a nurse by the way she looked and acted. It so happens that Y. Psychiatric Hospital is located right next to my apartment, and I've seen the patients and the nurses there many times. Many of those patients were sort of fat and slow-moving, or they would move their legs or. arms hesitantly. They would always be in a group led around by a woman giving orders. You knew she was in charge. That's the nurse. It was the same with that group at the garden."

Suddenly a phrase popped out from the bottom of my memory: "head nurse."

"I just remembered something. The patients were lined up for a group photo. One of the patients was yelling to a woman — a little on the heavy side — 'C'mon head nurse, get in the picture.'"

"That is memorable. Most people would just say 'nurse.' That patient was literal-minded. This is an important fact." Mr. Akutsu had been jotting down notes. Now his hand stopped and he affixed me with his clear-eyed gaze. It was slightly dazzling. When he started blinking again, it felt like being caught in a strobe light. "Was this group of patients a women's group?" he asked.

"No, there were women and men. It was a very large group. There were quite a few nurses around. More than ten. It was like half the patients in the hospital were out for a stroll."

"Could it have been people from the psychiatric hospital near your apartment?"

"It's possible, but I don't really know. That hospital is close to the botanical garden and they do take the patients for walks during the different blossoming seasons. Whether it's plum, cherry, peonies, roses, bush clover, chrysanthemums, or whatever. I love to do the same thing, so I have run into those people quite a few times."

"Of course it must have been Y. Hospital! No doubt about it!"

Until this moment, Mr. Akutsu had been calm. Now his voice went shrill and his face reddened. "Think about it. You're running a hospital, you know when the plum blossoms in Jindai Botanical Garden are in full bloom, and you are in a position to take many of your patients for a walk in that garden. Now what hospital fills those conditions? The one that is near the garden, of course. Unless there is more than one. I will check into that."

"Okay, but even if we know that, they don't know me. None of those people could be a witness that I was there."

"They took photographs. It is possible you appear in one. I will see if I can find any photographs."

"Photographs?"

"If there is just one photo we know was taken that day in the gardens, that would be unassailable proof."

"Uh-hmm. Okay, but there isn't much chance there is such a picture with me in it."

"We don't know that, and we don't have the luxury of overlooking small chances anyway."

The mental hospital patients walked leisurely among the plum trees blooming red and white. They didn't really stand out from the other people around them, but, having observed them for all the years I lived at that apartment, I could spot them as patients. They looked as if there was something missing in them. There might be a line of saliva running from a corner of their lips. Their movements were slow. They threw fretful looks at their surroundings.

443

The path through the plum trees led to the camellia woods. I was hurrying toward some scattered early blooming camellias I had spotted. I heard a shutter click, off to the side. Patients standing side by side beneath a plum tree were casting critical looks at me. I was about to cross in front of a nurse pointing a camera. That was when I heard that patient calling out "C'mon head nurse!" to a chunky middle-aged woman.

"You know, I just remembered I was crossing in front of a nurse pointing a camera just as she pressed the shutter. But that would have been a no-good shot, as far as they were concerned. I would think they must have thrown it away. A patient called out 'C'mon head nurse!' just as I passed by. Now that I think about it, it is amazing I didn't recall that before."

"We all have a great deal of information in our memories, but are actually able to recall only a part of it. No matter. That 'no-good photograph' would be a major piece of evidence. I will look for it. What did that head nurse look like? Did she have any distinguishing features?"

"Ahhh . . . About all I can tell you is she was chunky, in her fifties, I guess. Not very tall. I don't really remember her face, but I guess she was the cheerful type. She would crack jokes that made the patients laugh."

"It sounds like the patients were fond of her, the way they called to her to get into their group photo. You have given me enough clues to track her down."

Mr. Akutsu was smiling. By that time I was seeing that shiny badge of his differently. That attorney's badge modeled after a sunflower was starting to look like it held a new kind of power.

Chapter 8

Sunflower

Jun Akutsu emerged from a taxi and looked up at the building before him, identified by a name plaque as Y. Hospital. A concrete building prettified with imitation brick walls, it might have passed for a condominium at a casual glance, but iron grills over the windows of the wards that extended to the rear were telltale fixtures of a psychiatric hospital. Beside the entrance was a flower bed planted with two rows of small roses arranged in an unnecessarily regular pattern of white and pink blossoms alternating at equidistant intervals.

Akutsu pondered how he should proceed as he watched, first a group of patients pulling weeds from the flower bed, and then the nurse directing the activity. Upon returning to his law office the day before from his visit to Atsuo Yukimori at the detention center, he had immediately consulted a map, and then called the Japan Association of Psychiatric Hospitals to confirm that Y. Hospital was the only psychiatric institution in the vicinity of Jindai Botanical Garden. That morning, he had decided it would be best to simply show up at the hospital, lest he fail to properly convey his objective over the phone. So there he was, but he still hadn't formulated a strategy for his investigation.

"Oh, well, I could stand here thinking about it forever," he told himself to muster his resolution, then strode inside. Beyond the entryway, he found a broad corridor that doubled as a waiting room. There were examination rooms, a pharmacy and an office, with more bustle and activity than he had been expecting. The office sofas were fully occupied, and some people were standing. Nurses and pharmacists called out patient's names at frequent intervals. The scene was no different than one would find at any general hospital. Akutsu proceeded to the reception desk.

"Are you here for an examination?" a woman asked him tonelessly.

"No," he began impulsively. "I would like to meet with the head nurse."

"Which head nurse?"

"Um . . . There are several?"

"There are five, one for each ward, A through E."

"I see. Is one of them a jovial sort of person?"

"What!" The woman regarded Akutsu suspiciously. Then her expression became compassionate, befitting one accustomed to dealing with psychiatric patients. "Just what is it that you need?"

"It's a bit too complicated to explain in a few words." Akutsu hesitated over how to proceed. He could briefly summarize his business, but he didn't want to do that surrounded by a waiting room full of strangers. The woman's eyes narrowed, and she was again looking him over suspiciously. Apparently, she didn't recognize the significance of the attorney's badge Akutsu wore. He held out his business card and said, "I would like to meet with the hospital director concerning a certain case."

The word "attorney-at-law" on the business card had the desired effect. The woman retreated to a desk behind her, consulted with someone, and then made a phone call. After a few moments, she emerged through a door into the corridor and politely escorted Akutsu to the director's office on the second floor.

The hospital director was a man of generous size in his fifties, wearing outstandingly thick tortoiseshell glasses and a crisply starched white uniform. By his side was an older, balding man who was introduced as the office manager.

"Now, please tell us what it is you wish," the director began, with a tense expression. Akutsu read from the man's manifestly deep concern and suspicion that he was under a misapprehension. Generally, people in a position like the director's would react to an unexpected visit from an attorney by steeling themselves for a demand that compensation be paid over some alleged fault on their part. Akutsu consciously relaxed his face into a smile as he hastened to make the purpose of his visit clear.

"I am the legal representative of a defendant in a case who needs to have his alibi proven, and to do that, I would like to have testimony from one of the head nurses at your hospital."

"In a trial?" The director's expression expressed open distaste. "That's a lot to ask. The head nurses here are all extremely busy. To expect them to accommodate you . . ."

"Does this hospital have a practice of taking patients out for walks in Jindai Botanical Garden?" Akutsu continued, untroubled by the protest. "For flower viewing, I mean, seasonally, for the different kinds of blossoms."

"Yes, we do, but it isn't just going for walks. It is a kind of recreational therapy. The objective is to make positive changes in the patients' frame of mind, from the standpoint of mental health."

"I see. That is really admirable. I would call that a wonderful kind of therapy, and a very good way to take advantage of the hospital's location."

"Quite so." The director was finally smiling. "This area used to be one big cultivated field. Now, it is pretty much filled up with residences. Fortunately, Jindai Botanical Garden preserves the natural environment that once existed everywhere across the Musashino Plain."

"Do they go to see plum blossoms too?"

"Of course. Plum blossom viewing is the first event of every year. After that, cherry blossoms, double flowered cherry, tree peonies, azaleas . . . Now we are in the rose season. Flowers are scarce in summer, but in autumn we have bush clover and chrysanthemums. We could not be in a better location for therapy." The director winked one eye affably, as if to say Akutsu would be welcome as a patient, if he liked.

"When do you schedule days for plum blossom viewing?"

"Well, we work that out every year when the time comes round."

"Yes, of course you would. When did they go the year before last?"

"Why the year before last?" The hospital director looked wary once again.

"Let me explain everything, quite frankly. The defendant I am representing tells me that he was in Jindai Botanical Garden the year before last, on Foundation Day — that is, February 11. He went to the plum wood. It was afternoon. He says he saw patients from this hospital while he was there. If I can prove what he says is true, that will establish his alibi."

"Just what kind of thing was he supposed to have been involved in?"

"The decision in his trial was handed down just recently. The Shinkansen bombing."

"Those radicals! That horrible crime!" The director stared at Akutsu in horror. His demeanor showed he was genuinely afraid.

"The defendants were falsely charged. My client, Atsuo Yukimori, and Wakako Ikéhata were charged with putting the bomb on the train, but they had nothing to do with the crime. They both have alibis."

"We will not have any dealings with radicals!"

The director rose and gestured toward the door with his chin, as if telling

Akutsu to get out now. The office manager also stood. Akutsu remained seated, reflecting on the fact that he was an inch away from being driven out.

"Please listen just a little more." Akutsu's voice was calm as he remained seated, but his face was reddening and he began perspiring. He was telling himself, don't get excited, just say what has to be said.

"A person's life is at stake. Atsuo Yukimori has been sentenced to death, but the truth is he didn't commit the crime. The trouble is that we still don't have enough evidence to prove his alibi. It needs to be corroborated. If his alibi can be fully proven, it will show he is not guilty, and that will be a historical event. The credit will go to you."

"Hmph." The director sat down in his seat. The office manager returned to his place and sat down as well.

"Forgive me, but are you really a lawyer? Oh, don't be offended. It's just that you are so young-looking, I was wondering, is this some student who just now became lawyer, and then all of a sudden you start talking about that radical affair — I was kind of startled. The fact is, this hospital was taken over for a time by some young doctors in a radical sect a little while back. We were having quite a hard time. It was giving us a bad reputation."

"I really am a lawyer. I belong to the Dai-ichi Tokyo Bar Association. You are welcome to call there and confirm it."

"No, that isn't necessary. I can see from your badge that you are a lawyer . . . We have lawyers in the Chofu Rotary Club. They have the same attorney's badge, but you know, they are all on in years, and their badges are dull yellow. Yours is the first I have seen that is so shiny. Sorry."

The director undid a button on his white uniform, removed a handkerchief from a pocket of his suit and dabbed away sweat from his brow. The office manager passed a handkerchief over his balding crown. Without missing a beat, Akutsu removed his handkerchief and passed it over his face and brow. The three laughed in unison.

"When did you become an attorney?" the director inquired.

"Last year."

"That figures. If you don't mind, how old are you?"

"Twenty-six."

"Uh-huh. Nothing like being young. Where'd you go to school?"

"C. University."

"Oh, my, that is a very good school. My son will be up for entrance exams next year, but schools like C. University are probably out of the question."

"Getting to the matter of the alibi," Akutsu began by way of resetting the

448

conversation. "My client says on that day a group of your patients were lined up for a photograph in front of the plum trees, and a sort of heavy-set head nurse was in the middle. He says she was cheerful, laughed a lot, and it looked like the patients really liked her."

The director looked over toward the manager, as he said "Hmmm! Who might that be?" The manager inclined his head to one side and spoke solemnly.

"'Cheerful and laughs a lot' — that would fit Nurse Shimizu in B Ward. For that matter, Nurse Oúra in E Ward would also fit that description."

"All our head nurses are cheerful, you know," the director said brightly, with another wink. "They are all well liked. Our patients trust them."

"Could I meet Nurse Shimizu and Nurse Oúra?" Akutsu asked.

"Do you want them to appear as witnesses?"

"No, at this stage I only want to ask them one thing — if they took patients out for a walk in Jindai Botanical Garden on the afternoon of February eleventh, two years ago."

"Well, if that's all . . ." The director picked up a telephone and set up an appointment for Akutsu with the two nurses. The director's secretary escorted him to one of the wards.

He first met with Ms. Shimizu, whose tall, thin figure did not fit Atsuo Yukimori's description. A brief conversation established that she was not the witness he sought because she had only joined the hospital staff near the end of the previous year.

Nurse Oúra met Yukimori's description of a short, stout woman. She accepted Akutsu's business card and peered at it curiously. Then she stared up at him and emitted a soft gasp of surprise.

"My, goodness! I didn't even know they had such adorable-looking lawyers — I thought lawyers were all old fogeys. Ask me anything you like! Delighted to help!"

Akutsu explained the issue briefly. The head nurse pulled a binder from a shelf labeled "E Ward Rec Therapy Logbook," and began turning pages.

"Lessee . . . Showa 44, you said? February 11 . . . Oh, here we are, 'Plum blossom viewing. Participants: all patients (63)' How's that?"

"Was that the afternoon of the eleventh?"

"It doesn't say. Sorry, no way to tell!"

"Weren't you with them that day?"

"Oh, dear! I just can't remember a thing. My memory's no good at all!"

"Would you have taken commemorative photos that day?"

"I'm afraid I . . . No, I don't know about that either . . . Oh, but there is a possibility! Last year was the hospital's fifteenth anniversary. We were preparing to print up our history, and one thing we did was take pictures of outings and events to put in the book."

She pulled another volume from the shelf. *Y. Hospital — The First Fifteen Years*, opened to the section beginning Showa 44, and found a picture whose caption identifying the event as a plum blossom viewing outing. The picture showed what looked like patients posing in front of a blossoming plum tree, but it was small and grainy. No faces were clearly distinguishable.

"This does seem to be what you are after," the nurse said, but without conviction.

"You can't make out people's faces," Akutsu said with disappointment.

"It's intentionally printed that way, to protect people's privacy. The original photos should show more detail than this."

"Do you have the original photos?"

"Well now . . . The rec therapy technician took these pictures. She may still have them. She took all the pictures used in this history."

"Who is this rec technician?"

"She majored in psychology. She conducts the physiological testing and oversees the recreational therapy program."

"Can I meet with her?"

"She was in the ward a little while ago. She may still be there," the head nurse said, gazing through the office window, out into the spacious room beyond.

Until that moment, Akutsu had been focused on informing the nurse about his objective. Now his attention turned for the first time to his surroundings. He was inside the nurse station, enclosed by glass panels on three sides that afforded a full view of the corridor and the entire floor of the ward. The arrangement was quite like the guard station at the detention center.

There was a man pacing up and down the corridor. He would reach the end, turn on his heel and retrace his steps. It looked as though he would be repeating this journey many times. Three people were seated before a television set, watching a samurai slice-'em-up. A boisterous clatter of tiles issued from one corner where a Mahjong game was in progress. Elsewhere, people were playing table tennis. Akutsu soon noticed one outstanding human situation amidst this confusion of activity. A large number of people in the room were standing or sitting vacantly, essentially doing nothing but staring into empty space through eyes like clouded glass. Having supposed a psychiatric hospital to be a place where agitated patients ran about, Akutsu watched in wonder at people for whom time seemed to have been suspended, who thought of nothing and had no reason to even move. It looked as if they would spend the entire day at the same locations, in the same postures.

Failing to spot the person she sought among the patients, the nurse gripped a microphone on the desk and spoke into it. Her summons emerged from loudspeakers above the ward floor.

"Ms. Yoko Mizuno!"

A young woman near the end of the corridor looked up. "Please come to the nurse station!"

The young woman hurried to the station. She had long hair, wore blue jeans, and had a nice figure. She looked about twenty-four or twenty-five.

"Yes, ma'am. What can I do for you?"

"I have a question about the February before last. You went picture-taking in the botanical garden that month, didn't you?"

"Sure did. I took a lot of pictures."

"Do you still have them?"

"Let me think. That's a long time ago. They should be around somewhere."

The woman showed awareness of Akutsu standing there by giving him a sidelong glance. She wore no makeup, allowing her dark complexion to show a velvety, lustrous tone. A well-formed pair of lips resided beneath the delicate bridge of her nose. She was a beauty by any standard.

"This fellow here is a lawyer. He says a picture you took could be useful for defending his case."

"Oh, a lawyer!" The woman fixed her gaze on Akutsu, looked him up and down, then raised both hands to her face with a contrite expression. "I'm sorry, I was thinking you were probably one of those insurance salesmen. I'm Yoko Mizuno — *Yo* as in 'sun.'" With this self-introduction, she lowered her head politely.

"Jun Akutsu. *Jun* as in 'purity,'" Akutsu said, and returned the bow.

The woman had a faintly pleasant odor. Akutsu was a bit sweaty. Realizing his own face was reddening again, he launched into an explanation of the photograph he needed.

"You mean if that person shows up in one of the pictures I took, he'll be found not guilty?" Yoko Mizuno asked.

"That's right."

"Wow! That's beautiful!" she said, laughing. "I love that kind of story!"

Akutsu followed Yoko Mizuno outside to a single-story wooden frame building. It had a nameplate on its door bearing the words "Occupational Therapy Center."

"This building used to be one of the hospital wards."

The building was divided into a number of rooms along a corridor. Inside each of the rooms were patients engaged in such activities as woodworking, sewing, and adding appendices to periodicals. Yoko invited Akutsu into the room at the end of the corridor.

"The room is a mess, but do come in." She showed him to a small chair. He sat down, and the chair lurched unsteadily to one side. With a slight giggle, Yoko explained, "The floor is off kilter." He laid a hand on the desk, only causing it to teeter in the same manner as the chair.

On the desk were papers that looked like psychological testing sheets. The small space available in the room was crammed with wooden building blocks and various kinds of printed pasteboard diagrams.

Yoko opened a cupboard and rummaged through such paraphernalia as colored construction paper, celluloid clown masks, and balloons. Finally, she found five photo albums that she pulled out. Doing so caused a few sheets of construction paper to slide from a binder to the floor. Akutsu hastened to retrieve them.

"We had a parade with everyone wearing costumes just before that flower viewing outing. As the rec therapy director, I organize costume parades and field day games, teach square dancing, take pictures of activities . . . you name it. I also do psychological testing."

"That's a lot of responsibility. I understand you majored in psychology. What school did you go to?"

"R. University."

"No kidding! That's a coincidence." She was arranging the sheets of construction paper as Akutsu spoke. "One of the defendants in my case is from R. University. I wonder if you know her. Wakako Ikéhata."

"Mmmm, I don't think so," Yoko Mizuno said, tilting her head to the side.

"She's a defendant in that Shinkansen bombing case."

"Oho! Now I'm trying to remember if I heard anywhere that a woman from our school was involved in that. I'm not really interested in politics. I'm so busy with my job . . . Even on Sundays, there are meetings with patients' families . . . OK, here we are!"

It was an album of mounted photographs, the same as those appearing in the printed book *Y. Hospital — The First Fifteen Years*. These photos were all properly in focus. One could make out the individual faces among the crowds of people shown walking beneath the blossoming plum trees. His pulse racing, Akutsu searched through the photos.

It was looking as if the search would be in vain. He couldn't find any figures that looked like Atsuo Yukimori. Each page had about twenty L size prints of photos, all from the same day of shooting. He scrutinized each one meticulously. When Yoko Mizuno handed him a large magnifying glass, the operation suddenly became easy to perform.

"Are you looking for that woman student?"

"No, I'm looking for her boyfriend."

"I understand he's like a legend as criminals go. What was his record . . . more than ten offenses?"

"No, he had five convictions, and he's no desperado. He is basically a good person who happens to be very weak-willed. In this case, the police grilled him morning till night until he finally gave a false confession. He denied the charges at trial, but the judges believed the false confession and convicted him. But he was really in Jindai Botanical Garden at the time the crime was committed. If I can find his face in these pictures, that will get not guilty decisions for him and the woman student as well."

"Really? Will she get off too?" Yoko's expression became animated. She brought her face up close to the album.

"Here he is!" Akutsu exclaimed excitedly. The photograph in his hand showed the profile of a man to the side of a row of patients. He was passing by the stationary line of people, from the far end. The face was cut off at the ear, but it was unmistakably Atsuo Yukimori. He wore a necktie with red polka dots on a dark blue background, and his buff-colored duster coat showed up clearly.

"Is that him?" Yoko Mizuno asked. "You're right, he does look like a good person. Looks sturdy, manly . . . young-looking too."

"He was forty-nine at the time."

"He doesn't look it! He looks like he's about thirty-five or six."

"Yes, he is young-looking. And now we have decisive proof, thanks to you."

"This proves him innocent? And her too?"

"They were charged with committing the crime together. And now we have proof of one of the alibis. Naturally, she is innocent too."

"That's terrific!" Smiling, Yoko Mizuno patted her long hair onto her shoulder. "Kind of thrilling, like a mystery story. I'm a big mystery fan. But this story is 'Whodunit?' upside down. And it is completely outrageous! Arrest an innocent person and pin the crime on him. That is unforgivable, and, guess what? I'm going to expose it! I have a friend who is a crime reporter for *A. Shimbun*. I'll tell her the truth about this. It'll be a scoop for her. She'll write all about it!"

"Not so fast, please!" Akutsu said in alarm. It looked as if the next moment would find her reaching for the telephone.

"Please don't tell anyone about this until it is presented as evidence in court. We can't let the prosecutor know what we're up to. Any time we present some evidence, you can be sure the prosecutor is going to try to destroy its value. We've got to be very cautious. But let me ask, would you have the negative of this photograph?"

"Yes, but finding it will be a major operation. The negatives are not in any order. The project was for fifteen years of history. I took hundreds of pictures, and they ended up just being put away without ever sorting them out."

"That's fine. If they're all together, it's just a matter of looking in that one place until it turns up."

Yoko extracted four paper bags filled with negatives from a shelf. Akutsu began the process of holding up each negative against the light from the desk lamp to search for the one matching the photograph. Yoko did the same. When they had gone through about two-thirds of the negatives, Yoko found the right one.

"Can I borrow it?"

"Of course."

"This is a life-saver. I'll have it enlarged to use as material evidence. Do you remember the day and time you took this?"

"I am certain it was in the afternoon on National Foundation Day, the year before last. We left about two o'clock, so I guess it was around three o'clock. Wait now! . . . It would take thirty minutes to get from here to the garden entrance, because our patients move slowly. The plum wood is at the far end of the garden, so that's ten minutes from the entrance. So, around two-forty . . . Oh, now I remember. We have to be back in time for supper at four-thirty, you see. That meant I had to take the pictures all very quickly. It must have been somewhere between three thirty and four o'clock."

"Bravo!" Akutsu said heartily. "It so happens that covers the interval when the time bomb was set."

"I wonder if you blew it up to poster size, maybe you could read someone's watch. That would really nail it down!" Yoko seemed to have become infected with Akutsu's fervor. Her voice was getting shrill.

As he exited Y. Hospital, Akutsu had a sudden inspiration to drop by Atsuo Yukimori's old apartment. He knew the landmarks to look for, and thus was able to find the two-story apartment building, located beside a thicket of trees. It was a light modular type ferroconcrete building. According to the case documentation, the first floor was the owner's residence, with six apartments on the second floor. There was a steel staircase. Akutsu walked to the Number 2 apartment, where Yukimori had lived. The name of some other occupant was on the doorplate. Akutsu stood still and listened. The only sound to reach his ears was the wind through the treetops. Nothing could be heard from inside the apartment.

Treading softly, Akutsu descended the steel stairway, and caught sight of a first-floor window opening and a pair of eyes upon him. Facing the direction of the disembodied gaze, he called out "Hullo there!" The eyes vanished for a moment and reappeared as the face of an old woman wearing an expression that reproached him for taking the liberty of climbing the stairs. Akutsu gave a cordial nod of salutation.

"Pardon me. Do you remember Mr. Atsuo Yukimori, who lived here a long time ago?" Instead of replying, the old woman opened her window a little more.

"Um . . . Mr. Atsuo Yukimori . . . That person is not here."

"Oh, you do remember! Actually, I am Mr. Yukimori's attorney."

As if on cue, the woman wrinkled her face and waved her hand side to side in a gesture that signaled, "I won't have anything to do with it!"

"I don't know any Mr. Yukimori."

"Well, Mr. Yukimori has fond memories of you. He told me that if I was in the neighborhood I should give you his regards. He said that the seven years he lived here were the happiest in his life, because he had a thoughtful landlady, the surroundings were quiet, the air was clean, and the apartment building was as well. This apartment house was paradise, as far as he was concerned."

The woman's face relaxed, and the window opened wide. "How is he?"

"He is well, but a little blue from being in jail for so long. If I may, I would like to ask you about that day two years ago, on the eleventh of February when that bomb exploded on the Shinkansen."

"I've forgotten all about it. It was so long ago."

"The truth is that Mr. Yukimori had nothing to do with that explosion. Did you know that he went plum blossom viewing in Jindai Botanical Garden that day? Take a look at this!"

Akutsu held out the picture that showed Yukimori. "Oh, my, that is him. This was taken that day?"

"Yes, it certainly was. I have just come from Y. Hospital to borrow this photograph. I believe you told the prosecutor that on that day Mr. Yukimori returned home at about five-thirty in the evening. Since you knew the time he returned, I wonder, can you tell me what time he left here?"

"My, my . . ." The old woman peered closely at the photo. "You know, that necktie he's wearing — he really liked it. Once I told him he looked good in it, and he never forgot. He put it on again and again after that. I knew he had it on that morning too because I said he looked good in it when he was going out. If there's anything that man likes, it's being praised for his clothing."

Akutsu was not able to get anything more from the old woman. Nevertheless, he had obtained from her a statement that Yukimori's clothing on that day marched the clothing shown in the photograph.

As a newly minted attorney, Akutsu made his living drawing a base salary at a law office headed by a senior graduate of his alma mater, Sadanosuké Ishikawa, who had earned a solid reputation through many years of law practice. In his employment, Akutsu received day-to-day advice about the nuts and bolts of routine law practice and how to handle difficult cases.

After returning to the office, located on the second floor of a building in Shimbashi, Akutsu had lunch, then went to see Ishikawa, who had both feet up on his desk and was puffing on his pipe.

"So how did it turn out?" Ishikawa asked, brushing back white, tousled hair and emitting a long stream of smoke. His nickname among friends was "the lion," in reference to his hair. Ishikawa hated barber shops, preferring to let his hair grow out, occasionally cutting it himself, as he thought necessary. He had wiry, stubborn hair that resembled the great mane worn for kabuki lion dance programs. Unusually for a lawyer, Ishikawa would appear in court without a necktie, but he nagged Akutsu to dress like a "proper jurist," adding for consolation, "You can do as you please when you get as far as I have."

"It turned out very well." Akutsu gave a brief report on the result of his visit to the hospital, adding that he could now prove Atsuo Yukimori's alibi.

"Don't be so sure," Ishikawa answered dryly, knocking ash from his pipe into an ashtray. "The question is, how is that picture going to hold up when the prosecution attacks it. To begin with, you can't prove when it was taken."

"I can . . ."

"The rec therapy woman will testify, yes?"

"Yes."

"How do you know she has an accurate memory? Maybe it was taken some other day."

"The hospital has a daily log of rec therapy activities, and there is a record of taking the patients plum blossom viewing in the botanical garden on February eleventh, 1969."

"Was that the only day they ever went plum blossom viewing?"

"There were two other excursions that February — on Sunday, the twenty-ninth and Friday, the fourteenth."

"Well?" Ishikawa held a flame to his freshly filled pipe and pulled at it energetically, then intentionally expelled a heavy cloud of smoke toward Akutsu, whom he knew disliked tobacco smoke. Akutsu held his breath to weather the stream.

"I called the Meteorological Agency and found that the weather on the twenty-ninth was clear, and there was a cloud cover on the eleventh, classified as 'very cloudy.' That matches the sky shown in the photo."

"I see," Ishikawa said with an approving nod. "Good work. What about the fourteenth?"

"Yukimori was on an 8:40 a.m. flight from Hanéda Airport, bound for Kushiro."

Ishikawa looked closely at the photograph Akutsu had handed him. "So does that mean this was shot on February eleventh?" he asked, more to himself than Akutsu.

"This is one valuable piece of new evidence. Be forewarned that the prosecution will move heaven and earth to demolish the alibi. You yourself will have to be ready with double and triple defenses."

"Yukimori's landlady says she saw him in the morning the day the bomb exploded, and she complimented him on his necktie. She recognized the tie in this photo. She says it was the same tie he wore that day," Akutsu said proudly.

"You don't suppose her memory could be mistaken, do you? Is she one for remembering necktie patterns?" Ishikawa asked sarcastically. "Hmmm, I wonder . . ." He said as if at a loss to say more, but then continued after a couple of beats.

"See if you can find somebody at that company where Yukimori worked who can confirm that necktie pattern. With luck, you might turn up a woman with a sharp eye for that kind of thing."

"I will," Akutsu said, nodding obediently. "If we assume Yukimori's alibi is established, that throws Wakako Ikéhata's guilt into doubt as well, so I want to look into her alibi — after getting Mr. Tsukioka's approval, of course." Then Akutsu inhaled some smoke and choked on it.

"That will be a hard call," Ishikawa said. He dropped both legs from his desk and looked at Akutsu. "Tsukioka's not the kind who's likely to accommodate you. Number one, you're not going to find any alibi he didn't know about long ago. Second, his defense was all about his client's diminished responsibility, so he is most likely cool about proving an alibi."

"Arguing non compos mentis bought a life sentence. It is clearer than daylight that the only way to win the appeal trial has to be by disputing the facts of the case."

"I have not yet done a full reading of the case documents. Just what has Tsukioka put out as evidence on Wakako Ikéhata's alibi?"

"Only Professor Matsuda's psychiatric testing report. It contains her testimony that she was in the R. University library the day of the bombing. There is no corroboration. As things stand, Onuki squelched it by arguing her testimony has no value because she's a schizophrenic patient."

"What you have there is simply sloppy defense work." Ishikawa lay down on his sofa and began stretching exercises with his pipe in one hand, while casting a glance at his son Einosuké, back from lunch, who did work that would otherwise be handled by a secretary. He vigorously thrust out his legs and arched his upper trunk. "I've known Tsukioka . . . ever since . . . we were in the same . . . judicial training class . . . The thing about that guy . . . he goes flat . . . doesn't see things though . . . aah . . . OW!" Ishikawa grunted and stroked his lower back. "Went a little too far."

"Are you okay?"

"No, of course not. I'm old. Going on sixty." Ishikawa resumed his exercise, this time moving cautiously. "That wasn't Wakako Ikéhata . . . It was Kotaro Ikéhata . . . that engaged Tsukioka . . . right?"

"That's right. Professor Ikéhata engaged him."

"Tsukioka came out with that . . . non compos mentis stuff . . . because Professor Ikéhata told him to . . . So the quickest solution . . . is talk him out of that defense . . . before you see Tsukioka."

"I'm thinking about seeing the expert witness, Professor Matsuda, first of all. I'd like to ask him about schizophrenia patients' memories and their ability to testify. That's important because it was his diagnosis that was the basis for Mr. Tsukioka's defense."

Ishikawa was on his belly, like a grasshopper, rotating his butt with both legs extended. His pipe smoldered throughout the exercise. Take a breath, twist, puff smoke. He executed this cycle a dozen or more times, looking like a wind-up novelty toy. When he finished his stretching exercise, he sat up on the sofa facing Akutsu.

"You're going to ask questions about schizophrenia? Do you know anything about psychiatry?"

"Not a thing," Akutsu said, the tip of his tongue momentarily visible. "But I'm going to study about it, starting now."

"'Starting now.' I see." Ishikawa said, rolling his eyes. He ran a comb through his hair, but it stubbornly resisted discipline, standing defiantly at haphazard angles.

Akutsu returned to his desk and began reading the hefty report on Wakako

Ikéhata's psychiatric analysis. It followed the standard format for such reports used as evidence in criminal trials: family history, personal history, psychological state at the time the crime was committed, present psychological state, diagnosis, analysis and "main text," i.e., the conclusion. It was no easy read, with its extensive use of specialist jargon, but it was nevertheless quite interesting because it contained records of question-and-answer sessions with the defendant and her family members, and included informative notes on the speakers' gestures and facial expressions.

Akutsu read, underlining unfamiliar terminology and passages that raised questions in his mind. When he arrived at the main text section that presented the diagnosis in summary, he fell to pondering. From the portrait of Wakako Ikéhata that emerged in the report, she could easily be taken for an ordinary young woman, if it were not for a sudden emphasis on her abnormal aspects when it came to her diagnosis. At least, it seemed that way to Akutsu.

Akutsu didn't have any particular knowledge about schizophrenia beyond what he knew from popular books on psychology and general interest articles. Now he decided he would have to do some serious reading of specialist texts, then go back and decide what to make of this expert witness report.

Ishikawa called him into his office. "Yessir?"

"I have some books on psychiatry for you." Ishikawa pushed a stack of books at him. They were all specialist works: *Clinical Psychiatry, Schizophrenia, Psychiatric Assessment, Introduction to Criminal Psychiatry*, etc. They were exactly the kinds of books Akutsu had been thinking he wanted to read.

"If this isn't enough, go to the T. University medical library. It has a full collection of books and journals. It would be worthwhile to have a look at Professor Matsuda's latest papers too."

"Well, thank you . . ." Akutsu began, but Ishikawa abruptly turned his attention elsewhere and hustled away. The next instant he had picked up a telephone just as it began to ring, before his son could react, and began speaking into it, casting a meaningful glance as he did so at a young lawyer who had approached.

Seated at his desk in the busy law office, Akutsu began reading his reference books. He was still at it late at night when he recalled something he had been told by his childhood friend, Tetsukichi Jinnai.

"I don't know the first thing about what this psychiatrist's report has to do with that bombing. But Professor Matsuda knows better than anybody that girl Wakako had nothing to do with it. She kept her mouth shut straight through in front of the police and the prosecutor and that lawyer too, but for some reason, she told the truth to Professor Matsuda."

Once he began a research project, it was Akutsu's nature to follow through to its natural end, without cutting corners. The texts occupied him fully through all of Saturday and Sunday. By Monday, he had finished reading the books Ishikawa had lent him. He visited the T. University Medical library on Monday and searched out papers by Professor Matsuda that had appeared in magazines. He made a careful reading of two — *Crimes Committed by Schizophrenic Patients*, and *Mental Disorders and Criminal Responsibility*. With this preparation, he made a telephone call to Professor Matsuda to request a meeting.

On Tuesday afternoon, the fourth day since his visit to Y. Hospital, Akutsu was in the faculty room of the N. Medical University Criminal Psychiatry lecture room. Most of the wall space was taken up by shelves holding massive volumes of specialized technical literature in criminology and psychiatry from domestic and foreign publishers. There were imposing steel book cabinets as well, filled with reference materials.

Professor Matsuda's hair was thinning. He had a round face and old-fashioned, round eye-glasses. Although he had told Akutsu that he would have no particular business during the time period allotted for their meeting, they were interrupted by someone who seemed to be an assistant with information to convey, a secretary with papers needing approval and a telephone call from a newspaper asking for a comment about some crime. Akutsu got to the point quickly, thinking his best bet with such a busy person would be with the questions he had prepared in advance.

"Professor, do you believe that Wakako Ikéhata was not involved with the crime?"

"Well, that is what she told me." Professor Matsuda said warily.

"What do you think about that statement?"

"What do I think of it? I am not a judge and so I would like to reserve judgment."

"Well, you did say in court that you recognize the defendant's statement as true."

"Yes, I did, but . . ."

"The prosecutor completely denied the truth of her statement, the judges concurred and she was found guilty."

"The whole thing is appalling, completely."

"Yes, appalling. I believe the shortest route to winning a not guilty decision will be to prove in court that she was telling the truth. I am here today as the attorney for Atsuo Yukimori and Yukichi Jinnai, to request your assistance."

"Have you spoken with her Attorney, Mr. Tsukioka?"

"Not yet. I thought it best to visit you first to ask some questions about what she told you, and then check that against the facts of the case before discussing matters with Mr. Tsukioka."

Professor Matsuda frowned. A tiny bead of sweat glistened at the side of his nose. "I must tell you that Mr. Tsukioka has told me not to say anything about what Wakako Ikéhata told me while I was examining her. You see, Yukichi Jinnai's older brother had come to visit me, and he asked me what relationship there had been between Yukichi and her. I told him she had said there was never any relationship between them. That made Mr. Tsukioka extremely angry. He said that if the prosecutor knew that, he would use it to make it look like everything she said was a lie."

"There isn't anything in your report about her and Yukichi. In fact, there is very little about her relationship with Atsuo Yukimori."

"That is because Mr. Tsukioka's position is that Wakako Ikéhata was sick, that Atsuo Yukimori was manipulating her and that she was only being used by the Q. Sect." Professor Matsuda seemed abashed, like a child caught in the act of a naughty deed.

"I don't think those arguments are enough to undermine that fantasy story spun by the prosecution. Why? Because Wakako Ikéhata had a relationship with the Q. Sect, and she had a relationship with Atsuo Yukimori, too. That's right, her relationship with him was of her own choice. Your report does not contain much about her recollections of that."

"Well that comes down to what Mr. Tsukioka . . ."

"Professor, Wakako Ikéhata and Atsuo Yukimori had a very close relationship. They were in love with one another. That is a beautiful kind of relationship, wouldn't you say? For Mr. Tsukioka to define that relationship as an ex-con with a radical agenda using sex to seduce a young woman away from a life of luxury — that is a ridiculous distortion of the facts. They were two people of a single mind. That is why it is necessary to prove Atsuo Yukimori's innocence, in order to prove Wakako Ikéhata's innocence. I have found indisputable proof of Atsuo Yukimori's alibi for the day of the crime. Here it is."

Akutsu displayed the photograph and explained how it had been obtained. "Then this means . . ."

"Yes, it is just as you see. It means Atsuo Yukimori did not commit the crime. Therefore, Wakako Ikéhata was not involved in it either. What she told you was the truth. And she has not given any other testimony. As things stand now, your report contains her only affirmation of her own innocence. But you have heard a great deal more of her statements than what appears in your report. I would like to know what she said. That will enable me to prove that Atsuo Yukimori and Yukichi Jinnai are not guilty of the crime, and doing so will reflect right back on the truth of Wakako Ikéhata's own statements."

"Well, nevertheless, the fact remains that Mr. Tsukioka is her attorney."

"He is not her attorney. He is the attorney that Professor Ikéhata assigned to her. She never once gave any indication in court that she wanted Mr. Tsukioka to conduct her defense. How could any attorney provide an adequate defense under those circumstances? Professor, I would like for you to consider this question as an expert in psychiatry and criminology, and just don't worry about what Mr. Tsukioka thinks."

"'That is all very well for you to say."

"Professor, you undertook Ms. Ikéhata's examination at Mr. Tsukioka's request. You fulfilled that mission, and the first decision has been handed down. I think at this stage there is no reason for you to refrain from expressing your own views as a free individual. There is good reason for you to speak out, because it is very much in Ms. Ikéhata's interest for you to do so.

"You diagnosed her as schizophrenic. According to your findings, the first condition of that nature she exhibited is described as a 'self-odor delusion,' that appeared while she was attending a private school to prepare for university entrance exams. Then, soon after starting as a student in the science department of R. University, she found herself unable to attend classes. By that time, your diagnosis was that she was clearly manifesting abulic-autistic tendencies, and she progressively fell into a delusion of persecution."

"That is correct. There are full details of that progression in my report."

"I have read it. Now, I think that even after Ms. Ikéhata's disorder appeared, there were still periods when she could be regarded as normal." Akutsu looked deep into the professor's round eyeglasses.

"Normal? No, she had schizophrenia all along."

"Yes, she did. I got the idea that might nevertheless be true by reading your paper 'Crimes Committed by Schizophrenic Patients.' It says that schizophrenia has active phases in which the condition worsens, and passive phases, like a tide that rises and ebbs."

"Oh," Professor Matsuda gave a start of surprise and smiled in a way that clearly showed favor toward his visitor. "You read that."

"Yes, as I understand your thesis, symptoms of schizophrenia have changed in recent years, most notably since the high-growth era, in the sixties. They tend not to exhibit the 'first rank systems' set out by Kurt Schneider, like audition of thought, auditory hallucinations, thought withdrawal, passivity experiences or delusion of control. To borrow your terminology, 'non-standard' or 'broken-form' symptoms have become common, and at the same time there has been an increase in non-standard, manic-depressive-like cases that are diagnosed as only showing abnormal symptoms during the active phase, while they return to normal at other times."

"I see you read carefully. That is quite correct."

"And could you say that Wakako Ikéhata belongs to the new types of schizophrenia, or at least that she is a 'non-standard' type?"

"Yes, one could say that. It would be reasonable."

"I see. That point was not strongly emphasized in the report. I think that was a natural consideration at the time, when Mr. Tsukioka was strongly arguing a non compos mentis theory. The judges don't know anything about psychiatry. They wouldn't have understood about schizophrenia, much less the concept of it taking non-standard forms."

"You have quite a good understanding of psychiatry. Do you have a medical background?"

"No, no" Akutsu reddened with embarrassment. "I studied law. That was just from a surge of reading over the past three days."

"To get that accurate an understanding in three days . . . There are some medical students I would like to have following your example."

"If Ms. Ikéhata was a non-standard case of schizophrenia, couldn't it be said that outside of the times her condition required hospitalization that she was normal? For example, that she was normal in January 1969, around the day of the tower, or February 11th, when the bomb exploded, or when she was traveling in Hokkaido? To put it more exactly, could you say that when she participated in a demonstration and fell in love with Atsuo Yukimori she was acting on her own normal volition?"

"Yes, you could." Professor Matsuda was listening with narrowed his eyes, and he nodded repeatedly, as if to acknowledge that Akutsu's reasoning was undermining his own courtroom testimony.

"The problem is the issue of her silence after her arrest. You testified that it was not a willful refusal to speak, but a kind of selective mutism that was a symptom of schizophrenia. Your report contains a similar observation, but wasn't that a slight exaggeration for the sake of emphasizing that her present condition was abnormal? The prosecutor seized on that to unilaterally declare that her condition made her incompetent to testify, and therefore her declaration of her own innocence was meaningless."

"Yes, that was meaningful testimony, but, unfortunately, it served no useful purpose." Professor Matsuda nodded twice.

"In order to make it serve a useful purpose, she has to have been normal all during the time after her arrest, including when you examined her. She needn't be completely normal. All we have to do is show that she was competent to give testimony. You deal with that issue in 'Mental Disorders and Criminal Responsibility.' That paper clearly states that there is a difference between criminal responsibility and competence to give testimony. The example you give is that a child under fourteen years of age has no criminal responsibility, but would still be competent as a witness to a murder. The same principle could apply to Wakako Ikéhata. Her statements to you can be used just as they are as viable evidence of her innocence. The thing to keep in mind, however, is that presenting this in court means we will have to arrange for her to respond to the prosecutor's cross-examination so that her statements won't be just hearsay, but will have the same probative value as a confession."

"Does this raise a possibility of her winning a not-guilty decision?" Professor Matsuda, asked, as if the question was for himself as much as Akutsu. Then he sank into thought, while Akutsu waited patiently. Finally, Professor Matsuda spoke again.

"If her statements can be used to her benefit, I will show them to you. Some of the recordings have still not been transcribed, so some of the material is not in order . . . But there are two conditions. For the sake of future trial strategy, Mr. Tsukioka must give his approval. In addition, this material contains a great deal of private information. Wakako Ikéhata herself must also approve."

"Understood," Akutsu said, realizing there was no possibility of making further demands. "I will come to visit again after those two conditions have been met."

The next day, Akutsu paid a visit to the Tsukioka Law Office in Yotsuya at ten in the morning, to confer with Tsukioka. The Ishikawa Law Office could not compare to this spacious, well-lit office that occupied the entire first floor of the building. Several female secretaries were busy operating Japanese typewriters and copy machines. From the looks of the array of desks, more than ten salaried attorneys like Akutsu were employed here. The atmosphere suggested a trading company or a travel agency. Akutsu had called to make his appointment, but there were people waiting ahead of him. Akutsu was ushered in to one of several reception rooms. After a time, he heard hurried footsteps and Tsukioka, short and plump, appeared in the doorway.

"So sorry to keep you waiting! Do have something to drink. Coffee, tea, oolong tea? Or how about a beer?"

Akutsu asked for coffee, and Tsukioka picked up a bell from the table, rang it and a young woman appeared. Tsukioka gave her the order.

"This bell was a present from a group of American lawyers who came to visit last year. They said Indians use them for communication. I've never seen anything quite like it. Well, now . . ." Tsukioka abruptly quit talking and gazed at Akutsu from behind his lightly tinted glasses.

But before Akutsu could announce his reason for visiting, Tsukioka again began talking effusively.

"Ishikawa was telling me all about you the last time I met him at the Judicial Institute class reunion. He had nothing but praise. He said you're more enthusiastic than anyone. Enthusiasm is a good thing. We have a lot of young people here, but they are not very aggressive. You have to get them all set up before they will even move. Well, of course, it's Ishikawa's style to let his people do their thing. That's why they call him 'the sleeping lion.' Having your people run the whole operation — I don't know about that. But anyway, about your proposal on the telephone that we make a joint defense . . . If that is what you want, I'm more than happy to listen. It's just that . . . I'm sure you know, there are a number of problems that would get in the way if we tried going at it together. Do you understand that?"

Akutsu kept quiet instead of answering. He guessed Tsukioka would go on talking, and his expectations were met as Tsukioka launched into self-justifying polemic.

"First of all is the issue of the client's feelings. Kotaro Ikéhata hates Atsuo Yukimori because his confession got his daughter arrested. As far as he is concerned, joining with the attorney for Atsuo Yukimori is out of the question. Secondly, Wakako Ikéhata hasn't spoken yet, and she may not be speaking in the future either. She didn't say a word to me throughout the entire first trial. Of course, she has every right to keep quiet, but there is a major problem with a defendant who won't even say she's innocent, who won't even defend herself. I don't think your joining the defense will improve the situation. I hate to say it, but I don't think a young fellow like you will be able to handle someone like Wakako Ikéhata.

"Problem number three is how to deal with the lawyers for the Q. Sect. That might be the biggest problem of all. As you know, the Q. Sect members confessed to being accessories to Atsuo Yukimori's crime, but at the trial they switched to claiming innocence. Their lawyers said Atsuo Yukimori and Wakako Ikéhata did it by themselves and the Q. Sect had nothing to do with it. They care about the Q. Sect and don't care what happens to anyone outside of it. If you try to mount a joint defense for Yukimori, Ikéhata and Jinnai only while you're at odds with the Q. Sect, that is not going to amount to an adequate defense. This case is about as troublesome as they get. To be honest, I've got my own doubts about it. I would have parted with it long ago if it wasn't for my friendship with Professor Ikéhata."

Akutsu had been listening carefully to all this. He gave a slight nod, as is customary to do before the judges in a courtroom as a sign of respect, and began speaking at the same rapid pace Tsukioka had taken.

"Difficulties number one and number three have the same roots. Both Professor Ikéhata and the lawyers for the Q. Sect think that if Atsuo Yukimori committed the crime, or, even better, if he is the sole principal offender, that diminishes the responsibility of Wakako Ikéhata and the three Q. Sect defendants. That is why they refused to mount a joint defense. But if there is decisive proof that Atsuo Yukimori did not commit the crime, then the way is open for a joint defense on the grounds that all the defendants are innocent. Very well. Here is the decisive proof." Akutsu took out his photograph from his briefcase.

Tsukioka took one look at the photograph, sprang to his feet and began pacing the length of the room, back and forth, taking tiny steps and reversing direction when he reached a wall.

"This is Atsuo Yukimori. The plum trees are in full bloom. Looks like a holiday, with all those people. Is this a picture of him in Jindai Botanical Garden, like he says? If it all fits, this is quite a discovery. Who took the picture and when?"

"The picture was taken by a woman in charge of recreational therapy at Y. Hospital. That hospital is near Jindai Botanical Garden. The date is February 11, 1969. The time is between three thirty and four in the afternoon. I met the woman and got a verifiable statement. Nurses took the patients plum blossom viewing that day. The outing is recorded in the hospital diary."

"Hot damn! This is getting interesting." Tsukioka quivered while he beheld the picture in his hand, as if he might begin to dance. "This is new evidence, and it can break down the prosecution's story of the crime! . . . You know, I'm embarrassed to admit it, but I had doubts about Atsuo Yukimori right up to this very moment. That had me doubting Wakako Ikéhata too. As her lawyer, I argued for her innocence, but, you know, when you have doubts in your own mind, that is bound to take the edge off what you are saying. So I let that smart-ass prosecutor roll right over me." Tsukioka reddened with excitement and stamped his feet, looking far younger than a man approaching sixty.

"Getting to difficulty number two," Akutsu continued in a level tone. "Don't you think you could get Ms. Ikéhata to break her silence and testify in court if you told her that new evidence has been discovered, and persuaded her that, by giving testimony, she could benefit Mr. Yukimori? She loves him ... My understanding is that she said precisely that to Professor Matsuda. There is an enormous amount of material from his examination of Ms. Ikéhata that he did not use in the report submitted to the judges. It seems the extra material includes her confession about her relationship with Mr. Yukimori, in explicit detail.

"Now, there is another thing I heard from Professor Matsuda. Her silence was not a case of selective mutism related to schizophrenia. In other words, it wasn't abnormal and it didn't have to do with mental disease. She was mentally normal. She was keeping quiet of her own free will."

"Her own free will? ... Look, she didn't come out and declare in court she's innocent. She had any number of chances to do that."

"I think that's because of her distrust of organizations. According to the report on her psychiatric examination, she has her own concept of organizations and a strong aversion to them. It isn't a case of not wanting to talk to individuals. She doesn't want to talk to any person she sees as a representative of an organization. Policemen, prosecutors, and judges all fit the description. As far as she is concerned, a courtroom is just a stage play where the organization makes up any rules it pleases for judging people."

"Even so, refusing to talk to her own lawyer only creates trouble."

Yes, Akutsu was thinking. That fact that she sees you as one more organization tool is a major problem. She won't talk to you because she doesn't trust you.

Tsukioka returned the photograph to Akutsu and ceremoniously seated himself on a ludicrously big sofa that made his small form seem child sized.

"Be that as it may, this single photograph is going to turn the whole damn trial around. I'll hand it to you — this is a coup. Now we have to all get together and use this as a lever to get a not guilty decision for all the defendants. You are quite right that all the defendants should be together on this. And that takes us right to the three problems I mentioned. Number one, I will have a talk with Professor Ikéhata. He'll come around when he sees we are talking about freeing his daughter. Number two is Wakako Ikéhata. Would you please talk to her? I'll get Professor Ikéhata to agree to you being on the defense team, so please go visit her at the detention center. Number three is the Q. Sect lawyers. There is a question whether we can get them in on this as easily as you may be expecting.

It is not a done deal that we will all be marching in step . . . I've had nothing but difficulties with them."

"That story about the Q. Sect doing the planning and Mr. Yukimori and Ms. Ikéhata carrying it out is just a fantasy the police and the prosecutor made up. If those two didn't commit the crime, there won't be any way to tie Q. Sect to it anymore. There is certainly every reason we should be able to have a joint defense."

"Yeah, we should, but when it comes to those guys, all bets are off." Tsukioka leaped from the sofa and again began pacing the room restlessly. "As I said, they don't think in terms of the interests of people outside the Q. Sect. They see you and me as outsiders, not fellow lawyers, because they consider themselves revolutionaries. They call us 'bourgeois lawyers.' They have their own supporters. There is a group called the 'Shinkansen Bomb Defendants Support Committee.' Many of its members are hardcore radicals. It's bitterly critical of the defense."

"It might have been in the Q. Sect's interest for Mr. Yukimori and Ms. Ikéhata to have been the culprits, but now there is proof that they aren't. The situation has changed. If the defense gets together on the line that the charges against all the defendants are false, ordinary people will start agreeing with the support group. There won't be any need to draw lines around Q. Sect members for exclusive support."

"Well, maybe I'm stuck in the past." Tsukioka stopped pacing and folded his arms. Then he cocked his head to the side like a rooster. "You're a believer in movements and citizen participation, aren't you? That makes sense, coming from someone of your generation. When did you graduate from the university?"

"1968."

"That puts you in the Joint Struggle generation."

"The beginning of it. I guess the C. University Struggle was starting at the time. But I was a non-political student, so . . ."

"Well, anyway, we will have to be very careful about how we deal with that third issue, if we want to get around it. Let's just pray this new evidence puts things on the right track for us."

Tsukioka excused himself at that point, explaining that he had another visitor waiting. He saw Akutsu off to the exit.

As he often did, Akutsu took a stroll through the Kanda bookstore district on his way back to the Ishikawa Law Office in Shimbashi. The neighborhood had been the scene of raucous student demonstrations for two or three years, but now it was as quiet as it always had been in years past, a special place when men and women placidly browsed the shops in search of old books. But the scene nevertheless bore dismal black scars where the old-time paving stones of the sidewalks had been replaced by asphalt, lest they be dug out for use as weapons against riot police during demonstrations.

Akutsu still belonged to the same generation as the students he saw, carefree in their blue jeans, but his own business suit and necktie gave him the feeling he had abruptly aged. He stopped into a law book specialty shop he often frequented, where he leafed through the revised version of Kotaro Ikéhata's *Code of Criminal Procedures*. Not long ago, he had studied it carefully, as required reading for students facing the national bar examination. Now, as a lawyer with one year of experience, he already understood how far it diverged from the realities of legal practice.

For example, Article 319 of the CCP provided that "Confession under compulsion, torture, threat, after unduly prolonged detention, or when there is doubt about it being voluntary may not be admitted as evidence." Professor Ikéhata praised the article as the product of postwar democratization that emphasized the protection of human rights, but he failed to mention anything about how the law actually works in practice. The unjust, unlawful interrogation the defendants in the Shinkansen bombing case had undergone under police detention were but one glaring example of that contrast. Evidently, long years shut up in his university office poring over law books had allowed him to lose sight of the real world.

Article 37.2 of the Constitution says, "The accused shall be permitted full opportunity to examine all witnesses." Professor Ikéhata explained that this provision guaranteed the right to cross-examine; statements not subject to cross-examination are treated as hearsay evidence having no probative value. Outside the books, in actual criminal trials, judges do not place high value on cross-examination. They commonly admit evidence from prosecutors not subject to cross examination — confession statements that have the blessing of CCP 321.2 as "documents containing statements given before a public prosecutor." Professor Ikéhata's writings paid no attention at all to the yawning gap between the provisions of the law and the way it is practiced.

The date of the book's last revision was April first of this year. That placed it after the defendants in the Shinkansen bombing case had been subjected to numerous instances of unlawful interrogation that were fully supported by the prosecutor and judges at their trial. Despite outrages that reached into the bosom of his own family, Professor Ikéhata was still touting the law's respect for human rights. Feeling pity toward old ways of thinking, Akutsu replaced the new edition on the shelf. Then he remembered his original intention in coming to Kanda had been to visit the shop where Atsuo Yukimori had been employed.

Fukawa Motors' gas station caught the eyes of passersby with arrays of triangular multicolored flags that fluttered ostentatiously, like a display of national flags at a sports stadium. Young people in army fatigues moved about briskly, shouting welcomes to customers as they arrived and thank-yous as they left.

Akutsu walked over to the pay parking lot. He went through the entrance and located the car maintenance shop. From the corner of his eye Akutsu took in a couple of cars resting on lifts and assorted grease-covered machine parts as he strode to a door that displayed a plastic sign marked "Employees Dormitory." He had intended to ring the bell, but the door was half open, so he stepped inside and called to a woman in working kimono washing dishes at a kitchen sink.

"Excuse me, is Ms. Sonoko Kanéhara here?"

The woman turned and regarded him with a look that said, "What are you selling?"

"What is your business with Ms. Kanéhara?"

"Please forgive me for barging in. Actually, I'm the attorney for Mr. Atsuo Yukimori. There is a private matter I would like to discuss with Ms. Kanéhara."

The woman had begun drying her stack of dishes. Both her hairdo and dress were neat and sober. She accepted Akutsu's business card, rested it on a dishcloth, read it, and took a good look at him. She said in a low, secretive tone, "I'm Kanéhara. What is it you want to talk about?"

Akutsu whispered back to her, "There is new evidence that proves conclusively Mr. Yukimori is innocent."

"All right. This is not a good place to discuss that. Come inside. It's almost lunch time, and the boys will be coming back."

She showed him to the dorm mother's room. It was a spacious eight-tatami room filled with the fragrance of an arrangement of white blossoms in the tokonoma. Akutsu sat upon a zabuton cushion at a tea table across from Sonoko Kanéhara

"What a lovely fragrance. What are those flowers?"

Sonoko Kanéhara gave a short gasp of surprise at the young man's ignorance. "Why, they are freesia," she said with a patient smile.

"Oh, yes, I do recognize the name."

"You know all about the law, but not so much about flowers, I see."

"Yes, not a thing about flowers. I'm from Hokkaido, you see. I suppose I know a little bit about north country flowers, but certainly nothing about flowers in Tokyo."

"Freesia come from Africa . . . Mmm, Hokkaido! I wonder if you're from the same town as Mr. Yukimori."

"That's right, I am. We are both from Nemuro."

"For goodness sake. And is that why you took his case?"

"That's part of it. You see, I was in the same class in elementary school and middle school as the older brother of Yukichi Jinnai, who also worked at Fukawa Motors."

"Really? Isn't that something! You know, Mr. Yukimori and Mr. Jinnai were both good people. Then that crazy thing happened. It is all beyond me."

"I'm also defending Yukichi. They're both completely innocent of the charges, and now there is full proof of Mr. Yukimori's alibi. I would like to request your kind cooperation in corroborating that proof."

"I would be happy to help! But why me?"

"Because, in reading through all the trial records, I saw that your testimony showed the most goodwill toward Mr. Yukimori and Mr. Jinnai."

"You are so right!" Sonoko Kanéhara's eyes darted meaningfully toward the maintenance shop and gas station outside. "As soon as they were arrested everyone else had nothing but bad things to say about them, even the ones who had been their good friends. I'll say this just between us, because it's your job as a lawyer to keep people's secrets. The worst of all was the company president."

"Mr. Ichiro Fukawa."

"Right. This company started off as a small repair garage with Fukawa, two mechanics and me as the only employees. It grew into a business doing vehicle inspection and maintenance work, with a pay parking lot and a filling station, all thanks to Mr. Yukimori's hard work. Besides knowing all about machine tools, he has a sharp sense of how to run a sales business. He has the build for working with heavy machines, and he's the hardest worker you'll find anywhere. He was an NCO in the army and he had what it takes to lead our young people. That is how we got to where we are today. In three or four years we built up a crew seven, eight times the number we started with. He was our number one achiever, and what does the boss do? Fires him, and then, when he gets arrested, has nothing but bad things to say about him. Says he built that barricade to give the radical students a hideout, that he only pretended to like hunting so he'd have a way to get gunpowder. That is all wrong! He built the barricade to protect our customer's cars, and he liked hunting because his father was a hunter. The boss likes hunting too, and thanks to Mr. Yukimori, he had many enjoyable hunting trips to Hokkaido. Then he turns around and treats him that way . . . But, no, the boss wasn't the worst. Someone else outdid his underhandedness — Kimiko Fujiyama!" Sonoko Kanéhara shifted in her seat and leaned forward.

471

"She was the president's secretary and clerk, right?"

"Yes, you really know the facts of the case. She is simply what you would call a bad woman. Married, with children and middle aged, she came in and seduced the boss."

"Hmmm. What is the situation now?"

"Just listen, it's a disgraceful story!" Sonoko Kanéhara was on the edge of her seat now, with both hands on the tea table. "Since Mr. Yukimori was fired, she has been carrying on with his replacement, a man named Tatsuro Shiomi."

"'Tatsuro Shiomi.' You didn't mention him in your testimony."

"That's right. He doesn't know anything about Mr. Yukimori. He became the foreman after Mr. Yukimori. He is just under thirty, single, a good man. That Kimiko, with all her lard, and aged forty-something — she managed to seduce him. Of course, the boss was jealous. He blew his top and there was a scene, but he can't fire the man. Shiomi is a computer expert. With all the electronic this, electronic that devices they put in today's cars, we can't do maintenance without him. Well, Kimiko quit working here and moved in with Shiomi. She left her husband and children to live with a man ten years younger. What do you think of that?"

"If they like one another, there isn't much to say about it."

"It isn't a case of their liking one another. Mr. Yukimori was the one Kimiko really liked. I know that for a fact."

Sonoko Kanéhara seemed overjoyed having Akutsu to hear her out. She continued as if transported, her eyes luminous.

"Kimiko was taken with Mr. Yukimori. I could sense it, being a woman myself. Kimiko would become agitated when Mr. Yukimori came into the office. Her eyes would light up. That's a very exceptional way to react when someone simply walks into a room. But Mr. Yukimori greatly disliked Kimiko. He wasn't about to take up on any advances from her. So at some point she started hating Mr. Yukimori. You know, it's my opinion that Kimiko is behind those two thefts of money that were blamed on Mr. Jinnai. Pinning a robbery on him was a way to strike out at his uncle, Mr. Yukimori, because he was the one who got Mr. Jinnai his job at Fukawa Motors. It amazes me that the police never suspected Kimiko. I thought it was very peculiar that the boss didn't report the thefts to the police, so I went to the nearest police box and did it myself. As soon as I did, all of a sudden the boss announces he found the money. That was a lie to cover up for Kimiko. The truth is that money never did turn up, and Mr. Jinnai was arrested for it. That is the absolute truth. You're a lawyer. Would you please check into this and expose Kimiko's crime? She's the one who told the detectives that Mr. Yukimori was behind that bombing when they came around questioning us. She had just come back from Hokkaido, where she got into a big argument with Mr. Jinnai's father and she had already stolen that four hundred thousand yen. She saw it a golden opportunity to pin crimes on Mr. Yukimori and Mr. Jinnai, and the boss went right along with it, as he always did when it came to doing what Kimiko wanted . . ."

There was no sign that Sonoko Kanéhara would finish any time soon. She seemed to have forgotten the purpose of Akutsu's visit in her preoccupation with vilifying Kimiko Fujiyama. Akutsu was thinking, "This woman is in love with Atsuo Yukimori." When he thought the time was right, he took out his revealing photograph. Sonoko regarded it ardently.

"It's Mr. Yukimori! And so young-looking! He was looking so much older in court. Yes, I didn't miss a single hearing."

"Do you know when this picture was taken?"

"I certainly do. The duster coat is English made, by Chester Barrie. He was proud of it. The polka-dot necktie is Italian, by Angelo Litrico. This was taken the day he was fired."

"Do you remember the pattern of the tie?" Sonoko glared at Akutsu as if offended.

"I should remember it. I gave it to him as a present for his forty-eighth birthday. It made me happy that he was wearing it on that last day. I was the last person he went to see before he left. I told him just wait, I'll start a petition against your dismissal, but he just said, 'Thanks for everything' and left." Sonoko was holding back tears.

"If he was wearing this outfit on that day. Mr. Yukimori has an airtight alibi. He was in this park right at the time that explosion occurred."

"Of course he would have an alibi. There's no way he committed that crime. That poor man, sentenced to death. It's just too much." Sonoko's face wrinkled up and she began to sob. At the same moment, sounds of doors opening and closing and the shop workers in conversation were heard, meaning the lunch hour had begun. Someone appeared at the door.

"Hey mom, got a minute?"

"Go away! I have an important visitor just now." Sonoko dismissed him in a shrill voice. Akutsu waited as she dabbed at her eyes and the crying subsided.

"Can I count on you as a witness?"

"Of course."

"Please keep this photograph an absolute secret until I submit it to the court as new evidence. We don't want the prosecutor to know about it ahead of time."

473

"That's no problem," Sonoko answered with a red-eyed laugh. "I never have much to say. I'm the silent type."

As Akutsu was being escorted by Sonoko to the workshop door, a pair of men talking and laughing looked over at them. One was balding and portly, with the look of a sea lion. The other had a prominent nose, suggestive of a fox. Sonoko informed Akutsu it was the company president and Tatsuro Shiomi.

"Hey, Sonoko!" Ichiro Fukawa called out boisterously. Few would have taken him for a company president. "I was just about to go looking for you."

"Oh, no, not when I look like this," Sonoko muttered, annoyed. But the next moment she was beaming smiles at the company president as he approached.

"Got a new boy for the dorm. He's nineteen, from Yamagata."

"I told you we're full. We've got three men in two-man rooms as it is."

"Try to fit him as best you can. He's a good kid. High school grad and a year of maintenance experience. He's from Shiomi's hometown."

Ichiro Fukawa stared openly at Akutsu, then turned back to Shiomi. The shop foreman gave an exaggerated bow to Sonoko.

"Oh, well, if he's from Mr. Shiomi's hometown, we'll just have to shoehorn him in somewhere." The foreman smiled broadly and bowed once again.

Sonoko introduced Akutsu to Ichiro Fukawa. "He's a lawyer. He's handling Mr. Yukimori's defense."

Fukawa's face turned suspicious, as if to ask what sort of individual the said Yukimori might be.

"He says they have found Mr. Yukimori has an air-tight alibi. He wasn't in Tokyo Station at all. He was in a park, and they have a picture that shows it. There's no mistake about it. The picture shows the necktie and the duster coat he was wearing that day."

Akutsu had been desperately sending Sonoko eye signals intended to shut her up, but she triumphantly retold everything she had heard.

"No kidding? There's a picture?" Fukawa asked Akutsu.

"That's right," Akutsu confirmed with composure. "Decisive proof of Mr. Atsuo Yukimori's innocence has been found."

"That's good to hear," Fukawa said, rubbing a belly that protruded like a volley ball. "This is a big deal as far as we are concerned. If there is anything we want, it's for him to be found innocent. We have been losing business ever since he was arrested."

"He's wearing a tie I gave him in the picture. It shows up clearly," Sonoko added proudly.

Sunlight falling on her hair showed traces of white, revealing it had been dyed. "The necktie he was wearing that day?" Shiomi asked.

"That's right," Sonoko said happily, after flashing a look at Akutsu. "It's Italian, by Angelo Litrico. I gave it to him for Valentine's Day."

Sonoko seemed to have forgotten that she had called it a birthday present a moment before. This raised anxiety for Akutsu. Such slips in detail would be easy targets for a prosecutor's impeachment of a witness. He decided to get this point straight.

"It was a present for Valentine Day and not his birthday?" he asked. Sonoko seemed startled, but she answered emphatically.

"That was a memory slip. It was for February 14th, Valentine's Day. The day everything happened was February 11th, right? Suddenly he was fired, the poor man, so I rushed to give him the necktie I had bought for him and he said, well, this is goodbye, so I'll put it on now. I'll never forget how sad he looked. Hey, boss, what did you fire him for? That's how he got to be a suspect in that bombing."

"The firing's got nothing to do with the bombing," Fukawa said testily.

"No, it has a lot to do with it," Sonoko said, with startling lack of delicacy. She may have wanted to demonstrate her own influence with the president to Shiomi.

"If you hadn't fired him he would have worked all that day and that would have been a perfect alibi. He was a suspect because he left at lunchtime. You're the one who sent him off, aren't you?"

"No I didn't. I said he could work through the end of March. He decided to leave on his own."

"You had no business talking to him the way you did. You tell him out of the blue he's fired. That's cold blooded. You were talking to the one who made Fukawa Motors what it is! Then you fired him in one breath. It's inhuman, that's what it is!" Sonoko pounded her fist against Fukawa's chest and began to cry. Shop workers and customers outside in the parking lot stood still at the startling emotion-filled outcry. Fukawa stepped aside with an embarrassed grin. When Shiomi approached Fukawa protectively, she glared at him, and shouted with abandon. "Kimiko's the real troublemaker! That woman stole money and set up someone else to take the blame. You tell her something! Tell her that when Mr. Yukimori and Mr. Jinnai get out, she is the one who will be hauled up for an accounting!"

"Now Sonoko, calm down," Fukawa said placatingly. "We shouldn't be upsetting our guest."

"Excuse me," Akutsu said with a bow to all and left the parking lot. The story about the tie being a Valentine's Day gift was awkward. If Yukimori put on the tie for the very first time just before he was fired, that invalidated the landlady's story that she had seen him wearing it that morning.

It was past one in the afternoon when Akutsu returned to the Ishikawa Law Office. Acting secretary Einosuké told him that in his absence there had been four telephone calls from Tsukioka.

"He called four times?"

Startled, Akutsu immediately dialed Tsukioka's office. Tsukioka's voice came booming through the receiver so loudly Akutsu had to hold it well away from his ear to listen.

"Professor Ikéhata just isn't buying it. He says the credibility of that picture is dubious, and even if Yukimori does have an alibi, that doesn't mean anything as long as Wakako doesn't. That's how he sees it. It's within reason."

"No, it's unreasonable," Akutsu said unequivocally. "If Atsuo Yukimori has a firm alibi, the prosecution's argument that he and Wakako Ikéhata committed the crime falls apart."

"Yes, I told him exactly that, but he's still not convinced."

"Look, we've got new evidence on Yukimori. Evidence on Wakako Ikéhata is bound to turn up."

"Well . . . It hasn't turned up yet."

"I think it will, once we've looked for it. We might be able to pick up a hint from what she said about what she was doing that day in the unreleased part of Professor Matsuda's record of her testimony."

"Maybe it's possible something will turn up there. But Professor Ikéhata believes his daughter is crazy and he thinks Yukimori is the number one reason she went crazy. He says the ex-con drove her to it."

"That's nonsense."

"Hold on. There's more to it. He says the ex-con dragged his daughter into his revolutionary plot, then set her up as an accomplice with his phony confession. Now, that doesn't even square with the facts. I did my best to persuade him, but I can't give him a precise explanation why the alibi you found will hold water. That's where the conversation gets complicated. So how about you going to see him and getting him on board?"

"All right, I understand. I'll do that. But before I do, I'm going to see Wakako Ikéhata. There are a few things I absolutely have to ask her about in person. And I want her consent to me reading the entire record of her analysis. Please get in touch with Professor Ikéhata now and tell him to expect my visit within the next two days."

Akutsu put the telephone down and was about to set out for the detention center when he was stopped by Ishikawa, back from lunch and puffing on his pipe.

"I presume that was Tsukioka on the phone and he was telling you all about how stubborn that Professor Ikéhata is. I talked to him when he called for the third time, and he made me listen to a tedious list of reasons why it won't work. But I suspect he neglected to mention to you one of those reasons."

"What might that be?"

"You're too young. The professor and Tsukioka are agreed that it wouldn't be smart to have you holding up one end of a joint defense. It's a lame argument. You can win the case." Ishikawa laid back on the sofa, grasped both calves, bent forward and began his stretching exercises.

Akutsu sat across from Wakako Ikéhata, on the far side of a reinforced glass partition. He had seen that face in numerous newspaper and magazine articles. Most stories featured photos selected to fit with the adjective the media most commonly applied to her — "brazen." But his first impression was of that a prim young woman with long hair. Akutsu introduced himself as Atsuo Yukimori's attorney.

"How is he?" Her large eyes became animated as she asked.

"He's getting along fine. And he's concerned about you. He told me to send you his regards. He's written you many times, but his letters are all banned because of the rules against communications between detainees. He also said he regrets all the trouble this case has caused for you."

"He hasn't caused me any trouble. Organization people put us in this place. Please tell him not to blame himself for that."

"I will give him the message. You seem to be doing well yourself."

"Well enough. I don't get all the exercise I should, but I do have plenty of time to read. When I get tired of reading books, I switch to music scores. Music is fun. I do zazen and practice dancing too. There is more than enough to do, but there's no freedom here, and that does get depressing."

"I have some very good news for you. The fact is, hard proof of Atsuo Yukimori's alibi has been discovered." Akutsu held out his photograph.

"That's him!" She said in a loud voice. Her lively eye movement ceased as she gazed upon the photograph.

"Do you know when this was taken?"

"I think it was around the time he was fired. That coat he's wearing was his favorite."

"What about the necktie?"

"This is the first I've seen it. He prefers more reserved designs. He doesn't go for straight lines and circles. He likes patterns of plants or animals. Polka dots aren't to his taste. I would guess someone gave it to him."

"It was taken the day of the Shinkansen bombing, between three thirty and four in the afternoon, in Jindai Botanical Garden. It firmly establishes Mr. Yukimori's alibi. That means the prosecutor's allegation that you two committed the crime together has collapsed. Now I want to take the next step and prove your alibi."

"My alibi? Does that mean you believe I am innocent?"

"Of course I do. Mr. Yukimori is not the culprit. That fact overturns the decision of the first trial, which found that the crime was committed by a man and a woman acting together. It means you could not have committed the crime either."

"Absolutely?"

"Yes, absolutely."

"I am glad to hear you say that. That other attorney, Mr. Tsukioka — he doesn't believe anything I say. There was no point in even talking to him, so I didn't. Professor Matsuda was open-minded — to a degree, not completely. I told him the simple truth. I had my own reason — I had to know about my own disorder. But tell me something. What is the purpose of your wanting to prove I'm innocent of the charges against me?"

"Because the truth is you are innocent of the charges." Somehow, Akutsu's answer came out in a voice that did not sound confident.

"The truth," Wakako Ikéhata muttered, and her expression filled with anguish, furrows crossing her attractive face.

"In this world, no one can know what the truth is. That is my conclusion from this trial. I didn't do any of those things they said I did. I know I haven't done everything right in my life. Maybe I was some freak from outer space compared to whatever the average girl is supposed to be. But I never had so much as a thought about putting a bomb on a Shinkansen. Organizations will arrest someone like that, put her on trial and give her life in prison because it believes it knows the truth. That is utterly absurd. I kept quiet through it all because organizations always twist people's words around so they mean whatever they want them to mean. What else was there for me to do but keep silent?"

"You kept silent by your own volition."

"Yes."

"But don't you think it would have been better to assert your innocence? As an accused person, you have every right to defend yourself."

"What evidence was there that I could have used to base a claim of innocence? Excuse me, but I have been around law books since I was a baby. I know a good bit more than the average person about how criminal trials work. For one thing, I know there isn't any evidence to prove my alibi."

"Is there really no such evidence? Evidence is something that could be hiding where you least expect it to be. It took a good bit of searching before that picture of Mr. Yukimori turned up. Won't you try to do some deep concentrating on recalling what you were doing on February 11, 1969? All I know comes from your statements in Professor Matsuda's psychiatric analysis report. You leave your apartment in West Shinjuku in the morning, go to the R. University library to read chemistry journals, have lunch in the student cafeteria, and you are back in your apartment at three thirty. In other words, you were in your apartment when the crime was committed, which was somewhere between three thirty and four o'clock."

"That's right up to a point, but I didn't say I returned to my apartment at three thirty."

"Ah-ha! It is quite true the report says no such thing. But Professor Matsuda testified to that in court. That is odd, isn't it?"

Akutsu was mentally running through his recollections of the relevant documents. There was a police officer's examination record from the superintendent of Wakako Ikéhata's apartment building to the effect that she returned to her room that day at about four pm. Professor Matsuda had picked that up from Mr. Tsukioka and given testimony to match it. Akutsu took out his pen and notebook.

"Well, then, about what time did you return to your apartment?"

"I don't know. I don't own a watch — never have. It was well after dark."

"The sun set at 5:17 on February 11th. It must have been past that time. If you can give me a detailed breakdown of what you were doing, starting from before that time, we will know what we need to be looking for. Incidentally, why don't you wear a watch? That's unusual for a student nowadays."

"Is there something strange about a student not wearing a watch?" Wakako blinked at Akutsu inquisitively, as if she could not understand the meaning of his question.

"Well, there are lecture starting times, ending times, exams — all sorts of occasions when you need to know the time, aren't there?"

"Oh, I get you now. I don't need a watch for any of that. A bell rings at the start of lectures and again when the time is up. It's the same for exams. I never need to know in between how much time is left until a session ends."

"How about going to classes? Say you have a lecture in the morning. You must at least have an alarm clock to make sure you get up on time."

"I don't have an alarm clock either. I'm pretty regular about waking up in the morning. If I was still sleepy in the morning for some reason, I wouldn't force myself to go a lecture I probably wouldn't learn much from anyway."

"All right, that makes sense. But still you sometimes have to know the time, like if you've got an appointment to meet someone."

"Just arrange to meet at a place where there's a clock. A train station. A coffee shop. Any public place. There are clocks everywhere. You can't escape them."

Akutsu laughed. "That's a relief. You do consult clocks when the necessity arises."

"Yeah." Wakako giggled. She found it amusing that Akutsu would make such an issue of someone not having a watch.

"Let's get to what you did on February 11th. First, what time did you get up?"

"I don't know. I guess it was still morning, but probably close to noon. At the time, I was leading an outrageous way of life. Dance until late at night, drop acid and fly to the dawn, or whenever. There was no distinction between day and night. So I can't really answer the question, 'What time did I get up?' At any given time, I might have been way up or way down or spaced out."

"Even so, I believe it was morning when you left for R. University."

"I had a custom of strolling through Shinjuku after getting up. So I think I must have been doing that. Wait, I just remembered. I was flashing on some acid I had taken about a week before. The high-rise buildings in west Shinjuku were looking like they were going to collapse, then suddenly they were coming apart and falling to the ground. I could see the expressway was rotting away. A big hole opened up and the cars were falling through it like a meteor swarm. A moment later I was back in the peaceful, normal, boring street. The circuits in my head were shorting out, then connecting again. There was a department store like a monster that would open its mouth and swallow crowds of people, then vomit them back. I guess that was close to noon time. I walked around Shinjuku Station's west exit, the east exit, and up around Shinjuku 3 chōmé. Then I took the subway to Yotsuya and walked to R. University. The idea was to do some reading in the library. Well, it was more like a way to kill time. But that day was a holiday . . . Oh, right, I realized it was National Foundation Day. The library was closed. So I went to the student cafeteria. I was hungry."

"The cafeteria was open on holidays?"

"There are student dorms in the university, so the cafeteria is open on holidays. It was pretty crowded. The first thing you noticed was all the students wearing helmets. In the afternoon I went to Shimizudani Park. It's not far from the campus. I remember there was a rally opposing the revival of National Foundation Day and one guy was screaming through a bullhorn. I didn't see anyone I knew. It looked like there were a lot of students from schools other than R. University. Then I went to the chemistry reading room. It's in a very peculiar place in a basement."

"What do you mean, 'very peculiar?'"

"It isn't a regular one-room library. The books are at one end of a professor's office."

"What's peculiar about that?"

"Not the reading room, but the office. It belongs to Professor Kirikaé, of the physics department. It is not your typical professor's office. If you go to visit, one look will show you what I mean. To begin with, it has almost a hundred old clocks. Professor Kirikaé fished them all out of garbage cans and repaired them. Every one keeps perfect time. So you walk in and hear all those clocks ticking. He has water tanks, supposedly for experiments, but he raises fish in all of them. There are goldfish, carp, crucian carp and trout. There is a big pile of personal seals on the professor's desk. One of his hobbies is carving seals."

"Well, he is a peculiar sort of professor."

"He really is. Besides that, he's a devout Catholic. Oh yes, he came to visit a while back, out of the blue. He believes in my innocence. He prayed a long, long prayer and left."

"Were you on friendly terms with this professor?"

"Very much so. He is popular for his eccentricities. Students come to his office just to hang out. I dropped in frequently myself. He would be there even on holidays. That was why it occurred to me to go down into the basement to visit his office that day."

"About what time was it that you went to that reading room, or should I say professor's office? Or don't you know the time?"

"I know the time. As I said, there are a hundred clocks in that room. All the chimes and cuckoo clocks sound the hour together. It is lovely music. There are students who come just to hear it. I got there just before one o'clock, and the first thing I heard was the one o'clock hour sound. Then I started reading chemistry magazines. Reading papers with a lot of chemical formulas and math was a good way to calm down and get focused when my mind was unglued by acid."

"Was anyone else there?"

"Yes, I thought about that too. There wasn't anyone else when I got there just before one. The door to that office is never locked. I went in and sat down in the reading room in the back. Around two o'clock Professor Kirikaé came in with a group of women students. The reading room is partitioned off with plywood panels, so it's separate. You wouldn't know someone was inside if you didn't go in and look. I wouldn't have minded meeting Professor Kirikaé, but I didn't want to deal with other students, so I was careful not to make any sound. I kept reading, and, by and by, things got quiet. I came out of the reading room, and there was Professor Kirikaé taking apart a large grandfather clock. He said he found it in the university's oversized refuse dump, and it was originally in the university president's office."

"You talked with Professor Kirikaé."

"Yes. We talked about the origin of clocks, how it was unforgivable for the president to throw out a clock with a history going back to the university's founding — that kind of thing. I know for sure I was there until three o'clock because I waited until then to hear the chorus of clocks strike the hour."

Wakako unexpectedly cut off her narrative. Akutsu looked up from his notepad and saw her head hanging downward as if all strength had drained away. Hair clung to a deathly pallid face that bore a desolate expression.

"What is it?"

"It's no good. I didn't meet anyone after that. I left Professor Kirikaé's office and walked up onto the Yotsuya embankment outside the university. While I was strolling along the embankment, I had a sudden urge to go to church. I went into the church near Yotsuya Station. I was baptized when I was very young, but somewhere in high school I stopped going to mass. By then, any kind of faith I might have had was long gone. But I have the habit of going to church when I am feeling sorrowful. That is how I felt that day. The church was holding someone's funeral."

"Whose?"

"Well . . . It was a woman. There was a framed picture of an old woman on the altar, and a coffin covered with flowers. About the front half of the pews were occupied. The choir sang hymn number 656. That is one of the most well-known hymns. 'Trust patiently, my soul, trust in the Lord. Let God your burdens hold, and loving help afford . . .' That one."

"Next, the priest began giving benedictions to the coffin with incense and holy water. He walked around the coffin shaking the censor and sprinkling the holy water. It's a beautiful ceremony. Watching this made me want to pray, so I did. It was my first prayer in a very long time. The next thing I knew, the funeral was over and everything was quiet. It was getting dark, so I went outside. Then I went back to my apartment in Shinjuku. It was pitch dark by then."

"Did you meet anyone you knew at the funeral?"

"I caught sight of someone I knew, but I didn't meet him. The priest, Father Okuda. I know him very well. He is a professor of theology at the university. He's a Catholic, but he practices zazen and runs a school zazen club. But he was far away from me at the altar, and I was all the way in the back row. That's a big church. I don't think he recognized me."

"What makes you think so?" Akutsu took pains to enunciate these words for maximum effect. "If you could see him, he must have been able to see you. This was a case where everyone else was concentrated in the front pews. If you were sitting all by yourself back there, you would have stood out. Don't you think so?"

"I wasn't all by myself. There were a number of sisters. It looked like they were involved in the funeral and arrived late. Besides that, it is dark in the back. I don't think I would have stood out."

"The seats all the way in back do stand out. I taught at a high school when I was in university, to get a teaching credit. The most conspicuous students are the ones in the back row. The last row looks like the closest. Didn't you yourself tell Professor Matsuda that when you sat in the back row the instructor's face seemed so close up you couldn't handle it?"

"You know, that's right, it really is!" Wakako's eyes brightened as if somewhere a flame had been lit. "At the time I was seeing everything as compressed images that had no depth. The result was things far away looked as if they were right in front of me. I took it as abnormal visual perception, but when you think about it, maybe I was only experiencing an exaggerated version of normal perceptions."

"Whatever the case may be, I'll go see Father Okuda and ask if he recognized you. Don't worry, I would guess there is a ninety percent chance he did. But about that old lady the funeral was for, even if you can't remember her name, do you have any idea about what kind of person she might have been?"

"It was someone I didn't know. The photograph was far away, so I couldn't make out the face very well, but I got the impression she was a sister. Many of the women attending the funeral wore veils, and there were many sisters too. Oh, wait a minute! Those sisters just might have been wearing the same habits the sisters wore at the Catholic school I attended, F. School. Black hood and white hem around the face. Yes, yes, I think they belong to the Mercedarian order."

"If so, you might know one of those sisters."

"All I saw were their backs."

"After the funeral ended they turned around and walked past you on their way out while you were praying. Maybe someone noticed you. Of course they would not address someone engaged in prayer, so they would have just walked past. At minimum, the possibility cannot be denied."

At that, Wakako Ikéhata burst into laughter, and it exploded into something she could not stop. Her slim shoulders quaked as she laughed on and on.

"Forgive me, Mr. Akutsu. That's such a show of confidence, it seemed so comical. It's just me. I react that way when I see that kind of self-assurance. My father shows it all the time. He'll spend the day poring over legal documents, then try to make small talk and sound like he's reading out a bill of attainder."

"I do get carried away sometimes."

"'At minimum, the possibility cannot be denied.'" Wakako's imitation of Akutsu's manner was flawless.

"Hmmm, I guess some pompous stuffed shirt must have said that."

"Mr. Akutsu, I'm wondering if you're the same age as me."

"I'm a year younger. Born in 1945. The wartime generation's last gasp."

"I'm the elder sister and you're already a lawyer. I'm still a student — or would be, if I wasn't in jail."

"We're going to fix that!"

"It took me two years before I passed the entrance exam. That put me the year behind your class, and still I wasn't even on the road to graduating. Now the only thing happening is that I'm getting old."

"Well, you're not old yet. I guess it's a funny thing for a kid brother to say, but I'll say it anyway. You have everything to look forward to, and I'll tell you why. You're being kept here by an unjust decision based on a mistaken determination of fact. So let's you and me overturn that decision."

"Can we do that?"

"We have to. That prosecutor and those judges are from the wartime generation. It's up to us to start writing a better history." Akutsu raised a fist and made a gesture of smashing the glass panel.

"Sounds good." Wakako returned the gesture and slid her fist along the panel until the slim fingers were eclipsed by Akutsu's fist.

"I need your consent for something. I want to read the complete record of what you said to Professor Matsuda."

"What for?"

"I want to get all the details on your relationship with Atsuo Yukimori."

"I didn't tell Professor Matsuda everything. There's a lot of private stuff that's nobody's business but ours. But if you want to read that record, so ahead."

"That was confirmation of your consent?" Wakako began to laugh again.

"Right. I hereby confirm my consent. I'll even confirm that you confirmed it."

"As long as we're on that topic, I have some other things to confirm," Akutsu continued, this time in an utterly serious tone. "You're in love with Atsuo Yukimori."

Wakako's laughter evaporated and was replaced once again by helpless sorrow.

"When you say love, the concept is so wide it doesn't have much meaning. Here's how I would put it. He is carrying around a long history of suffering, worry, strength, weakness, hope, despair . . . and all of it resonates in me."

"That tells me what I need to know. What about your relationship with Makihiko Moriya?"

"That's something else entirely. I don't understand him. He chased after me. I was always trying to get away. I could never understand him. There was always something about him that was strange and scary."

"He doesn't resonate in you."

"No, not at all. He lives in a different world than I do. That is why I didn't join his revolutionary movement."

"Your relationships with Shinichi Tagawa and Akito Shinya."

"I don't know them. As far as I could tell, the first time I laid eyes on them was when the trial started, but then the prosecutor said they were part of the group that ran into the Fukawa Motors employee's dormitory. I thought about that, and finally recognized their faces, but I've never even spoken with them."

"Moriya, Tagawa, and Shinya say they had nothing to do with the bombing. What are your thoughts on that?"

"I just don't know, Mr. Attorney." Wakako straightened her back and continued on as if performing a parody of a witness being questioned. "They spoke gibberish in court. What is this 'Q. Sect?' A bunch of guys who hung around with Moriya because they were into revolution, that's all. There was no particular organization. Anyone could come or go as their liked."

"But they call themselves Q. Sect members. They have two lawyers hired by the Q. Sect."

"That's what I meant when I said I just don't know, Mr. Attorney." Wakako was gazing directly at Akutsu. "Suddenly a sect springs into existence where no such sect existed at the time in question. People are found guilty of crimes they didn't commit. Just what is going on?"

It was past four o'clock when Akutsu exited the detention center gate. Though tired out from dealing with Tsukioka, followed by Sonoko Kanéhara in the morning and then Wakako Ikéhata in the afternoon, he was feeling exhilarated because he was starting to see the way forward to bringing the case to the settlement he envisioned. Dispirited-looking people returning from detention center visits walked with heavy strides along the narrow street, past shops specializing in goods for delivery to prisoners. Akutsu hurried along behind them, impatient to reach the train station. Each of those people had ties to someone held behind those high concrete walls, but they couldn't really know much about the inmates' lives on the inside. Conversations during brief visits could not convey that reality. Akutsu tried to think about the cell where Wakako Ikéhata was, but all he had to go on was an abstracted concept of a prison cell. He had visited detention centers and prisons as part of his training at the Judicial Research and Training Institute. At the time, he had been thinking of becoming a judge, and consequently did not pay deep attention to what he was observing. He considered confinement to be necessary and appropriate retribution for criminal offenders. He saw the blessings of civilization and democracy in the fact that individual and community cells were surprisingly clean and bright, not the realm of gloom and cruelty conveyed by words like "prison" or "jail." Now that he was handling a case in which the state was unlawfully confining innocent victims of false charges, those tall, sturdy walls with their steel bars appeared to him as appalling instruments for suppressing individual rights. This was one case where the police and prosecutors were turning the law to the pernicious end of unjustly locking up such a beautiful young woman as Wakako Ikéhata. As anger boiled up from the center of the life force below his belly, his pace quickened to a near run, causing him to collide with another pedestrian and be regarded as an oaf.

Kosugé Station is located upon an elevation that affords an overview of the streets and the iron bridge across the river Arakawa. He climbed the stairway. The outsized detention center loomed over the town, an uninteresting concrete rectangle, well designed for confinement of people and lacking any feature that even its staunchest supporter could call attractive. Almost any piece of architecture has some beautiful aspect to it, but this prison categorically rejected every kind of aesthetic. Inside that ugly mass, Wakako Ikéhata, Atsuo Yukimori, and Yukichi Jinnai were being forced to lead an appalling kind of existence. Akutsu stood in the wind from the river, lost in these thoughts.

The train pulled in. There were few passengers. Akutsu sat down, removed his attorney's badge and began rubbing it against the back of the seat. He was following advice received from Ishikawa several days before upon mentioning that he had been taken for a quack lawyer by the director of Y. Hospital because his badge was so shiny. His efforts to wear a respectable tarnish onto its surface in the course of several train rides since then were beginning to show results, as some whitish base metal began showing behind the plating. He wanted to wear down the surface to a more dignified silver color like the one Ishikawa wore. As he rubbed it, he realized the middle-aged woman sitting opposite was looking at him in wonderment. "Sorry to disappoint you, lady, but I'm allowed to do this," he thought, and mentally stuck his tongue out at her.

The Station Front Church was located by a traffic-choked boulevard, but was set off by shrubbery and a lawn in a quiet space of its own. Akutsu looked up at its crucifix, now beautifully alight in the rays of the setting sun. It was somewhat embarrassing that he had passed that way numerous times, including that very morning, on his way to Tsukioka's office, without a thought to the existence of this church.

He had seen quite a number of churches on a month-long tour of Europe taken in the spring of the previous year to commemorate his graduation from the Judicial Research and Training Institute. The great Gothic cathedrals of France had been especially impressive, as much for their soaring spires as the power of Christianity to motivate the people of the era to spare no investment of capital and ingenuity to achieve their longing to reach a little closer to the firmament. With no more than a commonplace knowledge of Christianity, the journey had not led him to any kind of soul-stirring experience.

The church now before him was incomparably smaller than those Gothic cathedrals. Its construction was quite modest, hardly a triumph of spiritual or financial investment. Despite this, Akutsu found himself captivated by its presence. Under the yellowed rays of the sun, it seemed to issue light of its own from within. The church stood up to the noise of the city and emanated serenity. It was an arresting sight, like a diamond gleaming in mud. He asked himself why the prison he had just seen that was dedicated solely to practical utility should be ugly, while this church that served no useful purpose — there only for the purpose of being there — should be beautiful.

Reception desks on the left and right sides of the entrance hall were attended by standing vestment-clad young men. He went inside. A wedding ceremony was in progress. A priest was giving his blessings to a young couple as an organ resounded. Akutsu had a brief glimpse of the scene over the shoulders of the guests before he went back outside. Having no idea how a church functioned, he decided to try taking a walk around this one to see what he could find. Noticing a priest moving rapidly toward the far side of the churchyard, he did not hesitate to call out.

"Excuse me, Father."

The man turned around. Akutsu saw that it was a white person, probably in his thirties. "Yes, what is it?" Blue eyes blinked in question.

"May I ask if you are a priest of this church?"

"Sure am! But I'm not a Father. I'm a Brother."

"Oh, all right. Brother . . . Does this church keep records of when funerals were held and who they were for?"

"Oh, yes, of course we do. We schedule them to keep funeral masses and wedding masses separate. There is a record book for that."

"May I see it?"

"Of course, of course." The Brother nodded and folded his arms with a sad expression. "Who died?"

"That isn't it. You see, I am an attorney. I would like to know the name of the person a funeral was held for in the afternoon of February eleventh, the year before last."

"Year before last. That's quite a while back. But we have it all in the record book. It is in the office. Let's go see."

After being shown into the office building beside the church, Akutsu offered his business card. The Brother responded, "Oh, yes, my business card," and looked over a pile of papers on a desk. Failing to find one there, he opened a drawer, extracted a card bearing a yellowish stain and offered it to Akutsu. "Sorry, this got wet in the rain. It's not pretty, but it's sanitary!"

Leopold Larra

Chaplain	Tokyo Detention Center
Inmate counseling	K. Juvenile Medical Reformatory
Volunteer	C. Prison, U. Prison

"Are you Spanish?"

"That's right! You're well informed. Did you study Spanish?"

"No, I just know the famous writer Mariano Jose de Larra was from Spain."

"You had a good education, I see. What . . . oh, yes, you're a lawyer. I have a little to do with lawyers. Because I visit prisons a lot. Now, let me see. Here is the church appointment record book. Mmmmm, 1969, February 11th, the afternoon, was it? Here we are. One o'clock, marriage mass for Sato. Three o'clock, funeral mass for Sister Teresia . . . hmmm, how would you read this name?"

"Must be 'Yugé.' There was a monk named Yugé-no-dokyo in the Nara Period."

"For goodness sake! Sister Yugé! I knew her well!"

"Do you know how long Sister Yugé's funeral ceremony took?"

"That I don't remember. The length of time isn't the same for everyone. The ceremony itself takes about thirty minutes, but there is a farewell ceremony after that, when people deliver eulogies and addresses. Some go on for a long time."

"About how long for a typical case?"

"I would say about an hour. We allow two hours for every booking."

"What is the name of the priest who officiated at Sister Yugé's funeral?" Akutsu peered closely at the record book.

"Says here Father Okuda."

"I thought it would be!" Akutsu looked up from the book in relief. "Father Okuda belongs exclusively to this church doesn't he?"

"No he doesn't!" Brother Larra raised bother hands palms up as he exclaimed this loudly enough to startle Akutsu. "Any priest can do a funeral. Father Okuda is a professor at R. University. He is not a priest of this church."

"If I want to meet Father Okuda will I have to go to R. University?"

"You will. Well, actually, no. If you want to meet Father Okuda, let's arrange for it. He is conducting a marriage mass right now, and he should be coming here pretty soon."

"I would be grateful for that."

Akutsu went to wait in a chair by the entry hall. On the wall were notices giving information on Bible study groups and Christian meditation groups. There was a poster on zazen sessions held by Father Okuda in Akikawa Valley. After a half hour's wait, the father entered the room, dressed in a black suit. He was lean and small of stature.

The moment a woman receptionist whispered something to the father, he moved soundlessly across the floor and appeared before Akutsu.

"I am Okuda. Is there something you wish of me?" The voice was serene.

"Yes." Akutsu arose and introduced himself as an attorney handling the Shinkansen bombing case.

"In that case, let us go to the minister's office." The father led the way. His back was straight, his footsteps soundless, like a Noh performer. Akutsu reflected that his manner of walking had probably come from practicing Zen.

When he was seated opposite the priest, Akutsu lost no time in explaining about the information he sought.

Father Okuda pondered.

"I don't remember . . . The job of a cleric includes conducting a great many funerals . . . Some days I will handle both. Just today, I had a funeral in the church in the morning, then a marriage in the chapel in the afternoon, and then a wedding here."

"It was a funeral for a Sister Teresa Yugé."

"Oh, yes, Sister Yugé — her I knew well. I do remember conducting her funeral. But I do not remember seeing Ms. Wakako Ikéhata."

"Do you know Wakako Ikéhata?"

"Yes, indeed. She belonged to my zazen group. Then she became a defendant in that case. I visited her just the other day at the detention center."

"On the day of the train bombing, she came to church at the time of Sister Yugé's funeral. She was sitting in the last pew."

"Really? In that case, I certainly wish I could remember."

"Don't you have a good view of the back row from the altar?"

"No. The altar is bright. One cannot see the pews well. Besides that, I look inward prayerfully during a mass. I lose sight of the church surroundings."

"Yes, of course." Akutsu felt his hopes dashed. There would be no testimony from the priest.

"I met with Atsuo Yukimori the other day," Father Okuda said unexpectedly. "He came to the prison chapel. He was also saying he did not commit the crime."

"It certainly is a small world! That is quite a surprise. The fact is, I am Atsuo Yukimori's attorney."

Akutsu gave a brief explanation about the proof of Atsuo Yukimori's innocence that had emerged and how proof of Wakako Ikéhata's innocence was needed.

"I regret not being of help to you." The father brought his hands together and bowed his head. "Sister Yugé's funeral mass . . . No, I cannot remember anything."

"Did Sister Yugé belong to the Mercedarian order?"

"She did, so there should have been many sisters from the Mercedarian Order in attendance, but I cannot recall that either."

There was a knock at the door, and a boy about three years old came into the room and called out an endearingly botched pronunciation of Father Okuda's title. He ran forward into the father's arms. Then the boy's mother came in and gave a respectful bow. Akutsu saw that the time was right for his departure.

Clouds obscured the sun. The darkened church rose to a sky that was still light. Brother Larra stood at the entrance stairway giving directions to workers packing up the equipment and supplies used in the day's wedding ceremony. Akutsu addressed him.

"Thanks very much for helping out. I see church ceremonies come with a lot of management work," he said as he watched people from the gardening concession carrying away roses and carnations. Then a question for Brother Larra occurred to him. "Do you have florists bring in flowers to the altar for funerals?"

"Sure do. And they're all fresh flowers. Catholics don't use artificial flowers. That's no good. Only fresh flowers. And they are set out without any name tags on them."

"Do you oversee the florists' work on those occasions?"

"Of course. It's part of my job."

"Does that mean you stay inside the church throughout a funeral?"

"Pretty much. There are all kinds of things that have to be done."

"Okay, now let me ask if you remember that funeral of Sister Teresa Yugé that you looked up for me."

"Well, you know we have funerals all the time."

"Yes, of course I understand that," Akutsu said earnestly. "It's just that at the time this particular funeral was being held, a defendant I am representing — a university student by the name of Wakako Ikéhata — was sitting all the way in the back row. Now if I can find proof of that, it will fully establish her alibi. I asked Father Okuda about it, but he says he doesn't remember."

"Wait a minute!" Brother Larra burst out in a loud voice, causing the men carrying out the potted plants to cast him startled looks. "I seem to remember something. There was something or other unusual about Sister Teresa's funeral. I'm trying to remember what . . . Ahh, what was it now?" He raised both hands against his face as if it sniff at them.

"You say it was a woman college student? What was she like?"

"She says she was wearing beige-colored jeans, a red sweater, and a navy blue half coat."

"I don't mean what she was wearing. What kind of impression did she give?"

"She is fair skinned, and I guess you would say she was kind of lonesome looking. She said for the first time in years she had a desire to pray, so she went into the church."

"The first time in years, huh? So she isn't someone who shows up often. Well, then maybe it was that girl . . ."

"Do you remember something?"

"I've got it now. When we were seeing off Sister Teresa, there was a strange girl wandering around outside the church. She was a little weird. She was looking up at the crucifix and muttering strange things to herself. Like, 'The cross is all rubbery, it's going to melt and fall down, look out!' I had things to do, but I was wondering what was with that kid. The next time I looked, she was gone. Then I saw her again after the funeral was over and we were putting things away. She was sitting all by herself in back of the church."

"Where was she sitting?" Akutsu asked urgently.

"I'll show you. Come on." Brother Larra led him into the church and pointed out a pew located in the third row from the back, on the right. Wakako Ikéhata had said she was sitting in the row all the way at the back.

"She was about here. Most people just sit, and when they pray, they kneel. This girl was sitting with her legs crossed. That made me think, 'Yeah, this one is nuts.'"

"She was just doing zazen."

"Zazen? Maybe that was it, but you know, no one does zazen in a church. She was very conspicuous. Then, when we finished getting things straightened away I went back to see if she was gone, but there she was, still sitting cross-legged. It was dark and cold. I said to her, 'Hey, you're going to catch cold!' but she didn't move. So I repeated it and this time she snaps into motion and leaves."

"About what time was it when she left?"

"It was completely dark by then. I wonder what time."

"If it was dark, it would have been about five-thirty. The funeral mass starts at three o'clock. Oh, yes, let me ask you this. When is hymn number 656 sung at a funeral?"

"Hmmm. Let's check. Come on." Brother Larra pointed toward several people in the church engaged in prayer and raised a finger against his lips. "We don't want to disturb them."

Behind the office building at the foremost end of the church was a rude shack. Brother Larra open the door and ushered Akutsu inside. There was a bed, a chair, and, for decoration, a plaster statue of the holy mother. A residence in the monastic spirit.

"This is my room. Here, take a look at this. It's the funeral program. It is about same for everyone."

One paper was entitled "Ceremony Program." On the right side was "Funeral mass" and on the left were the program particulars. Hymn 656 was scheduled at the start of the farewell proceedings. Following that was "Benedictions with incense and holy water."

"This is about the middle of the proceedings. If the mass starts at three, can we take it Hymn 656 was sung around three thirty?"

"Well, sometimes the mass takes longer. So it could also have been around four."

"That means Wakako Ikéhata was in the church from around four to five-thirty."

"Umm. Yes, that would be it." Brother Larra turned his blue-green eyes to Akutsu and scratched his angular nose.

"What this means is that we now have solid proof of her alibi. That offbeat girl you saw was Wakako Ikéhata. That is unmistakable. She has been convicted of planting a time bomb to blow up a Shinkansen train while in Tokyo Station, between three thirty and four o'clock that day. Brother, I'm sure you know about that explosion."

"Of course. That was big news. But this is certainly a surprising turn of events. Was that girl the R. University student in the Shinkansen bombing case? That day I went to six o'clock mass, and that bombing was on the TV when I came back. But I really wonder whether the girl I saw was really that R. University student. All I have is a vague recollection."

"It was her. Those things about 'the crucifix is rubbery, it's going to melt' nail it down. She had been taking LSD and was having hallucinations. It's the same kind of thing she said on other occasions under the influence of LSD. She belonged to Father Okuda's zazen group. That explains why she was sitting cross-legged in church."

"That was what you wanted to see Father Okuda about."

"Your testimony will win her a not-guilty decision. By all means, please agree to testify in court."

"I'll agree to that, if it would help her. But, you know, if I'm in a position to help her, it is a blessing. My involvement is the Lord's work."

A warm smile appeared on Brother Larra's face. He rose and announced he had to leave for six o'clock mass.

Though the sky was still a milky color, it was getting dark. Night was approaching. A multitude of students was moving from the universities toward the station. Akutsu felt tired, hungry and in the mood to find a place to have a beer. But being so close to R. University presented a golden opportunity to check on something that needed confirmation. He wanted to visit that chemistry reading room-cum-office of Professor Kirikaé to get corroboration of Wakako Ikéhata's testimony.

Passing through the university gate, his ears were greeted by the sounds of an orchestra out of tune. It was playing the introduction to Bruckner's Fourth Symphony, over and over again. He heard conversations between women students and cheers from a gymnasium. A group of men in sweatpants ran by. Black-clad priests and nuns walked together in a group, amidst male and female students. Akutsu felt a longing for the joys of the campus life he had left behind. He stopped to breathe in a full drought of the ambiance, pounding his chest with both fists to promote the air flow.

"Mr. Attorney!" A woman's voice was calling to him. It was Yoko Mizuno of Y. Hospital, her dark complexion alight with laughter.

"Hey! Thanks for everything the other day." Akutsu was embarrassed that his strange gesture had been witnessed.

"What were you doing?"

"Deep breathing. Nothing like the air on a university campus."

"What does beating your chest like a gorilla do?"

"That's a victory pose to prove you took it all in."

"Sounds like fun. I'll give it a try." Yoko took a deep breath, her small, well-formed nose twitching. "Feels good, like a battery charge," she said, stroking her own well-developed chest.

Akutsu was dazzled by the spectacle. "Well, Ms. Yoko of the sun, what brings you here?" he asked.

"Paying respects to former teachers. I graduated from this school. I come now and then to have a professor of the psychology department check over my interpretations of Rorschach tests. Now it's your turn. What brought Mr. Jun of Purity to this campus?"

"I came to meet Professor Kirikaé. It looks as if I can prove the alibi of Ms. Wakako Ikéhata, in that same case. A little while ago I found someone who will testify she was in a church from four o'clock until five-thirty that day. Before she went to the church, she was in Professor Kirikaé's office. I have to pin down what time she left."

Yoko responded with a hearty handclap. "Wow! Akéchi class detective work."

"Do you know Professor Kirikaé?"

"Of course. He's famous. I visited his office quite often when I was a student here."

494

"Even though he's in the engineering department?"

"I took physics under him as a general education requirement in my freshman year. It isn't easy to find his office. I'll show you the way."

Yoko started off. He soon realized the campus was kind of a maze. Besides having buildings of all sizes crowed willy-nilly into a small tract, paths were frequently cut off by stairways and arcades. He unexpectedly found himself in a courtyard laid out like a public park. They descended a staircase to a narrow passageway like a battlefield trench. At the end was a door with a sign, "Anyone is welcome to enter freely. Shiro Kirikaé."

Careful examination showed the spacious room to be a laboratory equipped with sinks and gas burners. One side was partitioned off by bookshelves. A whiskered man sat at a desk, engaged in some task. Yoko strode in, sat on a bench facing the man and beckoned to Akutsu.

Akutsu walked up to the whiskered man and presented his business card. He apologized for making an unscheduled visit and explained there was something he wanted to ask.

"Have a seat," Kirikaé said, and looked down. "I'll finish this up now." Then he looked at Yoko. "Whoa, haven't seen you for a spell. You're Ms. Mizuno, as I recall."

He was adroitly carving a pattern into a rectangular piece of stone, using a small chisel. On the desk was a line of stone seals of varying sizes, presumably his handiwork. He gestured to Yoko. "Try pressing one."

Yoko touched the seal to a cinnabar ink pad and pressed it out on a piece of paper.

"Here's how you do it." So saying, Kirikaé briskly stamped a seal to the ink pad and pressed it to the paper, producing a sharp impression. Some of the seals were names, others fragments of Chinese poetry. There were seals that made white character impressions. Many produced exquisite vermilion characters.

"This is fine craftsmanship," Akutsu said.

"Want to try carving one?" Kirikaé said, offering an uncut stone chisel.

"No, thanks. I'm all thumbs."

"It's finished." Kirikaé put down his chisel and blew powder from the cut surface, stamped the seal to the ink pad and pressed it to a piece of paper. The result was four characters:

石 火 光 中

stone fire light within

"It's like it was your pen name," Yoko said.

"You know, it could be," Kirikaé replied. Then, addressing Akutsu, he gave a commentary.

"This is from the Ming Dynasty *Vegetable Roots Discourse*. The characters mean 'In the light of a spark from a stone.' The entire stanza says something like '. . . to struggle and vie over differences in the light of a single spark.' In other words, human life lasts only a moment, so why spend it contending for trivial gain? . . . But, do tell me what's on your mind."

"I've come to see you because I am Wakako Ikéhata's attorney . . ."

"I see, I see! I know Ms. Ikéhata well. She was in a class of mine, and she visited this room many times. I went to the detention center to see her a couple of weeks ago. After that, I visited Mr. Atsuo Yukimori as well. Those two did not commit the crime. They received an unjust decision. I am praying every day that they be rescued. Let us pray for them together now."

Kirikaé closed his eyes, pressed his fingers together, assumed a pious expression and bowed his head. At a loss, Akutsu looked at Yoko Mizuno, whose tongue darted out playfully before she, too, assumed a posture of prayer. Annoyed, Akutsu ignored the two and looked about the room at his leisure. There certainly were a lot of clocks, on shelves, above the shelves, on the desk, on the floor — large and small, all ticking away together. It was twelve minutes to seven. Soon they would all sound the hour. The prospect of the event set Akutsu on edge.

There was a tiny splash in a sink, clearly caused by a living thing. It was a laboratory sink, filled with water. That would be the pond of goldfish, carp, crucian carp and trout Wakako Ikéhata had mentioned. Kirikaé looked up and Yoko Mizuno followed suit, with a look at Akutsu.

"It's just same as ever. Professor Kirikaé prays at the drop of a hat. Gee, I'm hungry!"

"There's spaghetti."

"That's just the same as ever too. Instant ramen and spaghetti. Hardly a meal."

"When you say those two are innocent, what's your proof?" Akutsu asked.

"I don't need proof," Kirikaé replied imperturbably. "I can tell by looking into their eyes. They were the eyes of pure, innocent people."

"I understand that, but nevertheless . . ."

"You mustn't cast doubt on people. That's wrong. They deny guilt — let us believe in them. I know Ms. Ikéhata especially well. She's the kind of person who couldn't lie if she wanted to."

"That's no good, professor!" Yoko Mizuno burst out in exasperation. "Judges don't care how much faith you have. They want proof. It's a good thing Mr. Akutsu is a crack detective. He found alibis for both of them."

Akutsu cut her off. "Professor Kirikaé, I would like to ask about what Wakako Ikéhata did on the day of the bombing. Do you remember what happened that day?"

"Yes I remember very well. Ms. Ikéhata popped in here that day for a visit. She was here all the time."

"What time was it that you met her?"

"It would have been three or four o'clock that I met her, but I saw her before that around noon, in the student cafeteria."

"You went to the student cafeteria that day?"

"I went for ramen with some students. Someone mentioned she was there, and I saw her. I thought of inviting her to our table, but decided against it. She has a thing about wanting to be alone — doesn't like being in a big group. A little while later, she was gone, so I guessed she'd gone to my office."

"Why did you think that?"

"I'm the only one whose office is open on holidays. Also, she had a troubled expression. It gave me the feeling she had something she wanted to talk over with me. So I returned here right away. I don't know if that was one or two o'clock. I wouldn't know."

"What are you saying?" Yoko demanded. "What are all these clocks for? You don't know if it was one o'clock or two o'clock — a whole hour's difference?"

Kirikaé grimaced and stroked his beard. "Yeah, that's a weak point of mine. No sense of time."

"Well, what do you have all these clocks for?" Yoko Mizuno picked up a clock on the professor's desk. "You went though all the trouble of repairing them."

"They are for my students. You can have any one you like."

"I like that one!" Yoko Mizuno rose and went over to a large grandfather clock in the middle of the room. "This clock is a marvel."

"It's German — a Siemens clock. The pendulum swings once per second in each direction. It used to be in the university president's office."

"I'd love to have it, but if I tried to put it in my apartment, the floor would give way."

The clocks throughout the room began to strike seven o'clock, in a hundred different tones. Most outstanding was the resonant bong-bong of the Siemens clock.

Yoko gave an exaggerated start in her seat. "I wasn't expecting that. It brings back my student days. Umm, it does sound good."

The chorus of chimes ended, only to be followed by more chimes starting up from a group of clocks in a corner. "Uh, huh, that's the corner for delinquents, like me,"

"Weren't you were repairing that Siemens grandfather clock on the day of the bombing?" Akutsu asked.

"I was consumed with clock repair at the time. I rescued that clock on Christmas of the year before last. I started work on it over New Years and finished at Easter time. I know that sounds like a contrived story, but it's the truth," Kirikaé said. "It was a major project getting it in shape. Some priests who thought they were handy with machines made up their own rules for the weights, and they skipped a few gears when they rigged it. I put it into working order, but no one will take it. I've offered it for marriage and graduation presents, but everyone says it's too big. How about you, Mr. Attorney, won't you take it?"

Akutsu was intent on putting the conversation back on track.

"On the day of the bombing, after you had ramen in the cafeteria, about what time was it you returned to your office?"

"That I don't remember. I am in the habit of taking a walk after meals, and I think that is what I did that day."

"You do recall that you had ramen that day."

"I always have ramen for lunch."

" . . . Was Wakako Ikéhata in your office when you returned?"

"She was. She was here until evening, and that means she could not have been the culprit. She has an alibi. I will testify to it."

"That isn't good enough," Yoko said. "Testimony has to be more precise than that. You can get on the train or take a taxi and reach Tokyo Station in thirty minutes from here."

"Wakako Ikéhata says she arrived here shortly before one o'clock and went to the reading room to read magazines. She says she heard you arrive in the company of some women students around two o'clock, and she came out a little before three, because by then you were alone. Where is the reading room?"

"I took it down. It wasn't a proper reading room — just a space sectioned off with plywood."

"Do you recall returning here with several women students?"

"No. I am always with students . . . I probably did return with some."

"Wakako Ikéhata says she left here after three o'clock."

"Seems like it was later than that. I was here when that bombing was reported."

The dialog began to go in circles and Akutsu despaired. If Wakako Ikéhata had left the office at three thirty, strolled leisurely along the embankment, then from around four o'clock, been in the church as Larra said, her alibi was established. But if she left Kirikaé's office at three o'clock, she would have had time to go to Tokyo Station, as Yoko had said. The prosecutor's presumption was that Ikéhata and Yukimori had bought Shinkansen platform admission tickets at three thirty. Wakako had said she left Kirikaé's office after hearing the clocks strike three o'clock. Kirikaé had been with her. If he couldn't remember anything about it, that left Wakako's story open to charges of low credibility.

"We're not getting a clear picture, Yoko said, irritation in her voice. I've been doing some re-reading of newspaper clippings about this case. It seems to me the basic issue is where she was at three thirty."

"That's it. The professor says she was here until evening. She says she left at three thirty. We can't rebut the prosecutor's argument without resolving the space between those statements."

Kirikaé hung his head. "What am I to do?" he said apologetically. "My fuzzy memory is a blight. The fact is, the very day Ms. Ikéhata was arrested I recalled that she was here that afternoon. I thought that would be helpful, so I called the attorney, Mr. Tsukioka. He said he couldn't use my testimony because the time was unclear."

"A statement that she was here until the evening would not only be unhelpful, it would be harmful to the case. But if you recall something, please do get in touch," Akutsu said, rising. Yoko did likewise.

There weren't many students left on the darkening campus.

"Well, Detective Akutsu, what are the prospects for this case?" Yoko asked in a mocking tone.

"We've come one hundred percent of the way to proving Yukimori's alibi. Ikéhata's is about sixty percent there."

"Is that all? That leaves room for worry."

"Average them together and you get eighty percent. That's good enough to go on."

"Spoken like an ace detective. Total confidence."

"Is that how I look? She said the same thing — Wakako Ikéhata. That I talk like I'm full of confidence. The truth is, I'm afraid of everyone — full of anxiety."

"I know. A little while ago you were looking like you were ready to kill yourself when you realized Professor Kirikaé's memory is no good."

"Can't hide anything from a fellow ace detective. It's time for an energy recharge. I'm ready to look for a place to eat. How about going along?"

"That's a wonderful idea. I'm starved."

Akutsu hailed a taxi and told the driver to go to Shinjuku.

The clamor of voices and popular songs in the restaurant enveloped the two, secluding them among the crowd. Yoko's voice had intensity, fit for lively engagement. She laughed with a resounding trill. Alcohol made it resound at a higher level still, and the sound was all the more pleasant to Akutsu. After several days of running from one appointment to another, trying to find viable witnesses, it was a pleasure to speak with a woman his own age like Yoko, with no need for circumspection or diplomacy.

" . . . Professor Kirikaé is such an oddball. He knows physics, he knows machines, he can fix a clock like new, but he's a mystic. He believes in prophetic dreams. One day he said he dreamed there would be an earthquake just past two in the afternoon, and there really was a big earthquake at two in Mexico. That made a lot of people believe in him, myself included. I wouldn't doubt he's convinced of Wakako's innocence because some voice told him so in a dream."

"The only trouble is that his memory is vague. It isn't much help for corroborating an alibi."

"With him, that doesn't matter. Belief comes first and the proof follows. Just believe what he says and eventually you will have the proof."

"You seem to be quite a believer yourself."

"I really am," Yoko said, nodding. "Even though I criticize that mystical stuff, I fall for it pretty easily. That might be why I majored in psychology. What I found out is that psychology doesn't really tell you much about how people's minds work. Not that I'm any authority in psychology — I barely managed to graduate. Still, I know that analyzing the unconscious doesn't tell you all that much. We know it's there, but it's like the ocean — practically limitless. Discovering the unconscious just gave a better idea of how little we know."

"That's fascinating. You sound like a psychologist to me."

Yoko trilled her distinctive laugh. "Actually, that opinion came from my professor, Dr. Nagai."

"You studied under Professor Nagai?" Akutsu recognized the name. Professor Nagai was distinguished in both psychoanalysis and criminology. Professor Matsuda of N. University was an orthodox medical scholar whose work in criminology focused on unspectacular themes, while Professor Nagai handled topical issues like domestic violence and crimes by juveniles. As such, his name was known in the media.

"Let me give you a little more of his views. He says there are as many theories in psychology as there are psychologists. Freud and Jung did extremely important work, but they did not uncover the truth. The most you can say of their theories is that they look like truth. You don't have the truth if there is no correspondence between different theories about the same things. Well, Freud's and Jung's theories don't correspond at all."

"That Professor Nagai is worth listening to."

"I've been doing all the talking. Now it's your turn. Tell me how you got to be a lawyer."

"I've been asked that before, but I don't think I have a particularly good answer. I wanted to be a judge when I was a student. The judge's job is to see that the law is applied fairly. And it's a secure position. When it was getting close to graduation, a lot of students I knew were being arrested for taking part in the Camp Oji and Narita struggles. Being on their support committees was enough work for ten people. It was an eye-opener to attend the trials and see how arrogantly the judges handled the cases. Even so, I still wanted to become a judge while I was at the Judicial Research and Training Institute, and I suppose I would have become one if Mr. Ishikawa hadn't invited me to join his law firm when I graduated."

"Are you satisfied now you made that choice?"

"I don't know. I'm just totally absorbed in doing the work."

"Total absorption is proof you are satisfied. I envy you."

"I'd say you have an interesting job, handling the mentally ill every day."

"It isn't boring work. But can I call myself totally absorbed? I started off that way. Now, three years after graduation, I don't feel that intense anymore. The fact that the pay is really low doesn't help."

"If it's been three years since you graduated, we're in the same graduating class. Born in 1945, right?"

"No, early 1946, so I started school the same year as the 1945 babies."

"Either way, we're in the same class."

"Three years already. I'm getting old."

"Hardly. I'm the one who's getting old. Although, actually, I'm happy about that. I can't wait until I'm thirty."

"That's a strange thing to want."

"Under-thirty lawyers are treated like idiots. Once you pass thirty you get a little bit of respect."

"Under thirty lawyers are just fine. You have plenty of dignity as you are." Yoko placed her saké cup down and glanced at her wristwatch. It was getting close to ten o'clock.

Akutsu observed this action with interest. "Hmmm, you wear a wristwatch."

"Well, of course. I need it for my work. Like for giving tests, for rec therapy . . . whatever."

"Wakako Ikéhata doesn't have a watch. She won't have anything to do with them, so it seemed funny you have one. But anyway, are you okay not going home yet?"

"I have my own apartment. No curfew."

"I was assuming you were born and raised in Tokyo and you lived with your family. Maybe that impression came from Wakako Ikéhata too. So you came to Tokyo from somewhere else. Where?"

"Take a guess."

"Your Tokyo dialect is flawless, so I would guess somewhere within the Kanto region. No further than Shizuoka."

"Sorry, I'm from Osaka. I lived there through high school." These words were the first she had spoken that were dressed in the distinctive Osaka dialect.

"You had me fooled. Until this moment, I didn't hear a trace of Osaka in your speech."

"It took a lot of work to get it that way. My job is all about talking with people. I had to get rid of the accent."

"Since you don't have to be home at any particular time, let's party a little. How about going dancing?"

They had emptied nearly ten saké servers between them, but they walked steadily. They were up to dancing as well, although the effects of the saké showed in their hampered rhythms and frequent collisions with other dancers. Yoko's vibrato laugh sounded frequently. As she approached, breasts swaying, Akutsu sought to draw her close, but she easily eluded him. Akutsu was not hiding his desire. Yoko accommodated by teasing, with provocative movement of her shapely hips and timely retreats from his grasp.

As a student, Akutsu had often indulged in drinking and dancing. Now it had been quite some time since his last opportunity to have fun with a woman. He forgot about time. It was probably past two in the morning when they emerged onto a street that had extinguished half its neon lights. They had jumbo orders of ramen at an all-night Chinese restaurant. As he was walking Yoko back to her apartment in Shin-Okubo, an unspoken consensus led them instead into a hotel along the way.

Akutsu awoke after Yoko had left. He recalled she had said she would be leaving at eight to be on time for a regular Thursday meeting of personnel in her hospital ward at nine-thirty. A strand of Yoko's hair beside the pillow reminded Akutsu of her superbly healthy body, and a wave of desire returned to him. It did not flare up, but remained as a pleasant glow within. On a side table was a page torn from an appointment book bearing Yoko's name and telephone number. He copied it into his own appointment book, then glanced at the time — ten forty-five, long past nine, when he was expected to show up at his office. He hastily called in.

Instead of Einosuké, Ishikawa himself answered. Akutsu had the feeling of being subjected to a heavy cloud of pipe smoke as Ishikawa informed him that word had been received from Tsukioka that Professor Ikéhata wanted him to show up at his home in Sendagaya.

"Got what? Your voice is hoarse. Drank too much, didn't you? Where are you?"

"A certain place in Tokyo."

"I suppose so. I just called your apartment and you weren't there. It doesn't matter. The issue is, are you prepared to meet Professor Ikéhata?"

"Not prepared enough. I met Wakako Ikéhata yesterday. She told me that after she left Professor Kirikaé's office at R. University she went to a church near the station, so I met with Professor Kirikaé and a brother at that church. That got me a fairly solid piece of alibi testimony."

"Does 'fairly solid' mean less than airtight? In any case, you're just going to have to consider that enough preparation for the meeting. Let it be your courtesy gift when you call on the professor."

"I wasn't thinking of the alibi when I said I wasn't prepared enough." Akutsu covered the telephone receiver with his hand and cleared his throat. Reestablishing his normal voice was enough to get his mind working at normal speed.

"I want to meet Professor Matsuda of N. University and get the raw data that didn't go into the psychiatric analysis submitted to the court. There are some things about Ikéhata family affairs and her relationship with Atsuo Yukimori that I want to know."

"That would all be worthwhile information, but there isn't time for that. The professor is in a hurry."

"Why is he suddenly in a hurry? There is still a month before the deadline for submitting briefs on the appeal."

"Professor Ikéhata is due to check into a hospital tomorrow. Tsukioka isn't saying what he's got, but it looks like cancer."

As soon as the line to Ishikawa cut off, Akutsu called Professor Matsuda and secured his pledge to turn over the analysis records. Then he called Professor

Ikéhata to tell him that unavoidable circumstances made a visit today impossible, but that he would like to call tomorrow. The professor seemed annoyed by this inconvenience. He said that he would be busy preparing for hospitalization the next day, but that he would make himself available for one hour at ten in the morning.

Akutsu felt reassured he had accomplished all that could be done for the moment. He took a taxi to his apartment in Tsukijima, freshened up and departed, carrying a large briefcase. He stopped at a nearby sushi shop and consumed a double portion of sushi. His hunger satiated, he felt ready for two thousand meters of laps in a swimming pool. He picked up a package of transcripts and cassette tapes from Professor Matsuda at N. Medical University. Back in his office, he put the reference material in order and began his review by listening to the tapes. There were six tapes, each a total of two hours on both sides — twelve hours in all. Listening to all that and reading the transcripts as well meant there would be no sleeping that night. Akutsu forced himself to begin. First up was a tape that began with Wakako Ikéhata's early years.

As a rule, Ishikawa did not speak with his salaried attorneys when they were preoccupied with their work. Each of Akutsu's young colleagues were engaged in separate projects of their own that had been approved. When Einosuké asked Akutsu if he wanted him to bring back an order of sushi or something, he just replied, "Yes, please," without remembering until later he had already had sushi that day.

When he tired of listening to tapes, he switched to reading transcripts. When he got sleepy, he stood and continued working. By the time the sky was beginning to show light, he had reviewed all the material. He didn't have much new information for the considerable effort he had invested. Wakako was giving Professor Matsuda answers to his questions that were more or less on the mark, but she wasn't being frank. It sounded like there was more to be said, and she had elected not to say it. In particular, she gave no details of her association with Atsuo Yukimori. He realized that Professor Matsuda had not been intentionally withholding information, but that Wakako herself had refrained from commenting.

What the overall record made clear was that Wakako was a strictly non-political sort of student, that she did not belong to the Q. Sect or any other sect, and there was nothing to suggest so much as the possibility she had ever acted on orders from Q. Sect. Akutsu thought regretfully that her testimony to this effect in court would have had a major influence on the decision. He was convinced that such testimony by her would be an indispensable part of the defense strategy henceforth.

On the question of whether she was psychologically abnormal, the level of understanding Akutsu had from his cram session in psychoanalysis was not enough to form an opinion. The more he pondered the information he had, the less clear it all became. She had once been obsessed with a belief her body smelled badly to men, and at another time, had lost visual depth perception. She believed organizations tracked her every move. It was all unusual, but it didn't add up to something Akutsu could understand. Wakako Ikéhata was a mystery to him. The fact that Atsuo Yukimori related to her perfectly naturally — not as one would relate to an eccentric character — was in itself a mystery, not explainable by the concept of love as he knew it.

Akutsu rang the doorbell of the Ikéhata home at 10 a.m., on the dot. When he recited his name into the inter-phone, a mechanism sounded, and the iron gate opened. Between the stone gate and the entrance hall was a magnificent stand of tall trees, richly verdant. Full wisteria blossoms hung luxuriantly from a trellis. But signs of the misfortune that had befallen the family could be seen in weeds overrunning the pathway and clapboard siding left in need of repair.

He was received by Mrs. Ikéhata, whose facial features were identical to her daughter — the only difference being age and the haggard look that comes with prolonged grief. But the gaunt appearance of her husband was a real shock to Akutsu, who had taken his lectures as a student at the Judicial Research and Training Institute. Professor Ikéhata moved slowly, supporting himself against the wall as he walked. He had aged dramatically, his hair whitened and skin covered with dry brown patches.

"I apologize for troubling you while you have other affairs to deal with," Akutsu said with humility.

"Not at all. I am the one who should be calling. I'm much obliged to you for taking the time to visit." Ikéhata's tactful reply was a turnaround from the annoyed tone in his response on the telephone the previous day.

"I understand you are not well."

"Yes, I have stomach cancer," Professor Ikéhata said, coughing lightly. "Ever since this case came up, I've had stomach trouble. A week ago it was confirmed to be cancer."

"That is . . ." The professor was being so shockingly open about his condition, Akutsu was having difficulty finding words of consolation.

"I had previously told my doctor — who happens to be from my high school class — to tell me if I have something malignant."

"I see," Akutsu said, and proceeded to change the subject. "I think you know that Mr. Tsukioka and I wish to form a joint defense that includes my clients, Atsuo Yukimori and Yukichi Jinnai."

"Yes, by all means, please do so. I am grateful for your assistance."

"Umm . . . " Having prepared for opposition, Akutsu was thrown off balance by the unexpected reply. Professor Ikéhata seized the moment to continue speaking in a manner of explanation, as if lecturing to students.

"I understand from Mr. Tsukioka that a definitive alibi for Yukimori has been discovered. I agree that is very much in Wakako's interest and have no objection to a joint defense for them. But I will not forgive Yukimori for seducing my daughter and then giving false testimony that dragged her into the worst imaginable trouble. I agree to a joint defense, but I want these facts of Yukimori's acts to be clearly stated throughout the defense."

Upon concluding this speech, Ikéhata was breathing raggedly, like one who had just run a long distance. Mrs. Ikéhata took on a concerned look, signaling that she wanted the talk to end soon. Akutsu had no desire to argue with someone in poor health, but spoke up for the sake of accomplishing the mission of his visit.

"I am afraid I must take issue with the view that Yukimori involved your daughter in this case. He is as much a victim as she is."

Noting that Professor Ikéhata was listening carefully, Akutsu felt confident enough to continue.

"Yukimori and Wakako were arrested because the police were biased against Yukimori. He was an ex-convict, he had access to gunpowder, and he had conducted experimental explosions. That combined with slanderous statements to the police from a former co-worker at Fukawa Motors, who had a grudge against him."

"I am aware of those circumstances," Professor Ikéhata said. "It's true that he is a victim in that aspect. But Wakako became involved in this because of her association with him. None of this would have happened if not for that."

"She was associating with him entirely of her own free will. He isn't responsible for the fact of the relationship itself."

"Look, that man is twenty-five years older than my daughter. He's uneducated, he has a criminal record. They are utterly incompatible. Even supposing she did approach him, simple common sense says he should have kept his distance."

"Atsuo Yukimori is a human being. He's a man. Men and women have freedom of association."

"In principle, that is true. But you are talking about someone who took a girl twenty-five years younger into his apartment and violated her."

"You're speaking of the night of International Anti-War Day, October 21st, 1968. He did not 'violate' Wakako that night."

"Do you expect me to believe that?" For the first time, emotion crept into Professor Ikéhata's voice. "No one would. Wakako had a relapse immediately afterward, and had to be hospitalized. That alone is proof."

"I have reviewed all of Professor Matsuda's records of his examination. Wakako stated clearly to him that nothing happened that night."

"She's lying to protect him."

"No." Akutsu took hold of his own feelings to keep intensity out of his voice. "Wakako has not told a single falsehood since her arrest. That is a major difference between her and all the other defendants. Therefore, her statement has credibility."

"That's right! Wakako was convicted on the lies of others." Professor Ikéhata's logic began to fray as mounting excitement set him to trembling. "Yukimori set her up as an accomplice to lighten his own culpability."

"No," Akutsu said, becoming ever more dispassionate. "He gave a false confession as the result of coercion and threats. It was not only him. The same was true of all the defendants, with the exception of Wakako."

"That argument was rejected in the first trial. The police officers and prosecutor both testified that those charges are groundless."

"The upcoming trial will tell a very different story. It is my intention to thoroughly demonstrate what goes on in those police holding cells that we 'substitute prisons.' What civilized country would allow its police to lock up everyone they suspect in animal pens so they can grill them day and night to force confessions? Policemen having absolute control over defenseless individuals, gang up on them and harass them with no lawyer present, with complete disregard for their rights as individuals. That is the reality of Japan, a country we flatter ourselves by calling an advanced democracy."

"You aren't telling me anything I don't know."

"Pardon me. I should not be giving lectures to one of the top authorities in the field." Akutsu realized he was facing a dilemma. He could quote chapter and verse from the professor's own textbook on criminal procedures to show how removed it was from the realities of actual practice. That would win his point, but that argument would take up time better spent emphasizing that he had evidence of high value to Wakako in the upcoming trial.

"Let me confirm for you what we have right now. Yukimori has an alibi. Mr. Tsukioka has been fully briefed on that. Now, my investigation will be able to prove Wakako's alibi as well."

"Wakako has an alibi!" Tension supporting Ikéhata's confrontational stance disappeared, and he began to breathe heavily.

"Yes. The day before yesterday I visited R. University and confirmed that on the day of the bombing Wakako was in the office of Professor Kirikaé all afternoon, and that she was in the church near Yotsuya Station from four o'clock to five-thirty. I received testimony on this from Professor Kirikaé and a Spanish friar named Larra at the office of the church."

"Testimony . . . Why wasn't Mr. Tsukioka able to find this?"

"Because Wakako wasn't talking to him. I visited her two days ago and asked her about what she did on that day. Then I went to R. University and the church, and found the witnesses she identified."

"You saw Wakako two days ago?" asked Mrs. Ikéhata from aside.

"Yes, I did."

"How was she?"

"She was looking quite fit."

"She won't see us at all," Mrs. Ikéhata said, drawing a deep sigh. "Whenever we try to visit, we're told she refuses to see us. She never looked our way in court. Why does she ignore us?"

Professor Ikéhata was regarding Akutsu with amazement.

"Mr. Akutsu, you and she had a normal conversation, didn't you? And that turned up her alibi. That is what we wanted to happen long ago." Professor Ikéhata looked very much like the powerless father. His thin shoulders drooped, and his head was bent.

Mrs. Ikéhata continued to sigh repeatedly, looking with unseeing eyes at the weed-choked garden outside. Then, spontaneously, she began speaking.

"She's the eldest girl. She took good care of her sister and brother. Her school records were good. She did housework, she listened to her parents. She was always a good girl. Things started going wrong after she finished high school, while she was going to entrance exam prep classes. She would run off with some man and not come home. If we said anything about it, she rebelled. Instead of studying, her head was always in the clouds on psychedelic pills and sleeping pills. After two years of trying, she finally got into university, but then all she could think of was to tear down the school, to start a revolution. She met up with a radical thug named Moriya and he infected her with his demonstrations and sect wars. By then, she was out of her right mind and hospitalized. Finally, she fell into the clutches of the worst thug of them all — Yukimori. He picked her up and took her straight to hell.

I don't know a thing about revolution or ideology, and I don't know about mental illness either, but I understand very well there were men behind that girl's downfall and illness. That's clear! When she was at home she was perfectly good. She only went bad when she left."

"That's right," Professor Ikéhata said, nodding. "Every man she met was some kind of villain. Yukimori was the worst of all, but Moriya really was hardly any better."

"It's true," Mrs. Ikéhata continued. "He started off looking like one of your best disciples. You did everything possible to help with his studies. Then, as soon as he found out we were against him marrying Wakako, suddenly you and the university are the people's enemy. That's his revolution. Harass the professors, make them negotiate, take them hostage. His final stroke was running off with Wakako."

"That's exactly right." Now Professor Ikéhata was glaring at Akutsu, as if he was seeing not his newly appointed attorney, but a student of Moriya's ilk. "That hooligan destroyed all twenty-five-years worth of my research papers. Do you have any idea what that means? The notes I took while studying in France, notes on readings since then, drafts of papers, records of surveys of prisons, not only in Japan but in many other countries as well, all of it wantonly destroyed. I am no longer able to conduct research. As you know, the study of jurisprudence has advanced slowly and incrementally by examining and surveying literature, and thinking through its meaning. It is the same as building a Tower — you must lay each stone upon the next, one by one. If the foundation is destroyed, the structure cannot be restored."

"I wonder if you can tell for sure Makihiko Moriya did that?" Akutsu said this in an undertone, as if putting the question to himself, but both Mr. and Mrs. Ikéhata shouted back as if they had been mightily insulted.

"I certainly can tell for sure!"

"There's no doubt about it!"

"It's a pity," Professor Ikéhata said, now returning to the feeble voice of an ailing person, perhaps chagrined at his own excitement. "I was on the faculty committee that dealt with the student disturbances. We surveyed the damage after the Tower takeover. It was the Q. Sect that took over the law department office. Moriya was on the Q. Sect Central Action Committee, and he had put what he called my bourgeoisie criminology on their target list. He's a full-blown lunatic, and his insanity infected Wakako. He drove her crazy."

"Excuse me, but it's wrong to demonize people with words like "lunatic" and "crazy." I'd say that young people have a clear-eyed view of the world." Akutsu had dropped his reserve and was speaking bluntly. "When I met Wakako the other day, I came away with a strong impression that her ideas about all that has happened are valid. It's probably true that she showed symptoms of mental abnormality in the past. But from the time of the Tower takeover through the day of the Shinkansen bombing and all through the trial, her view of the proceedings were as clear-eyed are they are today. Professor Matsuda has the same opinion."

"If that's true, why does she refuse to meet us, her parents?" Professor Ikéhata said with anguish.

"Because you have been treating her as a lunatic from the outset. To be honest about it, Mr. Tsukioka has been making the same mistake. The proof of that is Wakako was happy to meet with Professor Matsuda and me. We both had normal conversations with her."

"That's very strange," Mrs. Ikéhata said tearfully. "To treat even one's own mother as a stranger!"

Akutsu faced Mrs. Ikéhata. "The only men Wakako associated with treated her as equals. That was Makihiko Moriya and Atsuo Yukimori."

"A pair of good for nothing crooks!" Professor Ikéhata said with disgust.

"Nevertheless, it is the truth. Please understand this point, for her sake. If you do, I think Wakako will reciprocate and open up to you."

"Dear, are you in pain?" Mrs. Ikéhata hastened to her husband's side. He was leaning wearily against the back of his chair.

Akutsu rose. "I will be leaving now. Before I do, allow me to make one thing clear. Mr. Tsukioka and I will be working together as your legal counsel, but I do not wish to proceed on the premise that Yukimori or Moriya seduced Wakako or brought her to ruin. Instead, we will make every effort to establish the innocence of all the defendants."

"Wait a moment, please." Professor Ikéhata struggled for breath as his wife wiped cold sweat from his brow. "Please be seated. If you say so, and it is in the interest of the defense, I withdraw my conditions concerning Yukimori. But Moriya is another matter. I absolutely cannot agree to cooperation with him or the Q. Sect. That means I do not want a joint defense with them."

"That won't work. There will be no prospects of beating the prosecution's case if our defense does not cover all the defendants."

"Well, if the Q. Sect didn't bomb the Shinkansen, who did?"

"That, I don't know."

"There you are." Professor Ikéhata cast a look of pity for the young lawyer's limited vision. "It's unrealistic to claim all the defendants are innocent. Even if Wakako and Yukimori and that boy, what's his name? Jinnai? — even if they are innocent, that Q. Sect gang is another matter. There's a very high probability that they are the culprits. I don't have long to live. Please lend an ear to a fellow being soon to die. Please draw the line at those defendants. It would be a mistake to trust them."

Professor Ikéhata again struggled to catch his breath, as if this speech had exhausted his energy.

"I think you should take a rest," Mrs. Ikéhata told her husband. As Akutsu rose to leave, she cast him a look that implored him to remain, then escorted the professor from the room.

Akutsu went to the window and gazed idly out at the garden. Tall thickets of weeds gave the scene a rustic look. Crepe myrtle and paulownia trees sported fresh new leaves. A classic style bamboo fence was oriented as a setting for a distant view of a neighboring temple roof and woods — a subtle bit of landscaping artistry not often seen in the heart of Tokyo. The black luster of the outer corridor reflected the white of the shoji. Such touches suggested that the home had been built before the war, and may well be very old. Akutsu examined the eaves and roofing tile as he might if he had been in an old temple.

He had read that a temple built during the Edo era was one of the Ikéhata residences and the second son, Kotaro Ikéhata, had inherited the temple's neighboring retirement residence. Akutsu could imagine the kind of feelings that had made Wakako want to flee this home.

"Forgive me for making you wait," Mrs. Ikéhata said when she returned, politely inclining her slim, fair-skinned neck. " . . . and please forgive my husband's rudeness to you. We have had much to worry about with the legal affairs, and now, this illness has made him irritable."

"Of course. Serious illness poses a terrific burden."

"Oh, not really. He believes he has cancer, but his doctor says it is just a simple ulcer. So he probes everyone he meets to test if the doctor has let the truth out to someone. Mr. Tsukioka fell for it, and now he's talking as if he heard from the doctor himself that it's cancer . . .

"As you can imagine, we were thrilled to hear that our daughter has an alibi. Please do see it through to a not-guilty decision. To be honest, we don't have much confidence in Mr. Tsukioka. Of course, he is a very talented attorney — it's just that he has a very big case load. At the moment, his office is focusing on defending a politician on a bribery charge. He does not seem very interested in leftist radical cases. May I ask your thoughts on my husband's theory that the Q. Sect students may be the culprits in the Shinkansen bombing?"

"To be honest, I don't know yet. What I can say for sure is that the police investigation did not turn up any evidence implicating them. The possibility is great that the story of a Q. Sect conspiracy to bomb the Shinkansen is nothing more than a frame-up by the investigators."

"If that's the case, it would really be best if you mounted a joint defense with their attorneys."

"That's what I would like to do. That would make the defense much easier. It would be the most effective way to break down the prosecutor's false allegations."

"Then, please do so." Mrs. Ikéhata suddenly began to cry.

"To have your daughter receive a life sentence when she didn't do anything — It's horrible, a nightmare. My husband knew the prosecutor in charge of the case. They are from the same graduating class. He said he would talk to him. I felt relieved, but the worst happened." Mrs. Ikéhata began to sob uncontrollably. Akutsu stolidly waited for the tears to subside, searching the while for an opportunity to escape.

Chapter 9

Stars

The state still hasn't made a final decision on what to do with me, but it has handed me a death sentence, and that makes me a condemned prisoner. As proof of my changed status, I have been given a new residence among the other inmates under death sentence, in a corner of the building set apart from the prisoners with life sentences. There is pure and simple discrimination even within zero cell block, the home of the serious offenders. Inmates having death sentences and those having life sentences receive different treatment. Now I share in the glory of being one of the condemned. Atsuo Yukimori has moved up in the world.

One good thing has come with my new status. My associates during exercise hour are Mikio Wakabayashi and Mitsuo Takasaki. Both are in the execution queue, having had their sentences confirmed. I had believed Takasaki had already been executed, but there he was, still among the living. I don't know why I was put with two inmates whose sentences are confirmed. My guess is it has to do with Wakabayashi and me both going to Father Okuda's sermons, and my previous friendship with Takasaki. If my theory is right, the authorities see me as pious, and they want my influence to inspire the other two to be submissive about their fate.

This morning's exercise hour passed quietly. None of us took any exercise. We just talked, while the chilly autumn wind blew steadily. We stood in the warmth of the sunlight, three men having a friendly conversation in low voices. And what kind of talk was exchanged between the one-time mechanic, his head shorn, the former carpenter with deep-set eyes and the former foundry man, still young, fair skinned and handsome? Women? Crime? Dreams of freedom? Most anyone's imagination would run along those lines, but actually, we talked about what we wanted done with our bodies after death. Wakabayashi, from the snow country, killer and derailer of a passenger train, lamented that he could not be interred in the cemetery where his forebears slept.

"That's where I want to be, but my ancestors, and my father too, wouldn't like being with someone who was executed. And you don't want to write 'cause of death: execution' into the family register. Really, the best thing would be cremation after I'm dead, and have my ashes scattered from an airplane."

Takasaki didn't have any relatives. He said he had arranged to donate his body to a medical university for medical students' vivisection practicum.

I'd been keeping quiet. Wakabayashi caught me unprepared when he asked me, "What are you going to do?" Being innocent of the charges against me, I had not regarded that as an issue for me to deal with. I made up an answer and hoped it would sound like the product of careful consideration.

"My parents' graves have a beautiful view of the Sea of Okhotsk. Of course, I can't be there, even though I would want to be. So, what I want is to be put on an ice floe. In the spring, the ice moves south, then melts. The sharks will get my body."

Takasaki laughed. "You think the prison's going to take that much trouble for you?"

"If it comes to that, I'll have my body cremated and ask my sister to put the remains on an ice floe."

A guard came and put an end to our talk. Back in my cell, I got busy making baggage tags, with a vivid picture in my mind of my body riding an ice floe. There was a strong wind whipping across the concrete walls. Its roar drowned out Furukawa's rants. That was the next best thing to real quiet.

Mr. Akutsu came to discuss the first hearing of the appeal trial next week. He wears a strong pair of eyeglasses that give him a studious look. He is a young man, and thin enough to still be a teenager. Nevertheless, he is so businesslike he inspires confidence.

A second lieutenant fresh out of officer's school believes the war will be won if you follow the orders laid down in the army's strategic training manual. He will lead a head-on attack into a hail of bullets without flinching. Such a young officer wins the hearts of the troops more than any seasoned non-commissioned officer. He can score a victory before you know it. But the war goes on and on. You advance, you retreat. You find yourself in a protracted struggle where you can't tell your friends from your enemies. That is when the experienced NCOs are best prepared to make the troops perform.

I think this young lawyer is trustworthy. At the same time, something in me sees his weaknesses. Does this cynicism come from the many treacheries I have been dealt? In any case, he is full of confidence and smiles, and I have responded by obediently allowing him to proceed as he thinks best.

Mr. Akutsu favors me with frequent visits. He has briefed me fully on the new witnesses and the agreements reached among the different lawyers. I am now being apprised of the fine points in the state of the war, like an important trooper on the battlefield. My last lawyer, Mr. Iino, gave me no such consideration. He visited me once in a while, and then only to cry about how the defense wasn't going well. There is a vast difference between these two lawyers. Mr. Akutsu wants to question the new witnesses as soon as possible. He said he wants to show up the prosecutor's lies and make the hearings proceed to our advantage. That made me smile, because what he said was so like the army's official strategy directive. To wit, "The key to victory in battle lies in gathering a combination of tangible and intangible combat elements and applying them in essential places with force surpassing that of the enemy."

After we got through the strategy conference and were down to general conversation, I asked how Wakako was doing. He said she intended to speak out at the second trial and she was practicing by going through the trial proceedings. The fact that she does not have hard feelings against me brightens my outlook. However hard a battle it will be, fighting it together with her is my idea of happiness.

"How is that memoir coming along?" Mr. Akutsu asked.

I had started writing a record of my past when I arrived at Kosugé. I soon realized it was going to be an agonizing mission to fulfill. Most of what is in my past if the kind of thing anyone would want to keep quiet about — frolicking in brothels, stealing, embezzling, running away from police, lying, battlefields, slaughter. I am at the bottom level as far as men go, hardly worthy of Wakako. I am not even much at writing, but I am writing the memoir to fulfill the promise I made to her at the hot spring in the mountains at Raúsu.

"I write a little bit every day, while I make baggage tags. It is not a pretty thing to write about, but I have to do it."

"Why do you have to?"

"I promised Wakako I would. Maybe part of it is wanting to understand what kind of person I am, even if it is unpleasant. Sitting in that tiny cell all day long makes me confront myself. I guess that's where the desire came from."

Akutsu nodded his encouragement. When he does things like that he looks dignified enough to be older than I am. Maybe it has to do with that gold attorney's badge he wears. The shine has faded lately. Now it's a somber silver color.

Trial number two had a hearing. The courtroom is smaller than the district court's. It feels almost as if we were all sitting around the same table with the judges. It isn't mandatory for the defendants to be present at the appeal trial, but we were all there. All six are white as sheets, having been long deprived of much time in the sunlight. The lightness of Wakako's skin stayed within my view throughout the hearing. Following the motion of her breast as she breathed, and watching her other body movements was very much like the feeling of embracing her. Tetsukichi and Suéko and Sonoko Kanéhara were in the spectators section. Surprisingly, Torakichi's stocky figure was a part of the scene. It was the first time he had come to a hearing.

It is one of those inexplicable wonders that so many prosecutors are look-alikes. The one this time is named Shunji Domaé. He's tall — a hundred seventy-five centimeters — and at forty, he's only slightly older than Onuki, the prosecutor in the first trial. He has the same dark complexion and the same penetrating gaze. He gives off the impression of being from a wealthy family. And he's a smooth talker — just like Onuki.

Wakako spoke for the first time in response to the routine confirmation of identity question. It was the first time I heard her voice in two and a half years. It echoed through me. Two and a half years since we were together. We were at the pinnacle of happiness then; now we undergo torment through no fault of our own.

We have a defense team of four lawyers: Kida and Uzawa for the Q. Sect, Tsukioka for Wakako, and Akutsu for me. Tsukioka is the only one who is not young. Kida and Uzawa look to be in their early thirties. Mr. Tsukioka read out the statement of reasons for appeal on behalf of the entire defense team. There were serious errors of fact in the decision of the first trial. First of all, there was no conspiracy between the Q. Sect, Yukimori, and Ikéhata to bomb the Shinkansen. The evidence purporting to show there was is inadequate. Second, Yukimori and Ikéhata were not engaged in planting a bomb between three fifty and four o'clock on the afternoon of February eleven. Trustworthy witnesses will testify that Yukimori was in Jindai Botanical Garden and Ikéhata was in the Station Front Church at that time.

Mr. Tsukioka's reading had the emotional overtones of a staged ballad recital, with shamisen backing. When he got to the alibis, his gestures grew quite dramatic. I looked around the courtroom and saw that Mr. Domaé sat motionless, with a blank expression. The reading took over two hours. Then Domaé rose and began reading the prosecution's response. It was a rehash of the closing statement in the first trial, even to using the same text that Onuki had read out. The only thing new was where he flatly declared the alibis and Yukimori and Ikéhata were groundless. He concluded by saying "Therefore, the defendants have no reason for appeal." Then he abruptly sat down again and returned to his state of suspended animation.

Without missing a beat, Akutsu asked the presiding judge for permission to be heard.

"The four witnesses whose names appear in the evidence examination request form are all present in the courtroom. I would like to conduct their questioning right now."

The presiding judge, a man in his sixties, regarded the young attorney with widened eyes. "What is the questioning of the witnesses intended to prove?"

"Witnesses Yoko Mizuno and Sonoko Kanéhara will testify to the alibi of Atsuo Yukimori, and witnesses Leopold Larra and Shiro Kirikaé will testify to the alibi of Wakako Ikéhata."

"What is the opinion of the prosecution?"

"In consideration of appropriate steps for the calling of witnesses, I would like to have witness examination conducted at the next hearing."

"Your honor," Akutsu began spiritedly. "Witness Yoko Mizuno is in charge of recreational therapy at Y. Hospital, witness Sonoko Kanéhara is a dorm mother at Fukawa Motors, witness Leopold Larra is the administrator of the Yotsuya Station Front Church, and witness Shiro Kirikaé is an associate professor at R. University. Each is engaged in a demanding job. It would not necessarily be feasible to arrange for them all to appear at the next hearing. It so happens that they are all present now, giving us an excellent opportunity to question them."

"What is the opinion of the prosecution?"

"In that case, I would like for the defense to conduct its direct examination today and reserve the prosecution's cross examination for the next session."

"That's no good!" Tsukioka muttered, and whispered to Akutsu. At least it seemed to be his intention to whisper, but I caught everything he said, quite clearly.

"Do only the direct questioning today and you show all your cards to the other side. There's no reason not to put it off to next time. Just do it so direct and cross questioning happen on the same day."

Akutsu agreed to do witness examination at the next hearing. His face was red, and he was sweating. Then the defense and prosecution disagreed over when to schedule the next hearing. Akutsu wanted it to be as early as possible in the next week. Domaé was firm about scheduling it a month later. The judge questioned each of the witnesses about their schedules, then set the date for the hearing at October fifteenth — one month later. It is galling to me, a defendant, to be made to wait that long.

Torakichi, Suéko, and Tetsukichi paid me a visit.

"I apologize to you," Torakichi said, with a deep bow of his head. "I had it all wrong. I'm sorry I doubted you."

"Aw, don't be bowing like that. There's no need to. It's me that's in the wrong. It's what I get for confessing to lies."

The glass between us made it impossible for me to shake his hand, but it felt like we had a hearty handshake. Suéko dabbed at tears in her eyes upon seeing her husband and brother reconciled.

The conversation turned to all that Mr. Akutsu was doing. To Tetsukichi I said, "Hey, thanks for finding a guy like that for me."

An expression like an abashed schoolboy came over Tetsukichi's tanned features, and he gave an answer as if his broad arms were prepared to strike blows.

"The government is what put you here! Somebody's got to see that government gets what coming to it!"

Torakichi was regarding Tetsukichi as if unnerved by the sight. Never before had he shown such an attitude. The father had grown apprehensive of the son, now a young man who had profited handsomely from illicit dealings with Soviet fishing boats, and was bent on proving the innocence of his uncle and brother.

I can see pigeons on the roof of the cell house across from mine. They roost in an exacting alignment. If two are spaced fifty centimeters apart, the next pigeon that lands comes to rest just fifty centimeters down the line. The spacing rule holds for any number, even when several birds arrive together. Fifty-centimeter spacing is not in itself a rule — it could be thirty centimeters on another occasion. I observe such rules of pigeon society as I make my baggage tags. The pigeons observe with wonder the strange rule by which human beings here are spaced at regular intervals behind iron bars. Of course, the pigeons' rules have been in effect from antiquity. They mock human come-lately imitators.

"Cross-examination," the presiding judge said. Mr. Domaé approached Yoko Mizuno on the witness stand.

"What was the date and time this photograph was taken?"

"I explained that to the attorney just now. February 11th, 1969, between three thirty and four o'clock."

"Why do you remember so clearly?"

"It's one of the pictures in an album I kept for the Y. Hospital's Fifteen Year History. They are arranged in order by year. It was in the February, 1969 section, so I know for sure it was taken on that day."

"In other words, it is not that you remember the day the photograph was taken, but that you inferred the date."

"Well, of course!" Yoko Mizuno said in a voice that carried well across the courtroom. She seemed to have been annoyed by this statement. "There is no reason why anyone would remember all the days pictures were taken two and a half years ago. The plum trees are in full bloom in this photo. It shows a large group of people. We went plum blossom viewing three times in February, 1969 — the hospital schedules these outings as a kind of therapy. I can infer with certainly that this picture belongs to that group."

"Three times. What were the dates?"

"February ninth, eleventh, and fourteenth."

"Did you remember those dates?"

"No, I checked them from my rec therapy diary."

"What is the basis for saying this photo was taken on February 11th and not on one of the other two dates?"

"The cloud conditions. The ninth was clear skies, the eleventh was highly cloudy — that is almost an overcast condition — and the fourteenth was just cloudy. The sky in this picture is highly cloudy, so it must have been taken on the eleventh."

"Inference once again. You did not remember the day this photograph was taken, and yet you remember the time? 'Between three thirty and four in the afternoon' is an awfully detailed recollection."

"Yes, I do remember the time. We arrived at the park at two thirty in the afternoon. I wanted to be back in time for supper at four thirty. We wanted to take a group photo and had very little time to get it done. The patients move slowly. It takes them thirty minutes to walk from the park back to the hospital. So, it had to have been before four o'clock — somewhere between three thirty and four — that the picture was taken. That is not inference. I remember it clearly."

"You say you don't remember the date, but you nevertheless do remember the time of day?" Domaé asked, sarcasm in his tone.

"That's quite natural," Yoko Mizuno said, wriggling her well-endowed body. "It is a principle of memory that people remember fine details of time more readily than they remember days. As a rec therapist, I have responsibility that patients' activities be carried out within a certain time frame. It is part of my job to be mindful of the time."

"I see. As a psychology specialist, you are knowledgeable in this area. One's recollections of the time of day are good, but not so good about days, and when it comes to the year, they become vaguer still. Do those principles of memory apply?"

"Well, yes, they do."

"A moment ago you said you inferred that this photograph belongs to the February 11th section of an album you keep. Wouldn't it be fair to say that you had no actual recollection that the album is for Showa 44?"

"Showa 44 . . . I do not use Showa . . . era names for dates."

"I am saying that you had no recollection this photograph was taken in 1969, that you only inferred it."

"Instead of calling it inference, you can say that there is certain proof that it was taken in 1969. All the photos in this album are arranged by year."

"I visited your hospital at the end of this July to be shown that album. The photographs were not arranged in any order at all. It took you a great deal of time to even locate the album."

"The pictures got all jumbled when I showed them to Mr. Akutsu. Then you showed up, all of a sudden. I was in such a hurry to get it, they got even more mixed up."

"Let's turn to something else. When did you start working at Y. Hospital?"

"April, 1968, right after I graduated university."

"Did you begin taking photographs for the Y. Hospital Fifteen Year History immediately after you began working there in April, Showa 43?"

"No, I started in late May, when the hospital had a field day. I was a member of the university photography club, so it seemed natural to take pictures at the event. The hospital director took notice and put me in charge of the photography for that history."

"Well, then, was there someone taking pictures for the Y. Hospital Fifteen Year History before you?"

"Ms. Nemoto, the occupational therapist, took pictures."

"Does that mean there are photographs taken by Ms. Nemoto in the album in your charge?"

"There certainly are."

"About what proportion of the whole?"

"Oh, I would guess about half."

"Then it is by no means certain that this photograph was taken by you.

Pardon my bluntness, but your room at the hospital and its shelves are far from orderly. The room is disorderly and your album was in more of a jumble."

"As I said before, the album was in order before that."

"Anyone can put photographs into that album and take them out again as they please. Just because this photograph was in the Showa 44 section doesn't mean it couldn't have been moved there from some other section."

"I didn't do that and I would never do anything that dishonest."

"It's something that could be done unintentionally. When I went to see this album, didn't two or three photos fall out onto the floor?"

"There are negatives that go with the pictures from the shoots of plum blossom viewing outings. You can tell which set the photo was from."

"There is no correspondence between numbers of the negatives and the print numbers. There are gaps, negatives from other sets are mixed in. Therefore, it cannot be said with absolute certainty that this photograph was taken on February eleven, Showa 44 or that you took it. To the contrary, doesn't your inference have an extremely low probability of being true?"

Yoko Mizuno bit her lip, at a loss for a response.

"Objection, your honor," Akutsu protested. "The question imposes a conclusion on the witness."

"Sustained," the presiding judge said.

"I withdraw the question," the prosecutor conceded lightly. "I will proceed to the next question. Have you been meeting with Mr. Akutsu very much?"

"Yes, we meet occasionally."

"Is that for the purpose of discussing this day's testimony?"

"Yes."

"Near the end of July you stated that you first met Mr. Akutsu in May of this year. Correct?"

"That's what I said."

"How many times have you met him since then?"

"Well, I haven't been counting."

"Maybe more times than you could keep track of, eh? When was the last time you met him?"

"The day before yesterday."

"October third. That was Sunday."

"Is there something wrong with meeting on Sunday?"

"The Ishikawa Law Office where Mr. Akutsu is employed, is closed on Sunday. What is the reason for your meeting with this attorney countless times since May and even on a holiday?"

"If the court please!" Akutsu burst out.

"I have the floor, counselor," Domaé said with equanimity and continued. "Police officers of the Onarimon station on patrol observed you and Mr. Akutsu on October three, at 10:05 p.m. entering P. Hotel at West Shimbashi 3 chomé, and again at seven o'clock the next morning leaving together. Were you conferring about your testimony for that very long time period?"

"That is despicable!" Yoko Mizuno shouted. Domaé continued to maintain his unruffled tone.

"You and Mr. Akutsu have been positively identified by police officers staying together at hotels with great frequency — at least ten times since May."

"You had them following us!" Yoko Mizuno shouted, her body trembling. "Low-down, sneaking . . ."

"Wouldn't you say it is low down and sneaky for an attorney to stay in a hotel with a witness whose appearance he himself requested for the purpose of obtaining favorable testimony?"

"My testimony has nothing to do with whatever purely private, individual activities I may choose to do."

"Can you prove that?"

"I have the freedom to associate with whoever I like and do whatever I like, as long as it isn't against the law."

"I'm asking whether you can prove your individual activity, in other words, your staying in hotels with the defense attorney, bears no relation to the act of giving legal testimony."

"How on earth could I prove it? It is a private matter between two people. But I can swear to this. There is absolutely no relationship."

"That is all." Domaé sat in his chair and closed his mouth tightly. His precise movements gave the impression that his internal engine had gone into neutral. The swell of his jaw muscles projected resolve that nothing more would be said.

The presiding judge said, "Will the defense re-examine?"

Akutsu looked back to Tsukioka and the two lawyers began to confer. I could only catch Tsukioka's voice.

"That was a kick in the balls." . . . "You've got to rework your strategy." . . . "Whatever else there is, see that you keep it under wraps."

Akutsu rose, flushed and visibly sweating. He said, "No further questions," as he wiped his glasses. There was no mistaking that he was a young man overcome by frustrated anger.

Akutsu called Sonoko Kanéhara as his next witness.

Sonoko Kanéhara had been appearing faithfully in the spectators' section at every hearing of our trials. For some reason, she had always sat in the back row, inconspicuous, but this day she was extravagantly dressed in a black pongee kimono with a red batik sash. She did not look like the Sonoko I knew, always preoccupied with running the men's dorm at Fukawa Motors. As our eyes met, a faint smile creased the corners of her eyes.

"Do you recall the day the defendant Atsuo Yukimori was fired from his job at Fukawa Motors?"

"Yes. It was National Foundation Day, Showa 44."

"About what time was it that you met the defendant for the last time that day?"

"A little before two in the afternoon. I left the dormitory to see him off because it was a last goodbye. I watched him as he crossed the parking lot."

"Do you remember what he was wearing at the time?"

"Yes, a red polka-dot necktie and a light brown duster coat."

"You recall the tie's pattern?"

"Of course I do," Sonoko Kanéhara said with a smile at me spreading across her face. "That tie was a present I gave him. It is a top Italian brand — Angelo Litrico. I had bought it for thirty thousand yen as a Valentine's Day gift."

"Is the necktie in this photograph that same tie?"

"That's the one I gave him."

"Is the duster coat the same as he wore on that last day?"

"Yes. This is the coat he wore. Mr. Yukimori is very particular about overcoats and jackets. He only wears foreign made brands. This is an English Brand, a Chester Barrie." As Akutsu sat down, nodding with a satisfied look, Domaé sprang to his feet.

"Your honor. I request you have the witness leave the courtroom while we prepare for her questioning."

"How much time do you need?"

"Just two or three minutes."

The presiding judge conferred with the associate judges, then granted the request. After the courtroom doors had closed behind Sonoko Kanéhara and her plainclothes bailiff escort, the prosecutor gave instructions to his assistant officer, who proceeded to lay out three duster coats and five neckties on a table. The duster coats were all brown colored, and as far as I could tell, they were mine. Three of the five neckties were polka dotted, one had plum-colored stripes and one was a white print of grass on a peony background. Those I recognized for sure as mine.

"The defendant, Atsuo Yukimori, testified during the investigation phase that the coat he wore on the day of the crime in question was Exhibit 37, and the necktie he wore was Exhibit 38. The other items are all possessions of the defendant. I request permission to show them to the witness for the purpose of verifying her recollections."

"Granted. Please have the witness return to the stand."

Sonoko Kanéhara returned to the witness stand wearing an anxious expression. She looked with apprehension at the coats and neckties as she nervously patted down stray hairs.

"The witness will please stand before the table," Domaé said as he rose from his seat and went to the table. In his proximity, Sonoko looked like a small pigeon beside a raven.

"All of these items belong to the defendant, Atsuo Yukimori. Please point out the coat and necktie worn by the defendant on February 11th, Showa 44. No, you may not touch them. Just stand one meter away . . . Yes, that's fine."

Sonoko Kanéhara was trembling, almost imperceptibly. She folded her arms and clasped her shoulders to control it, but to no avail. After much indecision, she pointed out the correct coat, then shook her head and pointed to another one. When it came to the red polka dot ties, all three were so similar I couldn't tell one from another either. She finally pointed to one.

The prosecutor held up the photograph and asked, "Is this the duster coat and necktie shown in the photograph?"

"I think so . . ." Sonoko Kanéhara's voice was trailing off as she spoke, making the last word barely audible.

"Did you give the defendant, Atsuo Yukimori, any other presents prior to that one?"

"Yes, I started giving him neckties every Valentine's Day, I suppose a couple of years before then."

"Neckties are among the gifts you gave him?"

"Yes." Sonoko Kanéhara pointed out the three polka dot ties.

"Why always red polka dots?"

"I thought they were becoming to Mr. Yukimori."

"Neither the duster coat nor the necktie pointed out by the witness were worn by the defendant Atsuo Yukimori on the day of the crime. The questions have demonstrated that the photograph was not taken on the day of the crime, but at a previous time. That concludes cross examination." The prosecutor spoke rapidly, bowing to the presiding judge and ignoring Akutsu, who seemed about to raise an objection.

"Will the defense again conduct direct questioning?" the presiding judge asked.

The defense attorneys conferred, then Akutsu stood and stated weakly there would be no redirect examination. Instead, he called Atsuo Yukimori to the stand. He whispered to me, "Just relax and answer the questions, please," with a look of encouragement from behind his powerful eyeglasses.

"Is this a photo of you?"

"It is."

"When was it taken?"

"Showa 44, February 11th, in the afternoon."

"How do you know it was the afternoon of that day?"

"That day has a special meaning to me, so I remember it well. It was the day I was fired from the company where I had worked for over seven years. I got my things together and left the place a little before two o'clock. I was feeling about as low as could be. I took the National Railways rapid service express from Ochanomizu to Mitaka, then took a bus from the south exit of Chofu Station. It was about three when I arrived at my apartment. I went out again right away — to Jindai Botanical Garden."

"Did you change clothes in your apartment?"

"No. I was in no mood to stay there. I left immediately, dressed just as I was."

"You could have gone straight to the botanical garden without returning to your apartment. Why stop off there at all?"

"I was carrying a paper bag with everything that had been in my locker at Fukawa Motors — work uniforms, a toilet kit, my mechanic's license, an English dictionary, and some other things. I didn't want to be carrying that while I was walking in the park."

"About what time did you arrive at Jindai Botanical Garden?"

"Probably about three thirty. I know every path in that park. I headed straight for the plum wood. That is where I saw a group of psychiatric hospital patients with a nurse leading them."

"How did you know they were psychiatric hospital patients?"

"Y. Psychiatric Hospital is located close by my apartment. I'm used to seeing its patients and the nurses. Someone in the group I saw at the park called out, 'C'mon head nurse!' That told me the group was the psychiatric hospital patients. The patients were lined up for a group photograph. A middle-aged woman, kind of stout, ran up to the group and sat down in the middle."

"Do you think this photograph was taken then?"

"I don't know that it was, but since it shows the plum blossoms and seven or eight people squatting down with me at one end, it seems to me it was taken just when I was passing by that group."

"What time did you leave Jindai Botanical Garden?"

"At about four thirty I heard the announcement that the park would close at five. I headed for the gate at a leisurely pace, so I was a bit before five."

"So you were in Jindai Botanical Garden from what time until what time?"

"From three thirty until a little before five."

After Mr. Akutsu finished, the prosecutor, Domaé said he had questions for me. Mr. Akutsu warned me, "Careful, he goes for the jugular." Even so, I was feeling upbeat, thinking it was a good opportunity to give a clear statement of my alibi.

"Defendant Atsuo Yukimori, do you go to Jindai Botanical Garden often?"

"I do. It is near to my apartment. Convenient for taking a stroll."

"Do you go to see different flowers blossoming in season?"

"Yes, I like flowers. I have the seasons in mind when visit the park. Plum, peach, cherry, double cherry, magnolias, roses . . . That park has wonderful variety."

"Did you go plum blossom viewing previously?"

"Yes, I make it my business to catch the plum blossoms every year."

"Do you see the psychiatric hospital patients and workers very often?"

"Once in a while. I suppose they come to see the flowers too."

"How do you know they are from Y. Hospital?"

"I don't know that's where they come from. It isn't as if they carry a flag. But I can tell they are psychiatric hospital patients. Many are fat, slow-moving, some even have the shakes, maybe because of medication. And there is always some energetic woman leading them. That's the nurse."

"All right. This is a photograph of you. You go plum blossom viewing every year. You encounter people from the psychiatric hospital often. So how do you know this picture was taken in Showa 44, on February eleven?" Domaé's expression did not change as he looked at me. He might as well have been a big bronze statue. I saw him as exactly like Onuki, the prosecutor from the first trial, except that Domaé was one size larger than Onuki.

I felt as if I had to push aside that heavy statue. "Well, that's like I just said, I can tell by the clothes I'm wearing in this picture." My voice was suddenly hoarse.

"But this photograph is focused on the people in the group shot. You are slightly out of focus. The necktie does not show up clearly. As the witness Sonoko Kanéhara has testified, you have received neckties of the same pattern year after year. You have more than one duster coat of the same color. Couldn't this photograph be of the previous year, or the year before that?"

In order to answer that, I was forced me to say something I would normally refrain from saying. "Ms. Kanéhara means well, but the fact is I don't really like polka dot patterns. It isn't just polka dots. I don't go for any kind of geometrical pattern on a necktie, whether it's dots or lines. I like designs that show something from nature — trees, flowers, crickets . . . that kind of thing. So, I didn't wear the ties I got from Ms. Kanéhara. The only exception was the day I was fired. I went to the dormitory to say goodbye to her. She had bought that tie to give to me on Valentine's Day. I opened the box and put it on as a way of showing my gratitude. I left the company wearing that tie."

Domaé held up the two neckties registered as supplementary evidence. "You say you never wore these ties, but they show unmistakable signs of use."

"I opened up the boxes and tried them on in front of a mirror. But I never went outside wearing them."

"Is there anything to prove that?"

"Proof? Look, I'm not lying."

"Did the defendant put on a necktie on the morning of February 11th, 1969 before leaving for work?"

"Yes."

"If you put on the necktie the witness Sonoko Kanéhara gave you as a present upon leaving the company, what became of the necktie you put on that morning?"

"The other tie . . ."

I didn't remember anything about it. I put on the gift necktie in the dorm mother's room. Did I leave the other tie there? Did I stuff it into my pocket?

"Isn't it strange that you should remember putting on a tie and not remember the one you removed to change ties?"

"I have no recollection."

"Do you remember what tie you put on when you left your apartment in the morning?"

"I have no recollection of that either."

"If not, then what we can conclude is that the defendant can recall only the allegation in his interest as he knows from seeing the photograph and hearing the recent testimony of the witness Sonoko Kanéhara."

"That's not true!" I was so excited, my voice was came out in a pitiful undertone. "I remembered that Ms. Kanéhara gave me that polka-dot necktie. It left a strong impression because I knew she gave it to me on the day of our final parting."

"Fired from your job, leaving the company. Your strong impressions of that day should include what you were wearing. Going to the locker room, taking off your work clothes, then changing into your necktie and coat for the last time."

"You've got it wrong!" I was nearly screaming.

When the prosecutors questioning ended, the strength in my legs suddenly vanished. It was a shaky walk back to the defendant's seat. The judge announced the hearing would adjourn until one thirty p.m. The guards handcuffed the defendants and led them from the room, one by one. Suddenly Wakako faced me and yelled out. "It's all right! We can fight this!"

Her female guards reacted together with a merciless jerk on the handcuffs that made Wakako pitch forward and fall to the floor. Raw violence from two hulking uniformed women forcing a sweet young girl into submission — the perfect picture to symbolize this trial. I made it my business to walk slower than the pace of the guards on either side of me, so they had to drag me along back to the court holding cell, where I had a dismal cold lunch.

Mr. Akutsu came up with a beautiful attack plan, only to have it shot down by a master of dirty tricks on the other side. I'm just a useless old trooper who wants to save the platoon commander, but can't do anything. That thought raised an ironic laugh from me. Here I am overcome with worry for a bright young man, as if I was nothing but an observer watching the battle from the sidelines.

~

"We lost that one," Ishikawa said, clapping Akutsu on the shoulder and shaking his white mane at his face.

"I lost that one," the dejected lawyer replied, looking at the floor.

"Your glasses need cleaning," Ishikawa commented as he nodded to Tsukioka, then launched into a chummy conversation with the other two lawyers, Kida and Uzawa.

Akutsu wiped off a layer of sweat and fingerprints from his glasses. Yoko Mizuno, who had been sitting alone in the observer's section, approached, smiling brightly.

"You look dejected. Hey, it's all right. We can fight this!" she said, in a creditable impersonation of Wakako.

"I feel bad that I've caused such unpleasantness for you."

"There's no need to feel that way. I don't blame you for anything."

"But your privacy was violated."

"That's just how it goes. It doesn't bother me because we've harmed no one. The evildoer is that prosecutor, with his bag of dirty tricks. Sending out two policemen to follow law abiding citizens. He's the one with something to be ashamed of, not me. All he did was make me good and angry. That picture was taken the day of the Shinkansen bombing and he answers that fact with quibbles and snide insinuations. I am not going to let him get away with it. I'm going to prove it was taken that day and no other."

"How?"

"I'm working on that now. The first thing for me to do is sort every single negative by year. I know that room is in total disorder. The fact is, I'm a perfectionist about putting things in order. I didn't want to even start arranging things unless I knew I could do the job right . . . Well, I guess that doesn't amount to an excuse. Listen, I'm staying for the afternoon session, and I want to see you again when it's over. Stay strong."

As Yoko Mizuno withdrew, Mr. Tsukioka, looking fretful, hurried to Akutsu's side as if he had been waiting for the moment.

"It's been decided that we should all have lunch together to work out this afternoon's strategy. Your sponsoring attorney says he'll be there."

"Is that so?" Akutsu's expression showed displeasure. Though a guest attorney at the Ishikawa Law Office, he had handled this case independently to date. For Ishikawa to turn up at a strategy session without so much as an advance word to him would be a denial of that independence. Before Akutsu could respond, Ishikawa beckoned him aside.

"You look like your dog peed on you. Brighten up! You can't let a little thing like that get you down."

"It hasn't gotten me down. It happened, though."

"Don't underestimate that Domaé. He's been prosecuting public safety cases for Tokyo from way back. He and Onuki are joined at the hip. What one of them knows, they both know. He's got a reputation for tripping up witnesses on the stand. Look, I give you credit for bringing in those witnesses. Your trouble is your own security. You go to bed with your own witness and get nailed for it. They followed you ten times and you never caught on?"

"No. Didn't have a clue."

"A lawyer who goes to bed with a witness inside a police net is no lawyer at all!"

"I went to bed with a woman, not a witness."

"Who do you expect that argument to convince? You can't count out anyone in this judicial system. You got your head in the clouds, boy! . . . Today's hearing was too much to have to watch. You've got a lot of reeducation coming, and I'm going make sure you get it!"

"It's all right. I can handle this alone."

"You damn fool!" This was the first time Ishikawa gave Akutsu a taste of his raw anger. "You've got a man's life in your hands. Suppose you go it alone and fail. Atsuo Yukimori is under a death sentence. We've got to undo that no matter what. It's the same as being a doctor. You can't let your patient die because you botched the treatment."

"There's a straight path to winning the case. Reinforce the evidence we already have."

"Yeah, that's the right theory. The trouble is, it's never easy to make it work. I know what I'm talking about. I've handled two or three of these false charge cases."

"We're leaving now," Tsukioka said, marching off with fellow attorneys Kida and Uzawa. "Room Four of the Daiichi Tokyo Bar Association building. I'll order lunch."

"Now pay attention," Ishikawa resumed, pushing back at his bristling white hair. "Defense lawyers turn up what they consider to be sound, crystal clear evidence and prosecutors make it look dubious and fuzzy. That's the theme of every hearing. Were you anticipating that counter-punch you took this morning?"

"No. I thought I was making a surprise attack, but the surprise was on me."

"That's because he knew exactly what you were up to. Any time you put out an argument about the facts, make yourself aware of how it can be refuted. That's the same as a doctor anticipating a drug's side effects. Are you going to do the witness questioning again this afternoon?"

"Yes. This afternoon will demonstrate Wakako Ikéhata's alibi. I'm the one who found the witnesses."

"All, right. I said what needed to be said. You take it from here. This afternoon I have other business. I'm out of here now," Ishikawa said, and left abruptly.

~

The first witness in the afternoon, Shiro Kirikaé, I recognized as the one who visited me this spring. Such whiskers! His mustache was trimmed, but his mouth was still buried in the other shrubbery. It must get in his way when he's eating. He read out the printed witness pledge, "I pledge to tell the truth, following my conscience, concealing nothing and adding nothing." Then he added, "I don't know just what conscience is, so I will only follow the lord, Jesus Christ," and drew a cross in the air.

Before Mr. Akutsu could say a word, he blurted out, "Ms. Wakako Ikéhata is innocent!" The judge told him, "Wait until you are questioned to give your answers."

First question: Was Wakako in Professor Kirikaé's office on the afternoon of the bombing? He said she was with him from two until past three in the afternoon. Then Domaé rose to cross-examine.

"When you say 'past three o'clock,' does that mean you looked at a clock?"

"As you know, having visited yourself, my office is filled with old clocks. They have all been repaired to run accurately."

"Very well. How many minutes past three o'clock was it when the defendant Wakako Ikéhata left your office?"

"That I don't remember."

"Isn't it strange to remember the hour of three o'clock, but not the minute?"

"The three o'clock chimes rang. That is how I know the hour. Ms. Ikéhata left sometime after that."

"Let me ask you this. About what time was it that I left the day I visited your office?"

"You came in the afternoon, at two or three o'clock. We discussed the events of the day in question while I was carving out a seal. You left around three or four o'clock."

"Well, was it three o'clock or four o'clock?"

"One of the two." There was a ripple of laughter from the observers' seats.

"At least please say if it was before or after three or before or after four o'clock."

"I don't remember that."

"I left your office that day at ten minutes past three o'clock. It appears that you are well accustomed to hearing the hour chime and therefore do not pay attention to it. Questions concluded."

Shiro Kirikaé spoke as the prosecutor sat down. "Excuse me, that is not the end of your question."

"The witness will request permission before speaking," the judge said. Kirikaé ignored him.

"When my clocks announced the hour at three o'clock, Ms. Ikéhata said something. She said, 'How wonderful to be hearing all these clocks again, singing "Three o'clock, it's three o'clock." That tells me the world is still turning.'" That is why I remember it was three o'clock. She left right after that."

"About how many minutes past three?" the judge asked.

"We talked for ten or fifteen minutes, so three ten or three fifteen."

The next witness was a Franciscan brother by the name of Leopold Larra. He was Spanish, with a fine beak of a nose and crinkly black hair. After Professor

Kirikaé had established the time Wakako left R. University, Mr. Akutsu's questions began having impact; a young man on the rebound from the morning's despair.

"You told me that during the funeral mass and farewell ceremony for Sister Teresa Yugé held at the Station Front Church on the afternoon of February eleventh, 1969, you encountered a strange girl. Is that strange girl in this room?"

"There she is," Larra said, turning a hand toward Wakako, as if to introduce her. "When I saw her this morning I was sure it was the same girl I saw that day. She was a very distinctive sight. It was cold, but she was carrying her coat. She had on jeans and a reddish sweater. I was busy getting everything ready for a funeral and there she was wandering around and getting in the way. Sister Yugé must have been popular, from all the flowers that were sent. There were too many for the altar, so I had to put some of them at the church entrance. I was directing the people from the funeral service provider where to put them when she came wandering around and getting in their way. I was wondering how to handle this when she suddenly pointed to the crucifix and saying, 'Watch out! It's going to melt and fall down!' I was thinking, 'This one's a mental case.'"

"About what time was it?"

"Sister Yugé's funeral was supposed to start at three o'clock, but it was delayed. I was trying to get the show on the road. It was nearly three thirty — maybe twenty after."

"Did you look at the time?"

"Oh, yes! I sure did! It was going on three thirty. I was in a hurry to get those flowers set out. At some point, she disappeared."

"When did you next see her . . . No, before I ask you that, what time did Sister Yugé's funeral begin?"

"It was a good thirty minutes late. So I guess it must have been about three thirty."

"What time was it over?"

"Normally, the funeral mass and the farewell together take one hour, so it would have been four-thirty."

"Brother Larra, did you see the defendant, Wakako Ikéhata inside the church during the funeral?"

"I did. It's my job to see that the votive implements go on the altar for the father's use and check that everything is right inside the church. So in the course of making arrangements I spotted her all the way in the back, and that was another surprise. She was sitting cross-legged, with her hands together, in zen meditation. Who in the world does that in a church? During a funeral, mind you! And when the funeral was over and the equipment was put away, I went back to the seats and there she was all by herself, still meditating."

"Around what time was it?"

"The ceremony ended at four-thirty, and it was after cleanup, so I guess it was past five."

Akutsu bowed to Larra and his face took on a satisfied smile. He had placed Wakako in Kirikaé's office until three ten or three fifteen, doing zazen during the funeral from three thirty, and still in the church past five o'clock. Her alibi was complete.

Domaé rose to cross-examine.

"Mr. Larra, what is the program for the church funeral ceremonies? Are there different programs for different people?"

"No, the ceremony program is pretty much one size fits all. First there is the funeral mass, then the farewell ceremony."

"You were saying that the two together take one hour."

"Right. Thirty minutes for the mass and thirty minutes for the farewell. It could differ on occasion, though."

"What about when Father Okuda gives the ceremonies?"

"Father Okuda gives long sermons. He would probably take a bit more time."

"Meaning the funeral mass might take more than thirty minutes. Could it possibly take forty-five minutes?"

"Yes, it's possible."

"What ceremony was in progress when you saw defendant Ikéhata?"

"The funeral mass was over. That was a relief. I went back to the office for a while. I guess it must have been the beginning of the farewell ceremony. She was sitting in the back of the church."

"The start of the farewell ceremony. That would be four-fifteen. What happens at that point?"

"Choral Hymn 656. It's always the same."

Mr. Akutsu called Wakako for questioning. This was the first time for her to speak in court. You could tell everyone was listening carefully. Clearing of throats ceased. The room was still. Her voice was the return of a welcome memory. I felt it flowing from my ears though my whole body like warm life blood.

She said that on the day in question she went to Kirikaé's office before one in the afternoon, left past three o'clock and went to the Station Front Church.

"Why did you go to the church?"

"As I was walking along the Yotsuya embankment, I was feeling desolate.

I wanted to do zazen. The church seemed like a good place for that, so I went there."

"Did you meet anyone there?"

"Yes, I met Brother Larra, who just testified, outside the church. Well, I don't know if you could say I met him. I was having an LSD flashback. The church was like soft rubber. Both the steeple and the cross looked like they were going limp and were about to come crashing down. I was frightened. When I tried to let everyone know there was danger, the friar came over and asked if I was all right. He didn't understand what I was saying. I could tell he thought I was crazy and a nuisance. I was afraid the church was going to break up, so I went back to the embankment. I just watched for a while and finally my flashbacks stopped. The church had become a solid building, so I went in again. A funeral was being held. They were singing Hymn 656. Father Okuda was conducting the rites. The sight of the flowers on the altar and Father Okuda incensing the coffin just banished my anxiety. That was how I went into meditation. The funeral ended, everyone left, and it was quiet. The stained glass was getting darker by the minute when Brother Larra called to me. He said I was going to catch cold. So I left."

"About what time was that?"

"I don't know. It was getting dark."

Domaé announced he would cross-examine Wakako Ikéhata. She complied after telling Mr. Akutsu, "I will answer anything. I'm not keeping silent anymore."

"Professor Kirikaé has testified that when you were in his office and the clocks rang the hour at three o'clock, you said 'How wonderful to be hearing all these clocks again, singing "Three o'clock, it's three o'clock."' Why did you say that?"

"There are about one hundred clocks in that office and about a third ring the hour. It's beautiful music that I was hearing for the first time in a long while. I always enjoyed hearing them when I was there."

"Wasn't it more like impressing Professor Kirikaé that it was three o'clock? Isn't it unnatural to say 'three o'clock, three o'clock?'"

"Meaning what?"

"When you have a hundred clocks before your eyes, there is hardly any need to say, 'Hey, look, it's three o'clock.'"

Wakako looked at the prosecutor with wonderment in her large eyes. Expressionless, Domaé proceeded to the next question.

"Why did you go to the church that day?"

"As I just told the counselor, I was feeling lonely."

"How long had it been since you had gone to church before that day?"

"Two or three years."

"Did you ever feel lonely during those two are three years?"

"Yes, I did, being human."

"But you didn't go to church. So why did you suddenly decide to go to church on that particular day?"

"Why do you keep asking why? I went into a church that was there before my eyes just as I was feeling lonely."

"Preparations for a funeral were under way. The area around the church entrance was crowded. With all those people outside, why did you approach Brother Larra and say mysterious things about the cross melting?"

"I didn't approach Brother Larra. He approached me. I said the cross was melting because that's how it looked to me. I wanted to warn everyone."

"You weren't trying to make Brother Larra remember you being there?"

"That's another ridiculous question. I certainly wasn't doing what you allege." Wakako's eyes showed anger. Her reaction was fully justified, given the malignancy of the question.

With a gaze that took in each of the three judges equally, Prosecutor Domaé began a statement of his opinion.

"In the foregoing, first of all, the witness Shiro Kirikaé has testified that the defendant Wakako Ikéhata left his office at the R. University Engineering Department between 3:10 and 3:15 of the afternoon of February eleven, Showa 44. Witness Leopold Larra has testified that he encountered the defendant at the Station Front Church at 3:20 on the afternoon of that day. In each of these cases the defendant's words and actions accorded with those of a person intentionally confirming the time of day with others. I think this demonstrates sufficiently they were in fact a strategy to establish an alibi.

"Secondly, the testimonies of the defendant and witness Leopold Larra have established that the defendant was inside the church when Hymn 656 was sung at approximately 4:15 on the afternoon of the day in question. The evidence establishes only the actions of the defendant at approximately 3:20 and 4:15 that afternoon. There has been no certain evidence at all that the defendant was inside or nearby the church for the 55 minutes between those two times.

"Next, I request that the results of an investigation conducted by an assistant officer of the Tokyo High Public Prosecutors Office with the cooperation of officers of the Onarimon Police Station be entered into evidence. The findings concern the time required to get from the Station Front Church to

Platform Eighteen of Tokyo Station, which is reserved for Shinkansen use. If one takes a taxi on a holiday afternoon, that would be a 15 minute ride from the taxi parking areas in front of Yotsuya Station to Tokyo Station's Yaésu Exit. It's a three minute walk from the Station Front Church to the taxi parking area, and a four-minute walk from the Yaésu Exit to Platform Eighteen. Total travel time is 22 minutes. If one takes a train instead of a taxi, the rapid service National Railways train from Yotsuya Station to Tokyo Station takes 10 minutes. Allowing for time walking to the respective destinations and waiting for the train, gives 20 minutes travel time. Therefore, getting to Platform Eighteen and back to the Station Front Church requires 44 minutes by taxi or 40 minutes by National Railways. In either case, the round trip can be made within the aforementioned 55 minutes."

An oppressive silence settled in after the prosecutor sat down. I heard Mr. Tsukioka mutter "Damn it to hell." Otherwise, there were no voices from the defense's seats. Instead, a murmur ran through the spectators' seats like ripples from a stone cast afar. The presiding judge offered to schedule the next hearing in two weeks, but it was the defense that had it set for November second, one month later.

I was returned to my cell by the last courthouse run of the day. I was so tired out I wanted only to lie down, but the guard said I couldn't do that without first getting an examination and written permission from the doctor. So I leaned back against the wall and began writing this entry. Now I am finished. It is the middle of the night. I was making do under a dim light bulb to keep writing after the lights were turned down. My exhaustion is at the limit. I feel cold and heavy, like dead meat. Still, I am in such turmoil, I can't get to sleep.

A courtroom is supposed to shine the light on crime, not make innocent people into criminals. Prosecutors are supposed to be representatives of the public interest, there to find out the truth. They are required to handle cases according to a consistent set of rules that apply from the justice ministry on down. In our case, that only means Domaé uses the same twisted logic in our appeals trial as Onuki did in the original trial to make every piece of evidence pointing to our innocence look irrelevant, if not backhanded evidence of guilt.

Neither I nor Wakako were involved in any bomb plot, but here I am sentenced to death and Wakako to life imprisonment. Wakako . . .

~

I shift my full weight to my right leg, go into a deep crouch, then shoot upward with all the power I have. My body goes into a spin around an axis inside me. It is a fast spin that turns on flashing whirls of light. Once, twice, three, four times around and then my left leg meets the ice surface and I go shooting backwards. I hear applause at my successful Salchow jump. There are cheers.

A light-filled rink of silver to skate across as I please. I am free of home, school, prison. Every kind of organization lays far behind. Like a gyrfalcon aloft in a howling blizzard, my body takes me where I choose to go.

Atsuo Yukimori slips through the silvery blizzard, emerging like an Olympic athlete with a hand wave in response to a cheering crowd.

"Nice to see you again. Is it okay for you be out here?"

"Absolutely!"

"You don't have to get permission?"

"Permission? Whose permission?"

"The organization's, of course."

A look of anxiety appears on Atsuo Yukimori's face and he suddenly slows down. "I shouldn't have asked that. Don't let it get you down."

Atsuo Yukimori has slowed almost to a halt. The tip of his skate caches on the ice and he goes down.

"This is the first I've ever seen you fall." She moves to raise his massive body. "You're too heavy. I can't raise you. You must get up yourself."

"It's all right! We can fight this!"

Then I woke. I think I was actually shouting.

~

It's still night. Half the tiny window looks out to the dark sky, and the other half to a sheet metal wall. On the other side of that wall are the male prisoners. In other words, I am in a space made into a female cell by partitions within a prison for men. A small cage inside a large cage.

My name is Female Prisoner, answering to number 74. Why in the world am I here, inside a small cage inside the inside of a prison made by the Greater National Organization of Japan? Well, now, I just don't happen to know the answer to that. If anyone does, please clue me in.

Picked up suddenly one morning and put into a police station prison, where, from morning to night, day after day after day, they said *You are a criminal, You are the criminal who put a bomb on the Shinkansen that killed two human beings. You are a murderer. Confess it, confess it, confess it now.* They yell, they bellow, they shriek. It was all so crazy I just didn't say anything. So they took me out of the police prison and put me in a detention center. Then they dragged me into a courtroom and identified me as the worst sort of criminal, the kind who doesn't show a shred of remorse. They put me to a psychological examination I never asked for and took it as proof I was just the sort of crazy person who would kill. But, because it would be meaningless to put a crazy person to death, a special act of mercy was ordered. They downgraded the penalty to life imprisonment, meaning forced labor in prison until natural death.

I was born in a string of islands that has a thriving organization the world provisionally calls Japan and recognizes as the territory of said Japan. I was given the name Wakako Ikéhata — though I never asked for it — taught Japanese and raised as a Japanese. None of this was anything I wished for.

I am a car. Of all the abilities people have, cars augment only one — the ability to go forward. All other abilities — to dream, to stop, explore byroads, squat down where you are — are discarded. They put me in school for the sole objective of advancing to the next school, where the objective again was only to prepare for the next advance. Eventually I got tired of the pushing and shoving along the narrow path I was on. I wanted to stop and take a side road. When I tried to stop being a car, the organization people pushed back. They fussed that I was a nut, a dropout. It took me two years to get into a university, only to find out it was nothing but another manufacturer of cars. You get into an assembly process called a curriculum that gives you knowledge that is the engine to keep you on the organizations' networks. It was all about moving forward and nothing else. The head engineers called professors and their artisans, called assistant lecturers, drill the holes and put the screws into their cars, run performance checks, stamp their approval, and shunt them into the next assembly process.

The campus conflicts that were occurring was the revolt of the cars. I was all for smashing the factories. It became my purpose in life. The organization watchers and the engineering chiefs went into panic mode to control all the cars that were going off into all the side roads. The Tower symbolized all the factories. The day of the Tower symbolized the war between the organizations and the cars. The organizations won, of course. Lamentable, however inevitable it as. By their nature, cars can only run forward. They just kept running toward destruction until they crashed into a giant wall.

Suddenly one morning, I found myself under arrest. I was one of the cars that rebelled, but they said I did more — that I was the one who placed a bomb on the Shinkansen train, which is one thing the organizations prize highly. All I actually did was join a demonstration on the day of the Tower. Those hot-headed, self-assured agents of the organizations in their blue suits claimed to know all about what I was doing on the day the Shinkansen bomb exploded, and they were determined to make me confirm what they had already decided was the truth of the matter — that I was at the scene of the crime.

Organizations are obsessed with numbers. Their idea of the truth is all about what year, in what month, on what day, at what minute. One makes a thing true with numbers and repetition: *You were there. You were there. You were there.*

A day that was ordinary to me the organization wants to make special by plastering it over with numbers. Time is one thing that should not be reduced to numbers. Another is the wind, invisible and elusive, infinitely more interesting than a set of numbers about direction and speed. That prosecutor's head works like a monotonous machine that turns everything into cars.

That day I left Professor Kirikaé's office and was walking along the embankment, I had a vision of the entire super-organization falling apart. The hotel, the bank, the school, the train station; it all just dried up and came down in roiling clouds of dust, like great mountains of dry sand. Flames fell down like rain, and everything burned away. The crowd of people gathered outside the church were crushed under the falling tower. I ran down from the embankment, feeling like alarm bells were screaming.

As I was telling people they should run away because the green cross on the bell Tower was going to melt and fall, the vision faded. I suddenly realized I was getting puzzled looks that said I was a mental case, so I got away from the scene.

Finally, the vision went away. The hotel, bank and station were back in their original forms. I knew the vision had come from the LSD I had taken before. I also knew the vision would come true, whether it was a hundred or a thousand or ten thousand years later. From God's point of view, the greatest hotel, bank, school, or station winks out of existence in a day, in an instant. It's all the same, whether that instant happens in a day or a thousand years. The vision taught me how foolish it is for human beings to be complacent about their institutions. I went to meditate in the church. I was free to do as I pleased. Organizations be damned. The church and its rites disappeared. There was nothingness — *Sunyata.* Now the organizations are trying to force their meaningless numbers — in this case meaningless in the ultimate sense — on that liberated time. "The defendant proceeded to Tokyo Station during the 55-minute period from 3:20 p.m. until 4:15 p.m. in order to place a bomb on a Shinkansen car."

There is an agonizingly cold, penetrating wind blowing in through the crevices. Atsuo Yukimori's words in court are a ghostly echo in my ears. His temples are noticeably grayer. He has undeniably aged. The half-light from the window shimmers through tears that come welling up. For myself, I don't cry, but for him, yes, I can cry.

I was able to recall that model of health, Yoko Mizuno, when she turned up as a surprise witness. She graduated R. University, and I know she and I were together in Professor Kirikae's office a number of times. She was the center of attention, with that wild laughter of hers. I'm the type who looks for a place to hide when the room starts filling up. Normally, I would be out of sight in the reading room. Wherever she was, her presence took on a life of its own. Now she and Mr. Akutsu are making love. He is quite a lively one too. They make a good pair. I would like to send them my congratulations. The only thing is, there is a nasty little feeling inside me that would unfortunately leave an ugly stain on any goodwill I might show. It is the same feeling I get from the young female guards I have encountered. It's the bad feeling all prisoners get from people their own age who are walking about freely outside their cells. She is a psychological therapist in a mental hospital. There were people like her working in the hospitals I was in. Many of them take pride in their work. They empathize with the patients. They understand the patients. They are dedicated. I wouldn't doubt that description fits Yoko Mizuno. What she has in common with all hospital workers, whether they are doctors, nurses or therapists is being fundamentally different from the patients. It is the same as the relationship between guards and prisoners. The hospital workers stand above the patients, looking down from their safe positions, extending a hand to the mental patients crawling around in their holes. Yes, that fundamental difference is the keynote of my feelings toward Yoko Mizuno.

~

"I wouldn't know it was the same place."

Jun Akutsu stood in the middle of the room, glaring. He struck his fist against his chest, gorilla-like. The desk was in perfect order. No miscellaneous objects littered the floor.

Yoko Mizuno wore a triumphant expression, breasts proudly to the fore. "Things are all in order now. Take a look." She held out one of the albums. Where there had been five albums, there were now twenty. She extracted a companion file of photo negatives. "Here's how it's arranged. I checked with the manufacturer, F. Corporation. These negatives are arranged according to the emulsion numbers. The prints are in the same order. From that we know your evidence exhibit photo is on a piece of film manufactured in May, 1967."

"That's no good. They'll just say, for all you know the picture was taken in 1968."

"Hold on," Yoko cut him off in a heavy tone that bespoke confidence. "There are more parameters. The picture itself was taken in either 1968 or 1969. It couldn't have been any time before. I made a table of all the patients with the dates they were admitted and the nurses, with the dates they started working and when they left the hospital. There are three patients in this picture who were admitted in April of 1968 or later. There are also two nurses who started work in April, 1968. See, this one and this one. That means this picture couldn't have been taken in February, 1968. It has to be February, 1969."

"Great work!"

"It gets better than that. Our other plum blossom viewing outings in 1969 were on February ninth and fourteenth. This nurse here is an assistant nurse. She was hired February tenth. On February fourteenth, as we well know, Mr. Yukimori took a plane to Hokkaido. This picture couldn't have been taken any time other than February eleventh!"

"Perfect!" Akutsu hugged Yoko and kissed her forehead. "This does the deal. There is no way the prosecution can counter this. I'd like to hear him claim the picture is a forgery, though."

"I don't think he would try. We have the negative." Yoko separated herself from Akutsu, sat in a chair and trilled with laughter.

"I turned up something useful too. I found a nun from the M. Order who tape recorded Sister Yugé's funeral, from start to finish. With narration, no less. 'The requiem mass held upon Sister Teresa Yugé's ascendance to heaven has begun.' Like that. I timed the tape. Hymn 656 that Wakako testified about begins at 3:55. The doors to Hikari 33 opened at 3:50. Unless Wakako knows how to ride light beams, there is no way she could have gotten to Tokyo Station in time to put a bomb on that train."

"Perfect!" Yoko said, mimicking Akutsu. "No way the prosecution can counter it!"

"Basically, no. But he'll do what he can to muddy the water. Maybe the tape doesn't start at the very beginning. Maybe it was copied over with imperceptible blank spaces slipped in. He's not interested in getting at the truth. He is interested in his own face. As far as he is concerned, that requires getting away from the truth. We've got to show him up for what he is."

"I've learned something about how it works too. We find what looks like the perfect alibi and the other side moves heaven and earth to tear it to pieces or make it look vague."

"That's the game. Atsuo Yukimori has a colorful way of looking at it. He says most of what happens in a war is sudden raids and disorganized firefights repeated over and over. If there's a thinly guarded enemy encampment, you raid it and take it over, but then you are counterattacked from the direction you least expect and driven away. You are pretty much assured victory if your base of operations is secure and you have the firepower to subdue your enemy. That takes overwhelming logistical support, like America had. In this parable, of course, America is the prosecution that has investigative power and can use the police. We're the Japanese army, under-equipped and unsupported."

"The truth is bitter."

"It is, but thanks to you, I think our next attack will be very effective."

"I don't have all the credit coming. Ms. Oúra is the one who arranged the negatives and finished up the albums. Do you remember her? She's the head nurse on E ward. You met her the first time you visited the hospital. She's the one Mr. Yukimori said looked like a cheerful type. She saw that write-up in A. Shimbun about your work on the case and started coming to help on her days off. She's a terrific asset to this hospital. She knows everyone here — every nurse and every patient. That encyclopedic knowledge of hers was exactly what was needed for this project."

"It's good to know there are people like that you can count on."

"There's more where she came from. The word is getting around the hospital that this case stinks. I'm getting encouragement from all kinds of people."

"The basic story from the newspaper coverage was that the prosecution blew away the defense's alibis."

"With one exception. A. Shimbun has been giving decent coverage of the defense arguments."

"Yes. A. Shimbun's coverage had a big impact. Especially that feature, 'Seven Unanswered Questions About the Shinkansen Bomb Case.' It brought out what the police interrogation was like and the prosecution's phony structure of evidence. That article was a little bit revolutionary. I was interviewed by the reporter who wrote it, a woman by the name of Yoshié Wada. It was clear she wanted to dig down below the surface. Did she come to talk to you too?"

"I have a confession to make. She and I were in the same graduating class from the psychology department at R. University."

"Does that mean you set up that article? Well, well! You know, it's kind of surprising that a reporter covering national news was a psychology major."

"She says newspapers don't care what the people they hire majored in."

Yoko was getting ready to leave as she spoke. She put away the negatives and photos to be used as evidence, combed her hair, picked up her handbag and beckoned Akutsu to the doorway. It was getting past five in the afternoon. Nurses were beginning to take their leave on bicycles and motorbikes. A stout woman wearing a bright smile was approaching from the wards. It was Nurse Oúra.

"Hey, there's our favorite attorney. Keep up the good work!"

Akutsu bowed his head. "I am very grateful for all your help."

"Looks like you two are stepping out." The nurse looked from one to the other. "You have a good time! How I envy young people!"

When Jun Akutsu and Yoko Mizuno arrived at Professor Kirikaé's office at R. University they heard raucous voices from the other side of the door. Someone was cursing out someone else, as if spoiling for a fight. Catcalls were followed by applause. The couple looked at each other, then at a large paper taped on the door. "Shinkansen Bomb Defendants Support Group — Session No. 2." They had come to the right place.

When they entered the room, there was momentary quiet. More than fifty people sat in a circle. A bearded man in the middle stood and beckoned them forward. It was professor Kirikaé, dressed formally in black, like a pastor.

"Let me introduce you to Mr. Jun Akutsu, of the defense team and Ms. Yoko Mizuno, who discovered Mr. Yukimori's alibi."

There was brief applause that quickly subsided.

"We are having a big difference of opinion just now on something that should interest you. The view has been expressed that it isn't enough to just prove the defendants' alibis, because there are more fundamental issues to be addressed."

As he said this, male and female voices called out. "That's right!" . . . "No objection!" They were answered in confrontational tones from another quarter: "That's not the issue!" . . . "That's got nothing to do with the trial!"

The shouting match consisted almost entirely of young people in their twenties on both opposing sides. Fists were raised, faces were angry. The ones wearing helmets were especially loud. Presumably, they were from the Q. Sect.

"Quiet down!" Professor Kirikaé picked up an orchestral cymbal that lay beside him. He raised it to eye level and struck it, causing it to resonate loudly. The sudden shock to the ears had the desired effect of quieting the jeering voices.

"Statements will be made by one person at a time. All right, you," he said, pointing at a helmeted woman. She had thick lips that gave an impression of a female goldfish. She screamed rather than spoke, in a terrifyingly high voice that emerged from a large mouth set with jagged teeth.

"I've got a question for Attorney Akutsu, who entered just now. Why do you deal only with alibis for Yukimori and Ikéhata?"

"Well, those two people are innocent. Their alibis prove it."

"Yeah? What about the other defendants? Mr. Moriya got a death sentence. Mr. Tagawa and Mr. Shinya got life. I don't see much defense of them going on!"

"Mr. Kida and Mr. Uzawa are handling their defense." Akutsu recognized Kida at the far end of the helmeted group. "Please ask Mr. Kida over there about that."

"I don't need to ask him. I'm asking you. I'm taking issue with your attitude as a defense lawyer. The fundamental question is whether planting a bomb on the Shinkansen is criminal or revolutionary! That's the big issue! You don't even understand that! You don't understand that all crime is revolutionary!"

"You're right. I don't understand that." Before Akutsu could continue, he was interrupted by the goldfish woman's high-pitched voice.

"What is the Shinkansen? It's the product of that high economic growth rate the state is so proud of, isn't it? It is revolutionary and heroic to place a bomb on the Shinkansen and smear the state's reputation! That's why a real defense would see punishment for that act as unjust, even if the client actually did the deed! What kind of defender do you think you are? 'Please, sir, my client has an alibi. He begs your forgiveness.' That sniveling attitude is the real problem!

"Do you know what kind of trouble that attitude of yours is causing? Q. Sect comrades are getting hauled in for questioning because you put out that alibi rap. The Man wants to frame up someone else in case your clients get off. Don't you see it's counter-revolutionary to say you want to find the real culprit? That's the basic problem in this case!"

"No, that's wrong. It's absolutely wrong!" Akutsu said. During the goldfish woman's rant, he had risen so that he was facing off with her and her helmeted colleagues, who shouted out angry retorts as soon as he spoke.

"Who says it's wrong?" . . . "Bourgeois lawyer!" . . . "Smartass nonsense!"

"You're wrong." Akutsu stood and began speaking again. Instead of trying to match the fevered pitch of his opponents, he was calm, speaking in a quiet voice. Experience in his student days doing emergency support work for classmates arrested during demonstrations told him this approach would have a quieting effect by inviting listeners' curiosity.

His strategy worked. Others in the room spoke out. "Hear, hear!" . . . "Listen to what the lawyer has to say." The clamor subsided.

"Now listen. The six defendants in this case are accused of conspiring together to commit the crime. In other words, the charge is that some of them plotted the placing of the bomb while the others actually carried out the deed. That means the ones who were not the executors of the plot are still guilty of the same crime because they belonged to the joint conspiracy. That's why there were sentences of death and life imprisonment to both the executors of the plot and the ones who only conspired. The prosecution's indictment says there was close-knit cooperation among the six defendants. But we have found alibis for Mr. Yukimori and Ms. Ikéhata. In the last hearing the prosecutor used leading questions and phony arguments to try to argue down the evidence, but thanks to support work from all of you and cooperation from the press — especially the *A. Shimbun* — it is becoming more and more clear that the charges are false. We can see that the prosecution doesn't get away with this. I want to make it clear that when we have proven the alibis of Mr. Yukimori and Ms. Ikéhata beyond doubt, that means the indictments of joint conspiracy against Mr. Moriya, Mr. Tagawa, Mr. Shinya, and Mr. Jinnai no longer hold."

There was applause. "That's it!" ... "The lawyer is right!"

"No, he's not right. He's just changing the argument," the goldfish woman said. She was no longer screaming, but in step with Akutsu's tone.

"Arguing alibis will get Yukimori, Ikéhata, and Jinnai off, but it will increase guilt on Moriya, Tagawa, and Shinya. You don't have a strategic understanding of these vectors."

"That isn't a problem. The prosecution hasn't made any charges in that direction. There is no reason at all to worry about charges the prosecution hasn't raised. As long as the Q. Sect can't be convicted on the bombing charges, there's nothing to fear. The battle is only inside the courtroom. It doesn't matter who says what on the outside. But I would say that claiming bomb attacks are justified would be apt to make the judges dubious about the defendants."

"We don't expect anything of those judges. They are all state running dogs. The issue is to radically disavow the trial. Your weak-kneed approach of worrying what the judges think is no good!"

"What's that you say?" This statement came explosively from Yoko Mizuno, a sudden presence looking like the Winged Victory. "Everything you've been saying is just for the sake of your sect's benefit, isn't it? Maybe you think that stuff about radically disavowing the trial sounds good, but the trial is going on now, isn't it? And it has already handed out death sentences to two people, life sentences to three, and a five-year term to one. If we don't rescue them on appeal, their situation will be pretty much hopeless. When you have sick people in pain you treat the sickness, you don't chase fantasies about disavowing the sickness. I don't know where you get those theories. They have no practical use." Like an alto singer, Yoko's voice had reach and vibrancy. It seemed to overwhelm the goldfish woman and her helmeted friends, because they kept silent.

Stroking his beard, Professor Kirikaé moved the program along.

"Let's get back to our agenda. First, I would like to know if we can confirm that the support group will establish a system of full cooperation in the effort to discover new witnesses and new evidence to affirm the alibis of Mr. Yukimori and Ms. Ikéhata."

Numerous declarations of "no objection" were made.

"All right, now about our media strategy. The *A. Shimbun*" reporter Ms. Wada is with us, so I would like to ask her views about something. As you know, Ms. Wada wrote the first newspaper article raising the theory that the charges in this case are false."

A slim, sun-tanned woman of twenty-five or twenty-six stood up. She seemed not overly concerned about personal appearance. She wore no makeup, her hair hung freely and her skirt was noticeably wrinkled.

"I'm really not in a position to express opinions. I am not a support group member. I'm here as a reporter to find out about the activities of your group."

"I do think you could advise us of some things, like how our support group should make our appeals. On that point, I would very much like to ask you how you came around to considering the charges in this case could be false."

"I started out like most others, simply accepting everything the police said, which was that the bombing was the work of an extremist conspiracy. That was the basis for my coverage. I am ashamed to say the articles I wrote for the first trial were along that line. But the last hearing changed my mind."

With that, Wada stopped talking and sat down. Professor Kirikaé hastened to pose a follow-up question.

"How did it change your mind?"

"Allow me to stay seated to answer. I've been walking around and standing all day. My legs are tired. Mr. Yukimori and Ms. Ikéhata have sound alibis. The prosecutor said they were no good, but his arguments were just so much quibbling. That raised doubts in my mind. The other thing was that neither Mr. Yukimori nor Ms. Ikéhata look anything like people you would expect to be involved in an extremist political movement. That is what set me to do investigating on my own and led to changing my mind."

"One quick point for the reporter," the goldfish woman said. "Would you stop using the word 'extremist?' We're students involved in a political movement, as you said. We aren't extremists. We are true to the answers that come naturally from scientific analysis of the present day political situation. I give you credit for having the courage to look back at your own past and change your view of this case. I'd just like you to mature a little more and stop using discriminatory labels like 'extremist.'"

The helmeted group chorused a resonant "No objection!" as if cued by an invisible conductor.

"That takes you to the fundamentals!" The goldfish woman was excited again. She raised her voice to higher pitch. "There's no denying the police just assumed people they call extremists planted the Shinkansen bomb. That's how they arrested Mr. Moriya, along with two more of our people, and Yukimori, Ikéhata, and Jinnai, for having contact with them. The arrests were illegal. They used torture and threats to get confessions. All these police frame-ups come from the prejudice of labeling a group extremist and assuming they set the bomb."

"Wait a minute there!" Yoko was standing again. "You keep contradicting yourself. Weren't you just saying bombing the Shinkansen was revolutionary and heroic? If that's what your sect believes, what's prejudiced about thinking it actually did it?"

"How about stating the case accurately? I'm saying there is a difference between someone wanting to blow something up and the actual culprit in a bombing case. Yeah, we wanted bombings to take place in the past and we still do. But we ourselves haven't done that. Absolutely not! The Man doesn't make that distinction. He's jumping to the conclusion that people who want there to be bombings must be the culprits. Look, anyone who wants revolution might think about putting a bomb on the Shinkansen. If you're going to call everyone a criminal who gets that idea, you've got thousands, tens of thousands of people to arrest. And then guess what? It's back to the good old days of the Peace Preservation Law!"

"Okay, let me ask you this. What happens if the real culprit is found. Say someone turns himself in and says 'I'm the one who did it.' Is it okay to indict that person?"

"No. That would be a great injustice. All crime is revolutionary. It shouldn't be punished. No so-called 'real culprit' should be charged for anything."

"That doesn't make any sense at all. Is that what extremists consider logical?"

"I told you, don't use the word 'extremist.' You still don't get it, do you?" The goldfish woman was shrieking.

"You're beyond reason. That makes you extremists. You're the one who doesn't understand. This support group was formed to clear false charges against the defendants. That means letting the general public know they are innocent, letting them know they aren't forgotten and helping their lawyers. Criticizing dedicated lawyers and sowing divisiveness in the support group is extremism."

"You say you're helping the defendants, but you're only helping some of them, not everyone. That's the trouble. Mr. Moriya is dissatisfied with the support group's activities. The last time I visited him, he said with the kind of support the group is giving, Q. Sect people should get out of it. What the support group should be concentrating on now is opposing the new investigation the police have started, looking for the real culprit. They have taken in support group members for so-called voluntary questioning, and they have started a new round of questioning the Q. Sect defendants. But the support group has its eyes closed to all this, because it is totally preoccupied with proving the alibis of just some of the defendants. That's the trouble with this support group."

"That's right!" ... "No objection!" ... "Reorganize the support group." ... "No confidence in the group leader." ... "Fire the bourgeois lawyer!"

All members of the helmeted group stood up. Shoulder to shoulder, they advanced to the front of the room and forced Professor Kirikaé to retreat. Clocks were swept from desktops and thrown from shelves, crashing and breaking on the floor.

"Stop this violence! Let's talk out our differences!" When Kirikaé attempted to halt the takeover, his cymbal was snatched away and he was pushed backward. The sleeve of his black coat caught on a vise and suffered a rip.

"This is too much." As Yoko started to her feet, Akutsu grabbed her hand and pulled her back. "You can't stop them. It's better not to try."

"They should be stopped. It's outrageous!"

"Those dissatisfied with the support group," Akutsu shouted angrily, "please leave. I say that with regret. And stop breaking things. Have some respect. This is a place of study."

"Who are you to tell us to leave? We don't take orders from bourgeois lawyers." The goldfish woman waved her fist in Akutsu's face. Broad lips opened wide, her ferocious expression hinted she would attack with her teeth. Akutsu stepped out of her path.

With a ten-member helmeted escort, the goldfish woman occupied the central position where Kirikaé had been and began a speech, as if the right to moderate proceedings had fallen to her.

"First of all, we demand that the support group's objective be set to opposing the police investigation for the Shinkansen bomb culprit. With that investigation now extending to support group members, this is the most urgent item of business. What does everyone think? I want to hear your views."

There were no answers from the more than thirty other members. Professor Kirikaé sat in a chair and began to carve a stone seal. Three sisters from the Mercedarian order were looking away from the spectacle before them. The eyes of several young people — probably non-political students, were downcast. Yoko Mizuno and Jun Akutsu looked at one another and sniffed dispiritedly. The goldfish woman spoke.

"If there are no opinions, I take it that the proposed group objective has been unanimously approved."

"That's a phony vote count if ever there was one!" Yoko called out in a loud voice. The goldfish woman frowned, but ignored Yoko and continued.

"Secondly, we demand the dismissal of Professor Kirikaé as leader of the support group. We recognize his contribution in founding the group. But his persistent chasing after reactionary illusions like God and Christ and his forcing group members to participate in primitive prayer rites is unforgivable. I would like to get everyone's view on this."

Professor Kirikaé spoke quietly, as he continued to apply chisel to stone. "No one appointed me group leader, so there is no need for anyone to dismiss me from that post. I would be thankful for someone else to do the job. One more thing. God and Christ are no illusion to me, but the most substantial reality in the world. I suppose the world is the illusion."

"The professor's unscientific, illogical way of thinking is wrong," the goldfish woman said, curiously using the appropriate honorific in addressing the professor. "Believing in an invisible being like a god is religious fanaticism."

"That which cannot be seen, measured or reduced to numbers, in other words, the objects of science, are what God is not."

"Nonsense!" said one of the helmets. Kirikaé did not refute this, answering with only with a slight shake of his head.

"Item three is we demand that the support group take more direct action. It has got to declare itself for more than just supporting the defendants. Like putting out a newsletter on attendance of hearings, collecting funds and defending members rights by opposing the new police investigation with street demonstrations."

"No, I'm against that," Yoko said. "This is no political group. There is no need for demonstrations. To begin with, the last thing I would ever do is be seen as part of your group, with its helmets."

"There is only one truth," said Professor Kirikaé. "All the defendants are innocent. That is the only thing we need to tell people about. As Mr. Akutsu was saying before, all we should concern ourselves with is winning the trial. We have different kinds of people here for that, not only students. There are company employees, housewives, sisters, and nurses. They have different beliefs and different positions. Q. Sect members are one part of many."

"Once again, you are repeating issues that have already been dealt with," the goldfish woman said, stamping a short leg. "You don't even realize the situation we are dealing with. Your approach is not going to win the trial. Everyone, listen! Three of the six defendants are Q. Sect members. I want to declare right now that we have fifty percent of the right to speak for this group. And I am telling you to confront the fact that the two false confessions from the others is what got our people convicted!"

"Let's not be mistaken about this," Yoko said, standing. "Those two were not the only ones who gave false confessions. Ms. Ikéhata is the only one who did not confess. The other five did, including all three Q Sect members. If you are going to go reckoning accounts on responsibility, it's heaviest on the Q. Sect side."

"I would like to hear Mr. Kida's opinion," Akutsu said, addressing the lawyer who was standing behind the helmeted group as unobtrusively as possible. He and Uzawa had handled the defense of the three Q. Sect members from the first trial. Kida had put up the most steadfast opposition to Akutsu's proposal of a joint defense for the second trial. "The three Q. Sect students have a low opinion of Yukimori and Jinnai," he had said, and spelled out their objections: "They are not sect members or students, and they have criminal records. They see themselves as completely unlike those two. They expect to be betrayed by them sooner or later. They believe Yukimori is the real culprit. I don't see how we could mount a joint defense under the circumstances." It had taken a full week of Akutsu and Tsukioka arguing that there was no hope of winning the case without forming a defense team until he was finally persuaded.

Kida stepped forward and the helmeted group cleared a path for him to the front. He began speaking in a small voice, as if muttering to himself.

"Mr. Akutsu demonstrated the alibis of his client and Ms. Ikéhata, and the prosecution disputed them in the same hearing. On the surface, the prosecution seemed to have a valid argument, but it wasn't really convincing. The logic was strained. The proof of that was that the prosecutor began a new round of interrogating all three of our defendants, and the police are questioning Q. Sect members on a supposedly voluntary basis. This proves they are now assuming the executors of the bomb plot were someone other than defendants Yukimori and Ikéhata. I am seeing some indications of psychological stress in Moriya and the other two Q. Sect defendants. It's not at the point where they are close to giving more false testimony, but the situation is very serious. My opinion is that the joint defense for the six defendants we set up is the right way to proceed. I agree with Mr. Akutsu that there is nothing to be gained by going our separate ways. I think the defense should continue on as it has. Frankly, I do not see any way to avoid a split between the Q. Sect supporters and the others."

"No way!" one of the helmets shouted. This was followed by "Traitor!" and "There's something wrong with this lawyer," from others in the helmeted group.

As the group's representative, the goldfish woman bore in on Kida. "You're a Q. Sect attorney. Why are you opposing our demands?"

"There's something I should make clear. I am not a Q. Sect attorney. Mr. Uzawa and I are private lawyers selected by the families of Makihiko Moriya, Shinichi Tagawa, and Akito Shinya. Because the defendants all happen to be Q. Sect members, we have been keeping in touch with all the Q. Sect members."

"Are you saying you have nothing to do with us as attorneys?" the goldfish woman asked, a shadow of worry appearing over her brash demeanor.

"Not at all. I'm saying that the defense team and the support groups are separate, independent bodies that can cooperate. Let's just not hurt our independence by interfering with one another."

"Mr. Kida is quite right," Yoko said. "Nobody in the support group knows law. It takes specialized knowledge to mount a defense. Every time the defense wants to get some testimony on the record, they've got to watch their backs so they aren't outmaneuvered by the prosecutor. It's for us to leave that to the attorneys, while we attend to giving moral support to the defendants. Those six people have been in prison for two years and eight months since they were unjustly arrested. They are isolated, hated by the general public and facing heavy sentences. If you understand that and want to extend your hand to them, that's why you join a support group."

"Yeah, but we can't be satisfied with that tepid level of activity," the goldfish woman said. "Moral support isn't enough. If we don't take direct action to stop the prosecution's investigation of the Q. Sect, that serious situation Mr. Kida was talking about isn't going to get any better. We demand . . . ahh, we declare that we are no longer part of this support group. We are forming our own support group."

"From now on, there are two support groups?"

"That's it. That is Mr. Moriya's wish. We want to respond to that wish."

"Anyone who wants to leave is more than welcome to leave. This group doesn't have any manifesto or anything like it. It's just a group of volunteers."

"We carry on our struggle independently. That means we publish our own support newsletter, monitor defense activities, have street demonstrations, attend hearings and collect contributions. If the need arises, we will take direct action to crush your support group's activities."

"Of all the . . ."

Yoko's voice was drowned out by a loud round of slogan chanting suddenly issuing from the helmeted group, punctuated by right arms thrust aloft.

"Free the Shinkansen Six!"

"No to bourgeois lawyers!"

"Stop the Shinkansen witch hunts!"

They upset desks, kicked over chairs, threw clocks from shelves and trampled glass cases. Then they formed a double line and began circling the room in zig-zag procession as they chanted "Wasshoi!-wasshoi!" in husky voices. After three circuits, the door was kicked open and the procession exited.

The remaining group members immediately rose from their seats and began the cleanup. Clocks strewn on the floor were set aright, broken glass was swept away, and desks and chairs were returned to their original places. When the room was in proper order once again and everyone had returned to their seats around professor Kirikaé, a wave of laughter arose spontaneously. Yoko's distinctive trilling laughter set off renewed bursts of laughter, and when that had subsided, numerous clocks suddenly began to toll the hour. The Siemens clock, with its pendulum ticking off each second sounded an authoritative *bong! bong!* Alarm clocks blared urgently. Clocks that had been thrown to the floor made muffled sounds. The torrent of sound triggered yet another laughter explosion. Yoko was in convulsions, hands across her belly in helpless distress. When silence finally settled in, Professor Kirikaé stood up.

"Now let us pray that the defendants' innocence will be proven."

"Please, don't make us laugh any more," Yoko said, herself laughing and brushing away a tear. But then she placed her hands together and bowed her head reverently. In the ensuing silence, the ticking of countless clocks began to resemble the breathing of the living earth.

The last business that remained for the support group after the helmeted student group had gone was deciding on appointments of the newsletter editors, the members who would handle correspondence with the defendants and those responsible for visits to the defendants. When that was taken care of, most of the members left, leaving the room to Kirikaé, Akutsu, Yoko, and Yoshié Wada.

Yoko regarded the pile of broken clocks atop the desk and sighed.

"You did such a lovely job fixing these clocks and now they're broken again. Half of them are no good at all."

"No, they can be fixed. They will be," Kirikaé replied.

"Not something this bashed in."

"Unlike human beings, machines don't reach the point of no recovery. If it's bent, you straighten it out. If its cracked, you glue it together. Parts that disappeared you replace. Eventually, you can get it working again, somehow or other."

"You're going to fix them all again?"

"Of course. Actually, I'm more than happy to. Having so many broken is all the more fun in the fixing."

"Our good professor is one of a kind. I'm hungry. Is there something? My, we are well-stocked!" Without so much as a by-your-leave to Kirikaé, Yoko was into the rusty, old-fashioned refrigerator Kirikaé had rescued from the dump, briskly setting about to preparing a meal. She extracted eggs, thin-sliced pork, potatoes, and cabbage. "Just wait a bit. Spaghetti with sauce *Yoko à la mode Kirikaéaise* is coming up."

"Shall we drink to that?" From a bookshelf, Kirikaé pulled aside several volumes of the Catholic Encyclopedia to reveal a hidden shelf in the back. He put a hand inside and reverently pulled out a bottle of French wine. "Hospices de Beaune, 1961. This is a little special. I have a weakness for wine. There is a French pastor I extort a bottle from every time I carve a seal for him. There is a lot more left."

Yoko came to peer inside. "Imagine that, a secret stockpile."

"I learned that trick in the campus struggles. This office was going to be inside a barricade, so I spent a whole night building it. The students tore everything up, but they didn't find it."

"That's what you call 'Dantès' Dodge.'"

"Hah?"

"Edmond Dantès hid the treasure of Monte Cristo in his own secret cupboard on his yacht."

Yoshié Wada extracted the cork from the bottle and filled glasses for all. Shortly, Yoko's meal was ready.

"Unfortunately, the cooking isn't up to the class of this wine," Yoko said happily, as she ate and drank. In a short time she was looking slightly intoxicated. She giggled, suddenly recalling the scene in the room not long before, "What a laugh! What is the world goes on in the minds of those Q. Sect people?"

"It's no joke and it won't go away," Akutsu said, frowning as he wound spaghetti around his fork. "The fact that we are working together on the defense of the three Q. Sect defendants means we can expect they will be leaning on the defense any way they can."

"So, how do you see the trial going from here?" Yoshié Wada asked, in the level tone of an interview question.

"We win some, we lose some, most likely."

"Aw, don't sound so weak-kneed about it," Yoko protested. "Not when we've got new evidence that's airtight!"

Akutsu slowly closed his eyes as a caution sign to Yoko. He had already told her not to talk about new evidence to any reporter, even one who is a close friend.

"We lay out the evidence for the alibi. The prosecutor presents whatever he's got to knock it over. We can it expect it to go back and forth that way for a while," Akutsu said solemnly.

"Will the trial continue for long?"

"As long as the prosecutor keeps trying to tie the story up in knots like he did in the last hearing, yes, it will. I don't expect to see this being settled in one year or two."

"That guy is one low-down rat!" Yoko shouted. "Anyone could see the evidence we presented was good, and he dumps out all that niggling stuff to make it look like we don't know when the picture was taken. And he goes snooping into my private life, as if it proves I'm lying. I wonder if there is anything he's above trying. You can bet I'm annoyed. Damn, stinking rat. I'm not finished drinking. Professor Kirikaé, give us another bottle!"

Kirikaé slowly raised a bottle that was on its side in the compartment and laid it down in a basket.

"This is Château Margaux, 1953. I was keeping it in reserve. It is old, so there are lees. Set it down without disturbing it. Please remove the cork Ms. Wada."

Yoshié Wada performed the task smoothly and filled the glasses. "How many years do you think the trial will take?"

"At least five. It could be ten."

"That's hideous," Yoko cried out and coughed violently, as if choking on a swallow of wine.

"That's exactly right. Japan has a rich culture, it's industrially advanced, a major economic power, and it has a trial system as inefficient and irrational as you can find anywhere. The system ignores basic rights and selectively ignores facts, too. That's where the wrongful convictions come from. Cases based on false charges occur time and again, and if they are corrected at all, it takes a terrifyingly long time. The Sachiura case took ten years, the Yakai case 17 years, the Oúme case, 15 years. We can't expect to be finished with our case any time soon."

"Ten years? . . . That's too much to take. Wakako Ikéhata was twenty-four when she was arrested. She is still young. It's just awful . . . awful." Yoko started to cry. She raised her face and wept on, not moving to dry the streaming tears.

"I wish our sleuthing could get our people exonerated as quick as it happens in crime thrillers, like *Dial M for Murder*. Or *Phantom Lady*. Or *Black Path of Fear*. Et cetera."

"I do too, but it doesn't work that way, at least not in Japan," Akutsu said, again lightly dabbing Yoko's eye.

"Hey, Yoshié," Yoko said, then snatched away Akutsu's handkerchief and vigorously blew her nose into it. She grabbed the wine bottle and upended it over Wada's glass. "You've got to write more about this case. Just keep churning out articles. Use media power to pour some oil into that rusty trial."

"I'll write about the case, but there is always push-back. My editor is okay — he's from the fifties' student movement. He'll suspect a police frame-up any time student radicals are defendants. Otherwise, this case draws a conspicuous lack of interest from anybody in government or politics — the ones in parties on the left, in particular.

"It's when you go out and talk to ordinary people that you start finding sensitive reactions. Average people are normally considered conservative, right? The ones who don't really care all that much about politics, maybe they're students, housewives — they're the ones who can look at this case with a clear eye, and they're the justification for doing articles about the case." Wada ran a hand over her disheveled hair.

"Write about false charges in criminal cases in general, apart from this one case. Make it a campaign," Akutsu said.

"It's true, there are an awful lot of those cases. You mentioned the Yakai and the Sachiura cases. It's just astounding the total manipulation behind them. Pick them up on one charge, hold them in the station jail and make them confess to some other charge, then send the case to trial. You see so many TV dramas with scenes of police shouting down the suspects to make them confess. The message is, that's what police do, that's how they solve crimes. People see it and absorb that message, without ever having an occasion to see how it works when the cops get it wrong. The majority just don't think in terms of suspects having any rights. That's the culture that keeps the cycle alive."

"That's it. Here we are on our way to the twenty-first century, and the people who run the country prefer police station prisons. They want to preserve them for posterity, and don't worry about what goes on in them."

"I think that's because as long as you have police station prisons you can turn out the culprits of crimes when you need them."

"I've got a question for Ace Detective Akutsu," Yoko said. "When it comes to Wakako Ikéhata and Makihiko Moriya, I have some idea about their how they're thinking, just because they're the same generation as us. But there are some things about Atsuo Yukimori I don't quite understand. What's going on in that old guy's mind? He's been through war and prison. He's had all kinds of experiences we haven't."

"To be honest, there are things I don't understand either. He doesn't like to talk about his past. He doesn't say much anyway, and there's the age difference. But his nephew was in my class in elementary and middle school, so it isn't as if we were from separate worlds. He and I both come from that port city way up in the north, where it gets colder that you'd believe. That makes for a certain empathy. I can understand that feeling of always being an outsider, the kind of person who just can't be in the center of things."

Professor Kirikaé crossed himself.

"Yes. He's a person who has suffered from living on the far side of the blessings of prosperity. He knows the deceptions and evils and flaws that underlie everything that supports that prosperity. Seeing his face makes me want to pray."

"He wouldn't talk to me," Wada said. "Ms. Wakako Ikéhata agreed to talk to me, and so did all the other defendants, but not Mr. Yukimori. So I can't very well write about him."

The clocks began striking eight o'clock. Akutsu invited Yoko to join him for a night in Shinjuku.

~

Got a telegram.

"FATHER DIED OCTOBER 30 6 P.M. STOP MOTHER"

Mr. Akutsu told me of my father's sickness and that he went into the hospital, but I didn't think he was on the verge of death. I didn't meet him once after I was arrested. I had decided I didn't want to meet him anymore. But he was my father. I wouldn't have expected it, but the tears started when I read that telegram. Little teardrops of a girl isolated in a solitary cell. I guess I'll meet with my mother the next time she comes.

There was a single star in a grayish sky, and then it trailed out of sight. I wondered if it was blurred by a tear. I looked hard, but it was gone. Maybe it was a shooting star. I can remember that blazing night sky over Lake Furen, sparkling with shooting stars. I can't believe this poison painted sky is the same one I saw that night. But this is the sky that Father departed into.

I'm thinking about his life. Raised as the second son of the priest of a big temple, he became a famous scholar of criminal law and the father of one boy and two girls. I was his troublesome daughter, bringing him sorrow by running away from home, turning mentally abnormal and finally getting into big trouble with the law. All I wanted was to get away from the organizations, but they got me while I was on the run. Father would not believe in my innocence. He wanted to get me pardoned for being insane and not responsible for what I do. That's why I didn't want to see him. My true feeling was I wanted him to understand. But he died.

Nights are long when one cannot sleep. I open *The Ways of Mental Prayer* by Vital Lehodey, but in the dim light my eyes tire after reading three lines. Suddenly I recall the dark eyes of Atsuo Yukimori, eyes that watch over my own innermost darkness. For some reason, he understands me as I really am. Talk about organizations to a psychiatrist and I'm looked down upon with an expression that says I have delusions of being victimized. He, who has his own strong sense of what organizations do, smiles gently.

Morning. The sky is still gray, but it is no longer non-living silver. It has life, and it looks like rain is coming. There are gulls, slowly descending to water somewhere. A flock of crows has come. Their black feathers are wet and shining. The effect is ghastly.

The prison day has begun, with its morning inspection. Female Prisoner Number 74. Here.

The orderly delivering breakfast normally appears only as a pair of hands through the door grating, but this morning he looks inside, staring. An obnoxious someone. I was about to tell him to get moving when the eyes began laughing and I recognized him. The gang boss, Ginji Sato. His mocking laughter is like having mud thrown on me. His false testimony was used as evidence against me. He's in for a minor offense.

I lost all desire for the meal. I felt as if he poisoned it, and dumped everything into the toilet. Anger has charged up my pen. I have a strong desire to write. No volunteer labor for me today.

Wakako, today I write for you. And my writing will continue.

Chapter 10

Hamlet Bleak

I was born in a cold little village near Cape Kiritappu. I only passed that way once on my own, when I was going to take my induction physical. It was just a cluster of about a dozen weather-beaten houses, huddled together in a narrow bog by a runt-sized river dribbling into the sea. There is no trace of it now. I learned from someone of the region that it was washed away by a tsunami one winter.

I have a memory that must be from being in a little house beside the sea. Part of the wall was broken away, to a view of sheer whiteness. It was eerie whiteness, as if it held countless squirming creatures in seething waves. I don't know — maybe it was something I actually saw.

The family moved to Nemuro when I was two, in 1921, the year the Nemuro Trunk Line was completed. The reason for the move was my father had given up fishing to open a bath house. It was business on a very modest scale. The only workers were family members, and there was not much in the way of equipment. My father fed firewood into a wood furnace, and my mother and older sister took turns sitting at the reception stand, watching over the customers. The building had previously been a diner that went out of business after two years operation. The family bought it and eventually built up a clientele, but, just when the business had started to run smoothly, something happened that made them give it up and open a diner in another location, even though they had no restaurant experience. My older sister Yoshiko told me what happened. My mother, Misa, went to her grave without uttering a single word about it.

Every bath house opens at three p.m. There was a widow who was always the very first customer. Her age was uncertain, but she was a fair-skinned beauty

558

with a nice figure who looked young. She enjoyed taking her time to luxuriate in the hot springs water while it was still pristine. She would always take her leave before the house filled with customers. Misa would sit watching her from the reception stand, fascinated by her affluent-looking dress and slightly lonesome expression.

One day, the widow was the first customer in, as usual, but she suddenly rushed from the bath room, dressed hastily, and hurried away. Alarmed by this, Misa called out her children's names. Little Atsuo — me — came running in immediately, but my brother Yuzo, who was one year older, was missing. I told and we went looking for him. When Yoshiko's gaze fell on the bathtub, she spotted the child under the water.

Looking back on that scene, Yoshiko said she was impressed with the strength her small-sized mother summoned from somewhere. She grabbed the child by both legs, pulled him from the water, and in the next instant was swinging him in the air as if shaking water from a sheaf of mustard greens. Then she began pounding on her son's back and crying out his name. Misa ordered Yoshiko to alert her father to the emergency. Father and daughter returned to find Misa crying uncontrollably before the inert child.

The widow had stepped into the bathwater and was astonished by an unfamiliar something inside. Maybe she would have claimed she lost her presence of mind and fled instead of looking to see what it was, but it is hard to imagine she did not realize it was a child. The probable truth is she was overcome with revulsion and it never occurred to her to summon the mother sitting at the reception stand. Misa must have thought bitterly that a word from her would have saved the child. The widow never showed up again. My parents didn't know who she was or where she came from. They quit running the bathhouse immediately after that.

I don't actually remember anything from the days of the family bathhouse, although I do recall wondering what kind of upbringing would make a person go to some far-off bathhouse instead of using one in their own neighborhood. It wasn't until much later, when I was in elementary school, that I knew I had a brother one-year older named Yuzo who had died by drowning.

The diner was located near the fish market, amid strong odors of fish and kelp, where cries of herring gulls never ceased, day or night. The front of the store faced the sea. It had a bay window that was used to sell shaved ice in summer and oden in winter. Customers would pull open the lattice door to a kettle over a fire, a homespun cooking counter and a long table with benches for seats. In the back of the diner was a four-and-a-half-mat tatami room with a tea table.

Two six-mat rooms on the second floor were used for dinner parties or when the first floor was filled to capacity. Behind the cooking space, a narrow corridor led to the main building, which only consisted of one three-mat and one two-mat room. That was where our parents and we five children slept. A tin-roofed shed served as our father's workroom.

Business was good. Of course, baby Suéko and I — still an infant — only got in the way, so we were given to a neighborhood nanny to be looked after. She would show up in the morning and take us to her house, Suéko in one arm and leading me by the hand. The nanny brought us back in the evening or at night. I don't remember her face. She lived in a gloomy house, with no children of her own. Once Suéko began to cry, and that greatly angered the nanny. When she hit Suéko with her open hand, that started me crying, so she hit me, too. I remember that it really hurt.

The nanny was a great saké fan. She was delighted with her privilege of getting one server of saké on the house whenever she came to the diner. According to Yoshiko, she would come in with me in tow and ask her or Mother for saké, and she seemed to have trained me as well to fetch her saké. I have a vague recollection of her smacking her lips when she emptied her cup. She treated me nicely when I was useful. Instead of hitting me, she would do things like take me to the shore to pick up red shellfish or take me to Takahira Shrine to look out over the harbor. My mother was too busy to give me attention, so I developed affection for the nanny. I wanted to do anything I could to please her. That was probably the background to a very bitter experience.

I've thought about it more times than I can count, and every time the memory comes out slightly different. I may have been four or five. My mother came at me with a completely unaccustomed angry expression and took me into the three-mat room where a woman who helped at the diner was sitting. She held my arm down and put a white powder — moxa — on my index finger while I howled in fear. My mother ignited the powder. It was hot and it hurt, but I wasn't crying out of pain. I was angry because I didn't understand what was going on. Later on, my mother told me it was a charm to prevent me from doing wrong. It left that little scar on my finger. My mother's explanation of the wrong I had done was taking some copper coins from a change basket in the diner. I have no recollection at all of doing it.

That change basket hung from a string on a post by the cooking counter, within a child's reach. My theory is that the nanny told me to bring some of those coins to her. If that isn't the explanation, it doesn't make sense why I would have done it, because I had been warned the basket was out of bounds for children. I didn't even know what the coins were for. But maybe the story is that I had already learned to take pleasure in violating a taboo. Perhaps that incident was the germ that developed into full willingness to pick people's pockets, years later (that's right, I had a career as a pickpocket), not despite the danger to me of breaking the law, but because of it.

My mental image is that the lady who helped in the diner was the one who held my arm down when the moxa was being applied, but it could have been my sister Yoshiko. She was twelve years older than me, and from my perspective, that was a grown-up. She had looked after me when I was a baby, and now she was serving tables, delivering orders, and otherwise helping Mother. From the time the nanny began looking after me, Yoshiko was easily angered by my attempts to please the woman or imitate her mannerisms. "We don't teach children such things in this house," was her standard line. She certainly would not have been inclined to forgive my stealing change from the basket to give to the nanny.

My two living brothers were Shinichi, who was four years younger than Yoshiko, and Keiji, born the year after Shinichi, making him seven years older than me. They, too, were more like grown-ups than brothers, from my perspective. They were in elementary school and got along together famously. They would go out together in town or into the countryside, leaving me behind. I got used to playing with Suéko, two years younger than me. We would play house or with dolls, quietly in a corner of the yard or by the clothes drying rack. There were hardly any other children in the neighborhood, which had only a ships' carpentry shop and a few pubs. Suéko was my only friend until I started elementary school.

At first, my father Ishizo manned the cook's counter ambitiously, but his unsociable personality was no good for dealing with customers. The day he got into an argument with a customer was the end of his career behind the counter. From then on, he worked as a fixed-net fisherman over the summer and a hunter during winter. He would go into the field for days at a time carrying a rifle and wearing a rubber lined rain cloak with an otter-skin hood. He shot deer and bear, then skinned them in our shed. He was also a taxidermist, who produced stuffed specimens of duck, snow grouse, and various other birds and animals.

My own image of him was as a hunter, although he later worked at other jobs. He was a hand on a steam passenger boat in the bay, and on a whaler too, but as far as I was concerned, my father was a hunter. It pleased me to be the son of a hunter.

It was fun to quietly handle Ishizo's rifle when he wasn't around. I would gaze into the barrel and turn myself into a tiny explorer who could walk down its luminous tunnel. I would put my finger on the trigger and pull back gently, imagining the feeling of setting off a thunderous blast, unleashing power far beyond my own child's strength. I pressed my cheek against the smooth wood stock, my head filled with images of myself stalking animals in the forest. Knowing I would catch holy hell if Ishizo ever caught me, I kept those sessions short and secretive.

Ishizo was uncommunicative by nature, but his tongue loosened quite a bit when he drank. Those occasions were not at all infrequent. He would talk hunting as he cleaned his gun or did some other chore. I would huddle down beside my big brothers around a stove flickering bright red to hear stories about shooting bear or killing foxes with muzzle bombs. Nowadays, muzzle bombs are banned. You make a paper casing about three centimeters long, fill it with gunpowder and crushed pottery as a catalyst, set it out and cover it with a piece of duck or salmon meat. A fox comes along, chomps on the bait, and bang! he's bagged. At times there would be several fox carcasses, their muzzles blown apart, strung up in the shed.

Making muzzle bombs was one of my father's important tasks. I loved to watch his intense expression while he was carefully grinding up the red and white granules in a mortar and making the paper casings out of damp Japan paper, then slowly drying them by the stove. We had to keep perfectly still while we watched these proceedings. Questions from children would only elicit an angry command to shut our mouths.

By the time I started Hanasaki Ordinary Primary School, Yoshiko was working in a paper manufacturing plant in Nemuro, Shinichi was working in a warehouse in Otaru, and Keiji was a longshoreman at Hanasaki Harbor. My mother ran the show single-handedly while my father was both a shiphand in Nemuro Bay and a hunter. Everyone was working except for me, and we still couldn't make ends meet. When it got close to the end of the month, Mother would get busy with the abacus, moving the beads and sighing over the results, again and again. It had taken a series of loans to finance shutting down the bath house and opening the diner. The repayments, plus interest, took a major bite out of the household budget. I didn't know anything about it, though. All I knew was being dissatisfied that my daily allowance of one sen was so very little.

There was a candy store near my school. It stocked hard candy, rice crackers, pastries, menko cards, paper balloons, flat marbles, marbles, and similar stuff. All you could buy with one sen was one piece of hard handy. Sweet adzuki beans wrapped in cellophane were seven sen — a whole week's worth of saving up. A sweet roll or a *dorayaki* cake went for ten sen. Those items were beyond reach of my savings.

The first time I visited a classmate's home I found out that afternoon snacks are served in normal households. There was a kid named Yuji Harazaki, the son of a doctor, who happened to sit next to me in class. We became friendly and he invited me to his house. I was impressed to see the big medical clinic outside. Then I got a surprise when I followed along in back to see there was a gabled roof and a plant-lined path that led to a really impressive front entrance to the home. Harazaki had his own room, just for him. It had a desk and a chair and a bookcase with books in it — books that cost one or two yen each. There was a shelf that had a tinplate ship and a horse-drawn wagon. Everything I saw amazed me. My three-mat room was shared with two brothers. For a desk, all I had was an apple crate. My toy collection was a few *menko* cards and dolls shared with Suéko.

When the maid came in with chocolate rolls and black tea, I was flabbergasted.

"Hey mom, how about a snack?"

I tried saying that one day when I came home. My sense was that I would be told "What are you talking about? You're getting one sen every day for that!" That was exactly what my mother said. I stole money right after that. I remember the first time clearly. It was the first in a long career of theft.

The change basket had been taken down. The diner's cash was now kept in a drawer with a lock that my mother always kept watch over. I set my sights on a savings box that sat atop a chest of drawers. It was a hand-made box with a padlock my brother Keiji kept for savings from his pay as a longshoreman. I supposed locking it up gave him a feeling of security because he flashed a smug smile when he caught me watching him drop money inside. I made a careful study of techniques for removing the box's contents through its narrow slot. I discovered that if you rattled the box with motions parallel to the slot, whatever coins happened to fall next to it could be shaken outside. My reflexes were well attuned to this kind of operation.

My first success was a fifty-sen coin. That was a home run, but I put it back inside, fearing the disappearance of such a large sum would be immediately noticed. I shook some more, and this time a silver ten-sen coin fell out. I ran out with that coin tight in my fist, straight to the candy store. With the money, I bought a bag of sweet adzuki beans and a *dorayaki* cake.

The next problem was where to eat the loot. Kotohira Temple was near our house, but I would be seen there. I just couldn't bring myself to eat standing in the street. I ran around, searching for a place to hide and finally came to a pasture with a brick silo. It was called "Meiji Pasture." There was a small Sakhalin fir woods just beyond the gate. I remember the needles were a rich green and there was smoky mist, so it was probably summer. I ran into the woods, looked around to check no one was there to see, and started eating.

Now I realize all that furtive searching for cover wasn't really necessary, but at the time I thought there would be very big trouble if I was caught with something purchased with stolen money. That was the same as being caught with stolen goods. The probability of being subjected to another moxa burning treatment if my mother found out was also on my mind. At the same time, I relished the taste of my stolen sweet beans and cake. It tasted far, far better than the chocolate roll I had eaten at Harazaki's house.

My thefts continued. I pilfered ten sen one time and five sen another, and always spent everything and ate my purchases immediately. My brother seemed not to have caught on. That emboldened me to make off with a fifty-sen piece.

The day came when the savings box was no longer in what had been its usual place. I looked in the closet and drawers, but couldn't find it. The greatest likelihood was that my brother was on to me and had hidden the box. I was prepared to be called out on my thefts. But my brother said nothing, and neither did my mother or father. Their silence haunted me. It was worse than being confronted. It felt like all eyes were watching me, lest I reach for more money that didn't belong to me.

One day, there was a village funeral. Our diner would occasionally be asked to do the catering for funerals and ceremonies. On this day, my mother went out serving rice to people attending the funeral. When I came home no one else was there. I tried the drawer containing the diner's earnings and it opened. Mother had forgotten to lock it. There were ten-yen and five-yen notes — enough to make me feel giddy. I didn't touch them, instead pocketing several five-sen and ten-sen coins.

I should have limited myself to that, but then I got greedy, adding three fifty-sen silver coins and a fistful of one-sen coppers to my take, then moved around everything in the bottom of the drawer so it wouldn't look like anything was missing. Next, I looked for a place to hide my stolen money. I found an empty jar for jam, put the money inside and ran to Meiji Pasture and buried it in the pine woods.

My mother discovered the theft immediately after returning home. "Atsuo, you didn't take the money, now did you?"

"What money? I don't know anything about it."

"But you were the only one in the house."

My father and brothers returned while this exchange was occurring. Keiji took me into our three-mat room.

"You're the thief. Where did you hide the money?"

"I didn't steal any money."

"You're lying. You robbed my saving box too, didn't you?"

"I didn't!"

"Damn fool!"

With that, he hit me in the face hard enough to knock me down. Keiji had been growing huskier by the day since he started working as a stevedore. A very strong arm had delivered that blow. He grabbed my arm, pulled me up and hit me again.

"I did it. I stole the money. I'm sorry."

I was crying, not from remorse, but fear that I was about to die at my brother's hands.

That night, my brother carried a lantern and accompanied me to the fir woods. It was frighteningly dark. I dug up the jar. When we got back home I opened it before my parents, lowered my head and said, "Please forgive me. I won't do it again," as I had been instructed to do by Keiji. Father sat with his gaze fixed elsewhere, arms folded. Mother was in tears. "No, you will not steal again. You must not," she said. Then she lectured me about how deeply in debt the household was to pay back loans for opening the diner, and how scarce money was.

I suppose it was shortly after that incident that I started helping out in the diner. When school was out and most of the kids went running around the fields or the streets of the town, I was in the diner washing dishes or running orders to customers. It is a terrific hardship for a third-grader to have to make deliveries hither and yon toting a heavy wooden box laden with prepared meals in bowls and dishes. But my allowance went up to two sen a day, and it was gratifying that my parents and brothers were dealing with me in an agreeable way. Moreover, no one would come down on me when I ate an extra piece of pork cutlet or some leftover noodles. That meant I was liberated from the unbearable hunger that would otherwise visit me every day around three in the afternoon.

Another job I handled was packaging and sending gifts at money-lenders homes in the summer Bon festival and year end seasons. Our home also received such gifts from our own associates, like the house where we did the funeral catering, the gun shop, and the grocers. All those gifts were immediately repackaged and used for our own gift-giving. No one at our house ever sampled any of the cake, confections, or canned goods we were given.

It was interesting to encounter the same greedy expressions on the faces of the wives and the household help at every money-lending home I entered. They were all conceited over their status in service to the wealthy. I could speak to that conceit very well, just by delivering a subservient self-introduction when I showed up at the door and doing a bowing and scraping act when I left. No one taught me how. Even a little kid can understand that you can avoid trouble just by giving the person dealing with you lots of room to feel superior. Once is a while my performance even got me a five-sen tip.

I always spent any money I got right away. It never occurred to me to save up for something big. My nature was just the opposite of my brothers in that regard.

The elementary school was close to the downtown area. Many of its students were from the homes of merchants, bureaucrats, or military men. It was the kind of school that cultivates a reputation for graduates that go on to higher education, so it attracted high performers. Some of the kids lived far outside the school district, coming all the way from Bekkai or Hamanaka. Some were expensively dressed. Kids like me in my hand-me-downs from two brothers were the conspicuous ones. There were times when I stood alone in the school yard just so the other kids wouldn't see that my trousers were torn.

After I returned home I had work to do that took up all my time. I didn't really put in study time, but I had good grades anyway. I liked arithmetic and Japanese, and I was better than anyone else at manual arts. I made an accurate model of Nemuro Harbor that stayed in a glass case in the school entrance hall for something like ten years.

My best subject was geography, which started in fifth grade. Looking at a map starts me imagining what the mountains, rivers and towns look like, as if they were set out in a miniature display. I enjoyed learning the names of railways and stations. Tokyo, Osaka, Kagoshima . . . All the places I headed for when I was wandering around the country later on. I might have been anticipating all that as a child.

Despite my good grades, I never got to be class president, or even vice-president. That friend of mine, Harazaki, the doctor's son, was good in science, but not in writing kanji, and in math class, I had to explain to him how to solve cranes and turtles problems. Even so, he was chosen class president several times.

In sixth grade I finally realized the class was divided between the kids bound for middle school and the others, like me, who would go into higher primary school. The middle school group all got a turn at being class president or vice-president. The graduation order was skewed the same way, so kids far and away below my class performance were ranked higher than me. We primary dead-enders didn't count.

My homeroom teacher from fourth through sixth grade was named Mr. Ogawa. He had a shaved head and looked very much the part of the monk he would eventually become. He was the son of the head priest of a temple in Nemuro, destined to inherit the post. Mr. Ogawa was fond of sake, and his breath always smelled of alcohol. I recognized the smell, being from a home that served liquor to customers, but the other kids seemed to think that was just a smell peculiar to that teacher.

One day I was on the street delivering year-end presents for a money lender and ran into Harazaki carrying a bundle of something wrapped in a *furoshiki*. I'm sure this happened when we were in fifth grade.

"Where are you headed?"

"Mr. Ogawa's."

He was delivering a present too, not as an errand for someone, but for himself. That solved the riddle for me about why he got to be class president again and again.

When the issue of what happens after sixth grade graduation came up, I tried mentioning to my parents that I wanted to go to middle school. Father turned me down flat. "You can't. We don't have that kind of money," he said.

My sister and my two brothers all went to work as soon as they finished higher primary school. I could understand that our situation precluded me being the only one to go on to middle school. Yoshiko spoke up for me. She said it would be a good thing if one of the family got a better education and offered to help finance it from her salary at the paper plant. The proposal met silence from everyone else. I returned the survey sheet on post-graduation intentions the teacher passed out with a circle around the "higher primary school" option.

The students on the middle school track received supplementary lessons from the teacher. I was extremely envious. At the same time, it was nice not having to study. I didn't work very hard in the diner either. I tried skipping one day of school, then two days, and when my mother didn't say anything, I went out frolicking around every day. I wasn't amused by things considered normal for kids my age, like being in a gang playing soldier, or hide and seek on the drift ice, or running around in a pasture. I liked to get away from the town and go off by myself exploring in the marsh, which was out of bounds for little kids because it was dangerous. It suited me very well. The rivers froze in winter, under an ice cover forty or fifty centimeters thick, turning them into highways navigable by sleds pulled by horses or dogs. The weather was harsh in winter, but getting around the marsh was easiest then. When April came around, the ice pack would loosen up and become progressively fragile, until one day it would start breaking up and drifting. Water from the melted ice would flood fields, hills, and rivers, submerging much of the marsh. By then the ice that had the harbor locked up would break apart and let the wind take it to sea. Fishing boats that had been dry docked would start going out to sea and the spring fishing season would begin. That was the time when I started venturing into the area around Lake Furen.

My first destination was Shunkunitai, which is a peninsula (you know it — we went there on the snowmobile). I explored that Sakhalin fir forest, chasing after red foxes and jackrabbits and squirrels, walking through flowers blooming everywhere across the marsh and listening to countless bird calls. It made me feel wonderfully light being by myself, away from school, the diner, my friends — everyone and everything. But there was a limit to how far I could go while still on the shoreline. I needed a boat before I could go wherever I wanted on Lake Furen. I wanted to get out and travel up the river that emptied into that lake, so I started work on a boat.

I cut off a log about four meters long from a dead tree I found in the Sakhalin fir forest along the Furen river shoreline and went to work hollowing it out with a hatchet. I was still just a kid, so I couldn't accomplish very much in a day's work. I had Ishizo's bark canoe in mind. He said "You can't get around the marsh if your boat doesn't have a flat bottom. It's full of driftwood underneath. An ordinary boat would get stuck." So I resolved to make a flat bottomed boat. As I said, I'm suited for doing that kind of work. A wood carving I did in class got praise from the teacher. Physically, I was pretty much up to the job too, for a sixth grader, at least. Anyway, it took me about two months to hack out a flat-bottomed canoe from that log, like an imitation of a south seas style dugout canoe, and a paddle to make it go. With that vessel, I was suddenly able to take a trip down Furen River, go out into the lake and explore any of its narrow waterways.

So I set out on the water and found myself in another world, the beautiful world of the marshland. It was early spring. Most of the trees were still bare, but bird cherry were in bloom, casting a white reflection on the water having the appearance of fog that had morphed into flowers. When breezes blew, showers of pearls would go cascading down and decorate the water surface. And there were no people.

It was a marvel to me how much fun it was just being alone and free. It seemed to me that friends my age who went into in town just to hang around together were wasting their time with child's play. I would pretend to be going to school, but would really head straight for the riverbank, push my boat into the water and have a ball all by myself. No one was keeping watch on me at the time. My father was on a steamboat crew at the time and my mother was busy at the diner. Once in a while, my kid sister Suéko would give me an amazed look and ask, "Where did you go today?" She must have thought it funny because she could see I wasn't going to school, but, kid that she was, she just seemed to take it that as something big brothers do and didn't say anything about it to our parents.

I was playing hooky every day, but I worked in our diner in the afternoons. Sometimes I got sneaky under my mother's eyes. One day I filched ten sen from payments for noodles I delivered. A few days later I took five sen. All the money I stole was spent on things to eat. But then I got a yearning for a fishing pole and hook. That required about five yen. I started looking for a chance to get it.

It happened that my brother Shinichi was home at that time. I didn't miss it when he tossed his wallet into the chest of drawers. The wallet was made of dark blue canvas. It contained ten-yen and five-yen notes. The only money I knew was coins. I was used to silver and copper, not paper money. I counted out ten silver fifty-sen pieces, put them in my pocket and ran to the fishing supplies shop, where I bought a pole, hook, float, and sinker.

"What kind of fish are you after?" the man in the store wanted to know.

"I don't care. Anything's fine," I answered. I got away from the store as quickly as I could. I didn't even know there were different poles and hooks for different kinds of fish. All I knew was Ishizo always took a small bamboo pole, a hook, and worms for bait when he went fishing in the marsh. I thought that was all you need for any kind of fish. I brought the fishing gear I had bought to the boat I had hidden in the Sakhalin fir woods.

I was expecting to get caught right away, but several days passed and nothing was said. I stopped worrying and began preparing for my adventure. From Ishizo's workshop I took some mosquito repellent salve, dried rice rations, and a small knife. From the store I took miso, salt, and matches. I wanted a rubber raincoat, but that was beyond my means, so I took an old rice straw raincoat. Every day I pretended to set off for school, head straight for the boat and had fun in the marsh until the evening.

I was caught the day school ended for summer recess. I needed a compass, so I went for Shinichi's money again. His wallet wasn't in its usual place. I was searching for it when the fusuma unexpectedly slid open and Shinichi came into the room. He didn't ask for excuses, instead bringing up the five yen I had stolen previously. He told me that the fishing gear shop owner had informed Ishizo of my purchases and that everyone thought I was up to no good. Shinichi was not one to slap me down as Keiji had done. He sighed, genuinely troubled over my waywardness.

"Atsuo, listen. Why do you take other people's things? Don't you know it's wrong?"

"I know."

"Well, if you know it's wrong, why do you do it?"

"I want the stuff."

That exchange is the basic pattern for questioning sessions with me that were later repeated by my parents, brothers and sisters, policemen, prosecutors, and judges. People say if you know it is wrong to steal you shouldn't do it. But I was weak-willed. If I got to wanting something, that desire was stronger than the will to resist wrongdoing. It's not true that I did not hesitate to steal. But the hesitation I felt when I was looking at money and no one was around was much weaker than the urge to satisfy my desire for it. There is a moment when hard currency and banknotes take on a blinding brilliance, like a fountain of pleasure. Later on, I became acquainted with many criminals, men who committed every sort of crime. If you talk to rapists or arsonists, for example, they will tell you that if they see a woman who can be taken by force, or a house that will go up in flames just by lighting a match, that woman or that house takes on an irresistible glow that mesmerizes them.

The power contained in a single silver coin held my child's heart in thrall. I knew as a child that everything has meaning and that things have the power to control people. So when I simply said "I want the stuff" when asked why I stole, I was expressing only a part of the reality, due to the insufficiency of my expressive ability. It isn't simply a matter of stealing because I wanted something. Rather, the reality of the hard currency before my eyes generated my desire for it. The real cause and effect relationship is just the reverse of what I said. Detectives, prosecutors, judges and the learned people of our world always put desire first. As they tell it, crime starts with evil desire in the hearts of human beings. The afflicted people see the money, evil desire does its work, and the crime is committed.

I know differently. Anyone can understand the impulse to steal, but if there was something especially evil in little Atsuo, it was only that I knew the power a single silver coin held. Taking that coin instantly transformed me into a bigger, more fulfilled version of me, very different from the aimless me of the moment before, living in the everyday world. I suddenly found myself in a dream world, where nothing was ordinary and where pleasure existed in its true form. Of course, a little kid like me couldn't possibly have given a complete answer to Shinichi's question. It would have taken much more analytic ability than I had. I actually understood essentially what the desire to steal was all about, and it was frustrating that I couldn't explain it to him any better than to say "I want the stuff."

That night my father took over from Shinichi and proceeded to berate me. He bemoaned the fate that had given a man like himself, who had never turned from the righteous path, such a wicked boy as Atsuo. He slapped and kicked me, over and over. My face grew swollen and purple. I owned up to my wrongdoing and begged forgiveness, but did not reveal where I had hid the fishing tackle I bought with the stolen money.

I left home the next day and set out for the Furen River. I got into my boat determined never to return. It was the first time I ran away from home. My father had told me I was a child who didn't belong in his home, who should never have been born, and I agreed. I was not despondent to the point of wanting death. My idea was to just keep heading upriver and go roaming through the wide-open marsh, away from home, town, school, and every human being that ever had anything to do with me. But there was one person I did want to meet. He was right there, hidden away, somewhere deep in the marsh.

Of course I mean the Furen hermit. Ishizo had told me about him, among stories of foxes, rabbits, and birds. The old man with white hair down to his shoulders, lithe and light as the wind sweeping across the marsh, close by for just a moment, and then nowhere to be seen. The man who lived by hunting and fishing, his ancient musket and bamboo pole slung, soldier-fashion, from his shoulder.

Ishizo had met the old hermit many times. He was well educated, with knowledge of all the flora and fauna of the marsh, including their Latin names. But he didn't like people and wouldn't have anything to do with them, although he did make an exception in Ishizo's case, but only for a shallow kind of association. Where did this riddle of a man come from? What was his purpose in living all alone? No good answers to these questions came to mind.

I had been wanting to meet the Furen hermit for a very long time. It was one of the reasons for carving out my boat. Thus far I had only been paddling around the river mouth, knowing the chances of meeting the hermit at the outer perimeter of his domain were slim. Now I had decided the time had come to penetrate deep into the marsh with a mind to find his hidden lair. I would go as far upriver as my strength would take me.

The Furen is a river of twists and turns. Dense thickets of reeds grow along its shoreline. Alders with double trunks and poplars that have extended their roots beyond the shore to grow half submerged are a memorable sight. As I recall, the current was a pleasant murmur in the quiet along some sections of the river, but mostly it was a running flow of thick mud. Nevertheless, my immature strength was enough to keep moving upstream. The hard part of the journey was driftwood that would get into the boat. It took much effort to throw it back out. If I became too preoccupied with the beautiful scenery, I would find myself buried in driftwood.

Eventually, the fog came in. Fog that hits that marsh forms out at sea. It is the kind of heavy white cloud that forms in the water when you wash rice. It hangs over everything, so you can't tell the river from the land. While I was drifting about aimlessly in that thick mist, I scraped my head on the branch of a poplar and almost fell out of the boat.

The fog on the marsh is really an incomparably beautiful sight. Misty patches of purple, yellow, and white float into view, then shimmer into focus — dark purple irises, light yellow bush clover, cotton grass that looks like rows of capped spears, and a vast field of bright yellow star shaped day lilies. The spectacle of these brilliant colors slowly taking form inside the sheer whiteness of the fog must be seen to be fully appreciated.

I brought my boat up to a section of shore, took out a worm for bait and threw out my fishing line. I wanted to pull in any fish I could catch and cook myself a meal on land. Unfortunately, it started to rain.

It was as if the fog had a bottom that suddenly sprung ten thousand leaks, releasing a deluge. My rice straw raincoat was no defense. In no time at all I was soaked to the skin, cold and hungry. I ventured out into the reeds, intending to build a fire, but everything was wet. After a while the rain was falling so hard it got dark. The water was rising all around me. At such times you find out the marsh is not just an open field; the river overflows the shore so far that there is no land any more — only a lake.

I started paddling desperately, but all sense of direction was gone. It was evening when I finally arrived at a Sakhalin fir woods on real land, the kind you can walk on. It was a wonder I hadn't drowned or frozen to death. Some hunters found me and took me home. Once again, I caught hell from Ishizo. That was to be expected, given my string of punishable offenses. I went to bed with a fever, and it was my mother who nursed me, taking free moments during her work in the diner to come back and change wet compresses on my head. When I confessed to her I had bought a fishing pole and hook with the five yen I stole, she was silent and held up a finger across her lips.

I started Hanasaki Higher Elementary School. It was April 1932, the year Manchuria became Manchukuo. The kids who started middle school looked self-conscious in their uniforms, school bags slung over their shoulders, but we were the same as ever, the only difference being that we were going to a different classroom, off in a corner of the school grounds. Even so, because the students came from many different elementary schools, I did get to meet a slightly wider cross section of humanity.

All the smart kids having gone to middle school, the way was clear for me to test first in the class at the end of the first term. For that accomplishment, I was praised by my father for the first time ever. I didn't even have to study, so I devoted myself to helping at the diner. When it was getting close to graduation time in the winter, I took a job as a salesman with a local pharmacy called Nintendo.

The job was to carry a lantern with the name of the pharmacy written on it and walk the streets hawking their products: "For fevers, take Convalescence Pills, for frostbite, apply White Dragon Salve." The pay was fifteen sen for three hours work, plus thirty percent of the take if I sold over fifty sen worth of goods.

When the ice reached the shoreline, it was as if the whole town was frozen stiff. Everyone was shivering in their houses while I was out trying to make a little money selling medicine. At first, I was hardly yelling loud enough for anyone to hear, and I didn't know the neighborhoods. My sales weren't any better than about twenty sen a night. I had reached the point of thinking the job wasn't worth the effort when I finally developed a feel for how to move the goods and suddenly found myself making sales of nearly a whole yen a night. That restored my enthusiasm for the work. I had learned where to find customers. Kitchen workers in pubs and restaurants bought the White Dragon Salve, with its powdered seashell content, ships deck hands who stayed in cheap hotels bought ointment for cuts. I learned to march right into the different shops and businesses, changing my pitch to suit the clientele.

I handed over all my earnings to my mother, and she put it into a small saving box she called the "Hades jar." I didn't know why until the winter recess was over. She told me to take the box to the town hall and donate the money to the military affairs section.

I didn't know what that was, so I went to the town hall and said I wanted to give my money to the soldiers in Manchuria. The man at the desk directed me to the Servicemen's Benevolence section. He said, "You're donating all your earnings to your country? That's an admirable thing to do." He broke open the box and counted out the money. It was a little over six yen. He wrote out a receipt and wrote in a double circle, like a teacher puts on an exceptionally good composition.

Two days later Mother said excitedly, "You're in the newspaper!"

The headline was "Exemplary Lad Shows His Love of Country." The article was about my noteworthy deed, contributing all my earnings selling medicine in the biting cold, all for pure generosity. It was accompanied with remarks by my teacher saying I was a model boy who not only got the highest grades in class but always helped at the diner run by his family.

My father was overjoyed. "Way to go, Atsuo, boy! You've got good in you, that's sure." That newspaper article did much to boost my status with him, and with the Nintendo Pharmacy as well. They said they wanted to hire me on as soon as I graduated primary school. I was to be their live-in apprentice.

The pharmacy was in a good location downtown, where it drew a healthy level of patronage. The owner was a fat woman in her fifties with good business sense. She hired a young pharmacist to fill prescriptions and make sales. My jobs were taking orders, making deliveries, and pounding the pavement at night peddling remedies. It wasn't very hard work. There was nothing to distract me from worrying about the future when I was inside my futon in the pharmacy storehouse, lying in pitch blackness because flammable materials stored there forbade use of a lamp.

My parents had told me I could learn about drugs in the pharmacy and become a pharmacist. That had been my expectation when I took the job, but every day went by without a chance to learn about anything. I found out there would never be learning opportunities when I tried asking the pharmacist what he was doing. He told me, "Don't interrupt. I'm busy" in a tone that indicated I wasn't allowed to ask questions. When I tried asking the housemaid about my problem she said you have to graduate from a pharmacy school to become a pharmacist and that takes a lot of time and a lot of money.

On my first payday I got five yen. I considered that to be a ridiculously small sum for doing thirty days work, day and night, including street peddling, considering that I had made six yen for ten days street peddling alone during the winter break. The store was paying its "apprentice" a pittance while it was taking in handsome profits. The pharmacist sold bottles of something called "glycerin water." It was just a tiny drop of medicine in a lot of water. The bottles were labeled and sold for thirty sen each. To me, it looked like nothing other than a way to turn water into money. Glycerin water sold like hotcakes as an instant remedy for frostbite.

In the evenings after work the pharmacist went to his room and played a record of "Kagoshima Ohara Air," which was the big hit of the day.

> *Kirishima's lovely blossoms,*
> *Kokubun's tobacco fields*
> *Smoke rising from Mt. Sakurajima*
> *HA!*
> *YOÍ! YOÍ! YOÍ! ya!*
> *SA'-tto!*

He played it over and over again.

Looking through the window in the pharmacy storehouse where I slept, I could see a small room in the next house. Once day I noticed a young man in a futon. He was lying down all day, meaning he must have been sick. It seemed to me I recognized him, so I decided, why not try talking to him?

As I was calling out, "Hey there," I realized it was my brother Keiji's classmate. His name was Katsuhiko Ishibashi, but Keiji just called him "Kachi." I remembered that he had come to our house often when we were little. He was the one who had shown me where the pasture was. One time he got me to smoke a cigarette. It tasted horrible and I choked on it.

I just went in through the back gate to get to Kachi's room. I guess he was bored. He went on and on, telling me about Osaka, where he had been a dockworker. Osaka is a great city, there's no comparing it with a dinky place like Nemuro. There were streetcars, tens of thousands of factory chimneys. Great steamer ships were always arriving from abroad. You never saw so many beautiful women in one place. My brother Shinichi was a dockworker too, in Otaru, but he never said anything like this to me. Listening to Kachi filled me with a strong desire to see the big cities.

When I mentioned to my mother I had met Kachi, her face showed frank displeasure. "You mustn't go near that person!"

"Why?"

"He has lung disease. He caught it in Osaka. Other people can catch it from him. Once you get that disease, there's no curing it."

"Is Kachi going to die?"

"He certainly is. He doesn't have long."

The next time I looked in through my window at Kachi's pale, tired-looking face, I felt as if his room was seething with great invisible swarms of germs. When Kachi spotted me, smiled and said, "Hey, come on over!" I suddenly became nervous. I pulled away from the window and tried to keep from making a sound.

For all its wonders, the great city of Osaka was a scary place that gave young men horrible diseases. I quietly shut the window and locked the door. Then I used wrapping paper for powdered prescriptions to seal off all the places where breezes might blow in disease-ridden air from the room next door into my room. Of course I never visited Kachi again. Nights when I was laying out my cheap futon, I kept quiet lest he catch on I was in the room. When I asked the pharmacist if there was medicine for lung disease, he answered in his usual beleaguered tone, "Who says there should be?"

In late June, when I had been at my live-in job just about three months and thoroughly fed up with it, Mother told me about a job opening in Tokyo. A cousin of mine (the son of Mother's older sister) who worked at a realty office in Yokohama knew a scribe in Tokyo who had written him a letter saying he was looking for an assistant. The offer was to work during the day with an opportunity of taking night classes. Just being told that I could not only go to Tokyo, but could also take classes in school was enough to set me burning with excitement. I could get away from home and a boring little town like Nemuro. Instead of doing manual work on the docks, I would be sitting in a nice office. Everything about the offer sounded good to me.

On the morning of my departure, my father Ishizo called me into a room where he sat wearing his uniform as harbor vessel crew member. I faced him, trying to project a respectful demeanor.

"You have given your parents all kinds of trouble so far. Listen to me, now. Keep your hands off other people's money. If you don't, this time you'll be heading for jail. Don't forget that. And see that you aren't back in Nemuro before its time for your induction physical."

I had been handed two imperatives. My army physical examination was five years down the road — 1939. I was to get serious and put in an honest five years of work in Tokyo until then. I answered up with a vigorous "Hai!" as I had been taught at the pharmacy.

As far as I was concerned, I didn't have to be told to stay in Tokyo for five years. I thought I would be happy to stay there forever.

Father continued, "Son, you can do things with your hands. You can do calculations. The thing for you to do is go to a technical school or maybe a school of architecture."

Not having any particular future goal in mind, I answered "Hai!" two more times.

I arrived at Uéno Station in early July and got scared out of my wits when I stepped into a scene of vast crowds of people in the steaming rain, all wearing shrewd expressions, as if completely confident about where they were going. I told myself it was no place for losing my way. Following the instructions I had received, I took a one-yen taxi ride to the scrivener's office in Joto Ward, Kameido. The word "scribe" was written in eye-catching gold letters on a glass door to an office. Behind the counter sat the owner, a man in his forties named Sakai, and his younger wife. This childless couple operated the business.

Mr. Sakai was the short, round-faced type you would expect to find in a downtown business office. He wore round glasses and his hair was short. His wife was slim and very white complexioned. She had an air of sophistication. Later on I found out she had a history in the pleasure quarters. Being in the company of this suave, citified couple, speaking their smooth Tokyo dialect made me conscious of how unrefined I was. I couldn't relax because I was desperately concentrating on controlling my shaking knees.

The next day Mrs. Sakai took me to the Uéno zoo, and to the Buddhas at Asakusa temple. I couldn't get over the elephant's trunk and the giraffe's neck. Same for the size of that temple. It made me think of Kotohira Shrine in Nemuro as a little nothing building way out in the country. After all my expectations toward the big city, a feeling of deep disappointment was setting in. My disappointment was not in Tokyo — that exceeded my expectations — but in myself. I was just so totally unprepared to deal with life in the big city.

The work was easy enough. There were forms to fill out and sort according to Mr. Sakai's instructions, and various errands to run. On Sundays we went out surveying land. Mr. Sakai would peer through a small theodolite and direct me where to stand and hold up a pole. His business was a matter of checking the survey data against the land register. If he discovered there had been any discrepancies, he would notify the landowner and make out the papers needed to apply for a new land survey. The business depended on sending presents to land registry clerks so they would send us timely notices of useful information. One of my jobs was taking documents showing changes in land category classification to try to get survey orders over landholding rights questions. I would try to convince landlords to commission new surveys by telling them about cases where new surveys found as much as twenty percent more land than the current register showed.

My salary was ten yen a month, plus fifty sen for movie going. That was better than I had been doing at the pharmacy. I learned the work quickly. What got to me was the weather. Hokkaido doesn't have a rainy season, so it was hard getting used to rain day after day, or else vaguely dark and clammy weather.

One day it suddenly wasn't raining anymore and had turned sweltering hot. Mr. and Mrs. Sakai took me swimming at Enoshima. In Nemuro it's too cold to swim even in summer. The sight of people in bathing suits and beach umbrellas was another novelty. Mr. and Mrs. Sakai went swimming off together as if heading for the high seas. That impressed me and hit a sore spot at the same time. It suddenly hit me what a reckless thing it had been to take a little boat into the marsh for someone who couldn't swim a stroke.

When September rolled around I enrolled in night classes at a school of engineering affiliated with N. University, at Honjo Yokoamicho. If I got through three years there, I could get into the N. University high school, and that opened the possibility of getting into a university. I had given up dreaming about such things, but now the opportunity was in my grasp.

It was a fifteen-minute bike ride from Kameido to Honjo. Mrs. Sakai bought me a school uniform and paid my first month's tuition payment of 4.50 yen. Suddenly I was in blissful dreamland. Giving up on the pharmacy in Nemuro had been the right decision.

Conscious of how much I owed the Sakais, I worked at my job with enthusiasm. I learned how to fill out the land survey documents and how to take measurements with the theodolite. I absorbed enough that I could take over for Mr. Sakai at the front desk. I was on the road to a successful future.

My undoing occurred in pace with some chance occurrences that seemed minor to me at first. I was destined to be derailed again and again by apparently minor chance events.

I sent my sister Suéko the New Year's edition of *Children's Club*. At fifty sen a copy, the only way we had ever been able to read that magazine at home was by borrowing old copies from friends. I knew she would be delighted to get her own, brand-new copy, with all the tear-out attachments intact.

Sure enough, I got a letter back about how she was overjoyed. The fold-up warship model had caught Ishizo's interest, and he had set it on display in a corner of the room. She loved the smell of the ink as she turned the pages. Wasn't it wonderful I could buy such a lavish present!

Always the avid letter writer, Suéko's letter was long and filled with family news. Keiji was home, sick in bed with the same disease as Kachi Ishibashi. Like Kachi, he had come down sick while working at the docks. Keiji had developed a relationship with a girl working as a hairdresser. Though he was due to get married when the New Year began, there was trouble with his fiancée's parents. They were against their daughter marrying a stevedore. When Keiji visited the home he would always remove his happi and tabi dockworker's garb and change into a business suit. Ignoring Mother's warnings, Keiji would go to visit Kachi. Mother was tormented to think Keiji had caught the sickness from him.

I wrote Suéko a long reply. Naturally, I didn't forget to emphasize that I was going to school and studying hard to become an architect.

I paid a visit to my cousin in Yokohama over the New Year's holiday, traveling by bicycle. Back then, the roads were not at all crowded. I traveled everywhere around Tokyo by bicycle, to save on train fare.

Like most everyone in my mother's family, my cousin was fair skinned. He looked every bit the modern city person in his wire frame glasses. His employer was a fairly big real estate company. He had his own home. It was small, but it had a neat little garden. He was just married. His young wife served spiced saké and lots of special New Year's dishes, including the *kamaboko* my mother had sent. At first I was shy about serving myself, but the seasonal refreshment eventually loosened me up enough to chat about one thing and another about my home life in Nemuro.

My cousin recounted his own success story, with a little bit of pride. He had come to Tokyo when he was just about my age, as an apprentice at his real estate company. He took night classes, got through university, and the company hired him as a full-time employee.

"You can do that, too," he told me. "Go for it!"

"That means a lot, coming from you. You've done well compared to anyone else in the family." I knew how to turn on the flattery. He told me to stay the night. We shared one room and his wife slept in another room. He told me, "She graduated a woman's college. That's a valuable asset for a man. You would be smart to marry a college girl too."

The next day, my cousin and his wife showed me around Yokohama and a hotel restaurant overlooking the harbor, where we could see little boats and deluxe steamers coming and going. It was a grand sight. It outclassed Nemuro Harbor a hundred times over. We had the house specialty hotcakes. I sat there thinking someday I would like to have the money to stay at a hotel like this and treat someone to hotcakes. Back in Kameido, the scrivener's office was suddenly looking third rate to me.

From the time I started at the school of engineering I realized that for some reason I couldn't really concentrate on the lessons. That was slightly incredible, in view of the heartfelt encouragement I had just received from my cousin. It was a time to rise to the challenge before me, but I was thinking about whether I really wanted what this study promised to give me. Take the tough slog, working and studying, get through university and get hired by a company, live in a charming little house, married to women's college graduate. Did I want that life? It seemed to me there had been a little sarcasm in mind when I told my cousin "You've done well."

My thoughts didn't go any further than that, however. Whatever doubts I may have had about my cousin's life, I wasn't really thinking about what kind of future I did want.

One night when Mr. Sakai had given me my monthly tuition payment of 4.50 yen, I used some of it for a bowl of Chinese noodles before classes. That was all it took to get me accustomed to having a snack before classes began. One night it was Imagawa cakes, the next hotcakes, and the next udon noodles. Shortly, the 4.50 yen was gone. I intended to make the January tuition payment with the money I got for the February payment, but I neglected to stop buying snacks every night. I would get off work at five-thirty. There wasn't time for a meal, because I had to ride my bicycle to school in time for classes at six o'clock. I would be ravenous by nine o'clock when classes ended. During breaks many of the students were going somewhere in the neighborhood to get something to eat. At first I would grit my teeth. I was bearing up admirably. Then that overwhelming hunger I was feeling suddenly took over.

In March I was due to start at the second level of classes, but I wouldn't be able to without paying my tuition. Mr. Sakai would find out what I was doing with the money he was giving me for tuition. What to do?

There were books about real estate in the office bookshelves. I remembered my father had sold books about animals he had to a book shop when he needed cash. I pulled out a couple of volumes and got two yen and something from a used bookstore for them. I sold another five volumes and got five yen plus. It was enough to cover January's tuition, but no more, and the book selling strategy had been taken as far as it would go. I was still in a fix.

A search of the office turned up Mr. Sakai's savings account bankbook, together with his seal. I have a thief's sense for quickly smelling out where people put their valuables. It served me at home and Mr. Sakai's office as well. His savings came to about two hundred-fifty yen. I withdrew fifty yen. Now it seems amazing that I didn't withdraw it all. I suppose I must have been telling myself fifty yen wouldn't be such an inconvenience to the Sakais.

Though the purpose of taking the money had been to cover my school tuition for February, this unexpected windfall changed my mind. Now I was thinking of going somewhere far away. That is my standard behavior whenever I have a substantial sum of cash in hand. Thoughts of what I might do with it fill my head, with no room for thinking about where the money came from or how it really should be used. There is no anxiety about what will happen after the money is gone either. Money is the magic wand that makes dreams come true. I can't see anything beyond the dreams. I left the house wearing my student uniform, as if some business claimed my attention. Mrs. Sakai saw me, but said nothing.

I went to Asakusa, when I bought a pair of lace-up shoes and a raincoat. Then I boarded a train at Tokyo Station for an overnight journey to Osaka. My idea was to go somewhere far away from Nemuro and Tokyo.

In Osaka I went sightseeing at the harbor, thinking of Kachi Ishibashi's talk of "tens of thousands of chimneys and big steamships from overseas." I didn't find any sights there that seemed very special, though, having already seen Tokyo and Yokohama. I was also worried that Osaka was so close to Tokyo I might be caught right away. I decided the thing to do was take off for somewhere still farther away. That made me think of "Kagoshima Ohara Air," the record the pharmacist had played again and again. Like Nemuro, sitting way out at one far end of Hokkaido, Kagoshima was all the way south at the far end of Kyushu. Okay, I thought, that's where I want to go.

Spring had come to Kagoshima. I wandered around Shiroyama under trees sporting new leaves. Next, I found many local attractions new to me in Kajiyacho. It felt good walking around in warm breezes, gawking at whatever caught my attention. This went on for a week, until my last sen was gone. The fifty yen I had stolen had lasted two weeks. My raincoat was only getting in the way, so I went to sell it off. There was a second-hand clothing store on Tenmonkan Street. It was run by a couple who appeared to be in their sixties. The man examined the coat.

"Hmm, this was made in Tokyo . . . and you are not a Kagoshima child. Let me just ask, what are you going to do after you sell this raincoat?"

"Spend the money."

"And after you spend it all, then what?"

"I haven't thought about that."

"A problem child, if ever I saw one. Your papa and mama are worried about you, kid. Where are you from? . . . Nemuro? You are a long way from home, aren't you? Well, there is only one thing to do. You write home and have someone come get you."

Handed a post card, I wrote the essentials to my mother as the man watched. I took it to the post box, had a vision of my father, his face burning red with anger, tore up the post card and threw it away. Then I went back and told the man I had sent the post card. He told me to stay until my mother came for me and showed me to the second floor.

Three days later, of course with no telegraph and no one from my home, I grew tired of pretending to wait, stole fifty sen from the old woman's purse and headed for Kagoshima Station. I bought a ticket to Kushikino, which was as far as fifty sen would take me. I did not get off at Kushikino Station, however, intending to go all the way to Kumamoto, the last stop, but I was caught by a conductor's ticket inspection one stop before my destination. I was handed over to a station "police box" on a charge of fare jumping.

It was my first stay in a police station holding cell. I remember it all vividly, the steel bars, the dark, dank air, the lice, and fleas. There was a straw mat on the wood floor. Your bed is a blanket that you roll yourself up in, and there is no pillow. Besides me, there were five or six adults in the cell. They were all unshaven and they all scared me. They were laughing over an "Amida-kuji" lottery game.

The winner had tattoos over his whole body. He took off all his clothes and the next thing I knew he was rolled up with me in my blanket, saying nothing and pulling off my clothing. What he pressed against my backside was hard and hot. He pushed again and again, but it wouldn't go inside. I was scared and hurting terribly. I wanted to cry out, but his hands were around my throat, squeezing it so that I stopped resisting. After that, I couldn't have made any noise if I tried. He was pushing harder and harder while his hand was groping at my crotch. After a time, I was overcome by a strange feeling as I ejaculated. Shortly the man ejaculated too. He repeated, "Good boy, that's a good boy" a few times.

Every night the same thing happened with a different man. I was taught that a young boy used as a woman in this way is called an *anko* and the one taking the male role is the *kappa*. On the fourth day the first man who had made me into an *anko* tried again, and this time succeeded in penetrating my anus. Hearing his overjoyed reaction gave me a feeling of actually being transformed into a woman, shivering with passion.

On the tenth day I was taken outside. My mother was sitting next to a detective. She froze stock still when she saw me, clearly astounded.

" . . . You're alive . . ."

I had pulled my head back reflexively, expecting a tongue-lashing, but Mother only wept speechlessly. After we were on the train she explained that when the police has contacted her with an order to "receive me" in custody, she thought it meant she was to go retrieve my corpse. She had taken the journey in mourning dress.

The return from Kagoshima to Nemuro took five days by train and ferry. Mother kept silent throughout, except that in Tokyo she made this one brief statement: "I returned the fifty yen."

Though spring had come to Kagoshima in the south, winter still reigned in Nemuro. Thick ice layers covered its rivers and lakes, and the sea was filled with drift ice. When I appeared before my father Ishizo, he wouldn't say a word. My brother Keiji followed his lead and wouldn't talk to me either, and my sister Suéko was the first to speak when I met her. I, the wrongdoer, occupied a small space in the dark and cold of my home.

In fact, there was cold and darkness in the house above and beyond what my behavior had brought. Keiji lay in bed in the three-mat room, stricken with the same disease Kachi Ishibashi had contracted. Keiji suffered from continued coughing and painful hemorrhoids. These symptoms had afflicted Kachi when he died in early spring. We were prepared to watch Keiji meet the same fate. His face looked as if was painted red. The hollow cheeks and sunken eyes made him hardly recognizable. In Kachi's case, Mother had asserted abhorrence for dangerous germs, but she never shrank from being at her son's bedside. At the same time, Suéko and I would be chased away with a fierce look we if tried to enter Keiji's room.

There is no doubt that Keiji's health had been destroyed by work at the docks that was too demanding. He had married his hairdresser fiancé during the New Year holidays and the couple had set up their household on the second floor of her house, but when his disease came to light the girl and her parents offered Keiji a choice of amicable separation or a lawsuit for annulment of the marriage. Mother expressed bitter indignation at their callousness when Keiji returned home, but Father only voiced quiet resignation. He said, "Nothing we can do," with eyes downcast.

~

There was much fog from the sea that summer and a reddish-brown sun that was giving no warmth at all. Navy men would sit in our diner shivering in the cold as they downed containers of warmed sake.

One day, a gentleman of about forty called "Chief" by his companions cast his eyes on me and asked, "Hey, there sport! How would you like to work for the railroad?"

Mother came over, bowed and said, "Please do take him on."

Mellow with warm saké, the chief gave his agreement. Accustomed as I was to the things adults said when they were drinking, I was thinking there was a fat chance anything would come of that promise, but it turned out I was wrong. The chief meant what he said, and it was arranged that I would go to work as a junior employee of the Kushiro Railway Management Office's Nemuro Railway Management Division.

"Junior employee" was the lowest rank among company workers, distinguished from full employees, who were middle school graduates, according to a clearly defined system of discrimination by educational level. My job responsibilities were to perform odd jobs for other workers. I went to the Railway Management Office shack at seven in the morning, got coal from the coal dump at the end of the terminal and brought it to the potbelly stove in the passenger carriage. I cleaned the office, dumped out cinders, put in fresh coal and lit the stove so the room would be warm when the other workers arrived at eight. Fifty men worked at the management office, and they could all summon me, the office boy, to serve tea, buy cigarettes, stoke the fire, help collate the pages of contracts for work projects, get matches, etc., etc. My services were constantly in demand. I was on the run non-stop until five in the afternoon, with never enough time for lunch.

A junior employee received eighty sen for a day's work. That came to twenty yen a month, twice what I was getting at the scrivener's office. After three months, I had sixty yen saved, not having had any occasion to spend money. One day near the year's end I heard a junior employee who had been on the job longer than me talking about the local sporting houses. Never having been with a woman, hearing this was like having a line to a new world. My thoughts returned to experiences of being embraced by the men in the Kumamoto holding cell. I didn't think of anything else as I put ten yen in my pocket and headed for the pleasure quarter.

Heavily powdered girls siting together behind latticed windows called out to men strolling by. The sight alone made me light-headed. I went inside the third parlor I encountered. I was greeted by a woman who called me the "railway gentleman." I was wearing the cap from my uniform. One could tell at a glance where I worked.

The madam sat me down by a charcoal brazier, served me tea and asked what kind of girl I wanted. "I'd like a pretty one." I told her.

A petite girl of about twenty appeared and showed me to a minimally sized room lit to vermilion by a lamp with a bare light bulb. There were two pillows on the futon and a chest of drawers. Feeling like a balloon floating in the sky, I had sex with a woman for the first time, at the age of sixteen. The cost of this pleasure was 1.50 yen.

It's my nature that once I get started on something there is no stopping me.

I visited the pleasure quarter every night. My sixty-yen savings was shortly all spent. I discovered that it was possible to buy goods from the city purchasing department on company credit. You write out an invoice for a clock or something and the cost is deducted from your salary. I bought a clock for ten yen, took it to a pawn shop and got three yen for it. Fifteen kilos of rice cost 2.5 yen and I was able to sell it to an inn for two yen. At that rate, my pay at the end of January was slightly more than nothing.

Too mortified to face my parents, I wandered the streets instead of going home and finally showed up late at night. I was surprised to see the house brightly lit and filled with people eating and talking. Wondering what was going on, I found out that Keiji had died. I had walked into his wake. My brother's face was bluish white, like drift ice. It shone with Mother's tears.

My nightly excursions to the pleasure quarter were uncovered that very night. Father demanded my salary to cover funeral expenses and examined my empty pay envelope. Pressed by his questions, I confessed to everything and received a terrific slap in the face. When that was followed by a punch to my chest, my brother Shinichi intervened.

"I'll look after him, Father. Don't be too angry."

Thus, my career with the railways ended after four months work. Shinichi took me with him to Otaru. Behind a line of warehouses along a canal was a shack where about twenty workers lived. The air stank of sweat, fish, pulp, and pickled vegetables. I found a corner where I could be as inconspicuous as possible and went to sleep.

Shinichi was the keeper of a warehouse, meaning that it was his job to keep track of the goods hauled in by the crew for storage there. In dock workers jargon, Shinichi was called the "Gampi." Though I don't really know, I guess it was because he was a bookkeeper, and that is the name of a plant was used to make paper, long ago. I wanted to do that job too, but the supervisor put me on as a dock hand.

That is the simplest kind of manual labor. You shoulder a futon over your *happi* and haul steel machine parts, pulp, cotton, rice, barrels of herring roe or whatever else comes in. Your move the load from the ship to the warehouse or from the warehouse to another ship.

I had confidence in my own strength, but I was still immature, no match at all for the grown men around me who were used to the work. I was puffing and panting just to keep up. The first week was the hardest. Every muscle in my body hurt like needles were piercing it all the way to the bone. Sweat poured out and froze, so I would have to scrape it off.

Days when it rained or snowed were eagerly anticipated because on those days we received thirty percent of regular pay just for showing up and doing nothing. If it began to rain or snow after the day's work had begun we were paid seventy percent. My pay was not the same as everyone else's. Pay for every worker was a portion of the warehouse's monthly earnings. The foreman's portion was one and a half the regular share, while in principle, all the other shares were divided up equally, except that my pay was sixty percent of a regular worker's.

Shinichi held my earnings in custody for me. I didn't have any spending money for drinking or women. There was nothing to do when I was off but sit around the shack. Though I wanted to read books, the tiny light bulb in the shack was too dim for reading. I did a lot of sleeping.

One night will always remain sharp in my memory. It was cold, and snow was falling. Everyone got up when word started getting around that something terrible had happened in Tokyo. I jumped out of my futon and went to Shinichi's office.

"What's this terrible thing that happened in Tokyo?"

"They're saying some army men killed a lot of ministers and government officials. An agent from Tokyo told the supervisor about it."

"There's nothing in the newspaper about it."

"Yeah. We're always the last to hear about everything up here."

Shinichi was excited about this news. He fiddled with the radio dial, but all he got was a lot of static noise.

The rumor was passed around for a while and the dock workers quickly forgot about it. The incident claimed no greater level of our attention than would have been given news that a herring boat had capsized at sea.

~

I was making a mighty effort to win the right to get full pay for a day's work, the same as my fellow workers. By the time summer came around, my shoulders and arms had filled out. It was no longer a struggle to haul heavy loads. I became enamored with the image of the sturdy young man that reflected back at me when I entered the public bath. My legs and back were so up to performing the work that I didn't mind hauling steel parts, a commodity that others hated to deal with.

The supervisor must have taken notice because I was promoted to full worker status at fall's end. That change in status was accompanied by a change in the way everyone treated me. One day I suddenly found myself accepted as an equal rather than as a child by everyone — including Shinichi. Now he was handing over my pay to me, meaning that I was free to go drinking and whoring.

I soon discovered that my belief that Shinichi was all probity had been mistaken. When on the town he wasn't shy about drinking and dallying with women. In serious moments he would lecture me on the part of wisdom in the pursuit of pleasure. "When it comes to saké and women, moderation is the mark of adulthood. The way you were going wild back in Nemuro is what kids do."

Many of my fellow workers had been on the job anywhere from ten to thirty years. Their build resembled the best sumo wrestlers. They had the same elephantine way of walking. The other workers were mostly in their twenties. There weren't many like me, still in their teens.

When the New Year was approaching, we pounded out rice cakes in a warehouse, drank sake, and ran races. The supervisor refereed as each of us pushed a wheelbarrow loaded with a pulp barrel. It is very hard to maneuver a wheelbarrow without dumping the load. It takes strength, concentration, and good reflexes. Unexpectedly, I came in first.

Next was sumo wrestling on the dirt floor of the warehouse. I easily pushed a man in his thirties out of the ring and beat the next seven challengers in a row. The ninth challenger was Shinichi. We had played at sumo together as children. Back then, he would send me sailing out of the ring. This was our first serious match. I got him in a right-handed belt grip and did an over-arm throw. My brother went down hard, hitting his back against the ground. His face showed pain and he didn't get up right away. Simultaneously surprised by my own strength and seized with concern for Shinichi, I ran to help him up. One hand on his back, he managed a smile as he said, "Well, Atsuo, you certainly have come of age."

As the winner of both competitions, the supervisor said I got the gold prize. I opened the envelope he handed me, expecting a piece of gold inside, but it was a five-yen bill. I bought saké for everyone. That insured popularity for yours truly, "the kid."

It was the following summer that the Lugou (Marco Polo) Bridge Incident touched off war in China. Dock workers were shipped out to fight one after another. Shinichi received his induction notice in mid-December, the same day the whole city turned out for a lantern march through the street in celebration of the fall of Nanking. Shinichi had already fulfilled his military obligation and returned as a private first class. Now he was going back, pledging in a loud voice to the crowd of people holding Rising Sun flag as they saw him off to the station "I will do all I can for the country." That was the last time I saw him.

I inherited the job of warehouse keeper that my brother had held. I kept the record book showing the inventory on hand and schedules of receipt and delivery. It required constant attention to where things were to make sure shipments could be made with a minimum of lost time. Of course, I wasn't exempt from the actual work of helping to move the goods. The job came with a lot of responsibility and a lot of work to accomplish. I took satisfaction in the hard work. The crew of men would listen to what I told them even though they were all older than me because Shinichi had built up a reputation for reliability over the years and because the supervisor was on my side. Of course, there were some who resented working under someone so young, but my own physical strength gave me the upper hand. None of them could whip me if it came to a fight.

I had put in three years as a dock worker when 1939 rolled around. That was the year I was due for my induction physical. I had been working conscientiously until then and had achieved a position of responsibility. But now it seemed to me that if I would have to just walk away from my job to go into the army, it had all been for nothing. Suddenly, I no longer saw any reason to take my work seriously. My feelings are like that, swinging from one extreme to the other.

It was the end of April. The wind was still chilly, but springlike sunshine brightened the snow-covered roofs of houses. The peculiarly sweetish tang of a paper mill drifted in from somewhere. Dock workers waited idly in the sun for a shipment that hadn't arrived on schedule. The supervisor called me into his office. He ordered me to run an errand to the bank to fill in for a clerk absent with a cold. He handed me a brown envelope. Looking inside, I saw it was stuffed with ten-yen bills. "There's five hundred yen in it. Go deposit it in the station front bank. You get the job because you can be trusted," the supervisor said.

The station was located on an elevation that gave a view of the city and the sea. A train pulled in as I was looking over the panorama. It was bound for Hakodaté. Seeing the train's destination written on its side triggered a store of geographical knowledge I had taken pleasure in learning. One could take a ferry from Hakodaté to Honshu, and from there, a train to Tokyo.

I bought a ticket to Tokyo and boarded the train. Having reverted to standard behavior, I did not think at all about the probable reactions of my supervisor or fellow dock workers. I was preoccupied with the fact of having five hundred yen in hand and the feeling of power it brought.

Not much was going on in my mind about what actually to do. I did recall hearing, however that long distance rail lines served excellent rice curry. I went to the dining car and ordered some. Then, well satisfied, I returned to my seat and went to sleep.

Traveling south took me to the spectacle of trees laid barren by winter shortly before showing new buds and fresh leaves. Spring had come to Tokyo. Women's kimonos blazed with color. It was scarcely believable that I had come to Tokyo five years before as a child apprentice to a scrivener. Now I knew the city. I strolled here and there as whim dictated. In Asakusa I bought a suit, a necktie, and a wristwatch to transform myself into a businessman.

My next stop was the Yoshiwara pleasure quarter. The women found my physique a marvel. I told them I had been on a university rugby team. The harsh cold of Hokkaido had so roughened my complexion I was taken for being three or four years older than my actual age. Sexually, I could perform strongly enough to interest the women to come back repeatedly for more.

Yoshiwara held my interest for a week, and then I grew bored and continued traveling south. From Wakayama I crossed over to Shikoku by ferry. I drifted about Shikoku for a time and returned to Honshu. I was wandering around aimlessly. By the end of May, I had spent four hundred eighty yen. The cost of third-class fare from Tokyo to Nemuro was about eighteen yen. I could just barely stretch the money I had left to cover that and meals. Somewhere in my mind was a vague awareness that I was up for an induction physical in mid-June, meaning it was time for me to get back to Nemuro.

When the train rolled into Nemuro Station, my father's face popped into my mind. He was not the sort of parent who would receive me quietly after having stolen and spent the tremendous sum of five hundred yen. No, I had better not go to Nemuro, I thought as I descended to the platform.

At that point, I had only five sen left and no particular place to go. It came to me that I might go visit my sister Yoshiko, who worked in a paper mill. The only trouble was that I didn't know her address. There were paper mills all along the Kushiro River. I went asking around and finally, that night, I located Yoshiko in a very old dormitory that stood listing at an angle to the ground. "...Atsuo?...Do you know the police are looking for you?" With this, my sister's voice abruptly rose in register. "Look, you have to turn yourself in. There's no other way." She said she would go with me to the police. I should wait there at the door while she went inside to change.

I could feel curious glances from female mill workers passing by. I edged back into the darkness to get cover for my escape from those women, then set out into the darkness of the town. Stumbling upon a police station with a red light outside, I turned around in a panic and ran while footsteps behind me rang in my ears. I crossed beyond the houses to the harbor. I passed a humble looking restaurant with good smells wafting outside, but however reasonable its prices might have been, five sen would certainly not have covered a meal there.

There was nothing for me in town, so I took the narrow road along the coast. The starlight showed a vista of dark blue waves laced with white lines. Once in a while I passed a hamlet, but never saw traces of people. The houses were dark, but I didn't feel lonely as long as the sea was beside me. It spoke to me like a friend.

But the road wound upward toward the mountains, where it disappeared into a forest. A little way into the wood the starlight was swallowed up into near perfect darkness. Ubiquitous weeds made it uncertain if there was still a path underfoot.

Fears assailed me. What if a bear happened by? Listening carefully I could make out a soft *whoo-whoo* of a bird. It sounded like a fish owl. I caught the glint of a pair of eyes high up in a tree that seemed to reach all the way to the black sky.

The fish owl is a big creature. As birds go, it is like a bear, and it has a piercing gaze. When I tried to run, there was a *whooosh!* The bird's wing had clipped my face. I went face down on the ground to evade the next assault. The bird flew off, shining silvery in the night sky. I had felt the wind from that powerful wing before it hit me, but there wasn't a sound. That uncanny silence in flight is unique to the fish owl. I hugged the ground, paralyzed with fright.

Something alive rustled the bamboo grass. I could hear it breathing. It might have been a deer or a rabbit. I finally relaxed enough that I could jump to my feet. I went back to the shoreline and sought a fishing boat to sleep in. It was cold. I covered myself with a sail and eventually went to sleep, listening to the waves' lullaby.

Mosquitoes were deep drilling my face. It was daylight. Summer nights in the north are short. I jumped to my feet and started walking. Afraid to be seen, I fled to the mountain road and went into the woods. I was hungry, but there wasn't anything I could do about it. I gathered bog rhubarb stalks and drank their water. The morning light filtering through the leaves lit the forest spectacularly. That uplifted my spirits. I set out to push through the bamboo grass, having just then decided upon my destination.

I would follow the coast to Nemuro without a thought about what awaited me there. My psychology serves me well at such times. Anxiety and care went into a box, shut up as if they did not exist for the time being. The issues that I now faced were the difficult going on the path ahead and my empty stomach. My full attention was taken with the business of placing one foot in front of the other.

Venturing too deeply into the woods would only get me lost. I resolved to avoid straying too far from the sea at my right. Woodcutters had opened a wisp of a path along the top of a cliff. It was cut off by a rocky slope. My left shoe was ripped, and the little toe had a cut from a rock. Down below, the main road that joined one hamlet to the next was visible. The going there would clearly be easier, but I was afraid to meet people, so I stuck with the craggy path.

There was a house on the cliff with a drying rack outside. Two women were tending to a row of saffron cod laid out on the rack in the sun. The white meat of the dried fish was an appetizing sight. I hid behind a white birch and settled down to await my chance. The women went inside, and I went to the rack, treading softly. I had picked up two fish when a dog started barking. The women — one was old, the other young — came running out yelling "Thief!" I threw a rock at the noisy dog so it wouldn't chase me and ran. Something cold hit my neck. When I had put some distance between me and the house, I stopped to find out what had hit me. It was a dead crow in an advanced state of decay. It had been strung up to deter thieves. The stench was horrible and the gore from the crow had gotten on the fish. Hungry as I was, I had to throw away the fish with the dead bird.

Now flies were swarming around me. I ran to a brook to wash my hands and face. Mercifully, I was able to remove the foul-smelling filth.

It occurred to me that I was penniless, having lost the jacket with my last coins in its pocket the previous day. As I tramped through the forest, the sole of one shoe started to come off. I tied it with my hand towel and learned to walk by shuffling one leg. I trudged on.

In the evening I spotted a small shrine atop a hill. It was deeply overgrown by grass and its veranda was broken. I approached and confirmed the building was abandoned. I laid down inside. A column of mosquitoes swarmed in the air, but I was able to drift into sleep, with a brief thought that death would be agreeable. The low sound of waves reached the far edge of my consciousness. Morning brought the sight of a big blue expanse of water — Akkeshi Bay. I also saw there was a town I would have to pass through to get to Nemuro, no matter how much I wanted to avoid being seen. Though it was like jumping from a bridge, I walked toward the town. I must have looked like the living dead, but no one even glanced my way.

Boats large and small were moored to piers and fishing catches were being unloaded. Small boats were returning fully loaded with vegetable kelp, the fresh-tasting kind that could only be taken from fast-flowing currents for a limited time in June, in advance of large scale kelp harvesting in July. Entire households were turning out to take away the kelp for drying. The smell of miso soup was in the breeze. I was savoring it when someone called to me.

"Hey buddy, the ferry's fixing to leave!"

I scrambled to get on board and only recalled I didn't have a sen on me after the barge was chugging toward the far shore. It edged to the pier and everyone filed out without a word about collection of fares. Most of the other passengers were young men who no doubt worked on the herring, salmon, and cod fishing vessels. I had been mistaken for one of them. There was nothing out of the ordinary about my sweaty shirt, seedy trousers and tanned face.

Beyond the village I came to a temple set upon a modest hill. It had a large, complicated roof, befitting a temple with a distinguished history. Going around to the monks' living quarters I sang out a loud "Hello there!" but there was no answer. I went inside to be greeted by the glorious smell of cooking. Something was boiling in an earthenware pot while a pressure kettle was making music of its own.

I was expecting a monk to show up so that I could appeal to his sympathy with my story of not having eaten in two days. I called out again. This time a lovely girl emerged. And I do mean lovely. Her bearing bespoke grace and dignity quite unlike women in the pleasure business. Suddenly, I was speechless with embarrassment.

"May I ask your business?" she said.

"Could I have a drink of water?"

The girl ladled water from a jar into a cup and offered it to me. Her hands were slender and fair. The cold water gave my stomach a jolt. Never had a drink of water given me such happiness.

"That tasted good!" I said with feeling.

The girl's face brightened into a big smile. "It's from the mountain spring outside." She showed no trace of alarm at my muddy, scruffy appearance. I thanked her and left.

Starved and weary, my body was so much dead weight that my legs could just barely support. But in spite all this, a wellspring of strength had come bubbling up from within. That drink of water received from a young girl seemed to have tapped into an unlimited source of strength. Her smile stayed in my mind and gave me an amazing feeling such that I had never experienced with women I had paid for. It was a different kind of pleasure, a gladness that brought inner warmth.

Fog that had come gliding softly over the waves swept in through the trees, cloaking everything in milky whiteness. Fog from the sea, thick and heavy, is a distinctive feature of eastern Hokkaido. I walked on, taking care not to stray from the road's course. In the afternoon I reached a vast field of reeds.

The reeds were yellow and dry, but fresh green leaves reaching up from their base proclaimed summer's arrival. Alders stood like sentries all around. An indeterminate mass of red would appear, slowly take form and crystallize as flowers, lose shape once again then fade away. I was trying to recall the names of flowers learned in elementary school when I came upon flowers of yellow. They were a type of pond lily distinctive to Nemuro. Next were white trifoliate flowers known as bogbean. It was delightful to behold the many types of flowers of the marsh stretching on and on into the foggy distance.

I came to a river. Along its banks was a path used by people who come to fish. It is the only passageway in the marsh that people can stroll along. I set out upon it.

A snipe — a bird with long legs and a very long bill — was making its uncanny *jiiiiiii–jiiiiiii–* cry. My approach did not trouble it at all. It stayed right where it was and continued making its strange cries. For my part, I ignored the many mosquitoes that were repeatedly biting me. I was concerned with edging quietly toward the waterfowl so that I could seize it. The snipe took flight a split moment ahead of my hand's arrival at the place where its neck had been. The meal was lost. Exhausted, I drank some water. My hunger had passed the point of even feeling hungry. Now I was overcome with drowsiness that permeated my body. Having one split shoe made walking all the more difficult but my strength was still not so depleted that I couldn't continue. "You're not down for the count yet," I told myself, gazing at some white objects bouncing up and down.

They were plants — cotton grass growing in tussocks — that looked like white-tipped spears swaying in the wind. Instead of bending with the breeze, each stalk had a white head that nodded left or right of its own accord. Like me, there was no rhyme or reason to what they did.

Again, I recalled that girl with the lovely face and was suddenly seized with a desire to place myself into her custody. I would go back there and tell her everything. I am about to starve to death. I am a thief who stole five hundred yen. Please give me something to eat, then turn me over to the police.

I was stopped from actually going back to that temple by the sudden disappearance of the fog, like a great curtain pulled back to the sea. The vista that met my eyes was a familiar cape jutting into the blue sea — Cape Kiritappu. I had been there a number of times before.

When I arrived there, I looked over the vast Biwasé marsh. I got an energy boost from the realization that I was standing not far from the hamlet where I had been born. It was dusk when I reached that lonely spot. I couldn't find anything recognizable to me. I asked an old woman walking along the road. She told me that a tsunami had carried away every trace of the old hamlet. As always, the waves washed the lonely beach. The wind was cold, I guess because the area had been foggy all day. Looking for a place to sleep brought me to an elementary school. It was dark inside, suggesting there wasn't a teacher to mind the building overnight. The door wasn't locked either. I went into a classroom, gathered up about twenty cushions from chairs and made myself a place to sleep on the teacher's dais. The cushions were too small. Every time I moved my bedding came apart and I woke up on the cold floor. Once I awoke from the fright of a dream about myself as a small child crying because a furious white wave was coming.

The next day was again shrouded in heavy fog, with occasional rain that seemed to come welling up from inside the fog. Exhaustion, lack of sleep, hunger, and cold kept making me want to just lay down and die, but still I walked on. I must not have been in my right mind. I saw bizarre landscapes without knowing if they were real or not.

Dead birds on a black shoreline, crows pecking at their reddened bellies. As more and more dead black birds appeared, the population of crows pecking at them grew. The waves heaved rapidly, like a wounded animal gasping for breath.

The heads of horses suddenly appeared from the fog. They were joined by ponies running toward me, as if to attack. I jumped to the side and they ran past. One fell, its leg broken. It cried piteously, but its mother didn't return.

A pasture with no people. Foghorns sounded from the lighthouse and somewhere close to my ear. Waves broke on a towering peak. A forceful wind wearing down the words on gravestones. A Sakhalin fir woods . . . The streets of a town . . .

I finally reached Nemuro, although I don't have a single recollection of where I walked or how. I opened the door of my house and my mother's eyes opened up wide. She yelled out "Atsuo!" and I fell to the floor.

I was in a hospital bed when I regained consciousness. The first image I recognized was the worried face of my sister Suéko. My mother came over to me. My sister Yoshiko turned to look at me. There was also a man I didn't recognize. I guessed he was a policeman.

I had been mistaken about the police. They were looking for me, but as a missing person, not a thief. My father had returned the entire five hundred yen.

He had put the money together by borrowing from friends and relatives, then settled with the supervisor at the cargo handling company.

I was greatly relieved to hear that. I ate voraciously and was fully recovered three days later. My mother was overjoyed, but, as usual, my father kept silent. At my mother's instruction, I went to him to apologize.

"Damn fool!" he said, looking away.

My induction physical in the middle of June was nearing. My one consuming thought was to pass it and join the army. I had been nothing but trouble to my parents and the whole family. I was wicked, worthless. The army was the only place for me, as I saw it. If I just got into the Imperial Army, my parents could be proud of me. Then for sure I would be of benefit to our country.

One week before the physical I wrote a letter in my blood to the Regimental District of Nemuro. I cut my left ring finger with a knife and filled a new fountain pen with my blood to write it. I want to serve my country. I have been a burden to my parents, but now I have a new outlook and want to be a soldier in the Imperial Army, I wrote. I did not forget to add that when I was in elementary school I had donated six yen earned as an itinerant peddler of medicine to the army for the welfare of soldiers. I concluded with a plea that my examiners look into my heart and grant my induction.

The day before the physical I went to the barber shop and got a monk's fuzz cut. I put on the loincloth my mother had made for me. It was the kind that just hangs in front and leaves the buttocks bare.

Hanasaki Higher Ordinary Primary School gymnasium was the venue of the induction physicals. It brought back memories to be at my old school. Veterans Association members had set up the facilities and were there giving directions. Military police stood guard. I observed my fellow naked inductees while they measured height, weight, chest, lung capacity, etc. It was to be expected that the sons of fishermen would be well built, but thanks to my career as a manual laborer, none was better than mine. This was an area of human affairs in which one's body is all that matters. Our honorable country was examining and classifying our bodies for its use.

A first lieutenant sitting at the teacher's dais told me, "You are accepted as a conscript with a Grade One classification."

"Thank you, sir."

I was overjoyed. The nation had accepted me as one of the top level of its men. "Do you have any preferences?"

"I do. I want to be an infantryman in the China expedition."

"Why the infantry?"

"I like to walk." I was recalling that I had walked two hundred kilometers from Kushiro to Nemuro without drinking or eating.

"I read that you wrote a letter in blood to the regimental commander."

"Yessir."

"That is very commendable."

"Thank you, sir."

Informing my father Ishizo I had made Grade One brought a broad smile to his face, the like of which I had not recently seen.

"Is that so? That makes you a full-fledged human being. Congratulations. I'm proud of you." The next evening, Ishizo got a surprise from the newspaper. He called me in.

"There is an article in here about you!"

It was a short article about my petition in blood. The headline was "A Young Man's Oath of Allegiance to Serve — Written in Blood." It said I was a praiseworthy youth who would probably become a model soldier in the emperor's army.

"Atsuo, I didn't even know you wrote a blood petition!"

"I kept quiet because you'd have been mad if I came out Grade Two."

"Crazy kid!"

Father was in high spirits. He delivered a slap on my back and was silent for a few moments while he ran a hand through hair that was showing traces of white, then he placed his fingers on his forehead.

"I'm proud of you. Atsuo, give it all you've got. What you do is for your country, for us all," he said.

It was early October when I received my notice for induction to active service into the Asahikawa twentieth regiment on December first. I decided to spend my last two months as a civilian getting back into good physical shape before induction. I got a job as a dock hand once again with the company where my brother Keiji had been employed. The work served my purpose well; back, arm and leg muscles tightened up quickly. By the end of November I was back to the condition I had been in when I was working at the Otaru cargo handling company.

It was still dark in the early morning of November thirtieth when a large crowd of people gathered around our diner. I was standing in the middle of the floor wearing my brother Shinichi's army uniform beside a banner I had set up that read "Call to service." The white-haired president of the Veterans Association gave a little speech.

"Congratulations on your induction. It is an honor to become a soldier in the Imperial Army in this time of national emergency. We are all looking forward to your gaining distinction in service to the country."

The neighborhood association chairman stepped up and said pretty much the same thing. I gave my responses, memorized in an intensive study session the night before, in my loudest voice.

" . . . and during my absence this house will be watched over only by an elderly couple. I therefore request the kind favor of all in our community." This was delivered with a low bow of the head. My mother's eyes were downcast. My father was nodding emphatically. Suéko was nowhere to be seen.

Everyone rose and started off for the Hanasaki Ordinary Primary School, where new inductees from all over Nemuro had assembled in the schoolyard. The crowd stirred restlessly. The rising sun flag and a white "Congratulations Inductees" banner fluttered in breezes from the sea.

There were a dozen or so inductees, each with their own ideas about how to dress for the occasion. Some wore uniforms from a certain young adult school, some suits — and one fellow was in haóri. At some point I was singled out as the most conspicuous one in my army uniform, so the village chief and the others faced me with their congratulatory remarks. I was out in front, singing in full voice when the parade began, led by the youth association brass band.

> Striking down the unrighteous, in Heaven's service
> Soldiers without peer, brave and true,
> Send them forth with exultant cries!
> Land of our fathers and mothers, the hour has arrived!

People from the village had gathered outside. Elementary school children holding flags lined the streets shouting "Banzai!" The Patriotic Women's Association and the Women's National Defense Association vied for prominence among the voices raised in song. Members of the Veterans Association, the Youth Association and the neighborhood associations all cheered. All the village celebrated our induction.

As the procession moved uphill from downtown toward the Gokoku shrine to the war dead, my own state of transport set the mood. Everyone admired my knowledge of martial songs like "Brave Bombers Three" well enough to sing each one from the first line all the way through to the end. By the time we arrived at Nemuro Station after visiting Gokoku Shrine to pray for good fortune in battle, I was getting frightened by the size of the gathering crowd. The festival at Kotohira Shrine had never been this big. Cries of "Banzai!" arose and fell like raging ocean waves. The inductees lost their way among the vast swarm of people. We probably wouldn't even have gotten onto our train if it hadn't been for the non-commissioned officers from the regiment who met us and did an efficient job of guiding us to it.

The train started rolling at precisely seven o'clock. I searched for Mother's face, but all the faces I saw outside the window were unfamiliar. The faces of this crowd were flushed, with bloodshot eyes. I had not been expecting such a frenzied celebration for village youth going into the army. It also occurred to me that if the induction physical had turned up some problem that called for my non-acceptance, I would have found myself in such a situation of shame it would not even be possible to return home. We reached Asahikawa at eleven pm. All that I remember of that night is that it was dark and cold and that I was in a hurry to get to sleep to prepare for the next day.

I was placed in Company 4 of the Second Machine Gunner Corps. The company commander was a corporal who had graduated a military school. My life began as a new second class private with one star, subject to hazing by the older troops, from the Pfcs on up. That life was governed by meticulous rules of conduct, from wake-up time at five until lights out at nine. Even so, it was an easy life compared either to my time as a junior employee on the railroad or as a dock worker. My only concern was to do whatever I was told. Just walk, run, flatten on the ground, eat, take care of your shoes, sword or clothes as ordered by the squad commander and you receive praise. Praise makes you happy. My first discovery was how good it is to be a soldier.

I already knew from being a dock worker that the key to recognition in an organization is having your name known. The idea came to me to go to the non-commissioned officers room to clear away the dishes after the squad commander's meals. I would drop everything eighty percent of the way through my own meal and run off to do it.

"Company Four, Private Second Class Yukimori, sir! I have come to clear the commander's table." With this announcement, I would carry away the dishes, deferential as you please. I did this with every meal. The squad commander learned my name quickly.

One day the company commander called together the new recruits and asked if any of us knew the Imperial Rescript to Soldiers and Sailors. Of course everyone knew that it had five articles and they were about allegiance, decorum, bravery, fidelity, and reserve, but the company commander was asking if anyone could recite the whole thing — introduction, main text, and addenda. None of us could. I decided I would be the first to learn it. That would be no easy task for a new recruit who didn't have a single moment of free time during the day. I read the rescript in bed after nine o'clock lights out by the light from the hall that remained on all night. It takes twelve minutes, forty seconds to read the rescript at normal speed. I learned it all in ten days by reading it twice a night and during defecation time during the day. It happened that the company commander asked "Is there anyone here that's learned the Rescript?" on the tenth day. I was the only one whose hand went up and could recite it.

Basic training was over in two weeks. Our machine gun corps special education began in mid-December. We had to learn operation of the Model 92 machine gun. The barrel weighs twenty-eight kilograms and the mount weighs an additional 27.5. I went with the older troops to the armory to help with disassembly and cleaning of the weapons, hoping to learn the mechanism as fast as possible, and preferably faster than anyone else. My curiosity and manual ability served me well in the effort.

The weapon has to be fired with the mount fastened down on the ground. Again and again we practiced point shooting at targets and sweep shooting, where you cover an area with a sweeping motion. In addition to shooting, we practiced breaking down and transporting the weapon. It takes two men to carry the twenty-eight-kilo barrel and two men to carry the 27.5-kilo mount. The other troops carry the twenty-kilo munition box. We would be carrying this ordnance along snow covered paths in the dead of winter. Physical strength was in demand. We were in for fifty-kilometer treks in territory where your boots sink into the snow with every step.

Out on a mountain road, we kept getting stragglers. The company commander handled this by blasting the rule breakers verbally and slapping their faces. Those who had fallen would get up and push on, gasping desperately. Machine gun companies cannot fight when even one man is absent. Having been a dock worker hoisting one hundred kilo loads all day, carrying a twenty-kilo munition box was light work as far as I was concerned. If a man went down, I would take his load and lend my shoulder to help him walk. When I did it for someone who hadn't liked me until then for playing up to the commander, suddenly he and I were buddies.

The army was an agreeable place to me. In two months, I was an old trooper. The commander called me out in front of the other troops for commendation as an outstanding performer.

We trained right up to the end of the year and into the next, without a holiday break. One day in February they had every man fall out on the parade ground at two in the morning. The new troops wore casual fatigues and still didn't have weapons. The regiment commander told us we were shipping out to China. After paying a visit to the regimental shrine, we formed ranks and marched to the station. Even though it was snowing and the middle of the night, a great number of people from the town turned out to send us off with cries of "Banzai!" I was amazed that they knew we were going. It was supposed to have been a secret troop movement.

Chapter 11

Mire

My outfit, the Asahikawa 20th Regiment, had been transferred from Manchuria to the north, to protect that area, but some new troops were being sent to other regiments in central China the year I joined. There seemed to be a plan afoot to build up our forces from the center to the south. The ten-thousand-ton cargo ship I was on departed Otaru in early February and disembarked fresh troops at two or three ports before we reached the Yangtze River at the end of February.

The sight of junks with sails unlike anything you would see in Japan drove home the reality that we were in another land. The Yangtze is so broad I didn't even realize we were looking at a river before someone mentioned the fact. It was no ordinary river in any case, not with so many merchant ships and warships from all over the world coming and going. At Nanjing we were transferred to a small boat that took us upriver. We reached our port of landing on the morning of the second day after that.

We had left Otaru in a blizzard, but it was already spring when we landed on the continent. We found a landscape of green wheat stalks and bright yellow rape blossoms on rolling hills reaching all the way to the horizon. I had been expecting blood and chaos, since it was a war zone. It seemed curious to see Chinese peasants peacefully driving their cows and wielding their hoes. They kept to their work, displaying no interest in the Japanese troops marching past them.

We arrived at B Enclosure in the evening. Throwing down a straw mat in a wood floored room lit by a kerosene lamp of the private house our machine gun company had appropriated as our barracks, I wrapped myself in a blanket and went to sleep. A cock crowed at dawn. The cattle slept until it was fully light before they started making noises that sounded strange to me. One of the older troops told me it was water buffalo.

Our combat training began the next day. Machine gunners don't carry small arms. If it comes to hand-to-hand fighting we have the same short swords that are used as bayonets. For our training we used short wooden swords. Machine gun training was held in a wheat field. Trampling through the wheat farmers had been cultivating, we set up our mounts and took our positions. Then we practiced running up several different hills carrying our weapons, pretending we were pursuing enemy troops. By evening, we were covered in sweat, but there was no bath. We didn't even have time to wipe ourselves down with wet towels before night fighting training began. That became our daily schedule.

One day in April when I was going back to the barracks I passed a storage shed that had been made into guardhouse I saw an old Chinese was there, inside a cell built of steel bars. He wore a long white garment and his face looked gentlemanly. He gave an impression of being a person of some importance. I quietly asked the superior private on guard duty what was up. The prisoner was the mayor of the next village. He had been arrested on suspicion of passing information about the Japanese army's movements to Chiang Kai-shek's army.

The next morning a sergeant major in charge of personnel called together the forty recently arrived troops on our parade ground. Shortly, the man on duty at the guardhouse brought in the mayor, his hands bound behind his back. His garment was muddy and his face was swollen purplish. His nose was out of shape and his lips were split. He had plainly been tortured.

The sergeant major was smiling self-importantly.

"All right, men. We have made special arrangements for your benefit. This is the target for your bayonet practice, to give you experience with a living human body."

The mayor had been tied between two posts, the same as the empty straw bags we used in bayonet practice. His swollen eyes glared fiercely at us.

"There are forty of you. Everyone gets a chance, so when it's your turn be sure you keep away from the throat. You are not to let him die anytime soon. Private Second Class Yukimori, commence!"

I was unsheathing my sword as I went into a run. By then, I was the complete military man, who could be switched into motion by an order. As a practice target rather than an enemy soldier, it didn't matter whether my objective was a straw bag or a human being. I didn't look at the old man's face or think of anything as my sword pierced his chest on the right. The blade went through the clothing, the tip hit bone, then soft muscle, and the man gave an agonized cry.

His eyes were open wide, glaring at me. If that had met a qualm of conscience in me I might have had some small claim on humanity, but I was quite untroubled, even proud of having carried out my order with distinction. I withdrew the sword smartly and blood stained the man's clothing. I turned, took my place among the other troops, and the next man ran forward and elicited another scream of pain by piercing the old man's stomach.

Probably it was the sound of screaming that caused a number of men to emerge from the barracks to come to watch our bayonet practice. They came close, watching the spectacle with interest. Some sat down on the bare ground. When two coolies we had drafted showed up, the NCO yelled angrily, "Don't let the Chinese watch! Get them out of here!"

The old man's screams became weaker and weaker each time he was stabbed. He was silent after the tenth time. His right hand came loose from its binding and was feeling at his bloodied breast. A soldier stabbed the palm of that hand, splitting it open.

"Next! Next!" The sergeant-major ordered the assaults in turn. It was around the twentieth man who inadvertently violated the prohibition by piercing the prisoner's neck. At that, the head fell forward, not to rise again.

"Fool! Why did you stab the neck? Have you no consideration for your fellow soldiers?"

"It was a wrongful act."

The soldier said this with a formal bow, inclining the upper half of his body precisely fifteen degrees. His carelessness had deprived the remaining soldiers the experience of bayoneting a living human being. Nevertheless, the sergeant-major continued ordering "Next! Next!" to one solder after another.

After the last man had his turn, the old man's corpse was thrown into a hole the soldier on guard duty had dug. The guard covered the hole with dirt, stamped down the surface and covered it with grass, intending to erase all traces that the earth had been disturbed. He was not successful. It was plain that the spot differed from its surroundings. I had previously noticed a number of places that looked as if holes had been dug and then refilled. Now I realized they may have been places where corpses had been buried.

"Listen up!" the sergeant-major shouted. "That concludes your practice. You were given this opportunity because you will be facing real combat with real enemy troops. It might not look like much is happening around here, but this is a war zone, and don't forget it. And don't forget that if you are ever captured, you would be lucky to get off with the kind of treatment this Chink just got. They would probably have a lot worse ways to kill you. Understand?"

"YESSSS!" Forty rookie troops chorused their answer like grade school children.

About three days later some men who looked like peasants paid us a visit, asking what happened to the mayor. The company commander flatly denied knowing anything about such a person. When the young men persisted with their questions, he pulled out his sword and chased them away.

I came to realize that the peasants in the area were making a show of allegiance to the emperor's army and at the same time watching us very mistrustfully. However peaceful this agricultural region might have seemed, it belonged to a foreign country occupied by force. The vast territory that extended as far as the eye could see was inhabited by people hostile to us.

We were occasionally ordered to move as information was received about the appearance of Chinese troops, but no engagements resulted. The enemy had always withdrawn upon our arrival. We would break into houses abandoned by farmers and carry away rice, vegetables, chickens, and eggs, then cook up a banquet. In fact, looting and feasting was always a part of our expeditions. It wasn't honorable, but the expectation of being able to eat our fill made us look forward to them. Older troops boasted of raping women who hadn't fled in time, but there was never anyone left in the villages our company attacked. That impressed me how wary the people were of the imperial army.

The local river would occasionally flood its banks. It was explained to me that the water level of the Yangtze had risen at those times, the result of snow melting in Sichuan Province and Tibet. Snow melting in Hokkaido would reach downstream rivers the following day, but the same phenomenon was playing out on a far greater scale in China. Things like that made me think about what an immense country it was and how much military power it would take to conquer it. It didn't look like the imperial army had that much power. The proof of that was the fact that it didn't order an all-out assault Chiang Kai-shek's stronghold in Chongqing.

At the end of August water levels in the canals began declining rapidly. Earth baked in the sun day after day turned into yellow dust clouds that caked on our sweaty faces like a strange kind of makeup. The most troubling thing of all was that the dust got into our machines gun and interfered with their functioning. Cleaning them after returning from the field took twice the time and twice the careful attention that normal conditions required.

One evening the dust was like a heavy fog obscuring vision. Our company was heading back for a break from maneuvers when we heard a rumor, its source unclear, that another outfit was going to do beheadings. Our company commander sent out a messenger to the unit. An exchange of messages resulted in a decision that we would go to watch.

At the summit of a hill a line of guards was keeping strict watch. We went down the slope to find an open area of ground where a group of Chinese in peasant garb was digging ditches. There were eight of them. The ditches were two meters long, four meters wide and about one meter, fifty centimeters deep. They were surrounded by troops, who opened up spaces for us to sit down and watch. I sat down near the ditches. We spectators took the proceedings as an entertaining show. We were in a hollow, with reddish dust swirling by far above our heads.

When the Chinese finished digging, their hands were bound behind them. The first lieutenant in charge of the company came out before them. He was in his thirties, having probably started as a cadet school graduate. He rattled the decorative chain on the sword he was wearing as he delivered an inflamed lecture to the prisoners.

"You have killed two members of our imperial army, two sons of the emperor. This act of murder absolutely cannot be forgiven. Accordingly, I will now give you honorable death by a Japanese sword."

Unable to understand what the officer was saying, the prisoners watched his oratorical display in amazement. Their clothing fluttered as the wind picked up. Afterwards I got the details on what it was all about. Late the previous night, the first lieutenant's men had been suddenly fired upon. They returned fired and the enemy fled. After that, they had rounded up this group of peasants at random. Having lost two of his men, the first lieutenant had requested and received the regimental commander's permission to conduct executions of the villagers.

As a pair of soldiers brought one of the prisoners forward and the first lieutenant had drawn his sword, a young medic came forward.

"Sir, I wish to conduct an experiment for the benefit of our military medical research."

"What kind of experiment?"

"It is said that injecting air into blood vessels causes death. I would like to test that theory."

"All right, go ahead." The first lieutenant returned his sword to its sheath and folded his arms.

The young medic removed a large syringe from a first-aid kit and filled it with air. Three soldiers untied the rope around the prisoner and held him while another rolled up one of his sleeves. The arm was slender, with the kind of hard muscles that manual labor produces. The young medic brushed away dirt with his fingers and abruptly jabbed the needle into the arm without bothering to sterilize the skin. The prisoner coughed as air was injected into his arm. That was all. The young medic injected air a second time, and again the prisoner coughed, with no other visible effect. "Private, it doesn't seem to do anything at all," the first lieutenant said with a derisive laugh.

"Yessir. I have found that it has no effect."

Laughter arose from the spectators while the young medic gave an embarrassed smile.

The first lieutenant ordered the prisoner's hands bound once again and held so that his neck was above the ditch. He unsheathed his sword and swung down. The neck was cut deeply before the prisoner screamed, but bone prevented complete severance. The first lieutenant clucked his tongue and kicked the prisoner's backside, making him fall into the ditch. Blood welled up from the prisoner's neck and he was still.

The first lieutenant wiped gore from the sword and attempted to sheath it, but it had been bent and would no longer fit. He ordered the medic to wrap it in gauze and laid it down on the ground. He had demonstrated both lack of swordsmanship and lack of attention to keeping a proper edge on his sword, but no one laughed. We all looked away, fearing his wrath.

The prisoners were not blindfolded, so they had to watch their fellow villagers be slaughtered, one by one. The sergeant major approached the second prisoner, held in position by two soldiers, raised his sword and brought it down on an inclined path to the back of the neck.

The head severed cleanly and rolled into the ditch like a watermelon. Blood welled up from the trunk of the body, but didn't spray the surroundings as samurai movies typically show. The volume of the flow was only about the level you would get by opening a water faucet a little way. The third and fourth prisoners were similarly dispatched. The fifth man sprang away from the ditch and ran in fear. Some soldiers chased him in the spirit of a game of tag. The prisoner — a young man of about twenty — was seized screaming and taken back for execution. A sergeant from the automotive company was waiting with a "spring sword" crafted from a leaf type suspension spring. This type of sword was made from good quality steel and reputed to hold a good edge, but a blow to the neck only cut the surface flesh. The prisoner wailed in pain. The sergeant tried a second stroke that landed on the shoulder and again only slashed surface skin. Another man, unable to stand the spectacle, finished the prisoner off by running his short sword through the man's heart.

The sixth and seventh prisoners were executed. The last remaining prisoner was a boy who didn't look much older than ten. Fear might have driven him to insanity, because he was expressionless, looking more like a doll than a living human being. Just as the soldiers had him positioned for execution, the yellow dust cloud dispersed, and in its absence the setting sun brightly bathed the boy's slender neck in a red glow.

The first lieutenant came forward, thinking, I suppose, of restoring his honor after his initial display of ineptitude. Borrowing an NCO's well-honed weapon, he swung it down, and this time and the head easily flew from the body. Smiling triumphantly, he kicked the body into its ditch. Surprisingly little blood spilled, as if there wasn't much blood to spill. The child's headless body lay still.

We hastened to fill the ditches and cover the bloodied ground with dirt until the field looked as if nothing had happened there. Presently, the local farmers were again permitted to pass. Old people shouldering bamboo poles and baskets, and an old woman driving a water buffalo traveled by, casting long shadows on the ground. The scene was peaceful.

I did have misgivings about the looting and mass killings the emperor's army was committing. But I believed what most everyone else in the army believed — that we were fighting a sacred war on His Majesty's orders, that destroying the army of Chiang Kai-shek would bring peace to China. I did not have the courage to doubt that. By that mindset, looting and mass killing happened because the army was corrupt; it wasn't living up to its own standards. If it had good leaders, that kind of thing could never happen. It was up to me to rise through the ranks and become a leader myself.

I don't mean to claim that my mind was full of glorious thoughts. My reality was that I had no confidence there was a place for me outside the army. Suppose I went back home after my two years of active duty was up. I knew very well I couldn't get a decent job. I wasn't like the troops who had been in school or running their own businesses when they were drafted. They wanted to be out of the army and back to their former lives. I was the opposite of that. I wanted to stay in the army.

The regimental commander put in a recommendation for me to be an NCO candidate. They sent me for six months training with the Central China Non-commissioned Officers Education Corps at a school outside Nanjing. By June 1941, I was back in my outfit as a lance-corporal, outranking the other men who had joined the same time I did and were either superior privates or first-class privates. In October I got to put on a gold stripe with one star, having been promoted to corporal, the second-to-lowest ranking NCO. The climb up from there is sergeant, with two stars, and sergeant-major with three. After that, if all went well, the road was open to becoming a warrant officer or second lieutenant, in other words, a commissioned officer.

Be that as it may, the Greater East Asian War started just when I had rejoined my company.

It was December twenty-fourth when the army launched the Second Changsha Operation. Our mission in central China was to attack the Chinese army in the south while our South China Expeditionary Army hit Hong Kong and Singapore. The company's new strategy for maximizing its machine gunners' effectiveness included my relocation, meaning that I had to part company with the men from Hokkaido who had been my companions since induction. My new outfit consisted largely of troops from the Kinki and Shikoku areas. I didn't like having to move, but there was no sense in letting it bother me. They made me the leader of Squad Three, in the Second Platoon. Our squad had ten men, two horses and one heavy machine gun.

Though I had been in China close to two years, this was my first time to be part of a major troop movement. Our advance began with a train ride, and then a march in a formation longer than the train. There was excitement to being a member of a great army in motion. I was getting first-hand experience of the tumultuous transition from peacetime to war that was set in motion when the nation decided on a course that led to the establishment of a great military force.

One of our horses carried the gun and its mount, and the other carried four cases of ammo. That arrangement was comfortable for us humans where the going was easy, but when there were obstacles to passage, people and horses had to share the load.

It was highly probable there would be snow. Our faces were stung by a cold wind that blew across the open ground. We were following what had once been a path between rice fields, but was far too narrow to accommodate the army marching across it. It had become a broad strip of slippery mud. In some places you would sink in up to the knee and it was no easy matter to take the next step. If a horse bearing a heavy load went down under those conditions, we would lose time waiting for it to recover. To avoid this, we had to carry half their burden, which made it all the more difficult for us to walk through the mud. We slogged on and on all day, eventually covered all over with mud. When we finally arrived at the village where we were to spend the night, we didn't have any way to get our clothing dried. The best we could do was throw some muddy water on rice, make a fire, and gulp it down plain as soon as it was half edible, then grab every moment of sleep possible. We were shivering all night long.

Soldiering was above all a matter of physical suffering. The hardship we were enduring demonstrated the folly of believing that our training had amounted to preparation for real battle.

A blizzard hit on the second day. We were traveling on a road of thick mud, the same as ever. One after another coolie bearing our food supply fell by the wayside and was left to await death by freezing. To be Chinese was to receive the same treatment as an animal. As the sun went down, the snow stopped, and it became colder and colder. As squad leader, it was up to me to keep counting heads. There came a time when the count was one short — a new trooper. I went looking for him in the squad ahead, then found him in the squad to our rear. I was heading back with him to our squad when an orange pillar of fire suddenly rose up ahead. Thinking we were under mortar fire, I yelled "Take cover!" We all hit the ground and waited for an attack that didn't come. I got to wondering what was going on, went to the spot where the explosion occurred and heard someone groaning. I played my flashlight around and found a private with one arm torn off from the shoulder. He had already expired by then. Lying on the ground next to him was Superior Private Eda, who kept repeating "It's so cold." His trousers were soaked in blood. I pulled them off. His thigh was split open and blood was pouring out. His belly was cut too, and his intestine was swelling out through the opening. Next to him the pack horse with our gun was on its side with half its belly blown away. That told me it had stepped on a mine. All together, one horse and seven men were killed instantly, and two were injured. Of those, the horse and the two injuries belonged to my squad.

The squads were reorganized. The old third and fourth squads became the new Squad Three, with me as its leader. It gave me more responsibility than before because we had three horses and fifteen men. I assigned four men to carry Superior Private Eda on a stretcher made out of bamboo poles and a field tent. He kept complaining he was cold. The next day I got the word that he had died. I had been walking next to him all day. If I hadn't gone looking for the missing private, that mine would have taken me out too.

After we crossed a river called the Miluo Jiang, the territory became hilly. From then on we were getting enemy attacks from all directions. Messages from our squad up ahead kept coming in. An advance party sent to conduct raids in Changsha was surrounded by a bigger enemy force and retreated back to its squad. The word "retreat" was not used, though. In the emperor's army that tactic was called a "position change." It was up to our company to back that party up by engaging with the enemy.

I have no desire to go into a detailed battle chronicle here. The only point I want to make is that there is nothing heroic about what happened. War is about suffering and nothing else.

Enemy troops popped up from the hills ahead of us. We could hear the bouncy musical sound of Czech-made machine gun fire. I made a split-second decision to order placement of our heavy gun in the cover of a berm. The enemy fire was accurate. I watched it kill three or five of our troops who were flat on the ground ahead of me. Squad leaders are only supposed to issue orders, not fire weapons, but we were desperate to boost our gun's hit rate, so I took over from the gunner and started shooting. I could see enemy troops going down. But more and more kept coming down the slope. That hill was covered with running figures. It was a full-scale company. I kept laying down blanket fire. The enemy troops were close enough that I could see individual faces, and I watched as their chests and bellies became covered with blood under my fire. Our side went to meet them in hand-to-hand combat. We went at each other with knives, swords, and hand guns. I kept shooting at the enemy's backup forces coming down the slope. The barrel of the gun I was shooting was glowing red hot. When an enemy soldier came at me, I used the short sword sheathed under the mount to stab him. A second one attacked, and this time one of our men stabbed him from one side while I stabbed him from the other side. Finally, the enemy began to withdraw.

My squad had lost two horses and three men. Another two men were badly wounded. The impact was huge. We could not afford the luxury of even burying our dead, much less cremating them. The enemy's main forces had caught up with the tail end of one of our companies as it was relocating. The best we could do was cut off a hand of each of our dead so we would have some of their remains — and leave the rest. Our squad was already carrying the hands of five comrades in mess kits hung from soldiers' necks in slings. The two wounded men had to be carried. It took four men to transport each and two more to carry their gear. In other words, each injured soldier lowered our fighting force by six men. The gun had to be carried, so I took over transporting the twenty-eight-kilo barrel myself, which two other men had been carrying together. When the squad leader does something like that, it inspires his men.

We walked without eating or drinking anything, I can't even remember for how many days. Many of the men fell over from exhaustion. I would pull them up and lend my shoulder. It started raining and we were drenched. Then it turned to snow. Then the snowfall became a blizzard. Walking through so much mud started tearing up our boots. Unshaven, beards caked with mud, I suppose our faces were like wild animals. The enemy hit us with mortar and machine gun fire. We no longer had the will to fight back. We just fell to the ground, exhausted.

We got back to B enclosure on January twentieth, one month after we started out.

I got through that month of battle on my own physical strength. It was amazing that I came out of it without a scratch. We had suffered five battle deaths — six dead in all, counting Superior Private Eda — and four were wounded. I don't know how many of the enemy I killed. It wasn't ten or twenty, more like fifty or sixty that I shot to death. Men shot through the face, falling down clutching their bellies. Some went down as easily as target practice dummies, one after another — people I killed. That is what war is: killing people and nothing more. At home you are a criminal if you kill one person, but if you kill ten in the war theater you are a hero.

The imperial army's Second Changsha Operation was a total loss for our side. We could not take the city and were driven from the area. The Chinese army was strong, it was brave and it was big. I had underestimated the Chinese resistance when I was part of the suppression operations around B Enclosure. Now I realized I had been wrong. Most troops took news of Hong Kong, Manila, and Singapore surrendering with simple delight, but our ordeal told me that our future in this war would not be bright.

I was in the NCO office reading announcements one day in April when I spotted a notice that the Air Corps was taking applications for new personnel. It said physical examinations and oral testing of applicants was being held at the army hospital in Hankou. Training would be conducted back home. I told the company commander I wanted to apply. It seemed like the best chance I would have for a while to be sent back to Japan. Noncoms sometimes got that opportunity, to go take charge of new recruits or oversee delivery of soldiers' remains to their families, but, being a new noncom, I presumed it would be quite some time before my turn at that kind of duty would come up. I didn't have any particular desire to fly or get into aircraft maintenance. I really only made the application on a sudden whim.

I passed the physical and the oral, and I was back in Japan in early May, arriving at Hiroshima on a government contract ship. The MPs made a close check of my bag, looking for photos of massacres, jewelry, and narcotics. A large contingent of National Defense Women's Association members greeted the ship in white aprons when we docked at Hiroshima harbor. They served us tea and cakes. That gave me a warm feeling of really being home.

The first thing that struck me when I was in town was the empty showcase in a bread shop. Loaves of bread were stacked up in the back. I asked for one and was refused because the only bread they had was for distribution as food rations. It was the same story in butcher shops and grocery stores. In China, food supplies were plentiful, while the home front was facing miserable shortages. When I bought twenty boxes of hard jelly in Hankou, I had not realized what precious commodities they would be at home.

I visited the home of the late Superior Private Eda in Abéno, Osaka. It was a large house, with a nice entrance and garden. I had sent the family a letter, so Eda's parents and his younger sister were expecting me. They showed me to the family Buddhist altar, where the late soldier's black-framed picture was displayed. It showed him in front of our quarters in B Enclosure. I started talking about how he died, but couldn't bring myself to say a horse had stepped on a land mine. I said we were under attack and he was the gunner, so the enemy directed their Czech machine guns at him. He was shot in the left shoulder, but he still continued returning fire until the second shot hit him in the abdomen. I said that he had met a gallant death.

His sister began crying audibly. I recognized Superior Private Eda in her features. She was slender and pretty. Her body shuddered as she wept.

When I gave the family my presents, it was clear the hard jelly was a rare treat for them. The talk turned to daily life in Japan and how meals were sparse. Inevitably, the next topic was how the war was going. The father asked me a lot of questions, putting me in the uncomfortable position of a perceived expert.

Mr. Eda worked for an insurance company. The girl's name was Takéko. She had graduated a school for women and was learning the koto. She was eighteen — I would have guessed nineteen — and showed a dimple when she laughed. After all that crying, my impression had been she was the timid type, but she didn't hesitate to break in on her father's conversation.

"My brother was in school when he was drafted. He said he took a lot of hazing his first year in the army. He was satisfied to be an enlisted man instead of volunteering for officers training. He just wanted to get out of the army as soon as he could."

Takéko concluded her remarks with a smile, having ignored the pained glances she was getting from her parents.

"Isn't she just awful, saying all that shameful stuff about her brother," Mrs. Eda said.

"No, not at all. Mr. Eda was a soldier to be proud of. He was brave, and he had a strong sense of responsibility. There is no contradiction that he didn't like being in the army. That's only sensible. There is plenty to dislike about the army. It's smart to want to leave it behind when you can."

"Do you really think so?" Takéko asked.

"Yes I do. I am only in the army because there is no other place for me . . . What did Mr. Eda study in university?"

"French literature. He was doing research on Paul Claudel. Do you read novels, Mr. Yukimori?"

"I'm afraid not. I came from a poor home. There wasn't any time for reading books."

I realized this visit was stirring up gloomy feelings for me. Eda had lived in a totally different world than I. He had education, he could go to some French salon and talk the language. He grew up in a beautiful house where he could spend afternoons reading novels. Everything you need in life, he had. It was the same for charming little Takéko. She had graduated a women's school. She could put on a formal kimono and play the koto.

Mr. Eda rose. "Come on, let's go for a stroll." We three went walking along Mido-suji Avenue, while Mrs. Eda stayed home. We turned into Takashimaya and went downstairs into the restaurant. There was a mural by Ryohei Koiso on the wall, *The Fall of Singapore*. The background music was martial songs, and many of the customers wore the uniforms of enlisted men. When they saw I was a corporal, they would give a hasty salute. I had the impression Takéko enjoyed being in the company of a noncom.

Strangely, although it escapes me now just how it happened — I wonder if alcohol was the reason — Takéko and I ended up in a movie theater minus her father. It was a full house. Mindful that she was short, I pushed ahead of people to get a seat where she could have a good view of the screen. People must have resented my obnoxiousness, but everyone moved out of the way without complaint when they saw I was military.

I don't remember the movie at all. I remember clearly the young woman sitting beside me and sensing a sweetness to the warmth of her skin. I accompanied her back to her home in Abéno. Her parents came to the door and thanked me with much courtesy.

My new assignment was XXX-Corps in Kakamigahara, Gifu Prefecture. There were hangars and barracks. Training started with piloting basics and combat shooting exercises. Airplanes are far more complex than machine guns, but I thought that they are still man-made machines, and if I could understand one kind, I could understand the other. The trouble was that the names of the parts were all in English, which for me might as well have been Martian. I didn't know abc, cat, or dog, much less aircraft part names. My only option was rote memorization of hundreds of what were to me were meaningless strings of katakana. Most of my classmates had received at least some kind of secondary education, even if they weren't university graduates. They all looked pretty smart to me, as I was struggling and fumbling with the strange vocabulary.

Nevertheless, I managed to get through the introductory courses. Maybe my instructors gave me points for trying hard. I was promoted to sergeant, effective December first, and scheduled to enter the Gifu Army Air Force Maintenance School as a drafted non-commissioned officer in June of the following year.

~

In July, I was spending one rain-soaked day after another squatting on the floor of a hangar, taking apart an xxx-horsepower Model Ha-25 engine for the Type 99 Light Bomber, all the while brushing away mosquitoes that swarmed around my hands and face. The assignment was to completely disassemble one engine all the way down to its constituent parts, put it together again and get it running. Not far from me was a corporal who had come from a tech high school and had been in this line of work from the time he joined the army. He was easily working twice as fast as I was. I looked around, and saw others who had already finished. I was the only dunce who hadn't yet so much as touched a cylinder. I was despairing about not having what it takes to be an aircraft mechanic.

My depression was deepened by a letter from Suéko. I had been exchanging letters with her after I arrived in the war zone, but we lost touch after I was reassigned a couple of times. I finally got a long letter from her for the first time in a year and a half. It said our brother Shinichi had been killed. She said he had been in some South Sea island and there were no remains, just a letter that said he had returned in spirit as a war hero. It was after the war was over when I met a man who had known Shinichi in the army. He told me that seventy percent of Shinichi's regiment — the Asahikawa 28th — had been killed in the battle of Guadalcanal. I thought of Shinichi at Otaru Station when he left to ship out, looking sharp in his uniform — that had been my last glimpse of him.

I also got letters from Takéko, written before and after Suéko's letter. They came in a bundle forwarded from Kakamigahara Corps, and were completely unexpected. I had sent her a courtesy letter right after the day I met her in Osaka the previous May. Never having received a reply, I had been having bitter thoughts: She was out of my class, she wouldn't be interested in anyone with so little going for him, etc., etc. But she was telling me all about her life. Her father had been paralyzed by a stroke and she had been nursing him until he died on January seventh. Having lost father and brother — the two men of her household — she didn't know who she could turn to. I wrote back and received another letter from her immediately. That was the start of almost daily exchanges between us.

I might have used common sense when I wrote, but instead I told Takéko how well I was doing in school. When I wrote I was up for getting the Aviation Inspector General's Silver Watch Award for scholastic achievement, she wrote back, that's wonderful, I'll get you a chain for it, and she really did send me a gold chain. I received it right after that engine breakdown exercise that proved my ineptitude.

I stopped brushing away mosquitoes, waited until they attached themselves, then squashed them with the flat of my hand. Next, I decided I would go see Takéko.

The following Sunday I applied for a late-night curfew extension pass and went to Osaka. Takéko was looking truly haggard. Grass at the entryway and in the garden badly needed trimming. I did that, cut away old branches and generally got the exterior looking shipshape. That wasn't all that needed doing. Algae had killed all the carp in the gourd-shaped pond. I drained it, washed the stones, and put in fresh water. While I was doing this Takéko and her mother put Mr. Eda's possessions in order and cleaned the house.

"This day has been a spirit booster," Takéko said. "I finally feel like I have a tomorrow again."

"That's good to hear," I said.

"It's like this is a new house. It would be just right for newlyweds," Takéko said laughing. I pulled her close and kissed her on the lips. Startled, she went rigid, but only for a moment. As she relaxed in my arms, I relished the sensations of her breasts and hips.

"Let's get married," I said. Takéko's eyes were closed. She opened them just a little and nodded. We were standing side by side, looking out at the garden when her mother came downstairs from the second floor.

Takéko invited me upstairs to her brother's room. There were about three shelves filled with foreign language books. The titles I could read all looked like reference material for someone's advanced research.

"Here's a present for you," she said, extracting the two volumes of the Iwanami pocket edition of the Manyoshu. "This was one of my brother's favorites," she said, turning pages. The book took on the aura of a priceless treasure.

I spoke up about what was on my mind, though it required an effort to overcome a sudden feeling of insecurity.

"What I said a little while ago — I don't even know if I should have said it. I just made sergeant last month, so I'm not getting a decent paycheck. And I'm going back to the war zone . . ."

"I know all that," she said, smiling. "You have to earn that award, and you want me to wait for you. Isn't that right? I'm in no hurry. I have things to do too. I started working at the post office last week. We won't be able to eat if I don't work. We may have to sell the house. Right now, none of us knows what's going to happen, what tomorrow will be like, how the war will go . . . It isn't really a time to be making everlasting vows."

"No! That is the one thing I can do. I want you, and that won't change." Once again, I pulled Takéko close to me, this time with enough vigor to make our teeth touch. I didn't want to release her. At that moment I was feeling such an urgency I would have had her then and there if her mother had not called to us, "Hey, you two! Come down and get some sliced watermelon!"

I left the Eda home a little before five o'clock so I could make the last train at six-thirty. Takéko went along to see me off. Again, I sensed her pleasure when I was saluted by a passing enlisted man, but a short time after that, the military ritual played out in the other direction, when I saluted a commissioned officer. He also had a lady at his side, and as they passed, Takéko's eyes followed the other woman with a look that might have spelled envy.

I caught sight of a signboard for an inn beside the station, and turned into the entrance as if that had been our destination all along. Takéko followed without a word. We were shown to an eight-mat room with pillows and a futon laid out. Our brief time there left me with vivid images of the two of us standing beside the bedding, then lying in embrace and of her beauty unclothed. There was perspiration in the vicinity of her hips. One strong push made her cry out in pain, but after that moment everything was easy. She curled up modestly as I dabbed away little spots of blood.

We had to run. The train started to move and I jumped aboard. When I turned in her direction, she was climbing the stairs. As she turned, I waved, and she waved back hard enough to shred her handkerchief to pieces.

The following Sunday I went again to apply for a curfew extension pass. The warrant officer in charge of personnel beckoned me to his desk.

"Go on, have a seat."

I sat.

"Hate to bring up stuff like this, but you found yourself a little girl friend, no? You bought a military discount ticket to see her in Osaka, and since then you two have been trading love letters. It's time for you to do some hard thinking. You're in school. The most important time for you is right now. You have a test coming up in December that's going to decide the rest of your life. Stay away from your girl until then, and put a stop to those letters."

This warrant officer was about thirty-four or thirty-five. He was already more than ten years into his army career, and he was as hard core military as they come. He had read every one of my letters and clearly knew every secret that had been written in them. I didn't have any choice in the matter.

"Yessir," I replied. Then I wrote to Takéko saying it would be my last letter until the year's end, and I wouldn't be able to see her until then either. She must have understood the situation, because she sent no further letters.

The warrant officer's concern about my study was well founded. After the engine assembly competition came a competition to repair a damaged engine. I placed 192 among 200 student noncoms. The principal called the bottom twenty students into his office. He informed us that we would be out of school and back to our previous units if our next test scores did not show improvement. Dread of the prospect of a return to the living nightmare of the battle front accompanied my regret at having established intimacy with Takéko on the basis of a ridiculous lie about being an honor student.

In late December — I think it was the twenty-sixth — my turn came to do a number of routine transactions for the school at several locations outside our base. I was given a red armband with the words "official business" lettered in white. Students were normally allowed off base only on Sundays and because this was a weekday, I was asked by other students to take care of personal business that had to be done on weekdays. I was handed five watches needing repair and one military sword to sharpen. I left the base carrying these items and ten yen for expenses.

My first stop was a sword dealer located near Nagoya Castle. My intention was to ask to have it sharpened, but once I was inside the shop, another thought occurred to me. I asked what the sword was worth.

The man behind the counter seemed to take the question to mean I meant to sell the sword, because he examined it carefully and removed the hilt rivet to check the manufacturer. He looked up and said diffidently, "This is a one-hundred-twenty yen item."

That was a surprise. I had been expecting something more like fifty or sixty yen. My monthly pay as a sergeant was twenty yen. The man was talking big money. Abruptly, he spoke again.

"Since you're in the military, I'll make a special offer. I'll give you one-hundred-fifty yen."

"Sold!" I replied. Where did my words come from? A demon had taken control of my voice.

With that act I became a stone tumbling downhill. My next stop was a jewelry store where I sold the five watches for twenty yen. I also had a leather pouch, borrowed from that warrant officer to carry the watches. I took it to a "used goods exchange" booth in a department store, where the clerk said, "For a serviceman, I'll make a special offer of ten yen. The people's hearts are with you."

I could not return to the school anymore. I was a deserter. I presumed the penalty for being caught would be death. That was what I had heard from others in the army. I decided I would stay on the run for as long as I had money, then slit my belly with my short sword when it ran out. The first thing to do was say goodbye to Takéko.

The next morning I visited the post office where Takéko was working. "I'm on my way to Kyushu on Army business. Just wanted to say hello." She rose to go outside with me, but I told her to stay where she was. "Take care," I said with a smile and a wave. I thought the smile she gave me in return sealed our final parting.

With a view to putting as much distance between me and Gifu as possible, I went south by rail, then crossed over to Shikoku.

On New Year's Day the streets of Takamatsu were thankfully filled with returning soldiers, so I was no unusual sight. I paid a visit to Kotohira Shrine. I was eating a mandarin orange outside the shrine when I caught sight of an MP climbing the stone stairway in my direction. I fled to a mountain path and spent the day hiding in a shrine deep in the woods.

I roamed to Tokushima, Kochi, and Matsuyama, always with the feeling of being hunted, never staying in one place more than two or three days. Time spent on trains offered no respite from anxiety. I would sit fretting an MP might come walking down the aisle and ask me what outfit I belonged to. Ordinary people, however, were as kind as could be to a soldier. Innkeepers raised no objections when I asked for a room without having my own rice ration. They would bring my meals, as if there was no such thing as a rice and grain ration book. If there was a waiting line in a restaurant, people would hasten to show me to the head of the line.

I made several abortive suicide attempts. First, I bought two bottles of Calmotin, the bromine compound marketed by Bayer. I went into the woods and stuffed white pills into my mouth. The bitter taste alone made me gag and spit them out. Next, I thought of jumping into the sea from the cliff over Cape Ashizuri, but despite my will to jump, my prudent part dragged me down from the craggy, windswept height.

Realizing I was not able to do away with myself, I decided to turn myself in to the school and let them shoot me. With my remaining money, I bought a ticket back to Gifu.

I called the school from the station. The regimental commander took the line.

"Oh, is this Sergeant Yukimori?" he said genially. "It's good to know you are all right. We will come to get you. Just stay put." The personnel officer and the district corps commander came in a car. Once the regimental commander had me before him, he roared angrily.

"You're a disgrace to the imperial army! You will be court marshaled. Until that matter is settled you are ordered to be held in the guardhouse."

The date was February fourth. I had been on the run for a little more than a month.

The guardhouse prison, located behind the base guard station, was built entirely of wood, with broad slats for bars. Prisoners sat in formal *seiza* posture on the rough, unfinished floor. Our sole occupation all day long was to copy the Rescript for Soldiers and Sailors with ink and brush, over and over, using the obsolete kana that was prescribed. The experience burned those peculiar characters into my memory forever.

I was brought to the Gifu military police headquarters. My sergeant's stripe was removed and I was handcuffed for the first time in my life. My interrogation was conducted by a short, thin sergeant who looked exactly like General Tojo. He wouldn't believe me when I told him I ran away because I couldn't keep up with the aircraft mechanics lessons. He suspected some kind of skullduggery had been going on in the company and I had been set up to take the blame. As he saw it, that was why I went back to the school instead of turning myself in to the military police. He slammed a bamboo sword on the desk where I sat as he expounded this theory, but he didn't hit me with it. I admitted to all my misdeeds and gave a full account of what I did throughout my period of flight, with the exception that I mentioned nothing about Takéko Eda.

My court martial was held in late February at the Third Divisional Head-quarters in Shiroshita-cho, Nagoya. The prosecutor was a legal affairs captain, wearing a white-collar ensign. The judges were three field officers who were not legal specialists. There was no defense attorney. It wasn't much of a trial — they just reviewed the record of my interrogation. The prosecutor asked, "Is that all true and correct?" and I answered simply, "It is all true and correct," the better to hasten the death sentence I awaited with equanimity.

"Sergeant Atsuo Yukimori, due to your lack of the imperial soldier's spirit, you disregarded your obligation to provide an example to soldiers as a non-commissioned officer, by committing the crimes of unauthorized absence, fraud and misappropriation of goods and monies. You are therefore sentenced to imprisonment with labor for one year and six months and reduction in pay grade to the rank of first-class private."

Actually, that was the sentence the prosecutor had requested. Having come to the trial prepared for death, this penalty was anticlimactically light. My court martial had played out in one day. Three days later, I was sent to the army prison in Ishikiri, Osaka, and placed in a common cell holding fourteen other inmates. We were all dressed in shabby army fatigues without insignia.

The cell was about six meters square with four meter square latticeworks of thick wooden bars on two sides. Guards patrolled corridors about three meters wide running outside the grid-covered sides. Low doors were set in the grids. In front of the grid on the far side was a row of wooden toilets. The cell was always dark, lit only from windows high up over the corridors outside. All there that was visible inside were the lattice posts and stark walls of rough wood.

At six in the morning we prisoners arose and formed a double line facing the door for morning inspection. Immediately after inspection it was out into the yard, marching by twos to the place for body inspections. We threw down all our clothing to march one at a time stark naked before the guards. Next, we changed into a coarse garment called a "workshop uniform." We were then permitted to wash hands and face before entering the cafeteria for breakfast. The cafeteria held about two hundred prisoners from all the cells.

Talking without permission was strictly forbidden. Sounds heard inside the cafeteria considered mainly of clattering of dishes and the sounds of eating. Any indication of a word spoken or even a look given to the man sitting next to you would earn a reprimand from a guard. After dish washing, we were hustled to a line of porcelain urinals. In the morning the only form of elimination permitted was urination. Defecation during the day was a prohibited act. The rule was that defecation had to be done in the cells at night.

At eight o'clock we arrived at our workshop, where we sat in narrow cubicles partitioned off by plywood, sewing leather ammunition pouches. You sit in the cold, blowing on stiffened hands that must run a giant needle through pieces of leather. You have to be careful with every move you make lest the needle go into your hand. You have to continue the operation for the four hours until noon, with no breaks in between and no toilet trips. Because peeing isn't allowed you're careful not to take too much liquid for breakfast, but by nine or ten o'clock your body starts telling you it's time to urinate. When it gets to the point you can't control it any more you pee in your loincloth. Worse than that is when you have diarrhea. That is almost impossible to control, so you do that in your pants too. You want to clean it up, but you don't have anything to clean with, and even if you did, the guards wouldn't allow you to stop doing your work for a single moment anyway. I am one of many who have had to go on working while sitting in their own feces and putting up with the smell. It wasn't just once, but many times.

At noon you stop work, have lunch, and urinate. Work resumes at one and continues until four.

Then it's supper and full toilet privilege, defecation allowed. Then you run to the bath.

You get to take cold water baths from a wooden bucket three times per week. On three alternate days, you get guard-controlled shower baths. There is no bathtub. Two lines of prisoners stand naked, with towel in hand, over footprints marked on the floor. The guard opens a cold-water faucet over your head for exactly one minute, during which time you must use the towel to wipe yourself down. Over time, you cultivate your own technique for getting as clean as possible under the circumstances. If you don't move fast, you just come away with your hair wet, feeling worse than when you went in.

Once a week you get ten minutes to bathe with whale oil soap and lukewarm water. For men used to cold water showers in the dead of winter, this kind of bath is a luxury beyond words.

From the bath you went to have your body cavities inspected. Your work uniform went on a peg. One at a time the prisoners came before the guards, stark naked. First you open your mouth, then march while straddling an iron bar to demonstrate you don't have any concealed some object stolen from work-shop in your anus. When you pass your inspection you put on your jail cell uniform, then repeat the morning routine in reverse, marching in twos through the yard, back to the jail.

At six o'clock is the evening inspection, after which the fifteen prisoners are divided in two groups to sit facing the wall until nine o'clock, half the time in the *seiza* posture. Sitting in *seiza* for a prolonged time on a wood floor causes considerable pain to the thigh bone. Numbness of the legs is another kind of agony. The smallest movement is forbidden. You are not permitted to change the position of your hands on your legs. If the end of your nose gets itchy, you can request permission to scratch. You do this by calling out your number.

"Number 12."

"What is it?"

"My nose has an itch."

"All right, you've got three seconds."

You can't ask permission more than once a day. Whatever else happen you just have to put up with it. It's natural for a human being to scratch and change positions. Forbidding all such movement imposes terrific suffering under any circumstances, but much more so in a jail cell infested with fleas, lice, and bedbugs.

After thirty minutes of *seiza*, we were allowed to change to sitting with legs crossed, for thirty minutes, again, with no further movement of any kind permitted.

Alternation of the two postures every thirty minutes continued until nine o'clock, when we were allowed to bed down by wrapping our bodies with a single blanket, thereby allowing the bugs it was infested with to lunch on our bodies. Toilet time then began, in order, beginning with the longest-serving prisoners. That was the only time you got in a twenty-four-hour cycle, so in cases of constipation, you would have to insert a finger to promote expulsion.

Lights went out at ten o'clock, although it was only a matter of a couple of naked light bulbs in the corridor being turned down, but not completely off. Because it was very cold, the guards marched noisily up and down the corridor at a fast pace. It was not a good environment for sleeping, but the prisoners tried their best to sleep, even as they desperately scratched their numerous bug bites, to rest up for another day of exhausting routine exactly like the one they had just endured. The army prison was nothing other than a web of compulsion and prohibition that permitted not the smallest shred of freedom. Bodily movement of any kind, conversation, visits with family, letters and any other form of individual human expression was wholly forbidden. Work, movement, and sitting posture were all subject to compulsion by guards who demanded complete submission. It was a kind of perfect world, wholly of itself, even though it was a part of the army. In fact, it could be described as a distilled form of army life, in which the harsh regime is carried to the farthest extreme. Imprisonment in the army showed me that the army itself was a kind of prison.

Dislike of prison-like army conditions had driven me to run away, and when I was caught, irony of ironies, I was put into the place where those very conditions exist in super concentrated form.

By the end of the first week, I was close to insanity. Submitting to rules, jumping to orders, apologizing when rebuked, absolute obedience, absolute abasement . . . It was more than I could stand. I wanted to make it all go away. My brain seethed with thoughts of self-destruction, of biting off my tongue, stabbing myself through the heart in the workshop with the leather work needle, standing up and screaming during a *seiza* session, seizing a guard, and raining blows on him — no, beating him to death. My head felt near to exploding. But I didn't have the courage to go crazy. Through the turmoil inside I could see the guards watching us every moment with eyes like tongues of fire that said there would be no mercy for anyone who went over the line.

One day, my worst fears were confirmed. A prisoner sitting in *seiza* posture collapsed to the ground with a loud cry. He was instantly set upon by a guard who used his bamboo sword to beat the man's head and back as he lay quaking on the ground. A whistle sounded and several other guards came to support the operation of carrying him away.

Two days later, he returned, his face swollen purple. It was clear that he had been tortured into an extreme state of weakness. Nevertheless, he responded to the guard's order by assuming a correct *seiza* posture. Torture had banished all trace of the man's insanity. He had been transformed into a model prisoner.

In two or three weeks, I had grown accustomed to prison. My distress subsided. I had adopted the view that existence would be easier by being a good prisoner, who does what he is told and follows every rule. In four or five weeks, I had become the complete prisoner. A guard had only to form an expectation of the prisoners in his mind for me to instantly internalize it. I knew that if a guard's forehead creased while we were being marched somewhere, we weren't raising our legs high enough, and if a bamboo sword was brought to the floor, our *seiza* posture needed straightening. By the eighth week, I had acquired such advanced prisoners' skills as ventriloquism for exchanging words with one's neighbor and using the fleeting moment a guard's attention was diverted to scratch an itchy spot.

It was around the last week in April when the warden called me into his office with an unexpected announcement.

"Your enlistment is up. You're civilian, and this prison is only for soldiers. You can't stay here anymore, so we're sending you to civilian prison."

This was a bombshell. They were sending away a man who had aspired to the part of non-commissioned officer, with the intention of spending his entire life in the army. Feeling somewhat dissatisfied, I posed a question.

"I have a question. Am I being dismissed because I was demoted to private first class?"

"Nobody said you could ask questions, dummy! You're not a soldier in the imperial army as of today. That's all there is to it."

"Yessir," I said, standing at attention.

And so, suddenly one day in April 1944, I stopped being a military man. Now I was a civilian once again, a "provincial" as they said in the army. I was still a convict, mind you, but no longer a private first class convict. My army career had lasted four years and five months.

I should have been pleased to receive this notification, having run away from the army fully expecting the escapade would lead to my death. Instead, my heart was telling me it didn't want to stop being a soldier. It was proud of being a former sergeant in the emperor's army.

~

My battered uniform with no insignia was taken away and I was transferred to the Sakai prison in Osaka. There, I was given a red prison garment that labeled me as a class 4 inmate, the lowest in the prison.

What first surprised me about the civilian prison was how easy life was there, compared to the army prison. In the solitary cell, as long as you didn't lie down, you were allowed to stretch your legs, lie back against the wall, scratch your nose or talk to yourself. For me, that was not the only attraction. Being a former sergeant carried weight there, even with the guards. I could sit there and masturbate all day, and they wouldn't say a word. It only took me a few days before I pretty much had it down how to make the best of life at that prison. The trick was to take every opportunity to play up my army sergeant reputation.

At the end of May, they put me in handcuffs and waist rope, then sent me to the Aioi City Shipbuilding Corps. From the name of the place, you would think it was a military facility, but it was just an ordinary prison. In other words, it was a dockyard that operated on forced labor. Its workers lived in six large scale barracks with wooden bars on the windows that ran up a slope inside the western shoreline of Aioi Harbor. Each barracks housed three hundred convicts. The buildings were emptied out every morning by marching the men in columns of four across a temporary bridge to the far shore. There they labored in the shipyard until the day's end.

At first, I was placed in a training center for new inmates. They gave us basic training to inculcate the discipline necessary in a shipyard: things like marching, saluting and calisthenics, all of which were second nature to someone like me, fresh from the army. It showed. The head of the guards spotted me as a sharp performer and called me over.

"I see you're a sergeant. You do any training in the army?"

"Yessir! I ran basic drills for new recruits."

"Yeah? Want to try doing that as my assistant? Let's see what you can do."

I ordered a rabble of new men into ranks. That was simple enough. All that had to be done was follow the field manual from "individual drill" through "company drill." There weren't even rifles or swords to manage, so it was easy as pie. In one hour I had them marching in perfect order. Poof! A company was born. The next item was calisthenics, to get them into the right frame of mind. I thought I'd try the exercises I learned in aircraft mechanics classes, and it was a hit. All my troops mastered the moves in no time.

"Ummm, umm! Yes, that's how it's done. You know what you're doing, Yuki-mori." The aging guard chief made several admiring comments, then concluded by saying "Okay, good enough. I'll put in for you to be my assistant."

I was designated for "latrine cleanup" duty. It is one of the barracks details. The job is to carry out human waste from the latrines in wooden buckets balanced on a pole across your shoulder and discard it in the mountain behind the barracks. Two thousand men produce a prodigious quantity of excrement. Climbing and descending the slope all day, seven days a week is extremely arduous labor. Except that I didn't have to do it. I got a special pass to permit my working as the guard chief's assistant. As the one barking out the orders, the other prisoners took to calling me "Chief," which gave me a little bit of status.

One day, the assistant warden came in while I was running new arrivals through the aircraft mechanics' calisthenics. The chief of guards proudly provided commentary. I suppose that helped my early promotion to class three prisoner. In addition to that, I got to be on the instructor's stand every morning to run the aircraft mechanics' calisthenics.

The inmates wore different colored garments according to their classes. Class four was red, three was white, two was sunrise pink and class one was the standard prison uniform gray. From my dais, the inmates looked like a bed of dirty flowers that rippled in the wind when I called out my commands. It made me feel like some kind of a wizard to be in control of that movement.

In October I was abruptly kicked up to class one, skipping the two intermediate classes. Having dispensed this favor upon me, the chief of guards gave me a wink and said, "It doesn't look right for someone directing the men to be wearing red or white or pink."

This elderly chief of guards suffered from asthma. It seemed to require much effort for him to move. Much of his time on the job was spent in his office. He was responsible for directing the men on latrine duty, the medical orderlies, and cooks, but the majority of that work was delegated to me.

As a first-class inmate, I had the privilege of walking freely around the prison yard, provided that I informed a guard where I was going. Until then, it had never entered my mind what a joy it is simply to be able to go somewhere of your choosing. I found many reasons to go hither and yon. Latrine orderlies scurried across the stairways between barracks, shouldering buckets of excrement. Beside the barracks were the bathing station, physical inspection ground, mess halls and assembly hall. All were crude, hastily built structures. There were pig pens atop a slight rise that were being kept by the latrine orderlies. The area had quite a distinct aroma that I realized was a mixture of pig essence and sea breeze. A cacophony of clanging metal echoed from the shipyard. The workers were all dressed alike, making it impossible to distinguish between prisoners and civilian workers, but close to half the number had to be prisoners. Angry whistle blasts occasionally assaulted the ear like jabs from a sharp needle.

Beyond the harbor it was barely possible to pick out ships threading between the islands of the Inland Sea. Among the cargo ships and warships were boats with white sails raised that glided in the direction of Osaka. I thought of Takéko Eda. Her garden in Abéno was likely overgrown with grass once again. The image of her face when last I saw her at the post office merged with the sails. She wouldn't be thinking anything nice about a runaway soldier fallen to the status of convict. Whatever she remembered about me she probably wanted to forget. There was not much chance I would ever see her again.

When I came down from the rise I found thirty newcomers just arrived. They were all kids from the Himéji Juvenile Prison. I was to give them their training. Being young, they picked up everything quickly, and easily fell into a proper formation. I went through the flight mechanics' calisthenics and didn't have to say anything twice. We finished up early and took a break. One of the boys with a fair complexion was coughing frequently. His cheeks were unnaturally red and his forehead was hot. It looked like he had influenza. I notified the medical orderly chief and was told to take him to the clinic.

"This your first time in a place like this?" I asked him.

"Yes."

His face had a childlike charm. The whiteness of his skin accented a small mole beside his lip. "What are you in for?"

"Stealing sweet potatoes."

"Theft during wartime. That would get a heavy sentence."

"Two years."

I became friends with the boy on the way to the clinic. When he undressed for the examination I saw he was smooth skinned, without much hair, as lovely as a woman. Below his slight hips were buttocks soft and supple, like a woman's breasts.

The medic said, "There may be pneumonia. You're to stay in a room here," and immediately sent the boy to a room in the clinic.

I had a hard time getting to sleep that night. I couldn't shake the image of the boy's sumptuous nates. Sensations experienced when I had been the boy possessed by grown men sharing my holding cell in Kumamoto returned to thrill me to the core. I wanted to somehow make that boy my own. During the day, Takéko had filled my mind, but at night I fretted for love of this boy. Faithless heart of mine.

Being a class one inmate did not exclude me from being put into a common cell for the night like any other prisoner. They all smelled of machine oil from the shipyard and most snored. The cell was kept darkened by black cloth wrapped over the lamps because we were under a blackout.

An air raid siren sounded and the lights went off, plunging the cell into blackness. We don't get to hear any radio broadcasts, so we did not really know what was happening, but the grapevine said the Osaka area was being hit. The guards shouted, "Keep quiet!" but in the pitch dark, that did not still the commotion. A man nearby me called over his *anko* and proceeded to mount him. The man was a supervisor in the shipyard and the unchallenged boss in the cell. He could choose his bed mate. The anointed one would comply quietly because crossing him could result in being assigned dangerous, arduous jobs in the yard. Listening to the man's breathing go ragged intensified my longing for that boy.

The next day I had caught a cold, enough to raise a fever. I went to the clinic and was told I had a very high temperature of forty degrees and was immediately put to bed in a room of the clinic. It sounds like I had been plotting this outcome, but I really hadn't.

The boy came in to visit. "Are you sick, Chief?"

"Yeah. It looks like I caught it from you."

"I'm sorry."

"How are you doing?"

"I still have a fever."

We were the only two in the room. Unlike the rest of the prison, the clinic was not subject to close supervision. The boy undressed, turned up the blanket and invited my embrace. Thinking of his young, smooth limbs as those of a woman invited desire. The next moment, desire turned to love for the flesh inflamed by his fever. I knew the ecstasy of sex with another male.

We had sex every night of the few days we were confined to the clinic. I regretted it when our fevers subsided and we recovered from our disease. We were both released the same day, but sent to separate cells.

"I want to be with you always, Chief."

"I want it that way too. But I don't have the power to make it happen."

We went our separate ways and never met again. I felt jealousy for whoever was taking his pleasure with the boy. That feeling lasted for only a short time, however. Prison is no place to be preoccupied with worries or resentments. Survival requires that you just keep forgetting burdensome thoughts. Achieve that state, and the time goes by like stones falling into the void.

~

I had been at the prison for more than a year. Daily life went on without newspapers or radio, but new arrivals brought in fragmentary information that told me the war was not going in Japan's favor. Germany had surrendered. Iwo Jima and Okinawa had fallen. Tokyo, Nagoya, and Osaka had been turned into burnt out fields. Sooner or later, the Aioi shipyard was bound to come up on the list of air raid targets as well.

There was no getting around that the quality of our meals went down. Instead of having normal servings of rice with oats and miso soup, we were getting a little rice with potatoes and grass, and warm water with a little miso. Everyone was hungry, thinned down and listless. New recruits were doing aircraft mechanic's calisthenics like a spiritless, slow dance, and the guards stood by quietly. They were all old and had reached the point of not caring enough to get angry.

One day I was released, with no prior notice. There was still two months left to my sentence. My release was called a special dispensation parole. I suppose they were letting me go to reduce the number of mouths to feed. The day was July 4th, 1945.

Having arrived at the prison in winter, I had nothing suitable for summer to wear. The chief of guards gave me an old khaki guard uniform and a send-off as far as Aioi Station. He even waved his cap, although it made him look smaller. Exposing his bald head made it look to me like he was twenty years older.

Some time after leaving the station, the train came to a stop for no visible reason. All the seats were filled, and there was nowhere else to go to wait out the delay. It was a hot, humid day, and the car became increasingly stuffy. We were left to puzzle over what was going on for about an hour before the train started moving again. We understood all when we arrived in Himeji.

The city had been turned to blackened ruins. From the look of the smoke plumes still arising from numerous locations, the bombing must have taken place the previous night. People covered with ash and soot slowly picked their way among the rubble, while heat continued to rise from the ground. Himéji Castle alone was untouched, rising over the ruins like a white mirage.

Akashi and Kobé had been similarly razed. For the most part, Osaka as well no longer existed. In its place were wide swaths of scorched ground. A great city that dazzled the senses had vanished. Standing at Osaka Station, you could see all the way across the Saibashi-suji and Mido-suji promenades. The Takashi-maya store Takéko Eda and I had gone to was still recognizable, all by itself. I walked the area, muttering to myself over and over that there wasn't anything left between Tennoji Park and Abéno City.

It was a task of many hours to search out what remained of Takéko's house. I was finally able to identify it by the outline of what had been the gourd shaped fish pond. Many of the burned-out houses had bills posted in front by survivors that gave the addresses of places where they were staying, but the Eda house had no such message. Where was Takéko? Was she still alive? I went back to the station with no answer to these questions.

It took a week to get back to Nemuro. On the way, the train was held up again and again by bombing raids, and then ferry runs were canceled. I quickly ran out of money and didn't have anything to eat. I went four whole days without food, subsisting on water only. After the train had passed Akkeshi, I got my first taste of home — a pea soup thick fog from the sea that gradually enveloped the surroundings. At the station, the familiar town was overcast by a smokey gray sky. There was no one to greet me, of course. What a contrast to the festivities on the day the town had turned out to see off the new enlistees! Word of me going AWOL and being imprisoned had doubtlessly circulated through the town. I set out on the downhill road leading past the harbor, hoping not to meet anyone who knew me. Fortunately, the fog thickened still further to a near whiteout state, making it impossible to make out the faces of anyone I passed. The sun was a red disk in the sky, there for decoration only, not to send warmth. Though it was mid-summer, a cold wind was blowing.

The town had not changed, except that the roads had been dug up in so many places to make bomb-shelter trenches it made walking difficult. Outside the houses, people had installed concrete water reservoirs, sandbags, and shovels for fire fighting — stark reminders of the lurking threat of death dealing enemy aircraft.

I walked around to the side of the fish market and turned into the quiet path leading to my house.

It didn't look at all the way it used to look. The sign "Yukimori Diner" was not there. The sliding door to the public part of the house was closed and there was a heavy layer of dust on the windows. I went around to the back. An old woman with bent back sat on the deck outside the three mat room where Keiji had died. It was my mother, Misa. "O-kaa," I called to her.

"Atsuo! It's you!" Amazed, Mother tried to stand, but her legs didn't respond to the sudden effort, and she sank back down.

"I'm back. I have caused you worry for so very long." I mouthed this formality, being at a loss for better words.

"Sit down. I'll bring tea."

"No, don't do that," I said before she started to rise again. I sat next to her on the deck.

"I don't suppose you're on the run again."

"I was paroled. I'm a free man."

"If that's so, it's good to hear." Mother was close to tears. "We've been so worried for so long. You caused so much grief."

She told me about what the family had been through. Military police had come to the house time and again. Because of me, the whole family had been labeled traitors. Rocks had been thrown through windows. People had come into the diner and upended tables. They were left no choice but to close the store. Suéko was helping to support the family by working for the Railway Welfare Association.

"How's Father?"

"The same as ever. He joined the Home Defense Corps. He is out at their observation post with a rifle now."

The Home Defense Corps was an organization of about thirty hunters. They had received thirty rounds of ammunition from the police. They were taking turns on watch at a post in Kotohira Shrine, ready to fire upon enemy planes if they approached.

"I guess he's angry with me."

"He certainly is."

"As usual, I'm in the doghouse."

"He won't say anything. He hasn't been himself since Shinichi was killed. He's an old man now."

When Suéko came home, she threw her arms around me. "You're back, safe and sound! What a relief!" She laughed and cried simultaneously. Her unadulterated welcome made me so happy I placed my hand on her back and kept stroking it.

When my father Ishizo saw me, his expression froze. He went silently to his workplace. Dinner was a poor gruel of potatoes. Ishizo spoke to me while he looked at the wall.

"We can't afford to feed you. Go to the regimental district headquarters tomorrow and ask them to take you in the army."

I couldn't get a train ticket to the Kushiro Regimental District Headquarters. Suéko tried unsuccessfully to get one through someone she knew in the Railway Welfare Association.

Ishizo told me, "You're a disgraced traitor. Don't show your face outside."

So, in lieu of a doghouse, I spent my waking hours cowering in a corner of our abandoned diner. Outside, the sea was wrapped in fog, day after day. When it thinned out a bit, Benten Island appeared by the harbor entrance. Ships requisitioned by the military carrying full loads of drum cans moved unsteadily across the water. Flocks of herring gulls that had waited out the fog swooped down to begin harvesting fish.

One morning, the fog vanished to reveal a completely blue sky that I will certainly never forget. It was July fourteenth.

As I was looking out over the harbor I heard explosions. The sound came from the right, off Kotohira Shrine. It was a bright day, with good visibility. A short time later, five black shadows appeared. I had learned to recognize different aircraft in air mechanic school. I knew they were Grumman F6Fs. The stubby fuselage and square cutout wings were unmistakable.

"Air raid!" I shouted.

"Nah, there's no sirens," Misa said.

Ishizo was brushing his teeth. He glared at me contemptuously. Suéko laughed.

"Father is in the defense corps. If it was an air raid, we would be the first to hear about it."

The explosions were getting closer. The ground was shaking. Pillars of water were rising like the spikes of a sea urchin in front of and behind the ships bearing drum cans. The second of the five aircraft suddenly plunged downward — I could plainly see the bombs on its underbelly. They were 450 kilo bombs made especially for the Grumman models. They hit a ship smack in the middle. Drum cans flew upward like sand scattered in the air. The ship burst into flame and sank in a very short time.

The sound of a light machine gun came from somewhere . . . It was a supply ship in the harbor. A shirtless trooper wearing a helmet was doing the shooting. Another Grumman dropped a bomb on the ship and it went up like fireworks. There was no more shooting. The soldier had probably burnt to a crisp in an instant.

About a company's worth of soldiers appeared from somewhere. They were not carrying guns to resist. They were running in various directions — for their own lives, out of harm's way. The next moment a Grumman began shooting at a warehouse that must have stored flammable material because it soon burst into flame.

I heard shooting close by myself. Ishizo was straddling the roof with his Winchester in firing position. He fired about ten rounds, hitting nothing. A Grumman turned around and came nosing toward us. Ishizo seemed to realize this.

"Father! Look out!" I screamed. "Get down from there now!"

Wearing an expression of fierce determination, Ishizo fired again at the monstrous black attack bird. Some roofing tiles came loose and slid away. Ishizo fired another round. The aircraft had circled around and was heading away from the scene. I scrambled up on the roof and grabbed Father's arm. "The enemy will be back. Get down from here, for Mother's sake."

Ishizo looked absentmindedly at a large hole in the roof and slowly began to descend.

Misa and Suéko were quaking under a pile of futons in the closet. Ishizo silently blew air through pursed lips as he regarded a hole in the tatami floor from a bullet that had passed through the roof. Perhaps surprised at the might wielded by the enemy plane, he shook his head again and again.

A look at the bullet hole in the roof beam allowed an estimate of the caliber of the weapon used. "This is from a 20 mm machine gun. It went through the tatami and buried into the ground."

"Damn! Came down too quick." Ishizo was gritting his teeth. "A little more shooting and I would have hit him!"

"It wouldn't have helped if you had," I explained. "That was a Grumman F6F, the latest fighter-bomber. It does 600 kilos an hour and is heavily armored. An ordinary rifle bullet would just bounce off."

"Ah . . . yeah, I guess so." Ishizo seemed impressed with my knowledge. "Right, you were in the Air Corps."

There were no further sounds of explosions and no signs of enemy planes. Fire brigades were fighting fires at several warehouses.

"Will they come again?" Misa asked.

"They'll be back. That was a reconnaissance squad. They're coming back in force. That's a carrier-based plane. The enemy has a task force close to here."

"So we need a bomb shelter. Shall we start digging?"

"No, we'd best get out of here. The harbor's their number one target, I suppose, but there are warehouses all around here. We're in a dangerous spot."

"Don't tell me to show my backside to the enemy! You're talking to a member of the Home Defense Corps!"

With this declaration, Ishizo picked up his rifle, clearly resolved to spend the day at his lookout post.

I dug a trench in front of the garden, then covered it over with some steel reinforcement mesh I found in the wreckage of a warehouse, and covered it with dirt. Misa spread straw matting inside and brought in her emergency supplies of dried biscuit, dried rice, and canned food.

"We're all set," she said, well pleased with these preparations.

"This won't stand up against bombs and 20 mm rounds. We should abandon this house and run," I said.

"Maybe so . . ." Misa said with a sigh. I knew very well that sigh meant Ishizo's perversity stood in the way of every other consideration.

Suéko came back from her job with word that the entire village had begun to evacuate. It was expected that air raids would begin shortly and would be followed by a land invasion by the American army. Early flight was recommended. People were loading up their valuables and heading for the Onneto Bridge. If that bridge was destroyed Nemuro would be cut off from the mainland.

Misa answered brightly.

"That's all right. We'll stay where we are. Tonight is the Bon Festival. I'll be making red rice, and we are going to have a good time."

We sat down to a holiday meal when Ishizo returned home, after dark. We had red rice, salted salmon, boiled eggs, and saké. Ishizo let the saké do his talking.

"No sign of the enemy since this morning. If he shows up tomorrow, he won't like what we're going to give him."

I didn't take issue with him. I was savoring each deliciously sticky grain of the red rice, thinking it a shame to have to swallow it down.

Ishizo went to bed early. Misa talked to me as she cleared away the dinner table. "Shinichi, Keiji, Yuzo — they all died. Atsuo, you must go on living!"

The next morning an intermittent siren's wail set our fears on edge. Air raid alert! I sprang from bed. Ishizo was standing in the garden, dressed in his civilian uniform. "Enemy attack!" he shouted. "Everyone up and out!"

Two military requisition ships were burning in the harbor. A third exploded and unceremoniously slid under the waves. Seven Grummans flew over us so low they seemed close to scraping the rooftop. A short while later, seven more came over the horizon like flying fish to attack transport ships anchored in the harbor. The ships began burning so fiercely their sinking was almost inevitable.

"Hmmph! They're just going after ships," Ishizo laughed.

Our mouths were stuffed with rice balls for breakfast when the sirens sounded again. We stayed at the table, believing they portended no major event, but there was a bone-shaking explosion that collapsed the fish market next door. The next moment, our house pitched forward. Shattering windows sprayed the room like scatter shot. Ishizo fell to the ground. His head and face had been pierced with slivers of glass. I raised him up and picked out the slivers. There were more than ten. I dabbed tincture of iodine on the cuts, then swathed his head in bandages that shortly became stained with blood.

"You all right, Father?"

"Yeah, okay." Ishizo stood up and shook his head, then shook it twice more. "Death to the enemy!" he yelled, with surprising vigor.

"The shop's on fire," Suéko said, running out to fill a bucket with water. I grabbed another bucket and followed her. The kitchen, the dining area and window were aflame, red tongues dancing before our eyes, as if to mock our efforts. Throwing a couple of buckets at the conflagration convinced me it was out of control. A roar close by was followed by the roof crashing down in a rain of dust and sand.

"Time to get out!" I yelled, taking Suéko by the hand and pulling her outside.

I put some emergency supplies into a bag, wetted down a futon and lined up the four of us, with me in front and the futon over our heads. Our only avenue of escape was the path to the house, already surrounded by crackling flames. I clasped hands with Mother, Father clasped hands with Suéko, we took deep breaths and ran down the path. It disappeared in a jagged forest of flames just as we cleared it. The diner and house were no longer visible.

I thought carefully about which direction to run. Every warehouse on the harbor was burning. The wind was southerly, that is, blowing in the direction of the town. But the enemy planes were targeting the facilities around the harbor and its ships, the same as the day before. I decided the place to run was into town. I thought my alma mater, the Hanasaki National Elementary School, would be the best place of refuge.

The four of us ran in single file. Our progress was first impeded by a fire brigade trundling a pump cart, then by a disordered band of soldiers. The soldiers had a formidable appearance, with rifles on shoulders, but they scattered in all directions at the sound of enemy planes taking a sudden dive.

Then Ishizo stopped in his tracks. "I forgot my gun."

"It's gone. Burned up," I said.

"No it ain't. I put it all the way at the bottom of the bomb shelter." He turned, about to start running back toward the house.

I got in front of him. "Our house is in a sea of fire. Your gun is a burned potato."

"I'm in the Home Defense Corps. I can't fight without a gun."

"Father, listen, please. The Home Defense Corps' job is soldiering, right? You just saw what the soldiers are doing. Get it? There's nothing they can do!"

"Hogwash! The government issued me live ammunition!"

"What's the government? What about Mother? What about Suéko? Start thinking about them!"

"I don't listen to talk from traitors!"

My hands moved of their own accord. I hit my father until he fell to the ground, punching his chest and stomach while avoiding his bandaged head. As soon as he was down, I scooped him up with both arms and placed one of his arms across my shoulder. Suéko got on the other arm across her shoulder and we ran for all we were worth toward the downtown area. Mother followed, crying all the way. We were putting on quite a show, but we didn't catch anyone's attention. Everyone was focused on running ahead of everyone else, pushing, shoving, screaming, and ranting.

The schoolyard of Hanasaki Elementary School was wrapped in silence. There weren't any schoolchildren because it was Sunday. We rested in the shade of the gymnasium where I had taken my induction physical. Ishizo made himself unobtrusive, like a scolded child, silently eating the red rice ball Misa handed him. Suéko poured tea from a canteen into aluminum cups. Plumes of smoke rising from fires around the harbor twisted together to form a black column that hung in the sky. I had seen the wind was coming in from the sea, but now it looked as if there wasn't much wind at all, meaning the spot we were in was all the safer. I was not alone in making this assessment. There were soldiers posted in the school looking idly from the windows at the fires.

Misa's head was downcast, her spine curved like a cat's. "The house burned away to nothing."

"That's for sure. We just have to let it go. There's nothing we can do," Suéko said consolingly.

"Oh, well. It's not such a big loss. We'll just have to make it up," I said.

"Who are you to call it no big loss?" Ishizo growled. "Whose fault is it we went out of business?"

"You're right. I shouldn't have said it. I guess I'm just a traitor at heart." I couldn't help adding the extra barb to my apology.

"Stop that talk," Misa said with dignity. "We won't have another word of that talk in our house."

Little by little, refugees gathered. There was a woman with no belongings beyond the blouse, pantaloons and charred air raid hood she wore. There were families that brought handcarts loaded with household miscellany.

The harbor was completely destroyed. Big ships on the water had been sunk. The wooded bridge over Lake Onneto from the Nemuro Peninsula to the Hokkaido mainland had been knocked out. People gathered to hear the story told by a man who had fled Cape Nosappu the night before. There had been a mobile enemy force off Kunashiri Island that looked like it would be landing on the island today. That news alarmed a group of families, who hastily gathered their things and hurried outside.

The distinctive roar of the Grumman engines grew ominously closer. A merciless flock of monster birds was heading in our direction. As we watched, black objects fell from beneath their bellies. Everyone went down to the ground, shielding eyes and ears. Deafening roars shook the earth, one after another.

Before our eyes, great billows of smoke rose from the business district. Every house in sight was on fire. The enemy was methodically wiping out the town.

"They're going to hit us next. We've got to get away!" I said. Mud spattered rice balls were dropped half-eaten. Suéko scooped them up. There were more explosions. These blasts weren't just a matter of noise and shaking, but rippled painfully though our bodies. The thought "second wave assault" had formed in my mind when part of the roof of the gym flew off, leaving pieces of tin roofing dancing in the sky. One fell atop the futon covering Misa's head. She wasn't hurt. The windows of the building hadn't broken.

The four of us ran. "Head for Meiji Pasture — that's best!" I told them. Meiji Pasture was a large piece of land to the east of the town. I thought we would be safe there. I looked back to find white smoke rising from the roof of Hanasaki National Elementary School. Through the windows, I saw fire raging like the inside of a stove. We would've been in dire straits if we'd lingered there a few more minutes.

We reached an elevation that looked out over all of Nemuro. Every facility on the harbor and every house nearby it was burning. It looked like the entire downtown business district had been decimated as well. We arrived at the Sakhalin fir wood at the entrance to the pasture, where I had once buried a jar of stolen money. Like many trees of that part of the country, they had developed under wind conditions that had bent the trunks so they hung over the ground, making it an ideal refuge. A great many people had gathered there, making it hard to find an open spot, but we did, and we sat down on the ground. Mosquitoes swarmed as we settled down, but none of us had the energy to brush them away. Ishizo and Suéko were soon sleeping. Misa spoke forlornly.

"We've lost everything. Our house, our diner, three boys . . ."

"Ma, I'm alive. Don't worry. You've got me."

"You're the only one left. But what about . . ."

"Suéko's here. Yoshiko's here. Don't worry, Ma."

"What happens to Japan now?"

" . . ." I had an answer to that question, but I was worried about being overheard. "Japan's going to lose the war pretty soon. Then it will all be over."

"That's what I want!"

Misa kept the same excited tone, and said exactly what she was thinking. "I want it to be over before they take you in the army again!"

She was voicing what they called "dangerous ideas." It was alarming. I took a careful look around to see who might have heard. All I saw was exhausted people lying around like so many wet gunny sacks. A great brick silo rose up to a blue sky. Larks trilled above where we sat. Lustrous hillocks of green grass decorated the pasture. It should have been a refreshing scene, but not while the town was being razed by enemy planes.

The futon I had taken for our protection was covered with burns and holes. I had burns and scrapes on my face and hands. Ishizo woke up around noon and I went over him again with a pair of tweezers, extracting shards of glass that remained in his skin. The count went up to over twenty pieces. One piece was just over his left eye, a good 5 mm long. He would have lost his sight if it had hit his eye.

Air raids continued the following day, about once every two hours. In town, the fires spread from the central district to the surrounding neighborhoods. In some places the flames were powerful enough to raise objects like tatami mats and tin roofing into the air and toss them about. I watched it all, assuming it was my last view of the town where I had grown up. Perhaps the fires had all subsided by dark. The buildings were blackened hulks. The roaring of the enemy planes had given way to the sad sound of locusts in the grass.

The war ended a month after the air raid on Nemuro. On that particular day I was doing volunteer work digging an air raid shelter in the ruins of a neighborhood temple. After Hiroshima and Nagasaki were hit with a new kind of colossal super bomb, it was expected that the naval facilities at Nemuro would again be hit. We were told we needed deeper bomb shelters. Ten of us had dug six trenches, each two meters deep, when the emperor's announcement of the surrender came on the radio at noon. The head of the neighborhood association had a radio that, incredibly, had emerged relatively unscathed when his house had burned the day of the air raid. Everyone sat on his veranda to listen, but we couldn't make out what was being said for the static noise. The neighborhood association chief explained he was sure His Majesty was saying he understood how hard it was for his subjects, but we should remain steadfast.

I went back to digging trenches. Having had nothing to eat but rice gruel since the air raid, I was in a weakened condition. All that manual labor was quite a hardship, but I knew very well I was the village traitor, so I made it a point to work harder than anyone else. I had been digging holes every day since we had been burned out of our home. The first one I dug was about four and a half mats in area, enough for the four family members to live in. Then I went around Nemuro with my trusty shovel, earning small fees digging bomb shelters for others.

We found out what the emperor had been saying from Suéko, when she came back from work. It was getting dark by then.

"The war is over. Japan lost."

"Well, what I am doing with this thing?" I said, and threw the shovel outside. We didn't need any more bomb shelters, thank goodness. I stretched my aching back, then thrust both arms high up into the hazy sky.

People returned to their homes from wherever they had taken refuge. Lights went on in burned out buildings. Barrack construction projects began among the ruins. Gradually, it became more and more common to see veterans back in their homes. Like many, I wandered around the ruins, picking up bowls, spoons, pots, helmets, wires, scorched rice — scorched anything that was still usable. Helmets I refashioned as kettles. Wire was washed, bundled, and sold on the black market. The money from that was taken to Abashiri or Obihiro to buy vegetables, rice, or potatoes, and that too was sold on the black market.

This operation depended on riding trains for free. I managed that by changing Suéko's name for mine on the train pass she had as an employee of the Railway Welfare Association and buying a second-hand railway workers uniform from an old acquaintance of my days at the Nemuro Railway Management Division. Besides getting me through the train entrance wicket, the forged pass and uniform exempted me from baggage inspections when the police checked for black market runners. I pursued this racket single-mindedly, day after day. It was necessary to keep the four of us fed, because Suéko's income would not stretch that far.

Ishizo quickly got over being burned up over Japan's defeat. He stopped vilifying America. As the result of his reading the newspaper inside and out every day, he began saying things like, "The day of militarism is past. Now is the time for democracy."

I was too busy to read newspapers. I didn't have a clue about what democracy might be. I was dealing in the black market for the same reason I had joined the army — it was the only way to keep eating. I wasn't really interested in any kind of ideology.

My black-market dealings returned a very respectable sum of money between late December and the New Year holiday season. I thought of using it to visit Osaka so I could find out what had become of Takéko Eda. Leaving the house saying I was going to Obihiro to make some purchases, I used the Railway Welfare Association pass to go as far as Sapporo. From there, I bought a ticket to Osaka and went straight to Abéno from there.

Much of Osaka was still burnt-out fields, but the amount of rebuilding that had already been done was very impressive. Even after being razed by aerial bombardment, it was still a great metropolis. New wooden residences stood out among the bomb shelters and barracks. I found the place I was looking for identified by a nameplate reading "Eda" before a one-story house. It was far more modest than the building it replaced, but it was a home, with a sheet-iron roof, glass windows and a front entrance. I announced myself with a "Hullo!" and none other than Takéko answered the door, as young and beautiful as ever.

"For goodness sake, Mr. Yukimori! Whatever became of you?"

"I'm sorry. I've been wondering about you for so long! I only wish I could have come sooner." She invited me inside. It was a small house that consisted of one six mat room, one four-and-a-half mat room, and a kitchen. There was a veranda that looked out over the pear-shaped pond and a garden that was barren at the time. Takéko explained her mother was out delivering a kimono she had been working on.

I told her I had been transferred from an army prison to the Aioi Shipbuilding

Yard and had come looking for her when I was released, but found only ruins, so I returned home to Nemuro, where I was caught in an air raid. My explanation of why I was imprisoned was only that I had gone AWOL, with nothing about the fraud and theft charges.

Takéko explained that she and her mother had gone to live with relatives when they lost their home in an air raid. When the war ended, they had used her father's estate to build a new home.

"We've both been through a lot," I said reflectively.

"But your being in army prison — that's horrible. I had no idea! I hadn't heard from you for so long, I finally went to the air mechanics school in Gifu and asked about you. They told me they couldn't reveal anything about the whereabouts of persons involved with military craft. I thought you were involved in some secret mission."

"You went looking for me?!"

That made me so happy I wanted to hug here then and there, but I just brought her hand close and patted it. It was a thoroughly enjoyable small intimacy.

"Do tell me about the army prison."

"Do you really want to hear about that kind of thing?"

"I do. I'm seriously interested, and I'll tell you why. Some friends and I have formed a group to study militarism. An army prison is just the kind of thing we want to know about."

"Sounds like stuff that's over my head. I didn't like the army, so I ran away. They caught me and put me in prison. That's the whole story."

"It's a wonderful story! Going against the authorities while there's a war on! That's not something the average person could do. It takes an authentic war resister to do that!"

"Hardly." The unexpected praise had me feeling abashed. I let go of her hand and started scratching my head. It certainly felt good to hear such things from a woman, but it was totally undeserved.

"We're having a meeting of our group tomorrow night. Please come and talk about the army prison. Everyone will love to hear it."

I was searching for an answer when Takéko's mother returned home. I went through my story again for her. They invited me for dinner and to stay the night. Takéko and her mother slept in the six-mat room and I got the four-and-a-half mat room.

The following day was a Monday. Takéko went to her job at the post office. I spent the day exploring the black market in the Sen-nichimaé and Dotonbori districts. It was like nothing imaginable in Nemuro — countless street stalls and an unbelievable variety of high-quality goods. Canned foods, cigarettes and sleeping bags from the occupation forces; vendors of military decorations — you could get an Order of the Golden Kite decoration for a song. Among women's wear, there was everything from evening dresses to work pantaloons — thousands of garments swaying in the wind. It made me happy to be one of the masses in the new era just beginning. If you stayed in a place like Nemuro, way out in the country, there would be no way to experience that new world. You had to be in the big city. I did recall my parents and Suéko, whom I had left in Nemuro, but their image faded in the distance before the magnetic power of the crowds I saw about me.

Takéko took me to a barracks near Tennoji Park. Around twenty young men and women sat around a charcoal stove. Some wore student uniforms, some overalls, and some dress jackets. Dressed as I was, in my railway workers uniform, they received me with warm expressions. Takéko introduced me to them.

"Comrades, I give you a working man, Mr. Atsuo Yukimori. In the era of militarism, Mr. Yukimori was imprisoned by the army for fleeing military service. He's an antiwar fighter."

It wasn't hard to sense the mood of this gathering, and what they expected of me. I made up a story of how Atsuo Yukimori, antiwar fighter, rebelled against the inhuman conditions of the army by escaping, how the military police arrested him and how he suffered under confinement in an army prison. I received a rousing hand of applause, followed by a series of eager questions. I gave my audience a richly detailed account of the court martial and the army prison.

One of the listeners in student uniform applauded with especial gusto. He came up to shake my hand. "Mr. Yukimori, you're a true revolutionary. It is an inspiration to meet you," he said.

The names of Marx, Lenin, and Stalin came up time and again. The name of Stalin in particular inspired awe when it was invoked, with just the same effect as when someone would refer to the emperor during the war. Just quoting something Stalin wrote was enough to silence anyone who had voiced disagreement, as if the fear of being purged for heresy had been raised. All this made me want to read something by this Stalin, with his miraculous powers. On the way back, I asked Takéko about him.

"Is Mr. Stalin a great person?"

"He is the god of revolution. He hasn't once said anything that was not correct."

"I'd like to read his stuff."

"Not much has been translated yet. A comrade made some mimeograph copies, I'll give you one."

"Thanks," I said. She invited me to stay the night again and I refused. I stayed at a cheap hotel in Kamagasaki that I had spotted earlier that day. Once upon a time Takéko had been cheering me on to reap glory as a soldier, and now she was selling me as an antiwar fighter. I wanted to know what was at the bottom of that turnaround. I was too tired to read any of Stalin's wisdom. I was out like a light as soon as I climbed into my tier of the double-decker bed for which I had paid one yen for a night's sleep.

Thereafter, I found a spot among the ruins of Kamagahara and dug myself a trench to live in. I didn't know whose land it was. If the owner shows up, I thought, I'll just leave. All my neighbors — squatters like me — shared my point of view. The advantage of living in such a place was the trucks that showed up early in the morning looking for hands to clear away rubble from lots. I don't remember what the pay was for a day's labor. I do remember that inflation pushed down the value of money every day. The money I had brought from home was soon gone, so it was work or go without eating.

Living in the trench next to mine was a former lance-corporal who gave me some very interesting business information about workers' footware. You buy black market *jikatabi* footwear, transport it to farming villages, and trade it for rice. Then you sell the rice on the black market and buy more jikatabi. Profits are guaranteed, but only if you can hold down transportation costs. Drawing on my experience in Nemuro, I proposed forging an Osaka Railway Welfare Association train pass and use my railway workers uniform to get free train rides. We decided to work together. The "lance-corporal" would buy the goods and the "sergeant" would handle transport and rice-purchases. The profits were to be split four to six, in my favor.

The operation worked as planned. We made good money because there were no transportation costs. I bought rice in Kyoto, Hyogo, and Okayama. Spot checks for black market rice were common occurrences, but I always slipped by, thanks to my railway uniform.

I attended Takéko's study group meetings, from a desire to be with her. I mixed in with the students and workers and listened to their bewildering discussions. Takéko seemed to be something like a group leader. If the discussion took a confused turn, she would invoke the name of Stalin like a magic wand that always hushed dissent and produced the right conclusions. Takéko held the entire group of men in the palm of her hand because she was smart, articulate, and knowledgeable, but above all, because she was beautiful. She made inflammatory statements about things like the great leader of the Soviet Alliance, historical necessity, and violent revolution with complete confidence that everyone would support whatever she was espousing.

I just could not believe this was the same woman I had once possessed. What had become of her soft voice and endearing way of looking at people? Now her voice seemed to explode from the top of her head. Her eyes raged at their objects, as if to tear them apart. In other words, she was exactly like the wartime right-wing stalwarts, those walking, talking crystallizations of emperor worship, filled with the indomitable belief that their credo was the only truth, and that opposing views had to be obliterated. My understanding of Takéko was that the erstwhile Land of the Gods was for her the Grand Soviet Alliance, His Majesty, the Commander in Chief was her Stalin, the Holy War to liberate Asia was her revolution and the Greater East Asian Co-Prosperity Sphere was for her the communist monolith.

One day Takéko gave a speech to the effect that the revolution is led by organized proletariat and intelligentsia of high consciousness. I rose to ask a question.

"What happens to men like me, who don't have regular jobs and don't have an education?"

"People like you in the black market are called lumpen proletariat. Because you have low consciousness you must study diligently."

The laborer comrades who worked in corporations and factories and the student comrades looked at me with pity in their eyes.

Spring came. The rice trade kept me as busy as ever. Like everyone else, lumpen proletariat cursed with low consciousness had to work if they wanted to eat. Realizing that people like me would be among the first to be purged if the revolution envisioned by Takéko and her friends came to pass made me distance myself from Takéko. Curiously enough, it was infuriating not to have gotten to sleep with her even once, but it worked out that way because of my rising loathing for her — body and all. Once I had been away from her for a while, I no longer minded not seeing her.

The landscape was picturesquely littered with petals fallen from cherry trees when I was pinched. I was carrying eighteen liters of rice from Okayama. Just outside Kobé, a conductor examined my train pass and caught on to the forgery. I was handed over to the Sannomiya police station. The old criminal procedure laws were still in effect — I didn't get a lawyer and the whole process went by quickly. I was charged with forging a public document and violation of the Staple Food Control Law. The prosecutor asked for three years. The judge gave me eighteen months, but he had something to add.

"You were sentenced by a court martial to eighteen months. By order of the American army, your desertion offense is canceled, but your convictions under regular criminal law for fraud and misappropriation remain as prior offenses. Because you are a two-time, repeat offender, the two months that remained on your prior sentence will be added to the current sentence."

I listened to this with head hung down. A year and a half plus two months is a long sentence, but I consoled myself that life would be easier in jail than on the outside, where both food and work was scarce. With that, I quit worrying about anything. After all, there wasn't even all that much difference between what I got for my first and second offenses.

I was thinking ahead about life in prison. My experience in the shipyard told me that if you are going to do time, get yourself assigned to an easy work station. When the time came to declare my working experience, I emphasized the job I had at the pharmacy and lied that I had been a field medic in the army. That tale did the trick. Instead of being sent to a factory, I was made a medical assistant at the Kobé Detention center.

The work consisted of general cleanup and being a helper to the chief guard, an older man who was working as an assistant nurse. We made the rounds of the cells, me pushing a wagon loaded with medicine ampules for injections. We did minor surgical procedures as necessary and gave injections. It wasn't long before I demonstrated to the guard I was handier at giving injections than he was. He was more than happy to let me take over half his work; he did the rounds on the second floor, and I did the first.

There was a gang boss from Kobé on the first floor. I gave him a 5cc shot of ethanol, having received an order from the nursing assistant to do so. He quickly settled into a mellow mood and gave me an assortment of confections and cigarettes. Both those items are forbidden to prisoners, but this boss had an ample stock. I later found out that a member of his gang was paying my boss to keep replenishing his supplies.

I tried giving myself a 1cc shot and immediately felt a wallop across the back of my head. It made me tipsy enough that I couldn't walk without tottering. The nursing assistant gave me a dressing down, but didn't give me any penalty.

At the time, the prisoner population was experiencing a rapid rate of growth. New residents were being stuffed into cells like marmots into cages at laboratories. Besides the overcrowding, meal quality was extremely poor. The rule was that prisoners who didn't participate in any kind of labor were given Class Five meals, which were supposed to contain 1,600 calories, but by the time a meal reached a prisoner, it would usually have only half the prescribed volume because the cook and the guards had shaved off portions to sell on the black market, if not consume themselves. In summer, we suffered from an insufficiency of the bottled water provided in lieu of running water. There was also a shortage of guards to watch over a prisoner population aggravated by hunger and thirst. Guards who had recently been in the army managed to stoke inmate resentment by trying to maintain control through indiscriminate violence and verbal abuse.

Things came to a head one boiling hot afternoon in early August. One community cell ran out of bottled water. The inmates demanded refills, but the guard on duty wouldn't move because it was so hot. When he finally opened the cell about an hour later, one of the men punched him, setting off a chain reaction among others hungering for that kind of action. They tied up the guard, took his keys and went down the corridor opening cell doors. A group of guards ran into the cell block when they heard the commotion, then turned around and fled in panic when they saw there was a large number of angry prisoners on the loose. Prisoners were streaming outside the cell house and running to the front gate. I looked out the clinic window to see what the tumult was all about just as the inmates were climbing over the gate and flocking outside.

A formidable mob of prisoners had seized their freedom and were milling around in front of the gate, while fellow inmates watched from the other side, regarding them with a mixture of envy and misgivings. They gathered themselves together defensively before the security guards that approached with handguns drawn. When a single warning shot was fired, they scrambled back to their cells and waiting guards swiftly banged the iron doors shut.

Meanwhile, more than two hundred inmates were freely roaming the corridors and open cells, with no more than a dozen or so guards on duty. Order would not be restored until the mob was dispersed back into the cells. The security division chief barked orders through a megaphone until he was hoarse, but the prisoners only gathered outside the cell doors and glared back defiantly at him.

The uniformed security chief went to the office of the warden, in his business suit, for a conference. The two faced each other with expressions of anxiety and hesitation etched in their faces. They had to get the rebellious prisoners under control and begin searching for the escapees, but they wanted to do it without having to call in support from another prison, thereby exposing their faulty prison management.

Time went by with nothing being accomplished as the two men simmered under the hot summer sun and the cicadas chirped loudly. Watching this, I stepped out in front of the nursing assistant to address the security chief.

"Sir, let me talk to the men. I'll get them back into their cells."

"What's this?"

The nursing assistant was looking at me dubiously. Then he talked with the clinic chief and the clinic chief talked to the warden. Having bided my time, I finally presented the warden with a demand.

"I have to get your promise that everyone who goes quietly to their cells won't be put on trial and won't get any kind of punishment."

The warden agreed. I went to the cell house gate. "Hey, guys, let me in, will you?" They backed away and I stepped inside.

I walked over to the stand where the head guard was normally posted and got up on it. I told the men about the warden's promise and asked them to go back into their cells. The first one to do what I asked was that gang boss who was chummy with the assistant medic. By then, I knew he ran the gang that shook down street vendors. He had the key that was stolen from the guard. He shooed the men back into each of their cells, starting from the back and turning the key when they were inside. He was the last one back to his cell. When he was inside, he tossed the key to me. The moment he did, the guards came rushing in. Now they were brave and in cover-up mode, strutting about and whistling.

"Good work, Yukimori," the security chief said to me.

"Don't mention it. You've done me a lot of favors," I said, feeling self-righteous. I was thinking he owed me something, and the time would come when I could collect on it.

I was a hit with the security chief and the guards in an additional way by helping them make a list of the prisoners who had escaped. Knowing many of the men's faces from making daily rounds of the cell house, I could pick out the names of the missing men.

I used the security chief's register to make a list of the registered domiciles, home addresses and addresses of relatives and friends of the runaways and make mimeograph copies of it. While I was doing that, they started getting calls from police reporting arrests of runaways. Some turned themselves in to the detention center. Most cases were cleared up by that night.

Several days later, when the last escapee had been rounded up, the security chief called me into his office to caution me about the thing that most worried him.

"See that you don't talk about what happened the other day. You're the one that knows most of the inside stuff. We don't want it to get out."

"Who cares about something like that?"

"Number one, the occupation army. Also, the press. There's plenty of jerks who would make a big thing of it."

"Understood." I gave a sly smile.

The thing that had him most worried was spot checks by the occupation forces. He had good reason to be afraid that the Americans would find out about his past as an "Emperor's policeman," torturing thought-crime prisoners and harassing Koreans. Once he had a GI who looked like a schoolboy come in, accompanied by his girlfriend, on the pretext of making a "hygiene inspection." It was clear that the kid didn't know anything about hygiene inspections — he was just having a good time showing his girl around a Japanese prison — but the security chief submissively gave them a guided tour.

I was released from the Kōbé Detention Center on parole in early February 1947. That was ten months earlier than my full term, including what was left from the first sentence. There is little doubt my role in the prison escape had influenced the parole board. The trouble was, turning me loose on the streets in mid-winter with no place to turn for clothing, food, or shelter was not a favor at all — it was condemning me to suffer from the cold and starvation. I did not want to ask for Takéko's sympathy, and I certainly did not want her to see me dressed as shabbily as I was. That is why I left Kōbé and headed straight for Tokyo.

The only thing I had to wear was my faded, grime-stained railway worker's uniform. I didn't have a single sen in my pocket. I stalked the streets like a wraith, fishing out any discarded food I could find in garbage. I feasted on half-eaten scraps of bread and clumps of rice soaked in sauces of unknown content.

My roost was the street passageway running under Shinjuku Station. There, drifters and war orphans lived in stench, mud, and filth seething with lice and bedbugs. The bright side of that existence was that it was peacetime. Otherwise, the cold and exhaustion was much the same as it had been during the Second Changsha Operation. The only cooperation between us was when someone froze to death and we carried the body outside. Otherwise, we were pretty much like a community of vegetables, having nothing to do with one another, and rarely exchanging words.

One afternoon the Revolutionary Party came to the station for a speech session. A famous revolutionary delivered fine-sounding oratory from atop the party's mobile speaker's stand on how he would save the starving poor. He made some comments that sounded good to me. He said crime is revolutionary and criminals are on the front lines of the revolution.

I crawled out from my roost to get closer. The Revolutionary Party members were like all the other listeners to the speech; my strange appearance and bad smell bothered them. When they tried to shoo me away, I got mad. I went over to the speaker's stand and yelled at the party leader. "Hey, Governor, I'm hungry."

He ignored me and went on with his speech. I yelled at him again. This time two students jumped out in front of me. They were well nourished, with good skin tone.

"You shouldn't be here."

"Don't you see you're interfering with free speech?"

"I'm hungry!"

"You've got a big, strong body. You should go to work."

"People who don't work don't eat!"

"I can't work. I'm too hungry."

While this exchange was going on, another party member showed up carrying some sheets of newspaper. He wrapped the newspaper around my arm and pulled me away from the truck. I was getting the cockroach treatment. The party member threw me away by the road. I didn't have much strength left, so I just sat where I was, like a piece of rotten meat.

"Hey, comrade! I'm the damn proletariat!"

Instead of answering, the revolutionary party member gave me a hard kick in my side. I just thought about that, without groaning or flinching. I was fantasizing that Takéko Eda had delivered that kick. I could hardly complain about it, not after I had abandoned her. Besides that, it was pleasant to be kicked by a woman, strangely enough. I felt more pleasure than pain while being kicked.

Passersby avoided me, just as they would avoid excrement on the street. The cold of the pavement assailed me. I was on the way to freezing to death. My eye fell upon a bicycle leaning against the revolutionaries' truck. It was shiny silver, apparently new. I ran to the truck, leaped on the bicycle, and rode away as fast as I could.

"Thief!" A Revolutionary Party member yelled and ran after me. Of course, the bicycle was faster. I was drawing on a reserve of strength I had not been aware existed. I got away. From Shinjuku, I peddled on and on to Yotsuya. Nowadays, there would be too much traffic to go sailing along such a route, but back then there weren't many cars on the main road. I finally ran out of energy and stopped at a police booth, where I toppled to the ground.

"Officer! I just stole this bicycle. Arrest me!" I passed out.

It was mid-February 1947 when I was arrested in flagrante delicto. I had resided in the outside world following my previous release from prison for no more than two weeks. The trial was quickly over because I did not dispute any of the charges against me. In early May I was sentenced to two years and two months for theft. To that sentence, the ten months remaining on my previous term were added, bringing my actual term of imprisonment to three years. Although it did seem to me a too steep penalty for one bicycle, I nevertheless considered it a major blessing that for three years I would not have to worry about clothing, food, or a place to live.

In mid-May I was transferred to Urawa Prison. This prison is located in the main part of the city of Urawa. It is known as the place for first offenders and short-term inmates from the Tokyo area. I looked over the high concrete wall that surrounds it and the cell houses with their iron bars feeling strangely reassured that the government had become the guarantor of my minimum living requirements. It was the same feeling of stability I had when I became a second class private in that Asahikawa regiment.

They made me a shoemaker. That assignment might have been decided based on my experience making leather ammunition belts in the army prison. I would have preferred being a clinic assistant or storekeeper, but I could hardly complain. Every morning, I would change from my red prison uniform (short sleeves and pants for summer) into a blue factory workers uniform and go to my workshop.

The guard in charge of the shop sat at a stand near the entrance — one man overseeing forty prisoners. The tasks were divided according to the steps of the manufacturing process: clicking, closing, welting, heel edging, sole stitching, finishing. I was put into the heel edging slot. Being fairly deft when it comes to manual operations, I fully mastered this skill. You cut away the extra leather that sticks out without leaving any surface marks from the cutting tool. The foreman, who had actually been a shoemaker on the outside, praised my work — you could have a future in the trade, he said.

If you think the work you do is meaningless, it becomes an unbearable grind. You can get some enjoyment from it if you look at every detail as interesting. My efforts to do that made the time go rolling by. Pretty soon it was lunch time, and pretty soon after that it was time to quit.

Compared to the leather working I did in the army prison, this shop was downright comfortable. I could pause in my work if I wanted to. If I had to use the toilet, I could. It was possible to talk in a low voice when the guard wasn't looking. There was even a trifling payment, according to volume of work accomplished.

In the evenings, I returned to the cell, and relationships with fellow inmates began.

The man everyone in the cell called "boss" was not quite the overlord type boss like the one at the Aioi shipyard, but he certainly had clout. He was the boss of the gambling rackets in Asakusa.

Normally, the strongest and smartest man in the cell gets the role of boss. This *oyabun* commanded respect on the basis of his quiet charisma. He spoke softly, and had a smile that did not put one off. The first impression he gave was a short old man with a large face that you might see on a retired patriarch who goes around the streets of his neighborhood watering flower beds. Closer inspection would turn up the scar on his cheek, and the fact that his entire third finger and the top half of the middle finger — up to the second joint — were missing.

He explained one day, in his own quiet way of speaking, why he had cut off sections of his fingers. He would use a well sharpened kitchen knife to sever the joint. The finger segment would be preserved in salt and set upon one of those stands made of unfinished paulownia wood they use for Shinto offerings, and it would be sent to the oyabun of whichever gang his own gang was battling. Provided it was the kind of dispute a formal gesture could settle, that would do the trick. By this grisly ritual, one boss would gain face and the other's legend grew. It follows the procedure handed down from Edo times, when the severed finger of an oyabun recognized by the Shogunate would be delivered to the other party in a turf feud. The oyabun explained that you can use one finger three times — thirty times for the whole hand. His point was that making the sacrifice saves many lives.

There was none of the braggadocio you normally expect from a yakuza. He spoke quietly, in the manner of someone's grandfather explaining things to a young person. The bright red scars on his finger stumps lent a powerful impact to his words. His aura would enable him to put a decisive end to some argument over trifles simply by saying at a timely moment, "That's enough. Quiet down now."

This oyabun was doing time on a charge of "providing a place for gambling." Specifically, he was hosting hanafuda card games at his residence. Many of the inmates were intensely interested in hanafuda, but he rebuffed them when they asked about fine points of *koi-koi* or *ato-saki*. "Respectable people don't get mixed up in that kind of thing," he would say.

At bath time, I discovered he had a tattoo on his back of a woman, a breath-takingly beautiful likeness with the kind of exquisite detail seen in works by Utamaro. It was hard to believe such delicate nuance could be achieved on a person's skin. There was a certain seductiveness to the sight of steam rising from the girl's cheeks and shapely neck as the oyabun soaked in the bath. Rumor had it that he had obtained the model by paying her ransom to a Yoshiwara brothel.

There was a man called the "Fox" who had set himself up as the oyabun's personal valet. The Fox did every possible service for the oyabun, like bringing his meals, doing his laundry, and putting away his futon. He was called "Fox" because the top half his face was wide, and the bottom tapered down to a narrow chin. He had parlayed that face into a career as a comedian at a striptease theater in Asakusa. His ventriloquist routine using his left hand as a puppet would draw laughs from the whole cell.

Fox had stabbed a man to death while colossally drunk one night. He was drinking with friends from the theater when someone in the party announced that something was up and police were outside. Fox staggered out the door to see for himself. He looked up and down the street, but couldn't spot any action. That annoyed him. "Ain't nothing happening out there!" he said. Then he added, at the top of his voice, "BAKA YARO!" to show how annoyed he was. Just then, a man who happened to be passing by in the company of a woman mistakenly thought the epithet was meant to taunt him — for who knows what reason. The man threw a punch at Fox, who reflexively pulled a knife from his pocket and stabbed the man in the chest. The man fell to the ground and did not move, but Fox continued stabbing indiscriminately, in the neck, chest and numerous other places. He was still engaged in stabbing the man when a patrolman appeared, so Fox was arrested in the act of committing the crime.

"The prosecutor said I stabbed the guy because I wanted to kill him, but that's not right. I wasn't even thinking about that. I was having fun sticking the knife in, so I kept doing it — that's all. I knew he was already dead. If I just wanted to kill him, I would have stopped, right?"

"What's it feel like to stab a person?" I asked.

"Same as sticking a piece of meat. I was thinking, gee it's amazing how soft the human body is."

Laughing uproariously, Fox attacked a futon with an imaginary knife, pretending it was his victim. I averted my eyes because I was having a vision of his hand being stained scarlet, and it wasn't his hand at all, but my own, once again in China, stabbing that village chief.

There was a man sitting in a far corner of the cell. He was short and thickset, with a long torso, like a fireplug. He didn't speak much and didn't seem to enjoy mixing with people. The latter quality curiously emphasized his presence in the cell; your eyes would fall upon him in spite of yourself. He had been an alcoholic farmer in Saitama Prefecture who broke into the home of a wealthy family in the neighboring village to get money for saké. Having never before committed a burglary, he had prepared for it by imitating the burglar stereotype you see in every crime melodrama. He covered his face with a furoshiki, held a hatchet in one hand and a kitchen knife in the other, and told the couple inside the house to give him money. He got away with one thousand yen, but even the victims spotted him as an amateur. The close proximity of his house to the crime scene and his reputation for drinking led to his early arrest. Fox ridiculed Fireplug Man.

"Did you go to clumsy school, or does it just come natural? Getting five years for taking a lousy thousand yen — that's fabulous. I killed a guy and only got six years. That's one for the books!"

The Fireplug Man didn't answer, leaving no openings for further attack. Fox abandoned the venture as fruitless.

There was a roofing construction worker whose hobby was collecting women's underwear. He started his collection by stealing from clothes lines, then decided underwear that had been washed lacked the female aroma. He began sneaking into homes where young women lived to get slips and brassieres they had removed before retiring. One night he hit a women's dormitory and was discovered by a student returning late. He was seized by three women, who tied him up and called the police.

This pantie thief clearly had taken pleasure in having three women restrain him. He boasted of the experience.

"Every one was a looker. I wanted to rape all three. If it was just one, I would have. Next time I get the chance, I'm going to find me another girls dorm, go in there, and rape three of them dolls!"

He said he had a good look at the thighs of the three women as they were punching and kicking him. When they were tying him up, he had managed to shoulder the breasts of one. He became excited as he recounted the experience and ended the tale by exposing his erection and fondling it until it emitted a jet of white semen.

Fox was captivated by the spectacle. "Wow, you're just like a fountain," he said admiringly.

There was a bandsman who had thrown concentrated sulfuric acid into a woman's face. He had left a wife and children in Yamagata to find work in Tokyo. He got a job at a cabaret and became intimate with one of the dancers. They began living together in an apartment until the woman decided she wanted out of a relationship with a married man who became violent when drunk. She attempted to escape one night, only to be pursued by the man, a bottle of concentrated sulfuric acid in hand. He threw it down over her face from behind, disfiguring it so badly it was hardly recognizable as a face. He received a term of two years on a charge of bodily injury. The bandsman was only about thirty, but he tried to cast himself as an old man by talking about how age had caught up with him, or framing a story from his past as an event that happened "when I was young."

"I'm going to marry her," he said. "She wants me to take care of her for life, and I will. I love her. That bottle of acid fixed everything for me. My wife took one look at what happened and agreed to a divorce, and that woman certainly isn't going to find anyone else to love her."

The fox with his bloody knife, the pantie thief roofer and the sulfuric acid bandsman talked on and on together about their adventures tirelessly. Their favorite topic was their sexual adventures, with richly detailed descriptions of the act itself, from start to finish. They were fully confident that all the other men in the cell were interested in these stories. They would cast glances and nod at each of us in turn. Fireplug Man was the only one who wouldn't respond. Everyone else would return an acquiescent smile. I did too, at first, but after a while I became bored of hearing their unvarying renditions of grunts, moans, panting, and cries. At one point Fox threw me a glance and I ignored it. They was all it took to put him in a violent mood.

"What's your problem? You don't like my story?" I glared back at him in silence.

"You just got here, shithead! It looks to me like you don't know the rules!" Fox said, pushing his jaw out and posturing as if to advance on me.

The pantie thief stepped up the voltage. "Say something, you!"

I glared back at him, too.

It was Sulfuric Acid who actually jumped me. He grabbed my arms and held them behind me. The next moment Fox was punching me in the chest and belly, while the pantie thief kneed me in the groin. They had a strategy of avoiding hitting the face so there would be nothing for the guards to see that they would have to deal with. They went on hitting me until the oyabun said, "That's enough. Let him go now." They stopped, morosely.

Pain lodged in my chest and groin spread throughout my body. I moaned softly once, but I made sure not to cry out. I had been through as much when I got punishment as a new soldier.

I got threats from every one of that gang: "You've got a thick head!," "You're not getting off that easy next time!," etc.

I did not answer any of this or show any other kind of reaction, not moving, like a stick of wood. That seemed to spook them enough to make them stop antagonizing me altogether. I went to sit next to the fireplug farmer and together we faced the world with our backs forward and mouths closed.

The gang of three established themselves as a force in the cell, under the oyabun's control. Everyone else either toed their line or stayed out of their way. When a new inmate would come in they would wait for the opportunity to assert their power.

One day, an old man came into the cell. He was clearly older than the oyabun. He might have been around seventy. His shaggy eyebrows were half white. It was plain he had never been in prison before. He eyed his cellmates uneasily and sat in a corner. He had a hard time adjusting to prison life. He would not have his futon in order when it was time for morning inspection or do things like dropping his meal tray when it came through the delivery slot, spilling miso soup on the floor. On his first day I tried to explain the rules of life inside the cell to him, but he was still lagging behind everyone else on the second and third day. Worst of all was his inability to get used to taking his turn defecating. He sat on the toilet seat fretting about everyone else seeing him instead of doing his business and getting off.

At night, when the gang of three gleefully started up their usual tales of women, I went over and addressed the old man.

"What did you do? You don't seem to be the sort of person to be here."

"I'm very ashamed of myself," he answered in a small voice, hanging his head as he spoke.

He told a rambling story, with a lot of beating around the bush, but the point of it all was that he had killed his second son, a troublemaker.

He had been operating a small machine shop in Urawa for forty years. He lived in a place that wasn't hit by air raids during the war. When peace returned, he began making pots and pans, and soon was doing extremely good business. The trouble began when his son returned home from the army.

The son had belonged to a unit of commandos scheduled for suicide pilot missions, but the war ended before his mission came up. Instead of finding peacetime employment, he drank and chased women. When he ran out of money, he came to his father, asking for more. If he didn't get it, he would beat his mother. He threatened to kill both his parents if they didn't give him money. Once he started a fire in his bedroom. He took a radio and furniture and sold it off.

The old man consulted with a psychiatrist, the police, and a welfare office, but could find no solution. One day after his son had again raised his hands to his mother, the old man ran into his workshop, picked up a hammer and used it to strike his son on the back, knocking him to the ground. Then he got down and strangled his son to death with a towel.

"What was your sentence?"

"Three years."

"Three years for homicide! That's very light. The judge must've taken the circumstances into account and didn't think you were in the wrong!"

"No, it was wrong to kill my son . . . I never did anything wrong before . . . and I was never in prison before."

The old man started to cry, pathetically. The gang of three stopped talking and came over to us.

"Say, what's the matter there?" Fox asked familiarly.

"Leave him alone," I said, waving him off. "He's got family trouble."

"You keep out of this," Fox said threateningly. "I'm not talking to you. Butt out! Hey there, old man. Tell us why you're crying."

"Crying like a damn baby," the pantie thief said. "I can't stand listening to it," Sulfuric Acid added.

The old man sat, surrounded by the gang of three, cowering and wiping his tears. "Hey, tell us why you're crying!"

"It doesn't matter."

"What doesn't matter? Answer the damn question!"

"Please just forget it."

"What kind of shit is that? We're asking you in a nice way and you give smart ass answers! You talk like you don't know where you are."

"Leave him alone," I said, and punched Fox in his side before he could turn on me. The poke sent his short body staggering backward until his shoulder slammed into the wall.

The next moment I was fighting his two buddies. I could move fast at times like that. They tried to grab me from both sides, but I stepped aside and kicked high, clipping Sulfuric Acid on the hip. Someone punched me on the lip, making it bleed. Then I took a punch in the right eye. Just as the guards came running in, I landed a full force punch squarely on the pantie thief's jaw. For violent behavior, assault, and disobeying orders, I was sentenced to one month in solitary confinement, one month of no reading privileges and forfeiting of all remuneration for work performed. The gang of three got off with one week in solitary. I got the heavy penalty because I landed the first blow.

The solitary cell was dark and musty. Regardless of that, the privilege of being suddenly taken away from the community cell and placed all by myself felt to me as refreshing as a bath after a hard day's work. Of course, I was under the constant scrutiny of guards through their observation window, but they left me alone so long as I didn't commit infractions like lying down or trying to talk to someone in another cell.

All day long, my eyes looked upon walls and iron-clad windows, while my mind was at ease and free to recall the feeling of liberation that had been mine in childhood, when I ventured into the marsh. I remembered my quest for the Furen hermit, and all the joys and dreams since then. At the same time, it seemed to me that every vision I ever had about what might happen in my life was fading, because, at twenty-eight, it was all over. I was in prison for being a thief, existing at the bottom of society, where I could do nothing but writhe hopelessly in the mud. My life had peaked when I was an army sergeant, in love with Takéko Eda. From that moment on, it had gone straight downhill.

What should I do to escape from the mud? Did I have what it takes to make the upward climb, to pull one leg and then the other from the muck, and keep doing that for as long as it took? Just asking myself these questions was enough to discourage me. When I was in the world outside, I wanted to go to prison. In prison, I was happy to be separated from everyone else in a punishment cell. It was hard to see any hope that such a man might go out in the pernicious world of people and succeed in getting along.

I had a strange dream one morning. I was walking down a street that was all gray, and I suddenly felt that my chest was completely empty, as if the wind could blow right through it. I looked down and, sure enough, there was a big cavity. My heart had fallen out. I looked down and there was something lying on the ground that was twitching. It was soft and red, so it must have been a heart. I grabbed it and tried to put it back in the cavity, but it wouldn't fit. It was shaped the exact opposite of the cavity's shape. I kept trying unsuccessfully to fit it, and finally, I realized that for some unknown reason, my heart had turned inside out. I panicked, believing the only way I could put my heart back where it belonged was to turn my entire body inside out. I was puzzling over how to accomplish this — maybe by shrinking down inside my own skin like a caterpillar in its chrysalis, then emerging again in a new skin — when I woke up.

The world had undergone a major change. Outside the window was a high concrete wall, and beyond it was the city. The prison was supposed to occupy an unobtrusive place in the shadows. enclosing but a small plot of land where unclean individuals resided. Its function was not much different than an outhouse behind someone's home. Now, everything was reversed — or so it seemed to me. The real world was the prison, and the city was the place hidden away in the back. The sun shone brightly on the concrete wall and in the prison courtyard, while the streets of the city were shrouded in gray.

I thought it was a lingering effect of the dream distorting my perception, but blinking and taking another hard look didn't change anything. The inside-out city beyond the walls remained just as it was.

Something had changed inside me for sure, but I no longer had time to ponder what it was all about. I was released from the solitary cell and put into a different communal cell. I was also assigned a different occupation to work at every day. This time, I was employed at a metalworking shop, manufacturing items like tin dippers, buckets, and hoes. Once again, there was a single guard-supervisor overseeing forty inmates. I was the shop storekeeper, sitting next to the supervisor and keeping accounts of quantities of materials and products and the inmates' per capita production. Besides that, I was also in charge of the wall display of name tags of inmates currently away from their workstations, either using the toilet or on errands to the warehouse.

"Request permission for bowel movement!" an inmate would say. When the supervisor gave permission, I would deal out five or six sheets of toilet paper and move the inmate's name tag to the space marked "toilet."

My job was easy, but my concern was keeping busy. If I had free time, I would do cleaning, meal delivery, dish washing, or even help with transporting the materials I had inventoried. I kept moving constantly, occupied with one task after another. The supervisor commended me for this, but I wasn't trying to impress him. I kept busy because I was afraid of having idle moments to think about the change that was taking place in me.

I was a model prisoner — obedient, servile, and industrious. When I returned to my cell, I tried to avoid conflicts with others. The facts of my fist fight with the gang of three in my previous cell had gotten around, with the result that I was seen by the others in the cell as one to be feared. Before my arrival, there wasn't anyone to play oyabun to settle issues among the inmates, whose offenses covered the usual spectrum of theft, fraud, rape, homicide, etc. They handed me the role of cell boss, and I managed to do a decent job of playing it. Mainly, it was a matter of giving the order to wind up a fight at the right moment. When I said, "All right, that's enough," the cell quieted down. Of course, my model was the oyabun in my previous cell. Instead of his charisma, my newly minted reputation for packing a strong punch and not hesitating to use it, backed by my credentials as a two-time convict and former army sergeant impressed the other inmates, who were mostly in their twenties.

Time went by fast. I passed my second New Years in that prison — 1949.

Since everyone there sent New Year's greeting cards, I thought, okay, I will too, and sent one to my younger sister Suéko. It was the first time I had written to her in three years — since New Year's 1946. I just wrote that I was sorry for my long silence and that I was fine. The return address from the prison didn't have the prison name, so I assumed she would not catch on, but she did. Her reply came promptly, and it was a long letter.

"It didn't take me long to find out where your card came from. I just looked up the address on a map in the library. What did you do? Thinking about what kind of bad thing you might have done is keeping me awake at night. I won't tell Mother or Father, so please, tell me. As for me, you're my brother no matter what you did. You couldn't have a bigger fan than me! So, tell me the truth about what happened.

"All kinds of things have happened since you went away. I got married. It was soon after you disappeared. I didn't tell you, but I was pregnant. The baby was born in February 1946, a boy. We had a quick marriage soon after. My husband's name is Torakichi Jinnai, and the boy's name is Tetsukichi. We opened a diner, the Jinnai Diner. It is just a shack with an iron roof, located a little bit closer to the business district than Yukimori Diner was. Mother and Father are living with us.

"Father is sick in bed. He had a stroke and his left side is paralyzed. He can't see from his right eye. He needs help with meals and using the toilet. Mother looks after him constantly. Her back is bent way over. Father cries and yells, just like a little child. Mother has a terrible time comforting him. But his memories of long ago are fresh as yesterday. It can get downright scary. He talks about when we ran the bath house, about the day Yuzo died in the bath water, as if he saw it a moment ago. Then he cries so pathetically. You can see why I couldn't tell them about you. I don't know if he'd cry or get angry, but it would be sure to make his condition worse.

"Yoshiko just got married over New Year's to a Kushiro fisherman. He was married before. Yoshiko is 42. That's pretty old to be getting married, and I'm so glad she finally found happiness. It wasn't her fault she got married late. It was the war's fault.

"When will you get out? I want to see you so much. You're the only brother I have.

"I suppose it must be very hard for you, but try hard to reform, for us both!"

~

I didn't write a reply to Suéko. I didn't think Suéko would take it well if I told her the grim story of my life from the time I disappeared from Nemuro. Since she already knew I was in prison, I thought the time would come when I would have to tell her some of the story, but right then, I couldn't find the courage to go into it.

Then, one blazing hot day in mid-summer I was called away from my workshop and informed I had a visitor. I was thinking something was up, because it was a general rule that inmates weren't allowed visitors. I went to the visiting room, and there was Suéko on the other side of the wire net. She looked like the typical woman from the countryside, in her monpé, with a dirty rucksack by her side.

"I came to tell you that Mother and Father have died." She spoke with unnatural formality because she was very conscious of the guard next to her, writing notes on what she said.

"Is that right?" I said, stupidly, with my eyes downcast. It felt like I had a vast, white snowscape inside and nothing else. I didn't know what else to say.

Suéko suddenly flew at the wire mesh and grasped it in both hands. Her words poured out in a rush.

"Father died on May third. He was talking and looking well in the morning. Mother left him for just a moment to use the toilet and phlegm caught in his throat and he died. His funeral was just so sad. Most everyone he knew had moved far away after the air raid. There was only two members of the Home Defense Corps, Yoshiko and her husband and me and my husband. Mother wanted a proper grave, so we bought a plot in the town graveyard overlooking the sea and buried Father there. Mother went down fast after that. She was more bent over than ever. She just lay down and died on July third, the same day as Father, two months later."

"Is that right?" I said for a second time. I had not been reacting at all, but the tears shining in Suéko's eyes got to me and something melted inside, like the ice floes in spring slowly starting to break up and move out to sea.

"Mother kept talking about nothing else but you. 'I wonder where he is, what he's doing. If he's still alive, I want him to come back, I want to see him again.' She said that every day. So I told her. I told her you were still alive. One day I just told her. I guess it was about a month ago."

"You told her I was in prison?"

"Yes."

"That must've hurt her."

"No, you're wrong. She was happy to know you were alive. You could see it was a big relief to her. She took a turn for the worst right after that, and didn't have the strength to live."

"It was because of me. Her no-good son."

"I told you, that's not right. Listen to me. Mother was overjoyed. She just regretted that she wouldn't be able to see you again because she knew she was about to die."

Suéko began crying, with both her hands gripping the wire mesh. She broke up suddenly, like a sand hill under an onrushing wave. I cannot bear to see a relative cry. I looked away. Then, without realizing what I was doing, I was on my feet. I rushed outside the visiting room. There was a large keyaki tree, shining in the sunlight. All around, cicadas were chirping. I brought my face close to the trunk of the great tree. The bark was split open and armies of ants were marching up and down the tree. Suddenly, I was being shouted at. The guard who had been taking notes on my conversation with Suéko was standing there with sweat pouring down his face, furious.

"What do you think you're doing, walking off by yourself?"

"I'm sorry."

"You're going to be a lot sorrier!"

Three guards came running and grabbed my arms. They brought me to the area office and began to interrogate me. Unsupervised walking was almost as serious an offense as fleeing confinement. The area supervisor's interrogation was harsh. What was the motive? I was thinking of escaping, wasn't I? Seeing my sister's face incited my desire to escape home, didn't it?

"No, that's not it. I don't know why I got up and left the room. I just found myself doing it."

"That's no excuse! You're lying!"

"I didn't know what I was doing. I wanted to be alone."

"Nobody cares what you want! You don't move an inch here until you're told to! Understand?" I was sentenced to two weeks in solitary confinement and no reading privileges. The grief finally came pouring out when I was left by myself. The tears were more for my mother than my father. She was the one who suffered when I disappeared, and I let her die without hearing my apology.

Mother . . . forgive me, please.

I was called into the area chief's office one week into solitary to be told I was being transferred to Fuchu Prison. That's where they send repeat offenders. I didn't get an explicit explanation why, but my impression was they were handing me off to the hardcore criminal specialists because I was too troublesome for a prison intended for first offenders.

Fuchu Prison is an imposing building complex. You enter through a tall gate with a guard station suitable for admitting high officials. My first sight of the inside, looking out from the van transporting me, was of a long road lined with keyaki trees rustling pleasantly under summer breezes. We finally reached the main building, looking like a great reception hall. It's big scale architecture that makes you conscious of the state's power. Beyond it were stone cell houses like fortresses.

I was taken along a narrow corridor watched over by solemn uniformed guards to an enormous three-story cell block building. There were more guards and a pair of iron doors that opened to a very long corridor. A ventilation shaft in the ceiling above the corridor extended all the way up through the top floor, with wire netting over the openings at the second and third floors to stop any falling bodies. The entrances to the inmates' residences were lined up along both sides of the corridor. Nowhere else were there such vast numbers of cell doors, each exactly the same and spaced the same distance from the next.

The long corridor opened to a great hall that looked out over three more long corridors. That's to say the vast hall afforded a view of four corridors, all the same, on each of the building's three stories. There was a central station where guards were posted, ready to be dispatched at a moment's notice to any spot in the building where they might be needed.

My transfer through central station was a vivid demonstration of the power relationships among the guards. The guards from the corridor I was bound for were like mere footmen until they had me in their own jurisdiction. Accustomed as I was to being a prisoner, it was still somehow shocking when my status changed in an instant from new guest to slave, the same as when a free citizen first becomes a convict.

After the war, when everything supposedly changed, new terminology was adopted for the old system of imprisonment. The basic prison law of 1909 stayed in effect, but other laws changed the term for prisons from *kangoku* to *keimusho*. Both words mean the same thing; the only difference is that the new word isn't from the musty feudal past. Now, when they throw you in jail, they say it is all about "correction" instead of punishment, but what has not changed from the old system is the minute web of rules concerning detention, work, clothing, haircuts, visits, letters, and everything else concerned with daily life — rules that don't recognize the prisoner's free will to decide anything, do anything, or show a personal attitude about anything.

Fuchu Prison's notoriety as the ultimate place for hardened criminals had me feeling acute anxiety as I entered there.

Someone decided the auto maintenance shop was just the right workplace for me to report to from my communal cell every day. The main work done at this shop was repair and assembly of old car engines. The skills I had learned at the army aircraft maintenance school proved very useful. Together with that, the experience at Fuchu led much later on to my becoming an auto mechanic on the outside.

The shop's operation and rules were the same as at the shoemaking shop in Urawa, so there's no need for me to go into that.

What was different about Fuchu were the inmates.

The average person's mental image of criminals comes from the sensational press coverage given to perpetrators of especially fiendish murders or spectacular fraud operations. They are not the type I met at Fuchu, because that class of criminal is usually not a repeat offender; some do get out of prison and then kill someone else or pull off another big con scheme — but I've never met that kind of criminal. The many repeat offenders I did meet at Fuchu were the true criminal archetypes, quite different from the criminals I had known until then.

Anywhere in the world, at any time in history, crime is mostly a matter theft — taking the belongings of others, without their consent. The criminal population always consists mostly of thieves. I read somewhere about a theory of crime as a great tower in which theft is the cement that holds it all together. The rooms and windows draw people's attention, with no notice going to the cement, even though that is what makes it possible to have rooms and windows.

My reading of the Ten Commandments of Moses is that theft is the real basis of evil. Theft is forbidden only after the commandments about worship, home life, murder, and adultery are set out, but actually, murder and adultery are forms of theft. One is stealing a person's life and the other is stealing the fidelity between two people. In one book of Saint Augustine's *Confessions*, he does battle with his qualms of conscience over stealing a neighbor's pears in his youth. I laughed about that when I first read it because it seemed like a trivial crime to make so much of, but thinking about it more leads me to conclude that Augustine's insights about theft being the root of evil were correct. War is theft on a grand scale committed by a state — the theft of the territory and the lives of the people of another state.

As I write this, I am looking at the scar from an old burn at the base of the index finger of my right hand. I am a man who began his life by stealing. The scar is the record of my theft of the contents of a small change basket. Thereafter, I committed I don't know how many exactly, but a tremendous number of thefts. I belonged to a great army of thieves dispatched by my country to China, where I stole life from scores of people.

In Fuchu I found myself among a vast assembly of thieves. There were five men in my cell and four of them, including me, were there for theft.

The oldest was about sixty-eight or sixty-nine, a short, stout, genial old fellow. With a record of thirteen offenses, he had spent most of his life in prison. When he was an infant, his father had failed in the textile business and sent him as an apprentice at a kimono store. After completing his term of service, he started his own fabrics business, only to suffer a terrific loss when the bottom dropped out on textile prices.

His first criminal act was a classic bag snatch. He set down a bundle of something wrapped up in a furoshiki atop someone's briefcase at a train station, then walked away with the bundle and the briefcase together. Overweight from youth, he could not run fast, so he made up for that with a nonchalant manner and leisurely way of walking. That was the pattern for all his subsequent thefts. As time went on, he became quite adroit at the game. He made a bottomless briefcase and developed a technique of placing it over some other briefcase at a train station and lifting it inside with a hook.

When he was in a good mood, he would give a demonstration of the maneuver. He used a blanket as his supposed briefcase, walking a little unsteadily, as if it was heavy. Then he set it down to take a rest in a place where there were many people. Casually, he set the blanket atop a pillow that represented a Boston bag. A moment later when he picked up his blanket, the pillow had disappeared from sight. His performance looked so much like a theft being committed that he got spontaneous applause. Although he was normally cheerful, this expression of admiration from his cellmates only made him downcast.

"It's a damn shame to be spending your life learning sly tricks. I started off honest, working hard at my trade. When that fell apart, I tried doing day labor, but I just don't have the right body for that kind of work. Next thing you know, I got a record and no one will hire me. It came down to stealing baggage. That was the only thing I could do. So it became my job."

"I know what you mean. A man can't live if he don't have a job."

A middle-aged fellow with fifteen offenses to his credit said this. He was a purse pickpocket who specialized in moving trains and only one single train station. He must have been in his mid-forties, but smooth features and light skin created a youthful effect that was emphasized by animated body language. He was left-handed, with long, slim fingers that were so limber they gave the impression of octopus arms when he flexed them. He used an audacious cover for his crimes. He would surreptitiously fondle women's bodies with his right hand while he extracted valuables from their handbags with his left.

"How come you only do women?" someone would ask. Once he answered, "Because men might get violent."

Another time he said, "When I was a kid, I had a fight with my stepmother and she told me to get out of the house, so I did. I've been a woman hater ever since.

"I'm very specialized. I only work Shinjuku Station. There are detectives that only work Shinjuku, too and one of them has busted me — I don't know — several times. He told me to go work some other station because he was getting sick of seeing me. I should do what he said, but for some reason, for me, it's got to be Shinjuku. I try some other station, and I can't bring myself to do anything. When I'm in Shinjuku, and its crowded, I can just go wandering around, and the next thing I know, my left hand goes for a dip in somebody's bag, all by itself."

The old bag snatcher was thunderstruck by this tale.

"That's amazing! You're some kind of genius — or your hand is, anyway. It took me weeks to invent my trick bag, work out the right technique, and polish my act before I got it working. And you just do it all just naturally. That's really something!"

With an envious look, the old man took Octopus Fingers' hand in his own and examined it carefully.

There was a fellow in his twenties who considered himself the only intellectual in the cell. He read one book after the next from the prison library. He wore eyeglasses, and, when he was poring over some Buddhist text, he did have the air of a scholar. He mostly stayed aloof from conversations, but we knew he was listening. The proof of that came one time when Octopus Fingers was saying, "You know, that what-do-you-call-it temple in Ueno," and without missing a beat, he interjected, "Kaneiji Temple, founded by the monk Tenkai during the Kanei era." That's how he earned the nickname "Scholar."

The scholar specialized in stealing books from research library collections. His father had been an army officer — I think he said a lieutenant general. When he found out I had been a sergeant, he suddenly approached me and started talking in a friendly way.

"I was born in Taiwan. My father was in the military. We had three maids. We were living a posh life. Then my father was killed by bandits and my mother died of grief. I wanted to get into a university, so I came to Japan. I became an apprentice to a tailoring business and went to night school in Kanda. One day, I shoplifted a book in a used bookstore and sold it to another used bookstore for a good price. After that, I learned how to put on a student uniform and go in university libraries, boost foreign language books and sell them to pawn shops. That kind of book is a hot item among pawn brokers around universities. Another gig I had was sneaking into dormitories or student boarding houses and lifting dictionaries or foreign books. Sometimes there would be watches or cash there too. It was pretty good business."

"You look the part. With those glasses, all you need is a student uniform, and anyone would think you're a student."

"It's not enough to just look the part. There's a lot you have to know, too. You need to be able to tell the difference between English, German and French, for one thing. Worse than that is picking up some of the stuff students talk about. You've got to sound the part too. It took a lot of study to do what I was doing." There was pride in the scholar's voice as he told me this.

"Do you need to know this stuff for business too?" I asked, looking at the book he had been reading with evident interest.

"Not that business," he said, with a slightly sheepish expression. "I'm too old to pass for a student anymore. The last time I went into a student dorm, I was hit with suspicious questions. They wanted to know where I came from because they didn't believe I was another student. I got out of there. Now I know better than to try passing for a student again."

All three of these thieves, the baggage snatcher, the octopus fingered pick-purse, and the scholar, had much in common. They were specialists who took pride in their work. They had invested efforts over time to hone their skills. That's why they could get along together well, even though none of them were generally prone to open up to others. They had contempt for the kind of thief who couldn't do any better than try to grab whatever wasn't being watched because he lacked any particular knowledge or skills. From that perspective, I was a worthless kind of thief. There was no pattern to my random crimes, and no skill had been required to commit them. When the scholar found out about my criminal background, he assumed a very serious expression and gave me a warning.

"You shouldn't imitate other people. You can't use somebody else's system. You need your own. Get your act to where nobody else can do it better than you. When you get there, you won't ever have to worry about keeping fed."

"Weren't you saying your act went out of business?" I asked.

"That's right. I need a new one. That's what I'm working on now. I sneak into temples and go after Buddhist statues and altar goods. I know dealers in used goods that will buy them."

"Is that why you're reading books on Buddhism?"

"Of course! You want to make money, you got to know what you're talking about," the scholar said and spat on the cover of his book, which was titled something like "Transcending Life and Death with Buddhism."

One thing that could disturb the tranquility in a cell that is a community of thieves is when it is joined by an inmate with a record of assaults or murders.

One day a big fellow, about 1.8 meters tall came in. When the elder baggage snatcher went to the toilet, he returned to find that his centrally located place had been taken over by the newcomer. The two men glared at one another for a moment.

"That's my place," the bag snatcher said.

"You don't say? They got a seat reservation system here?" The man folded his arms. A tattooed likeness of a gourd shone on the left arm.

"You ain't no stranger to what goes and what don't go on in here. We got a custom that says first-comer gets the good spot. That's my place."

Standing, the baggage-snatching elder was just a trifle higher than the seated man, but he held his ground — and it was the bigger man who gave in.

"Okay. I get it," he said, and moved to another spot.

The man with the gourd tattoo was a medium official in a gang from Fukagawa. His yakuza credential was a missing middle fingertip of the left hand. From what he said, he was an organization strong arm with a long history of run-ins with the police for assault or injury, but only two formal arrests. His current charge was the result of cocaine addiction. He had assaulted a doctor who refused to give him a cocaine injection, and then fled with a supply of cocaine ampules. He related this story in booming tones, evidently pleased with himself.

Rolling up a sleeve, he revealed an arm covered with countless black needle marks.

"When you get hooked on cocaine, you get to seeing little animals squirming around — like mice and frogs. They disappear when you shoot up. Trouble is when you're in the pen and them critters start swimming around your head, and you can't shoot up . . ."

The man enjoyed talking, and seemed to believe that everyone admired him. He talked nonstop, probably fancying himself in the role of cell oyabun. Had it been a prison for first offenders, he would easily have filled the basic qualifications, but things were different in the land of with long records. The situation got worse for the yakuza as the baggage snatcher, pick-purse, and even scholar studiously ignored him and began a conversation about women. Morosely, the yakuza approached me, sitting in a corner with my mouth shut.

"Ever try shooting up goodies?"

I was feeling no warmth for the guy, so I just said, "Nah."

"Well, it's a damn good kick. Tell you what, I'll fix you up when you get out of here. Just come around my organization."

"Once you get hooked, you can't stop and you get the agonies when you don't have the shit, right?"

"You get a badge when you're in the organization. It gets you all the shit you want. There's no worries."

He was clearly happy to have me to talk to. He taught me all about his organization. It fronted as an association of open-air stall vendors. He was part of the oyabun's guard detail that was sent out when there were turf wars and when it was time to collect protection fees from stall vendors. He also talked about a Model 94 Nambu pistol he said he had hidden.

When he had finally finished talking, the bag snatcher came over. "Just asking, but what's your skill set?"

The yakuza's expression indicated he didn't quite understand the question.

"A criminal with no skills is good for nothing."

Fuchu had a brisk turnover. Some inmates were paroled, others left when their terms were up, and there were always newcomers. There were also periodic rotations from cell to cell. You could be sent elsewhere if a guard was in a bad mood. It was common to see new faces in your cell. I don't remember all the names and all the faces of the men I shared a cell with. The most likely explanation for my being able to recall the bag snatching old man, the octopus fingered pick purse, and that big yakuza with the gourd tattoo is that they were in my cell when my stay at Fuchu began. To generalize, Fuchu was a den of thieves, as I said at the start. Or maybe a concentration camp for thieves would be a more apt way to put it.

Each individual was different, with a different personally and different things he could do. It was certainly common for pairs of inmates to face off in mutual hatred, but we were all tight when it came to dealing with guards. Even though guards watched us constantly, there was still a separate world among us that they knew little or nothing about.

Smoking was a common example of this. Cigarettes were always forbidden, but we had them in the cells anyway. The simplest way to get them was bribing underpaid young guards, but in most cases, cigarettes were smuggled over more complicated routes. If they were obtained from civilian contractors at work-shops, they would reach the cells by somehow circumventing the network of body inspections. Cigarettes stolen from desks or guards' pockets by prisoner assistants in storage rooms or the medical clinic would be distributed to cells by prisoners on meal delivery details. Individual cigarettes passed from hand to hand this way lacked the firmness they had when still fresh from the pack. Sometimes they arrived at their final destinations hardly more than limp scraps of paper twisted around loose strands of tobacco. No one knew the exact routes from end to end, but there was never even one informer at any stage. Informing was the lowest possible act, the one sure to earn a prisoner the intense hatred of his fellow inmates. No one considered trying it.

Prisoner solidarity maintained the integrity of cigarette traffic, but the profit motive moved it. Cigarettes had high value because, unlike other countries, Japan bans them in prisons, for some reason. Consequently, cigarettes take on the same value as hard cash. They can be used to purchase such necessities as towels, washbowls, soap, underwear and belts, or such forbidden items as hard candy, confections, sleeping pills, razor blades, or even metal files. In cold weather, cigarette traffic steps up to meet the demand for high priced items like fluffy new cotton padding or sweaters.

Of course, prisoners actually smoke cigarettes too. They enjoy the slightly ceremonial practice of passing around a cigarette inside the cell without guards catching on. It takes a light to make this pleasure possible. Matches being an extremely difficult commodity to obtain, alternative fire making methods are required.

You need to grind or chop up a piece of celluloid into powder. Get the celluloid from the earpiece to a pair of glasses or the bristles of a toothbrush or something else. Spread out some cotton from a futon, put the celluloid powder in the center, roll it up into a tube, then roll that up in a piece of straw matting from a tatami and tie it tight with string. Now you've got the tinder — the word for it is a "gori." You get the gori to spark by striking it hard against a block of wood. The thing that is commonly used for this purpose is the bottom of the wooded sandals provided for toilet use.

My father Ishizo used a similar method to make muzzle bombs for killing foxes. My heritage from him gets the credit for my gori-making ability, which was celebrated at Fuchu. Everyone would watch my deft fingers at work, noses twitching in anticipation of the aroma of tobacco smoke.

A lookout would be posted by the cell's observation window to observe guard movement during smoking sessions. The cigarette's owner got the first drag. Then he would pass it around. Etiquette required making sure not to get your spit on the end, and security required that you hold the smoke in your lungs long enough for most of it to be absorbed so that only light smoke emerged when you exhaled. Because everyone observed these precautions, there was nothing to make the guard catch on when he looked through the window. He couldn't smell anything because the air holes in the door were too few and too small. The bad ventilation of cells was in this case an advantage.

I suppose the main reason for smoking was that it was banned. I can't think of any other explanation. Passing around the fag was resistance to the authorities that brought a feeling of pride in belonging to an underground. It was a ceremony as well, that no prisoner could very well forego, even if he had been a nonsmoker on the outside. This ceremony brought a smile that bespoke solidarity and contempt for the guards. Everyone participated in the rite for the pleasure of wearing that smile.

Cigarettes were stolen and smoked for the same reason the forbidden fruit was stolen and eaten. Violation of a taboo brings satisfaction. The pain that caused the scar on my index finger notwithstanding, I had a long career as a thief because I sought the joy of violating the laws banning theft.

If you get caught smoking in prison, you are punished for breaking the rules and disturbing the prison order. Why do they have punishable rules in prison for acts that aren't punishable on the outside? Many of the rules are arbitrary. Someone makes up a rule, it's adopted, and it becomes a part of the crime paradigm. In the Bible story, the rule was set out by God.

It's forbidden to possess cigarettes in prison. This rule was imposed in 1941. Disobeying orders, assault, battery, arguing, theft, possessing unauthorized articles, defacing property, reclining at unauthorized times, communicating with other cells, lewd behavior, engaging in games similar to gambling (gambling being impossible because prisoners have no money), non-performance of labor, making unauthorized articles, malicious slander, incitement, planning to escape, and other acts, among them, possession of cigarettes, are all prohibited.

Every rule violation that the state has specified actually occurs. As an example, take the rule forbidding the unauthorized making of articles. There is a flourishing practice among prisoners of fashioning miniature *geta* and *zori* as small as matchsticks, called geso. They would filch the wood from the woodworking shop and get silk thread from the tailoring shop and stitch in the thong, so small you need a magnifying glass to see it. It would take at least a month to make one pair. A well-made pair would have currency value, like cigarettes.

A more bizarre form of unauthorized craftsmanship was the embedding of beads in the foreskin. Inmates would polish beads of glass or celluloid, two to five millimeters in diameter, and implant them under their foreskins. The objectives were to increase size and sensitivity. Performing the operation on oneself under the gaze of cellmates was a way of proving one's daring. One incidental advantage to this practice was that men wearing a number of these beads would sometimes remove one for use in a gori when no other source of celluloid was at hand. It was very handy to have this source available. The demand for those beads increased as plastic came to replace celluloid in manufactured goods.

Some prisoners would implant a bead to commemorate the start of their term when they first came to the prison. A more elaborate system of using beads to record prison stays was to use smaller beads for short term detentions and larger ones for long terms. That made it possible to do sums of prison terms by touch. Inmates skilled at making implants were in great demand. They could do a thriving business.

The "lewd behavior" rule was about sex between inmates. I had already experienced that in the Aioi shipyard. It is no easy matter to have sex in a prison, where guards frequently conduct inspections. Inmates took it as a challenge to be met, and they often succeeded. In Fuchu, sex was impossible in cells. Guards kept strict watch through the night to ensure that the mandated spaces between sleeping prisoners were maintained. During the day as well, there were no blind spots in cells safe from the guards' watch.

Opportunities came during time in the workshops. The shop floor itself was no good because it was always under watch, but storehouses and toilets offered the possibility. There was a case of fleeting moments seized while kitchen operations were suspended for cleaning of the water tank. And there was the bath. As an example, I will tell of my own experience.

Mild breezes were bringing in the scent of plum blossoms from somewhere far away. Buds on trees in the prison courtyard were swelling by the day, and so were the carnal interests of the prison inhabitants. All the young inmates were already someone's anko. The inmates' own code of conduct placed them out of bounds to everyone else. No prospective outlet for my carnal interests was available.

As the days went by, frustration swirled around my head like spring haze. Then a slim young boy came into the cell. He was good looking, though a bit dark. I lost no time engaging him in conversation. Then I gave him cigarettes, a towel, soap, and a few geso that were up to prison currency standards. Soon we were on familiar terms. He responded positively when he realized he was the object of my ardor. All we needed was an opportunity. We strategized that the bath would be the scene of our love's consummation.

If you imagine that a prison bath chamber is like your neighborhood bath house, you have it all wrong. The prison bath is run like a factory assembly line that moves the inmates through the process quickly and efficiently. You start in an undressing room, where prison clothes go onto shelves that are rotated through a door in the wall and dumped out into a separate dressing room. There are ten bathtubs in five columns of two, used by one man at a time. The guard's stand is in the middle, at the far wall. Inmates wait their turn in single files, each holding a towel and soap. When your turn comes, you get into the first bath. The next phase is your rubbing and scrubbing time, and you'd better hustle if you want a thorough wash, because the time is short until you take the place of the man taking his post-scrub soak in bath number two. You take his place while he moves on to the drying off station.

Everyone changes places together, on command from the guard. You get five minutes at each stage. There are ten men in each line, for a total of fifty naked men moving through the bath chamber as the rumbling boiler pours out steam. It is an impressive, one-of-a-kind spectacle. The men are all of ages and sizes, although, of course, you are only supposed to see the back of the one ahead of you, which may be adorned with a tattoo for your admiration.

I exchanged glances with the boy and we joined the line farthest from the guard. I had paid out a tidy sum in cigarettes and pairs of geso for the services of two accomplices: a big man standing nearby was to act as our "shield" by blocking the guard's view as best he could, and another who was game to put his chutzpah to the test by distracting the guard's attention. (That role is called the "curtain.") At the proper moment, he was to start singing a pop tune of the day, "Tokyo Boogie-Woogie," in a loud voice.

I began the mating ritual in line for bathtub number one by stroking my partner's anus to dispel tension. At the washing station I applied Vaseline. "Tokyo Boogie-Woogie" began as we stood in line for the second bathtub and I was I making my entrance. I vaguely saw the guard reprimanding the singing inmate. I breathed easily, feeling assured my activity was under good cover. The inmates around us were playing dumb. My excitement rose. Together the boy and I slipped into a separate world. Then the guard was upon me, shouting an order to desist immediately. His face was a study in self-righteous fury.

Too late, I realized my planning had overlooked a crucial element. Our escapade should have been scheduled under the watch of a young, inexperienced guard, thus avoiding the kind of guard like the one who was raking me over the coals as I stood naked before him. The man clearly had sufficient job experience to recognize a ruse and go looking for what was being covered up.

I was given solitary detention with no reading privileges for three weeks and no compensation for work performed. To that, they added cancellation of early release on parole, meaning I would have to serve my full term. The conditions also meant that I would be penniless upon my release. Had there been a possibility of getting an early release I would have been a submissive prisoner, but under these circumstances I soon grew accustomed to being passively disobedient. Guards said that kind of prisoner had the "short-timer attitude." Of course they didn't like it, and of course I assumed it, but only to the extent that I could rebel without incurring fresh penalties. My resistance was a matter of not giving answers during inspections, doing a sloppy job of folding up my futon, not performing my work properly, speaking in a loud voice, etc.

When there were just ten days remaining of my prison term I found that fate had arranged for me an offer of employment upon my release from none other than the middle aged pickpocket with the octopus-like fingers. He was also up for release, only a few days before me.

"Got any work waiting for you when you get out?" he asked me.

"No. There's no way I would."

"What do you think about teaming up with me?"

"You mean for some of this?" I asked, crooking my index finger into a hook shape, meaning thievery.

"That's it. You have the touch for my kind of work, you're quick on your feet and you got the balls to bait a guard — you'd be a natural."

"I don't know. I've never done that kind of thing."

"I'll teach you. We'll start from the basics. Anybody who can make a pair of geso like you won't have any problems learning."

"How do you work? Two-man team?"

"Three man — one more guy's our tool. If it comes to a trial, the story is we all worked alone, but it's actually teamwork."

"Okay, I'll think about it."

"Uh-uh. I told you that much because I need an answer right now. I'm out of here today. I'll go do what I have to do to take you in. I'll be waiting for you."

The part about taking me in hit a soft spot. I didn't have anywhere else to go. I thought I might as well go along and see what happened.

They turned me loose on the last day of May 1950. I walked out of Fuchu Prison wearing the same old railway workers uniform I had been wearing in Shinjuku three years and three months before. I wasn't quite penniless. I had slightly over two hundred yen on me, which the state had kindly given me as carfare for visits to the Japan Rehabilitation Aid Association.

The moment the iron doors of the prison closed behind me, I felt as if the density of the atmosphere had changed. It was like being left atop a high mountain, where the air was thin and hard to breathe. The long road lined with keyaki trees, heavy with green branches, was just as I had seen it the previous summer from the window of the prisoner transport bus. I was about to give a servile greeting to a group of approaching guards in uniform, then laughed at myself when I realized that was no longer necessary.

I was waiting at the front gate bus station for the bus to National Railways Kokubunji Station, as I had been told to do. A man short enough to still be a child was standing there too. He suddenly addressed me.

"Would you be Mr. Atsuo Yukimori? Boss G. sent me." He gave a bow of his head.

"G." was the name the octopus-fingered pick-purse went by. I nodded and the man told me to call him Yasu. Besides being short, he was thin. His face was dusky and angular. His earlobes and nose were pointy, and seemed bony. He smoked the short cigarette brand, revealing nicotine-stained teeth. He would smoke a cigarette greedily down to a tiny butt, manipulating it with wiry, nicotine-stained fingers. He might have been thirty, the same as me, or perhaps younger; I couldn't tell.

Yasu escorted me to Shinjuku, which had sprouted many impressive storefronts in the three years I had been away. There was no more black market on the main streets. We went into a used clothing store on a back street and Yasu bought me a full business suit, a necktie and three white shirts. He had me change clothes there in the store. In prison, they had let me start growing out my hair before my release, but it was still short. The image that started back at me in the dressing booth mirror looked like someone on a sports team.

Next, Yasu brought me to a cheap apartment near Shin-Okubo Station. It was a single four-and-a-half mat room that was poorly lit by a small window facing another apartment scarcely one meter away. Yasu brought in a cheap futon and pillow from somewhere. He said the cost of the clothes, the futon and the apartment was all a loan from G.

Shortly thereafter, the great man showed up. G. was dressed in a suit and soft cap that looked like a corporate uniform.

"Hey, great to see 'ya! Been looking forward to this."

"Thanks. I appreciate all this stuff," I said, fingering my lapel.

"Don't mention it. We got work to do. That'll cover it," he said, flexing his long, pale fingers. Then he got down to business.

"Atsu, you're going to be the shield. All you have to do is plant that big carcass of yours in front of the customer. Yasu is the draw — he draws the customer's attention to him while I do the job. Let's just start with that for beginners. If the heat's around, I wrinkle my forehead, like this."

Our first customer was a broad beamed lady who got on the train from Shinjuku Station, both hands full with bags of things she had bought. Her handbag was on her left shoulder. As the train went into motion, she was looking in vain up and down the car for an empty seat. When the train opened its doors at Shibuya Station, she hustled to get a seat that had opened up, but Yasu beat her to it by a hair. While she was throwing an envious expression at him sitting there, G.'s fingers went into her handbag before my eyes and extracted a coin purse. The handbag made an audible snap when he closed it, causing the woman to look back, but she couldn't find anything out of the ordinary. By the time she got off the train at Shinagawa Station, G. had already discarded her coin purse, after extracting the cash it held.

The effortless success of the first job had me thinking that picking pockets was easy work, but I soon realized I was wrong. As I approached the woman we had marked as our second customer, she regarded me with open aversion and clutched her handbag tightly. Number three ran to claim an open seat just as G.'s hand was homing in on her handbag. Number four had to be passed up due to the proximity of a detective. By the time number five had been selected we were swamped by an evening rush hour crowd that interfered with our ability to stake out positions for a joint operation. By then I was able to appreciate why the first customer had been a success. Both her hands were full, G. and I were able to get on either side of her, a vacant seat suddenly appeared in front of her and when she lunged for it, G. moved fast enough to do the job before she regained stability. All those random events had to happen in the right order to create that brief moment for G. to spring into action without her catching on. Such a confluence of fortuitous random events is naturally rare. The day ended with only that one initial success. Half the take went to G. and the other half was split fifty-fifty between Yasu and me.

We went to work every day. In addition to working inside moving railway cars, we worked crowds on train platforms. We stayed away from Shinjuku Station because it had at least one detective who would recognize G. Another consideration was that it would be too conspicuous for the three of us to be seen together day after day. We decided on breaking up and working individually every third day. Any profits we made on those days were all for ourselves. Yasu set out with high ambitions on those days. Being short, it was natural for him to specialize in women's handbags. He was proving himself a pro in the field by showing respectable profits at the day's end. But as for me, I was not being successful at all as a would-be pickpocket working alone. I tried to imitate G., but my hand just would not take on a life of its own as his would.

It took two or three months of utter frustration before I began to form an image about who my natural customers were. The number one consideration was finding a customer the same height as me. G. targeted women's handbags because he was short and women's bags were most likely to be within his easy reach. Those explanations he gave when were in the can together, that "men might get violent" and "taking revenge on women" seemed to be just made-up stuff, not a real reason. The real reason was the same as for why Yasu went after women's handbags: they were in the right place for him to reach. That being the case, I was too tall for that. For my height, men were the natural target.

Men keep their wallets in the inner pockets of their business jackets — or at least many of them do. Of those, two-thirds put the wallet in the right-hand pocket, so they can pull out the wallet with the left hand and use the right hand to extract bills from it. Very well. Now how do I extract that wallet from that right hand inner pocket? Of course I have to face the customer's right side while supposedly reading a newspaper in my left hand (the newspaper is doing what is called a "forward shutout") while I do the job with my right hand. The operation is a matter of supporting the bottom of the wallet and slowly easing it all the way up until it falls from the pocket, then catching it under the jacket hem with the same hand. G. explained the procedure to me and I practiced with a jacket on a dummy made of a rolled up futon. Sometimes there is a button on the inner pocket. There is a technique for undoing it that involves pinching the fabric, but I was unable to master it, so I just resolved to give up when I encountered a closed button.

Autumn winds had begun to blow and business suits were everywhere when I set out on my first campaign. Three months experience had taught me the importance of finding the right amount of crowding on a train station platform or inside a train car. The "right amount" means enough room to approach your customer or flee if necessary, but crowded enough that it is impossible for anyone at a distance to observe what you are doing. The right conditions occur somewhere in between the midday hours when relatively few people are using the trains and the height of the rush hours.

The morning rush had eased, the big execs were on their way to work, and crowding conditions were favorable. Dressed in my business commuters' outfit, I pretended to read a financial newspaper. I spotted a likely customer. His face had an alcohol induced flush. He yawned repeatedly as he read a banner ad hanging above, to his left. He was grasping the hand strap with his right hand, leaving his jacket front flapping open. I went to work without hesitation. He had a smooth leather wallet that rose and then went into free fall almost by itself. I just barely caught it in time and slipped it into my pocket.

The gentleman put his hand to his breast pocket. He was suddenly desperate, realizing his wallet was gone. But it never occurred to him that the thief who took it was standing in front of him. He was lost in thought about where he could have dropped it, but I was too absorbed in reading my newspaper to notice him. I got off at the next stop, walking at my leisure. I discarded the wallet in a public lavatory. The take was sumptuous: One hundred thousand yen.

That was my initiation to the ranks of the professional criminal. Now I inhabited the realm where the city presented itself inside out before my eyes.

Order in the city follows rules of ownership. Every house has an owner, people wear clothes they own and carry around their own money. The rules give people a sense of security — that no one will sneak into their homes and steal their property, that they can walk about the city and not be attacked by someone bent on stealing their property, lives, or dignity. Nevertheless, criminals lay in wait just outside those homes, so peacefully bathed in sunlight, as the people of the city go about their shopping in confidence.

To the criminal, a home is there to be snuck into and plundered; doors and locks on a house are obstacles to be broken; valuables are meant to be stolen; any person who stands between you and your objective naturally deserves to die like a noisome cockroach; women exist to be raped and ladies and gentlemen who have money are charitable providers of donations.

I do not mean to suggest that criminals are all the same, that you needn't think of any one as being different than another. Quite the contrary — there are some points in common, but not many. From my prison experience, I know that one striking aspect of criminality is that people who commit crimes are stubbornly resistant to simple classification by their traits. G., Yasu, and I were three entirely different people. It is unfortunately common for people to discuss groups of fellow human beings about whom they know little as if they were all the same, be it mentally ill people, Americans, or criminals. The mistaken belief is that the supposed traits of the group define the individual.

My only point about criminals has to do with the professionalism of the true criminal who considers himself a specialist in some well-defined type of work. Whatever his specialty is, he pretty much sticks with it, whether it's burglary, shoplifting, baggage snatching, or picking pockets. There is an unwritten code among true criminals that one specialist does not intrude upon the territory of another.

My gang of three under G. as oyabun abided by that principle. Our exclusive territory was railway cars and station buildings. In other words, we were hakoshi. We considered our skills and experiences second to none in our field.

G. was explicit about his professional pride. A fence that usually handled goods we appropriated once showed him an elegantly crafted piece of hardware that he said came from Osaka. It was a tiny knife designed to be worn concealed between the fingers, for use in cutting fabric. A tool like that would eliminate the need for the extremely difficult art of undoing buttons. G. flatly declared he would have no part of it.

"The only tools I use are my fingertips. I take things from pockets, but I would never damage the clothing of a valued customer."

Another principle G. lived by was not to work any more than you needed to. "A pickpocket should never have too much money on him. If he does and gets busted, it's his loss," is the way he put it.

G. didn't tell us where he lived or what his life was like away from the job, but it was possible to piece together an image from things he was wont to say. It seemed that he had a house, wife, and children. If we had a good day's take, he might declare that he would be taking the next three days off. On those occasions, we were free to work any way we liked, without his interference. The only directive he gave was "When you get busted you don't tell the names of your buddies."

When we worked together, I called G. boss, followed his orders, and left to him the work of selling off goods we stole. I did not, however, use any particular honorifics when addressing him. We were equals in speech, and when we went drinking and eating together, the rule was that everyone paid his own bill. In other words, we were mere acquaintances when we weren't together on the job, and not even particularly close acquaintances. If we were working and knocked off for lunch, he would go off by himself somewhere and show up again later.

G. enjoyed drinking. One night Yasu and I had a chance encounter with him at some bar in Shinjuku. He was drunk and red in the face. We pretended not to see him, and he didn't join us.

Having been in the same cell with G. in Fuchu, I knew his real name, but from the time I joined up with him, I never called him by any name other than G. or let on that I knew more. The fences in the black markets of Asakusa and Ikébukuro also knew him only as "Mr. G." Their manner indicated they had long been accustomed to dealing with him.

Yasu and I frequented establishments in the barracks that still remained around the west exit of Shinjuku station and the blue line quarter to the east of the station. We often discussed G. on those occasions.

"How old do you think he is?" I asked.

"I don't know. Past thirty, I guess."

"He ain't in his thirties. I'm thirty-one. That guy's got at least ten years on me, I'd say."

"He don't have a single gray hair."

"He's young-looking, but you can see deep wrinkles. I would guess he's forty-five."

"Eh, that old?" The startled voice had jumped a good two octaves. Yasu's pointy ears seemed to quiver. Because his voice was naturally high, he normally held it down, but it would soar uncontrollably on certain occasions. By then I knew that Yasu had been born in 1930. He was twenty years old and looked ten years older.

"Where did you meet him?"

"Met him in Shinjuku," Yasu said, his eyes narrowing. Teaming up with G. was an event of a lifetime to this skinny little man. Yasu liked to tell of the encounter. Though its details would vary as he embellished the story upon retelling, here is the basic outline.

"The March tenth air raid made me an orphan. I went to relatives in Yamanashi, but they didn't even bother hiding that they didn't really want me around. I couldn't take that. When the war ended, I came to Shinjuku and got by shoplifting and snatching stuff. I didn't want to get mixed up with yakuza black market rackets like the Otsu and Wada gangs were running, so I basically stayed with grabbing what I could get around sales stands in department stores. Just take stuff and run. Short guys like me can get away with that kind of thing if they're fast, which I am. So, one day I was in the basement of Isétan. I glommed on to an old lady's change purse and went zooming up the stairs. 'til then, I would be home free once I got that far, but this time somebody was on my tail. Thought it was a guard, but I got to the door and no bust. I ran outside and headed toward Sankocho, still running, and that's where somebody grabbed me by the wrist."

Yasu reenacted the event by taking his right wrist by the left hand and pulling it up to eye level. "When he grabbed it and raised it up like that, there was no way to shake him off. My hand felt like it was inside some kind of rubber trap. It was creepy."

"Like an octopus wrapped an arm around it?"

"I never thought of it that way, but, yeah, that's it. Once it puts those suckers on, they don't come off easy. Anyway, it was G. Here's this good-looking guy, you could almost mistake for a broad, but he's fast as hell, and strong too. I was thinking, Okay, I give up — Here, I'll give you the damn change purse. I look in my pocket and it's not there. G. not only got it away from me; he'd already dumped it somewhere, and I never saw a thing. And that's not all. He lifted my wallet besides.

"Then he starts giving me a sermon, starting in with what a bum I was. I got no technique, no timing, no planning, no control, he says. Then he gets into the main message — the art of stealing. If a thing is worth stealing, he says, it's a job for an artist."

"'The art of stealing.' He says that a lot."

"Yeah. That's the great thing about G. Being artistic . . . That's what I wanted. The first thing I ever shoplifted was a book. A novel, to be exact. Every novel I really wanted to read I stole. Next time, come up to my place and I'll show you. Got lots of books. Not to brag, but I shoplifted every one . . . Anyway, I went to work for G. He taught me everything, right from the start. Back then, there were two others. We were a four-man hakoshi team."

"Where are those two now?"

"Slammer. They'll probably be back, by and by. I was up three times myself. Did all three stretches in juvenile prison. What about you?"

"Got three priors."

"Okay! That's championship class."

We went on drinking shochu, well satisfied with one another. Yasu's voice went higher still as it steeped in alcohol, until it verged on screeching. Small as he was, being drunk with a dark red face was no obstacle to his penchant for adding rich detail to narratives of his exploits. His walk was not even a bit unsteady as we roamed from bar to bar.

One night I took Yasu's invitation to visit his apartment. As advertised, he had a library of impressive size. The bookshelves dominated the room. Nearly every volume was a novel. I hadn't been prepared to believe he had been able to shoplift a large collection of books, but a look at its sheer size was persuasive. He never had the kind of money it would have taken to buy a tenth that many books.

Surrounded by his many books, Yasu's eloquence rose to greater heights. He spoke of each title as if introducing a close friend. In this way, I came to hear the names of authors of literature and the titles of their works. Encouraged by Yasu, I read one novel after the next. At first, I was leery of the books. The texts were strewn with unfamiliar kanji. I had to keep leafing through previously read pages because I couldn't remember who the different characters were. Progress was slow. In both elementary school and aircraft mechanics school, just trying to keep up with the textbooks had kept me so completely occupied that there was no room for any other kind of reading. I would keep giving up on a novel and then going back to it. Somewhere along the way I started to find that reading had a way of infusing me with memorable ideas that made the effort seem worthwhile. Ultimately, I was reading novels for hours on end. It was time well spent, and nice to have as an alternative to going out drinking or whoring.

My preferred novels depicted the war. Having participated in the war in a role that consisted primarily of killing people, I was interested to see how others described what was going on at the time.

War literature was the product of strong anti-military sentiment that arose after the war. The novels did a thorough job of showing what is bad about that hierarchical organization called an army. They cast the officers and NCOs as heavies to be criticized for being militarism personified. The protagonists were invariably opposed to the war. They participated only because they had no other choice.

After reading many of those novels, disappointment began to creep in.

I don't assume that the protagonist of a novel is none other than the novel's author. War literature is usually written from a point of view that makes it easy for the reader to identify with the central characters, but at the expense of neglecting fundamental issues. The novels focus on privileged kinds of men who found themselves in the army. They had the benefit of higher education, so they are a little better informed and a little more able to take a critical view of things than the other troops. They hate the war and anticipate Japan's defeat. Surrounded by Japanese who support the war from the bottom of their hearts, they look down on that vast majority, keep their mouths shut and suffer in silence.

Much is made of the bravery of Japanese troops in the war. But if a man had an informed perspective on the doomed war effort but declined to share it with others, even though he understood that prolonging the war was causing unnecessary death and suffering to his own people, I would call that cowardly.

I don't deny my own cowardice. I know as well as anyone that back then, the surest way to finding yourself jacked up by military police and being labeled a spy was to say anything that smacked of disapproval of the war. That was undeniably a practical reason for ordinary people not to speak out, but it is equally undeniable that the failure of knowledgeable people to speak out was non-resistance to a war that we can now justifiably call criminal. There is no need to condemn people in the past for that. The important thing now is to know how it came to be that nobody could resist the march to self-destruction.

War literature for the most part continues to keep mum about the massacres and abusive treatment of the inhabitants in the countries we invaded, even though they were a very common occurrence. The army killed and plundered on a vast scale, but the novelists don't write much about it. Instead, they write about protagonists who are models of purity and victimized by the militarists. It seemed to me that stuff was distorting the realities of the war.

It annoyed me that the authors of all these war novels didn't seem to realize or care that their characters lacked consciences. I reached the conclusion that such novels have little value. My enthusiasm for novels waned as I came to realize they are just a bunch of lies that the novelist makes up at his own convenience. That did not dampen the enthusiasm for reading I picked up from Yasu, however. I just became more discriminating about which books I selected.

Autumn winds were blowing cold enough that people were beginning to turn out in overcoats. That kind of dress interfered with my work. G. and Yasu could get on without regard to the season, but I was suffering from a lack of customers. I suppose I let it make me become overanxious. That was a fatal mistake.

I was glumly surveying my fellow passengers inside a moving train. As far as I was concerned, I might as well have been standing in a department store among racks of overcoats. Then I noticed a man in a suit who filled the bill perfectly for my purposes. He was a white-haired, refined looking gentleman who might have been an important executive somewhere. He seemed to be the type that is oversensitive to warm environments. Even without an overcoat, perspiration was visible on his forehead. There was a bulge in his right inner pocket that looked like a fat wallet. I let the flow of passengers ease me close to him. The gentleman held the hand strap in his right hand while reading a book in his left hand. I could not have asked for better positioning. I eased the wallet upward. The moment I caught it as it fell, there was a cold sensation on my wrist. It was a gleaming silver handcuff. I should have been suspicious about such an ideal customer. The gentleman was a detective working as a pickpocket decoy.

Back in Fuchu Prison, a guard I knew frowned with disapproval. "You back again, Yukimori?"

"Thought I'd come visit. It's wonderful to see you again," I said in the servile tone of the model prisoner, while smiling a submissive smile.

"How long were you out?"

"Six months."

"They gave you three years this time?"

"The sentences get longer for repeat offenders."

"Well, you're one of the hardcore crooks now — the guys who've been in the can longer than they've been out in the world."

After placement in a fourth-class community cell, I reflected on the guard's words, feeling bitterly remorseful. He was quite right. In the seven years since being arrested for going AWOL, I had been a free man in normal society for a grand total of about eighteen months. My life was being spent in prison, with occasional interludes on the outside. I was a hardened criminal, with four offenses to my credit, a man who stole other people's property without hesitation. I knew theft was a punishable offense, but the notion that the act is wrong had disappeared from my mind. The prosecutor of my last offense had lectured me about this. Stealing is wrong. Reflect on that, listen to your own conscience telling you it is wrong, he said. His words persuaded me of precisely nothing. Apparently, the dream in my previous incarceration of my heart falling from my chest had indeed been about my conscience. It wouldn't fit back inside because I had turned into a completely wrong-side-out human being.

My life proceeded from one rigorously timed event to the next, every day, without variation.

06:00	Get up, clean cell, wash up, stand inspection
06:30	Exit cell, strip search, march to work (auto shop, same as last term)
07:00	Breakfast
07:30	Start Work
09:50 — 10:00	Break
11:50	Lunch
12:30	Resume Work
14:50 — 15:00	Break
16:30	Stop work, strip search, march back to cell, supper
17:30	Stand inspection (After this the radio goes on until lights out)
21:00	Sleep (Dec. 1–March 31: OK to lie down after 1900)

All three meals are eaten in the cell on days off from work.

Time flew by under this completely unchanging daily routine. This prison term was quite unlike the previous one due to my enthusiasm for reading during free time. I absorbed myself in books from the prison library while cellmates had conversations and the radio played popular songs or baseball games. I didn't mind being the cell heretic, even when other prisoners intruded by commenting to me in loud voices or reading my book over my shoulder. What did bother me was that the prison library didn't have many of the books I wanted to read: modern history and books about the war. Most of the collection consisted of books on religion and poetry.

I presented myself to the other prisoners as a common thief and kept quiet about being a pickpocket. I took a certain pride in having lived beyond the young first-timers who liked to boast of the jobs they pulled off. This was the period when I met a lone wolf pickpocket named Ginji Sato. He had an incredible facility for "badge unpinning." That means undoing the button on the inside pocket of someone's jacket, extracting the wallet inside the pocket and re-buttoning the pocket, all in one pass. Veteran pickpocket that G. was, he couldn't do that. Being an inner pocket specialist was a skill I very much wanted to acquire.

I ingratiated myself with Ginji, calling him "boss" at every opportunity and doing what I could to persuade him to give me a lesson. I suppose he regarded me as a complete novice. He was relatively amiable about showing me the essentials of badge unpinning. The knowledge wasn't enough, though. My body wouldn't absorb it, however much I practiced. It was a rare gift Ginji had been endowed with by nature. One day Ginji mistakenly lifted a guard's pocket notebook when he had been after cigarettes. He was quickly caught and put into solitary. That was the last I saw of him until we met again fifteen or sixteen years later, on a day in mid-October 1968. It was about three days before I went with you to Shinjuku. He was riding the National Railways and picking pockets, as usual.

I worked at maintaining a distance from other inmates, avoiding fights, and not breaking rules. In the shop, I was industrious. In other words, I did all that I could to appear to the guards as a hard worker with a good record and good behavior, so they would label me a model prisoner.

For my trouble, two years and six months later, my parole was approved six months before my term was fully served. I walked from the front gate of Fuchu Prison one morning in June 1953, under an overcast sky.

Parole comes with strict requirements: get a respectable job, don't associate with disreputable people and pay a visit to your probation office for an interview. I intended to do that until the moment I stepped outside the prison gates. From then on, survival depended on resuming work as a pickpocket. I wanted to meet up with G. and Yasu as soon as possible. Just as I had undergone instant conversion to model prisoner when I re-entered Fuchu, departure instantly converted me back to a hardcore criminal.

I arranged to meet up with G. through a fence in Ikébukuro, according to a longstanding arrangement. I wasn't waiting long before Yasu showed up, grinning and ears twitching.

"Yo! Good to have you back!"

"How's everyone?"

"G.'s the same as ever. I got busted and did a one-year stretch in Urawa. One of the boys is back. A guy named Ono. He said he was in Fuchu. Did you bump into him?"

"I'd need to know a little more than just 'Ono.'"

As before, we found an apartment for me near Shin-Okubo Station. Then I went to a coffee shop in Shinjuku to meet up with my coworkers: a slightly older version of G., who had the same gang boss gravity as ever, and I got to meet Ono. My first impression of him was that he had a square face that didn't look very nice. He was about my age, past thirty. Since we were both just back from Fuchu, we got as far as exchanging smiles. It looked as if we would get along fine.

We started plying our trade inside a local commuter train, which felt like a steam bath in the muggy weather. I wore a business suit provided by G. My first customer was an expensively dressed woman carrying a dazzling lizard-skin handbag. While she was casting a suspicious look at swarthy little Yasu, G. got her wallet and quickly passed it to Ono, who handed it off to me. As I slipped it into my pocket, a man shouted "Pickpocket!" He was standing next to the women — he was probably her husband. A sweaty smell emanated from the middle-aged man's white shirt as he pointed to me.

"I saw you! You put her wallet in your pocket!"

"Please stop making wild accusations," I said, determined to bluff it out. Unfortunately, my voice had a nervous edge.

In the meantime, the woman was checking her handbag. She confirmed that the wallet was gone. Three male passengers grabbed my arms. One recovered the wallet from my pocket. The next thing I knew, Ono had given me a resounding slap in the face.

"You're the thief! You are under arrest for flagrant commission of robbery!" Ono said this as he clamped a pair of handcuffs to my wrists. The three men withdrew, leaving me in custody of the supposed detective. He dragged me off the train at the next station and we melted into the crowd.

"You're badly out of practice!" Ono said, removing the toy handcuffs.

"Yeah, my touch went dead on me. Spent too much time taking apart car engines." I nodded to Ono, showing him a look of gratitude. Instead of thinking he didn't look nice, I should have realized his broad jaw, thick lips, and surly expression made him a dead ringer for a policeman. I had seen countless examples of that type of face. It was no wonder the train passengers had taken him for a detective.

In two or three weeks I was again comfortable in my work, including the days when I worked independently and could keep the entire day's gains. When I had enough money, I stayed away from work and spent most of the time reading. On those days I would go to the public library in Naitomachi because it would look suspicious to be in my apartment during the day. Nights would be spent drinking and walking along the blue line quarter near Hanazono Shrine (or "Golden Lane" as it is now called). Insofar that I had work, leisure and amusement, my life was stable — almost, but not quite the same as normal people working at honest jobs, when their work is going along well.

From the time I realized that novels, especially war novels, only deceived readers for the benefit of the authors, I kept away from them and developed a fondness for history and nonfiction works about the war. I would refer to maps as I read, to heighten the effect of being on the scene. I rediscovered the enthusiasm I had for geography in elementary school. I wanted to travel, not only throughout Japan, but throughout the world. One day, I told myself, I will realize that dream.

One afternoon I picked a copy of the Bible from a bookshelf. What attracted me about it was not the text, but the maps of Israel and Egypt. It was an easily understandable, colloquial translation. I found myself enjoying it, and shortly after I was hooked. I spent about two weeks reading straight through from Genesis through Revelations of St. John. It was very interesting stuff. Countless villains turn up. There is plenty of killing, stealing, slander — exactly the same stuff that goes on right now. I especially liked the story of how human history starts in the garden of Eden with one of God's apples being stolen.

It was a case of theft because God claimed the apples as his property and forbade humans to touch them. The only reason Eve took an apple was for the fun of violating the prohibition, or so it seems to me. Why did God declare apples off limits to people? I think because he knew that of all the things humans might do that they shouldn't, the most probable would always be some form of stealing. God strongly asserted his own existence by demonstrating that stealing is the fundamental human vice. It finally came to me that the whole purpose of the Bible is to keep reaffirming God's presence by staying unwaveringly on the theme of the long, sordid history of human thievery.

Unfortunately, pitifully, I was a thief — a professional pickpocket, to be precise — evil, forsaken by God, and ripe for punishment.

I began to get strange feelings immediately after I had read through the Bible. While I was preparing to lift someone's wallet I felt as if I was being watched.

The observer was not a detective, nor was it anything awesome like God's gaze. It might be best described as the searching look of ordinary people toward an object of disdain. In other words, I had changed. Theft was no longer coming to me naturally. I was hesitant about doing it, as if having pangs of conscience. Ono was the one who quickly recognized that something was up with me.

"Atsu, are you feeling okay? You seem a little heavy handed lately."

"Is that how it looks? I've always been kind of clumsy anyway."

"Clumsy you ain't. Normally, you're the fastest of us. You need to have more confidence. That's something you can't do without in our business." Disaster hit just after this exchange with Ono.

We were inside a train approaching Shinjuku Station. G. pulled a red wallet from a shoulder bag on a tall girl in trousers and passed it to me. I thought I had it, but it dropped to the floor. It rested half-open next to G.'s feet, bright red and conspicuous as could be. Fortunately, the young woman was oblivious. I was trying to think of a way to recover it when a middle-aged lady sitting in front of me spoke to the young woman.

"You dropped your wallet. At least, I guess it must be yours."

Clearly at a loss to understand how her wallet could have possibly fallen to the ground, the young woman picked it up with a suspicious look, then realized the zipper on her shoulder bag was open. She turned her suspicious glare to G., standing beside her with a blank expression. About two beats later, a pair of men approached from roughly five meters down the aisle. They virtually smelled like detectives. The older one of the two addressed the young woman.

"You run into a pickpocket ma'am?"

"He's the one who took it," the middle-aged woman said, looking at G. The detective unhesitatingly clamped a handcuff on G's wrist.

"At it again, are ya' . . ." he said, using G.'s real name.

Having lost G., Ono took over as our provisional boss, but his skill level wasn't really up to it. He would do things like catch his sleeve on the clasp of a handbag or mistake a commutation ticket case for a wallet. Days went by with us having nothing to show for our efforts. Yasu was the first to announce he was splitting off to work independently. As a duo, Ono and I weren't any more successful. We finally arrived at a decision to break up until G. was out of prison. The three of us gathered at Yasu's apartment to drink rounds of farewell saké to mark the event. It was March 1954.

As usual, Ono put his finger on harsh reality.

"G. got two years. He won't be picking up where he left off when he gets out."

"Why not?" I asked.

"He slipped up bad. That's why he got busted," Yasu said.

"I'm the one who dropped the wallet, like a dummy."

"Uh-uh," Ono said. "He made a sloppy pass to you. He never messed up like that before. It would have been a miracle if you didn't drop it. Then he got excited and tried to zip up the bag again, but he muffed that too."

"That's it. G. messed it up. He's over the hill," Yasu said.

Yasu advanced the view that fingers lose their sensitivity and speed past the age of forty. Once a pickpocket starts fumbling the job, he just can't do the work anymore, Yasu said, and Ono agreed. As I was approaching my mid-thirties, I could not help but take their talk seriously. Ono had told me that G. had just turned forty. I had thought he was older. He certainly did not look young anymore — far from it.

Spring came and people began leaving their overcoats at home. Conditions were perfect for harvesting commuters' wallets. I should have been getting fat on my earnings, but in fact I didn't have any earnings. Whenever I was primed to extend my hand, that feeling of being watched came over me. Eyes that watched, criticized, and disparaged me came from all directions. My hand grew numb, and it would only quaver if I forced it to move. Prey that should have been mine for the taking escaped me time and again. Every night I returned home empty handed and disheartened. This went on for about ten days.

Inside my apartment I dressed my rolled-up futon in my jacket and practiced the crucial technique. Under those circumstances, I could extract my targeted wallet stealthily. My dilemma was that I no longer could do the trick anywhere but in the privacy of my apartment. With no savings to fall back on, the cupboard was shortly bare. One becomes very hungry in an occupation like mine, which requires walking all day. My strength was waning. By then I was too hungry to even attempt to work. I holed up in my apartment to save what little strength I had left. All I could do was drink water and sleep.

There was a student living next door to my apartment on one side, and an old man on the other. Presumably, the student studied all day; the only sounds coming from his side were his sighs and the rustling of paper. The old man was living on welfare payments. In the first days after he received his monthly allowance, he would give spirited renditions of *enka* songs that were clearly fueled with saké. When he ran out of money, the radio would be on constantly. The family of the landlord lived below. From those rooms emanated sounds of the toilet flushing, dishes being washed, cursing — in other words, the myriad sounds of family life. Outside the window, the screeching of railways cars on steel made the whole apartment creak, over and over again.

All these sounds reached my ears from the world of the other side, where people lived in the security of morality and ownership, and would have nothing to do with people like me. I felt that the only place for me was prison.

Something told me as I kept sliding downward that an extravagantly walled citadel was waiting to give me a warm reception and put an end to the anguish I was feeling. On the third day I recovered my spirits enough to venture outside. It felt as if my hunger had peaked and my body had begun to consume itself. I didn't feel hungry anymore, but the muscles in my legs felt unreliable, as if they had turned to water. I staggered in the direction of a shopping district, filled with confectioners, bakeries, and grocery stores, all displaying nourishing food. I was in no condition to try walking into a dining room or a sushi shop, ordering a meal, then running away. I had the idea of lifting what I could from some shop, and if I was caught, well, maybe that's what I really wanted to have happen. But even in that state, I was once again frustrated by the feeling that the eyes of the world were upon me. I came to the food section of a department store, but all the stares pushed me outside again. I fled to a back street.

There was no need to run away, but I felt pursued. I hurried into a shady, damp alley, where I found a foodstuffs shop on a corner with a showcase holding stacks of sweet rolls and enticing arrays of cheese and canned goods. No one was minding the store — a highly inviting happenstance. I entered the store, picked up a paper bag from a pile of them on a counter and threw a package of cheese and a container of milk inside. I was looking through the canned goods when someone shouted, "Just what do you think you're doing?"

It was a short, middle-aged man wearing an apron. That was another happenstance that determined how events unfolded. If it had been a hardy young man I would probably have simply fled.

"Shut up and hand over the money!" I said, picking up a bread knife. My voice was unsteady and the knife was shaking.

"You know what you're doing? I'm calling the cops." He backed up and reached for the telephone.

"Shit! Gimme the money or I kill you!" I held the knife up.

Suddenly, he was grappling with me. Seeing that I was unsteady, he pushed me hard. It was all I could do to flail at him with the knife. It had a flimsy blade, but nevertheless, it put a cut on one wrist that began bleeding. I shoved him backward, making him fall on his butt, after breaking a glass shelf. I picked up the paper bag and ran out, with the man shouting and running after me. I looked back and saw his furious face and three men behind him, all coming after me. I wanted to reach the main street and disappear into a crowd, but emerged into another back street. A throng of people alerted by the commotion surrounded me. Someone grabbed my legs from behind and pulled me to the ground, face down. There was heavy weight on my back and legs. I couldn't move an inch.

That escapade bought me a sentence of eight years, for robbery and bodily injury. I argued that the injury should be treated as incidental to my attempt to escape rather than the result of a planned armed robbery because I had entered the shop believing no one was present and could rob it without harming anyone. The circumstances of the injury offense were heavily against me, however. The crime had been committed while I was still on parole without once showing up at my probation office. Moreover, I was recognized by a pickpocket squad detective who testified I had been on his list of suspects. The judge sized me up as the kind of criminal who can't be rehabilitated.

I was sent to Chiba Prison in late June 1954. Chiba is for long-term prisoners. It has an elegant red brick main building in a forest surrounded by a woodland. The setting is suitable for aristocrats, which is what the inmates are, in the sense that their robberies, rapes, or homicides are generally distinguished by uncommonly atrocious circumstances.

It took only a few steps inside the high walls when I got the sense of being in a prison unlike any I had previously experienced. There were the same barred windows, the same uniformed guards, and the same prisoners in light green prison garb. The difference was a heavy silence that hung over each of the inmates. It was a dominating, unnatural silence that robbed the environment of any sense of human habitation.

A group of prisoners led by a guard approached where I stood. They walked in a double file, so perfectly formed their necks might have been held by an invisible yoke. This group was also shrouded in that strange silence.

I was put into a communal cell of Class Four inmates and immediately felt how different prevailing conditions were in Chiba. In Urawa (where they put the first offenders) and Fuchu (serial offenders), cell newcomers attracted much attention. The other inmates wanted to know their criminal histories, hometowns and whatever else they considered relevant. Here, I merely received a few sidelong glances. No one even addressed me. There was little conversation between cell mates. All were stone silent during evening inspection. When the radio came on with a baseball game, the men listened quietly. There were no reactions, even if someone hit a home run. The heavy silence weighed down on my spirits, forcing me into silence as well. I had the feeling that if I had tried making normal conversation, the kind exchanged between people who have a lively interest in something, I would have been shunned as someone who didn't know where he was.

I was put into the woodworking shop where furniture was made to sell to the public. Desks, chairs, and shelves of various kinds were the most common items. My job was shaving down chair legs to specification. Using a plane all day made my skin peel and my back hurt. It took two weeks to become re-accustomed to such manual labor. The man in charge of my unit was in his sixties. He had been in that prison for over forty years — since the last days of the Meiji era.

"Forty years! Straight? Right here?"

"No. I was out twice, on parole. Both times I couldn't get a job. No way to keep eating. Both times I shoplifted in department stores and the parole was canceled, so I was back with my life sentence." He said this with a sad smile.

"That must have been hard, after being free."

"No. Hard was being outside. Out there, you've got to have a job, and always be worrying about cooperating with somebody or other."

There was a real sense of history to hearing this old prison veteran talk about how prisons had changed from the Meiji to the Showa era, then from wartime to peacetime. In the early Showa era, a lot of ideological offenders came and went. With the 1933 law on "progressive treatment," prisoners were sorted into four classes — the bottom two classes had to wear red uniforms until 1947. Under the system, you get a better chance for parole if you can persuade the guards to promote you to a higher class.

"The rule is a man with a life sentence gets the possibility of parole when he's served ten years, if he's a model prisoner all that time and he's got a clean record. In actual practice, it's something between ten and twenty-years time. That's how it was with me. The trouble is, after you've been in twenty years, you have trouble coping on the outside. You get used to prison life. They give you clothes, food, a place to sleep. Everything's taken care of. You don't have to think about a thing, just obey orders. It's the same as being a little kid. So, you come out of that, you can't get by on the outside anymore." He nodded to himself, silently reflecting. His face was deeply wrinkled.

The wood shop chief had committed a robbery-murder at the age of nineteen. He used a hunting rifle to waylay a man walking through the mountains. He had only been after money, but wound up shooting the man when he resisted. He made off with twenty sen. To put it another way, he threw his life away for twenty sen. Both his bearing and his mild expression were gentlemanly. There was nothing menacing about him or anything else in his manner to suggest a criminal nature. His sole ambition was to pass the remainder of his life quietly in prison.

I was on my way to the supply storeroom one day when he asked me, "How many years did they give you?"

"Eight."

"That's not so long. You can get out early if you just keep straight. The law says you have to serve at least one third of your sentence in prison. The way it actually works is they'll consider you for parole when you've served three-fourths of your sentence. In your case, that's six years."

"Could I get out in six years?"

"It all depends on how you do your time. It's all about looking like a model prisoner to the guards. There's a knack to that."

Then, with the confidence of Jesus delivering the Sermon on the Mount, the old man laid down the guidelines for me to win my early release:

+ Don't form friendships with other prisoners. Friendships hold the seeds of quarrels, because you and your friends are different people, with different opinions. Always allow for a little distance in relationships, and keep conversation to a minimum.

+ Don't let anyone rope you into a confrontation. There are people who love to annoy others. They can't get any satisfaction if they can't sucker you, and they'll leave you alone.

+ Follow the guard's orders precisely, without overdoing anything. If you try to do any more than you're told, they'll just think you're a smart ass and they won't like you.

+ Don't even think about the world outside, least of all, politics and crime — which are nothing but different ways of talking about the same thing anyway. Be interested in all the trivial things right here, like the dinner menu or your work record. Forget about everything else.

+ Don't look back on the past. Even though prisoners don't have much of a future, just pick out any one small hope you can possibly to hope to have — just one. Hold onto it. Cherish it. Live for it.

It's absolutely true that the old man's sermon brought me to some kind of understanding. I started thinking about my future. I was thirty-four. If I served my full sentence, I would be forty-two when I got out. There wasn't that much future left, and that was all the more reason to get out as early as possible. I wanted to try making a fresh start, a new life for myself out in the world. I settled on parole — early release, even if it only came a short time before the full eight years was up — as my one small hope to embrace.

I took the sermon's directions to heart. My relationships with others stayed within reasonable boundaries. I obeyed the guards. It was only an act, of course, and I did not forget that overacting stinks. It was almost a pleasure to do a good job in the workshop every day. In time, I discovered that I had absorbed all those traits of the long-term prisoner that had been so unsettling when I first arrived at Chiba. I was one of the silent men with expressionless faces, the minimalist human robots who moved only when a guard switched them on.

When you're facing ten or fifteen years to life in prison, the way to deal with it is to drive away all your own feelings, all your capacity for joy and sorrow. The old man told me not to care about what goes on in the outside world. That is because caring is painful and not caring is easy. So I decided it simply didn't make any difference to me if there was a new cabinet running the government or what was in fashion out on the streets, or if the big corporations were doing good business. I was satisfied to stay in my own little world, where I worked in the wood shop during the day, then went back to my cell and read. I did exactly the same thing every day, but I was not especially bored by it. Time flowed by without any turbulence, like in thin air.

I had been in Chiba about two years when one day there was a spot inspection of the workshop by the chief of the prison's general management department. That's the man who holds the second most important post in the prison, under the warden and above the security division chief, who is the boss of all the guards. The general management chief lives in a realm above the clouds, as far as the prisoners are concerned. It was a rare event for us to even see his face. Of course, I was tense with anticipation of the visit as I concentrated on planing desk legs.

A voice beside me asked, "How's your job going? Got the technique down?"

"Yessir. I'm getting used to it now." I gave my answer standing ramrod straight, military style. A glimpse of the man's face gave me a surprise. He had been the chief of security at the Kobé Detention Center right after the war ended, when a group of prisoners escaped. Wheels started turning in my head. I was wondering if I could call in the favor I did for him then, in the interest of getting an early release. Without breaking my sober expression, I spoke up.

"Atsuo Yukimori. I haven't forgotten your kindness at Kobé Detention ten years ago."

The management chief stared me hard in the face, and, thankfully, he finally remembered. "Oh, yes. Yukimori! You still wallowing in the mire here?"

"Yes, I'm sorry to admit."

Three days later I was called into the management section chief's office. The guard who escorted me tried his best to solve the mystery of what there was between such an important person and me, but I wouldn't tell him. He took me into the spacious room, was dismissed and then it was just the section chief and me together. I sat unsteadily upon a lavishly upholstered sofa while a heavy aroma of nicotine excited my nostrils.

"I read your record. You're doing just fine this time around. How is the wood shop? Hard work?"

"It isn't hard, but if I had a choice, I would want to work as a librarian."

"Why?"

"I love to read. Books make me happy."

"Yeah? What kind of books?"

I reeled off the names of some postwar authors of novels and history. That seemed to impress the section chief. His mouth popped open and he looked at me with a blank expression.

He didn't tell me why he called me to his office and I didn't ask. But when I was pulled from the wood shop and reassigned as a librarian a few days later, I concluded he wanted to pay me back, and just maybe make me not want to talk to anyone about that prison break.

Working in the prison library involved going around the cells lending out books and editing submissions to the prison journal, which was named *Hope*. The work was much easier than in the wood shop, and it gave me a lot of free time as well. In the morning I went around the cells and collected paper slips with the titles of books prisoners wanted to borrow, went back to the library, and fetched them from the shelves. In the afternoon, I went around with a wagon loaded with the books, delivering them and collecting returned books. Not many prisoners used the service. It didn't take very long to finish my daily tasks. The journal was issued monthly, and didn't require much time either. I could use my free time to read anything I liked.

. . . and marvel at how vast is the world of literature. I did a lot of reading. It gave me the delightful experience of feeling my world get bigger. At the same time, I felt regret that I hadn't reached that stage sooner, when the war ended and I was still young. I started reading Manyoshu", probably due to my memory of Takéko Eda. During my flight from the army, I had lost the copy she gave me, but I did have the strong memory of red lines carefully drawn by Superior Private Eda throughout the text that showed how thoughtfully he had read it. It occurred to me that at my advanced age I might finally have reached the level he had been at when he was very young.

Strangely or not, of all the images that arose as I read those poems, Takéko was not among them. Instead of her, the girl who appeared in my mind was the one who had ladled out for me the best cup of water I ever tasted, inside an old temple in Akkeshi, where I had been wandering in the woods, ragged and hungry, immediately before my induction physical. Images of her appeared with extraordinarily clarity: a slim, white hand holding the ladle and a beautiful, delicately featured face that modestly blushed red as she offered me the water. At the age of twenty, I had loved that girl and no other.

The birds, flowers, trees, and grasses celebrated in the Manyoshu do not belong to Hokkaido, but

they do, as far as I am concerned; to me, Manyoshu sings of the flora and fauna of the fields and marshes of Nemuro. I began writing imitations of its verses. Perhaps they were not very good verses, but much pleasure came my way just by writing them.

About one in three of the new inmates that came to my cell were serving life sentences. Some had been sentenced to death and had their sentences reduced on appeal. Their offenses were generally robbery-murder, rape-murder, or just plain murder. You would imagine such men as cold-blooded monstrosities, but the ones I shared a cell with were fairly ordinary people. If anything, Fuchu prison, whose population consisted largely of professional thieves, was the place that had many usual characters. My cellmates at Chiba gave me a lot to ponder on the subject of crimes that start out with the simple intention of stealing money or human dignity, but play out in a way that ends in the theft of someone's life. Fortunately, I had only injured my victim, but it would have been entirely possible to have ended up killing him. In fact, under the circumstances, there was a very high probability of that actually happening.

As a general rule, thieves pay no attention to their victims, and certainly not to what their victims are feeling. The same rule applies in cases of murder and rape, when victims suffer pain and fear before the perpetrators' eyes. When you think about the situation of crime victims, you realize their experience is basically the same for all crimes, including cases of simple theft. I began thinking about the people whose pockets I had picked, and experienced remorse for my many crimes. The general impression I received from my cellmates, however, is that remorse was in short supply among them. It looked to me that they regarded the issue as settled because they had been handed heavy penalties for their crimes. They, too, wanted to get out someday, and rejoin society. Their goal was to win recognition for serving ten or fifteen years with a clean record and be paroled. They waited for the decision to be granted parole, but such decisions did not come as easily as the old woodwork shop chief had suggested. In practice, it was a matter of only one of many being selected.

I received notification that I was being considered for parole when I had been incarcerated for nearly five years. The conditions were that I have a fixed place of residence and secure a gainful occupation. I sent a letter to Suéko asking her to be my guarantor. I received an immediate answer, as if from an alert partner returning the ball in a game of catch.

"To my elder brother:

"You're still among the living, I see. I didn't know where you disappeared to. I was so worried. Hope finally ran out, and I got to thinking you must have died. I wrote to Urawa time and again, and the letters all came back stamped 'addressee not in residence.' I kept wondering what happened to you. It's been ten years. The time sure does go by fast, don't you think?

"Of course I'll be your guarantor. Do come back home to Nemuro. Make a new start in our hometown. The economy has really picked up lately. We'll see if we can find some kind of job for you. You could always help out with our dining room.

"Come on home, and I don't mean maybe. Come home for sure. I want to see you. You are my one and only brother."

A short time later, a hand knit sweater and a three-piece suit arrived. Suéko also sent photos of her family. Torakichi Jinnai was a man with a very sturdy build. He was posed in the center like a stone pillar, cradling a Winchester on one arm. Tetsukichi was a tall, healthy-looking boy. The little boy Yukichi was square shouldered, like his father. Suéko was young-looking, no different than ten years before. Though surrounded by males facing the camera with sullen expressions, her rounded cheeks framed the smile of one who had found happiness. Benten Island in the bay was in the background, calling up fond memories. Herring gulls flew in a clear sky. I could see white waves out in the open sea. As I took all this in, I made a firm decision to return to Nemuro.

My parole came down. On February 5, 1959, I emerged from the iron gates once again into the world of free people. White plum blossoms had already fallen from their branches onto the hill slope. In their place, fragrant double-blossom plum was dazzling in bright red profusion. Other tree branches were budding. Breezes were warm. In five months, I would turn forty.

It was still winter in Hokkaido. Beyond the snow-covered pastures and forests, the sea was packed with ice floes. The closer my train came to Nemuro, the heavier the snow fall became. Cold wind and powdery snow blew into the railway car.

Suéko appeared from a distance as I exited the Nemuro Station ticket gate.

"*Ani-san!*" she called out as she approached, and caught my arm with both hands. We found a corner somewhat removed from people coming and going, and she threw both arms around me. Her tears dampened my jaw.

"Now don't you go anywhere again! I'm going to look after you!"

A blizzard was blowing outside. We walked hand in hand, making slow progress and sinking into the drifting snow with each step. Reconstruction of the city was complete. It felt like being transported back to the time to before there was any war.

"This is the same route we took the day of the air raid — you and me and Father and Mother. Remember?" I said.

"Um-hmm. Father had me by the hand."

"I was holding Mother's hand."

"You're getting to look just like Father."

"Yeah? Well, you look a lot more like Mother."

We were broadsided by a strong wind that blew up so much snow visibility went to zero, and we tumbled into a drift. We struggled to our feet, laughing all the while.

Chapter 12

Gateway

Dawn

Atsuo Yukimori awoke to the frustration of rediscovering his existence in a narrow space, tightly constricted by four walls. He had emerged from a sunny dream of early summer, in a great, open field carpeted with flowers. His companion was Mikio Wakabayashi, the man who had set off a bomb on a Yokosuka Line passenger train. Wakabayashi had been speaking to him in a low voice that sometimes faltered, though his round, deep-set eyes were shining. Pleasant breezes rustled the fluffy flower heads of a vast expanse of cotton grass and made the petals of marsh lilies tremble. Wakabayashi's face faded away as the moment of awakening came. Atsuo was calling, "Hey! Where are you going?" but the scarred visage of dark walls maliciously blocked his field of vision, like mocking laughter.

He was in a three-mat solitary cell — more like a narrow box than a room — as he had been for longer than he could even remember. He could never get used to it. His dreams all took place in wide open, unrestricted spaces.

The day was breaking. Light had banished darkness from the bars of the cell house facing his own. Without knowing the exact time, Atsuo supposed there would yet be time before the six o'clock get-up. Turning over in his futon, he dourly surveyed the cell. It looked the same as ever, despite all his efforts the day before to put everything back to the state it had been in before he had taken up residence there, in preparation for the decision in his appeal trial that was to be handed down this day.

(This is the big judgment day. Maybe today they throw out my appeal and

697

endorse the death sentence the lower court handed me. Or maybe the death sentence gets kicked down to life. And maybe, just maybe, they will throw out that decision and admit I'm not guilty.

(Spent yesterday putting my affairs in order — as if that amounts to much. It was mainly a matter of putting all my books back into storage — with the exception of my dictionary, Bible, and *Manyoshu* — and counting up all the baggage tags I made. I finished up by cleaning every crevice of this cell, including the sink and toilet, with soap. You wouldn't know I did anything at all, though. You can't break anything in here, and no amount of cleaning makes any noticeable change in how it all looks. Everything fits together in one unit: the iron door with the air vent and windows for observation and passing dishes in and out; the speaker; the guard call box, with its button and plastic tag; the steel mesh covered clothing case; the combination wash basin and desk; the combination toilet and chair and the small window covered with iron bars.

(Sounds of sparrows and pigeons have started up, together with steam pipe sounds from the kitchen and miscellaneous sounds of movement throughout the building — the same sounds heard every morning.

(Time that speeds by invisibly, like an enchanted wind can suddenly suspended itself and present vivid images that exist outside its flow. That is how, I recall the morning Mikio Wakabayashi was executed.)

The sudden shock of the cell door opening. Surrounded by guards, Mikio Wakabayashi stands up unsteadily, his legs barely able to support his wasted body.

"Time to say goodbye."

(His voice was quiet and calm. I was about to say, "Goodbye. Be well," then stopped myself when I realized that would be denying reality. Instead I just said "Yeah," in a voice that was far from calm. I didn't see anything about him to suggest he would be killed in the next thirty minutes. Incredibly, he had a warm smile and a bright gaze. He gave me a nod and walked on. At the next chapel, Father Okuda said he had met death admirably, as a Christian fully prepared by his faith. The pastor prayed for the dead, and then added, "For Christians, death is not followed by darkness, but light. Let us pray for Mr. Wakabayashi in the world of light."

(I just saw Wakabayashi's face in a world lucid and bright, where he did indeed live on. Working as a carpenter had made his body strong. In prison, inactivity and poor nourishment had left him thin and weak. He had already gone far toward separation from his physical self when he melted away to that invisible world. Could I match his performance in my own passage to death?)

Atsuo Yukimori reflected that the sentence due to be handed down that day could well result in his having the same end as Mikio Wakabayashi, hanging beneath the gallows in handcuffs, an object of contempt, put to death by the state on behalf of the people.

(I did not plant that bomb inside the Shinkansen car, but in the course of a long trial, the people's representative, Prosecutor Shunji Domaé, rebutted every defense argument with quibbling and twisted logic that led to the same conclusions as those of the first trial decision, which was itself nothing but a slight rewording of the first prosecutor's arguments. After Domaé had concluded his presentation with supreme confidence, the arguments from our attorney, Jun Akutsu, sounded meek in comparison. Most unfortunately, the prosecutor, which is to say, the state, wants to kill the citizen named Atsuo Yukimori. Having spent my life in the army and prison — both institutions that exercise complete control over the citizens under their authority — I have undergone a long process of being tooled and cut down to specifications, and now the state wants to dispose of me as a being of no further use. I didn't choose to be born to this country. Who decided I would?

(How many times did I attempt suicide? I had reached the conclusion it was the only way I could escape the state's clutches, escape these unyielding walls.) Atsuo Yukimori ran a hand across one wall, then struck the flat, cold surface with his fist.

(This wall is the perfect symbol of the state's will, in solid form. Dying by battering my skull against it is the most revenge I could take on the state. Start two meters away — the farthest I can get from it — run as fast as I can and smash into it. That will do it, I thought. There should have been an explosion of sparks, followed by my soul breaking through the wall and soaring off into free space. What actually happened was that I regained consciousness to discover that a lump had appeared on my head. On my second attempt, a guard realized something was up, and the next moment two guards had rushed into the room and grabbed me before I could move. The third time . . . ahh, that's enough. I couldn't do myself in. I couldn't believe that the world I would enter following my suicide was the world of light that Mikio Wakabayashi had joined. Eventually, I gave up my suicide attempts.

(Wakabayashi fully owned up to his crime of placing a time bomb onto a Yokosuka Line railway car. Moreover, he accepted the state's verdict that said he deserved the death penalty for the crime. "I killed one person and caused serious injury to eleven people. It is appropriate to put me to a humiliating death. Your case is different. You didn't commit the crime. You are a victim of injustice. Of course you should fight it."

(He had ended up giving me encouragement. A guy fully prepared to die giving a pep talk to one with a history of suicide attempts. Every word he spoke carried terrific weight. Years have passed since his death. How many years? I gave up counting years after I had stopped caring about such things. Time goes sweeping by, like the wind.

(My colleagues, my fellow condemned prisoners, were killed, one by one. The judges had given them death sentences, eminently secure in the belief that they were carrying out the will of the state, and so, each went to the gallows. Mitsuo Takasaki, the handsome young man with a background in die casting and coal mining, disappeared one day forever. Many rumors about his execution circulated. He punched out a guard; he wasn't executed, but was only in solitary because he did something spectacular again, like the time he bit his own arm and bled a river. In fact, that rumor had circulated previously, and it had proven correct, but this time he really had been sent to his death. It is certain that his corpse had been sent to a medical university for student vivisection practice, according to his wishes. Those lucky students would surely have learned much about the beauty of the human body, by dissecting such an exemplary specimen.

(Eiji Furukawa, the irrepressible chatterbox of the "Shinkokyu" murder, went to his death in the same way he had approached every day, only maybe a little more exuberantly. He walked down the middle of the corridor, talking nonstop at the top of his voice so that everyone in their cells knew what was happening.

"Hey, gang, hear this. Shinkokyu, the legend of the golden age of high growth, is going to meet the rope! Shinko, you beautiful bitch, I loved you! Goodbye! Bye to all! Everybody gotta' go — going on the rope is better than a lot of ways I could name, 'cause it's quick. Hey, Yukimori! Why don't you quit playing innocent, be a man and own up to your crime like me! . . . Damn it!"

(It sounded like the guards did something to make him quiet down. Suddenly, his voice was much quieter. A short time later, we could hear him singing from the vicinity of the stairway. Whether the cheerfulness was real or feigned, the singing voice faded away.

(Katsumi Kamimura, the man with the nude woman tattooed on his arm, showed the guards who came for him his famous trick of making the woman's breasts shimmy. Then he punched the head guard on the jaw with every ounce of his strength, knocking the man out. He offered no resistance when the other guards rushed him, merely shouting vilification of the guard he had struck. Shunta Ueda, who had raped and killed a fifty-year-old woman, put up what was probably the fiercest resistance of all prisoners being taken for execution. He held onto the iron bars desperately. When the guards pried his hands away, he wailed like a baby and was put into leather handcuffs and a leather "voice suppressor" (a gag that makes it impossible to make any audible sound with your voice; this device is the foremost invention to come from the prison system). He struggled like a pig to the slaughterhouse as the guards bore him away. He was probably crying and screaming up to the moment of being hung; perhaps the gag was still in place when the trapdoor opened beneath his feet.

(Keiichi Morita, the condemned prisoner who had the longest record of time in detention awaiting execution, finally escaped hanging by dying of a misdiagnosed medical condition. Steadfastly denying the charge of overturning a train, he had repeatedly submitted requests that errors in his decision be corrected and a new trial granted, all the while eating garlic daily to maintain his health. One day he was overcome with a headache and nausea. The medical officer had diagnosed prison psychosis and done nothing about it. Morita ended up dying of a ruptured cerebral tumor. His death could have been prevented if he had received treatment for the condition in time. In other words, he was killed by medical negligence.

(A few of my fellow prisoners survived. For Yusuké Okayasu, who had killed his father, the life sentence he had received at his original trial was reaffirmed on appeal by the prosecutor. He was sent to Chiba Prison. Even aside from the special circumstances in his case, the ruling made sense on the general grounds that his crime had not involved theft or rape. In contrast to that, Yoshio Yamaishi getting away with a life sentence for his theft-murder case did not square with my sense of justice.

(Yamaishi claimed he was innocent, that the real killers were a drug smuggler and his lackey, and they had pinned the rap on him. That story lacked credibility, just as Eiji Furukawa had said. It was pretty easy to tell it was a fiction Yamaishi had made up to evade his own culpability. The judges weren't taken in by his story. I think they saw through his lies, but believed he was psychologically abnormal enough to diminish his responsibility for the crime. It is true it was abnormal to tell such a story with such composure, and raise a fuss about it like a small child, with tears and screams, which he did repeatedly, in the courtroom and the detention center. A psychiatrist was commissioned to examine him. Shortly before the doctor was scheduled to visit the detention center, Yamaishi began crying and screaming as if his mind had been seized by demons. He quieted down as if nothing had happened when his examination was over. He dropped his play-acting completely when his life sentence was affirmed with no further prosecutorial appeal. Shortly before his transfer to Chiba Prison, he bid me a gleeful farewell.)

"Take care, man. Ha-ha. I really gulled the doctor and the judges both. You'd better do like me if you want to get out of that death sentence. Just act crazy. The law says you can't hang a guy if he's nuts. Ha-ha-ha."

(Looking at Yamaishi's grinning face gave me a galloping case of revulsion mixed with envy. I had contempt for him because he did not admit to his crime and, of course, I was jealous that his death sentence had been reduced to life. He seemed to be expecting praise and congratulations for outwitting the judges, but I only glared back at him vindictively, without saying a word.)

~

Atsuo Yukimori cast an angry look at the wall, which repulsed his gaze so forcefully that pain shot through his retinas as if they had been struck. He closed his eyes. The commotion of residents getting up in the cells all around reached his ears. Shortly thereafter, the soundless rush of time stopped for the moment of transition everyone anticipated. Then the six o'clock chimes began.

> *Frère Jacques, Frère, Jacques Dormez-vouz? Dormez-vouz?*
> *Sonnez les matines, Sonnez les matines, Ding, ding, dong.*
> *Ding, ding, dong.*

It was Atsuo's custom to spring from his futon and promptly fold it away, but this day drowsiness lingered in his head. He shook it heavily, then languorously began washing up. The sun was shining and a blue sky was visible, but there were also many clouds threatening to take over in the near future. In late March, lurking winter was rudely intruding on spring's arrival. It had been cold the day before under a sky that was cloudy and sometimes rainy, but then it cleared up at night and presented a bright, round moon, pretty as any autumn moon, ushered in by a mild breeze. That had given him an expectation of nice weather for decision day that was so far being met by cold.

"Wish the damn weather would make up its mind," he muttered. Then, facing in the direction of the women's section, he called out, "mornin' Wakako!" That reminded him he had been cuddling with Wakako in the flowery field a short time before joining up with Mikio Wakabayashi. Dismayed, he checked his shorts, to see if that part of the dream had been wet.

A bound manuscript rested atop the clothing case. It was his memoirs, written down, little by little since the latest incarceration had begun. The final copy consisted of three hundred pages. The original version had been scrawled into university notepads and then reworked. He had put a cardboard cover on it and imitated Augustine by entitling it *Confessions*, with the subtitle, "To Wakako." Then he vacillated about sending it.

There was, first of all, an issue with prison censors. He had consulted with his attorney, Mr. Akutsu, who said he thought permission to send it would be granted because it was a creative work of literature and not a direct communication. In that case, Atsuo had answered, I request that you give it to her. He did not bring it, however, when next Mr. Akutsu visited.

"I can't quite bring myself to send it now. I'm worried how she'll react when she reads it," he had explained, and the matter had been left pending for years. Dust collected on the manuscript. Eventually, he noticed the title was a bit faded. By that time, he didn't even want Wakako to see it. His original intention had been to fulfill his promise to her made at the hot spring in Raúsu: "I'll give it to you to read as soon as I get it done." He had been writing it with the feeling of speaking to her directly of his "cold-blooded past."

That story had been too grim, too dark; more than he could shake off. Now he thought it would be so profoundly startling to such an innocent girl that it was sure to crush her hopes in him. The manuscript remained on his clothes case instead of being discarded because he was also unsure of his own thoughts about it. Guards had eyed it and teased him about it. "Is that your masterpiece?" they would ask, among other things, all of them unkind. Still, he could not bring himself to throw it away any more than he could muster the courage to have it given to Wakako. He also feared the consequences if anyone else — say, for example, Suéko — read it. He didn't want prison censors to read it, and not even Mr. Akutsu. Therefore, his *Confessions* had gathered dust. Now he used a duster to clean it off, then wrapped it in old newspapers.

His diary had been among the items slated for storage the previous day. The diary took up thirty-two university notepads. Leafing through them before packing them up had been an exercise in self-amazement at how much there had been to write in an environment that underwent so little change. He had made entries a little at a time, despite being quite busy every day.

Too busy, really. Each day wasn't long enough. He had to keep at his baggage tag manufacturing job because he needed the income for necessary expenses. Tetsukichi was covering his lawyer's fees, but he didn't want to receive a single sen from anyone, including Suéko, for anything else.

He was receiving material support, though — quite a bit. Suéko sent him sweaters, underwear, and suits to wear in court. Professor Kirikaé's support group sent him books and magazines. Keeping up correspondence with them took up much time. The members included students, housewives, newspaper reporters (in particular, Yoshié Wada of *A. Shimbun*) and Professor Kirikaé (he had become a full professor several years before). Before now, he thought, it would have been inconceivable that I would be associating with so many people.

He cherished the time for reading that was his after dealing with all that business. He had been avidly reading novels since his arrival at Sugamo, though he had previously avoided them. He had first read novelists of nineteenth century Russia and twentieth century Europe and America, then he went to modern Japanese and Latin American literature. There were many more novels he wanted to read. All of this kept him very busy.

~

"Number 74, Wakako Ikéhata," the uniformed woman said self-importantly.

"Here." She gave her reply in a small voice that showed the tedium she felt. Not answering at all would only bring on more pettifoggery, and with it, more tedium.

"Your cell isn't in order," the uniform said, raising an eyebrow at the music scores, papers, books, and a sweater on the tatami. "I think you were told to put it in order yesterday. You appear in court today. The bus leaves at eight o'clock," she said and loudly slammed the door shut.

Wakako Ikéhata took a deep breath, then expelled it forcefully against the door to dispel the afterimage of the uniform with lips like poison mushrooms and creases about the eyes framed in swirls of powder. Then she set out her blanket, folded to double as a zabuton, assumed the posture for meditation and opened a book of Beethoven's complete piano sonatas, to Piano Sonata in A-Flat Major, Opus 110. The moment she began reading the score, music filled her ears and her heart. The music was accompanied by an outpouring of sights, bits of conversations and ideas.

(It was the same when I would play piano. My teacher always said listen to the music, concentrate on the beauty of the pure tones. I listened, but it always came with a rush of images to see, and all kind of conversations to hear. For me, music is always accompanied by many other sounds. For some reason I don't fully understand, I have gotten around to really liking Beethoven's late piano sonatas. Most especially, the last five make all the sense in the world to me now. My teacher wouldn't let me do them on the grounds that I was too young. He said you need life experience to understand these works. Well, now I've had abundant life experience, so I understand them . . . Yeah, fabulous life experiences I've had. Look where aging has landed me, now at age thirty-three. You see, once upon a time I ran afoul of a particularly nasty organization that puts people in jail for no reason and keeps them there while they get older and older and older.

(Beethoven was completely deaf when he composed this wonderful music. It came bubbling up from inside, and he heard it in his head. I wanted to find out what makes this music so good, so I tried reading his late string quartets, but that didn't work very well. No matter what music I read, it only comes out as piano sounds in my head, because piano is all I can do, and that's not enough to hear his string quartets properly. Even so, I could still tell what it is that makes the C-sharp Minor and A-Minor string quartets so very special. You can't listen to records or tapes in prison. I really want to hear those works performed. Unfortunately, they put me in here for life, so that won't ever happen. Being the lowest form of humanity, I don't get permission to hear the music I want to hear.

(Breakfast is served. I don't want any of this stuff. No, wait, I'll take just the tea, if that is what you call this warm, slightly tinted water. I see, as usual, you won't take no for an answer and insist on leaving it all. Your organization says every prisoner gets a tray, and that's all there is to it. Miso soup with shriveled lees of tofu and some dried pickled vegetable that smells bad. First movement: Moderato cantabile molto espressivo. Father started me on piano when I was very little. Piano lessons were by far the best thing he gave me. I learned to distinguish tones and read scores, thanks to him. Maybe he wanted to make a musician of me. Kotaro Ikéhata, the great law scholar, was delighted that his little girl, the piano prodigy, could play Mozart sonatas, one after another.

(Father is dead. Ah, those broken chords in low register! His students put together a memorial collection of his papers, and they even included his diary. It says he believed in my innocence, but he was going to win a not guilty decision for me by proving I had no responsibility for my actions because I was psychotic. I would have accepted him when he was still around if he had stopped treating me as crazy and instead considered the possibility I was wrongfully indicted. Just as he when he was alive, his diary takes every opportunity to inveigh against Makihiko Moriya and Atsuo Yukimori.

(Second movement, Allegro molto . . . no it isn't — it's the third movement already, Adagio, ma non troppo. Atsuo Yukimori has had such an amazing life, way out in a marshland in the north, living among those monster fish they have up there . . . He went from an army prison to a civilian prison. Wow, has he ever had life experiences. "I committed crimes and was sent to prison again and again," he told me in the middle of a blizzard. We were upstream on the Furen River. The wind was whipping up snow from the river surface and it got into the cinders of the can we were using for a stove. Allegro ma non troppo. That outing was really fun — we were together all the time. I seem to remember we were on a glacier playing tag. Yes, and we ice danced on the frozen lake. We were in a cave with pillars of ice like the thousand images of Buddha in the Hall of Thirty-Three Spans in Kyoto.)

Wakako Ikéhata felt rather than recalled the sensation deep inside of the moment when Atsuo Yukimori had entered her body. It was like turning into a flowing stream of molten wax. The sudden emergence of that experience caused her to drop the music score she had been holding. The music vanished and all was wretchedness again, a cramped concrete box, shared with tofu lees and desiccated pickled vegetables, where the only freedom permitted was to grow older.

Talk among the women in the cell across from hers proceeded in unrelenting cascades. The women talked on and on, untiringly, all through the day, about nothing in particular. (I don't suppose people so preoccupied with talk as they are would have the time to do any reading or quiet thinking about anything.) A baby began to cry. Arrangements are made for women serving prison terms to have infants under the age of one year together with them in their cells. The baby stopped crying, possibly because he or she was nursing. A uniform was reprimanding someone . . . No, that wasn't it; she was breaking up a fight.

(Being regarded as the perpetrator of an especially heinous crime, they have me in a special cell to keep me isolated from the other prisoners in the female block. The typical crimes committed by women are shoplifting, arson, and killing newborns. They usually serve a year or maybe a few. When someone like me showed up, a radical who got life for murder, attempted murder, injury, and overturning a train, the uniforms had to give me special treatment. At first, I played the depraved criminal: no polite language, laying around in the daytime, leaving things around on the floor — that kind of thing. This enraged the tubby section chief, with the result that I was suddenly confronted with four uniforms hauling me up, and me resisting. When you resist that kind of treatment, they say you're one who's violent, and resisting orders, which is a grave offense. That's when they put on the leather handcuffs, with both hands strapped down at your sides, and the leather gag, so you can't open your mouth and throw you into a pitch-black soundproof cell.

(By and by I had to pee. There is no way to pull down your pants when your hands are strapped at the waist, no matter how much you struggle. Realizing the futility of my efforts, I wanted to call a uniform, but that isn't possible either, with a leather strap over your mouth. The only sound that comes out is a muffled "oooh oooh," through your nose. I was just about to start peeing in my pants when the door opened, with the uniforms all in a row, looking down at me.)

The tubby section chief sneered. "It looks like Wakako Ikéhata wants to piss. Okay, let's take her pants down for her."

(The uniforms gathered around me and removed my panties. They were much too strong for my resistance. They held me, legs apart over the toilet — a square hole in the floor — while the section chief coaxed me: "Now we go pee-pee!" And that is just what I did, with abandon. The uniforms stared at my crotch, while one wiped it with paper, taking her time and wiping much more thoroughly than necessary, apparently enjoying the fact that I was shaking with anger and shame.

(The evening meal was delivered. I could not feed myself, being handcuffed. A uniform brought a spoonful of food to my mouth, which I kept tightly shut, in refusal. Thus, I ate nothing. At night, they brought a futon and blanket, and removed the gag only. They rolled me onto the bedding and left me curled up with my hands strapped to my sides. It was impossible to assume a natural position for sleep. Attempting to turn over made the harness creak. My hands hurt. The blanket had slipped down and I couldn't pull it up. Cold, pain and the return of an insistent urge to urinate kept me from sleeping. Finally, I yelled out angrily, unable to stand it. Two uniforms were immediately inside the cell. My underwear was again removed, as in the afternoon. Instead of being held, I had to squat by myself and be closely observed while I urinated. They refastened the leather harness gag, on the grounds that I had to be punished for disturbing the other prisoners by raising my voice. One of them tightened the band so severely it was obstructing my breathing, then she hastily loosened it when she saw I was in the process of suffocating to death. The leather device clamped my jaws tightly together. Biting my tongue was out of the question — I couldn't open my mouth at all. About a quarter of the area of my nostrils were covered over as well, so breathing continued to be difficult. The leather stank of the sweat and saliva of I don't know how many prisoners who had been subjected to this instrument of torture.

(In the morning the tubby section chief came sneering and rolling her massive breasts. She removed the gag. As I breathed deeply, she said, "Well, Wakako Ikéhata, are you beginning to get the message?"

(She became infuriated when I didn't answer. "It's courtesy to answer when you're asked a question! I would say you still have days and days to go on your stay here," she said and closed the door. Again, I wouldn't have what they brought for breakfast. The uniforms left me with the waist handcuffs on and my underwear off so I could use the toilet, but I couldn't wipe my backside after defecation. The only thing to do was wait for it to dry and flake off.

(Tubby, the section chief, took me back to my cell in the evening. Both my wrists were bruised purple. I could hardly stand up straight; my spine hurt and made popping noises when I stretched. I continued refusing to eat. I meditated all day without saying a word. When I got tired, I played Mozart piano sonatas or danced Japanese dances, all in my head. On the third day, the medical officer tried to force-feed me. The uniforms held me down spread eagle while he put oil on a rubber tube and twisted and forced it through my nose and esophagus, then pumped liquid nutrients in with a big syringe. Just as I had done when the police subjected me to force feeding, I spewed it all right back at him, doing my best to also hit each one of the uniforms too.

(The struggle between me and the uniforms continued — they pumping in the nutrients, followed by me spitting it back at them. When they tired of cleaning my vomit from the walls and floor, they transferred me to an isolation cell in the medical section, where they tied me to the bed to force-feed me. It's impossible to resist in those circumstances, unfortunately. Day by day I grew fatter and fatter, like an inflated balloon. I tried walking around and jumping up and down in the cell in an effort to lose weight. It didn't do any good. Finally, I gave in and announced I would eat, so they took me back to the women's section.

(At this point I was very quiet. I answered at inspection time, didn't lie down during the day and kept my cell more or less in order. All of this made a big hit with Droopy, the new section chief when Tubby was transferred elsewhere. She rated me as a prisoner remorseful for formerly bad behavior, and rewarded me with permission to have four books in my cell at once, write in a notebook, and even have a flower vase in my cell. She enjoyed handing out dispensations. You see, there's a base of rules about things no one would suppose would be subject to rules. Like you can only have up to three of your own books in your cell, you can't have a pen or a writing pad or anything for writing, you can't have a flower vase. Given all these rules, the section chief has the authority to change them. If you're a good girl, you can have this, you can have that, you can have an extra one of these, etc., etc. Of course, if you're naughty, the largess is taken away. The uniforms can control everything affecting the prisoners' daily lives in the same way. Everything is subject to limitation. The limits are arbitrary, but it all makes sense in that they increase control over the prisoners' lives at the convenience of the uniformed overseers: you can have only one visit a day, you can write only three letters a week, each letter can't be longer than seven pages, you can't purchase instant ramen or coffee, you can only dry clothes three times a week.

(One night I dreamed of a giant tower. It had innumerable rooms that were all semitransparent. A vast population of people worked inside the rooms. Each

708

floor was slightly smaller than the one below. The tower reached way up into the sky and out of sight. When I woke up, I realized the walls around me are what organizations are all about; that everyone working inside are just prisoners. In other words, those uniformed women dominating us are not the organization, but merely its prisoners. Their hatred of us is the hatred one feels for close relations, and is the same kind of hatred that falls upon them. They are identified as section chief, head guard or plain guard, and they think those roles are their identities, but the people in the roles are interchangeable. The roles themselves are important to the organization, not the people who happen to be in them. If it doesn't need the tubby section chief any longer, the droopy one will do just as well, and her role could be fulfilled by the prison warden, or for that matter, the Justice Minister. The message here is that however much I might resist any of the individuals in the organization, it doesn't make any difference at all to the organization itself.

(On another night I dreamed of many towers, including even bigger towers than in the first dream, but small ones too. They were everywhere, lined up side by side or stacked one atop another. Each tower had numerous rooms, but the entire tower was also like a single room unto itself, with slightly smaller rooms on top of it and slightly larger ones supporting it from below. The towers could change around their positions in relation to one another, they could fuse together into new towers one moment and disappear into thin air the next. The entire complex of towers was constantly changing, like countless soap bubbles forming themselves into mountains that duplicated themselves into other soap bubble mountains, fissioning, and breaking apart. The thing about those towers that are different from soap bubbles is the towers have rooms and rooms full of people confined as prisoners. They were being thrown out into space as the rooms suddenly merged into others or disappeared altogether. What that means is all the people were complete prisoners of the towers and could not live apart from them. In my dream, I saw a group of people who had been expelled from their tower trying desperately to slip into another one. They gradually lost their strength and ultimately dried up and were blown away by the wind.

(I became increasingly docile, that being the ultimate virtue for a prisoner. By no means was I trying to show subservience or obedience to the section chief or the other uniforms. The droopy section chief was taking me as a model prisoner, but of course I did not respect her or the other uniforms, and I was not afraid of their authority or their violence. To the contrary, I felt compassion for them as fellow prisoners. I saw their guard uniforms as a kind of prison uniform and their swagger as the sorrow of the prisoner. The organization that was currently being called a detention center would not exist forever. I was originally held in a detention center in Sugamo, but that is gone, having morphed into a completely different kind of tower they call Sunshine Sixty. This one, too, will someday disappear, as will Sunshine Sixty, proving again the emptiness of human endeavor.

(The meaningless intimidation I am being subjected to derives from a court decision to put me here. Maybe I will eventually be found not guilty and be released, or for some other reason I will stop being a prisoner. For the uniforms, though, their imprisonment goes on and on because they have pledged loyalty to their organization and because they are under the delusion that they are the ones ruling the prisoners.

(Be that as it may, being a fellow prisoner, I came to understand a little bit about what makes the uniforms so confident, taking pleasure in throwing their weight around, being satisfied with their situation, and in particular, taking delight in wearing uniforms, while they demonstrate that they themselves are the ultimate prisoners. My own treatment as ultimate prisoner was given to me by section chief Tubby, when she had me gagged and bound in leather harnesses, my underwear removed and held up like a baby to pee. I was trembling with anger and shame, but paradoxically, deriving the kind of pleasure felt when being taken sexually by a man. Throughout the entire abuse I suffered in having my underwear snatched off, my hands bound in waist handcuffs, rolled onto the floor like a trussed-up chicken, helpless, exposed and unable to say a word because my mouth was in a gag harness, I felt pleasure, and even thought I wanted more torment, to be made more thoroughly a slave. I suppose being a woman makes the pleasure of being captive all the stronger. God made things so that domination accompanies the woman's pleasure in intercourse. Observation tells me that this tower also has a lot of uniformed men who take pleasure in being prisoners in the same way as the female uniforms. The male uniforms make the same display of self-confidence and show the same delight in bossing and dominating. All of this agrees with what I have read about men knowing masochistic pleasure in being a prisoner.

(In other words, human beings take pleasure in being imprisoned in one single room, even though towers have many rooms. When I found myself in a situation of being a kind of ultimate prisoner among prisoners, I felt the pleasure come up from somewhere deep inside. One conclusion I can draw from all this is that maybe, just maybe, my attempts to escape from the organizations and break down their walls was nothing more than the delusions of a female Don Quixote.)

Wakako Ikéhata emerged from her reverie with cascading conversational accompaniment by the women in the opposite cell. She turned to putting her things in order by closing her complete Beethoven piano sonatas and placing them atop her notes. Then she filled the water basin and used the surface as a mirror to comb her hair. She was not permitted a real mirror, due to the possibility that she might break it and use the glass shards to commit suicide. Also, she was permitted only ten grams of perfume a month and no other cosmetics because — well, just because. She applied a dab of perfume to her hair and ruefully regarded her own soft, pale features in the water's reflection.

~

7 a.m.

Jun Akutsu stepped from the shower. He had been out in his neighborhood running for exactly thirty minutes. The workout had provided an invigorating rush of blood through his head and body, critical for dealing with the day's agenda. That particular day had an especially heavy one. The appellate court decision in the Shinkansen bombing case was to be read at ten o'clock. He would have to visit his law office beforehand and do a quick rereading of the key lines in the trial proceedings. His afternoon schedule depended on the morning's decision, but whatever it was, he had to appear at a press conference and give a report to the support committee. There were conferences with the defendants and their relatives. Actually, there simply were not enough hours in the day to deal with all the relevant issues. Most could be left for handling in the days ahead. In any case, Akutsu wished from the bottom of his heart the case could be done with on that day.

There was no question that his clients were innocent of the charges. The right decision was not guilty on all charges. He had devoted all his energy to this case from the time he had accepted it from Tetsukichi Jinnai in May 1971 to this day, March 23, 1978. He wanted it over today. He was fully prepared to take the case to the Supreme Court if the day's decision threw out the appeal and upheld the lower court's decision. But he wanted it over today.

As he toweled himself, Akutsu examined his own reflection in the mirror, appearing a bit fuzzy because his glasses were off. He saw a man of thirty-two, whose skin had loosened a trifle. Thanks to daily jogging, he did not have a paunch, but the body looking back at him was no longer youthful. He put on his glasses and closely examined the face. Eye creases had deepened, and there was a small spot on one cheek. He pulled down his lower eyelid.

"What are you doing?" his wife, Yoko asked. She had suddenly pulled open the door.

"This is the gents' room and you are a voyeur."

"Sorry. Coffee's on. Ahh, for goodness sake, you just got a haircut and it's a mess already."

"Okay, okay."

Akutsu did a few final vigorous licks with the towel, then turned his attention to his hair, which was indeed disheveled. He could see he was in for a hard time as he applied a comb. It snagged.

"Let me do it." Yoko dashed inside and picked up a hair drier. She took her time combing the hair down with one hand while pointing the drier with the other.

"Why nannies go on strike. You don't use a wet comb after you apply tonic." There was a scream from Reiko in the living room.

"Mama. The milk spilled!"

Yoko ran in the other direction, setting aquiver breasts that had grown larger than ever. "It didn't spill by itself, did it?" she said sternly to the little girl in a loud voice.

Akutsu Jun inspected the inside of his lower eyelid once again, then began to shave. He was ravenously hungry.

They lived on the ninth floor of a condominium built atop a hill. Their windows afforded a long-distance view of central Tokyo. The most prominent figure of the cityscape was Tokyo Tower. Otherwise, it was a vast sea of buildings, sparkling at that moment, like salt crystals under oblique sunlight. Observation of this panorama was a major attraction of the morning breakfast table.

"Buildings keep sprouting up," Akutsu said. He had been surprised by the sight of a crane and scaffolding that had at some time materialized around one of the buildings. "Well, I'll be . . . We can't see the Diet building anymore."

Yoko brought sausages, natural cheese, and carrot juice. Reiko sat in her highchair with a ring of yogurt around her mouth. "Wal-al bee," she said, imitating her father.

"Oh, yes," Yoko said, picking up a leaf from a memo pad by the telephone. "You had four calls: Ms. Wada from *A. Shimbun*, Attorney Kida, Mr. Tetsukichi Jinnai, and Professor Kirikaé. They were all surprised you weren't home so early in the morning, and they are all going to call your office in Akasaka after nine. Ms. Wada's message was simple: check out her piece in the morning paper. She says she expects to get priority for an interview, after all the plugs she's given the defense arguments in the Shinkansen case."

"Give her priority? That sounds like something you would put her up to say."

"Actually, you're right. I would have done that much for an old classmate anyway, but just look at the papers. None of them come even close to the *A. Shimbun* article."

"Me priming her with a lot of choice intelligence should have something to do with that."

Akutsu took sips of coffee as he scanned the morning newspapers. Each one had a prominent article on its front page about the Shinkansen bombing case decision, due later that morning. Each had its own take on which way the decision might go. *A. Shimbun* flatly declared it was fully expecting not guilty decisions for all defendants. You could tell that *B. Shimbun* and *C. Shimbun* were expecting another guilty decision by their emphasis on the exhaustive detail in the prosecution's evidence; they seemed to think the most the defendants could hope for would be lighter sentences. *D. Shimbun* took the third-party position, simply giving a balanced presentation of the arguments advanced by the respective sides. Akutsu was surprised that the press was leaning toward the prosecution by two to one. Yoko instantly read his expression and gave a disappointed sigh.

"I just don't know about these other papers. I mean, almost everybody agrees with what we've been saying."

"Oh, well, everything depends on the decision. What's your agenda for today?"

"Take Reiko to the nursery in Y. Hospital. I have to set up job interviews for two patients there. After that, it's straight to the courtroom ASAP. There is zero chance I will get inside, but I have to be in on the drawings for tickets to the observers' box. Everyone in the support group will be there, and any of us who get tickets will give them to the defendants' family members. Every one of them should be let in automatically. It's just not right to limit them to one ticket per family . . . Uh-oh, if I don't run the washer right now, she won't have a change of clothes tomorrow. She goes through them so fast, just like you know who."

Reiko was in the living room, running in place, recognizably imitating her father's jogging. The child's stamping resounded in the apartment below. Complaints about the noise had been made on numerous occasions.

"Reiko, stop that running!" Yoko scolded, but Reiko ran even more recklessly, until her skirt caught in the branches of a potted flowering peach tree in full bloom, pulling it down, scattering petals and breaking the delicate branches.

Yoko held her anger in check while her face turned crimson, and Akutsu swept Reiko up. She smelled of milk, jam, and yogurt. Greatly pleased to find herself up high, she surveyed her surroundings in delighted wonderment.

Akutsu patted the soft bundle of motion in his arms and recalled his conversation with Yoko Mizuno three years before, when he had decided on marriage. "I turn thirty next year," she had said.

"Well, what would you say to getting married while you're still young?" he had answered jokingly.

"Hmmm . . . okay, let's give it a try!" she had said in a like tone, settling the matter. The condominium in Hongo was purchased on a loan. Reiko was born the following year, and even the child's existence felt like some kind of strange joke. Making a living was no joking matter, however. Akutsu had withdrawn from his position at the Ishikawa Law Office and set up his own practice in Akasaka, with two young lawyers in his employ, assisting in work on the Shinkansen bombing case and extending their range of operations to civil lawsuits. As Yoko continued working at Y. Hospital, the family income was within the bounds of adequacy.

Jun Akutsu put Reiko down and carried the newspapers into the study. He gathered up a notebook labeled "Shinkansen Bomb Case Overview," a file of papers relating to the support committee and a fundamental document entitled Statement of Reasons for Appeal. He stuffed them into his briefcase, then began searching through the trial proceedings that took up most of the space in his four bookshelves. Seven years worth of trial records occupied many thousands of pages. The sight of them recalled the many hours he had devoted to fencing with the prosecutor over the complicated, tedious minutiae of the facts they contained. Akutsu realized the futility of trying to carry away only those volumes containing the key points. He decided it would be more practical do the best he could right where he was, using all available time until he would have to leave for the courtroom.

He sat down and opened the notebook. Then it occurred to him Yoshié Wada had written a very competent summary of the trial for the morning edition. He opened his copy of A. Shimbun.

"Shinkansen Bombing Case: Tokyo High Court Decision Today
    "In the nine years since the original trial began, prosecution and defense have each spared no effort disputing virtually every major point. The decision in the second trial on the defense's appeal will be handed down today. The defense has argued that all of the state's charges are unfounded, and all the evidence against the defendants is false.
    "Following is a summary of the essential points argued by the respective sides:

"Disputed Issues in Shinkansen Bombing Case

"1. Conspiracy to commit the crime

"Prosecution — Fifty Q. Sect members under the leadership of Maki-hiko Moriya, Shinichi Tagawa, Akito Shinya, and Wakako Ikéhata met at an inn located in Hongo 1-chomé on April 22, 1967 to plan the bombing of a Shinkansen passenger train.

"Defense — Such a meeting of Q. Sect took place. There was no discussion of any kind of bombing plan."

(By sheer coincidence, that inn was only a short distance from Akutsu's condominium. He could see its rooms from his study.)

"2. Bomb testing

"Prosecution — As a chemistry student at R. University's Department of Science and Engineering, Wakako Ikéhata was highly knowledgeable about explosives. She became acquainted with Atsuo Yukimori at a skating rink and learned he had access to gunpowder because he had a license for a hunting rifle. She used sexual favors to induce him to become a Q. Sect member, then asked him to conduct tests of bombs. He agreed, and conducted three explosions in the area of Lake Furen, on November 17 and 19, 1967 and November 18, 1968. These tests laid the groundwork for the Shinkansen bomb.

"Defense — The relationship between Wakako Ikéhata and Atsuo Yukimori was a purely individual affair that had nothing to do with Q. Sect, or its radical ideology. Ikéhata was close with Q. Sect member Moriya, but she herself was not a Q. Sect member. Like many students at that time, she identified with radicalism on an emotional level, but that was all. Since she was not a sect member, there would have been no reason why she would ask Yukimori to conduct bomb experiments even if the sect did have a bombing plan. Yukimori did set off explosions in Hokkaido as the prosecution said, but they had nothing to do with the bomb that exploded on the Shinkansen. The first two explosions were done for his own amusement. He set off the final explosion to scare off a bear that was roaming the vicinity close by.

"3. Thefts committed to finance Q. Sect activities

"Prosecution — Q. Sect had been suffering from a shortage of funds ever since student protest at T. University turned to large scale strike activities in the fall of 1968. The members enticed Yukichi Jinnai, who shared radical ideology with his uncle, Atsuo Yukimori, to commit thefts for the sect to provide money for its activities. Jinnai committed two thefts from Fukawa Motors, his place of employment, of 170,000 yen from the president's office in the evening of October 10, 1968, and 427,540 yen from the company's filling station on February 7, 1969. He gave the money from both thefts to Q. Sect members.

"Defense — The claim that Atsuo Yukimori infected Yukichi Jinnai with radical ideology is fiction. Jinnai did not commit either theft. Jinnai had no part in any Q. Sect activities or the Shinkansen bombing."

Well then, who did commit those two thefts? Akutsu had pondered that question many times. Yukichi Jinnai had steadily denied the charges from the outset of the original trial, and there was good reason to believe him. He had been sentenced to five years and told that if he appealed, he could expect to stay in detention for around ten years, because that was how long the appellate trial in this case could be expected to take. He had unhesitantly signed on to the appeal, and fiercely disputed the charges for nine years. If he had been the true culprit, he would have accepted the sentence and been discharged long ago. Someone else had stolen that money, and the most likely culprit was Kimiko Fujiyama, the mistress of the president, Ichiro Fukawa, who had placed her in full charge of the company's money, he being the only one who could give that authority. As soon as the company dorm mother, Sonoko Kanéhara, reported the 170,000 yen theft to the Kanda police station, Fukawa had hastily prevented a police investigation by claiming he had misplaced the money. That looked a lot like a cover-up for Fujiyama's sake. Maybe the 427,540 yen theft had been nothing more than a plot hatched by Fukawa and Fujiyama.

If that was the truth of the matter, it was an inspired use of the fact that Yukichi Jinnai had abruptly left Fukawa's shop without telling anyone he intended to leave. If Jinnai was absconding with stolen money, Atsuo Yukimori would fall under suspicion of being an accessory to the crime. That could be taken as justification for dismissing him, which Fukawa did, shortly thereafter. Akutsu recalled Fukawa with distaste — that crass, goggle-eyed walrus. Fukawa seemed to take pleasure only in making money.

"4. Credibility of the confessions
"Prosecution — The defendants' confessions contain detailed, secret information that could have only have been acquired by personal

experience. They agree with objective evidence and testimony. Hence, they have a very high degree of credibility. The confessions were given completely voluntarily. There is no evidence of coercion, threats, or the use of leading questions by the investigating officers.

"Defense — Important parts of the confessions undergo change from one questioning session to the next, but show unnatural agreement among all the defendants about irrelevant objective evidence. This is the result of investigation using coercion, threats, and leading questioning under unjustly prolonged detention in police station 'substitute prisons'for the purpose of obtaining confessions. Hence, the confessions were not given voluntarily and therefore are not valid evidence."

There had been no end to difficulties in defending the case because the five defendants other than Wakako Ikéhata had all confessed to the charges before the first trial had begun. Akutsu had not been able to understand why Makihiko Moriya — the militant revolutionary, the theoretical and operational leader of the Q. Sect who had played a central role directing the Tower takeover — had proven to be the weakest police suspect, giving the police their first false confession. Shinichi Tagawa and Akito Shinya had followed him. The confessions of all three were almost exactly the same. They said Q. Sect had planned the Shinkansen bombing, and it had been executed by their secret member, Atsuo Yukimori. The early confessions of all three said Yukimori had done it alone. By and by, Moriya's story switched to Yukimori and Ikéhata carrying out the deed together. In a few days, Tagawa and Shinya were saying the same thing. In other words, the policemen interrogating from the podium had arranged Moriya as first violin and the other two as second violins repeating the melody.

Next came Yukichi Jinnai's confession. According to it, he had first become acquainted with Tagawa and Shinya, who had introduced him to Moriya and Ikéhata. He became a secret member of the Q. Sect, conferred with his uncle, Yukimori, then committed the two thefts to get money for dear old Q. Sect. Atsuo Yukimori's confession came last. It followed the story laid out by the other four. In fact, it meshed so well, providing such neat explanations for everything, that it ended up out of sync with evidence that emerged afterwards.

If nothing else, it was at least clear that Atsuo Yukimori had been cast in the role of executor of the bombing plan together with Wakako Ikéhata by the four other suspects who had confessed, and that his confession had been the last of the lot.

The media had painted a baleful image of Atsuo Yukimori on the basis of his notoriety as the Shinkansen bomber. One much discussed theory of the crime was that his confession was filled with lies that falsely implicated the Q. Sect members and Wakako Ikéhata. The minority who did not accept this theory was comprised largely by Yukimori's family members. The other defendants' families believed it, and Professor Kotaro Ikéhata had consistently vilified Yukimori as his enemy. Many support committee members also believed it unquestioningly, most prominently, the Q. Sect students, who denounced Yukimori for being a "lumpen proletariat criminal of low revolutionary consciousness who sold out our revolutionary fellow students to the state." They were suspicious of Yukimori's defense and opposed efforts to establish his alibi. They ultimately split from the support committee and formed their own "revolutionary support committee." Akutsu had patiently explained to both the Q. Sect students and Professor Ikéhata that their assessment of Yukimori's confession was wildly inappropriate, but the more passionately he corrected them, the more they pushed against him. The professor had castigated Akutsu for being so ill mannered as to discuss a habitual criminal on the same level as his daughter, and the students had ridiculed him as a "bourgeois defender of anti-revolutionary elements."

Why had Makihiko Moriya been the first out of the gate to confess? It was true enough that he was an excitable young man with a weak personality who had simply folded under pressure from the police, but why include his woman (former woman, really), Wakako Ikéhata, when he was naming co-conspirators? Maybe there was some truth to his confession. Maybe Q. Sect really did hatch a bomb plot and one of their members carried it out. If that was the case, you could say the best thing for Q. Sect would be for Atsuo Yukimori and Wakako Ikéhata to be branded the culprits. It was hardly coincidental that when *A. Shimbun* launched a media campaign that cast Yukimori and Ikéhata as innocent of the charges, the police raided Q. Sect headquarters and hauled in members for questioning. There might have been some truth after all to the goldfish woman's "vector analysis" that a defense strategy of establishing the innocence of Yukimori, Ikéhata, and Jinnai would make Moriya, Tagawa, and Shinya look all the more guilty.

Akutsu had of course argued in the courtroom for the innocence of all the defendants, including the Q. Sect members, but when it came to Moriya's case, his defense would sometimes sound equivocal. That had earned him protests and sarcastic remarks from Kida and Uzawa, the Q. Sect attorneys.

The defense environment worsened immeasurably when six members of the K. Sect, armed with steel pipes, stormed into the Q. Sect headquarters. In the ensuing battle, one Q. Sect member died and three more suffered skull fractures serious enough to disable them for life. Police found a blood-spattered room and a paper pasted to the wall that said, "Divine punishment for the Shinkansen bombers." Shortly thereafter, the Q. Sect attacked the K. Sect's hideout, seriously injuring two members. This escalation of the war between the two sects had thus far resulted in 13 deaths, 700 injuries, and 400 arrests.

Yoko appeared at the door to the study. "Aren't you going to your office?"

"I'm going to stay here a little longer. More of the papers I need to look at are right here."

"If you're not going to the office, please call Ms. Wada, Mr. Kida, Mr. Jinnai, and Professor Kirikaé who are expecting to reach you there. I'll switch over the phone so you can call out from here."

"Gotcha."

"I'm taking Reiko. Oh, and just before you leave, check that the washer isn't leaking."

Yoko hurried off. Akutsu noticed that the roof of the inn was no longer shining, and the sky was graying with clouds. His mood a trifle heavier, he resumed reading the newspaper.

"5. Alibis

"Prosecution — Sometime between 3:50 and 4:00 p.m. on February 11, 1969, Atsuo Yukimori and Wakako Ikéhata entered car No. 2 of Shinkansen Hikari No. 33 from Tokyo Station's Shinkansen Platform Eighteen, placed a time bomb on an overhead luggage rack and then exited the train. They were witnessed boarding the train by two newspaper stand workers and one passenger. Neither defendant has an alibi proving they were elsewhere at the time.

"Defense — Atsuo Yukimori was in Jindai Botanical Garden in Chofu City from 3:30 until 4:30 p.m. on that day. He appears in a commemorative group photograph of patients and nurses from Y. Hospital, taken between 3:30 and 4:00 that day by the hospital's recreational supervisor, Yoko Mizuno. The group was there on a plum blossom viewing outing. Wakako Ikéhata met Brother Leopold Larra outside the Station Front Church near Yotsuya Station at approximately 3:20 p.m. on that day, and subsequently sat inside the church during a farewell ceremony for Sister Teresa Yugé until past five o'clock."

Those alibis were the number one item of contention in the case. Proving them amounted to kicking away the underpinnings of the Shinkansen bombing case that cast Atsuo Yukimori and Wakako Ikéhata as the executors of a plot hatched by Makihiko Moriya and company; the investigation would be back to square one. The hearings in the case had been largely concerned with the prosecution's attempts to undermine new evidence that supported the alibis presented by the defense.

When Akutsu had submitted the photograph of Atsuo Yukimori striding past a group of hospital patients assembled under a plum tree in blossom, the prosecutor, Domaé, had argued it was a picture taken before the day of the crime. Yukimori had owned the distinctive necktie and duster coat shown in the photograph prior to that day, and by his own admission, he had visited the park and encountered patients from that hospital on several occasions. Therefore, Domaé had announced smugly, it could not be determined that the photograph was taken on the day of the crime.

Yoko Mizuno then uncovered counter evidence. She contacted F. Corporation, the photographic film manufacturer, and inquired about the emulsion number appearing on the photograph's negative. It meant that the film had been manufactured in May 1967. Therefore, the blossoms on the plum tree appearing in the photo had to have been those of either February 1968 or 1969. Next, she checked the records of admission and discharge of the patients and the dates of employment of the hospital staff members appearing in the photo. That information pinned down the date the picture was taken to one day only — February 11, 1969.

The factual support of this defense evidence was precise. Two nurses who had begun working at the hospital in April 1968 and three patients admitted after that time appeared in the photograph, so it could not have been taken in February 1968. That left only February 1969, and no later than February 13, because Atsuo Yukimori had taken an airplane to Hokkaido the following morning, as the prosecution had demonstrated. Y. Hospital had taken patients plum blossom viewing on February 9 and 11 that year, but one of the nurses appearing in the photo had only begun employment on February 10. That eliminated all possibilities other than February 11.

Thus, the prosecutor, Shunji Domaé, had to concede that the photo was taken on the day of the crime. He proceeded from the view that Yoko Mizuno's saying the photo was taken at a certain time didn't make it so. She had testified that on that day, she had left the hospital at two o'clock in the afternoon, with the head nurse, other nurses and sixty-three patients, that they had arrived at Jindai Botanical Garden at two-thirty and left again at four o'clock in order to be back to the hospital in time for supper at four-thirty; the photos had been taken hastily within a thirty minute period before leaving the park, in other words, between three and four o'clock. Domaé seized on this testimony.

"Why do you say you arrived at the park at two-thirty?"

"Why? . . . Recreation therapy time begins at two o'clock at Y. Hospital. At the rate the patients walk, it takes thirty minutes to reach the park from the hospital."

"What did you do when you arrived at the park?"

"We headed straight for the plum blossoms. Show beautiful flowers in bloom to people who have slow emotional responses and you put them in touch with the flowers themselves. It is a technique called inductive therapy."

"Why were you carrying a camera?"

"To take pictures of our activities to go into the fifteenth anniversary history of Y. Hospital."

"Including pictures of inductive therapy?"

"Yes, of course."

"Did you take pictures of inductive therapy by plum blossom viewing?"

"Yes, a few of the pictures show that."

"Then you began taking pictures when you arrived at the park at two-thirty. Did you continue to take pictures until you left the park at four o'clock?"

"Yes, but most of the picture-taking was between three-thirty and four o'clock. This photograph in evidence is one of those taken in that time period."

"How can you be sure of that? There is no record of the time each photograph was taken. If your objective is a photographic record of inductive therapy, the natural approach would be to take pictures at every stage. You made an album of all the photographs taken that day arranged in the order you took them. This photograph in evidence was among the first several photographs in that album, wasn't it?"

"Most of the pictures were taken just before we left the park. We were in a hurry to get back in time for supper at four-thirty."

"People normally take a lot of pictures at first and fewer later on. Your approach to taking pictures is very unusual."

"Not at all." Yoko's voice had risen in excitement. "That day I was so focused on induction therapy I forgot to take pictures at first. When time was getting short, I remembered I needed pictures, so I started shooting one after another."

"Is all that part of your recollection?" Domaé regarded her placidly, his imposing frame stock still.

"What does that mean?" Yoko asked darkly.

"You went on plum blossom outings three times in 1969, on February 9, 11, and 14, and you took photographs on all three occasions — altogether, there are two hundred photos from those excursions. I wonder if it is possible to remember when one of those pictures was taken."

"It was! That day was . . ."

"All three of those excursions began in the afternoon. You had already done one, on the 9th. February 11th was the second time. Is it possible, despite this, to remember what was going on in your mind on that particular day? Aren't you just saying you took those pictures between three-thirty and four o'clock because that time slot is in the interest of proving the defendant has an alibi for that time?"

"Your honor!" Jun Akutsu exploded. "The prosecutor is forcing his opinion on the witness!"

The presiding judge nodded. "Mr. Prosecutor, please be a little more careful about your manner of expression."

"Forgive me. I will be more careful." Domaé conceded offhandedly.

Akutsu took his turn, for redirect examination of the witness. Once again, he asked Yoko about the time frame when she took the photograph, and, of course, she could only give the same answer she had given the prosecutor. Nothing changed the fact that, Yoko's spirited testimony notwithstanding, only the approximate time of day was certain about what time the crucial photo was taken.

Shunji Domaé instantly rose to present his opinion.

"Three points, your honor, concerning what has been shown. First, according to the present witness testimony, the photograph of defendant Atsuo Yukimori was taken between two-thirty and four o'clock on the afternoon of February 11, and possibly early within that time frame. Secondly, it takes twenty minutes to get from Jindai Botanical Garden to Mitaka Station by bus, and thirty-seven minutes from there to Tokyo Station by a rapid-service train. Allowing fifteen minutes for making connections means the distance to Tokyo Station could easily be covered in one hour and ten minutes. Point number three: If the photograph was taken by two-forty, there was plenty of time to be on Platform Eighteen at three-fifty as the doors opened to Hikari No. 33."

"Who do you expect to buy that story?" Yoko yelled angrily. A moment later she was hanging her head, having been sternly silenced by the presiding judge.

Domaé dealt with Wakako Ikéhata's alibi by first conceding her meeting with Brother Larra outside the Station Front Church that day, and that she had been present at Sister Yugé's farewell ceremony later, provided that the former event had occurred at three-twenty in the afternoon, and that she had only been inside the church after four-fifteen. He then explained that she would have had no trouble trysting with Yukimori on Platform Eighteen during the interval, because the trip from the Station Front Church could easily be made in twenty minutes. This reasoning was based on Brother Larra's testimony that Hymn 656 that Wakako Ikéhata had heard when she entered the church had been sung at approximately four-fifteen.

Akutsu's investigation of the sisters of the Mercediarian order who had attended Sister Yugé's funeral brought him to a sister who had recorded the entire proceedings on a cassette recorder, with narration:

"The time is three-twenty in the afternoon, February eleventh, 1969. We are at the Station Front Church, where the requiem mass for Sister Teresa Yugé is about to begin. Father Okuda is conducting the ceremony."

With this, the beginning of the requiem mass is heard on the tape, and is followed by the farewell ceremony. Counting up from the time spoken by the sister, the farewell ceremony that opens with Hymn 656 should begin at three-fifty-five, and, sure enough, five minutes later, the sound of a clock chiming somewhere can be heard, with no room for disputing it is announcing four o'clock.

If Wakako Ikéhata was in the church at three-fifty-five, that fact was by itself fatal to the prosecution's case that required her to be on Shinkansen Platform Eighteen in Tokyo Station between three-fifty and four o'clock. One could hardly hope for a stronger alibi. But Domaé was untroubled over such a trifling matter as producing counter evidence on this point. He raised issue once more with Wakako Ikéhata's actions and her memory.

"You have stated that when you went into the church Hymn 656 was being sung. How did you know it was number 656?"

"It is a very well-known hymn. Every Catholic knows it."

"What are the lyrics?"

Wakako Ikéhata began to sing in a more than competent soprano voice.

> Trust patiently, my soul, trust in the Lord
> Let God your burdens hold and loving help afford
> Abandon not hope, but hear the trumpet sound
> Morning breaks and springtime follows winter's chill
> Depend on God's protection; his truth is your salvation

Domaé stopped her when she began the second verse.

"That's enough. Let's continue. When you entered the church did you receive a pamphlet entitled 'Program of a Requiem Mass and Farewell Ceremony for Our Deceased Sister Teresa Yugé'?"

"Yes. A sister standing at the entrance gave it to me."

"Do you remember what the program included?"

"Yes, most of it. I'm always interested to know what hymns are sung, so I usually read that kind of program carefully. I'm pretty sure it was the Requiem, Number 602, Number 75, and 'May everlasting light shine upon them — Lux Aeterna.' The farewell ceremony was Number 656 and Number 660."

"You learn the numbers of hymns besides the names?"

"Yes. I find that helps learning, for me, at least."

"For example, what is Number 602?"

My Jesus, as thou wilt! . . .

"You don't have to sing it. You certainly have a remarkable memory. Now, when you entered the church, Hymn 658 was being sung."

"No, it was Hymn Number 656."

"Well, with a memory like yours, you could identify any hymn being sung. Of course, all you had to do was look at the program for that day and remember the number of the hymn scheduled for the time closest to when the crime was committed."

Domaé's handsome features highlighted the drama of his questioning. He cast a harsh stare at Wakako Ikéhata's profile in silence. She was facing the judges from the witness stand, unable to see the prosecutor looking at her, but at that moment, she stirred, as if struck by his gaze.

"According to Brother Larra's testimony, you were sitting cross-legged in a zazen pose in the last row at the back of the church during the funeral ceremony — not the farewell ceremony. Wasn't it the requiem mass, rather than the farewell ceremony that was in progress when you met Brother Larra?"

"I was not there for the mass."

"Hmm, I wonder. Brother Larra had occasion to come into the church several times during the mass, and he says he saw you then."

"I don't know anything about that. There is no way I could, because I was not there during the mass."

"You were outside the church immediately before the funeral began. Why didn't you go inside?"

"I answered that before. I had taken LSD and was experiencing hallucinations. The church seemed to be made of soft rubber. It felt dangerous, so I ran up onto to the embankment across the street to get away."

"February eleven was cloudy and cold. You went out on that embankment where there was a cold, blustery wind and stayed out in it thirty minutes?"

"Correct. I waited it out until the visions stopped."

"What kind of visions were you having?"

"The city was crumbling, there was a sea of flames burning it up. The church was collapsing and crushing the people inside. The crucifix melted and fell down."

"It's funny that you would have such a fantastic hallucination over that thirty-minute period. You're saying you were normal, then suddenly you had thirty minutes of hallucinations, but the scientific papers available on LSD say the hallucinations continue for a set period, not go on and off as you described."

"My hallucinations go on and off."

"Please give truthful testimony. You entered the church while the funeral mass was in progress, as Brother Larra testified, then you looked to see what the program would be between three-fifty and four o'clock and then you left the church no later than three-thirty."

"Objection!" Akutsu said. "The prosecutor has made a purely speculative statement on no grounds whatsoever."

"The objective is sustained," the presiding judge said.

"I withdraw the statement. Nevertheless, I think I have demonstrated some important points. There is no objective evidence to establish that the defendant was present in the church to hear Hymn Number 656 as she has testified. We've seen that she saw the program for Sister Yugé's funeral and has it memorized, down to its lyrics. That is all."

As Akutsu put down the newspaper, an image arose in his mind of Domaé's cold features, like a profile carved in steel. Suddenly the telephone on his desk began to ring.

It was Yoko, speaking at a high enough level to cause eardrum pain. "I'm calling from the lobby."

"Is that as far as you've gotten? What's the hold-up?"

"I just happened to run into Yoshié here. She has something to tell you. Give her a quick listen, will you?"

"I don't want to give individual interviews. There will be time to handle everybody's questions at the press conference this afternoon."

"She doesn't want an interview. She has some very important information. She just told me. I can't say what it is over the phone. It's that big."

"All, right, I get it." Akutsu held down his copy of *A. Shimbun* with the palm of his hand. "I'll meet her, but it has to be brief."

725

"Thanks."

"If you don't get to the hospital in a hurry, you won't be on time for the spectator gallery ticket lottery."

"I'll make it. They won't have the lottery until the last minute. There isn't any advantage to getting there early."

The study was too far from the entrance to hear to hear the door chime. Akutsu hurried to the living room and cleared away the breakfast remnants from the table. In a moment the chime rang. "Sorry to barge in on you like this." Yoshié Wada, in a pants suit, strode inside and got straight to the point. She wore no makeup over her suntan.

"I got to meet with assistant police inspector Hino yesterday. I was finally able to find out where he lives last week. I kept calling him for an interview, and he kept refusing. Then suddenly yesterday afternoon he agreed, on a certain condition. That condition he set is what I want to talk to you about."

"The great assistant inspector Hino! I should say the notorious Hino. He's the guy who made Atsuo Yukimori give a false confession. He has more responsibility than anyone else for the whole frame-up. What does he want now?"

"Now he says the confession was completely involuntary because the interrogators forced it on him with coercion, threats, and leading questions."

"That's hard to believe. He's on record in the first trial testifying the confession was completely voluntary."

"He says that's what he believed at the time. After the press started running with the theory that the photo proves Mr. Yukimori's alibi and the defendants are innocent, he says he read over all the statements and his own notes on the investigation, and that brought him to recognize he was mistaken."

"It doesn't make much sense. If that's true, why did he let his lies stand? Why didn't he give us a statement of the truth?"

"Because he wasn't that brave. He didn't want to say anything that would reflect poorly on fellow police officers still on the job. He was afraid his old buddies would turn against him. There are lots of reasons, but to hear him, it seems the biggest one of all is loyalty to Superintendent Noseh, who was running the investigation on that case. Since then, Noseh became a chief superintendent, and now he is running N. Prefecture police headquarters. He retires at the end of this March. Everyone at Hino's station worked under Noseh, so . . ."

"Cops have to stand by their fellow officers' honor, and they have to be loyal to their chief. Therefore, they are not free. Seems like I've heard that story before."

"It's the same wherever you work."

"Except that in this case looking after that old gang of mine means sending innocent citizens to the gallows or putting them in jail for life. It is not excusable . . . So what is the condition our intrepid assistant inspector has set for talking?"

"I can only run the story if today's decision is not guilty for all defendants."

"And keep quiet if they are found guilty again. My goodness, such bravery."

"It's to be expected, I guess. He's wavering about the whole thing. Going public about a thing like this is a life-changing event for him."

"Yes, I can understand that. Well, what is my part in this?"

"Assuming this story goes into the evening edition, I would like to include a comment from the defense side. It's sure to get special feature handling. Heavy criticism of an investigation like this from one of the core investigators is very hot stuff."

"Indeed. That's what they call a bombshell. But just be careful to avoid getting him hit with a charge of violating the National Public Service Law. Article 100. 'Public service workers shall not divulge secrets learned in the course of performing their duties. This prohibition shall continue to apply after public service workers leave their positions.'"

"I'd like to have your advice on that point. But, you know, the only secrets we are talking about is how the police interrogated their suspects, and that violates the law, too — the Constitution."

"Article thirty-eight, paragraph two: 'Confession made under compulsion, torture or threat, or after prolonged arrest or detention shall not be admitted in evidence.' The Constitution is something to be proud of. The police are supposed to abide by it, but they don't. In which case, I don't see that there should be any issue made of Hino violating the public service employee's obligation to secrecy."

"You would think so, but if Mr. Hino does run into trouble, could he ask you to be his lawyer?"

"I couldn't do that because of the way I am already involved in this case. But I could refer him to a lawyer I know who would be very good."

"That is a major encouragement. This has been a very worthwhile visit."

With that, Yoshié Wada visibly relaxed, as if a camera had stopped rolling, leaving her off duty. Akutsu was feeling a hint of desire for this unmarried woman with a willowy figure that contrasted intriguingly with Yoko's ample proportions. Yoshié's suntan came from springtime skiing. She blinked self-consciously under the other's gaze.

"Actually, I have another request. After today's decision, and of course after the press conference, I would like to hear your assessment of the whole trial, in detail."

"For you, yes, I would be glad to," Akutsu said brightly, completely forgetting he had told Yoko earlier he didn't want to deal with individual interviews.

"That will be a big help . . . Oh, well, might as well ask just one more, teeny favor," Yoshié said, tilting her face to the side and lightly winking. "Tell me your gut feeling on what today's decision will be. Not guilty? Reduced sentence? Appeal rejected?"

"That's a tough question," Akutsu said. Dropping his eyes to her slim waist and thinking, here is a woman I would like to bed, he said, "I would say six to four, not guilty. Of course, I'm supposed to expect victory, but a look at all the papers suggests that, as usual, weather conditions favor the prosecution. The worst possible outcome is our appeal gets thrown out."

"If that happens, at least some of the public won't keep quiet about it. I can push back hard with Mr. Hino's admissions, and I will."

"Wouldn't that be against his condition for going public?"

"That's not really a big issue. He just said that for the sake of saying it. He's got a book he wants to sell — The Untold Story of the Shinkansen Bombing Case. He's been working on it ever since he retired. The game plan is to get famous by spilling his story in the papers, collect manuscript fees from some weekly magazine for a series of articles, then publish the articles as a book and collect more royalties."

"This is all about his own fame and fortune?"

"Not entirely. He wants to settle old scores too. He never rose any higher than assistant inspector. He has no higher education, he spent his whole career in homicide at the bottom level, on the street chasing down suspects. His senior on the case was Inspector Magara, who has the university degree that put him on the fast track. Magara's still in his thirties, and already he's Onarimon station chief. Hino is full of resentment about one thing and another, but especially about Magara. It was Hino who made Mr. Yukimori confess, but Magara got the Metropolitan Police Chief's award on the case. Hino says he got no recognition at all. According to him he was approached by Noseh, who was Inspector at the time and told him Magara was going to get the award because he had a big future and Hino was up for retirement. Noseh put it in terms of Hino doing a personal favor for him: 'Okay, sure, happy to help you out, sir. Let Magara take the credit.' So, Magara got the award and a promotion to superintendent, which put him into the echelons of Osaka Prefecture Police administrators. The year after Hino retired, Magara started claiming credit for single-handedly solving the Shinkansen case with some kind of advanced investigation method. He was setting himself up as an expert on terrorist cases. He got an article published in the Police Science Journal, 'Investigating Bomb Cases.' He stopped talking about the case when the media began raising the possibility the defendants are innocent. When the wind started blowing in that direction, everyone who was involved in the case laid the blame on Hino for steering the investigation in the wrong direction. Noseh keeps Hino informed about all this. Noseh has been paying visits to Magara's home lately."

"This is like following a soap opera."

"Exactly. Assistant Inspector Hino is casting himself as the muckraker. He wants to tell all, lay it out in the open. *The Confessions of a Confession Maestro.* Now, these are his words about what he did: He had Mr. Yukimori on the grill from morning to night, with no breaks. He used threats, promises, lies, and misinformation. He says he hypnotized Mr. Yukimori to make him confess."

"I'd like to hear him talk about that sometime. I can imagine what that kind of interrogation is like, but, just like everyone else, I've never actually seen it. It doesn't make any difference that I'm a criminal lawyer."

"I listened to him for six hours last night. He gives a very impressive performance. Hino is a virtuoso. You wouldn't believe a man shorter than I am could be so intimidating, but he is, because of his energy. He gave me a demonstration. 'We already know everything. We're just giving you the chance to come clean and get a lighter sentence. Just say what happened and don't hide anything — You hear me talking to you, girl?' First he's purring like a cat, then suddenly he's giving you verbal abuse. I knew it was just a show, but I was trembling anyway, like I'd done some terrible thing and he'd caught me at it. He keeps you guessing where he's going to come from next. You listen to his nonsense in spite of yourself. If I had to spend every night in jail and listen to that every day, I don't doubt I would be blurting out confessions to anything at all.

"Another thing that impressed me about Hino's technique is the way he made imaginative use of the few facts the investigation turned up about what Atsuo Yukimori had been doing. Hino connected the dots into a pattern that didn't exist before. Having majored in psychology, I know you could call that 'Gestalt formative ability' — 'gestalt' meaning 'percept.' In other words, he has a creative way of perceiving reality. That Shinkansen bombing unearthed a lot of random facts that didn't naturally tell a story by themselves, but Hino saw a pattern no one else saw. He believed in it implicitly and conveyed that belief to his suspects. That's what he means when he says he hypnotized them, and I guess that's as good a word as any. The hypnotist has charisma and keeps sending the same monotonous stimulus over and over until the subject's in a trance and starts accepting the hypnotist's suggestions as his own thoughts. That is exactly how those confessions materialized. Hypnosis is not a particularly advanced technique. Assistant inspector Hino picked it up on his own through long experience."

"Would you say that you could make anybody give a confession that could stand up in court, just by letting a policeman like Hino keep your suspect isolated long enough for him to play games with his mind?"

"Yep. Mr. Hino is a virtuoso, but I think most, if not all, police stations in Japan have the basic ability to do what he did. I presume the techniques are learned in on-the-job training. The police don't talk about it, but any psychology undergraduate would know the principles well enough."

"Japan is a backward country when it comes to the rights of criminal suspects, although the government insists that we're advanced. America has the 1966 Miranda Supreme Court decision that says suspects cannot be subjected to coercion while in custody and they must be informed of their rights to remain silent and have legal counsel present during questioning. Police can't even question a suspect without a lawyer present, unless the suspect waives that right. In this country they just haul you into a little room where there is nobody else but policemen like Hino who don't take no for an answer."

"Incidentally, about that piece on Mr. Hino; it's my own feature — top secret, at least until two o'clock, which is the deadline for the evening edition."

"Understood. I won't tell anyone. Where does that guy live?"

"His address is secret, but he's not home anyway. I spirited him off to a certain place. He needs to be hidden right now . . . Well, I guess that's all. This was a good morning blitz for me."

"A what?"

"It's something reporters do. Night and morning blitzes. Hitting a source just when he's getting off work, or just before he starts work. Bye, now."

Yoshié Wada departed, not quite running, but covering ground quickly. From the window, he saw a large black car flying the *A. Shimbun* flag slipping into traffic. It was seven-forty-two. While he was thinking it was about time for him to get going too, the telephone rang. It was attorney Kida. Though Kida always spoke in a low voice, it would become lower still when he was tense. This time he was so gravelly, his voice had the disquieting effect of an anonymous threatening call.

"Are you having some kind of trouble?"

"The K. Sect released a declaration. Someone stuffed it into our mail slot yesterday. It says 'Harsh judgments will be meted out today to the support group outside the courthouse. If any among the anti-revolutionary traitors Makihiko Moriya, Shinichi Tagawa, or Akito Shinya are released, their fate is in our hands. We will never forgive the leaders of the Q. Sect, which carried out the criminal killings of so many brave revolutionary comrades.' The same paper was delivered to attorney Uzawa and the members of the Q. Sect defendants support group."

"That does sound like trouble. What is that stuff about harsh judgments to support group members supposed to mean? The regular support group is one thing and the 'revolutionary' support group is quite another. What about that?"

"I think those guys make that distinction, but that doesn't mean there's no danger of ordinary people getting hurt."

"There will be riot police around the courtroom looking out for exactly that kind of trouble. They couldn't do anything violent there if they tried."

"I think you're right. At least, I hope so. What has me worried is what happens if we get our not guilty decision and the defendants are released. How do we assure their safety?"

"I hate to be coldhearted, but that's the Q. Sect's problem. I don't think it is up to the attorneys to worry about things like that. Do you?"

"I'm worried about family members, most especially Makihiko Moriya's mother. There's no father. She came to Tokyo from Togi on the Noto peninsula, and has specifically requested that the defense lawyers look out for her son's safety. She knows that him being on the Q. Sect's executive committee makes him a prime target for K. Sect terror operations."

"'Look out for his safety.' I don't know how we do that." Akutsu fumed inwardly about the knotty problems that kept popping up in this case. He struck his chest with a fist as he pondered. "Say we get him a hotel room . . . That's it. Put in a request to the detention center to keep the time of his release secret. Make it late at night, so no one sees. That's a common tactic for releasing yakuza bosses."

"That's good. I'll call the detention center right now. Although the K. Sect is watching the center. I don't suppose they won't notice, whatever time he's released."

"In any case, there is only about a fifty-fifty chance of our getting a not-guilty decision. Did you see the morning papers? Public opinion is still on the prosecution side. They're having the victims' families say they want stiff penalties for the defendants. Well, see you at Akasaka at nine."

Jun Akutsu put down the receiver and prepared to leave. He was pledged to meet with the other attorneys on the joint defense at his office in Akasaka at nine o'clock.

About the same time, Makihiko Moriya finished packing all his possessions into a cardboard box. He had been suddenly ordered to do so, and received no answer when he asked why. Do I get turned loose right away if it's not guilty, he had asked again, but the guard would only shake his head. The guard was a disgusting middle-aged running dog of state power, whom he would gladly kill one day. On this day, it was best to obey his orders. There was no question that the decision would be not guilty. They didn't show a single piece of inculpative evidence against me. (My comrades will join me in taking my revenge upon every one of those class bigots, for sneering at "the radical," after I'm freed. We'll break their necks, one after the next. Laugh, you slaves of state power, for your remaining hours of vainglory are few.)

Enough of those thoughts. An unflattering image arose in Makihiko Moriya's mind of himself carrying his cardboard box and making a dash for safety. He clucked his tongue sharply. The lives of himself, as the Q. Sect central executive committee member, and those of operations squad chief Shinichi Tagawa and operation squad member Akito Shinya were in the sights of their arch-enemies at the K. Sect, who restlessly awaited their opportunity to attack. All three Q. Sect members would have to go underground immediately upon their release. The attorneys Kida and Uzawa had informed him their comrades had readied a safe house for them in Tokyo, but he could not believe such a place would be safe. He had to assume they would be under the K. Sect's watch from the moment they stepped out from the detention center.

Attorney Kida was also doubtful we could stay safely concealed. "We'll take precautions to keep your whereabouts unknown to them, but to be honest, there is no real way to be sure they aren't following."

It was laughable irony. "In other words, what it comes to is the safest hideout is the detention center?" I asked.

Kida was, as usual, utterly straight-faced, now with a touch of pessimism in his expression. "That's it. The state can provide far better security than the Q. Sect."

"I guess we have to be grateful to our detention center," I said, even more sarcastically, staring straight at him.

Kida would go straight to hell before he would abandon that deadpan expression of his. "That's right. If it wasn't for this Shinkansen charge — say, you were just convicted on the Tower takeover, which would be maybe two years, for storing weapons, trespassing, and interfering with officers' performance of duties; you would have been out long ago, and you probably would not have escaped harm after they let you go."

Makihiko Moriya's thoughts turned to a tentative plan to live out of sight in a certain cave. It was located at the end of a precipice on the Noto Peninsula, hollowed out of the rock. He had discovered it as a child, halfway up a rocky peak, beyond where a woodcutter's trail petered out. The cave looked out over breaking waves and resonated with the whistling of the wind through a hole in the rock. There was a narrow entrance that opened to a chamber about thirty meters across — the equivalent of a twenty-mat room. The rock facing formed surfaces serviceable as a bed and a table. A pathway along the rocky shoreline had recently been laid out for people coming to hike and fish, but the cave was not at all visible from there, and remained undisturbed. From the time he started going to T. University, he had continued coming back to the cave, bringing in food supplies each time. He would be safe there, listening to the wind and the cries of the seabirds.

No, no — that was no good. Such thoughts were defeatist. He clucked his tongue sharply a number of times, then began pacing with long strides, from wall to wall to wall, back and forth, approaching the wall, then withdrawing, like ocean waves at the shore.

Who is behind the Shinkansen bombing? Whoever did it is out there somewhere. At first, I fell for that cop story that Atsuo Yukimori did it. They said he was a machine gunner way back when, that he had a long record and a fixation for blowing things up. I thought, yeah, he must be the one. That led to me saying a lot of made-up stuff, and then they cornered me into saying the Q. Sect planned it all. Fine law student I am — it didn't even occur to me the "joint principals in a conspiracy" principle would apply, meaning we don't have to have actually done it to be charged with the crime. Call it instant reprisal for cutting lectures on crimlaw and burning Professor Kotaro Ikéhata's research papers.

It is true enough that the Q. Sect had thought — vaguely — about bombing trains — Shinkansen among the possibilities. The cops reheated and ran with that story. At that meeting in Hongo at the inn on April 22, 1967, maybe ten sentences were spoken about bombing trains — if you include jokes. It was one item of a long agenda that included street demonstrations, issuing pamphlets, closing down campuses, and attacking police stations. There were about fifteen people — not fifty! — and Wakako Ikéhata wasn't even there, much less on the central committee. There were a few things said about bombing some train, but that was all. There wasn't any planning, none of that shit about timers and manufacturing and experimenting. But the cops knew about that little exchange on bombing a train, and that can only mean there must have been a spy among the fifteen who were present at that meeting. There's more: that spy was not only peddling information to the cops, but to the K. Sect too. Attorney Kida sees a relationship between those targeted by the K. Sect for their terror operations and the list of who attended that April 22nd meeting.

The K. Sect has issued countless tracts denouncing the Q. Sect for being degenerate criminals against the people and committing crimes like the Shinkansen bombing. As far as the Q. Sect is concerned, they are the betrayers of the revolution and the phony opportunists. Thence continues the feud between the two sects, consisting of pitched battles, raids or assassinations that occur every so often.

There is widespread misunderstanding about us. I testified about it in court time and again. We didn't call ourselves the Q. Sect. There was no clear-cut organization. Nobody said anything about "the Q. Sect" at that April 22 meeting. There wasn't any membership log, then or afterwards. We were just a bunch of people who would get together for whatever action was coming up, be it a meeting, a demonstration, or a scrap. The membership was always fluid, sometimes more members, sometimes fewer. The name for the organization was just something we used when there had to be a name. Sometimes Wakako Ikéhata was there, but the cops are the only ones who ever called her a Q. Sect member. As for that organization name, it took on a life of its own, and the more it stirred up hatred by the K. Sect, the more it became a distinctive presence.

Being attacked by the K. Sect brought us together, and made each one of us see our identity as a Q. Sect member, however, we might have seen it previously. You beat a guy up, and the pain he feels won't let him forget his own existence. The terror operations between the two sects brought horrific damage to both sides. The press and the law always have great fun jeering at what they call "internecine fighting" between the radicals. Well, we are radicals, in the most honorable sense of the term, whereas the K. Sect is nothing but a bunch of opportunists who aren't qualified to be called radicals of any kind, and probably are in secret contact with the state's security apparatus. It doesn't make any sense to call our war with a group like that "infighting.")

Makihiko Moriya stopped his pacing and wiped sweat from his forehead with the palm of his hand. His physical strength had fallen off in the recent past, to the point that even a little walking was enough to make him breathless and break out in a terrible sweat. By nature not very strong and prone to illness, lack of exercise and many days of sleepless nights pondering the future of the Q. Sect had taken a heavy toll on him. He sat down on the tatami and leaned back against the wall. He closed his eyes in defiance of the creeping darkness that hung over the cell.

The K. Sect did not lose a single moment to declare the Shinkansen bombing had been the work of the Q. Sect, using it as a pretext for terror operations against us, serving the interest of the state's security forces in its own way. But we didn't have anything to do with that bombing. The real perpetrator is lurking somewhere, and the K. Sect is suspect. It is entirely conceivable the attacks on the Q. Sect were intended to cover up the fact that it committed the crime. Whatever the truth is, it is up to me to get to work finding the perpetrator, without delay. The state has squandered unbelievable resources for nearly a decade to prove five innocent people guilty, without lifting a finger to find the real perpetrators. By now, any middle school student can see the case against us is a bunch of lame lies, but the man in the prosecutor suit doesn't mind repeating the same tired litany, even though it stopped meaning anything long ago. Who knows? Maybe they know very well we are innocent. That has nothing to do with it, as far as they are concerned. The only important thing to them is, stay on the original line and save face. They don't care — they are perfectly willing to use all their power to make sure the real perpetrator is never found.

If these trials have proven anything, it's the inherent violence of state power. A country that calls itself advanced accuses innocent people of a serious crime on trumped up evidence, steals their freedom, subjects them to psychological torture, and calls it fair criminal procedure. It's no different than the witch trials of the Renaissance period, the Nazis' concentration camps, Stalin's POW camps. Their only reason for doing this to us is that the Q. Sect's goal was to abolish the state.

We started from the premise that Engels was way too optimistic with his formula in *Origin of the Family, Private Property and the State* that says you can do away with the state just by destroying the class system it uses to maintain its rule. In *The State and Revolution*, Lenin says the state is an evil that the proletariat maintains after it has seized control, but he clings to the illusion that it will wither away in the future. All you had to do was look at state power growing ever stronger in the Soviet Union he built to see that the truth is just the opposite.

Contrary to what Engels and Lenin prophesied, the twentieth century has seen no countries fade away, but rather the births of many new ones. For places that had once been colonized by imperialist powers, the new states were bastions of independence achieved through national liberation. In that sense, the state was an organization of precious value that was well worth protecting, but what followed was wars over national frontiers, confrontations over conflicting claims and ideologies, demonization of rivals and rampant nationalism. Worst of all, instead of having colonies, some countries were maintaining nuclear weapons to intimidate other countries. Now countries were no longer a necessary evil as Lenin said, but an abiding evil. The way to avoid the nuclear threat and insure the survival of humanity is not getting rid of nuclear weapons, but ending the existence of the evil of states willing to use nuclear weapons. When there are no states, young people won't have to pick up weapons to defend them. There won't be any reason for them to sacrifice their lives. There won't be any need to use the bomb or have it used against you. Abolish countries and have only regions: the Soviet region, the American, Japanese, and Chinese regions. Get rid of borders, armies, and customs, and set up a world federation with a single currency, where everyone comes and goes as they please. The first step on the road to that goal was taken by the Q. Sect.

Simultaneous world revolution will put an end to the state and to war. The greatness of Che Guevara leaving Cuba to die in a Bolivian jungle lies in his work for revolution not in one country, like Lenin, Stalin, or Mao, seeking instead to bring freedom through revolution to other countries. The road is long and hard, but the light of Che's ideals burns steadily throughout the suffering world, and inside me.

The concept of simultaneous world revolution held out by the Q. Sect is exactly what is lacking in the K. Sect. It came out on a line of patriotic revolution against American imperialism and Japanese monopoly capitalism. It could only see revolution on a small, national scale. That is no good. Yeah, that is no damn good! Break down these walls! Bring down the state!

Makihiko Moriya resolutely struck the wall with his fist. Searing pain shot through his hand. He had struck with too much force. He cocked a leg back and delivered a solid kick against the iron door. Instantly, the guard on duty was at the observation window, peering inside with eyes gleaming.

"What was that?"

"Nothing."

The sound of a key turning in the lock filled the air and the door opened. A brawny running dog of state power rushed inside, poised to impose submission. He pushed Moriya back from the door and gathered the front of his prison shirt with both hands.

"There's a dent in the dish slot cover. Damaging prison property is a punishable offense."

"So punish me." This guard was another target for revenge. His residence and family were known to the Q. Sect. The first step to abolition of the state would be his abolition.

"Moriya, you're leaving this cell now and getting on the bus to the courthouse. Bring that cardboard box over here."

"Why? Are they going to turn me loose?"

"We don't know that yet. You could be coming right back here this afternoon," the running dog said, with the malicious sneer all state running dogs had. It was the standard outcome of their mental processes.

About the same time Yukichi Jinnai lay abed in a psychiatric cell of the detention center's medical cell block. He was turning over again and again, trying to dislodge a wire in the core of his body. He had retired the night before with no such affliction, but had awakened to find that some kind of foreign object had been inserted into the core of his body as he slept. It was like a stiff rod somewhere in front of his backbone that made a creaking noise when he bent forward. When he tried bending backwards it pushed back, so he could not move freely. It was a piece of steel wire inside — that much was clear. The guard for the night had slipped into his cell and used acupuncture to insert it from the base of the neck. Presumably, there was an opening in his neck where the wire went in, but there was no mirror in the cell he could use to see it. He voiced a protest without delay. They guard was a half-senile old man who regarded him vacantly, as if he had already forgotten what he had been up to. The old fox was faking, of course.

It was impossible for Yukichi Jinnai to remove the wire. Fearing he might end up breaking blood vessels if he struggled too much made him half-resigned to the situation. He sat on the bed and looked through the window at the ground outside. There were three pigeons, then four pigeons pecking at grains of rice he had flung outside. He waited for them to fall over and emit foam from their beaks. The rice and oats breakfast he had been served had stank of poison. He had thrown a handful from the window to test its effect on pigeons. They were not falling over. A fifth pigeon joined in, peacefully eating the rice grains. Could he conclude the odor from the meal was simply because the rice was old? The miso and tofu soup also stank of what seemed to be some new kind of poison, but there was no way to test it on pigeons. In any case, the odor from the food was so bad that he had no desire to eat it.

Yukichi Jinnai dumped the entire breakfast meal into the toilet. As he flushed it, the wire in the core of his body suddenly creaked. He became alarmed that straightening up again would tear blood vessels, so he held his bent over position and laid back down on the bed that way. It was a crying shame that he would have to appear in court in such a state. The guard had done this to him with that in mind. He heard footsteps approaching. It was the psychiatric medical officer. The footsteps from outside went past the internal medicine cell and turned into the corridor outside the door. It was the steady pace of a self-confident man. Then he felt the stinging hotness of radio waves running from his cheek to his neck. That doctor carried a miniature transmitter in his pocket that sent out the waves whenever he pushed its button. It gave him control over the very feelings of others. Yukichi Jinnai had made many protests about it.

"Doctor, please stop sending radio waves."

"I'm not sending radio waves."

"You are. I feel my face get hot when you come this way."

"You are quite mistaken."

"It gives me a strange feeling, inside and outside, like I'm floating. It only happens when you are around." The radio waves intensified. The heat ran through his spine as if the wire in the core of his body was acting like an antenna.

The doctor and the guard on duty were standing beside him.

"Doctor, you are doing it again, aren't you? I can't stand those radio waves anymore. Everyone's coming around trying to kill me."

"Why did you want to see me? I happen to be on duty now. I have rounds to make, but I hurried over here." He was slightly out of breath.

"Like I said, everyone's trying to kill me. Breakfast was poisoned. They put wire in my back while I was sleeping."

"Who do you mean by 'everyone?'"

Yukichi Jinnai answered with a silent scowl. (I know very well who is behind all this. He orders the guards and the medical orderlies, and they do things like putting this wire in my body and poisoning my food. The only one in a position to do that is Prosecutor Domaé. He is even nastier than Prosecutor Onuki in the first trial. He started saying Yukichi Jinnai did not commit theft only to finance Q. Sect activities, but also took an active part in the bombing, so he should get the death penalty, the same as Atsuo Yukimori. That had me worried, so it was a relief when I asked Attorney Akutsu, and he said that wasn't anything to worry about because the second trial was only on the defense's appeal — since the prosecution didn't appeal, it couldn't ask for stiffer penalties than were given by the original decision. But the nasty tricks started immediately after that. If Domaé couldn't get a death sentence passed on me, he was going to pull strings to get me assassinated. I can't tell anyone on the side of the detention center about that. Of course it would be dangerous to confide in any doctor, who's only there to do what the prosecutor says. This one doesn't want to fix what ails me — he's bent on driving me completely crazy.

(I'm already neurotic, thanks to the night orderlies. They start stamping around loudly whenever I try to sleep. If I close my eyes, they stare at me through the window in the door. When it gets to be too much and I complain, I hear them laughing. So I ended up with insomnia. The doctor examined me and wrote out a prescription for sleeping pills. As soon as I swallowed one, the nerves in my skin began to act abnormally, and I started feeling radio waves on my bare cheeks, neck, and hands. I complained to the doctor, and it stopped for two or three days. I guess he turned off the switch. But it started up again. I kept complaining about it, and he turned it down far enough that I only felt it when he was close by. Thinking through all these things that are happening, you can see the doctor is carrying around a miniature transmitter in his pocket that he can control. I told him what I knew, and he said, oh, that's big-time neurosis. So he put me under watch in this psychiatric cell.)

The doctor took a look around the cell and said, "I suppose you have gotten your things together to get ready to appear in court, haven't you?"

"I ordered him to do that, but he hasn't lifted a finger," the guard said.

"Why bother? They're just going to turn down the appeal, and I'll be right back here. There's no need," Yukichi Jinnai said to the doctor.

The doctor was about thirty years of age, the same as Yukichi Jinnai. He dropped his eyes under Jinnai's intense gaze. Then, unexpectedly, he switched off the transmitter, giving immediate relief to Yukichi Jinnai's turmoiled condition. The burning sensation in the core of his body vanished.

(After they throw out our appeal, I'll just kill myself. I've had it. I'm not going to take any more of Domaé's plots. Okay, it's decided. I will put my things together, in preparation for my suicide.)

Yukichi Jinnai stood up. "I'll pack up everything now."

8:45 a.m.

Jun Akutsu arrived at his law office on the eleventh floor of a building in Akasaka. As he opened the door he received a hearty "Good morning!" from Einosuké Ishikawa, who was busily operating a copy machine. Akutsu's expression showed displeasure at not seeing the other attorney in his employ, Shoichi Nomoto. He had told them both to be there at eight-thirty. No sooner had he set down his briefcase on the room's centrally located desk than Einosuké Ishikawa approached. His father, Sadanosuké Ishikawa, had been his own mentor.

739

Einosuké had graduated the Judicial Research and Training Institute four years previously, at the same time Akutsu opened his own law office.

"There was a call from the courtroom reporters' association. They wanted to know where and when the press conference will be."

"That happens after the hearing is over. We don't know when that will be."

"That is what I told them. I just said that the venue would be Tokyo Bar Association auditorium. We also had visits from C. *Shimbun* and D. *Shimbun*, asking for comments. I turned them down. The other thing is I made up handouts for the press conference — a table showing the positions of the prosecutor and defense on each issue." Einosuké Ishikawa held up a neatly printed copy of the reference material he had prepared with a Japanese typewriter.

"A. *Shimbun* had a similar chart this morning. It was pretty good."

"Yeah, it was exactly the information I gave their reporter, Ms. Wada. The original here has more details, and it compares what the two trials were all about. I'd like for you to be my assistant at the press conference, in case I get something wrong."

Jun Akutsu considered the young attorney a reliable hand. Like his father, he had wiry hair that rose up impressively — a young version of the lion's mane that was the elder Ishikawa's trademark. Though he was still a relative newcomer to the profession, the gold plating of the attorney's sunflower badge Ishikawa wore was disproportionately worn down to dull silver. Noticing that raised an image in Akutsu's mind of himself sitting on a subway car, earnestly rubbing his badge in an effort to tarnish his own sheen of youthful inexperience. Through the window he noted the sky had a smokey look in the vicinity of the prime minister's residence, meaning probably that it had started to rain.

"I went to visit Yukichi Jinnai yesterday morning. He's acting strangely. They have him hospitalized. He expects to be found guilty, but what was really worrisome is he was saying weird things about how the prosecutor is trying to assassinate him."

"The prison doctor wrote up an evaluation of his state that said he had prison psychosis. So is that still it, an abnormal mental condition?"

"That was three months ago, and he hasn't changed since. Delusions of being poisoned, of being persecuted, confusion and something about being under attack by radio waves."

"You couldn't see any of those signs in court, though."

"I was wondering about that too. Actually, I went to N. Medical University yesterday afternoon to ask Dr. Matsuda's view about it. He said it is common for prisoners who are psychotic from being locked up to appear normal as soon as they are taken outside the prison. But he said Yukichi Jinnai is in danger of going from psychosis to full-blown schizophrenia. He said there are cases when simple psychosis triggers the more serious condition."

"Ouch! And Yukichi's family has been living for the day when he is released."

"If he's released today, he should be examined by Dr. Matsuda. I called his brother, Mr. Tetsukichi Jinnai, yesterday evening to ask that he have that arranged."

"There was a call to my house from him yesterday. I guess it was about that."

"I think it was. I said I thought it would be for the best if he asked you to refer Yukichi to Dr. Matsuda for examination."

Attorney Kida entered the room, as usual like a silent shadow, and addressed Akutsu in his customary sepulchral tone, with a courteous bow of his head. "Thanks for your advice. I asked the detention center to delay the time of release and keep it secret."

He was shortly followed by Attorneys Tsukioka and Uzawa, chatting volubly as they strolled in. The telephone rang. Einosuké Ishikawa instantly lifted the receiver, and a moment later passed it to Akutsu. It was Professor Kirikaé. A bullhorn squawking nearby him made it extremely difficult to make out what he was saying.

" . . . in front of the high court building . . . chaotic . . . support group . . . tickets for spectators' seats . . . they cut into the line . . . that's the situation."

"I got part of that, but I can't hear you very well."

Attorney Tsukioka was gabbing unconcernedly at a very noisy level. That manner of speaking was partly by nature, but it had become worse as aging had noticeably taken its toll on his hearing. Akutsu inserted an index finger into one ear and listened intently through the telephone receiver with the other.

" . . . so we'd like you to come now . . . reason with them . . . at all!"

"Hello? Reason with who? . . . hello? . . ."

Professor Kirikaé had hung up. Akutsu put down the phone and waited for it to ring again, but it didn't.

"Mornin'!" Tsukioka said, his face beaming.

Loss of weight in the near past had rendered Tsukioka quite wrinkled. On top of that, his hair had turned completely gray. Nevertheless, his visible aging had not in the slightest affected his active involvement in numerous criminal cases, among which his defense of a certain conservative politician's graft case had brought him renown. His partner on the Q. Sect defense, Attorney Uzawa, had inherited a share of attention in the press after Tsukioka had taken him on board in that case. Inevitably, the revolutionary faction of the Q. Sect support group had denounced Uzawa for taking the case, but the defendants' family members assessed his involvement favorably, taking it as certification of his ability and connection to power. Thus, Uzawa remained with the defense of the Shinkansen bombing defendants.

"Well, m'boy, the big day's come," Tsukioka said, pushing past Uzawa to clap Akutsu on the shoulder. "There's just one thing. Let's drop that business with the hired car company. I have two Rolls Camargues on reserve for us. They'll be our chariots for today. For a case this big, we can't have the defense team arriving in rinky-dink taxi cabs. Not live on national television. We'd never live it down if we came on looking stingy at a time like that."

"Camargues, eh?" Akutsu's brow furrowed as he spotted Shoichi Nomoto quietly enter past the appointed time. Nomoto had come from a corporate career and had just obtained his bar license the year before. He was past forty — older than Akutsu. It was no drawback that his oddly brownish complexion made for a less than personable appearance, but as his employer, Akutsu did not care for his casual approach to work — especially the lack of punctuality. "Nomoto, you did make a reservation for the hired cars, didn't you?"

"Oh, sorry, I forgot," Nomoto said, unnecessarily scratching his head.

"Well, that's a fortunate coincidence," Tsukioka said, nodding importantly and throwing his shoulders back. "No reason not to make our entrance from Camargues. It's still a little early. Getting out of here about nine-forty will be just right."

"The fact is I just had a call from Professor Kirikaé. There's some kind of disturbance in front of the courthouse. He says he wants me to go there right away. Something to do with people pushing in the line for observer seat tickets."

"That's the Q. Sect. They rallied about five hundred supporters in Hibiya Park this morning and they were pumping themselves up. They would be the ones raising hell in front of the court room. They were on the news earlier. Wait, let's see if they are still on."

"I haven't seen any TV."

Einosuké Ishikawa switched on the television, but none of the channels were showing news.

"If that bunch is the Q. Sect, Mr. Kida and Mr. Uzawa, won't you go over and talk to them?" Akutsu asked.

"Uh, sorry . . ." Attorney Kida said, shaking his head. "They are highly suspicious of everything we say. We've received notices of no confidence from them I don't know how many times. They resent us for not including their revolutionary principles in our court statements. They think our attitude is all wrong

— they call it begging for the court's compassion. If we went before that crowd, it would be like pouring oil on the fire."

"To state the obvious," Attorney Uzawa said, his expression plainly showing discontent, "we were appointed defense attorneys by the defendants' families only, not the Q. Sect."

"That's right," Attorney Tsukioka said, laughing without reserve. "We aren't getting paid very much for that defense either. Those clients have nothing like the generosity of the Ikéhata and Jinnai families."

"Okay, then, I'll have to go. The professor did seem highly stressed."

"No, that would be a mistake," Tsukioka said, spreading out both hands melodramatically. "Suppose you got hurt? That would be a disaster to have happen just before the decision. Besides that, it's important to show the world the six defense lawyers stepping out from those Camargues. That's not for anybody's ego, it's to show the importance of this trial."

"I'm very sorry," Akutsu said, lifting up Tsukioka's arm like a railway crossbar and stepping past him. "I'll go see what's up with the crowd outside. Ishikawa and Nomoto will accompany you. Mr. Nomoto, you serve coffee to everyone."

When Akutsu left the building, the rain had stopped, but the dark of the sky and dampness of the wind suggested it would start up again at any time. It was nine twenty-five. He hailed a taxi. There was a line of armored police cars at the perimeter of Hibiya Park. Riot police stood outside the Tokyo Public Prosecutors Office, helmets and shields gleaming despite the gloomy sky. A vast procession of demonstrators wearing helmets of many colors filled the sidewalk and street to overflowing. Traffic was at a standstill. Akutsu alighted from his taxi, got through a riot police checkpoint on the strength of his lawyer's badge, and made his way to the table where the lottery for observation section seat tickets was being held. A court clerk was overseeing a wooden vase filled with sticks. Applicants who drew sticks with colored paper at the ends were given tickets.

A demonstrator shouted slogans through a power bullhorn. "Keep open trials open!" "Stop unfair limits on trial observers!" "Crush the reactionary trial system!"

Akutsu easily picked out the exceptionally tall figure of Tetsukichi Jinnai among the crowd.

"I hear you tried to reach me earlier." Akutsu said to him. Rain started to fall. Suéko Jinnai held an umbrella over Akutsu. Torakichi Jinnai, standing a slight distance apart, nodded to Akutsu in greeting.

"It was about Yukichi. From what Mr. Ishikawa said yesterday, he's acting very strangely. His parents and I went to see him yesterday morning, but we couldn't. He told the guard he didn't want to see family."

"What has gotten into him? Honestly!" Suéko Jinnai said plaintively. "He is absolutely terrible about corresponding. I have written him letter after letter and never received a reply. Then suddenly this year he sent us a New Year's card, but it had a very strange verse written on it . . . Now how did it go?"

Tetsukichi recited:

> "Ere morning breaks
> This prison's fearsome cold
> The one marked for killing
> Shall in darkness freeze."

"Yes, that was it. What does he mean by that? I understand the part about the cold — the detention center cells have no heating. But what is that stuff about 'the one marked for killing?'

Tetsukichi says he's probably depressed. Well, we were saying he isn't under a death sentence, and he's being too pessimistic. Anyway, when we were finally going to see him for the first time in a long while, we got there and were told he wouldn't come out to see us!"

"All right, now." Tetsukichi Jinnai said to restrain his mother.

"Mr. Ishikawa said he's suffering from severe prison psychosis, so if he is released, we should have him examined by Dr. Matsuda at N. Medical University. I would like to have you write a referral to Dr. Matsuda for that."

"Happy to do it. But, you know, it all depends on today's decision." As Akutsu said this, he thought ahead about what he would have to do: write a letter of introduction of Yukichi to Dr. Matsuda, call him and explain the situation, set up an appointment for the examination, and if hospitalization became necessary, arrange for Yukichi's admittance.

"I don't want him being put into any hospital for crazy people," Suéko Jinnai said to her son.

"Well if he's ill, that can't be helped."

"No! I won't have it! We're taking him home to Nemuro."

"Auntie," Akutsu said, addressing Suéko the way he had as a child. "Of course, it's all right to take him to Nemuro. But when you do, he really should have an examination by a doctor recommended by Dr. Matsuda."

"Is he really all that bad?"

"His condition isn't good."

"Is he crazy?"

"He has prison psychosis. It isn't a big problem."

"What made him crazy?" Suéko Jinnai said, breaking into tears and tipping the umbrella such that rain ran down into Akutsu's face. "They take a boy who didn't commit any crime and put him in jail for years and years until he goes crazy! Those prosecutors . . . those fiends . . . snakes!"

"Ma," Tetsukichi Jinnai patted his mother's slight shoulder. "There's no sense in getting steamed up. Mr. Akutsu, we'll leave the matter to you."

"Understood. I'll do everything I can. At least that's one issue you don't have to worry about." A megaphone began to blare. This time, it was the riot police.

"Move away from here! You're blocking traffic!"

From the demonstrators, another megaphone gave a defiant answer. Exchanges of this kind continued for a while. The noise was intolerable. It frightened Suéko Jinnai, who edged close by her broad-shouldered son.

Torakichi Jinnai looked stolidly elsewhere as his wife and son discussed his younger son's difficulties. The typical northerner, he wore a fleece lined coat even though it was nearly cherry blossom time. He stood apart from the others, showing his discomfort with his surroundings. Though still broad shouldered and sturdy, he was developing an old man's hunched over stance. Tetsukichi Jinnai had also aged. White flecked his frizzy hair, probably from long exposure to strong winds at sea in the north. His face was creased like the bark of a tree — Akutsu could hardly believe he and Tetsukichi were the same age. The only one of the group who had not changed at all was Suéko Jinnai. She had the same white-as-rice-cake cheeks, rounded and full. Her hair was only a trifle thinner than it once had been . . . Then the sound of Yoko's twittery laughter rising above the awful squawking of the megaphones reached his ear.

Yoko was in conversation with Yoshié Wada. The reporter faced Jun Akutsu's direction, gave a formal bow, and in the next instant silently approached to hand him a document written in a compact hand and whisper, "This is that Hino interview. Would you read it while you're in the courtroom, then give me a five-minute interview immediately after the session is over?"

"Okay." Akutsu wore a bland expression as he slipped the manuscript into a pocket.

Yoko launched into an explanation of the morning's events. "People were lining up to get seats by six o'clock. When I got here a little before nine, there were about two hundred. The court clerks came out and announced there were already too many applicants, so they were limiting the lottery to people who arrived no later than nine o'clock. Then the revolutionary faction showed up in force after nine and started screaming how the clerks can't change the rules, it's discrimination, the non-revolutionary support group put them up to it. They started pushing ahead in the line and causing general confusion. There's about two hundred of us and they have around five hundred. Well, Professor Kirikaé came out and said, look, there are just too many people who want to get in, so how about each side puts up one hundred people. For that, they started beating up on him."

"What? Was he hurt?"

"Yes, but not very badly." Yoko darted a glance to where he was standing. The professor's head was wrapped in a bandage like a turban. With his beard and his completely black suit, he might have been a character from the Arabian Nights.

"Well, the riot police started pushing out the revolutionaries. That was riot number two. Professor Kirikaé stepped out in front again and tried to get the police to hold back. So the police roughed him up."

"Oh, no!"

"Yeah, he was knocked down on his beam. He had to crawl away. It was outrageous. But anyway, the police drove the revolutionaries away from the courthouse and into the street."

Professor Kirikaé spotted Akutsu and swam through the crowd to reach him. "Sorry for disturbing you with my phone call," he said, rubbing his whiskers.

"I couldn't make out everything you were saying, but I thought I had better come."

"The trouble was resolved, but, unfortunately in a very undesirable way — by violent suppression."

"I understand you also gave me a call early this morning."

"Yes, that was because the main people of the support group will be coming to my office at six o'clock for a final meeting, and we would like you to attend as an observer."

"I'll be there, of course."

"You should be aware the decision will unquestionably be not guilty."

"Um — all right."

"I have prayed hard on this. It is a certainty."

Akutsu could not discern if Professor Kirikaé was joking or serious, so he simply repeated again, "All right."

"Ge'cher observer seat ticket here," a man mumbled as he passed by. His hair was heavily slicked down with pomade and his eyes had a sharp glint.

"Whups! There goes a scalper," Yoko said.

"Let's see if I can wheedle it from him," Yoshié Wada said over her shoulder as she chased after the man. She was back again shortly waving a blue scrap of paper.

"Got it for twenty thousand. Pretty cheap. Let's find a good person to give it to."

"The support group has twenty tickets. Why not give it to one of the defendants' families?" Yoko said. "They only give one ticket to each family. I know Tetsukichi Jinnai wants to get in." Yoko accepted the ticket and sprinted away.

"That courtroom is way too small for this case," Yoshié Wada said. "One seat for defendants, twenty for the press and fifty for the public. It's not right to keep out the families of the people on trial."

"Hey, everyone, there are some people you must meet." Professor Kirikaé shepherded over a motley group of about ten men and women. "This is the P. Itinerant Theatre Company, and they are support group members. They came up to Tokyo today from Hokkaido just to be here for the decision."

All the troupe members were in gaudy costume: bright red cheek rouge, yellow eye shadow, Tolstoy shirt, false eyelashes, Pierrot shirt, plastic nose, etc. One sightless man in dark glasses carried a guitar.

"I'm sure many of you know that Mr. Yukimori and Wakako stayed at a lodge by Lake Furen nine years ago. It so happens these people were staying at that same lodge, at the same time, and they actually met them at night in the dining room. I hear there was a howling blizzard that night. When they read about the trial, they thought the defendants must have been those two, and one call to the lodge confirmed it. They became supporters from that moment on."

This introduction drew applause. The blind guitarist expressed his thanks on behalf of the group. The rain began falling harder, and the theater company members put on plastic raincoats. Professor Kirikaé addressed the falling rain. "One sure fire way to raise up the energy level around here would be to just get these people all singing together, but it's just no good with all this noise."

"Sensei, you're getting wet," Yoko said, extending an umbrella to the professor, who only waved it away.

"I don't need that. The rain will stop soon, and the weather will clear up."

"But the weather reports say it's going to be raining all day today."

"The weather will clear by my prayers," Professor Kirikaé said, crossing himself.

"Oh, Mr. Akutsu!" A woman in kimono approached timidly. It was Sonoko Kanéhara, the dorm mother at Fukawa Motors. "I've been wanting to talk with you, but I was putting it off because so many people were gathered around you."

"I owe you my thanks for helping us out," Akutsu said, with a polite bow.

"I wish I could have been helpful. I wasn't much good as a witness."

"That isn't true. Your testimony was valuable evidence for Mr. Yukimori's alibi. It was really just fine."

"Could I ask a favor? I had no luck with the lottery. I wonder if the attorneys could get me a ticket for an observer's seat."

"I'm afraid we can't. We don't have any say about that."

"Oh, I see. Yes, of course, you wouldn't. Oh, dear, what can I do?" Sonoko was colorfully dressed for someone well past fifty. She absentmindedly twirled her umbrella — pink with a floral pattern — sending a spray in Akutsu's direction, as she recognized a figure at some distance. Her eyes fixed upon it, like those of a cat on its prey.

"Is something the matter?"

"That women parading along in her red raincoat and boots. That's her. Kimiko Fujiyama. You know, President Fukawa's kept woman. That relationship lasted until she left him for the shop foreman, Tatsuro Shiomi. He was her second husband for a few years, and when that went bad, she tried to go back to her real husband, but he wouldn't have her. So what did she do? Latched on to Mr. Fukawa again! And now there she is, looking for more trouble to cause. It's just too much! I know what she wants. She wants to see Mr. Yukimori. If he's found not guilty, she wants to turn back the clock. The sneaky, scheming . . ." Sonoko Kanéhara appeared to have forgotten Jun Akutsu, facing her, she was so absorbed in what she was saying.

"She was the one who informed on Mr. Yukimori to the police and had him arrested in the first place. After that treachery, she shows up for the decision now, even though she never came to even one of the hearings. I can just see her putting on a devoted friend act if she gets the chance."

"I have to be getting on." Jun Akutsu looked at his watch. Seven past ten.

"Sensei, wait!" Sonoko Kanéhara was determined to make Akutsu listen to the end of her complaint. "That Kimiko got a seat at the decision! How unfair can you get? I haven't missed a single hearing and now I don't get to hear the decision. Sensei, can't you do something?"

Jun Akutsu finally managed to separate from Sonoko Kanéhara and join the tide of people filing into the courtroom. Yoshié Wada was ahead of him.

Two Rolls-Royce Camargues slid into place before the courthouse entrance, flanked on both sides by a waiting battery of cameras. A white gloved chauffeur reverently opened the door of the first vehicle, and out stepped Attorney Tsukioka, followed by Uzawa. From the second vehicle Kida, Ishikawa, and Nomoto emerged. Flash photography of the leading players in the day's drama continued from the moment of their appearance until they were inside the building. Though Nomoto was a newly minted lawyer, he had the appearance of a seasoned legal strategist for this one moment.

Yoshié Wada called to Akutsu, "Sensei, it's time! Go on in!" but Akutsu shook his head.

10:04 a.m.

"The main text of the decision will be read first. Main text: All the defendants are not guilty."

Cheers erupted from the observers' gallery. People sprang to their feet, and messengers from the respective newspapers ran for the door. Atsuo Yukimori turned to his left to face Wakako Ikéhata, who was already looking at him. Her pale cheeks had become flushed. Her eyes were laughing but the next moment, tears were flowing copiously, and she looked away. He thought her face in profile was supremely beautiful. He wished to drink her tears. He actually was thirsty. He recalled the young girl he had met long ago at the old temple in Akkeshi. (Thirst was even worse than hunger. She gave me a cup of water that tasted better than anything I had experienced until then, or any time later. There she is again, but this time she is Wakako.)

Atsuo Yukimori was feeling the presence of Wakako's soft body in every nerve cell as he regarded the ill-favored face of the presiding judge. He looked closely, marveling that such an ugly being could exist together in the same world with Wakako. There was a mole like a piece of dog waste at the corner of his mouth, in the center of which a single hair sprouted. It wriggled like a snake as the judge read out the decision. Bits of dandruff glistened upon the judge's black robe. Atsuo Yukimori passed the time by looking beneath the black robe that symbolized the state and taking a raw look at the man in his sixties reading the decision. It was quite inappropriate to look that way at a judge who was affirming his not-guilty status. He should feel gratitude to him and the two associate judges to either side of him, but no such warmth or friendly feeling would come to him. To the contrary, he was of a mind to curse the judges for their incompetence and lack of compassion that they would waste seven years of his life — seven years that he might have shared in happiness with Wakako — before they would recognize the obvious fact that the charges against him were utterly false.

Joyous feelings did not arise at being found not guilty. He was instead overcome with irresistibly heavy sorrow that pressed him inexorably downward, like an incautious hunter fallen into an "eye of the bog" in the northern marsh and being drawn downward into viscous peat mud. (Wakako is probably feeling the same thing. Those tears express the same sadness as mine.

(I am fifty-eight years, seven months old. Youth is far gone. My life has no more future. As always, yesterday's diary entry ended with the date and the time elapsed since my arrest: nine years, one month, three days. I followed that up with an accounting of how much of my life has been spent in prison. I included the time spent in the army, that being much the same as prison.

Army induction — going AWOL: 4 years 1 month
Urawa and Fuchu prisons: 3 years 3 months
Army prison — Aioi shipyard: 1 year 5 months
Kobe detention center: 10 months
Fuchu Prison: 2 years 7 months
Chiba Prison: 5 years
This time: 9 years 1 month
Total: 26 years 3 months

(At age fifty-eight, that comes to forty-five percent of my life spent living as a slave to the state. Service to the state made me live a life of killing wholesale, killing one at a time, imprisonment and forced labor. None of it happened by my own choosing.

(It goes without saying that I'm an evil human being, an unmitigated thief and worse. In the army I took part in massacres, killed scores of Chinese people, and then as a civilian I was as criminal as they come, committing fraud, forgery, theft, robbery, and injury. Now I have spent nine years in detention for no reason, but you might very well call it just desserts for the kind of life I have led. That's where I can't quite subscribe to the beliefs of Makihiko Moriya and the Q. Sect bunch, who call the state an oppressor that is evil incarnate. The state is evil, no doubt about it, but so am I, for doing what the state told me to do. Besides that, I consider myself all the worse for all the evil I did on my own. I would never feel self-righteous enough to denounce the state.

(I am just very tired of dealing with the state. I am fed up with being ordered, restrained, watched, informed upon, reprimanded. And I am sick of being the object of phony smiles, rumors, gossip, treachery and all the other things that dealing with people makes necessary. If possible, I would like to spend the little time remaining of my life with Wakako. Yeah, sure I would. There is the source of my sorrow. She is still young. To me, thirty-three is very, very young. It would be cruelty for her to live with an old man like me. All the more, an ex-con who's

750

spent forty-five percent of his life in jail. It's a pathetic idea. No, it is a hopeless idea. Hopelessness that cannot be healed, even by the nectar of her tears.) Wakako Ikéhata listened to nothing of what was being said. When the defendants had been told they could be seated while the reason for the decision was being read, she returned to her place on the wooden bench and promptly lost interest in the judge's unpleasant drone. It would hardly be worthwhile to know the reasoning by which the court had found insufficient evidence to support the supposed "facts" the prosecutor had presented. (It's beside the point that I have not uttered a single falsehood since they arrested me. Everything in the prosecutor's indictment is taken as fact. Everything I say is taken as suspect. After all my statements are subjected to every possible form of doubt, they condescend to recognize a small particle of the truths I have stated. Organization people believe nothing and doubt everything. Only when they have disbelieved, doubted, and suspected to full measure are they willing to grant their suspect the favor of a little bit of belief. It's exactly the same with doctors. They examine people they call patients, meaning people who are presumed ill, and suspect them of having this, that, or the other illness, and only when they can't find anything that matches their catalog of illnesses will they exercise their authority to declare them healthy. People in these sorts of organizations have to demonstrate their authority because that's the only way they can get recognition from the people who have authority over them. Look at that pompous judge playing lord of the realm. It's pitiful. He's just another prisoner of the system.)

Wakako Ikéhata recalled Atsuo Yukimori's broad chest rising and falling as he slept, and then his sad smile of a moment before. (We're not guilty he says. That isn't what I would call a very meaningful way to conclude a meaningless farce of a trial that took seven meaningless years. If I was walking down the street and a man suddenly pushed me into a hole and left me there for a long time, then showed up and helped me get out again should I be grateful to him? Is it up to me to be happy for being saved? You certainly understand what I am saying.)

Suddenly, Beethoven's Hammerklavier piano sonata began to resound. Movement one: Allegro. Her mother's eyes upon her produced the same sensation in Wakako Ikéhata she had once felt when her mother had warmed her clothing by blowing upon it. (Mother is overjoyed that the false accusations against me were dispelled. Well, I must be happy about it too. The prodigal daughter will return to hug her mother in gladness. I don't hate my father now. Or my mother. I am told my sister graduated university and works at a gallery in Ginza, and my brother recently began working at a small, foreign-owned company. I'm the only one who is still a student. A thirty-three-year-old student. The organizations stole my youth. I am fed up with university life. No doubt those friends of mine from R. University will tell me I should go back to the chemistry department. "It's not too late," they'll say. But that's the last thing on earth I would want to do, because it would be a return living as the prisoner of an organization. Scherzo — a merry chase. Beethoven speaks in free and easy terms, but he knew the emptiness of human existence. He knew in his soul what vile things the aristocrats and the church did via their organizations, and created music that laughed at them and kept on going, soaring off into the sky — like that infinitely clear blue sky in Hokkaido. The only things in this world that aren't subject to the organizations' restrictions are music, pictures, poems . . . art, in other words. That's why art will always be with us, so long as people form organizations that imprison other people. Those aristocrats and bishops and even Beethoven himself are gone, but this piano sonata remains.)

Third movement: Adagio sostenuto. Wakako Ikéhata recalled her hallucinations when strolling along the embankment at Yotsuya. Organizations of every stripe fell apart like a great mountain of dry sand: a hotel, a bank, a school, a railway station, an office building, a fire station, a police station, a sports club, the state guest house. Fire fell from the sky. People fleeing from the organizations burned to black cinders. Like Sodom consumed by fire and brimstone or Babylon falling under thunder, lightning, and earthquake, she saw the city, its sturdy structures of cement, steel and glass, being smashed to powder and vanishing. That vision might have inspired the dream of towers she had later on. It was a vast city, like a mountain range of towers, each consisting of individual towers of all sizes, built one atop another. This city of towers melted into a sea of darkness that was larger still. The darkness was infinite. It underlay all things — towers, earth, sun, and the vast space filled with what humans call stellar clusters; upon some chance occasion, all things quite easily melted and disappeared into the darkness. Of course, any structure that could be made by human beings living upon their planet had but the flimsiest existence, and could, as she had seen, disappear in an instant. Emptiness within emptiness, all is nothing. Let all things become nothingness, like the captured wind.

Wakako Ikéhata grew sleepy. As she nodded off, someone elbowed her. But the boring monotony of the presiding judge's non-music swept her along until she slipped into sleepy darkness.

Makihiko Moriya was startled to observe Wakako Ikéhata peacefully going to sleep. How could anyone sleep at such a time? He was inspired by the audacity of it. At the same time, he began having a vaguely uneasy feeling that it was ridiculous to be so excited as to listen to every word and phrase uttered by the judge, in order to know how full of deception this document of state power was, and where it should be rebutted. Then, an alternate track of consciousness momentarily switched him from following the judge's analyses to look back at the observers' gallery, where he met his mother's eyes, causing him to blink. The proprietor of a small seaside inn on the Noto Peninsula, she wore a somber kimono and had a thoroughly haggard appearance. "If the decision is not guilty. You will be free. If that happens, come back to Togi. Leave Tokyo behind. Come back and take over management of the inn for me." His father had died while he was in middle school. His mother's efforts to maintain a household that made up for the void had only made him feel stifled. He had fled to Tokyo and became devoted to revolution. Ten years had passed. The mother had spent them living a solitary life, clinging to the belief that her son would grow disillusioned with revolution and return home to become whole again. She had sold her beach-front property to cover her son's legal fees, waiting and hoping. (Of course I could never go home. My comrades in the Q. Sect are waiting for me. Their hopes and expectations have far more meaning and substance than those of my mother. She does not know that the K. Sect has a team of assassins who are also waiting for me. Or that the prosecutor will appeal this not guilty decision and kick it up to the thoroughly reactionary Supreme Court. I know very well the reactionary positions of each Supreme Court justice. This decision will infallibly be annulled and returned to the original trial level, and the defendants will ultimately be found guilty. This trial is not over by a long shot. The farce will continue for another ten, maybe twenty years, and conclude with a death penalty for me. So, no, I cannot feel very happy about this decision. At the moment the words "not guilty" were spoken, Shinichi Tagawa and Akito Shinya had gleefully risen to their feet to exchange a hearty handshake. They extended their hands to me, too, but I turned away, leaving them to grasp the air. Hey, guys, how naive can you be?)

Wakako Ikéhata was perilously close to falling from her bench. Suppressed laughter arose from the spectators' gallery. Makihiko Moriya gave serious thought to the idea of taking her underground with him. (The guard had told me to pack up my cardboard box and take it with me from the cell, but then the guard in the personnel processing roofm told me to leave the box there. When I asked him why, he whispered, "Attorney Kida put in a request to keep you here even if your decision is not guilty." I knew what that was about right away. He wants to keep me out of the K. Sect's sights. I don't know where in Tokyo the lawyers set up a safe house for me, but it probably won't be safe. Maybe Ryujiro

Nakajima's hospital would be safe. He had been a med student at T. University. He was arrested on the day of the Tower, indicted, and did two years. He went back to school, graduated, and now he is the director of a surgical hospital in Omé. He never was a Q. Sect member, and has stayed away from the movement since then, but his friendship with me is the same as it always was. He visited me often in the detention center, so we could reminisce about being young and in the Tower on that day in history. No doubt he would be happy to let me — no, me and Wakako — hide out at his place.

Makihiko Moriya recalled the image of Ryujiro Nakajima and a woman embracing in the nude that night in the tower. They made love unashamedly under the eyes of a great crowd of people. (I didn't understand until then how beautiful the sex act is. It was a liberating moment for me, freeing me from the bourgeois prejudice that sex is shameful and should be done in secret. In detention I indulged in self-gratification under the guard's eyes countless times, with no concern and no shame. The imagined partner was always Wakako. Nude Wakako aroused my desire in an assortment of positions, bringing pleasure and finally, orgasm. The most satisfying times in detention were passed hitting the cell wall with white semen. Wakako's sleeping face, indifferent to the judges, the spectators, and, regrettably, to me as well, has me aroused this very moment. She is adorable beyond words. Being seriously into breaking down bourgeois prejudice about monogamy, I balled just about every female in Q. Sect, but Wakako was always special. I always wanted her, her alone. I want her now. She, fast asleep, and I, with my hard erection, together laugh at this pretentious buffoon of a judge. We are a well-matched pair of revolutionaries. Yeah, we can hide out at Ryujiro Nakajima's hospital and pass as a couple of nurse trainees.)

Makihiko Moriya pondered contacting Wakako Ikéhata by telephone about his plan for going underground. He took the peaceful rhythm of her breathing as proof of the plan's feasibility. The big obstacle was Atsuo Yukimori. He cast a hard glance toward the man close to sixty sitting at the right end of the bench, eyes filled with hatred and envy, but not jealousy, because that word was not a part of Makihiko Moriya's vocabulary. He recognized that Yukimori's physique far surpassed his own and that his sexual vigor was probably adequate. From his courtroom testimony, he was in love with Wakako. Very well, he recognized that passion. (I don't have any right of denial against someone other than me wanting her. Her feelings are the issue. Which of us will she choose? Will she go for a revolutionary working for simultaneous world revolution to abolish the state and establish a global federation, who has a historical perspective that looks to the twenty-first century and beyond? Or does she prefer a mechanic with no education and no ideals, but who does have a long record of arrests for theft and fraud, and an environmentally destructive taste for hunting? I was a fool for believing in the thesis that crime is revolutionary. Atsuo Yukimori is a criminal who has nothing revolutionary at all about him. He's just a petty thief, without the slightest interest in revolution. Me falling for the mistaken idea that crime is revolutionary was bad enough, but that prosecutor tying the two of us together in the same indictment was worse. I have to rescue Wakako from the hand of that non-revolutionary criminal. Even if she does choose him, her error must be corrected. She must be set upon the right road to revolution. That will require her kidnapping. Yes, indeed. I will make a revolutionary of her. Just as the heart of a K. Sect woman was changed by tying her to a steel desk and applying the whip. Whatever is necessary to do the job.)

Yukichi Jinnai was watching the prosecutor. It was annoying that Domaé did not move. His large nose, prominent like an occidental's, did not so much as twitch. He might as well have been a ship's figurehead. There should be some kind of motion, the sound of breathing, anything! (He sends all those radio waves my way and has a face like it's made of steel. Or maybe it's an iron mask. If there was any doubt about who was behind those radio waves that psychiatric medical officer was sending out, this day's court session has dispelled them. The moment the not guilty decision was read out, Prosecutor Domaé turned on the switch and stepped up the voltage. It sent a shock through my forehead and cheeks. A little later, the wire in front of my spine started to heat up. It's not just a wire, but a heat conductor. Even so, it doesn't get so hot I can't take it. It's a message, from Domaé. He's telling me, don't think you can relax just because they said you're not guilty. I am right behind you, wherever you run. That's what he's saying. Well, why don't you just come out and say you're going to kill me and quit making sly innuendos? Take off that iron mask!

(I've got it! Domaé knew what today's decision would be because the judge had already told him, so he sent out an emergency order to that guard to implant the wire inside my body. That's the only explanation!)

Yukichi Jinnai experimentally hunched forward to feel for the wire, and sure enough, he heard its creaking sound. (It takes someone like Domaé, one of the smartest prosecutors to come from the nation's top university, to think up that kind of underhanded trickery . . . Ah ha! That pointed beak of Domaé's finally moved, and now it's pointed my way! He's looking me over, real good. Now it's over — he's back to that stone face, like he sees nothing and feels nothing.)

But then Yukichi Jinnai realized the wire had turned red hot. The heat was enough to fry the core of his body. "It's hot!" he screamed. Once more, "It's hot. Turn it off!" he screamed again. Two guards rushed to his side.

Atsuo Yukimori was taken aback by the sudden screaming. It was Yukichi, his voice strong. The judge gave an order and Yukichi was escorted from the courtroom by a guard and the bailiff, with several reporters chasing after them. What was the matter with Yukichi? He had always been a self-possessed kid, not easily upset. It was beyond belief that he would start screaming in a place like this. After Yukichi had left the courtroom, burly Tetsukichi and Suéko, looking paler than ever, were exchanging worried looks where they sat, near the exit. "The courtroom will be quiet," the presiding judge said sternly, but the commotion raised by Yukichi's outburst did not subside. The judge resumed reading out the text of the decision. Atsuo Yukimori turned once again to Suéko's direction, and this time succeeded in meeting her eyes. They nodded and smiled at one another. All at once, he was filled with warm serenity. He had been found not guilty. He would be freed. He could be with Suéko. Not that the prosecutor would refrain from appealing the decision. The trial was surely not over, and he might very well be ultimately found guilty. But for a brief moment, at least, he would be free. He would return to Nemuro. (Right now, the old place will still be all ice and snow, but it won't be long until the ice melts and spring comes. Being there is bound to bring some consolation to this despair.)

Five minutes past noon

Having concluded the reading of the decision, the presiding judge asked Prosecutor Domaé, "Will you release custody of the defendants in the courtroom?"

The prosecutor rose slowly, quite out of keeping with his customarily animated manner. "Yes, your honor," he said, setting off applause from the observers' gallery. The court was dismissed. The men who hurried away with ill-humored expressions were the police investigators. The defendants were surrounded by family and supporters as they walked outside into the corridor, where the many who had been unable to attend the court session greeted them with more applause. Small groups of people laughing and chatting formed around each of the defendants.

"We did it!" Attorney Tsukioka exulted, delivering a loud slap upon Jun Akutsu's shoulder. "They accepted about eighty percent of the defense's arguments. More than anything else, the alibis turned the tide, thanks to the fine work by Mr. and Mrs. Akutsu."

"Did you read it?" Yoshié Wada said in a small voice.

"Yup," Akutsu said and slipped a paper to her. It was his comment concerning Assistant Inspector Hino's confession, written during the court session. Wada wore a blank expression as she melted back into the crowd of reporters.

Professor Kirikaé approached, head bandaged and stroking his whiskers.

"Instead of a final meeting, we will have a party at six o'clock for the defendants, attorneys, and supporters. It's time to celebrate. I have some choice wines saved for this occasion. One of our members is a restaurant owner who will supply the food. Music will be provided by the P. Itinerant Theatre Company. Let us all have a good time. Please inform the defendants and the other attorneys."

"Understood! I'll do that gladly."

Professor Kirikaé was crossing himself as he walked away, but then he did an about-face. "My prayers were answered, weren't they?"

"Um, yes they were."

"The prosecutor will not appeal. The matter is settled. I prayed for this. That makes it a certainty."

"Oh . . ."

Tetsukichi Jinnai, Suéko Jinnai, Torakichi Jinnai and Atsuo Yukimori approached. There was a similarity in the facial features of Suéko Jinnai and Atsuo Yukimori, as one would expect from siblings.

"Yukichi is completely out of his mind, isn't he," Tetsukichi Jinnai said. "What do you think we should do?"

"Right now, he is in the court's custody, but he will be released. We can do whatever we think best. I will arrange for him to be examined by Dr. Matsuda."

"I'll talk to Yukichi and get him to go along with it," Einosuké Ishikawa said. "I will need a written referral to Dr. Matsuda, though."

"Here it is," Jun Akutsu said. He had written the letter as well during the court session. Wakako Ikéhata and her mother were with Tsukioka, thanking him. Wakako addressed Akutsu. "We're both very grateful to you!"

"Congratulations! I'm almost as happy about it as you are."

Jun Akutsu was once again astonished by the youth of this woman. She was about the same age as Yoko and Yoshié, but she looked like a girl in her late teens. It was as if time had stopped for her in prison. Now free, she was once again a very desirable young woman.

Atsuo Yukimori received the cardboard box containing his personal items from a guard and pressed his thumb print on a receipt. That transaction marked the end of his relationship with the detention center. Tetsukichi insisted on carrying the box. He tucked it under his arm, but Atsuo said "Wait a minute. There's one thing in there I need." He extracted the manuscript entitled *Confessions* from the box and wrapped it into a furoshiki Suéko had brought. While he had been watching Wakako in the courtroom he had suddenly mustered the resolve to give it to her.

Her hair flowed freely halfway down her back. Naturally fair skinned, lack of sunlight in prison had bleached her complexion to glowing whiteness. She was smiling at her mother. The young woman who closely resembled her would be the younger sister. The tall man to the side wearing a suit might have been her younger brother. Perhaps the others were friends from university. All the people around Wakako Ikéhata had a sophisticated look — intellectuals who led enviable lives. The people with Atsuo Yukimori were quite different. They had the somber, earthy atmosphere of working people from the countryside. Suéko wore a kimono, Torakichi an old, fox fur lined overcoat, and Tetsukichi, in an oil-stained navy-blue jacket, looked very much a man of the manual labor class. The evident differences between the two groups deprived Atsuo Yukimori of his courage to say something to her. Instead, she looked his way and they were immediately smiling at one another wordlessly. He felt as if the moment would be damaged if he spoke. The moment continued until, finally, the conversation began.

"Hey."

"Hi."

That was their first exchange of words after nine long years.

"I wonder if we could meet today."

"I want to, but my mother has a lot planned. Today is no good."

"That's natural enough. It's been a long time. You have to be with your family. I'll give you a call."

Wakako was called over by her mother and she turned to go. Atsuo hastily called her back and held out the furoshiki. She returned a puzzled look, and he said in a quavering voice,

"Would you read this? It's addressed to you. You know, my promise in Raúsu . . ."

"Ahh, that! Got it. Thanks."

Wakako grasped the furoshiki like a runner receiving a baton and withdrew, her long legs taking her across the room in a few strides. Atsuo felt as if he had shed an oppressive burden, and that doing so had put an unequivocal end to . . . everything. This was their final parting, the inevitable outcome. He understood and accepted this. Handing over that furoshiki had been his conscious act of letting go. (I am an inveterate criminal who has no business in Wakako's world. She will come to understand that, and I will depart from her before she gives up on me.)

"What was that?" Suéko asked.

"Farewell letter," Atsuo Yukimori in a tone like one who had thrown away his cares. "It's back to Nemuro for me — just as fast as I can get there."

A middle-aged woman approached. She was heavily made up to look young. "Congratulations," she said. It took a moment to realize who it was — Kimiko Fujiyama.

"You came to the trial?" Atsuo Yukimori said with nostalgia in his voice.

"I sure did! I've been coming to the hearings all along," Kimiko Fujiyama said, laughing in a voice register close to a shriek. The laughter emphasized the creases in her skin.

"What are you doing nowadays?"

"Same as ever!" Atsuo Yukimori was left in a cloud of perfume, unable to infer what "the same as ever" might mean when she whispered, "Won't you come back to Fukawa Motors? As foreman, of course. The boss wants you back. He asked me to tell you so."

"What about that . . . what's his name?"

"Tatsuro Shiomi. He quit. He had a big argument with the boss."

"I left because I was fired."

"The boss regrets that terribly. Shiomi was smart, but he didn't have what it takes to run a crew. He says he was crazy to let go of a valuable leader like Yukimori."

"I'm not bright, but I know how to give orders, in other words."

"No, of course not. Your experience and your integrity are what make you valuable."

" . . . integrity . . ."

By "integrity" was meant "fidelity," "allegiance," "fealty." These were not words that resounded well in his mind. He associated them with servility.

"Are you still the president's secretary?"

"Me? No, but I have influence with the boss. I'd be a help to you."

"I haven't thought anything about the future."

"When you do, please think of me and Fukawa Motors."

Attorney Akutsu had come to where they were standing. Kimiko Fujiyama gave a deferential bow of her head and walked away.

"Mr. Yukimori, your supporters are having a rally in Hibiya Park. Would you please come with the defense team and address them? You don't have to give a speech. Just 'Thanks, folks,' would be fine. Because their support was a big factor in the not guilty decision. Also, there will be a press conference at one o'clock. We would appreciate it if you were there for it too."

"Fine, please count on me."

"Thank you very much, Mr. Yukimori."

They were interrupted by the booming voice of Tsukioka, who had come up beside Akutsu. "You and Ms. Ikéhata will be the only ones of the six defendants who will be attending. The three Q. Sect members are staying at the detention center for the moment to protect them from their rival sect, and Mr. Jinnai will be hospitalized. You two are the most important defendants in the case, so the support group and the reporters will both be satisfied if you are there. Well, it's time to get going."

The rain had ceased. Sunshine reflected up from the puddles on the sidewalks. A breeze, warm and moist blew. The car entered Hibiya Park. The leaves of dewdrop laden camphor trees rustled heavily. About three hundred people had gathered at the Hibiya Public Hall outdoor amphitheater, sitting on plastic sheets laid out on the ground. They all greeted the arrivals with applause. Many of the attendees looked like students, but there were also older men and women, and some nuns as well. It was likely that some attendees were not support group members, but only curiosity seekers. The words "Not guilty" appeared on a large paper banner held aloft by a flagstaff that flapped briskly in the breeze.

Thirty minutes past noon

Jun Akutsu shooed Atsuo Yukimori from his seat to stage center.

"Thanks to all of you, I am back among the living, instead of waiting my turn on the gallows. Thank you, with all my heart — thank you, thank you!"

This was followed by the sound of press photographer's shutters and applause that went on and on. Several familiar faces of young men and women were smiling at him. He was able to pick out Father Okuda, Professor Kirikaé, and Sonoko Kanéhara. Atsuo Yukimori caught his breath time and again. Until that morning, he had been shut up inside a narrow solitary cell, breathing from a narrow cube of stagnant air. Being turned loose in an open space where the wind blew gave him a consciousness of air pressure and a feeling of difficulty in breathing. It was difficult to believe that everyone was paying attention to him and wishing him well. He recalled the sendoff he had received from the townspeople the day he was inducted into the army. Then he was effusively happy with himself. This time he was filled with sadness, despair, and resignation. He was smiling at others and feeling powerless inside. He did not expect Mr. Akutsu, or Suéko to understand. He thought the only person in the world who could understand was Wakako. Atsuo Yukimori complied with the photographers' requests to smile while feeling as lonely as anyone could all the while.

Next it was Wakako's turn. "Go ahead," attorney Tsukioka said, and she stepped forward and said, "Thanks to you all, thanks very much." She said in such a soft voice, the listeners didn't catch it, and they all sat quietly waiting for her to begin. Then she returned to her seat and applause finally began. Photographers hastily began shooting and giving her requests: "Smile, please, over this way." It was not lost on Atsuo Yukimori that Wakako complied with a smile subtly shaded by loneliness that deepened with each burst of blue-white flash.

1:00 p.m.

The press conference was held in the auditorium of the Dai-ichi Tokyo Bar Association. Seated around a long table on the podium were Atsuo Yukimori, Wakako Ikéhata, and their defense lawyers. Many of the reporters' questions were simplistic and the defendants answered in kind.

"How did it feel when you heard the words, 'Not guilty?'"

"Extremely happy."

"What kept you from losing hope for nine years?"

"Belief that the truth must come out."

"What was your happiest moment these nine years?"

"When I received a not guilty decision."

Shortly after the question-and-answer session began, Wakako Ikéhata fell silent and left the responses to Atsuo Yukimori. In his three-piece suit and conscientious manner of dealing with the reporters, he had a professorial sort of presence that was more than adequate to the job. His hair was as black as ever, but the deep wrinkling of his face showed he had aged considerably. The biggest difference about him was how well he chose his words. He was presenting ideas very intelligibly. The impression was that he had used nine years in the can to do a lot of reading. She felt for the furoshiki bundle resting in her lap and found an impressively thick writing paper manuscript. She could hardly wait to see what was written.

"What do you most want to do now?" a reporter asked. Atsuo Yukimori answered.

"I want to be alone."

Ahah! Wakako Ikéhata thought, tuning up her hearing.

"For example, what do you mean by that specifically?"

"I mean literally be alone. In a detention center one is never alone, because he is under watch every moment."

"Ah, I see. Well, what about Ms. Ikéhata. What would you most like to do now?"

This was asked by a middle-aged reporter who was serving as the primary questioner for the reporters assembled for the conference. He was leaning back in his chair with his legs crossed so the bottom of one shoe was visible. A filthy piece of chewing gum was stuck to the heel. When the man spoke, the shoe bobbed up and down, drawing attention to the gum.

"Just the same as Mr. Yukimori. I want to be alone."

"What would you like to do all by yourself?"

"Go skating."

"Skating? Roller skating?" The chewing gum stopped bobbing.

"No. Ice skating."

"That's a very childish ... Sorry, I mean it's kind of offbeat. You people were unjustly detained for nine years, and now you've been freed because journalists and many ordinary people took an interest in the injustice. They supported you, so ..." The chewing gum was again bobbing restlessly.

"I see. You mean to say the number one thing I should want to do now is show my gratitude to journalists and all those ordinary people."

"I wouldn't go that far, but ..."

"It happens I do have something to say to journalists. When Mr. Yukimori and I were arrested as suspects in the Shinkansen bombing, journalists treated us as the perpetrators of the crime. They described us as cold-blooded bombers. They wrote that when I was in high school, a chemistry experiment I did at home that caused a fire showed I was an arsonist at heart. Journalists revealed to the public that I was admitted to a mental hospital twice. That is private information that anyone would want to keep secret, wouldn't you agree? It was journalists who did not hesitate to reveal it, and offer up their analysis in the bargain — that I had delusions of being persecuted, therefore I hated everybody, therefore I resorted to indiscriminate murder. You were the people who said I started my rebellious career when I was small, I was egotistical, cold blooded, I didn't see other people as human beings, I was a crazy radical and therefore I set a bomb on a train to murder innocent people. Worse things than that were written about Mr. Yukimori — a great many. You took it for granted that if Mr. Yukimori and I traveled together, it must have been to plan an attack, because that is what the police told you. They were telling you lies, but you didn't seem to mind. Your journalism was mainly about finding colorful details to add to the stories the police fed you. You didn't mind overlooking our rights of presumed innocence, privacy, and simple human dignity, either. There was no difference between you and the police — and the prosecutors — on that score as well. You followed the lead of the investigators and called it serving justice and the people's right to know. Your unconscionable reporting served both causes poorly. It was unforgivable, completely unforgivable."

The chewing gum was no longer visible. The shoe drooped listlessly, showing instead a dusty toe that was now still. The middle-aged reporter was tapping his pencil on his writing pad as he glared at the speaker with an embarrassed expression. Wakako Ikéhata recognized that her words had bought extreme disfavor among the reporters. Just as she was thinking she might as well end there, her mouth opened again of its own accord.

"When people are arrested in connection with some crime, they are only suspects. They have not been found guilty of the crime. Does the people's right to know include digging up and revealing private information about people you don't know are guilty of anything? It happens that in our case we were not arrested as suspects in the Shinkansen bombing. That was impossible because there wasn't any evidence connecting us to the crime. We were arrested on minor, trumped up charges. I was arrested because the police said they thought I was involved in stealing money from Fukawa Motors. Just lock up suspects for long enough, surround them with surly policemen yelling at them to confess from morning to night, without any lawyer to stand up for them, and when they finally make a false confession, write in up with big headlines. 'They confessed! They're guilty! We knew it all along!' That kind of journalism doesn't leave any room for protecting the rights of the accused. We all know there are cases of false charges and mistaken judgments, and the fact is, everyone who is falsely accused or falsely convicted suffers terribly from the kind of treatment you journalists gave us.

"Let me say that I certainly do recognize there was also journalism that saw the truth about the phony charges against us. Some of that coverage was very creditable. I am grateful to the reporters who took our side after they paid attention to our attorneys' work in actually finding the evidence that proved the prosecutors' stories were lies. One or two journalists did a competent job of reporting that, and their work had a big impact. Eventually, the media at large started campaigning for us. The only trouble is that only happened after the press completely ignored our side of the story through the whole first trial. We didn't start saying anything new when the second trial began. We were saying exactly the same things from the very beginning of the first trial. If you had paid attention then and did objective reporting of what we were saying about the prosecution's case, we might have been spared seven more years in jail while our convictions were being appealed."

"Can you make it briefer?" one reporter asked.

"Great speeches of our time," another remarked, drawing snickers. The reporters were talking among themselves, clearly bored with what they were being told.

A woman reporter put up her hand. The face was familiar — Yoshié Wada. She had persistently visited the detention center, asking for an interview. Wakako had refused to meet her again and again before she finally gave in, only to find that *A. Shimbun* was running a series of articles on the premise the Shinkansen defendants were probably innocent. Reporter Wada had again been persistent about writing constructive articles on the case.

"For my part, your criticism hits home. The reporting I did on your case in the first trial was completely on the side of the police and the prosecution. But once I realized that was mistaken, I did all I could to show the world it was a case of unjust prosecution. Not that it cancels out the mistakes made out the outset . . ."

"I am very much aware that *A. Shimbun* was foremost among the newspapers and magazines that reported on the side of truth. I am sincerely grateful. Nevertheless . . ."

"Crime reporting almost inevitably starts off with reporters basically taking announcements from the police at face value. After that, it becomes difficult to turn around and criticize the investigation. Readers sympathize with crime victims, and that makes them want to see suspects treated as criminals. So, there is pressure on reporters to meet their expectations. That is the basis for reporting that overlooks the rights of the accused."

"Yes, I understand that. Maybe I went too far just now. I'm not accustomed to addressing people like this. I've spent the past nine years in solitary confinement. Some of the things I was thinking all that time in my cell just came out all at once."

"No, no, that's quite all right. If I can ask a question, what would you like to tell the police officers and the prosecutors who investigated you and interrogated you?"

Atsuo Yukimori cleared his throat.

(Wow! That's something he never did before.)

"There's one point I would like to make clear. Ms. Ikéhata consistently remained silent in the face of interrogation. Unlike me, she did no such disgraceful thing as make a false confession. Not a single word. For myself, I feel very ashamed that I allowed myself to be lured and bullied into doing the bidding of my interrogators."

"What do you think of the way they conducted your interrogation?"

"It was brutal. The people who do the interrogating can walk into your cell anytime, just so you know you are always in their power. The interrogation starts early in the morning and continues until late at night. All the while, you're handcuffed in a chair and being harassed one way or the other every minute. It is mentally and physically exhausting. I was in a state of extreme mental torment when I told the interrogators the lies they wanted to hear."

"Is there an officer who especially stands out in your recollection of that experience?"

"There is. Assistant Inspector Hino. He enticed and praised while he manipulated me. I would very much like to ask him how he feels about it now. No, I wouldn't. I would like to hear his expression of regret at what he did to me."

"Thank you." Reporter Wada sat down. Another reporter spoke.

"If the prosecution appeals this decision, the trial will continue. What would you do if that happens?"

"Then I would have to continue the same struggle in court, as if more proof was needed that we did not commit that crime. But the truth is, I am very tired of that struggle. It won't be long before I turn sixty. I don't have any future. If the decision is appealed, I might die before the not guilty decision is affirmed. It would be an extremely cruel fate for a person to have to spend his whole life on trial for a capital crime."

Attorney Tsukioka leaped to his feet as if he had been awaiting that cue. "The defense team has prepared a declaration that addresses that very point. Here are copies for each of you. It basically says the defendants' innocence is abundantly clear, not guilty was the only conceivable decision, the trial has demonstrated criminal abuse of power by the police and prosecutors, and the only conscientious choice for the prosecutor is to acknowledge this, apologize to the defendants and, of course, refrain from appealing the decision."

"Where are the other defendants?" another reporter asked. "Mr. Moriya, Mr. Tagawa and Mr. Shinya."

Attorney Kida replied in his somber voice.

"They have told me they didn't want to attend today, for personal reasons."

"Does it have anything to do with sect infighting?"

"No, not at all. It is a matter of purely individual circumstances." Attorney Tsukioka was suddenly tight-lipped.

1:32 p.m.

The press conference over, Atsuo Yukimori was on his way to the auditorium exit door when someone grasped his arm from behind. Stunned, he turned to look behind.

"Wada, from *A. Shimbun*," the woman said softly, speaking rapidly. "Please give me just one minute. The fact is, Assistant Inspector Hino has spoken out to admit that he was wrong to have interrogated you in the way he did. He says he regrets using force, threats, and suggestion to entrap you."

"What? . . . I don't believe that."

"It's true. The story will appear in tonight's evening edition."

"It's entirely too late for him to be coming out with that stuff. He put me in prison for nine years for a crime I didn't commit. It's outrageous, although I suppose him regretting what he did is better than not regretting . . . But why now?"

"Various circumstances came together. Okay to get your comments?" Wada asked, showing him a small cassette recorder.

A few reporters from other news organizations spotted Atsuo Yukimori and Yoshié Wada off in a corner in conversation, realized something was going on and approached them, but Wada was already walking away.

"I'm from *D. Shimbun*," the middle-aged reporter who had been the main questioner at the press conference proffered his business card. He was smiling congenially. "Won't you write a personal account of your experiences for us?"

"Sorry," Attorney Akutsu was signaling Atsuo to cut off the conversation. "We can't keep your families waiting like this." He ushered Atsuo away. The reporters followed, trying to set up appointments, but Atsuo was resolved to follow Akutsu's directions, and did not respond.

The Jinnais were waiting at the entrance to the bar association building. Suéko Jinnai addressed the two as they approached.

"I don't know about you all, but I'm ready for lunch. What do you say we all have a meal somewhere? Do you know any place good?"

"I'm not really the best person to ask," Atsuo said. "I've been out of town for a while."

"I know a good place in Ginza," Akutsu said. "I just hope we can get there without an entourage of reporters. It looks like they mean to follow us."

Wakako and her lawyer Tsukioka were surrounded by Wakako's relatives.

Atsuo wanted to exchange a few more words with her, but he couldn't think of a way to insert himself into her congregation.

Mrs. Akutsu came running up.

"Mr. Ishikawa has taxis waiting for us. Let's go!"

As expected, a contingent of reporters resolutely pursued them. Mrs. Akutsu got into one taxi with Mr. and Mrs. Jinnai, while Attorney Akutsu ushered Tetsukichi Jinnai and Atsuo Yukimori into another. As they pulled into traffic, they were followed by cars flying the standards of the respective newspaper companies.

Akutsu directed his taxi to turn left as the other turned right. A zigzag route through several back streets finally succeeded in eluding the media vehicles.

"I'll bet those guys are harder to shake than Soviet patrol boats," Akutsu said to Tetsukichi with a satisfied laugh.

3:27 p.m.

. Atsuo Yukimori was on a gravel path, with no one else in sight. Alone, I am finally alone, he was thinking, oblivious to the freshly green treetops that swayed gently. The breeze gave its blessing to his obliviousness and left him. The sun cast his shadow tall ahead to lead his way. Greenish flowers danced about the periphery of his view. They were buds on the branches of a winter hazel, swollen and heavy. He had long taken this flower's appearance as his cue to acknowledge spring's full arrival. Countless peach blossoms in the process of blooming had the riotous look of frolicking children. Caramel boxes and candy bags littered the ground, but there was no one about. He sat upon a bench to smell the fragrance of flowers bathed in warm breezes and narrow his gaze upon braids of golden forsythia that reflected slivers of light like a running brook. More than anything in prison, he had longed to engage in the simple act of walking around as he pleased, under no one's watch, with no one giving orders, asking questions, berating, sympathizing, or covering him for the news. He could do anything at all. He could take off his belt and use it to hang himself from the branch of the cherry tree just above where he sat. He stood up and reached out to the branch to run a fingertip along the slick surface of a red bud that would soon be bursting open. The branch looked sturdy enough to keep him suspended until he breathed his last. (Good old cherry tree. You would see me through in the greatest freedom still open to me. Might as well do it. There's nowhere left for me to live any kind of life.)

After lunch with Mr. and Mrs. Akutsu and the Jinnais in Ginza, he had gone off by himself to Ochanomizu and strolled past Fukawa Motors. There was a new building behind the gas station. It filled up all the space that had existed between the parking lot and the employees' dorm, with the shop occupying its first floor. He hadn't recognized a single face among the many shop workers. He had half expected to see Ichiro Fukawa's goggle eyes looking out from somewhere, but only discovered a stout pillar standing incongruously where Fukawa's office had once been.

He had then taken a ride on a National Railways train to Mitaka to look over the apartment he had once called home, but it had morphed into the tennis court of a newly built high school. No trace remained of the little patch of woods next door or the small, cultivated plots here and there that had previously served as a suggestion of a bygone pastoral time. Now it was a residential district no different than central Tokyo, where houses, apartment buildings and condominiums stood chockablock. The hospital was there, but hardly recognizable, having expanded twofold or more, with a line of new wings. Nine years had wrought breathtaking change. He had finally fled to this botanical garden, where at long last he encountered familiar sights.

Atsuo Yukimori snapped out of his reverie and edged away from the cherry tree branch that had captured his attention. (Uh-uh — there are things yet to be done. For one thing, I want to retrace the path Wakako and I took one rainy day. We passed through a brambly-looking rose garden with no flowers and emerged from the back gate to the All Souls Monument for departed animals. A tea shop was closed for its off-season break. There was no one else but us. Camellias were withered on the branch, and their petals were strewn about the ground like severed heads. The late blooming plum blossoms were blood-red.)

At last he encountered other souls — a few visitors to the main building of Shindai Temple. He thought it was an appropriate time for a forecast of his fortune. A white-robed attendant handed him a well-thumbed hexagonal wooden box. He gave it a shake, and out popped a bamboo stick with a label signifying "good fortune to come:"

"Young bamboo bent low under heavy snow rights itself in spring sunshine."

Lest the oracle's words puzzle a visitor, interpretation followed:

"Like bamboo that straightens itself when spring comes and banishes the snow that made it bend to the ground, your fortune is destined to rise after misfortunes you have suffered."

Atsuo Yukimori laughed aloud upon reading this, earning an annoyed look from the temple attendant. Snow laden bamboo was far too delicate a metaphor for his nine years in detention. The fortune reading was not very satisfying, but it made him feel a little better anyway. He was happy at not having drawn an "ill fortune" prophesy.

The restaurant with rainbow trout in its pond was open. He was delighted to discover the same table Wakako and he had shared, and that it was in its old place. He sat there and that stormy day came back to him vividly. Driving rain had intensified the waterfall from the pond's miniature mountain under long droplets that raised numberless waves. Once again, he heard the sound of the rain beating down and saw Wakako's smile, its radiance never fading. Just as he had felt the presence of God close by when Father Okuda had baptized him in prison, he was feeling her close by him at that moment. I want her, he told God prayerfully. (That's it — I can't live another moment without her. At fifty-eight, I'm no different from any kid praying that his first love will blossom.) Then he was overcome with regret that it was all much too late, no matter what he wanted.

He left the restaurant, abandoning his order of *kuzumochi* half-eaten, and went back to Mitaka Station. It was getting past five o'clock, and his thoughts had coalesced to an intention of attending Professor Kirikae's party, scheduled to start at six, where he could perhaps meet up with Wakako. He had actually turned down the invitation on the excuse that he would be celebrating with family, but really because of embarrassment at the thought of an old man like himself with no academic background being among the support group members, who were mostly students. But at the last moment, his feelings had changed abruptly. Now he wanted to get there as quickly as he could.

He was stopped by the sight of the vertical banners hanging below the counter of a station newsstand proclaiming the top headlines of the evening editions: "Shinkansen Bombing Case Decision!" His exchange with Reporter Wada in mind, he bought a copy of *A. Shimbun* and began skimming the summary of the decision and the article on the press conference while standing on the platform as he awaited a train. Then he opened the newspaper to the second page, and his attention was seized by a photo of Assistant Inspector Hino — instantly recognizable even though his hair had turned all white. His picture appeared with a special feature article that occupied a full double page spread: "Mea culpa: One Investigator's Explosive Admission." As he read the article, Atsuo Yukimori shivered at his recollection of the squat, hunch-shouldered detective yelling in his obnoxious growl and emitting specks of spittle through a snaggled row of teeth, "Start talking! It's for your own good! You hear me mister?"

A train arrived. Atsuo stood in the aisle, reading the startling article.

" . . . The truth is I got the impression Yukimori was not the perp a number of times. First of all, he didn't have a motive. He was an auto repair shop foreman making good money. He didn't have radical ideas. It just doesn't fit to say a man like that wanted to blow up a Shinkansen for some crazy political reason. Number two, there was reason to think his story about what he was doing that day was true. In other words, it looked like he had an alibi. So, I took it to my superior officer, Captain M. I said I didn't believe in what I was doing, I wanted out of the investigation. But Captain M., he was completely confident. He said Yukimori's the perp, no doubt about it. He also said, you know, once you arrest a guy for the crime, it doesn't look too good to turn around and say he wasn't the guy after all . . ."

That just might be the way it really was, Atsuo Yukimori thought. (Hino was the main interrogator, but that tall, young Captain Magara showed up occasionally, reeling off minute details about my supposed criminal acts from that computer memory of his. Now that Hino says so, it would make sense that it wasn't him, but Magara who came up with that smooth logic they used in their frame-up.)

" . . . When you get an order from the top, you follow it to the letter. That's the way it is in every police force. Even if I thought it wasn't right, I couldn't go against Captain M., when he was so sure about saying Yukimori did the deed. I was the low man on the totem pole. The way I thought about it was, even if Yukimori wasn't the perp, that's Captain M.'s concern, not mine. If that's how it is, there's no point in going against Captain M.'s opinion and getting him sore at me. It's better to go along with him and make out Yukimori as the perp — well, to put it in plain words, frame him up. That's what I thought. Once that was on the agenda, I went after that guy Yukimori with everything I had. I had a reputation to live up to. It sounds funny for me to be saying it, but they called me 'Make'em Sing Maestro.' I earned it. In all the years I spent in the force, I never once failed in getting a suspect to confess after I put the mark on him. In order to make a man confess you have to believe he committed the crime. It just won't work if there is something inside you saying maybe he didn't do it. So you get that total belief, and it's all the stronger when the word from on top is that you've got it right. I am a weak-willed person by nature. If they only told me 'Just do the interrogation according to what you believe; it's completely up to you,' I would waver. Doubts would creep in. I wouldn't have the confidence you need to do that job. But that would have been the opposite of what Captain M. told me. I built my own confidence on top of his orders. The result was I got Yukimori's confession."

(So the other side of that show of total confidence Hino put on was nothing but servile acceptance of his boss's orders. That's what I fell for. That's how big a fool I was. It cost me nine years of my life.) Atsuo Yukimori gazed at the smiling picture of Assistant Inspector Hino playing the role of an ordinary person, mild-mannered and well-intentioned. He sighed deeply.

The interview with Hino was followed by Attorney Jun Akutsu's comment. Next was the comment from Mr. Atsuo Yukimori.

"Even though I was under extreme duress, I regret that I allowed myself to cooperate in writing my false confession. It cost me a death sentence and nine years of suffering. I am grateful that Assistant Inspector Hino had the courage to admit the truth. I hope we can count on his cooperation from now on, especially if we have to go back to trial and prove our innocence all over again."

The last sentence had not come from Atsuo's statement to Yoshié Wada. She had written it for him. (Okay, I'm grateful to you too, even though it is another case of putting words in my mouth.) He opened to the "national news" page in the back. He and Wakako Ikéhata were standing in front of the support group people. He compared their two figures in the photo. Side lighting from the sun brought out the creases in his face. Wakako hardly looked different from the majority of her female supporters — university students not yet twenty, or not much past it. Venus and Pruneface. Their age difference was more pronounced that it ever had been.

A boy of about high school age occupied the seat Atsuo was facing. He stood up and said, "Won't you have my seat?" courteously. As if he had been sent to confirm Atsuo's awareness of his own elderly appearance, his timing could not have been better. "Thank you," Atsuo said, matching the boy's politeness, and sat down to steep in depression once again. I'm an old man and everybody knows it, he thought.

As he passed through the entrance gate to R. University, Atsuo felt an impulse to flee. One look at the campus filled with young people of wholesome upbringing convinced him that he was very much out of place. He held his panicky feeling in check and walked past several large buildings, then descended the staircase to Professor Kirikaé's basement office. Mrs. Akutsu was outside the door. She waved to him. "Welcome, Mr. Yukimori. Ms. Ikéhata is already here!" Her cheerful voice resounded through the open concrete chamber.

5:57 p.m.

Professor Kirikaé was stroking his beard as he stepped forward, somewhat unsteadily. "Ladies and gentlemen," he began, but before he could continue, Yoko ran over to him. "Sensei, your bandage is coming undone." She took up the bandage end trailing down his back and deftly rewound it about his head neatly and fixed it in place with a bandage clip.

"Ahh . . ." The unexpected assistance had derailed his thoughts. "What was I about to . . . Oh . . . Ahh, Let us now welcome Mr. Atsuo Yukimori and Ms. Wakako Ikéhata with our celebration of their not guilty decision. The first item of business is to pray that the prosecutor does not appeal the decision. All right now, let us pray."

Instantly, Father Okuda and the nuns of the M. Order immediately stood up, followed a half-beat later by Atsuo Yukimori, Wakako Ikéhata, and the P. Itinerant Theater Troupe. Jun Akutsu rose upon an eye signal from Yoko, with Einosuké Ishikawa and Shoichi Nomoto following suit. The students and housewives rose as well, looking somewhat ill at ease.

Professor Kirikaé addressed the reporters and photographers clinging together in a tight group by one wall. "Come on now, please join us in prayer!" They hesitantly pressed their hands together and bowed their heads. Professor Kirikaé closed his eyes and began silently mouthing a prayer. Clock noises were audible; countless spring mechanisms of all sizes were metallically ticking off the time. The clock faces read 5:59. How many more seconds until the grand chorus proclaiming the hour? If you looked closely, you would have noticed the tip of Yoko's tongue protruding in gleeful anticipation. She had set up the timing of this moment with the professor for a prank on the media people. First, there was a splash in the water-filled lab sink, startling a few reporters. A large fish — perhaps a carp, perhaps a trout — had jumped. Then the clocks began chiming all at once. Wall clocks, ponderous pendulum clocks, raucous alarm clocks. There was a strobe flash as a startled photographer reflexively pressed his shutter button. Yoko lost control and burst into her twittery laugh. The next moment there was a general explosion of laughter. Professor Kirikaé crossed himself and clapped his hands above his head.

"Okay, let's drink up. We have some of the world's finest wines I've been saving for this occasion, all these long months and years. Will you start with a white Bourgogne? We have Mazis-Chambertin Hospices de Beaune 1976 and Romanée–Conti Montrachet 1976. The year before last was a great harvest year. Whichever you choose, you will have a consummate vintage."

Professor Kirikae delicately twisted out the corks of two bottles with his long, slender fingers and went around the room filling classes. Jun Akutsu led a toast to Atsuo Yukimori and Wakako Ikéhata as the photographers snapped image after image. In a response to a reporter's question Atsuo said, "Let me say to everyone in this group I am deeply grateful for all you have done. It was your support and encouragement that got me through seven years under death sentence." To this, Wakako added with a radiant grin, "I am grateful to you all. This wine sure does taste good!" Their remarks brought hearty applause.

In accordance with prior agreement, the media people cleared out after getting their interview and photography session. With that source of tension gone, the group members settled into amiable conversations. By and by, the master of a French restaurant located in Akasaka appeared in chef's attire, received a round of applause, and began bringing in platters of food. Professor Kirikaé was equally busy opening wine bottles and filling glasses. He announced the name and year of each vintage in an uncharacteristically loud voice.

"This is . . . ahh Château Haut-Brion, 1961. An excellent wine, brought to you by a dear friend who happens to be a French pastor."

"Sensei, isn't this very pricey stuff?" Yoko asked.

"I wouldn't know. Wine is not something to buy. It is something to be given. Here, now Father Okuda, let us drink!"

The P. Itinerant Theatre Troupe received applause as they appeared in the center of the room. They began a performance with no preliminaries. Pew, the blind pirate from "Treasure Island," played a guitar accompaniment to five dancers. Long John Silver, with a long, spiky nose, was recognizably Prosecutor Domaé. The presiding judge was incarnated as Eeyore the stuffed donkey, sporting a mole the size of a cherry. A bespectacled Winnie-the-Pooh was Attorney Akutsu. Atsuo Yukimori appeared as the Wizard of Oz wearing cardboard armor, and Wakako Ikéhata was Peter Pan. The characters identified themselves by their idiosyncratic behavior: Domaé getting onto and rising from a chair like a mechanical man, the judge delicately scratching his mole with a pinkie, Akutsu beating his chest like a gorilla, Atsuo Yukimori standing at rigid attention and Wakako Ikéhata assuming zazen poses in unlikely locations. It was a mystery what source material the players had used to master these individual traits, but all were unmistakably identifiable.

"Did you read the evening edition?" a woman asked Jun Akutsu. She had brown hair and was wearing sunglasses and a purple suit. Akutsu was wondering who she might be when she removed her sunglasses and laughed. It was Yoshié Wada.

"For goodness sake, I was wondering if you were some actress or what."

"There's no need to flatter me. I was just wondering what you thought of my piece."

"If this is an interview, it's against the rules. I distinctly remember asking the media to leave."

773

"I'm not using press credentials. I'm a support group member in good standing."

"A support group member with a tape recorder running somewhere, I'd guess."

"Of course," she said, patting her handbag.

"I give up. Actually, I don't think I've ever gotten more of a kick out of reading a newspaper article. That story of Hino, the fainthearted detective, makes sense. Police work is all about following orders, even when it means forcing a phony confession. Every police station in the country wants to have the number one arrest rate. Japan has the highest arrest rates, and it doesn't care that it got there by ignoring people's rights. Hino was a model detective. We all have good reason to be afraid of policemen like him. Police, prosecutors and judges are the three classes that changed their way of thinking the least after the war, and the police are the most antiquated of them all. The law says the people's rights are supposed to determine how police deal with them, but the way it actually works, arrest rates get priority." Akutsu's passion was rising as he spoke.

Atsuo had finally managed to detach himself from toasts and meeting people and answering their questions. He went to talk with Wakako.

"So how was your afternoon?"

"The house was flooded with reporters and people from magazines. It was awful. Trying to keep them away and they kept coming back like flies. We couldn't have a quiet meal together. The front door interphone kept ringing. We finally said, all right, and let them into the tatami guest room so they could ask their questions and take their pictures. We ended up having to deal with that while we had our meal."

"We were lucky. The press was following our taxi, but Mr. Akutsu succeeded in shaking them off. We had a peaceful lunch in Ginza."

"They all know where to find my house. The worst part is Attorney Tsukioka loves reporters. He says things like, 'Hey, get a shot of me having lunch with my client.' When they finally left us in peace, I snuck out for the beauty parlor."

"Ah . . . !" Atsuo realized Wakako had a completely different hair style. The long tresses down her back were gone. Now her hair was short and permed, as it had been when they were arrested. "You had your hair cut short."

"For going skating."

"Would you like to go skating together tomorrow?"

"That sounds good."

"Ten in the morning, just when they open, is the best time. At least, I don't think opening time has changed."

Wakako's emphatic nod brightened his mood. He had been thinking that if he did see her this evening, it would be their last encounter, and he would return to Nemuro. Her wanted to hurry off, out of her life, because a rogue like himself was simply not suitable for her. The other side of him wanted desperately not to lose her. He regretted giving her his *Confessions*, and wanted to ask her to return it if she hadn't yet read it.

"After lunch I went off by myself and visited Jindai Botanical Garden. The peach trees are in full bloom. I followed that path we took to Jindai Temple."

"Ah..." As Wakako broke off, a woman in sunglasses appeared. "Wada, from *A. Shimbun*," she said. Makeup and a different hairdo had changed her appearance enough that she was completely unrecognizable.

"Have you people seen today's evening edition of *A. Shimbun?*" Wakako shook her head. Atsuo nodded.

"What did you think of it?"

"It gave me a very horrible recollection of the interrogation I endured nine years ago. That article told the truth. I was railroaded into agreeing to a lot of lies. I regret very much that I was weak and foolish. I should have resisted, like Ms. Ikéhata. But I know I am the same weak-willed person. If I was put through that wringer again, maybe I could be driven to making another false confession. In any case, Hino's admission came much too late. I greatly resent his not admitting to the truth at the first trial."

Atsuo was about to comment to the reporter that her article on his interview had quoted him as saying something he had not actually said, but she spoke first.

"What will you be doing from now on?"

"I'm going back to Nemuro. I intend to live a quiet life there." He made this explicit declaration of intentions upon noting from the corner of his vision that Wakako was watching him with a look of burning curiosity.

"What will you do in Nemuro?" Reporter Wada pressed on.

"That isn't settled yet, but I will have to work at something. Otherwise I wouldn't have anything to subsist on."

Atsuo Yukimori suddenly remembered his promise to Suéko. He had promised to show up at the inn they were staying at in Ueno at six o'clock to have dinner with them. It was already six-thirty. He had to call them and apologize.

"Mr. Yukimori, I have an offer I would like you to consider." Every inch the gutsy reporter, Yoshié Wada was not shy about intruding upon people's private affairs. "Why not write a book? Start off with the miscarriage of justice, then go into a memoir of your life."

"No, I don't have any talent for writing."

"I've heard that you write tanka. All you have to do is write out your extraordinary life experiences. You kept a diary while you were in detention, didn't you?"

"Yes, I did, but it certainly isn't anything to show to people."

"Rewrite it into something you can show to people."

"My life has been a long string of regrets — one wretched affair after another, and it all comes to nothing. Zero. There isn't anything to write." Atsuo Yukimori had Wakako Ikéhata very much in mind as he said this. (If she reads *Confessions* she'll know what a low-down villain I am. She as the one, solitary reader is just fine.)

"Well, it's a shame," Reporter Wada said in a tone suggesting she wouldn't give up that easily. "But if you decide you would like to give it a try, please make me the first person you contact."

Professor Kirikaé was holding a bottle of wine aloft as he led a group of young people over to where Atsuo Yukimori and Wakako Ikéhata were standing. He introduced them to the couple, one by one. There was the editor of the support group newsletter, the person in charge of collecting contributions to finance the organization, the restaurant owner who had cooked, served, and donated all the food for the party and others who helped run the organization. Atsuo and Wakako each recognized the names or faces of several who had visited or written them letters when they were in detention.

"They all did dedicated work because they believed in your innocence. They all have things of their own to do, but they gave their time. Come to think of it, Ms. Yoshié Wada over there wrote lots of very helpful things. Everyone said if you aren't found not guilty, there's no God. I had to pray hard to make sure God didn't go away."

The newsletter editor said, "I would like to request both of you to write something for the newsletter."

"Understood. I will write something," Atsuo replied without hesitation.

Wakako said, "I'm no good at writing things . . . What I can do is give you the score of a piece I composed in jail."

"I would certainly like to hear it," said the guitarist in dark glasses made up as Pew.

"It isn't much — it was just way to pass the time when life was very tedious," Wakako said. She borrowed the P. Players' accordion. "It's called 'Swan Reel,'" she said and began playing. The guitarist clapped time and the pair fortuitously fell into a duo. People gathered to listen.

Einosuké Ishikawa whispered to Jun Akutsu.

"Yukichi Jinnai is in the hospital. Dr. Matsuda examined him. He said the case is urgent and referred Yukichi to Y. Hospital."

"Yoko's hospital?"

"Yes. Your wife and Dr. Matsuda conferred about it, and that is what was decided."

"Hmm. She didn't say anything about it to me."

"I was just about to tell you," Yoko said in an uncharacteristically low tone. "Dr. Matsuda has a full schedule. It was about three o'clock when he got to the examination. He called me at the hospital after four. I just now checked with the hospital and found out the patient arrived a short time ago, with his parents and his brother. It seems he was perfectly willing to be admitted because he felt safe going to a place that has bars on the windows. He thinks that's the best protection against nasty things the prosecutor wants to do to him. There is also a message from his mother to Mr. Yukimori. She says to tell him the situation with Yukichi made it impossible to go ahead with the family dinner they were planning. It would be best for you to tell him that."

"I wonder just what the diagnosis was."

"Possible schizophrenia," Einosuké Ishikawa answered. "At least, something more serious than prison psychosis."

"That's heart-sickening . . ." Akutsu approached Atsuo Yukimori to give him the message. He was watching Wakako Ikéhata playing the accordion with half-closed eyes, the better to take in the music.

"Isn't that something! Ms. Ikéhata is a wonderful musician. To think she created something like that in prison. I couldn't do anything like that. For me, those nine years amounted to nothing."

"She really could make it as a composer. Not only in this pops style, either. I understand she produced a great many classical piano pieces as well."

"You mean, in prison?"

"Yes, of course."

"And without a piano . . . without any instrument. That kind of talent is beyond my imagination. I can't do anything. No schooling . . . no nothing."

The creases in the corners of Atsuo Yukimori's eyes suddenly deepened and his head hung helplessly. Jun Akutsu felt stricken by such a display of despair. Even though he knew his next words would only increase the anguish, he could not avoid passing on the message from Suéko Jinnai.

"Yukichi . . . ? I see. Well, it is a good thing he is in the hospital your wife is associated with. Is Suéko . . . Suéko Jinnai at the hospital now?"

"I think she probably is," Yoko said. "Wait, let me check to be sure. I'll just tell Professor Kirikaé I have to use his phone." She ran over to the professor, who was dancing unsteadily to Wakako Ikéhata's accordion. In a moment, she was back, dialing the telephone, and got Suéko Jinnai on the line. Atsuo Yukimori fell into what appeared to be an involved conversation with her. Wakako Ikéhata had finished playing "Swan Reel" and was receiving spirited applause when he put down the receiver and looked up, his eyes shining with tears.

The blind guitarist extended his hand to Wakako Ikéhata, and she gripped it enthusiastically. "That was great fun. You really know how to put together a melody. Won't you play some others for us?"

"Thank you." Wakako Ikéhata said, reaching again for the guitarist's hand. The face with the dark glasses took her back to the blizzardy night at Peken Lodge on Lake Furen. He had played guitar as they sang one Beatles song after another. She had forgotten the name of the P. Itinerant Theatre Troupe, but vivid images of the faces and figures of its members came flooding back. The man in the judge's getup was the troupe leader, who had been wearing a red nose. The well-proportioned woman with the false nose impersonating Prosecutor Domaé was the troupe leader's wife. Carried away with Beatles songs, she had suddenly noticed Atsuo Yukimori standing in a corner with a sullen expression. But now she took a closer look at his face and was struck with alarm; he was a study in extreme despair. She ran to his side.

"What's up? You look unhappy."

"Yukichi's been hospitalized," Atsuo Yukimori said grimly. "I'm going to see him now."

"Oh, dear . . ."

"Solitary confinement did it to him. That kid's nerves just couldn't deal with it."

"I understand that. I understand it completely." She stroked his broad hand, feeling its warmth. It was shaking.

"Yeah. Well, I'm going to that hospital. Mrs. Akutsu is going with me. She says her daughter is in the hospital's day care."

"I have to go to dinner with my family at eight . . ."

"My regards to them. Let's see, your phone number's the same, right? Here's the number of my inn." He wrote out a number on a slip of paper and gave it to her.

After his silent departure, everything darkened, as if shadow had fallen upon the sun. All was different than before. Now the P. Itinerant Troupe seemed to be tragedians telling a tale of prosecutor and judge pursuing the attorneys and defendants to their destruction. The students, so plainly naive in their drunken disport, seemed to be ridiculing her as an old lady. Suddenly she was distressed to find the madness that had tormented her so often in prison was showing signs of escaping once again from its lair, hidden deep in her mind. Her body emitted unpleasant odors. Everyone was suppressing their displeasure. She caught Attorney Akutsu pinching his nose — stark proof!

(He was edging away from me because my body smell repelled him. That was why he would sometimes throw me a look of hatred and push me down. Oh, no, now the whiskers on Professor Kirikaé's face are writhing, close by me. It felt as if they brushed against my face. How can the whiskers of someone standing ten meters away do such a thing? Something funny is happening . . . I had made up my mind this time I would not argue with my mother, no matter what. It happened anyway. When I came back from the beauty parlor, I could tell someone had looked at Atsuo Yukimori's *Confessions*. I had tied it up in a furoshiki with a square knot, and when I came back, it was done up in a feminine style granny knot, which is what Mother ties by habit. I confronted her angrily.)

"You looked at it."

"Yes, I looked at it. You didn't say I shouldn't."

"It is a letter to me. Prisoners aren't allowed to exchange letters among themselves. He spent all those long years writing this instead."

(She wrinkled her nose like a police dog on the scent of a crime scene.)

"That is all the more reason for me to be concerned. I wanted to know what that man was trying to say to you. He happens to be the man who ruined your life. You might expect an apology, but no, he gives you an overblown piece of junk he calls *Confessions*. That's quite a title! Does he think he's a movie star or a saint? I only glanced through it. That was enough to tell it is just what you would expect from a man like that. He started stealing at four. That is what you call a born crook. Girl, I'm pleading with you. Don't have anything to do with that man! Stay away from him. He isn't fit to do so much as look at you!"

"You are mistaken about him!"

(I said that because I wanted to set her straight about our relationship, but I knew right away I didn't even know enough of the facts of my own case to be able to show her that all those things she had been believing for the past nine years were just not true. Defendants in trials only get to see random scraps from the mountains of paperwork being passed back and forth, even though it is determining their fate. Sometimes they even made me leave the courtroom when one of the joint defendants testified about me. Presumably, that was so the judge could test the credibility of my testimony. That's standard procedure; they took pains to insure I was only shown a small part of details of the case that have to do with me. So I didn't get any kind of understanding of the overall structure of the Shinkansen bomb case. All I really have is my own belief that I was not indicted solely on Atsuo Yukimori's confession, and that comes from my own strong faith in him as a person, not on anything objective that I could use for argument's sake.

I was seething, but I got an iron grip on my impulse to explode into angry words.)

"You really are mistaken, but, Mother, I do not want to fight with you now. There is just one thing I want you to know. I do not have any resentment toward him at all. I like him. I love him. I want to marry him."

"Uhh . . . !"

(She yelled in pain as if she had been punched in the chest. I regretted my words instantly. I had never discussed marriage with Atsuo Yukimori, and what I had said to my mother made the word "marriage" have an awfully vulgar ring. Mother instantly sensed my regret and took it as an opening to attack.)

"You'll be unhappy if you marry such a man. Everything that possibly could be wrong is wrong — upbringing, birth, and age for starters, and that is just the beginning. He's poor, he's an ex-convict and he has no way to make a living."

(Mother continued pouring out her dissatisfaction with Atsuo Yukimori. I put a filter on my ears and just quit listening.)

"Ms. Iké-ata," Professor Kirikaé called out, happily tripping over syllables. "We've got three bottles of red Bordeaux that are out of this world. Château Mouton Rothschild, Château La-tour, Château Lafite-Rothschild! Can you believe it? Open them up, please and celebrate!" he said, handing her a corkscrew.

All three bottles were vintage 1945. They were decorated with red labels to celebrate France's victory. At the professor's urging, Wakako Ikéhata extracted a long cork deftly and made short work of opening the other two bottles.

"Exquisite!" said Father Okuda, repeating the appraisal just about everyone was making. "Wine was a commission of mine at home. My father was quite a connoisseur."

The glasses of everyone were filled. All were merry, all carefree. Everyone — boys and girls in university, middle-aged housewives, nuns, the P. Itinerant Theatre Troupe — all were delighted to have Wakako pouring out their wine. "Congratulations!" they said and applauded. Camera shutters clicked. Everyone in the room celebrated the not guilty decision. Wakako realized the sickness that had attacked her was buried away somewhere. She was a bit drunk. Her feelings ballooned and shriveled erratically. Long years of enforced sobriety in prison seemed to have done away entirely with her tolerance for alcohol. A mouthful was enough to affect her.

(Everyone is happy for me. They believed in our innocence. They worked hard for us. When that rusty iron gate at the detention center opened up this morning and the bus took off, I threw a dirty look at those stone walls and thought about how much I wanted never to return to that hell. I wanted to smash it to dust for taking a young girl for no reason at all and keeping her there for nine years, stealing her youth, love, hopes, dreams — everything. Now, Wakako Ikéhata, you are free.)

She took up the accordion again and faced the blind guitarist.

"What'll it be?"

"That's just what I was thinking. My head is full of music and it's all playing at the same time."

"Yeah, that can happen. The way to deal with that is start playing from one end and just keep going."

"Okay."

Wakako Ikéhata began transferring sounds she was hearing to the accordion. It was a bright dance piece. (One of many pieces heard in prison darkness — lively tunes, the kind of brightness you think about when you want to emerge from a cave. They were my heartfelt dreams.) They played a second piece, then a third. The P. Itinerant Theatre Troupe started dancing. Others joined them. The nuns were dancing. Halfway into the fourth piece, the storehouse of music was all emptied out. She could hear no more.

"That's all," she said, and returned the accordion. The audience was silent, everyone with a quizzical expression, but applause soon followed.

"Are you okay?" the blind guitarist asked, concern in his voice.

"A little tired. Not really used to using the fingers."

"Take a rest, please," the guitarist said gently. "Our guys will play for a while."

Guitar, accordion, saxophone, and tam-tam were taken from cases. Professor Kirikaé was consulted about whether that much firepower was permissible.

"Sure, go ahead. It's Easter break now. We're in a basement. There's a student hall near here that gets a lot noisier, I assure you."

It was a feeling was like being left in the darkness of a cavern when the brightness at its far end has disappeared. She heard the P. Troupe people playing, but it was all incomprehensible noise to her. (Everyone is looking at me because they are disgusted by my body odor . . . Yes, the sickness is there, doing what it does.) Wakako Ikéhata forced herself to drink the red liquor in the glass. It became a hot presence in her stomach that just sat there without dissipating. She laid a hand to her belly as she experienced slight nausea. Realizing she was exhausted, she collapsed into a chair like a wet rag.

She remembered the scene that immediately followed when she told her mother she wanted to marry Atsuo Yukimori. Her younger sister, who had been listening silently until that moment, suddenly was raging tearfully.

"How can you say a thing like that? Don't you understand what that does to me? Don't you know that you being put on trial ruined my engagement? I'm thirty! No one wants to marry me. No one wants the sister of a homicidal mental patient. No one would hire your brother after he graduated. Every company did a background check and turned him down. It took him two years after he graduated before a third-rate foreign owned firm took him. I understand you're not to blame for that — the prosecutor who indicted an innocent person is. But none of it would have happened if you weren't going with that Yukimori. Thanks to him, our whole family has been ruined. Will you please give some thought to how much we have gone through? I am overjoyed that you finally got the not guilty ruling. Really, you have my heartfelt congratulations. But when you start talking about marrying that man, that's just too much. It's too self-centered. No one is going to marry someone whose sister married an ex-con. Just stop putting me — putting all of us through this suffering!"

(My sister blurted all this out in a loud, tearful rush of words, as if she had been saving up all her grievances for that moment. I had no idea of what I should do about it, so I just stood there under the cold shower of words. Thankfully, my sister returned to herself before she was finished, and the tirade turned to a tearful apology.)

"I'm really sorry. I hope you'll forgive me. I wasn't planning on talking that way. Just don't blame Mother for looking at that man's journal, or letter, or whatever it is. She's worried about you. We all are. Listen, please. Don't go back to seeing him. Don't have anything more to do with him. Get married to someone decent."

(I didn't say a word. I took Atsuo Yukimori's *Confessions* into Father's study, put it in a steel drawer, locked it, put the key in my handbag and left for here.)

"You don't look well at all, Ms. Ikéhata," Yoshié Wada said.

"I'm not. Just tired."

"Let me take you home. I have a company car waiting. You're welcome to use it."

"Let me go with you," Jun Akutsu said, and the three departed together.

7:30 p.m.

Chief Superintendent Noseh and Prosecutors Onuki and Domaé were having a meal sent to their room in Hotel O., located not far to the rear of R. University. Domaé had proposed this gathering to his colleague Onuki in the Public Safety section of the Tokyo High Prosecutor's office. Onuki had contacted Noseh at the N. Prefecture police headquarters office, where he was in charge. Noseh had been in the courtroom that morning to hear the Shinkansen bomb case decision. The ostensible purpose of the meeting was to exchange views on the decision, but the conversation had naturally settled upon asking the opinion of Noseh, who had been Police Assistant Inspector Hino's immediate superior, about the interview with Hino that had appeared in *A. Shimbun*.

Superintendent Noseh showed his discomfiture by chewing his lower lip.

"He did not consult with me before he gave that interview. I am surprised and angry about it."

"Had he shown any signs he was about to do something like that?" Onuki asked with a dead-serious expression, as if questioning a witness. He seemed to have slipped into his professional persona.

"Not really. He retired eight years ago. He's been farming land owned by his present old lady in Sakura. He would show up at my place on holidays and he did talk generally about that book project of his, but he certainly gave no hint he was suddenly going to put out something like that!"

"You can't help but wonder, why now?"

"From what I gather, he wanted to write a memoir about the cases he handled. He was putting together the reference material he needed, and he was meeting former colleagues, to refresh his memory, I guess. I remember him checking with me about dates and facts in the Shinkansen bomb investigation. But he didn't say a single word to suggest he was going to turn against his own investigation of a suspect like that. I'll tell you what I think may be at the bottom of it — resentment of Inspector Magara, who is now chief of Onarimon Police Station. He would have hard feelings, because when the press came up with that hokey 'miscarriage of justice' campaign and started naming names in the investigation, Magara suddenly lost confidence and came out with his own story that it was Hino who had dragged everyone on board his theory that Yukimori and Ikéhata were the perps."

"Mr. Noseh," Onuki said, lowering his always proudly straight upper trunk, bringing his dark, rugged features close to the inspector. "Do you remember the day I conferred with you, Inspector Magara and Assistant Inspector Hino in my office just prior to my decision to bring the indictment?"

"I remember it well."

"My impression of that conference was that Mr. Hino was driving the investigation and Mr. Magara, who was his superior, but younger than him, was not in control. How was it really?"

"Hino took on that case like a fireball. He zeroed in on Yukimori and Ikéhata. He said they did it. But only one of the eyewitnesses identified them, the motive was flimsy, and Yukimori was saying things that sounded like an alibi, so the investigation team was wavering. That was when Magara came out with a show of full confidence. He said those two and nobody else are the perps and I want their confessions. That push from Magara fired up Hino like never before. He went into that interrogation like nobody's business and got the confession. But that stuff from A. Shimbun about brutal questioning is baloney. That never happened. No one could get away with that kind of stuff in the democratic police force I run."

"I saw that Atsuo Yukimori was making his statements completely voluntarily in my own interrogation of him. I am not convinced by these sudden charges from Assistant Inspector Hino. For a man to engage in slander that violates his obligation under the Public Service Employee Law, it seems to me there must be some hidden motive. Maybe a fat payoff from A. Shimbun."

"Sure, that's possible. The thing about Hino is his heart is in the right place when it comes to justice, but he is very interested in fame and fortune. He's quite proud of the outstanding service awards he's received. He was still complaining years after the fact that his retirement pay was too little and the farewell gift from someone or other wasn't enough."

"All right then, now let me ask you frankly about your own feelings on this case. Are Yukimori, Ikéhata, and that Q. Sect bunch the real perps or not?"

"No question about it. They and nobody else did it. I went through fifty or sixty records from eyewitnesses, canceled out every one that didn't fit, and they are the ones who remained."

"It's a relief to hear you say that. I don't think there is any doubt about it either. The conviction I received from reading your investigation report and referral records did not waver when they denied everything in the first trial, and after carefully reviewing the trial records in the appeal, I found nothing there either to make me change my view."

At this, Onuki smiled at Inspector Noseh and looked at Domaé, who had been listening to the conversation between the two with a bright smile. Domaé was a level five judo black belt Onuki had often encountered at the MPD gymnasium. He had a heroic physique that made for an awesome presence in a courtroom, but normally he was reserved and spoke little, listening to others with a cheerful expression that told you he was a sociable person. Inspector Noseh, himself a level two judo black belt, had faced him several times in free practice judo sessions and had exchanged pleasantries with him at the MPD coffee shop as well.

Prosecutor Domaé's nose had reddened from drinking white wine. At last, he offered his own words.

"Like you both, I find today's decision completely unacceptable. Those alibis the defense put out are full of holes, and I proved it, not once, but again and again. The first decision was one hundred percent correct in finding that the crime was planned by Q. Sect and carried out by Yukimori and Ikéhata. For the prosecution to be handed total defeat, that is of course due to my own inadequacy, but aside from that, I'd say we were tripped up because the defense successfully manipulated the media. That interview with Hino was done by that female reporter with *A. Shimbun* — Wada. Well, she was in the same class at R. University as Akutsu's old lady, and those two are tight. Don't forget Akutsu is the kind of snake who fornicates with witnesses to get the testimony he needs. He didn't stop there, either. He made his big witness his old lady, then used her to get that Wada on his side. There's nothing he won't stop at. He's probably behind those crazy accusations from Hino. A detective who used to be with the Fuji police station spotted Wada coming from Akutsu's condo early this morning. You can bet that was all about that clearing with him what to run in that piece."

Domaé drank the white wine in his glass as if it was water. Inspector Noseh was a teetotaler who observed this with the feeling of being in the presence of a ferocious imbiber. Onuki had a fairly high threshold as well, and the two had emptied the wine bottle from room service. Domaé lifted the telephone receiver. "Send up some wine — any kind. I don't care if it's red or white. Give us three bottles of cheap stuff, like about a thousand yen a bottle."

As Inspector Noseh rose from his chair, he said, "Well, gentlemen, I'll have to ask you to excuse me. The last train back to N. Prefecture departs Ueno Station at six minutes past nine."

"Thanks very much for coming all this way," Prosecutor Domaé said with a respectful bow. "Your comments were very informative, but even more than that, they were encouraging to me."

"Mr. Noseh, I understand you will be leaving the police shortly," Prosecutor Onuki said.

"Yes," Noseh said, suddenly downcast. "I retire in another week. My second career will be vice principal of a driving school in N. Prefecture."

"My congratulations on a long career of outstanding work." Prosecutor

Onuki shook hands with Noseh. "I certainly have good memories of investigations we have done together."

"Yeah, me too."

"Thanks to your fine work, the criminals behind the Shinkansen bombing were brought to justice. Your honor is one more reason why I do not want that investigation to go to waste."

"Thank you. I appreciate your consideration." A porter showed up bearing wine, providing Noseh with a convenient opportunity to depart.

Alone together, Onuki and Domaé drank again from refilled glasses and exchanged remarks on a subject both found repugnant.

"That Noseh's taking it hard, like his own dog bit him. Hino was supposed to have been his most trusted subordinate."

"Once a cop goes out to pasture, he doesn't pull any weight at all. Hino knows that very well. He pushed all the right buttons with his boss when he was on the job, and now when the boss is retiring, Hino doesn't mind sticking it to him. We both know what that's all about. Police organizations look like a straightforward up and down power structure, but the truth is there's infighting wherever you turn, same as it was in the army."

"Noseh can't do anything to pull the plug on Hino and his confessions."

"Don't forget that Chief Magara is our ace in the hole. Of course, anything Hino says outside a courtroom wouldn't make any difference to the trial proceedings. If the case does go to the Supreme Court though, the thing to watch out for is that some of those justices will want to look good in the media. In other words, we need our own media strategy, and that's where Magara comes in. He'll cooperate. He's burned up over today's article, you can be sure. There's nothing like having a good man on the job, standing behind the dignity of the men in blue. The fact is, I told Magara to be here at eight o'clock. All I had to do was say it's about the *A. Shimbun* article, and he said okay right off the bat," Domaé said, laughing and throwing back his shoulders.

Onuki always showed respect for Domaé, as a fellow graduate of the same university, senior by five years, but far more than that, for the brilliance of Domaé's work. There was something awesome about his unwavering attention to detail. Onuki liked writing research papers more than doing the tedious paperwork involved in prosecution. He could not match Domaé's mastery of the complexities of any given case; his careful unraveling of each thread connecting the defendants to their crimes. It was Domaé, standing backstage at the first trial, who gave Onuki encouragement when all the defendants denied the charges and claimed their confessions were forced. With his help, Onuki had won a victory, with a decision that handed out punishments close to what he had asked for.

"The prosecution of that case is getting some criticism over that decision," Onuki said as he filled Domaé's glass.

"Yeah, mainly from *A. Shimbun*," Domaé said with a sardonic laugh. "That crew was the big cheerleader for riots in the schools, like there was going to be a big revolution, and they were heroes for justice. They shut up quick after the United Red Army lynchings, though. Now they're trying for a comeback with this 'miscarriage of justice' campaign. Don't worry about it. Everyone but hard-core reds get tired of listening to that stuff for long. Here's what we do: let them squawk for a while, then give some choice inside dope on Hino to a couple of other papers, say, *B.* and *C. Shimbun*. Magara has lots of interesting stuff. Noseh didn't say anything about it, but Magara tells me Hino traded in his old lady for a newer model. He's got a live-in girlfriend with him in Sakura. He calls her his wife, but the real one is in his house in Yamaguchi, with his kids. That's one thing. For another, there just might be some hanky-panky behind that 'hypnotism' whoop-de-do he gave that reporter Wada. Chief Magara has a tail on her, and he already knows she put Hino up in a hotel in Ginza and spent hours and hours with him there. They're bound to let something slip. When that happens, we pass it on to *B.* and *C.* They can write up something about how she services her sources. Oh, yes, I just remembered, I got a report a little before you got here. If you take a look out that window you can see R. University over that way. Wada and her little friends are there now at a party put on by Professor Kirikaé. Akutsu and his wife are there, and so are Yukimori and Ikéhata. We have not one, but two plainclothes members in that support group, one on the treasury committee. In other words, we know everything they do."

"What are you going to do about appealing?"

"I don't know yet. A lot of that has to do with what we hear from the top about it."

"Well, it does seem to me there is adequate reason for appeal." Onuki was inwardly pondering what he had been taught by his mentor; the question is not whether the defendant is guilty, but whether there is an appropriate reason for appealing a not-guilty decision.

"Now is too soon to be discussing that. First we have to do a good, slow reading of the trial record, and I'll be needing your help."

"I'm at your disposal."

At precisely eight p.m., there was a knock at the door. It was Chief Magara.

Chapter 13

Spring Ice

Atsuo was surprised to find the Suidobashi Station front completely changed. In place of the giant quonset building that had housed the skating rink was a tall building painted a garish yellow that assaulted the eyeballs. He wondered where the skating rink might have gone, and was eventually able to locate it on the sixth floor. The only thing unchanged was the rink's ten o'clock opening time. When he stepped out of the elevator Wakako waved to him from inside the shop that sold and serviced ice skates.

"Aren't you the early bird."

"I just hope I'm not as rusty as my blades were. They were too far gone to use. I'm having new ones put on."

"Mine were okay. My nephew Tetsukichi kept them oiled, and he brought them to Tokyo for me. That guy is as thoughtful as they come."

"No such luck for me. My skates were thrown into a storeroom to collect lots and lots of mold, dust, and rust. But I did manage to save the leather."

The store owner smiled a greeting to Atsuo. He had sold Atsuo his skates many years before, then serviced them and sharpened the blades a number of times.

"Saw you on TV! Congratulations! What an awful thing to have happen! I was wondering where you disappeared to. Used to see you both all the time, then suddenly you were gone. Finally, yesterday I caught you on the TV news and realized what had happened."

"Kind of groping my way around. Everything's changed."

"From what I understand, Mr. I. doesn't teach here anymore." Wakako mentioned the name of their former skating instructor. "Now there is a place at Takadanobaba called the Citizen Skating Rink where he teaches — is that right?"

"Takadanobaba?"

"Yes, that's right. That new rink was built three years ago," the store owner explained. "Looks like there are new ice rinks in all kinds of places. Tokyo used to have only two — here and Shinagawa. Thank you," Wakako said, receiving her refurbished skates. The shiny new blades were a high-quality English brand that Mr. I. had recommended.

The couple were ready to go when the bell rang to announce the rink's opening, and they were the first on the ice. They were followed by four girls who looked like students.

The ice was a mirror reflecting the morning light. The moment their blades touched the ice surface, previously learned muscle memories were restored, and they were skating effortlessly once again. Bend the knees to lower your center of gravity, pick up speed and enjoy the wind as it caresses your earlobes. One turn around the rink was enough to fully acquire that flying sensation. There's nothing deceptive about ice; it is only flat and slippery. The freedom of being in a space consisting of nothing but self and ice is a profound joy. Go straight. Go on a curve. Zig-zag. Go forward. Go backward.

Wakako was approaching from afar. Her long, well-formed legs extending from beneath her short skirt were vibrant with life. She sped past Atsuo like a soaring bird. Atsuo went to the middle of the rink to observe Wakako glide. She dipped as if about to jump, hesitated, abandoned the plan, and went into a spin. Silver blades became a sparkling disk. She lowered her hips, transforming a rising spin into a sitting spin; then she rose again and crossed one leg over the other before finally leaping from the axis of the whirling top she had become.

"Very nice! You're as good as you ever were!" He clapped his gloved hands together.

"Not really. I was going to jump, but I lost my nerve." Wakako rolled her eyes. Her complexion was rosy, her chest rising and falling rapidly.

"It's really amazing how you can recover your feel after a nine-year gap."

"My body remembered for me. Even so, my legs and my back don't have the same strength."

"Same here. It's not too bad, though, thanks to all the leg stretches and flex exercises I did during exercise time."

"Aha! That's exactly what I was doing. I did it for the entire exercise hour, every day. I kept getting looks like I was blowing peoples' minds."

They went to doing circle eights. You trace out a figure eight on the ice having three times the diameter of your height. Atsuo's was slightly smaller that
Wakako's. He could never get the shape exactly right, and every time he corrected himself he left another divergent version of the pattern on the ice, shaking his head as he did so. Going in a circle does not come naturally to anyone;
your idiosyncrasies tend to show up when you train yourself to do it. That rule
did not apply in Wakako's case. She could go around and around any number of
times, and keep to within two centimeters of her original figure eight.

"You sure do that nicely. You have the knack. Me, I'll never get it right."

"One thing I did in zazen sessions in my cell was going in mental figure
eights. That might have helped."

Wakako began tracing circles backwards. Suddenly, three hurtling figures
came streaking from behind, and she hastily moved out of their path. It was
three boys of about middle school age in hockey skates. Next they came into
the area Atsuo was using to do circle eights and loitered there, blocking his way
and scuffing over his tracks. Their sneering expressions proclaimed they were
doing it intentionally. Next, the gang of three applied themselves to messing up
the patterns left by a group of housewives practicing compulsory figures. One
of the boys caused a woman to fall to the ground when their skates collided as
he cut in front of her. He fled to another area.

"That's despicable,'" Wakako said. I never saw anything like that here before."

"'There's no problem with kids being nuisances when they don't know better,
but it's another thing when they do it on purpose."

The woman who had fallen told the boy to be careful, and he answered back
with some kind of taunt. He circled the rink once and then was back to the
woman with his two buddies, all hurling abuse at her. "Drop dead, you old bag!
Fat ass! Stupid old bitch!"

"Let's leave. I've had it with this place," Wakako said.

"They're finished for now. They know they'll be in trouble if they keep it up.
Or should I go give them a talking to?"

"No, I don't even mean that. The music is too loud. I don't know why they
have the volume up so loud. It's hurting my ears. And I'd been looking forward
to the sound of blades on ice." She was covering her ears with her hands.

The giant speakers suspended from the ceiling were blaring pop songs at
an excessively high level, so loud one could not even make out the words being
sung.

"Okay, I'll see if I can get it turned down."

Atsuo went to the control room. He had often visited the previous rink's control room to have cassette tapes played for ice dancing. The person in change would adjust the sound level in accordance with user requests. A young man was sitting before the stereo equipment.

"Would you please turn the volume down a bit?" Atsuo asked. The man glared at him without replying. Thinking he hadn't been heard, Atsuo repeated his request.

"You got a problem, mister?" the man said loudly. "I'm controlling the audio, not you!"

"I know," Atsuo said, startled. "But it's too noisy for figure skating."

"Sound's got nothing to do with it. You wanna skate, skate!"

"The sound does have something to do with it. You need to hear your skates on the ice when you practice figure skating."

The man stared into space and said nothing more. Atsuo reflected that this was a public skating rink and the man was an employee of the facility. The world had changed, for the worst. He was more shocked than angry. Wakako was in the rink side area, gazing out the window as she covered her ears.

"Isn't that tower called the Sunshine something-or-other? You know, that was built on the site of the Tokyo Detention Center, where we were?"

"I think so. It's a tower that's too tall." It looked to Atsuo like a stick of wood standing precariously on end.

"Someday it will fall. Everything people build breaks down," Wakako muttered, distress in her tone.

"I went to ask to have those speakers turned down and met a guy with a hostile attitude. I don't like this place one bit."

"Me neither. Let's leave it behind," Wakako said with a malignant look at the loudspeakers.

On their way out they were approached by an old woman with white hair, who was wearing a conspicuously pink skating costume. She spoke in a piercingly loud voice.

"It is you two! Just as I thought! How are you!"

It was the "skater critic," thoroughly aged. Her wrinkled face was heavily layered over with powder.

"I recognized you right away, but it has been so long, I thought, well, maybe not. Neither of you have changed a bit, just as young as ever, and wonderful skaters. Were you taking lessons all that time?"

"No, actually, we were traveling," Wakako said.

"For so long! Somewhere overseas, I suppose," the critic said with envy in her tone. She seemed unaware of the couple's legal difficulties.

"Do you come here every day?" Atsuo asked.

"I come here every once in a while. You know, so many new rinks have opened recently, I go around to them all. There's this one, Shinagawa, Ikebukuro, Oji, Takasago, Takadanobaba . . ."

"Is there one that doesn't play music loudly?"

"That would be Takadanobaba. All the others are noisy. It's just awful!"

"What time does the Takadanobaba rink open?"

"At noon on weekdays. Ten in the morning on Sundays . . . Oh, my, that fellow over there — he just did a Salchow jump, but he wasn't completely on his back inside edge for his takeoff. That's why he had a shaky landing. Wouldn't you say?"

The gang of boys passed by, once again taking delight in annoying housewives with their repertoire of insults.

"They're in elementary school," the "critic" explained. "Many of them show up here on their spring vacation. They'll be gone soon, so it's best not to mind them."

Atsuo threw Wakako a glance, and they left the rink. Wakako extended her hands to the sun and made scooping motions to push its rays toward her face.

"What a disappointment. That was not the skating rink I was dreaming about revisiting for the past nine years."

"Let's go to Takadanobaba. Sometimes 'Seek and ye shall find' works the way it is supposed to."

The couple boarded a National Railways train. Their car had few passengers, and both adjoining cars were empty.

"How was Mr. Jinnai yesterday?" Wakako asked as soon as they were seated.

"Pretty bad. They said he's in a protective room because he was dangerously excited. It's hard on his mother, after everyone was working so hard for that not guilty decision. He's terrified the prosecutor's shadowing him to kill him."

"I know just how he feels." Wakako darted a glance at a man in a dark blue suit seated across the aisle from them, reading a newspaper. "He looks to me like a spy for our prosecutor."

"Gee, I don't know . . ."

"I think he's following us. He was standing in the entrance to that yellow building."

"He was?"

"Listen, it makes complete sense that Mr. Jinnai is afraid," Wakako whispered. "He's looking at facts, not delusions. Look what those prosecutors did to us! 'Hang this one and put the other one in a cellar for life!' They don't care that we didn't do anything, and they don't mind making up lies about us. Do you really think they will shrug it off and give up just because the judges freed us? I think the first thing they do in a situation like that is have us tailed, like they did to your lawyer! Don't you?"

"I wonder if they would go that far."

"Mr. Jinnai isn't the only one suffering that way. Yesterday I was getting the feeling I smelled bad, and everyone was avoiding me. They all had expressions like they wanted to hold their nose. That's a symptom of my old neurosis. The same thing was happening to me in prison, and it wasn't all just my imagination. Women in uniforms were watching me every minute, and they always looked at me with expressions that said 'this Wakako character is here because she is a stinking murderer.' There was no way for me to tell where the neurosis left off and where reality began. You can't be under that kind of pressure constantly without distress. It was hell."

Atsuo regarded the vertical lines deeply creasing Wakako's forehead, scarcely able to contain his own grief at the sight. The pain from long years of suffering in prison was inseparable from her whole being. He wanted to embrace her and somehow extract that pain. But they were arriving at Shinjuku Station, where they would have to exit and change to another train.

The Yamanoté line train was too crowded for conversation not intended for strangers' ears, so they stood gazing silently through the windows at the landscape passing by outside. In their absence there had been a conspicuous proliferation of office buildings. Each was adorned with signboards or eye-catching structures advertising things. That oversized "Sunshine" something-or-other building appeared in the distance. Though such high rises were regarded as symbols of national prosperity, this tower stood on ground occupied by the old Sugamo Prison, then by the Tokyo Detention Center, where the state had intended to execute Atsuo. The building appeared to him as a hideous monster that thrived on the blood of human beings, including himself and Wakako. He looked away and reflected that his understanding of that building's meaning would be beyond understanding to the laughing young people standing close by, or the housewives carrying paper bags filled with shopping purchases. Even if he had their attention and explained everything, it would all be too unfamiliar to readily get through to them. He glanced at Wakako and realized that she, too, had averted her eyes from the window.

"There's something nasty looking about that building."

"That's where tens of thousands — probably hundreds of thousands — of people endured what we endured, and worse. The thought of their suffering tears me apart."

The words resonated so strongly in Atsuo that he had his own feeling of being torn apart. An image of himself racked in pain flashed through his head.

The way from Takadanobaba Station led up a slight incline. The Citizen Skating building was situated in a corner of a shopping district. At five minutes before opening time, they waited in the lobby, looking through the glass entrance door at an ice resurfacing machine preparing the rink for use.

"There's our tail," Wakako said pointing with her eyes to a florist shop. Atsuo was surprised to see a man in a dark blue suit standing there. Not having gotten a look at the face of the man in the blue suit reading a newspaper on the train, Atsuo could not tell for sure if it was the same man, but he had the feeling it was.

"Do you suppose he's an organization spy?"

"I certainly do. It's a good bet he answers to Prosecutor Domaé."

A buzzer sounded, announcing the opening of the rink. They were the only two customers.

There was no music. White light gleamed like snow in exquisite silence.

"Finally, we found a quiet place!" Wakako skated out across the ice joyfully, and Atsuo followed.

Their blades sang *shissh-shissh-shissh* as they slashed across the ice.

"THAT's the sound I wanted to hear!" Wakako hopped exuberantly, then went into a letter perfect one-and-a-half-turn Axel Paulsen, landing on her toe pick with a satisfying clink. Next, her skates shaved the ice surface musically as she went into a spin. With no extraneous pop music blaring, they were free to enjoy the aural nuances of ice skating — and wonder at the thoughtlessness of the previous rink to have robbed them of that enjoyment. There are people who would carry a boom box into a mountain forest. Atsuo and Wakako each began to trace circle eights. You get a clean shearing sound if you stay on one edge of your figure, but the sound gets ragged if you come down clumsily on both edges. When you can hear that difference, your practice goes well.

"Hey, there they are!!" a voice called out loudly.

"I.-sensei!" Wakako responded warmly, as Atsuo bowed politely.

"I was wondering who the newcomers were, practicing so seriously! It has been much, much too long! And congratulations! I read the newspaper story. It was really awful what happened to you."

The coach had grown a mustache and a bit of a paunch, accouterments that played into the air of a dignified man in his prime. Back in his early thirties, he had been pleasantly boyish.

"Sensei, I have a question," Wakako said. "We haven't skated for the past nine years. What's the best way of practicing that will get us back up to our old level?"

"That would be the same as a recovery program any professional skater would go through after an illness. Number one is all about placing your axis on the edges of your blades. Number two is leg-bending exercises — lower your body and twist your hips. Your first task is recovering the knack of finding your axis and twisting your hips. Those are the basics of skating."

"Fabulous!" Wakako said in a little scream, as her face lit up.

"What's fabulous?"

"You said exactly the same thing in exactly the same way at my first lesson with you!"

"Well, of course I did. Truth is eternal," the coach said, winking. "If you people would like, I could use the next half hour helping get you back in the groove."

"Yes, please do!" Atsuo and Wakako said happily, in chorus.

They spent the next thirty minutes tracing circle eights, three-turns, double-threes, and loops on the ice. The coach showed the savvy one would expect of a national completion titleholder by pointing out each and every one of their errors. Atsuo realized how far his skating ability had deteriorated. He reconciled himself to a long regimen of hard practice.

A congregation of middle-aged women came out onto the rink. Their outfits showed as much variety as their skill levels, which ranged from the levels of complete beginners to those of accomplished skaters. The coach held up a beckoning hand, formed them into two groups, and began the lesson. Atsuo and Wakako moved aside to get out of their way and applied themselves to practicing the forms they had just learned. Their bodies had become like buoys that always aligned with an undulate lake surface. Time progressed with an enchanting rhythm. Atsuo was well satisfied with the feeling of Wakako close by, even as he abandoned himself to frolicking on the ice. If only it could always be like this, he thought.

"I'm starving." Wakako had approached, her face shining with sweat. It was close to two o'clock. Atsuo suddenly realized that he, too, was hungry and tired. Wakako glided off to where the coach was standing and exchanged some words with him. Then she was back.

"Just signed up for thirty-minute lessons every day."

"Daily lessons!"

"Um. Going to skate up a storm every day," Wakako laughed cheerfully.

They went into a German restaurant nearby the skating rink. All other late lunchers had left. The waiters, in dark red waistcoats, were standing in a row with bored expressions. Having scant knowledge of western cuisine, Atsuo was happy to leave the order to Wakako. He was deeply enjoying the sight of her pellucid finger picking out items from the menu as her eyes busily scanned its contents from beneath a profusion of silken hair. She blinked, as if reacting to his passionate gaze.

"Is that order okay?" Wakako asked.

"Yes, that's fine."

"It includes lamb. You don't even like lamb."

"Anything you order is okay."

"That makes it sound like you have no will of your own."

"You're right, I don't, when it comes to you."

"Oh, yeah? In that case, let's you and me live together."

"Hah?"

"Just as I thought. You have a will of your own, after all." Wakako wriggled her well-formed nose. "Oh, well, you don't have to jump out of your skin. I just wanted to throw out the suggestion."

"Well, you suddenly spring it on me out of the blue — something as important as that."

"Living together is such an important thing?" She opened her big eyes wide, and said it as a challenge.

"Of course it is."

Atsuo was at a loss about how to communicate thoughts he had mulled over vaguely while in prison, then with serious intent since the previous day.

"I read *Confessions*," Wakako said with a hint of a smile. "The whole thing. It took until dawn."

"And . . . ?" Atsuo said weakly. He was waiting for the ax to fall.

"I got a good understanding of the man named Atsuo."

"What kind of understanding?"

"You've gone through a lot of sorrow. Now I know just where it all came from."

"Every line is the truth. I did all of those horrible things, just as it says. I'm a big-time criminal, with a lot to answer for."

"Let the one without sin cast the first stone. That's not me. I don't qualify to judge you. Not at all."

"I'm glad to hear you say that. But I can't give you a happy life. I was under a death sentence, and if the prosecutor appeals, I could be facing it again."

"And I could be back facing a life sentence again. We're in the same boat."

"Or in two different boats that are both adrift. The state still wants to make mincemeat of us, and there's nothing we can do about it. We still don't know whether or not we'll get to keep our freedom. Maybe we will, if the prosecutor gives up on the appeal he wants to make. But as things stand, there's no telling what's coming."

"Don't talk to me about prosecutors!" Wakako said this with such vehemence the waiter who was serving their order flinched in surprise and fled as soon as he could. "I want to think about our future, and the hell with prosecutors and judges and all the rest."

"Do you remember when we were out on the Furen River in the middle of a blizzard?" Atsuo said sadly. "You said we should fight the people who pin labels on us that say criminal and mental patient. But those labels cost us nine years of our lives."

Wakako used both hands to push apart some invisible barrier between them, shaking her head as she did so. "That's not how I see it. The time was not wasted! Although I'm sure the prosecutors had great fun snickering over what they did, those nine years brought us together in a way that nothing else could have. We ate the same food. We were in the same ranks. It is a great blessing."

"A blessing?"

"Yeah. Romans, something or other: 'Where sin abounded, God's grace was more powerful.' Nine years in the can is beside the point. So's a life term and a death rap. 'O death, where is thy sting? O grave, where is thy victory?' . . . Oh, God, what am I talking about?"

"No, I get it now. I understand you." Atsuo folded his hands and regarded Wakako's face, flushed red by her impassioned flood of words, and thought it was beautiful. At last he felt there was indeed an inseparable bond between them.

"If you understand, there's nothing to dither about."

Perhaps not, but Atsuo always dithered at such a juncture as this. He hated himself for being mealy-mouthed, in addition to all his other sins.

"There's nothing I would want more than for us to be together, but there are too many differences in the way. You're going back to finish your studies. I'm going back to Nemuro to be a fisherman or a mechanic. You are young, with all kinds of opportunities — abilities. You can go into chemistry. You can compose music. I have no education and I'm old. It's all over for me, and I'm a loser. Even if we were in the same rank, we are still completely different, and we always have been. Apart from the fact that you have always led a privileged life, you have never been involved in anything crooked like me — all that stuff in my *Confessions*. That's the biggest difference of all."

Wakako listened to this soberly, eyes narrowed. When Atsuo was finished speaking, she gave a long, soulful sigh, then began speaking in a calm tone, quite unlike that of her previous words.

"I understand your point very well, but you misunderstand my situation entirely. First of all, I have no desire to return to university. I am not interested in chemistry anymore. I am interested in music. I want to compose and play the piano. One used piano and a supply of music paper is all I need. I don't want to live in Tokyo, or any other city. As far as I am concerned, that would be small improvement over the jail I've been in for the past nine years. I want to live in a quiet place. I don't want to hear the noise of the city, including its crass music. I don't care if you're a fisherman or a mechanic or a criminal or an old man. I just want to be with you. If you want to live in Nemuro, if you want to live in the marsh or anywhere else, that's fine with me, as long as we are together."

"Well, thanks." Atsuo's eyes were moistening. "I'm grateful as can be, but ..."

"That's enough buts. Let's eat." Grinning, Wakako poised knife and fork over her plate.

The food was no longer hot, but it tasted good to the hungry couple. Wakako's eyes rolled as she dealt with a large chunk of meat she had cut off over-ambitiously.

"Never had a better appetite."

"You said it!"

"This is the kind of meal I was dreaming about."

"The meals inside were horrid."

Meals in the detention center followed a rigid cycle. Rice was sooty from age. The limited menu was always unappetizing, whether it was greasy croquettes, noodles, or stewed vegetables. Prison meals supplied legally prescribed calorie levels with no regard for the inmates' satisfaction.

"I calculated the total number of years I was in prison. Twenty-six, including all the time in the army. That's about half my life."

"Ten years for me, including time in the mental hospital. A third of my life."

"Animals who lock up their own kind — that's one definition of humans."

"Lock them up, pass judgment, put them to forced labor, take away their lives, hang them ..."

"Still, I wasn't kidding when I said I understand what you mean about it being a blessing. I understand that very well."

Atsuo got that far into his thought, then gave it up. For some reason, he found it embarrassing. Wakako waited expectantly, but he dropped his eyes and continued with his meal. Then he noticed a large block print on the far wall. It was a scene from some foreign country. There was a cluster of houses on a hilltop with a big church in the middle, like a hen watching over her brood. The cross atop the church shone into a gray sky.

(Immediately after I finished my *Confessions*, I went to the chapel and posed a question to Father Okuda.)

("Father, will the Lord forgive even someone as evil as me?"

"Do you really believe deep down what you are saying? That you are a grievous sinner?"

"Yes, I do. I have committed theft, murder, mass murder, deceit. The worst sin of all was committing evil in spite of myself because I was too weak-willed to resist the people in power and the people around me."

"If that is the case, you probably will be forgiven."

"Everything?"

"Yes."

"It sounds too easy to me. I don't think I have done enough penance. At the least, I can't be really happy as it is. If I could be, I would have nothing more to ask."

(Father Okuda tried to persuade me that the Lord would forgive all. I went back to my cell and did a careful rereading of the four gospels, then I read them over again. On the seventh rereading I was in a very perverse frame of mind. I looked for places where Jesus says something wrong, something that doesn't fit. I couldn't find one. It looked to me that his reputation for perfection was the real thing. That seemed to me an amazing thing, because all his disciples kept making one blunder after another.)

Atsuo had undergone baptism shortly thereafter, but he continued being troubled by the thought that he was under-qualified for forgiveness. He reproached himself for having the arrogance to be baptized without ever attaining true faith. There were prisoners who had found their way to grace, peace of mind and happiness through Christ. He envied them as his own half-defined unease continued. There were times when he felt he had met a benevolent God and times when God appeared with a very scary persona that threatened him for his sins. If people who lived in warm, natural beauty could sing the praises of God, he who lived in a cold prison cell lived in fear of Him. He prayed for forgiveness, but another part of him was telling God, no, don't forgive me.

"What's on your mind?"

He was unnerved by Wakako's question.

"I was looking at that print — wondering what country it might be."

Wakako turned to look at the print. "Maybe Germany. Gee, I'd like to go someplace like that. I know lots of people who took trips abroad while they were students, but I was too preoccupied with things like my sickness and politics — then it was all over . . . Umm, I would like to travel — go somewhere that isn't this country."

"I'd like to travel too. Even though I have the feeling that any country you go to, there's sure to be a system that takes away people's freedom. I certainly get what you mean by organizations now. There are lots of them, and the one that sits on top of all the others is the state."

"Speaking of organization flunkies, there's one now," Wakako said unexpectedly, drawing his attention to a certain table with a glance. A man in a blue suit was sitting with his back to them, leisurely nursing a coffee cup, as if he had time on his hands.

"A stink that won't go away. Let's ditch him." Atsuo rose and headed for the door, Wakako following. The man stiffened, but didn't turn around to look.

The street was filled with people. They walked for a while and when they surveyed the scene behind, they could make out three men in blue suits, with no way to be sure which was the tail. They turned into a side street. There was an entrance exam prep school at the far end. A great many exam prep schools, large and small, were located in the district. They circled around in front of an ob-gyn clinic for a look behind, and spotted a figure in the shadow of a wall.

"Damn, he's still on us. Let's see, there's a station that way."

Atsuo started in the direction of the station, but Wakako stopped him. "I know the side streets around here pretty well. I went to a prep school nearby for two years."

They followed a serpentine path that took them around a pawnbrokers shop and outside a hotel with a price menu posted outside. "Short time: from ¥3,500; All night: . . ." A dimly lit entryway was open. After confirming no one was lurking outside, they went in. Both headed in that direction reflexively, neither one leading the way. Alone in their room, Wakako clung tightly in Atsuo's embrace. Their passion mounted slowly as they exchanged kisses for an endless moment.

~

Wakako stirred, half-awake, expecting the six o'clock chime would soon ring, starting another loathsome day inside her cell, the fortress of her imprisonment, where she lived under the constant watch of uniformed women. During those moments, she was accustomed to cast lingering looks over the textures of the ceiling, the beams, and the paper fusuma, not wishing to emerge from the twilight. Then her consciousness cleared, and she laughed ironically to find herself in the morning light and comfort of her own room. She stretched inside her soft futon. Some fatigue from the previous day's skating remained in her leg muscles. There was a glow deep in her nether region that brought back the previous day's lovemaking with Atsuo Yukimori. She was looking forward to the date she had made to meet him at the skating rink at noon. For reasons she did not understand, he persisted in making efforts to distance himself from her. He could not maintain hope for his own life or a life of happiness with her. (Even as we made love, his despair was such that it brought me to tears. It was as if he was falling into empty darkness or the bottomless peat marsh, and I just didn't have the strength to save him. That was what made me cry, and it's making me cry right now.) Wakako dabbed at her eyes with a corner of her futon.

(I will be with him again today. How many more days will we have together? . . . Nah, no point in thinking about future ill fortune.)

Wakako rose briskly from her bedding. She folded it all up and piled it neatly in a corner of the room. Then she realized her prison behavior had taken control again, and put it all into her closet, the way normal people do in their own homes. Deprogramming would take time. She was still primed to dress and wash in a few minutes, then sit beside the doorway, ready to answer up to roll call.

"Seventy-four!"

"Here!"

(Until the day before yesterday, I was Female Prisoner 74. Now I dearly wish to banish that number they instilled into me over nine years.)

She went out into the corridor. The garden was to the left. To the right was her father's study and her mother's bedroom. The eaves of the roof cut out a triangle of sunlight that shone upon the shoji. Her mother's tranquil breathing as she slept had the rhythm of waves washing to shore. Wakako crept silently to the bathroom. Sitting atop the upper rim of the kettle style bathtub she knew from her childhood was its inner wooden baseboard. Everything in the house was just the same as it had always been. Even the scratches on the wooden shelving, the cracks in the walls and the rust on the tub evoked a flood of images from the life she had spent in that house from her infancy. She arranged her hair, lightly applied makeup, and went into her father's study.

Her mother had instituted a strict policy of keeping everything as it had been when her father had passed away, down to the position of the Chinese ebony paperweight on the desk. The one exception was a photograph of him on the mantelpiece. The eyes of gray-haired Professor Kotaro Ikéhata bespoke great sadness. The snapshot had been taken two months before his death, at the Criminal Law Academy. He had sneaked away from the hospital to deliver a talk there, knowing by then that death was imminent. Long consumed with despair at the loss of his research papers during the Tower takeover, he had at last recovered his ambition to begin a new research project. The memorial collection of her father's papers her mother had sent to Wakako in prison had included notes on the research plan he had written. The topic was miscarriages of justice in Japan. The last item on the list of cases he meant to investigate was the Shinkansen bombing case.

Wakako sat down at the steel frame desk, propping her chin on one hand and thought about the days when she had served as her father's scribe, taking down notes he dictated. Days gone forever. (Let's see . . . I sat right there, my little brow furrowing over the stream of legal jargon Father was spouting.) The door opened behind her.

It was her younger sister, Kikuko.

"That's a relief. I was afraid it was a burglar in here."

Kikuko was wearing stylish violet half-rim glasses and an ornate velvet suit; business dress for her job at the art gallery.

"I was just thinking about one thing and another."

"Last spring, a burglar really did get in. It was dawn. I heard strange noises. I got up and the light was on in the study. I thought it was Mother, so I called to her, and all of a sudden he kicked out a window pane and escaped outside. I chased after him, but he disappeared somewhere in the graveyard. It was a middle-aged man, stocky. I thought he looked just like that Mr. Atsuo Yukimori. Then I got really scared, thinking about how I was running after him all by myself."

This spiteful invocation of Atsuo's name stung Wakako as if Kikuko had intentionally sought out a bruise and given it a jab. She had been on the receiving end of her younger sister's offensives many times since childhood. Being as uninhibited as she was talkative, Kikuko was accustomed to arguing back when Wakako became angry, persisting until she emerged victorious. Wakako nevertheless answered her in sharply measured words.

"Don't ever say that name in that way again. He is very important to me. If you insult him, you are insulting me."

"O-né-san . . ."

This time, Kikuko backed down. A streak of timidity never seen in her before showed up somewhere in the vicinity of her frilled shoulders.

"Kikko," Wakako addressed her in a subdued voice. It was the tone she was accustomed to using in prison when she wanted to present the uniforms with a reasonable demand. "I slept with him yesterday. We're happy together. We love each other. The past nine years were hard, lonely years for us. They brought us together. Look . . . . . . He's Christian. He was baptized. You and I are supposed to be born-again Christians, right? Well, stop passing judgment on him. Forgive him, not seven times, but until seventy times seven."

"But Mother can't . . ."

"I know. She's against the fact that we are bound together. Like when I skipped out on last night's family dinner."

"She was really upset. She had made tongue stew because you like it so much. We were waiting for you when you called and said you wouldn't be back for dinner."

"I realize that and I do feel sorry, but there is something I want you to understand. Right now, every moment we have together is very precious to us because he's leaving!"

"Leaving? You mean you're separating?"

"Yes, very unfortunately."

"If he's going to leave you, that means he doesn't love you."

"That's not it. Far from it. It's a completely different issue. He does love me, totally. I'm happiness as far as he is concerned, and he thinks he doesn't have any right to be happy, because he has so much guilt, because of his sins. Can you understand that?"

Kikuko shook her head vigorously. She might have been a dog shaking water from its head. Before she could speak, the telephone at the end of the corridor rang.

Wakako ran to get it, cutting in front of her mother, who was about to pick up the receiver. The mother glared, sending the message, "Horrid child!" and the child blinked back, meaning "Forgive me!"

The caller was not Atsuo, as expected, but Makihiko Moriya. "It's me! I want to see you right away."

"You can't. I don't want to see you."

"Why not? What's the reason?"

"There isn't any reason, except that I just don't want to see you."

"I left the detention center at dawn today. Right now I'm very close to where you are. I need you. I love you."

"Wait, just a moment." Wakako covered the receiver with her hand and addressed her mother and sister who stood beside her, watching. "Will you please do me a favor and go elsewhere?"

Then she returned to her would-be suitor. "I thought you were the one who had no interest in anything like love, since it can't be quantified. How do you square that with what you just said? If you thought you loved me, you had plenty of chances to say it way back when."

"I didn't realize it then. It came to me in prison. Love's the only word for what I feel for you. I do love you. I want you with me on the road to revolution.

I'm dedicated to abolishing the state to bring peace to all humankind . . . Ah, I guess that's a feeble way to put it, but that's what it is. I mean what I say."

"That stuff about revolution is meaningless."

"You're right, I take that part back. I want you, completely apart from that." Unusually for Moriya, he was sounding uncertain. She had a vision of his algoid hair and eyes that peeped out from slits like warily opened clam shells.

"You aren't making sense," Wakako continued on the attack. "You're the one who says he can't be anything outside of a revolutionary. If you're telling me you're in love completely apart from that, you're lying."

"I want to meet you once. It doesn't have to be right now."

"Like I said, I don't want to meet you."

"Well, that's a shame." The line went dead, unexpectedly, followed by an endless dial tone. He had probably been calling from a public telephone.

She put down the receiver and went to the dining kitchen, where her mother and sister were having a café au lait breakfast.

"Was it him?" Her mother's face was joyous. "You cut him loose, didn't you!"

"What him are you talking about?"

"Wasn't it Yukimori?"

"No, it was Moriya."

"They let him out, did they?"

"Early this morning. He wanted to meet me, but I refused."

"Of course you would, after all the trouble he caused. He's the one who burned all your father's research notes, then destroyed your life with a false confession . . . You know, I think it was his Q. Sect that really set the bomb, because it's having a war with the K. Sect. They're killing each other. It's a very bad situation." Wakako's mother set out café au lait, toast and Camembert cheese before her daughter and gestured for her to help herself.

"Thank you." Wakako was waiting for her mother to ask her about the previous night, in which case she was prepared to give the same reply she had given her sister. But her mother kept quiet, her slim, fair countenance bearing a loving smile that bespoke joy at the return home of her prodigal daughter.

Kikuko left for work after breakfast. Mother took a flower bouquet she had prepared and invited Wakako to join with her on a visit to her father's grave. They entered the temple that had belonged to her grandfather from the wooden door at the rear. Generations of Ikéhata monuments lay at the back end of the inner graveyard, and at the farthest point was a very conspicuous crucifix of Shirakawa granite. Wakako followed her mother's example by crossing herself, then prayed for a long while, feeling the sun's warmth on the back of her neck.

"Father," she said in a small voice, but the face that appeared before her closed eyes belonged to Atsuo Yukimori.

Later, she tried playing the piano, but it was grossly out of tune, so she gave up and called to arrange for a piano tuner to visit. Then she began listening to records. She took out the string quartets of Beethoven's later years, from her father's collection. She had been wanting to hear these recordings while in prison. Unable to decide which to pick, she closed her eyes, and her hand fell on Number 13, in B-Flat Major, Op. 130. She listened expectantly, because this piece is very close to Piano Sonata in C Minor, Op. 111, a work she had fell in love with while in prison. In no time, she was in her own world of music.

(First movement: Adagio, ma non troppo. The Furen River in a blizzard. Silver-white field of ice with a mighty side-wide blowing across. The end of the earth. There was Atsuo Yukimori. Oh, no, the figure of Makihiko Moriya has appeared. He's carrying a pistol, and an old-fashioned duel is about to begin. Hey, Moriya-kun, you'd better think twice, because there's no way you can win. Your rinky-dink ideas about revolution amount to nothing before his experience. Stop your nonsense . . . Now we're sweeping through the blizzard, across the ice . . . Second movement: Presto. We came back through the blizzard on that snowmobile. Great fun. So was skating on the lake. We had a special rink all to ourselves and we skated 'til the cows came home. Wow, did we ever skate! Skating has got to be the greatest pleasure there is. Movement three: Andante. There was ice dancing too. Fourth movement: German style dance. It's ten-thirteen, time to start getting ready to leave. Got a date at noon. Don't know how many more times we can meet, but, come what may, today we meet. Suddenly I'm all teary. Can't turn off the flood. I certainly have become a crybaby. It's because of the music. The fifth movement, Adagio molto espressivo. This is about the saddest piece of music in the whole world. The telephone is ringing. Mother has answered. Hey, wait a minute! It's not Moriya, it's him!)

Wakako cut in and took the receiver as her mother was saying "Wakako is not here!" in a venomous tone.

"Hello, sorry — I was immersed in music."

"It's Atsuo. I'm in the hospital. Something bad has happened. Yukichi . . . He committed suicide. We got a call from the hospital early this morning. Suéko and I got here fast as we could. Mr. and Mrs. Akutsu are here too. So that's how it is. I can't go skating today."

"It's all right. I'll go to the hospital."

"No." There was the sound of a deep breath being taken. "I don't want you to come. See, his mother's out of her mind. She won't let anyone get near him."

805

"What are you going to do?"

"I'm going to be by Yukichi. The hospital will keep him in their morgue until tomorrow. I suppose tomorrow will be the cremation. We'll take his ashes back to Nemuro and have a funeral there."

"Don't we meet any more?"

"No, that doesn't have to be. Once things get back to normal . . ." She waited, but his voice trailed off.

"Well, goodbye."

That was the end of the conversation.

Yukichi Jinnai was dead. This thought went through Wakako's mind, but she was standing in a daze. No thought came beyond recognition of this fact. Some kind of braking mechanism was acting on her mental processes. Her mother, standing beside her, took the telephone receiver from her hand and returned it to its cradle.

"What was it?"

"Yukichi Jinnai is dead. He killed himself."

"Oh, dear." Her mother's hand went to cover her eyes and forehead. "That poor fellow. He was acting very strangely. Why ever was he yelling, 'It's hot, it's hot' in the courtroom?"

"The detention center is a brutal place. Mr. Jinnai wasn't the only one. That place is enough to drive anyone crazy."

"Yes, I see that. You had a horrible time there too." Her mother turned away, lest she show her daughter the tears in her eyes. Wakako gently stroked the hair that was graying.

"Mother, I'm all right. It looks like my neuroses went away while I was in prison. The reality of prison was worse than anything my own mind was making me suffer. They watch you every minute; they control everything; they plant spies; they treat you like farm animals. That's just what it is. It's a place where human beings are just animals in pens."

"Yesterday, I guess I said things I shouldn't have to you. It was wrong of me."

"It's all right." Wakako said softly, using her handkerchief to dry her mother's tears. "I understand how you feel very well. It's just that I want you to understand how I feel. I'll take my time and explain everything."

"Explain? What?" Her mother used her fingers to comb back loose strands of white hair, as she scanned her daughter's face anxiously.

"There's much to say. Of course, lots of things happen in nine years."

"That Yukimori, what did he have to say?"

"He said he was going to take Mr. Jinnai's ashes back to Nemuro and have a funeral for him there."

"He's going back home?" There was relief in her voice as she asked this.

"That's right. He's going back without meeting me again. Listen, I'm going skating now. I signed up for lessons with Mr. I. Thirty minutes every day for a special two-week program. He says he's going to drill me until I am back to the level I was at before."

Wakako left the house carrying her skates in a bag. A warm spring breeze was blowing. The peach tree beside the Ikéhata home was in full bloom, presenting a glamorous floral display that seemed to proclaim pride in standing beside the home of a beautiful young lady.

Gliding over ice turns the passage of time into a delightful breeze. It was two in the afternoon before she knew it; time for the housewives' group lesson. The instructor made a sign, and they began skating dance steps to the music as they circled the rink. A pair of university students in speed skates sped along the housewives' outer perimeter. They were well trained for competition skating; their hips were down close to the ice and they swung their arms alternately, following a perfect orbit at rocket speed. Wakako recalled Yukichi Jinnai's skating. She had met him three times. The first time was in the fall, on International Anti-War Day.

(He skated very fast, in perfect form. He did several laps around the rink, and then he left abruptly, apparently in a bad mood. The second time was the day they took over the Tower and I took refuge from the riot police in the Fukawa Motors' employees' dormitory. He brought me a damp towel so I could clean up, and then me brought me a meal. We didn't exchange a single word then. The third time was early February. He had sent me a letter out of the blue. We met at the ice rink and talked while going around and around the rink together. He said hello, and then launched into a deluge of talk about how the Self-Defense Forces were no good and Japan needs an army. When he saw that I didn't know what to make of it all, he suddenly said, "I really like you. Please marry me." Everything he said, including this, took the tone of giving me a dressing down for not knowing things I should. Then he saw his marriage proposal had me dumbfounded, so he laughed and said, "Yeah, I'm pretty ridiculous, aren't I? That's me — just a ridiculous guy. So long." Then he left, without another word. I was thinking about calling him to come back, but he was gone, and I never saw him again. But his confession the prosecutor presented as evidence in court said he and I had been friends since before I even met Atsuo Yukimori; that I came to Fukawa Motors by prior arrangement with him; that we met at the skating rink after the Tower takeover to discuss where he would give me stolen money; that he had "sexual intercourse" with me in my apartment. The confession was the product of threats and leading questions. Everything he said about me was untrue, with one exception: it is certainly true is that Yukichi Jinnai was in love with me. Maybe his confession included talk about how he wanted things to be. In court he argued that his confession was all untrue, and he apologized to me, over and over again. It seemed that his love for me just kept increasing all that time. Unfortunately, I never had any love for him, and I really feel awful about it.)

Wakako joined the housewives' triple rhythm waltz steps. She skated around and around the rink to "The Skater's Waltz." On about the fifth lap, she was in covered in sweat, having exerted herself much more than is required for practicing figures. Spectators looked in at the rink through the glass doors. There was nothing unusual about that, but Wakako got a surprise when she caught sight of a male figure half concealed behind the railing on a landing of the staircase leading to the bowling alley on the second floor. Despite short hair and dark glasses, the diminutive figure was unmistakably Makihiko Moriya. How long had he been standing there? Why was he there? Assailed by these suspicions, her leg brushed against another woman's leg and she very nearly fell to the ground.

The housewives' group clustered around the instructor. Wakako went by herself to lean against the outer fence and look up to that stairway. Makihiko Moriya's form had vanished from sight. She pondered the possibility that her mind had been playing tricks, but the more she thought about it the more clearly she recalled the image of Moriya standing there. He had cut his shoulder length hair, put on a beret, dark glasses, a suit and necktie, and was carrying a black briefcase. All of that was presumably intended to be a disguise, but he couldn't change his distinctively oblong head and narrow shoulders. She knew him at a glance. Wakako stepped up from rink side, expecting he would be lurking somewhere. Her apprehension was almost instantly met as Makihiko Moriya emerged like an apparition from the hothouse in the florist shop by the skating rink.

"I knew you were prowling around here somewhere," Wakako laughed.

"You couldn't tell it was me, could you?" Moriya said with an affected pat on his beret.

"Sure could. That disguise is as lame as they come. You couldn't pass for anything in it, except yourself, looking silly."

"Was it that easy to tell?" Moriya's eyes went wide inside his dark glasses.

"Hey, there's something I want to talk over with you. Will you join me in a cup of tea?"

"And that's a lame come-on! Can't you come up with any good lines? I'm not going to field any pitch about love from you. I already heard more than enough of that on the phone."

"You don't have to be mean about it. What got into you this morning? You froze me out from the start!"

"My mother was standing next to me. You can't get into the kind of discussion you wanted in front of your mother."

"Ah, so that's what it was!" Moriya nodded, looking relieved.

"You look like you still don't get it, so I'll tell you again. I don't have anything to discuss with you."

"Look, I'm asking you as a favor. I just want you to hear me out on one thing. It's very important to me."

"It isn't important to me!"

Groups of housewives and middle school students walked by, casting curious glances at the quarreling couple.

"It's no good taking here. Isn't there a cafe nearby?" Moriya waved his hand as if to banish the glances from passersby, like bothersome smoke.

"The same old Moriya-kun. Oh, well, follow me." Wakako scanned their surroundings to confirm that the man in the blue suit wasn't there. He had been following her before her arrival at the skating rink. She led Moriya into a narrow alleyway, then turned into another side street where there was a small tea shop. They sat at a corner table at the far end of the shop.

"You sure know your way around here."

"Used to walk around this whole area every day. I haven't been in this shop for fifteen years, but it hasn't changed at all. It even has the same *du jour* blend menu."

She had frequented the shop with her prep school classmate Sa — the third-year *ronin* who never stopped drilling himself on English vocabulary with his handwritten word cards, even when he was in conversation with her. (He's the one I gave my virginity. For what that was worth.)

After the waitress took their order and left them alone, Moriya signified a changed attitude by placing both hands on his knees and lowering his head. "I have a favor to ask of you."

"If it has to do with love, the answer is no."

"It's not about love. You were right. I shouldn't have said those things this morning. This is about something else."

809

"I'm not interested in revolution either."

"That makes it harder." Casting an uneasy glance at a trio of girls students sitting two tables away, he lowered his voice. "It has to do with that in a way, but anyway . . . Without beating around the bush, I wrote a book-length thesis in prison. I want you to keep the manuscript for me."

"It's about revolution?"

"It lays out the ideals for mankind in the twenty-first century and thereafter. It's a proposal for a world federation that does away with states, which are the ultimate source of suffering in the world."

"That's a tough problem."

"No, it isn't, not at all. Look, nuclear war is the biggest worldwide threat. So you have an anti-nuclear movement that wants to abolish nuclear weapons. That's the progressive position, but there are also people who think limited nuclear war is okay, but you have to avoid all-out war because that would mean the end of the human race. Then you've got the anti-war position that says peace is the important thing, and we should cut armament expenditures and have disarmament agreements. But war occurs because every state has its own arms and its own right of self-defense, which comes down to a right to go to war. That's the source of the evil. The way to overcome it is for the people of the world to get together with a plan to do away with the organizations that have the right to make war — the states. Do away with arms and national boundaries. Make a common currency. Abolish nationality. Establish freedom of immigration and migration. In other words, set up a world federation. Put all the nuclear weapons in one place, under the management of the world federation, so we can use them if we're ever attacked by aliens from outer space."

"Abolish states! I wonder if that's possible."

"It is possible. It's the only way for us to survive. If the twentieth century is all about abolishing colonies and the birth of new countries, let the twenty-first century be about the glorious first steps toward abolition of the state and the birth of the world federation."

"Those are lofty ideals. Maybe too lofty to get enough people behind them."

"It's workable. People need ideals. That's a basic human need. The bigger the ideal, the more it is needed."

"Is that what you were thinking about in prison?"

"I was thinking about it because I was in prison. That is the state-owned place where there is less freedom than anywhere else. It gave me a good understanding of the true nature of the state. The people — humankind — have won their freedom in the course of fighting the state. They have won freedom from want, freedom of expression, freedom of religion. But it came to me that the one freedom they can't get by fighting the state is freedom from the threat of nuclear war. That's because the state itself is the creator of that threat. The nuclear threat is just the same as the threat of death when the state puts someone under a death sentence. It is a death sentence hanging over everyone. I realized that when I got a death sentence for a completely fabricated reason."

"What's the title of your thesis?"

"*The State and Freedom*. It's destined to go down in history as a great work."

"You're funny — calling your own thesis a great work."

"I'm that confident in it. This book is the work of nine years studying reference material and thinking it all through."

"You're going to make it a book?"

"I will. Well, that is, I want it published. That's the favor. If I die, I want you to get it published."

"That's an awful thing to be thinking about."

"I could be killed any time." Something made the girls sitting nearby burst into laughter together. Makihiko Moriya turned his face away from them, leaned forward and whispered. "The K. Sect wants me dead. They think the Q. Sect killed their members under my orders. They're out for revenge."

"Weren't those murders your orders?"

"No. I couldn't issue orders from prison. The comrades did it on their own. That's not to say I don't bear some responsibility, because they were being faithful to my principles. They're the disciples carrying out the leader's teachings to their ultimate conclusions. I told them to eradicate revolutionaries like the K. Sect, that only aim for revolution inside their own country — the K. Sect calls it 'Patriotic Revolution.' They took that to mean kill them all off."

"Are you okay now? By yourself in a place like this?" Wakako looked around the shop and the street outside uneasily.

"I can't say there's no danger, but I'm pretty sure they don't know where I am now. I've been going through very careful covering of my tracks since I left the detention center at dawn."

"What I can't understand is how you knew where I was. There's no way you would find out from my mother, and there isn't anyone else who would know."

"I have an intelligence network. The Q. Sect is very good at information gathering. To give an example, I knew you met Atsuo Yukimori at that skating rink yesterday."

"Well, that's pretty low-down, isn't it! We were followed yesterday. Was that someone from the Q. Sect?"

"You might very well ask that question." Makihiko Moriya showed his trademark gloating smile that stretched his thin lips wide across his face. He had used it often at triumphant moments in ideological debates with sect members who had attempted to oppose his views.

"Yukichi Jinnai committed suicide," Wakako said tersely.

"No." The gloat became a sneer, as if Moriya had taken the statement to be a joke.

"It's true. He did it this morning, at the mental hospital. I'd guess he was already dead by the time you were released."

"Did he hang himself?"

"That's right." She answered with a show of self-assurance, although she had not actually heard what the suicide method was.

"That's a surprise. I didn't know. One more murder by the state — that's what it is. Unjust arrest, unjust detention, and unjust trials drove him over the brink to suicide."

"I agree. There aren't many of your opinions I agree with, but what you just said is exactly what I think about Mr. Jinnai's death." Wakako glared into Makihiko Moriya's dark glasses as she said this. For a moment, the two were locked in a silent staring contest that ended when Moriya broke the tension by looking away.

"I had never even met that guy before I saw him in the courtroom, but we were in the same battle together because they gave him a part in that absurd frame-up of the Q. Sect, and I got to feeling a kind of solidarity with him over those nine years. He was in Masayoshi Taniguchi's Y. Brotherhood, which is ultra-nationalist, meaning it's for everything the Q. Sect is fighting against, but I liked him anyway, because he was straight. He didn't mind facing off against the power structure. There was nothing phony about him. He was a good man."

"I'm glad to see there are people you can have warm feelings about."

"Hey, I'm full of human warmth! How else could I be thinking about the happiness of all mankind? I'm for violent revolution, but the violence I'm talking about is nothing compared to the violence behind states that keep nuclear weapons — or the ordinary people who think letting states do that is good for national security. I've got enough human warmth to make you break down in tears!"

"Okay, I've got a question for Moriya-kun, the great humanist. How is it that you knew where I was, but didn't know where Yukichi Jinnai was, much less what happened to him?"

Makihiko Moriya raised a hand according to his gesture from long ago of brushing back the long hair he once had, but only succeeded in pushing his beret slightly out of shape. "Damn! That was a direct hit! . . . Okay, I might as well tell you the whole truth. I had a plan to kidnap you. I was waiting for the opportunity to pull it off. That's why I sent my comrades to follow you. I made the decision to go ahead with the plan when you turned me down on the telephone this morning. The fact is, there was a car waiting in the parking lot outside the skating rink, with two comrades waiting inside, with gauze pads and a supply of diethyl ether. The plan was that I would lure you to the car and they were going to drag you inside and keep you unconscious with the ether until we arrived at my safe house."

"This is a joke, right?"

"No, I was very serious about it. I needed you, even if violence was the only way to get you."

"You needed me . . . You mean something changed?"

"Well, yeah, you could say that. I was watching you skate . . . how you can just forget everything else and be totally absorbed in the joy of skating. I finally understood that you and I live in different worlds. So I called off the plan and had the comrades take the car back without me."

"I don't know what to say." Wakako was shivering.

"Well, so long." Makihiko Moriya abruptly stood up and handed Wakako the hefty black briefcase he was carrying. "Pay the check, for me, will ya'? I don't have money." With that, he walked away. Wakako watched his retreating figure, slim and lonely, until it disappeared from sight. Then she fell back in her chair, fully enervated, as if under full anesthesia. At the same moment, she was suddenly seized with a feeling of ravenous hunger.

~

There had been a spell of chilly days that delayed the season's cherry blossoms. Buds were beginning to open on the trees as April came. On Tuesday, April 4th, cold rain had been falling since morning. The cherry blossoms in the garden took on a waxy sheen, and then froze over, still a long way from reaching full bloom. When Wakako returned home from skating she found a thick special delivery letter in the mail box. It was from Atsuo Yukimori, in Nemuro.

> "I very much regret that I had to leave Tokyo in such haste, without being able to see you again. A great deal happened all at once after I got back home. Dealing with one thing and another has kept me from writing until now.

"I was in my room at the inn we were staying at in Uéno on March 25, when I suddenly got a call from Y. Hospital before daybreak, saying that Yukichi was dead. Suéko and I got to the hospital as soon as we could. Yukichi was laid out in the morgue with a purple welt on his neck. It seems he hanged himself by tearing up a sheet to make a rope and tying it to the bars over the window of his seclusion room. He had received an injection that had calmed him down. It all happened within a ten-minute period when the nurse on duty was attending to something else. Suéko would not come away from Yukichi's remains. She was crying loudly, blaming the hospital for letting it happen and getting more and more excited, no matter how much I tried to sooth her. Fortunately, Mr. Akutsu's wife Yoko came, carrying her sleeping daughter. She was a great help. Thanks to her, everything that needed to be done was taken care of. We had to order a coffin, get an altar set up and make a reservation for the cremation. It was about ten in the morning when the director of the hospital came to apologize. I called you right after that. Suéko and I, and Mr. and Mrs. Akutsu had a wake at the hospital morgue, then the next day we had the cremation. We were on a plane back to Nemuro that afternoon. Tetsukichi and Torakichi met us at the airport with a jeep. Suéko was still in shock, and so exhausted by the time she was back home, she went straight to bed. Torakichi just had a vacant expression all of the time, so Tetsukichi made the arrangements for a monk to come for the funeral the next day. We buried the ashes on the seventh day, which was April 1st, in our plot at the municipal cemetery. The Jinnai grave is close to the Yukimori grave, where my parents are, facing the sea. The shoreline was locked with sheer white ice floes and an ominous cold wind was blowing in from the sea beyond.

"Just when I thought things had settled down, Torakichi suddenly had a stroke. He lost consciousness, his left hand was paralyzed, and he was drooling. I called for a doctor located quite near to our house, but it was Saturday, and the doctor was on an outing. On the third call I finally found one — Dr. Harazaki. His clinic was mentioned in *Confessions*. His younger brother was my elementary school classmate who became a middle school teacher. I was relieved that he said he would come right away, but Suéko said no. She didn't want to have anything to do with the Harazakis out of resentment toward the doctor's brother, who had refused to write an employment recommendation for Yukichi because Yukichi had been in a reformatory. So I had to call back and turn down Dr. Harazaki. It wasn't until April 2nd in the afternoon that the doctor on call at the municipal hospital came. Torakichi was completely paralyzed on his left side. He was unconscious and snoring loudly.

"Torakichi was taken to the municipal hospital in an ambulance. Suéko is staying there, tending to him. Right now it's late at night. I'm alone in the house writing this letter as I listen to the creaking of ice floes in the sea.

"Was it a Russian novel that said 'trouble never comes alone?' I've got an anxious feeling that principle may apply to this house. Torakichi is stable for now, but even if his condition improves, he probably won't ever return to normal — at least not mentally. The doctor says the shock of Yukichi's derangement and suicide is what triggered the stroke. It would be another disaster if anything happened to Suéko, but as things are now, it's a good thing that taking care of Torakichi keeps her from focusing on grief for Yukichi.

"The cherry trees should be in bloom now in Tokyo, but Nemuro is still a world of ice and snow. The river is still frozen over, and the sea is filled with drift ice. The signs of spring are there to see, though. Snowmelt raises the river level a little bit, causing cracks to appear, and the ice floes out at sea are starting to move. As soon as the ice is gone, the fishing season will be on. Tetsukichi is out with his crew staying at a fishing post on the shore, repairing nets and getting their ship ready to go to sea.

"The ice blocks are very noisy as they grind against one another. Once in a while you can hear a whistling sound. That's air blowing out from crevices in the ice. I am all alone. That is the life I chose for myself at the very end.

"It won't be long before the two weeks the prosecutor has to file an appeal is up. If there is no appeal by April 6th, our not-guilty decision is finalized. That is what I want for you, very much. As for myself, a part of me thinks, so what? — it doesn't even matter. Even if the prosecution appeals and I continue to have the absurd role of defendant forced on me, that won't make any difference to my life in this dilapidated house in the far north.

"I do want very much to be with you, but that cannot be. Sad as it is, I believe just as strongly that the way it is now is for the best. It makes me very happy that we had that one day together. What I want now is to live quietly, in the comfort of that happiness.

"I wish deeply for your happiness. Your finding happiness will be the greatest satisfaction I could have.

"Goodbye."

Wakako finished reading the letter, then turned to her piano and began playing a Beethoven sonata. With no hesitation, the piece she chose was Sonata in E-Flat, Op. 81a, "Lebewohl," or "Farewell." Her tears began halfway through the allegro first movement. Rain began falling harder, spattering upon the corrugated roofing sheet projecting from beneath the eaves. Though it was well before sundown, the garden was completely dark. (I can't be happy without him. How do I make him understand that?) Wakako gave up thinking, the better to strike the keys forcefully, in competition with the rain.

Dinner included only herself and her mother. Her brother was living in a apartment provided by his company, located nearby, and her sister had left word she would be attending a party for a private exhibition at her gallery. Wakako said nothing, eating only a little. Rags had been placed at the base of the dining kitchen window to keep out the driving rain. Finally, the rain started to seep in. In addition to the dining kitchen window, two leaks appeared in the corridor, and another in the study. Wakako's mother said it was because the house was old, the sheet roofing was decomposing and the tiling was coming loose. After her father had passed away, the house budget no longer allowed for satisfactory repair work. Wakako returned to the piano, ignoring the sound of water dripping into a bucket and a water basin. She followed up the majestic Beethoven piece with a charming minuet by Ravel, then a frivolous piece by Eric Satie. Then, going wild, she began doing improvisations on a sonata she had composed in prison. Her mother sensed something was up, and watched her daughter for a time, then departed, shaking her head. Wakako quit the piano when exhaustion was finally making her fingers unruly. She took Atsuo Yukimori's letter into her room, spread out a futon and collapsed upon it. Rain soaking into the ceiling spread out into a shape like a map of Hokkaido. Wakako fell asleep and was awakened by her mother.

"Telephone for you!"

Wakako leaped up, suddenly filled with apprehension. "Who is it?"

"Ms. Wada, from *A. Shimbun*."

"I said I don't want to talk to any reporters."

There had been a flood of interview requests from reporters following Yukichi Jinnai's death, and Wakako had turned down all of them. Not one newspaper had printed even a single line about the criticism she had made of the press coverage of her case at the press conference held immediately after the release of the Shinkansen bombing defendants. That had dashed any hope she might have had of a conscientious response from the media to the issues she had raised. She had been avoiding reporters thereafter. Even though Ms. Wada had in fact given conscientious coverage of the Shinkansen case, Wakako was not inclined to make an exception for her. To the contrary, Wakako had developed a particular dislike for that reporter. After inviting her to be driven home from Professor Kirikaé's party in the *A. Shimbun* chauffeured car, she had used the occasion for some very out-of-place hand holding with Attorney Akutsu, who had invited himself along for the ride. The episode had given Wakako the distasteful feeling of being used by both for their own selfish purposes.

"I know, but she says it's about something serious that has happened," her mother said in a frightened tone. "She wants to inform you about it."

"Sounds like something bad."

"I don't know what it is."

Dourly, Wakako took the phone. "Yes? What is it?"

"Wakako? This is Yoshié Wada. I'm sorry to be calling at such a late hour. I have to tell you that Makihiko Moriya and Shinichi Tagawa have been killed. Akito Shinya suffered a crushed skull, and is in critical condition. All three were under care at the Nakajima Hospital in Omé. At about 1 a.m., three or four men broke a window of the residence hall and entered inside. It appears they beat the victims with steel pipes. Hello? I would like to ask for your comment on this."

Wakako slammed the telephone receiver onto its cradle and raised a hand to her forehead. What kind of horror was unfolding? Yukichi Jinnai goes deranged and commits suicide, and now Makihiko Moriya and Shinichi Tagawa, beaten to death, and Akito Shinya probably permanently disabled. Who would be next? Were all the defendants in for a grim fate?

Wakako immediately dialed the number of Torakichi Jinnai's home, where Atsuo Yukimori was staying. She counted thirty rings, but no one answered. Was it that Torakichi had taken a turn for the worse, and everyone was at the hospital to be with him? Wakako had decided she would not call if she did not receive a call. Having broken down and called anyway, without getting an answer, she felt regret at making the call, and at the same time was seized with unbearable anxiety. She changed into pajamas and buried herself in her futon, but restless thoughts left no room for drowsiness to set in. The sleeping pills she had received from the hospital years before must be around somewhere. She rummaged through a desk drawer until she found them, and took a dose.

The morning newspaper reported Makihiko Moriya's death on the front page. Akito Shinya had also died of his wounds. All three victims had died. No one had heard the sounds of the window breaking, or the cries of the three being beaten to death. Immediately after the crime, a man who identified himself as a member of the "K. Sect Revolutionary Army" called *A. Shimbun* to proclaim that his group had "annihilated members of the anti-revolutionary Q. Sect, including its top officer, Moriya." The Omé police station was investigating on suspicion of the K. Sect's responsibility for the crimes.

The national news page showed photos of the crime scene. The bodies had been removed, but the blood-spattered room told a grisly tale of the savage assault that had taken place. Futon, dishes and furniture randomly littering the floor suggested that the three victims had been attacked while asleep, meaning they could have offered only futile resistance. Wakako recognized a framed photograph fallen near a pillow that was none other than herself. She remembered it, having sent it to Makihiko Moriya ten years before, for his birthday. She was stung by the thought that she, too, would have been killed if she had been with him. There was a comment from Makihiko Moriya's mother, and another from Attorney Kida, who had defended the Q. Sect members, appealing for an end to "senseless sect infighting." Then the name of Atsuo Yukimori lept from the page, as if the characters were molded in relief.

"Mr. Atsuo Yukimori, one of the former Shinkansen bomb trial defendants, gave this comment from the municipal hospital, where his brother-in-law is undergoing treatment: 'Although I am in complete disagreement with the ideology of those young men, I realized in the course of nine years together with them in court as a codefendant that they were all genuinely well-intentioned, and they certainly did not deserve to die in such a manner.' (Nemuro Bureau)"

Nothing had befallen Atsuo Yukimori. He was among the living. Her awful premonition while falling asleep had been merely the product of exaggerated worry. Thank heaven. Wakako reflected that had she been kidnapped by Makihiko Moriya, she would certainly have been killed with him. She did not especially dread that thought, however. Atsuo's death alone would be a major issue to her. Makihiko Moriya's manuscript, *The State and Freedom*, was locked away in a drawer in her father's steel frame desk. Might the K. Sect show up looking for it? That was one thing she did not want to have taken away from her, because it was the only memento of him she had. She recalled the strangely moving effect it had had upon her when she had finished reading it. She could indeed confirm that Moriya had been a "genuinely well-intentioned young man."

Wakako's mother dutifully turned down each request for an interview with her daughter in the unending stream of calls from the media. Most wanted to get Wakako's reactions as the former lover of Makihiko Moriya. Some wanted information about Shinichi Tagawa and Akito Shinya. Never having exchanged so much as a single word with either of them, Wakako was appalled by the insensitivity of media people, who thought nothing of intruding upon private lives with no knowledge of the people involved.

Disregarding her mother's advice to avoid danger by staying home, Wakako headed for the skating rink. She arrived just after opening time, and had the whole rink to herself. It was a wonderful feeling. Wakako was taken with the desire to perform every trick she knew. Normally, she would practice figures in the center of the rink while the ice was in pristine condition, but this day she immediately launched into freestyle maneuvers. She skated straight ahead and then laterally. She executed a forward crossover, followed by a two and a half turn Axel Paulsen jump. She sped the width of the rink like an arrow, did a backward crossover figure, then tapped the ice with a toe pick and launched into a double spin Lutz jump. Next, she executed a complex step that magically started her spinning, her axis firmly at her body's center. The entire skating rink was transformed into gold, silver, and iron arrows that orbited about her. As she drew her arms and legs inward, all her momentum became terrific rotational force, and the arrows changed into a countless multitude of shining rings. Then she skipped out from the spin into a backward crossover, sailing into the distance as both perimeter fence and ice surface tilted away at angles to her blades. Next she executed a Salchow jump . . . but this one didn't work, ending with a single turn as her hips wobbled and she fell on her backside. She had been distracted by the sight of the instructor approaching. Wakako was breathing hard as she greeted him.

"You've been making good progress, but I'm afraid you've been over-reaching today. Your shoulders are all tensed up. You give the impression your suffering some kind of inner turmoil."

"That assessment is exactly right. Yesterday a dreadful thing happened that had me pretty upset."

"Might it be about that item in the newspaper? Those three people killed in a radical sect war?"

"Yes, that's it."

"At a time like that you should stay calm and do basic compulsory figures. You are more likely to get in better spirits that way. You'll only end up hurting yourself if you work yourself into a desperate state, like you're doing."

Following the instructor's advice, Wakako began tracing basic figures. The outside rocker is an exercise of considerable difficulty, in which the skater turns by emerging at the cusp of two intersecting circles, while staying on the inner edge of the figure. She was not experiencing success with it, although she had mastered it nine years before. Following instructions, she began by approaching the exercise in a calm state of mind. Soon, her tracks were aligning themselves neatly. At that point, a skating rink employee approached her.

"Ms. Ikéhata? There's someone who has an urgent message for you."

She saw the lanky Attorney Akutsu in the lobby, looking as if he had business to discuss. He was gazing her way intensely and beckoning with his hand. Wakako asked the instructor to cut short the day's lesson, did a rapid change to street clothes in the locker and hurried out to the lobby.

Attorney Akutsu dispensed with formalities to deliver his message.

"The prosecutor gave up on appealing. The not-guilty decision is finalized!"

"Oh, really?" For some reason, Wakako was not excited by the news; her mind was a blank. The next moment, however, she felt faint, unable to continue standing. A nearby sofa came in handy. She sat down, and suddenly her cheeks were moist with what could have been either tears or sweat.

Attorney Akutsu sat beside her, emphatically nodding his head. "Congratulations! This is a happy day!"

"Thank you. Thank you." Wakako had at last found her voice.

"I called Mr. Yukimori to give him the news. He was overjoyed, and asked me to convey his congratulations to you."

"He did? Is he at home now?"

"Yes, he is. He said that Mr. Torakichi Jinnai regained consciousness this morning. He was very happy about that as well."

"That is very good news." The emptiness that had been in her a moment before was being replaced by something like a core of incandescent living energy. It was rapidly restoring the strength that had left her only moments before. She tested her condition by standing, and discovered she could do it effortlessly. Attorney Akutsu also rose.

"There is an important item of business I must discuss with you. I want to file a request for indemnification under the Criminal Compensation Law. The law provides for maximum payment of 3,200 yen per day of detention in cases when the defendant is found not guilty. You were detained 3,319 days. That is an appallingly long period of time. It comes to about one hundred million yen, but the courts are miserly — they never order payment of the maximum amount, but we should certainly push the demand. In addition to that, we want to make a separate demand for compensation for legal fees. Let's say a claim for one hundred million — that will likely end up with a payment of around seven hundred million. It is pitifully small compensation for the fact that they robbed you of much of your youth."

"I leave that matter entirely up to you."

"All right then, will you join me for lunch?"

"No." Wakako looked up at to a clock on a pillar: forty minutes past noon. "I'm returning home." Her pulse quickened as she said this, and she was overcome with a feeling of urgency. "I have to get home right away."

"Okay, let me see you off."

They went out into the street. There was still a dampness in the air from the storm of the previous night, but the warmth of spring brightened things where the sun was shining.

"You're quite a good skater. Actually, I was watching your jumps. It seemed such a shame to call for you right away. I was waiting for a break."

"You were watching me all that time!"

Wakako realized she was being looked upon with admiration by a man who was far from unattractive. It momentarily occurred to her she could enjoy surrendering to his embrace. She looked away, and a taxi pulled up before them. Akutsu opened the door and invited her in.

"I'll take the train," she told him. When the taxi had gone, she ran into a book shop and bought a copy of the current book of national public transport timetables. She opened it while she rode the train. The next flight to Kushiro was at 1500.

Wakako arrived at her home at one-fifteen. She slipped quietly into her room so that her mother, who was in the living room watching television, would not hear. She had worked out her plan while on the train and was now cooly carrying it out. Into a small suitcase she packed music paper, clothing, cosmetics, and Makihiko Moriya's *The State and Freedom*. She placed some discount bonds her father had left to her, her savings account bankbook and fifty thousand yen in cash into her handbag. She looked around the room, set her desktop in order, then picked up the suitcase and hitched her handbag on her shoulder. The next step of the plan was to slip out the back entrance, but she suddenly changed her mind. She went to the living room and sat facing her mother in formal *seiza*.

"I am going to Nemuro to be with Mr. Atsuo Yukimori. Goodbye."

Mother regarded daughter in blank astonishment, her eyes widening when they fell on the suitcase.

"What ... What's your hurry?"

"It is urgent. I'm sure you heard that the prosecutor decided not to appeal our decision."

"I'm thrilled! So glad for you . . ." An actor was speaking in a strident voice from the television.

Wakako's mother finally recovered from her surprise. "We planned on having a celebration. Kikuko is all excited. She's going shopping at the big Tsukiji market. Won't you let us have a dinner party for you?"

"I hate to be a disappointment, but I have to go right now." There was joking and laughter from the television. "It is one-thirty now. There is a flight at three that I must be on."

"Did that man tell you that?"

"No. I decided to go. Mother, please understand. I want to see him today. If I don't, I'm going to kill myself."

". . . Don't say that!" This came out as a barely suppressed scream. Wakako's mother had recalled Wakako's many suicide attempts in the past. She switched off the television and regarded her daughter afresh, watching her face closely.

"Go and be on time for your flight. But do come back home again, please. I want you to live."

"Thank you, mother." Wakako aligned her hands on the tatami before her knees and bowed deeply. "But I cannot make any promises. I won't know what will happen until I get there." Wakako went to the entrance door, her mother following.

"Do you have money? Take this," her mother said, handing over twenty thousand yen. It was all the cash she had on hand. "Do you realize what you look like? You're dressed like a schoolgirl of ten years ago! If there was time, I would get you proper clothing for a wife. You don't want Mr. Yukimori to laugh at you!"

Wakako turned and smiled. It was the first time her mother had prefaced that name with "Mister."

"Take good care, Mother." Wakako put down her baggage and hugged her mother. The tiny, angular body was quaking with sobs.

She ran all the way to the station. It was two-thirty when she arrived at the airport. When she had her boarding ticket in hand, she called Nemuro.

"I'm going to board the 1500 flight to Nemuro now. Just come to meet me, and we can talk later."

Atsuo was startled by the sight of her slender figure, carrying a small suitcase. Her outfit was guaranteed to make her catch cold in short order: only a tee-shirt and jeans, with no coat and no muffler. Taking long strides, she walked forward to greet him, her big eyes shining.

"Hey!"

"Hi!"

With that, both broke into laughter, as they realized they had reenacted their first exchange of words upon meeting in the corridor outside the courtroom in Tokyo.

"Your call was totally unexpected. I had to hustle. I only got here about ten minutes ago. You know, you're not exactly dressed for this territory. You'll freeze in no time in that outfit. It has been getting a bit warm during the day over the past two or three days, but it still drops below zero at night . . . Is that all your baggage?"

"This is everything. I left home pretty abruptly. I just now remembered I should have brought winter clothes."

"Let's get in the car, then we can go look for a place where we can get you a parka, sweaters and whatnot."

He had come in a jeep. Wakako got into the passenger seat, and off they went, into a wintry landscape of barren Sakhalin fir and brown meadows. Slopes facing north still had more than a meter of snow cover remaining. Cold wind stirred greenish brown bamboo grass.

"Where should we go?"

"You decide."

"Well, east, anyway."

"Right! East, to the end of the earth."

"Here we are."

Their first stop was a supermarket in Kushiro, where they acquired a parka, thermal trousers, sweaters, and gloves, all for a good price because the entire winter wear inventory was on sale. Finally attired suitably for the environment, Wakako went to sleep inside the heated car. Atsuo glanced occasionally at her sleeping face and reflected upon her long years of suffering. He had the feeling that he could absorb that experience with each breath she took, so he inhaled deeply, again and again. He continued east along the national highway. When he came to a bridge over one of the rivers that wind through the marsh, the sinking sun was casting a dramatic spotlight on great slabs of ice floating upon it. Atsuo pulled up to the side of the road, woke Wakako, and they went to the riverbank.

"It's gorgeous!" she said, taking a little bound in childlike delight.

"The ice is breaking up. Snowmelt from the mountains raises the ice farther upstream. The breakup starts there, and moves downstream. Take a look. The water level is so high it's flooding the banks."

The biggest ice blocks were five or six square meters. They crashed and ground against one another. The big chunks were destined to become progressively smaller, wearing down to one square meter and less. Ice slabs of every size caught the light like flashing, dancing flames. The water level was rising steadily even as they watched, creeping higher and higher up the bridge piers.

"Aren't those sounds marvelous!" Wakako said, and squatted down by the water to listen closer. Atsuo joined her. Mixed in with the murmuring of the river were delicate clinking sounds like crystal glasses lightly striking one another. Sometimes a great ice chunk would produce a heavy basso tone that reverberated in the pit of the stomach. Shimmering reflections and musical sounds continued on and on, according to some inscrutable harmonic pattern.

"The sounds of spring," Atsuo said admiringly.

Rivers are not all the same. The ice cover on the river before them had begun to break up, but the next one they passed over was still frozen, even though its volume had swollen tremendously, bringing its surface up close to the bridge girders. Reeds withered and colorless had been flattened and submerged by the overflow, except where some of their tips projected from the surface. Alders were under water almost up to their tops.

Further downstream, the ice was locked, with no open crevices. After the orange sun had sunk beneath the horizon, the forest ahead fell under darkness heavy like black ink. When they reached Lake Furen, stars had begun opening points of light in the darkness. Wakako gazed up at them in simple admiration of their beauty.

"See there," Atsuo explained. "The stars in the upper right are the Ursa Major dipper. At the bottom left is Cassiopeia's 'W.' There's the North Star. It's higher up than in Tokyo because we are further north."

"In Tokyo, it's unusual to see it like that at all." Wakako's breath tickled Atsuo's earlobe.

Atsuo had the idea of going to the Peken Lodge. He had considered and rejected staying at Torakichi's house. With Suéko staying at the hospital, the house wasn't as clean as usual, and master chef Tetsukichi's time was more than taken up with getting his boat ready for the start of the fishing season. When he had tried calling Peken, he had only to mention his name to evoke a warm and enthusiastic response from the lodge master.

"The Shinkansen Mr. Yukimori? Congratulations to you!"

When Atsuo said he wanted to make a reservation for two, the response he got was "With Ms. Ikéhata?"

This opened up a long conversation, through which he learned that the master had been questioned by police immediately after he and Wakako had been arrested. That experience had piqued his interest in the case. He had joined with the P. Theatre Troupe people, who were regular guests at the lodge, to participate in Professor Kirikaé's support group, contributing money and distributing the group's newsletter. He was delighted that the prosecutor had waived his right to appeal the not guilty decision.

The jeep pulled up in front of the lodge, sliding on a patch of snow that remained. A light instantly went on inside, and the master emerged, stouter than before, belly rolling as he ran to greet his guests. His head was completely bald. With him was a woman of around thirty-three or four, and a boy of about eight who resembled his father. The master introduced his wife and son, then remarked "Oh, my, you certainly bring back memories!" This left Atsuo searching the man's face for hints from the past.

Recognizing this, the master nodded his understanding. "I've had many opportunities to see your face in the newspapers and on TV. It is very good to see you again in person."

The room was warmed by a kerosene stove, and a hot bath was ready for use. Atsuo invited Wakako to use it first, and he went into the foyer. The central stove with tables arranged around it and the large window looking out on the lake was just as it had been. What was different were the picture books and toys there for the child in the household. Another item not previously part of the scene was an upright piano. As the master threw sticks into the stove, Atsuo raised his palms toward its warmth and gazed out at the lake's white surface under the stars and moon.

"The lake's still frozen," Atsuo said, rubbing his hands together in the stove's warmth.

"The water level has been rising since this morning. I expect there will be enough push from underneath by tomorrow that we will be seeing it all break up and go rolling out to sea."

"I'd like to see the moment when that happens. Where would be the best place to watch the show?"

"Up that hill over by the salmon roe extraction station. If you want to see the river ice heading out to sea, that's your front row seat." The master's eyes narrowed as he watched a log of white birch crackle and snap in the fire.

By the time Atsuo emerged from the bath and returned to the foyer, Wakako was chatting and laughing with the master and his family like an old friend.

"This lad's name is Koíchi — the -ko is for 'lake' because he was born here. He's in second grade. His mom's from Tokyo and she likes it here, but she thinks it best for Koíchi that they go back to Tokyo."

"Well, that's not the only thing," the master's wife added. "My father's not well, and he gets lonely. He has a bad heart, and he's always been a city boy. He wouldn't do very well in a cold place like this."

"Still, this is the best kind of place for children growing up," Atsuo said. "You have forests and lakes, the marsh, birds, and stars at night."

"Well, there are a lot of drawbacks. This is the only house around. He doesn't have any playmates, and he gets bored. He stays in the house and watches TV all the time. He's overweight because he doesn't get any exercise."

"Is that how it is?" Atsuo thought about how he had played in the woods or the marsh every day as a child. It was sad to think that changing times should have that kind of effect on the way children played.

"It makes me feel kind of snookered," the master said, with an ironic expression. "He and his mother are both Tokyo people. When summer vacation comes around, he gets all excited about going to visit his grandma and grandpa in Tokyo, and going to the amusement park. I finally gave in and found myself a job in Tokyo. It's a desk job in a little company. I'm the guy who ran away from that life in favor of the forests and the marshland. But now I'm going back to the city. I suppose it's too much to expect everything in life to go the way you want it to."

"What happens to the lodge?"

"We're going to close it down pretty soon. We haven't been getting many off-season guests lately, so you folks just might be the last ones. I've already sold the snowmobile. We don't have a car either."

"What a shame." Wakako crossed her hands over her breast and sighed. "I have very fond memories of this place. I'd be happy if I could keep coming back to visit."

"I'd second that." Atsuo cast a disconsolate gaze over the tables, bookshelves and ceiling of the old building he and Wakako had visited nine years before.

They had a lavish dinner featuring delicacies like scallop sashimi, walleye pollack roe marinade, dried sea-skate, and deer meat stew. There was a generous selection of drinks as well, from the master's assortment of fruit wines and liquors, made from crowberry, monkey pear, wild grape, and magnolia berry, each in a neatly labeled bottle. He held up a bottle of dark red magnolia berry liquor.

"This is really an herbal medicine, what they call a 'performance enhancement tonic.'"

Atsuo sampled the bitter liquor. It definitely tasted like something from the wild. He liked it enough to ask for a refill. Wakako eyed the cartilaginous seaskate and gave it a cautious nibble, then smiled as she discovered it was tender and sweetish. Mellowed by the exotic liquor, Atsuo urged his hosts to drink up, and soon they were all under its spell.

"I see a piano," Wakako said.

"I was starting our son on learning it, but we couldn't continue sending him to Nemuro for lessons. So I'm afraid it's not being put to use," the lodge master's wife said sheepishly.

Wakako opened the cover and played a scale, starting from the end. Then she abruptly began playing a piece. It had a fast tempo, raging like turbulent waves at sea. The master's wife was startled.

"Who would imagine music like that coming from this derelict piano?"

When Wakako finished the piece, she said "I'm a classical music fan, and I have a fair-sized record collection, but I never heard that piece before. Was it Chopin, or maybe Liszt? It sounded like something of that sort."

Wakako smiled, but instead of replying, she began playing another piece. This one was slow. Though bright, it had a quiet sadness, like a snowscape under the last rays from the sun as it sank on the horizon. Eventually, stars were twinkling in darkness that had settled in. The night was clear and quiet; once in a while a high register chord rang out and hung suspended in silence.

"This piece is called 'Star Sonata,'" Wakako said.

"Aha!" Atsuo said. "That was shooting stars we were hearing."

"Right." Wakako turned to look at the dazzling starscape just outside the window. It was like an open treasure chest of fabulous gems.

"Who composed it?" the master's wife asked again.

"She did," Atsuo said.

"She did? Imagine that!"

Wakako had seen a shooting star for the first time through that window. Atsuo remembered her amazed cry, and the radiant look in her eye as she gazed after it. Then she had talked about her own life since her childhood as she continued looking at the stars. He recalled all this as vividly as if it had happened the previous night, so deeply was it burned into his mind, although it was really nine years in the past. It seemed to him he had declared his love for her that night. and then stopped her before she could reply. He had considered it necessary that he make a very, very long confession to her before hearing her answer. Now she had read his *Confessions*, and the time had come to hear her reply. Suddenly, the prospect of this set off an anguished tension in him.

Wakako finished playing her piece to the applause of the lodge master and his wife. Wakako caught sight of Atsuo's face and asked him in a worried tone, "What's the matter? Didn't you like it?"

"Of course I liked it!" Atsuo replied, disconcerted. "It's a beautiful piece."

"You have such a glum expression, like someone falling into bottomless well."

"I'm all right. It's just that your music is so beautiful it made me sad. I couldn't help that. It's a sad piece."

"Is it? I can't even tell." They went to their room.

"Let's talk and look at the stars again!" Wakako said.

Everything was just the same as it had been nine years before: electric lamp switched off, flickering blue flame inside the kerosene stove before them, sheer white field of ice in the still darkness, stars twinkling in profusion, and Wakako sitting by his side. She spoke as if his thoughts had reached her.

"Do you suppose we'll see shooting stars?"

"Sure, we're bound to. Just wait and see."

"They say shooting stars means someone died."

"So they do."

"Everyone is dead — Jinnai-kun, Moriya-kun, Tagawa-kun, Shinya-kun. It makes me feel like I'll be the next to go."

"That's not the way it's going to be. I'll be the next to go. I want you to live."

"When you die, I will die."

"Wakako," Atsuo whispered, and drew her shoulder close. As he stroked her lovely neckline, she grew restless. Shortly, they fell upon the bed together, each seeking the other's lips. The warmth of her tiny tongue was a delight. Her long legs were smooth, the calves youthful and sinewy, thanks to her daily regimen of skating. "Wakako," he whispered again, and she opened to receive him. "I love you," she said as he was reaching his climax, and both moaned in pleasure at the same moment. When desire ebbed, he said "Now I won't let you go. Not ever, even if I die." Her eyes were closed, but she gave a slight nod. When he woke, he found her sleeping peacefully atop him. As he lifted her up and placed her by his side, she was bright-eyed and snuggling close. When dawn was approaching a yellow, sickle shaped moon with sharp corners appeared in the east over the blackness of the forest.

"A new moon!" Wakako said.

"That puts us halfway through the lunar cycle that began the day of the decision. That night was just about a full moon. This happy day came exactly two weeks later."

"That's just the kind of thing my Atsuo knows a lot about."

"I've been big on watching the moon and the stars since I was a kid. It was important to know that stuff on the battlefield, because there was no other way to locate your position."

"Your generation is made of star people. I'm from the smog generation."

At that point, they fell asleep. Then it was Wakako waking him up. It was brilliant daylight, and she was calling to him in a clarion voice.

Water had risen beyond the stone embankment on the shore. The lodge master and his wife were hard at work moving boating and fishing equipment to higher ground, lest they be washed away.

"The water has risen thirty centimeters since yesterday. The level is much higher than usual for this time of year."

Atsuo easily hoisted a massive bundle of firewood and carried it up to the terrace. Wakako made herself useful by moving fish nets and fishing poles to high ground.

"Okay, now let's go have a look at the marsh," Atsuo said resolutely. "It should be flooded by now."

The couple had a hasty breakfast and then were off in the jeep. Atsuo turned off the national highway into the pine forest, and after a time came to a place deep in the marsh. Wakako cried out excitedly at the sight before them.

Ground that until the day before had been a field of reeds with scattered alder and bush clover was now a great lake. Water rushing in from the mountains, the river upstream and all other directions had submerged clover and, for the most part, the alders, leaving only their topmost branches barely above water. The water had the marsh's distinctive coffee color. Reeds swished and swirled in the surging flow. The torrent was unstoppable, like a great multitude of fish swimming single-mindedly. Flocks of geese, duck, magpies, and goosanders swam in the murky water, some beating their wings as if they were having an athletic meet. Some birds flew off to the horizon. The fact that they were not in formation suggested they were ducks, rather than geese. They seemed aware it was not hunting season, leisurely taking off into the blue sky without a hint of caution. Finally, there were out of sight. Ducks close by began honking boisterously, as if clowning at a party.

They came to the bridge over the Furen River. Upriver, the ice was already broken and moving downstream. Massive plates of ice ponderously moving downstream collided with stationary ice, causing the latter to rise up with the momentum, then come crashing down again. As pressure built up on downstream ice, it began breaking into chunks that joined the downstream cascade. Wakako ran from the bridge to the riverbank, squatted down and listened to the sounds of spring. Small ice blocks made high pitched crystalline sounds. Heavy mid-range tones issued from medium size blocks. The big pieces were ponderously low in register.

"Yesterday was chamber music. This is symphonic," Wakako laughed. Her laughter was sunny.

It had been a very long while since Atsuo had seen her so upbeat. "How would you like to see these guys ship out to sea?" Atsuo asked.

"I sure would!" she answered immediately, working her legs excitedly, like a small child.

Atsuo took the jeep as close as possible to the salmon roe extraction station. Deep snow blocked the way up the hill, so they had to get out and trudge through bamboo grass and snow. Finally, they reached the top of the little hill. It gave them a clear view to the extraction station and the Furen River beyond, surrounded by the great marsh, and, finally to the distant sea. He had climbed that hill when he had been there with Torakichi, who was acting as hunting guide for Ichiro Fukawa. It was the highest observation point in the area. In the morning light, the tableau of ice, snow, marsh, and river gleamed placidly, still in its winter attire, the river still frozen over.

"Nothing up here is moving yet," Wakako said.

"It's on the verge of moving. See there," Atsuo said pointing to the swollen waters of the marsh and the ice floes upstream.

They sat down together and Atsuo put his arm around Wakako. Her face was ruddy under the cold wind and morning light, as if she had been skating. They smiled at one another, waiting for the grand show to begin.

"This is exciting. I'm wondering what it will be like."

"So am I. I know this area, but I've never seen the moment when the ice breaks. I think that's probably true of most of the people who live here."

"God really does amazing things, bringing all this water and ice together every year, then sending the ice out to sea. Even when there's no one to see, he goes to all the trouble it takes to put on the show."

"And think of all the trouble he takes to freeze the rivers and put down the snow cover in winter to prepare for the big show in spring."

"Now I know why land developers can't do anything with the marsh. With this much flooding, any farms or ranches they tried to put in would all be washed away. Let me tell you about a book the late Makihiko Moriya wrote. It's called *The State and Freedom*. I thought it was going to be a hard read, but it turned out to be very interesting. He says the state is evil because it starts wars. Therefore states must be abolished, and the only way to do that is by simultaneous world-wide revolution. Well, one of the points he makes is there are territories the state isn't interested in, because they aren't useful to its purposes — places like this marsh and deserts that don't produce oil. He had the very interesting idea of separating those territories from the states and putting them under the joint ownership of a world federation."

"That is interesting. I like the idea of the state not controlling this marsh. Then we would be free here."

"That's it! True freedom in the marsh. You know, I think I could compose a piece about it . . . There's something else I was thinking about yesterday in the Peken Lodge. Why don't we buy it? Attorney Akutsu says we can each apply for something like a hundred million yen in compensation. If we put that together, we ought to have enough to buy it. Then we could operate the business together. As long as I can be with you, I don't need anything else . . . We could do it!"

"What an idea!" Atsuo looked at Wakako in surprise. She had suddenly spoken words that offered a bright vision of a future that had never occurred to him.

The next moment, an extraordinary sound began. Wakako screamed, and the couple jumped to their feet. The ice on the surface of the river was splitting apart, and water was suddenly gushing out from within. Without their realizing it, the ice upriver had vanished and a great wall of water was rushing downstream. Ice in its path broke apart, and the wave moved downstream — seemingly with enough force to move the earth itself — and onward toward the sea. Ice slabs large and small that had been swept aside came rushing along in a steady stream. The couple ran to the riverbank. The mighty flow in the Furen River was much broader up close than it had appeared when they had been driving past it on the bridge. The banks had all but disappeared in the torrent. Water swirled everywhere; when ice blocks collided, the lesser body would come apart and scatter. At last, the great array of ice blocks was in a sort of formation that gleamed in the sun as it sailed majestically out to sea.

"Is it possible to take a ride on the ice?"

"Sure!"

"That's what I want to do. I want to go out to the sea!"

"It's dangerous. It will melt away under you once you get out there."

Atsuo had a vision of going out to sea on the ice with Wakako. It was something they could actually do; those ice blocks must have been fifty centimeters thick, which was quite enough to bear them. A big ice sheet about three by four meters came up close to where they were standing — just the vessel for them! Wakako was crouched to leap atop it. Atsuo grabbed her arm and pulled her back in the nick of time, and she pressed her face against his chest. He embraced her tightly.

"Let's live here from now on. We'll both be the Furen hermit together!

Endnotes

Marshland is fiction responsibly modeled on real events and real people. These notes explain some of the novel's factual background, as well as features of Japan's society, culture and history touched on in the story. A version of these notes can be found on the standpointjapan.com website.

A

Ainu An ethnic population of Japan now residing mainly in Hokkaido that is genetically and culturally distinct from the dominant population. "Ainu" (pronounced, roughly, like "EYE-NEW") means "people" in Aynu itak, the endangered Ainu language.

The people we now call Japanese applied the Chinese world view to other peoples inhabiting their islands, calling them barbarians, and themselves "Wajin," according to terminology borrowed from ancient Chinese records. The word for Ainu was *Ezo*. Japanese historical records tell of some trade relations between Wajin and Ainu, but the main theme of the relationship was warfare that drove Ainu settlements northward, ultimately expelling most to the main northern island of Hokkaido, that Wajin formerly called Ezo.

Today, the word "Ezo" identifies numerous types of flora and fauna that are distinctive to Hokkaido. Several are mentioned in *Marshland*. Another trace of Ainu culture in the story is the "Traveler's Lodge — *Peken*" for vacationers who come to Lake Furen for fishing, ice skating, duck hunting or hiking. *Peken* is an *Aynu itak* word meaning "pellucid." There are Ainu songs using the world to describe rivers and teardrops.

When Japan first presented itself to the world as a modern nation-state in the nineteenth century, the new Meiji government renamed Ezo Island "Hokkaido" and adopted a "Former Aborigines Protection Act" that set out a framework for absorbing Ainu and other non-Wajin as Japanese subjects, eradicating their culture and colonizing Hokkaido by appropriating Ainu land and forcibly relocating its inhabitants. That law remained in effect until 1997, when it was replaced by the Ainu Cultural Promotion Act, a measure beneficial to tourism. Following the UN Declaration on the Rights of Indigenous Peoples in 2007, the government abruptly recog-nized Ainu as an indigenous people in a unanimous Diet resolution the following year. In 2019 a law was passed authorizing a budget for "measures to enable self-esteem among Ainu people." That marked a mean-ingful commitment on the cultural level, but it didn't address key issues concerning traditional salmon fishing or other self-government rights taken away by the Meiji government generations ago.

Air raids An air attack on Nemuro is describe in some detail in Chapter 11, and there are a number of other references to the many air raids against Japan's cities conducted in 1945. Atsuo returns home just before the air raids of July 14 and 15th, 1945 on Kushiro and Nemuro. A total of 579 people were killed and 4,075 homes were destroyed by air raids on those cities.

Like the nuclear weapons used against Hiroshima and Nagasaki, the bombing of Tokyo on March 9 and 10, 1945 by American low-flying airplanes dropping white phosphorus and napalm was an intentional act of killing non-combatants on a mass scale. More than 100,000 civilians were burned to death by the attacks.

Akéchi

"Wow! Akéchi class detective work."

(From Chapter 8)

—

Kogoro Akéchi is a Sherlock Holmes-like character in fiction by Ranpo Edogawa (1894-1965).

"All-Campus Joint Struggle" Zenkyoto The term is specific to a period from the mid-1960s through the 1970s or later. It applies to New Left activism in opposition to the US-Japan security treaty, the Vietnam War and a host of other issues. "Yoyogi faction" or "Yoyogi aligned" means New Left groups that didn't break with the Japan Communist Party. Yoyogi is the name of a district in Tokyo (the north part of Shibuya ward) where the JCP party headquarters is located.

"In order to circumvent the problems of sect rivalry and mobilize unaffiliated students for campus protests, students at Nihon University and the University of Tokyo developed a new horizontal form of student organization, the All-Campus Joint Struggle Committee (Zengaku Kyoto Kaigi, or Zenkyoto, which welcomed all students and operated on principles of mass democracy at open campus meetings. This form of organization for non-conflict spread rapidly to campuses throughout Japan, and the number of schools paralyzed by student strikes grew almost daily."

—*from "Student Protest in Japan in the 1960s" by Patricia G. Steinhoff*

ani-san This is a variation of the formal way of addressing ones older brother, *o-niisan.*

anko A sweet filling for buns or other kinds of confections, usually made from adzuki beans. (Pronounce it like "AHN-KO.")

anko has many colloquial or slang meanings, including an unsavory usage appearing in Chapter 10, ap-plied to a young boy in a police holding cell raped in turn by other prisoners. In that context, the slang word for the rapist is *kappa*, a word that is also inoffensive in itself. Kappa are mythical beings living primarily underwater in rivers or lakes, but sometimes emerging to cavort on dry ground. Stories and images of kappa (some salacious) are a fixture of Japanese folklore.

A-shimbun is the *Asahi Shimbun*, (as in "Morning Sun Journal," *shimbun*, meaning "newspaper.") It has the second largest circulation of Japan's five nationally-based newspapers, reporting from a stance a little more intellectual, a little less populist than average. It has had a cooperative relationship with the *New York Times* for close to a century. The *Times'* Japan bureau is located inside the *Asahi* head office.

Atsuo Yukimori The name Atsuo has meanings including "solid," "strong," "considerate," and "warm-hearted." The *-yuki* of "Yukimori" means "snow," and *-mori* means "forest."

ayu Ayu is a freshwater fish that is a favorite of Japan's anglers and anyone else who likes grilled fish. Also called sweetfish.

B

BAKA-YARO! Epithet to call someone a fool, stupid, etc., for confrontational or abusive use, or to express anger. By itself, *baka* ("fool," "dimwit," etc.) is heard in everyday conversation and used relatively innocuously in many contexts.

ballad recital (*rokyoku* or *naniwa-bushi*) A genre of traditional storytelling in song, accompanied by shamisen

Banzai! "Live ten thousand years!" From ancient times, this has meant "Long live the emperor," or an all-purpose "hurray!" It was a cry for victory in the context of the Pacific War. Today it is commonly heard in any kind of celebratory context.

belly band (*haramaki* or *stomach band*) Historically, haramaki was armor. Now it is a kind of girdle or belly warmer for both sexes and all ages, worn below the outer clothing. Women wear them during pregnancy. Haramaki sometimes come with pockets that can be used to hold valuables. They may also be worn as outer clothing. It was part of the costume of the hapless traveling salesman Tora-san, played by Kiyoshi Atsumi (1928-1996) in 48 feature films released by Shochiku between 1969 and 1995 in the series *Otoko wa tsurai yo!* ("It's tough being a man!"). Another form of abdominal fashion also having roots in Japan's military history may be used by members of teenaged gangs or ultra-nationalist gangsters who wrap their bellies with a broad band of white cotton called a *sarashi*. The function is protection when sword or knife play breaks out.

Benzaiten (or Benten) Japanese name for the Indian goddess Sarasavati; used in countless geographical names across Japan.

blue line quarter Licensed prostitution that operated largely as a debt-bondage business flourished in Japan long before and throughout its era of empire in east and southeast Asia. In response to a demand from the Allied (U.S.) occupation authority in 1946, the government issued an ordinance abolishing its system of reg-istering and regulating prostitutes. Another edict the following year set out penalties for managers of women engaging in prostitution. These measures removed legal protections for forced prostitution. In 1948, an act regulating "business affecting public morals" laid out guidelines for the always thriving sex industry. The anti-prostitution law of 1956 made the promotion of prostitution an offence, and provided measures to "protect and rehabilitate" prostitutes.

Prior to this legislation, the areas where licensed brothels could operate were known as the "red line" quarters because they were marked off in red on police districting maps. Japanese culture being traditionally friendly to the sex industry, the new regime classified cabarets, bars and private bath-and-massage facilities as "specialty" businesses, and the term "blue line" was invented to identify districts where their operation was permitted. The bar Atsuo and Wakako visit in Chapter 2 is close to Kabukicho, which is a famed blue line district in Tokyo's Shinjuku Ward.

bomb terrorism The Shinkansen bomb case describe in *Marshland* has many similarities to an actual series of linked trials for crimes that occurred between 1969 and 1971 involving a parcel bomb and three bombs packed in "Peace" brand cigarette tins (containers for fifty cigarettes). The parcel bomb killed the wife and gravely injured the young son of a Metropolitan Police Department official. The "Peace can bombs" targeted a building of Tokyo's riot police (with no damage), Japan's largest petroleum company (one injury), and the U.S. State Department sponsored American culture center in Tokyo (one injury). The state's case was based on false confessions coerced from sixteen of the eighteen defendants. The two holdouts were both women. The "confessions" described a complicated conspiracy that was ultimately proven to have existed only in the minds of police investigators, thanks to alibi evidence uncovered by defense attorneys.

Chapter 6 mentions other actual bombings of the nineteen-sixties. On June 18, 1967, a package placed on a luggage rack of a train receiving passengers at Shioya Station in Kobe exploded, killing one person and injuring many others. The bomb was similar to one that had exploded in a Kobe Daimaru department store five months previously. There was nothing to suggest either crime had a political objective. Both cases remain unsolved.

On June 16, 1968, the explosion of a package placed on a luggage rack in a Yokosuka line local train that was approaching Ofuna Station in Kanagawa Prefecture killed one passenger and injured 14 others. This case was solved by an unproblematic police investigation. A young carpenter named Yoshinori Wakamatsu had taken inspiration from past media coverage of bombing incidents to deal with his own unhappiness by attacking the train that his estranged girlfriend had frequently ridden. Wakamatsu was executed for the crime in 1975. By that time, he had converted to Christianity and produced a substantial body of poetry that won the praise of more than one literary figure, including Otohiko

Kaga. A volume of poems by Wakamatsu was published in 1995, under a pen name. Kaga wrote about Wakamatsu in a book of essays and cast him among the condemned prisoners described in *Marshland* (as Mikio Wakabayashi) and *Senkoku* ("*The Condemned*").

Bon festival (*o-bon*) All Souls Day, Festival of the Dead. Celebrated in Japan from immemorial, it is now a holiday of three days or so in Mid-August, a time for family visits to grandparents and the graves of ancestors. For people young and old, it is an opportunity to put on a yukata, (a light summer kimono that looks good on anyone, regardless of gender or ethnicity) or participate in a festival featuring outdoor group dancing.

"boss" (*oyabun*) The leader of a yakuza (criminal) organization; literally, one who assumes the role of a parent. Like a stern parent, the *oyabun* is expected to lay down the law to his underlings and look out for their interests. (See also sensei.)

bowing (*o-jigi*) Everyday Japanese etiquette normally includes various kinds of bowing or gestures that amount to abbreviated forms of bowing. The point of the formal bow from the waist is that you are lowering your head before whomever it is you are paying respects to. A slight nod amounts to an abbreviated bow, as a way of saying "thanks," "you're welcome," "excuse me," etc.

Buddhism In addition to the Bon festival above, here are some other Buddhist references appearing in *Marshland*:
+ Pure Land (*Jodo Shinshu*) one of the major schools of Buddhism, founded by Shinran in the thirteenth century
+ destruction of life (*sessho*) Avoiding destruction of life, including animals' lives, is one of the Buddhist Five Precepts (Japanese *gokai*, Sanscrit *panca-silani*).
+ seventh day (*shonanoka* or *shonanuka*) The seventh day after a persons death is one of many appointed occasions for a Buddhist memorial service to be held for the deceased.
+ Hall of Thirty-Three Spans *Sanju-san-gendo* Located in Kyoto (the capital of Japan long ago and its cultural capital forever), this temple is the designated repository of a thousand images of the Buddha. Its formal name is *Rengéoin-hondo*, meaning "Hall of the Lotus King."
+ Bon festival / namu amida butsu / poisoned arrow parable / shaba / sunyata / zazen (see separate entries below)

C

Camp Oji / Narita Airport opposition These were movements demanding return of expropriated real estate. The Camp Oji movement had an especially broad base of support. Support for the Narita cause was more traditionally leftist. Attorney Akutsu says in Chapter 8 that as a law student, he received a bad impression of judges' attitudes at trials of fellow students who had been arrested for protest activities in these causes. Makihiko Moriya, the complete radical, was of course deeply involved in both movements.

Camp Oji was a Japanese Army ordinance depot taken over by the U.S. Army during the occupation of Japan. It was being used as the headquarters of U.S. Army Security Agency Pacific. ASAPAC was relocated to Hawaii in 1966, but the real estate wasn't returned until 1971, as the result of much political pressure from the Japanese side that grew as American involvement in the Vietnam War escalated and Camp Oji began receiving wounded American servicemen for medical treatment. The American Vietnam War brought more opposition than support from the Japanese public.

The Narita Struggle sought to block the opening, and later, the expansion, of Narita International Airport because the project required government expropriation of land in Chiba Prefecture from farmers who had worked it for generations, and some refused compensation offers. The need for a new international air traf-fic hub was apparent by the nineteen-sixties. Hanéda Airport, located within metropolitan Tokyo on land reclaimed from Tokyo Bay, was then Japan's only international facility. It had begun operating in 1932 as a small airfield, and was expanded by the U.S. Army, after it demolished three villages and one Shinto shrine. The Americans had taken it over in 1945 and summarily expelled some three thousand residents, without compensation.

Faced with pushback from the farmers of Narita, the Japanese government adopted a conciliatory policy that was met with steadfast defiance by an uncompromising handful who received strong support from a broad leftist coalition that included radicals specializing in sabotage and violent clashes with police. When an airport authority was established, it dealt cautiously with legal challenges from a united opposition led by one of the farmers.

Narita Airport opened in 1978, about seven years later than planned, operating only one runway where five had been originally envisioned because some of the land the plan necessitated had not been acquired. A second air runway was added later, and three more international airports have opened. A few families of the farmers' opposition league continue farming land tracts they have successfully prevented being transferred to the Narita Airport Authority.

"center-of-life force" (*seika-tanden*) The area below the navel, according to traditional Chinese medicine.

char in Chapter 3, Kimiko hooks a huchen (see below) from the depths of Lake Furen. Huchen is a type of trout (*masu*) that can grow to monster size, and is much sought after by anglers, but Kimiko's catch isn't very large, and Atsuo mistakenly identifies it an *amé masu*, which literally means "rain trout," but is known in English as white spotted char. The only trouble with that name is that another type of freshwater trout found in Japan, *iwana*, is also called white spotted char in English.

Chinaman/chink (*shinajin*) The English word "China" may derive from the Qin dynasty of 221 — 206 BC. In Japanese, that ancient Chinese state is called *Shin*, and Japan referred to China as *Shina* from about the sixteenth century until sometime after its defeat in World War II. During the era of Japanese imperialism, when Chinese nationalists were calling their country *Zhōnghuá Mínguó* for Chinese Republic, *Shina* for "China" and *shinajin* for "Chinese person" pointed to a world view in which China and its people properly belonged under Japanese dominance.

Japan's 1948 Constitution renounced imperialism. Its leaders, textbooks and media adopted the word *Chugoku*, which is the equivalent of the Chinese *Zhōnghuó*, for "China." *Shina* and *shinajin* came to be recognized as pejoratives. Having been taught these words as children, many of the wartime generation who were not accustomed to pondering world affairs went on using them. A vocal minority of nationalist politicians and media personalities have employed them to provoke controversy at home and criticism from China. They find ways to play a similar game to target Koreans. Their utterances are especially incendiary because Japan's colonization resulted in a large Chinese and Korean minority population in Japan.

Unsuitability of the old words for the country and its nationals notwithstanding, the Japanese words *Higashi Shinakai* and *Minami Shinakai* for, respectively, East China Sea and South China Sea, are not considered improper.

Chinese zodiac

"About ten years back there was a dog year when purple futons were all the rage."
(Chapter 5)

—

The dog is the eleventh phase of the 12-year cycle of animals whose influences are said to be dominant for their respective years, according to a Chinese tradition that came to be adopted in other countries of East, Southeast and South Asia. The concept is known in Japanese as juniseisho and a few other terms. Its basic uses are to classify personality types, tell fortunes and provide animal themes for New Years observations. The 12 animals of a full cycle are: the Rat, Ox, Tiger, Rabbit, Dragon, Snake, Horse, Ram, Monkey, Rooster, Dog and Boar.

Chomé A numbered postal area unit. In most cases in Japan, postal address numbers are distributed among subdivisions of the town or city instead of along streets, because most streets that are not main thoroughfares are unnamed.

chopsticks *Hashi* (chopsticks) are just right for manipulating small pieces of food, such as separating bits of fish from fine fish bones. Japanese cooking is oriented to producing meals suitable for eating with them. Japanese use knife, fork and spoon for Western-style meals.

—

"Tastes best when it's hot," he said, pulling apart a pair of wooden chopsticks.
—from end of Chapter 2

The above bit of dialog refers to *waribashi*, or disposable wooden chopsticks, usually available at tables in public eating facilities. They are made in a single piece that is easily separated.

construction timbers Long pieces of wood frame material stolen from construction sites were among the standard weapons used against riot police and rival sects during Japan's era of campus strife (for example, as described in Chapter 1). The word used for them was *geba-bo*, a combination of the German *Gewalt* (meaning power, force, violence or control) and Japanese *bo*, for stick, club, staff or cudgel. The German term reflects Marxist ideology about revolution and the role of violence.

coup d'état attempt in Tokyo Wakako's erstwhile boyfriend Makihiko Moriya and Atsuo's nephew Yukichi Jinnai are opposites in some ways, but both idolize the junior officers of the Japanese Imperial Army who unsuccessfully attempted to overthrow Japan's government on February 26, 1936. The conspirators assassinated four government officials, but failed to get to the prime minister, and were suppressed in a few days. The ringleaders were hanged, but their goal of establishing an authoritarian military government bent on expansionism abroad was ultimately realized. Moriya dreams of a Marxist revolution while Yukichi just likes war, but both admire the resolution and ideological purity of the "2-26 Incident" stalwarts.

cranes and turtles problems Japanese elementary school math teachers typically challenge students to calculate how many of each critter there could be, given the total numbers of heads and legs.

"C. University" This is Chuo University, a private institution in Hachioji City, Tokyo, whose law department has a long record of rivaling or beating Tokyo University in the number of its graduates passing the national bar examination.

currency/Japanese Chapter 4 finds master pickpocket Ginji Sato counting paper banknotes in his pocket by touch. This is possible for highly experienced people because each denomination of bill is a slightly different width. At the time (1968), denominations of paper money in circulation were ¥500, ¥1,000, ¥5,000 and ¥10,000. Five hundred yen paper notes (phased out in 1994), were almost the same width as ¥1,000 notes, but much shorter in height. The total difference in width between the other three denominations (in general circulation today) is 10 mm.

In Chapter 10, little Atsuo gets a daily allowance from his parents of one *sen*. One yen equals 100 *sen*, which in turn consists of 100 *rin*. The latter two currencies were taken out of circulation in 1953, but can still be used as economic units.

D

debt of gratitude

> "I believe that 'overbearing father' you speak of so disdainfully happens to be a teacher to whom you owe a debt of gratitude."

(from Chapter 3)

—

The word being used here in the original Japanese is *onshi*, meaning, of course, a person to whom one is morally indebted for having given you instruction.

doburoku Milky white and lumpy saké. Easy to make at home, although in principle, that is against the law. Recipes are easily found

dorayaki a puffy hot cake with a filling of anko (see above).

E

Edo era (1600–1868) Edo became Tokyo (meaning "Eastern Capital") in 1868, when the Meiji parliamentary state was founded and the emperor got a new castle there, moving west, away from Japan's traditional capital of Kyoto. Edo (pronounce it like "EH-DOH") had become the *de facto* capital in 1600, the founding year of the military government or shogunate established by General Tokugawa Iéyasu. (Note that as a historical figure, his family name is given first.)

Employment Security Office Established by national law, Public Employment Security Offices are available throughout Japan to provide job referral assistance to job seekers.

era names Japan switched from the Chinese lunisolar calendar to the Western Gregorian calendar in 1873, but also numbers years according to the emperors' reigns. When a new emperor accedes to the throne, the Ministry of the Imperial Household announces the name of the new reign. The new reign can begin on any day of the Western calendar, but begins its second year on January 1.

Government issued guidelines for publishers of school textbooks are oriented to making students comfort-able with both dating systems. Documents issued by the national government or local municipalities may use Japanese dating exclusively or both systems, e.g. "Heisei 12 (2000)," as they deem appropriate. Banks and private businesses typically make use of both systems to accommodate the diverse preferences of customers. Newspaper articles may cite a Western year and give the Japanese equivalent in parentheses, or do the reverse, depending on the article's subject and the newspaper's position on the liberal-conservative spectrum. Articles on historical subjects would most likely include the Western system even if the subject is Japanese history.

Here are the Western calendar dates for the last five reigns. The first day of each reign is given in parentheses:

Reiwa: 2019 (May 1) – the present

Heisei: 1989 (Jan 8) – 2018

Showa: 1926 (Dec 25) – 1989
Taisho: 1912 (Jul 30) – 1926
Meiji: 1868 (Jan 1) – 1911

exam prep school *yobiko* means "preparatory school," but the term doesn't refer to private secondary schools offering full curricula. *Yobiko* are short-term commercial "cram schools" whose sole purpose is drilling high school students or graduates for university or college entrance exams. That *yobiko* market is reflected on a smaller scale by *yobiko* for middle school students competing for entrance to high schools having outstanding records of graduates who gained admission to top universities.

Over half of all Japanese students now go on to higher education, and competition for admission to a high-ranking school is always keen, providing good business for the *yobiko* industry.

Ezo (see Ainu)

F

fish owl (or Blakiston's Fish Owl) The largest owl species, with a wingspan on the order of six feet, it inhabits old-growth forests in Japan, China and Russian islands north of Japan. The Japanese name is *shimafukuro*, meaning "island owl." A silent predator with excellent night vision and auditory sense, it swoops down on rivers and lakes to pluck fish from the water or other prey from the forest floor. The English explorer and naturalist Thomas Blakiston introduced the species to the English-speaking world. Habitat loss and climate change have made it an endangered species. In 2021, National Geographic described dedicated conservation efforts being made on behalf of this impressive bird, estimating the global population at only 1,000 – 1,900 birds.

Fuchu Fuchu is a city in the Tokyo greater metropolitan area where Japan's largest prison is located.

furoshiki A woven wrapping cloth with a thousand uses. Said to have been invented in the thirteenth century for use in public bathhouses. You wrap your clothing in a furoshiki decorated with your family crest so you can identify your bundle when you emerge from the bath (*furo* or *o-furo*).

futon quilts suitable for spreading out on a tatami (rice straw mat) floor, consisting of a mattress type quilt and a cover type quilt. In warm weather, one dispenses with the top futon. Sheets, blankets, and pillows are used with futon.

G

geso is a slang word for gesoku, meaning "footwear," such as geta and zori, which are different kinds of thonged sandals.

gori One meaning in some regions of Japan is a kind of small freshwater fish, but its usage in Chapter 11 is prisoner slang for an ad hoc tinderbox for lighting contraband cigarettes when no lighter or match is available. No doubt this slang existed in the nineteen-fifties, but it doesn't seem to be widely known now. It is a likely guess that it comes from the Japanese expression gori-gori, which is onomatopoeia for the resistance offered by a hard object as you try to impose your will on it, for example, by sawing through a piece of hard wood. Producing fuel for the tinderbox requires vigorous scraping of anything that will catch fire easily if transformed into ultra-thin shavings. Gori-gori expresses what it feels like to do the scraping.

Japanese has a vast vocabulary of onomatopoeic and mimetic words for sounds, tactile sensations, sights, smells, states of mind, emotions and people's attitudes.

Greater East Asia Co-Prosperity Sphere The name of the new economic order Imperial Japan sought to impose on East and Southeast Asia, announced in 1940. The idea was the Japanese empire would replace the British empire, thereby bestowing contentment to all Asian peoples through life under the benevolent rule of the Japanese emperor. Few Asians wanted any part of the plan.

gyoza A kind of Chinese dumpling, fried and encased in won ton skin. Gyoza is the Japanese reading of the Chinese jiaozi. Also known in the English-speaking world as pot stickers.

H

hai means "yes," but is also a generalized affirmative used in various contexts. In the following, it is a formal response indicating understanding and acceptance:

> *I answered up with a vigorous "Hai!" as I had been taught . . .*
> (Chapter 10)

hakoshi Criminal slang for a pickpocket who works passenger trains. Hako means "box," but in this and other slang expressions, it refers to a car of a train; the suffix –shi means a "specialist" or "master" (of some discipline).

Hall of Thirty-Three Spans (see Buddhism)

hanafuda "Flower cards," or Japanese playing cards. A deck consists of 48 cards, divided into 12 suits of four cards each. Each suit is a kind of flower, tree or grass. There are numerous hanafuda games. Three of the most common are koi-koi, ato-saki and oicho-kabu. Nintendo has supplied hanafuda to many countries.

Hanafuda are associated with yakuza gambling lore. The standard explanation for why Japansese gangsters are called yakuza derives from the game of oicho-kabu. The worst hand you can get in 8-9-3. Though it has a face value of 20 points and combines the imperial chrysanthemum with that symbol of evanescent beauty, the cherry blossom and silvery susuki prairie grass that gives dignified grace to autumn fields, by the game's rules, you get no points for that hand. That is seen as a metaphor for gangsters, who are good-for-nothings with a propensity to put on an extravagant showing. The first syllables of words for 8, 9 and 3 are "ya-ku-sa," which becomes "yakuza" because that is considered easier to say.

happi / tabi

> *When Keiji visited the home he would always remove his happi and tabi dockworkers garb and change into a business suit.*
> (Chapter 10)
>
> —

happi: a half coat worker's uniform; *tabi*: mitten-like socks for thonged zori footwear.

high economic growth era The "high growth" sixties is generally thought of nostalgically as a golden age in Japan. The postwar era had begun in a state of desperation, with black markets for food staples, but the outlook was dramatically different in 1960, when Prime Minister Hayato Ikéda announced a long term Keynesian economic plan that he promised would double the salaries of the average worker (meaning, of course, male employees of mainstream corporations) in ten years time. It turned out that the early sixties saw an even higher growth rate than the government had envisioned.

The entire high growth period can be delimited between the outbreak of the Korean war in 1950 and 1973, when U.S. President Nixon ended the fixed dollar-yen exchange rate, long after America's backing of the yen had become an unrealistically low estimate of the currency's true value. Shortly after that "Nixon shock," the oil producing nations dealt another blow to Japan's ability to export at relatively low cost by dramatically raising crude oil prices.

Honshu the largest of Japan's four main islands; the others are Kyushu, Shikoku and Hokkaido.

housing lottery In Chapter Five, Atsuo's buddy, Yamamura the futoner says he was lucky enough to "Hit the urban development housing lottery." That means his application for a publicly subsized apartment was accepted, according to a lottery selection process. Such projects that provide quality low-cost housing are an important element in the widely supported goal of expanding the middle class.

huchen Fishing stories set in Hokkaido often speak of anglers pursuing the elusive *ito*, or Japanese huchen, a species of freshwater salmon. The *ito* is similar to the huchen, or Danube salmon, so named because the species was first recognized in the Danube River. The scientific name of the Japanese huchen is *Hucho perryi*. Also found on Sakhalin Island, the same species has the alternate name of *Sakhalin taimen*. The European equivalent is *Hucho hucho*. Both are on the International Union for Conservation of Nature and Natural Resources (IUCN) endangered species red list.

I

Ichi! Ni! San! Shi! "One! Two! Three! Four!" (Chapter 5)

"If" Coffee Shop This was identified by the author as "F. Teahouse," as in " A.

Shimbun," "C. University," etc. I opted for this name because it sounded appropriately avant-garde. Its real counterpart is Fugetsudo, which could be translated "Teahouse of the Wind and the Moon," but that would be too quaint. *Fugetsu* literally means "wind and moon." The phrase is evocative of poetry and the beauties of nature. It is used in expressions about communing with nature or engaging in aesthetic pursuits. Fugetsudo is the name of a confectionery company having a history of well over a century, and is associated with several spacious tea/coffee shops in major cities. The Fugetsudo of Chapter 5, located in Tokyo's Shinjuku ward, ceased operating in 1973. It was a famous hangout for foreign and domestic hippies until then, but lives on today in fiction, memoirs and Internet websites.

"Coffee shop" is the customary translation of kissaten, which really means "teahouse." *Kissaten* are ubiquitous across Japan. Decor varies widely, but all are Western style and most customers order coffee, Japan being the third biggest consumer of coffee, after the U.S. and Germany. That type of establishment is known as a "teahouse" in Japanese because its historical antecedent is the traditional teahouse. A conversational reference to "having tea" would as likely mean drinking coffee as Japanese green tea or other kind of tea.

ikema A perennial climber herb found in mountain forests, having medicinal properties; it is bitter, has a toxic root and be must thoroughly cooked before eating. See also tempura. Pronounce it like "EE-KEH-MA."

indefinite imprisonment (*muki choéki*) is the equivalent of a "life" sentence, with the understanding that parole after a long term is possible.

ink rubbing

> *"After she caught the fish I was helping her make an ink rubbing print of it."*
> (Chapter 1)

—

In a letter Atsuo receives from his sister Suéko, she mentions an "ink rubbing print" made from a trophy fish. She is talking about gyotaku, a way of making a direct print of a fish by painting it with *sumi* (the ink traditionally used by Chinese and Japanese artists for black-and-white paintings) or other kind of coloring medium, and impressing the fish on paper or cloth. There is also an indirect method by which the fish is covered with paper or cloth, and silk-covered cotton balls called tanpo are used to dab coloring medium onto the paper from the other side.

inn *Ryokan* or Japanese style inn. All travelers stayed at ryokan before Western-style hotels were introduced in Japan. They are still common. Like hotels, they range from modest to very classy. If you are traveling in Japan, it would be a loss not to stay at a ryokan at least once. Of course, the rule is always try to know what to expect before jumping into unfamiliar settings, but you can usually count on Japan's accommodations taking care to avoid situations of foreign visitors encountering inconvenient surprises.

International anti-war day October 21, 1968 In Japan, October 21 came to be observed as International Anti-War Day in 1966 by such prominent leftist organizations as the now defunct General Council of Trade Unions. Rallies marking the day usually consisted mainly of ordinary people, labor unions and the peaceful nonorganization Beheiren (Citizen's League for Peace in Vietnam), but in 1968 a violent demonstration spearheaded by Kakumaru (Japan Revolutionary Communist League) and a few other far-left groups culminated in a battle against police around Shinjuku Station. Chapter 2 includes a clip of the events that night.

The uproar that fell out at Shinjuku Station on the 1968 International Anti-War Day was the continuation of spontaneous demonstrations in summer of the previous year, following a spectacular cargo train accident at Shinjuku Station on August 8, 1967. A train run by the former Japan National Railways was transporting jet fuel for U.S. fighter planes based in Japan and used in the Vietnam War. As in many other cases of objections to U.S. military bases in Japan, there was both a public safety and political aspect. In this case, the safety issue was acute. The collision ignited four cars loaded with jet fuel bound for the Tachikawa air base, located in Western Tokyo. Remarkably, no one was killed or injured, because it happened a little before 2 a.m. Flames shot up high in the air and outside the station, into an area that becomes jammed with tens of thousands of people by 7:00 a.m. every day. It took until late afternoon to put the fire out.

The 1968 International Anti-War Day saw big turnouts for demonstrations at the National Diet (Parliament) building, the Defense Agency headquarters and Shinjuku terminal building. Demonstrators occupied Shinjuku Station, halting trains with rocks and fire bombs. The rioting continued into the next day, forcing extensive cancellation of train service. About 450 people were arrested.

J

Jiang-Qing Fourth wife of Mao Zedong and a key figure in implementing Mao's disastrous Cultural Revolution. She was arrested after Mao's death as a "counter-revolutionary" and imprisoned for life. Reportedly, she committed suicide years later.

jikatabi rubber-soled cloth worker's footwear, separated at the big toe to improve stability where having a good foothold is a concern; worn by farmers, carpenters and construction workers.

Jun-chan "Jun-chan" is a diminutive; *-chan* is attached to the names of very young children, close friends, etc. At some point, people become old enough for the standard honorific suffix *-san* (Mr./Ms.) In Chapter 7, Suéko feels slightly frustrated that etiquette requires her to call lawyer Jun Akutsu "*-sensei*," the honorific for teachers and other eminent people in leadership roles. Having known him well as a child, she is accustomed to calling him "Jun-*chan*."

To pronounce "Jun" correctly, think of it as being spelled "JYUN." It does not rhyme with "fun" or " moon." The Japanese vowel "u" sounds like the "u" in "put." See pronunciation hints below.

juvenile medical reformatory Japan has 52 juvenile reformatories, including four designated "medical reformatories" for offenders tried as minors and found to have some "physical or mental disability."

K

kamaboko A processed food made by steaming or baking ground fish meat, egg whites and seasoning into a firm roll having smooth texture and little taste of its own. It is sliced and served with noodles, in soups or eaten as a side dish, with soy sauce.

kanji Chinese characters. This Japanese word is written with two kanji: *kan* refers to China's Han dynasty (206 BC– 220 AD), which developed the writing system of ideograms that was adopted by Japan, Korea, Vietnam and the Ryukyu Islands. It also means the Han ethnic group. The second character, *ji*, means the units of any writing system, be they letters, ideograms or syllabic script (see below).

+ *kana:* Modern Japanese uses 46 kana to represent the sounds of spoken Japanese. Because each kana represents one full syllable of any word, the entire script set is called a syllabary rather than an alphabet. Modifications of the 46 kana allow for over one hundred syllable sounds. Kana is a Japanese invention. Its characters were developed by simplifying an assortment of kanji.

+ *kanji:* (Chinese: *hanzi*) Unlike an alphabet or syllabary, each of these characters has its own meaning independently. The Unicode Consortium that oversees encoding standards for all the world's scripts places the number of Chinese hanzi upwards of 80,000. This staggering figure includes many variations of the same characters. Chinese is written using this system exclusively.

Around the fifth century AD, Japanese visitors to China began studying the Chinese writing system, thereby opening the way for its adaption to the Japanese language. The system that emerged assigns separate "Chinese" and "Japanese" ways of reading/voicing each kanji. When using a Japanese reading, the kanji can be inflected to follow Japanese grammar rules by adding kana. By applying the quasi-Chinese readings assigned to kanji, two or more can be combined to make new words and expressions for the Japanese lexicon.

Knowledge of several thousand Japanese kanji or Chinese hanji is necessary for competence in reading or writing the respective languages. Non-speakers who advocate abolishing this complicated writing system in favor of the Latin alphabet overlook the value of a script whose individual characters have intrinsic meanings. The time spent learning it returns rich rewards in the form of deepened language understanding and expressive ability.

Kansai The western region of the main island of Honshu, including the cities of Kyoto, Osaka and Kobé

katakana Kana script is explained above under kanji. Kana has angular and cursive forms, each used for different purposes. Katakana is the square, or angular form. Nowadays, its most common use is for foreign names or words. Japanese uses vastly more foreign words that does English, and English is the number one source of loanwords to Japanese. Loanwords must be transformed from the language of origin to the Japanese syllabary. For example, "hamburger" becomes *han-baa-gaa*, in which the double letter "A" represents the conjunction of two "ah" sounds to make one long sound, because that most closely approximates the English pronunciation within the constraints of the Japanese syllabary.

kendo Japanese martial art of the sword, practiced using bamboo swords and protective armor.

keto (Pronounced "KEH-TOH") Japanese hate speech for foreigners, mainly Westerners, or white people. It derives from the history of Japan's contact with foreign traders arriving at its shores. *To* is the character meaning China's T'ang Dynasty, which lasted from the 7th into the 10th century. Besides applying to China or Chinese people, it also took on a meaning of "foreigner" in general, so that it could be applied to Indian traders as well. When Westerners entered the mix of traders arriving in Japan, *ke*, the character for "hair," was used to personify them by hair color or abundance of body hair.

Establishment of trade with the West in the 18th century led to sharpened perceptions of foreign powers in terms of valuable goods they offered and the national threat they posed. That led to keto being used pejoratively for Westerners. The word continues to be used today. It qualifies as hate speech, but has very limited usage and less social significance, first, because Japan never colonized a Western country, but also because the same kind of efforts at Chinese learning made many centuries ago have been directed to the West for the past couple of centuries, and this had resulted in more admiration than hate for Westerners. In sharp contrast to this, Japanese hate speech directed at fellow Asians that thrived during Japan's military adventurism has the same explosive effect as disparaging terminology used by Europeans and Americans toward peoples they have subjected to enslavement, colonization or domination.

keyaki a shade tree, also known as Japanese zelkova and Japanese elm

kimchi Korean style Chinese cabbage pickled in red chili pepper sauce

-*kun* A "familiar" honorific, affixed to a family name, the same as -*san* ("Mr."/ "Ms."), but used toward a social equal, such as a classmate or colleague. It is also used by adults toward children who are too big to be called -*chan* any more. Traditionally, this honorific was mainly for boys or adult men only, but gradual advances in women's social status have resulted in a greater tendency to apply it to girls and women in the same way.

kuzumochi A gelatinous dessert flavored with soybean flour (*kinako*) and molasses. The *-kuzu* of *kuzumochi* is a variety of arrowroot that is classified as an invasive plant in the American southern states, New Zealand and Australia, where it is known as kudzu. Whether this climbing vine it is actually harmful or not is open to question, however. It became widespread in the U.S. during the dust bowl era of the nineteen-thirties and forties, when the government paid farmers to plant it to prevent soil erosion.

L

Letter of apology An extralegal way of affixing culpability in cases of damage or harm caused by rule breaking, negligence or error. "Letter of apology" is a loose translation of *shimatsusho*, a document written by a person to take responsibility for an accident. It is a tradition in Japan for police or officials in authority to demand and get formal letters of apology as an alternative to more punitive action. If a public official is concerned, the submission of a letter of apology may accompany a reprimand or other penalty. Corporations tend to have a similar procedure.

The basic form of the letter is an account of what happened, why it happened, a statement of "self reflection" by which the individual writing the letter acknowledges error, pledges not to repeat it and explains how he/she plans to insure no recurrence of the problem.

love hotel This type of hotel offers rates for stays measured in hours, in addition to overnight stays. Some provide exotic facilities for high prices. By legal classification, love hotels are subject to regulation as a type of "business affecting public morals" because they can be used by sex industry workers, even though they do not themselves employ sex workers.

M

Manyoshu This anthology of about 4,500 ancient poems is like a mother lode of Japanese poetry, just as the eleventh century epic *Tale of Genji* is the exemplar novel for Japanese literature. Manyoshu includes poems by ordinary men and women, as well as important people. The title means "Ten Thousand Leaves" literally, and has also been interpreted as "Poems for the Ages." Children start learning it in elementary or middle school. Knowing it well is helpful for winning traditional poetry games played during the New Years holiday, and it offers consolation during life's difficult times.

A panel of scholars drew on a *Manyoshu* poem for the new era name of Reiwa to succeed the Heisei Era when that emperor abdicated in 2019. They weighed historical precedents to select two characters for the era name from a 22-character poem that was perhaps penned by the seventh century military commander Otomono-Tabito. The two characters have been interpreted to mean "Beautiful Peace." The poem is best served by a free form translation that disregards form:

> *When spring comes 'round and the air is lovely, the wind a soft caress; then plum blossoms appear like a beautiful lady powdering her face before a mirror, and the world is wrapped in the fragrance of orchids.*

May depression syndrome (*Gogatsu-byo* or "May sickness"). The term describes a condition seen among freshmen at highly competitive universities who find themselves overcome with apathy about everything. It follows the excitement of starting a new life as a student in April, the month when the school year begins. At the age of eighteen, they may have spent half their lives striving for their present status through long hours of daily study for one extremely competitive school entrance exam. After that success, they discover an inner emptiness. Having been preoccupied with that exam, they neglected to think about study as preparation for fulfilling any other ambition. Psychologists diagnose this malady as "adaptive disorder," if not simply "melancholia."

menko menko are cards, roughly like baseball cards in that they are collectable, but their primary use is a simple children's game. You hold a card in the flat of your hand and slam it down hard on other players' cards laid out on the ground. The objective is to make as many cards as possible flip over, backside up. You get all the cards you turned over. The cards are suitably heavy-duty for the game. There are rectangular and circular varieties.

"Met HQ" This slang doesn't really exist. The police colloquialism for the Tokyo Metropolitan Police Department headquarters in central Tokyo refers to its proximity to the emperor: "Sakurada Gate." The 18-story headquarters building faces that gate, located across the outer moat surrounding the Imperial Palace. It was the scene of a failed attempt to assassinate the emperor in 1932 and the successful assassination of a senior member of Japan's military government in 1860.

miso A paste of fermented soybeans that makes a nutritious soup and has countless other uses in Japanese cooking. Miso is one of the great basic resources in world food culture.

monkey pear / *sarunashi* (also called *kokuwa*) a grape sized berry akin to the kiwi fruit.

monpé The "work pantaloons" mentioned in Chapter 11 refers to *monpé*, which are traditional loose-fitting work trousers for women. They were a kind of uniform on the home front during the war with the West. Today monpé style casual wear is available for both sexes.

mountain god (*yama-no-kami*; mentioned in passing in Chapter 5) Japan has many folktales featuring mountain gods and goddesses.

moxa cautery Also called moxabustion, or, in Japanese, *o-kyu*. A basic technique in traditional Chinese, Mongolian, Tibetan, Vietnamese, Japanese and Korean medicine that uses a fine powder called moxa (*mogusa*, in Japanese) that is made from young leaves of a species of mugwort plant (*yomogi*, in Japanese). According to one common moxa cautery method, the person giving the treatment places a tiny pile of the power on the patient's bare skin at some point on the body, defined by traditional diagrams (the points are the same in acupuncture and shiatsu). The powder is ignited using a piece of moxa rolled up like a tiny cigar. Like acupuncture, this treatment is reputably good for numerous ailments. Best results are obtained on patients who believe in the practice. It doesn't hurt if done properly, but it can be used as a form of corporal punishment, as described in *Marshland* and some folk tales.

Musashino Plateau The Musashino Plateau is a large tableland to the northwest of Tokyo Bay. Small patches of its once forested environment have been preserved throughout the Greater Tokyo region.

N

names In Japanese, family names precede given names. The name of this novel's protagonist is written "Yukimori Atsuo" in Japanese, the family name being "Yukimori." Scholarly writing about Japan in English usually give names according to the Japanese order, but journalism and general-interest writings in English almost always present Japanese given names as the "first name," (e.g. "Atsuo Yukimori") for the sake of minimizing confusion. Everyone in Japan knows that the family name come last in the West, so Japanese people usually write their own names that way in English.

Honorifics are generally attached to Japanese names, and people older than small children are usually called by their family names, e.g. "Mr. Yukimori" (*Yukimori-san*) would be the most common usage even in informal settings between friends or colleagues. (Wakako's family members refer to Atsuo minus the honorific because they don't consider him entitled to common courtesy.) If someone is addressed or referred to by their given name, the honorific would attach to that name.

namu amida butsu A declaration of faith in the Buddha. The words are transliterated from Sanskrit to Japanese, meaning something like "homage to the infinite light of Buddha."

National Foundation Day February 11 was designated a national holiday in 1873 to celebrate the accession of Jinmu, the first emperor, according to the "Chronicles of Japan" (*Nihon Shoki*), a set of scrolls dating from the eighth century that describe the emperor's lineage as divine. Observance of that mythology had played a part in the imperialistic ideology that promoted aggression throughout Asia. The holiday was abolished by the American occupation authority, and was only re-established in 1966, despite opposition by the many antimilitaristic Japanese. The name of the holiday was changed to associate it with the founding of a nation-state, not the beginning of an imperial era.

New Years greeting cards (*nengajo*) are "seasons greetings" postcards sent to reaffirm family, social and business relationships. Customarily mailed early, for delivery on January 1, with the understanding that it isn't too late if they arrive by January 10.

noren A curtain between interior rooms or between the inside and outside of a shop or house. Most commonly, a noren is quite short, perhaps serving to give a little shade, but mainly there as decoration and to display a shop name or logo, not intended to hide the interior but invite people to enter. A noren outside a private home has a welcoming kind of appearance. Public baths typically have one noren for admitting everyone from the street and two more in the lobby, over separate passageways to the men's and women's baths. There are numerous Japanese expressions using "noren" that have to do with starting up and running a business, or the reputation of a business. A crafty swindler is called a *norenshi*.

Northern Territories An estimated 17,000 Japanese inhabited the four southernmost islands of the Kurile chain (Etorofu, Kunashiri , Shikotan and Habomai) until August, 1945, when Stalin declared war on Japan and Russian forces invaded them, together with their advance on Japanese held Manchuria. Russia occupied the islands and then forcibly expelled the Japanese. Today there is still no peace treaty between Japan and Russia due to the conflicting claims on them.

O

oden A popular meal for cold weather containing a variety of standard ingredients cut into large slices and simmered in a broth made from fish stock, soy sauce and cooking saké. To give a small sampling of numerous options, oden typically includes daikon radish, boiled potatoes, hard boiled eggs, *konnyaku* (a translucent cake made from the flour of a tuber known as konjak) and chikuwa (processed fish paste made into a hollow tube made to resemble bamboo). In cold weather, it is served by street push-card venders, stand-up counters near commuter train stations, bars, convenience stores and in most homes.

o-kaa ma, mom; less formal than *kaa-san*, which is less formal than *o-kaa-san*. "*o*" and "*-san*" are both honorifics. "*kaa*" is one reading of the kanji for "mother."

o-kaeri (short for *o-kaerinasai*) Greeting to family member or colleague returning from a short errand or a long journey. It could be translated as "Welcome back," "Hi!" etc.

Omura, Masujiro There is a statue of Masujiro Omura on the grounds of Yasukuni Shrine (see below). Omura was a high official in the national government established by the alliance of feudal domain leaders in 1868 that defeated the military shogunate. A village doctor, Omura had studied Western military science and played a key role in turning the army of the Choshu Domain (now Yamaguchi Prefecture) into a modern force that helped bring the alliance's victory. The new Meiji government tasked him with creating the national army.

At the age of 45, he was attacked by a faction of former samurai in the shogun's army and received a wound that was fatal two months later.

o-nésan The formal way, using the honorific *-o*, of addressing ones older sister.

oyabun See boss above.

P

pachinko Pachinko is a sit-down pinball game, and an industry supported by millions of fans who attend noisy, gaudy pachinko parlors that can be found in major cities across Japan. The estimated scale of the market in 2014 was about 19 trillion yen, or about 187 billion US dollars. It has since been declining. Most pachinko parlors in Japan are owned by ethnic Koreans, who constitute Japan's largest minority group. The novel *Pachinko*, by Korean-American author Min Jin Lee, is highly recommended for insight into the long history of abusive treatment inflicted upon this sector of Japanese society.

Peace Preservation Law A law adopted in 1925 that outlawed socialism, defined as any system that denies the right to own property. It also criminalized intent to promote socialism or undermine the socio-political organization of the state (*kokutai*). Tens of thousands of suspects were arrested under the law, and some were subjected to police torture. It was an effective system for silencing critics of the military government that smoothed the path toward foreign aggression. The law was abolished by the American occupation authorities in 1945.

Peken (see Ainu)

pigsty (*butabako*) Slang for police station jails. It is hundreds of years old, and "pig" is a not an epithet for policemen in Japan. Japanese radicals of the nineteen-sixties called policemen dogs because, according to Maoist ideology, they are "running dogs" (see below), i.e., servants of the capitalist class.

platform ticket One can purchase a railway platform ticket that is only good for entering the platform of the station where it is purchased, for meeting an arriving passenger or seeing someone off. Oversize or heavy duty platform tickets are sometimes offered as collectables.

poetry, Japanese In *Marshland*, Atsuo and his surly young nephew Yukichi each write poems, as does a fellow condemned prisoner Atsuo befriends at the Tokyo Detention Center. Atsuo explains that he likes poetry because "I like to read something that talks about the way things really are."

Japanese poems are terse sketches of reality as perceived by the poet. They exist as much for the masses as the elite. Most anyone who has been through middle school in Japan knows how to structure the three-phrase haiku and five-phrase waka or tanka poetic forms. Senryu is a haiku variation for humor or acerbic comment. Paid classroom instruction courses in poetry writing and free opportunities to join poetry circles are available most anywhere in Japan. Sunday newspapers have poetry pages featuring winning entries from various competitions. Part of the festivities each New Year is a live TV broadcast from the Imperial Palace of the reading of songs on the year's theme by His Majesty, royal family members and special invited guests, including the composers of winning entries selected from the thousands sent to the Imperial Household Agency during the year.

poisoned arrow parable In Chapter 6, we find that prosecutor Onuki likens his role to a doctor saving a patient's life by promptly removing a poisoned arrow. He's borrowing from a Buddhist parable, but cocksure Onuki considers only half of the parable and twists its meaning. It is not about punishing evildoers, but a warning not to be distracted from seeking the path to enlightenment. The poisoned arrow signifies mortality.

A disciple of Buddha is unable to dismiss his curiosity about the great metaphysical questions (Is there is an end to the universe? Is there life after death? Are spirit and body one or separate?, etc.). He resolves to put these questions to the Enlightened One, vowing to quit being a disciple if he can't get answers. He ends up satisfied with the Buddha's response, even though it leaves his questions unanswered. That response amounts to something like this:

"I am not here to explain things that are beyond human understanding. My teaching is about freeing your mind from anguishing over the pain that life inevitably brings. Pursuing these questions will distract you from the path that leads away from human passions, toward peace, wisdom, the holy life, and Nirvana. Your urgent task during your brief time alive is to follow this path. Don't be like the man who was shot with a poisoned arrow, only to become obsessed with finding out all about the arrow and who shot it, without ever coming to grips with his fast-approaching doom."

police booth *koban*: This word is a shortened form of *kobansho*, which means any kind of station where people rotate on-duty shifts, but when you say koban you are talking about a police substation or booth, which can be large, but is often quite small. If you want to report a crime or find your way to a local house or building, you can drop into a koban with confidence. Japanese police are unfailingly helpful when asked directions. Koban are typically located near major railway stations and other central locations. The word koban is understood by police organizations in many countries as one piece of an effective community policing strategy, together with bicycle and foot patrols.

pronunciation hints You can get the pronunciation of Japanese names and words approximately right just by (1) knowing the five vowels of Japanese, and (2) keeping in mind that the language is basically monotonal, meaning that every syllable of every word gets equal stress, with no accenting. All words are strings of syllables pronounced in short, unsustained tones. Words having long-duration vowel sounds achieve this with two vowel sounds pronounced together.

There are a couple of systems for transliterating Japanese *kana* script to the English alphabet. The result is called romaji (Japanese for "roman letters"). The romaji for the five Japanese vowels are: *a, i, u, e* and *o*. "Long vowel" sounds consisting of two kana characters can be written in romaji using macrons (*ā, ī*, etc.), or by just doubling them, like the letters "i" in the name of Atsuo's first lawyer, the fainthearted Mr. Iino (pronounced as in "eel").

This translation uses an acute accent, as in the French word *attaché*, like this: "saké," "Ikéhata," "Raúsu." Neither of the two official systems for transliterating Japanese into roman letters use this accent. I adopted it to mean that the accented vowels add a syllable to the word: "saké" is two syllables —"SAH-KEH," "Ikéhata" is four syllables —"EE-KEH-HA-TA" (the first "EE" rhyming with "key"), and "Raúsu" is three syllables —"RA-UH-SU." ("Atsuo" didn't get an accent, but that name has three syllables—"AH-TSU-OH.")

Japanese vowel sounds are like these letters (in kana order):

a   is like "ah," as in "achieve" or "pasta" (except that the Japanese "*a*" is a short, unsustained tone)

i   is like "long e" in English, as in "easy" or "tease" or "knee," (except that the Japanese "*i*" is a short, unsustained tone)

u   is like "u" in "push" or "ou" in "would"

e   is like "eh," as in "exit" or "ethyl"

o   is like "long o" in English, as in "own" or "loan," (except that the Japanese "*o*" is a short, unsustained tone)

859

Consonant sounds, etc.:

+ The Japanese syllabary uses consonant sounds similar to English consonants. Most of the 46 sounds that make up the syllabary are written in romaji using one consonant followed by one of the above five vowel sounds (e.g., ba, gi, ku, me, no). The main exception is the "n" sound, which can combine before and after vowel sounds, sometimes being romanized as an "m" sound in the latter case, when it precedes "B," "M" or "P" sounds (e.g., na, ni, etc.; kanji, but shimbun).

+ These hints cover most sounds of the Japanese syllabary, skipping over several sounds like "cha," "tsu" and others. If you are curious about them, you might try learning the forty-six kana, which will get your pronunciation into shape. There are online tutorials with videos that show the way.

Exceptional people aside, exposure to the language from an early age is generally necessary to acquire good pronunciation. The rest of us must be satisfied with good enough pronunciation, which is not hard to achieve, given many hours, not years, of practice.

R

red caviar Salmon roe. The Japanese word *ikura* is from the Russian *ikra*.

red rice *sekihan*: Glutinous rice (*mochigomé*)—the same used for making rice cakes—prepared with red adzuki beans; made for auspicious occasions from antiquity.

rice balls *o-nigiri*: Japanese rice can be easily pressed into mobile lunch rations, wrapped in paper-like sheets of *nori* (made from red algae seaweed). Rice balls are as handy as sandwiches, and have as have many variations. *O-nigiri* are handmade: the *o-* is the honorific prefix and *nigiri* is from the verb *nigiru*, meaning things like "grasp" or, in this case, "pack."

right to rebel "It is right to rebel," meaning that justice is on the side of the insurrectionist, was a slogan of Mao Zedong's Red Guard during China's Cultural Revolution. In practical terms, "rebellion" meant persecution of anyone in a position of authority viewed by Mao's inflamed followers as an "enemy of the people." The slogan appeared on many campuses across Japan in the late nineteen-sixties and beyond.

Rilke, Rainer Maria The most famous prose works of this celebrated Bohemian-Austrian poet are *Letters to a Young Poet* and *The Notebooks of Malte Laurids Brigge.*

ronin As manga or animé fans know, a samurai is a sword-wielding warrior from Japan's feudal era. A ronin is a samurai who has lost his affiliation with a clan for one reason or another. Nowadays, the word can apply to a currently unemployed corporate worker, but usually refers to high school graduates who haven't yet gained admission to a college or university.

"R. University" Though the letter name doesn't match, this must be Sophia University (*Jochi Daigaku*), founded by Jesuits in 1913, which is located near Yotsuya train station and a church —St. Ignatius Church —as described in Chapter 8. The author, Otohiko Kaga, belonged to the faculty of Sophia University where he taught psychology, specializing in criminology and incarceration, for ten years.

running dog Jargon used by Makihiko Moriya and the Q. Sect stalwarts, from an ancient Chinese term for a yes-man or lackey to the powerful. The image is dogs following humans, hoping food scraps will be thrown their way. Communists adopted it to refer to followers of capitalist powers. Its first recorded use in English was in Edgar Snow's 1937 reportage *Red Star Over China*. (adapted from Wikipedia)

S

"Sa" "Ah" "Eh" "Uh" and "Tsu" The names Wakako uses in her tales of people she encountered as a student and mental hospital patient (Chapter 5), are given pseudonyms from the Japanese syllabary (*kana* or syllable script). Women get vowel sounds: "Ah," "Eh" and "Uh" (the last is pronounced like the "u" in "push"— see pronunciation hints), and men are named with consonant sounds ("Sa" and "Tsu").

Sakurajima, Mt. Mt. Sakurajima is Japan's most active volcano consisting of three peaks, in southern Kyushu (Kagoshima Prefecture). It was an island until it was joined to the Osumi Peninsula by lava flow from a major eruption in 1914 that killed fifty-eight people. Since an eruption that killed one person in 1955, there have been several periods of high activity, with hundreds of eruptions recorded in some years, including one in 1974 that caused eight deaths.

samurai compassion (*bushi-no-nasaké* – Chapter 4): The samurai is supposed be unwaveringly loyal to his lord, never hesitating to risk his own life or kill all enemies, but his moral code is to never inflict unnecessary suffering on enemies and to show compassion to them where doing so would not harm his lord's interests.

sculpin *kajika*; a tasty, freshwater fish that is well camouflaged for lurking among rocks in mountain streams.

sea urchin roe *uni*; sea urchin are immobile sea invertebrates protected by a relatively soft, spiny shell. A few of the numerous varieties of sea urchin have orange-colored gonads that are a delicacy offered in sushi bars.

seiza formal kneeling posture, with thighs together, buttocks on heels and back straight; assumed at various kinds of ceremonies to show you are paying full attention.

This pose makes the legs go numb. Limber practitioners who started young might endure for an hour or more, but more commonly, twenty minutes or less is the limit. Endurance can be extended by surreptitious leg twitching. Of course, sitting seiza voluntarily for a tea ceremony session is nothing like being required to do it in a prison. In the latter context, it belongs to a regime of punishment and control.

Self-Defense Forces Japan's constitution renounces war as an instrument for resolving international disputes (Article 9), but since 1954 it has had an army, navy and air force called the Self-Defense Forces as a kind of adjunct to the U.S. military forces stationed in Japan under The Treaty of Mutual Cooperation and Security between the United States and Japan. This treaty had been mandated by the U.S. as a condition for the peace treaty with the 49-member Allied Powers, and both were concluded the same day in 1951, the year before the American occupation of Japan ended. The original security treaty gave America unilateral rights to protect its bases from internal attack with no explicit commitment to defend Japan from external attack. In 1960 the treaty was revised in Japan's favor, making the U.S.-Japan relationship a formal military alliance and removing America's ability to conduct police actions in Japan. Nevertheless, there was widespread opposition in Japan to the treaty in any form. Leftists saw it as an instrument of American imperialism, but many moderates didn't like it either because they didn't want Japan to become a theater of the cold war with the Soviet Union.

In *Marshland*, Atsuo's young nephew Yukichi is carried away by a distilled form of nationalism. He wants to replace the SDF with an unbeatable military as a matter of principle, apart from concern about aggression from abroad. His mindset aligns with a world-famous literary virtuoso of the time, Yukio Mishima, who considered it humiliating to have a constitution that pledges non-aggression. Mishima acted on his views in 1970 by leading a band armed with swords that invaded a Tokyo SDF installation, where he committed ritual suicide after calling on the troops to rise up against the peacenik government and restore the emperor's glory days. Mishima's novels and his well-crafted militaristic persona drew admiration. Ultra-rightists continue to worship him. This nationalist strain notwithstanding, the security arrangement is accepted because it supports prosperity and has enabled Japan to improve its status among the world's nations through its own peaceful efforts.

Those efforts are on display in a foreign policy that advances ambitious foreign development projects. The Japan International Cooperation Agency oversees technology transfer and infrastructure building projects in nearly every country or region. In the meantime, Japan's role in the security alliance has gradually expanded. It conducts joint military exercises with U.S. forces and picks up about 75 percent of the tab for the operating expenses of some 85 American military installations located in Japan (mostly in Okinawa), where around 56,000 GIs, plus their dependents, are stationed. The alliance now includes an agreement committing Japan to logistic support, supply and technical cooperation in developing military hardware. Apart from the U.S. alliance, Japan is party to defense framework agreements with Australia and New Zealand as well.

The SDF role has evolved gradually as each prime minister reemphasizes Japan's commitment to nonaggression. The respective defense forces have demonstrated professionalism at home and abroad for disaster relief, and in overseas missions, mine-clearing, logistics support and peacekeeping operations in Africa, Asia, Central America and the Middle East. Major expansion of SDF capability has been made inevitable by Japan's aggressive neighbors. North Korea's third Supreme Leader from the Kim dynasty, Kim Jong-un, has conducted a foreign policy featuring the launching of ballistic missiles that come hair-raisingly close to hitting Japan. The prospects of settling territorial disputes and concluding a peace treaty at last with Russia once seemed promising, but hope faded with Putin's aggression in Ukraine. China regularly engages in provocative behavior near Japan's territory, while the world braces for an attack on Taiwan that, given an American response, would involve the U.S. bases in Japan.

self-odor delusion In Chapter 5 Wakako explains the psychological difficulties she encountered before and soon after becoming a university student. One hurdle was her belief that her body emitted an offensive odor. She convinced herself this must be true to explain her own perceptions of how her presence affected the people she met. She eventually began visiting a psychiatrist for therapy, at her parents' urging. In Chapter 7, the psychiatrist explains in courtroom testimony that people becoming obsessed with the unreasoning belief that they smell bad is not a rare phenomenon. Worldwide, it is known as olfactory reference syndrome, meaning that the person who has it references his or her anxieties about social relations to other people's olfactory sense. In Japan this obsession is studied both as a psychological disorder and a consumer behavior pattern, the latter by companies that market body spray, mouthwash and even "body odor analysis" services.

sensei A standard honorific that literally means someone who is your elder. One is expected to use it when referring to or addressing (1) a scholar, someone recognized as being very knowledgeable in some field or your teacher in any kind of learning situation; (2) any professor or school teacher; (3) a doctor, lawyer or other person whose role is giving guidance to people. You can also use it in a sarcastic or teasing way to make fun of someone. Yet another usage appears in Chapter 6, where toilets in a police holding cell can only be flushed by guards from outside, forcing suspects to call out "Boss, please flush!" The "boss" in that case is really sensei.

shaba from Sanskrit *saha*: In Buddhism, the name of this world of suffering that must be endured by its human inhabitants; in prison or army slang, shaba means the world outside.

shabu slang for any drug covered by the Stimulants Control Law. It usually means methamphetamine. The origin of the term is uncertain. It is not related to the Japanese dish featuring thin sliced beef dipped in sauce, *shabu-shabu*. Other slang terms for meth include "S" (pronounced *eh-su*) and *su-pee-doh* (for the English "speed"), but those terms weren't prevalent at the time of the events in *Marshland*.

A wide variety of illegal drugs have been used for recreation in Japan, but methamphetamine has long been the most prevalent. The term used in the relevant law is: *kakuseizai*, meaning "stimulant drug."

shimbun "new communications" i.e., "newspaper;" commonly used in the names of newspapers. For example, the nationally distributed Mainichi Shimbun means "daily news."

Shinkansen Japan's "new trunk line," is a high speed long distance railway. The first Shinkansen running between Tokyo and Osaka went into operation in 1964. Today it has become a network linking most major cities on Honshu and Kyushu, and operates in Hokkaido as well. Shinkansen technology has been exported to Taiwan, mainland China and, the U.K.; there are contracts in the U.S. and India, and several other countries are considering Shinkansen projects.

"Shinkokyu" murder The condemned prisoner Furukawa, who first apears in Chapter 7, has a conceit that the murder he committed electrified the nation. He gave his tale this curious title consisting of the initial kanji (see above) from the names of his alleged girlfriend, Shinko, himself and Hisako, the stranger he killed, believing she was Shinko. The word is meaningful only to Furukawa.

shochu a clear liquor distilled from potatoes or grains

shogi a game something like chess, played on a board of 81 squares

shoji a framework of paper and wood on sliding rails serving as a room divider, door or window screen

Showa (see era names)

"silly putty neck"
> ". . . her neck was ridiculously long and thin, like it was made of silly putty."
> (Chapter 5)

—

In the original text of that passage describing Atsuo in an LSD fantasy world, Wakako's neck seems to have become absurdly long and infinitely flexible, just like a fantastic female being in Japanese folklore named Rokurokubi. Her head comes with such a very, very, very long neck that she can get in your face wherever you may be, or even go flying off from her body to chase after you.

A *rokuro* is a potter's wheel or any turning mechanism, like a lathe, pulley or windlass. Imagine a potter turning out a pitcher with a long neck. *Kubi* is a neck and/or a head.

Six Codes Japanese law is organized under the Six Codes (roppo: Constitution, Civil Code, Code of Civil Procedure, Criminal Code, Code of Criminal Procedure and Commercial Code. Condensed versions of the Six Codes are widely used as reference books. One edition runs over six thousand pages. "Pocket," "essential" and other editions are also sold.

steam locomotive
> *"At night I heard the sound of a steam locomotive."*
>> (Chapter 7)
>> —

The last steam locomotives operating in Honshu, Japan's main island, were phased out in 1974. They are an object of popular nostalgia. Steam locomotives cars are installed in a number of public parks and special runs of the beloved "SLs" are occasionally conducted.

straw raincoat *mino*; a cloak woven from rice straw, which is highly water repellent.

substitute prison *Marshland* tells how six innocent people are convicted of placing a bomb on a passenger train, resulting in deaths and injuries. The convictions are based primarily on meticulously detailed accounts of the crime presented to the court as full confessions given by five of the defendants. Each confession is the result of intensive police interrogation sessions totaling tens to hundreds of hours of grilling. Some people can weather such treatment, but most can't.

> *"The upcoming trial will . . . demonstrate what goes on in those police holding cells that we call 'substitute prisons.' What civilized country would allow its police to lock up everyone they suspect in animal pens so they can grill them day and night to force confessions? Policemen . . . harass them with no lawyer present, with complete disregard for their rights as individuals. That is the reality of Japan, a country we flatter ourselves by calling an advanced democracy."*
>
> *"You aren't telling me anything I don't know."*
>> (Chapter 8: Attorney Jun Akutsu to Prof. Kotaro Ikéhata)
>> —

As a law student, Akutsu had studied Professor Ikéhata's textbook on Japan's criminal law. By the time he was preparing to defend the legal scholar's daughter in the Shinkansen train bombing case, he understood that Ikéhata's textbook blithely overlooks "the yawning gap between the provisions of the law and the way it is practiced." Rather than question a criminal indictment built on coerced confessions, Ikéhata prefers to believe the charges and assume his daughter had been duped into helping commit the crime.

After Japanese police make an arrest, they are required to send their investigation findings to a prosecutor within 48 hours. The prosecutor must either release the arrestee or obtain permission from a judge for further detention within the next 24 hours. Similar procedures are standard among democratic countries. They are implemented to limit the time police have to "solve" crimes with forced confessions. For the rule to be meaningful, suspects must be transferred away from police jurisdiction when courts grant continued detention.

It doesn't work that way in Japan, due to a loophole built into its criminal law in 1908, shortly after a modern national government had been established. Under the "substitute prison" (*daiyo kangoku*) system, unsentenced detainees can be held in police jails. That provision in the prison law was adopted as a necessary temporary measure at a time when few detention facilities were available and the new Meiji government had limited resources. Unsurprisingly, the police considered it a treasure worth preserving. They have successfully managed to do that, as of 2023.

Under the system, suspects of any crime from shoplifting to homicide can expect to be imprisoned at a police station until they cooperate in the production of written and perhaps also video recorded confessions that satisfy the interrogating officers, or, barring that outcome, until 23 days have elapsed. The 23-day limit is the sum of the first 48 hours of police detention, plus 24 hours used by a cooperating prosecutor, plus a ten-day extension of legally permitted police detention, granted upon request by a cooperating judge, plus one additional ten-day extension, also permitted by law and granted by a cooperating judge. Prosecutors and courts occasionally demur, but usually support this system of police interrogation.

In *Marshland*, Atsuo's full confession to the Shinkansen bombing comes on the twentieth day of police detention. He had been arrested as a suspected accomplice to a theft at his place of employment, but his interrogation was all about the bomb, and his "confession" was the product of suggestive hints dictated to him by his interrogator.

Interrogation results in self-incriminatory documentation from most people arrested in Japan, usually within the 23-day limit, but 23 days is not an absolute limit in cases where police can find a pretext to "rearrest" a suspect already in detention on some separate charge. When that happens, the 23-day cycle begins afresh. One of the "Peace can bomb" defendants (see bomb terrorism above) underwent 330 days of police interrogation. The longest period of total detention time among the respective defendants in that case (including police custody time) was 10 years.

sunyata Sanskrit for the Buddhist concept of emptiness or void; the Japanese word used here is *kumu*.

T

Takadanobaba a district of Tokyo in Shinjuku Ward. It could just as well be written Takada-no-baba, where *no* is a possessive particle that makes the following word belong to the preceding word. The name means "Takada's horse corral" (or "riding ground"). There have been several film dramatizations of a samurai battle that took place at Takadanobaba in 1694. Its railway station is often called "Baba" for short.

Tales from the Inner Palace In Chapter 3, Atsuo catches an episode from early "Inner Palace" TV series. The inner palace was the living quarters of the Tokugawa shogun (top general and national dictator) at Edo castle. The women inhabiting this domain provide an unending source of tales for dramatic productions, novels, manga and games.

tatami a flooring material of tightly woven rush straw panels, each panel consisting of a surface component, an inner component about about 40 cm (1.5 in) or less in thickness, and a base. The panels come in a number of standard sizes; 180 x 90 cm, (5.9 x 2.9 feet) is common. With a history of about a thousand years, tatami floors are integral to Japan's culture. Tatami has nice fragrance, is pleasantly responsive to bare feet, stays cool in summer and retains warmth in winter. These qualities are conducive to sitting on the floor, instead of on furniture for everyday indoor activities. Ordinary homes in Japan typically have at least one room with tatami flooring. In *Marshland*, tatami shows up in a company dormitory's TV room, Atsuo's humble woodframe apartment house, a couple of restaurants having tatami rooms for customer groups and "protection rooms" in detention facilities for women and minors.

Tatami mats are made in standard sizes. Room area is normally measured in numbers of tatami. For example, Atsuo undergoes police interrogation in an extremely cramped two-tatami room. That is only the size of the interrogation room. It does not mean that it is equipped with tatami flooring.

tempura Tempura is fish, shrimp, vegetables or herbs, dipped into batter, oil fried for a few seconds, drained and served hot. The objective in preparing tempura is to adjust the temperature of the oil and the thickness of the batter so that neither obscures the taste of what should be crisp, fresh food in a light coating. In Chapter 2, Atsuo and Wakako dine on tempura of common forest delicacies, like bamboo shoots and a kind of mugwort called *yomogi*, and the more exotic herbs yuki-no-shita (meaning "under snow" and known as "creeping sasifrage" in English) and ikema (a word from the the Ainu language; the scientific name is *Cynanchum caudatum*; there is no common English name). See also ikema and moxa cautery.

The Japanese name of this cooking technique supposedy derives from the Portuguest *tempero*, meaning "seasoning." Portuguese Jesuit missionaries resident in Japan in the seventeenth century apparently used a kind of batter-fry cooking, but whatever influence came from them, there was a native batter fry cooking method in Japan even before their arrival.

tengu a mythical being from the mountains or the forest, with roots in Shinto and Buddhism. Tengu are almost always male, usually with a red face and a fearsome expression. Their trademark is an absurdly long nose. One common tengu likeness is masks for use in festivals, noh, kabuki or wall decorations. Tengu serve as guardians to shrines and temples, and appear as statues and in every kind of graphic art.

teshiroppu the Ainu (see note above) word for the sherbet-like state the sea ice reaches before it freezes into solid ice floes.

thousand stitch sash *sen-nin-bari*, meaning "stitches from a thousand hands," were tokens of moral support from women on the home front, typically sashes for soldiers at war to wear for good-luck as belts, but could also be vests, flags or other cloth items. The custom is said to have originated during Japan's first war against China in 1894. The stitching had to be performed by hand, perhaps ideally by a thousand women born in the year of the tiger (see Chinese zodiac), but, more practically, by many different women or girls. In World War II, the demand was met by sewing circles organized in communities across Japan and, in big cities, by teams soliciting participation of female passers-by in public places.

tofu a low-calorie protein source, and a basic item in Japanese cooking, made like cheese from curdled milk of ground soy beans (*daizu*). Fresh tofu is an almost tasteless, pure white block of delicate to firm consistency. It can be eaten as is, or used in a wide variety of dishes. Its versatility can be extended through processing by frying or freeze drying.

tokonoma a recessed space, slightly above floor level, in a Japanese style room for display of one beautiful object, such as a picture scroll or flower arrangement.

torii a wooden gateway to a Shinto shrine consisting of two columns joined at the top by an ornamental rail. Its purpose is to mark the boundary between the secular world and the sacred area of the shrine.

"Trust in the Lord" The lyrics given in Chapter 12 are based on an English translation by Peter Krey of *Harre, meine Seele*, by Friedrich Räder.

"T. University" For stylistic reasons Tokyo University, or *Todai (tokyo daigaku)*, is called "T. University" in *Marshland*. The characters are fictional, but the description in Chapter 1 of the clash between radical factions occurred as described on Todai's main campus, in Hongo, Tokyo. Similarly, the siege of the "Tower" in Chapter 4 adheres scrupulously to the facts of the events of January 18-19, 1969, at Yasuda Auditorium, also on the Hongo campus. The author himself was a medical student at Todai nearly two decades before the events described in *Marshland*.

From the time of its establishment in 1877, Tokyo University traditionally got the lion's share of government funding and occupied as much political prestige. It is still number one today, but many of Japan's other public and private universities have established considerable influence of their own.

typewriter, Japanese Japanese typewriters were used from 1915 until word processors pushed them into obsolescence in the nineteen-eighties. Early models had limited kanji capability, but eventually could accommodate almost any Japanese text. Operating a Japanese typewriter was a specialized, but not difficult skill. It was simply a process of selecting one piece of type at a time, from a font of thousands.

U

United Red Army lynchings (chapter 12): "Lynch" in this case means "arbitrary trial and execution." It refers to the murders of twelve members of a radical group called the United Red Army, in Dec./Jan., 1971-72. The victims were beaten, stabbed or tied to trees in midwinter and left to die of cold and starvation by order of the group leaders, as punishment for unacceptable ideology or insufficient dedication to revolution. Some were teenagers, and four were female, including one whose unborn child died with her. After the purge, five group members took hostages and barricaded themselves in a mountain lodge for ten days. They killed two policemen during the siege, but were captured alive and their hostages freed after the police used a wrecking ball to break into the lodge. The final hours of the siege were covered by live TV broadcast. The shock of these events generally reduced public sympathies for leftist causes.

Utamaro In prison, Atsuo encounters an unusual work of art on the body of a Yakuza boss:

> "At bath time, I discovered he had a tattoo on his back of a woman, a breathtakingly beautiful likeness with the kind of exquisite detail seen in works by Utamaro."

> (Chapter 11)

> —

Kitagawa Utamaro is among the most distinguished eighteenth century Ukiyo-é woodblock print artists of Edo, the thriving metropolis that was destined to become Tokyo. Ukiyo-é is a highly stylized, non-realistic genre that has influenced graphic art worldwide. An Utamaro specialty was women's beauty manifested in details of coiffure, gesture, pose, or the pattern and folding in the fabric of their kimono. Some of his works were pornographic. Kitagawa is the surname.

V

Valentine's Day In Chapter 8, Sonoko Kanéhara, the housemother at the dormitory for the young men working for Fukawa Motors, explains that she gave Atsuo a high fashion necktie as a Valentine's Day present. She was being unusually extravagant. In Japan women customarily give Valentine's Day presents to men they like, but chocolate is the prescribed gift. The tradition is said to have originated circa 1958 from a confectionery company's astute ad campaign. Such gifts are seen as no more than a friendly gesture as least as often as a romantic declaration. More than a few working women consider it a reactionary custom that gives their male colleagues unwarranted expectations of being handed token gifts of chocolate every February 15.

Vegetable Root Discourses *Saikontan* (Chinese is *Caigentan*): a Ming Dynasty book of aphorisms that blend the teachings of Confucianism, Daoism and Zen Buddhism.

W

war songs (*gunka*, "military songs") Verses from two formerly popular military tunes are quoted in *Marshland*: "Under falling snow our troops advance o'er the ice . . . " is from "The Snow March" (*Yuki-no-Shingun*), and "Striking down the unrighteous, in Heaven's service . . . " is from "The Army of Japan" (*Nippon Rikugun*). They were composed in 1895 and 1904, respectively.

wasshoi! This chant is a time-tested way of unifying minds and raising energy levels, normally heard at Shinto festivals, coming from dozens of hardy participants shouldering a litter bearing a weighty divinity shrine that they convey triumphantly past jubilant onlookers. It was also used by frenzied protesters in campus and street demonstrations of the nineteen-sixties and seventies. In Chapter 4, students at Wakako's university chant "wassho! wasshoi!" as they turn out for a street demonstration in support of "T. University" students battling riot police.

wrongful convictions Following Atsuo's conviction as chief culprit in the Shinkansen bomb case, attorney Jun Akutsu agrees to defend him because he is skeptical of the state's evidence, which consists essentially of interrogation room documentation only. Atsuo's "confession" is filled with details of events and descriptions of circumstances that only the perpetrator of the crime could have known— provided one rules out the possibility that the source of all those details might be the detectives who investigated the crime. The court that convicted Atsuo rejected that possibility.

In Chapter 9, Akutsu confides to a sympathetic reporter that he expects judicial appeals in the case will take many years, like other well-known homicide cases or train sabotage based on forced confessions in which the defendants were ultimately exonerated. He names three real-life cases (Sachiúra, Oúmé, Yakai) that took 10 to 17 years to be resolved, tactfully neglecting mention of many cases of dubious convictions that were never overturned.

Y

Yasukuni Shrine Visited by Atsuo and his newfound drinking buddy Yamamura in Chapter 5, this compound of imposing buildings graced by cherry, laurel, zelkova and ginkgo trees was built in 1869 at the dawn of Japan's transition from feudalism to a European style nation-state. This Shinto shrine has a register of some two and a half million servicemen (and a small number of women) who died fighting Japan's many internal and external wars since then. Because the enshrined include over a thousand convicted war criminals, formal visits to it by prime ministers, high government officials and national or local political representatives continue to prompt bitter criticism from countries once victimized by Japanese aggression, as well as a cross section of Japanese who wish to disavow the ideology that led Japan to acquire its empire in the twentieth century.

"Yo-" / "Jun-"

"I'm Yoko Mizuno – 'Yo-' as in 'sun.' With this self-introduction, she lowered her head politely."

"Jun Akutsu. 'Jun' as in 'purity,' Akutsu said, and returned the bow."

(Chapter 8)

—

They are explaining the kanji (see above) used to write their names. Kanji are designed for writing with a brush, each requiring anywhere from one to fifteen or more strokes. Japanese usually has two or more ways of reading any given kanji, i.e., it assigns different sounds to the same kanji, depending on the context in which it appears. For some names, one must guess how they should be read. "Yoko" is a very common girl's name. *-ko* is almost always the two-stroke kanji meaning "child," but there are twenty or more likely candidates and yet more unusual possibilities for how *Yo-* could be written, including kanji having such meanings as "lamb," "leaf," "song," "sun," "brightness," "willow," "jewel," "ocean" or "prosperous." For *Jun,* likely possibilities would be kanji meaning "purity," "falcon," "leader," "truehearted," "colorful," "felicitous" or "sincere and prudent."

yokan This is the "hard jelly" Atsuo buys, presumably from a Japanese commissary, for gifts when he returns to Japan from China in wartime (Chap 11). Yokan is made from adzuki or white kidney beans, agar and sugar. It usually comes in blocks, for serving in slices.

yomogi a kind of mugwort plant. See moxa cautery and tempura.

yukata A light kimono made of cotton or other light fabric for after-bath wear, like a robe. Hotels and inns provide simple ones for that purpose. There are also fashionable versions suitable for outdoor strolling. Yukata are commonly worn in summery, leisurely settings by both sexes and all ages, but most commonly young women.

Z

zabuton A square floor cushion, for kneeling (*seiza*) or sitting upon.

zazen Zen is a sect or school of Buddhism developed in China, Japan, Korea and Vietnam that teaches meditation as a way of clearing the mind, taming the ego, freeing oneself from attachment to things, and ultimately gaining enlightenment. The *za* of *zazen* means being seated, usually in a formal posture for meditating.

- *kyogo*: Walking meditation; a break during *zazen* sessions for standing up and walking a prescribed course, to banish sleepiness, or for exercise.

zenkyoto (see All-Campus Joint Struggle)

— Albert Novick
February, 2023

Otohiko Kaga (1929–2023), one of Japan's few Christian writers, worked as a hospital and prison psychiatrist before becoming a novelist. His studies in France inspired his 1967 debut novel, *Furandoruno fuyu* (*Winter in Flanders*), for which he received the Minister of Education Award for New Artists. *Marshland*, his second novel to be translated into English, was awarded the Osaragi Jiro Prize in 1986. In 2011, Kaga was recognized as a Person of Cultural Merit.

Albert Novick was born in New York City in 1948. He served in the United States Air Force and attended San Francisco State University. He studied Japanese at the Waseda University Language Research Institute, then graduated from Meiji University and received a master's degree in sociology from Saitama University. He was a columnist and reporter for English- and Japanese-language newspapers. For the past thirty years, he has been a freelance writer and translator.